A Secret for Julia

A Secret for Julia

A NOVEL BY

Patricia Sagastizábal

TRANSLATED BY

Asa Zatz

W · W · Norton & Company

New York   London

For information about permission to reproduce selections
from this book, write to Permissions, W. W. Norton & Company, Inc.,
500 Fifth Avenue, New York, NY 10110

The text of this book is composed in 12/15 Granjon
with the display set in Granjon
Composition by Molly Heron
Manufacturing by Haddon Craftsmen
Book design by Margaret M. Wagner
Production manager: Julia Druskin

Library of Congress Cataloging-in-Publication Data
    Sagastizábal, Patricia, 1953–
    [Secreto para Julia. English]
    A secret for Julia : a novel / by Patricia Sagastizábal ; translated by Asa Zatz.
    p.   cm.
    ISBN 0-393-05044-0
    I. Zatz, Asa. II. Title.
PQ7798.29.A356 S4313 2001
863'.64–dc21

                                                        2001030287

W. W. Norton & Company, Inc.,
500 Fifth Avenue, New York, N.Y. 10110
www.wwnorton.com

W. W. Norton & Company Ltd.,
Castle House, 75/76 Wells Street, London W1T 3QT

1 2 3 4 5 6 7 8 9 0

TO FRANCISCO AND HERNÁN

who give fullest meaning to reality

A Secret for Julia

▨▨ *A man of foreign nationality was arrested in London on
Wednesday in an operation involving a contingent of some
twenty police officers and an unspecified number of agents of
Interpol. The incident, which occurred at Hobbes' Place, a
restaurant located at Huntley and Capper Streets, Bloomsbury,
aroused considerable curiosity among the public inasmuch as
neither police nor government sources (also believed to be concerned) have released any statements to the press regarding the
event, nor what charges, if any, have been brought.*

*News agency sources hint at a possible connection between
the detained foreigner and smuggling involving Bonmayer,
adviser to the Foreign Minister on Security and Defense. However, other off-the-record sources suggest a possible association
with a network of mercenaries brought in to thwart the peace
negotiations in Ireland. For the victims of the assault—if the
incident at Hobbes' Place may be categorized as such—the
course of events remains unclear. Nine people were present at
the locale, of whom seven appear to have connections with a
foundation that provides advisory and support services to political parties and nongovernmental organizations. The other two
are the restaurant's proprietors, who have no police records; the
only complaint docketed against their place of business dates
back to the 1980s, when it was closed briefly after an incident
involving football rowdies.*

*Two persons were injured with gunshot wounds to the face.
The foreigner's identity continues to be withheld but unofficial
information indicates that he is an Argentine wanted by the
French authorities.*

I was there and can shed light on this incident, if not on the reason why the man was taken into custody. Since words fail me adequately to characterize this sort of individual, I should perhaps confine myself to saying that many years ago under other circumstances he was invested with minimal, yet monstrous power. And he wielded it against me as well as many others. "Fate," or perhaps "portent," would be a more appropriate word to apply to his having entered my life once again, here in England. My name is Mercedes Beecham and what I am about to recount is part of quite a convoluted tale.

He burst into Joyce's restaurant that night with the intention of extracting information from me that was evidently of utmost importance to him. Brandishing a gun and obviously in a state bordering on frenzy, he forced my friends to lie facedown on the floor, pushed me up against the bar, and launched into a disjointed harangue in which, by perverting the nature of certain actions committed in my country, he sought to justify those that were perpetrated by him along with so many others.

Vile monster!—I screamed to myself—as I listened to him hold forth like an unctuous politician. Then, all of a sudden, he came toward me, and in a tone of bitter, controlled fury said that he'd had it with the game I was playing. Evidently, he was obsessed by an uncontrollable need for the answer to a puzzle only I could provide. But, realizing that I was not about to respond to whatever it was he wanted, he

seized me by the throat and proceeded to choke me. My eyes fixed on his chilly glare, I was beginning to pass out. Expert that he was in such activities, he knew just when to relax thumb and forefinger enough to enable me to draw breath again. When I was able to speak, despite my quivering insides, I spat out that I had no answer to give. His face twisted into a grimace of enraged frustration an instant before his fist smashed into my face.

A moment later, there was bedlam: screams, the sound of fighting and glass breaking. Then, suddenly, a pair of shots. I could see blood, Eric and Todd sprawled on the floor, and the man gripping a gun. The sight exploded the pent-up hatred of years, and I leaped at him, tearing the gun from his hand. Where the strength came from, I have no idea. I think I can remember, yes, staring at the weapon, bewildered, calculating the possibility of letting Eric, or anybody else, take control. I could do nothing more.

I simply backed off to the center of the room, my eyes fixed on his malevolent face, obscene drops of perspiration coursing down the forehead. The brute was sweating. When I demanded that he beg me to forgive him, he let out a howl of laughter, a sound from the distant past, ugly as it was familiar. My reaction was so violent and visceral that I brought my hands together, gripped the gun, waited an instant, then pulled the trigger. The fraction of a second that elapsed gave me time to ask myself the question that had tormented me all these years: Could killing that man ever compensate for what he did to me?

As soon as I came to my senses, I realized I had done no more than shoot him in the leg. I watched him slither away and fall on the basement stairs. Eric's voice came through to

me, as I felt his hands pressing mine, the gun slipping from my fingers, then I heard steps, recognized the shapes of friends in the darkness. Exhaustion and the urge to burst into tears were overpowering. Yet I managed to stumble to the stairs and go slowly to within inches of the man's body grotesquely doubled over, his hands already tied behind his back, as he lay unconscious with his eyes wide open. Afterwards, I learned that in trying to escape being shot, he had fallen and struck the back of his head against the edge of the door frame near the bar.

A strange compulsion came over me, a need to dwell on the sight of that face: the same aquiline nose, white skin, eyes of a vague color, a mixture of off-blue and leaden gray. I lingered at this inspection a few moments, having struggled my way down for another reason. I had to get close enough to search him. My hands shaking, I fumbled frantically in his pockets: passport, other ID, credit cards, money; a tiny Blessed Virgin medallion pinned under his lapel. Finally, I found what I was looking for—photographs. A chill went through me as I recognized one of Julia in a park, apparently talking to Mickey and Shelley; others in the envelope of her, me, and friends of mine.

Then, leaving everything in his pockets, I climbed up the stairs, weeping. I recall Todd hugging me, unfamiliar voices, the commands of police taking over.

It's all over, I keep telling myself, and now I can look forward to a future without fear of being stalked. The house is quiet. I look out at the sky, at the floating white

clouds, not an unfamiliar sight anymore on this island. I must be patient, though. It is still too soon for my body to feel that it is at peace.

A few days have gone by and I've had time to think, to reconstruct the loathsome scenes I sought for years to put behind me. Incredible. The man who wiped out my identity and that of my friends and comrades was arrested for robbery or smuggling; petty crimes, in any case. And, as I contemplate the square in the twilight, the wet pavement, and the languidly swaying trees, I continue to feel uneasy. He won't be tried for those other crimes of his, the crimes of that unspeakable past. And what relief can I expect now from this unexpected denouement? Those in power thrust him into my life, and now others, equally empowered, are removing him. As haphazardly, as inconceivably, as that.

I have found no explanation for what I've been through. No simple one, that is.

Speculations come to mind—whether other's or my own is unimportant anymore. These conjectures concern impunity, that is to say, the impunity enjoyed by certain human beings who come to consider themselves exempt from punishment. These are individuals whose contempt for the fate of others enables them to avoid contemplating their own finality. Reality for such people is whatever they decide it to be. There is even a moment, perhaps, when conscience or spirit—the names we give to that nebulous zone where human values reside—makes its way into the flesh, filters through like a radiance ignoring the senses, to be transformed into an ethereal, almost unnoticed essence capable of being forever forgotten. And, in that case, of course, failure must become inconceivable. If there is a

threshold that sets good actions apart from bad, and it is crossed once, and then crossed again, the point may be reached when the difference between the two no longer matters.

:: But now my life, which had come to a halt during this period, had to be put back on track. I will be doing my book presentation this evening at the university at seven o'clock. I am picturing the faces of that audience as they merge with the image of that last expression on Julia's face.

I shall be leaving in just a few hours, but am unable to string together any thoughts or words unrelated to my daughter. One of Julia's dolls is on my lap. I stroke its hair as if it were she. I still long to see her walk through the door and into my arms. I must get her to forgive me. I can't leave without seeing her.

Julia now knows the truth. And though it may sound strange, I feel as though the meaning of life has been wrenched from me. Keeping that secret for so many years; hedging and inventing subterfuges in order to avoid the harrowing reply. Finally, the time came when my daughter refused to tolerate another evasion or lies. I had to speak out, bring everything into the open. It was a recapitulation of my life and hers—some of the scenes, the necessary words surfacing for conveying the enigma, dates, names, and places. I see her face in my memory. It expressed no jubilation, only calm deliberation. I would have had to make it clear to her that it was impossible for this account of mine to convey the utter unreality of the circumstances. It could never encompass all the motivations, nor the intimate conflict I had kept secret for so long.

My behavior was irrational, there's no denying it. Julia raked over the information in each word, in every gesture. She heard me out to the most insignificant detail. Then she told me she had to be alone to think it over. Watching her leave the house, little purse in hand, I wanted to stop her, but didn't. I now realize that I lived in perpetual fear for both of us. These recent events have made me reassess my behavior: blaming Julia for my desperation, I situated her at the locus of memory where obsession makes understanding impossible at any level.

I want to introduce myself into my narrative, but something happens to me with respect to time. It slips away from me, gyrates or expands, enabling me thereby to bypass consciousness and Julia's birth. I have the feeling that I'm inventing the sequence of events, doing so for her sake. I call up memory for her.

And now that I have set out to retrieve my past, I hope the words I choose will adequately convey my despair. Let me begin by saying, sadly enough, that life had been anything but easy before I came to England. I was forced out of my country and had to put up with difficult conditions here, but something terribly destructive had already invaded my body when I was exiled. Here I had to confront a world of anguish at a time when I was completely drained of energy. It was into this kind of setting that Julia was born sixteen years ago, on an afternoon in September. I tend to go back compulsively to those moments, as if there were a clue of some kind to be found in my labor contractions. To tell the truth, I blamed much of my misfortune on Julia for the sole reason that she had not been conceived in a union of love. But, of course, it was not her fault. Most of the time, I think it was mine. And so, although she brought another language into my exile's universe, it was not easy for me to accept her.

If I am to describe our relationship, I must confess that I looked on in disbelief as she grew up, continuing to suffer the same emotional block as when I first cradled her in my arms. I will have to be forthcoming about my ambivalence,

to admit my surprise as well as my pleasure, during the period when Julia began to walk and later on to talk. To be honest, very often I would look at her in consternation and, at times, even shut her brutally out of my life.

Julia respected my silence until she could bear it no longer. She began her cross-examining a few months ago. But I had become an expert at evading the inexorable reply.

Many things changed when she decided to find out the truth. Silence and concealment became my daughter's weapons. On one of these last nights, a little over two weeks ago, she made strange assessments of my behavior. When I asked her to explain what she meant by an unexpected remark (something about Argentina), she threw me a furtive, reproachful glare. Then she huddled in obdurate silence. I played along. Like a fool, I told myself that if she shut herself off, so would I. But Julia won that round; I got no sleep that night.

Early the next morning, I left the house and walked till I began to feel the cold air nipping at my body. I crossed the park, threading my way among the noisy children. It was a chilly, misty Sunday in September. My footsteps felt resilient against the splendid green lawn bordered by trees and sturdy privet hedges as the wind whipped the branches and ruffled the surface of the lake. It was early and few people were about. I thought up arguments I could make to Julia; each gave a different twist to the problem. An icy blast scattered leaves around my feet at the throne on which I sat that Sunday. Unexpected recollections congregated at a bend in my memory as though awaiting passage to my daughter's heart. But what should I be telling her? The truth? Where to begin and how?

I cannot describe the irrational state of mind into which my reflections had plunged me when a little girl approached me to tie her shoelaces. I looked all around but could see nobody. Uneasy, I asked where her mother was. Her answer—that she didn't know—upset me considerably. When Julia was that age (six or so, I calculated), I never let her out of my sight. In the park, I would peer about, checking everything. The people, smells, certain sounds, footsteps, were all points of spatial reference. If Julia moved out of my line of sight for even an instant, I would go out of control. And here I was this morning worrying over a little girl I didn't even know. I picked her up in my arms and was reassuring her that we would find her mother right away, when a pleasant-looking young woman in jogging clothes appeared and thanked me for watching out for her daughter. Apparently, the child made a habit of running off just to tease her mother and oblige her to chase all over the park looking for her. The little girl was smiling impishly as the mother scolded and tickled her at the same time. As they left, I couldn't help envying the peace that emanated from them. I was never able to achieve such serenity. Never, ever, did I relax my surveillance over Julia's living space, to the point where I would pick apart, and see things, in the most trifling details of the little anecdotes my daughter told me.

That morning, I went over countless images, mental snapshots of moments in my life with Julia. Yet, when I came home, I was incapable of formulating a coherent sentence or even an affectionate greeting. Had I been able to find the courage to reveal the secret I was concealing, I would have proposed a truce; but her eager expression and

the brusqueness of her body language put me off. Then I realized something: a child inherits certain characteristics and, in my daughter's case, one of them was irrepressible— Julia's wishes are non-negotiable.

The ensuing days were tense, strange, the two of us locked into a stubborn game of aimless maneuvering. We had developed a kind of absurd coexistence: when we were together, we either spoke not at all or got into arguments over the most trivial things. The presence of that man—I can't deny it—was what precipitated the denouement. In any case, I had already made up my mind to tell Julia the secret.

As I wait for her, holding my breath every time I hear footsteps outside the door, or when the phone rings, I recall her last appeals for help, and my failure to respond seems to me unforgivable. I keep thinking of the time Julia first began to hound me about her father.

That rainy April evening there was a sudden downpour. Across the street, people were crowding under the supermarket awning. I was looking out of the window as passersby milled around trying to keep from getting soaked when, all at once, the big Doberman from the corner bakery barged in among them. He knocked over an old lady as he shook himself, causing her bags of groceries to fall on the sidewalk and burst open spewing out oil, flour, eggs and touching off a tumult among those trying to avoid him or to keep from stepping into the messy puddle. As I watched at the kitchen window, Julia was pacing the floor impatiently with the thick leather heels of her boots clacking loudly against the wooden floor, to my great annoyance. She was very fond of those boots and wore them even in hot weather. I had told her any number of times that the noise they made set my nerves on edge, but she gets satisfaction out of my discomfort. Suddenly, she switched on her stereo to her favorite CD, the latest release of MEGADETH, a group whose music I fail to appreciate. Having to listen to it at all hours irritates me beyond words. But if I ask her to turn the volume down, she looks at me in disdain and informs me that loud is how this kind of music is supposed to be listened to.

She had it on especially loud that night and I remember staring at the apparatus with a mounting impulse to turn it off. But I didn't. My daughter had set out to bait me and was succeeding. That's the direction in which my thoughts were running when the bell rang. It was the delivery boy with the pizzas we had ordered. Julia answered the door. Then with brusque flourishes, she set out two plates, served a wedge on each, and sat down nervously at the table.

Instead of eating, however, she got up again and switched the music off. Returning to her chair, she sat for a time just staring at her food. I wasn't touching mine. We remained like that for a while, in silence, concentrating on our plates. When I looked up our eyes met. It was quite strange. Her expression defiant, she would not take her eyes off mine. Then, with a slow and I would say very precise movement, she pushed her plate aside, leaned over toward me, and bringing her face to within inches of mine, whispered: "Who is my father?"

"I told you . . . somebody I knew years ago. What prompts that question now?"

"Why don't you ever mention him?"

"Because there's no reason to."

"Yet you get on the defensive when I ask you, the same as always."

"I don't know what you're driving at. But is that what's bothering you?"

"Yes. Is it possible, Mother, for you to get anything that simple through your head?"

Her silhouette was reflected in the hall mirror. She had on baggy trousers and a blouse down to her knees; she kept tugging at the edges impatiently. Her long blond hair, gath-

ered up in a bun, made her look older and gave her adolescent features a cast of seriousness.

"I don't know," I answered.

"You don't know," she said with a nervous laugh, breaking off abruptly to stare at me. "You don't want to tell me and you figure that'll be that, right?"

"I told you what I had to tell you, as much as you need to know."

"You're cruel, Mother. You sit there, unflappable, looking the other way. You make me sick."

With that, she began to scrape the tabletop with a knife. I asked her to stop but she kept it up until I snatched the knife from her. At that, she got to her feet and turned up the CD player to full volume.

"Did you have a fight with Mickey?" I yelled as though I'd forgotten about her demand. "He left a letter for you." I took it out of my trouser pocket and laid it on the table.

"I asked you a question and you fobbed me off. Me, I'll answer your question. Mickey and I are good, very good. Now, you go. Your move, Mother."

"Turn that bloody set off," I yelled, now furious. "You're driving me up the bloody wall!"

"Only if you answer me, only if you let me in on the *secretito* you're keeping to yourself."

She was dancing, ignoring my question, as I had ignored hers. I'm disarmed when I hear her pronounce Spanish so beautifully, so much like my sister Alicia that I can't stand it. Of course, she doesn't know that.

After telling me it was my move, she began to walk, with me following her. When I reached out to touch her, she put up her hands to hold me off.

"Don't try any funny business. I want the truth. I know you're holding out on me."

I went into the living room and turned off the stereo. We were standing face to face. It was a long, infinitely long moment, after which I said, "Will you be satisfied with knowing some physical feature or other of somebody with whom I was alone just once and for only a very short time?"

"How long did it take?"

"What do you mean?"

"I want to know how many minutes it took; if it was good, or so bad you'd never want to see him again."

"It was fast . . . as if nothing at all happened."

Julia was stunned at my response and unable to speak for some time. Tears rolled down her cheeks. I went over to her and touched her face. She recoiled in displeasure and made straight for the full-length mirror on the pantry door, pulled up her trousers above the knee, flexed her legs as if to launch into a ballet step, and making a face, turned to me.

"Was he bowlegged like me?"

"You're not bowlegged. What are you talking about?"

"My legs are long but I always wondered why they didn't grow straight. Shelley complained all the time about her hair being kinky and was forever trying to straighten it. A couple of days ago she came to school with a mop of the neatest curls and a big smile on her face." Julia clicked her tongue, wiggled her eyebrows, and said, "Know what? She found out that her dad and granddad had exactly that same kind of hair. So, it's genetic. End of problem, that simple. Smashing, no?"

My daughter was looking at herself in the mirror again. I couldn't stand to watch her and went to the wine rack. I

uncorked a bottle of Sauvignon and gulped down a glassful. Soon I felt a hot flush beginning to rise.

"I must be at the university at seven o'clock tomorrow morning, and you have literature at seven-thirty," I said, as I put the remains of the pizza into the fridge and started tidying up the kitchen.

"Know something, Mother? I don't think I can go on like this—I really don't." Her lips began to tremble. "You have to tell me what he was like. I have to know."

She turned trying to reach me with her eyes. I poured myself another glass of wine, took a couple of sips, then went to the mirror and stood beside her. I asked her to stand up straight, shoulder to shoulder with me. I am of middle height, with a big frame, but have grown quite thin. My daughter is now taller than me, but we are built very much alike. Julia is slim and shapely, but disapproves of her looks. She muffles her body with loose clothes, puts her long, silky hair up in ribbons, and likes to wear it under a cap.

That night, she watched in the mirror with that sharp gaze of hers, eyes fixed on mine in the reflection.

"He was tall and had blond hair . . ." I blurted this out as if I would have no voice left to say anymore. "Not like yours. Yours is soft and straight, his was curly. He had blue eyes, but shifty, no resemblance whatsoever to your deep blues and your gracious expression. His nose"—I placed my finger on the spot in the mirror that reflected Julia's nose— "was aquiline. He was a tall man with small feet, an undignified deficiency on nature's part. I don't recall his legs at all, and his walk only vaguely."

I looked at her in the mirror, made a face that expressed my distaste, raising my eyebrows, at the same time, and

shaking my head repeatedly as though to expel the images from this exorcism of the past.

"Then you were with him more than once?"

"But on other matters."

"Mother, this is all a pack of lies, like that story of the Irishman you said was my father. Now I get it. You're remembering some other person. Why am I not using his name? Does he even know about me?"

My anxiety mounting, I moved away from the mirror. I felt chilly but my hands were perspiring.

"Julia, sweetheart, I cannot answer all the questions you ask me."

"Why not?"

"Because . . . I can't."

"You don't want to."

"No, I don't want to talk about him—and I'm not going to."

"But I am. You didn't love him, it's obvious, but what about him, Mother, did he love you?"

"No."

"What happened is that he mistreated you. Right, no?"

"Yes . . . he treated me very badly."

"Then why did you go with him?"

"I never went with him."

"No? How did I get here, then?"

"You're trying to upset me, that's what you want," I snapped at her nervously. "You keep badgering me with your questions and the way you stare at me."

"Tell the truth now. I never know if it's my presence that bugs you, or my questions, or what. That's what I can't get through my head."

"And what makes you think you'll be able to now?"

"I have to. I can't go on like this. Now, I can't even look at you. Who is he? Tell me once and for all."

"Enough, Julia, for God's sake! Stop this torture. If you can't bear it any longer, neither can I."

"Why, Mother, tell me, *why?*"

"He doesn't exist, or if he did, he was part of a nightmare. It's hard to explain."

"Try. I'll wait." With that she leaned back against the kitchen doorjamb as I nibbled nervously at the end of my pencil.

"There are some things that simply can't be explained, Julia."

"I have to know who he is!"

"You never had a father. He doesn't even know you exist."

I looked on as she shut her eyes and shuddered as though the information were causing her to fade, perhaps leaving her transparent.

"Where can I find him?"

"What are you talking about? You're out of your mind, you can't go looking for him. Stop it, Julia!" And I began to cry. "Have patience, I beg of you. I must think, because, you see, what happened is . . ."

I could no longer speak for the anxiety had lodged in my lungs and I felt it as an unbearable pain in the chest, hard and flat, like a heavy board lying across my diaphragm. I remember nothing else until I woke up the next day in the hospital.

When I opened my eyes, Eric's face was there before me. He was looking at me with an expression of tender concern

as a nurse beside him gave me an injection and, truthfully, I didn't even feel the needle.

::   No sooner was I out of the hospital and in his office the following day than Eric told me I was being cruel to Julia. I have great respect for his opinions, just about all of them. That one, though, annoyed me profoundly. He let loose a broadside of arguments regarding my character and how I could be ruining Julia's life as well as my own. Obviously, he knew about our quarrels through his son, Mickey. Eric doesn't expect such behavior from me and his attitude was reproachful. I felt ill at ease talking to him that morning. He unnerved me when we got to the point that so troubled Julia: who her father really was. With that, I excused myself, picked up my things, and got out of there as fast as I could. But I didn't miss hearing him say, "You'll hold back a secret at any cost, won't you?"

I sent him to hell, mentally, that is, flinging such arguments after him, as: "And what right do you have to offer an opinion? It's *my* life, and nobody, but nobody, can imagine the cost." But that word, "secret," brought me up short, like brakes suddenly slammed on. What did he mean by it? That my obsession was costing Julia her health? Eric didn't buy my argument that day. I had suggested that I was probably only waiting for the right time, the right way to tell my story in counterpoint with hers. What Eric didn't know was the extent to which the past had encroached on my life since I was speculating that this man was now in London. I was almost sure it was he. But, to tell the truth, there wasn't a

thing I could do, and it was only intuition. I was hoping to come out of this with my sanity reasonably intact because my own reactions were actually beginning to frighten me.

⁝⁝ My arguments were ineffectual, but I couldn't find a way out of my dilemma, at least, not readily. As if this weren't enough, Julia had barricaded herself behind a parapet of silence, giving me little opportunity to sound out her innermost feelings. If going on living sometimes signifies refusal to cope with thorny situations, that's what I had been doing for a long time, actually over a period of several months, during which my obstinacy provoked an even deeper rift between us.

As I wait for her, I'm wondering if I'll be able to explain my past. If I'm capable of conveying the essence of my worries and obsessions, the procession of ghosts that plague me with questions, my own unknowns, the doubts.

All at once, something that happened a few months ago flashed into my memory. No trifle, it changed my whole life. I had gone to Dillon's for a book that I had ordered. It was a theoretical work by a French author on the influence of law upon morality. It had gone out of print quickly and I was obliged to make do with photocopies, which I found irksome. Reading a book means turning the pages, touching the jacket, marking one's place with the flap when the day's stint is done. And so, when I was finally notified that they had obtained a copy, I hurried to pick it up. After finishing the transaction, I wandered over to the fiction section to see if my friend John Bronner's novel was out yet. He had told me that when he was finished, he'd be happy to see me. I was looking forward to lunch or a film with him. He had asked me out a few times. Perhaps it was time to put aside my phobias about men (Todd's counseling) and take a chance on one of them. Clerks were arranging the shelves. As I turned to ask one of them about the book, I noticed a man's silhouette. He was standing so that I could see him only in profile. But it was not his appearance that caught my eye as much as his expression: head tilted to one side, lips twisted in a scowl that froze half his face. Apparently, he didn't like what he was reading, but at the rate he scanned

the pages it seemed impossible he could understand what he read.

It was a grimace all too familiar to me. Impossible to keep my eyes off that face. Gray-haired and pudgy now, it seemed to match up with the image of my nightmares. But he was some distance away and there were several aisles of books between us. I couldn't tear my eyes away, I had to be sure it wasn't just a case of resemblance. I tried to move closer without attracting attention. I had maneuvered my way until there was only one aisle between the business section where he stood reading and me, but a clerk bearing an armful of books blocked my view. By the time he had placed them on a shelf and turned aside, the man was gone. I caught a glimpse of him going out of the store. Or, to be more precise, I saw a man in a raincoat leaving Dillon's. But by the time I ran into the street he had disappeared.

The next day, when I told Eric about the incident, he reminded me (I knew he would) of the time last year that I was absolutely convinced I had seen the man at the theater sitting in a box at *Phantom of the Opera,* of all things. It's true, I did think I saw him. I was with a group of our colleagues who were puzzled by my odd behavior in the lobby where I was casting around anxiously among the people crowded there during intermission. I offered no explanation and they discreetly made no comments. Even as I pondered the oddity of encountering such a marked resemblance, I promised Eric I would try to avoid that kind of behavior. Indeed, the man must have been a British double. When that happened—as it did several times—I invariably felt as though I had been suddenly seized and flung into a dreadful quagmire. The defenses aimed at lifting the

pall that hung over my life, while all perfectly logical, served no purpose. It was my body that took charge. Faced with the presence of the aggressor, real or imaginary, I was overcome by a sensation of relentless anguish, more menacing than tangible reality. In any case, I had developed a defense mechanism for dealing with those situations. I simply assured myself that it was an obsession and had to be treated as such.

On this occasion, however, the man at Dillon's with the characteristic grimace I knew so well brought me back to scenes from another time.

That night, I replayed in my mind the distinctive way in which this stalker would read. It went back many years, but I remembered every detail of the place—the pungent odor of damp, the squalor of that lair they called "the Archives." I had been assigned to duty there after somebody had recommended me for placement in a strange group of survivors. Treatment of prisoners was rumored to be better in the Archives. I couldn't stand the suspense. Who had done me the favor? Of course, I asked no questions and exhibited my usual stolid indifference whenever a guard approached.

When I started working there, I shut myself off entirely, focusing completely on my task. Since I had no idea what that "intellectual operation" was all about, I had decided not to talk to anybody. I was required to read and clip newspapers and magazines. This material was then used for a report which amounted to nothing more than a literal transcription of news. No interpretation was involved in its preparation, nothing beyond what appeared in the clippings.

Guards would appear at any point, take a seat, read the magazines, and talk to us, most of the time in a relaxed and even friendly manner. The whole thing was utterly unreal. Sometimes I heard voices and footsteps through the walls, like remote echoes from other offices which I knew adjoined the library and press office. I could make out the rumble of a telex machine and the clattering of a typewriter. Occasionally, I would look up from my work to see if some comrade was there, although I quickly suppressed my curiosity in order to avoid being subjected to further indignities; our jailers were animals, panting for information. And so, most of the time I did nothing but read and clip papers, read and clip, endlessly. I will never forget the piled-up papers, the cigarette smoke, the tedium of the unknowable, the guards' voices. In an ugly corner where the wall was covered over with newspaper clippings, vulgar messages, sayings, and "slogans," there was an armchair next to a lamp. The place was a hidden cellar, the ceiling so low it seemed to be falling in, the streets of the city alien to that world in which I—among others— was held.

On one occasion, I noticed this individual seated in the armchair, bent over the table. I was petrified, a speechless observer. He had been so absorbed in his reading that it took a while before he became aware of my presence. He then ordered me to explain a passage, after which I was told to retire and leave him alone. It became customary after that to see him sitting there, reading whatever had been drafted. I never could figure out if he tilted his head to one side as an indication of conformity with what he was reading or if it was merely a tic triggered by the position of

his head. But, yes, I do recall that he did it only while reading those "reports," perhaps as a convenient and precise way of closing off each syllable as he went along. Or, possibly, it was an involuntary gesture of the kind people make when considering whether to add something of their own to another's manuscript. The gesture of one who can't bring himself to do it, who foresees the possibility that if he were to jostle an adjective or adverb he might knock the whole structure out of kilter. The gesture of one who is driven by hubris because he would like to possess what is so highly prized by his superiors, the talent of those who write what he reads.

Memory can be utterly unreasonable. It focuses so inopportunely upon a particular person, as though the drama were centered in that man, the one I keep seeing on every corner in my nightmares, and now in the half-light of my wakefulness, as well. I couldn't see his face that day in Dillon's, but it was him. I knew it all the time.

London, winter, a few days before Christmas, sixteen years ago. I can still see the fog and feel the estrangement clinging to me. Willpower annihilated, I was shivering with the cold and isolation. The drizzle chilled my body, but although my senses had ceased to function, I was still able to think. It was a gray, dank Monday afternoon that etched dread and nostalgia in my spirit. A misty shower fell implacably on the cars and the pedestrians' heads. I can recall remaining completely immobile for a long while, images from my past merging with scenes of the gloomy,

alienating rainy day. And I remember pressing my nose
against the windowpane in an effort to find an opening in
the thick fog. But I was unable to see beyond the mist to distinguish the outlines of the simplest elements of my transitory existence. For some moments, I hadn't been aware of
anything but walking through the airport, disconnected,
my purse in hand with my passport and an amount of
money that would surely slip through my fingers in no
time. I felt lost. I can picture the little taxi perfectly that
dropped me at the bed-and-breakfast that was recommended as clean, cheap, and centrally located by the girl at the
newspaper kiosk. Nor will I ever forget the wild ride there
that had me fearing for my life.

All I could do those first few days was walk the London
streets, accustoming myself to the unfamiliar sounds of the
strange new geography, the rush of traffic, the loud noises.

I looked on through the window of a coffee shop at the
unending stream of variegated humanity that flowed by:
women and men in turbans; Hindus, Turkish children,
black young women, girls in skirts, short or long, some with
garishly colored hair; others, their ears sown with little earrings. Then, all at once, in the midst of this beehive of a city
that seemed nervous and at the same time sullen, I experienced the unexpected sensation that, yes, I could make a
place for myself here and that I might even aspire to be free
once again.

I had decided in the Madrid airport to change my desti-
nation, for I was seized by a sudden, overpowering desire
to flee everything. I was expected in Spain, but it would be
as strange there to me as the rest of the world: the rum-
bling of the airport, the anonymous faces to which I was

linked by nothing more than a common language. I felt that I was staring into an abyss the edges of which seemed to dissolve amid the heads of a throng of strangers. Once a person is convinced that those around him are not to be trusted, no token of brotherhood will allay the feeling of alienation.

My spinal column tingled with the sensation of being followed, spied upon, and that if I didn't run away immediately, I would collapse. I entered an empty office where employees found me behind a curtain, trembling. I had to hide. Since the whole experience was so senseless and I was dazed, I explained that I'd had a panic attack while my plane was landing and had wandered in there and fainted as I was exhausted, which was obvious from the rings under my eyes and my stammering. I was marooned in Spain for eight whole hours until my flight to London took off. England had occurred to me because my father was English and because I had a workable command of the language, having spoken it daily until I left home. Just at that moment, one of those mental quirks brought back some fragments of poetry. I couldn't remember the lines but I intuited the age-old, enigmatic meaning of a pair of words capable of demarcating life and, very likely, all of humanity—memory and oblivion—a synthesis of the Janus-faced aspects of another pair: past and future.

I was simply glad to be alive. And in view of what had happened, perhaps the solution would be to treat my body to a stay in a foggy land of leaden skies, a corner in which I might be able to find myself without fear of being found. Living in terror as I was, my nerves on edge, I suspected that it would be a good idea to lose myself in the ancient

cover of an island, the way a ship jettisons ballast, with a deep, deep sea to separate off my life.

Defenselessness darkened my spirit, a signal that would define the limits of my actions even more than I imagined. My persecutors, monitors of my conduct, who continue to tyrannize my future, had given me to understand that they would track me down no matter where I tried to hide. They reminded me of this for the last time at the steps to the plane.

London was a stopover for just a few days—I can't say exactly how many. A woman with a Spanish accent at the pub near my bed-and-breakfast suggested that I take a trip to Brighton. Even though it wasn't summer, she knew of two places that were looking for workers and told me how to find them. One of them was a bed-and-breakfast named Bloomy's, located a few blocks from the sea. That's how I came to know Joyce and Peter Sheridan, the proprietors, and how I began to live in a lost town at the edge of calm, blue waters. I walked the stony beaches, my thoughts benumbed by memories and frustrations.

I had nothing in the way of an outlook for the future and would have preferred to vanish into the obscurity of silence, into the afternoon mist that hovered over the unbelievably tranquil, soundless, waveless ocean. My days were saturated with the smell of brine. And they were not clear days, for the light emanating from a sun that hid behind a sheen of clouds did no more than mark the new morning's arrival. The weather was changeable and the sound of the water slapping against the gnarled boards of the fishing boats brought distant lands floating into my imagination. A kind of torpor overtook my senses and feelings. "They" had

changed my landscape, but I kept on searching stubbornly for the colors of other evenings, those I had left behind perhaps for good.

⠿ I was in an ambiguous state, a blend of melancholy and rage (I had been working at Joyce's place for two months), when, after ignoring the evidence for some time, I learned at the Royal Sussex Hospital that I was three months pregnant. Dazed, I ran to the street, overwhelmed, trying to convince myself that it couldn't be true. I was reminded of Juanse, my beloved Ernesto's friend. The resemblance was so striking, the way he had looked off to one side as he talked, one hand propped against the wall, as he let me know tenderly, in a whisper, that they weren't going to kill me. How I had needed to hear those words! Juanse's eyes searching my face, the brush of his hands seeking, possessively, the moistness of my vulva. I opened myself to him as if this were to consecrate my future. Suddenly, I was not feeling the oblivion of captivity, though the figure of Ernesto appeared fleetingly to me, as if he were alive, there, looking at us. I also had the sensation that my friend Nora was peeping. I believed I could recognize the expression of disapproval for an act that consummated a betrayal. But gratification took over and I let myself be carried away in the corner of that filthy cell.

Memory brought back other sensations, even odors and textures. For moments, I was back in the past, that tortured stretch of my life that had shattered my spirit. The chaotic state of my recollections made it impossible for me

to pin down the date of that experience with Juanse. I couldn't get the doctor's questions out of my mind. He had mentioned a specific date and, more than likely, a period during which gestation could have taken place. Suddenly, like a seizure, upon recalling the episode I felt an unbearable pain stabbing my breast. I needed to scream, but clamped my mouth shut in terror. I wanted only to escape to solid ground.

▪▪ I was faced with a townful of strangers and an insurmountable problem. Anxious as I was, I could not allow myself the luxury of desperation. To approach the nurses or doctors in the hospital was useless. I realized that, so I appealed to the girls at the pub and they gave me the address of a midwife who performed abortions. I needed money. On some feeble pretext, I got Joyce to give me an advance. If I close my eyes, I can see her observing me in just the way she had looked at me on the day of the interview when she hired me. Her attitude seemed to be saying, "What the devil does this girl think she's doing applying for a job with such lack of enthusiasm?" Yet, for some reason, Joyce responded gently, overlooking my apparent indifference, inquiring about where I was from and other personal details. She shook her head and regarded me with an expression of such commiseration, reflecting my own so intimately that I had to look away.

I was in a dreadful state at the time I asked her for the money. I hadn't been able to sleep for days, which was causing various problems with my physical reactions—keeping

my balance—and in communicating, struggling for words to the point where people would have to finish sentences for me. My speech was disjointed, but that hardly mattered anymore. And Joyce . . . she simply gave me the money, asking only that I be careful. I felt that I mattered to that fat woman with her crude ways. I knew nothing yet about her life or way of thinking. The one thing I did sense that day was that if I should ever need her, she would be there for me.

Two days later, I went to the midwife's place. It was a morning of strangely excessive heat, as if even the weather wanted to be in key with my own sense of unreality. It began to rain as soon as I stepped off the bus. In any case, I had to run no more than a short distance and suddenly found myself in a room with whitewashed walls, lying on a gurney covered with a sheet. Shortly after, a storm broke, with strong winds, and rain lashing at the window. I hate storms, and that was a particularly violent one. I was uneasy and fidgeted incessantly, which did not seem to bother the midwife, a good-humored woman in her fifties, who moved in and out of the room frequently, scraping her feet over the linoleum-covered floor to make an irritating sound, and whistling and singing as she went.

Time passed as the storm continued, the rain clattering on the galvanized metal roof. Then, all at once, the downpour slackened and a disconcerting silence descended both outside and inside the house. But worst of all was the stench of formaldehyde that had impregnated the walls, combined with that of the perspiring woman. When I complained that the smell disturbed me, she managed a vague smile and answered, "Country perfume, dearie. You're scared, that's normal." But the formaldehyde was unbearable; the place

was inundated with the hellish stuff. I went to a door near
my gurney and opened it. In a glass cabinet I saw a number
of jars of that awful liquid with a blob floating inside each.
Feeling an uncontrollable compulsion to get out of there, I
wanted to scream, to beg for help. I must have bumped
against a cabinet, for a jar fell over, spilling its contents on
the floor. I screamed, realizing that it was a fetus. I'm sure
even now that it was.

I was terrified, unable to breathe, and when I backed off
into the waiting room, the midwife was there, now wearing
a long white apron. She had rubber gloves on and was holding a scalpel. What followed was very quick and I remember only bits—exclamations—of it. She urged me to calm
down, but I was sobbing. I heard her telling me, "You must
calm down. You really must, you know." Her lips were
moving but I could no longer hear what she was saying.
The room began to spin as I noticed a table covered with
scissors, cotton, alcohol bottles, and at that moment I realized they would be rooting about in my body, but before
that could happen, I saw blood streaming from my insides.
I asked the woman not to touch me, I couldn't stand it.
Ignoring me, she kept coming toward me. I saw a hallway
and a door, and the only conceivable thing at that instant
was to flee.

I ached for a silent space inside my head into which I
could shunt the voices that were tormenting me. On the bus
back to Brighton, my mind was a blank. When I got to
Joyce's place, I returned her money.

I worked until very late that day; there were a lot of visitors. Unexpectedly, the act of getting out of that anonymous house had brought me some surcease. It was not until my encounter with the midwife that I became aware of my weakness, my utter inability to go on fighting. I must have had an inkling of something on the voyage that took me from my country to this beach. Then there ensued a decline—a progressive malaise that seeped in each morning, as well as a sobbing that wasn't crying, with which I relieved myself of every unbearable situation. But beyond that, nothing more. The days ran their course, slowly, and I came to no decision. Or rather, I was arriving at one but not taking it.

The midwife became a new specter. At night, I believed I was seeing her, a figure with grim features, swollen eyes, and the tremulous hands of death. The scalpels and scissors floated about in the darkness, their sharp edges terrifying me. Now I know that the pain, and fear of suffering anything like it ever again, had been driving me crazy every one of those nights and days. That pregnancy brought me face to face with my fragility, the mean and dark future that awaited me. I could return to that house, but was still struggling with the visceral rejection of a fresh violation.

I would remain awake till daybreak, as though there had been something unendurable about the night. One day, I stopped eating. I lost weight, began to bleed and have cramps, and at night my system went into some sort of tailspin. As if a miracle had materialized that early morning in March, Joyce was suddenly there in my room on the upper floor of her bed-and-breakfast. She rushed me to the hospi-

tal. The initial diagnosis was cardiac insufficiency and severe anemia. That was when she learned that I was pregnant, but acted as though she had known all along and made no comment. When I was discharged from the hospital, she continued in her role of angel and took me back to live with her and Peter.

:: Joyce and Peter took upon themselves the task of expediting my petition for asylum. Being an Anglo-Argentine was a strong point in my favor for obtaining residence. Initially, I was given a temporary visa, a document with seals and signatures sanctioning my stay on British soil until my troublesome case was decided. I was granted my permanent residency almost four years later.

I felt a part of me evaporate during those years. I'm referring to the energy that drives one onward, that stands in for loss of hope. Nevertheless, though I had been witness to unspeakable bestiality in the past, it failed to shake my faith in human beings. I would cling time and again to the certainty of that; and in fact, I lived under the illusion of having escaped unscathed, at least without major wounds to mind or body.

I smashed up against the truth during the first stage of exile: I hadn't come out of all that without paying dearly. They had managed to wreck a part of my character: my self-confidence had been damaged, and it would never be the same again. I ended up suddenly sunk in a welter of helplessness bordering on the grandiose, unable to ask for help in any way that did not spell anguish. I had cobbled together a platform within myself upon which self-pitying arguments could file by in slow procession, mimicking old wounds.

When Joyce and Peter took me in, I gave them an abbreviated, choked-up version of events, somewhat in the form

of a long telegram, that contained isolated dates and snip-
pets of my past necessary for putting a jigsaw puzzle together. They agreed to help me, according to their lights, of
course. With that Quaker-style severity, they pulled me out
of my despondence. Although they no longer were practicing members of the faith, their concept of morality had
remained unchanged. There was no room for even a
thought of abortion. The crackling of the logs in the fire-
place and the flames that brightened the twilight allayed my
panic to some degree, to say nothing of the awful sense of
alienation. I felt as though all doors were closed to me and I
was at the brink of disaster.

They were silent for a few moments. Peter watched me,
exuding serenity, and Joyce, after fidgeting in her chair,
decided to sit down next to me on the couch facing the big
window that gives onto the sea. Finally, with a heavy sigh,
she said, "Sometimes we have to cope with such challenges.
A painful test almost too difficult to face. There's no doubt
about it, we must overcome the frailty of our natures.
There's no other way out, Mercedes."

She stopped at that since I offered no comment. She tried
to go on while she was showing me my room, but the heart-
felt displeasure on my face brought her up short.

As the days fluttered off the calendar and time yielded to
space as an intrinsic mechanical function, the thought did
not seem alien to me that despite my paralytic state I was
making a choice. But it was a choice that threw my conscience into turmoil. To bear that child meant living with a
chunk of the past—the most dreadful part of it—before me
all the time. That child would keep the moments of my
humiliation alive in vivid sequence. Since life, however,

moves in pendular arcs, and diagrams are of little use in depicting reality, the fact of the matter is that in five months I would be giving birth to—what difference did it make?—a boy or a girl.

Joyce tolerated my self-absorption with a mixture of irritation and indifference. She seemed prepared for experiential processes of this kind, as though she believed that God set them out along the road in order to put His power and kindness to the test. It wasn't that she welcomed it or had no trouble dealing with it. But it did lend credence to the possibility of things being turned around. She harbored the strange conviction that a human being emerges strengthened by facing such obstacles. Arguing with those two would have been pointless, for their scale of values was so rigid there could be no valid rationale for certain kinds of behavior. Ergo, God gave life for it to be used in doing good.

The scene I described to them has remained frozen in time. Nothing of what happened will ever replay. But I would have wished to keep silent at the time, not to relive all that again.

▪▪ I remember Joyce's expression. She was trying hard to understand my story. I could see her gaze fixed on me, but I was far off in the past. My face, my gestures, must have conveyed a sensation of utter defeat, something I was no longer able to conceal from anyone. Our relation was tense in that period, for I was not about to accept advice of any kind, and Joyce knew this. I worked at Bloomy's until practically the last day.

A visit from Kate, Joyce and Peter's only daughter, with her protruding belly and smiling face, was the one thing that had a calming effect on me. Of all the people I know, Kate is the one with the fewest conflicts, if she has any at all. She looked so glorious, so flushed with health, in such constant good humor, as though expecting a child was a woman's ideal state. Listening to her talk about her belly, tell of her plans for the child to be born about the same time as mine, as if all the world was waiting, was for me a haven of tranquility. The splendid bulk of that belly of hers— forged with the marvelous precision of the atavistic power of the pregnant woman— synthesized the age-old mystery of gestation. She put into words her feelings for the child about to be born—words that had the weight and glow of joy. "They're going to be friends," she would tell me, as we strolled the beach at the water's edge, her coppery hair blowing into her gray eyes and her mouth as she poured out words of reassurance. She was going to name hers Frank if it were a boy and Shelley if a girl. I couldn't imagine any name at all for my daughter, not until the moment I had to register her. I said "Julia" as if that had been in my mind all those months. It's spelled the same in English and Spanish.

She had her Shelley a week later, after a short, easy labor. She left the nursery, rocking the newborn in her arms and cooing to it. When she showed it to me, I could hear the soft breathing. It was a beautiful little girl who looked "already weaned," as they say in my country. She weighed just under ten pounds, a redheaded doll with milky-white skin.

▚ Julia was born in September, on a mild night early in what was to be an unusual autumn. The breeze off the sea wafted in gently. The fishermen coming ashore from that soundless immensity commented that even the Channel was calm. Three days later, a storm broke that swept away every beach umbrella on the esplanade. The water turned deep gray and the stones on the beach took on a greenish opaline sheen. A chill and a silence now set in that marked the onset of a change in Brighton's geography.

When they set my baby down on my lap, I felt my heart shiver. She was fragrant as a rose, skin so smooth and velvety, high cheekbones, a little nose; all tiny, cuddling into my breast. She was born after a long wait, months without end, and ten hours of difficult labor. They were saying that I didn't want to push so the doctor gave up and ordered a cesarean. I remember that Joyce came over to me, a woman of decision, whispering into my ear, as she dried my forehead, that one mustn't gamble with life, encouraging me to be brave. When they lifted my back, she and the doctor between them, a tremendous surge forced my insides open with a rending and flapping, like a hot current that become a whirlpool in my innermost channel. I heard a cry and, then, "A girl, Mercedes, healthy and beautiful." With that I burst into tears as I had never wept in all my life.

They told me I talked to myself for hours. I don't remember. They said that I was speaking in my language, that when the time finally came to nurse my baby, I mum-

bled something they didn't understand. As soon as they put the baby to my breast, she seized the nipple with such a will to life that Joyce and Peter's faces lit up with joy.

I had lost a lot of weight during pregnancy, but gained back over thirty pounds. When I washed my hair during that time, some would fall out, but when it grew back after Julia was born, I pulled it out in tufts. It became curly, too. Once, when I saw myself in the mirror, I was shocked. That couldn't be me—no part of my reflection was recognizable.

The contours of my body, of my days, had changed. Whenever I looked out at the ocean, all I could see was the calm waters. Although the nights were enlivened by the songs of the fishermen, life for me was in a state of suspension, and I felt nothing but resentment and urgency to get out of there. Julia was a lovely baby, I must admit. I had to laugh out loud at the way she gurgled, my prejudices vanishing. Yet . . . almost instantaneously, guilt, her frightful origin, would break in. And so, I imprinted those contradictions upon her. Julia was subject to my fate. I reigned over her days, but later on, perhaps, not over her future. However, she was in my power for the time being. And I would find myself standing there, observing her, as if she were a character in a representation of some kind, unrelated to me.

From time to time, a scene involving my daughter comes to mind. We were on the beach one morning early in June, Kate with Shelley, I with Julia. Joyce had insisted that we take the babies for a bathe in the sea. It must have been

early, for the temperature of the water was ideal and the sun not yet very hot. There were no tourists to speak of, except the usual early birds at their morning calisthenics. Julia didn't care for routines that called for her to stay put; or, at least, that's what I claimed. Kate would keep telling me I had to be more patient, and was at it hammer and tongs that morning, when suddenly Julia slipped from my arms into the water before I knew it. I stood there paralyzed as I watched her float momentarily, and then, in no more than a second, go under. Kate's screams brought me to my senses, but by then she already had Julia in her arms and was talking to me from the water. I looked off to one side where Shelley, sensibly shod for that stony beach, had remained in her stroller, not making a sound.

As soon as I turned back to them, Kate went into a tirade about my behavior. I had never seen her in a fury and made no attempt to answer until finally I'd had enough. Snatching Julia away from her, I yelled at her to shut up and warned her, "Don't you ever again tell me how to take care of my daughter. You may be an excellent mother, but save it for your Shelley."

"What happened?" she asked in anguish. "You stood there just looking at her while—oh, my God!—she was drowning."

"I was taken by surprise, just like you," I answered as I dried Julia off. "I didn't realize what was happening until she was already in the water."

"That's no excuse. It's your daughter," she exclaimed angrily, "and you didn't react. You had the oddest look on your face. Mercedes, you were just watching her as she fell. You saw her in the water and didn't make a move."

"She's alive. That's what matters, isn't it?"

At that moment Julia stirred and began to slip away again, but I gave her a good shaking, at the same time yelling, "You must be a good girl and stay right here!"

Kate interrupted nervously, her voice trembling, "You mustn't talk to her that way."

"Leave me alone, Kate."

"You are supposed to give love, and what you did is sinful," she said with a deep sigh, as she looked off in another direction. She went on immediately, "I may not be educated like you, but I do know this much, your daughter is not only a concern of yours . . . if you don't look after her, when a person doesn't carry out their responsibilities . . ."

"Excuse me, Kate," I interrupted, as I stuffed Julia's clothes into a canvas bag while trying to keep the newspaper from flying away, "I've given you a chance to participate and express your opinion. You've helped me and I thank you."

I looked at her, nodding my head. Kate chose to turn hers away.

However, she did say, "I already told my mum, just yesterday"—her voice seemed to take on a flutey tone of self-importance—"not all women make good mothers."

I was bending over getting my things together, but those words and the accompanying gestures conveyed all the arrogance with which they were poured out, and they got to me.

"Oh," I said, "do I happen to have come before a messenger from God? What gives you the right to say who is better than whom? You aren't any better—you can't even lose weight, even though you keep saying you want to. Look at

you. You're fat, sloppy. But do I tell you what kind of figure you should have? Do I force you to step lively because walking with you is like marching in a funeral procession? Do I criticize you because you don't even read the daily paper and aren't interested in any subject other than your family? Did I ever tell you that you spoil Shelley?"

"But I don't." She was annoyed. "Children require love."

"And bathes in the sea, and prayers?"

People were about on the beach and Kate was uncomfortable with the argument. She kept looking around, and asked me to lower my voice as she greeted a woman who was approaching. I took advantage of the moment to make my exit, telling her the heat was bothering me.

"Wait, I'll come along with you," Kate said, and fell in behind me, making an effort to walk faster. "Wait," she called again, "here, you've dropped Julia's bonnet."

I stopped, took the bonnet, and looked at her. Obviously, she was still sitting in judgment. Her expression practically accused me of wanting to kill my daughter, and I suddenly had the impression that I had been expelled from the world. I began to speak in Spanish as I carried Julia, nude, folded the stroller and dragged it along the esplanade. I remember that Kate was following me, wild-eyed, as though she were seeing the devil himself. She kept repeating, "I don't understand. Talk English."

There I was, laughing, talking, and crying all at once. "I want out, to go home, now. I don't want to take care of anybody. God knows, I need to be taken care of myself. By somebody who speaks Spanish"—I touched an older man, who glanced at me with British phlegm, indifferent—"You're all perfect, and I'm drowning here. I'm . . ."

All at once a look from Julia buoyed up my spirits. In the
midst of this headlong frenzy, I had come to a halt, as we
did every day at that spot, to settle the children in their
strollers just before we reached the esplanade. So there I
was, Julia's bonnet in my hand, talking Spanish, when
something, a special warmth in those blue eyes of hers,
caught my attention. Kate was saying something. I gestured
with my head and she, annoyed, replied in kind. I had suddenly felt something. It was Julia's hand brushing across my
cheek. I turned in surprise to meet her insistent, bright-eyed
stare, as she stood up on the stroller stretching her arms out
to me. She was going to be ten months old in a few days,
and I rarely picked her up to caress her.

That morning, though, something changed—Julia's
hand touching my face that way produced an unexpected
reaction, a sensation of having had pleasure lavished upon
me. I can't explain it very well. I just picked her up in my
arms. And it was right there, that very morning, that I
taught her her first word in Spanish. I opened my mouth,
said, "Mamá," and repeated the word over and over again as
I stroked her fine hair and passed my fingertips over the
tender folds of her delicate face. I stopped short in stupefaction when I heard her repeat, "Mamá," and then I felt as
though a smile were making room for itself on my lips and
in my entire being.

Kate went ahead to the house with Shelley and I stayed
on the beach with Julia, since I had decided to take the day
off. That day I rocked my daughter for hours, talked to her
about my country, singing a song for her, one that goes,
"Duerme, duerme, negrita, que tu mamá está a tu lado (Sleep,
sleep, little darling, your mama's right here)." It wasn't so

much the words as the sound of my country, the cadence of the music, of a mother's lullaby for her daughter. I savored my language with Julia; she didn't take her big eyes off me. And I touched her, looked at her, as if recognizing her for the first time, until nightfall darkened the vista of my new life.

:: I heard noises at the door a little while ago, but when I opened it nobody was there. The hands of the clock keep moving. I count the seconds. I feel certain: Julia will be coming. I'm looking at my daughter's album; a few pages at the beginning are empty. An inscription, repeated in a nervous hand, says, "Past, no clues." True, there are only photos of Brighton and London, as if everything began here. It is an expurgated album, incomplete. I did what I could but it was insufficient. That is also true.

The telephone rang a few seconds ago. It was Mickey. If he's calling her it must be because she's on her way, I think excitedly.

When Julia and Mickey are together, harmony reigns; they are obviously in love. Sometimes I get to imagining them in the future, their lives surely growing as a couple. I was in love with Ernesto at that age. Not that they're similar, it's just that they are about the same age. Of course, Ernesto's image is my memory of it. His face comes to mind often: a tiny scar at the edge of his upper lip, his way of looking at me, of kissing me, his wonderful hands at the intimacies of my body, the virile contact of his body against mine. I became a woman at sixteen, and in subsequent years I felt that I had learned how to give myself. Something I never experienced again, and that was a long time ago. To this day, I feel that my trust in love had remained with the body I wept over on that tragic afternoon. It remained in Ernesto's bleeding body sprawled on the floor. I knew at the

same moment that, with his death, something vital and irrevocable had vanished.

Now, it all happens in my head, as if trusting somebody else might depend upon an acquired mechanism or possibly one's own will. I managed to remake my life in many ways but not that one. Much time has elapsed, enough perhaps to allow another man to occupy my thoughts, to shelter me with his hopes. Perhaps seeing myself in the mirror of another's eyes will make me giddy.

How long ago did all this take place? It was, in fact, so long ago that I wonder where in my body my sensuality and need for love has remained trapped. Perhaps I could be satisfied with the frisson from a certain glance, which I don't want to talk about now, as though it were something shameful, as though to feel this way would profane that immaterial space in memory.

And, again and again, I go over the sequence of events, the more distant and the most recent. While my daughter was growing up, I elected to give her a sketchy story with many loose ends. I knew it was incongruent, but stuck with it as though it were absolute reality. At any rate, up until a short time ago, Julia accepted my ambiguities, giving them the credibility I needed to continue down that road.

When she began to question me about her origins, the story I told her was that her father was an Irishman by the name of Ian, who was a sailor, and that he had been killed in a shipboard accident. I rounded out that lie with the explanation that the reason for there being no relatives and

the forgetting of surnames was due to our "relationship" having been very brief and intense. According to my elaborately embroidered tale, he had gone off to sea, thrilled with the news that he was going to be a father.

Children detect lies, being skillful trackers of what we try to hide. Perhaps my expression, the way my eyes would avoid hers whenever she brought the subject up, or maybe the flimsiness of the explanation, kept Julia on the alert ever since she was a little girl. She never understood and never forgave me for having been deprived of her grandparents' love. She could not understand why there were never any letters or telephone calls, never accepted the stubbornness with which I blocked off that connection. Since feelings tend to be inexplicable in the face of despair, I imagined embracing them and taking them to my heart, because my body continued to yearn for that contact, although the magnitude of the offense outweighed the urgency of my need.

Julia looks so much like my sister Alicia, accents the syllables in Spanish the way she did, frowns like her when she's annoyed, and although she hesitates before making up her mind, she resolves her inner conflicts quickly, letting the whole world know about them. That's what Alicia was like. And physically? Well, so far, almost the same height, hair color similar, although, actually, Alicia's was more on the chestnut side. If she were here looking at Julia, she would swear she was just like me, only perhaps lacking a certain characteristic expression in the photographs of Great-grandmother Mercedes. I would say she has less of the Beecham genes than those of my mother's side, a family of very mixed blood. Besides, Alicia would not have criti-

cized me, I'm sure; she always said that nobody was as severe a judge as I was of myself.

On one of the last opportunities I had to see my sister, she was wearing earrings—a pair of little pearls set in tiny gold petals, a present from my parents on her fifteenth birthday. Sitting over a cup of coffee at a table in the coffee shop on the corner of the college street, she told me that she was leaving our aunt's house and moving in with a girlfriend. She seemed removed, uneasy. When I asked her what was going on, she smiled strangely.

"You're as curious as ever, I'm glad to see," she said, looking tired, as she glanced at the people at other tables. "I've become a person of independent means, one of those who don't have to pay rent. Aunty is getting on and needs peace and quiet."

"Why don't you come back home then?" I asked ingenuously.

Alicia cut me off nervously, putting the earrings in my hand and asking me to take care of them for her. In fact, she urged me to put them on right then and there. Disconcerted, I refused.

"I want to see how they look on you. You're the only one who can keep them for me, the only one I'd trust."

Her expression was so sad that I couldn't refuse. They are the only earrings I have worn since that day, with a break now and then, of course. There was a time when I thought I hadn't been able to keep my promise. For a long time I was sure that I had lost them, until somebody returned them to me years ago.

A gust of wind just blew a shutter closed in the living room. On my way there, my attention was caught by a photograph that Joyce had framed some fourteen years ago. It was taken at the Brighton house, with the sea visible in the background. Julia is blowing out the candles on her second birthday. She is wearing a blue dress with lace edging on the collar, handmade by Joyce. Although not everybody is in the picture, the main members of the Sheridan family are there. It was stifling in the room, two wood-burning stoves throwing off an infernal heat. Perhaps that explains the redness of everybody's cheeks, but they are all smiling. I am a few steps from Julia, frozen in a gesture which may be interpreted as denoting surprise.

I remember that day so filled with activity, bursting with news of change: the closing of the sale of Bloomy's and the purchase of premises in London. The opening of the new restaurant was set for the end of October, which explains the hectic preparations of that time, a time of buying and selling, of the routine of contracts, schedules, and the anxiety of petty details that set my existence in turmoil.

Nevertheless, I returned to my tasks like a robot, and helped too with getting the bills out. That morning, on the day of the photograph, while I was piling folders and boxes on the table and floor and preparing a cup of coffee, a set of London telephone books caught my attention. The sun was streaming in through the big window in the kitchen. Without thinking much about what I was doing, I picked up one

of the phone books with the idea of checking through for the name Beecham. I knew that the original branch of the family lived in Devonshire, and because of trips my father had made to London, I was aware that he had visited certain relatives until only a few years ago. Flipping through the B's I found two names, both in the Mayfair district. I was uncertain about what to do with the information. I shut the book with mounting uneasiness and got busy putting the year's bills and receipts in order. Annoyed as I worked, I mulled over my thoughts regarding family names: a family name does not constitute a charter of brotherhood; it is an invention, a mere allegory for the unattached, which I repeated with the sadness imparted by lucidity. Balm for my wounds was not to be found in strange houses, with people to whom I was linked by nothing but seven letters in a row. It seemed impossible for me easily to bring any order to the chaos of my existence. There were moments in these years when I could have wished to be ingenuous, to play a little at make-believe, because knowledge is not a safety net over the void.

The change was upending me, and I grew uneasy that morning. I was trying to imagine what living in London might be like, for in Brighton, everything was predictable. I had already established a circular routine of some twenty streets, which included the bank, the supermarket, Bloomy's, the beach, and the amusement park. I was able to keep up with things there and, generally, I would get the latest town gossip from the guests. Amy, the owner of the supermarket, was in the habit of sending messages to Joyce, anecdotes about the behavior of Brighton denizens. Peter would bring back tidings of his family in London and, inci-

dentally, any newsworthy clippings. I read the local paper and plunged once in a while into the world of the British press, dawdling over the crime pages where the baseness of humanity, its frailty and madness, is exposed in a few lines. Reading that section made me feel less of a foreigner, as though evil, while it may wear many faces, remains essentially the same.

Joyce caught me talking to myself. She had come into the kitchen without my noticing to show me the sandwich she had prepared for Julia. She was already at my side when she said with an air of perplexity, "I understand you asked Amy for a job—how come?"

Her voice was soft, but the tone was that of a person who has been hurt, certainly not one dealing with a workplace complaint.

"Working for Amy might be a good thing . . . too bad she doesn't look at it that way."

"She's my friend, Mercedes. I'm quite surprised, particularly in view of all we've done for you."

I shut my eyes and said nothing for a few moments. Why would I want to remain in Brighton, and with Amy, a woman whose main interest in life was keeping her shelves looking neat? But, I had to admit that Joyce had a point; they had been kind and good to me and to Julia. So I said to her, "London is a city, this is a small town. I'm not sure you'll understand this, but I have trouble imagining myself living there."

"You'll get used to it. You'll even be able to resume your studies. Peter and I have discussed it. This kind of work is not for you. You have your career; you have to think of changing certain things . . ."

I must admit that Joyce made me nervous. She was thinking of my future; I couldn't even contemplate moving. I remember that I closed the conversation with a remark about modifications that would have to be made in our accounting system in the new place. Joyce just nodded, understanding that I didn't want to pursue the matter.

That segment of life in Brighton seems to me even now like something tacked on to reality. Since life had dealt with me so capriciously, and I was in fact alive, I had no expectations. At that point, it was not unusual for me to wake up sobbing over something I had been dreaming.

For years, I had a recurring nightmare in which I was being chased by a man in a circular maze that constricted to smother me for moments, only to expand again as though I were at the center of a beating heart. Panting, I saw blood, heard whispers, sobs, somebody muttering, and without being able to see his face I managed to run away, or thought I did. The way out was through a door of a room suspended in space. In it were a woman wearing a red dress and an adolescent girl in a school uniform, both standing, their eyes fixed on a huge painting that took up an entire wall. It was of a vast, green plain, the wind ruffling the crowns of some trees, and the sun in a sky bluer than one could possibly imagine. Suddenly, the man who had been chasing me in the maze brushed by and, ignoring me, stepped into the painting. He climbed a tree and was adding artificial flowers, yellow and inordinately large. The colors then turned more and more riotous until they faded. Immediately, great gluey drops began pouring into the room like a river, flooding it, sticking to the women's clothing, staining them, finally sliding off into the void. When night fell, sounds, voices, approaching footsteps could be heard, until a blinding light lit up an enormous rooster that made the walls

explode as he attacked the two women with his beak. Suspended from a white ribbon together with some yellow ducks and parts of the tree's branches, they both managed to escape. I stayed, looking at the picture, bewildered and alone. A drab, opaline patina had remained on the left side and the background had changed to a faded brown.

This was a mysterious language, surfacing from the very entrails of my being, perhaps in an effort to understand or not to forget. My fear and tortured past clung to my brain with barbaric cruelty. The persistence of images awakened the most disparate recollections. But I didn't want to talk; it was still too painful. I found that I was happiest when alone, holding few conversations and then only on essentials. After the altercation on the beach with Kate, nothing of moment happened. Life in Brighton remained on an even keel, orderly and easily forgettable. Nothing mattered to me outside my work at Bloomy's and bringing up my daughter. I was huddled in my shell; all that remained of a once sociable young woman was a friendly greeting for neighbors, and, as far as work was concerned, a smile for guests at the bed-and-breakfast.

But it was time for a change. Life followed its course, mine together with the Sheridans'. They opened their restaurant in London and I came with them as a waitress, balancing my tray with the best of them and trying not to think too much. The London rhythm was very different and it was hard to remain detached. As if that were not enough, as in the case of any new language, there was a burgeoning of strange faces and situations. In that populous city, my fears swelled to an almost uncontainable level, beset by out-of-the-way corners, blind alleys, new shouts and noises.

I worked at the restaurant for a year and a half. They sought my advice in picking a name for it and I suggested a philosopher's. It was installed above the newly painted entrance: "Hobbes' Place." I recalled some of his concepts: the need on the part of the state to prevent the worst evil by freeing its people from fear of violent death. Apparently, he was particularly sensitized to all issues relating to that topic. But he was not my favorite philosopher. I had read little on him, and at that period, I recalled his name just as a blip on my student past.

The streets smelled of books and paintbrushes. Bloomsbury was the home of artists, writers, and thinkers, intellectuals then and now. In time, Hobbes' Place became quite popular. The initial months, however, were disastrous. There was competition in the area since the same variety of food and drink was offered by most places. Lowering prices didn't work, revenues dropped, and we were on the brink of shutting down. Joyce cried at night and I couldn't find words enough to console her, for I saw no way out. It was a hard, chilly, desolate winter.

My daily walks with Julia were an experience. I would observe life on those streets, especially the young people out strolling, sunning themselves in the squares, sitting in their hangouts, smoking, reading, writing. That world, like a mirror, reflected my own, now buried beneath other experiences.

And on various occasions I wandered up and down the corridors of the School of Philosophy at the University of London by myself, unable to muster the courage to make inquiries. Finally, I ventured into the Admissions Office one day to ask about scholarships and was given application forms to fill out. At my interview, when the rather pleasant

woman on the other side of the desk asked why I was a refugee, the reason I gave her was not nearly as dramatic as the real one. She tried to pump me for further details but came up against my evasiveness. What won the day for me, perhaps, was the assurance with which I navigated the waters of ambiguity. However, I suspect that what really carried the most weight was my record, including, as I now believe, the attached file on my residence application.

In any case, I summarized my two most turbulent years as a philosophy student in Argentina. Most of my courses had equivalencies in the British curriculum and my interviewer seemed assured that I had received a good foundation at the university there. I remember that she remained silent as I expressed my feelings at length about what studying philosophy meant to me: thinking of our universe from a number of different standpoints, even though they were at variance with abstract concepts and entities disassociated from humankind. I believe that I succeeded in my interview in reawakening passion, my pulses quickening in the discussion, but only in my body and my heart, for the woman heard me out stolidly. Still, her manner at the end of the interview gave me hope. She said that the steps to be set in motion shortly could possibly be quite rewarding.

I left there buoyed up, and by the time I was back at Hobbes' Place I was feeling quite elated. In fact, it was one of my more communicative days. I described the interview (part of it) to Joyce, a moment she had apparently been waiting for. Several times that day I caught her eyes fixed on me, big green eyes, following me or Julia as we moved about the place. She was already envisaging the parting of the ways—and so was I.

Ever since that period, I have been driven by a pressing need to make something of my life. Delay was the inevitable counterweight. I needed a purpose and I now had it in the career I was about to pursue. In the midst of my daily routine, the days dragged on.

One morning, I took a bus that Joyce said would bring me close to a shop where I was to pick out a lamp. I got off at the corner but could see no sign of the place in any direction. The crowded street and a huge building looming up at me out of the fog made me nervous. A passerby told me it was the Imperial War Museum.

Confused, I went in without knowing why. In one room with light filtering through a glass ceiling I saw a platform with a pair of airplanes, alongside a cannon, relics of the First World War, and possibly the Second. I was about to leave, for I had no interest in those immobile machines, participants in what were once undoubtedly world-shaking events.

Near the exit, my attention was caught by some dimly lighted showcases, particularly one that contained pens, ink bottles, and brittle sheets of yellowed writing paper— frozen symbols that transported me hypnotically into the odious ambiance of war. Other elements contributed to the sensation of being present in a resurrected past: noises, bombs exploding, smoke coming out one corner, footsteps, sounds of panting, turmoil . . . John, only twenty years old, wrote to his sweetheart promising they would soon be together again; another whose name was illegible begged

God to get him out of that hell. This or that one sitting in tents on mounds of earth, yearning for an embrace, or hoping that the device of writing would miraculously connect him for a moment with the family he had left to plunge into devastation and madness. Distressing pages under glass in an inert wooden showcase.

My eyes then wandered to an opening from which strange noises emanated. A length of damp, tattered cloth covered the entry to a pathway without sky, a slot in the earth, a remarkable recreation of a World War I trench, choking with darkness and whispers, voices and the sound of guns, stinking of gunpowder and fear.

I walked in there as though descending into the bowels of hell, until, at a bend, I stopped before a dummy, a figure that looked almost alive in the haze of smoke and loneliness in that hollow in the earth. The voice of that soldier frozen in history emerged from somewhere. He was talking about his hope of seeing his parents. He described what had happened the day before, Christmas Eve, to be exact. A fleeting armistice had been granted for a vague period: under a star-studded sky, they had offered up a toast together with the enemy, had exchanged gifts with them, cigarettes, chocolates. He was saying:

> It was something truly remarkable, Mother. We drank with them as if we were just people and there was no war. I can't forget those faces, of the ones I am going to have to fight tomorrow . . . some of them practically lads like me. For a few hours we celebrated, what I don't know. Being alive, I suppose. . . . It's all so unbelievable. I'm sure I'll make it out alive, so I pray for you and you do the same for me.

I stayed in the trench for a while, looking out through an opening in the wall at the maze of a fake no-man's-land. A recording played out a background of sounds reminiscent of a faraway war. I remained listening to hand grenades exploding, the movement of crawling bodies, labored breathing. There was an expression of sad resignation in the dummy's eyes.

I left there exhausted, strangely disturbed and headed straight for the street and the nearest pub. Sitting over a pint of ale, I saw the headlines: England and Argentina were at war over the Falkland Islands. So, it was true. I had heard about it the night before on television. The Prime Minister announced that she would bring to bear all the forces at her command to repel this invasion of British territory. I remained transfixed by the aerial images of the islands and the maneuvers of the British fleet. The mock demonstration of armed might at the War Museum seemed to me almost more real than those voices and scenes on television. Chance had directed my steps to a special museum. It was as though chance once again had placed me where it was impossible not to dwell upon the news.

A loud conversation—an argument over a football game—brought me back to reality. A group of men—Brits, of course—were discussing this new confrontation over their beers. I couldn't understand them—they were talking among themselves. I remember thinking how senseless it all seemed, and since I had nobody with whom to exchange ideas, or even to chat with about unrelated, inconsequential matters, I stayed put. Then I went over to the cigarette machine and, for the first time in my life, bought a packet. And I stayed there smoking one cigarette after another.

Time stopped. All I know is that I entered in broad daylight and left when it was getting dark. But the one memory that has stayed with me was that of a profound sense of deprivation and, once again, an unbearable loneliness.

At that moment I wanted, as never before, to hear my name on the lips of my people, spoken in a very ordinary, everyday manner. Then something unusual happened. I thought I felt a familiar hand on my shoulder, and when I turned around expectantly, I saw it was the lad at the cash register holding out my change. I couldn't control my annoyance, despite his having been quite friendly. I ordered another pint. I had to stay there. I looked off vaguely at a point elsewhere in the room; everything was blurry—the people, the pictures, the wooden booths, everything. What was I doing in a country at war with mine? Nothing, of course, I immediately thought. That peculiar war had turned me into a foreigner in both places, in my own country and the country that had given me asylum. Thinking about that vast museum again, I was perplexed. Anybody who looked at that exposition could not help concluding that the British have had more than enough experience in waging war.

I was deeply upset for hours. I took a bus for one block, went to the Underground, got on a train and off again in the same station. I was badly disoriented but didn't want to ask for help. Wandering aimlessly, I was in and out of various bars, bewildered by the turmoil around me. It was close to midnight when I finally reached Joyce's house. I felt tongue-tied; words wouldn't come to mind readily. It was as though I couldn't speak English. Joyce let me in. I could see by her expression that she understood what was happening

to me. There was no need for words. She gave me some dinner and told me that I had better not come to work the following day, to get a night's sleep and take Julia for a walk in
the morning.

I stood staring at myself for a while in the bathroom mirror. The news had stirred up an inevitable procession of
yearnings, emotions, that massed demandingly in my body.
Again, I longed to see that look in certain eyes, the eyes of
one's intimates, charged with meaning, with the understanding of those familiar with my frailties and strengths,
those into whose dreams I was invited—the gaze of my
own people. All at once, light filtered in from the corner
street lamp, an unfailing prelude to rain borne on a gust of
wind. I observed that dark sky, a storm on its brow, always.
My body and my fate were bound to a city, a country in
which the sun is elusive.

◼◼ I changed . . . most certainly changed. I used to believe in immutability; certain habits, even one's own nature, don't change, I told myself. Well, true in a way. In adulthood, one develops another way of understanding actions, including particular behaviors. However, when people have gone through a variety of experiences and then find oneself obliged to live in another land, something dies inside one. I can't know nor venture to predict what will happen, but I sense a constant foreboding of unhappiness. I am certain that it will be impossible for me to avoid the descent in my memory to events cluttered there, because I also know that oblivion is impossible. Among the changes I recognize is that of mood. I keep quiet practically always, laughing only occasionally when I'm surprised by something, very surprised. I had not been withdrawn before but became so on this island. I never thought of myself as a dreamer until, after a long time, I realized that I had been off in limbo.

And so much is lost through migration of this sort. It would seem trivial if I listed what I am afraid I will forget, but intuition tells me that part of me has remained in those places. Hard as I try, I cannot bring back the scent of jasmine in the fields of the Azul countryside. Yet, my taste buds refuse to exorcise the flavor of bitter *mate*. During the first phase of my exile, I couldn't forget the dampness of Buenos Aires, that persistent drizzle that implacably sprayed Lake Palermo. And I wondered if the ducks were still there and if it was as dirty as usual. I was beset by the

most diverse memories, especially those of the common-
place kind. Of course, Paco, the factotum at the café on the
corner of the school, must still be there with his double-
entendres, taking charge of all matters related to traffic,
directing the jitneys, taxis, and pedestrians with the high-
handedness of self-imposed authority. How many potholes
would he have talked the authorities into fixing by now?

While I was living in Buenos Aires, I would complain
about its chaos, its irreverent facade. But here, from this out-
post, I earnestly wished that not a finger be laid on Avenida
Corrientes without my consent. Because here I had to give
up goat cheese and could no longer recall the taste of the
sweets or wonderful vegetable soups prepared at our country house by Aurora, my mother's cook, even when temperatures were in the nineties. No English cheese or candy can
match those particular flavors, nor did any of the sauces I
tasted even remotely approach the majestic tang of bay leaf
and other spices, mysterious mixtures, the magical spells of
my childhood. I began to forget the names of the streets parallel to Avenida de Mayo. Then I had to make an effort—I
keep notebooks with such jottings, my exile diary—to
imprint on my mind the names of the squares, the bus lines,
the memories of each strand and particle of the textures I can
no longer see. On many nights I wept. I still do now, when I
feel the absence of my perfumes, the streets I strolled in
hope. A city is the people who inhabit it and who put up
with it, too. Streets without inhabitants are impersonal. I
wanted to remember places, because that geography had
sheltered me in its nooks and crannies, found me in its
cafés—arguing, thinking, speculating, observing the hubbub of that city, now greatly changed, no doubt.

To say nothing of the odors. An English rose doesn't smell like an Argentine rose. The expressions on the faces of the people are unfamiliar, and even the jostling is different in my country. I spent years without getting the point of an English joke and, believe me, I tried, because I needed a laugh.

I was beset by deepest melancholy whenever I revisited my forbidden land through its images. To tell the truth, everything that was happening to me was alien, and ambivalence was one of my secret devices for survival. Very often, as I walked the crowded London streets, I would see images from the past. A face, a figure I followed for blocks, an accent, a tone, that finally turned out to be Chilean or Colombian. And I did have occasional opportunities to talk to Argentines, but only out of the habit of ordinary survival. I confined myself to listening to the singsong of their voices, to watching them walk, although some resembled my parents or my uncles and aunts—worldly people, in whom nationality is sometimes unrecognizable.

Frankly, after these years of British orderliness, I longed for the chaos of Buenos Aires, but I knew that going back was impossible. I felt powerless to change my transient fate; and since that's how it was, I couldn't bear it.

I began smoking that day in the pub near the museum and soon became heavily addicted, as if nostalgia could be turned into smoke, and anguish over my loss puffed away. I was to understand that staking out a future inevitably involves becoming embroiled in certain contradictions. I was to learn that following where fate leads is a more challenging and difficult task when one is living in exile. The everyday landscape was different, the horizon blurred by

the succession of buildings, parks, streets, and foreign impedimenta. I felt my innermost being betrayed, although I was no longer certain of its nature. There were moments when it seemed to me that reality was no more than bits of a dream—a strange, extremely bizarre dream. There was one point when I was sure only that I belonged nowhere. The ground had been pulled out from under me and I was lost in the clouds.

After almost four years, I was granted British residency. Some months later, the University of London notified me that my application for a scholarship had been approved for study in its philosophy program. I went to live there in a college flat with Julia. A new phase of my life was about to begin; I could feel my legs trembling. The world is asymmetrical. The rules in a London college would be a far cry from those at Hobbes' Place, but I was going to abide by them, no matter what.

And so, I put myself in the disquieting position of having to adopt a pattern of conduct laid out in a rigorously predetermined program, obsessively conceived and evaluated: living for what is to come, yes, but with everything prescribed, nothing improvised. There came a moment when I managed to situate myself outside my body. Having given a new twist to my old reactions, I was now ready for the main bout: to incorporate myself successfully into London. Julia adapted rapidly to our flat and her kindergarten. Moreover, Joyce did not relinquish her role as grandmother, nor Kate hers as aunt. Julia paid regular visits to play with Shelley. I began cutting back on my visits, pleading my heavy schedule. Now that I think of it, they never reproached me for my often curt and selfish behavior. But I had to cut loose from their output of advice and the critical glint in their eyes.

At the same time, I had no desire to make friends. And so I moved in solitary mode, existing more for remem-

brance than the reality at hand. My body retained the sensation of inching along a ledge, fear tugging at my sides. Faced with change of any kind, I stared into the void, cold sweat trickling down the length of my spine.

I thought I might be suffering from gastritis and went to see a doctor. He prescribed rest, a special diet, said he thought my problems were the cause of my condition, and suggested that I take life less seriously. I couldn't. Spasms continued that doubled me over with pain. I felt as though a thousand swordsmen were jabbing rapiers into the walls of my abdomen. And I had a habit of looking down as I walked, eyes fixed on the pavement, inexplicably seized by panic. I was almost convinced that a ditch would suddenly open in my path, or in the street, and, unable to call for help, I could be dragged into it by a force emanating from that void. I then imagined that the edges of that ditch would knit together over me and nobody would miss me. I continued to feel that I was being watched—a sensation I was unable to shake for years. I thought that any face or figure could be that lurking villain's. Nothing ever happened to justify my obsession, yet I remained alert and was thus always silent and withdrawn.

However, when classes began, I was obliged to adapt to existence at a different pace within a fairly large student body. I was plunged for months into the routine of hallways, classrooms, and classmates, into a student's reality for one whose age was out of sync. In class, I took notes and asked no questions. If anyone approached me in an effort to strike up a friendship, I took evasive action.

Speaking good English did not make communication any easier. After a few months at the school, I began to feel very

uncomfortable. My classmates' ways irritated me and I strove to keep aloof from any exchange of ideas. They annoyed me. The worst of it was that when their assumptions seemed off the beam, I couldn't find arguments with which to challenge them. I was in disagreement because I was in disagreement, as silly and unhinged as that may seem. When I listened to the professors and my classmates, I often did not get what they meant even though I understood every word. The thing is that certain topics cannot be translated, are not common to all cultures. It was unbelievable. After an almost exciting initial period in my studies, I plummeted into a phase of intolerance. I became a grotesque rebel, opposing everything, acting like an adolescent.

The autumn was drawing to a close when I saw a notice for a seminar in linguistics to be given by a Professor Todd Michaels. All I remember is that the course description— meaning of words in context, analysis of discourse, language in communication—attracted me irresistibly. Those classes became an oasis for me over a period of three weeks. Todd was the kind of lecturer who spoke slowly and simply. His ability to interpret complex concepts impressed me as brilliant. Furthermore, though he always dressed in classical tweedy English style, he seemed to me a man from anywhere, and I mean just that. His dark hair and eyes were the striking complement to a broad-shouldered figure over six feet tall. Since my concerns at that time were focused on getting settled, I cannot remember making any purely feminine value judgments; that is to say, although he was certainly a handsome man, my appreciation of his appearance was confined to the realm of aesthetics. He gave me a sense of confidence and that

surely was a relief from the sense of feeling lost and in a state of constant alert.

In class one day he was making an in-depth analysis of the word "resignation" when I reacted impetuously, getting into a tooth-and-nail argument with one of my classmates. I delivered a lengthy peroration on the uselessness of the philosophy of resignation. The gist of it was that since "resignation" was a word that helped keep nations patient in the face of hunger and violence, it should be purged from the dictionary and the language. When I finished my tirade, my fellow students looked stunned. I had unleashed an unexpected semantic hypothesis freighted with ideological values.

Todd, however, picked up a felt-tip pen and carefully made notes on the board of some of the points in my speech. Of course, one word of my passionate presentation stood out on the white surface of the board: *ideology.* That, according to him, slanted it toward a better explanation of each word from another perspective. That was much more interesting to study—he said—than isolated words. It was impossible to ignore ideology in the context of an analysis of communication. He added that every discourse has a particular logic, frameworks of beliefs that showed through in words; traditions and struggles filled out the same word with other essences. He quoted a phrase of Blake's—"the holiness of the particular"—and closed his argument with the suggestion that the use of analogies should not be discarded, since it was a pathway to finding the profoundest content in words. Since I did not wish to keep silent or to keep flinging darts at the least appropriate moment, I asked him for an appointment. It was for the purpose of discussing words, nothing more.

When I went to his office, I found out an unexpected piece of information: he was indeed a professor, but primarily a psychiatrist who worked in the field of psychology. I was perplexed. In that case, unless he gave another seminar I wouldn't be able to see him, or unless I were to change over to psychology—a profession unimaginable for a person of my character. However, I hit on the idea of seeing him as a patient. "Why not?" I said to myself almost triumphantly later that afternoon. Having made the decision, I felt a tremendous surge of relief. I wasn't yet aware of what analysis was all about. Not only that, if somebody had approached me at that moment when I was entering my name in the appointments book at his office, I would certainly have told a lie—a subterfuge for hiding my need to talk and be listened to, to confide in somebody, to unravel mysteries, to resurrect ancient anguishes and eternal conflicts.

Sometime later I attended our first session. I remember that my appointment was at six o'clock in the evening but I arrived five minutes ahead of time. I had left my logic class on the run stupefied by the talk. His office was two blocks away, a distance I covered in full flight. I did not want to change my mind, didn't want to think twice about the possibility of seeking help. I arrived out of breath and in unusually high spirits. I entered an enclosed patio in which there was a wooden bench and a doorway with a bronze knocker, a sign, and a plaque bearing Todd's full name and profession. The street noises were faraway. I was trying to maintain my composure. I should be entering—I was thinking—in a more tranquil state of mind, and I must be sure not to pour out my whole drama in the first few minutes. However, in a little while, my brain was caught up in a heated debate over conflicting ideas. I had a few minutes to kill and began playing with some pebbles at my feet to keep my nerves quiet as I waited.

Suddenly, I heard the door open and saw him appear. Quickly, I got to my feet. A young girl waved to him as though he were an old friend and disappeared. I remained standing there, not knowing what to do, until he made a gesture inviting me in. When he closed the door, I held out my hand to him in a very awkward gesture, as if I were about to ask for a job or something. He was obviously amused and told me he would never forget my impassioned statement at his seminar. I didn't know how to reply. I

remember that I smiled nervously, somewhat disconcerted by the tone he had taken.

In any case, there I was. To tell the truth, I had no idea what to expect in that room with its book-lined walls and ample, cosy-looking lavender couch. A warm breeze entered through the window, blowing the curtains and slowly shuffling papers about, to my psychoanalyst's utter indifference. A man of thirty-five or so stood before me, hands in his pockets. A few moments passed interminably. All at once, he turned his glance to the couch, indicating that I should sit there. I did so, settling down uncomfortably into what seemed like a featherbed, while he kept looking at something through the window. When he turned and asked my name, I answered quickly, "Mercedes."

"Are you comfortable that way?" he asked amiably. "If you settle in a bit further, you'll find that the couch has a back."

I was on its very edge, my rump in the air and my toes digging into the carpet.

"Oh, of course," I answered, with a forced little smile. "It's just that I don't really feel like sitting."

"And what do you feel like doing?"

"Well, I don't know. Walking, maybe."

"Then go ahead, and while you do that, you can tell me why you came here."

I remained on the couch, petrified. What had I come for? A veritable avalanche of thoughts thundered through my mind, but I kept my mouth shut. I made a slight movement with my head, a vague and indefinite gesture, and finally came out with: "To be frank, I don't yet know. I don't want to sound presumptuous, Todd, but I really don't believe psychoanalysis helps a person much."

"True, quite true," he answered, wrinkling his brow. "Perhaps just a little, or very little."

This appraisal disconcerted me, or rather, piqued my curiosity tremendously, and I asked, "Doesn't such a conclusion discourage you?"

"Sometimes, yes."

"I never did this before and I feel nervous." I raised my eyes and met his observing me serenely. "Where do I begin?"

"Mercedes, you want to talk about something. Then, I would say right there."

"I'm a foreigner. To be more precise, I was born in Argentina," I said, and remained waiting for his reaction, my eyes fixed on his face so as not to miss the faintest nuance of expression.

"I've been there, a vast country," he exclaimed with a smile. "I remember driving along a highway past huge fields of crops, cattle grazing under a violent sun, miles of plains with many animals, trees, birds. Yes, a beautiful and mysterious land."

The sky had darkened with the evening and I felt both confused and pleased by those last words of his. He was turning out to be not so mechanical and, perhaps, not so British. With mounting expectation, I asked: "When was that?"

"Let's see. When I made my first trip to Peru, and then, with a chance to visit Brazil. So, the first time must have been in 1970, and the second, three years later."

"Do you travel a lot?"

"Not so much now, but during one period, yes. We're talking about travels. You're here in London but you're an Argentine."

"I . . . was born there and now I'm here. I haven't visited any other place on earth."

"I see. And how do you feel?"

"A bit lost, actually." I shifted uncomfortably in my seat and heaved a sigh. "I'm putting up a fight, I think."

I began to consider that I had better go. I realized I was talking to a stranger. But when I looked up, I saw that the man was at ease and cordial. I heard him offering me coffee. I nodded. Then, I found a warm mug in my hand. Meanwhile, he had switched on a lamp.

"You're homesick, I imagine."

"Very."

I remember that I lowered my head and remained silent. I didn't want to stay there. Todd sighed, which caught my attention. He was looking out the window, his expression quite tranquil. We spent the rest of the hour discussing the philosophy curriculum.

I left quite disconcerted. I didn't know if I would go back. When I courteously indicated as much to him, his expression and his gesture told me he understood. He advised me to think it over; it was no obligation, he assured me, to submit oneself to something one doesn't believe in. But my life was growing more and more disorganized to the point where, finally, I could no longer handle it.

I ran into Todd again at the school almost a year later. He asked me how I was, I told him I was fine, which wasn't true. Estela, my classmate and now my roommate, was beside me, reading a poster. When he left, she looked at me in surprise, and teased me again about having my works overhauled, with special attention to springs not in operating condition. She often referred to me as the "out-of-order Swiss watch." I enjoyed her sense of humor. We had become close friends, but it wasn't until she told me that her parents had left the country shortly before Allende's murder and were living in France with her younger brother that I felt able to confide in her about the reason for my exile.

That day, Julia was cavorting with her toys, showing off one of her favorites, a huge duck with a red beak. At one point she went into the kitchen and could be heard playing among the pots, acting out a conversation between her dolls and the duck. Although I burst into laughter, the terrible scene suddenly flashed into my mind again. A pall must have suddenly fallen over my face, for Estela put her arms around me. When she asked me what was wrong, I told her about Julia, and even though it sounded awful, I confessed how difficult I was finding it to accept her.

"Estela," I said, "I wake up some mornings thinking I should never have had her. That . . . I did the wrong thing, that another woman in my place . . ."

"What are you saying?" she interrupted. "Nobody else

was in your skin, so nobody can have any idea what you felt in a situation like that."

"But I had an option, Estela, and didn't take it. Can you understand that I was in a panic about an abortion and in terror of having her? And the worst of it is that I love her." My eyes filled with tears. "I loved watching her walk and talk, teaching her to speak properly. It's such a strange thing because, at the same time, I keep feeling that I behaved miserably."

"Nothing is more beautiful than having let that little girl be born, Mercedes. What happened was not your fault and certainly not Julia's."

I had not felt such warmth from anyone, and her words that day were an enormous consolation. She was endlessly helpful to me after that in every way—in my life, my career.

I would wake up screaming, hiccuping with anxiety, and talking a blue streak. Estela would listen to me and, in words I can never forget, say, "One day you're going to remember these moments and think of them for what they are, nightmares." She and I were perfectly aware that it was not going to be all that easy; but in those days, her soft voice and kind words eased my pain.

And I gave her more than one scare. For example, the thing that happened a number of times, as I've already said. But on this occasion, Estela was very upset. One day, while we were walking near Piccadilly, I thought I recognized one of my former jailers. I began to tremble and feel breathless. Without thinking what I was doing, I begged Estela to take care of Julia if anything happened to me, and ran off after him in the crowd. I can't explain what went through my head right then. I do recall that something

forced me to do that, regardless of personal risk; a sensation completely divorced from sanity or logic impelled my legs to move.

So, I followed the man for blocks, until we came face to face at the entrance to the Underground. On approaching him, I simply stood there stupefied, paralyzed. Extremely annoyed, he demanded to know what the devil I wanted. I remained mute, unable to believe what I was seeing. There was not even the slightest resemblance. As he glared at me, waiting for an answer, I kept saying to myself that I must have been confused by the way he crossed the pedestrian walkway, rudely bumping people as he rushed ahead. I had tapped the man on the shoulder, or rather, in the dizziness of the pursuit, pushed him. I just stood there, saying nothing, he simply shrugged his shoulders and entered the Underground elevator. Absorbed in my thoughts, disconcerted, I watched as the elevator disappeared. I realized that my obstinate memory was making me commit acts of utter stupidity and that I could possibly endanger myself and Julia one day with my behavior.

A few minutes later, Estela was there, looking at me, Julia in her arms. I remember how worried she seemed. That was all we talked about that night. There was no explanation for anything quite as terrifying as fear of that kind converted into obsession. Estela asked me what I would have done if he had actually been that individual. At first, I said angrily that I didn't know. Then I had to confess that on such occasions, I was seized by fits of fierce thirst for vengeance, during which I imagined myself capable of any-thing—of hurting him, or worse. And so, when I told her about my consultation with Todd, she remained looking at

me solemnly. Since the chase in Piccadilly had taken place two days after our chance meeting at the school, she advised me to see him again. It was time I began to talk out my fears, in her opinion. I listened to her.

I asked for an appointment and a week later began consultations with Todd on a regular basis. Many things were to change in my life after that. It was a totally revivifying experience. There were difficult moments in which I got myself into mazes of quite unwelcome memories, moments in which I decided that flight was my most advisable course of action. It was hard. I was obliged to talk of events and people and to go through the experience of delivering myself up. But that spell of words and silences gave me strength, the mysterious power of repair inherent in a nonviolent struggle for a just life. In any case, it was then that I decided, almost with greater fervor, to give up the battle against myself. And that was what drew the line between what I had left behind and the future.

Although I told Todd only a part of the truth in the beginning—if there is a whole, I will probably never succeed in unraveling it—perhaps it was a mirror that did not reflect rancor. He listened calmly to my confession involving a story that was threatening to become alien to me but which was mine. I threw open the doors of identity with some information on my childhood, that included the Azul countryside, my parents, and my relationship with my sister Alicia. I mentioned Julia but cast a veil of silence over her. I thought at the time that it was the best way of protecting her. And so, at the beginning, Todd only knew her first name, age, and trivia about her character. Accustomed as I was to keeping quiet, our progress was slow and round-

about. His interpretations gave me hope that perhaps the cards were not as stacked against me as I had believed.

I had written about exile in my diary but never expressed my feelings out loud to a soul. When I actually began talking about it, however, I felt that I was beginning to pin down the implications of that term which—for me—encompassed expulsion and oblivion, a sentence and rare pardon. I was able to pin down the sensation of alienation as an unbearable suspicion that I had left the world, but with the additional factor of my being alive as an aggravating factor. I was able to tell Todd how that exasperating notion became reality when others did not understand me. I had no problem with talking about the sensation of panic that possessed me at times, its relentlessness and profound sadness. Todd was an interpreter of my incoherence, in which the behavior of my comrades or the British in general played no part. He allowed me to wander in that vague territory of those who wish to know about others in order to learn about their own afflictions. Now, I know that.

I confided to him the memory of my first approach to the strange world of university intellectuals. He was one of its graduates, and moreover, taught the subject of semantic analysis of discourse in the field of psychology. Many of the sessions in which we spoke of the meaning of words and of that which is relegated to silence were most welcome.

With each session Todd stanched a wound, lifted a weight of guilt from me, swells of anxiety drifting back to their realm without reverting again to mine.

And most of the time I emerged bewildered by the onslaught of the facts. At the end of one session, I told him that I couldn't bear the truth. Todd replied that it was not

easy but that I would soon be able to. I was tired when I got home and decided not to go to class. Instead, I stretched out on the bed, looking up at the ceiling, and closed my eyes. By a sort of magical spell, past became present, and it was as if I were back there years ago in that place I wouldn't have wished to set foot in ever again, even in recollection.

▪▪ Though I want to avoid calling it up, I am unable to, for the scene reappears in a rush: the long hallway with its scaly walls. Ernesto and Carlos are beside me, accompanying me to get my clothes from an apartment in Almagro. I had to get out of there. I can still see the mildew and soot on the ceiling of that hallway, the entrance, the door, can hear the rattling of the keys even now. I am nervous and trip over the few sticks of furniture. I try to hurry but my hands refuse to obey, aren't able to cope with the drawers. I put my things into a bag and go out to the courtyard, calling to Ernesto who looks at me from the kitchen door. I understand his signal and drop to the ground. I hear shouts, footsteps bursting through space, and everything changes. The abyss appears, I see it and am in it. I hear Ernesto screaming, "Run, *Gringa!*" "Can't!" I scream back. He crosses in front of me and shoots, gesturing to Carlos at the same time to cover him.

The enemy is a swarm of ants. The courtyard is too small for that many people and we are surrounded. Carlos falls and Ernesto drops beside him, cursing as he resists. Then he looks up at me in that blurred reality, separating his lips and mouthing my name without sound and I see blood spurt out as he shouts: "No, no!"

I go toward him, but as I reach him, his body crumples to

the floor and I cannot control my horror. I shake him, weep and implore. Immediately, something rains down on my body like a froth that thickens the air. Suddenly, I feel a burning sensation at my waist and legs and dampness spreading over my body. Everything is silent when a man makes time stand still with a movement of his hand, putting the muzzle of a pistol to my temple, and ordering me to count to five. I do so as a cloud of gunpowder fills the corner of that hell. I close my eyes, but that man orders me to open them and look at him. His eyes are black, glassy, and he is looking at me with a smile, of satisfaction, it could be said. In that smoking unreality, he declares that he is God and that I'm going to find out all about Purgatory. Then the air is thick with whispering. I feel a stretcher quivering under me as it lurches along endless corridors, a needle jabbing into me several times, and oblivion.

∷ The sensation that pervaded me that day still returns whenever I summon up memory of that scene. The bitter taste of tears that trickled slowly down my cheeks to my lips, pressed together to hold back a scream, though I was already weeping and unable to stop trembling. I had not relived those ill-fated events until that day. With nothing at all in mind, I went to the telephone, annoyed with myself, with Todd. He was to blame for making me go back to those places. I was not eager to reexperience that pain. Then I realized that my behavior was absurd and did not make the call. It was part of my life and the time had come for me to deal with it.

Yet the same sense of impotence still pervades me. Even today, I find it difficult to recall the situation without being overwhelmed by guilt. I didn't have to ask them to help me move, I keep repeating to myself. I cannot drive out the idea that they both died on account of my ineptitude. I couldn't even help them; I was unarmed. And I knew very well how to use a gun—my grandfather had taught me all the necessary skills, but I detested them and was against violence. I could have dropped out, but didn't want to. Not without Ernesto, not without my sister. I couldn't bring myself to or didn't want to. It's impossible for me to describe what I was feeling during those days. I wanted them near me, and everything happened at such a dizzying pace and so brutally that it was impossible for me to take time out to think. Events switched tone and color from one day to the next.

That I still cannot understand, simply cannot. Sometimes I think that maybe I don't have to force myself to. Violence and death cannot be understood; they are beyond redress.

It did me good to talk about my comrades. Some I knew were dead or presumed to be; of the rest I have no information. So, I talked of them: *Caro* (Carolina), with her wonderful gift for reciting poetry in the most unexpected situations and places; *El Chueco* (Bowlegs), high-spirited and warm, yet practical like nobody else; *El Chino* (the Chinaman), that is, Ernesto, I've already talked about him; *El Virrey* (the Viceroy), skilled organizer of almost anything, with a forbidding expression that discouraged intimacy of any kind; *Chuni* (Potato, a Quechua word), a twenty-year-old girl, fan of Fellini films, whom I didn't get to know very well; Nora, my close friend since childhood, who wanted to study philosophy like me; and others with

whom I played hooky or perhaps talked to only once. Faces
of long ago, aliases of another period. Nicknames to make
us anonymous: mine, *Gringa*, my sister Alicia's, *Angel*. All of
us betting heavily on the future; we venerated our struggle.
I remember the arguments, the abandonment, the temerity
of our actions, even certain contradictions that chipped
away at our beliefs. In fact, many of us (I was not alone)
were not convinced of the course we had set out on, not positively. I can't vouch for the group, or its discussions, as representing a meeting of minds, far from it. But we had ideals,
and judging from what I lived through, little experience
with horror.

As I had already told Todd, I would probably never be
able to write a conclusion for that story, that it was most
likely an impossibility. And to weep over it is barely a
momentary catharsis, serving only to dislodge infinitesimal
particles of pain, too tiny, too minimal to account for all the
suffering.

My approaches to the world of the unconscious were a
period of ramblings and uncertainties, a time in which
doubt became part of the texture. They were years in which
I submitted to the logic of the interpretation of acts and feelings. There were intense moments during which the curious interpretation of dreams, that strange delirium that
calls upon the device of convoked memory, dispelled the
shadows.

The fact of the matter is that I had succeeded in over-
coming all that, and in some way, I had reestablished the
strength to go on living in my body. And one day, I decided
that my treatment was ended. I wanted to think by myself,
felt in possession of sufficient strength to cope with reality.

In fact, most of the time I managed to be at peace, to function in accordance with my desires. I succeeded in reverting to my past, I know. And besides, I believe that in a certain way I converted Todd into the repository of my past: a distinguished-looking gravedigger, pleasant and quite sane, who would always be within reach if I should need him.

I am remembering Julia during the first years of her childhood. First halting steps, little hands building a tower of blocks, restless fingers pointing at things impelled by an urgency to know the name of this or that object. Her eyes following my lip movements, anxious to hear the sound of the letters that composed a cat and its meow.

I decided to teach her Spanish by telling her stories of my childhood experiences. Acting out the characters, getting down on the floor and changing my voice, I was able to come closer to her. And I imitated the songs of birds, the sounds of nature, describing with my arms the geography of the country of her ancestors. An assortment of personages, animals, and mysteries had inhabited my childhood and I transfused that different world into my daughter's heart. Of all the stories, Julia's favorite was the one about *La Cuca* (a nickname for María). I remember the first time I regaled her with that story as if it were yesterday. She must have been five years old. Smiling at me, she covered her mouth, her face pink, her eyes shining with wonder. I hugged her tight; my deduction was that if she understood that world, she was healthy and good. Besides, I considered it better than any Pinocchio story, better than the wonderful adventures of Donald Duck. Bugs Bunny would go to pieces with envy at the effect this story had on Julia. After that, I replaced it with others. But from time to time she would keep asking me to tell her about *La Cuca* again.

I remember a scene that took place four or five years

later. It was an afternoon of torrential downpour. She came
back from school soaked to the skin. By then, we were living in the same flat we now occupy. I had completed my
philosophy courses and was concentrating on my thesis. I
was still on scholarship but requested permission to give
Spanish lessons, since I wanted to decorate the apartment
and indulge myself in a few other directions. They were
pleased to agree. At first, almost all my students came from
the philosophy department. One of them, Martin Sheppard,
a distinguished philosopher and extraordinary person, was
with me then when Julia burst into the room crying, obviously very disturbed. The moment he saw what was going
on, he got up, put on his raincoat, took a candy from his
pocket, and gave it to Julia.

"*Hasta la próxima*," he said. "*Otro . . .*"

" *. . . día*," I finished for him, "*seguimos*. Yes, thanks,
Martin."

He nodded and left. When I turned around, Julia surprised me with a request.

"Mama, tell me about *Cuca* again."

"Yes, sure, darling, but first you tell me what happened.
Didn't you come home on the bus? You're drenched."

Julia didn't answer. She remained standing in the hallway,
and each time she blinked, new tears coursed down her cheek.
I understood that it was something only kisses and coddling
could take care of. There was no point in asking why she was
crying because I knew. It was the same thing all over again.
Julia went by my name—Beecham. Her schoolmates had
been teasing her once more about her father having left her
because she was ugly and bad. I knew there was nothing to be
done at school, no use talking to the teacher or the children.

I could only reassure her that what they were saying was not so and keep telling her all the things she wanted to hear. The truth is not so believable sometimes, nor what we need to hear. So, while I rubbed her down with a towel and changed her into warm pajamas, I told her the story she already knew by heart. Listening as though she had never heard it before, the color returned to her cheeks.

"Remember *Cuca*, Julia?" I asked as she sat in my lap. She nodded slowly. "*Cuca*, the girl who cleaned the big country house where we spent our summers as children, was positive that nothing would last if she didn't sprinkle holy water on it, even though the village priest did the blessings. She would sweep every corner of the house, clean out drawers and dust pictures, lamps, and the legs of the beds. As soon as the sun had gone in and the moon was just coming out, there was *Cuca* amid the shadows and zephyrs of the night. She would meet up with some confused bats and owls taking advantage of the night to perch in the trees. *Cuca* would talk in a low voice as she went about the fields sprinkling the cattle, the umbra trees, and the lemon grove.

"I followed her without her knowing it. That way, I heard her conversations with the animals. She imitated the croaking of the frogs and startled the owls by calling '*Hooah, hooah*,' as she stretched out her arms toward them. The owl would just look at her and sit there quietly. I enjoyed hearing her sing and talk to the flowers and the bees.

"One day, she appeared suddenly in the bend where the orchids grew, surprising me. She had a spider sitting on the palm of her hand, motionless. She held it out to me and before I realized it, the spider was in my hand. I let out a

shriek, but *Cuca*'s eyes told me to keep still. She approached and said something in Quechua that sounded just lovely. All I remember was the lilt, and the words '*Ona, eh! Ona, eh!*' I'll never forget that. She sprinkled her water on it and the spider went down from my hand by itself without hurting me.

"Another day, a thrush sat on my shoulder, tickling me on the neck with its little feet and beak. I went with her again one night, the two of us looking into the owl's eyes, though only she spoke to it. In a hoarse voice, she said, 'Listen, bad owl, don't frighten this little girl, she is my friend.' That night, my heart pounded as though there were a horse galloping in my breast. Two days before, the calf of *Cuca*'s favorite cow had died, and I heard a sobbing that filled the evening with a sadness that rebounded in the twilight and shook the moon. I saw her disappear among the shadows of the night. *Cuca* buried the calf under an umbra tree, sprinkled it with her water, and as a result, the most beautiful amaranths appeared and there were four-leaf clovers. The birds twittered for the calf to sleep in peace, as she wished, and so it was. I already told you, when we go to that country, *Cuca* will surely be there with her water and take you to visit the blessed land."

The rain was beating at the window, the London sky darkening while my country's sky made a blue vault over the figures of memory. Julia's eyes looked deep into mine, begging for caresses. It was impossible to resist that look. Suddenly, in the silence, I heard Julia's voice asking anxiously, "Did she have a daddy?"

"Who?"

"*Cuca*, Mummy."

"I don't know," I answered, somewhat annoyed, squirming in my chair. "Let's get on with the story."

Julia slipped from my lap and sat on the couch. She remained with her head hunched down for a few moments, then told me she wanted to go to sleep. I tried to get her to eat something, she refused so adamantly that I put her to bed. As I reached for the light switch, my daughter said, "Probably she didn't know him—like with me. But everybody has a daddy, isn't that so?"

"Of course, Julia," I answered without turning. "Go to sleep now, it's late."

I went downstairs, overcome by my child's anguish and by my failure to respond. I ate no supper, was not hungry. Left wondering what I would do if she questioned me again, I had no idea. I spent the night trying out answers.

■■ My daughter had a long restless spell until vacation time in Brighton deflected her worries, owing in part to fishing and long chats with William, an ancient neighbor, a veritable parchment of Old England, who spiced the afternoons by spinning tales of that singular region. And she enjoyed walks with Shelley and other children, playing with the sand and stones in that setting of seagulls and immense ocean.

Those memories of my childhood which I frequently transmitted to Julia were combined with others in which my parents appeared, their way of thinking about things, my upbringing, my sister Alicia. I often sought meaning for

my own existence among those ashes. They say that there is a tip at the end of a remembrance to which another circumstance is hooked, and that, if you keep pulling, more will appear in your memory to fill in the image of the past. And now that I think of it, Julia heard many of my stories and must recall one special night in Brighton. I know, am quite sure, she can't forget that moment on the breakwater and the question she put to me.

I made a habit of taking walks on the beach. During those days in Brighton while Julia was growing up and her features and even her voice were changing, I went back to reenacting ancient arguments with my family. Everything took place in my head—only certain questions can be resolved that way.

One night sitting on the breakwater, listening to music from the fishermen's pub, the last stop before turning back, I began to think of my parents. My mother's last gesture had been a slight brushing of my cheek in which the estrangement and strong disapproval of my behavior were evident. I was coming out of imprisonment, arrived escorted by guards. I had lost a lot of weight, had rings under my eyes and was depressed. There was no dialogue in that extremely brief encounter, nor an embrace. Only the look in her eyes and a silence that was even more hurtful in my vulnerable condition. I felt such pain, such abandonment. I turned around more than once as I went down the stairs of what had been my house with the perplexity of one who had only just discovered something profound and terrible. I stopped for a moment before the family photographs—my uncles and grandparents, my brother and sister. Then, although one of my guards was digging his fingers brutally into my

arm—I could hear him telling me to keep moving—I lingered before the wall of memories. And I went down the steps of that staircase one by one, pausing to look at each picture, my eyes photographing those images of my history to take away with me. My great-grandfather's saying resonated like an echo: "*Tierras las que veas, cosas las que quepan* (Lands—all that you can see; things—all that can be put there)" yours to take, yours to fill with things, a wonderful country, but not very cordial to those who are not "equals."

Standing out, in a yellowed photograph, was the disturbing glare of my great-grandmother Mercedes, the *criolla* who upset family tradition with her declarations that the inhabitants of those lands could not be considered inventory items. It was she who woke up one morning beside herself with rage, having decided that the country was turned upside down by injustice, and it was she who ended her days cloistered in the rambling old house of her beautiful countryside, surrounded by nothing but the twittering of the *benteveos,* which she could watch only through the slats of her shutters.

I closed my eyes, to imprint upon my memory the color of the fields in flower and to take away with me the immensity of the sky that insinuated itself so imposingly in those shots of my life. I did so in order to possess myself of that index to my identity, and I swear that it is all inside me, still flooding my life and my future with its presence.

I must have remained trapped in those memories that night in Brighton, with the charged atmosphere of scraps of stories redolent of wood, damp earth, and wheat fields. I must have stayed at that breakwater for a long time without realizing that Joyce and Julia were there, looking at me

with concern. "It's nine o'clock. We were waiting for you to play bridge," Joyce exclaimed, urging me to come home.

"I was about to leave. What's going on, Julia?"

She was standing there, studying me with that searching look of hers. Then, shifting her gaze to the sea, she sighed and posed a question that seemed to have been dredged up from the depths of her small body.

"Are we going to visit your country some day, Mummy?"

Julia's question tore at my heart. "I don't know, Julia. Maybe someday we'll be able to go."

"When?"

"Someday, Julia. I'll take you, I promise . . ."

I wasn't lying to my daughter. Deep within, I cherished the hope of setting foot once again in that measureless land. Perhaps because I have not totally lost hope, it would be unfair to deny that it is hard for me to imagine leaving this world without setting eyes on the pampa again and sitting in my city's cafés watching my people go by.

Perhaps Julia understands—if she remembers my stories—all that I suffered during this exile of mine. She gives no credit to my lies nor makes allowance for my concealment of the truth. She may, at least, grant this account a certain weight and, then, perhaps it will become possible to grasp the complex and contradictory emotions of exile.

I have often speculated as to what it was that made me stay on in England. I cannot attribute absolutely everything to that past or to my fear; it would hardly be honest of me to claim I did it for Julia, for that would be foolish. In fact, what developed for me over the years was good, and I can't complain. I worked hard and finally earned the degree I wanted so much. My daily life was overflowing with new challenges, with the stimulation of learning and the exploration of new avenues of study. Not only that, but vitality began to seep back into my body, albeit slowly. There was something more in my head—ideals, that other facet of hope. But I had to apply this to something specific and it was not yet clear to me what.

Aware that the degree was only the start, I set myself to pursue in depth the research I had begun months before graduation. It consisted of fieldwork in the course of which I interviewed nine individuals, in a study on the subject of hopes and dreams. The topic may sound pretentious, for it refers to utopias—not a particular one, but those designed by life, the everyday ones. I had already prepared a statement of my proposal, and even though it was heavy with subjectivity, my intention was to work on certain intuitions with the serious purpose of shaping them into conclusions that would be at the very least interesting.

I had some problems at the outset. The first people I approached as potential interviewees declined, alleging lack of time. I didn't want to draw premature conclusions, but

neither would I consider dropping the project. In any case, inevitably, I had to think up some explanations.

Generally, people don't care to get involved in interrogations about their private life or, what runs deeper, to discuss their tastes and hopes with a stranger. Then I came to realize that even though my surname was totally British, my first name put them on their guard, as, for example, when Joyce put me in contact with a highly educated woman who lives a few blocks from Hobbes' Place.

At ten o'clock in the morning, I was standing before a heavy oak door. There was a bell on one side but I used the old-fashioned option of the knocker. A middle-aged women opened the door, ushered me in with a twist of her head and, after hanging up my coat, led me in silence to a room in which Miss Pearson was waiting for me. Though it was a sunny day, the room was deep in shadow. What came immediately into view was a large library and a reproduction of a Turner on the wall nearest the windows. The Victorian-style furnishings were dark in tone, mainly blues and blacks. Except for one lamp which remained lit, there was no light in the rest of the room. The voice of Elizabeth, the mistress of the house, reached me from the armchair at one side of an upright piano. She pointed to another chair opposite hers and immediately launched the first question.

"You are not an Englishwoman, or am I mistaken?"

"I'm an Englishman's daughter, Miss Pearson."

She harrumphed and gestured to the woman who had shown me in and remained standing a few paces from her. She then signaled something by wiggling the fingers of her right hand. A few minutes later the woman returned with a tray holding a fine porcelain tea service—teapot and a pair

of magnificent teacups—and a basket of scones. With chilly correctness, Miss Pearson held out a steaming cup of tea. However, she remained silent for a few moments while keeping a penetrating eye upon me. Then, sighing heavily, she said: "My dear, that does not answer my question."

"I'm an Argentine."

"I am not familiar with that country," she commented with a certain tone of dismissal. "I would have thought you to be of Spanish origin."

"Well, no . . . I'm not."

I must confess that, given Miss Pearson's rather ungracious manner up to that point, I had written her off as a subject. I had no idea how I would be able to communicate with someone who showed such marked hostility from the very beginning. However, something in her manner left me indecisive, and I thought I sensed an overture in the way she invited me to try the scones. I ate in silence, feeling her eyes upon me, until I heard her voice.

"I do not talk to strangers," she began, and after a pause, added, "and even less when my personal affairs are concerned."

"We are of a mind in that," I answered unexpectedly, "and, of course, I wouldn't want anyone not convinced of its value."

"Well, then, why don't you try convincing me?"

With that, after I described the objectives of my thesis and the working hypothesis, Miss Pearson promised to think it over, which, in fact, she did and became one of my subjects. That slim little woman wrote poetry and reviews for a literary journal. A spinster, she is very reserved, and quite prone to periods of melancholy. Her days slipped

away in darkest gloom, as she put it. It took a while before
she confessed her more intimate sentiments to me. I was
able to deduce that Elizabeth harbored unrevealed illusions
of making a name for herself with a collection of essays she
had written some years ago. I was unable, initially, to
understand why her hopes had been pinned on her prose
writings when she produced really beautiful poetry.

Until one day when Elizabeth handed me a folder lined
with fine transparent paper. I read the opening paragraphs
of the handwritten manuscript with some anticipation. The
style was brilliant, arresting, the structure like clockwork
but the texture of a richness that made it seem like fiction,
which, of course, it wasn't. I continued reading under her
intent gaze. It appeared to be a series of reflections on love.
When I finally looked up, she was blushing so furiously I
decided I had best go no further that day.

Subsequently, I used more indirect methods. Since Elizabeth found it embarrassing to discuss the subject matter of
her writings, I could not help wondering why she should
want to publish them. For me, the obvious conclusion was
that they were aimed at reaching someone. But whom?
Elizabeth's character precluded my finding out the answer.

As far as my thesis proposal was concerned, at no time
did she let up on criticizing my plan, pointing out that
"utopia is unattainable, hope, however, is perhaps something more within reach." So, I explained that the process of
drawing conclusions from abstract concepts was terrain in
which I had little experience. Nevertheless, I put forward
the idea that in my opinion it was an approach that
embraced values and brought a constellation of behaviors
into play. That was what I was interested in investigating.

I recall her astonished look and her smile. "A semantic switch, Miss Beecham . . . carrying on an investigation with the purpose of twisting the meaning of a word. A brazen undertaking!" It was customary for her to express herself in ironies of that nature almost the whole time, except when she was overtaken by a fit of melancholy at some recollection that left her trapped in her particular world. Working with her to reach certain conclusions turned out to be difficult. Even so, it was quite enriching. I believe her answers contributed a very different vision of the intellectual world.

On that day of our first appointment she said goodbye to me with a vague gesture as she contemplated the afternoon light. She had been kind enough to see me out, offering the following observation: "The only thing that has come to my ears regarding Argentines is the mixture of races—what will be the upshot of such a bedlam of different beliefs and tongues?"

"We don't know yet, Miss Pearson, we are still a very young people."

I could hear her laughter as I went down the hall, but by the time I turned around, she had disappeared inside. It wasn't the first time the message got through to me—whether by means of a sarcastic remark or an actual insult—that being a foreigner puts you, a priori, in the judgment seat.

As on so many other occasions, that awareness set me apart, and I have behaved petulantly, been rude or arrogant many times probably. It may sound utterly stupid, but that was the only way I could get up the courage to face meeting a new person. It was not a good strategy. In some cases, at moments when I would have liked to pay people back in their own coin with the same disdain or indifference they

had no hesitation in showing toward me, I was barely able to avoid having anxiety seize control over my tongue. There were even times when I had to hold myself back from telling them to go to whatever hell they came from.

In any case, learning to survive is, of course, not a bad thing. I confess that I exchanged my pride for their stories and histories, disguised my disgust in the face of surprising replies, because what mattered was that I was entering into an interesting dialogue with many of them. And there is one thing I must be thankful for: if I had to adjust to their temperaments, they in turn had to put up with the irksomeness of my questioning, my persistence. In this light, to be truthful, I must conclude that on numerous occasions during which my feeling of foreignness was overshadowed by the intimacy of our purpose, the uneasiness was mutual. If the interviewees were reluctant to provide much explanation on certain points, I was overly troubled, myself. As a matter of fact, in many cases I was not clear in putting my questions to them.

I met some very interesting people through this fieldwork and was warmly received in their homes or workplaces. I recall one very strange couple, Juliet and Stephen, to whom Estela introduced me. Juliet was twenty years the senior, yet they seemed to be truly in love. However, it was not the age difference that impressed me but their ways. For example, to my surprise, they communicated through letters, almost never talking to each other. Greeting was a ritual consisting of an exchange of looks and brief phrases, barely audible to others.

Then, they talked to me separately, the interviews being held on different days. He was an archeologist and she

taught Greek. When I began to know them better, I found them to be highly sensitive people, perhaps to an extreme I was unaware of. Their outlooks on life were quite different, and on various occasions, I wondered what tastes they shared that led to that disturbing intimacy. Knowing them gave me a new slant on human beings.

Besides these people, I met others whom I decided not to include in my study. I selected only those whose social status provided me insights with respect to the objectives sought, who revealed hope in certain actions, in what sometime later I was given to call "Everyday Utopia."

Actually, the underlying purpose in this choice of discovering the utopias of others was the rediscovery of my own. However, I prefer not to discuss that until later on, because I want to relate how in doing this fieldwork, I discovered at the same time my need for getting to know the British more intimately. Most of the time their behavior either took me by surprise or, the opposite, I came to feel absolutely at home, as if I had been born in England. To be more specific, I felt an irresistible curiosity to decipher something of their nature.

Up to that time, there was little I could learn of their feelings, since they almost always kept their distance, maintaining a veiled procedure of differentiating themselves from the *others*—those of us who aren't British. I think I spied a tiny bit of their makeup: a hidden asceticism, great rigorousness, and a form of expressing their feelings through comments on the prevailing weather and/or the landscape. I think that living in the middle of the sea, in a frigid zone, with fog blurring the days, makes them reserved and little given to conversational dalliance. I would venture to say

that they are a people who get right to the point, even if they then decide not to answer or contradict themselves. In discourse, they choose their words as if aware beforehand of the impact of each one on the other person. I have noticed that they are annoyed by being asked to clarify, as if they had already been as clear as it is possible to be. And so it has occurred to me that perhaps we Latin Americans are afraid of not being understood, which may explain why we give our opinion over and over again. In any case, it is not my intention to define the character of a people; besides, I know that would be generalizing.

Almost every time I interviewed these individuals for my thesis, I think I picked up expressions that brought back memories of my father. Recalling him was to recover something of him—that moment of surprise, the expression of disapproval that would cross his face at the things we would say. As I was growing up, I had occasion to encounter that look of utter incomprehension as he watched us at play, as if we were absolutely alien to him. That raising of the eyebrows and blinking of eyelashes when present at our arguments. A kind of astonishment, causing his cheeks to flush, brought on by our grimaces and unruly behavior, as though he were discovering exotic elements in human beings. For, as I remember my father, only the immediate and tangible reached him. He was so accustomed to rules and regulations, to systematizing life, that things and people were arranged in categories in accordance with the position they occupied in the world. There was no place for any other view of reality, inasmuch as nothing not learned in childhood could get through to him.

Having married an Argentine appeared not to have

given him a better integrated view of certain aspects of morality and custom. Very often, my father would refer to the importance of a fair deal, a concept that disconcerted me, for in my country that term is perhaps a little more elastic and may even differ in translation. I suspect, now, with the years gone by, that England was not the only place where I felt like a foreigner. I believe there was a time when I also had the sensation of not belonging in my own country. And then I thought of situations that uproot us, even from our own birthplaces; perhaps irreconcilable differences, conditions and conduct that provoke expulsion even when attributable to persons of our own nationality.

After this journey of discovery, I reached the point of collating my material. Eager to correlate concepts for my thesis, I chose Eric Johnson, perhaps presumptuously, as my adviser. He was quite a famous philosopher at the time, had received various prizes, and continued teaching at the university. The reason I had singled him out was because his major field was behavior. To my delight, he graciously accepted. Later on, I was to confirm what others had warned me, that preparing the first draft of my manuscript was going to be the hardest part of the whole process. He was rigorous not only about the main subject matter but also the justification of my hypotheses. Time and again, I had to go back and rework my formulations and source materials, only to have him reject them. Since arguing would get me nowhere, I had no choice but to accept the challenge.

I was determined to obtain provisional acceptance of my proposal within the year. He returned my initial hundred pages accompanied by a little handwritten note advising me to "watch" my academic language. His attitude encouraged me to reformulate my premises and helped me learn thereby to research unrelentingly. Later on, my efforts were richly rewarded, for he ended up recommending my thesis to the university press for publication. Still, I have never forgotten the words with which he returned my manuscript: "You must be more explicit in your explanations." Then, at home, I received his report, brimming with suggestions. I still cultivate his habit of using colored marking pens, which has the effect of giving the text an avenue of reflections from which it is difficult to stray.

I was bogged down for months in the disquieting terrain of transforming my conjectures into a book, or rather, translating them into well-ordered words and chapters interesting to the reader. It was a most arduous task, which gave me the sensation that I was condensing much of my way of thinking.

After I defended my thesis before a jury of professors notorious for having rebutted and rejected interesting work of other colleagues of mine, and having now overcome the obstacle I expected to be my downfall, I enrolled immediately in the seminars required for the doctorate. It seemed that one challenge led to another—another effort, another step up, many tasks transforming my days into conceptual constructs, my mind jumping from research notes to supermarket lists. Practically all day long I was on the run between classes in philosophy I was taking and classes in Spanish I was giving. After that, I would shut myself off to work on the book.

I devoted very little time to Julia during that period. What is more, I think I practically fled from her. That's why I was not abreast of her studies. Whenever she asked me for help, I made sure to clear up her problems as quickly as possible and get back to my own concerns. The way Julia had shot up disconcerted me. This was no longer a child's body cavorting about the house; her voice and her mannerisms had given her a presence that was quite overpowering. This was a different Julia, no longer the little girl who came to me to be comforted or who giggled at my stories. And I was unable to avoid treating her like a stranger.

The fact that I forgot her birthday and made the discovery one morning when I asked her about a new jumper she was wearing was a clear demonstration of the way I was living at the time. Looking at me disdainfully, Julia replied: "A present from somebody who loves me."

"Don't tell me you have a boyfriend."

"Several," she snapped, and set about fixing herself some toast and jam. "One of them gave me this sweater. Like the color? Don't tell me, I know it doesn't go with the skirt that someone else gave me. This ring and bracelet are gifts from different admirers . . . and then, I have books and CDs upstairs from a cohort of followers who think I'm important."

"Julia, what's this all about?"

My daughter had moved to the table, buttered her toast, took little sips from a cup of hot cocoa. She did not look at me. Then, sighing suddenly, she said in a casual tone, "My friends threw me a birthday party at Sophie's house."

She made a dismissive gesture and I said nothing. There was nothing I could do now other than regret the irrepara-

ble situation. Even so, I considered inviting her out for supper and buying her a book, of course. But was that going to
make up for my forgetfulness? She had turned fifteen two
weeks before and I hadn't even given her a kiss. Didn't even
remember it. Nevertheless, I went over to her and said:
"Forgive me, dear, I had no idea. I don't know what I can
possibly say in my defense, but"—I brushed away a lock of
hair that hung over her face—"you've been wanting a new
CD player. I'll get it tomorrow. Agreed?"

"Awfully sweet of you," she said with a disdainful gesture, " but that date has passed into history, so you can hold
your concern over to next year."

"Julia!" I exclaimed with an edge of annoyance, "I'm
loaded up with work."

My daughter replied in the same tone: "Mother, you must
attend to your responsibilities, the player can wait. After all,
it makes no difference anyway."

With that, she went upstairs and shut herself in her
room. The following day, I bought her a handsome, imposing stereo with speakers—the most expensive in the place, I
believe—and left it in her room. Months passed before she
stopped using the old one and turned on the new. I remember the machine stayed in its carton for a whole semester,
whereby the evidence of my negligence and her annoyance
remained in full view in the hall upstairs alongside the door
to her room.

I met with the editor as soon as I considered the first draft of my thesis ready. Eric introduced us on a sweltering afternoon in June. I should say that it was so hot, I was so nervous, and my palms so wet that I tried blotting them against my clothing. The editor observed my movements through half-closed eyes, in silence, before acceding to the unavoidable handshake of courtesy.

When Eric left and I found myself alone with him, I had no idea what to say or do, other than observe the bookshelves, the orderliness, and a huge window which, while allowing the sunshine in, was shut tight against any breeze. Neither of us said anything for some time until he invited me to follow him into his office. Dr. Carlyle was sixtyish, a man who evidently spoke, walked, thought, and breathed with a professorial air. He predicted the weather for me as we made our way through the meandering corridors of the publishing house, but quickly interspersed observations about my book. It was an extremely unorthodox text, in the sense that the disquisitions on philosophical ideas were followed up by extensive exchanges of opinion with people (with the honorable exception of Elizabeth and the "peculiar" couple) who were for the most part "illiterates."

The editor's criticisms hinged on that point, since in his estimation, the subject under study was not one for discussion with just any class of people. In his humble opinion, those lacking academic background should have been excluded.

"How much could those who dehumanize their lives on a daily basis know of the vast and complex mechanisms of reality?" he declared with a sonority that made it an assertion rather than a question. "Perhaps they care about freedom, anybody might. But, surely, indifference has beclouded their thoughts, and unruliness and ignorance befuddled those heads that are functional only for purposes of watching football games on the television."

He seemed too crass and prejudiced to be an editor at a university press. I was politely cool in taking my leave of him. His behavior toward me had been decidedly cool, but what displeased me most were his criticisms. Not only were they hardly what I expected but they were totally opposed to my own thinking. When I told Eric about it the next day, he explained that Carlyle had gotten his Ph.D. two years ago for an excellent paper on the subject of time. I had to understand then that my approach was, to say the least, not quite orthodox and that I was using methods that were not yet mainstream. Professor Carlyle's hostility, Eric explained, represented nothing more than a rejection of new ways of articulating ideas.

Eric's explanation notwithstanding, my opinion of the distinguished editor remained unchanged. Be that as it may, a while later I received a letter from Professor Carlyle informing me of the forthcoming publication of my book, the number of copies, and, to my astonishment, a congratulatory postscript on the contents. "Well, now!" he wrote in surprise, "Your interviews contribute data of a highly interesting order." He also requested that I give him more details about my methods of eliciting information from two of the subjects: Evelyn and Florence.

The segment on Evelyn, a worker in a Manchester textile factory, yielded interesting interpretations and included, as well, a rather in-depth approach to the concept of freedom. "It gives the impression that she must have been reading Marx and Smith at the same time," Carlyle exclaimed in his note. She had surprised me, too, but for other reasons.

I discovered in the course of our conversations that the obligations imposed by society did not arouse the feelings I expected. What I called "resignation" were elements that, in fact, couldn't change. For that reason, Evelyn devoted herself assiduously to fighting for a new labor code. And I said to myself, "She doesn't want to leave the system, she's battling for the introduction of other standards." Evelyn's reactions were calibrated to her reality, located in a vast and unjust space of society.

All at once, I finally realized I could talk to somebody in this world without idealizing the responses, without presenting content that was other than real, without attempting to superimpose the features of a heroine. Evelyn knows what freedom of thought is, is familiar with the limitations of the social orientation. Since her husband is out of work, she is now the breadwinner. Pette, her oldest child, has finished middle school and will soon be able to lend a hand.

Her take on the workers' world was simple and emphatic. She was aware of how hard it is to change the rules of the game but, at the same time, had a positive view of the future. Evelyn maintained that the flaws in the system, more than obvious by now, were producing tremendous conflicts in society. Her desire was to collaborate in correcting those injustices, in being a catalyst of change. In a calm,

measured tone she insisted that to her, acceptance of the rules did not signify submission.

She demonstrated her solidarity with immediacy, with those close to her and those she knew she could help. And she was upset by other people's grief, but repeated that it was not within her power to do anything for them. As she serenely told me, she was able to fight for her world, that was already complicated enough. One day she assured me, with tears in her eyes, that no way was she going to give up fighting for her rights. Her voice choking up, she said, "I hope I never lose hope." I thought then, there are no big or little utopias, or whatever you choose to call them. They— Evelyn, their comrades and their families—feel that they are the creators of this workers' world, participants excluded from the formulation of the rules. In the exercise of their power to strike and hold union congresses, they seek to convert themselves into active members of this society. Perhaps, the fate of a major part of humanity is to suffer injustice but not to lose faith in the power of change.

I would, then, have to decide on a change in my thesis: not to bring in ideological concepts because, in the final analysis, they have nothing to do with the subject in question. I keep in mind, however, the withered faces of poverty, those images of my past—everywhere in this universe, blind chance controlling the existence of human beings. A world regulated by arbitrary criteria in which, at the same time that a healthy child is born with guaranteed shelter, food, and education, many others come into the world destitute, with the past eating their guts out and the future stoned into almost total disarray.

There are no stronger or weaker. The controlling factors

place us in a situation of winning or losing. I am absolutely convinced that some theories regarding the rich and poor are ideas that suit the purpose of many people for fashioning an "irreversible" reality of penury. A human being is capable of extremes of inhumanity and selfishness that terrify me.

I don't want to go back over all that I did in the past, but there is something I must confess: I suspect that I have been insufficiently rebellious against the system; and even now, what was taking place in the minds of those I wanted to "save," those upon whom I sought to impose consciousness of a different world, remains an enigma to me, an almost surrealistic mystery. As when one plays at understanding something that is impossible to grasp because it was never experienced. I think I took it for granted that these people agree with our beliefs. I remember their faces, can still see their expressions, for poverty wreaks havoc with hope. They knew a lot about brutality and injustice, learned through their stomachs, in the cold, in the anguish of their days without hope for the future.

Enough years have gone by since I've begun to dwell on this subject. I suspect that sometimes, along with the grand virtue of having ideals, the opposite aspect manifests itself, too, an omnipotence that tells us: it's only a step from the wish to its realization. Even if, at that, one crashes into a stone wall or gets trapped in a maze of misunderstanding lacking enough questions with which to find the way out. The games of fate, in short.

▓▓ The thesis is on track. As for Florence, I happened to meet her years ago in a supermarket. It was during a rather violent incident in which a man was harassing her, calling her obscene names, as she stood holding a small boy by the hand. A scene that brought memories flooding back of when I was humiliated and beaten. I couldn't bear what I was seeing and intervened. The man now changed his tactics from insolence to violence, pushing her against the shelves, calling her an "ungrateful bitch." When I tried to interfere, he threw a punch at me which I dodged and followed up with a kick in the groin. As he doubled over in pain, I grabbed him and whispered in his ear that he must never strike a woman, that women are to be treated with kindness, and then suggested he get on his way as fast he could, which he proceeded to do at once.

When I turned around, Florence was staring at me in admiration. I felt I had only done the right thing. She thanked me profusely, introduced me to her little boy, and told me that she had been in such situations before but that this was the first time anybody had protected her—the first time, she repeated. With that, she broke into tears. I put my arm around her, told her I lived just across the square, and invited her to have a cup of tea. After some hesitation, she accepted.

Her son, Jake, was the same age as Julia, and she had an older boy by the name of Simon who was in school. She seemed nervous, an odd, uneasy expression on her face, I

couldn't quite interpret. We spent most of the time talking about children.

Some time later, she telephoned and invited me to a performance at a place that turned out to be a strip club. At the entrance, there was a large poster of a woman, almost totally nude, in a suggestive pose. The place was called Mum's Club. I went through a long hallway, the walls covered with a velvetlike vermilion fabric. Although it was not yet dark, artificial light, the deep amber kind, held sway. Two half-naked women begged pardon as they squeezed by. They were laughing in high-pitched tones. A man in bright green trousers and a violent-orange blouse popped out of a door. The women stopped and listened in silence; then he disappeared round a corner under a staircase, and they continued talking and laughing more quietly, now. When I reached the end of the corridor, a large woman ushered me to a dressing room.

The door was open and I entered. Florence was behind a blue screen; I could hear her voice. The woman indicated that I should take a seat. I looked around for a while, admiring the unexpected orderliness of the room. There was a mirror; a table beneath, on it, neatly arranged, several boxes, and a number of combs in a row in order of their function, I assumed, some with heavier teeth for untangling, some for fluffing up the hair or curling, one with a long, thin handle for ringlets. Scissors of various sizes and shapes lay side by side. On a shelf were large, brightly colored bottles and jars which I imagined contained perfumes. There was nothing on the floor, not even discarded underwear.

When Florence emerged, pushing aside a section of the

screen, I could see more shelves, with wigs, shawls, and hats, and, draped on hangers, a variety of feathered, lacy, spangled garments.

She was almost nude, her body encased in lurid red-mesh leotards, spangles dancing on her nipples, and feathers that made a pretense of covering her pubis. She looked at me and I exclaimed, "My goodness, you really are what they call well put together!" She smiled. Her lips were painted a deep purple. Then she offered me a beer and handed me a little gift-wrapped package. It was a music box in the shape of one of those church towers that played tunes of Haydn. When I told her I couldn't accept it, she assured me that she would be offended if I refused it.

Florence was thoroughly composed that day, in her element, moving about with ease and naturalness. As we drank our beer, she told me that the man in the supermarket had been a regular client of hers, who became jealous and was pursuing her like a wounded lover, and after that incident, the owner of the place threatened to bring charges against him. However, the only thing really bothering her was that Jake had seen the man strike her.

Watching her as she spoke, it was impossible for me not to admire the expertise with which she applied her makeup. Her hands moved over her face with incredible speed and agility, eyeshadow on the lids, rouge on the cheeks, sprinkles of a kind of stardust on her shoulders. The room was soon filled with a fragrance of powders and perfumes. She was exceedingly tidy, leaving each container closed after use and continually running a damp cloth over the wooden surface on which her arsenal of beauty rested.

It was a quirk of fate that brought me into the life of a

woman who was preparing an assault on male senses. My experience with that world was nil. Not only that, but I realized then that I came from a family in which women went out with their "face washed." The girlfriends of my youth loathed makeup and feminine wiles. I spent my childhood and part of my adolescence climbing trees, riding horseback, and at the university I was scarcely ever out of my jeans, even for sleeping. The farthest my classmates and activist comrades would go was a pair of earrings. Getting a haircut in a beauty parlor was unheard of, and no perfume of any kind or even a speck of lipstick was ever applied. By then, everything had become so transitory that I would just throw on clothes with no regard whatsoever for the body beneath.

In that dressing room, I naturally felt a disquieting curiosity. When I asked her if I could stay for the show, she just nodded. It was an amazing spectacle. The audience whistled and howled at the sight of the swaying buns and naked breasts. But when Florence came on, they fell silent as she began slowly to flex all the parts of her sinuous body.

As she weaved among the tables, swaying her hips to the cadence of the men's heavy breathing, her fabulous backside became a magnet that drew all eyes along with it, letting them fall in supplication upon her firm thighs and torso. They followed her hands and fingertips as they touched, slowly and rhythmically, almost ingenuously, the sequins on her nipples, and then slid daringly down to the feathers. She ended with a wildly voluptuous grinding of her pubis that wrenched a single communal sob from out of the male depths.

I progressed from scholarly reflection to quite primitive

amazement, followed in a moment by a sense of total rejection and a feeling that I was, to say the least, thoroughly
uncomfortable and out of place. What was I doing here?
Nevertheless, I stayed on, trapped by curiosity and my
desire to learn. My eyes reverted to the tables, where the
men sat with the oddest expressions of expectation I had
ever seen.

A sweaty odor and strange silence emanated from the
tables as soon as Florence had left the stage. I made my way
across a space that reeked heavily of lubricity to the dressing
room, where I found Florence exalted. She was majestic, a
queen bee with a retinue of drones upon whom she had
unleashed lust at its purest.

It was in the early hours when I left, feeling, I must confess, that my universe had been turned upside down. At
home, somewhat calmer, I began working at the computer
in an effort to sort out my thoughts on prostitution, its code
and rules. I decided that I wanted to find out how that
detached and mysterious world operated. What could Florence's utopias possibly be like? She did not refuse to be
interviewed. My explanation was short and precise, and she
declared that she would try to be as frank as she could.
Although she did not warm up to my proposal, she had no
hesitation in cooperating. In fact, before beginning each
interview, she would refer to herself as "The Florence
Case." I went back to Mum's a number of times and discovered many sides of that reality and various facets of my own.

As for her life story, Florence did not give me many
details and was not, in fact, very forthcoming. She was
happy with her boys. She was a prostitute, but faced with
the question of what to do about those beings she was car-

rying inside her, she had decided to keep them. I could relate to that. Jake and Simon had different fathers, from among a host of anonymous men. The children had been conceived in rapid succession, at a stage when her sexual couplings had flooded like a river through the inebriation of long, plaintive nights. I learned that she was thankful for not having contracted AIDS or a venereal disease of any kind. She had indeed protected herself; resisting the temptation of abortion had not been easy.

Now, her sons were a joyful part of her life. She sent them to school and helped with their homework. She did all she could to ensure their growing up to be healthy, good people. Florence did not lie; she said that lying made things worse, that lies corrode. When they were a little older, she would tell them about how she earned her living.

She differed from her colleagues in that she was not religious. Her conception of morality was obviously at odds with that of most people. Actually, the subject is rather complex, and I want to be careful not to gloss over any aspect because it is so easy to fall into superficiality. I prefer not to enter into discussion of my questionnaire and the conclusions I reached in the fieldwork, mainly because something happened in the course of the interviews that affected me profoundly.

One afternoon I went to the club, feeling out of sorts. I don't know what was happening to me. I had a stack of notes in my folder, jotted down in a scrawl which even I had difficulty deciphering. When I sat in my customary chair to begin the session, I turned to ask Florence a question that came to my lips quite involuntarily.

"Does my hair look alright?"

Florence looked at me and, hesitating not a moment, beckoned to me to sit at the mirror under the lights.

"Well, it's clean," she said, teasingly, "but you haven't had it cut in years."

Proceeding to fluff up my hair, she said, between deep sighs, "There were bangs here once upon a time, after that you had it parted on the side, and then in the middle. It's a ruin of scissor-cut ends, all homemade."

And she burst out laughing, I thought because she was recalling something one of the girls said when she had gone to the door just before. But no, after coming back to my chair, she kept looking at me with a roguish expression.

"What's up, Florence?"

"Nothing. It's just that suddenly, after talking so much about being a woman, about makeup and all that—you know what I mean—about our condition, I take one look at you and . . ."

"And what?" I mumbled. Then with a nervous little laugh, I asked, nearly petrified, "Please tell me."

"Hmm, what you already know."

She poured a drink and handed it to me, glancing at my nails, my clothes, as I asked, "What are you thinking?"

"That no man has been around this female territory in a while—in quite a while."

"That's true. I don't have the time," I said, relieved.

"The urge?"

"Well, if you can't find the time, what's the good of getting the urge?"

"I see."

"Florence—"

She shrugged and swayed her head gently. "It's your

problem . . . I don't know how you're going to manage. To live without men is, as the philosopher said, a sin before God." She arched her eyebrows and added, "You must have some motive other than lack of time." Then, as she went to the mirror, she asked me playfully, "How would you like me to slap a little makeup on you and maybe give you a haircut?"

I got to my feet and, as I picked up my handbag and folder, answered nervously, "Maybe next time."

"Whenever you like. I'll be here."

I walked several blocks feeling an absolutely new sensation that made my legs shaky. At the outset I didn't contemplate learning what Florence's concept of womanhood was. She analyzed her behaviors on her own, considering the status of prostitution and what it had meant to her not only physically but emotionally. And she spoke of the feminine condition with an assurance that made me stop and think how I had neglected my own body. My mind was a virtual freeway of theories, on which hypotheses and shibboleths raced at full speed and with remarkable agility. I did feel, though, as if my body were severed from my head. On the way home, I kept thinking that I had ventured into unknown territory, imagining new capabilities on the sole basis of theoretical knowledge. Florence, without formal study, using ordinary language and a discreet approach, had made me aware of my neglected condition.

As soon as I got home, I went to look at myself in the full-length mirror on the pantry door ruined during installation by Bill, the handyman. I don't like mirrors and usually avoid them, yet there are so many that the house is inundated with presences, our presences. I stood there for a few

minutes, gazing at my clothes and my hair. It's true, it did look stringy and messy. I had on a man's T-shirt that hung on me loosely, below it a pair of those baggy trousers. Neither allowed any part of my figure to reveal itself. I picked up a comb and tried giving some shape to my hair but it wouldn't respond. I ended by tying it up tight with a ribbon and going to bed. But I was so restless I couldn't get to sleep. For the longest time my thoughts slid back and forth, my image on trial. In the semidarkness, I examined areas of my half-naked body again and again as if it were somebody else's. It had been so long since I had looked at my figure that I had actually forgotten about it. I became so discomfited it was as though I felt the situation was shameful.

The scars, the trail of another time, were there on my left leg, others at my waistline, several in my groin. Touching them always meant to me a return to the past, as it still does today, and that night it was impossible for me to rid myself of the sensation of pain and death. I had to keep repeating that I was alive, still alive, and I wept as though they had wounded me all over again.

A week later, I went to a beauty parlor and agreed to the style of haircut they suggested. Next, I did something totally foreign to me: I shopped. Not only that, I came away from the store with a couple of skirts, several pretty blouses, and a pair of sandals. The next thing I knew, I was clutching a bagful of stuff—jars of makeup, lipsticks, and creams. As soon as I got home, I stared at myself in the mirror, a bit dismayed at my new appearance. I wouldn't say I was disappointed at the change, but just a little frightened perhaps.

Julia came home toward evening. I had been waiting for her nervously, biting at my lipstick and pulling down the skirt which insisted on putting my thighs on view. After the initial shock, she dumped her folders and set about peering at me.

"You make me feel like one of those figures in the wax museum. Leave my skirt alone and stop poking at my hair!"

"Mother, I'm going to flip. What's got into you?"

I suppose I should have been more, shall I say, tolerant about my daughter's reaction, but I was feeling like a youngster myself. Those new clothes did indeed bring back my figure. I went to the kitchen to heat up some water as I peeped at Julia from the corner of my eye.

Without thinking, I said to her, "You should pay more attention to your hair and the way you dress."

I regretted it instantly. The thing was that Julia's appearance had changed so dramatically in the space of a few months. Her body, face, legs, and breasts told me that the little girl had gone, that this person was a woman. Her voice and features had taken on an unexpected cast. She had shot up several inches, and the physical transformation had brought with it a marked difference in demeanor, in the way she asserted her presence by the way she carried herself. Perhaps I should say that it was her growing up that induced the changes in me. Perhaps I could have been more honest, more forthright. But how could I explain to her how much her maturing dismayed me, that I was beginning to worry about how she was going to handle her sensuality? What could I say to her when I didn't know how to cope with my own?

"I just hope you catch somebody's eye," she exclaimed suddenly, "so then you'll have someone else to amuse you and leave me alone."

With that, she turned her back on me and disappeared upstairs. It was the most recent in a series of confrontations that were becoming increasingly frequent. Prior to this one, communication between us had been good. Though my opinions often displeased her, she would listen—I won't say very indulgently, that was not Julia's style, but she would hear me out and accept my advice, giving it at least token consideration. The way she looked at me that day was a different matter, and my unfortunate comment on her clothes stirred up a latent hostility.

A little while later, she banged down the stairs and came to a stop a few feet from my desk. I was playing a Ravel

recording as I erased interviews from my tapes. She switched on her CD to a singer howling in a loud, raspy voice that was maddening. Automatically, I got up and switched it off. I turned and stared at her. She made a face of sour displeasure, then, with a mocking smile, and in a lofty tone, said, "You're going to have to get with it, a little more in step with that new look of yours, Mother. If you'd like, I can give you some tips."

"Don't be disrespectful, Julia."

"Okay, then the same goes for you."

"What's going on? Why so . . . on the offensive?"

"You're the one being offensive. I'm just answering."

" Correct. I apologize. I won't interfere with the way you dress . . . simply won't."

Julia had moved toward the window, her figure in pajamas sharply silhouetted as she stood looking out, all her inner being emanating a strange serenity.

"What were you feeling when you found out you were pregnant with me?"

I closed my eyes and had a feeling as though I were taking off from myself. It was such an upheaval of memories. The question propelled me straight back to that time. I didn't know what to tell her. Something, of course, that had a normal ring of truth to it. To have brought my real feelings out into the open would have been inhuman, which is what I was thinking. There was a clarity in her tone of voice, and the moment she turned, I could sense in her softly searching expression that she was eager for answers. She was placing her hopes in me, and since I was on the spot, I would have to cobble together an inventory

of her life. The vehemence invested in her question, brimming with anxiety, made me consider my words; her future depended upon me; or more exactly, I was the repository of her data, her identity.

And, like so many times before, I wondered what would she do with the answers when she found out, what steps would she take? And so, once again, shuddering with horror, I let myself slide into the grip of deceit. Nonetheless, words came to my lips.

"It was surprising, unexpected. I felt quite strange during the first stage."

"And then?"

I could hear my breathing during those moments and my mind lost itself in memories, of my initial days in England, that most difficult time. At one point, I found myself summoning up the months during which Julia was growing in my womb.

"Then," I heaved a sigh, "my body began to change, my hips spread . . ."

"Change *how*?" She had sat down on the living-room couch and was scrutinizing me intensely. "Did it hurt?"

"Oh, no! How can I explain it? My shape changed, that's to say, the diameter."

I remained silent, and so did she. The word I chose was simply inappropriate. There's nothing geometrical about a pregnancy, and there I was talking to her about that body of mine as though it were a building. Holding my eyes on hers briefly, the images of the first moments of her life popped into my mind. That tender infant face now so changed. I sat beside her on the couch and took one of her hands in mine.

"Your skin is so soft," I said, as I ran my fingertips over the back of her hand. "I put all sorts of lotions and hats on you, you know, when we went to the beach."

Annoyed, she said, "Tell me how you were affected as the pregnancy developed—your emotions."

"Of course, that's what we were talking about." I fidgeted in my chair, not knowing what to say. Then I said forcefully, "You kept growing, very fast, so that before I knew it, you were filling my belly. You were making my skin stretch . . . yes, that's what it was like."

I was left wondering. I had told her something as if it had happened to another woman. I didn't dare to look at her. All of a sudden I heard her voice.

"But how did you *feel*, what were you thinking?"

I went over to her, took her in my arms, and said, "I was frightened, anxious, and at the same time—confused. But then you were born, and you were so beautiful and so delicate . . ."

Suddenly, that storm came back to me, the rain beating on the windows, my discomfort and anxiety. The darkness of the night, and the silence that was so tremulous and infinite. I had never before sensed silence so special and unfamiliar. I had been alone at very difficult and even dangerous moments, but that night, while the contractions grew stronger and stronger, I heard a deep sound, the melody of a quite different loneliness. Then, an unexpected question from Julia interrupted my thoughts.

"Didn't you ever think of an abortion, Mother?"

"Julia," I exclaimed, "whatever possesses you to ask that?"

My daughter went for her album, which contained quite a number of still unmounted photographs.

"Take a look at this one, the expression on your face. Remember?"

It was a shot Joyce had taken of me and Kate at the beach on a windy afternoon. We had both given birth not many days later. It was true, I looked very depressed. The contrast with Kate was impressive; she was glowing, smiling broadly.

"No. I hadn't seen it before, where did you find it?"

"Joyce gave it to me. She also made copies of some others I picked out."

I found myself replaying in my mind a time when my days were enveloped in a haze of shadows and uncertainties, of reflections that clashed with a harsh reality that imposed itself insistently on everything. There was no gentleness in that period. The aftertaste of trauma embittered my days—a punishment for my behavior, the most overpowering of my feelings. There was certainly no magic in that pregnancy.

"I never liked having my picture taken—I'm not photogenic," I remarked with some annoyance. "You can see it in my eyes."

"You're with me in this one. Notice, Mother, I'm in your lap and you're looking off in another direction."

I glanced away from that snapshot. It was from Julia's earliest days; I could hardly cope with my feelings, with her.

"What are you driving at, Julia?" I asked anxiously. Not wanting to hurt her. I touched her face. There were traces of tears on her cheeks.

"I'd like to know if you wanted to have me or if the idea

of an abortion entered your mind. I always felt something peculiar going on, wondering if whoever was my father actually died as you told me . . . and whether it was something out of the ordinary or very sudden, I don't know. You must have hesitated. It must have passed through your mind that bringing up a child all by yourself was not going to be an easy matter."

"What is it, Julia? Tell me."

"There are too many pieces missing from my history. I have no grandparents, or rather, I don't know them; an absentee father who left without a trace. Joyce says she doesn't remember him. William told me he was always on the road, but he's an old liar." She heaved a sigh heavy with anguish. "I feel an emptiness, as though there were a hole here inside me that's been there ever since I was little, that I was never able to fill. I asked you how you felt about your pregnancy. Your story is so thin that I prefer sticking with the photographs."

"Julia, I . . ."

"You've already answered me, Mother. Mary Pickering, a classmate of mine, is pregnant. She told us last week she's thinking of having an abortion. I watch her every day. Being near her makes me nervous. I don't know . . . there's something strange about it."

Julia had begun tugging at her eyelashes, a habit when she's truly upset. I was struggling to come up with something reassuring as she went on.

"I wake up with nightmares—one in particular. I can't recall the details but I do remember the sensation. Rather, it's when I sit up in bed that I feel it, that I'm bleeding from

between my legs and that I'm smothering. I even think I've seen stains on the sheets."

"My dear, you've never told me," I said with alarm. "It's just that you are becoming a woman, it's . . . that's what it is."

"No, it isn't that, it's something more," she exclaimed in pain. "My figure is changing, but I'm not happy about it. I see my reflection in the mirror and it looks horrible. And I cry. That doesn't happen with my girlfriends—they show off their breasts, are proud of them. They go out of their way to show their legs and I hate mine. And Mary, with her body like that . . . different, sets off something peculiar inside me. When she said she wanted to get an abortion, I couldn't keep from putting myself in her baby's place. Doesn't that sound crackers to you?"

"No," I replied, avoiding her glance because I was crying, "quite reasonable, it's a helpless being."

"But I wasn't thinking of that baby. I'm not judging her. There's a word you frequently use that explains it perfectly." She looked at me, her eyes brimming with tears. "Abortion is an *abstraction* for me, just a word without content. What I mean is that I felt as though . . . I was being killed."

I went to her, put my arms around her, and we wept together without a sound and remained silent for a long while. Suddenly, she got up and started off to her room. Pausing, she said, her voice steady, "You know something, Mother? I believe I'm beginning to understand some things."

"Which?"

"They don't matter now."

"Wouldn't you like to go on talking, Julia?"

"About what?" she answered on her way up the stairs, dispirited. "It does no good to talk if you're not told the truth, no good at all, now I know."

I shivered. My daughter had just informed me that she was determined to move forward. Julia had made a pact with herself that day. And now I had no arguments left, other than the pitiful, deep-seated fear of losing her. I was aware that keeping the secret would widen the rift between us—a rift I would have been able to avoid had I been brave enough to tell her about my past, the whole wretched truth.

I find myself in the attic now. I think I mentioned that Julia collects hats. They were all set up against one wall, making a colorful, striking mural. I can't say exactly when she began collecting them; she never mentioned when the hobby started. She simply fell into it one day.

I'm reminded of the time we went to watch the Changing of the Guard at Buckingham Palace and how special it was. She was impressed by the guards' great black, fuzzy helmets, more wonderful than anyone could expect. At five years of age, Julia's head was already abuzz with hilarious questions about all the many different kinds of hats she noticed around her.

William—the old fellow at Brighton, Julia's self-appointed surrogate grandfather—who accompanied us to Buckingham Palace—certainly knew his headgear and gave long lectures on the subject. He was a sailor, had traveled the world, knew all the oddities of his island and countless other places. I guess he was the one who gave her the first hats, after which Julia began visiting Portobello Road and other markets on Sundays to ferret out people willing to pass their treasures on to her. Age and rarity are important criteria for her.

I call it a collection, not only because there are a lot of different headpieces, thirty or so, but because she treasures them the way a museum would. Her collection includes caps, a mortarboard, a biretta, as well as a bonnet someone gave her that seemed to date back to the beginning of the

century—a particularly pretty, particularly special, one. It
didn't look like the kind that was worn on formal occasions,
or that I'd seen in photographs or engravings, that women
used in the daytime for outings. It was almost oval and flat
on the sides, had the texture of a fine felt, with silk and lace
attached, but it seemed to be intended for protection against
the sun and yet on closer examination there were signs of its
having been exposed to bad weather for a long time. I got to
thinking that it might have belonged to the kind of upper-
class ladies who went on safaris. But why use one like that
for ordinary wear?

I remember having talked to Julia about this bonnet and
I recall her mysterious, mischievous expression. She didn't
tell me what she was thinking or what she knew. Julia and
I played such guessing games. When I suggested to her that
I thought it might have belonged to a poor girl who got it as
a present and that she wore it for working in the fields, my
daughter just laughed and laughed.

"Why not, Julia?" I said. "Think about it. How else could
it have taken on all those different colors?" Useless my trying to worm any clue out of her. Wild speculations about an
odd hat. When an object or event is strange or out of the
ordinary, it stirs up all sorts of speculations, which develop
into full-blown hypotheses. All Julia's hats are special, some
from the thirties and the fifties, several outlandishly garish
headpieces of the sixties.

Julia cleans and classifies them, attaches tags with jottings as to their origin, date, if she knows it, name of owner,
and any other data that seem interesting to her. They are
arranged on the shelves in the attic where Julia spends half
her time. Julia has a theory about hats which she expounds

to a few people when in the mood. A brief and probably inadequate outline of what she thinks would be that hats are more or less indicative of class and occupation, and the user's need to dissimulate and at the same time conceal. I should add that I had something to do with this theory of hers, for I asked her how she drew so many conclusions, and she gave me a simplistic reply more or less to that effect. That is probably why I call it a theory. Julia, intelligent as she is, noted the aspect of dissemblance. Hats are a fascinating subject, almost paradoxical to me. Although an element in the study of custom and usage, they are the most mysterious of the articles of clothing. Their brims and folds have come to supplant speech in greeting. If an object becomes an intermediary force in communication, it evolves into a repository of nonintrinsic signs and symbols, to form part of a network in which the authentically personal disappears.

I miss Julia so much. I run my fingertips over things she has touched, as if that might somehow bring her back. This attic is special because my daughter is special. This is where she does her homework, listens to music; it is also her refuge. And since it has a bed, she sleeps there, too, a good part of the time.

I like to exchange thoughts with Julia when we're not quarreling. I enjoy her quick intelligence. It was always so, I mean, ever since she started to talk and put ideas together. It's not as if I was responsible for the development of her reasoning powers. Although we would chat about this sort of thing, my daughter and I, and at that level she had the benefit of my thinking.

I am alone now, observing the hats; one, lying on the floor, I return to its place. She bought it for herself last year

at Harrods. We had planned to go there to get Julia a hat. It was a really special day in that we had been sharing desires and exchanging opinions. As we were trying on clothing, scarves, and even jewelry just for the fun of it, Julia talked to me about Mickey, how they had met casually at the coffee shop near the school.

"He's so handsome, Mama, that my legs shake when I look at him. Can you imagine? The day we met, he noticed and, like a fool, said so. I asked him how he could tell what my legs were doing if I had them completely covered over, and he, with his best smile, stared down at my boots. When I followed his eyes, sure enough, it was absolutely hysterical the way one of my heels was tapping against the floor. So I burst out laughing."

The saleslady had taken up a position close by and was obviously keeping an eye on us. She asked if we were taking the jacket my daughter was trying on.

"That's what we are trying to do," I answered.

"I don't understand, madam."

Her expression made me think of my answer, but she was already jotting something down in a notebook. I hastened to mollify her. "Not without paying first, naturally."

Annoyed, the saleswoman moved further away. Julia laughed out loud.

"Julia, be quiet. We don't want to make a scene."

"It's that the silly woman thought we were going to walk out with it on and what you said confirmed her suspicion. Look"—she indicated the woman standing nearby stiffly, not having taken her eyes off us—"Let's make believe that's what we're trying to do. What do you say?"

I fell in with her, and we made our way toward the end

of the section. The saleswoman stood in our path, along with another woman who was looking at us with a distinctly disapproving expression. She didn't get to say a word because Julia took out the hat she had bought on the lower floor, tried it on before a mirror, and said in a very quiet tone, "See, like I was telling you, Mama, the colors clash. I'll leave it with this woman." Then, with a smile, she handed the jacket over to the reluctant saleswoman, adding dismissively, "Besides which, I couldn't find my size in this entire, huge section. Shameful, wouldn't you say, miss?" And we marched indignantly off to the elevator.

Then she told me they had done that once before with her girlfriends, but this time it was more fun. We ate together in a Japanese restaurant—Julia's choice. I don't know how to eat that food and Julia was amused by my clumsy efforts with the chopsticks, the rice falling back into the bowl and the sushi barely making it to my mouth. After staining my sweater with soy sauce and greeting the accident with some well-chosen Spanish expletives, we left the place.

Outside, Julia suggested that we go to Regent's Park, our favorite. It was a Sunday, people strolling about so seemingly carefree. There was a pleasant breeze and the sun was shining. Then Julia took me by surprise with a question.

"You like Eric, don't you?"

"I do. He's very intelligent, he's been a great help to me in my work . . ."

Julia looked at me with an impish smile.

"I get it," I exclaimed, "and the answer is no—not in the least. He was my tutor, now we work together and, by chance, we may become in-laws, or something of the sort. That's it. What else?"

"Every time we talk about him, you blush."

I began to walk faster, trying to avoid her question but not wanting to make an issue of it. In my most judicious tone, I explained, "It's that he commands respect. He's an important man, you know, and possibly I get nervous for fear of contradicting him."

"But I was there the day before yesterday when you were on the phone with him and you said, 'You were off the mark,' about something he said in a newspaper article."

"Oh, I remember. Yes, it was in an interview. He was in a hurry, I guess." I looked at her sideways and said suddenly, pointing to a nice-looking little lunch place under some trees, "Let's stop off there and have a juice or something. I'm thirsty."

Settled at a table, I sipping my apple juice, she her strawberry juice as she eyed me, Julia suddenly broke the silence.

"He's interested in you, but as a woman. I know it. He treats you in a very special way, only you don't want to admit it. I consider him a very attractive man, *guapo*, as the Spanish women say."

"Leaving a mistaken impression is the last thing I want to do," I said. "Eric . . . likes me and I like him. We're friends, and now colleagues. And that's all there is to it. Know what I mean? I think we'd better give them a call. I'm tired, I couldn't take staying up late."

"Don't give it another thought," said Julia, finishing her drink. "After all, he's just a man. I've never seen you go out with one as far back as my memory goes, or maybe I just forgot."

I stood up quickly, saying we would be late. My daugh-

ter put her arm around my shoulders and whispered in my ear that she wouldn't ask me any more questions.

"Silly," I replied. "Your questions don't bother me."

"No, of course not."

At supper that night at Eric's house, she amused Mickey and Eric by imitating the clumsy way I attacked the Japanese food. And she kept watching me as we played poker. I played well, rather better than I remembered I could, and beat Eric out of a couple of hands. I must confess, however, that I was disconcerted by the way he was looking at me.

In any case, we had a most pleasant visit. We arrived home quite late, singing one of those Spanish songs we liked so much, off in our own world, raising our voices Gypsy-style, indifferent to public opinion. I remember Julia, her eyelids drooping, telling me what a nice time she'd had. I remember her hug and kiss before going off to bed. Her expression radiated utter contentment. When I entered her bedroom to tuck her in, I saw that she was already sound asleep, and smiling.

Eric: I have been thinking about him. Something happened at a meeting in his office with another colleague. The way he kept looking at me made me so uneasy that when I left the room, inopportune feelings began to race through my body. Eric is my colleague, I kept thinking as he spoke to me, my nerves tingling and my muscles quivering slightly. I considered the possibility—as if it were in my power to shuffle the deck again—that it was only a fleeting sensation. I had kept this inconceivable emotion, now inevitably, it was troubling my senses, so carefully filed away.

A week after that meeting, Eric called me to his office. I had not been able to sleep the night before. I could not look him in the face; my greeting before dropping into a chair was barely a "Hello." I watched him out of the corner of my eye for a few moments as he moved about the office until he asked if I would like tea or coffee. I accepted a cup of tea while I flipped the pages of a magazine in as casual a manner as I could muster. Eric seemed to be ignoring my odd behavior, although he did turn to look at me a few times. I was irritated by this kind of mute interrogation—a typical tactic of his. I knew him.

At any rate, he then lost no more time getting down to the reason why I had been summoned. It concerned a project of his, a study on human behavior to be conducted by professionals in various disciplines. When he asked my opinion, I nodded assent. It was a gesture that annoyed him, I could see that. I wanted to leave that very moment with-

out an explanation. I was getting up from my chair when he detained me by saying that I was one of the people he intended to call upon. Standing in the middle of the room, I said nothing.

Eric went to the window and drew the curtains aside. The light blinded me momentarily. Looking to change the subject, I pointed out that it was the first time I had seen sunshine enter his room. He shook his head, puzzled by my remark.

"What is it, Mercedes? Just tell me the proposal doesn't interest you. It's as easy as that."

"I won't say that because I need the money." And I went on to explain: "I'm going through a difficult time, and I'm tired. I'll let you know tomorrow."

Eric, disturbed, got up and walked about the room, cigar between his teeth, chewing it nervously. I knew he didn't like evasion and that's the path I was taking. I tried changing the subject.

"My belief is that human behavior cannot be predicted," I said by way of apology; "how can you attempt to study it if we are basically unpredictable creatures?"

He continued to pace and I noted that he was wearing a very becoming corduroy jacket and beige gabardine trousers. He was a young man—I knew that, of course—only he dressed too formally. These clothes made him look like another person, or rather, I was struck by my having thought this. I shifted my glance to the bookshelves. Then I heard his voice, detached, explaining:

"We're going to approach our subject on the basis of certain hypotheses that will lead us to uncover new conflicts. The unpredictable element in human behavior is correct, as

you point out. At the same time, it's equally correct to say
that we live subject to written regulations and cultural man-
dates. But why am I trying to convince you?"

I can't say whether it was his vitality, the sun, the tea, or the
combination that gave me a sudden surge of energy. Without
thinking, I answered flippantly, "Because you think I'm so
brilliant and, besides, because you know . . ." I stopped,
cleared my throat, and asked him, "Actually, why *are* you?"

Eric burst out laughing. Then he looked out the window
and said, "Come on, let's take a walk. I need a stretch. I
want you in this group because you have that rare and
incandescent spark so lacking in academia. Although frequently"—he paused to relight his cigar and lock the
door—"it takes you up a blind alley, you sometimes draw
excellent conclusions."

Paying no attention to my protests about being in a hurry
to get home, he started off, with me trailing after. He
walked at a good pace, greeting acquaintances as he went. I
haven't said much about him other than that he was my thesis tutor and Mickey's father. As far as his temperament
goes, it's rather on the serious side but does have a sardonic
streak as well. He doesn't talk much. I have seen him
remain impassive at meetings or congresses, letting the discussion swirl over him. And I have then heard him express
his thoughts vehemently, but in an even tone, leaving the
listeners plunged in abstraction, and why not say it, some
doubt. He never raises his voice, always keeps a cool head,
even when directly alluded to by someone trying to dis-
member a theory of his. On that day, as we left his building,
I was able to get an inkling of how he behaved with others.
The assistant program director had caught up with him to

bring some problem to his attention. From his tone of voice, Mr. Jensen needed to talk to him urgently. Eric just stopped, put a hand on his shoulder, and told him gently he had no time to take up the issue. The poor fellow was surprised and displeased. Eric was unperturbed. However, he added a few words I didn't catch. Jensen then seemed to be satisfied and even said goodbye cheerfully. We continued our walk. As usual, Eric proffered no explanation.

Then, I remembered the time I gave him the introductory chapters of my thesis. Despite my nervousness—I had sat stiffly in my chair, my eyes fixed on him—Eric was detached. But he had no hesitation in marking entire paragraphs with the shattering question, "Meaning what?" in addition to notes in which he didn't spare criticism of the route I had used in dealing with one aspect of my hypothesis. When I ventured to ask him about a concept he had underlined, he dismissed me at the door with "You'll have to think; that's your job."

As we walked along, I was able to confirm that he was treating me with special consideration, that he was giving me his trust. Certain gestures—his way of taking me by the arm—conferred a state of intimacy I had not been aware of before. I have never been able to understand Eric very well. He has launched challenging theories, won numerous prizes, and is invited to all the important philosophical congresses that are being organized. It has never been very clear to me why he put up with my mood swings, the black ones, I mean, of course. Even though my other colleagues are very intelligent, he always seems to give me preferential treatment. That day, as I tagged along at his athletic, practically headlong pace, I wanted to sound him out on the

doubts that assailed me every time he tried to foist something new on me. Was he doing it because he knew about
my past history?

I was considering all this as I walked beside him, even
recalling occasions on which I aired my disagreement with
him. Actually, his theories on a new, latent social consciousness are innovative and highly disconcerting. I'm impressed
that Eric is able to support hypotheses in which theological
and fundamentalist metaphysics are not covered. In short,
as in all conceptual universes, such hypotheses are a part of
abstract and complex theories quite impossible to assign to
an earlier time frame.

The truth is that he has been unfailingly generous in his
efforts to further my career by actions such as bringing me
into this group of very competent specialists in my field.
Last term, he made it possible for me to travel to Italy and
Spain to give lectures. Through him, I was able to publish
in the two leading philosophy journals, and in general he
opened doors for me to reap the benefits of these connections. Not only that, but he took the trouble to review my
thesis again, now transformed into the manuscript of a pub-
lishable book.

That day, he gave me some background on the group in
charge of the human behavioral analysis project. It was to
be an interdisciplinary group whose work would be initiated by discussion on themes related to the autonomy of
morality; specifically, the intricate mechanisms utilized by
the human being to overcome obstacles and survive. He
handed me a folder containing the plan. I was to take it
home and analyze it that night, and with that he sped me on
my way with a handshake.

I was dismayed and at the same time inexplicably elated. The other members of the group were not big names but their considerable experience in their respective fields was quite evident. That of a mathematician caught my attention, but I wondered what sort of contribution could be made by someone who lived in a world ruled by exactitude. His field was statistics, which didn't tell me very much until we began working together.

I can now exchange ideas with them (they were the ones at Hobbes' Place on the day of the fracas). We met once a week to explain our proposals. The group's initial work brought out divergences and there were several areas of serious disagreement. Finally, however, the orientation was enthusiastically accepted. It was agreed that the initial task should be the first of a series of studies on values and behavior; on rules and their functions, on tics, standards and mores.

I have only now become aware of changes that have taken place in the world of my own concerns. By a quirk of fate, I am living in a land where another set of problems—economic, environmental, even those of violence—is on the agenda. My own country faces different challenges as do most of the rest of a region where protection and aid programs are nonexistent. Nonetheless, I am quite in agreement with the approach taken by our group.

Most of us appear in the specialized journals and have ventured into the mass media, as well. Eric contributes a Sunday column on political topics. The rest write sporadically, airing their opinions on ethical problems, social responsibility—brief and lush wordplay aimed, in my opinion, at the privileged few. I will occasionally do a piece on

urban behavior, although a week ago I wrote two articles for *The Times,* one on the language of politics, and another on the need for creating an ambiance more conducive to creative thought, a new take on the intellectual's role in an industrialized society.

These articles aroused a certain amount of antagonism. I was inundated with letters, some very angry. I must admit that these little forays into the anonymous world of readers has caused me no little irritation. An Oxford professor got really steamed and wrote to the newspaper, which published a letter of his that clearly referred to me. And so, I was caught up for months in the sporting event of replying to those letters. They have accused us of overstepping academic bounds, as though it were a crime.

▪▪ As for Eric, we continue circling each other on very shifting terrain. Sometimes I raise my eyes and meet his, which seem to me to be projecting a tender, intimate signal, and this scares me. Perhaps I'm misinterpreting, even though his hand brushing my waist couldn't be a more explicit signal. I like him and have feelings for him, but cannot respond to him spontaneously. Not yet.

⠿ It is early morning and the street noises filter through the slatted shutters. I can hear the footsteps, the automobiles. I have little time, but intend to wait for Julia, even though she won't tell me anything at all to explain her delay. I look at the handful of unfamiliar photographs. I haven't been able to get rid of them because they are snapshots of Julia, mine but not taken by me.

All at once, my thoughts revert to the last few days, almost as though everything were happening all over again with the same violence I most fear. Despite my quarrels with Julia, despite even an intense intuition that something seemed out of kilter—I had gotten into the habit of checking everything around me—the time went by in quite orderly fashion. I went through my daily routine, with my book on the verge of publication, I stayed up late many nights going over proofs. The quotes in the body of the text interrupted the flow of argument, making reading difficult. Professor Carlyle advised repositioning them all and suggested other changes, as well. As a result, I was spending much more time at the publisher's.

Two weeks before the book was to come out, I called Carlyle about some questions and we made an appointment to meet at his office. The publisher was in the same building as the library and two large assembly halls. The entrance was on the esplanade in front where the university flag was flying. When I arrived that day, it was closed. Dr. Carlyle had told me to ring the bell outside, but I couldn't

remember which one he had said. There were four bells and I was so nervous and timid that I couldn't bring myself to ring any of them and decided instead to go around to the teachers' entrance.

As I was approaching the back of the building, I brushed past a man, and before I could get to the door there, I came to a dead stop on hearing him call out a name I hadn't heard in years. I remained where I was, frozen, and did not turn until he came up to me and repeated the name.

"*Gringa,* this is a surprise and a half! An old friend right here in the middle of goddam Britain. Hey, it doesn't look like it's just me that's surprised. Well, well, how's life treating you, girl?"

What was happening was so incredible that I thought for an instant I was hallucinating, as if some hellish curse was being visited on me. Blinking, half-blinded by the midday sun, I shaded my eyes and saw that same sneering, sarcastic face staring at me. It took some effort to keep my eyes fixed on that humiliating grin, exactly as if the intervening years had not passed. With the reappearance of that man, I felt as though fate had destroyed any hope I might have had for a happy future.

With *El Zurdo* standing there blocking me, I felt as if a stake had been driven into my back. Scenes from the past, the legacy of my torture—dizzying, implacable apparitions—ran through my mind, as I imagine the kaleidoscope before death. Confounded, my thoughts in disarray, I had to act. In my stupefaction, I shouted at him wildly, with all the force I could muster, "Get away from me or I'll scream for the police!"

He guffawed but didn't move. Rather, he stood his

ground, inspecting me up and down as though I were an object, while he said, "You're not scared of cops now or else these aren't machos like ours. But you sure are still a beauty, dammit." And he began to jab his finger at me. "Like I always thought, this is the kind of dish that improves with age, like a good wine. The older, the mellower. And this little lefty here is the best I ever tasted."

I wanted to get past the man but his words held me back. The taste of bile had risen to my mouth—a fury mounting to summon the strength to knock him down. But I had to go on my way. In the most natural tone I could muster, I said, "The police here do their job. They go after criminals. You might attract their attention if you don't let me by."

"And what do you think you could say to them, *Gringa*? A couple of old friends meet up by chance and you don't want to say hello as would only be polite?"

"Possibly, or maybe I'd tell them other things. I could go to the embassy."

"Do that—and while you're there, tell the Ambassador, his first name is Martín, that I'll be seeing him at eight in the morning. If you could do me that favor, you'd be putting in a word for me; he's a very formal guy. We didn't fix an exact time. He wanted me to make an appointment. He's a bureaucrat, you know. They're all alike."

It was no hallucination, that much was certain. It was my recurring nightmare come true. I'd wondered more than once what I would do if a situation like this arose, if I really bumped into him again. I had fantasized running away, even planned a series of strategies involving the Argentine Embassy. And here he was, speaking to me as if the Ambassador were a close friend, a drinking companion, or worse,

one of that same gang of murderers now running free. He could very well be—I told myself—one of those types in hand-tailored clothes, with manicured nails, who uses not a wedding band but one of those wide rings with a little stone in it, the symbol of a man with a shady present and shadier past. All those things occurred to me at once. Then, suddenly, his voice again: "We should make up. Look how luck operates. Here I was, not headed any place special, and I meet up with you." He stretched out his arms toward me. "Somebody once asked me, 'What would you do if you run into one of those lefties you released?'" He grimaced and looked at me. "'Say hello to him,' I'd say. Don't you consider that a good answer, *Gringa*?"

"I wouldn't know—maybe the man wouldn't know what to do."

"No, that guy was sure, said that if he bumped into one, he'd put a bullet in him. A blowhard who doesn't use his head. I'm not one of those."

I kept quiet, not daring to reply, and he went on. "I'm chilly," he said, looking around. "Let's have a drink." With that, he took hold of my arm. I wrenched it out of his grasp. Clicking his tongue in annoyance, he added, "It's an invitation."

The image of that look was imprinted on my memory; the same glassy-eyed stare that he used for intimidation was still there. It occurred to me then that it would not be easy to get rid of him. Running would be useless; I would have to figure out what to do from now on. Accordingly, addressing him in the polite form, I asked, "So . . . what do you do, now?"

"I'm no *usted* to you. If you can't say *tu*, I can't go on talk-

ing. I appreciate your interest, though. I thought you might be holding a grudge against me."

After a moment, I found myself answering in the manner of those long-gone times, with the subterfuge necessary for survival in those places.

"Ah! I barely recall those days. I don't like remembering." I pulled a vague face, a combination of indifference and dismissal. "What for?"

"That's what I say. A bunch of the old lefties and the new ones are making a nuisance of themselves on the matter of the ones that left."

I felt a spasm in my gut, a violent mounting nausea. I swallowed saliva and took a deep breath. I had no intention of showing any emotion. I wanted to find out what he was doing now, what job had sent him my way. This was *my* terrain—I was thinking as I put on a friendly face, and I was going to defend this place to the death. It scared me to think about death, to have that word on the tip of my tongue, a word that had such special meaning for me, not the one that comes from having lived out a life, the normal human cycle. This fiend I was facing was filth incarnate; even more outrageous, anyone looking at us would assume that we were just having a friendly chat.

The sun came out sporadically. My shoes were very thin and the cold penetrated right to the bone but I was not budging. "Another chess game," I said to myself, "and I'm going to beat him, the son of a bitch, at this one." In due time, come what may, I would call checkmate. *El Zurdo* was not the kind who let go of a prisoner easily. At least, I doubted very much that the beast had changed his ways, for I had once again become the target of his obsession.

That lascivious, omnipotent expression of his confirmed my worst fears.

I calculated that in order to develop a defense strategy I had to obtain some information. First, I had to find out whether the boast about a contact in the Embassy was true. I had to check his name, how often he traveled to London. But the last thing he said had dislodged an ominous memory which prompted me to ask him quietly, "The ones that left? Like me, for instance?"

"No, a lot of those ingrates are causing trouble now but over there. Turning them loose was a mistake. Some of them, that is, *Gringa*." Every time he said my nickname, in his coarse, saccharine tone, I felt an almost irresistible urge to throw up. "They're yelling over people who're colder than an iceberg at the South Pole." And he burst out in laughter that distorted his face. "They're nagging, holding demonstrations; the mothers of dead lefties keep demanding they be brought back alive. You know what it means to resuscitate a dead one—impossible." There are no words to describe the hatred he aroused in me with his talk about the dead, the people he and other murderers had "disappeared." A sob was forcing its way into my throat and I began to tremble, not with fear but repressed hatred. As I looked at him, I said to myself: "Strategy, Mercedes, remember." Then his voice broke in.

"You want to know something—it's damn cold." He buttoned up his jacket and wrapped his elegant muffler around his ears. He had on an Italian silk necktie and his trousers and shirt looked very expensive. Apparently, he was doing well, enjoying freedom, traveling the world with no charges pending against him. "I already invited you to have some-

thing, but I'm frankly lost around here. Tell me, where's
there a goddamn restaurant or someplace a person can get
something warm in his gut?"

I was nervous. What I was doing didn't seem like the
greatest idea, but I had gotten myself into something and
had to see it through. I stole a look at my watch and remembered that Professor Carlyle would be waiting, disturbed by
my lateness. I imagined him wondering what happened to
me. Then, all at once, I realized that the date for the presentation of my book was two weeks away and it was to take
place in this same building. I knew I had to get him away
from here, so I pretended that I was just out for a walk and
had wandered off in this direction.

"I don't know this area either," I told him.

I looked around me acting as though I was trying to get
my bearings, and pointed away from Bloomsbury, where I
knew of a pub that catered exclusively to soccer fans. It was
usually filled with rowdies and the owner seemed surprised
to see us walk in. The customers were a raffish sort who
start drinking late in the afternoon.

We ordered a couple of beers, sat down at a table, and I
asked him, "What are you doing with yourself now?"

"I'm a business consultant, a little like what I did before,
but quieter."

"Ah, I see. And what kind of businesses would they be?"

"Are you interrogating or does it just seem like it?"

" It's been a long while since I last saw you . . ." I
shrugged and looked away as though to say I couldn't care
less. "If it bothers you, we can change the subject."

"You always did talk nice. Always refined and decent,
even when you were really bugged, you'd never let on. The

boys had no idea what to make of you, know what I mean? They said, 'That one's an icebox' and you even cried that day."

Remembering must have disturbed him for he carelessly tipped over his beer and flooded the table. As the bar girl mopped up and brought a replacement, he kept looking at me, fiddled with his tie, glanced at his watch and said, "I have friends in the Customs Service. I'm in with the cops and, well, now I represent an outfit that exports computers. We make clones, but I also import used machines. Then, I do other jobs, another kind of consulting, some commercial, some specialized. That's what I'm here for, to talk to this guy who looks like he's reliable. One of your people."

"I don't know what you mean."

"A Peronista, an old-lefty type, but reformed and clean. Now, he's only interested in what he can put in his wallet."

I made a face like I was thinking and snapped my fingers.

"What's on your mind, girl?"

"I was trying to remember your name."

"How could you remember if you never knew?" And he patted my head. I reacted with fright, which he ignored. Then he added, "Well, all that being water under the bridge now, I guess I can introduce myself. Mario Dapuontes, of Argentina. Tell me, how long since you've had a look at one of our kind? These gringos here are snobs. They must all be queers. Ah, you know something I'll never forget . . ."

He stopped short. Figuring he was going to bring back the vile past, which I knew would unnerve me completely, and not knowing what to expect, I dreaded that this would send me over the edge. I began to tremble, and without

stopping to think, I hurried over to the cigarette machine. I had stopped smoking two and a half years before, and didn't feel the urge now. The impulse, my behavior, was prompted by my fear that the disgust, the hatred would show through and that by looking in my eyes he would realize that I would kill him if I could, take pleasure in it. I got a packet of Marlboros from the machine and matches from the counter. I regained my composure to some degree and went back to the table, a cigarette between my lips.

"You didn't used to smoke," he said, and with an impudent motion tried to snatch the cigarette from my mouth. "I don't like women who smoke."

"What did you say my name is?"

"Have you got—what's it called—amnesia?"

He looked at me through half-closed eyes. Suddenly, he leaned toward the window, poked his head out, and began yelling in English at a couple of boys dealing drugs, youngsters no more than twelve or thirteen. I had noticed them before, I knew the neighborhood. After he pulled his head back in, he launched into a tirade turned into an excoriation of the British, who according to him had the highest number of homosexuals, transvestites, and drug addicts in the world, a people given to excesses, a bunch of degenerates— a logical outcome, in his opinion, for a country with a tradition of piracy that went back centuries. Then, suddenly, breaking off this intellectual discourse, he said to me, "Mercedes Beecham. Your parents held on to everything, didn't let go of a penny, so you and your brother, that useless brother of yours, are going to inherit a fortune."

"And how do you happen to know all that?"

"Because I sold some stuff to your father a couple of years

ago, and last month, by coincidence, the computer company closed a deal with the old man, who, I should explain, is doing exporting now, but not cattle."

I began to cough, the past choking me. Finding no ashtray on the table, I put my cigarette out on the floor. Suddenly, this vulture had turned into a carrier pigeon bringing me fresh news of home. But my behavior took a new tack, as if instinct were edging me toward the fire to finish with him.

"You're not in touch with them, they told me, and they've lost track of you. You know, at first I didn't believe them, but I checked with my intelligence contacts and they said it was true, there was no sign of you. No phone calls, letters, nothing. How about that? Disappeared, until I found you. And what are you doing here?"

"Visiting."

He made an angry face, banged on the table, looked at me again, leaning close. "Don't be playing games with me, girl."

"Stop calling me girl. I came here to work for the summer. I'm probably going to ask the owner of this pub if he has an opening."

"Ah, I see, you're playing hide-and-seek with me."

"And if I don't tell you?"

"I'll find out." He snapped his fingers. "Quick as that. You see, I'm a bloodhound at heart, Mercedes Beecham."

The way he pronounced my name outraged me, as did his threat. I knew that it was true. I sensed that his tale about the Argentine Embassy was true, that in no time he would have my address and my entire history in England. "Listen to me, you third-rate hooligan," I snapped as I put

money for my drink on the table, "I have my contacts too, and you're far from clean." And I dared go further as I leaned over and spat out, "This isn't over yet, and you're going to know it. So watch your step. It's slippery ground here for criminals."

"You're making a wrong move, Mercedes. I'm not trying to bother you."

"Then get out of my life. I don't want you around."

As I got up, he put his hand on my shoulder. "You won't get away." He clucked his tongue loudly. "You're not listening to me, I don't like for a woman to threaten me."

"You're the one in the habit of making threats. I'm warning you, that's the difference between us. Now, get away from me, I'm in a hurry."

I raced down the steps and out to the street, feeling as though I were smothering. Words were bubbling in my mouth that were not in my vocabulary. If I could talk like that it would be only by imitation. *They* were the ones with the foul mouths, who crush others underfoot, who had introduced me to a language of savagery. Old memories, an abyss under a leaden sky that made each day seem menacing, the initiation of a series of nightmares. He had been stalking me in that pub as if I were his prey, and would keep doing so, I was sure, for I was his obsession. I found no consolation in the argument that if he had not gone after me before, there was no reason for him to be doing so now. I suddenly thought of Julia, stopped at a phonebox, and called home. There was no answer. Distraught, I tried

Kate, Joyce, and Mickey, and finally located her at Hobbes'. After a brief, unpleasant exchange, she agreed to be home by seven o'clock. I then called Professor Carlyle, apologized for my lateness, and made another appointment for the following day.

I left feeling less anguished but with a sensation of being watched. I looked all around me but saw nothing disturbing.

As I hurried along through the city streets, I considered the possibility of seeking help, but no sooner did it cross my mind than I discarded it. That is, I would not do anything immediately, but if necessary, I would turn to Eric and his contacts in the Labor Party. I must admit, however, that my thoughts began to skirt the realm of violent action. In simpler language: if he dared to harass me again—and this was now being obsessive—I would literally kill the swine.

The worst of what followed was not the stalking in itself but the reawakening of panic, and with it the nausea and pent-up rancor, swirling about like particles congealing in my consciousness. Omnipotent forces had begun to take control of my reactions, my thoughts unrecognizable as mine. I would wake screaming at night, with the recurring sensation of suffocation, a racing heartbeat, and dizziness. And I was unable to weep or call out that a murderer was after me. I wondered whether he was alone or if several of them were involved. Was it a chance encounter or premeditated? He, of course, wanted to do me in. Or was it something else? If so, what? The succession of events in that period was anguishing. They were brutal, chilling days spent railing against infernos—my own and this fiend's.

I walked for hours that day, my thoughts plunged in variations on the same theme, stubbornly calling up remnants of the past that had reappeared as my present, as live reality now. My mind, accustomed to developing assumptions, was sunk in a kind of paralysis, as though insecurity had frayed my nerves to the edge of obliteration.

Without warning, I found myself subject to a new space, the limits and contours of which were largely unfamiliar to me. I sensed his stalking but was unaware of his movements, and whether or not they were prelude to an act of

any kind that might soon occur. I could not predict when or
how the harassment would unfold, for one who is inured to
siege knows that most panic is instilled through anticipation
of surprise.

I was home by five o'clock, beset by fear. I inspected the
buildings that surround the block of flats in which I live. I
had never considered the possibility of my house being
entered anywhere but through the front door. But that
evening, I checked out all the possibilities with our superin-
tendent and a locksmith. Keeping a straight face as though
under interrogation by Scotland Yard, they answered all my
questions dutifully.

With the information I gathered about stairways, windows, cellars, and roofs, I prepared a rather rough plan of
the layout of my corner of the neighborhood. To get in
through the top attic window, it would be necessary to cross
the roofs of adjoining blocks of flats, and to my good fortune, there was an abyss between my building and the next
one. When I stood at the window, I could see it would be an
invitation to suicide for anybody.

I should explain that I conducted this examination
together with Bill, the bumbling handyman who was
responsible for the disaster of the mirror door that was
such a trial to me. He was a burly man, an asthmatic with
a breathing problem. Climbing up and down stairways,
over obstacles in hidden places on the top floor, I felt
oddly reassured by the companionship of the man's
wheezing, swearing, and complaints—directed not at me
or what I was doing but at indifferent neighbors who did
not pay proper attention to their flats and the exteriors,

which are ignored until a disaster strikes such as seepage or a leak.

As the two of us stood at the edge of the terrace, I was reassured by the thought that it was inaccessible without ropes and elaborate climbing gear. This made me reconsider the decision I had reached moments before to have bars installed on the window. I had figured that although it was not possible to enter very easily, to climb out, hang from the railing, and reach the stairway, although risky, would, in case of extreme emergency, be a definite possibility. Julia was on my mind in all of this, and how I could help her escape if it came to that. I consulted with Bill and he confirmed that, although dangerous, entry would be possible; in fact, quite feasible. Then, with a mysterious air, he asked: "Missus Beecham, was you robbed and I didn't hear about it?"

"Oh, no, no. I just like to play safe."

"I see," he muttered as he helped me down the last few steps. Then, his face a study in concern, he handed me a paper and said, "Here's my phone number, and underneath I wrote down my son's who works at the supermarket, just in case."

I smiled at him in appreciation. He was blissfully unaware of the anxiety his ineptitude caused me. No matter, I resorted to him regularly, complaining all the time about his creativity in modifying the instructions I had given him—whether it was using a paint color different from the sample I had given him, or whatever. There he was, with his bushy eyebrows, graying hair, and shuffling gait, acting as my guardian angel. I thanked him for his thoughtfulness. He nodded, and ambled off.

At home, I was checking out the whole place microscopically when Julia came back. Unfortunately, I didn't hear her come into the living room. Seeing her suddenly, out of panic I gave her such a shove that I knocked her to the floor. I rushed to help her up but she pushed me away angrily, exclaiming, "What's with you, Mother?"

She was looking at me in dismay as she got to her feet. I hadn't realized that hyperalertness had invaded my muscles, my nervous system, in short, my behavior. Now, I edged around the curtain, peeping furtively out of the window, having already double-locked the door and put the window guards in place in the kitchen. All this went on in Julia's presence. Finally, she intervened, when I was half off in another world and only vaguely aware of the consternation my actions must have caused her. But there was nothing I could do to control myself. She took my hands in hers and exclaimed in a tone of voice I hadn't heard from her in a long time, brimming with tenderness and anxiety, "You're trembling. What's going on, Mum?"

I was moved by her expression and felt like hugging her. "I love you very much, my darling," I said. "I know my behavior is upsetting you. But we may be in danger." I began to stroke her hair, her face so touched with concern. Then she let go of my hands and moved away a bit. "You must take care of yourself," I cautioned, "something strange is going on. I don't know what, but it scares me."

I realized that I was provoking her curiosity while offering her no information. So I invented a political situation concerning my work with my group at the university. I hadn't taken into consideration that such an explanation would only stir up further questions.

"Danger of what kind? Does it have to do with the situation in Ireland?"

"Well, I don't want to let you in on the whole business. It's much less risky if you aren't aware of . . . anything."

Julia's eyebrows lifted in surprise. Then she asked me with considerable indignation, as she began pacing the room, "What are you saying? We're in danger but I'm not supposed to know? You talk as though we're about to be kidnapped or something, and when I ask a question, I get the regular treatment. You hide . . . I can't live like this . . ." Her lips began to tremble. "You're sick. I don't understand, don't know what to do about it."

I didn't answer. We stood face to face for a few moments. Suddenly, Julia took a few slightly unstable steps toward the kitchen, opened the refrigerator, took out a can of fruit juice and sliced off a piece of cheese. She remained thoughtful, looked at me, about to tell me something, then changed her mind. After sighing deeply a couple of times, she excused herself and went up to her room. She was very tired; her face showed it.

When I sat down in the living room, I could feel my heart pounding at a tremendous rate. I felt terrible about the coldness of the way I had distanced myself from Julia, *my* Julia. Was it perhaps that I had reverted to the conduct of another time, readying to face high-tension situations? "Yes"—I said to myself—"that's what's happening to me." That devil's presence had put me into a time machine. I'm back in my 'militant's uniform' in the urban jungle again, trying to come out unscathed from the young revolutionaries' crusade." But while I attached lit-

tle value to life in those days and did not consider fear a sensation to be taken into account, right now I felt an overpowering urge to live.

My daughter was my main concern. I must have fallen into a long sleep, because when I awoke the light from the street lamp was filtering into the room. The telephone rang, frightening me. Should I answer? Could it be him?

Since the ringing persisted, I thought it might be Eric, or an emergency. It was Professor Carlyle, always the solicitous gentleman; he thought he had detected an anxious note in my voice. Obviously, he was attributing it to my looming publication date and offering me his unconditional support. I thanked him for the friendly gesture. Actually, the man's kindness was truly touching.

A couple of minutes later, the phone rang again. I answered nervously, but Eric's voice calmed me instantly. He was asking me to call him back regarding a matter concerning our project. Unable to get Julia out of my thoughts, I went upstairs, tapped on her door, called out, and getting no answer, entered. I found her asleep, sprawled out on the bed, the light on, a book in her hand. On the few occasions when I had come upon her as she was reading, she would act as though she were trying to hide something. She was holding a book of Sylvia Plath's poems. With my own special brand of aberrant reasoning, I made a connection between the author's suicide and Julia, as though a death wish were contagious, thinking that she might be identifying with the book for that reason.

I looked at her lying there placidly asleep, her hair cascading down her back; she was so tall now that it no longer

covered her as it used to when we would pretend that she was my teddy bear and I her tickling friend. She no longer let herself be hugged the way she did when she was little, listening, eyes wide, mouth open, to my fantastic stories. No more sitting in my lap, learning to read, or seeking my help in her first footsteps; no more tugging at my skirt in her desire to move on from wherever we were, no more bed-time lullabies.

During the course of her upbringing, I had established limits. I had been flexible in imposing them—aspects, I thought, of the profession of motherhood—and I tried to be a companion as well along the way, setting priorities and aware of inconsistencies. There was the matter of calling attention to an error, of pointing out the inevitability of mistakes and, at the same time, their reparability, and the virtue of admitting a mistake; the task of translating the symbols of reality, of people's behavior, of helping to decipher sentences, metaphors, with words and gestures. I took missteps in my endless search for content and its forms, and guilt feelings over a punishment, even when well-justified, often flooded through me.

In the course of learning rituals there are moments when we founder, even as the criteria of order, of liberty, are imposed. Given the inadequacy of words, even paraphrasing will not synthesize arguments, and I often find myself unable to reply to Julia's questions. I'm not referring to our particular conflict but to day-to-day incidents, those that we incorporate into expressions of our own experience for the benefit of our children. There was no diagram or recipe book, no introductory text to turn to in time of need. I was

conscious of having practiced motherhood out of devotion
to my daughter. But I only administered information. I was
unable to decipher the code for opening the casket only
because I didn't consider it the right one.

With time, a wall had built up between us. Now I didn't
know if I could touch her, if Julia would allow me to take
her in my arms, cradle her body with mine, but I wanted to
ask. Even though she was sound asleep, I lay down beside
her without thinking, purely on impulse. It was a delight
just to listen to the sound of her breathing, to smell her
scent, to see the outline of her body, and to feel, deep inside,
my pride in her. It had only been a few minutes but it was
enough to calm me.

I left on tiptoe, with my spirits revived. I was suddenly
hungry and even felt like listening to music. I skipped
downstairs, treasuring the closeness I felt with my daughter.
In the kitchen, I was taking a package of pasta and a jar of
sauce out of the cupboard when the phone rang.

"Hello," I said, but there was no answer, although I could
hear voices on television and what sounded like breathing.
I stayed on the line but there was no reply. I hung up as a
cold chill traveled my spine. The phone rang again immediately. Again nobody answered and the same sounds came
through. There were four such calls. Others would
undoubtedly follow, so I disconnected the apparatus. As I
did so, I realized that I was also afraid that my phone was
being tapped. I thought I would talk in code from then on
but quickly decided against it. I noted with displeasure that
a new scenario had already begun to form in my mind. I
was plotting out the blueprint for my resistance.

In view of the sequence and nature of events, I could not underestimate the possibility—almost certainty—of finding myself in danger again. I had to be prepared and show no signs of apprehension. Even in the midst of my anguish, I realized that it would be most inadvisable to show my fear. I didn't know his plans. How long would he be around? Where was he calling from? Finally, I fell asleep on the couch.

The shutters banged against the window as it began to rain. When I went to fasten them to the hooks in the wall, I stayed looking out into the street. Water was streaming down the gutters, and a woman in a yellow raincoat suddenly appeared, trying to make her way around the puddles. After closing the window, I brought my fingers up to my earlobes for an instant. Something in that woman's gait reminded me of somebody, and the gesture of touching my ears was automatic. I was wearing my sister Alicia's pearl earrings. A friend turned them over to me some years back and I haven't seen her since.

Perhaps this is the moment for me to tell you about something that happened a long time ago. Estela had taken Julia for a walk, and I was waiting for them with strawberry juice and cheese sandwiches, Julia's favorites. I had bought some jars of varnish and a can of paint to touch up the bedroom and bathroom doors. Brushes and all the paraphernalia were scattered around the small living room in the student flat I shared with Estela.

That Sunday, while waiting, I was busy putting them to use. The sun was pouring in and I was perched on the ladder in a very good mood, whistling, when the doorbell rang. Estela had said they would be back around four o'clock. It was now just three. I climbed down, put aside my brush and gloves, and opened the door. In my bewilderment I did not recognize who it was at first. What I saw was a face that looked familiar, but by the time it dawned on me who the

woman was, her greeting was uncomfortable. Nora was wearing a yellow dress, I remember. She had put on weight since I last saw her, and her curly hair reached down to her shoulders. After a few moments of looking at each other in silence, she repeated her greeting, "Hi, how are you?"

Seeing her was a shock. In an automatic reaction, I slipped out the door and peered around, still not fully aware of what I had seen. Except for some students going through the little square between the buildings, there was nothing out of the ordinary to be seen. Her voice came through to me, "Aren't you going to ask me in?"

I paused for a moment. Then, after finally managing to focus on her, I gave her a senseless answer. "I'm painting."

"Mercedes!" she exclaimed irritably, "it's me, Nora."

I asked her to come in, closing and double-locking the door behind her. In the next few minutes, I kept watch at the window. Finally, I asked, "What are you doing here? How did you find me?"

Nora remained standing, looking very annoyed. Making a face, she pointed to her backpack, which had a number of stickers on it, and asked, "Can I set this down someplace?"

"Over by the table. Be careful of the paint."

Nora had been a comrade activist in the movement. She had ended up in the cell next to mine when we were captured and, like me, was one of the survivors of the group. We had been close friends, struggling together to survive the cellars. The last I remember of our time together was a vague rumor about being liberated shortly, which is what happened; her release came two weeks after mine, according to what she told me.

After that, nothing. I knew I was being unfriendly, and

regretted it at the time, just as I do when I recall the incident. To make my apprehension at all understandable, let me explain that it was impossible for me to explain how she had managed to get here. How could they have traced me when I had left no trail whatsoever—none? The realization was unavoidable: that if she had been able to find me, my former jailers should have no trouble at all.

"I'll fix you some coffee. Or would you prefer juice?" I opened the refrigerator nervously. "There's beer also."

"Mercedes, for heaven's sake . . ."

My head inside the refrigerator, I angrily repeated the list of drinks.

"It's hot. I'll have a beer." And she snapped, "Is it alright if I sit?"

"I'll make it two. That chair's not safe." I pointed to another one as I handed her the beer. "Let's drink to this reunion."

"It doesn't feel like much of a welcome. Your tone is so distant."

"It's coming from over six years ago. My sound got turned off along the way."

"I don't want to inconvenience you. I'll leave, if you prefer."

"No, wait . . . I don't mean to say that. Are you alone?" I got up suddenly and examined the stickers on the backpack. I exclaimed in surprise, "These say—"

"Yes, I've come from Argentina."

"You stayed on? I mean, they let you live there?"

"I'm catching on now that you haven't been in touch with anybody over these years. They put me on a plane, I took it in Brazil, they threw me out of there. I was working

in Spain, nothing steady. We have comrades there, you know?"

It was moving to hear the word "comrades." Such a long time since anybody used it to me, and coming from Nora, it had a very special ring.

"Ah, and what did you do there?" I looked at her closely and was surprised to see a scar, more like a seam, at one side of her neck, but I looked away quickly so as not to make her feel ill at ease. "Did they give you any guarantees? No, forgive me, I don't want to talk. It's . . . absurd."

"But I want to talk. I came back with Victoria and Juanse. Remember them?"

I nodded. I didn't know they were alive. They were leadership and they had survived. But my sister was one of them and she's dead. Obviously, I couldn't help thinking of this irony, unfair as it was any way you look at it.

"They're almost all coming back. Democracy . . ."

I interrupted her quite rudely as though talking to myself. "Sure, democracy. And what about the military? Up until just recently, they were out there destroying lives—the army, the regular police, the port police, the navy, gangs of monsters." My voice rose as I went on. "The enemy is assumed to be . . . what, hibernating, their vicious instincts dormant?"

I looked away through the window, heaved a sigh, then continued, "Well, be that as it may, I'm glad. Somebody told me the President is an intelligent man. I was impressed to learn that he's been riding around in an open car."

I was lost in thought, far away. I hadn't banked on the possibility of running into anybody and had completely removed myself. And, if I must be frank, I was also thor-

oughly annoyed. I couldn't think clearly that day, which may explain why what I am saying sounds so ridiculous, even crazy. But that's how it was. At that time it was impossible for me to conceive of such overwhelming developments. I was still remembering the torture, waking out of nightmares in which the setting was invariably awash in blood. Nora interrupted my abstraction.

"The government appointed very well-known, democratically-minded people to take affidavits from those who were imprisoned and managed to come out alive."

"Ah. Very courageous people." I smiled nervously. "Admirable. I'd be terrified they would kill me."

"They can't. We are protected now, the whole world knows."

"Yes, it's possible . . . You know what I thought while we were down in those cellars?" I looked into her eyes. "That the world out there knew, but nobody was coming to set us free."

Nora closed her eyes and nodded. It gave me an opportunity to study her closely. Even her hair was all different colors and her very flashy dress didn't quite succeed in lightening her look of exhaustion, which was so extreme that it gave me a chill. We were silent for a little while, brooding on our own recollections, until, calmer now, I finally ventured to ask her something.

"The places—you know what I mean—did they find which ones were used, where they were located?"

"Well, that's where we're at now. Identifying the prisons with the people willing to testify."

She became anxious, each word growing more emphatic as she spoke in the heat of conviction. "A report is in the

works on the atrocities committed during the dictatorship. Even army officers who didn't go along with it are coming forward; the fiends will not go unpunished."

Nora's words took on a new fervor as she went on talking, but I couldn't help feeling dubious. Monsters like those were ready to step down from their posts and go to jail, just like that? Nora's expression was telling me that something new was in the air: justice. Society was finally taking action. Nevertheless, my mind became caught up in a series of questions without answers, a haze of inevitable assumptions, the arguments of which clashed with reality. All to the good, it's true. They can't remain in power. But all that sinister structure—was it just going to disappear under democracy's magic wand? What had happened in Chile seemed the most clear-cut to me, with Pinochet untouchable. That was indeed a sinister transition, although the way I see it (I was thinking as I continued biting my nails), brutally conceived, but real. And that swine travels around the world with no problem, unpunished as yet. The world knew what he'd done; he carried out the dirty work himself, took responsibility and accepted the blood-soaked laurels. Why not? He'd won. My mind pulsed with terrible thoughts, Nora's voice coming through to me as though from very far away.

"Mercedes, are you listening?"

"Yes, of course, go on."

And so, I listened to her argue in favor of the people who were offering testimony—first before that group, and then before a court that would certainly try the criminals. The murderers were going to pay, they had to. But there was something I wasn't able to justify in my mind. So much

power, and now jail? I put no store in the armistice, although the outcome of the conflict, or rather the war, could not be looked at in that light.

"You'll appear, right?"

"Nora, I'd like to get something clear. Do you think this deal is really solving anything?"

"If it wasn't, I wouldn't be here."

"How did you get my address?"

"What difference does it make?"

I hiked my body forward, and in a rather curt, rude manner, said, "Listen to me carefully. Every little detail is important in this. You come through that door into my life and you throw me a proposal that you're sold on. Okay, let's go on. I want to know how you managed to locate me. Then, we can talk."

"The Commission on Human Rights made inquiries. You applied for asylum, Mercedes."

"I see."

I began to pace restlessly, trying to keep my wits about me. I looked at my watch. Four o'clock; time had whirred by too fast. My daughter was about to arrive and I didn't want Nora to see her. I had little time. I tried to come up with a reply of some kind that wouldn't sound aggressive, or wishy-washy. The truth is, I had no intention of testifying, I had my reasons, in addition to my personal reservations about that new buildup for avenging us. But no way was I considering confiding anything to her, to them, or to anybody else, absolutely nothing that would give a clue to my movements after prison.

As I have already said, I think I was being unfair, but at that moment, old wounds were opening and terror was

seeping into my ordinary life. I thought about it every waking moment. I could not move out of my terrain, a space
fenced off and with many retaining walls. Everything still
had life-or-death importance for me.

I said nothing for a while. And then, I did something
horrible: I reproached her harshly for her action. She was
putting me in danger. I opened the window; the sky had
blackened. I was convinced I was going to see figures lurking about. I listened desperately to every little sound I could
make out. But an unexpected mist suddenly came up, coating the sidewalks. It was surely about to rain, and all I could
see was the breeze fluttering the tops of the trees in the little square. Again, Nora's voice broke into my thoughts.

"You must testify, it's your duty."

"My duty," I retorted as I nervously shut the window and
covered the jar of paint, a thickened layer already harden-
ing on its surface. "My duty is to try to live . . . to live a useful life. My duty is not to collapse into madness, as I was on
the point of doing. I know what I went through and I have
no intention of reliving that hell. What for, Nora?"

"They'll be in jail."

"What about the ones who tortured us?"

"They'll get them too, they'll all be put away."

"Don't be so damn naive, Nora."

"What's the matter with you, Mercedes? You're letting
your bitterness blind you."

"There's a whole flood of feelings involved in these
things, including bitterness. But, now, that isn't what it's
about. I got myself into that hell, wasn't able to look out for
myself, and if anybody could have, they didn't . . ."

"I'm confused. I had the idea we were on the same side,

that we swore that we would find the way for justice to be done. Did you forget?"

"I haven't forgotten anything, it's just that I still don't trust them. Can't you imagine how I feel, can't you accept that this time I'm scared? I can't put those beasts out of my mind, the ones who killed Alicia, Ernesto, the ones who tortured defenseless kids, who tortured us. I was in the same place you were. There were a lot there, Nora. Too many. And it all went on practically under everyone's noses. How can I not be doubtful? If those guys had it all sewed up until only little while ago—how long ago was it? A year or two ago they were the masters of the present and the future. What do you expect me to think? That they are going to just let themselves be put on trial?"

"Democracy won out. They're going to try the top instigators, and then . . ."

"But, Nora, democracy is a newborn infant." I looked at her. Not wanting to hurt her, I sat down beside her. "Does anybody know where the weapons are, the rank-and-file murderers? Tell me"—I was yelling at her, I couldn't help it—"can you swallow that those monsters are going to turn power over to civilian hands without making sure who's in the rearguard? Sure, they'll put them in jail, and let's hope it'll be a goodly number. But it was all just a project. How long do you think they'll stay in the coop? A couple of months, a year; and the others?"

Her eyes filling with tears, she interrupted, "Don't shout at me. They couldn't turn us against one another before; please, don't let them now."

"You're right, yes." I embraced her. "Are you alright? I mean, you're going to stay there to live, obviously."

"Yes," she answered as she dried the tears that had trick-led down her cheeks to the corners of her mouth, "with my parents, until I find work."

"Has the city changed much?"

"No, not much. Very little, actually. Except for a new freeway, everything looks shabbier. I know you haven't been in touch with your parents."

I didn't reply. Her eyes revealed she understood why. The strange thing was that I stopped glancing at my watch as she told me about the activities of the Mothers of the Plaza de Mayo. Nora had gone with them on their demon-strations every Thursday. She described them as vast protests, block after block jammed with people, made more dramatic by the placards and blowups of photos of the dis-appeared that the women carried. The country had changed. Perhaps I was mistaken in my reservations about democratic power.

Skepticism is a mask for cowardice, which I realized at the time but wasn't able to act otherwise. When I said that I couldn't testify, I couldn't, not at that moment. Nora just nodded. Embracing her, I wept as I told her. I begged her forgiveness. It's a terrible thing; one cannot apologize for not having the courage to do something and so must accept the punishment befitting the behavior. But I needed her forgiveness as if it were a blanket pardon from a throng of unknown strangers who had died in that hell. This is the plain, unvarnished truth about my behavior. Any other explanation is mere speculation.

All at once, I heard Estela and Julia at the front door, call-ing to me. Before I could react, my daughter was up on my lap, saying, "Mummy, we went to the amusement park and

I won this bear. Ping! I knocked over the pins on the first shot."

I introduced Nora to Estela, who was standing in the kitchen doorway. Suddenly galvanized, without introducing Julia, I told her to go take her bath, and since I was busy, I asked Estela to help her.

Pointing out the obvious, Julia said, "I had a bath already this morning." Then, pointing to Nora, she asked, "Who's she?"

"I'm Nora, an old friend of your mother's," Nora answered in English, which she had always spoken fairly well, but it now sounded much improved. "What's your name?"

"I'm Julia Beecham," she answered, arching her little eyebrows. "Are you going to stay and . . . ?"

I picked Julia up and held her under my arm. She enjoyed my playing with her like that. I started up the stairs and beckoned Estela to follow us. I told Julia she could play in the bathtub for a while, handed her the bubble bath and brought out some plastic boats and ducks.

Back downstairs, I told Nora that we would have to be leaving in a little while and that I still had to put away the paint and clean my brushes. Julia had repeated her full name, as she usually did, and I was sure it would start Nora thinking, which is just what happened.

"I didn't know you had a daughter."

"Oh yes. Why would you know?"

"Why does she say her name is Beecham?"

"Is that what she said? Her name is Julia. When are you leaving?"

"How old is she?"

"Four and a half," I lied. Julia was going to be six in a few months. "Oh, excuse me, I'll walk you to the door."

"I understand." She picked up her backpack, zipped it open, and handed me a package. "You left this in Juanse's house."

I was bewildered, couldn't move for a few moments, my eyes on a smallish package wrapped in brown paper.

"When did I leave it . . . in which of the houses?"

"Boedo's, Mercedes. Here, it's yours."

"What is it?" My hands were shaking. I made a face and added, "I took only my handbag, I have nothing more."

Nora handed me the package, closed the bag, and started for the door.

"Nora—thanks."

She turned. Nora knew me well and my eyes betrayed my feelings despite my efforts to hide them. We had been childhood playmates and remained close friends ever since, our innocent secrets and dreams, a pleasurable part of growing up. We had shared a lot, but nothing like this. And I believe she sensed something that she conveyed to me with her eyes when we parted.

"You must have your motives, though I don't share them," she said as we held each other tight in a swift, uneasy embrace. "Maybe you'll be able to confide in me again some day. So long."

I had no reason at that moment to doubt that Nora would keep her mouth shut. I was, in fact, practically positive that she would. I knew her, missed her. Terrible things can separate people, or bring them closer together. In our case, that experience had opened a vast gap between us. Something so intense that it cannot be forgotten.

I had to cope with my own perceptions of my delirium because there were moments when I couldn't bear to live with the absurd trajectory of my history. I was afraid of losing my mind. In fact, I became involved in a sad series of contradictions in which deficits from my past began oozing to the surface of my consciousness, and not even the best of arguments had a cleansing effect. Old wounds reopened; the ghosts, relentless, gave me no peace. I felt hounded by my persecutors and by others, bent over in the shadows, the innocent ones, and I'm not exaggerating when I say that my torments multiplied.

At night, I opened the package. It contained a book by Hegel; another by Fanon; a volume of poetry by Neruda; some letters; two photos of Alicia; one of Ernesto, when we were kids, of course; a bracelet engraved with my nom de guerre . . . and Alicia's earrings. I spent an agonizing night. Estela stayed next to me. She knew she could do no more for me than hold me tight, and when I mentioned my conversation with Nora, she said nothing. I don't forget the generosity of her understanding. I needed it so badly.

⠿ The encounter with Nora left a wake of bitterness. I didn't change my mind. I had good and sufficient reason not to show my face back home—not to mention my lack of courage, let me not hide that. But now that I reconsider, that space held over from the past is flooded with life by the figure of my little daughter and her beautiful smile. Always at the center of the swarm of my contradictions, she gave me the strength that I lacked to stick to the resolution I had made. Were I able to maintain the joy that I felt when I saw her come in and announce her name and surname, would it have made a difference in my relationship with Julia? I don't know. Inevitable thoughts that pop into my mind at such moments. Opportunities did come up for me to have told her everything straight out, but I did not take them.

Now, when I think of Julia at sixteen, I realize that my youth was quite different from my daughter's. Her values are similar but they have taken a different form, and she is of another time, unlike mine, and possessed of a need so genuine that it has wrenched my soul.

I was dwelling on those thoughts when the phone rang. Alarmed, I answered. It was a friend of Julia's asking for her.

⠿ I've gone for my handbag, am combing my hair, staring blankly into the living-room mirror. Something, a shadow, appears in it and, fearfully, I turn around. Nobody is there.

I'm alone and safe. When I try to open the outside door, I am unable to. The lock seems to be jammed and I'm stuck inside.

Agitated, I remain standing at the window. The wind is blowing strongly, rustling the leaves. I am afraid, don't want to live through that again, but it has come alive in my consciousness, the memory implacable.

It was something incomprehensible during a violent time in my country, when nothing made any sense, that I should have been released that day years ago. It was a sixth of December, proclaimed by the headlines as a day of record-breaking heat for the decade. It began at four o'clock in the morning. I came out in street clothes. They gave me a handbag, my own. How upsetting when I recognized it. I felt around inside it: my toothbrush was still there and the Spanish comb Ernesto gave me. It would soon be two years since his murder and I invoked it at night, silently, but upon touching the comb, it was not his face but his death that appeared to me.

I came out of there bathed in sweat, gasping for breath, not realizing what was happening until I found myself sitting in the backseat of a van with *El Cordobés* (the Cordovan) peering into my face and asking me if I was alright. *El Cordobés* was a nineteen-year-old boy who had been picked up while slogan-painting. He was intelligent, well informed, and the military had made good use of his kind. He had been brought into the Archives a few months before. He was such a little fellow that seeing him thrown in with us made me feel particularly bad. But he had shown fortitude and the ability to adjust—the key to survival in such a place. Whenever he talked politics, it was always in a

low voice. In any case, I would never confide in him; the habit of silence was ingrained in those days.

That morning, we were together with *El Zurdo* (Lefty), *El Chancho* (the Pig), and *El Loco* (Loco), three murderers transformed into seemingly harmless citizens by dint of nicknames. "Released" was the one word we both heard, and nothing more. We turned our heads as the van drove along the inner roadways. We were able to see the building. At that moment, loud shots could be heard and I jumped. *El Zurdo* tapped me on the shoulder as he pointed out a little field where conscripts were target-shooting. Chalk-colored columns, large windows of palatial dimensions, a broad, white facade set in a grove of trees. Nearby, a flag-pole with a flag barely fluttering in the warm breeze.

My eyes lit on some openings, ventilators for the cellars. In the delirium of that unreality, it seemed to me that I could make out the faces of some comrades coming out. I had to cover my eyes because if I opened them, I would see them crossing the road at the edge of the pathway of magnolias at the main entrance, to one side of the statue, on the same side as the fence. They were motionless and just stared. I began to weep disconsolately for the first time in almost two years. And I repeated, holding my hand over my heart, that I would never forget them. I swore that, somehow, I would bring them back to life. I had one clear, sound thought in the midst of my madness: that I would bring that thought to reality afterwards in my own way. No question about it, I was going to write a book.

My weeping brought immediate disruption. The question arose as to whether I should be taken back. They pulled

up beside the road and parked. Obviously, my behavior was worrying them. Was I sufficiently recuperated? Thinking about it now, it is clear to me that for *El Chancho* and *El Loco,* the group of rehabilitated patients were an enigma. If the prisoners had been given treatment, what was this symptom of busting out crying all about? *El Zurdo* counseled keeping cool, that it was nothing serious, and consulting his watch uneasily, suggested continuing on our way. We never knew what his line of work was, although some figured he must be an accountant because of the way he could manipulate numbers. Whatever the case, compared to the others, he had a much more sophisticated mind.

El Loco calmed down after *El Zurdo*'s explanation and started the motor. Then, as though a light had gone on, illuminating the unknown in his brain, he snapped his fingers, looked at me as though I were a specimen of some kind, donned his dark glasses, and began to pontificate.

"She's worked up. This is typical female behavior. What do you expect? Say something serious to them and the waterworks goes on. Happens to me all the time, like I been saying, a woman is no good for war."

Unpredictably, I felt a panic attack coming on, a paradox, as though leaving there was putting me in danger. I remember trembling, my mind defying my perceptions. That situation had me on edge, not just then but for years. It's strange, but I cannot explain the sensation, even when I've tried to give a name to what I was feeling, I couldn't. More so when what happened subsequently exceeded the imaginable, by far.

I still remember the first hours; the monotonous music

and hoarse voices on the van radio, annoyance rather than entertainment, as I looked out in fascination at the streets of my city.

Then something changed. Toward afternoon, following a frugal lunch, their voices took on a cheerful, friendly tone, and a new, unexpected activity began to play out. They took us sightseeing through the city, as though we were tourists. *El Chancho*, with his hoarse voice and fluid gestures, took on the role of tour guide, announcing all the points of interest, including public buildings. He called particular attention to the excellent impression made by the riot police at the Casa Rosada (the presidential palace) and the statues of the forefathers at City Hall. His harangue included a running commentary on the age and architectural style of the various buildings. Cobblestones, narrow streets, moldings carved by famous artists, the Nereids' Fountain, the statues.

They had been almost too predictable up until that time. We were familiar with them in their sleepless nights and ours. Now we were getting information on architecture, the French, baroque, or colonial styles, provided by *El Chancho*. *El Loco*, however, seated to one side of the van, held forth on the current status of the city's sewage system and the population of rats in the cellars. Although they quarreled constantly, there appeared to be a relationship beyond friendship between the two of them. They were indeed like brothers; yes, that was the impression I had of them after that sojourn in the cellars.

El Zurdo, who had been guarding me so far, kept quiet almost all day, until night, when we went to a restaurant that belonged to an acquaintance of his. He became talkative then. And so, for that entire day and until ten o'clock at

night, we visited every corner of the city. It isn't easy to describe the surrealism of the scene, those men relating anecdotes of the history of the streets with a vocabulary and set of gestures I didn't recognize in them. Although some of their mannerisms did show through, they seemed different, that is to say, decent, educated people. They were anything but and taking themselves seriously.

El Chancho was called by his nickname because of his off-beat predilections, not to say perversions. He was tall and skinny and for some reason hated appetizers, going directly for the main course and then dessert. He had indeed been a specialist in thinking up the bloodiest types of torture and was known, in another period when it was still permitted, for having raped many prisoners. It was not only the violations in themselves, but the accompaniment of certain tortures that excited him tremendously. His record includes the cases of two adolescents he had killed during the act. At night, the guards would leave the door open so we could hear their discussions. It's hard to describe the gamut of depravities I overheard in that hellish pit. I suppose they did these things so that we would have no illusions, so that hearing their stories would leave us no room for question as to who held power.

Fostered by the abnormality of the circumstances, everything became even more macabre. Some mornings, we merely stared up at the ceiling, speculating endlessly on how we were going to end up. Ideas ranged from painful death to silent submission to the will of the masters of life and thought.

El Chancho, reeking of blood and hell, was a scorpion spawned by the devil; he had stepped outside the bounds

of humanity. *El Loco*, a small and skinny fellow with mad eyes, who roamed the halls drunk or on drugs, enjoyed describing how he laid *chinas* (servant girls) in his *barrio* (neighborhood). The verb "to bang" is the one he used which, I assume came from the vocabulary of firearms. He banged any poor lost wretch that crossed his path. That was *El Loco* for you. He could numb your soul with blood and death, boasting to handcuffed prisoners and to us. Judging by the circles under his eyes, and the fact that he was in the habit of spending the night telling different stories to the *chinas,* it seemed like the guy never slept. Apparently, he banged them in the subway, the elevators—practically a Superman. Sometimes we laughed. Only sometimes.

I recall the time we heard *El Loco* come tearing down the stairs panting, spitting, and apologizing. It seems that the filth of corruption had finally come down on his head and he was being consumed by the dunghill of crimes perpetrated with his riffraff coworkers. But now, apparently, this murderer was biting his nails over something else. A nervous little giggle and a horrible little sob kept interrupting the nasal voice as he told what happened the night which he confessed to somebody when he thought he had killed his girlfriend, *La Chueca* (Bowlegs). He thought so because when she stopped breathing, he took off, leaving her tied to the bed. *El Tartamudo* (the Stammerer) nodded and sort of made fun of *El Loco* until *El Chancho* walked in.

The cracks in *El Loco*'s voice became more pronounced, his tongue seeming to bounce against his palate like a defective spring. The story would get lost for moments in the interrupted vocal rebounding, as if every syllable were resonating with incredulity. They hadn't been seeing each

other for months because *La Chueca* was going with the neighborhood butcher. But, according to what he had heard, she missed him, and so he looked her up again. Word was that she took on the fat man for his steaks, on account of her little brother, who was so severely malnourished he had stopped growing. She was made out to be such a heroine that he was caught off guard and ready almost to offer her matrimony. She was wearing one of those skirts that exposed her well-shaped thighs and spoke to him with that little singsong note in her voice that got him so turned on. She was Paraguayan and prepared typical tamales of her country that "overwhelm" a person.

That was another verb, not very common, that *El Loco* was in love with, which most people didn't get, but it sounded good, elegant. "Don't overwhelm," he would say if he was being rushed. Or, "That's an overwhelming feeling." He overwhelmed everything. And when he saw her naked in the room, he said, "You overwhelm me." Such niceties on his part charmed *La Chueca*. He insisted that they play a little game. First she would tie him up and he would let himself be choked. Then, when it was her turn, it seemed like she was being tickled because she was laughing a lot until she stopped making any sound at all. The *negrita* was looking at him, eyes vacant, a glint of surprise in them. He shook her, slapped her a few times, but *La Chueca* was silent, not breathing. This time he had screwed her to death. *El Loco* didn't appreciate that usage of the verb, but it fit the circumstances for he had certainly screwed up. He remembered having tied her to the bed. Then there was the choking game. Did she lose it? Her eyes, blank, looked at him in fear—no, no, not possible—then suddenly the taste of

bleach in the back of his throat, and he dropped her on the
bedspring. It was as if he had been kicked right in the balls,
because nothing remained of his excitement but the wraith-
like shadow that accompanied him home at night.

There are certain corpses that leave you with a funny little aftertaste which he swore had never happened to him
before. He could be heard reflecting that the whole thing
was on account of the game. Since he loved her, it was just
that he had gone too far. He didn't remember anything, and
didn't want to have to explain to anybody, so he jumped the
fence at the rear of the shack and beat it around the garbage
dump. Fats was blamed because he was laying her for
money; because he was a butcher, and a brute; because *La
Chueca* told him he smelled like a dog that needed a bath.
At the end of the story, we could hear backslappings and
"Don't worry about it," and *El Loco*'s nervous giggle fading
away as he went down the hall.

And that's who was at the wheel of the van. To make me
even more nervous, the others began telling him, before we
started, that he shouldn't try showing me how he could
drive with his eyes closed. The guy was considered really
crazy, so crazy that he was capable of poking a lollipop stick
through the skull of a newborn. He and *El Chancho* sometimes debated military strategy with our group. They liked
to read about the Vietnam War. Police dramas and war
movies were discussed endlessly as real events.

El Zurdo was another case. This was a different mentali-
ty, a kind that really terrorized me, for he was a theorist. He
maintained a composure that was almost metaphysical and
he never betrayed emotion, not even while being reviled in
the midst of a torture session. Coldly, he would get on with

his task. He changed tactics frequently. He conducted himself in those cellars as though he were in the jungle, prepared to kill. He ventured an opinion only when asked, and sometimes we had even seen him give an offhandedly vague reply to a question from a superior. He was wily, materializing like a shadow behind one's back, and there was a certain gleam of contempt in his glance. As for his nickname, nobody could explain the reason for it. Inasmuch as he wrote, tied knots, and ate with his right hand, the nickname became not so inconsequential in view of the fact that one of our favorite pastimes to keep from losing our sanity was playing guessing games. The rumor began to go around that his father had been a Communist. Finally, we came to the conclusion that he had been infiltrated into our organization. For that reason he was up on philosophy, politics, and Marxism. He was an avid reader of our reports. Besides, he was the only one who dared suggest to his superiors that other subjects be investigated in the Archives where that strange Brains Trust Operation was conducted.

⠺ I did not know how to interpret the events of the final days. Under siege by that monster, I lost all notion of time. One morning during the last week, I awoke in a fright. A terrifying silence seemed to be permeating all the spaces of my house. Julia was not in her room. Half-asleep, I looked at my watch: already eight o'clock. I brushed my teeth; a quick, warm bath seemed momentarily to allay the chill in my bones. When I went down for breakfast, it caught my attention that everything was in place, the tabletop clear. Julia always left things in a mess and I had to follow her tracks with the vacuum cleaner. Now, there were no crumbs, no bits of cheese, no sign of Julia.

Had she gone out alone, or worse, had Dapuontes broken in and forced her to go with him? Oh God! I began to scream her name and raced up to her room, looking desperately for any clue. Everything was in order. Then, I noticed that her briefcase was gone and, suddenly, remembered with a sigh of relief: she had a standing appointment on Thursdays for early breakfast with classmates at a coffee shop near her school. She would be there for less than an hour. I dressed quickly, berating myself for having overslept and left my daughter in danger. Although Dapuontes had shown no signs of life all day yesterday, that meant nothing. It was entirely possible that he would confront me out on the street, anywhere. First and foremost, my daughter had to be protected. I decided that the best way to watch over her was to keep abreast of her activities.

Then, if I had to deal with that character again, my strategy would be to keep him in doubt, unsure whether I was capable of bringing charges against him before the Human Rights Organization, accusing him of robbery, or whatever. But, in addition, what happened was that besides unleashing panic in me, he had moved my mental gears into high gear. Among the possibilities I had not discarded was that of killing him, assuming I was capable of it. But on that day, it was not at all clear what could be done about the murderer. I didn't know.

I went to the coffee shop and saw Julia coming out with her friends. I followed them as far as the school. She would be safe there for the next few hours. I continued on to the publisher's to keep my nine o'clock appointment with Professor Carlyle. On the way, I observed the same extreme caution as when I left my house, peering on all sides.

There was nobody in Professor Carlyle's office when I arrived. A door was ajar in the next office and I thought I recognized his voice as I approached. I peeped in and he was there, but the person he was talking to was not his assistant, John Dickens. It was Dapuontes. My breathing stopped, my brain went numb, my eyes flooded with tears. When I could breathe again, I had a wild impulse to break into their conversation and face the son of a bitch. But reason quickly restored a semblance of calm, and the issue became one of not betraying weakness.

I stood there, mute. While I was trying to formulate my opening words, I listened to their conversation. Carlyle was answering the stranger's questions brusquely but amiably, sizing him up, sagacious and cautious as usual, expressing his displeasure at the interrogation to which he was being

subjected by providing vague, then inexact, and finally deliberately false information. Despite my panic, I couldn't help smiling at what I heard him saying.

"You must be referring to the Beecham manuscript, I understand. Well, it isn't ready for publication yet. It is"— there was a prolonged pause during which he blew his nose—"a muddled subject, very badly written, besides. Let me see if I can find it here in this pile, my assistant is quite sloppy. Look at this, for example, that I was sent last week. Can you imagine trying to work with material presented in this form? Well, be that as it may—what did you say was the name of the publishers you represent?"

"It is a new publishing group, not yet public as such," Dapuontes answered. "But, excuse me, Professor, according to my information, the book is to be published in two weeks."

So, he had that information as well. Those cowardly telephone calls, then, were being made by him. He knew my address, had studied my movements and Julia's, too. I shuddered at the implications. By following the same rigorous tactics he had used on that previous occasion, he was now familiar with my daily habits. I recalled the stories of his relentless hounding of Alicia, whom he was able to locate on a couple of occasions when she had managed to get away under his very nose, recalled his exultation over the result of a chase that ended in the detaining of my sister and two really important members of the group. I can still hear the words with which he concluded the pitiless description of Alicia's slow, lingering death: "She died looking into my eyes with an expression of primitive wonder." *Primitive wonder*. Twisted words to describe her death throes. Upon

my release, he was the one who made sure I knew all the details, such as the exact time of Alicia's death and how they had disposed of the body. I still remember it, as if it were yesterday, despite the panic and hatred of that night, the way his bloodshot eyes lit up with the telling of the macabre story. He kept them fixed on me as he told it, even making a gesture with his hands, a gesture as of discarding trash. The coward knew that I was defenseless and had no qualms in telling me what was the most excruciating thing that had happened to me until then. I never forgot that moment and kept the bitterness alive in my breast.

But I could not allow my life to be destroyed by harboring that deranged memory. As the minutes went by, I felt a tickling in my throat that was rapidly becoming uncontrollable. I swallowed and resorted to every method of self-control I knew. I wanted to hear how much more he knew. If I was not mistaken, Professor Carlyle was getting wind of something, so the next question would go further. But Dapuontes went on.

"It is a book about utopias of this century, according to the note I saw. Actually, the reaction was favorable and apparently . . ."

Carlyle cut him off, his tone curt. He was becoming annoyed and could show his rugged side when he had a mind to. "I cannot give out information to anybody I am not acquainted with, whether he be the representative of—well, no matter what important organization. Nor am I able to show any original material, even if the writer is, frankly, an utter disaster. So now, if you will excuse me, I must get on with my work."

He called to John Dickens who, to my bad luck, was

already coming in my direction and not only waved to me but called out my name. He walked in and said, "There was no answer at her house, but Professor Beecham is already here."

I went in and without preamble apologized for my tardiness. Professor Carlyle did not miss my expression of disdain as my glance traveled from the visitor to him. He frowned and said, "This gentleman wanted to see you, Mercedes. I don't like the idea of publishing this sort of rubbish in the newspapers and I'll have a talk with the Program Director if I see him. So, take heed. If I see that you decide to publish anything so . . . disastrous . . . By the way, your name is . . . ?"

"Mario Dapuontes"—holding his hand out—"pleased to meet you, Doctor?"

I did not take it, but greeted my editor effusively. Though he was not accustomed to an embrace, he accepted it, and even patted me affectionately on the back, taking advantage of the moment to say, "I don't like it." I replied with a gesture of affirmation.

"Professor Carlyle," I assured him, "I have absolutely no intention of publishing a line." I then turned toward Dapuontes with a smile and said politely, "But I am pleased to hear that you are keeping up with my career and, what is more, that you seem to know more about me than I do myself."

"No, nothing like that." Then, including himself absurdly in the dialogue, he went on to say, importantly, "The point is, I seem to have some loose ends." With that, he took out a pocket electronic organizer, consulted it, then jotted down something with an expensive-looking pen in a

tooled leather memorandum book. Then, with a masterful
air of self-confidence, he glanced at the editor and his assistant, and turned to address me. "I have the title listed as *Fin-
de-Siècle Utopias*. The subtitle, *New Concepts of Freedom*.
Also, at the author's suggestion, an alternative title, *Freedom
of Thought, a Feasible Utopia*. This without any subtitle, am
I correct?"

Since I did not reply, he went on, "Ah, how lucky you
are, Doctor, because . . ."

I cut him short with a clarification he didn't expect. "I
haven't received my doctorate yet."

"Well, in any case, you are just as lucky," and to the surprise of the three of us, he took out a copy of the dust jacket. "As you can see, the first proof is already out, and as I
understand it, the printers will have the entire edition ready
in four or five days."

I no longer had any idea if that other meeting had been
by chance or if the hunt had begun at an earlier point. But
none of that mattered. Events were moving at a headlong
pace, with little clarification of the role of chance in trigger-
ing this nightmare. As if nothing out of the way had transpired, he added, "We could probably suggest some other
illustration for the dust jacket."

"You are a specialist, Mr. Dapuontes," I said with a deep
sigh. "I see no 'loose ends.' On the contrary, you seem to be
quite aware of everything."

"Yes, but here on the flap, it doesn't say where you were
born. Only information on your academic career is given. I
mean to say, having been born in the same country as you,
it sounded like an oversight that is—how shall I say?—
inexcusable . . ."

Carlyle looked at me, while John slipped out to his office, visibly disconcerted. The situation had become untenable. I decided to end it by interrupting him. "Excuse me, Dr. Carlyle, I'll show this gentleman to the door, if I may, and be right back."

He put his pen back in his pocket as we walked down the hall, he with a doctoral air. I asked him, in the softest tone of voice I could summon, "What's next?"

"I don't understand."

"Now you know my editor, you have the dust jacket, and perhaps the text of my book. Well, is interference in other aspects of my life to be anticipated?"

"You know, I hadn't thought," he answered with a malicious smirk. "Would you like me to pay you a visit?"

"Didn't you get what you wanted? Wasn't that enough?" I spat out at him, "Obviously, harassing people fascinates you. You enjoy seeing a person suffer, it's something that goes way back, isn't it? It's in your nature."

The monster continued along as though he hadn't heard me. On the landing outside the main entrance, he threw me a disquieting glance. Before he could leave, I said, "The British consider the repression in Argentina an important subject, little studied as yet. If you are interested, I can put you in touch with some organizations that consider it genocide, not to mention those whom, as you say, are 'still around.' I'm not sure, but I believe some are living here in this country."

He turned completely around toward me and I managed to catch a glint of alertness in his eyes. "I'm protected. Do you think I would have been able to survive otherwise until now . . ." He straightened his expensive jacket. "Don't you

realize you are talking to one of the winners." Then he came up to me and whispered in my ear, "You should get up to date on life in your country, girl. We won; you're all fighting windmills."

At that moment, Julietta, the Italian sociologist from the behavioral group, appeared on the street, waved a greeting, and gestured to me to wait for her. He looked toward her, then said something unexpected.

"You had a daughter. Her name is Julia, a nice name. Talking about loose ends, she uses Beecham. How come? Were you left holding the bag?"

A bitter taste of bile rose in my throat. Before I could answer, Julietta was upon me, giving me a hug and planting a couple of kisses on my cheeks, ignoring the stranger. "I was calling you." she said, "Don't you listen to your messages? Well, now that I've got you, you won't get away." She looked at her watch and with a sidelong glance at Dapuontes, went on, "I have to see Sheppard and I'm free in half an hour. Don't say no, we'll have a cup of coffee. I guess you're here about your book, so you'll be with Carlyle. See you there."

Despite being in her eighth month, Julietta was quite agile. She pressed my two hands and rushed off into the building without another word. Subsequently, she was to tell me that she realized something unpleasant was going on with that man because I was standing there so stiff and pale.

Then, Dapuontes's voice again, asking, "Who's the father?"

"None of your business. I have to go."

"You know, I've never forgotten that night, how the smell of your body comes back to me and the way the fierce

lioness fought me . . . it was just great. The best fuck I ever had. Yes, I still remember, so well it makes me feel like having a repeat."

I realized that he was holding all the aces. He had no intention of letting up, he was going to persist in torturing me. Right now, he was celebrating something that made my guts writhe. I turned around, dizzy, and hurried off straight to Carlyle's office. I asked to use his telephone and called Julia's school. The principal promised to hold her there till I came. Then I spoke to Eric and told him I was very busy with my book. The call turned complicated and absurd. He was unable to understand my refusal to attend a session on the work we had to present the following day and I became harsh, impatient at his insistence.

"I can't! Aren't you familiar with that word?" I shouted at him. "I've got too much to do and I'm tired, yes, tired. I have to hang up, Eric."

Carlyle had been watching me. When I looked up, I saw his expression filled with concern.

"As I told you yesterday, you can confide in me. Do you want to talk? Are you able to?"

I shook my head, made a limp gesture of impotence. Carlyle put his hands on my shoulders and said, "I see. You'll have to calm down a little bit, at least. Here's comes your coffee." John was bringing me a mug and a glass of water.

I drank the coffee as though my life depended on it, and then, unable to control myself, I began to cry. Immediately, I was wracked by spasmodic sobs, a mixture of grief and rage, gushing from my eyes, my lips. I could feel the fury pressing at my rib cage. It was a tumult of violent emotions. I didn't want to cry, had no desire to be sobbing like this,

feeling like dirt. I cried but couldn't conquer the sensation of repulsion, of nausea. At that moment and during the days that followed, the sensation of violation turned into a rebirth of hatred that took possession of my body anew.

When Julietta came into Professor Carlyle's office, I had calmed down considerably and was giving the pages a final check and taking a last-minute once over at the cover. Only by looking into my eyes could anyone have suspected what I was feeling.

As we sat in the little coffee shop near the building, she tried to get at what was happening to me. Of course, my evasiveness quickly convinced her of the uselessness of questions. We parted shortly afterward and her warm words of encouragement accompanied me as I rushed on to the school. Julia was waiting indignantly, left with me in an angry mood and wouldn't say a word until we were home. All the way there I felt that I was being watched.

⠿ Buenos Aires, December 6: a terrible day. A few worried-looking passersby in the dim early morning light. The streets empty, the sidewalks littered, a handful of people waiting, expressionless, for a bus. That is the image that sticks most in mind, although there were others, the Florida swarming, Avenida Corrientes, at midday when we went for something at an office near the courthouse. I was off in another dimension, convinced that I was living out a part in a movie with a fantastic plot. Even now, I still think of that period as a fictional exaggeration of horrifying reality. They allowed me to see my parents; my brother was in the United States.

A delay with the papers and, I might add, a calamity awaiting me right at the very frontier of hope, to tear at my entrails—a countermanded order that opened up a timeless, shapeless gap that was to last two days. And that was when the truly unexpected happened. I was waiting quietly for them to kill me, prepared even to disappear under the concrete with a bullet in my head. But no. The group was put up in a hotel. *El Cordobés,* the intelligent one with the sad eyes, was with *El Chancho* and *El Loco* in one of the rooms. I, with *El Zurdo*, in another dimly lit room with damp, whitewashed walls.

When I saw *El Zurdo* appear on one of those days with bottles of beer and a crazed expression in his eyes, I feared the worst, which is actually what was soon to happen. I had never seen him behave like a madman before. Although he

was a murderer, he never went out of control. He tossed some documents on the one table in the room and proceeded to inspect them with apparent uneasiness. Suddenly, he stood up, went out, and returned at an even more advanced stage of derangement. I remained silent, almost riveted to the chair, in a position my body unconsciously assumed, hands clasped behind the back of the chair, my feet together, ankles touching. There were no common borders of understanding between us. The only history we shared were the two years in those cellars, I as a prisoner, he as my guard.

How absurd, at that moment to be thinking of that boy, *El Cordobés*, sleeping with those two notoriously debauched individuals. My guard came in and out of the room several times. At one point, he took a paper from his pocket and raised his glance to me. He kept staring, his eyes fixed on mine. Then, with a nervous laugh and a drag on his cigarette, he left the room, slamming the door. Since he did not return and it was eleven o'clock by then, I settled into the armchair in one corner of the room.

It was very hot. I had wandered the city for two days without showering and was giving off a heavy, sweaty smell. Also, I hadn't slept in two and a half days, yet I was alert, wanting to be awake when they killed me. The hands of my watch crept exasperatingly. Inevitably, suppositions of all sorts crossed my mind. I have no recollection of feeling depressed or apathetic. Freedom was still only a step away, and all I wanted was for the end to arrive. I was so tired that, even though my eyelids drooped, I remained awake. I did one of those exercises in which you had to concentrate on a chessboard in your mind.

It was a mental game my grandfather taught me. Practicing with him, I developed a respectable ability to visualize and locate the pieces on the board. The game was not only amusing but it kept me awake. I never did like to be checkmated. Chess and solitaire were the games with which I occupied my mind in periods of tension. I went into a kind of trance in which whatever was happening around me remained in suspension, my thoughts were focused on the imaginary pieces fighting it out as long as the game lasted on the imaginary squares for the glory of winning.

That night I remembered my grandfather's chessboard, a huge wooden affair with black and white marble pieces. He always let me play the whites. Every afternoon before the sun went down he would set up the board, put on music, Bach preferably, and teach me all he knew about that fascinating game.

As I look back now, I believe that I lost that night because my brain was tired and my moves sluggish. What I am describing may sound like foolishness and undoubtedly is, but it does help me escape reality. When I closed my eyes, the board vanished and the faces of my parents appeared to me: the uncertain outcome of that hot day, the suddenness of my unexpected release, the conversation with them over the telephone downtown and then our meeting, so impersonal, so lacking in any signs of familiarity other than their wrinkled faces and certain characteristic gestures from an earlier time. All of us trapped in an absurd reality.

Then, the shell of the city, its sweating people, a movie theater—nothing related to what was going on. Not even the leaden sky that evening as we passed through nearly empty streets. I could not help thinking that perhaps the

events and the people who crossed my path were unreal, and that I must be dreaming. I could identify aspects of the city—signs, buildings, even the moisture that slid down my back. But something was out of joint, and I was just another lost citizen in a strange neighborhood, unequipped to set it straight.

Finally, I must have fallen asleep, because at some point I was awakened by a hot breath on my neck and *El Zurdo* on top of me. I struggled up and began to beat at him with fury. But he continued fighting me, unbuttoning my blouse and grabbing at my breasts. I screamed at him to stop and bit him on the neck as hard as I could. He pulled away in pain and, putting his hand to his neck to stop the bleeding, went to the bathroom. He returned with a wet towel. As he was holding it to his neck, I yelled at him that rape was forbidden and that if he knew what was good for him he'd better stay away from me. This reference to one of their own rules seemed to work like magic, disconcerting him momentarily. After standing there for a moment he vanished from the room.

I thought I had won. But no. In half an hour, like a predatory animal, he was back and in a state of tremendous agitation, his eyes glassy. I recognized the ferocity; I had witnessed it before. I knew there was little time left. If I needed any further proof, all I had to do was look at the armchair jammed up against the opposite wall. Snorting like a bull, he tore off my skirt and then the rest of my clothes. I kicked at him wildly, while he retaliated by punching me in the nose. Despite the blood spurting out, my agonized screams, and my efforts to resist, he continued trying to force me. It didn't take very long before he had me

stretched out on the bed, naked, as when he had tortured me the first time.

And then he started to slobber frenetically over me, making my very entrails recoil in disgust. I landed him such a kick that it knocked him against the headboard while I tried to get to the door. But I changed my mind and scrambled to the armchair over which his jacket was draped. I knew he kept his revolver there, found it, turned, cocked it, and pointed it at him. His response was maniacal laughter. Then I realized I couldn't shoot. I would be sealing my own death warrant. I tossed the weapon aside and tried bringing him to reason by insisting that he couldn't do that to me, that he would be held responsible. It was forbidden by his superiors, and I knew it. I relish the memory of that conviction, relish it because, even as I was delivering this absurd speech, I considered myself already hopelessly condemned.

Although those men had gutted my hopes, and wielded enormous power over me, I thought I could still save myself from this one ultimate outrage. I had resisted torture and they had never succeeded in breaking me. I had been able to use a made-up language of phrases and silences that made them think I was defeated and that they had taken my soul from me. Each agony I was subjected to had been grimmer than the one before. I remember once when *El Chancho* came to my cell and imitated for me the way he had made Alicia beg. I remember that my feeling of impotence was so overwhelming that I broke down in a flood of tears, and in that infamous cellar I swore never to give in to them. I must admit, at the time, it was only the thought of vengeance that kept me alive.

However, between this murderer and my freedom, I chose (if it can be called a choice) the latter. In a spontaneous, involuntary reaction, I made a dash for the door, thinking of running to the street nude as I was and without money. He reacted just as quickly, grabbing me and throwing me back on the bed. And there I lay, his prisoner. He tied my hands to the back of the bed, forcing my face down; then with his legs he applied a scissors hold on mine, and from that point on, I can recall only the shock. When he penetrated me, he let a darkness into my insides the agony of which I have not ceased to suffer to this day. It is like the night, not dead-of-night blackness, but foggy, silent night, a darkness of shadows that weigh upon body and spirit, and I sink into a deep pit that never ends, that has no bottom.

Out of that night came Julia's life. My body transformed into a coffer of scum. Because of the vicious instincts of a beast, ill termed a man, I was obliged to hold my rage in check, to be sensible, to seek a structured rationality amidst chaos, if I were to go on living. I was given no slack, had to silence my indignation, my helplessness having left a wound on my body and my mind, indeed, on all my actions.

The monster had now given me to understand that he intended to hound me even more relentlessly. What followed was unpredictable, opening up another brutal and violent chapter in my life. Was this the moment to rethink things? No, action was urgent.

The tempo of my life accelerated at a feverish, jerky pace. I followed my daughter every day, not giving myself a moment's rest. It was a time of constant tension during which my mind seemed to find no place for anything. What is more, although he provoked nothing, I kept changing my schedule and the pattern of my movements.

As I said, I began to follow Julia, waiting for her to leave school. I think I didn't really care whether she saw me or not, as long as I found her safe. No matter, I took precautions. My plan was a long and tedious one. Estela was brought into it, accompanying me several times. I liked having somebody along, and no one knew as much about the source of my agony as she did.

During those turbulent days I also came to a decision, or several. I finally decided to reveal to my daughter the motive for my silence and constant vigilance, the cause of the pain and anguish that has been my lot for so long; to explain about her identity and her name and the bestiality of that man, the malevolent bearer of the genes arbitrarily deposited in her. There was so much for me to tell her, and as I walked, the confession scene began to take form, the words and gestures, the reasons for my secrecy, an endless

litany teeming in my brain. I would tell her that I forged my new existence because I felt that doing so was my only option. And that she wasn't the cause of my overwhelming grief. She would have to understand—I told myself—I wanted her to give me that opportunity. At the same time, the sensation of anxiety never ceased plaguing me. And even though the extraordinary thrust of desperation, of agony, of horror seen and experienced opened a furrow in my life, I was determined to challenge, to give battle. And I intended to win.

These revelations accompanied me in the course of each day of my life. I went to Regent's Park last Sunday, where I saw Dapuontes walking along a path. I could tell that he was heading toward my daughter, who was roller-skating on the park's main road. I looked about for Mickey nearby, could not find him, but then saw him bending over on a bench adjusting his rollers. That was where Dapuontes appeared a few moments later; but meanwhile Julia had gone on to the maze area, smiling happily.

I can't explain what happened next. All I know is that I ran to prevent her meeting Dapuontes but was slowed down on a bridge. To my disgust, I saw that they were conversing, she nodding as he spoke. At one point, she looked down, frowned, and covered her mouth. The villain was saying something that disturbed her. From what I could see, this was not the first time he had approached her, for she showed no indignation. On the contrary, it seemed to me that although she may have greeted him with surprise she

did not react as though he were a stranger and continued talking to him.

Julia seemed worried as she said goodbye to him. Dapuontes disappeared along the pathways of the maze. Mickey caught up with her and they sat talking on a bench. All I could see were perplexed expressions, Mickey glancing over the park, Julia saying something, and Mickey finally nodding and stopping his search. They set off again on their skates, but the smile on Julia's face had vanished.

Half an hour later, I appeared before the two of them, feigning a casual encounter. Of course, Julia did not swallow that, certainly not after I asked her to tell me what Dapuontes had said to her. She refused, warning me to stop interfering in her life, even though, beginning to lose control of myself, I told her that Dapuontes was an extremely dangerous character, that she should be extremely wary of him. Julia threw me an angry look and stalked off without a word.

I remained frightened but determined to keep myself from sinking into depression. In any case, there were moments in which I felt that life was slipping out of my grasp. Perhaps what one learns is how to fight the ghosts, to seize them and to set them a limit; a useless course, to be sure.

Those days were filled with a search for guidance. I realized how deeply rage had penetrated my being. What Dapuontes did was to bring it to the forefront, to rub salt in the wound that hurt the most. All my thoughts were tinged with fury; the feeling I had managed to pacify within my spirit now changed each day's aspect, upsetting my actions. Sooner or later I would have to deal with the question of the identity of Julia's father. But here he was forcing the issue, stalking, just as he had done before.

It was inevitable, then, that disappointed hopes should come to the fore, and something strange came over me. All the predators of my fate, like that of so many others, became concentrated in the face of *El Zurdo*.

I realized that I had never gotten over the feeling of being persecuted by my captors. It had remained latent even though I had come to put my life together again. That is the explanation for the obstinacy with which I guarded my secret. But then, suddenly, in the park that day when I was feeling so terribly anxious, I looked at the figure of Dapuontes and thought: "This creature is on the prowl again, but now, he's on his own." Without the government machinery behind him, there was little he could do beyond threatening and unnerving me. The tracks of my past were sufficient motivation for the scoundrel to strike a final blow. The situation now had a new twist.

I understood so many things during those final days of such deep anxiety. The shadows of that hell were fading away, little by little. Still dubious and hesitant, I gradually began to put together the building blocks of my history, and, ultimately, Julia's. It was difficult and unpleasant, but I sought beyond the barricade and discovered other words, new devices for revealing the hidden plot to my daughter. I felt a consolation of sorts entering my spirit.

▪▪ When I found her at home later, she looked at me furtively. I remember the slow steps, her silhouette in the corners of our house, the silent passages replete with gestures and movements which hinted that she had undergone

a change. I suddenly had the sensation that a denouement, lilting and tremulous, was impending. I had no idea what form it would take, but the moment that could more accurately be called a new stage in my daughter's life, in both our lives, was imminent. Yet she hovered in the shadows of night, seeking no communication.

At one point I got to thinking that after these intrusions into my life, it would all be over with. Actually, that was what I fervently desired. But the next day, the opposite was true. I left the university at about five o'clock carrying a book, a few folders, and of course my handbag. I was about to hail a taxi when Dapuontes's voice stopped me, telling me to keep walking. He was annoyed and pushed me toward a bench in the square. After making sure nobody was around, he made me sit down, saying, "Curiosity killed the cat." He let out a guffaw, followed by an intimidating gesture. "I want you to tell me about the girl. I saw her . . . two or three times, and today I realized something, you know? I think there are no loose ends anymore, get me?"

I kept quiet. He went on, "So, you bettter talk. Take your time—but not too long."

"Obviously you have some kind of an obsession, but I don't think I can do anything about your loose ends—"

He cut me short, "Don't provoke me, Mercedes. For some time I've been holding back the urge to wipe that look off your face."

"What are you talking about?" I answered defiantly. "You're flying off the handle. I don't think that will get you anywhere."

"Julia doesn't know anything. The pretty little thing needs to be brought up to date about this and that, wouldn't you say?"

I held my breath, a knot in my throat, and finally said,

"And what do you intend to tell her? Where do you start?"

"No problem. You were a subversive, plotting against your own government. You and your gang fought and lost. And the winner spared your life. Well, after that . . ."

"You raped me, you vile coward. You took advantage of a helpless person, beat me and raped me like a wild animal."

"What am I? Go ahead, tell me."

"Say it yourself and leave me alone."

"You enjoyed yourself, Mercedes. Don't play the victim now."

I stood up, but he forced me to sit again, as he whispered into my ear, mockingly, slurring the words, "You had a good time that night, admit it."

I looked at him as he stood in profile. For a moment, it seemed to me like an unbearable nightmare I had never thought it possible for me to dream. In fact, it was something even more horrible. Suddenly, as I looked at his profile, I saw Julia's superimposed. The insubordinate gene had left a slight mark, and yes, she did resemble this creature. An invisible factor had brought the elements together and linked events, making him come after the information now. Our paths had crossed. The man's presence seemed an impossibility, but it was real. And for an instant I thought there must be some primordial justification for this. He was no longer a ghost, he was a tragic factor imprinted on my life, on my daughter's life, seeking to confirm his intuition or his truth. I tried not to cry or show the hatred aroused in me by his presence, and even more by his words. I heard his voice.

"She's my daughter, isn't she?"

"Is that what you think?" I heaved a long sigh and looked at him. "Better think again."

"Don't be putting me on." Annoyed, he stood up and began to rock from side to side. Suddenly, he took some photographs from his pocket, separated one, and holding it up to his face, exclaimed wildly, "You can't deny it! Look— my color eyes, this part of my face, everything!" Then, proudly, "Just like when I was young."

I couldn't believe it. Not only was he hounding me but he had taken pictures as well, a number of which I didn't get to see. I didn't want to do anything rash, but I wanted so badly to humiliate him that it was almost unbearable.

"What a surprise! You want hope. You need reassurance. You touch my heart . . . with disgust."

"Answer me."

"Sorry, I can't do you that favor."

"I checked it out. She was born on September 10, 1979, nine months later exactly. She's mine. You didn't have time to . . . for anything, and besides, you're not that kind of slut."

"And what kind of slut am I? How would you know?"

I watched him lean over violently toward me, his face distorted. I found it hard to believe the man really was anxious for my answer. He had suddenly shrunk to become a small, maniacal cur.

"I'm not going until you admit it, and you have to. I'll keep on your tail, Mercedes Beecham, you're not getting rid of me so easy."

"I know," I heard myself answering him calmly. "If you'll excuse me, I must get to work."

"Now, it's going to be worse, remember that. You can't even imagine—playing me for a sucker, where do you get the nerve? You'll pay for it, through the nose." And, jab-

bing his finger at me, he added, "For what you did to me today, the price goes up."

He grabbed my arm and put the palm of his hand against my face. Evidently, he was considering striking me. Something stopped him. He shook his head and walked rapidly away. I hesitated, still frightened but recovering. I stayed there for a while, needing time to think.

After that episode, the telephone calls continued. I would see him following me, or thought I did, I was no longer sure. Everything was proceeding at such a frenetic pace. My presentation was soon to take place and the editor was calling me constantly to supervise last-minute details. Then the secretary wanted me to go over the invitations to the ceremony in the auditorium. My friends began pushing for me to organize a celebration. And there I was, hardly able even to think. I considered postponing the whole thing but it was too late. It would be impossible to stop the process without a valid explanation. Moreover, announcements were already scheduled in one of the newspapers and a philosophy journal. The pleasurable excitement at the outset and the emotion I felt on seeing the first corrected originals of my book had evaporated disconcertingly. What was I going to say at the presentation? I was incapable of thinking of anything but how to protect my daughter.

And in the midst of all this, I had to continue my daily routine—classes at the university, writing for the specialized journals, the work of our behavioral group. The confusion in my life was translated into neglect of a whole series of things, people pressing me, surprised at my unreliability. Papers piled up on my desk, but I couldn't go near them. I had no excuse for my unfinished work. It was as if real life wielded astonishing power and intellectual abstraction seemed a joke. Everything was a regression, constricting and devious, that expanded over immeasurable time.

Those were intense days for a period (I can now say) of perhaps two weeks during which it all happened. But to measure time by days, or the appearance of the morning sun, is quite arbitrary.

A call from Eric two days, I believe, after the last of Dapuontes's incursions brought me back. I did not recall having missed the group's last meeting but apparently that was the case. Eric called it to my attention. I had to be present the following Wednesday because an important matter would be up for discussion. We had received an invitation to an international congress, and the idea was to present a paper on normative aspects of everyday life.

I argued over the phone with him that I might not be ready to think properly, that my head was very mixed up. He was surprised, but insisted on countering my protests. We were the most integrated group working on behavior. After all, I needed that money, and my collaboration in journals or magazines was insufficient. I felt myself at a dangerous juncture, seeing nothing but obstacles ahead. I said that I would attend and then make up my mind. I would listen, I would consider, and if I couldn't see my way clear, I would drop out of the group. I would decide later what I might turn my hand to. And that was where we left it.

Before going to that meeting, I asked Kate to have Shelley invite Julia to her house, not explaining my concern and evading her insistence on knowing the reason for my being on the alert.

I arrived at the meeting earlier than usual and lit a cigarette as I waited in the lobby. The days since my tormentor

appeared on the scene were endless, like years, and that morning when I opened the pantry door and looked at myself in the mirror, I saw deep hollows under my eyes. I had been paying no attention to my appearance, just taking a bath and throwing on whatever clothes came to hand.

After a few phone calls, and the threat in the square, I had seen no sign of him. This, to tell the truth, made me even more uneasy. Then I wondered if perhaps he was busy tailing my daughter and wasn't interested in anything else.

I was sitting on a bench in the patio, smoking, when Eric came over. Our recent conversations had been tense, my agitation further augmented by a call from the publisher on that very day. I had shouted at him, which I had never done before. It was a mistake, of course.

"You'd given up smoking," Eric said in a solemn tone. "What's happening? Would you mind filling me in a bit on what's going on?"

I could depend on this man. He had asked me a direct question. I had to answer accordingly.

"I'm going through a period of terrible tension." I put out my cigarette, turned, and said, "I need your help. I don't know if there's anything you can do, but . . ."

People began coming into the hallway punctually to attend the meeting; there was greeting, hugging, and banter. Eric told them to go ahead in, that we would follow. They got the message.

"Let me have it straight."

"The bastard who raped me in my country—the one who became the father of my daughter—" I was unable to go on, began to choke up. Eric immediately took me in his

arms. I looked at him and sobbed, "He's here. Harassing me."

Telling him did not lessen my torment one bit. A few moments later I was trembling, my body disobeying my brain. I felt as though I were about to go to pieces, as if talking in a loud voice would cause the brute to appear before me in the hallway at that very moment. Eric took my hands in his.

"Why didn't you come to me before?"

"I thought . . . I don't know, Eric. I thought I would be able to handle it alone."

"When did it begin?"

I quickly summed up the episodes of the conversation in the pub, at the entrance to the university, the day I went to see Carlyle, the information he had obtained, the phone calls, everything. My narrative was incoherent, but nonetheless, I believe Eric was able to get the whole picture. I could see him growing pale as I spoke, groping for something to say that would calm me.

At that point I said to him, in a fairly calm voice, "Don't worry. I'm under control. I won't go to the police . . . because I know that nothing is going to stop him. If I make a misstep he'll take advantage of it to harass me even more dreadfully."

"Did you go to the embassy?"

"He claims he's a friend of the Ambassador's, that he has dealings with him. I was standing at the entrance. What's more, I saw him go in, Eric."

"Did you follow him?"

"Of course, what do you think, I'm not about to keep quiet. I assure you he'll pay for it all, the monster."

"Now—my advice and, I hope, my help. I'm going to find out who he is, what he does, and you are going to calm down . . . if possible, of course."

Julietta stuck her head out, with a we're-waiting expression on her face. We had to get to work, that's what we were there for. I stood up, but Eric took hold of my arm, waved to her, and said, "Mercedes, you must tell your daughter. She has to know the truth. You must confide in her."

"How can I possibly do that?"

"You'll know. Besides, Julia has been asking you to; you no longer have any arguments. She'll help you. As for me . . ."

"I don't want you to talk to him, that would make it even worse. I know him, he's not a normal human being, he may do you harm. And besides, you may ruin everything."

"I won't talk to him. I'm going to check up, as I told you. And we'll have to keep in contact. Very well"—he added, a different note in his voice, one I had never heard before—"there's a lot to be done. To begin with, let's go in to the meeting, and you must take part in the discussion. You've been through worse—this can be taken care of. Yes, without going overboard."

I remember that I answered, "Sure, of course, I will." I went to the ladies' room and washed my face without looking in the mirror. I didn't want my reflection to tell me anything. Now I no longer felt so alone. At the meeting, I tried to listen when I felt Eric's eyes on me. He even asked me several times what I thought. I had to express an opinion. But my efforts to participate were really quite futile. Scenes kept cropping up in my mind all the time, the past blending with the present. Thoughts, discussions, images merged

and my brain was caught up in arguments, ideas unrelated to that place. My body was in that room but I was out in a nether world. Eric's voice interrupted my thoughts. He was standing at the blackboard writing words, connecting them with arrows, drawing question marks, flooding the surface with mathematical symbols.

At one point, I said what I was thinking and it sounded really off-key. Julietta tried to stop me and I answered irritably. I didn't want to talk about those things that day, my mental processes were so fuzzy. I was feeling unbearably sad, wanting only to stay home and tell my daughter the truth. Yes, this was the first time in sixteen years that I was going to be honest, and with my heart really open to the idea. Social dilemmas, world problems, humankind and its misfortunes seemed a faraway music tempered by abstractions that failed to draw me in.

My eyes kept straying to the clock, estimating the time Julia and Shelley would be spending together on their biology homework and adding the twenty minutes or so that separated our houses.

When I thought the seven minutes I had calculated were up, I looked at the clock again and realized that actually fifteen minutes had elapsed.

Unable to conceal my distress, I ran out, barely waving goodbye. As I stood at the doorway nervously, hoping a taxi would pass, Eric appeared with an umbrella. He told me he would call later. I threw him a little grimace to express the quandary I was in, all sorts of thoughts running through my mind. Then I glanced around and within a few moments doorways, cars, storefronts, had undergone a close check. I could see no trace of Dapuontes, even though I assumed he

was so trained in his profession that he was capable of disappearing from sight like smoke.

"Everything is going to be alright," Eric said to me. "Don't worry. You'll see how everything will be back on its normal course."

"I don't think so," I told him, as the raindrops lit insistently on my face. "Eric, I must get this over with, it's the only thing that matters to me."

Helping me negotiate a big puddle at the curb to get into the cab that finally stopped for me, he added, "I understand. I'll be taking care of it right away."

I waved vaguely to him as we said goodbye.

The rain had darkened what was already a foggy afternoon and I felt drained.

⠿ I sat there recalling my last discussion with Julia as the taxi traveled a roundabout route to avoid the afternoon traffic.

Faced with a direct question from my daughter—once again on the topic of her father—I had thrown out a slew of arguments for her. I thought of our conversation as I looked out the window. To dodge her question, I had told her that truth was such a definitive word that it left most actions without any possible explanation. As though I were giving a lecture before a group of colleagues, I reeled off one nonsensical rationale after another.

I waited for the phone to ring. If anybody came to the door, I had to be alert. That's what I wanted and that's what was happening to me. But meanwhile, what my daughter wanted was the truth. I blundered through that night, fouling the atmosphere with arrant stupidities. Nervous and excited, I told her that it was an enigma, and she replied, "My father's identity is?" her tone violent.

In exasperation I answered, "No, Julia, truth. To keep it from existing, it must be encoded into dogma or gospel. A topic in relation to which everybody has their own view, sometimes pertinent, sometimes not."

Julia interrupted me several times, but I failed to listen to her entreaties. I remember that she got out the corduroy hat she had bought at Harrods, threw it on the couch, danced a pirouette, lay down on top of it, and listened to me with an air of mock intensity. Nonetheless, I carried on.

"You see, Julia, I often think that in making a compari-son between truth and being right, there is a slight nuance which, in some cases, can make a huge difference."

"You see," I repeated as I strolled back and forth restless-ly in the living room, "reality seems to me to be an assump-tion, almost a detective mystery, a brainstorm of some suspicious lunatics whose game is to have a surprise waiting for you around every corner."

I opened the shutters, looked out at the night, turned around, and carried on with my lunacy.

I remember that she smiled only once, when I said that, for me, if something has eyes like a rabbit, ears and feet like a rabbit, it may not be a rabbit, it may be a clone of a rabbit, a sort of magical appearance that hypnotizes you and that you end up accepting—as a rabbit.

"Maybe I exaggerate," I went on excitedly, "but it wouldn't be an unreasonable thing at all that some day one of those scientists decides to clone a murderer, or some other kind of gene repository of new evil. And then we'll find ourselves in an even madder world, unexpectedly far more sinister."

Julia told me I was being crazy and not even that was going to save me from having to tell the whole story. I still remember the wild look in her eyes, her arms crossed across her chest as she watched me in terror. She was shifting about in extreme annoyance but I could no longer stop myself.

Suddenly, she reared up, begging me to shut up, and when I didn't, she screamed: "Enough!"

The only thought that went through my mind was that Dapuontes might get her away from me. The fact that I

hadn't slept in days was responsible for all this madness. The fiend had come into and out of my life with such impunity that he had driven me into a state of utter anguish.

The telephone rang and the two of us started to answer. Then something unexpected happened. We both grabbed it as though our lives depended on it. Suddenly, Julia yanked it out of my hands and hurled it out the window, smashing the glass to bits. I turned. Julia was staring at me with an expression that was part hatred and part stupefaction. All I could manage was to slap her in the face for the first time in her life.

"At last I know you don't love me. This finishes the whole business and I won't ever ask anything of you again." Her eyes filled with tears but she controlled herself. She glared at me contemptuously, went up to her room, and turned on her CD player full blast. I was in no position to hold back information from her, she was sixteen years of age. I knocked on her door and turned the knob. It was locked.

After a little while, Julia opened the door suddenly, threw me a disdainful look, put on her coat, and left the house. It was pouring. I saw her cross the street. She had run off in desperation. The trees in the square were sway-ing in the darkness. I ran out into the street but lost sight of her at the next corner. I returned to the house thinking that she was defenseless and that it was my fault.

She came back home around twelve, dripping wet and shivering. But she would not let me touch her. Just as she was, her body all wet, she sat down at the kitchen table and began drumming on it with her fingers.

In anguish, I stood leaning against the doorjamb. I was

utterly exhausted but determined that now was the time to
tell her the truth. I offered to bring her a towel and fix her
a cup of tea. On my way to the bathroom, she spoke, her
harsh, curt tone stopping me in my tracks.

"I made up my mind."

I turned to meet her blazing glare and said, "I'm listening, but I beg you not to go out into the night again. I have
things to tell you."

"I don't want any more talk, and now I'm the one who
doesn't want to hear anything out of you."

"It's that I can . . . tell you some things, Julia. I can't stand
seeing you all wet like that, you'll catch a cold. Take a bath,
and then we'll talk. What I have to tell you isn't easy."

Julia banged on the table. A glass of juice fell to the floor
and broke.

"No, it's too late now. When I asked you that night and
then you got sick, it frightened me. Then I watched you
going on with your life as if my anxiety didn't count at all.
Now, I think I'd rather see you dead . . . because you don't
give a damn about what worries me."

"You mustn't say that to me."

"I don't want any more talk, not tonight or ever again in
my life. To hell with you, Mother. I'm fed up with you and
your silences. I'm the one asking you to shut up. I'm setting
you a date, Mother, because you're going to be losing me."

"Julia!" I exclaimed in horror. "Don't ever say a thing
like that, don't threaten me, please, don't do it."

"Oh, if you only knew; you're a menace. I'm fed up, I've
had it with thinking, suspecting all sorts of things"—she
gestured to hold me back from interrupting—"I'm tired of
theories. I want simple answers. I want the truth."

▪▪ And that afternoon, after leaving the group meeting, I went into the house with that final sentence of Julia's weighing on my mind. As soon as I opened the door, I saw her. She avoided my glance. Every time I tried to approach her, she found a way to avoid contact. Our shadows crossed several times, in the kitchen and then in the bathroom. Dapuontes's words re-echoed, his threat in the square. Now, I was not the obsession, it was Julia.

After a while, I decided to take a bath. In the tub, my fingers strayed to my scars. I wondered whether Julia had ever seen them, and recalled that several times I had seen her eyes light on the ones upon my leg. She questioned me with a glance on those occasions, but got no word from me. My fingertips touched the seams as the soapy water ran along the channeled surface of clumsy sutures made by a nervous doctor working on my body, two guards with rifles looking on.

Then, Julia was knocking on the door. She had to go out and wanted to take a bath. Her voice was distant—not asking, demanding. I came out wrapped in a towel and she went in without even looking at me.

Distractedly, I began tidying up, with the sole purpose of keeping busy until my daughter should come down. Finally, she appeared, her hair wet, a comb in her hand.

I offered to comb her hair, but she ignored me. She stood at the window and I walked over to her. We remained there in silence. Then, all at once, I felt the words coming to my lips, docilely, and I found myself, at last, talking about my past.

Countless images inserted themselves into this present-

day setting. I expelled the terrible events buried in memory, mentioned names, gave nicknames, the hallmarks of the time. An entire stored-up alphabet of slogans, rituals, and symbols took on form and meaning that night. The degraded remained degraded and horror was not excluded from the scenes of brutality. Descriptive language was unnecessary when I told her how I had been raped, and as I reproduced those moments for her, I could not keep from crying.

Suddenly, in a hesitant voice, she asked, "Was that the man who spoke to me in Regent's Park?

"Yes." And I looked into her eyes. "That's him, the one who turned out to be your father."

The two of us remained uneasily silent, looking away through the window for a long time. The moon emerged, hidden briefly by fog. Julia drew the curtain back a little, smoothing it nervously with her hand, then shut her eyes. Tears began to roll slowly down her cheeks and I took her in my arms. Then, in a strange voice, she asked me to show her my scars. I did so.

My daughter remained thoughtful. Then, all at once, with an expression on her face I had never seen before, she said, "That is to say, you always thought of yourself."

"What do you mean?"

"The decision to have me, like this one of telling me the truth, are . . . let me think of one of your words, yes . . . *arbitrary*. If that creep hadn't showed up, you would never have told the truth, would you?"

"But now I *am* telling it."

"Sure, but right now it might not work."

"Aren't you going to forgive me?"

"See what I mean? You're not concerned about me,

you're looking for pardon. This has nothing to do with that."

"What else is there for me to do, Julia?"

"I have no idea. Do I have to show you the way now, too? But I can help, maybe by beginning to look at myself . . . really look."

"You see, that's why I didn't let you know before."

Julia covered her face with her hands, and by the time she took them away, she wore an expression of pure anguish. I went to her and with a gesture of deep pain, said, "Dearest daughter, let me try. I don't know . . . don't really know what you are referring to, but I want to find out. It's true, I thought of myself, years ago and now. I will have to reconsider many things, to learn."

Julia looked at me sadly. All at once, she said, "You're my mother. What I've just found out changes a lot of things, but for that reason, I'm not going to have a father. Not because I can't bear the idea that he is a murderer, but because he appeared now, and all the pieces are together."

"Julia, there's a difference between an evil person and one who hasn't done anything. If I didn't mention it to you before . . ."

"It was to protect yourself, because of the shame. That's why you hid, and why you kept me in the dark."

"That's true, but I love you, Julia."

"Yes, you do in your way, that I believe. But it's not enough."

With that, Julia went to her room. I remained with the thought that it was not going to be easy to regain her confidence. Actually, she was right. I had been thinking of myself all those years, although her opinion that I hadn't

done everything possible to understand her was not quite true. At that moment, I felt the situation as an unbearable weight pressing down upon me. Because I loved my daughter, always had. With all those contradictions, yes, but loving her, always.

▓▓ That evening, Julia sat down beside me on the living room couch. She told me that she had talked to Shelley. She had to get to Brighton, she didn't know why, but she had to. "I can't think here, Mother. I believe I want to feel the sand and stones under my feet. I miss the sea, or the seagulls." That's all she said. Then she left. I begged her to stay but she didn't. I called Joyce, who told me that Peter was outside waiting for her. He was going to take her and Shelley to Brighton. In a calm tone of voice, she added that they would keep an eye on them over the weekend. Nevertheless, I was worried. The fact that Julia now knew the story gave me no solace. I was aware that Dapuontes was on the prowl somewhere in London. It was driving me mad that I couldn't anticipate what he might do next. And something deep down in me had changed that night. My way of being served no purpose anymore, my daughter was no longer here. I had no idea what might happen from now on.

The incident at Hobbes' Place occurred the following night. A hidden design was woven that made events evolve almost in tandem. Different circumstances, different fates, tied together through a sinister past.

Three interminable days have gone by since my daughter left the house. I have recovered profoundly, in a way I don't believe I ever did before. The newspaper arrived a little while ago. The lead story was on the Bonmayer Connection—the Foreign Minister's main adviser who was mixed up in an arms-smuggling affair. The story contained nothing new except for an account of a ring of mercenaries that was recently broken up. Dapuontes's picture was on the front page, as one of the members, and apparently because he was also wanted in France and Italy for a variety of crimes noteworthy in their violence.

And I thought that in those days, as an instrument of others, motivated by no ideology, he killed simply because he was ordered to. Those in power introduced him into my life and others as powerful were now freeing me of him.

But that is no longer of any interest, for Julia just came home. She puts down her backpack, makes a gesture I do not understand, and hugs me. I start to cry, to tell her how she hasn't been out of my mind, and she answers that she knows.

"How do you know?" I ask.

"Because I know, and if there was anything I read in your face that night, it was an expression of weakness you never

showed before. I can't blame you for everything. You aren't perfect, I knew that already, and wanted you to know."

"I am going to change, I promise you."

Julia makes a gesture with her hand, touches my face. My daughter is protecting me, and I accept it. She is forgiving me. Suddenly, I am aware that I have brought up a daughter who is sure of who she is. She is placing the trust in me that I had begrudged her. She is able to set her anger aside, because it is the day of the presentation of my first book. And so, I realize, my daughter is taking pity on me, and I allow her to. It is even natural for me to behave that way. I suppose my conduct may appear strange, but for me it is an intense reencounter with my daughter. To tell the truth, I am completely disarmed, at ease as I never was before. There she is smiling at me. Then she looks at me for a moment, and tells me that we have to get ourselves ready for the ceremony. I hand her a copy of my book and she reads the dedication: *"For Julia, with a mother's pride."*

I'm laughing and crying. She asks me if it is a difficult book and I say yes, somewhat, and not to feel obliged to read it. But Julia tells me she wants to, and adds that maybe she'll have to ask me questions about some of the material she won't understand very well. Now, she wants to know how I am. I tell her that I'm fine. I ask if she is alright. She nods.

We open the shutters so that sunlight floods every corner and we are warmed as we talk about our feelings. Suddenly, she admits to having missed me, and I cannot help breaking into tears again. Then she takes a red hat out of her handbag and gives it to me. I ask what the occasion is, and she simply says, "Just because, Mother. It's best for the summer, for the beach. I figured you have to wear a hat."

I watch her as she speaks, the color mounting in her face as she blushes. Her glance is clear-eyed, direct, strong.

I see her as she goes about the house, walking with assurance, buoyantly, as she comments on the clothes she is going to put on that night. And she wants to know what I intend to put on. When I show her, she is pleased and smiles. In an instant, I feel as though my energy has been restored and I understand that this daughter is the embodiment for me of the future I looked forward to with such hope. The sudden realization provokes a surge of relief.

She resembles me, but is herself—quite different, more emotional than I, of greater integrity, with the gift of clarity in looking at life, and an extraordinary directness in conveying her feelings. She is healthy, at my side, and in this great paradox of life, in this Russian roulette, I have come through alive and winner of the grand prize of being Julia's mother.

We dress for the ceremony. We leave calmly, and being in no rush, decide to walk there.

My friends are already in the main auditorium—Estela and her children, many colleagues, newspeople, Eric and the rest of our group, Carlyle, Todd, the Sheridan family. Julia is in the first row. As I look out over the hall, I recall the time my daughter walked beside me asking me who this or that man was who looked so serious, Socrates, Hobbes, Leibniz, pictures and expressions projecting disturbingly from beautifully carved frames, with fine gilt edging. I remember my daughter running through these halls, the astonishment on her face when she went into the great hall for the first time, the hallowed precinct, velvet-cushioned, rigorous center of knowledge. The hall is full and a sensation resembling joy enters my spirit.

I am deeply moved when they speak of my book, proud to hear certain passages highlighted. I let the praise wash over me because I feel I deserve it, because the appreciation is for the rigorousness which I certainly put into the work.

My glance lights on Julia and at that moment I decide that I will drop some of my commitments in order to have more time with my daughter. When I think about it, I realize that she doesn't know any other country. We will go to France, or Spain since she likes the Spaniards. That is what runs through my mind as she looks back at me. Many things are going to have to change, many. Then, I observe the other faces, the familiar ones and those of visitors, of students. I begin to interpret the theorems of conflict for them; it is necessary to imbue them with the enthusiasm the

profession demands. At this point, I am thinking that professors teach through their experience, are never neutral,
always teach with passion—or at least that is how it should
be. I examine the place where the ceremony is taking place,
the same one in which I received my diploma from the university. My eyes travel over the moldings, the carved borders of the walls and the great oak doors, the domed ceiling,
the paintings, the institution's insignia. An austere velvet-
lined chamber, sown with secrets and stately touches of lin-
eage. At the rear of the hall, two columns bear sculptures of
the great geniuses of humanity on their capitals.

I take advantage of this opportunity to express my appreciation for the help received, the constructive criticism I
benefited from, the everyday collaboration of my colleagues, the honor of sharing that environment in which I
learned so much. I feel the warmth of their embraces, and
look upon them with confidence restored in my own worth.

Perhaps one of the most definitive conclusions is that I am no longer in transit, never again on the point of having to leave at a moment's notice. In fact, my daughter was born here, and in this land I was given the opportunity to be free. Julia gave me a chance to remake my life with her, and to concentrate all my energy on the task. I think that sometimes, geography is not the only thing that enables human beings to find their identity. Lands come with people and ideologies. Perhaps at some moments in the history of each one, it is for us to choose where to end our days. That is what occupies my thoughts now, convinced that this is my place in the world because I am no longer the same, and that is immutable. I have wondered on various occasions why I should want to go back, and I say to myself, to see the fields, the sidewalks, the streets. And I have wondered if one can go back to a land from which one was expelled, for whatever reason. My stubbornness has reached the extreme of wondering if it is necessary to do so, yes, necessary. And there really is no question of necessity in this matter. I have not forgotten my origins or my land. It is only that I have changed so much, and so have the avenues and the people. I have no friends there, no true friends. Now, the ghosts of the many, many "disappeared" inhabit the neighborhood, and those who remain there have other connotations in my life. That is why these pavements I tread here each day give me such peace.

What a paradox, to feel—as I stand at the edge of the

ocean, on an island—that I am on solid ground. There is nothing like personal perception, and there are no absolutes as far as decision about what to do with our life is concerned. I still believe that it is not wisdom but perhaps only a keen and subtle sense that impels us to make certain decisions.

I made my life here, yet many things remain there for me, although they no longer mean the same because of my absence. One does not always live with one's bags packed, even after having survived terror. Perhaps I will visit my country one day as just another ordinary citizen in order to show Julia my roots. And, surely, nostalgia will be the most powerful component of my life. I cannot imagine what sort of emotions I will feel at the sight of those horizons—the pampa, the trees, the big country house. Yet I yearn to sense the breeze on my body, to listen to the lapwings' call, smell the perfume of the jasmine and the orange trees in bloom. I imagine myself in a café ordering a cup of coffee, preferably the one on the corner of the School of Philosophy and Letters where I could see Paco, put my hand on his shoulder, and repeat one of his jokes to him that I still remember so well.

I would also like to walk Avenida Corrientes from end to end. I would hail the No. 60 bus and stay on it to the end of the line, like the guileless child I once was, and simply gaze out the window. And perhaps drink *mate*, although I don't know if I would still like it. But I do recognize now that I am no longer in terror of these monsters, these implacable demons, which not only fueled my nightmares but laid siege to my body and my daughter's as well. By simply recounting this convoluted tale, I have almost miraculously

succeeded in turning portent into promise, despair into acceptance, and causing the feelings of betrayal I allowed Julia to suffer to vanish with time.

My house is quiet again. I take pleasure now in knowing that I have not lost the past completely, for I have this way of bringing it back with a clarity I did not possess before. In retracing my steps, horrific as they were, it is as if I have been able to escape to a place strangely indescribable, far away in the upper reaches. But I must be patient, for it is still too soon for me to feel my body completely at peace.

About the Author

PATRICIA SAGASTIZÁBAL was born in Buenos Aires in 1953, and as a child was exposed to the violence and political repression that permeated the lives of all of Argentina's citizens. One of her most visceral recollections from her youth, in fact, is a scene when she was eleven of dozens of mounted policemen chasing women and children through a Buenos Aires barrio.

As a young adult, such scenes had become all too frequent. When she entered law school in 1972, she soon realized that to study law during a time of dictatorship was a "rather lunatic undertaking," for under the dictatorship, the Constitution that was studied was not enforced and political parties were forbidden. At the same time, Sagastizábal studied acting and play directing, where "the imaginary world operated under codes that were both welcome and hopeful."

After the 1976 coup, the repression instigated by the de facto government began anew, and the apartment that she and her husband, Leandro, shared became a temporary refuge for many friends who were persecuted, as well as fellow activists. A catalyzing event in Sagastizábal's life was the kidnapping of a close girlfriend, along with the girlfriend's husband, in the middle of 1976. To this day, nothing is known of how they met their end. *A Secret for Julia* is based on these events of the 1970s, but should not be construed as a work of nonfiction. For Sagastizábal, the atrocities of this time had the effect of paralyzing her imag-

ination, as they did for so many others of her generation. Such novels can only emerge after many years have elapsed.

A Secret for Julia, published in Argentina as *Un secreto para Julia* in the spring of 2000, won the prestigious *Premio La Nación*, judged by María Esther de Miguel, Jorge Edwards, and Tomás Eloy Martínez.

About the Translator

Born in Manhattan, Asa Zatz has lived much of his life there except for a brief (as he whimsically indicates) sojourn of thirty-three years in Mexico City. A graduate of the Yale Drama School, he began to work as a translator in Mexico, where necessity taught him to be a professional. His first paid translation was for the screenplay of a novel by B. Traven, and his career was launched soon after with his translation of *The Children of Sánchez* for the anthropologist Oscar Lewis, whose collaborator he remained for the following twenty years.

As a translator, his work, which he enjoys likening to bricklaying, has included stints for various international organizations (Organization of American States, the UN, and UNESCO, among others) and a wide variety of endeavors ranging from Mexican presidential state-of-the-union speeches to inaugural addresses. Not counting scientific and technical fields, his work has covered the basic categories of literature and the humanities: philosophy, art and art criticism, anthropology, drama and film, biography, essay, short story, and the novel.

Since returning to his native New York in 1982, Zatz has devoted himself almost exclusively to literature. Authors whose work he has translated include Carpentier, Fuentes, García Márquez, Galeano, José Luis González, Tomás Eloy Martínez, Sábato, Valenzuela, Vargas Llosa, and Valle-Inclán. Of particular satisfaction to him is his poetry translation of *Jaguar Eye*, by the Mexican Efraín Bartolomé. He is also completing the translation of *Recuerdos de Provincia*

by the legendary Argentine statesman, educator, and writer Domingo Faustino Sarmiento for Oxford University Press.

Zatz has given translation workshops at the City University of New York and New York University; he has received a grant from the New York State Council on the Arts, and an award for a short story translation from the Latin American Writers Institute.

early point in the project of the importance of honesty in America, and a few paragraphs from John Meyer helped me reshape central aspects of my argument. Frank Dobbin, Annette Lareau, and Robert Wuthnow provided very detailed comments on an early draft of the book. Special thanks to Jeff Alexander, Randy Collins, Natalie Zeman Davis, Paul DiMaggio, Wendy Griswold, Joe Gusfield, Marty Lipset, Barry Schwartz, Bill Sewell, Viviana Zelizer, and to the very intellectually engaging editor of the Morality and Society series, Alan Wolfe. These people showed a much appreciated support for the project at important times.

Finally, at the University of Chicago Press, Doug Mitchell proved once again that his wonderful reputation is well deserved. Lila Weinberg, of the University of Chicago Press, and Vicky Wilson-Schwartz provided excellent editorial assistance. In Princeton, Blanche Anderson, Donna DeFrancisco, and Cindy Gibson gracefully provided secretarial and administrative help as well as a friendly daily female presence.

The most personal thanks come last. I want to express my very special appreciation to those whose friendships greatly enriched my life while I was working on the book: Ziva, Annette, Kathy, Ben, and my sister Natalie. Finally, it is difficult to convey the depth of my feelings for my companion and colleague extraordinaire, Frank Dobbin. His generous kindness sustained me through this adventure; his sharp intelligence provoked me. He did not type, but he did more than his half of the second shift. For all this, thanks.

NOTE TO THE READER

This book compares how members of the French and the American upper-middle class define what it means to be a "worthy person," and it explains the most important cross-national differences in these definitions by looking at broad cultural and structural features of French and American society. The analysis draws primarily on interviews conducted with 160 college-educated, white male professionals, managers, and businessmen who live in and around Indianapolis, New York, Paris, and Clermont-Ferrand. I compare competing definitions of what it means to be a "worthy person" by analyzing symbolic boundaries, i.e., by looking at implicit definitions of purity present in the labels interviewees use to describe, abstractly and concretely, people with whom they don't want to associate, people to whom they consider themselves to be superior and inferior, and people who arouse hostility, indifference, and sympathy. Hence, the study analyzes the relative importance attached to religion, honesty, low moral standards, cosmopolitanism, high culture, money, power, and the likes, by Hoosiers, New Yorkers, Parisians, and Clermontois.

The book opens with descriptions of some of the upper-middle-class men with whom I talked. The Prologue gives a sense of the texture of the phenomena that I am describing, of what it means to be exclusive; only after going through the subsequent chapters will the reader fully understand how these descriptions take on a new meaning when looked at through sociological lenses.

Chapter 1 introduces the theoretical issues that this study addresses. Chapters 2, 3, and 4 explore differences between the cultures of French and American professionals, managers, and businessmen. Chapters 5 and 6 explain these variations, while Chapter 6 also compares differences

between various types of people. For instance, it contrasts the cultures of academics and businessmen, those of upwardly and downwardly mobile individuals as well as those of individuals who are first-generation upper-middle-class members and those whose families have belonged to the upper-middle-class for several generations. The last chapter brings together and explores further the theoretical contributions of the book. If the study properly addresses sociological issues and is primarily written for social scientists, it will also be of interest to nonacademics who wish to gain a better understanding of the culture of a greatly understudied group. i.e., of the men who, occupying the top of the social ladder, exercise considerable power in shaping the lives of their fellow countrymen and countrywomen as well as the characters of their respective societies.

Prologue

~~~~~~

SKETCHING THE LANDSCAPE:
SOME ILLUSTRATIVE VIGNETTES

Je juge donc que le sens de la vie est la plus pressante des questions.
—Albert Camus
Therefore I believe that the meaning of life is the most pressing of all questions.

CULTURAL SOPHISTICATION AS A SINE QUA NON

Sitting in his Paris studio, surrounded by walls covered with his art, dressed so as to totally express his individuality, the avant-garde professor of architecture talks about himself with great ease. He offers a very elaborate description of his identity, his friends, and his work. His romantic reconstruction of the family history is Proustian in style and replete with historical references; the family's colonial past is turned into an exotic and captivating story; the little rituals of bourgeois life are told in nostalgic detail. Didier Aucour creates his persona as he speaks.[1] His identity is embedded in images borrowed from the worlds of Andy Warhol, Rabelais, and Truffaut. He has a theory about himself, about his art, about the total role of art in his life. The phone rings constantly; students drop by to leave sketches; old friends who came to have lunch with him wait downstairs for a long hour while we conclude the interview.

In this environment, everything is carefully chosen to express something, an *état d'âme*. Didier explains that creativity gives him power: "I believe that there is a human nature which is not only concerned with material power but also with irrationality, something akin to the concept of superman, the Nietzschean superman, where surpassing oneself, whether it is religiously or creatively, is central. I believe in the desperate quest of the artist which is located at another level of reflection than pure matter."[2] Those living in a world of purely material values are scorned; this applies particularly to the *Français moyen*, the kind who drives to the ocean for his summer vacation. Accordingly, Didier depicts his friends as, above all, artistic, imaginative, intellectually stimulating, and active. Refinement is crucial:

I like refinement in the sense of subtlety in the way of thinking, subtlety in the way of being. I truly like people who are refined in their taste, the way they move, the way they present themselves, the way they think. And imagination [is] the most sublime dimension of the act of being.

Didier also likes people who are distant ("It is part of refinement, of the aristocratic dream, you see: *aristos-cratos: cratos* means the best. I like it: being distant means respecting others"). He is indifferent to people who are nice, considerate, religious, and well-informed, while he despises those he perceives as stupid and vulgar, or as leading boring lives and lacking in imagination.[3] Finally, Didier describes himself as pretentious and egotistical and declares that the essential in life is not money but pride (*l'orgueil*).

John Bloom is an economist. He lives in Summit, New Jersey, a posh New York suburb. In contrast to Didier, John does not perceive himself as aesthetically sophisticated. The tasteful English-country decor of his sumptuous home is "98.99% due to my wife": she inherited the antique furniture that decorates the room, and the drapes are made from a rich fabric she found in a shop on the Upper East Side of Manhattan. His wife, who has a perfect figure, has brought us Pepperidge Farm cookies and amaretto-flavored coffee.

After he got "burned out" by corporate politics at AT&T, John started to work for a consulting firm in Manhattan, to which he commutes everyday. He lives in a highly competitive professional world where peer respect is the name of the game: "What I find most enjoyable is when I get unsolicited calls, when business associates recommend me without any urging. My ego needs that. It's very much a desire, a need to feel that the thing that I do, that I believe that I do very well, other people also perceive I do very well. It's the endless quest for external validation." Peer respect for his competence gives meaning to his life, which is almost entirely structured around his work. The latter allows him to keep up his "high lifestyle."

John clearly defines himself by his intellectual curiosity: "I am somebody who would pass himself off as the intellectual type, absolutely." He says he really enjoys "intellectualizing." His friendships are built around exchanging ideas on a wide range of topics: "My whole point of view is

to attempt to answer certain basic questions about life. What is the purpose of it? The purpose is the development of your mind, of your thinking process, of your ability to reflect on things. So that, for me, feels like I have a meaningful existence, an untrivialful existence." He is trying to raise himself above the vagaries of the corporate world, and his intellectual power is a means to this end. It keeps him mentally alive and provides him freedom from the drudgery of everyday life.

John easily confesses to being intellectually exclusive and feeling superior to "people who I see are not as intellectually developed as I am, who don't have my natural curiosity or my wide range of interests. In a social situation, if I'm dealing with somebody who I think is very intellectually inferior to me, and he begs to differ with me, I probably won't be very tolerant or very decent about it at all." Being "nice" and "considerate" are peripheral to John's repertory of modes of interaction.

Peer respect and intelligence are not the only yardsticks of success used by John: "I would feel inferior in a social situation, if I meet somebody who initially appears to have it all: good-looking, well-dressed, articulate, knowledgeable, has traveled the world, and is successful. I feel very inferior to those kinds of people." The images of success John values are those offered to the American upper-middle class by popular magazines such as *Esquire*, *M.*, and *G.Q.* These images, whose enactment requires considerable material resources, assume a tangible character in John's gallery of desirable ideal types.

In contrast to Didier, John values worldly success as much as he values intelligence. His cultural standards of worth are compounded by social standards, for he feels inferior to people who are socially more successful than he. The boundaries that structure his perception of the upper-middle-class world are organized around both cultural and socioeconomic criteria.[4]

Fortyish, Lou Taylor is a tall, mild-mannered, tweedy-looking academic administrator who lives in Indianapolis. He comes from a well-established Midwestern family which includes three generations of Presbyterian ministers and theologians. When he was young, he used to listen on Sundays to his uncles debate fine scholastic points around the dinner table: "They used to have these great debates about God, and I thought it was wonderful. I was just fascinated by these discussions . . . . There just didn't

seem like anything else for me to do but go to seminary." He got his Ph.D. because "an advanced degree was important to me . . . it helped me be comfortable with other smart people." After working for a few years in an inner-city ministry on the West Coast, he took a position in an Indianapolis college.

Lou lives in a Presbyterian world of muted conflicts, mildly expressed feelings, and carefully chosen words. He declares that he gets along with everyone: "My wife says if people can't get along with me, they're in bad shape." His work requires that he interact with groups, and he feels that he is very good at it. He is a team player and others trust him.

Like John, Lou is more interested in individuals who see the world differently from most people, who "try to find other ways to understand things that are going on." He defines his friends as refined because "they are well-read, sensitive to suffering, careful about the ways they express their ideas—they would be honest but have some concern about how they are heard." They have culture, and they are open to the world. Because his old friends live far away, Lou feels very isolated, but "it would require too much energy to invest in new friends." In the meantime, his life is increasingly centered around his family. Despite the fact that he is not satisfied with this, he can't conceive of alternatives, and he feels trapped.

Feeling superior to people who have boring jobs, and particularly to manual workers, Lou says, "I'm sure glad I am not doing that . . . But they probably make more money than I do. So I don't know what superior and inferior means in this case." However, he feels inferior to people who "have more." A recent encounter with the president of an insurance company made him feel "not real comfortable in that great big office downtown. Because the guy has so much, I kept thinking: 'How come this person has all this and I don't?' 'What does that say about me?'"

Unlike Didier and like John, Lou does not question the relevance of worldly success as a criteria for assessing superiority. But like Didier and John, he attributes transcendental meaning to other realities: "In life there is something that one is, that has a 'being' dimension, beyond the external pile of money I get, that is internally satisfying . . . It gives satisfaction that I am participating in something that is beyond me, of ultimate worth." Lou's neighbor lacks this dimension of meaning. "The guy who lives next door to us has been working in the food industry all his life. Nice guy, good neighbor, unsophisticated in that his primary concern

is where his next sale is coming from, you know, just beating out a living . . . He's looking forward to retiring to have more of his own time."

These three individuals inhabit highly contrasted spaces: an artist's studio in a decrepit building at the periphery of Paris; a depersonalized office niche in a Manhattan skyscraper; and an old Indianapolis college, redolent of beeswax. They are all white, middle-aged, college-educated professionals. They belong to the upper-middle class, along with 10–15 percent of the French and the American populations. Members of this class have what most people desire and are what most people aspire to be.[5] Their lives are offered as a model to the rest of the population by the mass media and the advertising industry. They exercise influence on events, products, and people: they conceive, advise, hire, promote, judge, select, and allocate.

Didier, John, and Lou are similar in that they all practice *cultural exclusivism*: cultural standards such as intelligence, refinement, curiosity, and aesthetic sophistication are the decisive yardsticks they use in their everyday assessment of self and others. These three men are not very much concerned with moral standards: their definition of a "worthy person" assigns a minor role to honesty and altruism with a few exceptions. The cultural exclusivism of the academic administrator and the economist is, to be sure, complemented by their socioeconomic exclusivism, as suggested by the importance they attach to worldly success. They both are also somewhat less culturally Darwinist: they get along with most people, are more culturally tolerant, and less prone to order people along a sort of cultural "chain of being." In contrast, the architecture professor shows a great deal of intolerance for differences. For him, cultural sophistication is a sine qua non for interpersonal relations.

MORAL TALES

Paul Anderson lives in Indianapolis in a ranch house. He is a senior executive at Fort Harrison, a finance center of the Department of Defense. He is married and has two sons; his wife has been working as a part-time receptionist since the kids started school. He runs marathons and is highly competitive. Coming from a "hardworking background," he made his way up the professional ladder, and he is now widely respected by his

coworkers. "I am a great believer in human beings. I have always established a lot of pleasing relationships with the secretaries and administrative people, the chiefs that work for me and all . . . Now I do have an
awful lot of people that I think would stand behind me or select me as an
individual that they really thought a lot of."

Paul defines himself in opposition to his professional colleagues who
are "real aggressive, eager, climbers . . . they probably have many people
against them, and not that many for. [They are in it] only for themselves,
and don't sort of look out for their subordinates, and care for people first."
Paul says he is not very ambitious: "I have a theory that no matter what
your level of success is, what that ultimately translates into is happiness.
So if you're smart enough to be happy at whatever level you are, you've
achieved what you can achieve and you get more anyway."

The Andersons are very active in their church: "We get sort of a sense
of well-being, and contentment with the people, the friends, and those
groups of people who are concerned about their family, and are concerned about helping each other. It's a very warm church community."
Refined, artistic, and cosmopolitan people leave him indifferent. Being
religious, hardworking, and considerate is much more important. Accordingly, Paul strongly dislikes people who have low moral standards. His
feelings of inferiority are largely articulated around religion, and in particular around knowledge of religious matters: "If I had to say the groups
of people that I really feel a little inferior to, one of them are the people
in our church that are very well-read and devout in their religion. Again,
not fanatical people, but they have the ability to, if a question is asked in
Sunday school class, they are very knowledgeable . . . I sort of say to
myself, I'm not going to say anything now, all I'm going to show is how
little I know."

Michel Dupuis lives in Versailles, in the western suburbs of Paris. His
large apartment overlooks one of the chic "boulevards" in front of the
château. He inherited from his grandmother a furniture plant that at one
point hired up to a thousand workers. Brought up in a strong humanist
tradition and educated by Jesuits, Michel defines his mission in life as
helping his employees to develop themselves fully as human beings. He
assesses his success not only in economic terms but also in humanist and
relational terms. He explains: "Some people started with us at the bottom

of the ladder when they were nineteen. They have grown with the firm and now have important positions. For me, this precisely is the most important thing, that the firm was able to help some people to develop themselves as human beings . . . the goal was not to make money but to do something . . . Do you know Rogers, Carl Rogers? Well, my goal was to become 'someone' and to help others to become 'someone' . . . This means feeling that you are in a process of developing yourself, that you feel good about yourself and others. 'I am OK, you are OK.'"

Like many bourgeois Catholic couples, Michel and Mariette have a number of children—eight, all married and leading active professional lives. They are very involved in the Catholic organizations of Versailles. Mariette teaches catechism classes. They both have been participating over the last ten years in the Ligue Notre-Dame, a group that brings together couples to share their religious faith and family life. Michel's personal heroes include Antoine de St-Exupéry and l'abbé Pierre, a French exemplar of charity not unlike Mother Theresa. For years Michel was involved in an elite business association aimed at humanizing capitalism.

The Dupuis like to spend time and share good wine with their friends. They often have people over for a meal; their dining table easily sits fifteen. Michel likes people who are "true to themselves; they don't try to pretend that they are something else than what they are, to be interested in things that don't interest them. We prefer spontaneous people, who are what they are. And also people who like to share a good dinner, who appreciate the pleasure of being together." Like Paul Anderson, Michel is irritated by people who are always looking for an edge, who think only about money, who would do anything to advance. "Anyway, these people in general are not very interested in us."

Willy Pacino is first-generation upper-middle class. His parents came over from Italy to work in the Pennsylvania coal mines. Willy went to college on a football scholarship and completed law school in a Midwestern university. He is now a labor abitrator in New Jersey. Of the Midwest he says: "The greatest asset out there is the people, the sincerity, down-to-earth, good work outfits, and when they talk, they say what they mean, and I like that." In the East, on the other hand, "you're going to run into your pseudosophisticate . . . the one that appears to be what he is not

and wishes to be what he is not. He's not well-read, he is not well-cultured, and he doesn't have worldly experience, and yet he holds out this air that he has all of the above and you see right through him."

Willy describes his friends as "real people; some are working people, some are attorneys, some are officials of unions. But they all have to be real, real in the sense of sincerity, and share the values that I respect: family, respecting others, and, I guess, sincerity, compassion." Willy's friends are honest: "There is nobody bullshitting anybody else. I hate to sit around to listen to idle bullshit, irrelevant chatter . . . talk about what they've achieved over and over, and where they were, like [imitating a female voice]: 'I went to Switzerland and I got invited to this wedding and you should have seen this affair, and we're inviting them back and did I tell you that we saw that play? And do you know what that cost?' I can't stand that when people say 'Do you know what it costs?'; they got to tell you what it costs. If I like it, I like it. I know what's expensive, and what's inexpensive. Don't keep reminding me of what you're doing and how much it cost! I am never with my friends to start bragging. They like me for what I am, I am Willy Pacino." And Willy Pacino is "the sort of guy I click with you or I don't click with you, I respect you or I don't respect you. I'm not iffy-wiffy."

Willy is not very religious. He is a family man. He is proud of his boys and helped his nephews pay their way through college: now there are several Pacinos who are professionals.

These three also share common traits. In contrast to the previous group, they do not consider cultural sophistication important. More central to them are moral qualities: honesty, respect for others, charity, egalitarianism, and sincerity. Worldly success is secondary to "what kind of human being you are." They oppose those who judge others on the basis of their income, occupational prestige, or the status of their leisure-time activities. In brief, they all dislike social climbers. Their definitions of a "worthy person" revolves around moral rather than cultural principles.

THIS-WORLDLY WORLDS

Craig Neil is much more interested in worldly goods. He owns a car-leasing business on Long Island. Behind his house, adjacent to his back-

yard, runs a canal where he keeps his yacht during the summer. The kitchen has just been entirely redone at great cost. Craig and I are sitting on expensive-looking contemporary leather sofas. The poodle keeps running over the cream carpet with his muddy paws.

Craig is depressed: it takes too much money to live in this area. "It puts a lot of stress on a person, 'cause you've got to maintain that livelihood and that lifestyle." Yet he considers himself very successful because "financially, I've done well, materialistically, I've done well, and I've reached a level in my life that I'm happy, comfortable with, the comfort level I call that." If there is one person he respects, it is Lee Iacocca: "A successful man that came from nothing and worked himself up from studying engineering, joining Ford Motor Company, and look where he is today. That's a fellow right there. I mean there are many of them, but to give you a highlight, that's a successful person. I admire him. Absolutely, no question about it."

For Craig, success is the key to everything: "The person I like is a person that's an aggressive person, a doer, who will wake up early with a positive attitude, and move on and do successful things." Accordingly, he confesses that "highly motivated, highly successful, highly aggressive people, I would feel inferior to." He feels superior to people "who put in a forty-hour week and say, 'Well, I've put my forty hours in and I want to be paid my fifty or hundred thousand dollars a year because I've put my forty hours in.'"

Craig does not like to be associated with losers, "with someone who has low esteem for himself, is not aggressive, doesn't want to accomplish much for his family, or do better for himself." He does not care for ideologues; he prefers someone who is level-headed, "who looks at both sides of the story, leveling the pros and the cons and using his experience as a decision maker. And who says 'Gee, even though I'm for it, maybe I should say no because look at this.' And back and forth, it's a give-and-take ratio."

Craig says he is very materialistic: "I'm a materialistic person because that is the only sign that shows you how you're accomplishing. Like 'Gee, you went and moved from a two-bedroom house to a three-bedroom house, from a three-bedroom house to a four-bedroom house, from a quarter acre to a half acre.' You know what I mean? So the only leverage you have on anything is the scale of how much better are you doing: Have you bought a used car this year rather than a new car? Is your kid

going to a crappy high school or a better high school? Is she going to a better college or a worse? So materialistic things, yes, are very important to me, to see how I am doing. I have nothing else to."

In Clermont-Ferrand, an important city located in the middle of France, Charles Dutour, the chief executive of a large hospital, also delights in this-worldly success. I was able to talk to this energetic man after waiting for two hours while observing his secretaries authoritatively screen phone calls and visitors.

Mr. Dutour's yardstick of success is not money but power: "I cannot think that it is possible to say that we don't like power. If it was the case, we would not be there. I believe that there are two groups of people in life: those who are made to command, and those who are made to obey. We are among those who like power, because power also gives independence." In this context it is not surprising to discover that Mr. Dutour easily admits to having a "sense of the hierarchy," to respecting those who are above him, and to expecting respect from those below him. He says he cannot stand irony.

This hospital director is a proud member of the local elite. He participates in the fourteenth of July parade with the mayor and other dignitaries. People ask him for favors all the time. Like other local "notables," he makes a habit of "sending back the elevator," i.e., of returning favors. He feels more comfortable talking with the chief of police than with a simple cop: "When you arrive at a certain level of responsibility, you think differently, and if you don't, you encounter problems. You can talk about hunting and fishing with a cop, but I don't fish or hunt."

Son of *petits boutiquiers* (small-business owners), Mr. Dutour has moved up considerably on the social ladder. He has sacrificed to his work both his family (he is separated from his wife) and his social life (he has no friends, only professional acquaintances). The people he likes are hardworking, competitive, pragmatic, and competent. People who are refined, comformist, religious, and nice leave him indifferent. As he says, "You see, I reduce everything to my profession."

Mat Howard reminds me of Craig Neil, who owns the car-leasing business. Mat is a real estate developer in Indianapolis. He has made a lot of money and has also lost a lot. He is a gambler, a nouveau riche, and an

ex-playboy. A few years ago, he got married and things changed. He became a homebody but remained a wheeler-dealer. His closest friend is "fifty-two years old going on twenty-eight. You know what I mean: very well-to-do, very athletic, does all the triathlons, and everything else. Still living the lifestyle, just travels a lot; very much a ladies' man. Typically dates women in their twenties and thirties. He does not look fifty-two." Like Craig, Mat lives in a world that values success. And like Craig, when asked what his success gives him, Mat answers. "Lots of money, that is the reward of having made it. Let's face it, most men want to build their ego by saying, 'I made it, I've been successful.' Hell, how do you grade that success? You grade it by the amount of money you made." Strangely enough, Mat feels inferior to people who have made it with the help of their parents: "I've had to work hard for everything. This guy comes along, and he's making tons of money, and it was handed to him on a silver platter. I should not feel inferior to those people, but the tendency is to do that."

To various extents, these three characters live in this-worldly worlds. Their standards of hierarchalization are less organized around culture and moral character than around various measures of worldly success and social position, although their sense of boundary might at times combine multiple themes. The real estate developer and the owner of the car-leasing business use money as a yardstick of success. The hospital administrator values power and influence. The way he relates to others is explicitly affected by their class position, whether they be bakers, cops, or chiefs of police.

The first group of men I described, more inclined to value cultural and intellectual qualities, attach relatively less importance to worldly success, while the second group—the bearers of morality—vehemently reject the relevance of class position or social status for interpersonal assessment. These three groups of men live side by side. Yet, in another sense, they live worlds apart and to a large extent define themselves in opposition to one another. The way they assess themselves and others—the boundaries they draw between desirable and undesirable traits, inferior and superior human beings—dramatizes the classification systems that predominate in the French and American upper-middle class. It is these very systems that I wish to explore.

Chapter One

~~~~~~

THE QUESTIONS AND THE STAGE

Sans considération, sans pitié, sans pudeur autour de moi, grands et laids, on a bâti des murs.
—C. P. Cavafy
Without consideration, without compassion, shamelessly, around me, tall and ugly, they have built walls.

ISSUES AND APPROACHES

How do people get access to valued professional resources such as well-paying jobs, interesting assignments, and promotions? Degrees, seniority, and experience are essential, but also important are being supported by a mentor, being included in networks of camaraderie, and receiving informal training. Getting access to these informal resources largely depends on sharing a valued cultural style. Indeed, research shows that managers favor employees who resemble them culturally, and that corporate success partly depends on making other managers "comfortable" by conforming in cultural matters and not "standing out."[1]

The present study explores the cultural categories through which the upper-middle class defines valued cultural styles. This task is a particularly important one because upper-middle-class members tend to control the allocation of many of the resources most valued in advanced industrial societies. Moreover, the mass media and the advertising industry constantly offer upper-middle-class culture as a model to members of other classes,[2] who often come to emulate it or to define their identities against it.[3] Despite the influence of upper-middle-class culture in the United States and elsewhere, and despite the fact that much has been written on resistance to dominant culture, the latter has rarely been submitted to close scrutiny.[4]

What is primarily at issue here is the nature of the criteria that people use to define and discriminate between worthy and less worthy persons, i.e., between "their sort of folks" and "the sort they don't much like." To identify these criteria I scrutinize symbolic boundaries—the types of lines that individuals draw when they categorize people—and high-status

1

signals—the keys to our evaluative distinctions. More specifically, different ways of believing that "we" are better than "them" are compared by analyzing both the standards that underlie status assessments and the characteristics of symbolic boundaries themselves—their degree of rigidity, for instance. This contributes to developing a more adequate and complex view of status, i.e., of the salience of various status dimensions across contexts. It also helps us to understand how societies and social classes differ culturally. By contrasting the cultures of members of the French and American upper-middle classes, we will see that the disapproval that New Yorkers often express toward Midwestern parochialism, the frequent criticisms that the French address to American puritan moralism, the scorn that businessmen voice toward intellectualism, and the charges that social and cultural specialists frequently make against materialism and business interests can be interpreted as specific instances of a pervasive phenomenon (i.e., as boundary work) rather than as incommensurable manifestations of national character, political attitudes, regionalism, etc.[5] Using the framework presented here, it will be possible to view prejudices and stereotypes as the supraindividual by-products of basic social processes that are shaped by the cultural resources that people have at their disposal and by the structural situations they live in.

The book studies upper-middle-class culture using the comparative method, on the assumption that cultural differences—the shock of otherness—will make valued cultural traits salient.[6] The analysis is based on 160 semidirected interviews conducted with a random stratified sample of male college-graduate professionals, managers, and businessmen living in and around Indianapolis, New York, Paris, and Clermont-Ferrand, the regional metropolis of an agricultural *département* in the Massif Central that is not unlike Indianapolis (for a comparison see Appendix II). I focus on France and the United States because, being a Quebecer, I am an outsider to both cultures, and yet I know both of them from the inside, having lived in France and the United States for four and five years, respectively, at the time I conducted the interviews. Furthermore, as I will argue below, French and American cultures show somewhat different formal characteristics that illuminate important theoretical issues.

I have chosen to interview *white male* members of the upper-middle class because these individuals still hold most of the powerful positions in the workplace and are likely to have influence as gatekeepers.[7] With the goal of exploring gender differences in boundary work, however, I also conducted fifteen interviews with female professionals, managers, and

businesswomen residing in the New York suburbs. Gender differences will be briefly discussed toward the end of the book, even though more interviews are needed before firm conclusions can be reached. Future research should also consider differences in the boundary work of whites and the growing number of minority upper-middle-class members.[8]

Experts have suggested that the display of "cultivated dispositions," i.e., of cultural capital, is one of the most highly prized cultural traits among the upper-middle class. Most important, in his pioneering work on French culture, the sociologist Pierre Bourdieu has argued that members of the "dominant class" share distinctive tastes and lifestyles that act as status markers and facilitate integration into this group. These tastes are defined largely by cultivated dispositions and the ability to display an adequate command of high culture. According to Bourdieu, outsiders who have not been socialized into these aesthetic dispositions at an early stage in life cannot easily become integrated into high status groups as they are often excluded due to their cultural style.[9]

In the United States, sociologists interested in the cultural reproduction of elites have also emphasized how educational and occupational attainment is related to the display of cultivated dispositions and to familiarity with high culture (i.e., cultural capital).[10] This focus on refinement and high culture can be explained in part by the availability of survey data on the topic. While this research has contributed considerably to our knowledge of the effect of culture on inequality, however, it has defined a priori what status signals are most valued by adopting the analytical categories built into the survey questionnaires.[11] In contrast, by using open-ended questions, it is possible to allow people themselves to define what high status signals are most important to them. As the vignettes presented earlier suggest, these signals vary greatly across individuals as they range, for instance, from honesty and sincerity to competitiveness and material success.

So far no one has attempted to estimate the relative salience of various types of high status signals in the upper-middle-class culture despite recent calls for more research on this topic.[12] The present study fills this gap by analyzing the criteria of purity that interviewees use to describe, abstractly and concretely, people they perceive as "better" or "worse" than themselves, or to characterize individuals they don't want to associate with—as Kai Erikson has argued, boundaries exist only if they are repeatedly defended by members of inner groups.[13] I thereby chart the cultural categories through which upper-middle-class members perceive and

value others, stressing what differences are at the *center* of their maps of perception and what differences are *ignored*. Hence, my project is to illuminate the structures of thought through which upper-middle-class people organize (i.e., select and hierarchize) the "raw data" they receive on others.

At the outset of this project I intended to study differences in the ways in which French and American upper-middle-class members draw cultural boundaries.[14] However, I rapidly discovered while conducting interviews that the signals used by individuals to assess high status often pertained to moral and socioeconomic standing as well as to cultural attainment. Furthermore, it appeared that the large majority of these signals pertained to at least one of these standards; some signals, such as self-actualization, were taken to be simultaneously a proof of high moral character, strong success orientation, and cultural sophistication. Consequently, my study focuses on these three standards or types of symbolic boundaries:

Moral boundaries are drawn on the basis of moral character; they are centered around such qualities as honesty, work ethic, personal integrity, and consideration for others. Paul Anderson drew moral boundaries when he explained that he feels superior to people who have low moral standards and when he criticized some of his coworkers for not caring about people first. So did Michel Dupuis when he described his distaste for social climbers and for those who lack personal integrity.

Socioeconomic boundaries are drawn on the basis of judgments concerning people's social position as indicated by their wealth, power, or professional success. Craig Neil drew such boundaries when he explained that money is the yardstick he uses to evaluate his success against that of others and that he feels superior to people who are not high achievers. Similarly, Charles Dutour drew socioeconomic boundaries when he stressed that his friends are all very influential members of the local elite.

Cultural boundaries are drawn on the basis of education, intelligence, manners, tastes, and command of high culture. Someone who describes all of his friends as refined is drawing cultural boundaries. Didier Aucour and John Bloom both drew such boundaries when they talked about their feeling of superiority toward people who are less intelligent and less culturally sophisticated than themselves.

The most important contribution of this study is to enrich our grasp of mental maps and boundary work. It is also to provide a more complex understanding of cultural differences between nations and classes by ana-

lyzing these via symbolic boundaries, i.e., via the criteria that are used to evaluate status. The major empirical findings of this study, however, pertain to the relative salience of the three types of boundaries in both countries as revealed by the interviews, a survey of available research, and a quantitative comparison of the boundary work produced by all the respondents. First, I show that whereas in both France and the United States sociological studies of high status signals have focused almost exclusively on cultural boundaries, and more specifically on a small subset of the cultural signals that are used to draw cultural boundaries, again evidence suggests that members of the French upper-middle class draw boundaries on the basis of moral and socioeconomic standing almost as frequently as they do on the basis of cultural standing. Second, as suggested above, whereas sociologists also have often argued that cultural capital is a major basis of exclusion in the United States, the data I collected indicates that American upper-middle-class members stress socioeconomic and moral boundaries more than they do cultural boundaries; this is not the case in France where moral and cultural boundaries are slightly more important than socioeconomic boundaries; these differences are becoming less accentuated: data suggest that socioeconomic boundaries are gaining in importance in both countries while cultural boundaries appear to be losing in importance in the United States and possibly in France.

The implications of these findings for the metatheoretical assumptions of Marxist, structuralist, and rational choice theorists are discussed. In particular, my findings shed doubt on the ontological models of human nature central to these approaches, as the latter assumes that human beings give analytical primacy to socioeconomic resources (and boundaries or status) over other types of resources. The implications of my findings for the influential contribution of Pierre Bourdieu are also analyzed; the work of this French sociologist now represents one of the most influential trends in the sociology of culture and in cultural anthropology. My data suggest that Bourdieu greatly underestimates the importance of moral boundaries while he exaggerates the importance of cultural and socioeconomic boundaries. In addition, assumptions that are central to his concepts of power field are contradicted by my data. Some of these criticisms will be briefly introduced in the first chapters of this volume, but they will be brought together at the end of the book.

This study pursues three additional goals. First, it attempts to clarify the relationship between symbolic boundaries and inequality by specify-

ing whether and under what conditions the boundaries drawn by the interviewees could lead to class reproduction. Second, it provides a multicausal explanation for differences in boundary work across groups. Finally, it documents variations in boundary work *within* the French and the American upper-middle class in the process of explaining intergroup differences in boundary work.

To study the potential impact of symbolic boundaries on inequality, I discuss their formal features or structure, i.e., the degree to which they are rigidly defined and widely shared by a population. Comparing the French and the American cases, I will show that cultural boundaries, i.e., boundaries drawn on the basis of education, intelligence, refinement, and cosmopolitanism, are much more loosely defined in the United States than they are in France.[15] This directly influences the ways in which culture shapes inequality in each country as it affects whether boundaries create hierarchalization and exclusion rather than simply differentiation. Intead of assuming that symbolic boundaries directly lead to exclusion, we need to view them as a necessary but insufficient condition for the creation of inequality, and exclusion itself, as the frequent unintended effect of the process of defining self-identity.

In this context it should be noted that this study could potentially complement the neo-Durkheimian, and mostly American, literature on symbolic boundaries. This literature has tended to focus on social control and to predefine all symbolic boundaries as moral boundaries,[16] thereby neglecting to analyze differences between various types of boundaries.[17] This research tradition has also looked at symbolic boundaries to analyze cultural codes.[18] With a few exceptions, it has paid little attention to the potential role played by symbolic boundaries in group formation and in the production of inequality.[19] It has also neglected to study how *groups* draw boundaries in the process of defining their own identity, ideology, and status against that of other groups. This study brings together the neo-Durkheimian literature that focuses on cultural codes, with the French literature concerning class cultures and inequality.

Using comparative data, it is argued that the content of symbolic boundaries that people draw, and particularly the relative salience of moral, socioeconomic, and cultural boundaries, varies with the cultural resources that individuals have access to and with the structural conditions in which they are placed. These resources include those made available by national historical traditions (e.g., the core values of "Americanism": egalitarianism, individualism, and achievement) and by various

sectors of cultural production and diffusion (the educational system, the mass media), while proximate and remote structural conditions include the market position of upper-middle-class members as well as the general structural features of the society in which they live. While a number of social scientists account for the features of cultural systems that individuals uphold by their interests, the volume and composition of their resources (or capital), or the structure of their group,[20] these factors need to be supplemented by looking at the "cultural supply side," i.e., at the cultural resources that are made available to individuals for boundary work. As pointed out by neo-institutional theorists and others, individuals do not exclusively draw boundaries out of their own experience: they borrow from the general cultural repertoires supplied to them by the society in which they live, relying on general definitions of valued traits that take on a rule-like status.[21]

Finally, this book is also concerned with variations in symbolic boundaries across particular categories of interviewees. First, I assess the relative importance of cultural standards across groups that have different cultural resources at their disposal, i.e., that have unequal access to high culture.[22] I compare the responses of interviewees living in "cultural centers" (the suburbs of Paris and New York) with those of interviewees living in "cultural peripheries" (Indianapolis and Clermont-Ferrand), and I find only small differences across sites. Second, I analyze how boundary work varies with one's social trajectory by comparing the boundary work of the upwardly and the downwardly mobile, as well as that of individuals whose families have belonged to the upper-middle class for several generations with that of individuals who are new to this group. I find that social trajectory clearly affects definitions of high status signals. Third, I compare the effect of market position and the relationship that people have with economic rationality on boundary work, by contrasting intellectuals and nonintellectuals as well as social and cultural specialists (e.g., artists, social workers, psychologists, teachers, journalists) and members of business-related occupations. Expanding on the early work of Seymour Martin Lipset who showed that intellectuals and, more generally, social and cultural specialists are more politically liberal than for-profit workers, I find that this difference in attitudinal orientation extends to boundary work[23] and that these trends are reinforced by national cultures. For instance, the French for-profit workers draw stronger cultural boundaries than their American counterparts while the American social and cultural specialists draw stronger socioeconomic boundaries than their French

counterparts. The political insights suggested by these consequential findings will be discussed.

While this study examines a sample limited to narrow occupational categories, it provides us with a basis for understanding national cultures. When possible, I examine evidence from national surveys to compare the characteristics of my upper-middle-class interviewees with the French and American populations at large. We will see that my findings concerning the relative importance of moral, cultural, and socioeconomic boundaries often converge with studies of French and American national character,[24] and with the classic comparisons of French and American culture, such as Lipset's *The First New Nation* and Tocqueville's *Democracy in America*.[25] Most of the available work on national character tends to ignore the internal diversity of national cultures, and to explain differences primarily in psychological rather than social terms. Precisely because symbolic boundaries are supraindividual in nature and vary within groups, as an analytic tool, they allow us to avoid these problems and improve our understanding of national cultural differences. Moreover, most recent comparative research has centered on structural, i.e., economic and political, phenomena. Focusing on symbolic boundaries can renew interest in properly cultural comparative work and in the comparative stratification research that to date has tended to analyze transfers of social position rather than the broad features of status systems.[26]

It should be noted that in the process of examining the boundary patterns of the French and American upper-middle class, I indirectly document and explain national differences in the relative importance of high culture and materialism in France and in America. For instance, I advance that while cultural egalitarianism reinforces anti-intellectualism in the United States and generates forms of reverse cultural exclusion, materialism in France is weakened by the low level of geographic mobility characteristic of this society. These themes are explored only to the extent that they help us understand boundary patterns while using cross-cultural comparisons in lieu of a laboratory.

Boundaries and identity have occupied the center stage of recent poststructuralist, postmodernist, and feminist debates. All three currents are concerned with the role played by meaning in legitimizing differences and inequality.[27] In line with Derrida's thought—and, unknowingly, with the classical sociological contributions of W. I. Thomas—these writings conceptualize meaning and identity as plural, "decentered," and relationally defined, i.e., as defined through changing boundaries, in opposition

to other meanings against which they take on their own significance. Or else they are concerned with the fragmentation of definitions of reality, with how various groups (race, class, gender) contribute independently to the waving of disjuncted cultural codes.[28] Similarly, I analyze the polysemy of boundaries, i.e., the relative salience of various identities (races, classes, religions, genders, levels of education, or moral character). However, while poststructuralist, postmodernist, and feminist writings tend to focus their attention on the intersection between power and culture manifested in race, class, and gender boundaries, I also center my attention on the role of more diffused characteristics such as morality, refinement, and cosmopolitanism. Moreover, I specify the conditions under which differences generate inequality—a task too often neglected by poststructuralists and deconstructionists alike. I suggest that by studying the differences in the symbolic boundaries drawn by various groups, it is possible to better understand the nature of the dynamic between these groups, as we will see when we compare, for instance, social and cultural specialists with for-profit workers.

I now discuss the nature of symbolic boundaries themselves as well as some of the mechanisms by which they operate. This is necessary because symbolic boundaries have rarely been systematically explored in the sociological literature, although they are often alluded to.

BOUNDARIES AT WORK

Symbolic boundaries are conceptual distinctions that we make to categorize objects, people, practices, and even time and space. Here I am concerned exclusively with the subjective boundaries that we draw between ourselves and others. I pay no attention to other types of abstract boundary structures—e.g., spatial and temporal boundaries—or to the types of objective social boundaries that are revealed by the existence of ghettos, exclusive clubs, racial or gender segregation in the workplace, or the institutionalization of corporatist practices. Neither do I consider the institutional mechanisms that reproduce objective boundaries in specific institutions, such as religion, science, the family, the military, etc.

We know from Emile Durkheim and Georg Simmel that symbolic boundaries presuppose both inclusion (of the desirable) and exclusion (of the repulsive, the impure).[29] They also imply a third, gray zone made up of elements that leave us indifferent. According to Eviatar Zerubavel,

this model can be represented by two concentric circles mapped in a doughnut-like shape: the inside of the first circle represents elements that are appreciated and included; the inside of the second circle represents elements that leave us indifferent and are tolerable; the outside of the second circle represents elements that are intolerable and excluded.[30]

The people excluded by our boundaries are those with whom we refuse to associate and those toward whom rejection and aggression are showed, and distance openly marked, by way of insuring that "you understand that I am better than you are." This is done, for instance (in the words of one of my Indianapolis informants), by "being reserved, being quiet, not really openly discussing things, or being very formally courteous, not having much to do with you because I have no time or use for you and I try and send signals in that way . . . hands are quiet, the body position is, you know, very much in control." Exclusive behaviors are experienced as repugnance, discomfort, embarrassment for the excluder, and as snobbery, distance, and coldness by the excluded.

Distancing behavior is contrasted with what could be labeled "friendly behavior," or inclusive behavior. Behaving in a friendly way (*être sympa*) makes others feel "comfortable," which is particularly important in American upper-middle-class culture, where trust is the hallmark of inclusion.[31] It means ostentatiously giving up "fronts" and interacting as "human beings"—"relating." And inclusion is enacted through a range of everyday activities, such as "flirting, complimenting, flattering, honoring, introducing, initiating, debuting, exchanging gifts and secrets, promoting or electing to high office, taking into one's confidence, dancing together, hosting, eating together, playing together, corresponding, caressing, making love . . . [i.e., gestures/activities designed] to make people feel as though they have free and privileged access to highly valued social activities."[32]

Through our necessary involvement in a wide range of groups, we are all constantly participating in the production and reenactment of competing boundaries, both as we label others and we participate in communities whose shared beliefs make a specific definition of reality intersubjectively true. Indeed, we often carry out boundary work through our membership in professional groups, social classes, and ethnic and racial groups, or as residents of a community.

Some of these groups are more likely to generate influential boundaries than others. Since World War II, the labeling impact of ethnic groups has declined as their own identity has weakened.[33] Class divisions, too,

have become less significant as the class-specific contours of material and cultural life have broken down.[34] On the other hand, while the impact of social class, ethnicity, and religious socialization on marital choice has been diminishing, educational homogamy has been increasing.[35] In general, the college-educated population (which encompasses the upper-middle class as defined in the present study) continues to show a high degree of similarity in its cultural practices and attitudes over a wide range of areas.[36] The fact that a college degree remains the best predictor of high occupational status suggests that the boundaries that this population builds between itself and others are particularly significant.[37] These boundaries are likely to be more permanent, less crossable, and less resisted than the boundaries that exist between ethnic groups, for instance. They are also more likely to survive across contexts, i.e., to be carried over from the community to the workplace, and vice versa. We see again, therefore, the importance of studying in a systematic fashion the boundaries produced by college-educated people.

From what materials are boundaries created? As Weber argued, any characteristic can be construed as a polluting factor.[38] Yet boundaries are rarely created from scratch. They generally exist prior to situational interactions and are determined by available cultural resources and by spatial, geographic, and social-structural constraints, i.e., by the particular set of people with whom we are likely to come in contact. Indeed, most of the boundaries "have to do with public evaluation of behavior, with degrees of conformity to social codes, rather than with hypothetical inner states."[39] We often simply take them for granted and enact them unthinkingly.[40]

But why do we draw boundaries? Boundary work is an intrinsic part of the process of constituting the self; they emerge when we try to define who we are: we constantly draw inferences concerning our similarities to, and differences from, others, indirectly producing typification systems. Thereby we define our own inwardness and the character of others, identity being defined relationally.[41] By generating distinctions, we also signal our identity and develop a sense of security, dignity, and honor;[42] a significant portion of our daily activities are oriented toward avoiding shame and maintaining a positive self-identity by patroling the borders of our groups.[43] At a more macrosociological level, boundary work is used to reinstate order within communities by reinforcing collective norms, as boundaries provide a way to develop a general sense of organization and order in the environment.

Boundary work is also a way of developing a sense of group mem-

bership; it creates bonds based on shared emotions, similar conceptions of the sacred and the profane, and similar reactions toward symbolic violators.[44] More generally, boundaries constitute a system of rules that guide interaction by affecting who comes together to engage in what social acts. They thereby also come to separate people into classes, working groups, professions, species, genders, and races. Therefore, boundaries not only create groups; they also potentially produce inequality because they are an essential medium through which individuals acquire status, monopolize resources, ward off threats, or legitimate their social advantages, often in reference to superior lifestyle, habits, character, or competences.[45]

It should be noted that by documenting differences in symbolic boundaries across groups, I am documenting differences in the structure of potential exclusion across groups. In other words, I understand the criteria at work in an interviewee's description of his friends, his feelings of inferiority and superiority, etc., as reflective of the general mental maps and boundaries that he/she mobilizes in natural settings, and as subjective boundaries that only potentially can lead to the drawing of objective boundaries, i.e., to actual exclusion from groups, institutions, and so forth. For the sake of simplicity, however, I will use the concepts of boundary work and exclusion indiscriminately. The reader should keep in mind that, rather than focusing on inequality, the following chapters could as well have been framed as a study of inclusion and the making of communities, the two processes happening simultaneously.

Additional research is needed in order to obtain a clear understanding of the limits of this study. Indeed, we still ignore exactly how much the boundaries that people draw in interview situations correspond to the subjective boundaries they draw in real-life discussions; whether these boundaries reveal what high status signals qua high status signals are most salient, or, alternatively, what traits are most salient in a specific interaction; and whether these boundaries are indicative of the full range of an interviewee's high status signals or only part of it. More research is needed to see if these boundaries are those that respondents draw against "people like themselves" (i.e., other upper-middle-class people), or those that they draw against members of other social classes, and whether they reveal deeply seated categories or only those that are enough at the surface level to manifest themselves in interview situations. Moreover, we still ignore whether such boundaries are in fact always salient in routine inter-

actions, or only salient in situations of uncertainty and ambiguity. For now, given our general lack of knowledge concerning boundary work, it seems justified to assume for heuristic purposes that the boundaries that emerge during the interviews are illustrative of the categories most immediately salient, and therefore—hopefully—most central, in the interviewees' mental maps. It is unlikely that these boundaries are divorced from the respondents' fundamental mental maps even if situational factors can create distortions;[46] for reasons to be described below, I believe that the effect of the interviewer on these was minimized.

In conclusion, I want to emphasize again that many of the men I talked with wield considerable power. Some are responsible for fifteen employees, others for several hundred or thousands. Some are professors who affect the futures of generations of students, while others, as social workers, museum curators, priests, psychologists, financial advisors, lawyers, or physicians give advice and make decisions that can profoundly influence people's lives. Yet others are in charge of managing thousands or millions of dollars in their professional capacities as scientists, chief executive officers, bank executives, or academic administrators. These men frame other people's lives in countless ways as they conceive, advise, hire, promote, judge, select and allocate.[47] Therefore, their definitions of appropriate cultural style indirectly affect the opportunities of many working people. These definitions can be viewed as integral ingredients of the exercise of power in modern society because they play a central role in the framing of people's lives.[48] This is why it is important to study closely the symbolic boundaries these men draw.

Chapters 2, 3, and 4, respectively, map out the content of moral, socioeconomic, and cultural boundaries (the dependent variables) in France and the United States, documenting the relative salience of the three types of boundaries across sites—I start with a discussion of moral boundaries because these are important in both countries. Simultaneously, I analyze the nature of the interaction between these boundaries across national contexts, and empirically address the question of their relative degree of autonomy from one another. We will see, for instance, that the French often draw socioeconomic boundaries while drawing cultural boundaries, and that Americans more often subordinate cultural boundaries to moral ones. Chapter 5 compares the importance of boundaries within sites, considering differences between cultural centers and cultural peripheries. It also provides explanations for national differ-

ences in boundary work that take into consideration both available cultural repertoires and the proximate and remote structural conditions experienced by interviewees. Chapter 6 pursues the discussion of the causes of boundary patterns. It demonstrates that boundary work varies with the proximate structural conditions in which individuals live by analyzing the importance of moral, socioeconomic, and cultural boundaries across groups that have different relationships with economic rationality. The last chapter discusses the broader theoretical implications of the study. I now describe succinctly the methodological approach followed in this study. Appendix III contains a more detailed description of the research procedures.

PROCEDURES

The analysis is primarily based on four groups of forty interviews which I conducted with upper-middle-class men who lived in and around Indianapolis, New York, Paris, and Clermont-Ferrand. The participants from the Paris and New York suburbs were drawn from nine different communities. In the New York suburbs, residents were chosen from northern New Jersey and Long Island. In the Paris *banlieue* I conducted interviews in the very Catholic Versailles as well as in some of the slightly less affluent northern suburbs.[49]

For the purpose of this study, I define the upper-middle class as college-educated professionals, managers, and businessmen.[50] This group includes professionals and semiprofessionals such as social workers, librarians, elementary and secondary schoolteachers. The managerial group comprises executives, middle-level managers, and administrators in the public and nonprofit sectors. The businessmen include self-employed professionals and the owners of businesses of various sizes.

Occupations and levels of education are used to delineate the sample in order to avoid both nominalist definitions of the upper-middle class, and comparison of predefined abstract classes situated in different social structures: the mental maps of a French and an American dentist and those of a French and an American priest are more easily circumscribed than those of an ill-defined French or American upper-middle class, taken as a whole. Consequently, I am comparing occupational groupings located in four different sites, the samples being composed of people having similar occupations and levels of education.[51] This focus on occupation is

justified because it is a central dimension of the identity of upper-middle-class males.[52]

My goal is not to compare French and American professionals or managers from the standpoint of their career or work conditions, since French and American interviewees work under different conditions.[53] Instead, I am concerned with individuals who have at their disposal common categorization systems to differentiate between insiders and outsiders, and common vocabularies and symbols through which they create a shared identity. Interviewees who share such categories can be considered to be members of a same symbolic community even if they have no face-to-face interactions and if their work situations vary greatly.[54]

Respondents were randomly chosen from the phone directories of middle- and upper-middle-class suburbs and neighborhoods in order to avoid tapping into a specific upper-middle-class subculture. Availability and eligibility were determined on the basis of demographic information obtained through brief phone interviews. The final group of interviewees was selected from the list of available and eligible participants to match as closely as possible respondents from the other samples in terms of occupation, situs, and level of education.[55] The same sampling procedures were followed for the male and the female populations.

The male interviewees are listed by occupation, age, and site in table 1. The population has been categorized in two groups: on the one hand, cultural and social specialists working in the profit, public and non-profit sector and state-employed for-profit workers; on the other hand, salaried and self-employed for-profit workers (the theoretical rationale for this categorization will be presented when I discuss differences in boundary work across occupational groupings in Chap. 6). Information on the level of education and income of interviewees is presented in Appendix I.

The data was collected using semidirected interviews because the latter are superior to survey questions for studying symbolic boundaries, as they let interviewees themselves describe their standards of evaluation and lead the researcher toward the most appropriate analytical categories. Also, semidirected interviews allow us to infer how respondents draw boundaries by focusing on the implicit criteria of purity at work during the interviews; this is an important methodological advantage because people are rarely open about their exclusivism.

Semidirected interviews offer additional advantages: for instance,

TABLE 1
Occupation and Age of Male Interviewees by Sites and Category of Occupation

Paris Suburbs	age	Clermont-Ferrand	age	Indianapolis	age	New York Suburbs	age
		Cultural and Social Specialists (All Sectors): Profit-Related Occupation (Public and Nonprofit Sectors)					
public school administrator	50	public school administrator	50	public school administrator	45	public school administrator	58
academic administrator	57	academic administrator	41	academic administrator	49	academic administrator	50
music teacher	41	music teacher	55	music teacher	54	earth science teacher	46
priest	43	priest	55	minister	59	minister	51
museum curator	53	museum curator	41	museum curator	42	museum curator	44
musician	42	artist	43	artist	37	artist	48
science teacher	46	electronics teacher	50	professor of physics	51	science teacher	53
professor of architecture	31	professor of social work	41	professor of medicine	51	professor of social work	49
literature teacher	57	philosophy teacher	48	civil rights professional	41	professor of theology	57
social worker	35	athletics coach	37	recreational professional	51	recreational professional	33
diplomat	55	civil servant	41	staff assistant	43	civil servant	58
computer specialist	33	civil servant	41	computer specialist	39	computer specialist	34
professor of accounting	39	journalist	53	accountant (public)	44	economist	52
human resource consultant	38	physicist	35	medical researcher	34	human resources consultant	41
psychologist	44	psychologist	53	psychologist	46	psychologist	50
hospital administrator	60	hospital controller	36	manager human services	46	hospital controller	39
architect (public)	43	safety inspector	36	judge	40	labor arbitrator	47
human resources consultant	59	paramedic	40	bank examiner (public)	36	statistics researcher	46
dentist[a]	34	dentist[a]	55	science researcher	35	applied science researcher	42
physician[a]	46	physician[a]	48	research scientist	36	computer researcher	36
average age	45	*average age*	45	*average age*	44	*average age*	47

Profit-Related Occupations (Private Sector)

Occupation	Age	Occupation	Age	Occupation	Age	Occupation	Age
accountant	57	accountant	33	accountant	30	investment advisor	31
accountant	40	accountant	57	chief financial officer	48	chief financial officer	56
lawyer	39	lawyer	42	lawyer	32	lawyer	34
lawyer	45	lawyer	49	lawyer	37	lawyer	42
banker	45	banker	34	banker	43	banker	44
investment banker	40	banker	53	banker	54	banker	59
insurance broker	45	insurance broker	31	insurance company VP	47	insurance company VP	44
architect[a]	46	architect[a]	45	architect[a]	37	custom house broker	57
corporate attorney	36	financial advisor	34	corporate attorney	32	corporate attorney	41
business management specialist	46	plant manager	50	plant manager	32	plant facilities manager	40
senior executive manufacturing	58	senior executive manufacturing	58	marketing executive	45	marketing executive	45
computer engineer	51	computer marketing executive	53	computer marketing specialist	57	computer specialist	52
insurance executive	42	executive car dealer	43	used car dealer	39	proprietor car leasing co.	45
accountant	37	accountant	49	stockbroker	57	computer consultant	46
electrical engineer	42	chemical engineer	53	real estate developer	44	computer software developer	53
lawyer	47	financial advisor	43	realtor	58	realtor	51
proprietor engineering firm	47	architect[a]	45	architect	44	machine tool distributor	35
proprietor printing firm	56	proprietor surveying firm	53	forester	59	proprietor broadcasting co.	49
marketing executive	55	chemical engineer	42	data manager	55	portfolio manager	46
tourism executive	43	tourism executive	39	professional recruiter	52	wholesale distributor	55
average age	*47*	*average age*	*45*	*average age*	*45*	*average age*	*46*

[a] Hybrid Occupations.

they facilitate access to a more nuanced understanding of the interviewees' worldview. They are also less time-consuming than participant observation. This is an important consideration given that the comparative focus of this research requires studying several populations. Interviews force one to focus on the outer edges of classification systems, however, and to ignore finer types of behaviors that can only be tapped through observation. This is partly compensated for by the fact that the study also draws on behavioral data, i.e., on ethnographic notes taken after the interview, and on a questionnaire on leisure-time activities. Moreover, because symbolic boundaries are often primarily enacted at the discursive level—the crystallization of boundary work into institutional discrimination being an effect of subjective symbolic boundaries—the data generated in interviews can be interpreted as behavioral data, especially given that respondents are unaware of the existence of symbolic boundaries as a social phenomena as they tend to take at face value the standards of purity they adopt.

The interview schedule was constructed to tap symbolic boundaries. My efforts were aimed at obtaining an adequate picture of the labels participants use for describing people whom they place above and below themselves. Consequently, I asked interviewees to both concretely and abstractly describe people with whom they prefer not to associate, those in relation to whom they feel superior and inferior, and those who evoke hostility, indifference, and sympathy. Furthermore, I asked them to describe the negative and positive traits of some of their coworkers and acquaintances, regarding these descriptions as a template of their mental maps.[56] I also asked them to describe their perception of the cultural traits that are most valued in their workplace. Finally, to identify the interviewees' definition of high status signals, I set out to reconstruct their child-rearing values.[57] In this process, I often asked respondents to make explicit their standards and guide me toward a greater understanding of their cultural categories or schemes of definition of reality.

Each interview lasted approximately two hours; they were confidential and recorded. They were held at a time and place chosen by the participant, i.e., at work, in the garden, at the café, or preceding a family meal to which I had been invited. To insure greater comparability, I met all the interviewees myself. My being a foreigner in both countries turned out to be a major asset, as people were more prone to explain their taken-for-granted assumptions, not knowing the extent to which I might, or

might not, be familiar with their culture. I explain this in detail in the next section.

THE INTERVIEWING EXPERIENCE

Qualitative sociologists have seriously reflected on the nature and meaning of information collected using interviewing techniques. Many have suggested that the interviewees' answers are directly affected by what they perceive to be the interviewer's own values and definition of the "right answer."[58] Hence, the interviewees are liable to "construct" their identity or opinions so as to resemble, or to differ from, the perceived identity or opinions of the interviewer. For instance, in the present case, an Indianapolis plant manager might overstate his interest in high culture when he is being interviewed by someone associated with Princeton University. Alternatively, the same plant manager might strongly avow his total indifference to anything cultural as a way of asserting his own identity. From this point of view, interviews would produce nothing more than a template of the interaction between the interviewer and the interviewee's identity, or an original "text" to which no additional meaning should be attributed. Convinced that interviews nonetheless can yield valuable and textually rich data, social scientists have devised various techniques to minimize "distortions" and have continued to produce qualitative studies of great interest and importance.

To a certain extent, the conditions under which the present research was conducted minimized distorting effects. On the one hand, as an interviewer I tried to maintain a blurred professional and cultural identity. On the other hand, because the research was aimed at tapping high status cultural signals, I read the manner in which the interviewees dramatized their identity as potentially reflective of their own definition of high status cultural signals. To understand these two points, some background information is required.

1. I attempted to present myself to interviewees with a blurred *professional* identity from the time of their first contact with the project. They had received a letter on Princeton University stationery informing them that they had been randomly sampled to participate in the project. The letter was signed by myself. It mentioned my status (assistant professor) and announced that a research assistant would contact them to collect preliminary information and set up an appointment. The day of the inter-

view, I would pull into their driveway in an old Peugeot 504 (a small, rented Renault 5 in France). I, a woman in my early thirties, would engage them in a relaxed conversation.[59] Many were confused, perhaps expecting a university professor to be middle-aged and more formal in style. Instead, they were confronted with an inconspicuously dressed woman, who had few of the particular earmarks of the "academic" and who at times even made grammatical errors. This, along with the informality required by the interview situation, did not mesh with the image of the high culture officionado that is often attached to a Princeton University professor. Consequently, within a few minutes after we met, the middle-aged men I interviewed would often ask me if I was "the" professor or a research assistant—an uncertainty compounded by the fact that some Americans and many French interviewees did not know exactly what an "assistant professor" is. Others waited until the end of the interview to try to clarify my identity. Yet others looked me as if I were a fraud; a few asked me to produce my credentials, and a Clermont-Ferrand lawyer wrote to the chairman of my department to verify that I was really employed by Princeton.[60]

2. I presented the interviewees with a blurred *cultural* identity. This was due in part to the fact that as a Québécoise who has lived for several years in both France and the United States, I have an accent in both languages, but an accent that is not readily identifiable. Americans were often reluctant to ask me where I came from, assuming that I was French or being afraid of offending by making salient an ascribed characteristic; in Indianapolis, moreover, many were obviously not used to interacting with foreigners. To make interviewees comfortable, I would sometimes reveal my origins. Most of the men I talked to were aware of my foreignness but not sure of its extent, which allowed me to question them on taken-for-granted notions (e.g., the meaning of the concept *phony*) that a native researcher could not have explored as freely. Yet my familiarity with American upper-middle-class culture provided me with enough background information to get at subtle cultural nuances and probe interviewees in a fruitful way.[61]

The French reactions to my cultural identity also showed some repeated and characteristic features. Most participants expected to be interviewed by someone who had little background information on French society. Many did not know that I had lived in France for several years, had grown up in a family that was culturally and linguistically French, and shared a great deal of the interviewees' own cultural baggage. My slight

Canadian accent would often go unnoticed, or pass for an American accent. Again, interviewees could not decipher the extent, and in some cases the nature, of my foreignness. They often literally did not know to whom they had been talking until the very end of the interview, when I would finally provide them with information on myself. This confusion, I believe, was essential in order to decontextualize the "impression management" conducted by the men I interviewed.

3. Again, because the research was aimed at tapping high status cultural signals, I interpreted the way the interviewees defined themselves as reflective of their definition of what high status cultural signals ought to be. "Impression management" on the interviewee's part was not a problem: if he wished to make good impressions, so much the better, for I was looking for precisely the kind of signals he mobilized on such occasions.

The Indianapolis interviews led me to a country house in the middle of a tree farm surrounded by large lakes; to the twenty-third floor of the Indiana National Bank; to the Bohemian home of an artist, cluttered with drawings, old books, old cats, and sculptures; to a soft-drink plant manned with hefty workers and thunderous with noise; and to many suburban ranch homes, complete with dogs and an array of kids' bicycles in the driveway. I met with men who were carefully hanging on to their painfully obtained middle-class status, with others who had "prepped," and with still others who, behind their middle-aged and Midwestern sensibilities, were going through a mid-life crisis which sometimes they generously shared with me, making their middle-class values more apparent at the very juncture where those values were most seriously threatened. Most people were cooperative, friendly, and eager to participate.

Interviewing in the New York suburbs was a different experience. From the outset, the research assistants responsible for contacting the interviewees noticed that people were fairly suspicious and reacted aggressively to questions concerning their race or level of education—a problem we had not encountered in Indianapolis. Clearly, those contacted were more sensitive to status issues and less easily accessible. Many mentioned that they considered a two-hour interview to be extraordinarily long.

These interviews, too, brought me to various sites: the North Campus of the City University of New York, where most students are black or Hispanic; the twenty-second floor of a large office building next to Carnegie Hall and the New York Hard Rock Cafe; a hospital along the Hudson River in Westchester County. I met Jews from Brooklyn who had

moved to the suburbs, Irishmen from the Bronx, and polished and controlled WASPs. I visited the offices of Bell Labs located in the New Jersey suburbs, and was impressed by the large open areas in the Prudential office, where the private spaces of workers were only defined by movable screens. I also entered a number of homes decorated according to *Country Living* and adorned with trendy printed fabrics, decoy ducks, and other yuppy paraphernalia.

In contrast with American respondents, the French were more likely not to take the interview seriously. They were more often late, or had forgotten our appointment. Several insisted on being interviewed at lunchtime, and on treating me to lunch; they were reluctant to be interviewed at home, the sacred haven. These upper-middle-class men were frequently more difficult to reach than their American counterparts, as their wives or secretaries often carefully screened phone calls.

The French physical settings were markedly different from those in which I conducted the interviews in America: replicas of seventeenth-century furniture took the place of the American country style. It was not uncommon to see original works of art on the walls as well as contemporary "objets" displayed on carefully polished desks. The secretaries brought us coffee with no complaints (reluctance to perform this service had been expressed overtly twice during the American interviews). Several of the French interviewees were rather elegant in style. They had great presence, frequently enhanced by the faint flagrance of eau de cologne. The interaction was less clearly defined as a "professional" one than it had been in the American setting.

As for the houses, fewer French interviewees lived in single-family homes. Apartments were significantly more common, even among the most wealthy individuals. The furniture was less standardized. The settings for the interviews ranged from sober and traditional bank offices to an artist's studio, the baroque chambers of an old *château*, a psychologist consulting room, the Italianate park of a prestigious *lycée*, and the colorless cubicle of a mediocre accountant. Compared with the American interviews, the greater diversity of the physical surroundings was striking.

In contrast to both the American and Parisian interviewees, the Clermontois tended to offer a much less glorious vision of themselves. They described their lives with little romanticism and few garnishes; they were noticeably less verbally playful than the Parisians and treated the interview more seriously. And unlike the Indianapolis respondents, they made no effort to convince me that Clermont was not "culturally backward." It

was often evident, however, that they were proud of who they were, of the quiet solidity of the *auvergnats*, which presents a stark contrast with Parisian frivolity. Their sternness was frequently reflected in the decor of their homes and offices, which tended to be sober and functional. Here, the settings were somewhat less varied but nevertheless showed considerable range: from a sumptuous villa in the mountains overlooking Clermont, to an elementary school, a *café* facing the *bains thermaux* of Chamalières, the dusty rooms of an old museum, and the noisy offices of the local newspaper.

These scenes, then, establish the background essential for understanding my interviewees and their responses. We are now ready to enter the heart of the matter.

Chapter Two

〜〜〜〜〜〜〜〜〜〜〜〜〜〜〜〜〜〜〜〜〜〜〜〜〜〜〜〜〜〜〜

THE IMPORTANCE OF BEING HONEST:
KEYS TO MORAL BOUNDARIES

> Honesty is the best policy
> —George Washington

François Renault is a physician in his early fifties. This portly but nevertheless handsome man lives in a splendid villa in the countryside near Clermont-Ferrand. With the sounds of grasshoppers and the garden fountain in the background, I interviewed him on a veranda overlooking the surrounding hills. Dr. Renault summarizes his life by saying that he has always worked very hard. These days he takes more time to do things he really enjoys, like reading about technological innovations and computers. He keeps his professional and personal lives totally separate, spending most of his time with his devoted wife and their grown children. Nevertheless, friendship is very important to him. He described to me the kinds of people he likes thus:

> What I like in people is their simplicity. I don't take into consideration their social position. I think it is a mistake to do so. I know people from all levels. Some are not educated, but they are very intelligent, and they bring you something . . . I like people who are honest. I also like people who keep their word . . . people who won't try to exploit you, who will deal with others in a Christian way, who are sincere, truthful. This is a quality which is available to everyone. You don't need to be rich to be honest. I also like people who are generous, who help others, who are intelligent and nice, and who have humor. [Honesty means] to respect others. To know that it is a human being who is before you . . . What I don't like are people who try to impress, and are full of themselves because of their titles. I think that they lack charity and love. They don't like anyone but themselves.

The main objective of this chapter is to explore the ways in which individuals like Dr. Renault mobilize moral standards to evaluate people. The various criteria that are used by French and American upper-middle-

class men to assess the moral status of others are examined through several complementary lenses. More specifically, I compare the labels that interviewees use to differentiate between "honest" and "dishonest" people; I examine the traits that are valued in the French and the American workplace; and I discuss the role played by religiosity and volunteerism as high status moral signals. While influential books such as *Habits of the Heart* have been lamenting the decline of morality in the United States, I find that it is still very salient in the culture of American upper-middle-class men.[1]

"PHONIES," SOCIAL CLIMBERS, *SALAUDS,* AND OTHER POLLUTING CATEGORIES

Howard Becker and Erving Goffman have studied deviants and outsiders to sharpen our understanding of moral rules.[2] Following their lead, moral boundaries can be understood by looking at contrasted conceptions of honesty that are revealed when French and American interviewees explicate the labels they mobilize to describe "dishonest people." Americans use three rather well-circumscribed polluting labels: the "phony," the "social climber," and the "low-morals" type. On the other hand, French interviewees tend to define honest people in opposition to individuals who are "intellectually dishonest" or who are judged to be *salaud* (best translated as "bastard").

In a large modern hospital overlooking the Hudson River in Westchester County, north of Manhattan, I met John Bailey, a laid-back family man. John, who is about fifty, is the chief financial executive of the institution, with approximately seventy-five people working under him. While we were exploring his likes and dislikes in people, the category of "phony" kept popping up. So I asked John what he meant by a "phony" and how he recognizes them. He said:

> I'm thinking of an example: my old boss. I had a good relationship with him, but he was the type of guy who would always ask me, "How you doing? How's your wife doing? How's your kids doing?" and always look sincere, all right? But meanwhile, he didn't really give a darn, it was all show, all right? I'd rather a person, honestly, not ask me that question if they really didn't mean it.

When I asked John how he knew that his boss was a phony, he said:

> I know because I was around him for seven years. It would be the case when we went to meetings and that kind of thing, professional gatherings, I'd be next to him, and he would say, "Whose this guy coming up?" under his breath. I'd tell him the guy's name and he would go up and greet him like he was a long-lost brother, and he didn't even know the guy's name. I don't think it's real . . . I like people to be themselves. I don't have to put on airs, to be somebody I'm not when I'm with a friend. I'm just me.

The *phony* is a genuinely American category which has no adequate equivalent in French.[3] It was used again and again by John Bailey and others to describe people who are not sincere; who pretend to know more than they do, or to be something they are not; who have no substance and judge a book by its cover. They "do things that are totally without basis"; they try to put on a show. In contrast, nonphonies are "honest, they don't 'put on the dog,' they work hard, and they're not trying to scam the public" (informant, Indianapolis). In brief, the nonphony is a doer and not a "big mouth." He is who he is, "take it or leave it." He delivers the merchandise, judges others by their deeds, and keeps his eyes on the bottom line. Transparency is his middle name. Both Willy Pacino, the New Jersey labor arbitrator, and Paul Anderson, the Indianapolis senior executive in the Prologue, despise phonies. And they also despise social climbers.

As often disparaged as the phony, the *social climber* is criticized because of the way he treats his subordinates and the methods by which he achieves upward mobility. He is ambitious, which is good, but he overdoes it. Like the phony, he manipulates his environment to accelerate his professional advancement. Paul Anderson put it best: social climbers are "real aggressive, eager . . . they probably have many people against them, and not that many for. [They are in it] only for themselves and don't sort of look out for their subordinates and care for people first." They also have little consideration for their family's emotional needs as they put their own ambition above everything.

Neither the phony nor the social climber obey the Golden Rule. Because they are pushy and manipulative, strong boundaries are often drawn against them, as their unscrupulous ambition threatens others. There is a genuine feeling of moral superiority among those who condemn them.

Tales of coworkers who climbed the professional ladder at great speed, only to rapidly fall back, are told gleefully. Those who achieved mobility at the price of important personal sacrifices (e.g., mental health problems, divorce, or estranged children) are offered as negative examples, particularly by Midwesterners. In fact, a few Midwesterners equate New York with social climbing, divorce, and low moral standards, clustering these lexical terms within a single, all-encompassing polluting category. In so doing, they affirm the common rules for living by which they abide as participants in a symbolic community.

For American upper-middle-class men, dishonest people also include the *low-morals type*. Don Bloom, an Indianapolis consultant near retirement, offers his definition of the "low-moral type" when he tells us the sort of people to whom he feels superior:

> Well, I should say first of all, I don't believe in equality. I believe the Lord made us all very different individuals. But I feel superior to people who don't work and who expect that the world owes them a living, and I feel superior to people that have unclean minds and unclean bodies, and I feel superior to people who think they've accomplished something but they've done it immorally or illegally.

Like many Americans, Don Bloom gauges moral impurity by examining work ethics and obedience to the law and to the Ten Commandments, with particular attention given to the tenth which concerns "thy neighbor's wife." In general, given that American egalitarianism might militate against admitting feelings of superiority, my interviewees were extraordinarily prompt to affirm their superiority toward those who lie, cheat, and are not law abiding, i.e., toward people who have *low-morals*.[4]

How do these polluting categories contrast with the ones used by the Frenchmen I talked to? If the French share a noticeable dislike for social climbers and for people who are not sincere, rarely do they refer to sexual behavior as a standard for differentiating between "us" and "them." The contrast between American and French conceptions of honesty (and morality) is described by an intense intellectual who teaches literature at a *lycée* located in the Paris *banlieue* (suburb). I met him in a *café* catty-corner from Paris City Hall. Over his third *pastis*, amidst the hubbub of the dining room's noon rush, Denis Homier explains:

> For me, morality is not located between your thighs, but elsewhere. The Judeo-Christian education where morality is above all a sexual issue

is wrong . . . The individual is not essentially defined by his physical dimension . . . I am completely indifferent to whether or not the president of the United States has one, two, three, or ten mistresses, whether he likes little boys, or is homosexual or bisexual. I would simply ask him not to spend too much time at it . . . At this level, the situation in the United States seems unbearable. That society is completely based on money, and when a candidate for the presidency screws his secretary, it is the end of the world.

The definition of honesty that this literature professor promotes presents a stark contrast with this so-called American approach:

For me honesty in general, intellectual honesty, material honesty, honesty in relation to oneself, in relation to others [is essential]. In honesty, there is the idea of honor. The *honnête homme* [honest man] is a complex notion. There is certainly something more in it than the notion that you should not steal from your neighbor.

Clearly, Denis Homier himself is not very concerned with promiscuity and deviant sexual behavior. His position reflects wider trends: a cross-national survey revealed that 31 percent of the French respondents and only 5 percent of the American consider the Tenth Commandment which prohibits coveting one's neighbor's wife to be outdated (*dépassé*).[5] In this context, it is not surprising that, in the course of the interviews, three of the French interviewees offered, without probing, information concerning their extramarital relationships, while two mentioned being bisexual.[6] None of the American interviewees volunteered information concerning such relationships.[7]

In interviews, a few of the French men I talked to openly rejected Judeo-Christian conceptions of morality. For instance, Luc Dupuis, a short and balding man in his late fifties who organizes executive training courses, makes clear his opposition to traditional notions of honesty. I interviewed him in his apartment, which overlooks a park in St-Germain-en-Laye. He described honesty as a rule followed by those who have no choice:

People who are honest make me laugh. The word itself is a bit stupid: "Honest, he is honest . . ." I think that if people are honest, it is because they cannot be otherwise. When I am honest, it is because I don't dare be dishonest. I'd much prefer to be dishonest, truly . . . I think that stealing is fantastic. Lying too. There is no question that I lie, I know that.

Similar cynicism is expressed by Didier, the Paris architecture professor encountered in the Prologue:

> Honesty is important to me, but in a very, very general sense, that is, being intellectually honest above all. [This is] not at all, I mean *not at all*, honesty in the sense of money [because] everyone who succeeds is somehow dishonest and I think that it is fair game. I mean, the game of money is a dishonest game. Everybody knows it and everybody puts up with it. And in the end I think that it does not work so badly.

Didier justifies these attitudes by practical considerations:

> In a certain way, I have no problem personally with being dishonest. I don't want to destroy others, but . . . the end justifies the means. If you want to make money, you need to take it from someone else. To be a businessman is to be a little bit of a thief. You buy a watch for ten francs and you sell it for twenty. So you make ten at the other person's expense. If this is not to be dishonest! . . . It is the name of the game, so let's play it![8]

Both Luc Dupuis and Didier question Judeo-Christian notions of honesty when they affirm that the end justifies the means, and that being honest in the traditional sense of the word is *petit bourgeois* (i.e., lacking in guts, flair, and *panache*). Along similar lines, when asked to rank twenty-three qualities in terms of their desirability, only 35 percent of the French I talked to in contrast to 57 percent of the American ranked honesty first. Also, when asked which one of twenty-three negative character traits they considered to be the worst, 20 percent of the French chose "devious" compared to 31 percent of the Americans. Furthermore, of the French, only 6 percent chose "low moral standards" as the worst trait in contrast to 20 percent of the Americans.[9] These findings are reflected in a cross-national survey which asked respondents if the Ten Commandments still apply in their lives. This survey revealed that only 45 percent of the French male professionals, managers, and businessmen consider these commandments to apply to themselves, in contrast to 80 percent of the Americans in these same categories.[10]

Denis Homier, our literature teacher qua Parisian intellectual, mentioned the notion of *honnête homme* when explicating what he meant by honesty: the *rousseauistic* figure of the *honnête homme* who frequently appears in the novels of Balzac is one with which many French interviewees identify. As used in the seventeenth century, the notion of *honnête homme* describes an urban and well-mannered gentleman who knows how

to fully take advantage of life. He is good company because he is well read without being *fastidieux* (painstaking), as he absorbs culture effortlessly and inconspicuously. His *bel esprit* (fine mind) displays vast and often superficial knowledge. And our *honnête homme* is often *folâtre* (frisky) and promiscuous.[11] In this context, *honnête* takes on a meaning quite different from *phony*, with connotations of cultural sophistication (see Chap. 4). But the notion of *honnête homme* is also associated with "intellectual honesty, . . . honesty in relation to oneself . . . the idea of honor" (Denis Homier). This notion of *intellectual honesty*, which is quintessential to French upper-middle-class discourse on morality, is an interesting one.

When probed on the meaning of this concept, Julien, our Clermont-Ferrand physicist told me that to be intellectually honest, you have to "always be consistent with yourself, and not be ashamed of what you do and what you say. Not be ashamed of yourself in relation to others. Take responsibility for who you are." For others, being intellectually honest means "to be honest with your own ideas. To be able to sacrifice material interests to apply an idea you believe in. [To] refuse to deal with people you have no respect for. To refuse to lick other people's boots, . . . to lower [your]self before people, no matter what their title is" (manager of a car dealership, Clermont-Ferrand). It also means to refuse to "conform to what people who are our superiors would like us to do, in a servile way" (journalist, Clermont-Ferrand). Furthermore, intellectual honesty also implies "a notion of honor, a moral rigor: do not say 'yes' when you mean 'no'; always be faithful to what you think; assume responsibility for your life, in all circumstances" (lawyer, Clermont-Ferrand). These quotes suggest that intellectual honesty is not foremost an intellectual matter as it has to do with being faithful to oneself; this notion is antithetical to a pragmatic conception of morality that advocates adaptation to circumstances. These quotes also suggest that the often-noted lack of respect for authority of the "contentious French" (to be discussed in Chap. 3)[12] is related to matters as crucial as the maintenance of self-respect and honor. In the United States, personal authenticity is also emphasized but is framed differently. Americans also talk about truthfulness to oneself, about one's obligation to make ethical choices for oneself, "to be your own person," but these themes stem from a tradition of individualism rather than from a more Latin conception of honor.[13]

A second important polluting category mobilized by the French is the category of *salaud*. This label is used to refer to one who lacks intellectual honesty and who is ready to sacrifice the interests of others to his

own by repressing them politically or by being blatantly unfair to them if necessary. The *salaud* shows no group or class solidarity, informs on his schoolmates, underpays his workers, breaks strikes, and is ready to disown his friends for personal advantage. As perceived by a Parisian banker, the *salaud* thinks that his money gives him unlimited rights and the power to act arbitrarily toward the meek. He compromises and bends when pressured. In contrast to the social climber, he does not necessarily have overpowering ambition; he is simply unprincipled and feels little solidarity with other human beings. In other words, he is not politically or humanly correct. To a certain extent, for the French, this widespread social moralism seems to replace the more puritan moralism of Americans.

In post-Nazi France, the France in which my interviewees came of age, this notion of integrity, of faith in one's own convictions despite mounting external pressures, is particularly vivid: the recent historical experience has shown that a lack of political backbone can lead to dramatic consequences. In this context, political position is often used as a yardstick of moral character: one demonstrates one's moral stature by resisting oppression and power in general. A strong socialist tradition and the influence of existentialism among the age-group to which many French interviewees belong reinforced this notion that political positions are morally revealing.[14]

As pointed out by Seymour Martin Lipset, Americans also like to question authority, and political authority in particular.[15] As we shall see in the next section of this chapter, however, this tendency, as well as the cultural imperative to "be your own person," are more tempered for American interviewees than they are in France by the premium Americans put on teamwork, flexibility, and conflict avoidance. Also, Americans apparently do not, to the same degree as the French, regard their political position as a crucial form of moral self-expression. This might be reflected by their greater political apathy: French voter turnout for elections to the National Assembly is noticeably higher than the American turnout for congressional elections for similar periods.[16] Americans attach less importance to political positions and are more likely to read them as reflecting personal preferences and interests rather than broader class or ethical positions. On the other hand, this focus on personal interests implies a cultural model where market mechanisms are understood as a morally adequate way of distributing resources according to talent and efforts.[17]

We see that both the French and the American interviewees fre-

quently draw moral boundaries but use different criteria: Americans are more likely to reject the phonies, the social climbers, and the low-morals types. In contrast to the French, they are particularly concerned with the Ten Commandments, and they more clearly associate promiscuity with moral impurity. The French are less sensitive to Judeo-Christian notions of morality. They often exclude, at least at the discursive level, the *salauds* and those who lack personal integrity. They also object to the social climber and the insincere, but with less vehemence than Americans do. Finally, they are more likely to read political attitudes as a template of moral character. Therefore, independent of the specific moral signals that they mobilize to differentiate between "us" and "them," the French and the American interviewees alike stress moral character when probed on high status signals. The importance of moral categories is also substantiated by a quantitative evaluation of the salience of moral boundaries across the four sites.

Following procedures described in Appendix III, I located each of the interviewees on three five-point scales, pertaining respectively to moral, cultural, and socioeconomic boundaries. This ranking was done on the basis of answers respondents gave to a wide range of questions pertaining to such things as the attributes one appreciates in friends, child-rearing values, and feelings of inferiority and superiority vis-à-vis others. The ranking was determined relationally by analyzing each interview as a whole and by comparing it with similar and dissimilar interviews within and across sites.[18] While this ranking remains only approximate—differences between judgments cannot be exactly quantified—it provides useful information on the importance of various types of symbolic boundaries and on the magnitude of cross-national differences.

The ranking of interviewees on the moral scale reveals that moral status signals are roughly as highly valued as cultural and socioeconomic status signals by French and American interviewees,[19] and that both groups basically equally stress morality in their boundary work.[20] Therefore, contrary to recent claims, morality does remain quite salient in contemporary America, or at least in its influential upper-middle class. We will see that moral character is an important type of resource in the American workplace—and that moral boundaries are relatively independent from socioeconomic status—because individuals who rank high on one dimension do not necessarily rank high on the other.

The concluding chapter of this book will show that the evidence presented in this last section contradicts the Marxist and the structuralist

views that economic resources, and by extension socioeconomic status and boundaries, are by definition more valued than other types of resources (or statuses). We saw that many interviewees were very critical of individuals who put the improvement of their social position above human and moral considerations. The importance of morality has generally been underestimated in the recent social science literature, and particularly by rational choice and cultural capital theorists. I will argue in this final chapter that cultural capital theory adopts a narrow definition of morality, making it the privileged domain of particular groups and that it conceives morality as an ancillary resource while subsuming it to socioeconomic achievement.

MORAL CHARACTER IN THE WORKPLACE

We know that work occupies an extremely central role in the life of upper-middle-class men. In contrast to blue-collar workers, these men rarely live for "after work": work is the means by which they develop, express, and evaluate themselves.[21] In the interviews, the men I talked with underscored the pleasures they derive from their professional life. When asked to describe an individual they admire, they often talked about someone who has special professional competences or talents. These upper-middle-class men were very concerned with career development. Some saw a lack of professional opportunities as catastrophic, and most perceived the possibility of advancement as one of the more desirable job characteristics.

The way these men distribute resources, evaluate performance, and interact with their subordinates is most likely to be affected by how they draw boundaries and judge other people's worth, even if they make special efforts to base their decisions on work performance only. Their concept of boundaries often may determine if workers encounter a receptive environment and have access to critical on-the-job informal training. Consequently, to understand which norms act as a medium for power relations by framing people's lives and limiting their opportunities, it is crucial to explore the character traits that are most valued in upper-middle-class work settings.

These traits were identified by probing interviewees on their coworkers they consider to be the most successful, the traits valued in their corporation, and the qualities they look for when they themselves hire and promote. I also probed interviewees on their least favorite kind of co-

worker, and on the "impression management" they themselves direct toward their own superiors and clients. From their answers, I reconstructed what I call the elements of legitimate personality types which define the perfect way of acting that predominates in the value system of upper-middle-class workers. Only the most salient dimensions of such personality types, and only those revealing of moral character are described here. The analysis focuses more on the traits valued by men working in large organizations than on those valued by the self-employed, as the former group is more homogeneous and larger, and as the members of the latter group might have more freedom not to conform to surrounding high-status signals.

As suggested by Rosabeth Kanter in *Men and Women of the Corporation* (63), trust, which is allocated on the basis of loyalty and conformity, acts as an important regulating mechanism in work situations where uncertainty is high. Trust is what makes things happen, what makes it possible for people to work together in a productive way without being constantly on their guard, and what makes them able to relax and enjoy themselves in the process."[22] How we deal with others—in a straightforward or in a devious way, competently or incompetently, selfishly or generously, unpredictably or according to established rules of conduct—affects how people define our moral character and their willingness to allocate trust. But again, moral character is not clearly revealed upon first encounter and must be deduced from other external signals. Because there is always more than one plausible definition of a situation, the construction of others as "pure" or "impure" depends, as suggested by Kanter, on the display of homosocial characteristics. Hence the importance of operating style, lifestyle, personality, external appearance, modes of self-presentation, interactional behavior, and projection of general attitudes. Knowing how to read and signal trust is crucial to organizational life—and to the individual's chances for advancement.[23] While Kanter does point to this, she only stresses a narrow range of often external traits rather than documenting systematically the content of high status signals and the dynamic of symbolic boundaries. In other words, she only studies specific manifestations of the broader phenomenon with which the present study is concerned.

So how is trustworthiness signaled? The virtues valued in the upper-middle class can help us to answer this question. For Burton Bledstein who studied mid-Victorian professionals, these virtues included being ambitious, dependable, self-reliant, disciplined, patriotic, and a respon-

sible citizen. For Max Weber, who was more concerned with enterpre-
neurs, the crucial virtues are those that influence the ability to do business
with others: sobriety, courage, perseverance, audacity, sincerity, reserve,
self-mastery, humility, and long-term planning.[24] On the other hand, the
authors of *Habits of the Heart* suggest that self-reliance and individualism
are primary middle-class virtues, while Hervé Varenne adds to these virtues "community-mindedness" (or conformism).[25]

How do these portrayals of the ideal traits square with the ones depicted by the American men I talked with? One finds significant overlap,
even though my inquiry centered on virtues valued in the workplace, and
in large organizations in particular. The picture these men traced for me
revolve around honesty, which seems to be read via a number of other
traits. For instance, according to Denis Wilson, a New York computer
research scientist, "[Honesty] would probably be correlated with things
like being giving and unself-assuming and straightforward, rational, humble, not devious." I found that Americans think that honesty is signaled
through friendliness, conflict avoidance, team orientation, and flexibility.
On the other hand, moral character is revealed by competence and work
ethics, which themselves are related to competitiveness, dynamism, resiliency, long-term planning, and well-regulated ambition. But too much
ambition and one becomes a *social climber*. Too little and one is a *loser*.
These character traits need to be examined in turn before considering
their role in the French workplace.

Friendliness, Conflict Avoidance, and Teamwork in the American Workplace

In *Moral Mazes*, Robert Jackall writes that, for American corporate executives, it is important to "make other managers feel comfortable, a crucial
virtue in an uncertain world, and [to] establish with others the easy, predictable familiarity that comes from sharing taken-for-granted frameworks about how the world works" (56). From my interviews, it seems
that reliability and predictability are mostly signaled by the display of
honesty. This cultural trait is again central in discussions of hiring practices. For instance, when asked about his own hiring standards, John Bailey, our New York hospital administrator, says: "Honesty and being
straightforward, that's what I look for. I want people to be honest with
me and straight with me, and if they make a mistake, I want to know
about it." This position is echoed by Lou Fischer, a New York chief financial executive, who is at the top of a large international consulting firm
that contracts all around the globe. (Our interview was constantly inter-

rupted by phone calls from Brazil.) Lou says that he likes to hire "people who work hard, who are easy-going, and who will tell me what they think without being afraid that I'm going to hold it against them . . . Those are the biggest requirements for these two hundred people [who work under me]." But again, because honesty is not spontaneously revealed, other signals have to be used to approximate it; hence, the importance of traits such as friendliness, conflict avoidance, team orientation, and flexibility.

In the American workplace, friendliness is a key to integration because it is crucial in helping people feel comfortable. One manifests friendliness by being cheerful, easygoing, and "show[ing] concern and follow[ing] up by doing things that show that [you] are really concerned about [people]" (plant manager, New York). To not be overtly friendly is to risk being labeled cold, hard, and ruthless (i.e., something akin to "social climber"). Conspicuous friendliness is particularly important in an environment where neutrality or nonparticipation can be read as defiance or downright and conscious refusal of social intercourse. Indeed, because predictability is crucial in large organizations, executives and professionals avoid conflicts by ignoring altogether those with whom they differ.[26] This avoidance is important for the acquisition of a reputation for trustworthiness. Being overtly conflictual may lead to isolation, for one risks being labeled a troublemaker. Accordingly, it is not surprising that American interviewees often have problems talking about conflicts in the workplace, and often tend to ritualistically insist that they "get along" with all their coworkers. As explained by a young Indianapolis informant: "If I don't like you, you don't know the difference." This dislike of conflict frequently extends to relations in the private sphere. For instance, a New York radio station owner (who might be atypical) explains:

> Groups of people that I would dislike to be with socially are those who would disagree with me on anything that I would suggest or talk about. My feeling and my definition of a friend is somebody who will listen and support me. And if they think that I'm going in the wrong direction, they'll try to tell me in a very, very diplomatic way rather than to come down hard on me. I don't like to be challenged.

In this context, being "soft-spoken" and "balanced" is highly appreciated. A laid-back Indianapolis bank vice-president, e.g., says of his favorite coworker: "The way he states things is the way I would state things. Like, you would never know when a negative was up, that it was a negative. He would put it constructively. Automatically careful in the language." Being

balanced implies "being sort of middle-of-the road, no extreme, having the ability to deal with different aspects of life without being carried away in any particular aspects" (accountant, Indianapolis). This characteristic is associated with being down-to-earth and pragmatic, i.e., with avoiding theoretical problems that have no concrete impact. Along with conflict avoidance, humility and soft-spokenness seem to be more valued in Indianapolis than they are in New York.

Conflict avoidance results in the rejection of people deemed over-aggressive and in the inclusion of "teamplayers." This is why David Hart, a young, upwardly mobile New York data manager, had to "work on himself" when he took a job at the Federal Reserve Bank. He says:

> [I had to learn to be] less intense, less aggressive, to be a listener. I engaged in a relationship with a senior manager, and he would give me direct criticism, and I tried to use those things. [He told me to] be less intense. It's very easy to scare people or intimidate people. Especially supervisors. If you have the answer before they do, it makes people very uncomfortable. I've learned to let other people take the credit for solution, to be a teamplayer. Sometimes you don't get the credit . . . The advantage from my personal point of view is not to be disliked by others. If you're disliked, I think you're not going to do as well.

To make others feel comfortable, David had to learn to demonstrate team orientation, which goes along with friendliness.[27] Joe Cohen explains at greater length how this is done. Coming from a "Jewish immigrant background," Joe has been promoted from the inside in the large multinational corporation where he is now plant facilities manager. First-generation upper-middle class, he works hard to keep in touch with the ninety people he supervises. To do this, he tries to establish a "caring" environment. In his strong New Jersey accent, he explains:

> I invite [my collaborators] to my house at Christmas time, I take 'em out to lunch occasionally . . . I play golf with the wage guys that I played golf with fifteen years ago when I was their supervisor. So I've tried to let everybody know that my level has nothing to do with how we work together . . . I interface with everybody and let them know that I still am a team player and nothing's gone to my head, and I'm very humble about the whole situation. [Why?] Because if the situation was reversed, I'd want it that way. Why do you think Reagan was so popular? He went out in the crowd and said, "I'm president but I'm still the same old guy, and how are ya?" . . . If you don't work with your people and stay behind in that chair, and don't get out on the floor and into their

work area, when it comes time for that creative idea, when you need their help, they're going to say, "Who's that?" . . . Most of the time you find out what ticks. I'll walk into the shop and ask Ray how his wife's doing, 'cause her back is having a problem. And he'll tell me and that'll be it. They want me to be concerned about that. That's my job.

The goal is to maximize integration in the workplace by playing down power differentials. Friendliness is instrumental in achieving this.

You know, it's not how hard you work when you get into these situations, it's how smart you work. And I need to show people I'm interested in them, and this is genuine, it's not just for show. It's important that I tell people to have a nice weekend. I write them a note for every holiday, and say, "Keeping with tradition I would like to wish you and your families a happy and a safe Easter, and enjoy yourself" . . . , and it's Thanksgiving, Christmas, etc. I just wrote a letter to ninety people to say, "Springtime is coming, and that's when we have the most injuries, so please let's keep that in mind, and make sure, that we not only think about it here, but at home too, and let's be safe, we don't want you to get hurt." Sign my name and send it to ninety people. The little things go a long way.

Along these lines, bosses who are too pretentious and "stand-offish" are often said to "have a terrible time." Instead of indulging in narcissism, they are supposed to "channel [their] ego in something productive like getting the work done, making more efficient use of [their] time, learning more about the job" (portfolio manager, New York). And status does not justify domineering attitudes, as a premium is put on "being considerate," no matter who you are.[28] As a consequence, especially in the Midwest, only when associated with humility and at least formal egalitarianism does professional success become equated with moral purity.[29] A businessman in his fifties, a member of the Indianapolis elite, explains why he holds his friends in high esteem:

[They] are all very unself-assuming. I think they are all very well-positioned in their company; they have positions of responsibility. But it is not important to them; it is not visibly important to them.

Team orientation is expressed not only through friendliness, humility, and egalitarianism but also through flexibility, which is essential for professional mobility. As stated by John Bloom, the New York economist encountered earlier:

Most managers who are interested in career success are being promoted over their head, [especially] if you [are] perceived as someone who is cooperative, flexible, somebody who's not going to cause problems, who won't be difficult to work with. So it's very easy to get into a mode where you know what the party line is—what the president likes, what the president doesn't like.

In other words,

Inflexibility is really looked down on very much. A loner sort of person might go off by himself and do things, but I don't think that these things are valued. I think that we value more group-interaction problem-solving than individual problem-solving [public school administrator, Indianapolis].

While American upper-middle-class culture remains highly individualistic, it is also other-directed, and the lone wolf is not fit anymore for most upper-middle-class work settings as these increasingly turn into large bureaucratic structures. And to a certain extent, the cultural imperative for flexibility prevents American upper-middle-class men from putting personal integrity, which is so central to the French (at least at the level of discourse), at the forefront. Indeed, some might end up adopting a pragmatic approach to morality as they adapt their beliefs to the situation at hand. This is what happened to John Sherman, an old-time mortgage banker who has worked on Wall Street most of his life and who described himself as being hard-nosed and having a tough skin:

[I] always felt pressured [to be a yes-man]. Sometimes I did it, and sometimes I didn't. If it served the needs of where I was going and to make the department that I was running function, I did what was necessary to make the department go . . . I think that you do what you've got to do and you have your own standards.[30]

Living up to one's moral standards is often constrained by situational factors. Furthermore, maintaining moral standards might often conflict with pressures for conflict avoidance and team orientation. In light of these observations, talks of honesty could be read as ritualistic reaffirmations of the importance of moral purity, and as an indication that openly antimoral positions are taboo. Such talks might also express a type of "impression management" or "front stage work"—to use Goffman's concepts—aimed at reaffirming trust in the context of an uncertain and ever-changing environment.

The Proof of the Pudding: Competence, Ambition, Competitiveness, and Moral Purity in the American Workplace

Competence is most highly valued in the American workplace and is often equated with honesty. Indeed, some Americans go so far as to consider competence a guarantee against dishonesty, as if it had intrinsic purifying virtues. For instance, in Indianapolis a down-to-earth man who has been the proud employee of the federal civil service for over twenty years associates manipulative behaviors with incompetence. He opposes the competent and the unpretentious to the incompetent, the social climber, and the politically manipulative:

> I tend to respect people who I think are competent at what they do. And who I don't think are out for other ulterior motives, aren't really interested in pushing their way up the ladder, that sort of thing. I guess those are the people I admire . . . I just like people who are technically competent, who do the job. I would rather be around people who quickly get the job done than around those who don't get the job done, who manipulate others and take credit for it, that sort of thing . . . There are probably a lot of people who feel that way.

American interviewees often draw extraordinarily clear boundaries against incompetence, and they do so with a violence only equaled by French diatribes against stupidity. This is illustrated by John Sherman, the old-time Wall Street banker, who talks about his views of the French in a tone of moral superiority:

> I don't especially have a high degree of esteem for the French. I served in the NATO department of the Air Force with a group of French officers and enlisted men who were really bad people. They were slovenly about their dress, and they were cowards. They had a tendency to have a low technical knowledge in the area of expertise that they needed to stay alive. They just never mastered what they were doing. If there was a flight lieutenant, he was not a very good pilot. If he was navigating, he might miss. If he was a mechanic, the plane could crash. I mean, it was that kind of outlook.

As anticipated by Max Weber, a strong *work ethic* continues to be read as a guarantee of moral purity, at least by American upper-middle-class men. Hard work and competence are equated with moral superiority, especially if they result in professional success. This goes hand in hand with a widespread belief that authority should be functionally determined and based on competence.[31]

In the context of this cultural requirement for competence, it is crucial for American natives to know how to signal the internalization of an appropriate work ethic and a disposition toward "problem-solving activism,"[32] especially given that, as for honesty, competence is not often spontaneously revealed. The crucial signaling traits here are ambition, competitiveness, and dynamism, and also resiliency and long-term planning.

Ambition is defined as the ability to take advantage of all the opportunities that life offers, and to conceive every experience as a means to achieve this end. Along with its correlate, hard work, it was viewed by many of my American interviewees as a central component of moral character, whether it is motivated by a desire to develop oneself or to surpass others. Indeed, among the least respectable categories of people, those who are on welfare and "who think that the world owes them a living" (informant, Indianapolis) occupy an important place; the homeless are offered as negative examples, as are people who are assumed to lack ambition (e.g., janitors, garbage collectors, etc.). Laziness is condemned as one of the most despicable traits one could have, while self-directedness is seen as one of the main characteristics of ambitious people: one should not "sit there and wait for things to happen." Instead, one should "achieve his capability."[33]

Ambition is reflected in the fact of having a *competitive attitude*, fighting to be the best, to be "number one." John Turner, a former college basketball player who now works as a plant manager in Indianapolis, offers a telling illustration of the "competitive spirit" that he brings to both his personal and professional lives:

> I want to be the best in my profession, and I want to be the best basketball player at the Y on Saturday . . . It's always nice to be the best. I always strive to be the best. It keeps a certain drive in you, it keeps a dynamic going, it keeps you on an edge. You are constantly pushing yourself . . . [The best is] the one who can hit all his goals, who can manage his people, take them beyond the normal bounds. I don't want to stop here [gestures] because that's where we're supposed to be; I want to be out here [gestures].

This competitive attitude surfaces at work:

> I have set up not only competition between myself and other plant managers [but between my workers and other workers]. Whether they know it or not, they're in competition with the other plants. We are not going

to just beat them a little bit, we're going to *blast* them . . . We're going to be head and shoulders above them. I've called a plant meeting, and I've told the workers "Look, here's where we are, here's where they are. Let's go there and show them who's the best."

Competition permeates everything in the American upper-middle-class world. It even permeates the world of children: parents often make considerable financial sacrifices and efforts to have their children admitted to the "best schools," not only at the college level but at the elementary and high school levels as well. A science teacher working in the wealthy New York suburb of Scarsdale explains: "[Parents] want their kids to excel just as they excelled. They are all successful people. If the kids don't do well somehow, that's a reflection on them and somewhat detracts from themselves. So therefore their kids must be good, and they see to it. And if the kids are not, they see to it that they at least look that way."

Several men I talked with attempt to make this strenuous competition more human by distinguishing between various competing principles of hierarchalization which relativize one another. An applied science engineer, whose hobby is collecting miniature trains, explained it to me thus:

> The janitor where I work, I can meet him at a train show, and he'll know all the trains, and all the years, and how valuable each piece is, and I'll go "Huh! I didn't know that." And now you become inferior to him, so it turns around. It just depends on the situation . . . I might be good at tennis and he is a good singer. It all evens out.

By these shifts in hierarchies, equality can be maintained, at least at the symbolic level. Differences in performance can be explained away by factors other than innate superiority: excelling in a given field is presented as a personal decision on how to "invest" one's time. As our Indianapolis plant manager explains, "It's training, it's background, it's interest. I have no problem reconciling the fact that I am extremely competitive, and that I consider myself an equal." If Americans go to such lengths to maintain egalitarian beliefs, it is certainly because they associate them, along with other components of American civil religion, with moral purity.[34]

Dynamism also signals competence. Often the men I talked with confessed to feeling inferior to those who have more energy than they, to those who are more the "high-impact" type. For instance, a Fundamentalist minister explained his admiration for one of his peers in these terms: "I would call him a real high-powered guy. He's got a high energy level. His lifestyle is like that of a company president of Xerox. He's on the

phone with California and New York, and he's got all these things going; he's on national TV, he's meeting with TV producers." Self-direction is a central ingredient of dynamism, as is ambition.

Finally, *resiliency* and *long-term planning* are also highly valued. Resiliency, i.e., persistence, is used to differentiate people with a strong ethic of work from others. Over and over again, self-made men told me their story, emphasizing how their success is due to their resiliency and hard work. The following description is typical of these interviewees:

> I've always worked hard, I worked my way through college, through undergraduate school, and even through high school. My family didn't really have much in the way of assets. So I was kind of motivated to work hard . . . Everything was always hard work, and once I went to work for my present company twenty-three years ago, I was poised for an opportunity to succeed. If I failed, it was my own fault [chief financial officer, New York].

Long-term planning is associated with the ability to approach life rationally, this being another dimension of competence. Sitting in his posh living room, talking about the members of a motorcyclist gang, for instance, a New York machine tool distributor says, "Human-wise, they are not that bad, but their background is different. Their outlook on life and their aspirations are different . . . A lot of that type of people like to live day-to-day, paycheck-to-paycheck, that kind of thing. That's not the way I would live if I could at all control it."

Therefore, we see again that moral character is very important in the American workplace and that it is assessed not through indicators of personal integrity but through honesty, competence, and strong work ethics. As will be shown below, to the extent that moral character is valued in the French workplace, it is mostly estimated via the identification individuals have with the humanist tradition, whether it be Catholic or socialist in inspiration.

Work Ethics, Competition, Competence, and Brilliance in the French Workplace

Studies show that the French are overall less work oriented than Americans.[35] These cross-national differences are reflected in the way the Frenchmen I talked with approach work. While a number of them are as work-centered and hard-driven as their American counterparts, a significant minority of (mostly Parisian) interviewees hold antiwork attitudes:[36] either they ridicule workaholism and think that someone who is smart

should try to work as little as possible (museum curator, Paris; owner of an engineering firm, Paris; psychologist, Paris), or else they assume that a "hard worker" is "someone who lacks imagination and is too nice" (engineer, Clermont-Ferrand), or is a "lackey of the business class," "a sucker, the poor guy who can be exploited, who is asking for it" (engineer, Paris; science teacher, Paris). The antiwork ethic is epitomized by Luc Dupuis, the human management consultant whose opposition to Judeo-Christian views of morality was cited earlier in this chapter. He says:

> We are all exploited in one way or another. This means that I give as little as possible, which seems to me to be the most coherent attitude in relation to capitalism . . . because in the system in which we live it is the thing to do . . . I have the feeling that I am very well adapted in this respect.

The cultural differences between the two countries with respect to work are narrowing: the eighties saw a return in France to entrepreneurship and its associated virtues.[37] Despite these changes, my interviews revealed that the French still differ significantly from the Americans in the way they connect (or refuse to connect) work-related cultural traits with moral purity. The same holds for the way they understand the relationship between competence and moral purity. Indeed, overall, the French men I talked with do not see competence as a crucial sign of moral purity the way Americans do.

I became aware of the lesser importance attached to competence relatively early on in the French interviews, while I was talking with Simon Dutoît, the elegant director of a small Parisian bank, who has 100 people working under his direction. Dutoît explained to me:

> I have many incompetents working here, and what do I do with them? Nothing. I am not tough enough. I am basically a weak person . . . If it was my money, I could not stand seeing incompetent people making so much money doing nothing. It would be very hard. But as it is, they don't really bother me. I do nothing to get rid of them.

For the *banquier* Dutoît, incompetents are not so "polluting" that they need to be eliminated at all cost. The environmental requirement for efficiency, i.e., for running a lean operation, does not seem strong enough to force this banker to take action. He himself obviously does not read his passivity as revealing his own incompetence. While equivalents to

Dutoît can certainly be found in America, he presents a strong contrast with those of my American interviewees who forcefully described themselves as "real hard-nosed," offering this trait as a guarantee of their moral (and professional) purity, as a signal of their refusal to compromise with contingencies that reduce efficiency.[38] His attitude seems to indicate that incompetence is considerably less stigmatized in France than it is in the United States.

It should be noted, however, that in the homeland of Napoleonic technocracy a sizable number of interviewees maintain a discourse on competence that is as elaborate as the one offered by Americans. This is particularly true for those educated in the *grandes écoles*, which include high-level civil servants and private-sector executives.[39] Members of this group have passed very competitive entrance examinations, an achievement that has convinced them of their superior abilities.[40] They come to justify their authority by their "rigor, precision, and knowledge and respect for the rules" (hospital administrator, Clermont-Ferrand), by the "methodological approach" that they learned at the Ecole Polytechnique or elsewhere (insurance vice-president, Paris), or, more prosaically, by their capacity for leadership, or their mental or emotional resilience (academic administrator, Paris). And like their American counterparts, private-sector executives, and especially those employed by large multinationals, emphasize dynamism, responsibility, efficiency, and the other essential virtues of the modern business technocrat.[41]

However, as was the case for honesty, competence does not mean the same thing in the French and American contexts. As described by Ezra Suleiman in *Elites in France,* the education received by graduates of French elite schools values *general competence* over *specialized expertise* in narrowly defined domains. These schools teach students to synthesize information and to solve rapidly a wide range of problems.[42] In this context, the requirements for success have less to do with the facts mastery emphasized in America (to be discussed in Chap. 4)[43] than with the development of analytical skills, which in turn are measured by how well-read, articulate, versatile—in short, how "brilliant"—one is (183). The education given by these schools opens the door to a wide range of positions: their graduates are favored for employment in both the public and private sectors and can count on successful careers as politicians, bankers, industrialists, professors, or international civil servants. Here technocracy is separate from technical knowledge as authority is uncoupled from specialized expertise.[44]

Evidence suggests that to a certain degree this generalist approach to competence penetrates French upper-middle-class work settings at large.[45] Indeed, the elite, which again values general competence, often controls hiring and promotions of second-rank professionals and managers. In this context, many interviewees are very critical of their colleagues who have received too narrow an education (i.e., who received a "training" only), who lack versatility, or who are entirely pragmatic in their approach: these people "do short term calculation . . . [they] always sacrifice the long term to the short term . . . It is necessary to have idealistic objectives if you want to go further and do something great" (engineer, Paris). This focus on general competence would suggest that cultural boundaries, as distinct from moral ones, play more of a role in the French workplace than in the American workplace, since the evaluation of one's general competence is affected by one's level of general culture, verbal ability, manners, and style. This feature of French boundary work will be explored in Chapter 4.

It is interesting to note that to the extent that competence is valued in the French workplace, this emphasis does not seem to permeate upper-middle-class culture at large the way it does in the United States. Indeed, it is in general less important to the interviewees' personal life than it is to their professional life: few are those who pride themselves on being technically competent in as wide a range of domains as the Americans do (e.g., car and appliance repair, the real estate market, baseball statistics, and the operation of computers). Instead, they often coquettishly brag about their powerlessness when it comes to modern technology. Practical performance and technical competence are not as much at stake in male competition as are verbal duels in which each man showcases his wit and general culture.

These attitudes toward competence and work ethics affect the way French interviewees think about other types of status signals. For instance, many more French interviewees than Americans depreciate competitiveness: it is taken to mean "being the best by beating out someone else," which contradicts important humanistic values. This is precisely the opinion of Jean Deterrier, a slender and elegent diplomat whom I interviewed in his Louis XVI office at the Quai D'Orsay in Paris. Monsieur Deterrier sees the situation as follows:

> There is a good and a bad ambition: first, the ambition of the one who works because he wants to accomplish something and he wants to grow.

This is fine. But the ambition of one who simply wants to get ahead of others, for the sole pleasure of being ahead, this is bad ambition, because this is not *the* goal in life. *The* goal of life is to grow personally, to gain the respect of others.

Only three French interviewees—a Paris accountant, a Clermont-Ferrand surveyor, and a Michelin senior executive—openly sang the merits of competitiveness in terms somewhat comparable to the ones used by John Turner, our basketball player/plant manager. Even elite-school graduates who by definition have to be *bêtes à concours*, i.e., to have repeatedly succeeded at extremely selective examinations, remained much more discreet about their competitive instincts than the typical American interviewee. Clearly, competition does not play the part in the lives of French interviewees that it does in the lives of many American upper-middle-class men. Its lesser importance is revealed by a recent survey in which 55 percent of the private-sector middle-level managers and employees in France declared a preference for the civil service in the advent of a career change (this figure is 36 percent for those who have higher education). In contrast, only 31 percent declared that they would like to be self-employed. Another survey found that in response to the question "If your child was choosing a profession, what would you advise him to do?" 50 percent favored the civil service, while 28 percent favored the private sector.[46] These results indeed reveal a rejection of competition: one of the main reasons offered to justify preference for the public sector was that civil servants have guaranteed promotion and job security.

Several explanations might account for the fact that the French are less concerned with work ethics, competence, and competition than their American counterpart. First, one might suggest that these differences are related to the distinctive features of the French national character. Such a culturalist explanation was proposed in the fifties and early sixties and has been criticized often on methodological and theoretical grounds.[47] A second explanation, suggested by Max Weber in *The Protestant Ethic and the Spirit of Capitalism*, views these differences as having religious sources: Catholics greatly value detachment from the world for the pursuit of higher goals, whether they be spiritual or intellectual. Therefore, they do not conceptualize work as a means to salvation the way Protestants do. This explanation has been criticized in a recent exhaustive study of the link between religious affiliation and achievement.[48] A third, somewhat more satisfying explanation focuses on the conditions for profes-

sional mobility and on the greater job security that French professionals and managers experience in contrast to Americans. Studies show that the French often have considerable job security as strong social pressures are exerted against lay-offs.[49] Their competition is often curtailed by numerous monopolistic practices, especially in the case of the *professions libérales.*[50] Furthermore, their promotion, especially in the private sector, often depends on academic credentials (i.e., the school they attended) and seniority in the firm as much as on performance.[51] In the public sector, professional mobility in the elite is determined by one's capacity to get "nominated," which is mostly accomplished by mobilizing a social network of elite-school alumni. Among middle-level managers, it is determined less by performance on the job than by job title (i.e., rank) and by a national examination system. A Clermont-Ferrand safety controller who works for a state corporation describes the situation thus:

> The last thing I would do is work because of the promotion I will get. On the basis of this, I would do nothing. [The environment] is really not dynamizing—that's the problem of everyone who works for the state. People are not rewarded, or very rarely, on the basis of their work, but on the basis of the type of job you have, your *statut:* it is written somewhere that if you have this and that type of job, promotion is done this way, and people progress this way, and that's it! You are not asked to be dynamic, to perform, like in the United States—we often hear that in the United States, brilliant people are rewarded . . .

All these conditions militate to make the life of French professionals and managers somewhat more autonomous from market mechanisms. Indeed, promotion is not as closely linked to performance and depends more on the acquisition of privileges within bureaucratic structures, both at the top and at the middle level of the bureaucratic hierarchy.[52] Accordingly, many French interviewees seem to have a less aggressive attitude toward their careers. For instance, to the question "Where do you expect to be professionally five years from now?" many answered, "Right here," or "It does not depend on me." Clearly, few of these men manage their professional life as if it were an enterprise.

The Contentious French: Teamwork, Sociability, Conflict Avoidance, and Pragmatism in the French Workplace

The French put less emphasis than Americans do on signals such as friendliness, team orientation, and conflict avoidance. Instead, they value

highly a type of humanism that is an integral part of the bourgeois culture.

Thirty years ago, Michel Crozier suggested in *The Bureaucratic Phenomenon* that team orientation is antithetical to French organizational culture: the French tend to use formal rather than informal rules, thereby avoiding face-to-face relationships across hierarchical levels. They also tend to preserve their autonomy by resisting participation and relying on personal relations to protect themselves from higher-ups—who are assumed to be untrustworthy. According to Crozier, this system is incompatible with teamwork because it limits relationships across levels, relationships that would allegedly foster favoritism (215). Furthermore, it results in aloofness and a lack of collective spirit, as different strata fight for rank, status, and privileges. Teamwork is also limited because of an absence of feedback between levels. On the other hand, those who hold positions of authority remain distant and decorous in their relations with their subordinates.

The picture drawn by Crozier is somewhat outdated.[53] Many changes have occurred since he did his research in the mid-fifties. *Partenariat* (teamwork) has become popular as organizations put more emphasis on "quality circles" (i.e., horizontal control of performance), flexibility, consultation, negotiation, and participation of employees in benefits.[54] Several attitudes that obstruct teamwork, however, still persist. For instance, according to the European values/CARA surveys, whereas 69 percent of the American professionals, managers, and businessmen think that instructions received from superiors should be followed by employees even if they disagree with them, only 23 percent of the French take this position; furthermore, while only 24 percent of the Americans say that they need to be convinced first of the order's appropriateness before they carry it out, it is the case for 63 percent of the French. These data provide evidence of significant resistance on the part of the French to flexibility and cooperation with coworkers and, again, of their emphasis on personal integrity which is linked to intellectual honesty.[55]

Nevertheless, team playing was somewhat emphasized in the French interviews I conducted, if less so than in the American ones. Private-sector employees particularly tend to value this trait, especially those who work for large corporations that compete on the international market (Thompson, IBM, Michelin, Honeywell Bull, etc.). Here, people who are pretentious are strongly criticized, as are those who are in it only for themselves. In fact, in the French context, "teamwork" often translates

into loyalty to enduring networks of personalized relationships within the firm as well as loyalty to the firm itself and to its traditions. Elements of this general ethos are suggested in the comments of a Parisian senior insurance executive whom I interviewed:

> This is a country with an old civilization. The respect of people is important, as well as a certain formalism . . . To make someone part of the management group, you have to take into consideration a very complex network of relationships . . . Personal relations count a lot . . . we are not only determined by the market: it is a network of bilateral relationships . . . The bureaucratic structure is less important.[56]

The picture that emerges from the public sector is slightly different. Much has been written on conflicts and lack of communication across hierarchical levels within the French civil service.[57] This was confirmed to a certain degree by my interviews. This is how a Parisian science teacher described the situation—which might resemble the one that prevails in American schools:

> As soon as a teacher becomes a lycée director, he becomes the enemy. The other teachers do not remember that they used to be his colleagues, to drink with him, to converse with him. Instead of saying, "One of us has succeeded, maybe he will be able to understand us better," they are distrustful because they think that he is on the other side of the fence.

In such an environment, conflict is obviously not avoided; interviewees talk freely about their enemies at work, and they are very open about their lack of desire to make peace with them, an attitude hardly comparable to the conflict avoidance that prevails in the United States. Clearly, they do not see their moral worth as related to their ability to overcome differences. Instead, again, it is measured by their personal integrity, which works against flexibility. This is exemplified by a fifty-year-old Clermontois who explains his attitude at work:

> I don't get assimilated easily. At least I am not reducible: I cannot change my view of the basic qualities that for me define what a man is. I cannot compromise my behavior when it comes to being hypocritical, to kissing ass to gain something. Never. It's no merit on my part, because I'm absolutely unable to do it . . . It is important to show yourself as you are, with the authenticity of your failings, with your own little zany side and with your contradictions. You have to show who you are, live openly. Nothing is worse than to have to wear a mask.

While some American interviewees might be unwilling to make peace with their enemies, they seldom verbalized this feeling in interviews, for fear it would "reflect badly on them" (informant, Indianapolis). Overall, again, personal integrity in France seems to remain a more accurate sign of moral worth than conflict avoidance.[58]

But how do the other traits that Americans appreciate fare in the French context? Friendliness first. This trait is not valued by my respondents if it translates into familiarity, as this is considered more characteristic of working-class culture than of bourgeois culture. According to Bourdieu, for people of the working class, "Familiarity is . . . the most absolute form of recognition, the abdication of all distance, a trusting openness, a relation of equal to equal; for others [the bourgeois], who shun familiarity, it is an unseemly liberty."[59] In this context, managing relations with colleagues in upper-middle-class circles might mean not so much the display of friendliness as respect for formalities and conspicuous personal consideration: it might mean showing little attentions, exchanging small presents at Christmastime and flowers on the first of May, sharing le déjeuner, offering a drink after work. However, especially among the youngest respondents, being relaxed, informal, sympa is also valued.

Sociability is particularly crucial for self-employed professionals, who often develop personal relationships with their regular clients. For the dentist, it means taking the time to chat with patients and to get to know them personally. For the accountant, it means paying a personal visit to clients on the pretext of just happening to be in the neighborhood. A Parisian lawyer summarizes the situation when he says that the relation clients want to have with him is not unlike the personal relation they have with their priest or doctor: "They come to see a specific lawyer, and not any lawyer's office. They want personal attention . . . It is important that [I] take the time to see them personally. You develop a very personal relationship with them." Such contacts are also important in the United States, but a veneer of professionalism often neutralizes their personal dimension.[60]

Other traits are unequally valued in Clermont-Ferrand and Paris. In fact, the interviews suggest that in many respects the Clermontois are closer in their outlook to the Hoosiers than to the Parisians: they appreciate simplicity, pragmatism, hard work, and reserve (i.e., humility; "power, not glory" as one interviewee expressed it) more than the Parisians, who tend to put more stress on pizzazz and brilliance. François

Michelin, the head of the Michelin firm and an exemplary character, illustrates this similarity: he is known for "renouncing all ostentatious luxuries and ignoring titles and decorations." Like his top managers, he "lead[s] a discreet and hardworking life . . . all useless hierarchies are ignored, and those that must exist are not accentuated." Power differentials are minimized for the sake of efficiency.[61] Such a character would probably be esteemed by most of my Indianapolis interviewees as well, and in this similarity between the Clermontois and the Hoosiers, we might see the common influence of their agrarian roots: indeed, a significant number of interviewees on both sides are only first- or second-generation city dwellers. We know that the keys to success in an agricultural world are thrift, hard work, and determination, not instantaneous brilliance.

So far we saw that firm loyalty and integrity are more highly valued, while friendliness and conflict avoidance are less valued in France than in the United States. These patterns can be explained by differences in the frequency of job change in both countries and in the structure of the labor market. First, firm loyalty might be less accentuated in the United States because in this country mobility is a condition for success, as American upper-middle-class men are committed to career strategies that often entail a detachment from other workers and the firm.[62] Indeed, while French engineers tend to spend most of their professional lives in a single firm, their American counterparts have had a median number of four employers in a twenty-year career.[63] Also, conflict avoidance might be less salient in France in part because the French men I talked to have greater professional security than their American counterparts as well as guaranteed promotion.[64] These last factors favor the valuation of personal integrity in opposition to moral pragmatism. On the other hand, friendliness and ostentatious team orientation could be more central in the American upper-middle class than in the French because of the greater professional mobility experienced by Americans, which requires them to interact with a large number of people and to learn to constantly provide signals of trustworthiness. This is essential in order to decrease the level of uncertainty which is particularly high in American organizations, especially given that many American professionals and managers are part of a national labor market, whereas their French counterparts not only do not change employers very often but also are very stable geographically, since most recruitment is done locally.[65] The importance of friendliness and conflict avoidance are also reinforced by the decentralization of au-

thority in the American workplace. In contrast, in France teamwork plays a less central role at work since power is more centralized.[66]

Many of the traits that are most central for signaling moral character in the American workplace are less effective or simply inoperative in the French workplace. It is necessary to turn to the Christian humanist tradition in order to identify the moral traits that are valued in the latter case.

Michel Dupuis, the owner of a processing plant whom I described in the Prologue, exemplifies the humanist tradition: recall that this interviewee said that his goal in life is not to make money but to help his employees to become all they can be as human beings; when questioned regarding other business people he admires, he emphasizes their *qualités de coeur* (their inner riches and empathy for others) as well as their *soif d'humain* (thirst for genuine human relationships). And he is not alone in mobilizing such criteria: eight interviewees who live in the western suburbs of Paris (mostly in Versailles) follow the same pattern, as do nine Clermontois. Many of them attended private Catholic schools where they were socialized into France's humanist subculture. Several studied with the Jesuits for whom moral, cultural, and intellectual development go hand in hand. As explained by a Clermont lawyer, for these Jesuits, *"Eduquer veut dire bien faire l'homme"* (to educate means to form a man in his totality).

In this humanist culture, the moral value of people is assessed on the basis of whether they prove to be *hommes de principes* (men of principles) who hold strong beliefs and for whom truth is essential (public school administrator, Paris; senior manufacturing executive, Paris; dentist, Clermont-Ferrand), and whether they have a strong sense of social justice (*un sens social*) (business management specialist, Paris). Also valued are an *ouverture aux autres* (an openness to others), and a *sens du don* (an ability to give). The humanists often criticize the materialists and people who live in a self-contained and selfish way (e.g., the *jeunes loups*).[67]

Revamped by the Personalist school, which had a strong influence during the period in which many of my respondents grew up, this humanist tradition particularly values the socially, historically, and physically rooted person as against an increasingly anonymous mass society, narcissistic and hedonistic individualism, and the alienation and competition inherent to capitalism.[68] This is not surprising, as many people who identify with humanism belong to the old French Catholic bourgeoisie, whose subculture is defined largely by the rootedness of its members

within large family networks; by their attachment to household furnishings and effects, apartments, and country houses that have belonged to the family for several generations; and by their sense of duty, respect for the conventions, and love for tradition in general, of which religion is only one dimension. As we will see in Chapter 6, using in part humanism, the traditional Catholic bourgeoisie defines its identity against the *bourgeoisie de promotion*, i.e., the newer members of the upper-middle class. This humanist culture is also common mostly among right-wing, private-sector workers, and it has a strong impact on the workplace.[69]

The Catholic humanism of the group just described is opposed to a humanism that is socialist and atheist in inspiration, and also has a strong following in the upper-middle class, mostly among public-sector workers. These secular humanists, like their Catholic counterparts, value the full development of humanness and oppose capitalism because it results in the exploitation and alienation of the human race. Accordingly, they often gauge others morally on the basis of whether or not they contribute to political and economic oppression. They criticize capitalists as immoral by nature, and take political attitudes into consideration in the choice of their friends, a right-winger being by definition, a *salaud*. They favor workers' self-management as a way to counter the alienation inherent in our society.[70] This constitutes further evidence of the importance of moral boundaries in the French workplace. If, in the United States, obedience to the Ten Commandments, friendliness, work ethics, and competence are highly valued moral status signals, in France, personal integrity, political orientation, and humanism are more important. Attitudes toward religiosity and volunteerism afford us other perspectives on moral status signals, as many individuals directly associate these attitudes with morality.

THE RELIGIOUS SCENE

Historically, in France and America, many conflicts having to do with politics, class, region, or ethnicity have been framed in religious terms.[71] For instance, antimonarchist and republican forces in France have traditionally been anticlerical, while, again, the old bourgeoisie distinguishes itself from the *bourgeoisie de promotion* by its Catholic humanism. In the United States, religious differences have been the vehicle for conflicts between liberals and conservatives, between nativist WASPs and Southern European Catholic immigrants, and between prochoice and prolife

advocates in the abortion controversy.[72] Clearly, even if religion has traditionally been a "private" matter, especially in the United States, it is frequently mobilized in intergroup conflicts.[73] This does not mean, however, that it is very salient in the drawing of symbolic boundaries.

In *Economy and Society*, Max Weber had predicted that with the development of capitalism, religious and ethnic identities would lose their importance, since market relationships foster exchange above and beyond traditional group memberships.[74] If this prediction has not been altogether fulfilled (witness the comeback of Muslim and Christian fundamentalism), it proves to be largely consistent with our interviews: with a few notable exceptions, the men I talked to rarely mentioned religion in their description of the types of people with whom they would rather not associate.[75] And often they explicitly dissociated moral character from religious attitudes, pointing to the hypocrisy they have sometimes encountered in highly religious circles. In both countries, however, I talked with a few men who draw strong religious boundaries, identifying themselves with American Protestant fundamentalism or with the French Catholic bourgeois culture. I discuss these groups in turn.

Some of the members of the French traditional Catholic bourgeoisie have often very excluding (or closing) practices based on religious orientations. For instance, several of them make a point of sending their children to private parochial schools for explicitly religious reasons. Some also choose their friends on the basis of their religiosity and spend their free time almost exclusively by being involved in religious organizations (the Ligue Notre-Dame, e.g.). When asked who they feel inferior to, they do not mention capitalist heroes but saints such as St. Francis of Assisi—"someone who is simultaneously Truth, Intelligence, and Love itself, because this is what I want to be, and I am not succeeding very well at it" (journalist, Clermont-Ferrand).

In the United States, those who are very religious, i.e., mostly the fundamentalist Christians, also draw very strong moral boundaries based on religiosity. For instance, they also refuse to associate with people who are not strongly religious or with non-Christians, as this New York minister explains:

My wife and I are very careful about associating only with Christians. All of our associations are with Christians, not that we don't like anybody else, but again it's a matter of priorities. I find that I have in-

creasingly less and less in common with people who are not Christians
. . . We don't want to be someplace where people are drinking, for
example. So that 98 percent of the gatherings are a problem there.

These fundamentalists, as well as a Christian Scientist and a few others, feel superior to those who are less religious; they are convinced that
they are "way ahead" on a scale of hierarchalization that often remains
unknown to those being judged inferior. It is significant that French interviewees do not talk in terms of superiority in moral standards (concerning
drinking, marital fidelity, and so forth) but superiority in "humanness"
and charity. American fundamentalists believe that the teachings of the
Bible are the key to success and to gaining respect from others. As one of
them says: "[The goal] is to know God. If [our kids] do that, then hopefully the rest will fall in place when they're out in the business world.
Their morals are going to be high, and they're going to be noted, and
other people will have respect toward them."

Moral boundaries are particularly crucial for American fundamentalists because, according to R. Stephen Warner, being a fundamentalist
means defending not only a religious position but also traditional values
such as family life, neighborhood, community, and a Christian lifestyle against materialism, individualism, and elitist meritocracy, as well
as against the secular humanism and cosmopolitanism often associated
with the New Class.[76] For them, a lifestyle is a crucial template of moral
choices. Consequently, fundamentalists might signal their own moral
standards by being very involved in family life. Again, the same is true
for the members of the French Catholic bourgeoisie.

If only a small number of Americans identify with the fundamentalist
subculture, the church as a social institution has a strong influence on a
larger group of interviewees. Indeed, it provides them and their families
with a community, with a social matrix within which they have an identity and a reputation; this is less often the case for French respondents.
This function of the church is described by an Indianapolis resident:

A lot of our social life, a lot of just what we do, really revolves around
our church. The children have been involved in Sunday school. We
have Alpha Clubs, which was a group for younger children where they
would go on Wednesday afternoons, and they'd play games and do all
kinds of things. Dean, who is a senior in high school now, was what is
called a junior deacon, which is a kind of honor in our church. There
are only three children picked each year.

Being involved in church activities sends out a signal about respectability, moral character, and trustworthiness. There is an implicit association between "being good" and "being Christian" that reinforces boundaries against outsiders to this upper-middle-class culture, especially in Indianapolis, where the relatively small size of the wealthier northern neighborhoods allows for less anonymity.[77]

Both in France and in the United States, atheists also build religiously based moral boundaries but in a reverse way. Some of them said they were very uncomfortable with strongly religious people whose understanding of the world was diametrically opposed to theirs. Several of the French interviewees said they despise the traditional Catholic bourgeoisie because they consider it to be intellectually and culturally narrow, retrograde, and elitist. They also criticize it for defending private Catholic education and for supporting a church that collaborated with the Vichy Government during the Nazi occupation. In this context, strong religiosity might be a negative trait and a handicap in the workplace.

Both national groups contain a significant minority (roughly the same size in each case) of very religious respondents. Indeed, only 22 percent of the Americans interviewed and 18 percent of the French say that they are fairly often or frequently involved in religious activities, and only 23 percent and 28 percent, respectively, say that they very much like such activities.[78] Both national groups have a minority of respondents who show a strong antireligious attitude: 14 percent of the American interviewees say that they dislike or strongly dislike going to church, as do 12 percent of the French. Respectively, 20 percent and 37 percent of the Paris and Clermont-Ferrand interviewees declare themselves to be agnostic or atheist, in contrast to a mere 8 percent of the Indianapolis interviewees and 5 percent of those in the New York area.[79] In addition to this, a large number of American respondents described themselves as "not very religious," which might signify either that they are not strong believers or simply that they do not lead a very active religious life. These findings and the fact that many more French interviewees are not involved in churches lead me to believe that slightly fewer French than American interviewees take religiosity to be a moral status signal.[80]

To conclude, with some exceptions, French and American interviewees rarely made reference to religion in their discussions of moral purity, — apparently dissociating moral character from religious attitudes. While most were indifferent to the religious attitudes of others, a small group of atheists drew significant boundaries against people who are very religious.

Furthermore, a minority of both French and American interviewees drew strong boundaries on the basis of religious orientation. These were particularly salient among the few American fundamentalists and traditional French Catholics I interviewed for whom religious beliefs command a whole way of life, including a strong family orientation. On the other hand, the church as a central institution exercises some influence on a somewhat larger group of American interviewees because it provides them with a community. Overall, religion seems to be more important in Indianapolis than elsewhere, although the wealthy Paris suburbs have a strong concentration of highly religious interviewees.

VOLUNTEERISM

Even if volunteerism is associated with altruism and caring, it is also rarely salient in discussions of moral character. The American interviewees, however, were more likely than the French to take volunteerism as reflective of moral character and, therefore, to consider it to be a high status signal. In fact, many Frenchmen I talked to think about volunteerism within a framework that is very different in orientation from the one used by Americans. Didier Aucour, the Paris architecture professor, is in some ways representative of this group. He says:

> The relation that I have with humanity, it is not a relation with the mass, but with individual creation. I never vote, I never participate in associations, I never participate in anything, I never give money. If I give money in the subway, it is not because someone is poor. I never give to a homeless person. I am not charitable. However, if I hear a musician who plays an instrument well, I'll give him money because I like what he does. I don't like charity because it is complete demagogy. People make money out of that.

Similarly, several French interviewees object to charitable giving for political reasons: it makes poor people dependent on the whims of the rich. As stated by a Clermont-Ferrand philosophy professor:

> As long as individuals will give, social justice will not be realized. Receiving charity is an insult . . . The handicapped, the blind, their future should not be linked to the charity of individuals. [I am rather for] a political system that is not based on profit, on the exploitation of the Third World . . . Charity is a little perverse, it has nothing to do with Christian charity, with loving other human beings.

The support of the handicapped and other disadvantaged groups is understood here to be a collective responsibility that should be carried on by the state: these people have a right to be helped and should not be forced to rely on individual paternalistic sentiments. Therefore, few French interviewees take volunteering as a good indicator of moral character.

The American interviewees, and particularly the Hoosiers, offer a stark contrast with those of the French: several of them expressed a strong faith in the importance of giving, and this might affect their view of the role of altruism as a high status signal. The importance of volunteerism is stressed by this Metuchen human management consultant who describes the values he is trying to convey to his children:

> During Lent, we do a lot. We save money to give to the poor. Every night we have on the table a rice bowl, and we put some money in it. It's for the poor. When the kids get their allowance, they are supposed to spend part of it, save part of it, and part of it they can give away. Almost every Sunday, we'll go and put money in the poor box . . . We don't really hit it, the whole 10 percent. We maybe give 8½ percent of our income every year, but we try . . . We're trying to teach [the kids] to give to a number of charities, and we try to make them aware of the fact that we're doing it.

None of the French respondents expressed a form of altruism comparable to this. Instead, they seem to express compassion through their willingness to support a strong welfare system,[82] while Americans more often express compassion through private philanthropic activities, which they, in some instances, combine with conservative political positions.

As described by our friend Alexis de Tocqueville in *Democracy in America*, involvement in voluntary associations is an essential part of how Americans conceive their relationship to society. Besides the intrinsic satisfactions they might provide, voluntary associations often constitute a medium through which the elite can "give back" to the community.[83] They also provide an arena for gaining respect in the community and establishing one's reputation, while becoming socially constructed as part of the local elite. (In France, other institutions seem to be more central in performing this role.) Finally, as explained by Zussman in *Mechanics of the Middle Class*, participation in voluntary associations is an important source of friendship for upper-middle-class men with a high degree of geographical mobility. Many companies make it policy to encourage

their workers to get involved in local organizations as a way for these companies to maintain good relations with the community. Several authors, however, have suggested that, for Americans, moral obligations apply to an increasingly limited number of people defined by common blood, ethnicity, and religion, or by physical proximity, as "community" comes to be equaled with "people like us."[84]

The cross-cultural patterns in attitudes toward volunteering revealed by the interviews correspond to what we know of the attitudes of the French and the Americans toward philanthropic activities in general. Voluntary associations are weaker in France than they are in the United States.[85] Indeed, the total number of hours given in volunteer work in France equals the full-time work of only 1 percent of the employed population, as opposed to 3 percent in the United States.[86] The European values/CARA surveys also show that American profesionals and managers are considerably more involved in such activities than their French counterparts (45 percent as compared to 9 percent).[87]

CONCLUSION

This chapter has shown that moral boundaries are roughly equally important in both countries even if the dimensions of morality that are most salient vary greatly across contexts. Again, Americans are more likely to reject the phonies, the social climbers, and the low-morals types. In contrast to the French, they are particularly concerned with Judeo-Christian definitions of morality. On the other hand, the French often exclude, at least at the discursive level, people who lack personal integrity and who show little solidarity with other human beings. They are more likely to read leftist political attitudes as a template of moral character.

In both countries, moral status also is read from attitudes displayed in the workplace. While Rosabeth Kanter pointed at the importance of homophily in American corporations, she did not systematically study the high status signals that are valued in the workplace. Such signals are documented here. I find that for the American men I talked with, showing friendliness, being a team player and avoiding conflict are quintessential. Many interviewees value competence, work ethic, and their associated virtues—competitiveness, dynamism, self-direction, resilience, and long-term planning. In contrast, ambition and competitiveness are less crucial in the French workplace. In general, the French less frequently take a strong work orientation to be a template of moral character. They value

general competence over specialized expertise and do not stress conflict avoidance the way Americans do. They also tend to deduce moral purity from involvement in the humanist tradition, whether it Catholic or Socialist in inspiration. Overall, like most American interviewees, they rarely make reference to religion in their discussions of moral purity, dissociating moral character from religious attitudes. Similar patterns emerge for volunteerism, although Americans tend to stress private philanthropy while French more readily deduce moral character from one's willingness to support a strong welfare state.

While sociologists such as Bellah et al. suggest that morality is losing importance in American society, this chapter has clearly demonstrated that moral boundaries are still very salient at the discursive level in the culture of the American upper-middle classes. Morality, however, is less defined in terms of communalism than in terms of work ethics, humility, conspicuous honesty, and straightforwardness. In the next chapters, we will explore how moral boundaries mesh with cultural boundaries and socioeconomic boundaries and how autonomous from one another are each type of boundary in the two countries. We also will analyze whether the role given to morality in the workplace is comparatively more important in the United States than in France, given the importance that Americans attach to cultural and social egalitarianism.

Chapter Three

~~~~~~

THE WORLD OF SUCCESS, MONEY, AND POWER: KEYS TO SOCIOECONOMIC BOUNDARIES

<div align="right">

Ah! L'argent, l'horrible argent qui salit et dévore.
—Emile Zola
Ah! Money, dreadful money, that soils and devours.

</div>

A WORLD OF INEQUALITY

In his mansion in Summit, New Jersey, John Craig complains about the burdens of his life. He hates it. He cannot stand it anymore. He hates his job; he hates his boss; he hates the people with whom he works. This middle-age man craves a more meaningful life. After having worked as a top marketing executive for the same company for twenty years, he finds himself pushed aside because the boss wants to bring in his son-in-law. This triggers a crisis. There is an ego problem. His boss has a big ego, which he likes to flex. John would like to make a change, but there are a lot of social pressures to be reckoned with:

> To keep the pace up to generate a lot of income gets wearing. We live in a high-ticket town. I got caught up in the big house and the high lifestyle . . . Now I have become more conscious and aware of what is important to me. Some people never get to it . . . They lose sight of what's really important and they work, work, work, work, more money, more power, more this; and some people are happy with that, and others are not, but they are trapped. They become trapped by themselves [because of] Mr. Ego. Their value or their sense of self-esteem is the big house, the title, the Mercedes Benz. A great deal of people identify that with being successful as a person . . . The community we live in generates that . . . I would say my wife is caught up with that. What is important is not fur coats and rolex watches and diamond rings . . . [People here want to know] where you came from, where you went to school, what you're doing now, that sort of thing. Who you work for, how much money you make, where you live in town. The North Side syndrome.

John's world is a world inhabited by other-directed men who believe in worldly success. Like John, these men have "done very well for themselves" and have a high lifestyle. They are very involved in local country clubs, in civic or political groups, and in the Chamber of Commerce. John is now tired of it all. He questions the sacrifices required to pursue worldly success, the extraordinary amount of internal pressure and stress that he has had to endure, the burdens imposed by his wife who wants to "keep the lifestyle." To redefine what is important to him, he is reading *The Road Less Travelled*. A number of other upper-middle-class men in crisis emerged during the interviews: while describing their doubts and dissatisfactions, they often shed light on socioeconomic exclusion and helped me understand how the socioeconomically exclusive interviewees think.[1]

Whereas people who draw moral boundaries take moral character as indicative of an individual's worth, individuals who draw socioeconomic boundaries define desirability on the basis of social position as read through professional prestige, race, financial standing, class background, power, and visibility in prestigious social circles. Typically, people who fall in this category feel inferior to "highly successful, highly aggressive people" (proprietor, car leasing company, New York), which might mean "obviously people who are wealthy, in a higher position, just higher on a social-level type of thing" (staff assistant, Indianapolis). They might be envious of people who "succeed very well and very strongly" (banker, Paris).[2] As explained by John Craig, they judge people's worth by external status signals, such as "where you came from, where you went to school, what you're doing now, that sort of thing. Who you work for, how much money you make, where you live in town," and "whether you had the ability to achieve."[3] They don't like to associate with losers and they mostly choose their friends on the basis of "how well they have done for themselves"; they describe these friends as well-off professionals and businessmen[4]—"the other people you just put up with, but you don't want to be with" (corporate lawyer, New York). In short, people who draw socioeconomic boundaries are attracted by success. As a New York realtor, a "nouveau riche," explains: "I prefer dealing with people who are more successful than I am . . . I do work with them, I'm involved in politics; I've got lots of friends who are much bigger folks than I am and I enjoy being out there with them . . . Naturally, success breeds success; so I'm hanging around success."[5]

People who draw strong socioeconomic boundaries are consumed by

professional success, as measured by career curve and velocity. Success gives them a sense of self-worth, of psychological well-being, and of personal satisfaction; as a Clermont-Ferrand entrepreneur says, "[Success] is the full realization of oneself." These men sometimes see people who are less successful as "anxious, jealous, revengeful" (accountant, Clermont-Ferrand), because they conceive worldly success as the only real way to gain peace of mind. They take money to be the crucial signal of ability and desirability, and such external attributes as place of residence and type of car to be sure indices of success. For them, money is the key to everything, including social acceptance and membership.[6]

Chapter 2 showed that competitiveness, ambition, and resilience can be read as proof of moral purity, in which case successful people are admired because their success reflects the internalization of these moral traits. In this chapter I am concerned with individuals who admire the successful not for moral but for purely socioeconomic reasons, i.e., as members of a social elite who are superior on a properly socioeconomic scale. In other words, I am concerned with the ideal-typical socioeconomic excluders who value success per se for the social ranking it confers.

Whereas sociologists often tend to posit the predominance of ascribed characteristics (gender, race, ethnicity) in the creation of social closure,[7] or that of material standards of evaluation (i.e., income, ownership of durable consumer goods) in determining social status,[8] one of the goals of this chapter is to attempt to assess which standards of evaluation are in fact most salient in determining socioeconomic status, at least in the context of interviews.[9] Simultaneously, I analyze the relative salience of class in contrast to other aspects of social identity.[10] Important cross-national differences emerge with significant conceptual consequences for rational choice theory and other approaches that presume that economic resources are by definition more crucial than others. These implications will be discussed in Chapter 7.

For many interviewees, signals of high socioeconomic status are the only status signals that are really significant: our quantitative comparison of the ranking of respondents on the moral, cultural, and socioeconomic dimensions reveals that, overall, socioeconomic boundaries are slightly more important than cultural or moral boundaries.[11] Socioeconomic boundaries, however, are considerably more salient in America than they are in France.[12] Moreover, with only a few exceptions, the

French, and the Parisians in particular, rarely mention feeling inferior to wealthier or more successful people. In fact, the men I talked to were often uncomfortable with probes concerning their "success." They almost never describe their friends as "being successful," this notion itself sounding uncouth in French ("*ça fait prétentieux*," as a Paris dentist pointed out).[13] They also rarely take people who are very success-oriented as models, as illustrated by a young and dynamic Paris investment banker I talked to:

> I really am not envious of them. I find them limited, sad, even if often they have succeeded in doing impressive things. I think they are sad because they think that they're—I would not say the "masters of the world," but that nothing will stop them and they possess the truth . . . they are so small if you think in terms of the planet. For me, it is almost physical. I find them completely ridiculous, which is paradoxical because often they have succeeded very well.

In contrast, the American men I met with were considerably more prone to describe themselves as feeling inferior to rich, powerful, and successful people. For example, when asked to describe people they admire, they were more likely to point to Donald Trump and Lee Iacocca than the French are to point to Bernard Tapie. And when asked to describe qualities that leave them indifferent, only nine New Yorkers and four Hoosiers chose "successful," in contrast to seventeen Clermontois and nineteen Parisians. Previous research suggests that this stress on success is not confined to the upper-middle class alone in the United States.[14]

I now turn to the content of socioeconomic boundaries themselves and examine what signals of high socioeconomic status are most valued by the various groups of interviewees. If in France, success per se is downplayed, specific bases of social positioning such as power and social background are highly valued.[15]

THE IRON LAW OF MONEY

The French in general are clearly less money-oriented than Americans. Indeed, 93 percent of the upper-middle-class Frenchmen interviewed by the European values/CARA surveys, in contrast to 68 percent of the Americans, think that it would be good if people were to attach less importance to money. This undoubtedly affects the likelihood that people draw symbolic boundaries on the basis of income. Indeed, among the

men I talked with, 68 percent of the Parisians say that, in their evaluations of others, affluence is a feature to which they are indifferent, compared to 57 percent of the Clermontois, 51 percent of the New Yorkers, and 41 percent of the Hoosiers.[16]

Viviana Zelizer and others have noted that, far from having a simply utilitarian value, money has a wide range of meanings.[17] Indeed, while Frenchmen have an ambivalent attitude toward money, Americans see it as an essential means to control and freedom. This affects the role that money is likely to play as a signal of high socioeconomic status. Consequently, it is useful to discuss these various meanings at some length.

I have identified four distinct patterns in the way French individuals think about money. A first, rather important, group of respondents think of money as impure. The second group, the established traditional bourgeoisie, views money as a means of maintaining one's social position rather than of improving it. A third, smaller group, mostly concentrated in Clermont-Ferrand, is much more materialistic in orientation despite a certain asceticism. Finally, the last group conceives of money as the symbol and the reward of their upward mobility and as a means to reach a higher social position.

For many Frenchmen I talked to, money is unworthy of pursuit, for it has the power to desacralize life, infusing it with values that are purely instrumental rather than inherently worthy. Therefore, according to these people, money should not be considered the ultimate professional goal. As a successful Clermont-Ferrand architect states: "The aesthetic, the creative aspect, helping others to live better is really what is appealing. The goal is not at all to make money, but to reach a level of personal satisfaction."

For others, money symbolizes an embarrassing and profane relationship with customers and institutions. We see this in the case of a Parisian lawyer who can't bear the thought of having to bill his clients. This man is a bourgeois humanist of the type described in Chapter 2. He has six children and owns a very large nineteenth-century house which is in great need of repairs. He says:

> I am ashamed of asking for money. Charging a fee for preparing a case seems to me . . . I don't know, I'd rather do it for free . . . It makes me uncomfortable to ask. I am always afraid of asking too much, of making people feel uncomfortable. But when I analyze the situation, I know it is stupid, because I offer a service which should be paid for. I don't like money.

A third lawyer who works to support his passion (directing avant-garde plays) and the manager of a car dealership share similar feelings when they confess to having little admiration for people whose goal is to get rich. As the car dealer states it, "It is totally without interest." Many others, like the Paris literature professor, explained that they chose to make less money in order to have more freedom ("I much prefer to make what I make and to be free than to make twice as much and to have to follow orders and be subservient"). Those with antimaterialist attitudes of this sort are more numerous in Paris than in Clermont-Ferrand, which explains why overall one finds weaker socioeconomic boundaries in the capital than in the provincial city (see n. 12).

Such negative attitudes toward money, which might be associated with a Catholic disregard for worldly contingencies, are very rare among the Americans with whom I met. The few who partake of them do not go as far as repudiating the importance of money altogether. More typically, they emphasize the place of self-actualization and interpersonal relationships in their lives without belittling money the way the French often do.

A second group of French interviewees is more materialistic without, however, drawing socioeconomic boundaries on the basis of income. They frequently understand money as the nineteenth-century landed bourgeoisie did, that is, as a way to support a lifestyle, a way to live "not only honorably, but comfortably" (hospital controller, Clermont-Ferrand). In Paris, this means to many men being able to eat out on a very regular basis, to go to the theater and to various cultural events,[18] to offer frequent hospitality to a large number of friends and kin both at their city home and, on weekends, at the country house, and to support the country house itself. In short, money is a means of reproducing a traditional bourgeois way of life. It is a way of *maintaining* a social identity rather than of improving one's social position, of signaling one's progress on the consumption ladder. It is, therefore, not surprising that in these bourgeois circles "earned" money is deemphasized in favor of the *patrimoine* (i.e., wealth, especially inherited wealth, including real estate properties, art, and furniture, that incarnate the family history) of things which have always been there. As a Parisian human resources consultant puts it, "We had them, we always had them, and our children will have them."[19] These bourgeois rarely talk about prices and purchases (*ça ne se fait pas parmi les gens bien*"). They play down commercial relationships as if such considerations collided with their *"coté grand seigneur,"* i.e., their noble

appreciation for the disinterested and the gratuitous. Such attitudes did not surface among the American men with whom I talked.[20]

The ambivalence of many of the French interviewees toward money is not surprising given that a number of members of the French bourgeoisie are downwardly mobile economically and maintain a high social position mostly because their family has been part of the upper-middle class for several generations, because they are culturally part of the group, and because they have access to large resourceful social networks. Such downwardly mobile individuals will be discussed in Chapter 6.

A third group of Frenchmen are much more money-oriented than the majority of their compatriots. This group was mostly concentrated in Clermont-Ferrand. As is the case for many Auvergnats—the residents of the region where Clermont-Ferrand is located, who have a reputation for being hardnosed and astute businessmen—these men view the accumulation of riches as a major motivation in their lives. They talked to me about their awareness of the economic standing of their neighbors and their own interest in making their *patrimoine* grow. Like American participants, they consider making money to be the road to freedom. This is expressed by an upwardly mobile engineer whose father was a poor farmer, and who shows great pride in working for Michelin. This man's passion is to speculate on the stock market:

> The consumer is dominated; the investor wants to dominate. The consumer is a hostage in a ghetto, even if it is a golden cage. The investor dominates because he has the initiative. The consumer is the victim. On the one side, you have someone who wants to do things. On the other side, you have the one who swallows, who endures, who is conditioned and manipulated.

In contrast, people whose values are antimaterialistic see the drive to make money as a constraint, because it requires adapting to an organization's culture and norms and thereby losing one's individuality and personal integrity.

A last, very small group of the French participants, most of them first-generation upper-middle class, value consumerism as such—i.e., the spending of money rather than the mere making of it—as the symbol and reward of upward mobility. These men talk openly about the villa, the luxury car, and the other consumption goods they are now able to afford. Even in this last group, however, not a single interviewee equates a person's worth with his or her income. We will see that members of this

fourth group are often ostracized for their materialism by the traditional bourgeoisie, whose attitude toward money they are pressured to adopt, as if, unlike their American counterparts, this "bourgeoisie de promotion" had not yet fully developed a distinct and legitimate culture and was being pushed into mimicking the norms of the old bourgeoisie.

The ambivalence of the French attitudes toward money contrast highly with the more positive attitudes that were most frequently expressed by American upper-middle-class men. For these individuals money means above all freedom, control, and security, these being clearly circumscribed by level of personal income. In this context it is not surprising that money is itself more salient as a basis for socioeconomic boundaries for Americans than for French participants.

The first American respondent to associate freedom with control was a young, high-powered New York investment portfolio manager who makes around $200,000 a year. I interviewed him on the patio of his beautiful Riverside home. He explained his perspective in the following terms:

> I like to have control . . . I want to do what makes me happy and not feel that I'm being pushed around and forced into corners. [My job] is not a self-fulfilling job. The financial incentive is really what I'm here for. It gives me the freedom to do what I want, to go places, do things. I've never been good at budgeting. I would like to have enough money to retire in five years from now if I want to. To me this means freedom. A lot of people are saying to me, "You're too money-oriented." I'm just being honest. If the money went away on this job, I wouldn't be there more than another month.

Here freedom means being able to take off regularly for a weekend of skiing in Vermont, or being able to buy a luxury home in an exclusive area. For others, it simply means being able to afford a house in a safe neighborhood where their children will have access to good schools and be somewhat less exposed to drugs and other real or imaginary social evils, and where real estate values are likely to climb. It might also mean being wealthy enough to retire or become self-employed, a dream that looms much larger in American definitions of success than in the French.

For these American men, money is also seen as providing a certain "comfort level" that becomes the symbol and the reward of professional success. "Comfort level" is measured by the value of the items one can

afford, including cars, homes, trips, electronic equipment, and so forth. It is also measured by the kids' ballet classes and piano lessons, and their tennis and computer camps, as well as by the time spent at work versus the time the adults spend golfing or enjoying other leisure-time activities. And because "comfort level" reflects level of success, many are caught in an endless spiral of consumption.[21] A New York software developer who makes more than a hundred thousand dollars a year puts it best: "I find myself admiring the latest cars, the latest clothes, wanting to go to the nicest resort . . . I want these things even though I can rationalize and intellectualize it away. Those are not the things that make me happy, yet I still want the new car, the latest stereo . . . there are a lot of things that I'd like to have that I don't have." This infinite desire is echoed in a striking way by a middle-aged Indianapolis minister who also takes money to be a measure of his "professional " success:

> I would not be honest unless I said that economic success is important. It certainly is . . . It has been a sign value to how successful I am in the institutional church. Because that's important in determining or perceiving the level of success of a minister, i.e., by how much money he makes. I struggle almost constantly with the pressures of society, and particularly advertising and entertainment, which emphasize money and the things money buys as the most important thing in life . . . What television portrays both in its programming and news programs and advertising . . . is that there's an awful lot more out there that you should be able to buy, and things you should be able to do . . . It bothers me . . . But after a while [it] can make one feel that you really haven't achieved all that much . . . I am a child of my own culture and success has been worshipped, there is no doubt about that. Success is almost always defined in terms of either professional success or accumulation of material goods.

A valence foreign to spiritual salvation shapes in a significant way the sense of accomplishment that this minister gets from his work. As we will see in Chapter 6, his views are indicative of the fact that in America socioeconomic boundaries can be mobilized to evaluate even activities that are explicitly noneconomic in character, as conceptions of success centering on "comfort level" is diffused by the mass media to all groups.[22] It is, therefore, not surprising that overall, in the United States, socioeconomic boundaries are very frequently drawn on the basis of income. In France people more often associate a high income less with freedom

than with a loss of personal integrity, and less with "success" than with a denial of the intrinsic value of work.[23]

The importance of a high-income level as a signal of socioeconomic status for American participants can be explained by the fact that money is more central to their quality of life and to that of their dependents, the welfare functions of the state being relatively underdeveloped in the United States in contrast to France. Indeed, in America, the quality of schooling is less uniform than it is in France because it is more exclusively dependent on local taxes and, indirectly, on local real estate prices.[24] Also, health care and child care have to be privately purchased by the American middle class. College education is very costly, and most American upper-middle class men spend a considerable part of their life savings for the education of their children. This factor is important particularly because higher education is at the heart of the reproduction of the upper-middle class. In contrast, in France, higher education is less expensive and the quality of schooling tends to be more consistent across neighborhoods, because elementary and secondary schools are financially supported and controlled by the central government. Health care and child care, too, are free or available at low cost.

The importance of income as a signal of socioeconomic status in the United States is also sustained by the fact that professional success is measured more by income level than by nomination to prestigious positions. In general, market principles have more influence in the allocation of professional rewards, which strengthens the role of money—rather than, say, office—as a universal media of exchange.

POWER, FAME, AND GLORY: THE FRENCH DEFINITIONS OF SUCCESS

If the French attach less importance to money than Americans do, they seem to be more openly interested in power. A human resource consultant, whose job consists in helping French executives to deal with intra-organizational conflicts, provides us with a revealing description of the French attraction to power:

> What interests most French businessmen is power. I think this is characteristic of the French, this taste for power . . . The French businessman adores power, and prefers power to money, which does not mean that he does not like money, but that he likes power above all. It is sure that a French businessman would prefer to be ruined than to lose all

influence . . . Power is so much more invigorating. It is so much more fun to believe in, so much more romantic, so much more exciting . . . The idea of money does not replace emotions, pleasure, the Don Quixote side. It is much more fun to believe that you are the boss, that you have charisma. It's enlivening. It has to do with emotion, with passion . . . with romanticism. It gives you pleasure, sensations. What sensations can a growth index give you? To be in charge is so much more exciting.

A similar description is offered by the *banquier* Dutoît who, comparing French and American businessmen, also talks vividly about the role that power and money play in both groups.

What I lack is a sense of money. I am not a "moneymaker." This is typically French. The Frenchman likes to talk . . . He wants to grow personally . . . He has a strong sense of social responsibility. He wants power . . . but when it comes to business, to money—you can see it in the political speeches, in the mass media—we don't have a gut feeling for it . . . The Frenchmen are all a little bit like me . . . In France, the predominant philosophy or culture is much more: I am powerful, I am strong, I have connections, I can decide what will happen in my firm, I am well known in the Parisian microcosm, I make a good living . . . I think that 90 percent of the managers here are happy with this sort of thing. In contrast, you have the [American] managers who only think about profit, who buy, who sell, who fire . . . The [French] manager wants power, not money, or business profits.[25]

The type of power-obsessed French executive these two men are depicting is incarnated in Charles Dutour, the hospital administrator whom we encountered at the beginning of the book. Again, when asked if he likes power, he says:

I don't think that it is possible to say that we don't like power. If we did not like power, we would not be here. There are two types of people: those who are there to give orders, and those who are there to obey. I am of those who like power. Power is also independence . . . Power is when you can decide, direct, we feel better.

Similarly, a tough-minded academic administrator talked about his *volonté de puissance* (will for power), of the fact that as a high civil servant he exercises "a real power on events, on people, on situations" which gives him "the feeling of really existing, the feeling of finding ones' own justification or purpose in life"; also, an insurance executive described the

fascination exerted on him by the president of his company because of the way he wielded authority in the firm. For these men, power and glory often become one, the two faces of a single coin, for power gives them a sense of *grandeur* (greatness) and prestige. Power being greatly valued, it is more likely to be used to draw boundaries.

Both private- and public-sector managers participate in this power-centered culture, the national elite being above all a select group of technocrats for whom powerful and prestigious positions are the measure of success and to whom even top-ranking businessmen remain in many ways subordinate.[26] This fascination with power can be linked to a tradition of military leadership that until relatively recent times was still somewhat influential in the educational program of the "grandes écoles." These schools used to socialize their students into a romantic view of leadership, so that they saw themselves as charismatic men of action able to gain the loyalty of their subordinates. They had to "learn how to punish," to "serve and command," to "gain the sympathy of [their] men by [their] manner," to "look [their] men directly in the eye" and "impress them . . . with the force of [their] mind and will." They were also supposed to "give the impression of physical superiority" that can be achieved through gymnastics and sports, and, in short, to possess the "virile qualities that make an officer: frankness, a firm sense of reality, courage, tenacity, and dedication to his work."[27]

The fascination of power also can be related to the structure of the traditional French firm, with its "centralized authority, . . . [its] sharp divisions between strata and operating units, [and its] conservative and cautious management at [the] low levels."[28] Here administrators are trained to manage organizations, "their primary concern [being] hierarchy, leadership, the division of authority and work discipline."[29] We are worlds apart from more democratic models of human managements such as Theory Z and "quality circles" (i.e., Japanese-style work groups that contribute to decision making that are popular in America). But as shown by Luc Boltanski in *Les cadres*, the last thirty years have seen a marked shift toward more participatory types of management in the "human relations" tradition. The younger generation of managers is less explicitly concerned with power. Many of them say that they are interested in it only because it is the condition of their own independence. Others, coming from a radical or socialist perspective, are openly critical of the authoritarian model and support the concept of self-management by the workers.

In this context it is interesting to note that the French paradoxically

attribute less legitimacy to authority than Americans do. For instance, André Laurent found that, compared to managers from a number of other industrial societies, the French were significantly more likely to believe that "managers are motivated by gains of power—rather than by achieving objectives" (France, 56 percent; United States, 36 percent).[30] It is not surprising then that 26 percent of the upper-middle-class Frenchmen interviewed in the European values/CARA surveys declared that an increase in respect for authority would be a bad thing for society. Only 7 percent of the Americans shared this opinion.

We know from organizational studies that American corporate managers are also interested in consolidating their power and that they are often involved in corporate politics, in chains of loyalty which make or break careers, and in zero-sum games for influence.[31] They are less likely to talk openly about their will of power than the French, however, and more likely to emphasize teamwork. This is exactly the attitude of a New York chief financial officer who has two hundred people working under/ with him:

> I don't think of power in the sense of "having power." I think that in our profession, our power is as a group, as a team. If I'm a boss of something, I don't necessarily have any more power than somebody who's much more junior than I am. I think the power depends on what you do, not on the hierarchy of our business. I firmly believe that. I don't think in the sense of how you described it at all [i.e., "having power"].

The debonaire but commanding vice-president of an Indianapolis insurance company shares these views. I met him in his huge office located on the top floor of a large building where close to a thousand people work under his authority:

> I have never confused myself and my job. I exercise the power because it's my responsibility, and I have accepted that responsibility. I don't own that power. It does not come from me. In large measure all it is is power to enable others to exercise power. Who I am is the guy who happens to have this task that others have asked me to assume and I've agreed to take . . . It does not make me any better. It doesn't make me any different. It just puts me in a position where you are dealing with different responsibilities.

We see how some American individuals go out of their way to explain that they do not think of themselves as innately superior to others, and to dissociate power as an organizational prerequisite from charismatic or

personal power, as if these latter forms of power were illegitimate, or as if there was a stigma attached to the overt expression of these views. As suggested by Zussman, American upper-middle-class men see power less as a means of constraining others than as a resource for assisting others to get the job done; the engineers he interviewed perceive their boss less as exercising power than as offering assistance. For them, specialized competence ensures a rational use of authority.[32] But this does not mean that Americans rarely draw socioeconomic boundaries on the basis of power. A man such as Lee Iacocca is admired for his power as well as for his financial success. Maybe in contrast to the French, however, Americans might be more likely to reject powerful figures who have no claim to moral purity (i.e., to egalitarianism) and who are openly self-serving and self-aggrandizing. This might be a way of maintaining equality at the symbolic level in order to counterbalance the highly competitive nature of American society.

VARIATIONS ON THE INNER CIRCLE

Membership in prestigious groups and associations constitutes a third type of standard beyond money and power on the basis of which socioeconomic boundaries are often drawn. Belonging to such groups and associations provides information on socioeconomic status to the extent that it signals the fact that one has achieved a certain income level, that one is committed to its accompanying lifestyle, and that one has been accepted by the "right kinds of people." A description of people who use such memberships to draw socioeconomic boundaries is provided by an Indianapolis lawyer who discusses some of his acquaintances:

> Those people tend to choose their friends whether they belong to the Woodstock Country Club or the Marines Country Club and the amount of income. They tend to shun those of us who have a lower economic and social strata . . . They judge people by their material possessions, whether they conform, whether they are members of the right culture, the right political parties. Blacks are excluded. They would not allow their sister to date a Jew, because they are good Christians and very WASPy.

The interviews did not reveal clear cross-national differences concerning the frequency at which participation in prestigious organizations is used in boundary work. The Hoosiers and the Clermontois, however, seem to be slightly more invested in such organizations than the New

Yorkers and Parisians. Hoosiers engage in a particularly elaborate discourse on the importance in their lives of these organizations, which provide both an arena of interaction for the local elite and an avenue for social integration. An Indianapolis insider explains how it works:

> [People who are new in town] can get a lot of contacts with their church or through their banks. Your loan officer of the bank, he can help you out, he can put you in the right spots. Get the sense of who's who and who isn't through the Chamber of Commerce. You can't be pushy . . . Go to the Chamber and help out on this and help out on that and different drives . . . You don't just go in and try to take over . . . That's not kosher . . . They'll look at you, and they won't just rush you right through because they like the way you comb your hair.

Another informant describes the situation in similar terms:

> [When you move into town] you've got to work at it. You join the clubs, you join the church. My wife was a member of the Junior League; that helps. [People join] because they may have political ambitions. The ladies like to be president of this and that, the auxiliaries. It's an honor to be senior warden of your church; I was junior warden. My wife is really religious, she has been active there . . . Here it's the Bible Belt, and that also is a social deal. We happen to be Episcopalian. You know, they have parties, you make friends. My wife works on the altar now, the altar guild.

The churches, the Chamber of Commerce, the political parties, the alumni associations of the two most renowned universities in Indiana (Indiana University and Purdue University) are the theaters of action for the local elite. There is also a wide range of committees in which one can get involved, such as the committee "to raise money to make the Hoosier Dome, the Committee for Downtown, the committee to put Christmas decorations on Monument Circle, the hospital, people on business boards, etc." This profusion of organizations has to do with the fact that Indianapolis is small enough for the elite to constitute a self-conscious community which identifies itself with the city as a whole. As a realtor who is a member of the local elite expresses it, "The success or failure of the community is a direct reflection on you and on your life." The upper-middle class, "instead of opting out like they do in New York and mov[ing] on to the suburbs," has stayed in and "invested in the town" (marketing executive, Indianapolis).[33] This partly explains why membership in high-status groups is likely to be more salient in the drawing of

socioeconomic boundaries in Indianapolis than in New York. In contrast, New Yorkers seem to give to the "community" a narrower meaning that has less to do with collective life and more with the collective protection of real estate values. This is suggested by a young homeowner, a New York machine tool salesman who was asked if he cares about the community:

> I really do. It bothers me when people don't take care of their things, throw garbage all over the place . . . I want the place to look good. But I also want to be able to go away weekends and not spend all my money on my house. People who don't take care of their house are short-sighted.

Along the same lines, some New Yorkers seem to more often evaluate their community in terms of economic costs and benefits to themselves rather than in terms of a shared communal identity. As stated by the proprietor of a radio station:

> New Providence is a place where you can take advantage of all the services they have and not get affected by the politics . . . I can hide here. I can take advantage that I'm a mile from the shopping centers; I'm a short distance from New York City; my taxes are low; my services are high. I've got gas heat; I've got city water.

In the context of an anonymous community, level of income appears to be the predominant basis for socioeconomic boundaries, high status circles playing less and less of a role. As shown in Chapter 2, however, some New York interviewees do become involved in religious or other organizations to provide a community for their families and to counter a strong feeling of isolation.[34]

Clermont resembles Indianapolis because prestigious circles play similar roles in these communities. In both cases, the local elite is relatively small and has very dense social networks. Many respondents say that they know "everyone in town." As explained by a Clermont lawyer whose own family has been living in the area for a few generations:

> The circles are always interrelated . . . You don't need to know many people [and you] always see the same ones . . . We have been asked to participate in certain things, and we did not refuse, because we were asked. There is the Rotary Club, and little by little we have taken responsibilities in that. From then on, we are received, we have to represent the club, do this, do that, and then you find various circles, with

people who we already know. Quickly you discover that you know who everyone is.

Given such intertwined networks, membership in high status organizations is likely to have a stronger impact on the assessment of socioeconomic status than in areas where the population is more atomized.[35] Indeed, Clermontois attach a particular status to involvement in administrative and political committees in which the "notables" interact.[36] And they tend to identify strongly with their town, even though they have very sparse contacts with their neighbors.[37] In contrast to the Indianapolis elite, however, the Clermont elite seems to be less open, integration being regulated by old and relatively exclusive bourgeois families. Social clubs and fraternal organizations themselves are less important, maybe partly as the result of the lower rate of geographic mobility and greater family stability characteristic of French society (one out of six marriages ends in divorce in France, compared to one in three in the United States).

Finally, it is important to note that both in Clermont-Ferrand and Paris, much value is attached to social and family *relations* (connections), which play an essential role in getting access to jobs and to a wide range of resources, as clientelism is widespread and is, in many ways, a constitutive characteristic of the French administrative system. Several individuals mentioned how often they are asked to do or to return favors—i.e., to *renvoyer l'ascenseur*.[38] A hotel manager provides an example. Between several phone conversations with vegetable grocers, he explained to me:

> In my family, I have a high[-ranking] civil servant. Everyone knows it; it is an uncle. People ask me to talk to him to get things done. It goes from a speeding ticket to other more important things. I also grade exams for a local professional school. People ask me to get their kids in the school, because people know who I am. I really like to help others. It is my nature.

High status associations, and particularly the *associations des anciens* of the *grandes écoles*, play an important role in delimiting networks of support and clientelism. The same role is played in the United States by the alumni associations.

CLASS, RACE, GENDER, AND ETHNICITY

With a few exceptions American respondents almost never referred to class, race, gender, and ethnicity when asked about their feelings of in-

feriority and superiority. If people refer to these socioeconomic status or ascribed characteristics, they do so for the most part indirectly, by mentioning qualities often attributed to specific groups. For example, they might express their dislike for lower-class people (including lower-middle-class blacks or Hispanics) by talking about "lazy people who live in the inner city" (human service manager, Indianapolis). It is quite hazardous, however, to pinpoint euphemized expressions of race, class, or gender exclusion because by definition the latter are generally ambiguous.

Let's first consider class and occupation. In general, the American men I talked with downplayed the importance of these dimensions of their own and others' identity.[39] For instance, they often offered disclaimers of their own elite status, asserting that they are "ordinary Joes" despite their sometimes extraordinary professional power and success.[40] Overall, the norm that guides them seems to be one of egalitarianism and universalism, according to which it is illegitimate to explicitly take into consideration class,[41] or occupation when interacting with others.[42] Therefore, several men emphasize that they regard all types of work to be symbolically equal. As the Scarsdale science teacher who takes on various jobs during the summer vacations explains, "I have never in my entire life felt that any job was beneath me. I have done lots and lots and lots of things, and nothing, absolutely nothing I can imagine is beneath me. A job is a job, as long as you're doing something that is honest."

This egalitarianism is also stressed in relations with employees: a number of respondents consider it illegitimate to expect deference from subordinates. An Indianapolis plant manager who is very critical of his authoritarian boss puts it this way: "I'll work with him; I'll do the best of my abilities; but I'll be damned if I'm going to be subservient to him." Conversely, French sociologists have found that American managers attach less importance to subordination (i.e., loyalty and a sense of dependency) than do their French counterparts.[43] The chief financial executive of a multinational firm based in Indianapolis sums it up: "I figure anybody that I talk to, I'm equal with. It's critical in my lifestyle that I never put myself above anybody. I don't care who they are, because it's not up to me to do the judging." This explicit denial of class and occupational differences seems ritualistic when juxtaposed to the great salience of money and success-based socioeconomic boundaries in the interviews, and with the fact that, when probed, participants confess they feel inferior to people who are more successful or wealthy than they and superior to people who are less so.

The silence concerning racial differences when the American interviewees discussed feelings of superiority and inferiority is particularly striking given the high level of racial discrimination that prevails in American society. A number of explanations could account for why our interviewees explicitly downplay not only race but also class and ethnicity in the drawing of socioeconomic boundaries. First, it is possible that these factors have such a strong effect on choice of friends that interviewees simply take them for granted, the relevant traits remaining nonsalient at the discursive level.[44] Indeed, it appears that the interviewees' universe of reference mostly consists of people they come in contact with frequently, i.e., most likely white, middle- and upper-middle-class people like themselves.[45] In general, they omit to mention those with whom they have few contacts, i.e., those who are vaguely conceived of as "the other."[46] Hence, their discourse seems to focus on the finer categories of the classification system, ignoring the outer edges.[47]

Second, racially prejudiced interviewees might censor themselves in the interview situation, recognizing their attitudes as unacceptable to the general ethos of our time. Or else they might simply be open-minded: a college education is, by most indicators, positively correlated with tolerance.[48] Furthermore, because many respondents work in large organizations, they might be acquainted with a wide range of people, a situation that tends to generate more tolerance.[49] Finally, the nonsalience of ethnic and class differences in discussions of feelings of inferiority and superiority can be in part explained by the fact that the importance of these memberships are decreasing in America.[50]

It is interesting to note that while males never mentioned females when probed on feelings of inferiority and superiority, female professionals and managers often discussed males.[51] This finding supports the view that symbolic boundaries are experienced differently by individuals depending on the side of the divide they stand on.[52] It also leads me to believe that in interview situations members of racial minorities would be more likely than white people to point at race and ethnicity in their discussions of feelings of inferiority and superiority, these ascribed characteristics being more salient in their own identity.[53] The same mechanisms might explain why, while whites often think that blacks exaggerate the level of racism that prevails in their environment, blacks experience a wide range of situations as discriminatory.[54] We need more empirical studies of the mechanisms by which the same symbolic boundaries come to be perceived differently by the excluded and the excluders.

If the French interviewees are reluctant to draw socioeconomic boundaries on the basis of differences in income, in contrast to Americans they very readily use occupation or class, or class background, to distinguish themselves from others; this fits with the fact that in general the French are more aware of class identity than Americans are.[55] Some talk openly about their disdain for lower-prestige occupations—*boutiquiers*, policemen, butchers—as we will see in Chapter 6. They are also much more likely to think of themselves as part of an elite. This elitist orientation was expressed in a telling way in one of the interviews. The Parisian lawyer who hates having to collect his bills explains how he raised his kids:

> We tried to make them understand that they are part of the privileged class: they have had the opportunity to acquire a certain culture . . . The fact of being the elite for me means to be responsible, because of their knowledge and general culture. They have a mission on earth, a function . . . We have a responsibility toward those who have fewer advantages, to make them free men, more free than they are at the beginning. For me this is what it means to be the elite.

This consciousness of class differences extends to the interviewees' perception of their own class position. When describing their personal social trajectory, the French are more likely to emphasize limits that structural factors have put on their mobility[56] than Americans are.[57] This leads us to believe that class might be more salient as a dimension of the identity of French upper-middle-class men than it is for their American counterpart.

While the French debates on immigration and citizenship that concerned the integration of Arab workers into French society were at a peak at the time I conducted the French interviews, it is interesting to note that only two of the men I talked with mentioned race in discussions of feelings of inferiority and superiority. As was the case in the United States, race, like ethnicity, remained nonsalient in discussions of signals of high status. When juxtaposed with the omnipresence of racial and ethnic discrimination in both societies, this nonsalience suggests the importance of studying how objective boundaries result from subjective boundaries. More attention needs to be given to the process by which institutional discrimination is indirectly produced by the way various classes relate to ethnic and racial minorities, including the conspicuous ignorance of, or indifference to, ethnic and racial differences evinced

by my interviewees. Again, it is possible that the subjective boundaries drawn by the men I talked with are only informative of the internal boundaries that they draw within the upper-middle class itself, and cannot account for the processes of exclusion across classes. Unfortunately, the exploration of these questions remains beyond the reach of my study, as is the exploration of how members of ethnic and racial minorities do themselves draw boundaries against/with upper-middle-class white males.

ANTISOCIOECONOMIC BOUNDARIES

Several of the individuals I interviewed criticize people "who believe that they are more of a man than you because they are richer . . . who try to diminish you because they have their big car, their wallet, their house, their clothes" (philosophy professor, Clermont-Ferrand). They also criticize those involved in the "wine and cheese circuit" (minister, New York) and who only care about their status and prestige. In other words, they oppose those who draw socioeconomic boundaries, neglecting the moral dimension of life. This suggests that symbolic boundaries also can operate in a negative or reverse way.

Philip Buxton, a research scientist who works for the Lilly Pharmaceutical Company in Indianapolis, is the ideal typical "antisocioeconomic excluder." He explains that he likes his neighbors because they never make reference to social status in their conversation:

> I like their honesty. They are not pretentious. You know, you just go over and drink a beer with them, talk about football, and this and that, just anything. There's no different airs, no ranking. [I don't like people] who are going to make up their mind on what kind of relationship they are going to have with you depending on what you do, where you rank in society, how much money you make, what kind of person you are. It'd be better just to chat, get to know the person. Doesn't matter what you do for an occupation. It should just pertain to personality, pertain to your heart, your values. Occupation should be secondary, to get you by in life.

Philip's wife, Jane, agrees. She says:

> We probably lived here a year and [our neighbors] never asked us "What do you do?" We didn't know what Don did, where he worked, he didn't know where Phil worked . . . We lived here a long time before we even knew, and we didn't care. And it was so nice, and we'd just sit out in the

yard and have a beer together and talk. We never talked about money. Phil never talked about his job. It was never a Reagan-type thing: they'll see where you rank and see where we rank and we'll see. Throw all that stuff behind me. Be real! . . . At my son's school, people seem very competitive, very rank-oriented. They say, "What do you do?" and "How many sports is your child involved in?" and "How many extra-curricular activities is he doing?" That is a real problem, and I really dislike that.

Many condemn those who select on the basis of socioeconomic factors, whose success has taken them away from "real" human values. This opposition to socioeconomic boundaries on moral grounds was frequently voiced by Indianapolis respondents: again for several Hoosiers, it seems, worldly success needs to be accompanied by humility and egalitarianism if it is to serve as a proof of purity (see n. 64 below). This is particularly evident in their discussions of the Easterners: many Indianapolis residents expressed strong criticisms of New Yorkers whom they perceive as social climbers, "abrasive, uncaring, unfeeling—it's great to do business with you, but don't get in my way" (staff assistant, Indianapolis). Some disapproved of Easterners in general because of their excessive concern for "where you did your prep, what are your family ties, where do you stand on the ladder" (psychologist, Indianapolis). In general, the Midwesterners who reject the socioeconomic exclusiveness of New York emphasize the moral advantages of Indianapolis the same way New Yorkers criticize the cultural backwardness of the Hoosiers while emphasizing their own cosmopolitanism (see Chap. 4).[58] On the other hand, both the Hoosiers and the New Yorkers draw antisocioeconomic boundaries against the French, whom they view as too elitist and class-oriented, relating these attitudes to France's feudal past.

Overall, the French draw slightly stronger antisocioeconomic boundaries than Americans do.[59] They also often draw antisocioeconomic boundaries against the citizens of the United States, perceiving them as too materialistic and success-oriented.[60] They view America as the land of socioeconomic exclusion par excellence, as stated by this senior executive who has over two thousand people working under him:

> The United States is one of the few countries where I would not like to live. It is aseptic, and people are not interesting. They are only interested in status: the size of the car, of the house . . . In America, besides money there isn't much. I'd rather live in Mexico.

Along the same lines, a wealthy Versailles dentist says:

> The Americans are too attached to external appearance. They are interested in success, in how much money they have in the bank, in the car, the social rank. I think this is all very superficial . . . The American runs around so much after his ideal house, the car, that I think that he misses a lot of important things. He does not live much. There are a great many things that he does not see, which is really very sad . . . He misses a lot of people, a lot of things that are more interesting than having a big house, a big car and lots of jewels.[61]

The anti-Americanism qua antisocioeconomic boundaries of the French is often expressed under the cover of cultural, rather than moral, exclusion, as we will see in Chapter 4. This anti-Americanism, however, has become less predominant in the last few years. Indeed, a recent survey showed that, in 1984, 44 percent of the French population had positive feelings toward the United States, while 15 percent had negative feelings.[62] Today, this kind of anti-Americanism is confined mainly to certain segments of the intellectual elite.[63]

The findings concerning the anti-Americanism of the French and the American perceptions that the French are too elitist suggest that differences in patterns of boundary work across groups might partly explain regionalist, ethnocentric, or even racist feelings. Indeed, the rationale behind the negative reactions that the French and the Americans have toward one another correspond to differences in boundary work as documented in this study. For instance, while the French interviewees stress money less in their boundary work, they criticize Americans for being too materialistic. Therefore, differences in boundary patterns might help develop a better explanation of regionalist feelings and ethnocentric views: we can relate these to differences in shared cultural repertoires between groups rather than to individual psychological tendencies, moral failure, or ignorance.

CONCLUSION

We see that socioeconomic boundaries are important for many interviewees but less so for the French than for Americans, and essentially equally so for residents of cultural centers and cultural peripheries. Just as the French and the American interviewees stress different aspects of morality in evaluating moral status, these two groups do not value the same signals of socioeconomic status—the French stress power more

than Americans do, while Americans put more emphasis on success and money.

Analyzing the specific combination between types of symbolic boundaries across groups helps us understand the cultural outlook of each sites. For instance, evidence suggests that moral and socioeconomic boundaries are less autonomous from one another in the United States than they are in France: for Americans, and for Hoosiers in particular who draw stronger moral boundaries than their New York counterparts do,[64] only when accompanied by moral purity is socioeconomic success admired.[65] Therefore, if Americans attach great importance to success-related traits such as ambition, dynamism, a strong work ethic, and competitiveness, it might be because these traits are doubly sacred because they are read as signals of both moral and socioeconomic purity. By contrast it seems that in France moral status is not as directly read from social status.[66] Consequently, the French who are not "successful" in worldly terms might have more of a sense of personal worth, while those who are "successful" might have a less self-righteous and meritocratic view of their social position, with important political consequences for their support for welfare programs, for instance. On the other hand, socioeconomic status might be more easily converted into moral status in the United States than in France. Only by distinguishing between the three types of boundaries and by analyzing the nature of their dynamic comparatively is it possible to reach such conclusions.

In the United States, the social consensus on the importance of socioeconomic boundaries might be wider than that concerning cultural and moral boundaries: research shows that American working-class people often adopt dominant definitions of success that stress material achievement.[67] However, more research is needed on cross-national differences in the degree of influence that the signals stressed by the upper-middle class have on other classes. This might provide useful information on the degree of cultural autonomy of the lower and lower-middle classes toward the upper-middle class and on national differences in interclass dynamics.

Chapter 2 indicated that entrepreneurialism has become more popular in France over the last ten years. National trends would suggest that socioeconomic boundaries are likely to become increasingly influential in France and America as these societies become less differentiated. The growing importance of socioeconomic status is linked to the fact that it is more readily signaled than moral or cultural status: the durable consumer goods that we consume on a daily basis provide immediate infor-

mation about where we stand on the income scale. In contrast, cultural and, to a greater extent, moral status can be estimated only over time, information obtained through social networks playing an essential role in facilitating cultural and moral status assessment. Socioeconomic boundaries are particularly likely to gain in importance where geographic mobility is increasing. Their influence especially also will grow in cultural centers where more anonymous relationships prevail due to the size of the population.[68]

Analyzing the content that socioeconomic boundaries take in France and the United States leads us to rethink some of the images that Americans have of the French and vice versa. According to the popular wisdom that prevails on this side of the Atlantic, the French are more elitist than Americans. The picture that emerges from the preceding pages is more paradoxical: in some respects the French are less concerned with social position in general, and with financial success in particular, than Americans. Consequently, they could be viewed as less elitist. At the discursive level, however, Americans are less likely to draw socioeconomic boundaries on the basis of social background or occupation. If the French are very critical of individuals who overvalue success and wealth, they are more readily exclusive toward nonelite individuals who do not have the proper background or the right type of occupation. Therefore, if the French are more socioeconomically exclusive on some dimensions, Americans are more so on others. Rather than adopting popular categories that describe the French as more elitist than Americans, social scientists need to disentangle the dimensions of socioeconomic exclusion to obtain a more detailed and specific picture of national differences.

It should be noted that the findings concerning the greater stress that Americans put on success, achievement, and material possessions is consistent with much of the literature on the American national character. Indeed, classics such as Lipset's *The First New Nation* and Tocqueville's *Democracy in America* point to these very same characteristics. Lipset also discusses American universalism and egalitarianism which for our interviewees translates into the fact that Americans almost never draw boundaries on the basis of class.

The patterns of socioeconomic boundary work identified here are indicative of important differences in national cultural patterns in France and the United States. While studies of national character have been criticized for their essentialism, however, the present research suggests that the differences that have been identified are structural or supra-

individual because, again, they are linked to the existence of inter-subjective symbolic boundaries. Particular national characters can now be understood as specific patterns of symbolic boundaries and as historically constituted national repertoires that members of societies draw upon with more or less frequency. Stark national differences in such patterns also will emerge when we examine the boundary work of the French and American upper-middle classes in the areas of high culture, refinement, intellectuality, and cosmopolitanism.

Chapter Four

≈≈

MOST OF MY FRIENDS ARE REFINED:
KEYS TO CULTURAL BOUNDARIES

> Toute notre dignité consiste en la pensée.
> —Pascal
> *Our whole sense of dignity consists of our thought.*

AGAINST THE PHILISTINES

Julien Lafitte is a young scientist, born in Nice, who is studying the volcanos that surround Clermont-Ferrand. His parents are psychologists and lifetime militants in the French Communist party. He left Nice to pursue his graduate work in Bordeaux and has been working in Clermont for six years. He is vaguely punk-looking but carries himself with style.

Like Didier, John, and Lou encountered at the beginning of this book, Julien highly values the aesthetic dimension of life. He expresses great contempt for his culturally narrow scientific colleagues. He is easily bored and has no patience for people with poor taste. He selects his friends with great care; he wants to share intellectual experiences and political discussions with them. He cannot fathom being friends with a right-winger. This is partly why he does not get along with his research director, whom he depicts as radically different from himself: this director is interested in money, likes light opera and commercial movies, and has "no artistic culture."

Julien feels superior to people who "watch television everyday, everyday, everyday," and to conformists "who would never take a position in politics, who always talk about money, who would take their vacation in August at the beach, who would change their car every two years . . . who have no personal ideas, who would never say what they think of a movie, a record, a play, an exposition. They never express an idea, they are afraid to say what they think."

Julien is an ideal typical cultural excludor. Those who, like him, draw strong cultural boundaries evaluate status on the basis of intelligence, education, cosmopolitanism, and refinement. They feel superior

to "narrow-minded people who don't bother to pick up a newspaper, . . . who have nothing better to talk about than what the kids are doing and how their golf game is going" (lawyer, Indianapolis), to people who are "not intellectually my equal" or who "don't use their intellect to its capacity" (data manager, Indianapolis), and to "imbeciles who never think and never ask themselves questions . . . who are satisfied with everything and accept everything indiscriminately" (philosophy professor, Clermont-Ferrand). Like Julien, when discussing the qualities they appreciate in their friends, these people point less to their honesty or worldly success than to the fact that they have interesting minds, cosmopolitan views, and refined tastes. They appreciate things that ignite their curiosity and creativity, and they might even define success as "staying intellectually alive" (computer specialist, Indianapolis).

Interviews suggest that culture is central to French and American definitions of high status signals. The quantitative rankings of interviewees on the cultural dimension, however, reveal that cultural boundaries are slightly less important for the American men I talked to than for the French.[1] This pattern is reflected in the qualities that both groups select when shown a list of twenty-three character traits and asked which one they value most. Twenty-four percent of the French and only 6 percent of the Americans believe that being intellectually challenging is the most valuable trait on this list; showing a similar disparity, 22 percent of the French and only 6 percent of the Americans rank narrow-mindedness as one of the most negative traits one could have. Finally, a full 52 percent of the Americans describe cosmopolitanism as a quality that leaves them indifferent, in contrast to only 30 percent for the French. This is consequential because the American literature on cultural capital considers signals of high cultural status to be very central to American upper-middle-class culture.[2] My data suggest that this view needs to be nuanced: a sizable number of American professionals and managers are fairly critical of intellectualism, cosmopolitanism, and other signals of high cultural status.

The first sections of this chapter explore how intelligence, self-actualization, and cultural sophistication are defined by members of the French and the American upper-middle class, and how these dimensions are used in their discourse on status assessment. We will again identify important differences in the signals of high cultural status that French and American upper-middle-class men use—these groups mobilize different standards to evaluate intelligence and sophistication, while Americans

stress self-actualization more than the French do. We will also see that the range of high cultural status signals that most individuals mobilize is much broader than had been originally suggested by the literature. Indeed, whereas work on cultural capital stresses the importance of linguistic competence, command of high culture, and the display of cultivated dispositions, the interviews reveal that level of education, intelligence, and self-actualization also play a central role in the assessment of cultural status.

In the latter part of the chapter, characteristics of French and American cultural boundaries are analyzed by a comparison of their respective strengths and through differences in intellectual subcultures. Data suggest that the intellectual subculture is more cohesive in France than it is in the United States, which provides further evidence of the importance of cultural boundaries in France. Also, French and American cultural boundaries have different formal structures: French boundaries are more stable, more universal and more hierarchical, while American boundaries are weaker. Having a broader cultural repertoire than the French, Americans are more culturally tolerant and show more cultural laissez-faire, as the distinctions they make between "good" and "bad" tastes are less specific, more blurred, and less stable. This confirms the lesser importance of cultural boundaries in the American context. It also shows that French and American cultural boundaries differ in form as well as in content. As the last chapter will suggest, the cultural boundaries Americans draw at the discursive level are, therefore, less likely to translate into objective socioeconomic boundaries than those drawn by the French. But first I discuss the type of signals that are used to draw cultural boundaries in both countries.

CULTURAL EXCLUSION, BRILLIANCE, EXPERTISE, AND OTHER FORMS OF INTELLIGENCE

Given the importance that college education and expert knowledge play in defining the identity of members of the upper-middle class, it is not surprising that differences in level of education and intelligence are two of the most common bases on which my French and American respondents draw cultural boundaries. In fact, many people, including men who do not define themselves as culturally sophisticated, put a premium on intelligence when discussing the types of people with whom they want to

interact. Time and time again, they portray their friends and favorite coworkers as bright and intellectually stimulating. They describe the types of people they are interested in as people who "have a certain intellectual level" (lawyer, New York), and who "think well, or try to think well, rigorously, logically, with continuity. They are superior to those who think in a discontinuous way or who refuse to think" (literature professor, Paris). These groups also put a premium on higher education, which is the most important barrier to upper-middle-class status both in terms of access to job and of social integration,[3] as shown by the voluminous literature on educational and status attainment.[4]

The French men I met with appear to be especially concerned with intelligence, for they repeatedly acknowledge finding it very difficult to tolerate stupidity. Again, their diatribes against *la bêtise* reach a level of violence only comparable to American diatribes against incompetence. As Louis Dupont, a Versailles business management specialist, explains, stupidity is the worst sin of all, far worse than dishonesty:

> Thinking and trying to find solutions to problems is one of the greatest pleasures that life offers . . . There are surprising degrees of mediocrity and stupidity. I prefer to have to deal with someone who is devious and intelligent, because at least we will be able to understand each other. If they are devious, it's not my problem. Someone who is stupid leaves me powerless.

This opinion is shared by Julien Lafitte, the physicist encountered earlier in this chapter. For Julien, dishonesty is not as bad as narrow-mindedness because "it is still possible to converse with someone who is dishonest. It is possible to bring him back in the right direction. Whereas there is nothing you can do against someone who is narrow-minded." Not a single American interviewee expressed so clearly a preference for cultural over moral standards of evaluation.

The fact that the French participants are particularly concerned with intelligence is also reflected in their descriptions of their heroes and role-models: great intellectuals—Raymond Aron, Jacques Attali, Jean-Paul Sartre—occupy a place of choice. One of the French individuals I talked with, Jacques Mendel, a museum curator in Clermont-Ferrand, expresses a widely shared feeling when he admits that he often evaluates himself as "inferior to people who strictly at the intellectual level make me feel very small . . . because I think that they have succeeded at what I am trying

to succeed at." Ultimately, for these men, intellectual achievement is the achievement par excellence, beyond the money and the worldly success it can bring. Several features of French society reflect this belief. To take only one example, many top French politicians have written serious political essays; they are quite interested in gaining intellectual respectability and in deriving prestige from their involvement in Parisian intellectual life.[5]

The French and American men I talked with understand intelligence (like honesty) through strongly contrasted cultural categories. The French stress having *un sens critique* (a critical approach), which they take to be a measure of one's analytical power. They also read intelligence through intellectual playfulness, capacity for abstraction, eloquence, and style. In contrast, we saw that the Americans highly value competence. Hence, they largely read intelligence through expertise, attributing great importance to "knowing the facts," and most of all to knowing "relevant," i.e., useful, facts. I discuss these cross-national differences in turn.

In the French Cartesian tradition, knowledge proceeds from the ability to systematically doubt assumptions and accepted truths. Above all, gaining knowledge requires an ability to question authority and seek truth, regardless of personal cost and effort. Therefore, intelligence itself is signaled by the fact of having a *sens critique* and a certain intellectual honesty, i.e., "an absence of conformism, a capacity to appreciate situations and express personal opinions while keeping distance from all social conformisms" (social worker, Paris).[6] Having a *sens critique* is impossible for the boorish types who do not "nuance their thoughts, [who] don't think; they just secure themselves in morality. They know everything, they have understood everything" (lawyer, Paris). Cartesian skepticism—which from this side of the Atlantic might be viewed as indicative of an overcritical predisposition and a lack of flexibility—rarely appeared during American interviews, except in interviews with a few Jewish respondents who frequently had remained close to their European intellectual heritage.

The importance of this *sens critique* and the charismatic (and Promethean) view of the life of the mind it suggests is sustained in part by the philosophical education required for obtaining the *baccalauréat*, a selective terminal high school degree. The private Catholic *lycées*, where a sizable percentage of the upper-middle class send their children, particularly emphasize philosophical training.[7] In this context, students are implicitly

encouraged to approach rhetoric as an intellectual game in which to display intellectual playfulness, suppleness, and rapidity; reasoning capabilities, including one's capacity for abstraction, are crucial, as are articulateness and breadth of reading.[8] On the other hand, mastering facts is not highly valued, for students learn to develop complex arguments on theoretical grounds only. The attitude of Didier Aucour, the architecture professor, exemplifies a reaction to factualism that one often encounters. When asked if it was important to him that he be well-informed, he replies, "I could not care less. Current events are in the order of insignificant, transient knowledge."

"What is not clear is not French," says the dictum. The French intellectual tradition puts a premium on clarity of thought and expression, which are taken to be further signals of intelligence. One of the men reached an apex of lyricism when explaining to me the importance of "the equilibrium between the sentences, the attention paid to the selection of words and to their exact meaning, and to the thoughts on which they fundamentally rest" (human resource consultant, Paris). "Bad grammar reveals vulgarity of thought," I was told on another occasion. Many displayed their participation in the cult of the French language by noting with disapproval a spelling error on a questionnaire I submitted to them.[9] Competing conceptions of what intelligence consists of were also strikingly dramatized by the tone respondents used during the interviews: while the answers of Americans were short and to the point, the answers of the French, and particularly of the Parisians, were considerably more lengthy and more convoluted, richer in details and in self-reflexive comments.

The importance of these various signals of intelligence is reflected in the standards of evaluation used by French teachers. Indeed, style of presentation, accent, and diction have a strong impact on the assessment of the performance of students at all levels. Total mastery of the language is a key to being socially constructed as brilliant, especially given that national standardized aptitude tests are not used in the French educational system.[10]

This stress on eloquence carries over to the sphere of professional interactions, where verbal duels are frequent, just as competition through performance is an everyday occurrence for Americans. Hence, the art of outwitting the opponent is cultivated up to the highest level of sophistication.[11] Such a form of competition has its drawbacks. An old-time Pa-

risian diplomat describes to me the elite members of his administrative department who graduated from the prestigious "Ecole nationale d'administration." He does not hold them in high esteem because

> [t]hey are people who don't know everything, but who are able to talk about everything without knowing the problem. It is really unpleasant. You put them in front of a situation they don't know, and they'll talk about it as if they did.

In this context, expertise is not necessarily the key to becoming socially constructed as brilliant.[12] We saw that even in engineering schools specialized competence is not highly valued, as the most prestigious of these schools pride themselves on providing their students with a general method of analysis, a set of theoretical tools, that allows them to move freely from one problem to the next.[13] In recent years, many changes stressing specialization have been introduced into the curriculum of institutions of higher learning. Nevertheless, the Cartesian intellectual tradition seems to continue to influence the cultural categories through which the French understand and perceive intelligence. For instance, in the French workplace cultural resources such as the ability to express oneself abstractly with elegance are essential to success, cultural boundaries themselves playing an important role in the reproduction of inequality. These high status signals partly take the place occupied by honesty, friendliness, and conflict avoidance in the American workplace, making culture overall more important than morality for achievement. This is reinforced because the moral humanism, which is highly valued in the French workplace, is itself indissociable from humanistic culture itself, i.e., from cultural status signals.

The categories through which the French define intelligence are still strongly contrasted with the ones Americans use, the latter being largely organized around the mastery of facts and around practical knowledge. We saw that Americans admire competence. Consequently, they read intelligence largely through one's capacity to present, organize, and analyze specific facts in a coherent and clearly workable, if not necessarily elegant, way. This factualism emerges when the Americans discuss feelings of inferiority, as exemplified by this statement made by Craig Neil, the owner of the Long Island car leasing business:

> Somebody that knows an area that I am not familiar with makes me feel uncomfortable. If I sat down and had a long lengthy conversation, for example, with a stockbroker, I probably would feel uncomfortable be-

cause I don't know a thing about the stock brokerage business. If somebody sat down with me and started talking architectural design, I would
feel uncomfortable because I don't know a thing about architectural
design.

Expertise both opens and closes boundaries. Indeed, it can signal
superiority and can thus make others "feel uncomfortable." On the other
hand, the American men I talked with often define people they find interesting as having "a wealth of information"; they are "not necessarily
intellectually stimulating, but stimulating; they know things about what
they do, where they've been, who they've seen, how they fit into society"
(environment specialist, New York). The line dividing "us" and "them" is
less a *sens critique* and proper diction than the mastery of broad information
about the world. As explained by an Indianapolis recruitment specialist,

> It bothers me if somebody is not worldly enough to know much about
> history, geography, or current events. I don't even say that a person has
> to know a lot about sports. It helps, it helps, if they don't have any of
> those other things . . . I've got a good friend who's a neighbor, who
> doesn't know a lot about sports—he fell asleep during the I.U. [Indiana
> University] national championship game last year. I still like him be-
> cause he knows current events and he knows history pretty well. That's
> two out of three, or out of four.

The appreciation of expertise characteristic of American upper-
middle-class culture is revealed in the types of reading the American
participants say they do. More than the French, they are interested in
magazines and trade publications that help them keep up with recent
developments in their specialized areas of interest and to make informed
purchasing decisions. The reading tastes of this New York recreation specialist are representative of that of a number of American men: "[I] love
to read . . . sports magazines, clothing catalogues, housing catalogues;
you know, it's about housing, real estate, mortgaging, etc. For pleasure, I
like an occasional documentary book, an autobiography." *Consumer Reports, Car and Driver, Sports Illustrated,* and sundry computer magazines are
frequently mentioned publications, along with professional and current
events magazines. John Craig, the burned-out New York marketing specialist in the last chapter, described the reading habits of many as he
explained when and why his wife takes on a book: "She reads when something motivates her, when she needs to find out something. Like, her
mother is very ill and is under hospice care now, and she's reading a book

on hospices and what it's really all about." A questionnaire on leisure-time activities which was administered after the interviews revealed that a larger percentage of the French than of the American interviewees define themselves as frequent book readers (72 percent of the Clermontois and 77 percent of the Parisians, in contrast to 44 percent of the New Yorkers and 58 percent of the Hoosiers).[14]

This appreciation for information sometimes goes hand in hand with a quantitative approach to knowledge that underscores the number of books read and facts known. The popularity of this approach is revealed, for instance, by the high circulation of magazines such as *Reader's Digest*, of television game shows like "Jeopardy," and of party games such as "Trivial Pursuit." Of course, a large number of Americans do not partake of this quantitative factualism. It does, however, remain a distinctive feature of the American cultural landscape that is absent from the French;[15] the way the French focus on abstraction and diction is of comparatively little significance for Americans.[16]

I suggested above that the American men I talked with also have a more practical view of intelligence than the French. This is revealed, for instance, when Americans are probed on their heroes and role models: those who mention "great minds" are more likely to bring up a brilliant entrepreneur (à la Dr. Wang) than a pure intellectual (à la Jean-Paul Sartre). We will see, however, that there exists important variations across professions in this respect.

The reasons Hoosiers and New Yorkers put a premium on practical intelligence might relate to the fact that, in general, they more highly value success and often interpret success as resulting from having the wherewithal to use one's brains advantageously. As a down-to-earth Indianapolis realtor said, some smart people

> may have book learning, but when it comes to what I would consider a very simple practical judgment, they come up with ridiculous conclusions. In the business world, it's common sense in the extreme. There is no secret to it, it's not esoteric, you don't have to be a trained physicist to be a businessman.

In this context, intelligence is viewed as an "ability to recognize opportunities, to seize opportunities, to capitalize on them and to make them work. While other people at the same time, the same place, under the same circumstances, miss it all" (real estate developer, Indianapolis).

This practical view of intelligence is telling of the way Americans

draw cultural boundaries, in contrast to their French counterparts: while it is acceptable for a Frenchman to be incompetent in the organization of everyday life—in France, as mentioned above, men even vaunt their ineptitude concerning matters deemed prosaic—Americans are much more critical of those who are lacking on this sphere. However, again, I did of course encounter some Americans who had an appreciation of knowledge for its own sake, but even these generally valued competence and practical know-how in everyday life.

The main contrast between the French and American conceptions of intelligence is reflected in the way the two groups talk about one another. The *banquier* Dutoît and Louis Dufour, an engineer who often travels to the United States for business, encapsulate many of these differences. While referring to the French passion for eloquence, Mr. Dutoît explains:

> French managers are much more intelligent than American managers, easily . . . At the cultural level, the level of information, of education, of analysis, their wide-ranging interests . . . they are far more intelligent, without a doubt. But to succeed well, it is not enough to be intelligent, refined, and cultivated. You need to be pragmatic, to know why you are having a meeting, and which decisions need to be made and why, and how to go about it. The Frenchman does not understand this. He likes to talk too much. He has a desire for power, which he tries to take care of verbally. The one who speaks the most elegantly, who controls the French language the best, who has the last word, wins. Therefore, for us it is important to be more intelligent, more cultivated.

These views are echoed by Mr. Dufour, who sees American professionals as too specialized and too narrow in their interests:

> The Americans I know are not interested in anything besides their work and everyday life . . . [W]hen they go outside their country, when they come to France, they are mostly interested in the stereotypes [of French life]. [Their interests] are not very diverse and are very superficial . . . They want to take pictures, to be able to say that they saw the Eiffel Tower. They are not very curious about the [societal] differences. There are also positive differences [between them and us]. For instance, they do not take as much into consideration personalistic relations [and conflicts] at work. They have a much more serious conception of what professional life is all about. They are much more efficient.

The very same qualities that would allow one to be socially constructed as brilliant in the French workplace are likely to be useless in the

American workplace. While eloquence, general competence, *un sens critique*, and a strong capacity of abstraction are key in one case, factualism, efficiency, expertise, and pragmatism are more central in the other.

SELF-ACTUALIZATION

If the French seem to particularly emphasize intellectual style, Americans put slightly more emphasis than the French on self-actualization.[17] Bob Wilson, an Indianapolis computer specialist married to a musician, leads a very busy life, being actively involved both in sports and in the arts. He vividly exemplifies the meaning of self-actualization when he describes his conception of success in the following terms:

> I'm very much taken by activity . . . so people who are accomplishing things, I very much like. People who aren't doing much with their lives in my estimation . . . don't have much status . . . I am more comfortable with someone who is moving more in the direction of self-actualization . . . I see success as the ability to find a problem worth solving, and solve it . . . I don't see it as, you know, at forty-six, I want to be chief information officer at Hewlett Packard, and have three homes, an income of $487,000 a year, two kids, a dog, and a Ferrari. I don't see things in those terms. Again, as I said, in six months [my life] may change. I may find something that just absolutely ignites my curiosity. I just have to devour this, and my current success at that time may be defined around solving a problem and that may be a very specific thing at this point in time, like accomplishing this or that. So I think staying intellectually active may be my real definition of success.

For Bob, self-actualization means "doing things" and doing them "successfully," which he associates with curiosity and being intellectually active. More generally, in both countries, self-actualization is valued because it is equated with intelligence or curiosity. As one informant sees it:

> [Those who don't strive for self-actualization are] not real curious. I find that they're not very involved in anything, they don't have any passion. I see those people as less desirable. I try and reserve judgment until I find something out, you know: do I perceive this person as intellectually my equal or better? People who don't have that, I tend to dismiss them.

The non-self-actualizers are rejected because they indulge in passive and mediocre leisure-time activities, and particularly in television watch-

ing. Indeed, few self-actualizers hold television in high esteem. Their point of view is expressed by a bright Indianapolis professor of medicine:

> I think most of the sitcoms are stupid. Game shows are an insult to intelligence. I am totally disinterested in sports. I never watch sports at all. I don't see any purpose in it . . . I just don't find that much that is worthwhile.

In general, the self-actualizers have active and structured activities, their long-term goal being to develop their potential to its maximum: they play chess, learn a musical instrument, exercise, diet, go to the museum, get involved in the PTA, save the rain forest, take classes, and so forth. Like-wise, they describe their friends as people who are engaged in life, who ask themselves questions, who are curious, who will, e.g., build furniture "just for fun, buy a house, renovate it, become interested in all kinds of topics and read voraciously on them" (financial advisor, Clermont-Ferrand). As a handsome single yuppy Indianapolis lawyer explains:

> Those who tend toward mediocrity hold no fascination for me. I can't, I just can't find myself interested . . . You know, people who don't care about improving themselves, improving their minds. For one reason or another, whether it be sociological or psychological or economic, they tend to be stuck in a rut somewhere and it's just boring, boring, boring . . . I have no desire to associate with people who want to do nothing but go to bars and sit around in smoky environments and do that sort of thing.

These American upper-middle-class men set a high value on any kind of activity that can be read as a signal of self-actualization. This is par-ticularly true of dieting and exercising: several said that they feel superior to people who are in bad shape. A New York civil servant, for instance, explains that

> I like people who kind of take care of themselves, both physically and mentally, people who kind of stand above other people. I have this friend who is a carpenter and when he retired he took up running at the age of fifty-six . . . You really wouldn't want to be that friendly with those who just let themselves go, I mean physically. I tend to favor the disadvan-taged person in a way but still a person who takes care of himself.[18]

In many ways this focus on self-actualization could be taken as *the trademark* of the American upper-middle class: this group has the financial

resources necessary to get involved in many cultural and physical activities. Research on leisure-time and child-rearing values have shown that people with higher socioeconomic status are overrepresented in the population of individuals concerned with self-actualization.[19] While professionals and managers represent roughly 15 percent of the population in the United States, a study of patterns of leisure-time activities across socio-occupational groups found that 38 percent of the people surveyed who were interested in "cosmopolitan" activities and self-enrichment (defined as activities providing intellectual stimulation and opportunities for unique and creative accomplishments) were managers or professionals, while, respectively, 10 and 25 percent were blue-collar and clerical/technical white-collar workers, the remaining percentage grouping together homemakers and students.[20] Similarly, people with higher socioeconomic status watch less television.[21] Also, in contrast to working-class people, upper-middle class people consider it more important to transmit to their children a certain intellectual curiosity, a taste for discovery, and a need for self-fulfillment.[22]

When stressing self-actualization as a type of high status signal, people might simultaneously draw cultural, moral, and socioeconomic boundaries, equating self-actualization with showing proof of moral character and with having the "right" dispositions for being socially successful. The centrality of self-actualization in American upper-middle-class culture could be explained by the very fact that it can be taken to indirectly signal high ranking on the moral, cultural, and socioeconomic status hierarchies.

THE CULTURED WORLD OF EXCLUSION. THE CASE OF "BAD TASTE"

Both the French and the American participants stress sophistication, but again they define it differently, the French emphasizing refinement and humanistic culture, whereas Americans are more concerned with scientific culture and, to a lesser extent, with cosmopolitanism.

Boundary work based on cultural sophistication is a rather widespread phenomenon in France. Indeed, many of the French men I talked with resemble in this respect Jean de la Tour, an extremely elegant and distinguished fifty-year-old senior executive. De la Tour is a graduate of the Ecole Nationale d'Administration; he lives in Neuilly and is married to a social scientist. He describes the type of men he likes as *honnêtes hommes:*

The *honnête homme* is a person who attaches a lot of importance to culture, who has an open outlook on life, and not through television . . . I cannot stand people who don't have culture. The first thing I do when I go to someone's home is to look at their bookshelves. If they don't have books, I think they lack culture. They can be very good at what they do, but they lack something extremely important.

Jean de la Tour explains that he strongly dislikes vulgarity, the opposite of refinement. Vulgarity is signaled by

a lack of wit, of *recherche*, of personality. Vulgarity is a way of obscuring all forms of sensibilities, of human values . . . It is the worst failing because you cannot do anything against it. You cannot reason with it. It is simply there, and there is nothing you can do about it. If there is one large task that we have to pursue in life, if we have one mission, it is to try to be honest and not be vulgar.

Like Jean de la Tour, the French who draw cultural boundaries often define themselves in opposition to mainstream culture, to the lifestyle of the *Français moyen*, to "his taste, his activity, the way he organizes his life, the way he does things . . . with his house in the suburb, his Renault 21. He works thirty-nine hours a week; his wife waits for him at home; he takes his vacations at the sea and in the winter he goes skiing. At 8:30 in the evening, he watches TV." The *Français moyen* is a victim of society who lives in a caricatural way. Therefore, it is important to distance oneself from him. Didier Aucour, the architecture professor quoted at the beginning of this book has a strong urge to do just that:

I will tell you how much I am different from middle-class people. First, I hate to go to the beach during summer vacation. I cannot stand it. They all go to the beach—I go away. I am in the countryside where there is no one. Then they buy single-family homes, which I cannot stand. I like to be right in the heart of things. I need to have the Paris culture. As far as cars are concerned, I don't like to have the same car as everyone. So I organize my life differently. I take the subway. I have a car that is a sixties antique, a convertible, which I only use on the weekends. People go very fast; I go very slowly, because it is an antique car. Everything is different, because I am different. But I also refuse a certain way of life. I have no television. I listen to the radio.

Like Didier, Phillipe Duguy, a young Clermont-Ferrand lawyer, prides himself on the fact that most of his friends are culturally sophisticated.

Above all, Phillipe wants to learn from them; he needs to be intrigued by them; to discuss politics, the arts, culture with them; to exchange books and share reactions to movies or exhibitions.

For Phillipe, the aesthetic dimension of life is tremendously important. For instance, he cares a great deal about the physical environment in which he lives because it is expressive of his individuality. There is a *recherche* in everything he does, reads, or buys. He explains that he has a clearly defined opinion about "everything, everything that interests me. I know what I think about [Reagan's] Star Wars, about everything." Indeed, he is able to discourse at length on the type of writers he likes, on architecture, on movies. He scorns the conformists who are unable to create a lifestyle of their own and who have to follow formulas.

Refinement is *the* central value for the culturally exclusive like Phillipe. Members of this category generally describe their friends as refined. It is a question of "their manners, their speech, their vocabulary. It is a refinement which is not only measured in terms of manners, but [also in terms of] intellectual refinement . . . [They] know how to do things within the proper measure" (corporate lawyer, Paris). They define refinement as a *subtilité de l'être* (subtlety of being), "a style of life, but it is more than that. It is where you truly discover the qualities of the heart and the mind [of someone]. It presupposes a way of being that is elegant and perfectly measured" (journalist, Clermont-Ferrand). They also equated refinement with discretion, which means "not to mix up categories of people and situations . . . not to be in the way, not to impose yourself" (lawyer, Clermont-Ferrand). It also means "intellectually, not to have vulgar or simplistic ideas, [politically], not to confound the Bicentennial of the French Revolution with Progress; religiously, not to confound monotheism with religion; affectively, not to confound passion with the *richesse des sentiments* (richness of emotions). You see, it is the opposite of heaviness" (human resources consultant, Paris).

Someone who is refined avoids embarrassing himself. He never loses face. He is on top of social codes: he knows what form of introduction to use when writing a letter; he knows what title to use when addressing higher-ups; he knows when it is appropriate to initiate a conversation. He has tact and an infallible social antenna, a sense of how "not to do too much, not to do too little, not to talk too much" (priest, Paris); how "[not to] interact too abruptly, and [not to] think that you have to talk about yourself all the time" (owner of a construction firm, Paris).

Rejecting the *Français moyen* means distancing oneself from "common" tastes, i.e., from the tastes common to the middle and working class. The fact that French individuals often celebrate refinement over "common" or "vulgar" behaviors or values constitutes a form of euphemized socioeconomic boundary, i.e., a way to take distance toward other classes under the guise of cultural rather than socioeconomic differences.[23] Indeed, as Thorstein Veblen and W. Lloyd Warner have pointed out a long time ago, making distinctions on the basis of tastes and lifestyles is equivalent to making distinctions on the basis of class background.

The French respondents who draw the strongest cultural boundaries are acutely aware of clearly defined cultural codes and follow them conspicuously, adopting unconditionally the norms of behavior of bourgeois culture. A Clermont-Ferrand dentist describes certain features of this bourgeois world:

> [The women] wear a Hermès scarf with a white shirt, and if it rains, they also have a blue raincoat and a hood . . . The real [bourgeois] is totally centered on . . . things that you have to do, things that you should not do, things that are properly done and things that are not . . . For instance, you are supposed to go to see your family on Sunday, and you have to wear a tie for the occasion . . . Women will not buy tight dresses . . . My wife and I have received these same values, but we have integrated them, digested them, and relativized them in relation to what *we* want to do. In contrast they have absorbed everything, and they don't want to get out of it.

In this bourgeois world, as he says, there are rules for everything: when should one use *vous* instead of *tu*? Does one know at a glance the difference between a fish knife and a cheese knife? Of course, those who are in perfect command of bourgeois culture can make *erreurs de goût* (show bad taste) on purpose. Tastelessness, however, is accepted only as long as it is deliberate.

This bourgeois world is embedded in tradition, in the "cultural patrimoine, the general French classical culture," which pays "less attention to the modern culture of the 60s and 70s—by classical, I mean ancient authors and ancient languages" (social worker, Paris). This world also values "a certain concern with universalism; a taste for contact with foreigners, with foreign languages; a taste for travel" (social worker, Paris). Furthermore, in this bourgeois world as in much of the French upper-middle class, great importance is attached to humanistic culture. One must be

solidly grounded in past and contemporary culture, including music and literature, and have a keen awareness of economic and political issues at both the national and international levels. These traits are taken to be quintessential to a civilized person and affect evaluation in the workplace. Indeed, an unrefined, provincial person who lacks eloquence and general culture, who ignores the rules of graceful interaction as well as the rules of graceful self-presentation, and whose opinions are those of the *Français moyen*, showing neither originality nor individuality, is unlikely to be socially constructed as having impressive abilities and a promising future.

The French educational system has traditionally played an important role in diffusing this general humanist culture, or, in the words of a Paris public school administrator, in "preparing the ground, bringing culture, . . . [in teaching the student] as well as possible how to be a Man." This concern for culture, however, is not as widely spread across the population as one might think: a survey conducted in 1988 showed that only 9 percent of the French population attend one or more classical concerts a year, and that only between 10 and 15 percent of the population use public libraries, go to plays, play a musical instrument, or engage in similar cultural pursuits.[24] On the other hand, 76 percent of the population have never attended a dance performance, 71 percent have never attended a concert of classical music, and 55 percent and 51 percent, respectively, have never seen a play or an art exhibition.[25] Hence, those who are very involved in high culture remain a minority in French society.

How do Americans who value cultural sophistication compare with their counterparts in France? While the French who are culturally exclusive draw boundaries between themselves and the *Français moyen*, Americans tend to have a wide range of cultural repertoires within which they can encompass much of mainstream culture. This eclecticism is described by a rebel Indianapolis artist. During the interview which was conducted in his bohemian home, he described himself in the following terms:

> I am quite capable of dealing with the range of sensibilities that one finds in the Midwest. That is to say, I can be the typical American Midwesterner, rural-oriented. He talks like this and says, "Well shoot, I'm a home man," and stuff like that. You know, you listen to country western songs, and you play the guitar, and you say "fuckin" 'n "shit," I don't know. "Heck, you know!" [all in drawling tone]. Or I could go all the way up to talking like [voice change: high pitch] this. [I] change my voice and read natural history, and *The Visible Frontier*, the race to

synthesize the human being, and . . . the civilized French way. And I collect old dictionaries. And I have friends who are Rhodes scholars, and I have traveled around the world.[26]

Similarly, several American men told me that they get along with a wide range of people, regardless of background, and that they have many interactional patterns at their disposal, i.e., are very adaptable. They often explicitly refuse to select on the basis of cultural sophistication.[27] Partly, this might be because, in keeping with the populist tradition, drawing boundaries using such signals could be seen as undemocratic, the way selecting on the basis of religion or ethnicity is perceived by many as illegitimately bigoted. This pervasive, explicit nonexclusiveness is one of the characteristics that most drastically differentiate the French and American upper-middle classes.

The American individuals who do draw boundaries on the basis of cultural sophistication often tend to define as "different" or even as "undesirable" people they see as less cosmopolitan or refined than themselves.[28] This was particularly obvious during the interviews when the sensitive topic of regional differences came up. As noted earlier, some New Yorkers looked down on Midwesterners and Southerners for their lack of cosmopolitanism. A New York machine tool salesman describes the differences he perceives:

Los Angeles, Washington, there is something of a refined edge about these people. I don't know whether you'd call it a refinement or some type of extra these people have. In the Midwest, the people don't have it, although some of them will try to. When I do business in Maryland, and when I do business out in Western Pennsylvania, I have an edge even on their upper management. I don't know how to describe this to you. They are not as fast.[29]

A New York artist who is strongly committed to self-actualization says of the Midwest, where he was born:

They're blander out there. They are more willing to go along . . . It is all very suburban, and they are dealing with sort of a lot of mediocre things. I mean that's why I am not there. [They think] that things are pretty good . . . [They are] just doing something to make money to maintain the lifestyle, and that I consider mediocre . . . because you're not really trying to do anything different or better or expand yourself. I don't see a lot of that kind of thing going on out there. I don't see many of our great writers living in Indianapolis.

The cultural boundaries that Easterners draw against Midwesterners are particularly surprising because the quantitative comparison of approximative scores reveals that overall the New Yorkers I talked to are not more culturally exclusive than their Indianapolis counterpart.[30] Nevertheless, the issues of cosmopolitanism and regional differences are extremely sensitive ones: several men reacted defensively when these questions were discussed. Many Midwesterners affirmed the cultural distinctiveness of their region with vehemence. The Clermontois were less defensive: it is possible that they accept the cultural predominance of Paris as unavoidable, and even recognize that they are less culturally sophisticated than the Parisians are.[31]

Another contrast between the French and American respondents lay in the domains of cultural sophistication that they particularly value. There are similarities for sure: like the French, Americans highly value having a strong political and economic culture (i.e., being well-informed). Recent history is also important. Americans who draw strong cultural boundaries, however, put more emphasis than the French do on familiarity with scientific and technological developments, while overall they attach less importance to humanistic culture. For instance, John Bloom, the New York economist described in the Prologue, when asked if he was better educated in the sciences than in the humanities (literature, philosophy, history), answered:

> I am not sure what the humanistic culture is, but I would say certainly that my interests lie much more toward knowledge, toward techniques, through mathematics, astronomy, physics, quantum physics, and so forth. Those are the things that I relate to . . . See, one of the nice differences between Jane [my wife] and myself is I'm probably much more of a topic, subject-matter person, whereas Jane much more relates to people. To her, the world is filled with people. [For me] the world is filled with knowledge and techniques, you know, things coming up on computers and so forth.

The premium that the French, in contrast to the Americans, put on humanistic culture is reflected in a few cultural indicators: writers accounted for five out of seven individuals represented on the French bills in circulation in the late 1970s, while American bills depict political figures. Also, as of 1957, men and women of letters accounted for 6.4 percent of the names of Paris streets, in contrast to 1.2 percent in Boston, 1 percent in San Francisco, 0.9 percent in Chicago, and 0.6 percent in

Manhattan. While 8 percent of a sample of programs broadcast by French public television in 1976 concerned high culture, the same can be said for only 2.5 percent of a sample of programs presented by the Public Broadcasting System in the United States; similarly, drama and literature accounted for 3 percent of France's total television programming, as compared with 1.2 percent on PBS.[32] Finally, a comparison of the indexes of *Le Monde* and *New York Times* for 1988 also suggests the greater importance of humanistic culture in France: while *Le Monde* had sixty-eight entries under the heading "philosophy," the *New York Times* had only three.

Social scientists and education specialists have documented the general decline in literary culture in the United States and the weak interest that American students show in humanistic culture.[33] According to Bourdieu, command of high culture is valued in France over scientific or technical knowledge partly because it expresses the intrinsic quality of the person, i.e., his or her ability to invest in something that cannot be bought, and to use his or her time in a gratuitous, i.e., noneconomic way, this constituting the supreme affirmation of personal excellence.[34] It is unlikely that such an analysis could be applied to the United States, given the stress that Americans put on practical knowledge.

More often than the French, Americans who draw strong cultural boundaries define sophistication through cosmopolitanism, i.e., as having had a chance to travel, to learn languages, to discover various culinary traditions, and, more generally, to widen one's horizons—which goes along with the quest for self-actualization.[35] In this context, vacation destinations (as a respondent put it, "the California wine country versus Twin City, Tennessee") and eating habits (Northern Italian cuisine versus pork rinds) are used as signals of refinement. Also, unlike the French, several American respondents expressed a fascination with everything European, ranging from cars to wines, clothes, movies, perfumes, and kitchenware. Refinement and cultural sophistication are often equated with European goods and habits, some Americans being less concerned about the differences between types of European products than about their Europeanness itself. For instance, Pernod which is a working-class drink in France, is chic in the American context. The same holds for Italian pasta, capers, coffee grinders, or espresso coffee machines. A young Indianapolis curator whom I interviewed in the cluttered basement of the museum where he works, exemplifies this fascination with the exotic when he explains that his wife

came to this marriage with over 200 cookbooks. We probably do the basics but we're very exploratory beyond that . . . It gives us some sense of adventure. Our suitcases coming back from trips are not full of furs but they're full of anchovy paste and stuff . . . Food offers an opportunity, a focal activity around which the other aspects of culture and geography and all those things can be explored.

An additional difference between the French and American respondents is the purposefulness with which some Americans, and especially upwardly mobile Americans, are pursuing high culture. In the words of the Indianapolis artist, "They are appreciating art because art is important because it says so somewhere." High culture being seen as a positive thing to pursue, these Americans consume it in large quantities, rapidly and conspicuously, instead of taking it for granted. The success of cultural organizations and magazines oriented toward popularizing and democratizing high culture and cultural sophistication (e.g., book-of-the-month clubs, and periodicals like *Gourmet, Bon Appétit, Architectural Digest, Art in America*) bespeak this hunger for high culture and cultural sophistication.[36] This recent and accelerated cultural apprenticeship affects the way cultural products are appreciated. For instance, the relationship with European cuisine that people display when they have only recently internationalized their eating habits is different from the relationship that Europeans have with American cuisine; just as Europeans appropriate hamburgers using a cultural register unknown to Americans, i.e, associating the experience with a rejection of conventional bourgeois culture.[37]

Finally, some Americans also differ from the French in the emphasis they put on *buying* culture. A few respondents indicated that they interpreted the purchase of art as a manifestation of high *social* status, along with redecorating one's house, driving luxury cars, consuming expensive wines and meals, and staying fit.[38] It is as if high culture was more directly associated with high social status, i.e., had less autonomy, less independence from socioeconomic boundaries (or translated more directly into social status) in America than in France. Being involved in large social networks partly due to their high level of geographic and professional mobility, members of the American upper-middle class might have had to develop ways of rapidly signaling cultural and socioeconomic status.[39] In contrast, many French cultural consumers overinvest in high-cultural goods (books, movies, visits to the museum) as a way to compensate for their low income and blocked social mobility. In other words, for these

Frenchmen, consumption of high culture is not a signal of high social status but a way to signal cultural status in order to gain social status.[40]

At a more general level, the attitude that the American men I talked with maintain toward cultural sophistication tends to be less *blasé* than that of their French counterparts. For instance, several view high culture as a civilizing experience that elevates both the soul and the mind, as if it had purifying virtues.[41] According to Elizabeth Long who studied reading groups in Houston, Texas, great literature is conceived by her interviewees as providing a quasi-religious spiritual connection, as they strive for self-understanding and an objective view of themselves and their society; the act of reading itself is often seen as morally uplifting, a source for self-improvement and a reason for pride.[42] Likewise, according to a recent anthropological study of college life in New Jersey, college education itself is often seen as "a way to get broader horizons, to make someone better, more liberal, more knowledgeable."[43] This view of high culture and education as improving one's moral standing, or intrinsic moral worth, was never encountered in the French interviews.

The growing interest that Americans have in attaining cultural sophistication is reflected in statistics on cultural activities: a greater number of Americans were involved in high-culture activities in 1980 than in previous times.[44] In fact, 14 percent of the white Americans eighteen years of age and older, who were surveyed, attended one or more symphonic concerts compared to 9 percent of respondents fifteen and older who were surveyed in France.[45] In the United States, there has been a steady increase of interest in cultural activities on the part of a wide range of people from diverse backgrounds. As is the case in France, however, education remains the best predictor of arts participation:[46] in 1978, 69 percent of those interested in arts and cultural activities were college educated, as were 65 percent of those interested in activities oriented toward cosmopolitanism and self-enrichment.[47] It is noteworthy that blacks are increasingly interested in Euro-American culture while at the same time remaining very involved in Afro-American art forms.[48] On the other hand, Southerners are less involved in high culture than others, which might reflect the fact that their lifestyle is more oriented toward home, family, and church.[49] The group now most interested in high culture is the baby-boomer generation, now well into their thirties and forties.[50]

Differences in the importance that French and American participants

attach to cultural boundaries are indirectly reflected in the data I gathered on their involvement in high-culture activities. Evidence shows that on average Americans participate less frequently in the following types of cultural activities: creating works of art, going to the symphony and the theater, visiting museums or art galleries, and making use of the public library. While on average, respectively, 31 percent and 33 percent of the Parisians and the Clermontois are involved in these activities fairly often or frequently, it is the case for only 18 percent of the New Yorkers and 22 percent of the Hoosiers.[51] Residents of the so-called cultural periphery unexpectably are not markedly less high-culture oriented[52] than those who live in the so-called cultural centers.[53]

INTELLECTUALS AND INTELLECTUAL SUBCULTURES

Intellectuals, along with artists, can be considered the ideal type of those who draw strong cultural boundaries: indeed, ideas and high culture organize their mapping of the world to a very great extent. They put considerable importance on intellectual life as such, and as we will see in Chapter 6, they draw very strong cultural boundaries. For this reason, it might be interesting to examine more closely the subculture of the intellectuals. Indeed, it can inform us on the nature and importance of signals of high cultural status in both countries.[54] This subculture is more marginal to American culture at large than it is to French culture.

A considerable number of men I talked with can be defined as "intellectuals." It is the case for 21 percent of the American sample and 42 percent of the French sample.[55] To be classified as an intellectual, individuals need to meet one of two criteria: either they explicitly define themselves or their friends as such, or they make several references to their intellectual life during the interview. This second, looser criterion is used to supplement the first because the social category of "intellectual" is not as entrenched in the United States as it is in France, nor does it have exactly the same connotation, as seen below.

Jean Letellier is a rather eccentric Parisian psychologist who leads what he calls a "private intellectual life." Concretely, this means that he continuously learns new languages and writes for his own pleasure books that are partly art objects and that remain unpublished (he sent me samples of them upon my return to Princeton). He also spends his vacations visiting libraries "in various regions of France, in Portugal, in Ger-

many." His friends introduce him to new books ("I have never had a friend make me discover a book that left me indifferent. It happens that they always choose very well. I have this attachment to books; it is a craze of sorts"). A former student of Michel Foucault, Jean Letellier enjoys esoteric knowledge. He makes amateur movies as a way of expressing his individuality. He maintains an important correspondence, mostly with artists and intellectual friends who live in West Germany, Sweden, and the United States. For him, culture is a whole way of life.

Like Jean Letellier, the French respondents who define themselves as intellectuals do so because of their wide-ranging cultural interests, i.e., because they can "talk about anything, being very well-informed on all the books that just came out" (psychologist, Clermont-Ferrand). They pride themselves, too, on their "critical sense and ability to have personal opinions independent of the conformisms of the day" (social worker, Paris). They often choose their friends on the basis of their common political or philosophical ideas: "we make intellectual allusions, and the other one understands immediately. There is a lot of complicity intellectually and also on the philosophy of existence in general" (professor of social work, Clermont-Ferrand). Since they take ideas extremely seriously, they often have contempt for people who have "absurd political views."

These intellectuals do not distinguish intellectual life from pleasure, or from their sense of self. Some confess to having an almost visceral need for reading and intellectually exploring a wide range of ideas. They keep up with television programs such as "Apostrophes" where recent books are discussed,[56] and with weekly magazines such as Le Nouvel Observateur or L'Express which extensively cover new publications and cultural events, often including interviews with well-known intellectuals. Some follow the gossip of the Parisian intellectual microcosm, as relayed by these cultural magazines, with a passion akin to that of football fans following sports statistics.[57] Furthermore, these French intellectuals invest avidly in cultural goods (movies, books, art). They have at their disposal many cultural and institutional resources around which they can organize their common identity and culture.

With a few exceptions, many of these French intellectuals locate themselves to the left on the political spectrum. They try to incarnate a type of moral purity by defending egalitarian principles while backing their position with a sophisticated sociopolitical discourse. Many, how-

ever, offer a depiction of their political involvement that resembles that of Jean Letellier:

> Like all French intellectuals, I was a militant at some point, but I have never really been committed. I could regurgitate the ideas, the sentences which everyone knew. At some point I was really strong on the Communist party, and on the Italian left.

And many have stopped believing in the Socialist revolution, the end of domination and exploitation.[58] Indeed, since the 1970s, there has been a decline in the cultural prominence of this type of messianic French intellectual ideally exemplified by Jean-Paul Sartre.[59] French intellectuals are now less politically engaged and lead more privatized lives.[60] However, some of the intellectuals I talked with—a Parisian architect, for instance, and a social work professor, a lawyer, and a civil servant in Clermont-Ferrand—continue to define themselves against the power structure, though they read Foucault instead of Marx and are more interested in maximizing their own autonomy from the macrostructures in everyday life than in promoting collective solutions. These intellectuals still define themselves as nihilistic and somewhat distant from bourgeois (i.e., conventional) culture. It is often from this perspective that they adopt some of the antimoral positions that were described in Chapter 2.

The subculture of American intellectuals is different from that of the French. Indeed, several American men have a different frame of reference for understanding what an "intellectual" is. To the question "Why do you think of yourself as an intellectual?" again John Bloom, our New York economist, explains:

> My whole point of view is to attempt to answer certain basic questions about life. What is the purpose of it? The purpose is the development of your mind, of your thinking processes, of your ability to reflect on things. So that, for me, feels like I have a meaningful existence, an untrivialful existence. And to feel some sense of intellectual searching, intellectual curiosity, intellectual development is important to me. I can't imagine a time when I won't be interested in reading, in sports, or just in exploring.

John does not have at his disposal a clear view of what "intellectual" means as a social category, as he confounds "being an intellectual" with "being intellectual." This is also suggested by the way a human management consultant, who is attending Columbia University on a part-time

basis in order to complete a Ph.D., answered the question concerning whether he considers himself to be an intellectual or not:

> I wouldn't define "intellectual" as "cultural," because I work in the insurance business, which is very intellectually demanding, and I know some people who are very intelligent actuaries and maybe they lack something culturally. The way you raise the question, I would not say yes, [that my friends are intellectuals].

The cultural criteria Hoosiers and New Yorkers use for attributing intellectual status are blurred, partly because the category itself is not as often used by the mass media in the United States as it is by the mass media in France. Nevertheless, the American respondents whom I classified as intellectuals share a number of characteristics. They tend, like the French, to adopt abstract forms of discourse, especially when compared with other Americans who mostly appreciate a "down-to-earth" approach—this propensity for abstraction being evident in our discussions of their recent readings, for instance.[61] Judging by the tone of our interactions, a few obviously welcomed polemic discussions, as if in this subculture the principle of conflict avoidance discussed in Chapter 2 did not apply. On the other hand, in contrast to their French counterparts, these American intellectuals are more at the center of the political spectrum.[62]

The subculture of American intellectuals is not incompatible with mainstream culture as they consume more popular culture than do the French respondents who are intellectuals, including television, commercial movies, and mystery novels. Those who partake in this subculture, however, often say that they are alienated from the mainstream culture because of its pragmatic orientation, narrowness, and anti-intellectualism.[63] American intellectuals also define themselves and their cosmopolitanism in reaction to the parochialism that many of them see as pervasive in the United States.[64] In this context several intellectuals I talked with pointed out the importance of living close to a large city like New York, or to a college town like Bloomington, Indiana, if one wished to maintain an active intellectual life, as if special conditions were needed to survive as an intellectual in America. Along these lines, the literature on American intellectuals stresses how, overall, this group is alienated in American society.[65]

This same difficulty pushes American intellectuals to cling to their intellectual identity with more vigor than they would in more hospitable

environments, and this in turn might mean engaging in conspicuous intellectual practices and reinforcing cultural boundaries. In this context, a few of the men I talked with looked to Europe, and particularly to England and France, for role models to give structure and meaning to their identity. This was particularly the case for a handsome New York museum curator who has a fetish about French culture and frequently goes to Paris for long weekends:

> I collect towers and photographs, or anything that deals with Paris. We're buying an apartment this summer in Paris . . . I live vicariously. I am not French, and I don't speak French well enough, [as] I only took two years of French in college, so I never acquired fluent speaking ability. I can read French. So when I go over there I am always an outsider because I grew up an outsider . . . I can look at it from a distance and enjoy the full pleasure of it . . . But the beauty of Paris, the food, everything, the way I romanticize it . . . there are bookstores everywhere you go. . . . I relate it to the nineteenth century so I can look at it, at the streets that are still from that period, the buildings and so forth . . . I feel as if I am doing something every moment I'm there. Here, I'm just trying to get from one corner to the next to mail a letter, and I'm not enjoying it.

Such American intellectuals can be as much invested in cultural sophistication as are the French who draw strong cultural boundaries. They probably remain a small minority in the American context, however, and are certainly mostly concentrated in the cultural professions (artists, university professors, journalists). These differences reflect the lesser influence of cultural boundaries in the American context and the marginality of intellectual status markers in mainstream culture. It will be seen below that the marginality of American intellectuals is likely to be compounded by the strong presence of anti-intellectualist and anticosmopolitan feelings in the population. In this context the broadening of one's cultural repertoire to include popular culture might be the only viable alternative.

EXPLORING CULTURAL LAXITY: THE AMERICAN CASE

We saw that differences exist in the way the French and Americans draw cultural boundaries: they emphasize different aspects of intelligence (*sens critique* vs. competence), use different signals to read intelligence (eloquence vs. expertise and pragmatism), and set different values on humanistic and scientific knowledge. Also, my interviews and other studies

suggest that Americans have broader cultural repertoires than the French and are less exclusive in their attitude toward mainstream culture. Americans tend to emphasize cosmopolitanism and the broadening of horizons through culture more than the French, who stress refinement. Furthermore, some American participants seem to consume high culture with more intentionality and purposefulness than the French and to view it less independently from high social status. Finally, the most ideal-typical group of culturally exclusive Americans, the intellectuals, seem to have a less coherent identity and subculture and to be more alienated from aspects of American mainstream culture than their French counterparts are from their culture, even though they have a broader cultural repertoire.

Evidence suggests that the system of categorization used by Americans to draw cultural boundaries has a different formal structure than the system used by the French as it is not as differentiated (or detailed). First, Americans make fewer cultural distinctions, i.e., they draw fewer cultural boundaries, and in most cases they exclude only people who do not meet very basic and broadly defined cultural requirements. Second, the boundaries they draw appear to be more blurred and their hierarchalization of practices and tastes less stable. In other words, there is less consensus on what defines deviance and legitimate culture. Consequently, those who violate boundaries in the properly cultural domain are not likely to be as strongly criticized as they would be in France, as if the boundaries themselves were more permeable. Such a system can be described as having weak boundaries or as a "loosely bounded culture."

The notion of "loose-boundedness" refers to the sharpness with which the categories that make up a classification system are defined. In a loosely bounded culture such as American culture, one finds a high level of cultural innovation in lifestyles and in norms for interpersonal relations, and a high degree of tolerance for deviance.[66] In contrast, a tightly bounded culture has clearly coded and widely agreed-upon systems for evaluating attitudes and practices. Its classificatory codes are sharply defined and structured around rigid, bipolar, hierarchical oppositions (right and wrong, good and bad, and so forth).[67] Lifestyles are more traditional, cultural innovation less frequent, and cultural hierarchies more clearly defined.

Several pieces of evidence suggest that the classification codes that Americans use to draw cultural boundaries are loosely bounded: first, one finds more cultural innovation and a stronger tendency toward cultural laissez-faire in the United States, a greater tolerance for differences of

taste. This tolerance extends to the domains of ideas and politics. Second, the categories Americans use to talk about refinement and cosmopolitanism are less specific than those used by the French. Third, compared to the French, Hoosiers and New Yorkers tend to prefer laid-back or casual activities, such as home repair and watching television, to highly structured activities that require considerable exposure to a historical and cultural education steeped in aristocratic taste. Furthermore, when they consume high culture and literature, American men tend to emphasize the emotional and experiential dimensions of the aesthetic experience over intellectualist discourse on art. These various aspects of the loose-boundedness of American cultural boundaries provide more evidence of their relative weakness compared to French cultural boundaries.

Cultural Innovation and Laissez-Faire

The premium placed on cultural innovation and laissez faire in American society transpired in the fact that many of the American men I talked with often expressed their belief in the cultural sovereignty of the individual. They argued that "the way you choose to dress and spend your money is your business," that "if you feel comfortable with it, that's fine," and that it is wrong to be judgmental regarding other people's lifestyles and tastes ("If that's what they want, that's what they want"). This is precisely the position adopted by Willy Pacino, the New York labor specialist encountered earlier:

> "Bad taste" [means] my definition of "[bad] taste," and that does not mean that my taste is right and theirs is wrong . . . I don't feel qualified to judge your taste. What I like, I like. I might not like the way you do your hair or the clothing you are wearing. Coming to funerals in hot pants, that's bad taste. That's universal bad taste, because it is inappropriate for the occasion . . . I have this nephew who lives in New York, who has a special lifestyle (he is kind of a hippy). He wears an earring. That's what he does. Do I approve? No . . . But it is not to me to decide, so I accept it. It's me who does not like it. It's offensive to me, but it's his life. It's nothing that is going to cause him physical harm.

This relativism extends to the domain of ideas and politics where several men mentioned that they consider all opinions to be equally valuable and to be grounded in personal preferences. As explained by this Indianapolis informant: "Politics and religion, I don't like to talk about, because everybody has their own opinion and, you know, I'm as opinionated as you are about it and generally, you get nowhere talking about

religion and politics, I've found." Some people judge others as unpleasant if "they think that their opinion is more valuable and they're telling me something I don't know . . . that is a one-way street instead of a give-and-take" (professional recruiter, Indianapolis). Ultimately, this relativism results in anti-intellectualism, since it denies the possibility of reaching a more adequate analysis of reality.

American cultural laissez-faire also appears in the fact that, in contrast to the Frenchmen I talked with, more Americans express tolerant attitudes toward others: when probed on feelings of superiority and inferiority, they are slightly more likely to say that they do not feel inferior or superior to anyone, that their taste is not better than others', and that they like everybody.[68] They are also more likely to laugh off their friends' poor taste, seeing it as a superficial matter irrelevant to their friendship, and affirming that other considerations, particularly moral ones, are more crucial in the selection of friends. Also, overall, few Americans say that they put great emphasis on manners. On the other hand, they stress informality in dress and interpersonal relationships: the American men I talked with prefer clean, simple, comfortable clothes—as does the French working class.[69] Along with aesthetic and intellectual relativism, these observations suggest that a philosophy of cultural laissez-faire is more common in the United States than in France. This laissez-faire is sustained by norms of egalitarianism—and particularly cultural egalitarianism—and friendliness that also work to weaken cultural boundaries by favoring conflict avoidance and militating against the creation of clearly defined rules of behavior. This indirectly reinforces the relative role played by moral boundaries in the reproduction of inequality in America.

The greater American emphasis on cultural innovation is felt in several cultural domains. For instance, American cuisine features eclectic experiments, mixes between ethnic and regional traditions, and personal inventiveness.[70] In contrast, French cuisine has elaborate and well-established rules concerning the preparation and consumption of foods.[71] Similarly, in the area of lifestyle, Americans are constantly innovating and adopting new trends,[72] whereas the French tend to understand lifestyle as linked to deeply set cultural and personal preferences. In the area of interpersonal relationships, Americans tend to negotiate rules of interaction within groups, whereas the French might follow more rigid norms.[73] Furthermore, Americans encourage their children to define early on their own individuality and tastes, whereas the French are stricter with their children and have a more authoritarian concept of parenthood.[74] Finally,

Americans show less uncertainty avoidance than the French (they are less oriented toward rules). This is also associated with a greater tendency to laissez-faire attitudes in the culture as a whole.[75] Therefore, the boundaries Americans draw appear to be more blurred and their hierarchalization of practices and tastes less stable than the boundaries drawn by the French. From this, we can only conclude that one finds in America less consensus on what defines deviance and, consequently, greater cultural laxity. Therefore, those who violate boundaries would be more tolerated, boundaries themselves being more permeable, less defended, and less resisted.

Of course, this cultural laissez-faire is not all-pervasive in American upper-middle-class culture. A certain number of American men live in milieus where rigid classification systems prevail, where there is one right way to do everything. Jim Crutchfield, a New York banker, comes from such a milieu, which he describes in the following terms:

> My family are all, and I include myself, quite judgmental: there is a right way and a wrong way, and anyone who does not do it our way is wrong. This kind of definitiveness of judgment applies to everything, and that's from buying a car to choosing where you live. For instance, I would not have a crummy yard; I mean, I just would not do that. I would not feel right about it. Also I am very particular about dress. I know exactly what I want. I even know what I want before I go to the store. And they either have it or they don't.

These individuals, however, remain a minority, albeit a sizable one, among the men with whom I talked. Data suggest that even those whose family has been part of the upper-middle class for three generations—a group on the whole very likely to have tightly bounded systems of classification—define themselves as relatively culturally tolerant. This might be partly because, like other upper-middle-class people who are interested in high culture, they also have a broad cultural repertoire that does not exclude mainstream culture. As I will argue in Chapter 7, this has important theoretical implications because it contradicts an assumption often made in recent studies in the sociology of culture that the definition of legitimate taste is a zero-sum game, that differentiation necessarily leads to hierarchalization.

Differentiation in Classification Systems

The relative [or comparative] loose-boundedness of American culture is further suggested by the fact that the categories used by Hoosiers and

New Yorkers to discuss refinement and cosmopolitanism tend to be broader than those used by the French. While we saw that the French define refinement as *subtilité de l'être* (subtlety of one's way of being), "perfectly measured elegance," and "intellectually, not to have vulgar or simplistic ideas; . . . religiously, not to confound monotheism with religion," the vocabulary Americans use generally reflects a less fine-grained system of classification. They might simply distinguish between the college-educated and the non–college-educated instead of between the "subtle" and the "nonsubtle." Or they might differentiate between the appreciators of classical music and the nonappreciators instead of between the appreciators of romantic and of contemporary music. They might distinguish a refined from a vulgar person by external traits never used by the French to make this distinction. For instance, refinement might mean "wearing a suit and being careful with my language," "supporting the arts, and getting together for a dinner where you bring out the china and the white table cloth" (informant, Indianapolis). Or, as expressed by the chief financial officer of an Indianapolis firm, "Cosmopolitanism for a guy is not much of an issue unless you're a real Easterner that really wants to dress the style. We have raised our girls to be very cosmopolitan . . . appearance is critical, how they dress, their mannerisms, the clannishness of how they do things [is critical]." Conversely, the vice-president of a bank explained that in order to make Indianapolis more cosmopolitan, people have been "trying to get out of the county-seat mode, which is kind of hard. We're trying to get things like the symphony and things like that, the art museum, as opposed to entertaining on the back porch with the barbecue."

While most American participants seem to operate through categories that are less fine-grained than those in use among the French,[76] others seem simply not to be aware of the lifestyle universe in which they live, as is the case with an Indianapolis medical researcher who explains:

> [My friends] are probably sort of like me in that they don't know what social type they are. They're easygoing, and they don't, as far as I know, run in any social circles. Jim never tells me he's gone to such and such a party or anything like that. Jim has three children and one coming and that takes most of his time just like my family takes most of my time when I'm not at the office. So I guess we're just sort of in the middle. I think we're relatively middle-class and low-key types.

To summarize, Americans make fewer cultural distinctions than the French, they draw fewer cultural boundaries and they tend to only ex-

clude people who do not meet very general cultural requirements (e.g., who are too parochial or insufficiently cosmopolitan). This also tempers the hierarchical dimension of their classification system. This is precisely what makes American culture a loosely bounded culture.

Formalism and Loose-Boundedness

Further evidence of the loose-boundedness of American culture is found in the greater popularity among Americans of laid-back or casual leisure-time activities such as home repair, television watching, and sports that do not require considerable historical and cultural education steeped in aristocratic taste. It is also found in the fact that American high-culture amateurs stress less the intellectualist aspect of their aesthetic experience than its emotional and experiential dimensions.

A number of the American men I interviewed spoke of their greater enjoyment of casual leisure-time activities as compared to more structured and formal ones. For instance, they prefer casual hospitality—"Go over, have a drink, and cook out on the patio. Something like that. Watch an I.U. [Indiana University] basketball game,"—as opposed to formal entertaining. Male friendship is often expressed by mutual assistance with chores and home-improvement projects. A marketing executive whom I interviewed in his ranch house in Indianapolis describes a friendship organized around such activities:

> This friend of mine . . . he was very mechanical, very much of a crafts-man. And I really used to like to go over to his place and go down in the basement or out in the garage and tinker with things, this, that, et cetera . . . On Friday nights, you know, he liked to come over in my garage and tinker, because I know more about tinkering and doing things, and he got a kick out of coming over and helping me.

The popularity of casual activities such as home repair is a properly American phenomenon: among the participants, considerably fewer Frenchmen report being often or frequently involved in home repairs (22 percent of the Parisians and 28 percent of the Clermontois in contrast to 56 percent of the New Yorkers and 68 percent of the Hoosiers). Home repairs being typically a working-class activity in France, the greater hierarchalization and differentiation of leisure-time activities across classes in this country is further suggested by the fact that few members of the French upper-middle class engage in it.[77]

Watching television, another relatively casual leisure-time activity is

again more popular among Americans than among the French. According to the European values/CARA survey in 1984, 10 percent of the French professionals and managers never watched television in contrast to only 1 percent of their American counterparts. On the other hand, 15 percent of American professionals watched more than four hours of television a day in contrast to only 5 percent of the French.[78] These differences extend to the popularity of spectator sports which are considerably more appreciated in the American than in the French upper-middle class. Fifty-three percent of the Hoosiers and 36 percent of the New Yorkers watch sports fairly often or frequently as compared to 13 percent of the Parisians and Clermontois, while a full 66 percent of the Parisians never or rarely engage in spectator sports. In general, however, the number of men who enjoy watching sports events is greater in the "periphery" than in the cultural "centers."[79]

Americans are themselves more involved in sport activities. I used a questionnaire to survey interviewees on their enjoyment of and participation in the following types of sports: basketball, volleyball, bowling, working out, swimming, billiards, handball, hockey, baseball, football, golf, riding, skating, hiking, tennis. A considerably larger proportion of French people report that they rarely or never participate in any of these sports (80 percent and 74 percent for the Parisians and the Clermontois in contrast to 39 percent and 61 percent, respectively, for the Hoosiers and the New Yorkers). Paris respondents are slightly more prone to dislike sports than those from other sites.[80]

In the general American population, people who are most involved in sports are young, single, male wage workers with little formal education.[81] American upper-middle-class culture, however, does emphasize sports activities as a way to develop leadership, moral character, and a capacity for team work. As argued by various social scientists, watching spectator sports (e.g., baseball, football, basketball) provides men a forum for discussing competence and performance and for dramatizing and celebrating some of the values that are activated in upper-middle-class work environments—namely, competition, competence, male friendship, and masculinity.[82] The popularity of sports itself suggests a loosely bounded culture because enjoying or engaging in sports does not require as much high-cultural and historical information as does consumption of high culture. In other words, the enjoyment of sports is more democratic, despite the rising price of tickets to professional sports events.

This same downplaying of cultural information appears by the way

Americans consume high culture itself: they deemphasize the properly formal and intellectual aspect of the aesthetic activity to stress its emotional and experiential dimensions. This is suggested by several recent studies. For instance, in her analysis of the diffusion of abstract expressionism in the Midwest, Judith Huggins Balfe shows how the success of this movement was facilitated by its framing of art as an emotional experience available to all rather than as an intellectual experience requiring an elitist education in art.[83] Also, in his study of how New Yorkers give meaning to the art in their home, David Halle found that landscapes, the most common genre in all types of households, are mostly appreciated for the peace and quiet they represent. Again the discourse of the audience is emotional (rather than analytic), the views that amateurs have of art being very different from those held by art specialists and academics.[84] The study of reading groups in Houston mentioned above provided similar results: Elizabeth Long found that members of these groups subordinate formalism to more experientially based criteria of literary appropriation, and value personal enrichment over intellectualist analysis when describing why they like certain books. For them, the intrinsic greatness of books is secondary to (or subsumed by) its contribution to their personal enhancement; they look for "the transcendental experiential pleasure of deep emotional involvement rather than for the more rationalist pleasure which comes with analytic distance." The readers Long talked to did not identify with "the serious reader," because stylistic and narrative strategies left them indifferent.[85]

These studies stress the importance of emotion over intellect in the way Americans appropriate the arts; they document a refusal of the cultural hierarchies built by cultural critics on solely analytic criteria and a reliance instead on individual interpretation. Therefore, they provide indirect evidence of the loose-boundedness of American culture. In fact, the way several of the Hoosiers and New Yorkers consume high culture suggests that they often reject the isolation of art from society and, implicitly, the subordination of everyday life to art. This is suggested by a culturally sophisticated and extremely articulate social service manager who lives in Indianapolis:

> To me art is, you know, I think of a car as a sculpture, and I think of windows in a house as a Norman Rockwell [painting]. In other words, I don't want curtains over them. I want to be able to see trees and people and a person through a window; that's like Norman Rockwell showing life. I think of life as art. I think it's kind of one. And so I'm not really

into culture per se . . . If I get a chance to go to a play or a symphony, I enjoy that, but it's no big deal.

This quote suggests a desire to symbolically deinstitutionalize art and to integrate it within society at large. This is the ultimate form of cultural laxity, and a denial of cultural hierarchies, if there ever was one.[86]

As explained by a New York statistics researcher who is also a graduate of both Princeton University and Yale University:

I know plenty of sort of imaginative and interesting people around who are not high culturalists. Besides, what people call high culture is frequently very bogus. People who like classical music are thought of as having taste. Well, I love classical music but I actually don't think that it's got anything to do with taste.[87]

My Friends Are Boring and I Love Them: Anti-Intellectualism and Anticosmopolitanism as Reverse Cultural Discrimination

It is worth examining American anti-intellectualism in greater depth. Indeed, it provides us with additional evidence of the lesser importance of cultural status in American society as well as additional information on the nature of cultural boundaries; it can be interpreted as a refusal of complex, tightly bounded classification systems.

Intellectualism is correlated with being able to argue for clearly ordered choices about desirable ends, whether they be political, ethical, social, cultural, or spiritual. The evidence suggests that in America intellectualism is often seen as antidemocratic, since such an ordering process and such argumentation violates the principles of conflict avoidance and relativism described above. For instance, recent studies of high school and college students show that these groups often view intellectual interests outside course work as unegalitarian and threatening, and intellectualism as unfriendly and uppity.[88] Because intellectualism can be a social liability, it is important for students who are inclined to it to understate their intellectual interests and provide evidence that they are down-to-earth—as it is assumed that they are not.[89]

These attitudes are clearly reflected among those Americans I talked with who adopt the practical conception of intelligence discussed earlier in this chapter. Several of them do not value being well-read, "because I think that a lot of knowledge comes from personal experience" (staff assistant, Indianapolis). Others associate this trait with phoniness: "There are a lot of phonies in the world who would impress you with how bril-

liant they are. In some areas, maybe they are. Like none of that makes any difference" (marketing executive, Indianapolis).

This anti-intellectualism is often accompanied by anticosmopolitan attitudes, also fed by pragmatism. Some respondents describe the cosmopolitan person as someone who "lets reality slip from them," and who is somewhat limited, the kind of person who "could not appreciate the amount of work that is put in by a Four-H kid in raising a rabbit" (radio station owner, New York). The vice-president of an Indianapolis bank summarizes the opposition between cosmopolitanism and pragmatism while trying to explain to me why he does not like the former:

> To me the cosmopolitan approach would be a newly, it would not necessarily be a European approach, but more of a general, not necessarily down-to-earth approach. Maybe more a theory, an ideal, than a practice and hands-on implementation. And theory can run you up a tree. It's nice to have, but it can give you headaches . . . What is good for Indianapolis might not be what's cosmopolitan. It would be nice to know, but if they could use their cosmopolitan approach and net it down to the situation at hand, fine. But I can see many times when a person might overly sophisticate a simple problem by having too much input.

And like intellectualism, cosmopolitanism is sometimes seen as anti-democratic. As an Indianapolis informant explains: "Cosmopolitan is not important to me, definitely not, just be down-to-earth, just be a regular person. I think a cosmopolitan who is haughty or showy turns me off. Just be yourself."

Rather than expressing an actual opposition to intellectualism or cosmopolitanism, often respondents say that these traits simply leave them indifferent. For instance, while referring to people who are well-read, one of them suggests that "they come off being an expert in an area, and maybe they are, on one dimension. They might be an expert in what occurs on the dark side of the moon, but who cares." On the other hand, cosmopolitanism leaves some respondents indifferent because of its nebulous and intangible character. As a New Yorker chief financial executive says, "It is a much more qualitative quality. I can't measure it. So I mean, somebody who finds somebody with it, who speaks in a quote educated way unquote, that turns me no place."

We see, therefore, that the Americans in this study do not uncritically venerate high culture and cosmopolitanism. Also, many do not show

signs of cultural goodwill, i.e., an acknowledgment of the legitimacy of this culture. In other words, they do not think it is important to accumulate knowledge concerning high culture.[90] This anti-intellectualism is stronger in the Midwest, where populism and its associated values of anti-metropolitanism and anti-elitism have traditionally been more influential. In this context, being intellectual or cosmopolitan might be a handicap, and those who present these cultural traits might suffer from reverse cultural discrimination as they are socially constructed as "less interesting" or "less deserving" in the name of cultural egalitarianism and pragmatism, and in the name of the cultural sovereignty of the individual. This is likely to contribute to the feelings of alienation of American intellectuals from mainstream culture.[91]

Anti-intellectualism and anticosmopolitanism can be interpreted as a questioning of cultural standards of hierarchalization and as an attempt to subordinate them to moral ones, cultural sophistication being seen as a superfluous quality in comparison with sincerity or honesty for instance.[92] As an Indianapolis research scientist puts it: "I wouldn't mind associating with a boring, genuine person. I'd rather stick with a boring, genuine person than with a pretentious, interesting asshole." Along the same lines, an Indianapolis informant confesses, "I don't mind if my friends are boring. It's much more important that someone has a sense of morality that's positive and not destructive than the way they look, or how they choose to decorate their house, or where they take their vacation." Both individuals suggest that nothing is more important than "what kind of person you are," arguing for the sovereignty of moral standards of status attribution.

This anti-intellectualism is often doubled by a very pragmatic view of the role of education. Education is strongly emphasized by most American interviewees but often for financial reasons: many of them value education as a way of gaining access to an occupation that can support a comfortable lifestyle.[93] Consequently, they might develop a very instrumental attitude toward higher education, downplaying the properly intellectual element of the experience, and stressing the accumulation of credentials.[94] They might also encourage their children to choose a major that will lead to a well-paying job, steering them away from the liberal arts.[95] Students themselves often subordinate the properly intellectual side of the college experience to its social side.[96] This is illustrated by a Jewish nouveau riche computer consultant who lives on Long Island. He explains why his daughter chose to go to Indiana University in Bloomington:

She likes the university, she loves the kids, she loves the athletics, she knows most of the guys on the basketball team. She's having a good time. She went out there and took a look at it and said, "This is what college is." You know, big buildings, the ivy, the large stadium, a good business department, a good pre-law, a law school, the courses, and the quality of teachers.

This pragmatism is not surprising given that the American university system itself is less isolated from profit-making endeavors and from the market principle of supply and demand than the French. In America, tuition fees are much higher and universities are competing to attract good students—in France, students are not "competed for." Also, there exists a large number of private institutions in the United States whereas in France most universities and schools are public. Finally, American college presidents often resemble businessmen in that they need to spend considerable time raising funds for their institutions whereas their French counterparts expect the state to financially support their university in its entirety.

Opposition to cosmopolitanism is not as prevalent in France as it is in the United States. As noted by a Paris science teacher, "We are all cosmopolitan, so it does not matter." In this context, especially for large segments of the Parisian upper-middle class, cosmopolitanism is not isolated as a specific subculture but is part of a way of life. However, the Clermontois sometimes oppose the intellectual trendiness of the Parisians, while at the same time having a strong sense of cultural isolation and undoubtedly considering themselves to be less *au courant* than the Parisians. On the other hand, anti-intellectualism is frequent in both of the French sites. For instance, a Paris marketing executive explains that he does not appreciate people who are too sophisticated and who lack simplicity. He likes to discuss very ordinary things with his friends.

It is not big philosophical topics. I think there is nothing worse than that. When I was in the army, I knew a sociologist who was into that. He always wanted to debate for hours about everything: what was your attitude toward this and that employee, etc. I confess that I cannot stand this. It is too intellectual and not down-to-earth enough—too theoretical. I confess that it really bothered me. There are things in life that we naturally know. It is not necessary to ask ourselves philosophical questions.

Therefore, this same person criticizes people "who talk in a very complex way, with a lot of insinuations, who don't talk to be understood. This I cannot stand. These people always ask you if you see what they mean. I hate these people who have a completely esoteric language."

A few additional French respondents criticized "ideologues," i.e., intellectuals who are strongly invested in a specific ideological current, whether socialism, feminism, or some other "ism." Because most of these people are for-profit workers they will be discussed in Chapter 6.

CONCLUSION

Just as it was the case for French and American definitions of moral and socioeconomic boundaries, the picture that emerges from the interviews is one of stark national contrasts: not only do French and American upper-middle-class members read intelligence differently, but they also think differently about topics such as refinement, intellectualism, and cosmopolitanism. Furthermore, the French stress cultural boundaries much more than Americans do.[97] This is partly reflected in the fact that intellectuals have a less clearly defined identity and culture in the United States than in France. It is also reflected in the cultural laissez-faire and in the presence of strong anticosmopolitan and anti-intellectual feelings in the United States. The values of friendliness, conflict avoidance, and cultural egalitarianism all reinforce the marginalization of intellectual and high culture in American society as they stress the cultural sovereignty of the individual and the primacy of moral criteria of evaluation over cultural criteria. Similarly, pragmatism sustains a certain anti-intellectualism and anticosmopolitanism which results in a weakening of cultural boundaries. Consequently, familiarity with high culture is likely to have drastically different effects on mobility in the French and the American upper-middle class. Whereas in France this trait seems to be less unambiguously viewed as a positive one, in the United States it can be construed also as a sign that one is too uppity, not down-to-earth enough. In fact, in the American context, individuals who are interested only in high culture might suffer from reverse cultural discrimination in work settings because they can be seen as being too unidimensional. We see, therefore, that the cultural style that helps one to be socially constructed as professionally "promising" in one context can be ineffective in another context; we have some indication that in the French workplace refinement seems to partly

take the place occupied by honesty, friendliness, and conflict avoidance in the American workplace, making culture more important than morality for achievement. We also saw that French moral humanism is itself inseparable from humanistic culture, i.e., from cultural status signals. On the other hand, if in the United States a number of factors play against the importance of cultural boundaries, the greater association between high socioeconomic status and cultural consumption might reinforce these boundaries. There do not exist important differences between cultural centers and cultural peripheries, although the patterns are more differentiated in France than in the United States.

The issue of national differences in the degree of boundedness of symbolic boundaries that was discussed in the previous pages is an important one. the notions of tightly and loosely bounded culture helps us understand essential differences between the basic features of French and American culture. Until now sociologists of culture had largely neglected to study the structure of symbolic boundaries, focusing instead on the role played by command of elite arts in defining and maintaining class boundaries. They often adopted analytical categories that were too fine for most French participants. These categories appear to be too fine for American individuals as well. More specifically, even if the notion of cultural capital has proven to be a very powerful conceptual tool—as suggested by the fact that it is widely used in current sociological research—it might now prove to be too rigid because it unnecessarily narrows down the criteria used for judging cultural purity and pollution, downplaying the importance of sheer intelligence as a high status signal or exaggerating the importance of familiarity with high culture. Instead of using this notion indiscriminately, I hope to have shown the necessity of considering the content of symbolic boundaries themselves and of analyzing the place of various high status signals within these boundaries. The notion of symbolic boundaries is a useful dynamic concept because, not having a predefined content, it potentially encompasses all the different elements that make up signals of high status at different points in time and place. As will be seen in the next chapters, by considering the variations in the content of symbolic boundaries drawn by various groups, it is possible to study the dynamic and the nature of relationships between groups, i.e., their relative subordination and cultural autonomy.

Chapter Five

∼∼

EXPLAINING NATIONAL DIFFERENCES

> In [America], nothing is greater or more brilliant
> than commerce; it attracts the attention of the
> public and fills the imagination of the multitude:
> all energetic passions are directed towards it.
> —Alexis de Tocqueville

If the status signals that the upper-middle class uses to evaluate moral, cultural, and socioeconomic status vary, how much importance do the French and the Americans attach to each of these three types of boundaries? In other words, are the Hoosiers equally likely to draw cultural and socioeconomic boundaries? Are the Parisians more culturally exclusive than they are morally exclusive? And do the New Yorkers stress culture over socioeconomic status to the same extent that Parisians do? These questions will be examined below. Evidence shows that there is surprisingly little difference between the boundary-drawing patterns of residents of "cultural centers" and those of residents of "cultural peripheries." Our study shows also that while upper-middle-class men who live in the New York suburbs stress socioeconomic status much more than moral and cultural status, this does not apply to female interviewees. Moreover, moral and cultural status seem to have more autonomy from socioeconomic status in France than in the United States: the French who value moral or cultural purity are less likely to also appreciate high socioeconomic standing than their American counterpart.

The next pages also provide a more systematic explanation of the differences in the ways in which French and American upper-middle-class members draw boundaries. Combining structural and cultural factors, I offer a multicausal explanation that suggests that boundary work varies with the cultural resources people have at their disposal as well as with their structural situations and the characteristics of the societies in which they live. More specifically, on the structural side, a number of remote and proximate environmental factors have increased the probability of individuals drawing one type of boundary rather than another. These include features of nonlocal environments, such as the characteristics of

the French and American stratification systems and the level of racial and ethnic diversity of each society. They also include features of the structural positions of people, such as their job stability. On the cultural side, boundary patterns are affected by the national repertoires, or cultural resources, that French and American societies offer to their members, which are themselves defined by the historical national repertoire of each country and by various sectors and groups involved in the production and diffusion of culture (intellectuals, the educational system, the mass media, museums and other cultural institutions). This suggests that individuals do not draw boundaries out of their experience, interests, or social position alone: cognitive and structural factors often participate in shaping their perception of the latter.[1] Furthermore, values are rarely created anew: the boundaries we draw often have a rule-like status, being mediated by the cultural repertoires that our environment puts at our disposal. Therefore, phenomena such as the relative importance of anti-intellectualism in America compared to France can only be explained by the interaction of a number of cultural and structural factors.

NATIONAL PATTERNS IN BOUNDARY WORK

Previous chapters showed that moral boundaries are as important in France as they are in the United States, that socioeconomic boundaries are the most salient in America, and that cultural boundaries emerge most sharply in France. A comparison *within* sites reveals similar trends: the approximate quantitative ranking of all interviewees on the moral, cultural, and socioeconomic dimensions shows that cultural boundaries are the most salient type of boundaries for the Frenchmen I talked with, while socioeconomic boundaries are the least salient for this same group.[2] This pattern reverses that characteristic of Americans: both moral and socioeconomic boundaries are more important to them than cultural boundaries, the differences in emphasis between types of boundaries being more pronounced than in the French case.[3] It would appear, then, that standards of prestige do vary nationally in a significant but not very strong way, even if for both groups moral boundaries play a secondary role.[4]

These national boundary patterns are manifested in the ways Parisians, New Yorkers, Hoosiers, and Clermontois criticize the different forms of boundaries:[5] the French prove to be much more likely to oppose socioeconomic boundaries than Americans, whereas the latter more often

oppose intellectualism and cosmopolitanism.[6] Moreover, these patterns correspond to the types of boundaries that the French and Americans tend to draw against one another when given the opportunity to do so in interviews—we saw that several French participants viewed Americans as too materialistic, less intelligent, and certainly less cultivated, than themselves. Finally, national boundary patterns are also reflected in the relationship that each boundary has with the others in each country: the quantitative analysis suggests that both cultural and moral status are more autonomous from socioeconomic status in France than they are in the United States. Compared to the French who are very socioeconomically exclusive, more American interviewees who strongly stress socioeconomic status also strongly emphasize cultural status.[7] Accordingly, previous chapters indicated that in the United States consumption of high culture is often taken to be a symbol of high social status, along with such material status symbols as owning a luxury car and a house in an exclusive neighborhood. Also, moral and socioeconomic purity more frequently go hand in hand for the Hoosiers, who often take moral purity to be reflected in socioeconomic success by deducing honesty and moral character from success.[8] This is less true for the Parisians who tend to presume that money is corrupting and that moral and socioeconomic purity are incompatible.[9]

While some indicators could be interpreted as suggesting that high culture is slightly more democratized in the United States than in France,[10] cultural boundaries are not very salient in the boundary work of New Yorkers and Hoosiers: Americans who are culturally sophisticated seem to be less likely than their French counterparts to believe that they can legitimately expect to draw prestige from their cultural sophistication because the principles of cultural egalitarianism and cultural laissez-faire militate against this belief. In contrast, we saw that French participants more often make cultural distinctions as a way to gain socioeconomic status, i.e., to improve their social position; that they frequently draw socioeconomic boundaries on the basis of cultural status signals (e.g., rejecting working-class people as "vulgar"); and that signals of high cultural status play a more central role in the French workplace. Also, evidence suggests that Americans are more likely than the French to believe that cultural standards of evaluation should be subordinated to moral ones (i.e., to "what kind of person you are").[11]

What differences emerge when "cultural centers" and "cultural peripheries" are compared? The approximate quantitative analysis suggests that,

in general, strong moral boundaries are drawn slightly more often by periphery residents than by center residents; fewer Clermontois are indifferent or opposed to moral boundaries than Parisians.[12] The same contrast appears in the American case, with the Hoosiers being less antimoralistic.[13] It is surprising to find that the center/periphery differences are less pronounced in the case of cultural boundaries: while in France, residents of the cultural periphery are more likely to score low on the cultural dimension,[14] in the United States they are as likely as residents from the cultural centers to draw strong cultural boundaries.[15] On the other hand, center residents are not more socioeconomically selective than periphery residents. Overall, we find a small but significant difference in boundary patterns between people living in cultural centers and people living in cultural peripheries,[16] the contrast being more striking in France than in the United States.[17] This confirms the view that American cultural classification systems are relatively universal.[18]

Several indicators suggest that the national differences I have identified are diminishing. Again, French attitudes toward money and the private sector are becoming less negative. At the same time, French culture has been rapidly losing in international influence to the benefit of American mass culture.[19] Inside France itself, recent books have been lamenting the decline of high culture and the growing influence of American culture through television.[20] And the French, who have always been proud of their rigorous educational system, are now looking to the U.S. model to modernize their universities, which can no longer compete with their American counterparts in many domains of research.[21] In the United States, the yuppie era in the eighties symbolized the greater availability of cosmopolitan cultural goods (gourmet cuisine, fine wines, etc.), concomitant with the cultural consolidation of the professional and managerial occupations that have been expanding since World War II.[22] American cultural boundaries themselves, however, do not seem to be becoming stronger partly because, as Paul DiMaggio suggests, high culture itself is being eroded by factors such as "the transformation of local American upper classes into a national elite, anchored in organizations rather than community; [the] increased influence of commercial principles of classification with the rise of popular culture industries; the emergence of relatively autonomous and highly competitive high culture art worlds; and the growth of mass higher education and the modern state."[23] In other words, it appears that cultural boundaries are losing ground in the United

States while socioeconomic boundaries are gaining in importance in France; the traditional cultural hierarchies that glorify high culture are being threatened. Socioeconomic boundaries might also have gained in importance in the United States during the greedy eighties. Their increased importance over moral boundaries is suggested by the popularity of characters such as Donald Trump, by the savings and loans scandal, and other events. More research is needed to document these changes in national boundary patterns.

Gender differences have not yet been discussed. Although considerably more data are needed before conclusions can be drawn, the interviews I conducted with fifteen females living in the New York suburbs indicate that women tend to draw considerably stronger cultural boundaries,[24] weaker socioeconomic boundaries, and slightly stronger moral boundaries than men.[25] This is in line with the literature on gender differences which suggests that women have a stronger orientation toward morality and justice because their gender roles revolve frequently around taking care of people.[26] It is also in line with studies that show that females are less success-oriented than males[27] and that they are particularly involved in culture in general.[28] Randall Collins has even argued that the management of symbolic status is a feminine specialty given that females are often employed in occupations concerned with the presentation of self.[29] Accordingly, in their descriptions of the qualities they appreciate in their friends, the females I talked with were much more likely than the males to mention tastes in clothes, foods, books, art, travels, and so forth.[30] They also put more emphasis on self-actualization than the males, particularly when discussing child-rearing values: they often said that their main goal as parents was to help their children develop their talents and their mind to full potential. A focus on self-actualization and on psychological growth was also obvious in their discussion of their relationships with others. For instance, a New Jersey advertising accountant explained:

> I know a lot of men who cannot make an emotional connection and with whom you've only got two choices: you either play the subservient role or you play the dominant role. I don't find that very interesting. What I really like is some kind of more mutual involvement of equals that feels more like an equal relationship because you really can take a lot of risk in that relationship. People who can do that I think are the most interesting.

Psychological well-being in general seemed to occupy a more central place in the lives of female respondents. Such gender differences can be interpreted as reflecting institutionalized cultural repertoires within female culture rather than biologically determined differences. Again, more work is needed on gender differences in boundary work and their causes.

EXPLAINING DIFFERENCES

Previous chapters have introduced a few factors that explain differences in the content of symbolic boundaries in France and the United States. For instance, Americans might tend to measure moral character through friendliness, conflict avoidance, and team orientation because they are frequently required to provide signals of trustworthiness, as they change employers frequently and are often involved in large, revolving social networks. This generates much organizational uncertainty. The extent to which people read status through competence and work ethic is related to the typical conditions for mobility and the career structure of the French and the American upper-middle class. On the other hand, if money is more central as a status signal for Hoosiers and New Yorkers, it is partly because of the weaker development of welfare services in America. Finally, if cultural boundaries are drawn differently in France than they are in the United States, it is because of factors such as the influence of the Cartesian intellectual tradition in France and of pragmatism in America.

Considering these and other factors, following is an explanation of national boundary patterns that avoids the pitfalls of both the determinist/ reductionist and the voluntarist approaches to culture. Along with Bennett Berger, I consider that

> [t]he business of a generalizing sociology of culture is to understand as exactly as possible how a range of possible choices is presented to the consciousness of a potentially active agent, and how situational or intervening variables (i.e., microsocial structures) reinforce or undermine the predisposition to choose from among the range of possible choices; a process going from possibility to probability.[31]

Therefore, I analyze the structural characteristics of the French and American societies that increase the probability that individuals will draw one type of boundary rather than another. I also consider the cultural resources or repertoires that these societies make available to their members for use in their active boundary work. The effects of national reper-

toires need to be analyzed separately because, even if these repertoires are shaped by a wide range of economic, political, and sociohistorical factors, they take on a life of their own once they are institutionalized.[32] In other words, they become part of the environment, of the *structure* that facilitates or hinders the drawing of specific types of boundaries, or the "enactment" of specific configurations of historically deposited meaning.

In contrast to the voluntarist view of culture suggested by tool kit theorists, the multicausal explanation I propose takes into consideration how remote and proximate structural factors shape choices from and access to the tool kit—in other words, how these factors affect the cultural resources most likely to be mobilized by different types of individuals and what elements of tool kits people have most access to given their social positions.[33] In my view, the drawing of boundaries does not consist of voluntaristic processes guided by autonomous individual moral or existential programs, but of processes that are largely shaped by culturally available accounts of what defines a worthy person and what behaviors are reasonable.

In contrast to the determinist approaches, and like tool-kit theorists, I emphasize the possibility for individuals to actively choose among cultural resources, even if their choices are largely channeled by the "cultural supply side" of the equation.[34] Thereby I make room for the relative autonomy of symbolic boundaries from structural conditions. On the other hand, following neo-institutional theory, I am also fairly critical of approaches that consider boundary work to be mostly determined by the experience, interest, life history, or social position of individuals, because in their boundary work individuals routinely rely on the cultural rules that are provided to them by their larger environment. An analysis of remote structural factors is necessary to supplement theories that emphasize the influence of proximate structural factors (such as economic class position, volume and structure of capital, distance from necessity, or group structure and cohesiveness) on culture, because nonlocal environments often have as important an impact on boundary work as do proximate structural factors. Also, an approach that posits a direct correspondence between class, habitus, and cultural choices, for instance, or between group structure and degree of elaboration of symbolic codes, cannot account for the influence of national cultural traditions on individual tastes and preferences, as the last chapter of this book will suggest.

Whereas social scientists such as Michael Schudson, Dan Sperber, and Gary Alan Fine have been concerned with analyzing what causes

certain cultural resources to be used and mobilized by actors and to survive,[35] my goal here is simply to document what resources are supplied to
my interviewees, and what structural factors can potentially channel their
boundary work. Analyzing the full range of these resources and factors,
their respective weight in determining boundary work, as well as the specific interaction among repertoires, structural factors, and boundary work,
would require a more detailed and lengthy analysis than it is possible to
offer here. An in-depth study of these questions might draw in part on the
work cited above and on ecological models proposed by sociologists for
explaining the diffusion or success of specific ideologies or cultural forms.[36]

The following pages discuss in turn what historical national repertoires are made available in France and the United States; how sectors
and groups specialized in the production and diffusion of culture determine what cultural resources are available; and how remote environmental
factors—general social, political, and economic features of French and
American societies—favor or hinder the drawing of each type of boundary. I also consider the effect on boundary work of proximate structural
factors, such as the social position and work conditions of my interviewees in particular, and of the members of the French and American upper-
middle class in general. The influence of market position and of the
relationship that individuals have with economic rationality given their
occupations will be discussed in Chapter 6 by way of analyzing variations
in boundary work across various occupations.

Historical National Repertoires

This section concentrates on a few central historic themes that define the
traditional national values and ideologies of American and French society.
For the United States, the role of pragmatism, the role of populism, and
the ideology of "Americanism" are particularly important. In the French
case, the Republican ideals of the French Revolution as well as the influence of the aristocratic, socialist, and anarchist traditions are discussed.
The place of religion in both national cultures is also explored. It is reasonable to think that the presence of these themes in the French and
American repertoires affected the men I talked with by providing them
with readily usable cultural notions that could be mobilized in their
boundary work. Again, while the emergence of these themes is inextricably linked to the institutional and economic history of each country,
these themes have to be considered independently because they have a

life of their own as cultural resources, as Jeffrey Alexander and others have pointed out.[37]

The themes of pragmatism and populism occupy an important place in the American national repertoire. Pragmatism is defined here not as a philosophy but as a "'see-if-it-works' suspicion of dogma, of doctrine and of the rigid adherence to abstract principles of theories",[38] populism is defined as a tradition of grass-roots revolt against the idle rich. If pragmatism subordinates knowledge and intellectual pursuit to practical goals, populism glorifies "plain people" against self-indulgent and often effete elites.[39] Indirectly, both themes have shaped the place of high and literary culture in American society by widely diffusing the view that they constitute superfluous niceties.[40] As noted above, the men I talked with drew heavily on these themes to articulate their dislike of intellectuals and cosmopolitan people and to draw anticultural boundaries.

Many social scientists have written on the common vision of their society that Americans share. Terms such as "Americanism" and "American civil religion" have been proposed to refer to it.[41] Elements of this historical vision have affected in a contradictory way the likelihood of people drawing socioeconomic boundaries, reinforcing and weakening it simultaneously. For instance, themes such as achievement and individualism indirectly bolster the centrality of socioeconomic status, making widely available the idea that individual material success is one of the most, if not the most, important human goals. Others themes, such as egalitarianism and democracy, have weakened socioeconomic boundaries by promoting the idea of universalism and condemning socioeconomic exclusion based on ascribed characteristics. This tradition of egalitarianism has meant that American lower-class people have come to "expect and are accorded more respect in cross-class interpersonal relations than their European counterparts."[42] We saw that upper-middle-class Americans often draw on the theme of egalitarianism when opposing socioeconomic boundaries or discussing moral status.

The French equivalent of "Americanism" can be found in the Republican ideals of the French Revolution, which still survive today. These ideals include the Jacobin obsession with equality, universalism, and national unity that negates particularism based on locality, corporate membership, and birth, thereby weakening the probability of people drawing boundaries on the basis of ascribed characteristics. Another such ideal, inherited from the Enlightenment, is the idea that Reason is the only basis

for political order.[43] While Jacobinism destroyed local cultures, strengthening national symbolic boundaries in general by making them more universal, the cult of Reason is likely to have reinforced the centrality of cultural boundaries in national repertoires, and indirectly to have weakened socioeconomic boundaries, especially the role of money and competition as status signals. This cult sustains the view that society can and should be organized on the basis of a preconceived master plan that transcends idiosyncratic interests, and especially class interests. Thus it makes widely available the notion that human intellectual capabilities, as opposed to market mechanisms, are responsible for the organization of society through the action of the state. It defines the bourgeoisie, along with other classes, as particularistic, thereby enforcing a view of mercantile activities, and of the world of competition more generally, as corrupt and unworthy. Upper-middle-class men drew on these elements of the French national repertoire when discussing their ambiguous attitude toward power and when describing the pursuit of money as a trivial goal.

The place of cultural boundaries in the French national repertoire has also been reinforced by the presence of a deep-seated aristocratic tradition that prizes refinement and bolsters high culture. Over centuries, the court tradition has sustained the production of highly sophisticated fashion, foods, wines, and perfumes, helping to define France as a country of delicacy, elegance, and frivolity. As far back as the sixteenth century, "elements of the upper nobility . . . were deeply involved in [the] propagation [of high culture]," participating in a European cosmopolitan culture.[44] In the eighteenth century, the literary salons in which aristocrats were very involved became extremely popular. There, *hommes de lettres* developed stylish conversation into an art, often putting elegant wit above substance. Similarly, the Jesuit-run schools where the aristocracy educated its children promoted linguistic eloquence and knowledge of the classics over knowledge of the sciences and mathematics.[45] Aristocrats were instrumental in the creation of the academies of science and literature that established France's claim to primacy in Europe's intellectual life by bringing together a cultural class that aspired to influencing public events. Hence the aristocratic tradition helped sustain the view that high culture, refinement, and intellectualism are of ultimate importance.

On the other hand, the place of socioeconomic boundaries in the French national repertoire has been weakened by the presence of a well-established anarchist and socialist tradition that openly opposes the subordination of collective interests to the logic of profit making.[46] In the

United States, no important political party provided such a widely diffused fundamental critique of capitalism and of the cultural ideals of socioeconomic achievement and individualism. Accordingly, the French participants were more critical of materialism than their American counterparts.

A final element of national repertoires that is likely to have affected the makeup of symbolic boundaries in both societies is religion. In the French case, the Republican tradition, with its strong anticlerical overtones, has somewhat precluded strong religion-based moral boundaries. In America, the presence of a highly entrenched religious tradition, of a wide variety of sects, and of moralistic social movements, such as the abolitionist movement, the Prohibitionist one, and Puritanism itself, all have de facto sustained the view that moral issues are of great importance.[47] The Protestant tradition simultaneously could sustain strong moral and socioeconomic boundaries. In contrast, the French Catholic tradition militated against strong socioeconomic boundaries, finding difficulties in reconciling worldly pursuits and spiritual salvation. The American tradition of religious pluralism, however, might have increased the tolerance of (or at least indifference to) cultural and other differences, helping to define spiritual choices in particular, and cultural choices in general, as belonging to the private realm.[48]

The Influence of Sectors of Cultural Production and Diffusion

National repertoires are shaped not only by values that have been important in the history of a nation but also by the cultural messages that are diffused society-wide by the educational system, the mass media, and other institutions and groups that specialize in the production and diffusion of culture. The influence of these institutions is particularly crucial in affecting the availability of specific cultural resources. They limit the impact of proximate structural factors on symbolic boundaries by diffusing similar cultural messages over society at large, undermining regional and class differences, strengthening national unity, and universalizing national boundary patterns in the process.[49]

The Educational System. What schools say about a society has a strong impact on the way individuals within that society perceive it.[50] More specifically, mass education creates a whole series of social assumptions about the common culture of a society, thereby expanding the common view of society that people hold. It also "reifies a given national history," and, as John Meyer says, it

constructs a common civic order—common heroes and villains, a common constitution of political order with some shared cultural symbols and legitimate national participation . . . it validates the existence of a common natural reality through science and a common logical structure through mathematics and in this way constructs a myth of a common culture intimately linked to world society.[51]

The French and American educational systems have had different effects on the symbolic boundaries of their respective citizenries. In France, the educational system has bolstered the development of strong and universal cultural boundaries by making available a unified definition of high status culture, thanks to a tradition of administrative centralization. A single curriculum, with ample emphasis on the literary disciplines (philosophy, history, and literature), prevails nationally, being defined by the state and the academies.[52] In contrast, the American educational system militates against strong cultural boundaries because it does not diffuse a unified definition of high status culture. Instead, due to a long tradition of political localism, the curriculum is defined by local school boards. This political structure makes it possible for pressure groups to affect the content of the curriculum on topics ranging from evolution theory to the selection of canonical literary texts. In fact, in the last twenty years, the American educational system has become the terrain par excellence for contesting traditional cultural hierarchies—contesting the place of high culture—as minority groups have asked for the creation of a curriculum reflecting the cultural diversity of the American population.[53] This movement has weakened already frail cultural boundaries by questioning the value of the traditional canon as defined in the Western tradition. On the other hand, it has also weakened socioeconomic boundaries by further legitimizing racial, ethnic, and gender differences.

The American educational system undermines cultural boundaries in other ways. For instance, in sharp contrast to the French system, it diffuses a definition of high status culture that downplays history, philosophy, and the arts in favor of more marketable (and less clearly culturally hierarchalized) skills. But most important, this system is more subject to economic constraints than the French educational system. American school budgets depend more exclusively on local taxes, and are generally controlled by business-minded local elites, who have an interest in limiting their growth. This directly affects the salaries and prestige of American teachers. In contrast, their French counterparts have total autonomy

from their "clients," as their salaries and promotions are determined by the central administration.[54]

The fact that the French higher education system has historically played a central role in the recruitment and formation of the elite (namely, the role of the grandes écoles)[55] has reinforced a view of elite culture as important: such formation involves educating future members of the elite in the national cultural tradition by celebrating French grandeur, which is largely defined by French high culture, i.e., by its writers, philosophers, artists, and the like. These factors combine to increase the value of high culture, to make familiarity with high culture a more central type of high status signal, and to make cultural boundaries themselves dominant in French culture. Chapter 6 shows how this affects the boundary work of French social and cultural specialists.

The Mass Media. The effect of the French and American mass media on their respective national repertoires reinforces the patterns sustained by the two educational systems. Until very recently French radio and television stations were all state-owned, and many of them gave a relatively large time for cultural programming. This undoubtedly strengthened cultural boundaries by making high culture available to a wider audience at a time when television advertising was banned. It was only in the eighties that the state legalized private television and radio stations, largely under popular pressure for more entertainment programming.[56] This strongly contrasts with the situation on this side of the Atlantic. Most American cultural programming is diffused by the Public Broadcasting System stations, whose audience remains very limited, as we saw in the last chapter. The commercial stations make little effort to provide more culturally oriented programming. On the contrary, they play an important role in enhancing the perceived value of consumerism through their programming and through advertising.[57]

Cultural Institutions. State financing of culture and of cultural institutions, such as museums, monuments, universities, and conservatories, also helps to sustain strong cultural boundaries in France, as it makes high culture more available, providing artists, writers, and other cultural producers with more jobs and with more autonomy from market pressures.[58] In contrast, in the United States, most cultural institutions are nonprofit organizations, and they are much more vulnerable to market pressures than

state institutions.[59] While the availability of more financial resources might facilitate the diffusion of high culture and the arts in the United States, it also often constrains it by subordinating it more directly to financial considerations. Accordingly, as we will see in the next chapter, American social and cultural producers are more concerned with socio-economic status than are their French counterparts.

Intellectual Elites. One cannot account for the strength of cultural boundaries in France without referring to the cultural influence of contemporary intellectuals, who are following in the footsteps of the philosophers of the Enlightenment in attempting to shape the public sphere. Diderot, Voltaire, and Rousseau played an extremely significant historical role in bringing about a dramatic alteration in the values of educated Europeans, affecting social change with an efficacy rarely equaled by American intellectuals. They institutionalized a social role that was to be sustained during the twentieth century by such thinkers as Jean-Paul Sartre, Raymond Aron, and Michel Foucault. These modern intellectuals and their peers greatly contributed to diffusing French literary culture to the population at large. The existence of a considerable number of weekly magazines and daily newspapers that publicize the ideas of French intellectuals, while commercializing high status culture, is a measure of the intellectuals' effect on the French repertoires.[60] In particular, these publications play a crucial role in making the French intellectual culture known and available to the population at large.[61] Accordingly, the members of the French upper-middle class are much more likely than their American counterparts to interpret familiarity with the work of visible intellectuals as a signal of high cultural status.[62] In contrast, American intellectuals have had much less effect on the national repertoire, and their influence is diminishing, as suggested by the recent decline in the volume of publications aimed at the intelligentsia. In fact, while the population of college-educated Americans increased by 208 percent between 1947 and 1983, the average growth in circulation of a sample of intellectual journals and magazines was only 130 percent.[63]

A number of factors account for the fact that French intellectuals are able to sustain a relatively important level of cultural influence. First, using cultural indicators, Priscilla Parkhurst Clark has found that (1) compared to the American literary elite, the French literary elite is better supported, both financially and culturally, by the government and other powerful groups, with access to an important system of institutionalized

patronage, which includes the Académie française, the universities, and the Centre National de Recherche Scientifique; (2) French intellectuals receive more symbolic recognition, as there exists in France a large number of well-publicized literary prizes, for instance; and (3) again, the activities of this group are more widely covered by the media than the activity of their American counterparts.[64] Indeed, while American magazines aimed at intellectuals focus mostly on books (e.g., *The New York Review of Books*), French publications emphasize the presentation of intellectuals themselves, describing their tastes, lifestyles, and opinions, and their relationship to other intellectuals. Through their aggressive writing style, these publications diffuse a charismatic and hegemonic collective imagery of French intellectuals as a social group. Thereby they contribute to making the French intellectual subculture more lively and attractive, cultural boundaries more central, and intellectuals themselves better integrated in French society.[65]

The influence of French intellectuals is further enhanced by the old-boy networks of the French elite. First, top intellectuals and the members of other elites have often attended the same elite schools (L'Ecole Normale Supérieure, the lycée St-Louis, the Fondation Nationale de Sciences Politiques, etc.) and often participate in the same overlapping microcosms that constitute the *Tout-Paris*—this has become more frequent since the Socialists came to power in 1981. Also, certain leading intellectuals have been influential in political parties, which provided them with journals and with a platform from which to diffuse their ideas, and indirectly their intellectual subculture.[66] Finally, the sheer concentration of intellectuals in Paris has helped them to develop a more coherent and viable intellectual subculture.

Other factors explain the lesser influence of American intellectuals. First, increasingly, American intellectual circles either exist in parallel with the university or are confounded with it, to the point that intellectuals have come to resemble other upper-middle-class professionals in many ways, losing some of their subcultural specificity.[67] Indeed, the technocratic culture has gained considerable importance in academia, militating against the survival of the *homme de lettres*, as utilitarianism, pragmatism, and careerism are becoming more influential in this milieu.[68] In addition, as we saw in Chapter 4, the values of cultural egalitarianism and conflict avoidance have worked against the diffusion of intellectualism. The absence of strong left-of-center parties that can provide intellectuals with a forum and an audience as well as the geographical dispersion of

American intellectuals have further contributed to the decline of their cultural influence. In this context, it is not surprising that Lewis Perry concludes his comprehensive review of three hundred years of intellectual life in America by writing that the end of the twentieth century constitutes an all-time low point for American intellectuals, their influence being more limited than ever.[69]

Remote Environmental Conditions

The various cultural sectors discussed above play a crucial role in making specific types of cultural resources available to individuals for use in their active boundary work, thereby indirectly weakening or strengthening each of the main types of symbolic boundaries. But the structural features of French and American societies shape what resources individuals are most likely to use. While space limitations prevent me from discussing the full range of relevant structural conditions, I will compare both societies in terms of the relative presence of the public and nonprofit sectors, the characteristics of the stratification system, and the level of ethnic and racial diversity as well as the importance of geographic mobility and the standard size of communities. Many of the factors that answer the question "Why no socialism in the United States?" might be used to understand why socioeconomic boundaries are stronger on this side of the Atlantic than they are in France. These factors explain why "bourgeois ideology," as Gramsci called it, is more hegemonic in America than elsewhere.[70]

Public and Nonprofit Sectors. Many social scientists consider the early development of a strong state and the survival of strong political institutions to be the most distinctive features of French society.[71] Today the public sector is considerably larger in France than in the United States. Between 1970 and 1984, general government expenditures in France increased from 38 percent to 53 percent of the gross national product. And in 1985 central government expenditures represented 45 percent of gross domestic product, as compared with 26 percent in the United States. In the same year, 30 percent of the French active population was employed by the state (including local governments), in contrast to 12 percent in 1970;[72] in the United States, these figures were, respectively, 16 percent and 15 percent.[73] Many of the educational, cultural, health, and welfare services that are often provided by nonprofit organizations in the United States are a state responsibility in France.[74]

Because it provides the population with more distance toward economic rationality, the presence of this large public sector in France has weakened the probability of people attaching great importance to having a high income and consequently drawing strong socioeconomic boundaries. Indeed, the life conditions of French people are not exclusively linked to their personal market position, as the state makes available free health care, welfare, and educational services. In contrast, as explained in Chapter 3, in the United States resource allocation is accomplished less by the state than by market mechanisms. This means that Americans have to obtain day care, health care, and high-quality education at high costs. Consequently, they are more likely to value having a high standard of living, and to put more emphasis on income as a universal standard of status assessment. The role of market mechanisms in the allocation of resources is in turn likely to have important effects on a wide range of phenomena, which all weaken cultural boundaries. For instance, in the United States more than in France, in academia, the arts and the humanities might be given considerably less prestige and resources than preprofessional fields and more profit-oriented specialties. The salary and prestige of occupations that are not primarily aimed at profit making are also likely to be affected, as is the influence and presence of intellectuals and academics in the political elite. More research is needed on cross-national differences with respect to these issues.[75]

Stratification System. The effect of state intervention on the weakening of socioeconomic boundaries in France is reinforced by the greater stability of the class structure. Members of the French working class have historically experienced greater barriers to mobility than their American counterparts. Coupled with the fact that wealth is more unequally distributed in France than in the United States—the higher segments of the French population monopolize a larger fraction of the total national income (see Appendix I)—this factor has weakened socioeconomic boundaries by curtailing the extent to which people stress professional success and income as high status signals. In contrast, on this side of the Atlantic, a history of growing abundance and the absence of a frontier have reinforced the belief in the importance of mobility and achievement, making it more likely that people will draw strong socioeconomic boundaries.[76]

Geographic Mobility and Community Size. Simultaneously, the high geographic mobility and the large size of residential communities charac-

teristic of American society have also increased the probability that Americans will value signals of high socioeconomic status.[77] Indeed, as argued in Chapter 3, income is more likely to act as a central determinant of status in mobile and anonymous societies because consumption of durable consumer goods permits immediate signaling of one's status; the reading and signaling of cultural and moral status requires time, involvement in networks, and/or a growing personal familiarity with individuals themselves. Accordingly, we saw that socioeconomic boundaries are strong in the New York suburbs, where commuters remain anonymous, and that in Indianapolis strong socioeconomic boundaries go hand in hand with strong moral boundaries, this last site having a more stable and smaller population. We also saw that moral and cultural boundaries are strong in the French upper-middle class, whose members change employers much less frequently than their American counterparts. One might predict that socioeconomic boundaries will gain in importance in France partly because of an increase in the level of geographic mobility.

Ethnic and Racial Diversity. The last structural factor that affects the likelihood of people drawing one type of boundary rather than another is ethnic and racial diversity. In the United States, as suggested earlier, the sheer ethnic diversity of the country has weakened the importance of signals of high cultural status that pertain to the Western definition of high culture. This diversity might not affect the value placed on sheer intelligence and self-actualization, but it militates in favor of a greater cultural pluralism, which is in some ways incompatible with the predominance of European high culture. Indeed, members of ethnic minorities maintain a certain cultural autonomy vis-à-vis mainstream definitions of high status culture, reinterpreting within the logic of their own culture the main tenets of the American credo.[78] This is even more true for members of racial minorities, who through music, dress, and language celebrate their distinctiveness and develop subcultural pockets of autonomy or resistance, and thereby contribute to making American cultural boundaries less universal and homogeneous.[79] By contrast, the French population is much more homogeneous, both racially and ethnically. It is only recently that a major social movement contesting the view that being French meant being French-born and white has developed. French people are only starting to think of their country as a land of immigration, and French society has not yet developed a strong tradition of religious or racial pluralism.[80] This superficial unity has strengthened the dominance

of French classical culture and indirectly that of cultural boundaries; except for the Breton ethnic movement, minority groups have rarely claimed an equal status for their culture or representation in museums, concert halls, or school curricula. This is partly because many of the non-European immigrants are members of former French colonies and have themselves been socialized at an early age in the idea of the higher status of French classical culture. All these general characteristics of French and American society contribute to the likelihood that interviewees draw one type of boundary rather than another. Boundaries, however, are reinforced also by characteristics that are unique to upper-middle-class members, given their social position.

Proximate Environmental Factors

Previous chapters have discussed the effects of a number of proximate factors on boundary work. For instance, the weaker socioeconomic boundaries drawn by members of the French upper-middle class are in part attributable to the fact that corporatism curtails the role of competition in the French workplace. Furthermore, members of the French upper-middle class, who change employers less often and have greater job stability, are less likely to highly value professional mobility and economic status more generally than Americans do. On the other hand, since, like their American counterpart, upper-middle-class French men occupy the top of the social ladder in their society, they might be encouraged to stress social position as a basis for the evaluation of status. For both groups, autonomy at work and the fact that professional activity requires the intensive use of intellectual abilities might push interviewees to put a premium on self-actualization and intellectual development as types of high status signals than it is the case for members of other classes.[81]

Proximate factors also include a wide range of non–work-based solidarities, such as gender, age, race, ethnicity, religion, and urban or rural location. I consider these to be proximate factors because they vary from individual to individual even if they define their structural and cultural group memberships. The data provide information concerning the effects of some of these factors on boundary work. For instance, we saw that being male might increase the probability of drawing strong socioeconomic boundaries and weak cultural boundaries, while being female might slightly increase the probability of drawing strong moral boundaries. On the other hand, the data reveal that patterns of boundary work

performed by men in their thirties and men in their fifties are similar.[82] At this point, in the absence of comparative data, it is impossible to assess the effects of race, ethnicity, and rural location on boundary work.

Pierre Bourdieu has described other proximate structural factors that affect peoples' habitus and therefore their tastes and preferences. These include social trajectory as well as composition and volume of economic and cultural capital. In Chapter 6, the effect of these factors will be closely examined while variations in boundary work within the French and the American upper-middle class are being discussed.

CONCLUSION

The picture that emerges from this chapter is one where a range of cultural factors combine with structural factors to affect the likelihood that people draw one type of boundary rather than another. At times, individuals might automatically draw on the cultural repertoires that their environment offers; in other circumstances, their boundary work might be more directly influenced by their own social position and opportunities. The probability that individuals draw one type of boundary rather than another is structured by remote and proximate environments instead of being randomly distributed. More research is needed to specify the mechanisms in operation here and to understand the place of agency in boundary work.

The previous discussion helps explain not only national differences in boundary patterns but also specific and quite consequential substantive issues, such as the greater materialism of Americans and the greater importance of high culture and refinement in French society. Such difference in national cultural orientations (or, as some would say, in national character) are also accounted for by the combination of cultural and structural societal features. For instance, the greater importance of refinement and high culture in France can only be explained by simultaneously taking into consideration factors such as the role played by the state in diminishing the impact of market mechanisms on the life of cultural producers, the centralization of the educational system, the cohesion of the identity and subculture of French intellectuals, the greater ethnic and racial homogeneity of French society, and the lasting influence of the aristocratic tradition on the historical national repertoire. In the United States, materialism is sustained by a weaker Welfare State, historically higher geographic mobility, the privately owned mass media, the low influence of

intellectuals, and themes central to the ideology of Americanism (e.g., individualism and achievement). Some of the features of American society (as egalitarianism and weak state intervention) also work against the influence of high culture here. These explanations suggest again the necessity of considering the influence of remote structural societal features and of available cultural repertoires on boundary work rather than stressing only the proximate features of individual positions. On the other hand, given the growing influence of socioeconomic boundaries, these explanations also raise issues concerning the long-term vitality of intellectual subcultures in advanced industrial societies. A discussion of the differences in the boundary work of social and cultural specialists and for-profit workers in both countries helps to partly address these issues.

Chapter Six

~~~~~~

THE NATURE OF
INTERNAL CLASS BOUNDARIES

> Since social phenomena evidently escape
> the social control of the experimenter,
> the comparative method is the only
> one suited to sociology.
> —Emile Durkheim

The national boundary patterns that have been brought to light conceal important internal cultural variations within both the French and the American upper-middle classes. To unearth them, I compare groups of individuals who, due to their occupation or social trajectory, have different market conditions and different relationships with economic rationality: social and cultural specialists with for-profit workers, intellectuals with nonintellectuals, the upwardly with the downwardly mobile, and those whose family has been part of the upper-middle class for several generations with those who have recently entered the group. Examining these internal variations helps us gain a better knowledge of the role played by proximate structural conditions in shaping boundaries. It also permits obtaining richer knowledge concerning variations in the boundary work of various groups. While exploring such differences, I discuss further the causes of the greater French orientation to culture and American materialism. I show that national patterns in boundary work reinforce occupational patterns, distinct occupational groups having an impact on strengthening or weakening cultural and socioeconomic boundaries in their society.

SOCIAL AND CULTURAL SPECIALISTS AND FOR-PROFIT WORKERS

Chapter 2 pointed out that occupation is one of the main dimensions that define the identities of upper-middle-class men.[1] It seems likely that patterns of boundary work will vary considerably across occupational groups, and my interviews suggest that indeed they do.

Profit Making and Boundary Work

In *Economy and Society*, Max Weber distinguished between economic and value rationalities: economic rationality dominates contemporary life by organizing it around a systematic orientation toward profit and efficiency. In contrast, value rationality, which is antithetical to economic rationality, is "determined by a conscious belief in the value for its own sake of some ethical, aesthetic, religious or other form of behavior."[2]

In trying to explain fluctuations in level of political liberalism, social scientists have pointed out how political attitudes vary with the structural relationship that people have with economic rationality and with economic necessity more generally. For instance, some have suggested that people who grew up during periods of economic prosperity are more prone to favor postmaterialist values such as self-actualization, environmentalism, sexual permissiveness, and opposition to nuclear power and armament: these people have had more "formative security," i.e., they (or their families) had a strong market position during their growing-up years and are, therefore, less concerned with materialist values and with economic rationality.[3] Along the same lines, Seymour Martin Lipset has argued that intellectuals (in his definition, social and cultural specialists) have dissenting attitudes toward capitalism and the business class because their work requires that they maintain a certain independence from commercialism.[4] Following Lipset's lead, I have suggested that the political liberalism and dissent of professionals and managers varies with the degree to which their work is instrumental to profit making (i.e., is directed to and justified by the creation of goods and services that realize a profit), and with the degree to which these upper-middle-class workers depend upon the market system for their livelihoods (whether they are employed in the private sector or in the public and nonprofit sectors).[5]

Recent research supports this argument. For instance, a comparative study of American and British business, religious, media, and educational elites found that involvement in profit making explains more than half of the variance in the attitudes of elite members toward capitalism: this factor is a stronger predictor than gender, age, religious affiliation, race, income, and the size of the city where individuals are employed.[6] Along similar lines, another study showed that in the United States opposition to business interest in the new middle class is concentrated among professionals and managers who are disengaged from the market economy,[7] i.e., among the "social-science and arts-related occupations outside the

commercial economy."[8] Finally, Steven Brint, who in his early work had rejected the hypothesis that political liberalism varies with "distance from profit making," has recently integrated this factor (which he calls "employment status") in his cumulative trends explanation of New Class dissent. When comparing New Class politics in several advanced industrial societies, he found that social and cultural specialists and human services workers are more liberal than other occupational groupings on economic and welfare issues.[9] While these studies generally qualify the nature of the relationship between dissent, liberalism, and relationship to profit making,[10] they all emphasize the role of workers in the public and nonprofit sectors and/or social and cultural specialists in supporting liberal and dissenting perspectives.[11] Thus, they support the notion that proximate structural factors, and particularly the relationship that people have with economic rationality through their work—i.e., whether their work is oriented toward profit maximization or toward other educational, scientific, humanitarian, or religious goals—directly impinges on their political attitudes.[12]

I generalize this hypothesis to other cultural realms to suggest that the boundary-drawing activities of the members of the upper-middle class varies with the degree to which their occupation is instrumental to, and dependent on, profit making:[13] because the professional energies of artists, social workers, priests, psychologists, scientific researchers, and teachers are oriented toward attaining cultural, spiritual, or humanitarian goals, and because their professional achievements cannot be measured primarily in economic terms, one can expect these people to put more emphasis on cultural or moral standards of evaluation. On the other hand, because the labor of accountants, bankers, marketing executives, realtors, businessmen, and others like them is more dominated by the pursuit of economic rationality as they set goals based on cost/benefit analysis,[14] and because their success is measured in economic terms, these individuals are more likely to value socioeconomic standards of evaluation. For similar reasons, intellectuals might draw stronger cultural boundaries and weaker socioeconomic boundaries than nonintellectuals.

To examine these hypotheses, the respondents were divided in two groups: (1) those involved in capitalist production and distribution, i.e., in the institutional mechanisms of profit making (business ownership, management, sales and applied technology), and in market enhancement (banking and finance); and (2) those that are not involved in these mechanisms, i.e., those who work in occupations in the media, the academe,

the arts, etc. I further divided interviewees into two groups based on their sector of employment, positing that nonprofit and, to a greater extent, public sector employees are provided by their organizations with relative freedom from profit-making concerns, given that these organizations often depend on public funding and/or on donations for their existence and are not as directly dependent on the laws of supply and demand. On the basis of these distinctions, I classified respondents into four occupational aggregates depending on their sector of activity and the contribution of their work to the realization of profit (see table 2). These four categories could be represented as a spectrum of increasing dependency on, and utility for, profit making.

Category 1 of table 2 is comprised of salaried cultural and social specialists who work for the public or nonprofit sectors and who, therefore, have low dependency on, and low instrumentality for, profit making. This category includes those involved in religious, artistic, political, educational, social, scientific, and public service occupations (as priests, music teachers, academic administrators, diplomats, medical researchers, and so on).

Category 2 consists of cultural and social specialists working in the private sector and for-profit workers employed by the public and nonprofit sectors. This hybrid category encompasses individuals who are dependent on profit making yet are not very instrumental to economic rationality (e.g., pure scientists working in the private sector) as well as interviewees who have little dependency on profit making yet have a high instrumentality for the realization of profit (e.g., bank examiners and accountants employed by the state).[15] In this category we also find journalists working in the private sector, self-employed dentists, clinical psychologists, and the like.

Category 3 covers salaried for-profit workers in the private sector who are both instrumental to the realization of profit and dependent on it because they are employed by the private sector. This group includes engineers, accountants, corporate attorneys, actuaries, investment bankers, plant managers, etc.

Category 4 includes self-employed for-profit workers such as realtors and used-car dealers as well as self-employed professionals (lawyers, architects, financial advisors, and the like). Because these for-profit workers directly participate in the market, they are taken to be more dependent on profit making than their salaried counterparts.

For the sake of simplicity, individuals grouped under categories 1 and

TABLE 2
Occupation and Age of Male Interviewees by Sites and Detailed Category of Occupation

PARIS SUBURBS	age	CLERMONT-FERRAND	age	INDIANAPOLIS	age	NEW YORK SUBURBS	age
1. Cultural and Social Specialists, Public and Nonprofit Sectors (Salaried)							
public school administrator	50	public school administrator	50	public school administrator	45	public school administrator	58
academic administrator	57	academic administrator	41	academic administrator	49	academic administrator	50
music teacher	41	music teacher	55	music teacher	54	earth science teacher	46
priest	43	priest	55	minister	59	minister	51
museum curator	53	museum curator	41	museum curator	42	museum curator	44
musician	42	artist	43	artist	37	artist	48
science teacher	46	electronics teacher	50	professor of physics	51	science teacher	53
professor of architecture	31	professor of social work	41	professor of medicine	51	professor of social work	49
literature teacher	57	philosophy teacher	48	social service manager	41	professor of theology	57
social worker	35	athletics coach	37	recreational professional	51	recreational professional	33
diplomat	55	civil servant	41	staff assistant	43	civil servant	58
computer specialist	33	civil servant	41	computer specialist	39	computer specialist	34
professor of accounting	39	physicist	35	medical researcher	34		
				manager human services	46		
2. Cultural and Social Specialists, Private Sector; Profit-Related Occupations, Public and Nonprofit Sectors							
human resource consultant	38	paramedic	40	psychologist	46	applied science researcher	42
psychologist	44	psychologist	53	accountant (public)	44	human resources consultant	41
hospital administrator	60	hospital controller	36	research scientist	36	psychologist	50
dentist	34	dentist	55	science researcher	35	hospital controller	39
physician	46	physician	48	bank examiner (public)	36	statistics researcher	46
architect (public)	43	safety inspector	36	judge	40	computer researcher	36
human resources consultant	59	journalist	53			economist	52
						labor arbitrator	53
average age (cat. 1 and 2)	45	*average age*	45	*average age*	44	*average age*	47

3. Profit-Related Occupations, Private Sector (Salaried)

Occupation	Age	Occupation	Age	Occupation	Age	Occupation	Age
business management specialist	46	accountant	33	accountant	30	investment advisor	31
senior executive manufacturing	58	senior executive manufacturing	58	chief financial officer	48	chief financial officer	56
banker	45	banker	34	banker	43	banker	44
investment banker	40	banker	53	banker	54	banker	59
insurance executive	42	executive car dealer	43	insurance company VP	47	insurance company VP	44
corporate attorney	36	chemical engineer	42	plant manager	32	plant facilities manager	40
computer engineer	51	computer marketing specialist	53	corporate attorney	32	corporate attorney	41
marketing executive	55	chemical engineer	53	computer marketing specialist	57	computer specialist	52
electrical engineer	42	plant manager	50	marketing executive	45	marketing executive	45
tourism executive	43	architect	39	data manager	55	computer software developer	53
				architect	44		

4. Profit-Related Occupations, Private Sector (Self-Employed)

Occupation	Age	Occupation	Age	Occupation	Age	Occupation	Age
lawyer	39	lawyer	42	lawyer	32	lawyer	34
lawyer	45	lawyer	49	lawyer	37	lawyer	42
accountant	57	accountant	57	stockbroker	57	portfolio manager	46
architect	46	architect	39	architect	37	computer consultant	46
insurance broker	45	insurance broker	31	realtor	58	realtor	51
proprietor printing firm	56	proprietor surveying firm	53	forester	59	custom house broker	57
proprietor engineering firm	47	architect	45	professional recruiter	52	wholesale distributor	55
accountant	40	accountant	49	real estate developer	44	proprietor broadcasting co.	49
financial advisor	37	financial advisor	34	used car dealer	39	proprietor car leasing co.	45
financial advisor	47	financial advisor	43			machine tool distributor	35
average age	*47*	*average age*	*45*	*average age*	*45*	*average age*	*46*

average age (cat. 3 and 4) *47*

2 are referred to as "social and cultural specialists" while those grouped under categories 3 and 4 are referred to as "for-profit workers," even though category 2 also includes a few for-profit workers.

Patterns of Exclusion across Occupational Groups

The conversations I had reveal that, as suggested by New Class theory, social and cultural specialists and for-profit workers express somewhat critical attitudes toward one another. Indeed, by drawing antisocioeconomic boundaries in favor of cultural ones, social and cultural specialists often reject for-profit workers as impure: they often are critical of business types for their excessive materialism and lack of concern for cultural issues. For instance, a university professor in New York expressed his disappointment in his son, a business school student, for not being intellectual enough:

> It's very frustrating to see your own son walk away from all of your own values . . . [H]e can't read a novel and be impressed by it. He can't see something in the newspaper and recognize it as important. Even when he does well in school, it's purely a manipulative or mechanistic approach . . . He is probably well suited for the business culture. But I would prefer if he had ideas. If he went to Princeton, where he could pursue cultural wealth and achievement . . . Even when he rebels, he rebels in the way that is prescribed by the movies.

For-profit workers are not different: many expressed their dislike for the cultural style of social and cultural specialists, rejecting the cultural purity principle at the same time. For instance, a senior manufacturing executive who manages a large plant and several thousand employees in Clermont remarked that ideologues and intellectuals "have a bad reputation in France. They live on a cloud. They are not realists. They isolate themselves through their language." Likewise, a self-employed insurance agent who lives in St. Cloud criticized technocrats because "to tell you that this pen is red, they will talk for two hours, and at the end, we will learn that the pen is red. They like to listen to themselves." Along the same lines, a sporty-looking Clermont-Ferrand architect whom I interviewed in his stylish postmodern apartment explained to me that those who specialize in abstract thought are inadequate: "Intellectuals are disconnected from reality. They are too much into the cerebral dimension, they don't get out of it. This gets on my nerves. I think that the intellectual who only gets stuck in intellectual things does not try to help others. He is happy in his own little universe."[16]

The opposition between the two groups is often expressed under the cover of political attitudes, symbolic and political boundaries being drawn at one and the same time. This came up often during our conversations, but rarely as clearly as when a right-wing Clermont-Ferrand hotel manager described to me his hatred for the Socialists. He said: "I am anti-Socialist, completely. [Socialists] are all teachers . . . intellectuals. They have a bad attitude. They are bourgeois, i.e., very attached to their privileges . . . They are jealous, interested. I find in them many bad qualities."

The extent to which political attitudes and symbolic boundaries overlap cannot be explored here (this could well be the topic of an entirely separate study). Suffice it to say that attitudinal patterns such as opposition to capitalism, the business class, and unregulated economic activities as well as support for urban beautification, environmentalism, self-actualization, and income distribution could be taken as expressions of symbolic boundaries, i.e., as a way of drawing cultural (and moral) boundaries and of rejecting socioeconomic boundaries.[17] On the other hand, opposition to a strong welfare state might indicate a defense of socioeconomic boundaries and of another type of moral boundary based not on human solidarity but on a belief in the importance of strong work ethics. Just as social and cultural specialists (or intellectuals) differ from for-profit workers in their political orientation,[18] they also adopt different definitions of high status signals.

A comparison of individual scores on the moral, cultural, and socioeconomic dimensions reveals that social and cultural specialists are somewhat more culturally exclusive than for-profit workers;[19] that the latter group is slightly more likely to draw strong socioeconomic boundaries[20] than social and cultural specialists[21] and that moral boundaries are equally valued by both groups.[22] I am suggesting that the proximate structural positions of the men I talked to, as revealed by their relationship with the realization of profit, do shape their boundary work.[23] This is again confirmed by a comparison of the boundary work of intellectuals and nonintellectuals, the first group having a lower instrumentality for the realization of profit: the vast majority of intellectuals draw strong cultural boundaries compared to less than a quarter of the interviewees who are considered nonintellectuals.[24] Such occupational patterns might be reinforced by the market position of social and cultural specialists and that of intellectuals: those whose work is less instrumental to, and dependent on, profit making generally have market positions that are inferior to those of for-profit workers as their opportunities for mobility are often less abun-

dant and their income generally lower.[25] This might lead them to value forms of prestige other than socioeconomic status.[26]

Additional evidence suggests that proximate structural position affects boundary work: compared to social and cultural specialists from category 1, those of category 2 draw boundaries that are more similar to the boundaries drawn by for-profit workers.[27] This reflects their higher dependency on and instrumentality to the realization of profit as these interviewees are involved in the public sector or are for-profit workers.[28] Likewise, the self-employed for-profit workers score slightly higher than the salaried for-profit workers on the socioeconomic scale.[29] These patterns persist when the two occupational categories are compared within each site (for details, see Appendix IV, table A.5)[30] Further studies, however, based on larger data sets are needed before firm conclusions can be drawn on such comparisons.[31]

Chapter 4 presented evidence that suggests that intellectuals feel more marginal to American mainstream culture than French intellectuals do in France. Similarly, American social and cultural specialists seems to be more marginal in American culture than are their French counterparts in their own culture: Steven Brint indicated that in the United States, liberal sentiments are highly focused in a few predictable groups in the middle class, making these groups more different from the rest of the population than they would otherwise be in societies such as France where liberal and social-democratic views are more spread across various middle-class segments.[32] This pattern can probably be extrapolated to attitudes other than political attitudes: strong cultural boundaries are likely to be characteristic of only a relatively small segment of the American population, whereas in France such boundaries might be found among wider groups, including among for-profit workers. The next section provides support for these hypotheses.

National Patterns and the Dynamics of Occupational Groups

The national patterns brought to light in the last chapter reinforce boundary-drawing patterns across groups. Interviews and the quantitative ranking of respondents on the three dimensions confirm this:

1. French social and cultural specialists draw stronger cultural boundaries than American social and cultural specialists do.[33] In this context, it is hardly surprising that they often have a very charismatic view of their work, as is most tellingly expressed by Jean Lebleu, a bearded philosophy

professor who lives in Clermont in a small house cluttered with books. Talking to me through the heavy smoke of his Gitane cigarettes, he describes his *métier* with great gestures and emphasis:

> I thought I could give young people the pleasure of discovering the company of others, of intellectual giants, the company of poets, novelists, philosophers and eruditi, the very men who helped me to understand life in a new light at the time when I was really discouraged . . . I would like to do for [the students] what my masters did for me. I had teachers who were almost gods for me, because of the depth of their minds, their intellectual limpidity, their humor, their irony, the way they were able to synthesize, their ability to help me discover unsuspected things. My teachers are the ones who gave me faith in myself, who opened new horizons for me, who forced me to go further, to be more demanding toward myself.

Not a single American cultural specialist expressed half as strongly his devotion to the value rationality that animates his professional vocation.

2. The same French social and cultural specialists draw much weaker socioeconomic boundaries than their American counterparts.[34] Conversely, French teachers expressed fewer regrets for not having chosen a more lucrative occupation. Most take their small income to be the result of an active and positive choice on their part and of their decision to put freedom and self-actualization above money, as explained here by the literature professor who teaches in a *lycée* in the Paris region and whom we encountered in Chapter 2:

> I prefer to make what I make and be free rather than make twice as much and have to be subservient. I could not bear to be a butcher . . . the dependency on the customers, the fact of having to say "yes, miss; no, miss," of having to pay attention to her dog, while you should tell her to leave the dog outside because of hygiene. Or of having to be nice to a person who takes half an hour to get what she needs while there is a line of people waiting outside . . . But even more generally I don't like the notion that how you are doing financially depends on how you behave toward other people, with more or less insincerity . . . because it means a loss of freedom . . . I know that I make much less than my neighbors, including those whose professions require less of them intellectually. But this really leaves me indifferent. They can try to impress me with their Mercedes, but I go on my bicycle, no problem . . . For me, the value of things is not measured this way.

Along the same lines, a Versailles priest whose family is part of the most traditional French bourgeoisie explains that in his view his small income

> is a question of independence . . . The fact of not having a high salary allows me to choose to do what I do independently of what it gives me monetarily. When I worked in the corporate world, I made five or six times what I make now . . . But today I don't take money into consideration in choosing what I do or don't do, in deciding what activities I will get involved in . . . This allows me to avoid falling into mediocrity, and it allows me to do something interesting with my life . . . not to be only a widget in a large machine . . . to go further in experiencing things and in getting totally involved in what I do.

A French social worker whom I interviewed in the bare office of a charitable organization located in the Sixth Arrondissement offers a similar explanation for his professional choices when he says that

> the nonprofit sector gives you a chance to invest yourself personally in many ways . . . It gave me a chance to live according to my Catholic faith, my Christian faith. I made the decision to have an effect, even if a limited one, on our society, and more particularly on social inequality . . . Making money is not my professional motivation. I experience everyday how difficult it is for a family to live in Paris with a small salary . . . but I accepted that when I chose to work for the nonprofit sector . . . Honestly, I do not regret it. I believe that it is good to reduce income inequality. So in theory I personally live in coherence with that.

Like the Clermont-Ferrand philosophy professor, these men stress the value rationality that motivated their vocational choice over the economic rationality emphasized by "mainstream" society. This conviction that their comparatively low salaries are compensated by exceptional opportunities not available in the business world for service or personal fulfillment—are compensated by the fact that they are getting more out of life—was less frequently communicated by American social and cultural specialists. Indeed, members of the latter group more often denigrated their profession and voiced regrets for not having chosen a more lucrative occupation. Several told me that they hope to change their career course "because of the money issue." For instance, a second-generation Italian who works as a recreation specialist in New Jersey explained that he was in the process of finishing college courses in financial planning to pursue a new career because "I have to try to financially secure myself and my

little boy." Along the same lines, a Scarsdale science teacher told me that "I think if I had to do it all over again, I would put myself in a position where I had more opportunities to demonstrate my individualism . . . such as business . . ." A sizable number of American social and cultural specialists seem to believe that people who are really smart "go for the money" and that only "losers," people who are not "totally with it," and people who could not pay for the training that would qualify them for higher-paying work, would take a job with low monetary rewards. Along the same lines, echoing the Indianapolis minister encountered in Chapter 3 for whom money was the main yardstick of his "professional success," this New York teacher has also totally absorbed the principles of economic rationality, transposing them onto the educational and cultural worlds:

> I am not one of those sacrificial-teachers types that will spend inordinate amounts of time [working] for almost nothing. I really don't do anything in life, or hardly anything right now, that I don't get paid for. I'm a professional vocalist, and I never sing in any church or temple or concert hall without being paid. Also, a lot of teachers do an awful lot of volunteer work of all kinds. It's not doing their professionalism very much good. I have to admire them to a certain extent that they're willing to spend that much time, but I have a family and other interests, and I just really can't see spending the extra time. I work efficiently enough so that they're impressed enough with my work to pay me a lot. But I wouldn't be there if they didn't pay me, and if I change jobs it would be because of a combination of cost of living and a salary and so on.

While these few individuals do not represent the full repertoire of interpretations through which social and cultural specialists understand their place in American society, their views echo perspectives voiced frequently. They all hint at the fact that this group has not developed an alternative subculture as highly coherent as that of its French counterpart, an alternative subculture that would legitimate value rationality over economic rationality and clearly support cultural standards of status assessment. In this context, it is hardly surprising that American social and cultural specialists draw stronger socioeconomic boundaries than their French counterpart.

3. The comparison of scores on the three dimensions shows that French for-profit workers draw considerably stronger cultural boundaries than their American counterparts.[35] Accordingly, various French for-profit workers have joined social clubs and associations where they can

maintain a certain level of intellectual activity. The Freemasons are particularly popular because this organization puts a strong emphasis on philosophical and spiritual issues and provides individuals a forum in which "to ask oneself important questions beyond how to balance a budget or which car to buy . . . questions on the meaning of life, the meaning you give to your life, what actions you should carry out" (financial advisor, Clermont-Ferrand). An unusually charming and articulate Paris lawyer explains in similar terms that it is crucial for him to share ideas with people who have

> a similar search for truth, for spirituality, a detachment from materialism which is invading us more and more. [We need to] be able to take distance toward this, to attach more importance to other-worldly things that make us human . . . What I miss in my everyday professional life is the stimulation to push further certain ideas and topics that are not related to everyday life. I need to think about things like "Truth," otherwise I am living like an animal. I can't live only for my work. I have professional satisfaction when I win a trial, but this is only a technical satisfaction. The rest of my time is spent developing argumentations, and this is quite banal.

Not a single American working in the private sector indicated participation in organizations that would be the intellectual equivalent of the Freemasons, whereas at least ten Frenchmen revealed that they were involved with this group—largely for intellectual and spiritual reasons—despite the fact that as members they were sworn to secrecy.[36]

4. Finally, a comparison of scores shows that American for-profit workers are on average considerably more socioeconomically exclusive than their Parisian counterparts and slightly more socioeconomically exclusive than the Clermontois.[37] This, along with the trends described above, clearly suggest that national patterns in boundary work reinforce the patterns typical of occupational groups in both countries, French for-profit workers being more culturally inclined than their American counterparts, while American social and cultural specialists are more materialistic than their French counterparts. More generally, the dynamic between social and cultural specialists and for-profit workers in both countries reflects the dynamic between cultural and socioeconomic boundaries in France and the United States: cultural boundaries are strongest and are most stressed by a wider population in the context where intellectuals and social and cultural specialists themselves play a more active role in promoting value rationality and legitimating cultural standards of evaluation.

This is hardly surprising: as Weber suggested in *The Protestant Ethic and the Spirit of Capitalism*, types of rationality get carried on by specific groups who represent their objectification in the social world.[38] Similarly, the "hegemony" of socioeconomic boundaries in the United States certainly results partly from a propensity of American social and cultural specialists themselves to subordinate value rationality to economic rationality. Various remote structural factors that were discussed in the previous chapter (namely, a weak welfare state) promote their greater dependency toward profit making, therefore strengthening the proximate structural conditions that shape their distinctive patterns of boundary work; in this context, the promarket policies adopted during the Reagan years could be seen as indirectly creating conditions that weakened the importance of cultural boundaries in the United States.

TRAJECTORIES AND SENIORITY IN THE UPPER-MIDDLE CLASS

Social trajectory and seniority in the upper-middle class are other proximate structural factors that can affect the boundary work of its members. Again, market conditions and life chances explain at least partly differences in the status signals individuals value the most.

The Upwardly and the Downwardly Mobile

A large number of the individuals I met with are upwardly mobile: roughly 50 percent of them pursue occupations of socioeconomic status higher than that of their fathers.[39] This relatively high rate of upward mobility is largely due to the structural changes that have characterized postindustrial societies since World War II. This period has been one of rapid economic growth; in both France and the United States, the standard of living has risen; science and technology have come to play a more central role in the economy.[40] Simultaneously, professional and managerial occupations have increased in number (see Appendix I). Consequently, at the time many participants entered the job market in the fifties, sixties, and early- to mid-seventies, a large number of new jobs were made available. These men found themselves in very favorable market positions, their individual mobility inextricably linked to their collective mobility as a social group. While the percentage of those who have been upwardly mobile is roughly equal in the four sites—60 percent in New York, 57 percent in Indianapolis, 47 percent in Paris, and 50 percent in Clermont—the growth of professional and managerial occupations

since World War II has been more marked in the United States[41] than in France.[42]

Do these upwardly mobile individuals draw symbolic boundaries in a distinctive way? Their socioeconomic boundaries are moderately stronger than those of downwardly mobile individuals and than those whose occupations are of socioeconomic status equal to that of their fathers (who have had "stable" trajectories).[43] A stronger emphasis on socioeconomic purity is salient among very upwardly mobile individuals.[44] Having been relatively successful at improving their social position, it is likely that the upwardly mobile strongly invest this type of status and, therefore, stress it.

Only 12 percent of the men I interviewed have "come down in the world."[45] By definition, all these men come from families that have been upper-middle class for at least one generation; they have had successful fathers or grandfathers but are themselves not doing particularly well. This gives them a very distinctive outlook. Most important, like those who have had a stable trajectory, the downwardly mobile tend to be more culturally exclusive than the upwardly mobile.[46] Having inferior market position, it is possible that, like social and cultural specialists, these people tend to stress statuses other than economic status, either because they value them more or because they want to improve their social position via their cultural status.

Contrary to what some sociologists have suggested,[47] there is no relationship between mobility and the likelihood of drawing strong moral boundaries. On the other hand, again the downwardly mobile and those with a stable trajectory are slightly less likely than individuals with other types of social trajectories to draw strong socioeconomic boundaries. Furthermore, a substantially larger percentage of individuals opposing socioeconomic boundaries is found among the downwardly mobile than among the "stable" interviewees, the upwardly mobile and the strongly upwardly mobile.[48] Accordingly, the downwardly mobile tend to stress the fact that they find the most personal satisfaction in activities other than their work. For instance, a bohemian New York custom broker, who has not managed the company he inherited from his great-grandfather very well, explained that he spends most of his time playing jazz and reading:

> If I had put the same time and interest in my business as I have in my science reading and my music I think I'd be [in] pretty good [shape]. I might have expanded the company and bought up other companies.

But to me that's work, that's not fun; that's drudgery. I like to keep it as simple as possible.

Another downwardly mobile interviewee presents similar views. The son of a Clermont-Ferrand scientist, he became a paramedic because he failed the examinations for the school of dentistry. He now invests most of his time in the soccer team he coaches. He describes his friends as "not too hung up on professional success." He has lowered his professional sights and is finding meaning in spheres of activities other than his work.

A Foot in Both Worlds: The First-Generation Upper-Middle-Class Members

The number of men in each site that are first-generation members of the upper-middle class is slightly higher in the United States than in France: they represent 60 percent of the New Yorkers and 47 percent of the Hoosiers, as compared to 47 percent of the Parisians and 50 percent of the Clermontois. These individuals only partially overlap with the upwardly mobile given that people who belong to this last group often come from upper-middle-class families.[49]

Like Paul Anderson, the Indianapolis senior executive encountered at the beginning of this book, newly arrived members of the upper-middle class often come from a "hard-working background." Their parents were immigrants or blue-collar workers and were often poorly educated. Some of these individuals have known hunger, unemployment, the Great Depression, and World War II, and most of them have achieved mobility at the price of countless efforts, long work hours, and a stringent discipline. Does their trajectory affect the types of boundaries that they are most likely to draw?

These individuals are not significantly more exclusive, either morally or socioeconomically, than other people.[50] They are significantly less inclined, however, toward cultural exclusion, just as we found in the case of the upwardly mobile.[51] Many show great respect for education and competence, as these are largely responsible for their own mobility.[52] Few first-generation men, however, seem to view command of high culture as an important high status signal.[53]

These patterns are reflected in the feelings of cultural and social inadequacy that were often expressed by the men with whom I met. For instance, a few individuals confessed feeling that they had not acquired all the skills required to interact gracefully in upper-middle-class settings.

They admitted feeling inferior to "the ones that are good at cocktail parties at making chitchat, at diving into conversations" (artist, New York), and to "people who are able to be comfortable in all kinds of different milieux . . . This I don't know how to do, and I feel very inferior about it" (lawyer, Clermont-Ferrand). A workaholic recreation specialist from Indianapolis who thinks that he lacks culture summarizes the situation when he says that

> I had to work all my life, okay. I had to work when I was in college, so I did not socialize. I did not get involved in fraternities as a lot of other people did, and did not get involved in a lot of leadership roles that other people did, so I've gotten where I've gotten through hard work and common sense. So a lot of these young people that are leaders in high school and leaders in other places, they've been able to belong to a lot of different clubs, and their ease at conversation with people has been a lot easier. I've always accused myself of worrying more about what I'm going to say to a person next rather than what they said to me.

This experience is strongly contrasted with that of men whose families have been members of the upper-middle class for several generations and who often say that they feel comfortable in most settings and are not easily intimidated by people of higher standing or wealth. They have broader repertoires on which they can draw in social interaction. A Harvard-educated wholesale distributor who does not see himself as particularly sophisticated culturally summarizes the situation.

> Background education is a strength. If you keep an open mind and move within the structure of society, you can talk to the chairman of the board or the janitor. People in other strata of society tend not to be able to communicate at an upper level. They tend to be very good at their own level or at a lower level but not necessarily with others. Some have pizzazz to talk to anybody. That is what my education gave me.

Finally, it is interesting to note that individuals who are first-generation upper-middle class tend to be slightly more tolerant than others.[54] Because the mechanisms of the market have been the condition of their success, we might have expected them to tend toward socioeconomic exclusiveness. We find instead that they often use allegedly "transclass" standards of evaluation focusing on "what kind of human being you are," and that they frequently express a refusal to take social position as the sole measure of a person's value, which stances attenuate the force of whatever socioeconomic boundaries they do draw. This tolerance might

be explained by a desire to reconcile various milieux and to maintain relationships with professional colleagues as well as with less mobile family members who have not acquired upper-middle-class cultural styles and are perhaps not likely to do so. These interviewees have a foot in two worlds, for they have to juggle various definitions of high status signals that are at times conflicting—definitions that predominate in the milieu they come from and definitions that predominate in the milieu they have entered.

Solidly Upper-Middle Class: The Third Generation and Beyond

A considerable number of interviewees are solidly upper-middle class, at least culturally, as their families have belonged to this group for three generations or more. Such is the case for 25 percent of the New Yorkers, Hoosiers, and Clermontois, and for 37 percent of the Parisians. For convenience I will refer to this group as "third-generation upper-middle class."[55]

The most striking characteristic common to these men is that French and Americans alike are very culturally exclusive.[56] The greater cultural exclusiveness as well as the relative intolerance of this group—compared to first-generation members of the upper-middle class—are clearly reflected in the interviews.[57] Indeed, third-generation members are more likely to adopt very specific norms concerning what is acceptable and what is not. In other words, they function within a tightly bounded system that governs a wide range of cultural preferences, from the type of car one should buy to one's taste in clothes. Accordingly, these individuals frequently say that they despise vulgarity and bad manners and greatly appreciate charm and intelligence. Some exercise their exclusivism against the nouveau riche and against people who are acquiring high culture too rapidly, with too much purposefulness, or with the implicit assumption that they can buy their way into it. For instance, the New York museum curator who likes everything Parisian expresses this disdain for the cultural newcomer when he says:

> [I feel superior to] people I help here who come to the museum, who are doing fairly well. "Nouveaux riches," they come from the most uneducated background, but they have traveled a lot and so they have taken on superficial knowledge of things . . . They spend most of their time talking about things they've seen, but they don't know how to appreciate it. They might dress in ways that are a little startling and go and buy art from Woolworth's or something like that.

In contrast, individuals who are third-generation upper-middle class generally take high culture and cosmopolitanism for granted, viewing them as an integral part of their lives. In the family of our New York museum curator, for instance,

> we had this cultured background, and not a pretentious cultured background. It was just a way of life. [We] considered art as part of our life. And we had reproductions and paintings in our house . . . So it just became a natural way of life. It was never forced on us, it was just there.

The child-rearing values of individuals who are third-generation upper-middle class also contrast with those emphasized by first-generation members. The former group stresses self-actualization, intellectual curiosity, and aesthetic pursuit over more material and practical goals—and maybe more so in France than in the United States. The Clermont-Ferrand physician whom we encountered at the beginning of Chapter 2 illustrates this in a telling manner when he compares the way he and his wife raised their children in contrast to the way their friends raised theirs. These friends, or at any rate the wife, is third-generation upper-middle class. François deplores their child-rearing methods:

> They just overprotected their kids. Their children were supposed to be "happy," to "develop themselves" [ironic tone]. They chose to do what they wanted, they did not pursue college education, but they were "happy." The father teaches neurology at the university. Now these children, socially, they are nothing; they don't have the right level. Like me, he started from very low and succeeded very well because he worked hard. Now he is in conflict with his wife [over the children].

Along the same lines, some Frenchmen, who are third-generation upper-middle class, expressed a reluctance at the idea of sacrificing quality of life, intellectual playfulness, and self-actualization to upward mobility. Monsieur Lemaire, a senior executive in a French multinational specializing in telecommunication, is a notable case in point. His father was a certified accountant and his grandfather a small capitalist. A graduate of one of the elite engineering schools, he now lives in Versailles. He is tanned and handsome, plays tennis, votes Socialist, declares himself an atheist, and is involved in a consumer movement. He says that feeling superior to people for "cultural reasons" provides him with "more satisfaction" than feeling superior to them for "moral reasons." At fifty-one, he looks back on his life and describes his career as a "normal one." There were many compromises that he was not ready to make:

I did not want to optimize my performance all the time. If you do that you are frustrated, because you have no time to be intellectually playful. It is also frustrating in terms of your relationships with your coworkers. You don't allow yourself to spend more than five minutes talking with people because you have to do this and that. This is very alienating. Certain people don't mind living like this. I did not want to. There is a quality of interpersonal relationship that I am not ready to give up [for success].

Monsieur Lemaire's reaction reflects that of many third-generation men for whom *plaisir de vivre*—good food, good friends, good books, pleasant surroundings—is too important to be sacrificed to a little bit more upward mobility. Their attitudes contrast strongly with first-generation upper-middle-class members who need to make it on their own at the price of a great many sacrifices.

The difference between the new and the established upper-middle class seems to be particularly strong in Paris. This is exemplified by the way a marketing specialist, whose father was an employee of the national postal service, describes a cousin of his who is an aristocrat. This marketing specialist belongs to a sports club, also plays tennis and has a perfect tan, and goes to the United States on a regular basis. He is hip and does cocaine. Some of his friends race cars; others deal in art. His office is furnished with huge, bright purple leather sofas, and the walls are adorned with large contemporary paintings. He recently bought the slick postmodern building in which his office is located. He defines himself as an iconoclast, a nonconformist. He also defines himself in opposition to his cousin, the son of his mother's sister:

He comes from an older family than I, so it is completely different. His father is from an old family of the French nobility, and he is hooked into that. MacDonald hamburgers, he has not tried yet. His tastes are completely classical. He is classical in the way he dresses. Intellectually, he is classical. He does not follow the evolution of things; he does not even try to know. He rejects everything. I am completely different from him in the way I live. This is clear in my tastes in art, in music, and in cars. I started watching TV when I was six years old; I prefer American Westerns, or Walt Disney. My culture is more American than his.

This strong differentiation of the culture of someone new to the upper-middle class from someone solidly entrenched in it might be due to the presence of a particularly cohesive subculture among those whose families have belonged to the upper-middle class for several generations,

the subculture of the traditional Catholic bourgeoisie that was discussed in previous chapters. As noted earlier, this group has a culture that is clearly marked off and tightly bounded and that emphasizes cultural tradition, strong involvement in extended family networks, active religious involvement, and deep commitment to the defense of the "patrimoine."[58] Our hip marketing specialist sees this group as

> aging, with little money left. On the Versailles marketplace on Sunday morning, all their kids are dressed the same way, with Bermudas that the youngest brothers will be able to wear one day. They all have hand-knit socks . . . very conservative . . . They all imagine that they are the illegitimate sons of Louis XIV. Intellectually, this group has had very little renewal. Because they are always intermarrying, it even seems that they are declining intellectually. They don't follow what is new on the music scene. They are only interested in classical music. They are not interested in discovering anything new. The only thing that exists for them is what has always existed.

Another Versaillais describes members of this traditional bourgeoisie as

> very Old France. They are very nice with you, but if the mailman comes, they don't talk to him, they don't see him. If they receive the chief executive at home, they are on their knees. Their personality changes depending on who they talk to. They are very Old France in the sense that they think they are responsible for taking care of tradition. They are involved in Christian education, for instance; they have many friends who are in the clergy. [For instance, Mr. and Mrs. X] organize bridge clubs at the level of the city, and he [the husband] belongs to the Lyons club. She [the wife] has a maid because it is very Old France to have someone at home.

The members of this Catholic bourgeoisie are by far the most culturally exclusive of all the men I have interviewed, assimilating cultural impurity to lower social status. They can produce a discourse on cultural differences across classes that is far more elaborate than what we encountered among American interviewees. This is evident in the description that Luc Falquet, a Michelin engineer, provided of the main differences between himself and members of the *nouvelle bourgeoisie*. It is worth quoting him at length.

> I would say that my wife, like myself, is part of the group of the population that is well-off. You can go back to the beginning of the nine-

teenth century and you will find [in our families] ancestors who could live off their land with dignity. Other ancestors have very important filiations . . . My wife comes from a family of rich landowners. My family has always been a family of very important civil servants, well-known lawyers, capitalists who made a fortune. Now, [the heritage we will give to our children] is not so much the money as the values we are transmitting to them. This means mostly the values of the family, of the "milieu," the tribe, the extended family, who all have large houses where we can all be together . . . This is the kind of values that I have received from my family . . . Our friends mostly have the same background as we. Their fathers were engineers . . . Mostly, they don't belong to what we call the *bourgeoisie de promotion* . . . They come from the old aristocratic bourgeoisie. What I don't like with the new bourgeoisie is, first, their language. Then, how they deal with money. [In contrast] if we inherit money, we don't mention it . . . We don't buy a big house to show off. The new bourgeoisie fights too hard to get it . . . They talk too much about money. They spend a lot of money on their cars. All our friends have rotten cars . . . They are all very Catholic. Also, no one is divorced, because we don't accept that easily.

As illustrated here, the great exclusiveness of this traditional Catholic bourgeoisie is also reflected in the fact that they often explicitly refer to social background or occupation when discussing their desire to avoid associating with certain types of people. Again, as explained by this Michelin engineer,

Between a baker, and a pastry maker, and myself there is a huge gap. I cannot discuss with them. On the other hand, I feel good with people who are like me, who have the same type of responsibility, and who for the most part have received the same education. Because education is fundamental in life; if we want to be able to talk seriously about things, we have to have the same education, the same social background.

On the other hand, as noted earlier, these people define their class culture in part by the fact that they would never draw socioeconomic boundaries on the basis of wealth. This aspect of their ethos attenuates their socioeconomic boundaries, which would otherwise have been relatively strong given the importance they attach to social background. Their rejection of money as a basis for prestige is hardly surprising, however: the economic conditions that made traditional bourgeois living possible in France have been disappearing since World War II, with the result that many of the friends of our third-generation participants might

be from bourgeois or aristocratic families that are now "déclassés" and "désargentés." The strong cultural exclusivism of the traditional French bourgeoisie itself is reinforced by their own economic downward mobility, which strengthens their tendency to find prestige in cultural purity.

CONCLUSION

The philosopher, the nouveau riche, the marketing specialist, the "déclassé" Michelin engineer: the way these individuals understand status is inextricably linked to their contributions to the realization of profit and to their social trajectories. The influence of proximate structural factors on boundary work is, of course, mitigated by the broader environmental conditions that were discussed in the previous chapter. Positing a direct correspondence between such proximate structural factors and boundary work makes it impossible to explain differences in the boundary work of French and American upper-middle-class men who have the same trajectory and the same relationship with profit making, e.g., the stronger importance of cultural boundaries for French social and cultural specialists as compared to their American counterparts.

The analysis presented here and in Chapter 4 suggests that American intellectuals are more alienated from mainstream culture than French intellectuals are, even if they appear to have a broader cultural repertoire. This feeling is compounded by the fact that they are often unable to rank high on the very status dimension that strongly predominates in American society: the socioeconomic dimension. All this suggests that the relative "hegemony" of for-profit workers is much stronger in the United States than it is in France—as if in America this group had been able to legitimize more totally and exclusively the single criteria of hierarchalization on which their own social positions are based. Several institutional constraints, such as a relatively weak public sector, sustain this situation. By contrast, French intellectuals and social and cultural specialists are more likely to be in a better situation to affect the cultural outlook of their society than their American counterparts. These groups enjoy higher social status and consequently can more easily play a central role in politics, especially through the Parti Socialiste, where they often militate for solidarité sociale against profit maximization. However, again, with the growing materialism in France (discussed in Chap. 3), the situation might be changing.[59]

The preceding pages are rich in political implications. They help us

rethink the ways in which the conflict between the New Class and the business class have changed during the years of the Reagan and Bush presidencies. Is the relative actual powerlessness of the Democratic party linked to what looks like an internal cultural dismemberment of the American New Middle Class, its progressive cultural marginalization, and its growing adaptation to the mainstream materialism culture? Can any of the institutional conditions that sustain a strong French New Middle Class exist in the American context? And what type of boundary work underlies the political programs of the Republican and the Democratic parties? To what extent do the platforms of both American parties correspond to those of the population at large? For instance, can the recent successes of the Republican party be explained by the fact that Republicans have been able to impose a definition of moral boundaries that stresses work ethics rather than humanitarianism and social justice? What political program could strengthen structural and cultural conditions that foster value rationality? While these questions are beyond the scope of this study, they spontaneously emerge from its results, and they are particularly relevant for people who define "getting most out of life" by the availability of diversified and qualitatively rich experiences that are not solely defined by economic rationality.

Chapter Seven

〜〜

IMPLICATIONS, CONTRIBUTIONS, AND
UNANSWERED QUESTIONS

> Freedom is the recognition of necessity
> —Frederick Engels

The basic contribution of this book has been to make more complete and complex our understanding of the nature, content, and causes of the subjective symbolic boundaries that can potentially frame, channel, and limit peoples' lives in French and American society. At the most general level, the study has provided evidence that an analysis of differences in patterns of boundary work can enrich our understanding of how societies differ and help us get beyond the tourist's gaze. It also has improved our understanding of status assessment by identifying differences in the salience of various standards of evaluation of status.[1] National boundary patterns are a dimension of cross-societal differences that has been neglected until now, as comparativists have focused their attention on economic and institutional differences across societies. By shedding light on the structure of distinct class cultures, this study has also documented the cultural dimension of stratification systems, a topic that is too often neglected.

Before synthesizing the theoretical contributions of this research, it is appropriate to clarify what the implications of the findings are for our understanding of the relationship between symbolic boundaries and inequality; this central issue has not yet been addressed systematically. We will see that upper-middle-class men can unwittingly contribute to social reproduction by mobilizing in the workplace typically middle-class high status signals. Against poststructuralists who argue that meanings always generate inequality, I specify the conditions under which symbolic boundaries can foster objective socioeconomic boundaries, and I discuss the effect of variations in the strength of subjective boundaries on objective socioeconomic boundaries; this topic is only rarely explored. The findings finally call for a reassessment of rational choice, Marxist and

structuralist theories as well as of one of the most influential recent developments in French sociology, namely, the contribution of Pierre Bourdieu.

CLASS CULTURES AND THE REPRODUCTION OF INEQUALITY

To better understand the relationship between symbolic boundaries and inequality, we need to consider the relationship between the upper-middle-class high status signals that were documented in the previous chapters and other class cultures. Evidence suggests that many of the character traits that are most appreciated by the upper-middle-class men I talked with are more typical of middle- and upper-middle-class cultures. To judge worth on the basis of such traits could mean to use a class-biased gauge for all persons, under the guise of meritocracy and universalism.[2] Only under such conditions are lower-class individuals likely to be handicapped in the workplace for not having incorporated the cultural style that the upper-middle-class values. Being aware of this is crucial to our understanding of inequality because it makes us see how men who are not particularly taste-conscious participate unwittingly in social reproduction. It can explain also why so many opportunities are de facto closed to members of disadvantaged groups, and why achievement is so frequently uncorrelated with ability.[3] In other words, the class-bound nature of the high status signals that the upper-middle class values helps us understand exactly how symbolic boundaries, and the people who draw them, contribute to the reproduction of inequality. Consequently, we need to determine carefully exactly the extent to which the high status signals valued by economic, cultural, and moral excluders are more typically middle- and upper-middle-class traits.

First, the socioeconomic excluders: their contribution to the reproduction of inequality is direct and unmistakable because the high status signals that they value most unequivocally select people on the basis of their social position. By taking into consideration financial standing, class background, or power when evaluating whether people are interesting or desirable, socioeconomic excluders directly penalize working and lower-class people.

The potential contribution of cultural excluders to social reproduction is slightly less direct but nevertheless palpable. The signals of high cultural status they favor are also generally class-related. For instance, we saw that a high level of education, the upper-middle-class attribute par

excellence, is one of the most valued signals of high cultural (and socio-economic) status. Also, data for the United States shows that self-actualization,[4] intellectual curiosity,[5] linguistic ability,[6] and interest in high culture are traits that are more valued by the upper-middle class and that are more characteristic of middle-class culture than of working-class culture. As compared to Americans, however, the cultural traits the French use to read high cultural status more often seem to be unequally distributed across classes. For instance, the French value eloquence highly, a trait that cannot be dissociated from class-related cultural resources such as high-culture references and refined self-presentation. In contrast, expertise and pragmatism, which are more highly valued in the United States, are available to all, given a same basic level of ability. Also, as we saw, in the French context, rejecting vulgarity means distancing oneself from "common tastes," i.e., from the tastes common to the middle and working class. Consequently, cultural boundaries could have a stronger effect on class reproduction in France than in the United States.

Although morality apparently transcends class differences, moral excluders also often select on the basis of class-related traits: American data shows that several of the moral traits most valued by these interviewees are unequally distributed across social classes (less data is available for France). This applies to self-directedness,[7] egalitarianism, rationalism, and long-term planning.[8] It also applies to trustfulness and strong work ethics; having fewer opportunities to realize themselves through a meaningful occupation, working- and lower-class people are less trustful and show a weaker work ethic, i.e., do not give work too high a priority.[9] In fact, many lower- and working-class people think differently about achievement: while individuals with higher socioeconomic status stimulate their children to achieve in a conventional way, children of lower and working class frequently replace the standard achievement ideology with criteria of achievement such as physical toughness, emotional resiliency, quick-wittedness, masculinity, loyalty, and group solidarity.[10] They also often adopt unrealistic models of achievement offered by the mass media (e.g., Donald Trump, Oprah).[11] In other cases, they view job security as a form of advancement to compensate for the absence of real mobility, defining a good job as one that offers high wages, generous benefits, and steady employment rather than opportunities for mobility, advantageous career patterns, or a satisfying fit between job, personality, and interests.[12]

Finally, American lower- and working-class people emphasize toler-

ance and flexibility to a lesser extent than middle- and upper-middle-class people, especially college graduates—we saw that these traits are highly valued by professionals and managers in the American workplace. This difference holds true whether we consider attitudes toward deviant sexual behavior (e.g., homosexuality),[13] ethnic minorities,[14] or issues concerning freedom of expression and civil rights.[15] Furthermore, the non–college-educated give more support to "cultural fundamentalism," the cluster of values that motivate moral reform activists who support "adherence to traditional norms, respect of family and religious authority, asceticism, and control of impulse."[16] Because they require a certain level of moral rigidity, these values all militate against conflict avoidance which is also a signal valued in the American workplace.

Therefore, even if the secondary literature is not altogether conclusive—more recent studies on cultural differences across classes are needed—and even if the differences in class culture might be diminishing due to the homogenizing effects of the mass media and the educational system,[17] it seems fair to tentatively advance that many of the traits valued by my American interviewees are less common in the working and lower classes than they are in the middle and upper-middle classes.[18] This is why we might be justified in viewing the reproduction of class inequality as being, at least in part, the unintended consequence of the inadvertent use of class-related criteria of evaluation by upper-middle-class members whose jobs allow them to frame other people's lives in countless ways. This mechanism of class reproduction might be especially crucial in the United States given the presence of a strong norm of cultural egalitarianism that militates against the explicit drawing of some forms of cultural boundaries (e.g., of those based on refinement and intellectualism), and given the existence of a widespread taboo against the drawing of socioeconomic boundaries on the basis of class and ascribed characteristics.[19]

DIFFERENTIATION, HIERARCHY, AND THE POLITICS OF MEANING

Studies inspired by the writings of Foucault, Derrida, and, as we will see, Bourdieu, presume that cultural differences automatically translate into domination: the sane and the insane, the normal and the abnormal, the spoken and the written are viewed as cultural constructs that, by the mere fact of being defined in opposition to one another, generate hierarchies of meaning as well as discipline and repression.[20] In place of this model, again, we need more specific knowledge concerning the conditions under

which cultural differentiation can lead to hierarchalization and have political effects, i.e., effects on structures of power relations. More particularly, I view symbolic boundaries as a necessary but insufficient condition for the creation of socioeconomic inequality, and I suggest that only strong boundaries can generate inequality and that differentiation does not necessarily lead to hierarchy.

As we just saw, exclusion is often the unintended consequence or latent effect of the definition by the upper-middle class of its values and indirectly of its group identity and its nature as a community.[21] Not all symbolic boundaries, however, produce exclusion: for negative labeling to affect the objective positions of individuals, there must exist a consensus on the nature of cultural hierarchies and deviance. Only when boundaries are widely agreed upon, i.e., only when people agree that some traits are better than others, can symbolic boundaries take on a widely constraining (or structural) character and pattern social interaction in an important way, "conduct[ing] men with the same degree of necessity as physical force."[22] Only then can they lead to the exclusion of low status individuals, to discrimination, overselection, or more, to their self-elimination. Therefore, rather than considering that all meaning has political, i.e., hierarchical, implications, it is crucial to establish what meanings are significant, i.e., widely, shared.

Chapter 4 showed that cultural boundaries are much weaker in the United States than they are in France: Americans are more likely to defend cultural laissez-faire in the name of cultural egalitarianism; having a broad cultural repertoire, they define cultural deviance in many different ways. Their views on the hierarchalization of cultural tastes are also more variable, and their cultural distinctions are more blurred and less stable. Consequently, American cultural boundaries are less likely to lead to objective socioeconomic boundaries, i.e., to inequality, than French cultural boundaries. It remains to be seen whether socioeconomic and moral boundaries are less tightly bounded in the United States than they are in France.[23]

It is interesting to note that moral boundaries appear to be slightly more conducive to differentiation, and less conducive to hierarchalization, than other boundaries: especially in France, individuals who draw strong moral boundaries are more likely than those who draw strong cultural or socioeconomic boundaries to say in interviews that they do not feel superior to anyone, that they appreciate differences, and that they like everyone because they associate feelings of superiority and intoler-

ance with an immoral lack of humanitarianism.[24] Of course, some individuals who draw strong moral boundaries are very intolerant, believing that only Christians and morally clean folks like themselves are acceptable. However, again, my data suggest that moral excluders are slightly more likely to believe that differences in tastes and attitudes lead to a desirable diversity rather than to an inevitable hierarchy. In contrast, as we saw, socioeconomic excluders directly order people on the basis of social status. More research is needed on this topic before firm conclusions can be reached.

To fully address the issue of the extent to which subjective boundaries lead to inequality, it would be necessary to analyze how specific external traits are translated into social profits. This would require observational research that is also beyond the scope of this study. Analyzing the relationship between subjective and objective boundaries in the workplace would require analyzing (1) how expectations for self and others vary across settings according to the display of various external traits,[25] (2) what specific sets of signals are valued in specific types of organizations, (3) how individuals adjust their status expectations (for self and others) to the definitions of a "worthy person" that predominate in their environments, and (4) how this intersubjective process affects career trajectories.[26]

THEORETICAL REASSESSMENTS

My results suggest revisions for one of the main models of human nature currently in use in the social sciences. This model posits that human beings are essentially motivated by utility maximization, and that because economic resources are more valuable than other resources they are the main determinant of social action. This model is central to rational choice theory as well as to various Marxist and structuralist approaches. Pierre Bourdieu's rich and complex contribution also partly shares some of the metatheoretical assumptions of this model. These theories are discussed below.

Rational Choice, Marxist and Structuralist Theories

In recent years, a number of social scientists have taken issue with neoclassical economics in general, and with rational choice theory in particular.[27] There is no need to restate the complex arguments that have been presented. It will suffice to mention that the notion that individuals act

rationally to maximize utilities—their economic interest in particular—has been strongly criticized.[28] Social scientists also have taken issue with the neglect by economists of the role of culture in the process of preference formation, and with the implicit view that noneconomic behavior is irrational behavior, an abnormality in search of an explanation.[29]

In contrast to this perspective, sociologists have argued that definitions of rational behavior vary across context.[30] Instead of positing that self-interest guides behavior, they have argued in Weber's footsteps that valuation is not universally guided by economic necessity or the logic of profit maximization,[31] and that cultural factors determine whether instrumental and expressive considerations shape human action in a crucial way.

My research bolsters this argument. Indeed, interviews clearly indicate that preferences are not always defined by economic rationality and that moral and cultural values are often appreciated in and of themselves. In fact, many individuals are critical of (and potentially exclusive toward) the so-called rational man, i.e., the self-interested social climber. My research also shows that various types of cultural orientations operate across populations. By positing that the maximization of self-interest motivates all human beings, rational choice theorists universalize to the population at large the culture of specific groups, to wit, most typically that of upwardly mobile Americans working in the for-profit sector.[32]

A correlate to this maximization principle is the assumption shared by structuralists and Marxists that the control of material resources in general, and of economic resources in particular, are the foremost determinant of social life. The proponents of these approaches neglect to analyze the role of cultural constructs in filtering the value of resources,[33] their role in determining whether resources are desirable to others, and whether they can be mobilized as power bases.[34] They forget that, as William Sewell, Jr., points out, no resources are valuable per se, outside of the cultural context in which they are understood.[35]

In line with this argument, symbolic boundaries are viewed here as playing an important role in the constitution of power bases precisely because they are central to the process of valuation of resources. The notion of symbolic boundary is a conceptual tool that makes it possible to understand why, compared to moral excluders, socioeconomic excluders are willing to experience more deprivations to obtain economic resources; why very successful upper-middle-class men put their families' welfare above professional mobility even when they have an alternative; and why social and cultural specialists would sacrifice high pay to work

that allows them to "get more out of life." Instead of arbitrarily adopting metatheoretical assumptions concerning the relative explanatory power of ideal and material interests, or of socioeconomic needs versus other-worldly orientations, I take the issue of the relationship between these terms to be an open-ended question that should be empirically examined case by case. In fact, my study suggests that the role of moral, cultural, and socioeconomic considerations in shaping social life varies across time and space.[36]

French Social Theory: The Contribution of Pierre Bourdieu

My results provide tools for reassessing elements of the theoretical apparatus proposed by Pierre Bourdieu, one of the few leading contemporary sociologists concerned with high status signals. This study builds directly on Bourdieu's apparatus. Indeed, it adopts the Bourdieuian view that shared cultural style contributes to class reproduction. On the other hand, some of the patterns I have uncovered directly contradict Bourdieu's work. First, whereas Bourdieu posits that differences directly translate into hierarchalization, as we just saw, my research suggests that this relationship is somewhat more complicated because of variations in the strength of symbolic boundaries. It also suggests that we need to take issue with the view, implied in Bourdieu's key notion of power field, that individuals are involved in a zero-sum game and that they participate in relatively closed social networks. Second, while Bourdieu almost exclusively stresses the importance of signals of socioeconomic and cultural status, my results indicate that his work vastly underestimates the importance of moral signals and makes them the privileged concern of a small group of people; it also shares with rational choice theory the notion that socioeconomic status is by definition more important than other statuses; in contrast, again, my results indicate that the relationship between the three types of statuses changes across time and space. Moreover, in general, Bourdieu's work relies too heavily not just on French attitudes but on Parisian attitudes, thereby exaggerating the importance of cultural boundaries. Finally, while Bourdieu argues that worldviews are primarily defined by habitus (via proximate environmental factors), my analysis illustrates the importance of considering the roles of macrostructural determinants and cultural repertoires in shaping tastes and preferences.[37]

The core of Bourdieu's writings concerns the cultural and structural mechanisms by which inequality is reproduced. In *Distinction* and else-where, Bourdieu describes how individuals struggle to improve their so-

cial position by manipulating the cultural representation of their situation in the social space. They accomplish this by affirming the superiority of their taste and lifestyle with the view of legitimizing their own identity as best representing what it means to be "what it is right to be" (228). In other words, individuals compete to legitimize their definition of high status signals. What is at stake in this symbolic competition is the power to impose labels, to shape social definitions of reality, and to affect macrosocial classification systems.

According to Bourdieu, individuals who share similar tastes and preferences (i.e., the same definitions of high status signals) tend to spontaneously and automatically like one another and exclude those who have different tastes and preferences.[38] Because tastes and preferences are essentially determined by people's social trajectories and economic and cultural resources (or capital), they vary across classes. Consequently, when we select as friends people who resemble ourselves, we indirectly contribute to the reproduction of the class structure.[39]

Bourdieu's model is based on the assumption that tastes or preferences function as signs of distinction and signals of social position. Borrowing from structuralism, Bourdieu posits in *Distinction* and elsewhere that because meaning is defined within semiotic codes where the value of each element is defined relationally—meaning and value being inextricably linked—different preferences necessarily negate one another.[40] Therefore, expressing ethical positions means to sell "one's own virtues, one's own certainties, one's own values, in a word, the certainty of one's own value, in a sort of ethical snobbery or assertion of exemplary singularity that implies *condemnation of all other ways of being and doing*" (my emphasis) (253). All cultural practices "are automatically classified and classifying, rank-ordered and rank-ordering" (223). In other words, differentiation leads directly to hierarchalization.[41] Again, this presupposition is unjustified: the conditions under which cultural differences create inequality need to be specified.[42] As we saw, these conditions have to do with the strength of symbolic boundaries, a topic that Bourdieu does not address. Because some boundaries are weaker than others, and because many people are tolerant,[43] my data suggests that definitions of high status signals (or preferences) do not ineluctably involve a zero-sum game.[44] In fact, different definitions of polluting behavior often coexist and cancel each other out. In the American case, we saw that upper-middle-class men have particularly broad cultural repertoires and often appreciate diversity. In this context, it is unlikely that preferences are defined primarily

through a closed semiotic system of reference. Instead, especially in rapidly changing societies, they are more likely to be defined through invidious comparisons whose reference base changes across contexts.[45]

For similar reasons, the evidence forces me to question the usefulness of one of Bourdieu's key concepts, the notion of "power field."[46] Here Bourdieu transposes to social relationships and social positions the Saussurian view that meanings and values are defined relationally. Just as "high" is opposed to "low," "noble" to "vulgar," or "elegant" to "casual," Bourdieu advances the idea that the objective social positions of individuals involved in networks of relationships are defined relationally, i.e., by their respective social trajectories and by differences in the amount and nature of their resources (types of capital). Those who rank high given their resources automatically create low positions for others by the mere fact that they participate within a single social system.[47] This is a zero-sum situation: individuals are condemned to improve their social positions at the risk of being marginalized by the upward mobility of others. Hence, they compete to maximize their control over the valued resources in the field, whether these resources take the form of artistic renown or cash.

This theory presumes that social systems (or fields) are relatively closed and involve a stable set of actors. Only with this assumption is it possible to assume a zero-sum game, and only with this assumption is the notion of power field useful. However, again, we have reason to doubt that groups are stable especially in the context of highly mobile societies where various people are likely to compete for different sets of resources at various points in time. Such societies could generate a more dynamic system made up of a number of partly overlapping spheres of competition and comparison. Given the level of mobility of modern communities and the fact that individuals, and particularly upper-middle-class individuals, are often involved in a wide range of activities, it might be more useful at this point to think of the value of high status signals, and of the relative positions of individuals, as defined by open, changing, and interpenetrating semiotic and social fields rather than by stable and closed ones.[48] In fact, instead of using this notion of power field—which requires the creation of a methodological artefact[49]—it is more useful to simply compare how boundaries vary across contexts and across groups (not only classes), who boundaries potentially exclude where, and how they affect inequality.

My empirical findings also raise concerns for Bourdieu's theory of

human action: as is true of structuralist, Marxist, and rational choice approaches, this theory tends to predefine the resources, or high status signals, that are most valued. A close reading of Bourdieu's work suggests that this author conceives moral status as ancillary, subsuming it to socioeconomic achievement. It also suggests that Bourdieu makes it the privileged concern of a particular group.[50] These points are very consequential: because his work is primarily concerned with analyzing the effect of forms of capital (titles, habitus, etc.) on mobility, Bourdieu's conclusions can be questioned if his analytical focus is centered on forms of capital or status signals that are not highly valued; only if status signals are valued can they affect objective mobility.

In *Distinction*, Bourdieu discusses the role played in France by aesthetic and ethical preferences in the reproduction of inequality, pointing to the symbolic authority of honesty and trustworthiness (365). He argues, however, that those who value morality do so because they have no alternative, no resources other than their moral purity and asceticism to offer on the market: they realize their ambitions "by paying in sacrifices, privations, renunciations, good will, recognitions, in short, virtues" (333). People who can offer other resources than moral purity do so: they give "real" guarantees, such as money, culture, and social contacts. Therefore, the most morally inclined are "losers" who make a virtue of necessity.[51]

Along the same lines, Bourdieu allows no autonomy to moral discourse, which he implicitly conceives as necessarily subordinated to other principles of hierarchalization. He presumes that people stress moral values *only* with the goal of improving their social positions. He argues that all apparently disinterested acts, including the consumption of culture and the display of moral character traits, are in reality "interested" because they are ultimately oriented toward the maximization of one's social position.[52] By contrast, my interviews suggest that respecting one's moral obligations, particularly vis-à-vis one's family and friends, is often valued as a goal in itself.[53] Also, as seen in Chapter 2, a large enough number of successful upper-middle-class men mentioned in interviews that they do not respect phonies, social climbers, the intellectually dishonest, and the "salaud," to lead me to believe that high moral status is a crucial resource that is valued in and of itself. From these points we can only conclude that moral boundaries are one of the blind spots in Bourdieu's theory.[54]

Further evidence of Bourdieu's tendency to predefine valued resources is found in the fact that he understates the importance of moral bounda-

ries by making them only the domain of particular groups: he holds that those who are, to a marked degree, either upwardly or downwardly mobile are the privileged bearers of morality.[55] This hypothesis does not square with the evidence I gathered: while a sizable number of the men I talked to belong to the new "petite-bourgeoisie," as defined by Bourdieu (psychologists, data managers, recreation specialists, teachers, etc.), there is no relationship between their mobility and their tendency to practice moral exclusion.[56] In this context, it should also be noted that Bourdieu defines moral behavior rather narrowly, equating it with a limited set of virtues such as discipline, asceticism, legalism, puritanism, or propensity to save,[57] while ignoring such virtues as charity, peacefulness, personal integrity, and solidarity. Also when in *Distinction*, he analyzes the structure of the "bourgeois ethic and aesthetic" in terms of bipolar oppositions (à la Lévi-Strauss), the oppositions he looks at rarely have to do with morality: he opposes the heavy to the refined, the dull to the brilliant, the obscure to the intelligent, the ordinary to the rare, and the bland to the sharp. Terms such as *common, crude,* or *coarse* which could in principle be opposed to moral terms, are instead contrasted with *unique, elegant* and *fine,* which pertain more to cultural than to moral distinction. In addition, moral referents such as *honest, truthful, fair, good, peaceful,* and *responsible* are altogether absent from Bourdieu's semiotic analysis.[58] These observations clearly illustrate Bourdieu's tendency to downplay the importance of moral character as a status signal. This tendency is incompatible with any attempt to understand the full range of signals through which status in general, and moral status in particular, is assessed.[59] The "worldly maximization" principle should not prevent us from thinking about morality in its own terms; again, as the interviews demonstrate, moral factors constitute an important dimension of exclusion that merits examination.

This leads to my next point: Bourdieu shares with rational choice theorists the view that social actors are by definition socioeconomic maximizers who participate in a world of economic exchange in which they act strategically to maximize material and symbolic payoffs.[60] This universal worldly maximization logic is applied to cultural producers as well as to businessmen. Both groups are coerced by the logic of the power fields in which they are involved into maximizing social status or social position. Bourdieu even writes that walking away from this competition equals social death,[61] as if identity was only defined by social position.[62]

While scarcity of resources is an undeniable reality, the interviews suggest that individuals, and especially upper-middle-class individuals, are not continually, equally, and universally involved in a zero-sum game for the control of socioeconomic resources. Important variations exist in the extent to which upper-middle-class men value socioeconomic status, and by extension socioeconomic resources.[63] To disqualify as hypocritical the claims of those whose personal heroes include St. Francis of Assisi and Mother Theresa, and of those who declare themselves superior to atheists, is equivalent to engaging in a form of sociological ethnocentrism.[64]

In addition, the interviews suggest that by focusing on the role played in France by the educational system in the process of social reproduction, and by analyzing only the cultural boundaries that are institutionalized in the criteria of selection at work in this key social institution, Bourdieu has considerably overemphasized the importance of these boundaries. Indeed, in France cultural boundaries are only slightly more important than other types of boundaries,[65] and they predominate only in Paris and not in Clermont;[66] even if Bourdieu is not concerned with the American case, it is useful to stress again that many Americans do not show signs of cultural goodwill, do not acknowledge the legitimacy of high culture and the importance to accumulate knowledge about it.[67] In keeping with the populist tradition, drawing boundaries using such signals can be seen by Americans as undemocratic, the way selecting on the basis of religion or ethnicity is perceived by many as illegitimately bigoted.

All this suggests that in *Distinction* Bourdieu tends to generalize about the culture that prevails in the intellectual milieu in which he lives—arguing that it pervades the French population at large. Indeed, he is mostly concerned with the status signals that are valued by Parisian intellectuals and by cultural and social specialists generally. Like them, he stresses the importance of refinement and of cultural status signals.[68] Like the Parisians, he tends to minimize the importance of moral boundaries.[69] And like many high-powered intellectuals, he presumes that everyone is equally consumed with professional success. Again he writes that those who don't value success are making a virtue of necessity.[70] Similarly, he attributes to the population at large the high level of intolerance and cultural exclusiveness characteristic of intellectuals in general, and of Parisian intellectuals in particular.[71] The survey items he uses to compare class cultures are reflexive of the culture of intellectuals. This is notably the case when he probes respondents on their favorite painters and classical

composers.[72] While such items might operate as bases for distinction in the Parisian intellectual milieu, they are unlikely to be as salient to the French as a whole.

A last criticism can be addressed to Bourdieu's work concerning his view of the relationship between taste (in my terms, symbolic boundaries) and social structure. To summarize, rather than positing a direct correspondence between the conditions of existence and consciousness as Marx does, Bourdieu introduces an intermediate variable, the habitus.[73] He argues that the latter varies with class and is determined by "different conditions of existence, differential conditioning and differential endowment of capital."[74] More specifically, he writes, "The structures constitutive of a particular type of environment (e.g.: the material conditions of existence characteristic of a class condition) produce habitus," i.e., "a system of lasting transposable dispositions which, integrating past experiences, functions at every moment as a matrix of perceptions, appreciations, and actions and makes possible the achievement of infinitely diversified tasks, thanks to analogical transforms of schemes permitting the solution of similarly shaped problems."[75] In other words, one's class habitus shapes one's "prise de position," one's values, tastes, opinions, and the code used to classify others (i.e., one's symbolic boundaries). Although these "prises de position" are experienced by the subject as voluntary, Bourdieu argues that they in fact need to be explained by people's position in power fields, their social trajectory, and the likely return on their different strategies of investments that are mediated by the structure of the power fields in which they are involved.

The idea of habitus focuses too exclusively on proximate structural conditions. Bourdieu neglects to analyze how people's preferences are shaped by broader structural features as well as by the cultural resources that are made available to them by the society they live in.[76] Moreover, Bourdieu never makes room for the possibility that boundary work could be decoupled from interests. He provides no indication that people do not necessarily draw boundaries out of their experience alone, or that habitus is affected by broad features of society, whether they be a strong state or a high level of geographic mobility. Ultimately, his analysis could be read as implying that social actors with the same amounts of capital and the same social trajectories have similar tastes and attitudes, independent of the society in which they live.[77] We need not deny the importance of the habitus. Following cognitive psychologists and neo-

institutionalists, however, we need to recognize that people do not always perceive the world only through their own experiences and that they often borrow cultural models that are decoupled from their own lives.

SYNTHESIS AND AGENDA

At this point it is finally possible to clarify the theoretical and empirical contributions of this study and even to sketch the research agenda it suggests. Throughout the book, one of my aims has been to move our focus from one specific form of high status signal (cultural capital) and symbolic boundary (cultural boundary) to the nature and properties of symbolic boundaries themselves. To achieve this, I adopted an ap proach—which could be labeled the boundary approach—that does not predefine symbolic boundaries but instead analyzes their multiple contents and variable forms.[78] At the same time, I have attempted to incorporate theoretical considerations pertaining to national differences in the strength of boundaries, to the relationship between symbolic boundaries and objective socioeconomic boundaries, and to the autonomy that different types of boundaries have in relation to one another across contexts.[79] The resulting analysis can be contrasted to Bourdieu's theoretical framework. Again, while his framework posits that social actors value socioeconomic status equally, the boundary approach takes as an empirical question the extent to which individuals value social position over other types of status. While cultural capital theory posits that strategies of distinction are mostly organized around tastes and lifestyles, the boundary approach shows that cultural consumption constitutes only one possible type of high status signal. More generally, while cultural capital theory posits the influence of specific status signals, the boundary approach aims to determine how much importance is given to various standards by evaluating how people stress distinct status scales. In other words, this approach is more comprehensive and, I hope to have shown, in some ways more empirically adequate than Bourdieu's approach, although it is not entirely inconsistent with it. Also, this approach uses a more multifaceted theory of status that centers on the relationship between various standards of evaluation and, indirectly, on the dynamic between groups[80] that produce different types of boundary work.[81]

This approach complements the available literature in several ways. While social psychologists have studied strategic self-presentation and impression management, focusing on various devices that people use to

promote themselves in such a way that they will be socially constructed as having valued traits,[82] they have neglected to document high status signals themselves. Similarly, available studies of subjective dimensions of class have neglected to analyze the relative salience of class in contrast to other aspects of social identity;[83]—just as status is not always judged on the basis of work- or occupation-related characteristics,[84] class identity (or racial, ethnic, or religious identity) is not necessarily central to upper-middle-class boundaries. Along the same lines, the poststructuralists who are concerned with identity formation and with the dynamics between race, class, and gender have neglected to study the salience of identity dimensions across contexts, and have rarely accounted for differences in cultural orientation by explanations other than the rather unsatisfactory universal relational logic that Derrida and Bourdieu, among others, advocate. My analysis should be read as an attempt to fill these various lacunae.

In the preceding pages, I attempted to provide a convincing multi-causal explanation for the fact that Americans are less concerned with signals of high cultural status than the French, while the French put less emphasis on materialism than Americans do. In my view, these differences are best explained by the combination of cultural and structural factors that increase the likelihood that individuals draw on one type of cultural repertoire rather than another—as is the case, for instance, when the presence of a strong interventionist state provides individuals with greater autonomy from market mechanisms and thereby favors the drawing of cultural boundaries. In contrast to the most influential frameworks used to study national cultural differences (e.g., the "modal personality" framework),[85] this explanation considers national cultural patterns to reside not in individual psychological traits but in institutionalized symbolic boundaries.[86] Along these lines, studying national boundary patterns allows us to view national stereotypes as the products of differences in boundary work, or as the products of collective processes of the definition of identity. It also allows us to develop a more complex view of the differences between French and American society. More precisely, by disentangling various bases of the evaluation of socioeconomic status, it is possible to understand how the French can be less "elitist" than Americans on some dimensions, but more on others, by for instance putting less emphasis on financial standing but more on social background when evaluating socioeconomic status.

Many additional empirical findings and middle-range theoretical

propositions emerged from this study. For instance, I have found evidence that suggests that cultural and moral boundaries are more autonomous from socioeconomic boundaries in a society that has a large public sector, such as France; that socioeconomic boundaries are more important for people who are highly geographically mobile, and who live in environments where anonymity is maintained; that there are very small differences in the boundary work of individuals residing in cultural centers and cultural peripheries; and that the relationship that people have with economic rationality given their occupation significantly shapes boundary work. To push these contributions further, I would want to compare my results with the boundary patterns present in other advanced industrial societies and to determine whether these and other propositions hold when tested with larger data sets.[87]

What other research agendas for the sociology of culture does this study suggest? At the most basic level, we still do not know whether the types of boundaries described here are marginal or central to upper-middle-class life. Do these boundaries point only to superficial rules of interaction that are openly fought over, or do they also pertain to deep cultural rules, i.e., to taken-for-granted and cross-situational rules?[88] How can we interpret the fact that domains of identity such as citizenship, race, and gender were not more salient in the answers of my interviewees than were their identities as earthlings, heterosexual, mammals, or carnivores? Can domains of identity not be salient for different reasons? With new debates raging around the issues of multiculturalism, democracy, and nationalism, the tasks of studying how and why domains of identity are salient is more pressing than ever. This also holds for the role played by boundaries in identity formation and their impact on exclusion.[89]

Building on our findings, a second pressing issue are the differences in the cultural and political influence of intellectuals and social and cultural specialists (or the so-called New Middle Class) more generally across countries. Intellectuals and social and cultural specialists can contribute in a very important way to maintaining a diverse and rich collective life that is not totally subordinated to economic rationality. By comparing the structure of their boundary work with that of other segments of the population (especially, for-profit workers), we can assess better the extent of their political and cultural marginalization within specific contexts and develop a more complex understanding of these groups, while taking into consideration their subcultures in toto rather than focusing exclusively on political attitudes and behavior that can themselves

be viewed as expressions of symbolic boundaries: from a sociology of knowledge perspective, such an analysis could provide insights concerning the conditions of the diffusion of intellectual and cultural products in general. Finally, this could help us understand whether, and to what extent, it is possible to affect the conditions that now seem to be increasingly strengthening the influence of socioeconomic boundaries in American and French society[90] and consolidating the influence of the conservatives in many advanced industrial societies.

A third area that urgently demands more exhaustive exploring is the boundary structure that exists in parallel with the stratification system: we need to analyze the patterns of boundaries that dominant and dominated classes and groups draw, and to determine the extent of their similarities and differences in order to gain not only a richer knowledge of the cultural dimension of the stratification system but also a better grasp of larger theoretical issues.[91] For instance, by comparing the degree of differentiation between class cultures across countries, we could better understand national differences in the political behavior of the working class and the development of the labor movement: national differences could help explain variations in the popularity of labor parties or shed new light on the "American exceptionalism" thesis. We also need to estimate more precisely the extent to which the upper-middle-class culture, which is constantly diffused by the media, is hegemonic across settings, or is simply one taste culture among others. Probing class—or racial—differences in boundary work with the help of a comparative framework would enrich ongoing debates on the resistance of various stratas to the dominant culture by providing a more precise empirical lens through which to assess patterns;[92] most studies of the cultural autonomy of dominated groups are single-sites studies, and few of the researchers interested in resistance have had access to the type of comparative data that would allow a systematic analysis of new empirical issues.[93] Finally, documenting differences in class cultures—and race cultures—could help us develop a more complete explanation of poverty that combines cultural factors with more frequently studied structural factors. The growing social and geographic isolation of the American upper-middle class and the increasing marginalization of working- and lower-class African-Americans makes such a study ever more urgent.[94]

Based on the secondary literature on class and minority cultures and in line with the discussion of class differences presented at the beginning of this chapter, I would expect to find that, in France and the United

States, the white and nonwhite working classes (1) draw stronger boundaries based on morality than the upper-middle class; (2) more often use ascribed status characteristics (race, ethnicity, gender, religion) in their boundary work; (3) use different standards for assessing refinement, intelligence, and knowledge from those used by the upper-middle class; and (4) mobilize similar standards for assessing socioeconomic status, with more emphasis on financial success to the detriment of professional prestige, involvement in high status circles, and power. I would expect that compared to America, we will find in France greater differences between working-class and upper-middle-class status distinctions based on morality and socioeconomic factors; differences on the cultural dimension are more difficult to predict. Furthermore, I would expect French working-class men to put less emphasis on economic achievement than the Americans and to take class solidarity to be an important signal of high morality. Finally, compared to their white counterparts, I would expect African-American working-class men to use distinct standards for evaluating moral purity, i.e., standards that put more stress on egalitarianism and communalism and less emphasis on individual achievement. Similar differences might be found between minority members and whites in France.

Along these lines, the study calls for further analysis of changes in the salience of boundaries over time. Research supports the view that boundaries based on class-related characteristics (as education, familiarity with high culture, etc.) are gaining in importance over those based on universal traits (e.g., race, gender, religion).[95] In this context, are moral and socioeconomic boundaries increasingly used to euphemistically draw boundaries based on gender, race, and ethnicity at the same time that norms against boundary work based on ascribed characteristics are gaining greater legitimacy, and as we are assisting at the accelerated inclusion within the upper-middle class of individuals from sharply different ethnic backgrounds? Again, what looks like the growing balkanization of American society as manifested by the growing isolation of the American upper-middle class from other classes makes the study of boundary structures ever more important. Only by shifting our attention to symbolic boundaries will it be possible to reach an understanding of these changes. Only by recognizing the impact of cultural style on inequality is it possible to attempt to overcome its effects.

Appendix I

~~~~~~

SURVEYING THE FRENCH AND AMERICAN
UPPER-MIDDLE CLASSES

INTRODUCTION

Both in France and the United States, professionals and managers constitute one of the fastest growing occupational groupings. In America, they
have grown to represent 15 percent of the population by 1987.[1] In France,
the number of French professionals and high-level managers increased by
5.6 percent between 1954 and 1975–the greatest increase of all socioprofessional groups for that period.[2] In 1987, they comprised 9.9 percent
of the active population according to the Institut National de la Statistique et des Etudes Economiques (INSEE).[3]

   This expansion in both countries can be linked to phenomena such
as the growth of the educational system,[4] the development of internal
labor markets,[5] and the expansion of the service sector and the government.[6] In France in particular, the last forty years have been a period of
accelerated modernization: while only 32 percent of the active population
worked in the service sector in 1946, this sector employed 51 percent of
the population by 1975.[7] In line with the same trend, farmers made up
32.6 percent of the population in 1956 in contrast to 17.6 percent in
1976.[8]

   Given the growing demographic and social importance of professionals and managers, it is surprising that sociologists have not paid more
attention to the culture of the upper-middle class as such. In contrast,
much has been written on American popular and working-class cultures[9]
as well as on upper-class culture.[10] While French sociologists have been
equally interested in working-class cultures,[11] they have also paid some
attention to bourgeois culture[12] and to the culture of the new middle class

or the "middle strata."[13] They have also conducted survey-based comparisons of class cultures and class differences in political attitudes.[14]

It is useful to note that the culture of the American upper-middle class has been indirectly addressed by social scientists studying professions. For instance, researchers have debated such issues as the universalistic values and disinterested attitudes of professionals,[15] professional socialization processes,[16] the relation of professionals to authority,[17] and the role strains experienced by professionals working in bureaucracies.[18] But none of these contributions attempted to systematically trace clusters of values characteristic of the upper-middle class. More immediately relevant are recent studies based on interviews conducted with members of the American middle class[19] and studies concerned with the subculture of specific occupational groups.[20] Along with recent and not-so-recent studies on the formation of middle-class culture,[21] these studies add important empirical evidence to the few earlier[22] and more recent contributions on upper-middle-class culture.[23]

American sociologists have also explored middle-class attitudes in debates surrounding the New Class. These have focused on the adversarial attitudes of middle-class members toward the business class,[24] and on the class interests of the new middle class and its relations with the capitalist and working classes.[25] The distinctive attitudes of the managerial class, as contrasted from the traditional business class, also have been considered by students of technocracy.[26] Many contributions to the "New Class"/new middle-class debate, however, were speculative in nature and did not provide solid and specific empirical evidence on the attitudes and values typical of professionals, managers, and businessmen.[27]

It should be noted that because the present study is an attempt to illuminate the culture of French professionals, managers, and businessmen, it draws considerably on the French sociological literature to gain background information on these groups. Most useful for my purpose are French studies focusing on groups that are homologous to the American middle and upper-middle class and, more particularly, studies of the "cadres,"[28] the "patrons,"[29] the political and social elites.[30] Also useful are studies of the voting behaviors in the middle class,[31] the determinants of social mobility and the social reproduction of inequality,[32] and the role of intellectuals (broadly defined) in French society.[33]

In the following pages, I compare the French and American upper-middle classes from the perspective of their position in the French and American stratification systems. I also discuss the meaning of the term

upper-middle class in the United States and of its equivalents in France. Finally, I justify the use of this term in the present study and provide background information on the socioprofessional groups that belong to this *couche* (layer) in France, namely, the *cadres*, the *professions libérales*, and the *patrons*.

COMPARING SOCIAL POSITIONS

What do the French and the American upper-middle classes look like as groups? Statistical data on the education and income of professionals and managers in both countries can help us answer these questions.

Education

In 1985, 19.4 percent of Americans twenty-five years old and over had completed four years of college or more.[34] In contrast in 1987, only 11 percent of the French population fifteen years old and older had equivalent education, with 4.6 percent holding only the first level university degree (*diplôme de premier cycle*, roughly equivalent to the American baccalaureate degree), and 6.7 percent holding also a second- or third-level university degree (roughly the equivalent of a master's or a Ph.D.).[35] This data suggests that the American college-educated population—and our predefined upper-middle class—is less of an elite in relation to the global American population than is its French counterpart in relation to the French population, and this despite the lower cost of higher education in France.[36]

The elitist character of higher education in France is still largely maintained by the bifurcation of its institutions into a university system oriented toward the middle class and a more selective system of *grandes écoles*, which traditionally has had a monopoly over the distribution of degrees in areas such as engineering, business and government administration, political science, and military training. The public universities are considerably less prestigious and less selective. In 1980, 14 percent of the French students were attending the *grandes écoles* (including preparatory classes), while 86 percent were attending the university.[37]

Table A.1 summarizes the education levels of the men I interviewed and the types of universities they attended. A roughly equal number of American and French respondents completed a degree beyond the American baccalaureate (French *license*): 45 percent for Indianapolis and 51 percent for New York, 38 percent for Clermont-Ferrand and 40 percent for

TABLE A.1

Highest Academic Degree of Respondents and Types of University Attended by Sites

| | FRANCE | | | | UNITED STATES | | | |
| | Paris | | Clermont-Ferrand | | Indianapolis | | New York | |
	%	N	%	N	%	N	%	N
Low								
Some college	5	(2)	13	(5)	0	0	5	(2)
Medium								
BA/BS	15	(6)	18	(7)	55	(22)	45	(18)
High								
Masters	15	(6)	13	(5)	23	(9)	28	(11)
ABD	18	(7)	7	(3)	2	(1)	5	(2)
Ph.D.	7	(3)	18	(7)	20	(8)	18	(7)
Elite schools	40	(16)	31	(13)	15*	(6*)	37*	(15*)
Total	100	(40)	100	(40)	100*	(40*)	100*	(40*)

Note—*The total percentages for Indianapolis and New York do not include the graduates from the American elite schools as these are also listed in the degrees categories.

Low: This includes all French respondents who have the equivalent of 2 years of higher education (Bacchalauréat + 2). This comprises individuals who have the following diplomas: DEUG (diplôme d'études universitaires générales), DEUST (diplôme d'études universitaires scientifiques et techniques), DUT (diplôme universitaire de technologie), and BTS (brevét technique supérieur). This also includes two American respondents who said they had completed a college degree, but who later provided contradictory information that they had not completed their college education.

Medium: This includes all the American respondents who have a BA or a BS as well as the French interviewees who have a license or its equivalent (Bacchalauréat + 3).

High (Master's): This includes all the American and the French interviewees who have a master's degree, as well as French interviewees who have the equivalent of 4 years of higher education (Bacchalauréat + 4).

High (ABD): This includes all French respondents holding a DEA (diplôme d'études approfondies), a DESS (diplôme d'études supérieures spécialisées), or an engineering degree from a university as well as those who have completed studies in dentistry or pharmacology. It also includes American respondents who have completed all the Ph.D. requirements but the dissertation (ABD).

High (Ph.D.): This includes the French respondents who hold a "doctorat de troisième cycle" or a "doctorat d'état" as well as those who have completed studies in medicine. It also includes American respondents who have completed their Ph.D.

High (elite schools): These figures refer to American students who attended an elite university and French student holders of a "grande école" degree. These degrees are not equivalent to the degrees conferred by the university system and are therefore classified separately.

Paris. It should be kept in mind, however, that degrees from the *grandes écoles* are terminal, which means that their graduates are unlikely to pursue additional academic degrees. Respectively, 40 percent and 31 percent of the Paris and Clermont-Ferrand participants attended an elite school (grande école), whereas 37 percent and 15 percent of the New York and Indianapolis interviewees went to an elite private university.[38] Seven American participants attended Ivy League universities, while others hold degrees from a range of non–Eastern elite universities (Duke University, Emery University, University of Notre Dame, University of Chicago) and specialized schools (Massachusetts Institute of Technology, George Washington University Law School, and so forth). Of the French interviewees, seven graduated from the Ecole Polytechnique, the Ecole Centrale, the Ecole Supérieure d'Electricité, and the less selective Conservatoire National des Arts et Métiers; four graduated from the Conservatoire Supérieur National de Musique de Paris, the Ecole Nationale Supérieure des Beaux Arts, and the Ecole du Louvre, which are not all equally selective. Three graduated from the Ecole Nationale d'Administration and the Institut d'Etudes Politiques de Paris, the remainder having attended miscellaneous other schools.

Income

While the national median household income in the United States was $23,618 in 1985, the median income for people with four years of college or more was $39,506.[39] For managers, including executive, administrative, or managerial specialists, the median income was $36,155 for men and $21,874 for women.[40] By comparison, in France in 1979, the median household income before taxes for upper-level managers was 160,900 FF (approximately $35,000), and the national median household income was 93,116 FF (approximately $20,000).[41] The median income in the Auvergne is considerably lower. For instance, the 1989 per capita annual income after taxes was 183,300 FF ($39,000) for Auvergne's *cadres*, as compared to a national average of 209,700 FF ($45,000) (source: INSEE).

Data on income also suggest that French professionals and managers constitute more of an elite in the French context than their American counterparts do in the United States. Indeed, the income differential between managers and blue-collar workers is considerably greater in France: in the early seventies, the income ratio between a male manager with a college degree and a skilled worker with apprenticeship training was 2.65 for France and 1.43 for the United States.[42] The income ratio between

college-educated managers and the average employed male population was 2.53 for France and 1.87 for the United States. A greater percentage of the national income was concentrated in the top 5 percent income group of the population in France than in other advanced industrial societies (16.6 percent in the United States and 21.2 percent in France);[43] among the advanced industrial societies, only in the Netherlands was income more concentrated than it was in France. Accordingly, French society ranked 21 on the Schultz coefficient of income inequality while American society ranked 9.[44] Uruguay, Mauritius, and Syria are less stratified than France according to this indictator!

Table A.2 presents data on the annual household income level of French and American interviewees in this study. This table shows that respondents from Clermont-Ferrand have the lowest income, with 47 percent of the households making less than $49,000 a year, followed by Paris, where 24 percent are in this income category. In marked contrast, only 7 percent of my interviewees from Indianapolis and 5 percent of those from New York had income under $49,000 a year. On the other

TABLE A.2
Annual Household Income of Respondents by Sites in 1989 Dollars[a]

| | FRANCE | | | | UNITED STATES | | | |
| | Paris | | Clermont-Ferrand | | Indianapolis | | New York | |
	%	N	%	N	%	N	%	N
<$49,000	24	(10)	47	(19)	7	(3)	5	(2)
$50,000–$79,000	45	(18)	25	(10)	35	(14)	30	(12)
$80,000–$99,000	12	(5)	5	(2)	18	(7)	15	(6)
$100,000–$129,000	8	(3)	10	(4)	13	(5)	15	(6)
$130,000–$199,000	8	(3)	5	(2)	7	(3)	10	(4)
>$200,000					7	(3)	20	(8)
n.a.	3	(1)	8	(3)	13	(5)	5	(2)
Total	100	(40)	100	(40)	100	(40)	100	(40)

[a]The French income categories corresponding to these six income brackets are: <289,000 FF; 290,000–459,000 FF; 460,000–579,000 FF; 580,000–749,000 FF; and >750,000 FF. These categories were defined by multiplying the categories of income of American respondents by 5.80 (exchange rate as of 1 December 1987).

hand, New York has the highest percentage (45 percent) of households in the top income category ($100,000 or more), followed by Indianapolis (27 percent), Paris (16 percent), and Clermont-Ferrand (15 percent). These percentages should be interpreted with great caution, however: they reflect the fact that the French, and particularly members of the *professions libérales*, tend to underdeclare their income.[45] The net purchasing power of individuals earning $100,000 is approximately equal in both countries,[46] although there exists important regional differences.

In 1985, American families located in the top fifth income group (earning more than $48,000 a year) took in 43 percent of all U.S. family income. This suggests that all my American interviewees are located in this top fifth, taking into consideration changes in personal income between 1985 and the time of the interview (1988–89).[47] It should be noted, however, that social scientists differ in what they consider to be middle and upper-middle-income brackets.[48]

Differences between the two countries with regard to mobility are less than what one would predict based on the distributive structure of French society, as was borne out in a comparative study of *intragenerational* career mobility of men in Austria, France, and the United States. Max Haller and his colleagues recently compared the first job of their respondents to their job at time of inquiry, using representative mass data from each of the three nations.[49] They found that (1) the total percentage of mobile men was comparable for France and America (respectively, 76.9 percent and 75 percent), and (2) there was less upward mobility (40.7 percent) and more downward mobility (13.3 percent) in the United States than in France (48.8 percent upward and 6.5 percent downward). On the other hand, data on social mobility from one generation to the next shows more important cross-national differences: while the United States ranks fourth according to the mobility index (preceded by Israel, Canada, and Australia), France ranks seventh after Great Britain and Germany, with a score only half as high as the American score.[50] However, important differences in opportunity for intergenerational mobility exist between Paris and the *Province*: among the sons of Parisian private-sector managers, 73 percent remain in the upper-middle class versus 57 percent of those from the Province. This is linked to the fact that the social structure of Paris is more skewed toward the top: 33 percent of the Parisian population belongs to the so-called *classes dominantes* (i.e., professionals and managers) in contrast to only 14 percent in the Province. On the

other hand, 14 percent of Parisians belong to the *classes populaires*, i.e., to the lower and working class, in contrast to 46 percent in the Province.[51]

We see, therefore, that in general the French upper-middle class is more of an elite in French society than is its counterpart in American society. The French upper-middle class is smaller in size and controls a more sizable proportion of the national resources, as revealed by our comparison of the income of managers and of other workers in France and the United States. It is important to remember, however, that there exists important differences in income between the Paris and the Clermont-Ferrand upper-middle classes.

COMPARING SOCIAL GROUPS

The term *upper-middle class* is used for convenience and to differentiate between the college-educated population and the broader aggregate that appropriates the middle-class label in the United States. Indeed, according to Jackman and Jackman,[52] 33 percent of the blue-collar workers included in a national survey identified themselves as middle class, as did 35 percent of the operatives, 40 percent of the craftsmen, and 41 percent of the clerical workers. On the other hand, according to the same survey, 61 percent of American professional workers identified themselves as belonging to the middle class, while only 20 percent defined themselves as upper-middle class. Of the managers, including those without a college degree, 59 percent declare themselves to be middle class and only 18 percent upper-middle class. Despite these relatively high percentages of professionals and managers who identify themselves with the middle class, the term *upper-middle class* remains most appropriate as a designation for my sample, because of the heterogeneity of groups who identify themselves as middle class.[53]

It should be noted that the American label "upper-middle class" does not have a strict equivalent in France, although a few terms have traditionally been applied to the social groups located in a position in French society similar to the one occupied by the upper-middle class in the American stratification system. *Bourgeoisie* is one such term. However, it refers to a social group that has a distinctive historical identity and culture.[54] In the nineteenth century, this group included the members of liberal professions, landowners living from their rents, bankers, industrials, and merchants. Most important, these people shared a way of life defined partly by a strong attachment to family, religion, and tradition,

and a high regard for education. Even now, as Chapters 3, 4, and 6 explained, the term *bourgeois* connotes a cultural heritage that would not be shared by many first-generation professionals.

Another generic term used in France in lieu of "upper-middle class" is *cadres*, which refers to professionals and managers. The cultural importance of cadres as a social category is reflected by their presence in official statistics. It is reflected also by the existence of numerous books on this group—whereas one finds only a few books on the French middle and upper-middle classes. The absence of an adequate equivalent in the French context for the American term *upper-middle class* would suggest that the latter exists more as a distinct entity in the United States than it does in France.[55]

Now, along with the term *cadre*, I will briefly discuss a few distinctively French socioprofessional labels:

Again, the term *cadre* is used in France to refer sometimes to managers and professionals, but sometimes it refers to managers only. If these two categories (managers and professionals) are often brought together, it is because a great many French engineers are, in fact, executives.[56] Indeed, in French private industry, a degree from an elite engineering school is one of the most valuable credentials for promotion into the higher echelons, and it often leads to a managerial position. These *grandes écoles* degrees, along with seniority, largely determine mobility within private sector firms. On the other hand, French government agencies customarily categorize the *cadres* as follows: the *cadres moyens* include technicians, primary schoolteachers, social workers, office supervisors, and the like; the *cadres supérieurs* include engineers, while the *cadres administratifs supérieurs* include personnel managers, financial managers, lawyers, accountants, sales executive, and general managers. Private industry treats *cadres moyens* as non*cadres*.[57]

The *cadres* became a legal category under the Vichy government during World War II. People who are classified under this label have access to specific privileges, including pension rights. They also can belong to a *cadre* union, the most important of them being the *Confédération générale des cadres* (CGC), which defines itself as apolitical, even if it does, in fact, lean toward the political right. Traditionally, this union has fought for corporatist privileges such as reduced taxes and pensions. French *cadre* unionism is unique and is concentrated in the public sector.

2. The French *professions libérales* are more encompassing than their American counterpart, but they do not comprise all self-employed pro-

fessionals. Besides architects, physicians, lawyers, notaries, dentists, and pharmacists, it includes certified accountants and some paramedical professions (such as chiropractors and nurses)—i.e., all professions that have a certified state charter.[58]

These professions are defined as offering a public service. Consequently, their members are not allowed to advertise to potential customers. They are expected to put their clients' interests above the pursuit of profit. Competition between professionals is seen in France as contrary to the clients' interest, for the public should "seek [their lawyers or physicians] out in the same way that they seek out a priest."[59]

Because of this public contribution, the French liberal professions are subject to a greater amount of state control than their American equivalents, while at the same time the state gives them jurisdictional protection. For instance, the state, in collaboration with professional associations, determines professional fees; it organizes the professions and structures their jurisdictions; it acknowledges them, creates professional work by developing new administrative structures, referees disputes, and so forth. In other words, the state, not the market, is the dominant audience for professional claims.[60] In contrast, in the United States, specific occupational groups often have strong collective identities and corporate associations. They do not have unions like their French counterparts (e.g., the *Union nationale des professions libérales*).

It should be noted that while 8 percent of the American labor force is self-employed, professionals represent 15 percent of this figure.[61] In contrast, in France in 1982, 15 percent of the population was self-employed (including farmers and small shopkeepers), and only 5 percent of these were self-employed professionals.[62]

3. Unlike the term *professions libérales*, the term *patron* (literally, "boss") refers to a distinctive French reality which is difficult to pinpoint. Students of the *patronat* are often concerned with the French business elite, i.e., with the chief executive managers of the two hundred most important French firms.[63] However, the *Conseil national des patrons français* (CNPF) represents the interests of all business owners with 10 employees or more, of which there are 150,000 in France.[64] The French *patronat* also includes small craftsmen and shopkeepers who are de facto excluded from this study because none of those who were randomly contacted had the French equivalent of a college degree.[65]

The term *patron* is often used to refer to the traditional role of a business owner or manager who maintains a paternalistic relationship with his

employees.[66] The number of French businessmen identifying with this role diminishes as the proportion of chief executives drawing on rational legal models of authority increases, concomitantly with the growth of multinational French corporations, the proliferation of foreign companies in France, the decline of the traditional small and middle-sized enterprises (PME) and a reduction in the number of enterprises under familial control.[67] A growing proportion of French chief executives have access to their position not through family inheritance but through their *grande école* degree.[68]

Appendix II

∽∽∽

THE RESEARCH SITES

This appendix presents the context in which my research was carried out by describing the four areas where I conducted interviews. I first discuss the rationale behind the selection of the four sites.

SITE SELECTION

Indianapolis was selected as a research site because it is representative of one variant of American mainstream culture, that of the Midwestern culture.[1] On the other hand, it incarnates what New Yorkers consider to be a peripheral culture in the American landscape, just as Parisians consider the Auvergne, the region where Clermont-Ferrand is located, as illustrative of provincial culture.[2] Clermont-Ferrand was chosen because it presents striking similarities with Indianapolis. Most noteworthy is the fact that both cities are of roughly similar importance relative to the total French and American population. Both cities constitute important regional centers located in large underpopulated agricultural areas. Both are the sites of very important multinational industries that exercise a strong influence on the local economy: the Lilly Pharmaceutical Company in Indianapolis, and Michelin in Clermont-Ferrand. Both have important universities and medical centers. At a more superficial, but nonetheless interesting, level both cities have renowned raceways and are revamping their images using a "car and sports" trademark.

The physical proximity between my residence in the Princeton area and New York City, as well as my familiarity with Paris, made these metropolitan areas choice research sites for me. Also, both cities are important international cultural centers, and both have considerable national influence on their respective societies. Selecting respondents in the sub-

urbs of New York and Paris would guarantee that interviewees across the four sites would share relatively similar physical surroundings. This decision was further justified in the New York area by the ethnic and racial heterogeneity of the boroughs, by the increasing income bipolarization of the Manhattan population—where the middle class is underrepresented—and by the presence in the outer suburbs of a sizable proportion of professionals and managers.[3] Furthermore, the suburbs constitute the ideal-typical upper-middle-class habitat in America.

It should be noted that sampling from the suburbs is justified because the majority of Americans who are in upper-level income brackets now live in the suburbs. Also, as argued by the sociologist M. P. Baumgartner, suburban lifestyles and values are spreading elsewhere, as "standards to which those who live in the suburbs are held and the mechanisms whereby social control is exerted among them are already the most widely diffused in the nation."[4] Furthermore, as explained by Constance Perin who also studied American suburbs, middle-class people attach great meaning to these places: "Suburbs and city are each precipitates of American meanings, crystallizing American hopes and fears about families—children, women and men. They also capture American thoughts about the kinds of places promising the most satisfying size of community: Uniform or Varied, Small-town or Cosmopolitan, Friendly or Anonymous, Spread-out or Concentrated. The children and the barbecues: nurturing offspring and sharing suppers are what families are all about, and suburbia is all about families. And about being among 'our own kind' . . . In suburbs, that line between indoors and out fades, and the larger fund of trust there—the essential nutrient for gardens of children— account for Americans' honest albeit stock response: 'We moved here for the children.'"[5] The decision to conduct interviews in American suburbs determined my decision to interview French people who live in roughly similar settings.

I will now describe the social, economic, and geographic scenery that puts each group of interviews in perspective.

THE FOUR SITES

Indianapolis

Indianapolis is located in the core of the area culturally defined as the Middle West. It is a major agricultural and manufacturing center for the region, with a population of approximately 780,000. The median age is

31.2 years, and 20 percent of the population is black. Minorities are concentrated in the southern part of town, while most participants in my research resided in the northern part of town, which is wealthier.

Indianapolis has a very large superficies and is mostly suburban in character. In 1970, it was expanded to include almost all of Marion County, becoming one of the cities with the lowest population density in the United States. The cost of living is below the national average, as are housing costs.

In the nineteenth century, Indianapolis's main economic activities were processing and shipping of farm products, selling farm equipment, and transportation. The city grew considerably in the early 1900s with the discovery of natural gas reserves and the development of the motor car industry (between 1898 and 1934, thirty different makes of cars were produced in Indianapolis). Hardly hit by the Depression, this town entered a new phase of expansion and urbanization after the World War II. Today jobs are relatively diversified—in services (22 percent); manufacturing (18 percent); government (15 percent); retail trade (19 percent); finance, insurance, and real estate (8 percent); wholesale trade (7 percent); transportation (6 percent); and construction (5 percent). Major employers include the Eli Lilly Pharmaceutical company, RCA, Indiana Bell, and Fort Benjamin Harrison, home of the Army Finance Center.

Indianapolis became the capitol of Indiana in 1820. Located in the middle of the state and at several hours' distance from the nearest major cities of Chicago, Louisville, and Detroit, it remained isolated culturally until relatively recent times. The public school system is one of the worst in the country, according to official ratings.

As a community, Indianapolis has been developing at a fast pace in the last fifteen years. These changes are the result of a joint effort of the political and economic elite to expand the city's infrastructure and to improve its image. Working together in several committees (Greater Indianapolis Progress Committee, Commission for Downtown, Corporate Community Council, Indiana Sports Corporation), various groups have contributed to the creation of an enlarged civic infrastructure, including a convention center.

The culture of Indianapolis is very sports-oriented, as is reflected in the construction of a number of sports facilities and in the city's active involvement in the organization of several types of sports events, ranging from the PanAm Games to various amateur competitions. A scientific and technical culture also permeates the city, due in part to the proximity of

Purdue University, which has an important engineering program, and to the presence of the Lilly Pharmaceutical Company, which hires a great number of research scientists. In terms of cultural activities and resources, the city hosts an annual international violin competition and prides itself on being the home of the most important children's museum in the world.

Politically, Indiana has traditionally been a Republican state and Indianapolis a Republican city, especially in the more northern sections of the town. Indiana is also the fourteenth most populous state in the country; 32 percent of its population is still living in nonmetropolitan areas.[6] Furthermore, the Hoosiers form a very homogeneous population: they are overwhelmingly of German ancestry; only .4 percent of its population is Jewish and .8 percent Mexican-American. Compared with all the other states in the Union, Indiana ranked 32 in terms of individual income per capita and 42 in terms of state expenditure per capita in 1985. In 1980, 12.4 percent of the population had completed college (the national average was 16.3 percent). The state's legislative appropriation for its art programs between 1974 and 1986 was the twelfth lowest in the country.[7]

The New York Suburbs

In the New York area, I conducted interviews in nine communities of the regional metropolitan area, some very exclusive, others more middle class.[8] These communities include the upscale towns of Summit (21,071 population in 1983), New Providence (12,426), Madison (15,357), Metuchen (13,762), and the more mixed communities of River Edge (11,111) and South Plainfield (20,521)—all located in New Jersey. On Long Island, I conducted interviews in two middle-class towns, Merrick (24,478) and Massapequa (24,454), as well as in a more upscale community, the Rockville Center Village (25,412).[9] Most of these towns are very homogeneous racially; a few have a considerable Jewish population. These suburbs are located less than an hour's drive from Manhattan (see map A.1) and are concentrated in Bergen and Morris counties in New Jersey and in Nassau County on Long Island. All have a large number of professionals and managers.[10] It is more difficult to describe these New York suburbs than it is to describe Indianapolis, because the former are necessarily somewhat heterogeneous. Many are expanding quickly, as corporate headquarters move out of Manhattan to take advantage of cheaper electricity and lower taxes in New Jersey. While the population of the regional metropolitan area (RMA) in general increased from 14.7 to 16.8 million between 1956 and 1975, the population of the outer ring,

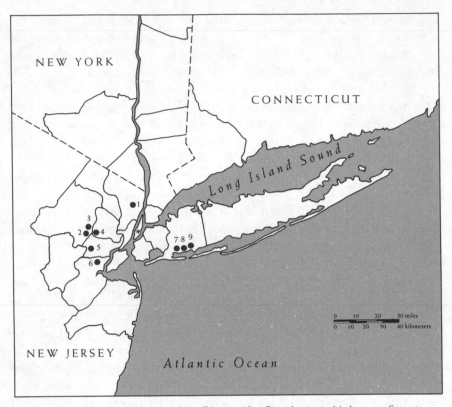

Map A.1. The New York Suburbs: 1. River Edge; 2. New Providence; 3. Madison; 4. Summit; 5. South Plainfield; 6. Metuchen; 7. Rockville Center Village; 8. Merrick; 9. Massapequa; *Manhattan.

where most of my interviewees reside, almost doubled in the same period to the point where it made up 31 percent of the RMA.[11] This increase has been particularly strong in Morris County, where New Providence and Madison are located. AT&T and Bell Laboratories have a strong presence in this area.

New Jersey is one of the smallest states of the Union, located between the Hudson and Delaware rivers. Historically, it has had an ill-defined identity, living in the shadows of New York and Philadelphia. The northern and central regions are constituted of suburbs, interspersed with rural areas that are being quickly transformed at the hands of the developers. The state has important oil-refining, electricity, and tourist industries. Ethnically and racially diverse, it presents clear patterns of residential

segregation, which reflect income differentials across racial groups. For instance, the populations of the towns where I conducted interviews are on average 2.6 percent black, the highest percentage being the Metuchen population with 5.8 (compiled from the 1980 U.S. census data).

The Summit–Madison–New Providence area, where many of the interviews were conducted, was at one point a summer resort for rich New Yorkers. After the construction of a railroad in 1830, it became one of the first commuter communities in the New York area. It hosts the foremost American Methodist university (Drew University) and many high-tech industries. The area has many cultural resources, including a summer Shakespeare festival, an arts center, and several theaters.

Metuchen, founded in the 1830s, is also one of the first commuter communities. It has attracted many intellectuals and literary figures (thus its nickname, the "Brainy Borough"), and has the reputation for being an exclusive community. South Plainfield is less exclusive. It is also largely residential and has served as a "bedroom community" since 1870. Like South Plainfield, River Edge played an important role during the War of Independence, while Summit was a sentry port in Revolutionary times. Washington fought in River Edge and rested in Plainfield after the battle of the Watchung.[12]

The three Long-Island sites are also residential communities. They are all located in Nassau County, one of the fastest-growing suburbs of New York. A large proportion of the population commutes; 40 percent of the active population worked outside of the county in 1980. Every morning the trains fill up with commuters heading for Manhattan. Approximately 25 percent of the population of Nassau County over the age of twenty-five has four or more years of college, according to the 1980 statistics.

Massapequa and Merrick are active resorts, located on the South Shore of Long Island. Here, boat channels roll behind single-family homes, where some residents keep their yachts. In the area, numerous harbors welcome boaters and fishermen. The flat terrain of the South Shore winds along the Atlantic Ocean, opening up onto wide beaches.

Paris

Interviews were likewise conducted in nine communities in the suburbs of Paris, most of them larger than the New York communities described above. Again I chose a mixture of middle and upper-middle-class communities. Neuilly-sur-Seine (population 65,941), Reuil-Malmaison (64,545),

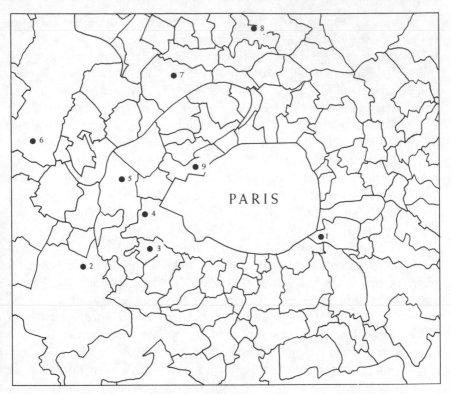

Map A.2. The Paris Suburbs: 1. Vincennes; 2. Versailles; 3. Sèvres; 4. St.-Cloud; 5. Rueil Malmaison; 6. St.-Germain-en-Laye; 7. Argenteuil; 8. Montmorency; 9. Neuilly-sur-seine.

Sèvres (21,100), St-Cloud (28,052), St-Germain-en-Laye (35,351), Versailles (95,240), and Montmorency (20,927) are traditional bourgeois towns, all but one located in the upscale western section of the Parisian suburban belt (see map A.2). Some of these communities are more similar to Greenwich, Connecticut, than to the newer New Jersey suburbs, in that they have been the home of an old bourgeoisie—and an aristocracy—since the nineteenth or, in some cases, the eighteenth century. The populations of Argenteuil (101,542) and Vincennes (44,256) have lower-income averages than Versailles, for instance, as was the case for South Plainfield and Merrick in comparison with Summit and Madison.[13] In contrast with the New York suburbs, these Paris suburbs are loaded with historical and cultural significance for their national culture. For instance, whereas New Providence is just one of many upscale suburbs of New York, St-Germain-en-Laye has a distinct historical identity aside

from that of a "Paris suburb." Its *château* has been inhabited by several of France's most illustrious kings. Argenteuil produces wines and is known for its cloister, where Héloïse, the lover of Abélard, took refuge. Vincennes, Versailles, Neuilly-sur-Seine, and St-Cloud also have *châteaux* which have made history. Vincennes is now the center of a major arsenal and military school which replaced the old prison. Versailles is of course a major tourist resort. Its population is noted for its strict Catholicism and its upholding of the traditional bourgeois and aristocratic cultures; one can find in Versailles, even today, people who favor the restoration of the French monarchy. Sèvres and St-Cloud house the major national porcelain factories and prestigious normal schools. Reuil-Malmaison is mostly known as the site of the residence where Joséphine took refuge after her separation from Napoléon.

The general aspect of these towns differs in many ways from that of their American counterparts. Physically, besides the admixture of local stores and cafés, the most striking differences between French and American residential areas include the presence of many apartment buildings, the smaller size of lots and houses, and the use of high fences to maintain privacy. Socially, the inhabitants of these French communities seem to have more clearly defined collective identity: their local elite (highly placed administrators of schools and hospitals, e.g.) often form a more or less cohesive group of "notables" and are more strongly identified with the town in which they live than are their New York counterparts. Along these lines, the proportion of commuters among the Paris interviewees is less than among the New York interviewees (37 percent in Paris, 52 percent in New York); because members of the American upper-middle class are very mobile geographically, and change employers or are relocated more often than their French counterparts, we would expect the residents of the New York suburbs to be less identified with their place of residence.

Clermont-Ferrand

Located in the middle of France (see map A.3), surrounded by majestic volcanos, Clermont-Ferrand is the capital of the Auvergne, a region known for its cheeses; for the stingy, hardworking, and stern character of its inhabitants; and for Michelin, the main employer. It is a region that has long been isolated, partly because of a poor highway system. Under these conditions, a strong regionalist feeling developed, not unlike what one finds in Indiana, and in Indianapolis in particular. The similarities

Map A.3. France.

between these two cities are striking. Besides those mentioned above, both cities are located in the physical or cultural midpoint of their respective countries.[14] Both city administrations are working at rejuvenating the local economy, renovating the downtown area, and making a traditionally isolated area more integrated in and central to the economic life of the nation.[15] Like Indianapolis, Clermont is trying to improve its image by hosting international sports events; it hosted an international fencing championship in 1981, a volleyball championship in 1986, and a boxing championship in 1987. Finally, like Indianapolis, Clermont-Ferrand has been thought of as a city with little to offer culturally,[16] although recently the situation has improved with the creation of an excellent string orchestra, a short film festival, and a science-fiction festival.

With 150,000 inhabitants, Clermont is the nineteenth largest city in France. The general metropolitan area has a population of 300,000. This is smaller than Indianapolis, which has 780,000 inhabitants (the metropolitan statistical area included 1,167,000 in 1980) and is the thirty-second largest city in the United States.[17] Given differences in the size of the French and American populations, I chose to compare Indianapolis with a somewhat smaller French city. In terms of sheer size, the metropolitan area which would be most comparable with Indianapolis is Marseilles; with its 878,689 inhabitants, Marseilles is the second most populous French city, ranking after Paris and before Lyon. But in terms of its national prominence, this city is comparable not to Indianapolis but to Chicago or Atlanta.[18] Furthermore, it does not share many of the geographic or cultural features of Indianapolis.

On the other hand, the similarities between Indianapolis and Clermont-Ferrand should not be exaggerated. Historically, of course, the two towns differ greatly. The town of Clermont was a metropolis from the first until the third century. It became an important episcopal city in the fifth century and remained so for the next ten centuries. Montferrand was created in the twelfth century and became unified with Clermont under Louis XV. In contrast, Indianapolis was incorporated in the nineteenth century.

Agriculture is the second most important industry of the Puys-de-Dôme, the administrative region (*département*) of which Clermont is the capital, but the agricultural sector is declining because of low productivity.[19] The alternative strategy for strengthening the economy is to develop high-tech industries, building on the presence of a good engineering school and an important university with 10,478 students. At this point, retail trade represents 17 percent of the local employment; manufacturing, 41.8 percent; government, 29 percent; finance, insurance, and real estate, 4 percent; transport, 5 percent; wholesale trade, 4 percent.[20] The manufacturing sector is larger than it is in Indianapolis, while the service sector is smaller.

The influence of Michelin on Clermont-Ferrand is an essential element of local life. By far the most important employer in the area since the beginning of the century, Michelin has openly opposed the implantation of other industries which would compete for the labor force and increase labor cost. Similar to many Catholic bourgeois families of the Third Republic, the brothers Michelin adopted a paternalist attitude toward their workers and built for them a wide range of facilities, including

schools, sports centers, and a hospital. They promoted traditional family values and did not encourage the urbanization of peasants from the countryside who came to work for them. The Michelin organizational culture is still known for "renouncing all ostentatious luxuries and ignoring titles and decorations . . . the top managers lead discrete and hardworking lives . . . all useless hierarchies are ignored, and those that must exist are not accentuated."[21] As this study shows, the culture of the American Midwest has features not unlike those promoted by Michelin. Up to the present, engineers working for Michelin are clearly perceived as Clermont's elite. They are world-class experts, and their salaries are well above the local average.

Foreigners, mostly Portuguese, represent 13 percent of the population of Clermont-Ferrand. Otherwise, the town and the region are ethnically and racially homogeneous. Also, Clermont-Ferrand is divided politically. The town has an old Socialist tradition, and the city's present mayor is a Socialist. The regional government, however, is controlled by the right and is presided over by the former French president, Valéry Giscard D'Estaing. The region's representatives in the Senate and in the National Assembly are mostly Socialists.

Geographically, Clermont-Ferrand proper is much smaller than Indianapolis. Consequently, the interviewees were also chosen from the Clermont-Ferrand metropolitan area, which includes seventeen "communes" (or boroughs). I conducted interviews in Chamalières, the town where Valéry Giscard D'Estaing served as mayor and which he now represents in the National Assembly. Interviews were also conducted in Royat, an affluent suburb, and Cournon d'Auvergne, a less prosperous town. Royat is particularly well-known for its spa. The elderly come from all over France to be treated there; the spa gives to the town the cachet of a turn-of-the-century resort, similar to Vichy in appearance, architecturally and otherwise.

In 1975, 60 percent of the top managers (*cadres supérieurs*) and professionals (*professions libérales*) of the Clermont-Ferrand area lived in one of its four rich western suburbs, which include Chamalières and Royat. They made up 18 percent of the active population of Chamalières and 13 percent of the active population of Royat (INSEE, 1982 census). Both towns have high proportions of retired people.[22]

Appendix III

∿∿∿

RESEARCH PROCEDURES

SAMPLING PROCEDURES

The research design calls for a culturally diversified group of interviewees, which is obtained by building four random stratified samples, drawing from the populations of Indianapolis, the New York suburbs, the Paris suburbs, and Clermont-Ferrand. The sampling proceeded as follows:

First, research assistants randomly selected from four hundred to six hundred names for each site. In the United States, these names were chosen from streets listed in criss-cross phone directories and located within the confines of census tracks with household income averages over $30,000; these tracks were identified using the 1980 census.[1] In France, names were chosen from the phone directory of cities with average household income above the national mean; these cities were also identified using census information. While selecting names, research assistants were instructed to reject those with female surnames as well as those that were conspicuously foreign. A large number of names were chosen in each site because it was anticipated that many potential respondents would not qualify.

Second, introductory letters were sent to all randomly sampled names. These letters described the research project, informed potential respondents that they would be contacted by phone shortly, and invited them to participate in the research. A few days, and in a number of cases, a few weeks later, these potential respondents were called by a research assistant to determine whether they qualified for the study and were willing to participate. Assistants were instructed to try to contact all potential respondents at least three times. Many remained unreachable, even though phone calls were made in the evenings and during the weekends.

Third, a relatively small number of interviewees were found using the professional listings of phone directories (the Yellow Pages) in order to increase occupational and sectoral match across samples. In a few rare cases, members of specific occupations were located by contacting the type of institutions where they worked (e.g., newspapers for journalists, museums for museum curators, hospitals for hospital administrators, etc.). A research assistant would ask the receptionist for names of employees who met the selection criteria. These professionals would generally be sent an introductory letter and then be contacted over the phone by a research assistant. Due to time constraints, a larger number of French interviewees were selected using this technique than were American interviewees. Except for one person, I never included in the sample names that had been obtained from my personal acquaintances.

Finally, after identifying a sizable number of people who were both qualified and interested in the project, I selected for inclusion in the final sample an occupationally diverse group of respondents. This selection was performed on the basis of social and demographic information obtained during the phone interview. It took into consideration the composition of each of the four samples in order to maximize the match between respondents across sites. I conducted interviews only with respondents included in the final sample.

The number of qualified respondents who agreed to praticipate in the research project varied across settings. The estimated acceptance rate for qualified respondents was 49 percent in Indianapolis, 42 percent in the New York suburbs, 58 percent in Paris, and 56 percent in Clermont.[2]

The criteria used to choose the respondents pertained to place of residence, occupation, sector of employment, age, level of education, gender, and race and ethnicity. I discuss these in turn:

Place of Residence

In order to be included in the final sample, potential respondents had to have resided in one of the areas under study for at least five years. This consideration was adopted to maximize the regional representativeness of respondents.

Occupation

The second criterion used to determine the eligibility of potential respondents was the type of occupation they pursued: the only qualified individuals were those who worked full-time in a professional or managerial

position or who were self-employed. In the rare cases where respondents held two jobs, eligibility was determined on the basis of their main occupation. While a few exceptions are made to protect anonymity, respondents are generally described by their main occupational title.

Because the research aims in part at comparing the boundary work of members of the so-called New Middle Class with the boundary work of business people, the selection process was directed at finding members of a wide range of social and cultural occupations (e.g., artist, teacher, priest, journalist) and of business occupations (e.g., accountant, banker, businessman).[3] Because social and cultural specialists make up a smaller proportion of the total population (10 percent of the professional and managerial class in the United States),[4] they are greatly overrepresented in the study as they make up 50 percent of the final sample.

Sector of Employment

For reasons described in Chapter 5, each of the four samples required approximately ten self-employed private sector for-profit workers, ten public or nonprofit sector social and cultural specialists, and ten salaried private sector for-profit workers, in addition to five to ten public or nonprofit sector for-profit workers or private sector social and cultural specialists.[5] Therefore, the sampling procedures took sector of employment into consideration in conjunction with occupation. The definition of each sector is self-evident.[6]

Age

The final sample includes only men who were between thirty and sixty years of age at the time they were contacted. This criterion of selection was introduced to minimize lifestyle variations due to age differences.

In the final sample, an attempt was made to match respondents from the four sites not only in terms of occupation and sector of employment but also in terms of age. Consequently, if from a pool of five Clermont-Ferrand self-employed lawyers I had to choose one person, I would select the one whose age was closer to the ages of the self-employed lawyers that were part of the Indianapolis, New York, and Paris samples.

Level of Education

For reasons described in Chapter 1, only college-educated men were eligible for inclusion in the final sample. For American respondents, this meant they had obtained a college diploma; for the French, it meant they

had obtained one of the following degrees: (1) a *diplôme de premier cycle,* which is equivalent to an American baccalaureate; (2) a *diplôme de deuxième cycle* (American master's degree) or a *diplôme de troisième cycle* (American doctorate); (3) a *grande école* diploma; or (4) a *brevêt technique supérieur* or a *diplôme universitaire technique,* which are the equivalent of a degree from an American community college (a few holders of such degrees were included in the sample because they often do in France the work that is done by engineers in the United States).[7] For more information on the equivalence of degrees, see the legend of table A.1 in Appendix I.

Gender

Because the main goal of this research project is to compare the symbolic boundaries drawn by residents of various cities and by members of pre-defined occupational categories, it was necessary to limit all other types of social and demographic variations among interviewees. Consequently, I chose to include in the sample exclusively *male* members of the upper-middle class. As explained in Chapter 1, this decision was theoretically justified because males still make up the bulk of the professional-managerial class.[8] Also, males in management and professional positions are more easily reached than their female equivalents because they constitute a larger group. For exploratory purposes I conducted fifteen interviews with female professionals and managers residing in the New York suburbs.

Race and Ethnicity

Members of minority groups were excluded from the final sample in order to minimize variations other than those pertaining to occupation and place of residence. Potential respondents not native to their respective countries were also eliminated from the sample for same reason. For the French sample, however, the native French citizens born in the former colonies were considered eligible.

The decision to exclude members of minority groups from the final sample is justified theoretically because they still occupy a marginal place in the upper-middle class. Indeed, in France, cadres are made up almost entirely of white males of native French extraction.[9] Again, in the United States, in 1987, only 6.2 percent of all executive, managerial, and administrative workers were African-Americans, and only 3.7 percent were Hispanics.

INTERVIEWING PROCEDURES

Five pilot interviews were conducted in Indianapolis in November 1987. After the interview schedule had been revised, a first wave of interviews was conducted in Indianapolis in December 1987, followed by a second wave in January 1989.[10] The New York interviews were conducted in the winter of 1989, while the Paris and Clermont-Ferrand interviews were conducted during the spring and summer of the same year.

The interview was held in the respondent's office, in his home, or in a public space of his choice. After introducing myself and chatting a little, I would install my tape recorder, have him sign a consent form, and answer general questions about the project while eluding specific probes that could influence his answers.

To get the interview started, I generally employed catalytic questions about work; these proved to be fruitful because they were not too threateningly personal. Generally, I made a conscious effort to limit the use of direct interrogation, except for such publicly verifiable items as age, occupation, father's occupation, etc. I also tried to relate the interviewee's answers to fragments from other interviews in order to entice him to be more explicit. Finally, I tried to keep the tone as informal and intimate as possible to avoid playing the role of the "expert."

In a few instances, the interviewee's spouse was present during the interview, either because she was intrigued and had asked to be included, or because I invited her to participate. While her presence might occasionally have encouraged the interviewee to censor himself, in most cases it greatly enriched the interview, because she could provide interesting insights on the tastes and opinions of her husband while discussing his preferences with him in my presence.

The interviews themselves lasted between an hour and a half and two hours and a half. After the interview, respondents were asked to fill out two questionnaires on their leisure-time activities and on their involvement in philanthropic associations.

DATA ANALYSIS

Immediately after each interview, I would generally isolate myself to take ethnographic notes. At that time or later on, I would also listen to the interview and describe it on a thirteen-page summary document that in-

cluded sociodemographic information as well as information on the boundary work of the interviewees. To facilitate comparisons, I noted some of the respondent's answers on standardized grids and summarized these on matrix displays.[11] I would determine also which sections of the interview needed to be transcribed (segments containing only background information were not transcribed). Thus I obtained close to three thousand pages of transcript.

It should be noted that this research project is a multiple-site case study designed to permit a controlled exploration of differences across specific groups. Therefore, each of the four groups of respondents are studied for the information they yield on themselves as well as for the information they supply on the other groups by providing a comparative perspective.[12] Consequently, interviews were first analyzed one by one, with a focus on the cultural orientation of the individual subject. Second, I compared individual interviewees with respondents that were similar to and different from them, both within and across site samples. Finally, I classified all the transcript pages thematically to perform a systematic analysis of all the themes that emerged from the interviews, approaching the latter as texts, as data against which emerging theoretical questions were explored. The structure of Chapters 2 to 4 reflects this thematic focus.

I located each of the interviewees on three 5-point scales, pertaining to moral, cultural, and socioeconomic boundaries, respectively. Again, this approximate ranking was done on the basis of answers respondents gave to a wide range of questions addressed, among other things, to choice of friends, child-rearing values, and feelings of inferiority and superiority. The ranking was determined relationally by analyzing each interview as a whole and by comparing it with similar and dissimilar interviews within and across sites. I attempted to identify as clearly as possible the principle of organization implicit and explicit in all of their answers. For instance, a man who said that the primary virtue he tried to communicate to his children was honesty and respect for others was considered to rank high on the moral dimension. One who stressed the development of the intellectual ability of his children and their openness to the world was considered to rank high on the cultural dimension. On the other hand, one who said that he primarily wanted his children to be successful was taken to rank high on the socioeconomic dimension. The same logic applied in the case of choice of friends: an interviewee who would describe his friends as above all cultivated, cosmopolitan, and re-

fined would be considered to rank high on the cultural scale, while one who would stress the high moral standards and religiosity of his friends would rank high on the moral scale.

It might be useful to describe the coding scheme with the example of the scheme I adopted for moral boundaries: respondents expressing very frequent antimoral attitudes were given no points at all, respondents expressing some antimoral attitudes were given one point, respondents expressing indifference were attributed two points, respondents making occasional statements of moral exclusion received three points, respondents making somewhat frequent statements of moral exclusion received four points, while those expressing such statements very frequently received five points. An interviewee who mostly associates with members of his church, who describes his friends as having strong moral character, and who says he feels inferior to Mother Theresa and superior to crooks, would receive five points on the moral scale. In the case of socioeconomic boundaries, one who said feeling inferior to wealthy people, who described his friends as members of the local elite and his favorite coworkers as powerful, would receive five point on the socioeconomic scale. On the other hand, an interviewee who mentioned having a mistress and declared himself indifferent to low moral standards would receive a score of 0 or 1 on the moral scale, while someone who had openly anti-intellectual attitudes, who criticized intellectuals and ideologues, who said that culture is less important than "what kind of person you are" would score low on the cultural scale.

The documents used to assign scores to each interview include a thirteen-page interview summary, the interview itself, the interview transcript, ethnographic notes taken during and after the interview as well as the questionnaires on leisure-time activities and achievement-related values. Each interview was coded four times by myself, and results from each coding were compared for greater reliability. Twenty percent of the American interviews were coded by both myself and a research assistant. We compared our results which were overall very similar. After discussions we also agreed on appropriate scores for the deviant cases. On the other hand, 50 percent of the French interviews were coded independently on the thirteen-page interview summary by a research assistant. I compared my coding with hers and again found a high degree of reliability.

Appendix IV

RANKING OF RESPONDENTS ON THE CULTURAL, MORAL, AND SOCIOECONOMIC DIMENSIONS

TABLE A.3
Ranking of Interviewees on the Cultural, Moral, and
Socioeconomic Dimensions

	CULTURAL	MORAL	SOCIO-ECONOMIC
New York			
Cultural and social specialists, public and nonprofit sectors			
public school administrator (1 + +)	2	4	5
academic administrator (1 + +)	5	5	5
earth science teacher (1 +)	4	3	4
minister (1 + +)	2	5	4
museum curator (3*)	5	2	2
(artist) (2*)	5	2	1
science teacher (3—)	4	2	5
social work professor (1 + +)	5	1	1
theology professor (2*)	5	3	4
recreation professional (1 +)	2	3	5
(civil servant) (1*)	2	5	2
computer specialist (1 +)	2	2	4
Cultural and social specialists, private sector; profit-related occupations, public and nonprofit sectors			
(applied science researcher) (1 + +)	3	4	3
human resources consultant (2*)	3	5	3
psychologist (4—)	4	3	5
(hospital administrator) (1 + +)	2	4	5
statistics researcher (3*)	5	3	5
(computer researcher) (1 + +)	3	5	4
economist (1 + +)	5	2	4
(labor arbitrator) (1 + +)	2	5	4

Note.—See legend to table A.3, p. 230.

TABLE A.3 (*continued*)

	CULTURAL	MORAL	SOCIO-ECONOMIC
Profit-related occupations, private sector (salaried)			
(investment advisor) (1 + +)	2	3	5
chief financial officer (1 + +)	3	4	5
(banker) (3*)	4	2	3
banker (1 + +)	5	2	5
(insurance company v.p.) (1 + +)	3	5	4
plant facility manager (1 + +)	2	4	5
corporate attorney (1 + +)	3	2	5
(computer specialist) (1*)	2	2	3
marketing executive (2 + +)	2	1	5
(computer software developer) (1 +)	2	4	2
Profit-related occupations, private sector (salaried)			
(lawyer) (3—)	3	5	1
lawyer (3*)	5	4	4
portfolio manager (1 + +)	2	2	5
computer consultant (1 + +)	4	3	5
realtor (1*)	2	2	5
custom house broker (3—)	5	3	3
wholesale distributor (3—)	3	2	5
(machine tool distributor) (3—)	2	3	5
prop. broadcasting company (1 + +)	1	3	5
prop. car leasing company (2 + +)	1	2	5

Indianapolis			
Cultural and social specialists, public and nonprofit sectors			
(public school administrator) (3*)	2	4	2
academic administrator (3*)	5	4	2
(music teacher) (1*)	3	5	2
minister (2*)	3	4	5
museum curator (1 + +)	4	3	5
artist (3*)	5	2	5
physics professor (2*)	4	2	4
medicine professor (2*)	5	5	3
social service manager (3—)	5	5	2
(recreation professional) (1 + +)	2	2	5
(staff assistant, federal) (1 + +)	2	4	2
computer specialist (1 + +)	5	3	4
(medical researcher) (3*)	4	3	3
(manager human services) (1*)	3	4	3

	CULTURAL	MORAL	SOCIO-ECONOMIC
Cultural and social specialists, private sector; profit-related occupations, public and nonprofit sectors			
psychologist (3*)	5	4	5
(accountant, federal) (1 + +)	2	5	4
(research scientist) (3*)	5	5	3
science researcher (1 + +)	3	2	5
(bank examiner) (1 + +)	2	4	4
judge (3 + +)	5	3	5
Profit-related occupations, private sector (salaried)			
accountant (1 + +)	2	2	5
chief financial officer (2 +)	2	5	5
banker (1 + +)	1	4	4
banker (1 + +)	2	3	5
insurance company v.p. (1 + +)	4	4	5
plant manager (2 +)	2	5	5
(corporate attorney) (1 + +)	3	4	3
computer marketing specialist (2*)	3	4	5
(marketing executive) (1 + +)	2	4	4
(data manager) (1*)	2	4	2
architect (1 + +)	2	2	5
Profit-related occupations, private sector (self-employed)			
lawyer (3*)	4	5	3
lawyer (1 + +)	5	2	5
stockbroker (2*)	4	4	4
architect (1 + +)	1	3	5
realtor (3*)	3	4	5
forester (2 +)	2	3	5
professional recruiter (1 + +)	2	4	2
real estate developer (1 + +)	2	1	5
(used car dealer) (2—)	2	4	4

TABLE A.3 (*continued*)

	CULTURAL	MORAL	SOCIO-ECONOMIC
Clermont-Ferrand			
Cultural and social specialists, public and nonprofit sectors			
public school administrator (1 +)	4	4	4
(academic administrator) (2 +)	2	3	5
music teacher (1*)	2	4	2
priest (1 + +)	4	3	3
(*museum curator*) (1*)	4	5	1
(*artist*) (1 +)	5	3	1
(electronics teacher) (1 +)	2	4	4
professor of social work (1 +)	5	3	2
philosophy teacher (1 +)	5	5	1
(athletics coach) (1 + +)	2	4	3
civil servant (1*)	4	4	2
(civil servant) (local) (2—)	2	4	3
physicist (2*)	5	4	3
Cultural and social specialists, private sector; profit-related occupations, public and nonprofit sectors			
(paramedic) (3—)	2	4	2
psychologist (2—)	5	0	1
(hospital controller) (1 + +)	3	3	5
dentist (3—)	4	2	5
physician (1 + +)	1	4	4
(safety inspector) (1*)	2	4	3
journalist (1*)	5	5	1
Profit-related occupations, private sector (salaried)			
accountant (3*)	4	2	5
senior executive manufacturing (1 + +)	3	3	5
banker (3—)	4	3	3
(banker) (1 + +)	3	4	2
executive car dealership (2*)	2	5	4
chemical engineer (4—)	5	4	5
(computer marketing executive) (1 + +)	2	5	2
chemical engineer (1 + +)	3	4	5
plant manager (1 + +)	2	4	5
tourism executive (2 + +)	4	1	5

TABLE A.3 (*continued*)

	CULTURAL	MORAL	SOCIO-ECONOMIC
Profit-related occupations private sector (self-employed)			
lawyer (2*)	5	5	1
lawyer (4*)	4	2	5
accountant (2*)	3	3	5
architect (3*)	2	3	3
insurance broker (3—)	5	3	3
prop. surveying company (2+ +)	1	3	5
architect (3 + +)	4	3	5
(accountant) (1 + +)	2	2	5
financial advisor (1 + +)	5	3	4
financial advisor (3*)	3	2	5
Paris			
Cultural and social specialists, public and nonprofit sectors			
public school administrator (1 + +)	4	2	5
academic administrator (2 + +)	5	1	5
(music teacher) (1*)	3	4	2
priest (3*)	5	5	3
museum curator (4*)	5	2	4
musician (3*)	5	3	2
science teacher (1 +)	4	1	3
architecture professor (3*)	5	0	5
literature professor (1 + +)	5	4	0
social worker (3*)	5	5	2
diplomat (3*)	5	2	2
(computer specialist) (1 +)	2	4	2
(accounting professor) (1 + +)	4	3	4
Cultural and social specialists, private sector; profit-related occupations, public and nonprofit sectors			
human resources consultant (3*)	5	0	3
psychologist (2*)	5	2	3
hospital administrator (1 + +)	3	3	5
(dentist) (2*)	4	2	3
physician (2—)	4	4	1
(architect state) (1 +)	3	4	2
human resources const. (3*)	5	1	5

	CULTURAL	MORAL	SOCIO-ECONOMIC
Profit-related occupations, private sector (salaried)			
business management specialist (1 + +)	5	5	3
(senior executive manufacturing) (1 + +)	4	5	2
banker (1 + +)	5	3	5
(investment banker) (2*)	2	4	3
insurance executive (1 + +)	5	2	5
corporate attorney (3*)	5	5	4
(marketing executive) (1 + +)	2	4	2
(marketing executive) (3*)	4	4	2
electrical engineer (3*)	5	5	3
(tourism executive) (1 + +)	2	4	3
Profit-related occupations, private sector (self-employed)			
lawyer (2*)	5	5	1
(lawyer) (3—)	2	4	4
(accountant) (1 + +)	2	4	2
architect (3—)	4	1	0
insurance broker (1 + +)	1	4	5
prop. printing company (3*)	4	5	3
owner engineer company (3*)	5	2	5
(accountant) (2*)	2	4	1
accountant (1*)	2	0	5
lawyer (1 + +)	3	0	5

Note.—Identification of respondents: very upwardly mobile + +, somewhat upwardly mobile +, stable *, downwardly mobile —, intellectual in italic, tolerant in parens. First generation upper-middle class 1, second generation upper-middle class 2, third generation upper-middle class 3, fourth generation upper-middle class 4.

Importance of boundaries: frequent drawing of antiboundaries (i.e., strong anti-intellectualism, antimoralism, or antimaterialism) 0, occasional drawing of antiboundaries 1, indifference 2, occasional drawing of boundaries 3, frequent drawing of boundaries 4, very frequent drawing of boundaries 5.

Example: *professor of social work* (1 +) = 5, 1, 1 (first generation upper-middle class, somewhat upwardly mobile, intellectual; draws cultural boundaries very frequently; sometimes draws antimoral and antisocioeconomic boundaries).

TABLE A.4

Average Score and Percentage of Participants Who Score
4 or 5 on the Moral, Socioeconomic, and Cultural Scales
by Occupational Groups and Sites

| Boundaries | FRANCE | | | UNITED STATES | | | |
	Paris	Clermont-Ferrand	Total	Indian-apolis	New York	Total	TOTAL
Social and cultural specialists							
Moral	35%	65%	50%	60%	45%	52%	51%
	2.5	3.5	3.0	3.4	3.7	3.6	3.3
Socioeconomic	35%	30%	32%	55%	70%	62%	47%
	3.0	2.8	2.9	3.8	3.8	3.8	3.3
Cultural	80%	55%	67%	55%	50%	52%	59%
	4.2	3.3	3.8	3.5	3.6	3.6	3.7
For-profit workers							
Moral	70%	35%	52%	65%	30%	47%	49%
	3.5	3.1	3.3	2.9	3.5	3.2	3.3
Socioeconomic	40%	70%	55%	80%	70%	75%	65%
	3.1	4.1	3.6	4.2	4.3	4.3	3.9
Cultural	55%	45%	50%	20%	25%	22%	36%
	3.4	3.3	3.4	2.8	2.5	2.7	3.0

TABLE A.5

Average Score and Percentage of Participants Who Score
4 or 5 on the Moral, Socioeconomic, and Cultural Scales
by Detailed Occupational Groups and Sites

	FRANCE			UNITED STATES			
Boundaries	Paris	Clermont-Ferrand	Total	Indian-apolis	New York	Total	TOTAL
Category 1							
Moral	38%	69%	53%	57%	43%	50%	51%
	2.7	3.8	3.2	3.6	3.0	3.3	3.3
Socioeconomic	38%	23%	30%	43%	66%	55%	43%
	3.0	2.6	2.8	3.5	3.4	3.5	3.1
Cultural	85%	61%	73%	57%	58%	58%	66%
	4.4	3.5	3.9	3.6	3.7	3.7	3.8
Category 2							
Moral	28%	57%	42%	66%	62%	64%	53%
	2.3	3.5	3.0	3.4	3.7	3.6	3.2
Socioeconomic	28%	43%	36%	83%	75%	79%	58%
	3.0	2.8	2.9	3.8	3.8	3.8	3.3
Cultural	71%	43%	57%	50%	37%	44%	51%
	4.2	3.3	3.8	3.5	3.6	3.6	3.6
Category 3							
Moral	80%	60%	70%	72%	40%	56%	63%
	4.1	3.5	3.8	2.9	3.3	3.1	3.0
Socioeconomic	30%	70%	50%	82%	70%	76%	63%
	3.1	4.1	3.6	4.3	4.2	4.3	4.0
Cultural	70%	40%	55%	9%	2%	6%	31%
	3.0	3.4	3.2	2.8	2.8	2.8	3.0
Category 4							
Moral	60%	10%	35%	55%	20%	38%	37%
	3.5	3.1	3.3	2.9	3.5	3.2	3.3
Socioeconomic	50%	70%	60%	77%	80%	79%	70%
	3.1	4.1	3.6	4.2	4.3	4.3	4.0
Cultural	40%	40%	40%	33%	20%	27%	34%
	3.4	3.3	3.4	2.8	2.5	2.7	3.1

NOTES

PROLOGUE

1. All the names in this study have been fictionalized to protect anonymity.

2. The French quotes have been translated by the author.

3. This information was elicited during an interview where I presented Didier with a list of qualities and asked him to comment on them.

4. The term *socioeconomic* refers to social background and social position as well as to variables defining socioeconomic status, such as income and occupational prestige.

5. Coleman and Rainwater, with McClelland, *Social Standing in America: New Dimensions of Class,* 125. For a discussion of the size of the upper-middle class in France and the United States, see Appendix I.

CHAPTER ONE

1. Kanter, *Men and Women of the Corporation;* Jackall, *Moral Mazes: The World of Corporate Manager.* On the importance of networks see Granovetter, *Getting a Job: A Study of Contacts and Careers.*

2. A recent study, which surveyed three decades of domestic sitcoms from the beginning of network television in 1946 down to 1978, found that these programs mostly depicted middle-class lifestyles: ". . . only 2.6% of series portrayed families headed by blue collar workers. Even including clerical and service workers the total percent rises to only 8.4% . . . By contrast almost two-thirds (63.5%) of television families were middle class." Similar results were found for the 1979–90 period. Butsch, "Class and Gender in Four Decades of TV Families: Plus Ça Change . . ." See also Butsch and Glennon, "Social Class: Frequency Trends in Domestic Situation Comedy, 1946/1978."

3. A recent study of television audiences showed that working-class women use entertainment programs to learn middle-class lifestyles. See Press, *Women Watching Television: Gender, Class and Generations in the American Television Experience.*

4. On this point see Appendix I.

5. The concept of boundary work is borrowed from Gieryn, "Boundary-Work and the Demarcation of Science from Non-Science: Strains and Interests in Professional Ideologies of Scientists." Gieryn refers to the "symbolic work" scientists produce to create a public image of science by defining it in opposition to religion. As used here, the term "boundary work" refers to the process by which individuals define their identity in opposition to that of others by drawing symbolic boundaries.

6. On the advantages of the comparative method for studying culture see Lipset, *Continental Divide: The Values and Institutions of the United States and Canada*, xiii–xviii.

7. A 1979 survey in *Fortune* magazine found only ten women among the 6,400 top corporate officers and directors of the United States. These figures were cited by Keller in "Women in the 21st Century: Summing Up and Moving Forward." While only 18.5 percent of working women occupied managerial, professional, or executive positions in 1970, this proportion had increased to 36 percent in 1985 (these percentages include low-level managers). See Blum and Smith, "Women's Mobility in the Corporation: A Critique of the Politics of Optimism," 528.

8. This group remains small: in 1987, only 6.2 percent of all executive, managerial, and administrative workers were African-Americans, and only 3.7 percent were Hispanics. See Hodson and Sullivan, *The Social Organization of Work*.

9. Bourdieu, *Distinction: A Social Critique of the Judgment of Taste*, 258. In his earlier work, Bourdieu had suggested that apparently neutral academic standards used in school settings are laden with specific middle-class cultural values. Not having been socialized within the framework of this culture, lower-class children are handicapped in the classroom with direct effects on their performance levels. See Bourdieu and Passeron, *The Inheritors: French Students and Their Relation to Culture*; also Bourdieu and Passeron, *Reproduction in Education, Society and Culture*.

10. See for instance DiMaggio, "Cultural Capital and School Success: The Impact of Status Culture Participation on the Grades of U.S. High School Students." DiMaggio and Mohr, "Cultural Capital, Educational Attainment, and Marital Selection"; Cookson and Persell, *Preparing for Power: America's Elite Boarding Schools*; Katsillis and Rubinson, "Cultural Capital, Student Achievement, and Educational Reproduction: The Case of Greece"; and Ryan and DeBord, "High Culture Orientation and the Attitudes and Values of College Students."

11. I am summarizing an argument concerning the cultural capital literature which was first formulated by Annette Lareau and myself in "Cultural Capital: Allusions, Gaps, and Glissandos in Recent Theoretical Developments."

12. See in particular Robert V. Robinson and Maurice Garnier, "Class Reproduction among Men and Women in France: Reproduction Theory on Its Home Ground," 278; Lamont and Lareau, "Cultural Capital"; and Farkas, Grobe, Sheehan, and Yuan, "Cultural Resources and School Success: Gender, Ethnicity, and Poverty Groups within an Urban District." This last study, which considered high status signals salient in the educational system, has confirmed the influence of extracurricular factors such as work habits on the evaluation of students.

13. Kai T. Erikson, *Wayward Puritans: A Study in the Sociology of Deviance*, 23.

14. Here and elsewhere I introduce a distinction between "symbolic boundaries" which is used to refer to all types of boundaries regardless of their content, and "cultural boundaries" which is used to refer to symbolic boundaries that are drawn on the basis of high status signals related to intelligence, education, refinement or cultivation.

15. I first explored cross-national differences in the formal characteristics of symbolic boundaries in "The Power-Culture Link in a Comparative Perspective." My discussion of the formal features of symbolic boundaries draws partly on Paul DiMaggio's work on the features of artistic classification systems. DiMaggio isolates four dimensions of these systems: hierarchalization, differentiation, universalization, and boundary strengths. He explains differences across systems primarily in reference to group characteristics, drawing on Peter Blau's structuralism. See DiMaggio's "Classification in Art."

16. This is true of most of the literature on deviance which analyzes how individuals come to be reclassified as morally reprehensible after moral boundaries have been moved.

See for instance Bergensen, "Social Control and Corporate Organizations: A Durkheimian Perspective"; Kai T. Erikson, *Wayward Puritans*; Becker, *Outsiders: Studies in the Sociology of Deviance*. See also Hunter, *Evangelicalism: The Coming Generation*.

17. One of the few sociologists concerned with the content of boundaries themselves is Arthur L. Stinchcombe. See in particular his "The Deep Structure of Moral Categories." See also his "Social Structure and Politics" where Stinchcombe discusses social change, social mobilization, and the making of boundaries. These topics are neglected in the present study. On the conduct of boundaries, see also the work of Beisel, "Constructing a Shifting Moral Boundary."

18. Robert Wuthnow describes this thematic approach in the following terms: "Where the structural approach differs is in emphasizing categories, boundaries, relations and the symbols that express these structures. For example, rather than pursuing a study of church-state relations by tracing arguments about church and state, [it] would begin by regarding both the concepts of 'church' and 'state' as problematic cultural constructs, and then proceed by examining what was categorized with each, how the boundary between the two was negotiated and how symbolic events contributed over time to changes in these definitions. Underlying this kind of study is the assumption that . . . structural relations among these categories are at least as important to examine as their content" (*Meaning and Moral Order: Explorations in Cultural Analysis*, 342).

19. These exceptions include Basil Bernstein, *Class, Codes and Control*, vol. 3; and the work of Cynthia Fuchs Epstein which is concerned with how traditional gender boundaries are reproduced in the workplace, for instance, "Workplace Boundaries: Conceptions and Creations." For a discussion of the neo-Durkheimian literature, see Alexander, ed., *Durkheimian Sociology: Cultural Studies*, chap. 1.

20. See for instance Douglas, *Purity and Danger: An Analysis of the Concepts of Pollution and Taboo*; and also her *Natural Symbols: Explorations in Cosmology*; and Bourdieu, *Distinction*, esp. chap. 3.

21. For a conceptualization of culture that focuses on the repertoires or tool kits that a society makes available to its members, see Swidler, "Culture in Action: Symbols and Strategies." See also the work of Wuthnow on symbolic codes: *Meaning and Moral Order*; and the neo-institutional approach described by Paul J. DiMaggio and Walter W. Powell in the introduction of *The New Institutionalism in Organizational Analysis*.

22. I recognize that the center/periphery metaphor is more appropriate in the French context than in the American, given the degree of decentralization of cultural life in the United States. Indianapolis and Clermont-Ferrand, however, do offer considerably fewer elite cultural events than New York and Paris. For instance, while Judith Blau's work shows that all forms of high culture are widely distributed throughout all regions of the United States, it also shows that New York offers considerably more high culture events per capita than the other major metropolitan areas. See her "The Elite Arts, More or Less de Rigueur: A Comparative Analysis of Metropolitan Culture."

23. Lipset, *Political Man: The Social Bases of Politics*, chap. 10. While criticizing the New Class thesis, Steven Brint showed that support for liberalism in the New Class was mostly concentrated among social and cultural specialists and public-sector workers. See Brint's "'New Class' and Cumulative Trend Explanations of the Liberal Political Attitudes of Professionals."

24. Hoffman, ed., *In Search of France*; Inkeles, "Continuity and Change in the American National Character"; Wylie, *Village in the Vaucluse*; Pitts, "The Bourgeois Family . . ."

25. Lipset, *The First New Nation: The United States in Historical and Comparative Perspective*; Tocqueville, *Democracy in America*.

26. For a review of the literature, see Ganzeboom, Treiman, Ultee, "Comparative Intergenerational Stratification Research: Three Generations and Beyond."

27. Agger, "Critical Theory, Poststructuralism and Postmodernism: Their Sociological Relevance." See also Rosaldo, "The Use and Abuse of Anthropology: Reflections on Feminism and Cross-cultural Understanding"; Joan W. Scott, "The Sears Case," and Showalter, "A Criticism of Our Own: Autonomy and Assimilation in Afro-American and Feminist Literary Theory."

28. For instance, West, "The New Cultural Politics of Difference," 93.

29. Durkheim, *The Elementary Forms of Religious Life*; Simmel, *The Sociology of Georg Simmel*.

30. See Zerubavel, *The Fine Line: Boundaries and Distinctions in Everyday Life*, chap. 2. I am grateful to this author for sharing with me, prior to publication, some chapters of his manuscript; they influenced my own thinking on boundaries.

31. See Jackall, *Moral Mazes*, 56.

32. Weitman, "Intimacies: Notes toward a Theory of Social Inclusion and Exclusion," 358.

33. Mary Waters has shown how ethnic boundaries have been loosened in such a way that ethnic identities are more blurred and increasingly result from individual preferences rather than from group action. See her *Ethnic Options: Choosing Identities in America*.

34. Hurrelmann, *Social Structure and Personality Development: The Individual as a Productive Processor of Reality*, 91.

35. Kalmijn, "Status Homogamy in the United States."

36. Collins, *The Credential Society*; Brint, "The Political Attitudes of Professionals"; James Davis, "Achievement Variables and Class Cultures: Family, Schooling, Job and Forty-Nine Dependent Variables in the Cumulative GSS."

37. On this topic see the work produced around signaling theory. See in particular Rosenbaum, Kariya, Settersten, and Maier, "Market and Networks Theory of the Transition from High School to Work: Their Application to Industrialized Societies."

38. Max Weber, *Economy and Society*, vol. 1, chap. 4.

39. Herzfeld, "Honor and Shame: Problems in the Comparative Analysis of Moral Systems," 341.

40. On the topic of the interaction between situation, identity, and labeling, see Alexander and Wiley, "Situated Activity and Identity Formation." The work pertaining to labeling, impression management, and attribution is also relevant. See Crittenden, "Sociological Aspects of Attribution."

41. As Alfred Schutz and Thomas Luckman note: "The action of others, and thus their willing, feeling and thinking is a constant problem for the practical hermeneutics of everyday life" (*The Structures of the Life-World*, vol. 2, 114).

42. Here I am drawing on Epstein, "Tinkerbells and Pinups: The Construction and Reconstruction of Gender Boundaries at Work."

43. On this aspect of identity formation, see Giddens, *Modernity and Self-Identity: Self and Society in the Late Modern Age*. I borrow the concept of "border patrol" from Brodsky, "Intellectual Snobbery: A Socio-Historical Perspective."

44. On this topic see Collins, *Theoretical Sociology*, chap. 6; on the issue of identity formation as discussed by social psychologists see also Rosenberg, "The Self-Concept: Social Product and Social Force," 593–624; see also Stryker, *Symbolic Interactionism: A Social Structural Version*.

45. Max Weber, *Economy and Society*, vol. 1, chap. 4.

46. For an analysis of the effects of situational factors on changes in orders of evaluation, see Boltanski and Thévenot, *De la justification: Les économies de la grandeur*.

47. Members of the working class are well aware of this framing power: their perception of the class structure is not organized around differences in occupational prestige but around differences in the distribution of authority in the workplace. See Vanneman and Cannon, *The American Perception of Class*, chap. 4.

48. Power is viewed here as the capacity to define norms and standards and to shape other people's lives, i.e., to act in such a way as to limit their opportunities. Inspired by Weber and Foucault, this definition assumes that the exercise of power affects people's lives in a negative way and that it occurs through a wide range of actions. For a more elaborate description of the approach to indirect power that underlies the present study and for a review of the literature see Lamont, "The Power-Culture Link in a Comparative Perspective." For a discussion contrasting the way American and European social scientists approach the relation between power and culture, see Lamont and Wuthnow, "Betwixt and Between: Recent Cultural Sociology in Europe and the United States."

49. The communities in the New York suburbs are the following: Madison (population of 15,357), Metuchen (13,762), New Providence (12,426), River Edge (11,111), South Plainfield (20,521), and Summit (21,071) in New Jersey; Merrick (24,478), Massapequa (24,454), and Rockville Center Village (25,412) on Long Island. In the Paris suburbs, interviews were conducted in Montmorency (20,927), Neuilly-sur-Seine (65,941), Reuil-Malmaison (64,545), Sèvres (21,100), St-Cloud (28,052), St-Germain-en-Laye (35,351), Versailles (95,240), and Vincennes (44,256).

50. This definition is borrowed from Coleman and Neugarten, *Social Status in the City*, 259.

51. As explained in Appendix I, the average household income of American interviewees is higher than that of French interviewees which reflects national differences in income averages.

52. In contrast, in the ghetto population studied by Suttles in *The Social Life of the Slum*, more focus is put on "age, sex, ethnicity, territoriality and personal reputation . . . these distinctions are emphasized to the exclusion of occupational, educational and other attainments that are more appreciated in the wider society" (223). On the importance of the organization of work as the basis of larger cleavages in society see also Lipset and Rokkan, "Cleavage Structure, Party Systems and Voter Alignments: An Introduction."

53. French engineers have greater job security and their career ladders contain more hierarchical levels. See Crawford, *Technical Workers in an Advanced Society: The Work, Careers and Politics of French Engineers*, 135. Appendix I provides an exhaustive description of differences between French and American professionals and managers.

54. Gusfield, *Communities: A Critical Response*.

55. A few interviews were conducted with men who do not meet the criteria used for sample selection. In the text they are referred to as "informants" in the rare instances where they are quoted.

56. The questions exploring feelings of superiority and inferiority were as follows: "Whether we admit it or not, we all feel inferior or superior to some people at times. In relation to what types of people do you feel inferior? Superior? Can you give me concrete examples? What do these people have in common?" To explore likes and dislikes in others, I asked participants, "What kind of people would you rather avoid? What kind of people leave you indifferent? What kind of people attract you in general? Can you give me specific examples? Which qualities do these people have in common?"

57. To explore child-rearing values, I asked participants to describe the values they try to impart to their children and to explain in detail the meaning assigned to each value. For instance, the participants would be asked to explain what they mean by "honesty" or "respect," and why these values are important to them.

58. Mishler, *Research Interviewing: Context and Narrative.*

59. My relatively young age and my gender might have acted as facilitator during the interviews because a sizable number of interviewees had daughters in their late twenties, early thirties. In order to entice respondent to assimilate me with their daughter/niece/sister and to see me as a confidente, I made special efforts to desexualize the encounter by paying special attention to my dressing style, for instance.

60. Of course, the "Princeton effect" did not play as much of a role in France as it did in the United States. Most Clermont-Ferrand interviewees obviously did not know the cultural meaning attached to Princeton University in the United States. A few Parisians did. The "Princeton effect" was most powerful among New York interviewees. They often told me they were honored to participate in the study, whereas most Clermontois indicated that they agreed to be interviewed because they wanted "to be helpful." Americanophile Frenchmen were the group most eager to participate, often inviting me for lunch, introducing me to their children, or trying to define the situation in such a way that the relationship could continue once I returned to America.

61. My life as an academic had put me in contact with upper-middle-class students and colleagues in various settings. I had had a taste of regional variations, having spent two years in Palo Alto, California, and two years in Austin, Texas, in addition to a few months in Cambridge, Massachusetts, and in Bloomington, Indiana, and then my experience at Princeton. I was intrigued by the variations in standards of evaluation I had encountered (see Lamont, "From Paris to Stanford: Une reconversion sociologique: de la sociologie française à la sociologie américaine"). I decided to explore the local rationales behind judgments about desirability—or importance ("greatness")—a problem I had previously explored by looking at a French philosopher (see my "How to Become a Dominant French Philosopher: The Case of Jacques Derrida").

CHAPTER TWO

1. Taking a close look at moral boundaries is especially timely given the dearth of empirical studies on morality. While an extensive normative and philosophical literature on ethics is available, sociologically informed studies of the concepts through which morality is thought and formulated are still few and often center on single issues such as pornography or abortion, or they analyze survey data to tap the distribution of predefined ethical positions instead of exploring variations in the very definition of these positions.

2. Becker, *Outsiders;* Goffman, *Stigma: Notes on the Management of Spoiled Identity.*

3. *Harrap's* French-English dictionary translates *phony* as "fumiste" and "imposteur." Neither term was ever used by my French respondents to describe dishonest people.

4. I interviewed a relatively small group of Christians who assess moral purity on the basis of attitudes toward alcohol, pornography, abortion, divorce, homosexuality, drugs, and atheistic humanism, but these issues did not come up often in interviews. Most interviewees put more emphasis on honesty and work ethics.

5. Source: European Values Survey/Gallup for the Center for Applied Research in the Apostolate (CARA). Information on the attitudes of French professionals and managers are based on the following occupations: the *patrons* from large, medium-size, and small businesses; the *cadres supérieurs* and *cadres moyens,* and the *membres de professions libérales* ($N = 256$). The American survey includes 192 professionals, managers, and businessmen. In the next chapters I will often draw on these surveys. They are based on the same questionnaire and were both conducted in 1981. The total number of respondents is 1,729 for the United States and 1,199 for France.

6. For instance, when asked what he does during the weekend, a Parisian human resource consultant answered: "It depends whether I am in love or not. If I am very much

in love, then I make love, which I think is the greatest thing in life. I am almost a mystic on this issue . . . It is not always with my wife . . . It can be with her. I can be in love with my wife, but not always. We have been married for thirty years. It can be with someone else. It has been with someone else for a while."

7. It is important to note, however, that studies of female and male adultery show that in the United States "one quarter to about one half of married women have at least one lover after they are married in any given marriage," as have "50 percent to 65 percent of men by the age of forty." Lawson, *Adultery: An Analysis of Love and Betrayal,* 75.

8. Didier is representative of a diminishing but sizable minority of Frenchmen: a study found that in 1974, 40 percent of the French thought that someone who did well financially "has had to work hard" while as much as 37 percent thought that "he must not always have been honest." Ten years later, 59 percent attributed success to merit while only 18 percent suspected that dishonesty was involved. SOFRES survey cited by Closets, *Tous ensemble: Pour en finir avec la syndicratie,* 434.

9. When the European values survey asked Frenchmen to rank a number of qualities in order of importance, 76 percent of them ranked honesty first. This was also the case for 73 percent of the interviewees of other European countries. See Girard and Stoetzel, "Les Français et les valeurs du temps présent," 28. The discrepancy between the French population at large and my interviewees might be accounted for by the fact that individuals confess stigmatizing information more easily during in-depth interviews.

10. The figures were 54 percent for French members of other occupations and 81 percent for their American counterparts. Respondents were asked to evaluate the relevance of each commandment separately. The percentages cited here are for the average of the responses taken as a whole. (Data compiled from the European values and the CARA surveys.)

11. Dens, *L'honnête homme et la critique du goût: Esthétique et société au XVIIe siècle.*

12. Here I am borrowing the title of Tilly's book on changes in forms of social conflicts in France, *The Contentious French: Four Centuries of Popular Struggle.*

13. Bellah, Madsen, Sullivan, Swidler, and Tipton, *Habits of the Heart, Individualism and Commitment in American Life,* chap. 3. On the Latin notion of honor, see Pitt-Rivers, "Honor and Social Status." Honor is defined as "the value of a person in his [or her] own eyes, but also in the eyes of his [or her] society" (21).

14. On the importance of the notion of political engagement in defining morality in postwar France see Boschetti, *The Intellectual Enterprise: Sartre and Les Temps Modernes,* chap. 4.

15. Lipset, *Continental Divide,* 59–63.

16. In France the average participation of the qualified voters was 77.5 percent between 1962 and 1981 in contrast to an average of 56 percent in the United States between 1965 and 1984. Thelen and Wilson, *Comparative Politics: An Introduction to Six Countries,* 75. Also Ehrmann, *Politics in France,* 125; and Wright, *The Government and Politics of France,* 290. It should be noted that other factors besides voters' apathy explains the low electoral turnout in the United States.

17. See Hochschild, *What's Fair? American Beliefs about Distributive Justice,* chap. 5.

18. Appendix IV describes the ranking of each respondent with regard to each type of boundary.

19. These scores are respectively 3.3, 3.3, and 3.6 for moral, cultural, and socioeconomic boundaries. The average total scores are relatively low because some interviewees oppose certain boundaries, and score 0 or 1 on these dimensions. For instance, a number of individuals considered intellectualism to be a negative status signal.

20. The average French score is 3.2 compared to 3.4 in the United States.

21. Weiss, *Staying the Course: The Emotional and Social Lives of Men Who do Well.*

22. According to Bernard Barber, trust refers to expectations that actors have of one another, which are related to the "meanings actors attribute to themselves and others as they make choices about which actions and reactions are rationally effective and emotionally and morally appropriate." See Barber, *The Logic and Limits of Trust*, 9. For a review of the concept of trust, see Silver, "'Trust' in Social and Political Theory," in *The Challenge of Social Control: Citizenship and Institution-Building in Modern Society.*

23. The type of trust that is not gained by loyalty but by displaying competence and reliability is particularly important for professionals because their ability to attract clients depends on people trusting their professional authority. As pointed out by Max Weber, this type of trust is also crucial for business people, as it affects their ability to gain business credit. See Max Weber's *L'éthique protestante et l'esprit du capitalisme*, 47.

24. Bledstein, *The Culture of Professionalism: The Middle Class and the Development of Higher Education in America*, 65; Max Weber, "L'ethique protestante," 71 and 238. Weber provides us with an indication of how high-status cultural signals get institutionalized when he describes that, with the expansion of capitalism, people are increasingly required to display these virtues, as the pursuit of profit itself becomes a moral obligation (79). Furthermore, he suggests that the type of trust that is not gained by loyalty but by displaying competence and reliability is particularly important for business people because it affects their ability to gain business credit (47).

25. See Varenne, *Americans Together: Structured Diversity in a Midwestern Town.*

26. On conflict avoidance as a general feature of American society see Baumgartner, *The Moral Order of a Suburb;* Perin, *Belonging in America*, 66; Varenne, *Americans Together*, 106; Greenhouse, *Praying for Justice: Faith, Order and Community in an American Town*, 68 and 106, which provides an insightful analysis of the way members of a Baptist community deal with conflict. Some aspects of this analysis might be extended to members of other Protestant denominations. Greenhouse argues that within the community she studied, conflicts are muted, or are conceived in highly moralistic and in personalistic rather than structural terms (120).

27. David's remarks echo one of Jackall's observations: "Striking, distinctive characteristics of any sort, in fact, are dangerous in the corporate world. One of the most damaging things for instance that can be said about a manager is that he is brilliant . . . What good is a wizard who makes his colleagues and his customers uncomfortable? Equally damaging is the judgment that a person cannot get along with others—he is 'too pushy,' that is, he exhibits too much 'persistence in getting the right answers,' is 'always asking why,' and does not know 'when to back off.' Or he is 'too abrasive,' or 'too opinionated,' unable 'to bend with the group'" (*Moral Mazes*, 52).

28. This is expressed by the vice-president of an insurance company, who says that he has no respect for people who "leave their shopping cart out in the middle of the parking lot. I feel superior to those people. They have behaviors that involve not treating people as equals, as well as saying that someone else is to be my slave. It involves being utterly inconsiderate."

29. This relation between egalitarianism and moral character resonates with the fact that Varenne's Midwestern interviewees conceive democracy, rather than Protestantism, to be the grounding of their morality. See Varenne, *Americans Together*, 55.

30. This quote resonates with Robert Jackall's conclusion that for corporate managers morality is not "a set of internally held convictions or principles, but results from changing relationships" (*Moral Mazes*, 101). See also Baumgartner's concept of moral minimalism as it relates to conflict avoidance in *The Moral Order of a Suburb*, 124–29; and the discussion, in Bellah et al., *Habits of the Heart*, of utilitarian individualism which defines subjective goodness as "getting what you want and enjoying it" (77).

31. Along these lines, a recent study found that a group of American engineers do not favor more participation in the workplace, because they see democratic decision making as incompatible with the principle of expertise-based authority. Zussman, *Mechanics of the Middle Class: Work and Politics among American Engineers*, 117.

32. This phrase is borrowed from Bellah et al., *Habits of the Heart*, 45.

33. Along these lines, while 31 percent of upper-middle-class Americans think that they have a great deal of freedom of choice in life, only 24 percent of Americans in other classes think so. These figures contrast with those gathered in France, where 11 percent of the members of the upper-middle class think that they have a great deal of freedom in contrast to 15 percent of the members of other groups. (Data compiled from the European Values and CARA surveys.)

34. On egalitarianism in America, see Lipset, *The First New Nation*, chap. 2. Hochschild found that Americans are mostly egalitarian in what she calls the political and socialization domains rather than in the economic domain. The first has to do with "citizenship, the effect of the federal government on one's own life, and the hopes and fears for the future of the U.S.," while the socialization domain concerns "everyday life" issues pertaining to the family, the school, the neighborhood (*What's Fair?* 81). On American civil religion see Bellah, *The Broken Covenant: American Civil Religion in Time of War*.

35. Seventy-one percent of the French professionals, managers, and businessmen and 19 percent of their American counterparts questioned in the European values/CARA surveys consider that a decrease in the importance of work in our lives would be a good thing; correspondingly, 29 percent of the French think it would be a bad thing, in contrast to 70 percent of Americans. While 89 percent of professionals, managers, and businessmen say that they take a great deal of pride in their work (77 percent for workers in other classes), it is the case for only 21 percent of the French members of this group (16.7 percent for workers in other classes).

36. A recent study also revealed that the French employees of a large multinational corporation do not value work more than the Iranian, Spanish, and Peruvian employees. These national groups rank approximately 43 on a work-orientation index in contrast to 62 for Americans. This index measures work orientation only indirectly. See Hofstede, *Culture's Consequences: International Differences in Work-related Values*, fig. 6.3.

37. This is revealed by two surveys conducted in April 1980 and February 1985, that asked respondents, "In economic terms, which of the following terms have positive and negative connotations for you?" The terms that gained most in positive connotation during the five-year period include liberalism (+11), profit (+10), competition (+4), and capitalism (+4), while socialism, unionization, and nationalization, respectively, lost 11, 10, and 7 points. The SOFRES survey, cited by Closets, *Tous ensemble*, 433.

38. The attitude of Mr. Dutoît echoes the fact that the culture of French upper-middle-class men is less bottom-line–oriented, i.e., less guided by the principle of profit maximization. On this topic see Granick, *Managerial Comparisons of Four Developed Countries: France, Britain, United States and Russia*, 78.

39. Forty percent of the Paris sample, 31 percent of the Clermont-Ferrand sample, and 35 percent of the French national sample. These figures compare to the 35 percent of American interviewees who attended elite private universities which includes 55 percent of the New York respondents and 15 percent of the Indianapolis interviewees. For details see Appendix I.

40. This argument concerning the relationship between selection and legitimation is developed by Suleiman in *Les élites en France: Grands corps et grandes écoles*, chap. 6.

41. On the importation of the American managerial model to France see Boltanski's *Les cadres: La formation d'un groupe social*. According to this study, which is congruent on this

point with my observations, those who attach the most importance to competence are *cadres* working for large enterprises involved in the international market (311).

42. Suleiman, *Les élites en France*, 170. On this topic see also Bourdieu, *La noblesse d'état: Grandes écoles et esprit de corps*, 210.

43. The importance of fact mastery is suggested by our New York economist when he describes how his clients verify his competence: "They check my competence by my knowledge of the industry: do I seem to know a lot in terms of what's happening, in terms of technology, what companies are good, what they do, do I understand their markets very well? My analysis needs to seem to be well thought out. The methodology can be described, the methodology seems to make a lot of sense. The findings are well-documented. When I present the results, I present them in a way that makes you feel comfortable. You seem like somebody who has done a lot of thinking, a lot of work, and who can articulate it in some manner that they find pleasing, the whole nature of it."

44. Granick, *Managerial Comparisons of Four Developed Countries*, 59.

45. Indeed, there still exists only a weak connection between field of study and occupation in France: for instance, a recent study reported by the magazine *Expansion* found that 46 percent of the computer specialists interviewed had no university degree, or only degrees in fields that have no relevance to computer science such as literature, law, political science, or commerce. Among respondents working in marketing, 44 percent had no university degree, while 24 percent had an engineering degree and 13 percent had degrees in other areas not related to commerce. Cited by Boltanski, *Les cadres: La formation d'un groupe social*, 322. The generalist approach to competence is reinforced by the public school curriculum, which is mostly theoretical and nontechnical in character.

46. Singly and Thélot, *Gens du privé, gens du public: La grande différence*, 30 and 36. These authors also discuss opposition to competition among public- and private-sector managers (13).

47. See the work of David Landes and others, who argued that historically the French business class had been less risk-taking and more oriented toward the preservation of the *patrimoine* (i.e., accumulated wealth) than other national groups. E.g., Landes, "The Entrepreneur and the Social Order: France and the United States"; Hoffman, ed., *In Search of France*; Pitts, *The Bourgeois Family and French Economic Retardation*. On this literature see Marin, "Qu'est-ce que 'le patronat'? Enjeux théoriques et résultats empiriques."

48. Riccio, "Religious Affiliation and Socioeconomic Achievement."

49. In France, some of the most powerful institutions, notably the state, the unions, the church, and the left-of-center parties, support the notion that the workplace cannot be regulated by profitability alone. In 1954, the "Association pour l'emploi des cadres" (APEC) was created to help the government labor department find jobs for managers. The unemployment rate for managers went from .7 percent to 2.3 percent between 1969 and 1984, while it went from 2.1 to 10.9 percent for nonmanagers. See Singly and Thélot, *Gens du privé, gens du public*, 87.

50. See Ségrestin, *Le phénomène corporatiste: Essai sur l'avenir des systèmes professionnels fermés en France*.

51. Granick, *Managerial Comparisons of Four Developed Countries*, 59.

52. On this topic, see Wickham and Coignard, *La nomenklatura française: Pouvoirs et privilèges des élites*. Closets, *Toujours plus*; also Crozier, *The Bureaucratic Phenomenon*, 208. Job security cannot explain all the differences in the French and American attitudes toward competition and competence. Other factors will be explored in Chapter 5.

53. For a critique see Suleiman, *Les hauts fonctionnaires et la politique*.

54. These changes are documented—and celebrated—in Closets's popular book, *Tous ensemble*. Recent studies, however, found that, in general, French employees are still

reluctant to express disagreements with their supervisors, more reluctant than Americans are. These groups, respectively, rank 68 and 40 on the scale which Hofstede designed to measure power distance. See Hofstede, *Culture's Consequence*, chap. 3.

55. According to the European values/CARA survey, only 33 percent of the French professionals, managers, and business people surveyed think that most people can be trusted, in contrast to a figure of 50 percent for Americans. Sixty-seven percent of the Frenchmen surveyed think that "you can't be too careful in dealing with people," in contrast to 50 percent of the Americans.

56. Loyalty to the firm which varies considerably across types of firm (state-owned vs. private; small vs. large) is more frequent in the traditional family enterprises, and decreases as careers become more rationalized, making employees less dependent on personal relationships. As late as 1975–76, 40 percent of French managerial jobs in small and middle-size firms were still found through contacts, as were 29 percent of the managerial jobs requiring an engineering degree (Boltanski, *Les cadres*, 391). In the United States a study conducted twenty years ago shows that 56 percent of the professional, technical, and managerial workers surveyed found jobs through personal contacts (Granovetter, *Getting a Job*, 11). Again, if Americans attach less importance to loyalty, it is in part because their professional mobility often requires a frequent change of employer.

57. See Dupuy and Thoenig, *L'administration en miettes*; Crozier, *The Bureaucratic Phenomenon*, 216–23.

58. Additional evidence concerning how the French and Americans deal with conflict is provided by the European values and CARA surveys which reveal that 77 percent of the French professionals, managers, and businessmen like "being with people whose ideas, beliefs and values are different from [their] own," in contrast to 51 percent of upper-middle class Americans. On the other hand, 41 percent of this latter group said that they "do not very much dislike" (*sic*) being with people different from themselves, in contrast to 16 percent of the French.

59. Bourdieu, *Distinction*, 199. Bourdieu explains that for the working class "it is free-speech and language of the heart which make the true 'nice guy,' blunt, straightforward, unbending, honest, genuine, 'straight down the line' and 'straight as a die,' as opposed to everything that is pure form, done only for forms' sake [as in bourgeois culture]; it is freedom and the refusal of complications, as opposed to respect for all the forms and formalities spontaneously perceived as instruments of distinction and power. On these moralities, these worldviews, there is no neutral viewpoint; what for some is shameless and slovenly, for others is straightforward, unpretentious."

60. In France, this neutralization could be a handicap on both sides of an economic exchange: a recent study of small shopkeepers in Paris revealed that some *boutiquiers* refuse to sell to customers who are distant or disloyal. On the other hand, these *boutiquiers* develop their clientele through extra attentions and a personalized relationship, as in an attempt to personalize exchange relationships that are market driven. See Mayer, *La boutique contre la gauche*, 172–73.

61. Mazataud, *Géopolitique d'une région: L'Auvergne* . . . , 158–59. When asked to describe the qualities valued at Michelin, an engineer replied: ". . . realism, sincerity, dependability, ability to work with others . . . It is important to start from facts, from observation . . . Michelin is exemplary when it comes to honesty, dependability."

62. See Zussman, *Mechanics of the Middle Class*, 170.

63. On French engineers see Crawford, *Technical Workers in an Advanced Society*, 135; on American engineers see the national survey cited by Zussman in *Mechanics of the Middle Class*, 138. While, in general, French professionals tend not to change occupations, in America, "by age 45, about 10 percent of a beginning cohort of pharmacists has left active

practice, about 30 percent of physicians, 25 percent of lawyers, 30 percent of architects. Rates for clergy, engineers, social workers and teachers are around 50 percent." See Abbott, *The System of Professions: An Essay on the Division of Expert Labor,* 132.

64. On the effect of modes of promotion on teamwork see Crozier, *The Bureaucratic Phenomenon,* 139–40.

65. Singly and Thélot, *Gens du privé, gens du public,* 17. According to the European values/CARA surveys, only 14 percent of French professionals, managers, and businessmen belong to professional associations, in contrast to 42 percent of their American counterparts. In the United States, these associations play an essential role in sustaining national labor markets by circulating information, organizing national meetings, providing a common forum, and so forth.

66. Authority is more concentrated in France, decentralization of power being viewed as dysfunctional. Consequently, power differentials are more salient then they are in German or British organizations, and there are greater wage differentials across levels (see Appendix I) as well as more material and symbolic perks for upper-level managers. Granick, *Managerial Comparisons of Four Developed Countries,* 59; Suleiman, *Les élites en France,* 154 and 161; Maurice, Sellier, and Sylvestre, *Shift Work: Economic Advantages and Social Costs.*

67. Additional virtues within this bourgeois world include being discreet, understated, serene, in control, responsible, ascetic, courteous, and having a strong sense of family tradition, duties, and conventions. Some of these other dimensions of the bourgeois culture will be discussed in Chap. 4. On this, see Le Wita's analysis of bourgeois education in *Ni vue ni connue: Approche ethnographique de la culture bourgeoise,* chaps. 3 and 4. Le Wita is mostly concerned with the education of women, but many of the principles that she identified apply to men.

68. Ulmann, *L'humanisme du XXe siècle.* French humanism is an old and strong tradition, going back to Rabelais and Ronsard, anchored in the philosophers of the Enlightenment, and again sustained by the cultural influence of religious education. Humanism (Christian or existential) was widespread after World War II as it constitutes a logical reaction to the Holocaust and to the irrationality of recent war experiences. Jacques Maritain, who was in this period the chief philosophical spokesman of the Roman Catholic Church, exercised considerable influence on the postwar generation: he defended a Catholic moral philosophy against Marxism, positivism, existentialism, and pragmatism, focusing on man's essence and nature as a way to get at true moral principles.

69. This group is also very politically conservative. See Le Wita, *Ni vue ni connue.* On the relation between wealth, religiousness, and political attitudes, see Michelat and Simon, "Déterminations socio-économiques, organisations symboliques et comportement électoral."

70. The European values/CARA surveys provide indirect evidence that this group represents a sizable proportion of the upper-middle class: 18.4 percent of the professionals, managers, and businessmen interviewed believe that firms should be run by the employees, who would themselves select their own managers, while 60 percent think that owners and employees together should select managers; only 21 percent believe that owners alone should run the firm and appoint managers. In the United States, 31.8 percent believe in joint management; 6.3 percent believe in total self-management by the workers; while a full 60 percent believe that the owners should run the enterprise and appoint the managers.

71. For the American case, see Hunter, "American Protestantism: Sorting Out the Present, Looking toward the Future," 55.

72. Wuthnow, *The Restructuring of American Religion: Society and Faith since World War II;* Luker, *Abortion and the Politics of Motherhood.*

73. Watt, "United States: Cultural Challenges to the Voluntary Sector," 261–64.

74. Max Weber, *Economy and Society*, vol. 1, 339–56, 385–99.

75. These exceptions are few enough to be described: a New York realtor mentioned not liking Iranians and other Muslims, not "knowing where they are coming from"; an Indianapolis marketing executive mentioned the low status given to Catholics and Italians, in particular, in his milieu; two of the French interviewees made racist statements concerning Arab immigrants. On the other hand, a few American Jews mentioned being discriminated against professionally (the French Jews did not mention any sort of discrimination against them). In all cases, interviewees seem to reject simultaneously members of religious and ethnic minorities as well as foreigners, the dimensions being fundamentally intertwined in their minds. The place of race and ethnicity in the drawing of symbolic boundaries will be discussed in Chap. 3.

76. R. Stephen Warner, "The Evangelical Ethic and the Spirit of Parochialism." See also R. Stephen Warner, *New Wine in Old Wineskins: Evangelicals and Liberals in a Small-Town Church*, 231.

77. As explained by Claude Fischer in his study of social networks in Northern California, "[I]t [is] small-town respondents who [are] especially likely to form or expand their relations within a church or church-based setting. They were involved in more relations of this sort than comparable church members living in urban places." Fischer, *To Dwell among Friends: Personal Networks in Town and City*, 113. While Indianapolis is obviously not a small town, many people I talked to described it as a metropolis that is conserving its small town character.

78. Fifty-nine percent of the French interviewees are Catholic compared to 24 percent of the Americans. Also, while only 5 percent of the French are Jews, it is the case for 18 percent of the Americans. Finally, none of the French are protestant compared to 46 percent of the Americans.

79. The high level of atheism in France is related to the convergence of two strong cultural traditions—anticlericalism, which dates back to the Enlightenment, and communism. Although it was only in 1905 that the French state and the Catholic Church were formally separated, the Jacobin tradition had always opposed the Church as an antirepublican force aspiring to spiritual and intellectual guidance of the population. One still finds a great many expressions of anticlerical feelings in popular culture: in San Antonio's novels, e.g., or in magazines such as *Hara Kiri* and *Le Canard Enchaîné*, and the songs of Georges Brassens and Jacques Brel.

80. The French interviewees are as religious as their national average—61 percent of the French say they never attend church; the European average is 32 percent. American interviewees are less religious than most Americans: church membership has been around 61 percent since 1974, with approximately 40 percent of the population declaring themselves regular church attenders. In 1985, about 55 percent of Americans felt that religion was very important to their lives. See Harding and Phillips, with Michael Fogarty, *Contrasting Values in Western Europe: Unity, Diversity and Change*, 42; and Wuthnow, *The Restructuring of American Religion*, 164.

81. Participation in volunteerism itself is not very popular among the French and American men I talked to. The questionnaire on leisure-time activities reveals that close to a majority of respondents are never involved in any kind of volunteering activities (46 percent for the United States and 47 percent for France). A small minority of 8 percent (United States) and 11 percent (France) volunteer very frequently, while an equally small group declares a strong dislike for volunteer activities (12 percent for the Americans and 13 percent for the French).

82. In *Culture Shift in Advanced Industrial Society*, Inglehart shows that the French express

very strong support for the Welfare State: of all Western European countries, the French population has the third highest percentage of people supporting measures such as reducing income inequality, more state intervention in the economy, and more nationalization (255). Only Greece and Ireland have a more pro-Welfare State population.

83. As explained by the coauthors of *Habits of the Heart* (Bellah et al.), "The self-interest demanded by the individualist pursuit of success needs to be balanced by voluntary concern for others. Without the joyful experience of support in such a community of concern, an individual would find it difficult to make the effort to be a success, and success achieved would likely turn to ashes" (199).

84. Wolfe, *Whose Keeper? Social Science and Moral Obligation*, 63.

85. On French voluntary associations see Roudet, "Bilan des recherches sur la vie associative," 26–27. It is only in 1901 that the French state formally recognized the right to freedom of association, with the exception of certain restrictions on religious associations.

86. Archambault, *Les associations en chiffres*, 25–27.

87. Studies indicate that participation in voluntary associations in the United States is strongly related to socioeconomic status as educated, affluent people are more likely to engage in volunteer activities. E.g., Fischer, *To Dwell among Friends*, 110. Older people are also more likely to volunteer than younger people. It is interesting to note that according to the European values/CARA surveys, French upper-middle-class men are likelier to engage in volunteer work for labor unions than Americans are, but proportionately fewer of them volunteer for charities, churches, youth groups, and the like.

CHAPTER THREE

1. Similarly, the downwardly mobile middle-class men interviewed by Katherine Newman made salient central middle-class values as they tried to hold on to them in the face of adversity. See her *Falling from Grace: The Experience of Downward Mobility in the American Middle Class*.

2. An Indianapolis civil servant talks about how his feelings of inferiority are linked to success: "There are times when I feel inferior to my brother because I think he's been successful . . . He's been personally successful—he is a doctor. And there are times when I feel that I should've done as well. There are probably a lot of times when I feel I should've done as well."

3. In *Social Standing in America*, Coleman and Rainwater give a systematic description of the *worldly* signals that are used to read status in America, using data collected in Kansas City and Boston. They focus less on distinctions within the middle class than on differences between classes. Earlier analyses, such as *Crestwood Heights*, are also useful for identifying symbols of worldly success, and especially the role played by professional associations and social and service clubs as arenas within which to acquire and enact status. See Seeley, Sim, and Loosley, *Crestwood Heights: A Study of the Culture of Suburban Life*, 292–302. See also Huber, *The American Idea of Success*.

4. An Indianapolis informant, e.g., describes his friends as follows: "One of them is president of the Illinois Gas Company, which serves two-thirds of the state. Another one is a chap just up the street whose wife is very active, almost pushy, socially. He was president of the Good Life Insurance Company. He's one of those fat cats who put money into the Republican Party and raises money . . . My wife belongs to two or three groups like the bridge club, and there's a golf-playing group and a church group. Some of [our friends] came from business, like Jack Grey, the fellow who's president of the Green Company. Another one is Charlie Black, who was with Mobil. And also, this other fellow who was editor of the paper, friends of my wife."

5. The ideal type of the socioeconomically exclusive depicted here corresponds to the success-oriented manager described in Bellah et al., *Habits of the Heart*. He has little concern for wider political or social issues, and he understands morality as the capacity to "do your own thing" if you have the money to do it (77).

6. On money and social membership, see Rainwater, *What Money Buys*.

7. See Murphy, *Social Closure: The Theory of Monopolization and Exclusion*; Parkin, "Strategies of Closure in Class Formation."

8. Chapin, *The Measurement of Social Status by the Use of the Social Status Scale*; W. Lloyd Warner and P. S. Lunt, *Status System of a Modern Community*; Veblen, *The Theory of the Leisure Class*.

9. One exception in this tradition of predefining status signals is the work of William Faunce which shows that status is not always judged on the basis of work- or occupation-related characteristics. See esp. "On the Meaning of Occupational Status: Implications of Increasing Complexity for How Status Is Conceived"; "Occupational Status-Assignment Systems: The Effect of Status on Self-Esteem."

10. This topic has been largely neglected by the available studies of subjective dimensions of class. See Mary R. Jackman and Robert W. Jackman, *Class Awareness in the United States*; Vanneman and Cannon, *The American Perception of Class*.

11. The average score for all interviewees on this scale is 3.6 in contrast to 3.3 for both cultural and moral boundaries.

12. The average score for the French is 3.2 compared to 4.0 for Americans. I find a weak positive relationship between the fact of residing in the United States and of drawing strong socioeconomic boundaries with a Somers' D of .26 at the .01 level of significance. The measure used here and elsewhere in this book is Somers' D, which accounts for the ranking of cases on an independent variable. In the present statement, Somers' D refers to the likelihood that American interviewees will score 3–5 on the socioeconomic scale. The level of significance is indicated by Tau C. It should be noted that 68 percent of the Hoosiers and 70 percent of the New Yorkers score high (i.e., 4 or 5) on the socioeconomic scale. Only 38 percent of the Parisians score this high on the socioeconomic scale as compared to 50 percent of the Clermontois.

13. Hofstede notes that the word *achievement* does not have a perfect equivalent in French (*Culture's Consequences*, 350). He also criticizes D. K. McClelland's theory of achievement as ethnocentric and as applying mostly to American society (171). See McClelland, *The Achieving Society*.

14. Contributing to the controversy around Merton's thesis of success orientation, L. Richard Della Fave found a weak relationship between success orientation and social class in the United States, which he interprets as indicating a considerable amount of overlap in level of aspiration from class to class. His conclusions are based on a questionnaire administered to high school students in the early seventies. "Success Values: Are they Universal or Class-differentiated?"

15. In *Social Theory and Social Structure*, Merton argues that each society has a culturally dominant frame of aspiration reference, and that in the United States success goals are defined in terms of accumulation of wealth and possessions. The following sections constitute an attempt to empirically document such frames within the realm of socioeconomic exclusion.

16. Studies provide mixed evidence of these cross-national differences between France and the United States. For instance, in *Culture Shift* (92), Inglehart showed that a roughly equal number of Americans in prestigious occupations—i.e., occupations with a prestige ranking in the top quartile—are materialistic as compared to their French counterparts (the figures are 30 percent and 33 percent, respectively).

17. Zelizer, "The Social Meaning of Money: 'Special Monies,'" 342–77.

18. On the importance of the *culture de sortie* (outings culture) in the French upper-middle class, see Donnat and Cogneau, *Les pratiques culturelles des Français 1973–1989.*

19. On this topic see Pinçon and Pinçon-Charlot, *Dans les beaux quartiers*, chap. 9.

20. More frequent disregard for money as such might have emerged from the American interviews if I had talked with upper-middle-class people residing in the Connecticut suburbs of New York City. Indeed, these suburbs are known to be the choice area for upper-middle-class families that have been part of this class for several generations. Many of my New Jersey interviews, however, were conducted in two historic summer resorts (Madison and Summit) that have traditionally attracted "old money"—a factor that helps to correct possible biases created by my limited sample.

21. On consumption goods as a sign of status see also W. Lloyd Warner et al. *Yankee City*; and Mills, *White Collar: The American Middle Class.* This last book discusses the status panic of white-collar workers who consume and follow rules out of uncertainty. See also Veblen, *The Theory of the Leisure Class.*

22. On the diffusion of an economic definition of success to the lower classes see Powers, "Second Class Finish: The Effect of a Working Class High School." Also Schwartz, *Beyond Conformity and Rebellion: Youth and Authority in America*, 193.

23. A study shows that 79 percent of Americans and 46 percent of the British surveyed use an economic criterion for class differentiation. See Wendell Bell and Robert V. Robinson, "Cognitive Maps of Class and Racial Inequality in England and the United States," 341. The American emphasis on money extends beyond the French-American comparison. Americans are nearly twice as likely as the English to specify income or wealth as a basis of class membership.

24. On the growing importance of the politics of residence in the United States, i.e., on the de facto segregation of the population on the basis of real estate prices, see Reich, "The Secession of the Successful," 16.

25. The *banquier* Dutoît adds: "When I see what is going on in New York, I think this is real business, but we are not doing real business . . . I am quite critical of the American model. It is too crazy, too crazy. They buy a firm one day, and the next, they take it apart and sell it for twice the price. I like profit, but not that much. You have to be concerned for the eighty people who lose their jobs too." It should be noted that this banker is a Socialist and that he worked for a while in a nationalized bank, which might account for his insistence on having a "sense of social responsibility."

26. Suleiman, *Les elites en France*, 178. This fascination for power and glory is also emphasized by Crozier in his description of the bureaucratic innovator, who, according to this author, is the only effective agent of change in the French organizational system, being located at the top of the pyramid. Others can only adjust to the existing system, through caution and submission. See Crozier, *The Bureaucratic Phenomenon*, 202.

27. I am quoting non verbatim from Boltanski, *Les cadres*, 129.

28. Zysman, *Political Strategies for Industrial Order: State Market and Industry in France*, 134.

29. Lévy-Leboyer, "The Large Corporation in Modern France," 133 cited by Crawford in *Technical Workers*, 131.

30. Laurent, "The Cultural Diversity of Western Conceptions of Management." Also, Hofstede observes that the French oscillate between complete rejection and complete acceptance of authority (*Culture's Consequences*, 320). See also Crozier, who portrays the French as alternatively rebellious and ritualistically obedient, as having difficulties in developing acceptable leadership models, and as conceiving authority to be universal and absolute, with no system of checks and balances (*The Bureaucratic Phenomenon*, 220).

William K. Shonfeld who analyzes antiauthoritarian tendencies among the French is also relevant. See *Obedience and Revolt: French Behavior toward Authority.*

31. For a particularly illuminating analysis of the dynamic of such power struggle in American corporations see Morrill, "Conflict Management, Honor, and Organizational Change."

32. "A few engineers do complain, often bitterly . . . but these complaints are directed at individuals, the 'bad boss,' . . . [who] represents an unnecessary interference, a style of management rooted in the character of an individual rather than in the structure of the organization . . . The bad boss is not bad because he exercises authority. He is bad because he makes technical mistakes, and he is bad from the point of view of the company as well as that of the employee." Zussman, *Mechanics of the Middle Class*, 113. This attitude is reflected in the American literature on the relationship between power and culture: American theorists are less likely than the French to insist on the coercive aspect of power. On this see Lamont and Wuthnow, "Betwixt and Between."

33. In general, wealthier and more educated people have broader social networks (Fischer, *To Dwell among Friends*, 252). They associate more often with coworkers off the job than do low-salaried workers (106). Working-class people are more family-oriented and put less emphasis on professional mobility than on interpersonal relations. They also are less involved in social and philanthropic associations. The same distinction holds true in France. See Héran, "Un monde sélectif: Les associations."

34. The following statement by a computer specialist in his thirties is not atypical: "In today's societies, with mobility being what it is, we don't have extended families. We find ourselves more isolated, literally a thousand miles or more from all of our immediate family. In each community where we live, it's quite a lengthy process, generally, of networking to eventually come up with a set of friends . . . that we can emotionally trust . . . Each move is so much more traumatic. It's not a matter of finding out where the K-Mart is. It's a matter of finding out a church that we can identify with; it's a matter of a community of people around us that we can interact with and form relationships." On this aspect of upper-middle-class culture see Margolis, *The Managers: Corporate Life in America.*

35. In New York, a lawyer thus describes the situation in the suburbs: "My social life in Rockville Center is almost nil, frankly. We haven't really had an opportunity to really develop any close friendships, and I think that's probably because everybody is very involved in their own life, business, family and whatever there is. There's not sufficient occasions to get together and get to know people, enough of a basis to develop anything worthwhile."

36. These committees are particularly important because they were institutionalized to mediate the central power of the state to the regions. On the notables and the local power see Abélès, *Jours tranquilles en 89: Ethnologie politique d'un département français.*

37. Based on a survey conducted in 1949, Lambert found that Americans attach more importance to their neighbors than the French do. Asked to rank various relationships in terms of their importance, Americans cite spouse first, then in decreasing order: friend, neighbor, colleague, and citizen. For the French, spouse comes first followed by citizen, friend, colleague, and neighbor. See Lambert, "Comparison of French and American Modes of Response to the Bogardus Social Distance Scale." For specific data on sociability with neighbors in France see Héran, "La sociabilité, une pratique culturelle."

38. On the importance of relations see Lerner's remarks on their role in obtaining interviews with members of the French elite in "An American Researcher in Paris."

39. The social salience of class as a dimension of identity seems to be diminishing as social class-based voting has been declining over the last three decades. Indeed, according to Alford's index of class voting, between 5 and 10 percent of the American vote

was class-based in 1989 compared with a high of 43 percent in 1948. In France, the percentage has gone from 32 percent in 1948 to approximately 15 percent in 1986. See Inglehart, *Culture Shift in Advanced Industrial Societies*, 260.

40. Along the same line, as shown by the ethnographic study of American blue-collar workers conducted by David Halle, members of this group do not perceive themselves as very different from middle-class people. When they are away from work, they do not consider their leisure, family, or residential lives [as] distinctly working class. On the contrary, most see life outside work as an arena where they can escape the humiliations and constraints of the factory. This attitude is reflected in a class identity based on the concept of being 'middle class' or 'lower-middle class' that refers to life outside the workplace and implies overlaps between themselves and others of comparable income, lifestyle, and material possessions. See Halle's *America's Working Man: Home and Politics among Blue-Collar Property Owners*, 395.

41. The lesser development of a distinct working class identity in the United States is related to the weaker political organization of this class, specific immigration and racial residence patterns, and cultural ideas about assimilation typical of the United States. See Katznelson, *City Trenches: Urban Politics and the Patterning of Class in the United States*. Lipset, "Why No Socialism in the United States?"

42. According to Varenne, universalism is very important in the United States. It is "defined in relation to a hierarchical view of the social world, and in opposition to it. It says that the distinctive social features of a person must be rejected as a valid basis for planning interaction with him and only his conduct must be considered" (*Americans Together*, 205).

43. Inzerilli and Laurent, "Managerial Views of Organization Structure in France and the U.S.A.," 112.

44. Homans, Lazarsfeld, Merton, Blau, and others have shown that similarity of attributes plays a central role in the formation of social groups. More recently, see, e.g., Fischer, *To Dwell among Friends*, chap. 14. Also, in *Class Awareness in the United States*, Jackman and Jackman found that most middle- and upper-middle-class Americans express a preference for their own class over other classes (47).

45. Edward O. Laumann has shown that the self-isolation of the professional and business elite is greater than for any other group as friendship choices are structured by class and as the probability of friendship declines with increasing occupational prestige distance. See his *Bonds of Pluralism: The Form and Substance of Urban Social Networks*.

46. In *Social Identifications: A Social Psychology of Intergroup Relations and Group Processes*, Hogg and Abrams note (40) that people usually compare themselves with out-group members most similar to themselves. Along the same lines, Jackman and Jackman provide evidence that "patterns of emotional differentiation among classes indicate that people do not make a categorical 'us versus them' distinction, but instead react to classes as a graded series of groups. People express successively greater emotional distance from classes as they become less proximate to their own" (*Class Awareness in the United States*, 218).

47. Coleman and Rainwater also suggest that "it is one of the characteristics of the class structure in the United States that lines of demarcation are not sharply or clearly perceived by the average citizen, and many are not known about at all by people whose lives they do not touch" (*Social Standing in America*, 120).

48. See Jackman and Muha, "Education and Intergroup Attitudes: Moral Enlightenment, Superficial Democratic Commitment or Ideological Refinement?"

49. This hypothesis is supported by the work of McPherson and Smith-Lovin, and shows that organizational size reduces status distance, i.e., that those who work in large organizations form friendships with a wider range of people. See McPherson and Smith-

Lovin, "Homophily in Voluntary Organizations: Status Distance and the Composition of Face-to-Face Groups." There is a voluminous literature on class consciousness and class identity in the United States that would be useful in explaining the attitudes toward class differences that I encountered among my interviewees. A discussion of this literature is beyond the scope of this study.

50. Waters, *Ethnic Options*. This book concerns mostly white ethnics. A recent study of high school students in California found that race and ethnicity are more central bases of association among students than class and gender. The population studied included a large number of Hispanics. See Gottdiener and Malone, "Group Differentiation in a Metropolitan High School: The Influence of Race, Class, Gender and Culture."

51. The fact that few males mentioned gender when answering these probes might be linked to the fact that they were interviewed by a female.

52. Anthony Cohen, *Symbolic Construction of Community*.

53. Research on class and racial identification shows that racial identification is always stronger for blacks than are other types of identity. See Patricia Gurin, Arthur H. Miller, and Gerald Gurin, "Stratum Identification and Consciousness," 37.

54. Feagin, "The Continuing Significance of Race: Antiblack Discrimination in Public Places."

55. For a discussion of the awareness of class in the French and American working class see Lash, *The Militant Worker: Class and Radicalism in France and America*, chap. 5.

56. When asked how far he thinks he will rise in his profession, a self-employed Paris accountant says, "I am starting from zero, so I don't think that I will be very successful . . . The person whose father was a businessman or a banker starts much higher. My father made false teeth." Another one described the values he transmitted to his children as follows: "You do what you can, not what you want. Everyone has a lot of projects when they start off . . . some are worse off, some are better off. But I think that overall . . . what is important is to be able to accept to just do what you can."

57. American upper-middle-class men are more likely than other Americans to think that their society is one of open competition, where mobility is determined by psychological and moral strength rather than by structural factors. See Kluegel and Smith, *Belief about Inequality: Americans' View of What Is and What Ought to Be*, 91–92; also Feagin, *Subordinating the Poor: Welfare and American Beliefs*.

58. It should be noted that a comparison of the scores obtained by the Hoosiers and New Yorkers on the socioeconomic dimension does not reveal important differences in the importance of socioeconomic boundaries: 17 percent of the Hoosiers express indifference or opposition to socioeconomic boundaries, as did 15 percent of the New Yorkers. These percentages were obtained by calculating the number of respondents who rank 0 to 2 on the socioeconomic scale. See Appendix IV.

59. Thirty percent of the Clermontois and 35 percent of the Parisians express indifference or opposition to socioeconomic boundaries.

60. A study of French perceptions of Americans based on a content analysis of textbooks showed that four of the most important characteristics attributed to the American way of life pertain to this orientation toward achievement and material goods. These characteristics include a high standard of living, a spirit of enterprise, and the individual's capacity for social success. See Wylie and Henriquez, "Images of Americans in French Textbooks," 201.

61. In *Cultural Misunderstanding: The French-American Experience*, 128–29, Carroll provides further examples of negative perceptions by the French of American materialism.

62. Survey by SOFRES for *Le Monde*, 16 November 1984, quoted in Rupnik and Humbertjean, "Image(s) des Etats-Unis dans l'opinion publique," 102.

63. On the anti-Americanism of intellectuals, see Rupnik and Humbertjean, "Image(s) des Etats-Unis . . . ," 120–21.

64. While 62 percent of the Hoosiers score 4 or 5 on the moral scale, it is the case for 37 percent of the New Yorkers. The average score on the moral scale for New York interviewees is 3.1 compared to 3.6 in Indianapolis. In line with the argument presented at the end of the previous section, if the Hoosiers perceive New Yorkers to be social climbers, it might be in part because the latter group draws weaker moral boundaries than the former.

65. Keeping in mind that the Hoosiers are considerably more morally exclusive than the New Yorkers, it is interesting to note that 50 percent of the Hoosiers and 66 percent of the New Yorkers who score 4 or 5 on the moral scale also score high on the socioeconomic scale. The same correlation is observed for only 35 percent of the Clermontois and 14 percent of the Parisians.

66. Accordingly, the correlation between the fact of scoring high on the socioeconomic boundaries is much more strongly negatively related to scoring high on the moral boundaries in France than in the United States; the Kendall's Tau are respectively $-.400$ and $-.273$, both significant at the .000 and .008 level.

67. See Powers, "Second Class Finish." Also Schwartz, *Beyond Conformity and Rebellion.*

68. It should be noted that the quantitative analysis does not reveal a significant relationship between cultural center and the strength of socioeconomic boundaries.

CHAPTER FOUR

1. The score of the first group on the cultural dimension is of 3.1 compared to 3.5 for the French. Accordingly, 59 percent of the French and 37 percent of the Americans rank 4 or 5 on this scale. The Somer's D indicates a weak association between cultural boundaries and country (.22 at the .01 level of significance).

2. For a discussion, see Lamont and Lareau, "Cultural Capital."

3. As suggested by Randall Collins in *The Credential Society,* by using educational credentials as a criterion of selection, organizations control for a number of character traits and habits that are seen as essential for adaptation in an upper-middle-class environment. For the excluded, the lack of a college degree has palpable consequences. Hence, in *America's Working Man,* David Halle argues that the non–college-educated are more conscious of their economic handicap which results in their inability to gain access to jobs than of the properly cultural handicap (e.g., not being familiar with the names of classical composers) that results from the lack of a college education.

4. On the role of French education in passing on privileges, see Girard, *La réussite sociale en France: Ses caractères, ses lois, ses effets;* Bourdieu and Passeron, *Reproduction in Education, Society and Culture;* Boudon, *L'inégalité des chances;* Thélot, *Tel père, tel fils.*

5. For a comparison of the attraction that intellectual prestige exerts on French and American politicians see Clark, *Literary France: The Making of a Culture,* 26–33.

6. In *Descartes, c'est la France,* Glucksman discusses the influence of Cartesianism on French culture.

7. As of 1982–83, 16 percent of France's schoolchildren were being educated in private Catholic schools. Data on the class background of these children, however, as for private school students generally, is not readily available. See Ambler, "Educational Pluralism in the French Fifth Republic," 10.

8. On the abstract character of the French curriculum see Crozier, *The Bureaucratic Phenomenon,* 242.

9. On the cult of the French language see again the insightful book by Clark, *Literary*

France, esp. chap. 5. She writes: "The cultivation of clarity and the exaltation of reason define the basic intellectuality of French literary culture. The French language, French writers and French literature appear 'intellectual' in ways that other languages, other literatures and other writers do not . . . the spirit of Cartesian logic suffuses the entire culture to this day . . . The *esprit de géométrie*, a sense of order, system and logic [are all crucial]" (99).

10. Eloquence is essential for gaining admission to many of the most prestigious grandes écoles. On this topic see the excellent analysis of Bourdieu, in "Epreuves scolaires et consécration sociale," 69. Also his *La noblesse d'état*, p. 1. While this emphasis on style and eloquence is most characteristic of elite education, it also permeates the university and the upper-middle class at large because, according to Bourdieu and Passeron, elite schools define what constitutes legitimate culture for French society as a whole (see *Reproduction*). The vocational schools (*lycées d'enseignement professionel* (LEP) do, however, put less emphasis on verbal skills and stress instead properly technical skills. On this topic, see Hamon and Rotman, *Tant qu'il y aura des profs*.

11. According to Bourdieu, apprenticeship in such skills is an intrinsic part of the preparatory courses for the *grandes écoles*, which courses are the "archetypical form of French academic culture" ("Epreuves scolaires et consécration sociale," 21.)

12. This last quote reflects many similar comments made by various respondents, all pointing to the fact that expertise is not crucial for success. For instance, a Versailles lawyer confessed that, in general, he does not carefully prepare the cases he takes on but counts mostly on luck: "It is instinctual. You put things in the machine, you think about it, and sometimes it works, and sometimes it is awful."

13. Crawford, *Technical Workers in an Advanced Society*, 72.

14. For information on the reading tastes of the upper-middle class in France see Parmentier, "Les genres et leurs lecteurs," and Donnat and Cogneau, *Les pratiques culturelles des Français 1973–1989*, chap. 4.

15. It is revealing that the distinction fiction/nonfiction that serves as an organizing principle in American bookstores is not used in France. Furthermore, the French never describe their reading interests as "facts" the way this New York computer specialist does: "[I read] facts, science, mainly. I could read a book on computers; I could read a book on relativity. I could read excerpts from medical journals, scientific journals like *Scientific American*. Those are the type of things I enjoy reading, popular science, popular mechanics, but mainly factual. I am not into fiction . . . Science by magazines, science by books, things of that nature, news, current events, uhm . . . anything factual."

16. While some American men I interviewed insist on the importance of proper grammar, this is never accompanied by a cult of language such as one finds in France. The extraordinary popularity of the televised French dictation championships reveals how widespread this cult is in France. They do not compare with American spelling bees because these dictations are a celebration of the beauty and the grammatical complexity of the French language; the "dictée" are generally taken from classical literary works.

17. Ronald Inglehart (*Culture Shift*) found that postmaterialism is slightly more important for the Americans than for the French, both countries being located in the middle of a spectrum that includes other advanced industrial societies. Postmaterialists are here defined as people who give top priority to nonmaterial goals, such as self-expression and self-actualization, environmental concerns, and social welfare. While in 1972 American materialists outnumbered the postmaterialists by 3.5 to 1, in 1987 the ratio had fallen to 1.5 to 1 (96). The highly educated make up a slightly smaller percentage of the postmaterialists in the United States than in France (42 percent vs. 50 percent),

this group being here defined as people having educational level in the top quartile for their nation.

18. Along the same lines, a New York machine tool salesman explains: "Now, my son plays soccer. I go to the game and I see some of the other fathers standing around, and I just don't want to look like that. It's just not what I want to be." On the cultural meaning attached to obesity in America see Millman, *Such a Pretty Face: Being Fat in America.* Obesity, defined as having 25 percent or more of one's weight in excess, is unequally distributed across social classes in the United States: 52 percent of lower-class women are obese compared to 43 percent of middle-class women and 9 percent of upper-class women.

19. Also, according to Viktor Gecas ("The Influence of Social Class on Socialization," 379), white-collar workers stress freedom, individualism, initiative, creativity, and self-actualization in their child-rearing practices, whereas blue-collar workers emphasize orderliness, neatness, and obedience. On this topic see also Lambert, Hamers, and Frasure-Smith, *Child-Rearing Values: A Cross-National Study.*

20. These results are based on a 1978 survey of patterns of leisure interests and activities (Greenberg and Frank, "Leisure Lifestyles," 448). On leisure-time activities and self-actualization see also Cheek, Jr., and Burch, *The Social Organization of Leisure in Human Society,* 51. On self-actualization and its growing importance as a cultural ideal, see Yankelovitch, *New Rules: Searching for Self-Fulfillment in a World Turned Upside Down;* Sennett, *The Fall of the Public Man;* and Bellah et al., *Habits of the Heart.*

21. James Davis, "Achievement Variables and Class Cultures," 584.

22. According to Alan Kerckhoff (*Socialization and Social Class,* 46), middle-class parents are particularly concerned with the psychological development of their children, as evidenced by their frequent use of reasoning and of positive reinforcement techniques such as praise. In contrast, working-class parents make greater use of power and show greater concern for external conformity.

23. The *Petit Robert* dictionary defines vulgar as follows: ". . . which totally lacks distinction . . . independently of social class"; "someone who has a mediocre or low social position, and ordinary tastes and ideas, in opposition to the elite." Quoted by Bourdieu and St-Martin in "Les catégories de l'entendement professoral," 76. According to a French survey on vulgarity, celebrities, artists, and writers are most often seen as vulgar when they are (1) old-fashioned and popular (e.g., Nana Mouskouri), (2) popular and perceived as right-wing politically (e.g., Sylvester Stallone), and (3) popular and appreciated by the youth (e.g., Madonna) (Donnat and Cogneau, *Les pratiques culturelles des Français 1973–1989,* 241–43).

24. Donnat and Cogneau, *Les pratiques culturelles des Français,* 12. According to these authors (184), only 5 percent of the French population are involved in three or more types of leisure-time activities that reveal a strong cultural orientation, or expressed three or more cultural preferences that reveal such an orientation (e.g., going to museums, exhibitions, art galleries, or historical monuments at least ten times a year; attending classical concerts, operas, plays, or dance performances at least five times a year; going to the movies at least twice a month; regularly reading *L'Express, Le Point, Le Nouvel Observateur, L'Evènement du Jeudi,* or a cultural magazine such as *Lire, Le Monde de la Musique, Première,* etc.

25. Donnat and Cogneau, *Les pratiques culturelles,* 105. See also Zolberg's "The Happy Few-en Masse: Franco-American Comparisons in Cultural Democratization," which shows that only 22.3 percent of the French population were highly involved in cultural activities outside the home in 1978.

26. It should be noted that this same person describes an uninteresting lifestyle as

the kind that can be gleaned from the latest issue of *People* magazine, which indicates that despite a broad repertoire he, like others, might harbor a certain contempt for conformism.

27. These findings concerning the nonexclusiveness of the highly educated support DiMaggio and Mohr in "Cultural Capital . . ." Similarly, Richard A. Peterson and Michael Hughes found that young, white, college-educated urban males engage in a wide range of leisure-time activities going from arts events to sports, hiking, and partying ("Isolating Patterns of Cultural Choice to Facilitate the Formation of Culture Indicators"). See also Ryan and Debord, "High Culture Orientation and the Attitudes and Values of College Students," which shows that people with a high-culture orientation know more about popular culture as well.

28. This is not incompatible with the fact that, as mentioned above, many American interviewees are indifferent to cosmopolitanism. It should be noted that the American literature on cultural exclusion, unlike the French, is relatively small. Also, a few studies provide detailed information on cultural professions (artists, intellectuals) where cultural sophisticates are concentrated. Others focus on cultural consumption communities (e.g., see Zukin, *Loft Living: Culture and Capital in Urban Change*).

29. In a less disparaging tone, a New York minister describes Hoosiers as people who "do fewer things for effect; they have simpler lives. They don't work at developing personality styles that are clever, fascinating."

30. The average score on the cultural scale for New Yorkers and Hoosiers alike is 3.1. Respectively, 38 percent of the Hoosiers and 37 percent of the New Yorkers rank 4 or 5 on the cultural scale.

31. The average scores of Parisians and Clermontois on the cultural scale are 3.7 and 3.3. On the other hand, 68 percent of the Parisians rank 4 or 5 on the cultural scale compared to 50 percent of the Clermontois.

32. Information on these indicators has been collected by Priscilla Parkhurst Clark (see *Literary France*, appendix A). National differences in the frequency with which the names of men and women of letters are used to baptize streets might be partly related to the fact that in the United States numbers are often used to identify streets.

33. American high school students know the correct answer to less than 60 percent of a set of basic questions about Western history and literature (Ravitch and Finn, Jr., *What do your 17-year-olds Know? A Report on the First National Assessment of History and Literature*; also E. D. Hirsch, Jr., *Cultural Literacy: What Every American Needs to Know*. On the decline in literary culture in the United States see Bloom, *The Closing of the American Mind: How Higher Education Has Failed Democracy and Impoverished the Souls of Today's Students*.

34. Bourdieu, *Distinction*, 281 and 330.

35. For instance, when asked whom he feels inferior to, an Indianapolis realtor answered: "I would feel inferior to somebody like you, for instance, because I don't know anything about what you are attempting to do, how to go about it . . . I also feel inferior to bilingual people who are fluent in my language as well as others."

36. In 1990, the circulation figure for *Bon Appétit* was 1,300,834; for *Gourmet*, 797,893; for *Architectural Digest*, 632,235; and for *Art in America*, 66,000 (*Ulrich's International Periodicals Directory 1990*). It is revealing that, unlike Americans, the French never use the term "Renaissance man," maybe because it suggests the notion of a purposefully exhaustive cultural accumulation rather than a cultural apprenticeship guided by one's particular tastes and naturally inscribed in one's lifestyle.

37. On this, see the interesting study of Fantasia, "Fast-Food in France: The Market in Cultural Change."

38. On this topic, see also Veblen, *The Theory of the Leisure Class.*

39. On the relationship between cultural capital and the size of networks, see DiMaggio and Mohr, "Cultural Capital . . ."

40. In contrast to this argument, Bourdieu interprets this cultural overinvestment as a way to "make the most" of what individuals have, i.e., a way of "making a virtue of necessity by maximizing the profit they can draw from their cultural capital and spare time" (*Distinction,* 287).

41. In *The Closing of the American Mind* (47–62), Allan Bloom compares the culture of French and American students along similar lines, focusing on the fact that American students are more excited by the intellectual discovery of the Great Books and less aware of intellectual traditions.

42. Long, "Reading Groups and the Post-Modern Crisis of Cultural Authority."

43. Moffatt, *Coming of Age in New Jersey: College and American Culture,* 274.

44. Blau, *The Shape of Culture, A Study of Contemporary Cultural Patterns in the United States,* 37.

45. The American data is for 1978. DiMaggio and Ostrower, "Participation in the Arts by Black and White Americans." The French data is for 1988: Donnat and Cogneau, *Les pratiques culturelles des Français,* 57.

46. Robinson, Kennan, Hanford, and Trippett, *Public Participation in the Arts: Final Report on the 1982 Survey.* See also DiMaggio and Useem, "Social Class and Arts Consumption: The Origins and Consequences of Class Differences in Exposure to the Arts in America." For France, see Donnat and Cogneau, *Les pratiques culturelles des Français,* 204.

47. Greenberg and Frank, "Leisure Lifestyles," 448.

48. DiMaggio and Ostrower, "Participation in the Arts by Black and White Americans."

49. Marsden, Reed, Kennedy, and Stinson, "American Regional Cultures and Differences in Leisure-Time Activities."

50. Blau, *The Shape of Culture.*

51. Fifty-one percent of the New Yorkers never participate in high-culture activities at all, compared to 38 percent of the Parisians, 36 percent of the Clermontois, and 39 percent of the Hoosiers.

52. Starker contrasts might have appeared if, instead of interviewing suburbanites, I had interviewed people residing within the city limits of Manhattan and Paris. We know that despite their high level of education, residents of the suburbs of large American cities show low rates of participation in cultural events (such as live performances of classical music, opera, or plays, other musicals) (Blau and Ouets, *The Geography of Arts Participation: Report Prepared for the National Endowment for the Arts*).

53. My finding contradicts those of Donnat and Cogneau which show that Parisians have higher rates of participation in high culture events (*Les pratiques culturelles des Français,* 67 and 216). For instance, while 44 percent of the managers and professionals who live in Paris go to concerts and the theater five times a year, they are matched by only 25 percent of the corresponding group in the provinces. Overall, the French upper-middle class consumes more high culture than other classes do: while only 14 percent of the French population as a whole declares a preference for classical music over popular music, jazz, and rock, fully 31 percent of those in managerial positions or in the intellectual professions declare such a preference.

54. Drawing from Zablocki and Kanter, I define a subculture as self-conscious lifestyle collectivity where there exists a "degree of consensus on prestige market concerning the ordering of values associated with [their] tastes" (Zablocki and Kanter, "The Differ-

entiation of Life-Styles," 271). I am following G. Webster in treating intellectualism as a subculture: see his *The Republic of Letters: A History of Postwar American Literary Opinion*, 212.

55. In New York, 25 percent of the sample are considered intellectuals compared to 17 percent in Indianapolis, 47 percent in Paris and 37 percent in Clermont-Ferrand.

56. At the time the French interviews were conducted during the summer of 1989, Bernard Pivot had just announced the cancellation of this program. It had played a key role in the diffusion of intellectual culture in France, partly because it displayed for the audience intellectuals in action, offered this audience role models, and enacted for them a complex universe of reference.

57. For a description of this type of French intellectual, see Louis Pinto, *L'intelligence en action: Le nouvel observateur*.

58. On the relation between intellectualism and radicalism see Bourdieu, *Distinction*, 420; also Donnat and Cogneau, *Les pratiques culturelles des Français*, 219.

59. On this decline, see Domenach, "Le monde des intellectuels."

60. On these changes, which parallel the rise of the "Me-generation" in America, see Lipovetsky, *L'ère du vide: Essais sur l'individualisme contemporain*.

61. The greater appreciation for abstraction among American intellectuals is noted by Irving Howe, who is cited by G. Webster in *The Republic of Letters*, 220.

62. This reflects the contrast between the political orientation of each national sample: while 50 percent of the American intellectuals classify themselves as conservatives or republicans, only 30 percent of the French intellectuals associate themselves to the center, the right or the extreme right. Eighteen percent of the French respondents classified themselves as belonging to the extreme left (including the Communist party), and 4 percent classified themselves as "leftist," socialist, or ecologist.

63. On this phenomena, see G. Webster, *The Republic of Letters*, 21; and Pells, *The Liberal Mind in a Conservative Age*, 403. On pragmatism see in particular Hofstadter, *Anti-Intellectualism in American Life*. The role of pragmatism in American culture will be further discussed in Chap. 5.

64. On the centrality of the theme of cosmopolitanism and European culture to the subculture of American intellectuals, see Hollinger, "Ethnic Diversity, Cosmopolitanism and the Emergence of the American Liberal Intellectuals"; Gilbert, *Writers and Partisans: A History of Literary Radicalism in America*, 59; and Wald, "The New York Intellectual in Retreat."

65. Lasch, *The Agony of the American Left*; Lipset and Dobson, "The Intellectual as Critic and Rebel."

66. Several social scientists have been concerned with the degree of boundedness of classification systems. Mary Douglas's work on cosmology, which borrows Bernstein's notion of restricted and elaborate codes to study the relation between social organization and social representation, has inspired many sociologists. In another vein, Claude Lévi-Strauss has built on the work of Emile Durkheim and Marcel Mauss to develop a structural method of analysis that highlights the structure of symbolic systems. See Douglas, *Natural Symbols*; Lévi-Strauss, *Totemism*; Merelman, *Making Something of Ourselves: On Culture and Politics in the United States*; and DiMaggio, "Classification in Art."

67. In short, to borrow the terminology proposed by Paul DiMaggio in "Classification in Art," such systems are highly differentiated and hierarchized; they have a relatively high degree of universality, being widely shared by members of a society; and they have great strength, the violation of their constitutive boundaries leading to unambiguous inclusion or exclusion.

68. Thirty-eight percent of the American interviewees are categorized as tolerant

in contrast to 31 percent of the French. See Appendix IV for a distribution of these respondents across sites. It should be noted that these tolerant respondents denied feeling superior to anyone or disliking anyone or anyone's tastes despite probes meant to reassure them that we "all feel superior to other people sometimes." On the importance of tolerance in American society, see also Riesman et al., *The Lonely Crowd: A Study of the Changing American Character*, esp. chap. 9.

69. See Bourdieu, *Distinction*, 194 and 381.

70. On American cuisine see Favreau, "The Emergence of American Cuisine: 'Alimentary' Forms of Domination."

71. On French cuisine see Clark, "Thoughts for Food: French Cuisine and French Culture." According to Clark, "The stylization of nature, its aestheticization and spiritualization, are the essence of French cuisine and an important part of French culture as a whole. French cuisine extended communal standards from the cadre of the repast to the content, reinforcing the social control of the dining ritual by the aesthetic control of the cuisine. In a France where literature and the arts were themselves regulated by highly codified standards, the correspondence is not perhaps so surprising. As in the arts, creativity was defined against, hence governed by, a set of rules" (35).

72. See on this topic the very insightful analysis of "lifestyle enclave" presented by Fitzgerald in *Cities on a Hill: A Journey through Contemporary American Cultures*.

73. For Varenne, "the absence [in the United States] of culturally defined norms as to the proposed composition of society leads to the possibility of small groups adopting ideological positions from an indefinite range" (*Americans Together*, 155).

74. Ibid., 44; Lambert et al., *Child-Rearing Values*, 318.

75. Hofstede, *Culture's Consequences*, chap. 4.

76. This might not hold for members of the upper-middle class who belong to what Herbert Gans calls the "user and creator oriented taste culture," a group that includes intellectuals. In *Popular Culture and High Culture: An Analysis and Evaluation of Taste*, Gans differentiates this taste culture from the upper-middle-class taste culture in which members are less interested in the formal aspects of art and are more interested in content, i.e., movies' plots and stars.

77. According to Cheek, Jr., and Burch, home improvement is an activity particularly appreciated by American men who are in the "middle level occupational prestige positions" (*The Social Organization of Leisure in Human Society*, 51). On home repair as a working-class leisure-time activity in France, see Donnat and Cogneau, *Les pratiques culturelles des Français*, 190. Also, Bourdieu, *Distinction*, 390. It should be noted that more French participants live in apartments, which could explain in part why fewer of them engage in home repairs.

78. These figures for the French and American populations at large are 24 and 6 percent, respectively. They certainly reflect differences in the quality and diversity of television programming offered to the French and the American populations.

79. Sixty percent and 73 percent, respectively, for Clermont-Ferrand and Indianapolis, in contrast to 45 percent of the Parisians and 51 percent of the New Yorkers.

80. It is the case for 23 percent of them compared to 19 percent of the Clermontois, 14 percent of the New Yorkers, and 10 percent of the Hoosiers.

81. Peterson and Hughes, "Isolating Patterns of Cultural Choice to Facilitate the Formation of Culture Indicators," 450.

82. On this, see Kanter, *Men and Women of the Corporation;* and Halle, *America's Working Man*, 281. It is interesting to note that only a few of the American men I interviewed, including the Indianapolis artist, said that they found sports truly boring: "Sports bore me . . . I mean every once in a while, if I'm with a bunch of people who are really into

it . . . I will enjoy their enthusiasm. Also, I'm enough of an American and a Midwesterner to . . . it's like going to see a cops-and-robbers movie. After a while, you just say it's meaningless, it's nonsense. But sometimes, in sports, there's some real skills and some real sort of intelligence and beauty as such. It's enjoyable, but I don't think it means a damn thing. I'd much rather look at paintings."

83. This movement defined itself partly in opposition to the intellectualism of the Parisian cultural world. It was less popular among Easterners, many of whom upheld notions of aesthetic purity, emphasizing the structured and the rehearsed in opposition to the improvised. See Balfe, "Social Mobility and Modern Art: Abstract Expressionism and Its Generative Audience."

84. For this study David Halle interviewed upper-middle-class suburbans living on Long Island's North Shore as well as upper-class residents of Manhattan's East Side and lower-class residents of Brooklyn, questioning the participants on the meaning they give to the art they have in their homes. See his "Class and Culture in Modern America: The Vision of the Landscape in the Residences of Contemporary Americans."

85. Long, "Reading Groups and the Post-Modern Crisis of Cultural Authority."

86. On the other hand, a wide range of institutional and cultural factors contribute to the creation of hierarchies between genres. On this see the work of DiMaggio, "Cultural Entrepreneurship in Nineteenth Century Boston: The Creation of an Organizational Base for High Culture in America."

87. Students of postmodernity would argue that this questioning of cultural hierarchies is characteristic of the culture of late capitalism both in Europe and in North America. Again, my interviews do not suggest that this loose-boundedness is equally present in both societies.

88. Moffatt, *Coming of Age in New Jersey*, 298.

89. An ongoing study of a high school in northern New Jersey found that the number of students who belong to the high school's intellectual subculture has been diminishing in the last ten years. This study is in part a replication of research conducted in the late seventies that found that the "intellectuals" constituted one of the main subgroups in the student body. The original study is Larkin's *Suburban Youth in Cultural Crisis*.

90. According to Bourdieu, French people who are not familiar with high culture show cultural goodwill and have a "sense of unworthiness" concerning their own class culture (*Distinction*, 320).

91. Phillips, *Post-Conservative America: People, Politics and Ideology in a Time of Crisis*. There has always been a strong streak of anti-intellectualism in the American artistic avant-garde, e.g., in the "Beat" generation as well as in the counterculture of the 1960s, and the New Left. Furthermore, the radicalism of the intellectuals often took a more cultural than political or economic focus and became alien to American mainstream culture. See Pells, *The Liberal Mind in a Conservative Age*, 403.

92. An executive staff assistant in Indianapolis declares that he admires people who are well-read as long as they are humble about it: "I feel I have a lot of respect for people who are well read but not who have to prove you that they're well read. People that, by virtue of your association with them, you're able to discern that this individual has done a lot of reading and he's done a lot of thinking. Not that they let you know, but where you're able, over a period of time, from the association, you're able to see it. Where you recognize it yourself, they don't have to prove it—that sort of thing."

93. As Coleman and Rainwater put it in *Social Standing in America*: "Income is the end, occupation, the means and education, the preparation" (68).

94. See Collins, *The Credential Society*.

95. A recent study of Stanford University undergraduates found, for instance, that roughly a quarter of the students interviewed in the late seventies had no concern for getting a liberal education. They were not open to intellectual experimentation and to exploration of new academic interests and valued a humanist education only because it "looks good" and helps you "to get into a conversation and feel comfortable" (Katchadourian and Boli, *Careerism and Intellectualism among College Students*).

96. Forty percent of a group of Rutgers University students surveyed in 1987 considered what they learned in their extracurricular activities more important than academic learning in their college experience (Moffatt, *Coming of Age in New Jersey*, 58).

97. In this context, it is interesting to note Michael Hout's recent finding that having a college degree cancels the effect of background status on intragenerational mobility in the United States. See his "More Universalism, Less Structural Mobility: The American Occupational Structure in the 1980s."

CHAPTER FIVE

1. As Paul DiMaggio and Walter Powell put it, "Institutionalized arrangements are reproduced because individuals often cannot even conceive of appropriate alternatives (or because they regard as unrealistic the alternatives they imagine). Institutions do not just constrain options: they establish the very criteria by which people discover their preferences. In other words, some of the most important sunk costs are cognitive" ("Introduction" in *The New Institutionalism in Organizational Analysis*).

2. The differences are not very important: 49 percent of the French rank 4 or 5 on the cultural scale, with 51 percent ranking 4 to 5 on the moral scale, compared to only 44 percent ranking 4 to 5 on the socioeconomic scale.

3. Sixty-nine percent of the American respondents rank 4 or 5 on the socioeconomic scale, compared to 49 percent on the moral scale and 37 percent on the cultural scale.

4. These patterns are weaker when differences within each country are taken into consideration: the three types of boundaries are equally important for the Clermontois, for instance. Fifty percent of the Clermontois score 4 or 5 on each of the three scales.

5. The term *national boundary patterns* is used here for convenience and with reservations, since patterns are identified on the basis of samples drawn only from the upper-middle class.

6. Thirty-eight percent of the Parisians and 30 percent of the Clermontois are opposed or indifferent to socioeconomic boundaries—i.e., score 0, 1, or 2 on this scale—compared to 18 percent of the Hoosiers and 16 percent of the New Yorkers. On the other hand, 45 percent of the Hoosiers and 43 percent of the New Yorkers are opposed or indifferent to cultural boundaries, compared to 23 percent of the Parisians and 35 percent of the Clermontois.

7. This suggests that the ideal type moral or socioeconomic excluder is hard to come by because most respondents express mixed standards of evaluation, with one standard predominating. The proportion of interviewees who rank high on both the socioeconomic and cultural scales are, respectively, for each site, 67 percent in New York, 60 percent in Indianapolis, 40 percent in Clermont, and 37 percent in Paris. The correlation between high cultural and socioeconomic score, however, is not significant in either country.

8. A New York radio station owner provides an example of this type of socioeconomic qua moral boundary: "If I look at somebody, no matter what field they're in, and I think that they've done it successfully, I admire that because, somehow, they had a sense of direction that made them succeed. They've been able to get it done, and they've hit that plateau, or that particular goal."

9. Forty-eight percent of the Hoosiers who score high on the socioeconomic dimen-

sion also score high on the moral one, compared to 34 percent of the New Yorkers, 35 percent of the Clermontois, and 20 percent of the Parisians. The correlation between high moral and socioeconomic score is significant and negative in both countries, but more strongly so in France than in the United States, with Kendall's Tau of $-.400$ vs. $-.273$ (.000 and .008 levels of significance). See also Chap. 3, n.65.

10. As noted in Chap. 4, 14 percent of white Americans 18 years of age and older attended classical music concerts at least once a year in 1978, compared to 9 percent of the French 15 years of age and older in 1988.

11. This is also illustrated by the recent scandals concerning the financial support that the National Endowment for the Humanities has given to art that some judge immoral. The percentage of Hoosiers and New Yorkers who are indifferent or opposed to cultural boundaries is greater than the percentage who score low on the other scales. In the case of the New Yorkers, the percentages who score 0, 1, or 2 on the moral, socioeconomic, and cultural scales are, respectively, 37 percent, 16 percent, and 43 percent. In the case of the Hoosiers, the percentages are (in the same order) 21 percent, 18 percent, and 45 percent.

12. The percentages are respectively 18 percent for the Clermontois and 38 percent for the Parisians.

13. Twenty-one percent of the Hoosiers are indifferent or opposed to moral boundaries, compared to 37 percent of the New Yorkers. Along the same line, 50 percent of the Clermontois and 62 percent of the Hoosiers score 4 or 5 on the moral scale, compared to 52 percent of the Parisians and 37 percent of the New Yorkers.

14. Forty-five percent of the Hoosiers and 35 percent of the Clermontois score low on the cultural scale, compared to 43 percent of the New Yorkers and 16 percent of the Parisians.

15. Thirty-eight percent of the Hoosiers and 50 percent of the Clermontois score 4 or 5 on the cultural scale, compared to 68 percent of the Parisians and 37 percent of the New Yorkers.

16. The Somers' D measuring the association between cultural center and moral and cultural boundaries is in both cases .11 (.01 level of significance). The Somers' D measuring the relationship between cultural center and socioeconomic boundaries is not significant for either case.

17. The difference between the average score obtained by residents of cultural centers and that obtained by residents of cultural peripheries on the three scales is larger in France than in the United States. In the French case, there is a difference of 49 points, whereas in the American case, there is a difference of only 18 points.

18. DiMaggio, "Classification in Art," 448.

19. Richard Bernstein, *Fragile Glory: A Portrait of France and the French.*

20. Finkielkraut, *La défaite de la pensée.*

21. Diana Pinto, "Toward a Mellowing of the French Identity?" 32.

22. Between 1962 and 1973 the proportion of white males between the ages of thirty-one and sixty-four who had college degrees rose 36 percent. See Hout, "More Universalism, Less Structural Mobility," 1383. On the place of culture in the consumption pattern and the lifestyle of yuppies, see Gielman and Wang, "The Year of the Yuppie"; see also Huntley, Bronson, and Walsh, "Yumpies, YAP's, Yuppies: Who Are They?" 39; and Piesman and Hartley, *The Yuppie Handbook.*

23. DiMaggio, "Classification in Art," 452–53.

24. The females have the same age average as the groups of men I interviewed. The sample comprises an equal number of for-profit workers and social and cultural specialists. The respondents have the following occupations: librarian, professor of social work,

teacher, psychiatrist, journalist, data processing manager, human relations manager, advertising senior executive, advertising account executive, portfolio manager, system engineer, banker, architect, accountant, and marketing specialist.

25. While males residing in the New York suburbs have obtained average scores of 3.1, 4.0, and 3.1 on the moral, socioeconomic, and cultural dimensions, respectively, the corresponding female means are 3.4, 3.0, and 3.8.

26. Gilligan, *In a Different Voice: Psychological Theory and Women's Development.* For a critique see Epstein in *Deceptive Distinctions: Sex, Gender, and the Social Order.*

27. In this respect it is paradoxical that some female interviewees drew boundaries against other females who were less achievement-oriented than themselves, i.e., who had chosen the "mommy track." It is also paradoxical that yet others measured the status of females by the achievement of their husband and children; the socioeconomic status of other family members was never salient in the boundary work of male interviewees.

28. See, for instance, Mohr and DiMaggio, "Patterns of Occupational Inheritance of Cultural Capital," 20.

29. Collins, "Women and the Production of Status Cultures."

30. When discussing their feelings of inferiority, females were also more likely to mention aesthetic appearance. For instance, a very successful self-employed female architect described her feelings thus: "I'm sorry I haven't had the time or the energy to maximize my looks and my clothes and my wardrobe and the whole bit . . . I feel intimidated by a very beautiful, very sophisticated female, particularly if she happens, in addition, to be a successful career woman." The topic of aesthetic appearance rarely came up during the interviews I conducted with males.

31. See Bennett Berger, "Structure and Choice in the Sociology of Culture."

32. As argued by Benedict Anderson, people who belong to the same society define their common identity by asserting a shared past and a common future embedded in specific traditions and values. See his *Imagined Communities: Reflections on the Origin and Spread of Nationalism.*

33. For a critique of the tool kit approach to culture see Bennett Berger, "Structure and Choice in the Sociology of Culture." For an exposition of this approach see Swidler, "Culture in Action." Michael Schudson suggests that Swidler's own work does not use a "tool kit" approach. See his "How Culture Works: Perspectives from Media Studies on the Efficacy of Symbols."

34. I am grateful to John Meyer for suggesting this term.

35. Schudson, "How Culture Works"; and Sperber, "Anthropology and Psychology: Toward an Epidemiology of Representations." For a microlevel analysis, see Fine, "Small Groups and Culture Creation: The Idioculture of Little League Baseball Teams."

36. See Peter Berger and Thomas Luckman, *The Social Construction of Reality: A Treatise in the Sociology of Knowledge;* Wuthnow, *Communities of Discourse: Ideology and Social Structure in the Reformation, the Enlightenment, and European Socialism;* Griswold, "A Methodological Framework for the Sociology of Culture"; Thomas, *Revivalism and Cultural Change: Christianity, Nation Building, and the Market in the Nineteenth-Century United States;* Lamont, "How to Become a Dominant French Philosopher: The Case of Jacques Derrida."

37. The issue of determination and voluntarism is central to the current theoretical debates in sociology. See Alexander, "The New Theoretical Movement."

38. Hollinger, "The Problem of Pragmatism in American History," 24.

39. Canovan, *Populism,* chap. 1.

40. Jacoby, *The Last Intellectuals: American Culture in the Age of Academe;* Perry, *Intellectual Life in America: A History,* chap. 7.

41. On Americanism as an ideology see Hartz, *The Liberal Tradition in America;* and

Harrington, *Socialism*; for a detailed and recent discussion of Americanism see Lipset, *Continental Divide*, esp. chap. 2. On civil religion see Bellah, *The Broken Covenant*.

42. Lipset, "Why No Socialism in the United States," 53.

43. Hunt, *Politics, Culture and Class in the French Revolution*, esp. chaps. 1 and 6.

44. Woloch, *Eighteenth-Century Europe: Tradition and Progress 1715–1789*, 184.

45. Ibid., 198.

46. On the strength of socialist politics in France see Dalton, *Citizen Politics in Western Democracies: Public Opinion and Political Parties in the United States, Great Britain, West Germany and France.*

47. Furthermore, as pointed out by Lipset and Rokkan, religion has often defined the central ideological cleavages of American society: "The struggles between the Jeffersonians and the Federalists, the Jacksonians and the Whigs, the Democrats and the Republicans centered on contrasting conceptions of public morality and pitted Puritans and other Protestants against Deists, Freemasons, and the immigrant Catholics and Jews. The accelerating influx of lower-class immigrants into the metropolitan areas . . . accentuated the contrasts between . . . the backward and the advanced states of the Union" (Lipset and Rokkan, "Cleavage Structure, Party Systems and Voter Alignments, 12).

48. On the effect of religious heterogeneity on tolerance see Weil, "The Variable Effects of Education on Liberal Attitudes."

49. Diana Crane has shown that the institutions that produce urban local cultures are losing influence to what she calls the core media—television, Hollywood films, major newspapers and news magazines—and the peripheral media (books and magazine publishing, popular music, and radio), with the peripheral media reaching specific taste publics, while the core media reach a large and relatively undifferentiated audience. "High Culture vs. Popular Culture Revisited: A Reconceptualization of Recorded Cultures."

50. See Meyer's "The Effects of Education as an Institution."

51. Ibid., 69.

52. Hayward, "Elusive Autonomy: Education and Public Enterprise," 191.

53. Minority members came to use the schools to contest the hegemony of Western and white culture in the educational world. Black leaders wanted "the public schools to legitimize cultural differences, to teach their own history, to use their languages in the classroom, and honor a diversity not encompassed by Anglo conformity" (Tyack and Hansot, *Managers of Virtue: Public School Leadership in America, 1820–1980*, 224–25).

54. Ringer, *Education and Society in Modern Europe*. Historically French teachers have had great prestige because they played a central role linking the local population with the central state and in acculturating the population into French culture by diffusing the language of the elite. See Eugen Weber, *Peasants into Frenchmen: The Modernization of Rural France, 1879–1914*, chap. 18.

55. Kamens and Ross, "Chartering National Educational Systems: The Institutionalization of Education for Elite Recruitment and Its Consequences."

56. "In the summer of 1982, many print media and, according to some opinion polls, many Frenchmen criticized the three public service television channels for an emphasis on educational and cultural programmes when the man in the street wanted entertainment as he ate and digested his daily bread. Such facile and carping criticism appeared to have carried the day when, in February 1986, the programme schedules of the two new commercial channels authorized by the socialist government of Laurent Fabius were announced: 'la Cinq' and 'la Six' promised entertainment with a vengeance" (Palmer, "Media and Communications Policy in France under the Socialists, 1981–86: Failing to Grasp the Correct Nettle?" 131.

57. See Schudson, *Advertising, the Uneasy Persuasion*; Gitlin, *Inside Prime Time*.

58. A measure of this support is the fact that three-quarters of the French Ministry of Foreign Affairs budget goes to the Direction générale des affaires culturelles, scientifiques et techniques, which is responsible for the diffusion of French culture and the French language. French cultural diplomacy has the explicit goal of increasing national prestige. See Tovell, "A Comparison of Canadian, French, British and German International Cultural Policy." On this topic see also Fumaroli, L'Etat culturel: Essai sur une religion moderne.

59. France has only one large private foundation, the Maeght foundation. In 1968, tax incentives were created to facilitate more private patronage, but with little effect. See Cabanne, Le pouvoir culturel sous la Ve République, 207.

60. In Literary France (p. 131), Clark compared the content of the American magazine Time and the French magazine L'Express, using a random sample of issues drawn from 1973 to 1974 and 1977 to 1978. She found that L'Express puts more emphasis on literary matters: 12 percent of its articles dealt with books, as compared to 6.9 percent in Time. Also, 24 percent of the articles in the L'Express issues analyzed by Clark pertained to culture, in contrast to 16 percent in the Time issues.

61. This popularization is discussed in several monographs on French intellectuals. For instance, see Debray, Teachers, Writers and Celebrities: The Intellectuals in Modern France; and Hamon and Rotman, Les intellocrates: Expédition en haute intelligentsia.

62. See Lamont, "How to Become a Dominant French Philosopher," 613.

63. This sample includes such journals and magazines as The Nation, The Public Interest, Dissent, Partisan Review, Commentary, and The New York Review of Books. See Lamont, "The Production of Culture in France and the United States since World War II," 172.

64. Clark, "Literary Culture in France and the United States."

65. On their access to the larger public, see Boudon, "L'intellectuel et ses publics: Les singularités françaises." It should be noted that according to George Ross the influence of intellectuals has been declining in France over the last decades. See his "The Decline of the Left Intellectual in Modern France."

66. Verdès-Leroux, Au service du parti: Le parti Communiste, les intellectuels et la culture (1944–1956).

67. Jacoby, The Last Intellectuals. On restraints imposed by the university system on intellectuals, see Finkelstein, The American Academic Profession: A Synthesis of Social Scientific Inquiry since World War II.

68. Coser, Men of Ideas: A Sociologist's View.

69. See Perry, Intellectual Life in America: A History, chap. 7.

70. See Lipset, "Why No Socialism in the United States?" esp. 50–120.

71. See e.g. Andrew Shonfeld, Modern Capitalism: The Changing Balance of Public and Private Power, chap. 5; Peter Hall, Governing the Economy: The Politics of State Intervention in Britain and France, chaps. 6 and 7; Dobbin, States and Industrial Cultures.

72. Mermèt, Francoscopie, les Français: Qui sont-ils? Ou vont-ils? 216.

73. Compiled from U.S. Department of Commerce, Bureau of the Census, Statistical Abstract of the United States 1987.

74. For a French-American comparison, see James, ed., The Nonprofit Sector: Studies in Comparative Culture and Policy; and Veugelers and Lamont, "France: Alternative Locations for Public Debate." On the American case, see Rudney, "The Scope and Dimensions of Nonprofit Activity." Generalizations about the importance of France's voluntary sector are difficult to make due to a lack of information. See Roudet, "Bilan des recherches sur la vie associative."

75. For an exploration of this issue see Lamont, "The Growth of the Social Sciences and the Decline of the Humanities in Quebec: A Macro Explanation of Recent Changes."

76. It should be noted that there exists contradictory evidence concerning the importance of intragenerational mobility in France and the United States since World War II. For a review of this literature see Lipset, "Why No Socialism in the United States?" 103–10. On the effect of abundance on American culture see Susman, "Introduction: Toward a History of the Culture of Abundance."

77. Craig Calhoun has shown that in the United States the importance of cities as communities has been declining because a decreasing number of them constitute communities of individuals linked to one another directly or indirectly by long-term social ties and committed to the survival of political and cultural institutions. See his "Populist Politics, Communication Media, and Large Scale Integration."

78. For instance, Ruth Horowitz analyzed how the mainstream American achievement ideology is attenuated in the Chicano culture by cultural requirements for familial and ethnic solidarity. See her *Honor and the American Dream: Culture and Identity in a Chicano Community.*

79. See Smitherman, *Talkin' and Testifyin': The Language of Black Americans.*

80. On these changes see Diana Pinto, "Toward a Mellowing of the French Identity?"

81. On this point see the work of Melvin L. Kohn and his collaborators.

82. This is surprising given that the literature suggests that older men tend to be less ambitious and to put less stress on money than younger ones. See e.g. Zussman, *Mechanics of the Middle Class,* 153.

CHAPTER SIX

1. See also Weiss, *Staying the Course.*

2. Max Weber, *Economy and Society,* vol. 1, 25. It is not my intent to engage in the debates surrounding Weber's concept of rationality. For a discussion of these and other types of Weberian categories of rationality, see Kalberg, "Max Weber's Types of Rationality: Cornerstones for the Analysis of Rationalization Processes in History." See also Wallace, "Rationality, Human Nature and Society in Weber's Theory."

3. Inglehart, *Culture Shift,* esp. chap. 9.

4. Lipset, *Political Man,* chap. 10.

5. Lamont, "Cultural Capital and the Liberal Political Attitudes of Professionals: A Comment on Brint."

6. Using multiple regressions, Hunter et al. also found that supporting traditional family structures and traditional morality are as strong predictors of attitudes toward capitalism as is occupational proximity to profiting. They take proximity to profit making to indicate the relative autonomy of different types of knowledge for the market. Furthermore, they read oppositional attitudes as reflecting a need to challenge not only the legitimacy of the market system but also the legitimacy of all other forms of bourgeois authority. See Hunter, Herrman, and Jarvis, "Cultural Elites and Political Values."

7. Macy, "New-Class Dissent among Social-Cultural specialists: The Effects of Occupational Self-Direction and Location in the Public Sector." Using analysis of survey data, Macy also found that relationship with the market economy, i.e., sectoral location, is a better predictor of dissent than level of self-direction at work.

8. Michael W. Macy explains (in ibid.) the dissenting attitudes of social and cultural specialists not by their occupation but by their sectoral location: "The causal pattern points to dissent emerging within the public and nonprofit sectors, among employees

whose greater tendency to disdain business and profit-driven activity reflects their disengagement from (if not competition with) the market economy. While more refined occupational categories . . . might reveal ideological influence net of sectoral location, there is no evidence here that the adversary culture emanates from 'humanistic' or 'social-science and arts-related' occupational activities." (347). Macy writes that his remarks on the lesser significance of occupation are inconclusive because the data he uses does not contain specific information on the occupation of his respondents.

9. Steven Brint's findings support the conclusion I drew from the Quebec case that oppositional patterns are particularly strong in countries with large public economies and strong left-of-center parties. See his "The Social Bases and National Contexts of Middle-Class Liberalism and Dissent in Western Societies: A Comparative Study," 17. For Brint's criticism of the "distance to profit making" thesis, see his "Classification Struggles: Reply to Lamont." See also Lamont, "New Middle Class Liberalism . . ."

10. For instance, Brint indicates that, overall, college graduates are quite conservative on economic issues and on basic system commitments, but that they comprise one of the "most liberal strat[a] on issues involving the protection of civil rights, on many social control and defense issues, and in their support for laissez-faire in personal morality" ("The Social Bases and National Context . . . ," 2). Because this chapter is not primarily concerned with political liberalism, I forego the task of describing how the authors just discussed qualify their analysis of the relationship between economic rationality and political liberalism, and also the task of discussing the importance of other determinants of political attitudes. For a review of the literature, see Brint, "The Political Attitudes of Professionals."

11. In an analysis of the New Class in the Netherlands, Hanspeter Kriesi found that support for new social movements was stronger among "young specialists in the social and cultural services and among young administrative specialists in public service." He argues, however, that the central conflict among professionals and managers does not oppose private sector workers to workers in the public and nonprofit sectors, but opposes people whose knowledge is instrumental to the running of large-scale organizations (technocrats) to specialists, i.e., people "who try to defend their own and their clients' relative autonomy against the interventions of the 'technostructure,'" this conflict superceding the one opposing occupations with high and low instrumentality to profit making. See his "New Social Movements and the New Class in the Netherlands."

12. French political scientists have also found that support for the French Socialist party is particularly strong among social and cultural specialists and public sector workers as well as among civil servants and teachers. See Capdevielle et al., *France de gauche, vote à droite*. Also Grunberg and Mouriaux, *L'univers politique et syndical des cadres*. I came to similar conclusions in an analysis of support for the Parti Québécois in Québec. See Lamont, "New Middle Class Liberalism and Autonomy from Profit-Making: The Case of Quebec."

13. Other authors have stressed relationship with profit making as a determinant of attitudes. Concerning the influence of situs on the internal segmentation of the professional/managerial class see in particular Daniel Bell, *The Coming Crisis of Post-Industrial Society*.

14. For instance, in the words of Stephen Crawford, engineers "value efficiency and economic growth, view the market as a natural mechanism for achieving both, and thus accept business considerations as appropriate criteria for economic and engineering decision-making" (*Technical Workers in an Advanced Society*, 236).

15. A few participants classified in this category could have been included in category 4. This is particularly the case for self-employed professionals such as physicians and dentists whose professional expertise is not directly instrumental to economic ratio-

nality. The same holds for architects who are classified in category 4. There exists no single appropriate way to classify these professionals because there are differences within these professions themselves in the extent to which their members are submitted to economic rationality.

16. French for-profit workers also draw boundaries against state employees who are often seen as morally flawed, and specifically as lazy and opportunistic. A Clermont accountant is quite critical of them when he says: "When I work forty hours in my office, I work forty hours minus five minutes. Civil servants are in their office for forty hours, but they work twenty hours. The rest of the time, they read their newspapers. My newspaper arrives in my mailbox, and I read it at night. [Also man] civil servants spend their days following the racing statistics to bet on horses, and the women do their shopping during their work hours [or] they go register their kids in courses. [They do] everything [but their work]."

17. I follow Etienne Schweisguth ("Les salariés moyens sont-ils des petits-bourgeois?" (692) in linking moral and cultural orientation to broader ideological systems which include religious and political attitudes.

18. In our French sample, 69 percent of the social and cultural specialists declared themselves at the left of the political spectrum, as did 50 percent of their American counterparts. On the other hand, 72 percent of the French for-profit workers positioned themselves on the right or at the center of the political spectrum, as did 69 percent of the American for-profit workers. The American social and cultural specialists are more divided than the French, given that 50 percent of them located themselves at the center or to the right of the political spectrum, compared to 31 percent of the French social and cultural specialists.

19. Their average ranking for this type of boundary was 3.7 as compared to 3.1 for for-profit workers. For details, see Appendix IV, table A.4.

20. This group scores an average on the socioeconomic scale of 4.0, compared to 3.6 for social and cultural specialists. The Somer's D measuring the relationship between occupational aggregates and cultural boundaries is $-.22$ at the .001 level of significance, in favor of social and cultural specialists.

21. The Somers' D measuring the relationship between occupational aggregates and socioeconomic boundaries is .16 at the .04 level of signification for socioeconomic boundaries. This means that in our sample the for-profit workers are less likely to draw cultural boundaries than social and cultural specialists are likely to draw socioeconomic boundaries. Available studies conducted by management specialists found that managers in the nonprofit sector are less likely to be highly motivated by economic success than their private sector counterparts. See Rawls, Ullrich, and Nelson, Jr., "A Comparison of Managers Entering or Reentering the Profit and Nonprofit Sectors."

22. These groups have the same general average score of 3.3 on the moral scale. The Somers' D on this dimension is not significant. Earlier studies have shown that professionals are generally more liberal on personal morality issues—abortion, sexual morality, divorce, and general moral nonrestrictiveness—than business executives (see Brint, "The Political Attitudes of Professionals"). If most of our social and cultural specialists are professionals whereas for-profit workers comprise business executives as well as professionals, we can only conclude that our findings do not support these earlier studies—assuming that the score on the moral scale reflects attitudes toward personal morality.

23. These patterns cannot be accounted for entirely by differences in the social trajectory of each category of interviewees: there exists a small difference in the number

of for-profit workers and social and cultural specialists who are upwardly mobile, given that 56 percent of the for-profit workers fall into this category, compared to 47 percent of the social and cultural specialists.

24. Respectively, 98 percent and 21 percent of both groups draw strong cultural boundaries. The previous statement is not tautological: people can rank high on the cultural scale without being intellectuals if, for instance, they stress intelligence and self-actualization rather than refinement or the fact of having a strong intellectual culture. The association between intellectuals and the drawing strong of cultural boundaries is .85 at the .001 level of significance, while the association between intellectuals and the drawing of socioeconomic boundaries is .22 at the .022 level of significance; the association with moral boundaries is insignificant.

25. While in Paris, 38 and 29 percent, respectively, of the social and cultural specialists of categories 1 and 2 are in lower-income categories (i.e., their total household income is less than 289,000 FF a year); only 1 and 20 percent of the Parisian self-employed and salaried for-profit workers had income comparably low. The contrast between the two occupational aggregates is even more striking in Clermont-Ferrand, where 85 and 57 percent, respectively, of the social and cultural specialists of categories 1 and 2 are in the lowest income category, compared to 20 percent of both categories of for-profit workers. Along the same lines, in Indianapolis these proportions are, respectively, 7 percent; 17 percent; 0 percent; and 11 percent, the lowest income category being defined in the United States as less than $49,000. In New York, only social and cultural specialists are in the lowest income group. For details, see Appendix I.

26. In *Distinction* (310), Bourdieu points at the fact that social and cultural specialists value culture more than executives. He explains differences in boundary work across occupational groups, not by their relationship with economic rationality or by their market position but by the amount of economic and cultural capital they have. The relative impact of these various factors in determining boundary work needs to be assessed empirically.

27. See Appendix IV, table A.5. People classified in category 1 draw on average slightly stronger cultural boundaries than those in category 2: 66 percent of them score 4 or 5 on this scale, compared to 51 percent of those in category 2. On the other hand, members of category 2 are slightly more socioeconomically exclusive than those in category 1, with 68 percent of them scoring 4 or 5 on the socioeconomic scale compared to 43 percent for those in category 1. It should be noted that these percentages and those presented in the following pages are based on a relatively small number of respondents.

28. Accordingly, Everett C. Ladd found that doctors (and lawyers) score next to social and cultural specialists on the "new liberalism" scale. See Ladd, "Pursuing the New Class: Social Theory and Survey Data."

29. Seventy percent of them score 4 or 5 on this scale compared to 63 percent of those in category 3. Interviews with self-employed for-profit workers partly reflect these patterns in boundary work. In particular, many expressed their feelings of superiority toward salaried for-profit workers by referring to properly socioeconomic criteria. For instance, they often view themselves as having more power than their salaried counterpart, because they are able to fence off corporate politics.

30. Only in France are cultural boundaries stronger among the salaried for-profit workers than among the self-employed. In the United States only 6 percent of them score 4 or 5 on the cultural scale compared to 27 percent for category 4 (these figures are, respectively, 40 percent and 55 percent in France).

31. It should be noted that the intensity of the opposition between social and cultural specialists and for-profit workers is analyzed by Brint when, using survey data, he

studied the magnitude of the antibusiness attitudes of social and cultural specialists. He found that the strength of the opposition has been greatly exaggerated by the literature on the new class. See Brint, "'New Class' and Cumulative Trend Explanations of the Liberal Political Attitudes of Professionals."

32. Brint, "Is the U.S. Pattern Typical? The Politics of Professionals in Other Industrial Democracies."

33. Sixty-seven percent of them rank 4 or 5 in contrast to 52 percent of the American social and cultural specialists. For details on the boundary scores of all groups, see Appendix IV, table A.5.

34. Their mean score is 2.9 on the scale of socioeconomic exclusiveness, as compared to 3.8 for Americans. The strength of the relationship between nationality and socioeconomic exclusion for social and cultural specialists from category 1 is .24 at the .06 level of significance. This signifies that American social and cultural specialists are slightly more socioeconomically selective than their French counterparts. The relationship is stronger for category 2 respondents: for this group the Somers' D measuring the relationship between nationality and the tendency to draw socioeconomic boundaries is .44 at the .02 level of significance.

35. Fifty percent of them score 4 or 5 on the cultural scale in contrast to 22 percent in the United States. This contrast is stronger if only salaried for-profit workers are considered: the Somers' D measuring the relationship between cultural boundaries and nationality for this group is − .51 at .001 level of significance. The Somers' D measuring the relationship between nationality and cultural exclusion is insignificant for occupational categories 1, 2, and 4.

36. This stronger cultural orientation of French for-profit workers is also reflected in their defense of general culture discussed in previous chapters. As an electronic engineer explains cogently: "We should not be handicapped. There is nothing worse than someone who only knows how to do his job and who cannot do other things. There is nothing you can do with someone like that. If you want to get the most out of what you do for yourself, or even for the firm, it is important to have a good general culture, and not only hire specialists . . . otherwise it is impossible to exchange. Professional expertise is fed not only by techniques and commerce but also by culture in general . . . a specialist will do a nice little job, but it won't get any further. One needs to have a broader view."

37. They average 4.3 on the socioeconomic scale, in contrast to 3.1 for the Parisians and 4.1 for the Clermontois.

38. To cite Steven Kalberg: "At times, owing to a sheer accidental juxtaposition of factors, interests crystallize to form a cohesive stratum. This stratum could, if another random configuration of historical forces congealed, carry a specific rationalization process. Civil servants, e.g., carried formal rationalization processes as a consequence of their typical daily activities in organizations. Other strata, as often as not, carried rationalization processes antagonistic to those upheld by bureaucrats, as, e.g., when religious intellectuals propounded substantive rationalization processes. As further carriers of still other rationalization processes became institutionalized in legitimate orders within a society, a labyrinth of such processes evolved" ("Max Weber's Types of Rationality," 1172).

39. The social trajectory of respondents is determined by comparing their occupation and level of education with that of their fathers', using Duncan's socioeconomic index. Respondents fall into four categories: the downwardly mobile (12 percent of the total sample), the stable (35 percent), the slightly mobile (10 percent), and the very upwardly mobile (42 percent).

40. Daniel Bell, The Coming Crisis of Post-Industrial Society, 167−265. During this period the position of the self-employed has become more precarious due to the increased

industrial and commercial concentration. This was reflected in some of the interviews I conducted with self-employed professionals and businessmen.

41. Using data from the early seventies, R. Erikson and J. H. Goldthorpe found that intergenerational mobility has been slightly greater in the United States than in Great Britain. They explain the difference by structural phenomena, and particularly the higher rate of growth of the professional segments in the United States rather than by an alleged American exceptionalism (R. Erikson and J. H. Goldthorpe, "Are American Rates of Social Mobility Exceptionally High? New Evidence on an Old Issue"). Their previous work had established that the British rates of mobility are similar to the French. See R. Erikson, J. H. Goldthorpe, and L. Portocarero. "Intergenerational Class Mobility in Three Western European Societies: England, France and Sweden."

42. It should be noted that some studies of intragenerational mobility show slightly more upward mobility in France than in the United States when all classes are considered. See Haller, Konig, Krause, and Hurz, "Patterns of Career Mobility and Structural Positions in Advanced Capitalist Societies: A Comparison of Men in Austria, France and the United States."

43. The relationship between mobility and the tendency to draw socioeconomic boundaries is a weak one at .2 at the .000 level of significance. Other studies support our findings concerning the fact that the upwardly mobile put a stronger emphasis on socioeconomic boundaries than other groups. For instance, in *The Managers*, Diane Margolis writes that her interviewees, most of whom are from blue-collar families, are often very impressed by social mobility (91).

44. Seventy percent of them draw very strong socioeconomic boundaries, compared to 62 percent of those who have been somewhat upwardly mobile, 53 percent of the downwardly mobile, and 36 percent of the so-called stable individuals.

45. The number of downwardly mobile participants is roughly equal in the four research sites: they represent 15 percent of the sample in New York and Indianapolis and 8 percent in Paris and Clermont-Ferrand.

46. Fifty-nine percent of them draw very strong cultural boundaries. So did 63 percent of those with stable trajectories, but only 33 percent of the very upwardly mobile and 35 percent of the mobile. I find a weak relationship between mobility and cultural exclusion with a Somers' D of − .24 at the .0001 level of significance. In *Distinction*, Bourdieu points at the fact that people who have a blocked social trajectory tend to be culturally exclusive (286).

47. Bourdieu proposes that the upwardly mobile are more morally exclusive than others. See *Distinction*, 333.

48. The respective percentages of individuals who draw antisocioeconomic boundaries in each of these groups are 22 percent, 10 percent, 11 percent, and 3 percent. In her book on downward mobility, *Falling from Grace*, Katherine Newman has documented how upper-middle-class men try to reconcile their old professional and personal identities with their new ones. Because she studied men who find themselves suddenly unemployed rather than men who are downwardly mobile in relation to their father's socioeconomic status, her findings do not directly apply to the men with whom I met.

49. The relationship between a respondent's mobility and the length of time that his family has enjoyed middle-class status is a a very strong negative one: − .63 at the .0001 level of significance.

50. There is no significant relationship as measured by Somers' D between how long the respondents' families had been upper-middle class and their tendency to draw moral and socioeconomic boundaries. On the average, 55 percent of the first-generation upper-middle-class respondents score 4 or 5 on the moral scale in contrast to 37 percent of the

third and fourth generation respondents. These percentages are, respectively, 60 and 50 percent in the case of socioeconomic boundaries.

51. Only 32 percent of the participants who are first-generation upper-middle class draw strong cultural boundaries compared to 78 percent of interviewees whose families have been in the upper-middle class for three generations and more. The relationship between the length of time that the families of respondents have enjoyed upper-middle-class status and the strength of the cultural boundaries they draw is .31 at the .0001 level of significance. In Paris and Indianapolis, more of the first-generation upper-middle-class participants are for-profit workers, whereas the opposite is true in New York and Clermont-Ferrand. Consequently, the identified boundary patterns for first-generation upper-middle-class respondents cannot be accounted for by their concentration within one occupational aggregate.

52. This is reflected in the fact that some of them tend to stress technical expertise and instrumental knowledge over high cultural attainment. The attitude of an Indianapolis accountant whose father was a blue-collar worker is typical: "In college I took liberal arts courses only to fill my requirements. My focus there was basically an honors business degree. I just focused on learning about my chosen area, so I was prepared when I got out . . . I did not want to spend any more time in the academic environment than I had to. I was ready to go out and get a job . . . The academics seemed to be a stop on the way, a place to stop to pick up knowledge before you go to what you're going to do for the rest of your life."

53. In their book on the undergraduate population at Stanford University, Katcha-dourian and Boli found that 29 percent of the students who were careerists (i.e., who in my terminology have showed a maximum degree of socioexclusiveness) came from families of lower socioeconomic status, compared to 14 percent of the more intellectually oriented students. On the other hand, 20 percent of the careerist students came from families of high socioeconomic status, compared to 36 percent of the students who are more intellectual in orientation (*Careerism and Intellectualism among College Students*, 93). This indicates that first-generation members of the upper-middle class have a more instrumental view of knowledge and do not value intellectual achievement as an end in itself.

54. The relationship between tolerance and the length of time that the interviewees' families were part of the upper-middle class is −.16 at the .005 level of significance.

55. In order to examine only the most clearly contrasted types of boundary-drawing patterns, the analysis focuses on first- and third-generations upper-middle-class respondents, while ignoring those who are second-generation upper-middle class.

56. Seventy-eight percent of them score 4 or 5 on the cultural scale, compared to 32 percent for first-generation respondents. Again, national patterns reinforce some of the group specific patterns as 93 percent of the Parisians who are third-generation upper-middle-class members more often score 4 or 5 on the cultural scales than other interviewees. These percentages are, respectively, 70 percent for the Clermontois, 70 percent for the New Yorkers, and, surprisingly, 80 percent for the Hoosiers. The cultural exclusiveness of third-generation members of the upper-middle class is underscored in *Distinction* (265), where Bourdieu discusses their epicurean attitudes. See also Boltanski, *Les cadres*, 125.

57. In *Social Standing in America*, Coleman and Rainwater note that those who have a higher socioeconomic status are more likely to take into consideration occupational prestige, family history, civic activities, cultural style and level, and membership in high status social circles when assessing status whereas other respondents focus more on economic success (49 and 79). This supports our finding that third-generation members of the upper-middle class are more culturally exclusive.

58. For a description of the culture of this group see Mantoux, *BCBG: Le guide du bon chic bon genre.*

59. This study has serious implications for Inglehart's postmaterialist values thesis presented in *The Silent Revolution: Changing Values and Political Style among Western Publics* and more recently in *Culture Shift.* Although I cannot present all of them here, suffice it to say that Inglehart's survey items unnecessarily limit the range of opposition between materialist and postmaterialists. Also, his studies do not adequately consider the role of morality in shaping political attitudes.

CHAPTER SEVEN

1. For individuals who stress socioeconomic boundaries, status and esteem are the same thing. This could be different for moral and cultural boundaries. More work is needed on this topic.

2. On this topic see also the work of Sherry Ortner who studies how class differences are reproduced by being displaced to other arenas, such as sexual discourse. She argues, for instance, that in middle-class families parents put down sexual attitudes associated with the working class, thereby reinforcing middle-class culture. See in particular her "Reading America: Preliminary Notes on Class and Culture."

3. Bowles and Gintis, *Schooling in Capitalist America,* 102–24. These authors show that socioeconomic background is a better predictor of economic attainment than I.Q.

4. According to Kerckhoff (*Socialization and Social Class,* 46), middle-class parents are particularly concerned with the psychological development of their children, as evidenced by their frequent use of reasoning and of positive reinforcement techniques such as praise. In contrast, working-class parents make greater use of power and show greater concern for external conformity.

5. Working-class people in general often show strong anti-intellectual tendencies as well as little interest in high culture (Jeffries and Ransford, *Social Stratification: A Multiple Hierarchy Approach,* 124–26; Gecas, "The Influence of Social Class on Socialization," 391; and Halle, *America's Working Man,* 48).

6. Lower-class members are less able to deliver abstract information than middle-class members: they lack distance from material necessities and economic urgencies and therefore tend to perceive the world in concrete and immediate terms. Leonard Schatzman and Anselm Strauss were the first to write on this difference in their article "Social Class and Modes of Communication." Other sociologists point at differences to the extent in which middle- and working-class parents work on developing the linguistic and cognitive abilities of their children as well as their use of reasoning. See Kerckhoff, *Socialization and Social Class,* chap. 7; Kohn, "Cross-National Research as an Analytic Strategy;" and Heath, *Ways with Words;* Basil Bernstein, *Class, Codes and Control.*

7. One's position in the social stratification system is linked to the structural imperatives of his or her job, which in turn are linked to components of personality. Members of the middle class value more self-directedness because this quality is needed to perform well in professional and managerial occupations. See Kohn, Naoi, Schoenbach, Schooler, and Slomczynski, "Position in the Class Structure and Psychological Functioning: A Comparative Analysis of the United States, Japan and Poland." It should be noted that the size of class effect on values is relatively small. However, in *Ain't No Making It: Leveled Aspirations in a Low-Income Neighborhood,* Jay MacLeod has showed that working-class members are more resistant and less conformist than studies in the fifties suggested.

8. On egalitarianism in middle- and working-class families, see Jeffries and Ransford, *Social Stratification,* 124–26. On the present orientation of the working and lower class, see

Schatzman and Strauss, "Social Class and Modes of Communication." Finally, on rationality in the working class, see Schneider and Smith, *Class Differences in American Kinship*, chap. 4.

9. As shown by Halle in *America's Working Man*, members of the working class tend to be less career-oriented, and more person-oriented than middle-class members (50). However, here again we find contradictory evidence. For instance, in *The American Perception of Class*, Vanneman and Cannon find that working-class men look down at middle-class white-collar workers who make a living by "pushing paper" instead of "really working." Sennett and Cobb make a similar point in *The Hidden Injuries of Class*.

10. For a review of this literature see Bronfenbrenner, "Socialization and Social Class through Time and Space."

11. MacLeod, *Ain't No Making It*, 117. This rejection of achievement ideology has been associated with the fact that members of the working class are often forced to do routine work. See Jeffries and Ransford, *Social Stratification*, 124–26, quoting Albert K. Cohen and Harold M. Hodges, "Characteristics of the Lower Blue-Collar Class." On the adoption of unrealistic models of achievement, see Powers, *Second Class Finish: The Effect of a Working Class High School*.

12. Kerckhoff, *Socialization and Social Class*, 45; Hyman, "The Value Systems of Different Classes," 492.

13. James A. Davis, "Achievement Variables and Class Cultures," 584.

14. Mary R. Jackman and M. J. Muha, "Education and Intergroup Attitudes"; and Stouffer, *Communism, Conformity and Civil Liberty. A Cross-Section of the Nation Speaks Its Mind*.

15. According to Steven Brint, civil liberties issues are notably more important for professionals than they are for nonprofessional workers and business executives. This is especially the case for issues associated with freedom of choice and self-expression, including sexual morality, divorce, and abortion. See Brint, "The Political Attitudes of Professionals," 389; see also Lipset, *Political Man*.

16. This "cultural fundamentalism" also provides guidelines on the use of alcohol and pornography, the rights of homosexuals, and "profamily" and "decency" issues. See Wood and Hughes, "The Moral Basis of Moral Reforms: Status Discontent vs. Culture and Socialization as Explanations of Anti-Pornography Social Movement Adherence," 89. Moral conservatism is also associated with factors other than class (e.g., age, region of residence, size of the city of residence, etc.).

17. Hurrelman, in *Social Structure and Personality Development*, questions the validity of assumption of class specific contours of social and material living condition. He argues that the class specificity has broken down in the last three decades.

18. It is interesting that according to Reeve Vanneman and Lynn Weber Cannon American middle-class people are very inclusive and tend to assimilate skilled and affluent blue-collar workers in a broad middle class, whereas the working class clearly differentiates between professionals and managers and themselves. See Vanneman and Cannon, *The American Perception of Class*, 284.

19. Most of these class differences are likely to hold and even be accentuated in the French context. The literature on French working-class culture suggests that the latter is more differentiated from middle- and upper-middle-class culture than its American counterpart.

20. Space limitations prevent me from carefully examining this literature here. For a review see Lamont and Wuthnow, "Betwixt and Between." See also the discussion of Bourdieu's work below.

21. Anthony Giddens's notion of the duality of structure describes the process by which inequality at the macrolevel is generated as an unintended consequence of micro-level interaction. See his *The Constitution of Society: Outline of a Theory of Structuration*, chap. 1.

22. Durkheim, *The Elementary Forms of Religious Life*, 260. The comments made by a fifty-nine-year-old Indianapolis forester exemplify that collective classificatory effects presuppose common definitions of status signals. The interviewee explains his indifference to signals whose meaning he does not know: "One day I met with a doctor and we were going somewhere and he said he was going to drive this Opel. Now, I still don't know exactly, but I do know now that an Opel is supposed to be something that, you know, you have some money, that you drive this. He was talking about this, and it didn't mean anything to me at all. I'd as soon drive my pickup trucks. . . . So, that didn't mean anything."

23. Moral boundaries are likely to be more strongly bounded in the United States given the tradition of moral restrictiveness and particularly the importance of fundamentalism. In France, however, a tradition of rigid ideological polarization also can be interpreted as a sign of moral rigidity.

24. The association between tolerance and likelihood to draw frequent moral boundaries is moderately strong, with a Somers' D of .25 at the .01 level of significance. The relationships between tolerance and socioeconomic and cultural boundaries is insignificant.

25. This can be studied using the experimental techniques developed by Berger and Zelditch in their work on the effects of ascribed characteristics on work performance and expectation. See Joseph Berger and Morris Zelditch, eds., *Status, Rewards, and Influence*. On the process by which specific clusters of cues are used to assign definite or diffused status characteristics to self or others, see also Nemeth, "Reflection on the Dialogue between Status and Style."

26. Studies that deal with this topic include Mehan, "Beneath the Skin and between the Ears: A Case Study in the Politics of Representation"; and Mehan's "Understanding Inequality in Schools: The Contribution of Interpretive Studies." See also Lareau, "Uncovering the Capital in Cultural Capital: Social Class and the Construction of School Careers." It should be noted that Pierre Bourdieu's early work did not concretely analyze how high status signals translate into social profits. It simply demonstrated the existence of an association between cultural capital and social attainment.

27. One of the most widely cited critiques is Sen, "Rational Fools: A Critique of the Behavioral Foundations of Economic Theory." For a recent sociological assessment of neoclassical economics, see Block, *Postindustrial Possibilities: A Critique of Economic Discourse*, esp. chap. 2. A review article that goes beyond the standard criticisms is Zelizer's, "Beyond the Polemics on the Market: Establishing a Theoretical and Empirical Agenda."

28. I am primarily concerned here with rational choice theorists who study economic rather than sociological issues. In my view, rational choice contributions that attempt to universalize the logic of maximization to all spheres of life, such as that of Gary Becker, propose a model of human action that is so general that it loses its utility.

29. From a rational choice perspective altruism and advocacy are explained by self-interest rather than by moral values which follow a universalistic rather than individualistic logic. On this point see in particular Paul Hirsch, Stuart Michaels, and Ray Friedman, "'Dirty Hands' versus 'Clean Models': Is Sociology in Danger of Being Seduced by Economics?" See also Etzioni, *The Moral Dimension: Toward a New Economics*, 34; and Wolfe, *Whose Keeper?* 32. For a sociological defense see Friedman and Hechter, "The Contribution of Rational Choice Theory to Macrosociological Research."

30. On this topic, see Granovetter, "Economic Action and Social Structure: The Problem of Embeddedness." See also Dobbin, *States and Industrial Cultures*.

31. One of the objectives of the growing field of economic sociology is to analyze "how does an individual weigh the relative value of more money against more leisure" and to criticize economists who have a "naturalized view of economy that ignores the cultural context of behavior." See Block, *Postindustrial Possibilities*, 23 and 28.

32. It would be interesting to analyze the social trajectories of the most influential neoclassical economists to see whether they share the same socioeconomic characteristics as individuals who value economic maximization highly.

33. Structuralists generally define their perspective against voluntarist approaches to emphasize how access to various resources (e.g., state capacity, social networks, property, military strength) shape social action and, particularly, the dynamic between classes, center and periphery, state and society. They conceptualize culture as located in independent subjective individual worldviews rather than in broad shared cultural repertoires. Therefore, their view of culture is essentially astructural. For a critique of such perspectives, see, for instance, Sewell's analysis of Theda Skocpol's theory of revolution. In "Ideology and Social Revolutions: Reflections on the French Case" (61), Sewell argues that structuralists such as Skocpol should conceive culture as "anonymous, collective and constitutive of social order."

34. Here again, I borrow an argument from William Sewell, Jr., who suggests that what transforms resources into bases for power and social action are the "schemas [mental structures] that inform their use." "Any array of resources is capable of being interpreted in varying ways, and therefore of empowering different actors." See Sewell's "Toward a Theory of Structure: Duality, Agency and Transformation."

35. See also Sewell's critique of Charles Tilly's work, "Collective Violence and Collective Loyalties in France: Why the French Revolution Made a Difference." It should be noted that Sewell's argument indirectly builds on a lively culturalist tradition that is both critical of and sympathetic toward Marxism, and that in part is defined by the work of Lynn Hunt, Roger Chartier, E. P. Thompson, Marshall Sahlins, and Natalie Zemon Davis. Among sociologists see also the recent work of Jeffrey Alexander.

36. Another argument, which suggest that the primacy of structure and culture should not be made into a presupposition but should be investigated from case to case, is presented by Somers, "Political Culture, Property, and Citizenship: An Epistemological Exploration."

37. Although my criticisms concern only these few key points, the analysis is based on a reading of the total sum of Bourdieu's writings published before 1988, and on a partial reading of his writings published since.

38. Bourdieu, "Social Space and Symbolic Power."

39. From this we could conclude that the greater the correspondence between social trajectory and social position on the one hand, and tastes on the other hand, the more cultural selection translates directly into the reproduction of inequality. It should be noted that Bourdieu does not use the concept of symbolic boundaries. The notion of symbolic boundary, however, is implicit in his discussion of legitimate culture and in his analysis of the institutionalization of boundaries between fields.

40. Bourdieu, *Distinction*, 194, 246, 247, and 250.

41. In his early work Bourdieu criticized structuralism for not recognizing that cultural systems constitute systems of differences that reflect the dynamic of power fields, i.e., the ability of specific groups to impose a principle of inclusion, exclusion, integration, and distinction that advantages them. See "Genèse et structure du champ religieux." In *Le*

sens pratique, Bourdieu even wrote that his only contribution to structuralism "was born from an effort to explicate . . . the logic of relational and transformational thinking . . . and to specify the conditions under which it can apply, beyond cultural systems, to social relationships themselves, that is, to sociology" (12, my translation).

42. Bourdieu simply states that logical differentiation becomes social differentiation. However, he does not demonstrate how this transition from the logical to the social happens. See his "Genèse et structure du champ religieux" (297).

43. Because Bourdieu believes that strategies of distinction are unconscious—in contrast to Veblen, he argues that deliberate searches for distinction are relatively infrequent—he would be unlikely to pay any attention to the statements of my interviewees concerning their tolerant attitudes. For him, distinction automatically results from differences in the relation that various categories of people have with their body, language, culture, and so forth. In my view, such mechanism functions, but only for people who are relatively taste conscious (See his "Social Space and Symbolic Power," 17 and 20).

44. Again, Bourdieu is very critical of subjectivist approaches that reduce the social world to the representations that agents have of it. For him, the causes of social life reside outside of consciousness because people's understanding of their action is necessarily inadequate: their involvement in structured networks of relationships (namely, power fields) in which they have specific positions prevents them from gaining a total (i.e., nonpartial) understanding of reality. In an early article titled "Structuralism and Theory of Sociological Knowledge," Bourdieu writes, "The anthropologist gives no credit to the representation the subjects form of their situation and does not take literally false explanations they give of their conduct; he, on the other hand, takes this representation and these rationalizations seriously enough to try to discover their true foundations" (705). On this topic, see also his *Le sens pratique,* chap. 2.

45. My position on the value of subjective boundaries is different than Bourdieu's: in my view individual perceptions of reality have to be taken at face value and should be studied in their own right, especially if one wishes to understand symbolic boundaries. These perceptions are the subjective conditions that make possible the creation of objective boundaries; only if individuals define certain characteristics as low status can these characteristics be used to actually exclude people from having access to resources.

46. On the concepts of field of power and social space, see Bourdieu, "Social Space and Symbolic Power."

47. "The emergence of a group capable of "making an epoch" of imposing a new, advanced position is accompanied by a displacement of the structure of temporarily hierarchized positions opposed within a given field." See Bourdieu's "The Field of Cultural Production or the Economic Word Reversed," 340.

48. I agree with John Hall, William Sewell, Jr., and others that Bourdieu's metatheoretical system needs a more "multiple, contingent, and fractured conception of society—and of structure." See Sewell, Jr., "Toward a Theory of Structure," 28; John Hall, "The Capital(s) of Culture: A Non-Holistic Approach to Gender, Ethnicity, Class and Status Groups."

49. The notion of power field requires defining the limits of groups which is most often an arbitrary decision because few groups have absolute natural boundaries. In addition, reconstructing the structure of power fields requires the use of correspondence analysis and the reduction of symbolic reality to the bipolar structure built into this technique. It also requires freezing for analytical purposes a slice of a virtual power field in time.

50. On this point, see Lamont and Lareau, "Cultural Capital." While Bourdieu's theory of cultural capital is not fully explicit, this article attempts to reconstruct it from Bourdieu's various writings.

51. In other words, they invest in morality because they do not have the ability to invest in any other type of resources. Bourdieu also considers strong morality a working-class trait when he writes that while the bourgeoisie can appreciate art through purely aesthetic categories, the working class "refers often explicitly to norms of morality or agreeableness in all their judgments" (Bourdieu, *Distinction*, 41). Linking aestheticism to moral agnosticism, he implicitly considers moralism to be a low status signal.

52. See in particular Bourdieu, "Le mort saisit le vif: Les relations entre l'histoire réifiée et l'histoire incorporée," 6.

53. Studies of altruism clearly demonstrate the importance of noneconomic factors in everyday life. On this point, see Wuthnow, *Acts of Compassion: Caring for Others and Helping Ourselves*.

54. Another indication that Bourdieu downplays the importance of morality is the fact that while he is very concerned with symbolic capital which he defines as a power of consecration, or a credit that one has because one has a legitimate social position, he grounds this authority in economic and cultural capital, and not on moral purity or esteem. See his "Social Space and Symbolic Power," 21.

55. More specifically, those who are vigorously moving upward (the new "petite-bourgeoisie") or downward (small shopkeepers and craftsmen) emphasize ascetic values (i.e., hard work and thrift) as a way to achieve mobility. Also, while the upwardly mobiles reject the religious, sexual, and political conservatism of the downwardly mobile in favor of a psychological approach to morality that focuses on personal needs, the downwardly mobile are repressive morally and conservative politically, "anxious to maintain order on all fronts, in domestic morality and in society, and [to] invest their revolt against the worsening of morals" (435).

56. My sample does not include small shopkeepers or craftsmen. The only site where there exists a significant relationship between mobility and moral boundaries is Indianapolis, where the most upwardly mobiles attribute *much less* importance to moral boundaries than do other groups. The association of $-.38$ at the .01 level of significance.

57. Bourdieu, *Distinction*, 331.

58. Ibid., 414, 445, and 468. It should also be noted that the questionnaire items that Bourdieu uses to gather data on ethical preferences are confined to a narrow range of topics only indirectly relevant to moral evaluation, such as preferences in interior decoration, furniture, food, clothes—in addition to the more directly moral probes on qualities appreciated in friends (261).

59. In his early work on the categories of perception and appreciation through which professors construct an image of their students and of their values, Bourdieu opens the possibility for a multidimensional view of high status signals. This possibility, however, is adequately exploited. See Bourdieu and St-Martin, "Les catégories de l'entendement professoral."

60. Bourdieu, *Le sens pratique*, chap. 2. It should be noted however that Bourdieu is critical of rational choice theory because it posits a form of voluntarist activism that overemphasizes the autonomy of individual action rather than conceiving individuals as largely constrained by the "power fields" in which they are involved. Bourdieu also criticizes rational choice theory for implying that individuals are consciously strategic rather than moved by the logic of the power field in which they are necessarily involved. See his "Le mort saisit le vif," 6. He also stresses symbolic profits more than rational choice theorists do, this latter group being more concerned with economic profits.

61. Bourdieu, *The Algerians*, 97. Also his "Le mort saisit le vif," 6.

62. While others, such as Axel Honneth, have argued that Bourdieu exaggerates the important of utility maximization, they have not provided empirical evidence demonstrat-

ing that this assumption was unwarranted. See Honneth, "The Fragmented World of Symbolic Forms: Reflections on Pierre Bourdieu's Sociology of Culture."

63. Bourdieu might argue that his notion of "causality of probability" suggests that individuals define as desirable what which is "necessary" given their capital and structural position, and therefore that people do not all value socioeconomic status equally. Implicitly, this notion again suggests that necessity, namely, material necessity, structures reality and indirectly gives precedence to socioeconomic interests over other types of interests.

64. On this point, see in particular Collectif "Révoltes logiques," *L'empire du sociologue.*

65. Exclusion on the basis of level of education can be considered a proxy for cultural boundaries. It is interesting to note that Robert V. Robinson and Maurice Granier have shown the effect of education on reproduction of class in France is much weaker than what had been suggested by reproduction theory. See their "Class Reproduction among Men and Women in France."

66. While in *Distinction*, Bourdieu emphasizes the fact that Parisians have more cultural resources than people living in the "Province" (e.g., 265 and 363), again, the research design of his study presumes that cultural boundaries (i.e., cultural distinctions) occupy a central place in French culture at large. Some might argue that if in this book Bourdieu neglects moral status signals, it is because this study concerns the role of cultural taste in the reproduction of the French stratification system. This objection does not hold because Bourdieu explicitly states several times in this book that his goal is to explain ethical as well as aesthetical dispositions.

67. It should be noted that in the preface to *Distinction* Bourdieu recognizes that French and American cultures are different, French culture being more homogeneous.

68. I found that the association between cultural boundaries and intellectualism is exceptionally strong, at .85 (.001 level of significance).

69. The Parisians I interviewed were the group least concerned with moral boundaries. As for the New Yorkers, 38 percent of them scored 0, 1, or 2 on the moral scale, compared to 17 percent of the Clermontois and the Hoosiers (the table A.5 in Appendix IV).

70. The intellectuals I interviewed drew somewhat strong socioeconomic boundaries, with a Somers' D of .22 (.001 level of significance).

71. I found a strong negative association between intellectuality and tolerance. The relationship is − .51 (.01 level of significance) in Paris, compared to − .32 in Clermont-Ferrand, − .21 in New York, and − .24 in Indianapolis.

72. For instance, using survey data, Bourdieu shows that the declining petite bourgeoisie and the downwardly mobile craftsman and small shopkeepers like "déclassé" works of bourgeois culture, such as the Blue Danube (350), while the "autodidact" attach great importance to minor cultural forms (*Distinction*, 329; see also 359 and 363).

73. He criticizes reflection theories of culture because they posit a direct reflection between culture and society (Bourdieu, *Question de sociologie*, 208). A logic of reflection or homology, however, is found throughout his work: he writes that some artists are enabled to produce daring work by their greater economic security and their access to wide social networks, that cultural producers and consumers who appreciate the same cultural goods occupy homologous social positions (Bourdieu, "The Field of Cultural Production," 325 and 349), and that the structure of the artistic fields determines the cultural practices in which people engage (Bourdieu, "The Production of Belief: Contribution to an Economy of Symbolic Goods."

74. Bourdieu, *Distinction*, chapter 5.

75. Bourdieu, *Outline of a Theory of Practice*, 83.

76. In *Outline*, Bourdieu defines the levels that determine habitus without ever mak-

ing reference to remote structural factors. He focuses on the "objective structure of the relationship between the interacting agents' objective position in the social structure (e.g., relations of competition or objective antagonism, or relations of power and authority, etc.)" and "the structure of the relative position [of agents] in the hierarchies of age, power, prestige and culture" (25). He also defines these levels as "the statistical chances objectively attached to social and economic conditions" (200n), and as the individual's life chance in the Weberian sense, e.g., his/her chances of access to higher education given his/her social position (21). Elsewhere, Bourdieu defines the factors that determine culture as permanent employment and regular income, i.e., distance from material necessity. See *Algeria 1960*, 49.

77. While Bourdieu argues that economic and cultural factors have the greatest power of differentiation and classification in French society, he also acknowledges that other principles of division also can be important. He notes, for instance, the potential importance of ethnicity, religion, and nationality. See "Social Space and Symbolic Power," 19.

78. For a sophisticated discussion of the multidimensional nature of equality and criteria of hierarchalization see also Walzer, *Spheres of Justice: A Defense of Pluralism and Equality*.

79. This approach complements neo-Durkheimian work that tends to focus on the content of cultural codes themselves without relating them to the structure of social groups that produce them. See, for instance, Wuthnow, *Meaning and Moral Order*. It also complements Douglas's work which links the degree of elaboration of symbolic systems to group structure and cohesiveness.

80. Symbolic interactionists have long shown that we define who we are by defining who we are not, the two processes happening simultaneously. In recent years, many have become interested in boundaries as a device for pinning down symbolic conflicts. For instance, in *The Great Cat Massacre and Other Episodes in French Cultural History*, Darnton showed how an eighteenth-century massacre of a pet cat dramatized a reversal of boundaries between a bourgeois and his workmen. Also, in *Society and Culture in Early Modern France*, Natalie Zemon Davis showed how the strengthening and weakening of boundaries between social categories (women and men, clerics and seculars) changed the symbolic order of sixteenth-century France.

81. Similar developments have occurred in anthropology. For instance, in her very powerful and influential book *Purity and Danger*, Mary Douglas discussed the danger of collapsing and violating conceptual boundaries and analyzed how they are used to maintain symbolic order. Other cultural anthropologists who have dealt with boundaries and pollution by studying rituals and other phenomena include Turner's *The Ritual Process*; Appadurai's *The Social Life of Things*; and Ortner's *The Sherpas through their Rituals*.

82. For a review of this literature see Jones and Pittman, "Toward a General Theory of Strategic Self-Presentation," 233. Also Goffman, *The Presentation of Self in Everyday Life*. For social-psychological approaches to self-identity, see McCall and Simmon, *Identity and Interaction: An Examination of Human Association in Everyday Life*.

83. See for instance Jackman and Jackman, *Class Awareness in the United States*. If Americans most often describe themselves and people like themselves by using terms bearing not on class or occupational identity but on personality traits—see W. Lloyd Warner et al., *Yankee City*—such pronouncements need to be viewed as more than "noise" hampering sociological research or evidence of false consciousness.

84. Faunce, "On the Meaning of Occupational Status"; and "Occupational Status-Assignment Systems: The Effect of Status on Self-Esteem."

85. See in particular the work of Alex Inkeles on the topic.

86. Whereas the debates of the sixties surrounding the culture of poverty thesis made a distinction between structural explanations and cultural (understood as natural or psychological) explanations, the approach used here takes cultural differences between classes to be structural, i.e., symbolic boundaries to be cultural rules that shape people's behavior. Indeed, along with neo-Durkheimians, symbolic interactionists, phenomenologists, and neoinstitutionalists I consider culture to be a form of structural constraint. See for instance Gonos, "'Situation' versus 'Frame': The 'Interactionist' and the 'Structuralist' Analysis of Everyday Life"; and Arthur Frank, "Reality Construction in Interaction."

87. If the sample on which this study is based is relatively small, it is not smaller than that which has been widely used to make strong empirical claims about the nature of the world-system.

88. On this distinction between surface rules and deep rules see Sewell, Jr., "Toward a Theory of Structure." To illustrate this distinction, we can differentiate between the violence of American debates concerning abortion, a highly contested topic, and the taken for grantedness of the notion that the private sexual conduct of politicians belongs to the public domain (a deep rule).

89. A very interesting discussion of the relation between boundaries and identity is presented by Pizzorno in "On the Individualistic Theory of Social Order." See also Taylor, "The Politics of Recognition."

90. For a very insightful discussion of the possibility of changing boundaries, see Wolfe, "Democracy versus Sociology: Boundaries and Their Political Consequences."

91. The boundedness of boundaries also could be compared across classes: they are likely to be more solidly established among upper-middle-class members than among members of other groups, given that the culture of the upper-middle class is likely to be more homogeneous, being constantly depicted by the media, and given the standardizing effect of college education. In contrast, the non–college educated might be less homogenously socialized.

92. I am referring here, for instance, to debates surrounding the work of James C. Scott, *Domination and the Arts of Resistance: Hidden Transcript.* See Tilly, "Domination, Resistance, Compliance . . . Discourse"; and Mitchell, "Everyday Metaphors of Power."

93. It is interesting to note that the relatively small literature on white American working-class culture, which is largely based on data from the late fifties and early sixties, is in great need of updating, while there has been very little work on the black American working class, although a rapidly expanding literature on the black underclass and middle class is available.

94. See Harrison and Bluestone, *The Great U-Turn: Corporate Restructuring and the Polarizing of America.* See also Reich, "The Secession of the Successful."

95. On this topic, see Matthijs Kalmijn, "Status Homogamy in the United States."

APPENDIX I

1. U.S. Department of Commerce, Bureau of the Census, *Statistical Abstract of the United States 1987,* table 666. The American managerial population grew twice as fast as did the total employment between 1972 and 1986. See Hodson and Sullivan, *The Social Organization of Work,* 288.

2. Bidou, "L'évolution de la structure socio-professionnelle en France depuis 1954," 175.

3. The number of engineers in America increased by 183 percent between 1950 and 1980, while in France it grew by 238 percent between 1954 and 1982. These figures contrast with an increase of 136 percent for nontechnical managers (Crawford, *Technical Workers in an Advanced Society,* 2).

4. Collins, *The Credential Society*; Craig, "The Development of Educational Systems"; Meyer, Ramirez, Rubinson, and Boli-Bennett, "The World Educational Revolution 1950–1970."

5. Doeringer and Piore, *Internal Labor Markets and Manpower Analysis*.

6. Cameron, "The Expansion of the Public Economy: A Comparative Analysis"; George M. Thomas and John Z. Meyer, "The Expansion of the State."

7. Fourastié, *Les trentes glorieuses*, 220.

8. Burris, "Class Formation and Transformation in Advanced Capitalist Societies: A Comparative Analysis."

9. Fantasia, *Cultures of Solidarity: Consciousness, Action and Contemporary American Workers*; Halle, *America's Working Man*; Komarovsky, *Blue Collar Marriage*; MacLeod, *Ain't No Makin' It*; Mukerji and Schudson, "Popular Culture"; Rubin, *Worlds of Pain*; Sennett and Cobb, *The Hidden Injuries of Class*; and Shostak, *Blue Collar Life*.

10. Baltzell, *The Protestant Establishment: Aristocracy and Caste in America*; Barton, "Determinants of Economic Attitudes in the American Business Elite"; Bonfield, *U.S. Business Leaders: A Study of Opinions and Characteristics*; Cookson and Persell, *Preparing for Power*; Domhoff, *The Bohemian Grove and Other Retreats: A Study in Ruling-Class Cohesiveness*; Ostrander, *Women of the Upper Class*; Useem, *The Inner Circle*.

11. Claude Grignon and Christiane Grignon, "Styles alimentaires et goûts populaires"; Claude Grignon and Jean-Claude Passeron, *A propos des cultures populaires*; Michel Pinçon, *Désarrois ouvriers*.

12. Le Wita, *Ni vue ni connue*.

13. Bidou et al., *Les couches moyennes salariées*; Grunberg and Schweisguth, "A quoi sert la sociologie empirique?"

14. Bourdieu, *Distinction*; Michelat and Simon, *Classes, religion et comportement politique*.

15. Parsons, "The Professions and Social Structure"; for a critique see Larson, *The Rise of Professionalism: A Sociological Analysis*.

16. Pavalko, *Sociology of Occupations and Professions*, chap. 4.

17. Derber, *Professionals as Workers: Mental Labor in Advanced Capitalism*; Derber, Schwartz, and Magrass, *Power in the Highest Degree: Professionals and the Rise of a New Mandarin Order*; Larson, *The Rise of Professionalism*.

18. Kornhauser, with Hagstrom, *Scientists in Industry: Conflict and Accommodation*.

19. Bellah et al., *Habits of the Heart*; Newman, *Falling from Grace*; Reinarman, *American States of Mind: Political Beliefs and Behavior among Private and Public Workers*; Varenne, *Americans Together*; Gans, *Middle American Individualism: The Future of Liberal Democracy*. This last study of the lower-middle class is mostly based on survey data.

20. Kanter, *Men and Women of the Corporation*; Jackall, *Moral Mazes*; Margolis, *The Managers*.

21. Bledstein, *The Culture of Professionalism*; Baritz, *The Good Life: The Meaning of Success for the American Middle Class*. Cultural historians such as Baritz have documented the process of by which American middle-class culture was constituted: after World War II, the WASP upper-class culture progressively lost its cohesion (see Baltzell's *The Protestant Establishment*). Simultaneously, sustained by the transition to a service economy and by the economic boom of the 1950s and 1960s, a middle-class culture consolidated, absorbing in the process immigrants and "talented" people able to demonstrate their professional competence.

22. Seeley, Sim, and Loosley, *Crestwood Heights*; Cuber and Haroff, *Sex and the Significant Americans*. Others traced some of the cultural dimensions central to middle-class identity: individualism, consumerism, materialism, conformism. These values embody American middle-class culture as a whole, along with a belief in progress, ambition, edu-

cation, optimism, achievement, and mobility. See Whyte, *The Organization Man;* Riesman, with Glazer and Denney, *The Lonely Crowd;* Mills, *White Collar;* Gans, *The Levittowners: Ways of Life and Politics in a New Suburban Community.*

23. See also Sennett (*The Fall of the Public Man*); and Lasch (*The Culture of Narcissism: American Life in an Age of Diminishing Expectations*), who explored the themes of narcissism and privatism.

24. Bazelon, *Power in America: The Politics of the New Class;* Brint, "'New Class' and Cumulative Trend Explanations of the Liberal Political Attitudes of Professionals"; Gouldner, *The Future of Intellectuals and the Rise of the New Class: A Frame of Reference . . . ;* Lipset, *The Political Man.*

25. Abercrombie and Urry, *Capital, Labor and the Middle Class;* Barbara Ehrenreich and J. Ehrenreich, "The Professional-Managerial Class"; Burris, "Capital Accumulation and the Rise of the New Middle Class"; Poulantzas, *Classes in Contemporary Capitalism.*

26. Daniel Bell, *The Coming Crisis of Post-Industrial Society;* Galbraith, *The New Industrial State;* Mills, *White Collar;* Touraine, *The Post-Industrial Society: Tomorrow's Social History: Classes, Conflicts and Culture in the Programmed Society.*

27. With a few notable exceptions such as Brint's "'New Class' and Cumulative Trend Explanations of the Liberal Political Attitudes of Professionals"; Martin, "From Class Challenge to Comfortable Collaboration?: The Politics of the Educated Middle Class in the United States, 1960–80"; Wuthnow and Shrum, Jr., "Knowledge Workers as a 'New Class': Structural and Ideological Convergence among Professional-Technical Workers and Managers"; Macy, "New-Class Dissent among Social-Cultural Specialists."

28. Boltanski, *Les cadres: La formation d'un groupe social;* Grunberg and Schweisguth, "A quoi sert la sociologie empirique?"

29. Bauer and Bertin-Mourot, *Les 200: Comment devient-on un grand patron?;* Bourdieu and St-Martin, "Le patronat"; Harris and De Sedouy, *Les patrons.*

30. Birnbaum, Baruck, Bellaiche, and Marie, *La classe dirigeante française;* Dagnaud and Mehl, *L'élite rose: Qui gouverne?;* Gaxie, "Les logiques du recrutement politique"; Suleiman, *Les élites en France.*

31. Lavau, Grunberg, and Mayer, *L'univers politique des classes moyennes;* Mayer, *La boutique contre la gauche;* and Capdevielle et al.; *France de gauche, vote à droite.*

32. Bourdieu and Passeron, *Reproduction;* Singly and Thélot, *Gens du privé, gens du public;* Boudon, *L'inégalité des chances.*

33. Debray, *Teachers, Writers and Celebrities;* Ross, "Where Have All the Sartres Gone?"; Hamon and Rotman, *Les intellocrates.*

34. U.S. Department of Commerce, Bureau of Census, *Statistical Abstract of the United States 1987,* 121.

35. Mermèt, *Francoscopie,* 63.

36. The average undergraduate tuition, fees, and room and board rates in American institutions of higher education in 1986–87 was $4,138 for public four-year institutions, and $10,039 for private institutions (U.S. Department of Education, Office of Educational Research and Improvement, *Digest of Education Statistics 1989,* 283). In France, the annual cost for university education is a maximum of 1,500 FF (approximately $300). The *grandes écoles* vary greatly in cost, from free tuition (with a future obligation to the state) to 25,000 FF (approximately $5,000 per year).

37. Magliulo, *Les grandes écoles.*

38. A list of American elite schools was produced by modifying the classification of elite schools used by Michael Useem and Jerome Karabel in "Pathways to Top Corporate Management." For France, I used the classification of elite engineering schools presented

by Crawford (*Technical Workers in an Advanced Society*, 142) as well as information contained in *Je vais en France 1989: Guide à l'intention des étudiants étrangers.*

39. U.S. Department of Commerce, Bureau of the Census, *Statistical Abstract of the United States 1987*, 432.

40. Hodson and Sullivan, *The Social Organization of Work*, 288.

41. Institut national de statistiques et d'études économiques, *Données Sociales 1987*, 204.

42. Haller, "Positional and Sectoral Differences in Income: The Federal Republic, France and the United States," 176.

43. Ibid., 189.

44. This coefficient measures how far a country is from complete income equality. The Schultz coefficient is empirically equivalent to measures of income inequality such as the Gini index. See Kerbo, *Social Stratification and Inequality: Class Conflict in the United States*, 164.

45. Villeneuve, "Les revenus primaires des ménages en 1975."

46. *Human Resources Management in France*, 4.4. It should be noted that a slightly larger percentage of French interviewees have a spouse who works full time: it is the case for 62 percent of the Parisians interviewees, 66 percent of the Clermontois, 59 percent of the Hoosiers, and 55 percent of the New Yorkers.

47. Income-based definitions of the American middle, upper-middle, and upper classes vary considerably. For instance, Blackburn and Bloom define (*a*) upper-class families as the 12.8 percent of all families with annual income exceeding $41,456 in 1983 (225 percent of the average income level for the nation); (*b*) upper-middle-class families as the 14.2 percent of all families with annual income between $29,840 and $41,456 (160–225 percent); and (*c*) middle-class families as the 23.1 percent of the population with income between $18,426 and $29,840 (100–160 percent). (Blackburn and Bloom, "What Is Happening to the Middle Class?"

48. Gans defines American middle-class families as those whose income ranged from $15,000 to $37,500 in 1984, which includes people located in the thirty-first to the seventy-first income percentiles of the American population (*Middle American Individualism*, 7). In *Fear of Falling*, Ehrenreich (205) defines the middle class as families with income between $20,000 and $50,000 in 1984. According to her data, the fraction of families with middle-range incomes declined from 53 percent in 1973 to less than 48 percent in 1984.

49. The comparison concerned occupational and sectorial positions. See Haller, Konig, Krause, and Hurz, "Patterns of Career Mobility and Structural Positions in Advanced Capitalists Societies: A Comparison of Men in Austria, France and the United States."

50. Tyree, Semyonov, and Hodge. "Gaps and Glissandos: Inequality, Economic Development and Social Mobility in 24 Countries," 416.

51. Gollac and Laulhe, "Les composantes de l'hérédité sociale: un capital économique et culturel à transmettre," 104.

52. Jackman and Jackman, *Class Awareness in the United States*, 73.

53. For an analysis of occupational class identification of professionals see Brint, "The Occupational Class Identifications of Professionals: Evidence from Cluster Analysis."

54. See Pernoud, *Histoire de la bourgeoisie en France*, vol. 2: *Les temps modernes*; Perrot, *Le mode de vie des familles bourgeoises.*

55. The new socioprofessional nomenclature developed by the French government to reflect how groups differentiate themselves from one another provides useful information on the native categories by which one refers to "professionals, managers, and busi-

nessmen" in the French context. One of the main differences between the new French nomenclature and the nomenclature used by the U.S. census (1985) is that the French nomenclature has two categories for managers while the American has seven. The French also has one category for scientific professions while the American nomenclature has four. See Desrosières, Goy, and Thévenot, "L'identité sociale dans le travail statistique: La nouvelle nomenclature des professions et catégories socioprofessionnelles."

56. In his important book on *Les cadres*, Luc Boltanski defines this group as part of the salaried bourgeoisie (111). See his first chapter on the categorization and representation of this group. While Boltanski is concerned with the constitution of the identity of this group in contrast to other groups, I am concerned with how identity is defined relationally, not at the level of socio-occupational groupings but at the level of definitions of legitimate behavior.

57. Crawford, *Technical Workers in an Advanced Society*, 246.

58. Vagogne, in *Les professions libérales*, provides an exhaustive listing (25–26).

59. Suleiman, *Private Power and Centralization in France: The Notaires and the State*, 53.

60. Abbott, *The System of Professions*, 158.

61. U.S. Department of Commerce, Bureau of the Census, *Statistical Abstract of the United States 1987*, 379.

62. Compiled from Desrosières, Goy, and Thévenot, "L'identité sociale dans le travail statistique," 65.

63. E.g., Bauer and Bertin-Mourot, *Les 200*; Bourdieu and St-Martin, "Le patronat"; Harris and De Sedouy, *Les patrons*.

64. Henri Weber, "Cultures patronales et types d'entreprises. Esquisse d'une typologie du patronat," 545. The CNPF was created in 1946. It is a confederation of associations of entreprises in the sectors of industry, commerce, and services. It includes a range of groups that represent the main ideological currents among "patrons" (e.g., the modernists, pro-Americans (*Entreprise et Progrès*) vs. the traditionals (*Association des cadres dirigeants de l'industrie pour le progrès social et économique*).

65. On this group, see the excellent study by Mayer, *La boutique contre la gauche*.

66. Elie Cohen, "Patrons, entrepreneurs et dirigeants: avant-propos."

67. Birnbaum et al., *La classe dirigeante française*, 33.

68. On these changes see Bourdieu and St-Martin, "Le patronat."

APPENDIX II

1. Indianapolis is located less than an hour from Muncie, Indiana, the town Helen M. and Robert S. Lynd studied in the twenties and described in their classical work, *Middletown*. These sociologists chose Muncie because they considered it to be "as representative as possible of contemporary American life." See Robert S. Lynd and Helen M. Lynd, *Middletown: A Study in American Culture*, 7. Experts consider Midwestern American English to be standard American. This also suggests that Midwestern culture can be considered as representative of mainstream American culture. See Hendrickson, *American Talk: The Words and Ways of American Dialects*.

2. On representations of the Midwest which predominate among Easterners see Shortridge, *The Middle West: Its Meaning in American Culture*.

3. On the structure of the population of New York City see Richard Harris, "The Geography of Employment and Residence in New York since 1950." See also Mollenkopf, "The Postindustrial Transformation of the Political Order in New York City."

4. Baumgartner, *The Moral Order of the Suburbs*, 7.

5. Perin, *Belonging in America*, 97.

6. U.S. Department of Commerce, Bureau of Census, 1986, *States and Metropolitan Areas: Data Book, 1986.*

7. U.S. Department of Commerce, Bureau of the Census, *Statistical Abstract of the United States 1987*, 222.

8. These communities were chosen because they included status tracks where the family income average was above $30,000 in 1980. Overall, these populations have slightly higher income than the Indianapolis respondents, though this differential tends to disappear in the face of regional differences in cost of living.

9. I choose to include in the sample interviewees who do not reside in exclusive communities (e.g., South Plainfield, Merrick) in order to reach members of the upper-middle class who do not live isolated from other groups, such as middle-income, skilled blue-collar workers.

10. Following the example of Hoover and Vernon in *Anatomy of a Metropolis: The Changing Distribution of People and Jobs within the New York Metropolitan Region*, Richard Harris measured the varying concentration of jobs by areas with an index of specialization, or location quotient, that measures the extent to which a particular type of employment is over- or underrepresented in specific areas. See his "The Geography of Employment and Residence in New York since 1950."

11. Harris, "The Geography of Employment and Residence in New York since 1950."

12. Westergaard, *New Jersey: A Guide to the State.*

13. In 1986, the average *net* annual family income was 73,894 FF (app. $15,000) in Argenteuil, and 93,838 FF ($20,000) in Vincennes, in contrast to around 110,000 FF ($25,000) for the other communities. Neuilly-sur-Seine is considerably above the mean, with an average net family income of 206,629 FF (approximately $40,000). In contrast, in 1980, the average family income for the New York suburbs was $34,000 (based on figures compiled from the 1980 U.S. census).

14. Indianapolis is the most centrally located of the hundred largest American cities.

15. Indianapolis is already well integrated into the American economy. In particular, it is the home of several important insurance companies.

16. This was stressed in a special issue on Clermont-Ferrand published by *Le Monde* on 21 January 1988.

17. U.S. Department of Commerce, Bureau of the Census, *Statistical Abstract 1987*, 29.

18. *Dictionnaire national des communes de France.*

19. Like Indianapolis, Clermont has traditionally drained farm workers from the surrounding region.

20. Ville de Clermont-Ferrand, *Clermont-Ferrand en chiffres 1988.*

21. Mazataud, *Géopolitique d'une région*, 158.

22. *Le point économique de l'Auvergne.*

APPENDIX III

1. Indianapolis, for instance, names were chosen from forty-six high and middle-level income census tracks. They were randomly selected from the *Indianapolis City Directory, 1985* and the *Indianapolis Suburban Directory, 1984.*

2. These figures do not include potential respondents who did not provide the information necessary to determine whether they qualified or not. These were more numerous in Paris and Clermont than they were in the United States.

3. I followed Glazer and Strauss in conducting theoretical sampling, i.e., in defining

sampling criteria on the basis of predefined theoretical issues. See Glazer and Strauss, *The Discovery of Grounded Theory: Strategies for Qualitative Research.*

4. Brint, "The Political Attitudes of Professionals," 401.

5. Specialists define the nonprofit sector as including organizations centered around religious, educational, cultural, historical, scientific, environmental and beautification activities; organizations concerned with youths, inner cities, communities, health, athletics, civil rights, legal aid and advocacy; and employee membership and benefit organization.

6. It should be noted that nonprofit organizations do not equally pursue collective goals. Using a "collectiveness index" based on source of income (gift, sales, dues), Weisbrod suggested that the most collectivist organizations are, in decreasing order; (1) cultural, religious, and public affairs organizations; (2) scientific, engineering and technical, social welfare, and educational organizations; (3) legal, governmental, public administration, and military organizations. See Weisbrod, "Private Goods, Collective Goods: The Role of the Nonprofit Sector."

7. Crawford, *Technical Workers in an Advanced Society*, 28.

8. Only a third of all executive, managerial, and administrative workers are female, and these are concentrated within specific areas, such as personnel and labor relations management. See Hodson and Sullivan, *The Social Organization of Work*, 290.

9. Boltanksi, *Les cadres.*

10. A few questions were added to the interview schedule for the second wave of interviews. Interviewees from the first wave were then recontacted and asked to answer these questions over the phone.

11. I followed a technique suggested by Miles and Huberman in *Qualitative Data Analysis: A Sourcebook of New Methods.*

12. On the multiple-site case study method see Yin, *Case Study Research.*

BIBLIOGRAPHY

Abbott, Andrew. 1988. *The System of Professions: An Essay on the Division of Expert Labor.* Chicago: University of Chicago Press.

Abélès, Marc. 1989. *Jours tranquilles en 89: Ethnologie politique d'un département français.* Paris: Editions Odile Jacob en association avec les Editions du Seuil.

Abercrombie, Nicholas, and John Urry. 1983. *Capital, Labor and the Middle Class.* London and New York: George Allen and Unwin.

Agger, Ben. 1991. "Critical Theory, Poststructuralism and Postmodernism: Their Sociological Relevance." *Annual Review of Sociology* 17:105–31.

Alexander, C. N., and Mathilda G. Wiley. 1981. "Situated Activity and Identity Formation." In *Social Psychology: Sociological Perspective,* edited by Morris Rosenberg and Ralph H. Turner. New York: Basic Books, 269–89.

Alexander Jeffrey. 1988. "The New Theoretical Movement." In *Handbook of Sociology,* edited by Neil Smelser. Beverly Hills, Calif.: Sage.

———, ed. 1988. *Durkheimian Sociology: Cultural Studies.* Cambridge: Cambridge University Press.

Ambler, John S. 1991. "Educational Pluralism in the French Fifth Republic." In *Searching for the New France,* edited by James F. Hollifield and George Ross. New York and London: Routledge, 193–221.

Anderson, Benedict. 1983. *Imagined Communities: Reflections on the Origin and Spread of Nationalism.* London: Verso.

Appadurai, Arjun. 1986. *The Social Life of Things.* New York: Cambridge University Press.

Archambault, Edith. 1984. *Les associations en chiffres.* Nanterre: Association pour le Développement de la Documentation sur l'Économie Sociale.

Balfe, Judith Huggins. 1981. "Social Mobility and Modern Art: Abstract Expressionism and Its Generative Audience." *Research in Social Movement, Conflict and Change* 4:235–51.

Baltzell, E. Digby. 1964. *The Protestant Establishment: Aristocracy and Caste in America.* Glencoe, Ill.: Free Press.

Barber, Bernard. 1983. *The Logic and Limits of Trust.* New Brunswick: Rutgers University Press.

Baritz, Loren. 1989. *The Good Life: The Meaning of Success for the American Middle Class.* New York: Knopf.

Barton, Allen H. 1985. "Determinants of Economic Attitudes in the American Business Elite." *American Journal of Sociology* 91, no. 1:54–87.

Bauer, Michel, and Bénédicte Bertin-Mourot. 1987. *Les 200: Comment devient-on un grand patron?* Paris: Editions du Seuil.

Baumgartner, P. M. 1988. *The Moral Order of a Suburb.* New York: Oxford University Press.

Bazelon, David T. 1967. *Power in America: The Politics of the New Class.* New York: New American Library.

Becker, Howard D. 1963. *Outsiders: Studies in the Sociology of Deviance.* New York: Free Press.

Beisel, Nicola. 1992. "Constructing a Shifting Moral Boundary: Literature and Obscenity in Nineteenth Century America." In *Cultivating Differences: Symbolic Boundaries and the Making of Inequality,* edited by Michèle Lamont and Marcel Fournier. Chicago: University of Chicago Press.

Bell, Daniel. 1972. *The Coming Crisis of Post-Industrial Society.* New York: Basic Books.

Bell, Wendell, and Robert V. Robinson. 1980. "Cognitive Maps of Class and Racial Inequality in England and the United States." *American Journal of Sociology* 86, no. 2:331–49.

Bellah, Robert N. 1975. *The Broken Covenant: American Civil Religion in Time of War.* New York: Seabury Press.

Bellah, Robert N., Richard Madsen, William W. Sullivan, Ann Swidler, and Steven Tipton. 1985. *Habits of the Heart: Individualism and Commitment in American Life.* Berkeley: University of California Press.

Bennett, William J. 1984. *To Reclaim a Legacy: A Report on the Humanities in Higher Education.* Washington, D.C.: National Endowment for the Humanities.

Bergensen, Albert. 1984. "Social Control and Corporate Organizations: A Durkheimian Perspective." In *Toward a General Theory of Social Control,* edited by Donald Black. New York: Academic Press, 141–70.

Berger, Bennett. 1991. "Structure and Choice in the Sociology of Culture." *Theory and Society* 20:1–19.

Berger, Joseph, and Morris Zelditch, eds. 1985. *Status, Rewards, and Influence.* San Francisco: Jossey-Bass.

Berger, Peter, and Thomas Luckman. 1964. *The Social Construction of Reality: A Treatise in the Sociology of Knowledge.* Garden City, N.Y.: Doubleday.

Bernstein, Basil A. 1977. *Class, Codes and Control.* Vol. 3. London: Routledge and Kegan Paul.

Bernstein, Richard. 1990. *Fragile Glory: A Portrait of France and the French.* New York: Knopf.

Bidou, Catherine. 1983. "L'évolution de la structure socio-professionnelle en France depuis 1954." In *Les couches moyennes salariées: Mosaïque sociologique,* edited by Catherine Bidou, Monique Dagnaud, Bruno Duriez, Jacques Ion, Dominique Mehl, Monique Pinçon-Charlot, and Jean-Paul Tricart. Paris: Ministère de l'Urbanisme et du Logement, 169–82.

Bidou, Catherine, Monique Dagnaud, Bruno Duriez, Jacques Ion, Dominique Mehl, Monique Pinçon-Charlot, and Jean-Paul Tricart, eds. 1983. *Les couches moyennes salariées: Mosaïque sociologique.* Paris: Ministère de l'Urbanisme et du Logement.

Birnbaum, Pierre, C. Baruck, M. Bellaiche, and A. Marie. 1978. *La classe dirigeante française.* Paris: Presses Universitaires de France.

Blackburn, M., and D. Bloom. 1985. "What Is Happening to the Middle Class?" *American Demographics* (January): 18–25.

Blau, Judith R. 1986. "The Elite Arts, More or Less de Rigueur: A Comparative Analysis of Metropolitan Culture." *Social Forces* 86, no. 64:875–905.

———. 1989. *The Shape of Culture: A Study of Contemporary Cultural Patterns in the United States.* Cambridge: Cambridge University Press.

Blau, Judith R., and Gail Ouets. 1987. *The Geography of Arts Participation: Report Prepared*

for the National Endowment for the Arts. Washington D.C.: National Endowment for the Arts.

Bledstein, Burton J. 1976. *The Culture of Professionalism: The Middle Class and the Development of Higher Education in America*. New York: W. W. Norton and Co.

Block, Fred. 1991. *Postindustrial Possibilities: A Critique of Economic Discourse*, Berkeley: University of California Press.

Bloom, Allan. 1987. *The Closing of the American Mind: How Higher Education Has Failed Democracy and Impoverished the Souls of Today's Students*. New York: Simon and Schuster.

Blum, Linda, and Vicky Smith. 1988. "Women's Mobility in the Corporation: A Critique of the Politics of Optimism." *Signs* 13, no. 3: 528–45.

Boltanski, Luc. 1982. *Les cadres: La formation d'un groupe social*. Paris: Editions de Minuit.

Boltanski, Luc, and Laurent Thévenot. 1991. *De la justification: les économies de la grandeur*. Paris: Gallimard.

Bonfield, Patricia. 1980. *U.S. Business Leader: A Study of Opinions and Characteristics*. New York: Conference Board.

Boschetti, Anna. 1988. *The Intellectual Enterprise: Sartre and Les Temps Modernes*, translated by Richard C. McCleary. Evanston, Ill.: Northwestern University Press.

Boudon, Raymond. 1973. *L'inégalité des chances*. Paris: Armand Collin.

———. 1981. "L'intellectuel et ses publics: Les singularités françaises." In *Français qui êtes-vous? Des essais et des chiffres*, edited by Jean-Daniel Reynaud and Yves Grafmeyer. Paris: Documentation Française, 465–80.

Bourdieu, Pierre. 1962. *The Algerians*. Boston: Beacon Press.

———. 1968. "Structuralism and the Theory of Sociological Knowledge." *Social Research* 35:681–706.

———. 1971. "Genèse et structure du champ religieux." *Revue Française de Sociologie* 12:294–334.

———. 1977. *Outline of a Theory of Practice*. Cambridge: Cambridge University Press.

———. 1979. *Algeria 1960*. Cambridge: Cambridge University Press.

———. 1980. "Le mort saisit le vif: Les relations entre l'histoire réifiée et l'histoire incorporée." *Actes de la Recherche en Sciences Sociales*, nos. 32–33:3–14.

———. 1980. *Questions de sociologie*. Paris: Editions de Minuit.

———. 1980. *Le sens pratique*. Paris: Editions de Minuit.

———. 1981. "Epreuves scolaires et consécration sociale." *Actes de la Recherche en Sciences Sociales* 39:3–70.

———. 1983. "The Field of Cultural Production or the Economic World Reversed." *Poetics* 12, nos. 4–5:311–56.

———. 1984. *Distinction: A Social Critique of the Judgment of Taste*, translated by Richard Nice. Cambridge, Mass.: Harvard University Press.

———. 1986. "The Production of Belief: Contribution to an Economy of Symbolic Goods." In *Media, Culture and Society: A Critical Reader*, edited by Richard Collins, James Curran, Nicholas Garnham, Paddy Scannell, Phillip Schlesinger, and Colin Sparks. London: Sage.

———. 1989. *La noblesse d'Etat: Grandes écoles et esprit de corps*. Paris: Editions de Minuit.

———. 1989. "Social Space and Symbolic Power." *Sociological Theory* 7, no. 1:14–25.

———. 1990. *In Other Words*. Stanford: Stanford University Press.

Bourdieu, Pierre, Luc Boltanski, and Monique de St-Martin. 1973. "Les stratégies de reconversion." *Information sur les Sciences Sociales* 12:61–113.

Bourdieu, Pierre, and Jean-Claude Passerson. 1977. *Reproduction in Education, Society and Culture*, translated by Richard Nice. Beverly Hills, Calif.: Sage.

————. 1979. *The Inheritors: French Students and Their Relation to Culture.* Chicago: University of Chicago Press.

Bourdieu, Pierre, and Monique de St-Martin. 1975. "Les catégories de l'entendement professoral." *Actes de la Recherche en Sciences Sociales* 3:68–93.

————. 1978. "Le patronat." *Actes de la Recherche en Sciences Sociales,* nos. 20–21:3–82.

Bowles, Samuel, and Herbert Gintis. 1976. *Schooling in Capitalist America.* New York: Basic Books.

Brint, Steven. 1984. "'New Class' and Cumulative Trend Explanations of the Liberal Political Attitudes of Professionals." *American Journal of Sociology* 90, no. 1:30–71.

————. 1985. "The Political Attitudes of Professionals." *Annual Review of Sociology* 11: 389–414.

————. 1987. "Classification Struggles: Reply to Lamont." *American Journal of Sociology* 92, no. 6:1506–9.

————. 1987. "The Occupational Class Identifications of Professionals: Evidence from Cluster Analysis." *Research in Social Stratification and Mobility* 6:35–57.

————. 1988. "The Social Bases and National Contexts of Middle-Class Liberalism and Dissent in Western Societies: A Comparative Study." Unpublished paper, Department of Sociology, Yale University.

————. Forthcoming. "Is the U.S. Pattern Typical? The Politics of Professionals in Other Industrial Democracies." In *Retainers, Merchants, and Priests: A Political Sociology of the Professional Middle Class.* Berkeley: University of California Press.

Brodsky, Jody Ellen. 1987. "Intellectual Snobbery: A Socio-Historical Perspective." Unpublished Ph.D. diss., Department of Sociology, State University of New York, Stonybrook.

Bronfenbrenner, Ulf. 1958. "Socialization and Social Class through Time and Space." In *Readings in Social Psychology,* edited by E. E. Maccoby, T. M. Newcomb, and E. L. Hartley. New York: Holt, Rinehart and Winston.

Burris, Val. 1980. "Capital Accumulation and the Rise of the New Middle Class." *Review of Radical Political Economy* 12:17–34.

————. 1980. "Class Formation and Transformation in Advanced Capitalist Societies: A Comparative Analysis." *Social Praxis* 7:1471–79.

Butsch, Richard. 1991. "Class and Gender in Four Decades of TV Families: Plus Ça Change—" Unpublished ms., Rider College.

Butsch, Richard, and Lynda M. Glennon. 1983. "Social Class: Frequency Trends in Domestic Situation Comedy, 1946–1978." *Journal of Broadcasting* 27, no. 1:77–81.

Cabanne, Pierre. 1981. *Le pouvoir culturel sous la Ve république.* Paris: Olivier Orban.

Calhoun, Craig. 1988. "Populist Politics, Communication Media, and Large Scale Integration." *Sociological Theory* 6:219–41.

Cameron, David. 1978. "The Expansion of the Public Economy: A Comparative Analysis." *American Political Science Review* 72:1243–61.

Canovan, Margaret. 1981. *Populism,* New York: Harcourt, Brace, Jovanovich.

Capdevielle, Jacques, et al. 1981. *France de gauche, vote à droite.* Paris: Presses de la Fondation Nationale de Sciences Politiques.

Carroll, Raymonde. 1988. *Cultural Misunderstanding: The French-American Experience.* Chicago: University of Chicago Press.

Centre National des Oeuvres Universitaires et Scolaires. 1989. *Je vais en France 1989: Guide à l'intention des étudiants étrangers.* Paris: Centre National des Oeuvres Universitaires et Scolaires.

Chalvon-Demersay, Sabine. 1984. *Le triangle du XIVe: Des nouveaux habitants dans un vieux quartier de Paris.* Paris: Editions de la Maison des Sciences de l'Homme.

Chapin, J. S. 1933. *The Measurement of Social Status by the Use of the Social Status Scale.* Minneapolis: University of Minnesota Press.

Cheek, Neil H., Jr., and William R. Burch. 1976. *The Social Organization of Leisure in Human Society.* New York: Harper and Row.

Clark, Priscilla Parkhurst. 1975. "Thoughts for Food: French Cuisine and French Culture." *French Review* 49, no. 1 (October): 32–41.

———. 1979. "Literary Culture in France and the United States." *American Journal of Sociology* 84 : 1047–76.

———. 1987. *Literary France: The Making of a Culture.* Berkeley: University of California Press.

Closets, François de. 1982. *Toujours plus.* Paris: Bernard Grasset.

———. 1985. *Tous ensemble: Pour en finir avec la syndicratie.* Paris: Editions du Seuil.

Cohen, Albert K., and Harold M. Hodges. 1963. "Characteristics of the Lower Blue-Collar Class." *Social Problems* 10 : 303–34.

Cohen, Anthony. 1985. *Symbolic Construction of Community.* London and New York: Tavistock Publications.

Cohen, Elie. 1988. "Patrons, entrepreneurs et dirigeants: avant-propos." *Sociologie du Travail* 4 : 509–14.

Coleman, Richard P., and Bernice L. Neugarten. 1971. *Social Status in the City.* San Francisco: Josey Bass.

Coleman, Richard P., and Lee Rainwater, with Kent A. McClelland. 1978. *Social Standing in America: New Dimensions of Class.* New York: Basic Books.

Collectif "Révoltes logiques." 1984. *L'empire du sociologue.* Paris: Editions La Découverte.

Collins, Randall. 1975. *Conflict Sociology: Toward an Explanatory Science.* New York: Academic Press.

———. 1979. *The Credential Society.* New York: Academic Press.

———. 1981. "On the Micro-Foundations of Macro-Sociology." *American Journal of Sociology* 86 : 984–1014.

———. 1988. *Theoretical Sociology.* San Diego: Harcourt, Brace, Jovanovitch.

———. 1992. "Women and the Production of Status Culture." In *Cultivating Differences: Symbolic Boundaries and the Making of Inequality,* edited by Michèle Lamont and Marcel Fournier. Chicago: University of Chicago Press.

Cookson, Peter W., Jr., and Caroline Hodges Persell. 1985. *Preparing for Power: America's Elite Boarding Schools.* New York: Basic Books.

Coser, Lewis. 1965. *Men of Ideas: A Sociologist's View,* New York: Free Press.

Craig, J. 1981. "The Development of Educational Systems." *American Journal of Sociology* 89 : 190–211.

Crane, Diana. 1992. "High Culture vs. Popular Culture Revisited: A Reconceptualization of Recorded Cultures." In *Cultivating Differences: Symbolic Boundaries and the Making of Inequality,* edited by Michèle Lamont and Marcel Fournier. Chicago: University of Chicago Press.

Crawford, Stephen. 1989. *Technical Workers in an Advanced Society: The Work, Careers and Politics of French Engineers.* Cambridge: Cambridge University Press; and Paris: Editions de la Maison des Sciences de l'Homme.

Crittendon, Kathleen S. 1983. "Sociological Aspects of Attribution." *Annual Review of Sociology* 9 : 425–46.

Crozier, Michel. 1964. *The Bureaucratic Phenomenon.* Chicago: University of Chicago Press.

Cuber, John, and Peggy Haroff. 1965. *Sex and the Significant Americans.* Baltimore: Penguin Book.

Dagnaud, Monique, and Dominique Mehl. 1982. *L'élite rose: Qui gouverne?* Paris: Editions Ramsay.

Dalton, Russell J. 1988. *Citizen Politics in Western Democracies: Public Opinion and Political Parties in the United States, Great Britain, West Germany and France.* Chatham, N.J.: Chatham House Publishers.

Darnton, Robert. 1984. *The Great Cat Massacre and Other Episodes in French Cultural History.* New York: Basic Books.

Davis, James A. 1982. "Achievement Variables and Class Cultures: Family Schooling, Job and Forty-Nine Dependent Variables in the Cumulative GSS." *American Sociological Review* 47:569–86.

Davis, Natalie Zemon. 1975. *Society and Culture in Early Modern France.* Stanford: Stanford University Press.

Debray, Regis. 1979. *Teachers, Writers and Celebrities: The Intellectuals in Modern France.* London: New Left.

Della Fave, L. Richard. 1974. "Success Values: Are They Universal or Class-Differentiated?" *American Journal of Sociology* 80, no. 1:153–69.

Dens, Jean-Pierre. 1981. *L'honnête homme et la critique du goût: Esthétique et société au XVIIe siècle.* Lexington, Ky.: French Forum.

Derber, Charles. 1982. *Professionals as Workers: Mental Labor in Advanced Capitalism.* Boston: G. K. Hall.

Derber, Charles, William A. Schwartz, and Yale Magrass. 1990. *Power in the Highest Degree: Professionals and the Rise of a New Mandarin Order.* Oxford: Oxford University Press.

Desrosières, Alain, Alain Goy, and Laurent Thévenot. 1983. "L'identité sociale dans le travail statistique: La nouvelle nomenclature des professions et catégories socioprofessionnelles." *Economie et Statistiques* 152:55–81.

Dictionnaire national des communes de France. 1984. Paris: Albin Michel.

DiMaggio, Paul. 1982. "Cultural Capital and School Success: The Impact of Status Culture Participation on the Grades of U.S. High School Students." *American Sociological Review* 47:189–201.

———. 1986. "Cultural Entrepreneurship in Nineteenth Century Boston: The Creation of an Organizational Base for High Culture in America." In *Media, Culture and Society: A Critical Reader,* edited by Richard Collins, James Curran, Nicholas Graham, Paddy Scannell, Philip Schlesinger, and Colin Sparks. Beverly Hills, Calif.: Sage, 194–211.

———. 1987. "Classification in Art." *American Sociological Review* 52, no. 4:440–55.

DiMaggio, Paul, and John Mohr. 1985. "Cultural Capital, Educational Attainment, and Marital Selection." *American Journal of Sociology,* 90:1231–61.

DiMaggio, Paul, and Francie Ostrower. 1990. "Participation in the Arts by Black and White Americans." *Social Forces* 68, no. 3:753–78.

DiMaggio, Paul, and Walter W. Powell. 1983. "The Iron Cage Revisited: Institutional Isomorphism and Collective Rationality in Organizational Fields." *American Sociological Review* 48:147–60.

———. 1991. "Introduction." In *The New Institutionalism in Organizational Analysis,* edited by Walter W. Powell and Paul DiMaggio. Chicago: University of Chicago Press, 1–40.

DiMaggio, Paul, and Michael Useem. 1978. "Social Class and Arts Consumption: The Origins and Consequences of Class Differences in Exposure to the Arts in America." *Theory and Society* 5:141–61.

Dobbin, Frank R. Forthcoming. *States and Industrial Cultures: Britain, France, and the United States in the Railway Age.* New York: Cambridge University Press.

Doeringer, P. B., and M. J. Piore. 1971. *Internal Labor Markets and Manpower Analysis.* Lexington, Mass.: Heath.

Domenach, Jean-Marie. 1981. "Le monde des intellectuels." In *Société et culture de la France contemporaine*, edited by G. Santoni. Albany: State University of New York Press, 321–71.

Domhoff, G. William. 1974. *The Bohemian Grove and Other Retreats: A Study of Ruling-Class Cohesiveness*. New York: Harper and Row.

Donnat, Olivier, and Denis Cogneau. 1990. *Les pratiques culturelles des Français 1973–1989*. Paris: La Découverte/La Documentation Française.

Douglas, Mary. 1966. *Purity and Danger: An Analysis of the Concepts of Pollution and Taboo*. New York: Pantheon.

———. 1970. *Natural Symbols: Explorations in Cosmology*. London: Barrie and Jenkins.

Dupuy, François, and Jean-Claude Thoenig. 1985. *L'administration en miettes*. Paris: Fayard.

Durkheim, Emile. 1965. *The Elementary Forms of Religious Life*, translated by Joseph Ward Swain. New York: Free Press.

Ehrenreich, Barbara. 1989. *Fear of Falling: The Inner Life of the Middle Class*. New York: Pantheon.

Ehrenreich, Barbara, and J. Ehrenreich. 1979. "The Professional-Managerial Class." In *Between Labor and Capital*, edited by Pat Walker. Boston: Southend Press, 5–45.

Ehrman, Henry W. 1983. *Politics in France*. 4th ed. Boston: Little, Brown and Co.

Epstein, Cynthia Fuchs. 1988. *Deceptive Distinctions: Sex, Gender, and the Social Order*. New Haven: Yale University Press; and New York: Russell Sage Foundation.

———. 1989. "Workplace Boundaries: Conceptions and Creations." *Social Research* 56, no. 3: 571–90.

———. 1992. "Tinkerbells and Pinups: The Construction and Reconstruction of Gender Boundaries at Work." In *Cultivating Differences: Symbolic Boundaries and the Making of Inequality*, edited by Michèle Lamont and Marcel Fournier. Chicago: University of Chicago Press.

Erikson, Kai T. 1966. *Wayward Puritans: A Study in the Sociology of Deviance*. New York: John Wiley.

Erikson, R., and J. H. Goldthorpe. 1985. "Are American Rates of Social Mobility Exceptionally High? New Evidence on an Old Issue." *European Sociological Review* 1:1–22.

Erikson, R., J. H. Goldthorpe, and L. Portocarero. 1979. "Intergenerational Class Mobility in Three Western European Societies: England, France, and Sweden." *British Journal of Sociology* 30:315–41.

Etzioni, Amitai. 1988. *The Moral Dimension: Toward a New Economics*. New York: Free Press.

Fantasia, Rick. 1988. *Cultures of Solidarity: Consciousness, Action and Contemporary American Workers*. Berkeley: University of California Press.

———. 1990. "Fast-Food in France: The Market in Cultural Change." Paper presented at the annual meeting of the American Sociological Association, Washington D.C., August.

Farkas, George, Robert P. Grobe, Daniel Sheehan, and Yuan Shuan. 1990. "Cultural Resources and School Success: Gender, Ethnicity, and Poverty Groups within an Urban District." *American Sociological Review* 55, no. 1: 127–42.

Faunce, William A. 1989. "On the Meaning of Occupational Status: Implications of Increasing Complexity for How Status Is Conceived." Paper presented at the annual meeting of the American Sociological Association, San Francisco, August.

———. 1989. "Occupational Status-Assignment Systems: The Effect of Status on Self-Esteem." *American Journal of Sociology* 95, no. 2: 378–400.

Favreau, Diane. 1987. "The Emergence of American Cuisine: 'Alimentary' Forms of Domination." Unpublished paper, Department of Sociology, University of California, San Diego.

Feagin, Joe R. 1975. *Subordinating the Poor: Welfare and American Beliefs*. Englewood Cliffs, N.J.: Prentice-Hall.

———. 1991. "The Continuing Significance of Race: Antiblack Discrimination in Public Places." *American Sociological Review* 56, no. 1: 101–16.

Fine, Gary Alan. 1979. "Small Groups and Culture Creation: The Idioculture of Little League Baseball Teams." *American Sociological Review* 44: 733–45.

Finkelstein, Martin J. 1984. *The American Academic Profession: A Synthesis of Social Scientific Inquiry since World War II*. Columbus: Ohio State University Press.

Finkielkraut, Alain. 1987. *La défaite de la pensée*. Paris: Gallimard.

Fischer, Claude. 1982. *To Dwell among Friends: Personal Networks in Town and City*. Chicago: University of Chicago Press.

Fitzgerald, Frances. 1986. *Cities on a Hill: A Journey through Contemporary American Cultures*, New York: Simon and Schuster.

Fourastié, Jean. 1979. *Les trentes glorieuses*. Paris: Fayard.

Frank, Arthur. 1979. "Reality Construction in Interaction." *Annual Review of Sociology* 5: 167–91.

Friedman, Debra, and Michael Hechter. 1988. "The Contribution of Rational Choice Theory to Macrosociological Research." *Sociological Theory* 6, no. 2: 201–18.

Fumaroli, Marc. 1991. *L'Etat culturel: Essai sur une religion moderne*. Paris: Editions de Fallois.

Galbraith, John K. 1968. *The New Industrial State*. New York: Signet Books.

Gans, Herbert J. 1967. *The Levittowners: Ways of Life and Politics in a New Suburban Community*. New York: Pantheon Books.

———. 1971. *Popular Culture and High Culture: An Analysis and Evaluation of Taste*. New York: Basic Books.

———. 1988. *Middle American Individualism: The Future of Liberal Democracy*. New York: Free Press.

Ganzeboom, Harry B. G., Donald J. Treiman, and Wout C. Ultee. 1991. "Comparative Intergenerational Stratification Research: Three Generations and Beyond." *Annual Review of Sociology* 17: 277–302.

Gaxie, Daniel. 1980. "Les logiques du recrutement politique." *Revue Française de Science Politique* 30: 5–45.

Gecas, Viktor. 1979. "The Influence of Social Class on Socialization." In *Contemporary Theories about the Family*, vol. 1, edited by Wesley R. Burr, Reuben Hill, F. Ivan Nye, Ira L. Reiss. New York: Free Press, 365–404.

———. 1982. "The Self-Concept." *Annual Review of Sociology* 8: 1–33.

Geertz, Clifford. 1973. *The Interpretation of Culture*. New York: Basic Books.

Gerson, Judith M., and Kathy Peiss. 1985. "Boundaries, Negotiation, Consciousness: Reconceptualizing Gender Relations." *Social Problems* 32, no. 4: 317–31.

Giddens, Anthony. 1984. *The Constitution of Society: Outline of a Theory of Structuration*. Berkeley: University of California Press.

———. 1991. *Modernity and Self-Identity: Self and Society in the Late Modern Age*. Cambridge: Polity Press.

Gielman, Eric, and Penelope Wang. 1984. "The Year of the Yuppie." *Newsweek* 104 (31 December): 14–29.

Gieryn, Thomas F. 1983. "Boundary-Work and the Demarcation of Science from Non-Science: Strains and Interests in Professional Ideologies of Scientists." *American Sociological Review* 48: 781–95.

Gilbert, J. B. 1968. *Writers and Partisans: A History of Literary Radicalism in America*. New York: John Wiley.

Gilligan, Carol. 1982. *In a Different Voice: Psychological Theory and Women's Development.* Cambridge, Mass.: Harvard University Press.

Girard, Alain. 1961. *La réussite sociale en France: Ses caractères, ses lois, ses effets.* Paris: Presses Universitaires de France.

Girard, Alain, and Jean Stoetzel. 1985. "Les français et les valeurs du temps présent." *Revue Française de Sociologie* 26, no. 1:3–31.

Gitlin, Todd. 1983. *Inside Prime Time.* New York: Pantheon.

Glazer, Barney G., and Anselm Strauss. 1967. *The Discovery of Grounded Theory: Strategies for Qualitative Research.* Chicago: Aldine.

Glucksman, André. 1987. *Descartes, c'est la France.* Paris: Flammarion.

Goffman, Erving. 1959. *The Presentation of Self in Everyday Life.* Garden City, N.Y.: Doubleday.

———. 1963. *Stigma: Notes on the Management of Spoiled Identity.* Englewood Cliffs, N.J.: Prentice Hall.

Gollac, Michel, and Pierre Laulhe. 1987. "Les composantes de l'hérédité sociale: Un capital économique et culturel à transmettre." *Economie et Statistiques* 199–200 (May–June): 93–105.

Gonos, George. 1977. "'Situation' versus 'Frame': The 'Interactionist' and the 'Structuralist' Analysis of Everyday Life." *American Sociological Review* 42:854–67.

Gottdiener, Mark, and Donna Malone. 1985. "Group Differentiation in a Metropolitan High School: The Influence of Race, Class, Gender and Culture." *Qualitative Sociology* 8, no. 1:29–41.

Gouldner, Alvin W. 1979. *The Future of Intellectuals and the Rise of the New Class: A Frame of Reference, Theses, Conjectures, Arguments and a Historical Perspective on the Role of Intellectuals and Intelligentsia in the International Class Contest of the Modern Era.* New York: Seabury Press.

Granick, David. 1972. *Managerial Comparisons of Four Developed Countries: France, Britain, United States and Russia.* Cambridge, Mass.: MIT Press.

Granovetter, Mark S. 1974. *Getting a Job: A Study of Contacts and Careers.* Cambridge, Mass.: Harvard University Press

———. 1985. "Economic Action and Social Structure: The Problem of Embeddedness." *American Journal of Sociology* 91, no. 3:481–510.

Greenberg, M. G., and R. F. Frank. 1983. "Leisure Lifestyles." *American Behavioral Scientist* 26, no. 4:439–58.

Greenhouse, Carol J. 1986. *Praying for Justice: Faith, Order and Community in an American Town.* Ithaca: Cornell University Press.

Grignon, Claude, and Christine Grignon. 1980. "Styles alimentaires et goûts populaires." *Revue Française de Sociologie* 21, no. 4:531–70.

Grignon, Claude, and Jean-Claude Passeron. 1985. *A propos des cultures populaires.* Marseilles: Cahiers du CERCOM.

Griswold, Wendy. 1987. "A Methodological Framework for the Sociology of Culture." *Sociological Methodology* 14:1–35.

Grunberg, Gérard, and René Mouriaux. 1979. *L'univers politique et syndical des cadres.* Paris: Presses de la Fondation Nationale de Sciences Politiques.

Grunberg, Gérard, and Etienne Schweisguth. 1983. "A quoi sert la sociologie empirique?" *Revue Française de Sociologie* 24:327–38.

Gurin, Patricia, Arthur H. Miller, and Gerald Gurin. 1980. "Stratum Identification and Consciousness." *Social Psychology Quarterly* 43, no. 1:30–47.

Gusfield, Joseph R. 1963. *Symbolic Crusades.* Urbana: University of Illinois Press.

————. 1975. *Communities: A Critical Response*. New York: Harper and Row.

Hall, John. 1992. "The Capital(s) of Culture: A Non-Holistic Approach to Gender, Ethnicity, Class and Status Groups." In *Cultivating Differences: Symbolic Boundaries and the Making of Inequality*, edited by Michèle Lamont and Marcel Fournier. Chicago: University of Chicago Press.

Hall, Peter. 1986. *Governing the Economy: The Politics of State Intervention in Britain and France*. New York: Oxford University Press.

Halle, David. 1984. *America's Working Man: Work, Home and Politics among Blue-Collar Property Owners*. Chicago: University of Chicago Press.

————. 1989. "Class and Culture in Modern America: The Vision of the Landscape in the Residences of Contemporary Americans." *Prospects* 14:373–406.

Haller, Max. 1987. "Positional and Sectoral Differences in Income: The Federal Republic, France and the United States." In *Comparative Studies of Social Structure: Recent Research on France, the United States and the Federal Republic of Germany*, edited by Wolfgang Teckenberg. New York: M. E. Sharpe, 172–94.

Haller, Max, Wolfgang König, Peter Krause, and Karin Hurz. 1985. "Patterns of Career Mobility and Structural Positions in Advanced Capitalist Societies: A Comparison of Men in Austria, France and the United States." *American Sociological Review* 50, no. 5:579–603.

Hamon, Hervé, and Patrick Rotman. 1981. *Les intellocrates: Expédition en haute intelligentsia*. Paris: Ramsès.

————. 1984. *Tant qu'il y aura des profs*. Paris: Éditions du Seuil.

Handler, Richard. 1988. *Nationalism and the Politics of Culture in Quebec*. Madison: University of Wisconsin Press.

Harding, Steven, and David Phillips, with M. Fogarty. 1986. *Contrasting Values in Western Europe: Unity, Diversity and Exchange*. Basingstoke, Hampshire: Macmillan, in association with the European Value Systems Study Group.

Harris, G., and A. De Sedouy. 1977. *Les patrons*. Paris: Éditions du Seuil.

Harris, Richard. 1991. "The Geography of Employment and Residence in New York since 1950." In *Dual City: Restructuring New York*, edited by John Mollenkopf and Manuel Castells. New York: Russell Sage, 129, 52.

Harrison, Bennett, and Barry Bluestone. 1988. *The Great U-Turn: Corporate Restructuring and the Polarizing of America*. New York: Basic Books.

Hartz, Louis. 1955. *The Liberal Tradition in America*. New York: Harcourt, Brace and World.

Hayward, Jack. 1973. "Elusive Autonomy: Education and Public Enterprise." In *The One and Indivisible French Republic*, edited by Jack Hayward. New York: W. W. Norton and Co., 190–226.

Heath, Shirley Brice. 1983. *Ways with Words: Language, Life and Work in Communities and Classrooms*. New York: Cambridge University Press.

Hendrickson, Robert. 1986. *American Talk: The Words and Ways of American Dialects*. New York: Viking.

Héran, François. 1988. "Un monde sélectif: Les associations." *Economie et Statistiques* 208: 17–32.

————. 1988. "La sociabilité, une pratique culturelle." *Economie et Statistiques* 216:3–21.

Herzfeld, Michael. 1980. "Honour and Shame: Problems in the Comparative Analysis of Moral Systems." *Man* 15:339–51.

Hirsch, E. D., Jr. 1987. *Cultural Literacy: What Every American Needs to Know*. Boston: Houghton Mifflin Co.

Hirsch, Paul, Stuart Michaels, and Ray Friedman. 1987. "'Dirty Hands' versus 'Clean

Models': Is Sociology in Danger of Being Seduced by Economics?" *Theory and Society* 16, no. 3:3170–336.

Hochschild, Jennifer L. 1981. *What's Fair? American Beliefs about Distributive Justice.* Cambridge, Mass.: Harvard University Press.

Hodson, Randy, and Teresa A. Sullivan. 1990. *The Social Organization of Work.* Belmont, Calif.: Wadsworth Inc.

Hoffman, Stanley, ed. 1963. *In Search of France.* Cambridge, Mass.: Harvard University Press.

Hofstadter, Richard. 1963. *Anti-Intellectualism in American Life.* New York: Knopf.

Hofstede, Geert H. 1980. *Culture's Consequences: International Differences in Work-related Values.* Beverly Hills, Calif.: Sage.

Hogg, Michael A., and Dominic Abrams. 1988. *Social Identification: A Social Psychology of Intergroup Relations and Group Processes.* London and New York: Routledge.

Hollinger, David A. 1983. "The Problem of Pragmatism in American History." In *In the American Province: Studies in the History and Historiography of Ideas.* Bloomington: Indiana University Press, 23–43.

———. 1984. "Ethnic Diversity, Cosmopolitanism, and the Emergence of the American Liberal Intellectuals." In *The American Province.* Bloomington: Indiana University Press.

Honneth, Axel. 1986. "The Fragmented World of Symbolic Forms: Reflections on Pierre Bourdieu's Sociology of Culture." *Theory, Culture, and Society* 3, no. 1:55–66.

Hoover, Edgar, and Raymond Vernon. 1959. *Anatomy of a Metropolis: The Changing Distribution of People and Jobs within the New York Metropolitan Region.* Garden City, N.Y.: Free Press.

Horowitz, Ruth. 1983. *Honor and the American Dream: Culture and Identity in a Chicano Community.* New Brunswick: Rutgers University Press.

Hout, Michael. 1988. "More Universalism, Less Structural Mobility: The American Occupational Structure in the 1980s." *American Journal of Sociology* 93, no. 3:1358–1400.

Huber, Richard M. 1971. *The American Idea of Success.* Wanscott, N.Y.: Pushcart Press.

Human Resources Management in France. 1986. Paris: Délégation à l'Aménagement du Territoire et à l'Action Régionale.

Hunt, Lynn. 1984. *Politics, Culture and Class in the French Revolution.* Berkeley: University of California Press.

Hunter, James Davison. 1987. "American Protestantism: Sorting out the Present, Looking toward the Future." *This World* 17:53–76.

———. 1987. *Evangelicalism: The Coming Generation.* Chicago: University of Chicago Press.

Hunter, James Davison, John Herrman, and John Jarvis. 1990. "Cultural Elites and Political Values." Unpublished ms., Department of Sociology, University of Virginia.

Huntley, Steve, Gail Bronson, and Kenneth T. Walsh. 1984. "Yumpies, YAP's, Yuppies: Who are They?" *U.S. News and World Report* 96, no. 15 (16 April): 39.

Hurrelmann, Klaus. 1988. *Social Structure and Personality Development: The Individual as a Productive Processor of Reality.* Cambridge: Cambridge University Press.

Hyman, Herbert H. 1966. "The Value Systems of Different Classes." In *Class, Status and Power,* edited by Reinhard Bendix and Seymour Martin Lipset. New York: Free Press, 488–99.

Indianapolis City Directory, 1985. Maldin, Mass.: R. L. Polk and Co.

Indianapolis Suburban Directory, 1984. Maldin, Mass.: R. L. Polk and Co.

Inglehart, Ronald. 1977. *The Silent Revolution: Changing Values and Political Style among Western Publics.* Princeton: Princeton University Press.

———. 1990. *Culture Shift in Advanced Industrial Societies.* Princeton: Princeton University Press.

Inkeles, Alex. 1979. "Continuity and Change in the American National Character." In *The Third Century: America as a Post-Industrial Society,* edited by Seymour Martin Lipset. Stanford: Hoover Institute Press.

Institut National de Statistiques et d'Etudes Economiques (INSEE). 1987. *Annuaire statistique de la France. 1987.* Vol. 92, ser. 34. Paris: Documentation Française.

Institut National de Statistiques et d'Etudes Economiques (INSEE). 1987. *Données sociales 1987.* Paris: Documentation Française.

Inzerilli, Giorgio, and André Laurent. 1983. "Managerial Views of Organization Structure in France and the U.S.A." *International Studies of Management and Organization* 13:97–118.

Jackall, Robert. 1988. *Moral Mazes: The World of Corporate Manager.* New York: Oxford University Press.

Jackman, Mary R., and Robert W. Jackman. 1983. *Class Awareness in the United States.* Berkeley: University of California Press.

Jackman, Mary R., and M. J. Muha. 1984. "Education and Intergroup Attitudes: Moral Enlightenment, Superficial Democratic Commitment or Ideological Refinement?" *American Sociological Review* 49:751–69.

Jacoby, Russell. 1987. *The Last Intellectuals: American Culture in the Age of Academe.* New York: Basic Books.

James, Estelle, ed. 1989. *The Nonprofit Sector: Studies in Comparative Culture and Policy.* New York: Oxford University Press.

Jeffries, Vincent, and H. Edward Ransford. 1980. *Social Stratification: A Multiple Hierarchy Approach.* Boston: Ally and Bacon.

Jencks, C., et al. 1979. *Who Gets Ahead? The Determinants of Economic Success in America.* New York: Basic Books.

Jones, E. E., and Thane S. Pittman. 1982. "Toward a General Theory of Strategic Self-Presentation." In *Psychological Perspectives on the Self,* edited by Jerry Suls. Hillsdale, N.J.: Erlbaum.

Kalberg, Stephen. 1980. "Max Weber's Types of Rationality: Cornerstones for the Analysis of Rationalization Processes in History." *American Journal of Sociology* 85, no. 5: 1145–79.

Kalmijn, Matthijs. 1991. "Status Homogamy in the United States." *American Journal of Sociology* 97, no. 2:496–523.

Kamens, David H., and R. Danforth Ross. 1983. "Chartering National Educational Systems: The Institutionalization of Education for Elite Recruitment and Its Consequences." *International Journal of Comparative Sociology* 24, nos. 3–4:176–86.

Kanter, Rosabeth Moss. 1977. *Men and Women of the Corporation.* New York: Basic Books.

Katchadourian, Heran A., and John Boli. 1985. *Careerism and Intellectualism among College Students.* San Francisco: Jossey Bass.

Katsillis, John, and Richard Rubinson. 1990. "Cultural Capital, Student Achievement, and Educational Reproduction: The Case of Greece." *American Sociological Review* 55: 270–79.

Katznelson, Ira. 1981. *City Trenches: Urban Politics and the Patterning of Class in the United States.* Chicago: University of Chicago Press.

Keller, Suzanne. 1989. "Women in the 21st Century: Summing up and Moving Forward." Paper presented at the first Radcliffe Conference on "Defining the Challenge," January.

Kerbo, Harold R. 1983. *Social Stratification and Inequality: Class Conflict in the United States.* New York: McGraw-Hill.

Kerckhoff, Alan C. 1972. *Socialization and Social Class.* Englewood Cliffs, N.J.: Prentice Hall.

Kluegel, James R., and Eliot R. Smith. 1986. *Beliefs about Inequality: Americans' View of What Is and What Ought to Be.* New York: Aldine de Gruyter.

Kohn, Melvin L. 1987. "Cross-National Research as an Analytic Strategy." *American Sociological Review* 52:713–31.

Kohn, Melvin L., Atsushi Naoi, Carrie Schoenbach, Carmi Schooler, and Kazimierz M. Slomczynski. 1990. "Position in the Class Structure and Psychological Functioning: A Comparative Analysis of the United States, Japan and Poland." *American Journal of Sociology* 95, no. 4:964–1008.

Kohn, Melvin L., and Carmi L. Schooler, with Joanne Miller. 1983. *Work and Personality.* Norwood, N.J.: Ablex.

Komarovsky, Mira. 1967. *Blue Collar Marriage.* New York. Vintage.

Kornhauser, William, with Warren O. Hagstrom. 1965. *Scientists in Industry: Conflict and Accommodation.* Berkeley: University of California Press.

Kriesi, Hanspeter. 1989. "New Social Movements and the New Class in the Netherlands." *American Journal of Sociology* 94, no. 5:1078–1116.

Ladd, Everett C. 1979. "Pursuing the New Class: Social Theory and Survey Data." In *The New Class?* edited by B. Bruce-Briggs. New Brunswick: Transaction, 101–22.

Lambert, Wallace E. 1952. "Comparison of French and American Modes of Response to the Bogardus Social Distance Scale." *Social Forces* 31 no. 2:155–159.

Lambert, Wallace E., J. F. Hamers, and N. Frasure-Smith. 1979. *Child-Rearing Values: A Cross-National Study.* New York: Praeger.

Lamont, Michèle. 1983. "The Growth of the Social Sciences and the Decline of the Humanities in Quebec: A Macro Explanation of Recent Changes." Ph.D. diss., Université de Paris.

———. "Cultural Capital and the Liberal Political Attitudes of Professionals: A Comment on Brint." *American Journal of Sociology* 96:1501–5.

———. 1987. "How to Become a Dominant French Philosopher: The Case of Jacques Derrida." *American Journal of Sociology* 93, no. 3:584–622.

———. 1987. "New Middle Class Liberalism and Autonomy from Profit-Making: The Case of Quebec." Unpublished paper, Department of Sociology, Princeton University.

———. 1987. "The Production of Culture in France and the United States since World War II." In *The Role of Intellectuals in Liberal Democracies,* edited by A. Gagnon. New York: Praeger, 167–78.

———. 1988. "From Paris to Stanford: Une reconversion sociologique: De la sociologie française à la sociologie américaine." *Politix* 3–4:22–29.

———. 1989. "The Power-Culture Link in a Comparative Perspective." *Comparative Social Research* 11:131–50.

Lamont, Michèle, and Annette Lareau. 1988. "Cultural Capital: Allusions, Gaps and Glissandos in Recent Theoretical Developments." *Sociological Theory* 6, no. 2:153–68.

Lamont, Michèle, and Robert Wuthnow. 1990. "Betwixt and Between: Recent Cultural Sociology in Europe and the United States." In *Frontiers of Social Theory: The New Synthesis,* edited by George Ritzer. New York: Columbia University Press, 287–315.

Landes, David S. 1952. "The Entrepreneur and the Social Order: France and the United States." In *Men in Business.* Cambridge, Mass.: Harvard University Press.

Lareau, Annette P. 1989. *Home Advantage: Social Class and Parental Intervention in Elementary Education.* London and New York: Falmer Press.

———. 1990. "Uncovering the Capital in Cultural Capital: Social Class and the Construction of School Careers." Unpublished ms., Department of Sociology, Temple University.

Larkin, Ralph W. 1979. *Suburban Youth in Cultural Crisis.* New York: Oxford University Press.
Larson, Magali S. 1977. *The Rise of Professionalism: A Sociological Analysis.* Berkeley: University of California Press.
Lasch, Christopher. 1969. *The Agony of the American Left.* New York: Knopf.
————. 1979. *The Culture of Narcissism: American Life in an Age of Diminishing Expectations.* New York: W. W. Norton and Co.
Lash, Scott. 1984. *The Militant Worker: Class and Radicalism in France and America.* Rutherford, Madison, and Teaneck, N.J.: Farleigh Dickinson Press.
Laumann, Edward O., ed. 1973. *Bonds of Pluralism: The Form and Substance of Urban Social Networks.* New York: John Wiley.
Laurent, André. 1983. "The Cultural Diversity of Western Conceptions of Management." *International Studies of Management and Organization* 13:75–96.
Lavau, Georges, Gérard Grunberg, and Nonna Mayer. 1983. *L'univers politique des classes moyennes.* Paris: Presses de la Fondation Nationale de Sciences Politiques.
Lawson, Annette. 1988. *Adultery: An Analysis of Love and Betrayal.* New York: Basic Books.
Lerner, Daniel. 1961. "An American Researcher in Paris: Interviewing the French." In *Studying Personality Cross-culturally,* edited by B. Kaplan. New York: Row and Peterson, 427–44.
Lévi-Strauss, Claude. 1963. *Totemism.* Boston: Beacon Press.
Lévy-Leboyer, Maurice. 1980. "The Large Corporation in Modern France." In *Managerial Hierarchies: Comparative Perspectives on the Rise of the Industrial Entreprise,* edited by A. Chandler and H. Daems. Cambridge, Mass.: Harvard University Press, 117–70.
Le Wita, Béatrix. 1988. *Ni vue ni connue: Approche ethnographique de la culture bourgeoise.* Paris: Editions de la Maison des Sciences de l'Homme.
Lipovetzky, Gilles. 1983. *L'ère du vide: Essai sur l'individualisme contemporain.* Paris: Gallimard.
Lipset, Seymour Martin. 1977. "Why No Socialism in the United States?" In *Sources of Contemporary Radicalism,* edited by S. Bialer and S. Sluzar. Boulder, Colo.: Westview Press, 31–149.
————. 1979. *The First New Nation: The United States in Historical and Comparative Perspective.* New York: Norton.
————. 1981. *The Political Man: The Social Bases of Politics.* Expanded ed. Baltimore: Johns Hopkins University Press.
————. 1990. *Continental Divide: The Values and Institutions of the United States and Canada.* New York and London: Routledge.
Lipset, Seymour Martin, and Richard B. Dobson. 1972. "The Intellectual as Critic and Rebel." *Daedalus* (Summer): 114–85.
Lipset, Seymour Martin, and Stein Rokkan. 1967. "Cleavage Structure, Party Systems and Voter Alignments: An Introduction." *Party Systems and Voter Alignments: Cross-national Perspectives,* edited by Seymour Martin Lipset and Stein Rokkan. New York: Free Press, 1–64.
Long, Elizabeth. 1987. "Reading Groups and the Post-Modern Crisis of Cultural Authority." *Cultural Studies* 1, no. 3:306–27.
Luker, Kristin. 1984. *Abortion and the Politics of Motherhood.* Berkeley: University of California Press.
Lynd, Robert S., and Helen M. Lynd. 1930. *Middletown: A Study in American Culture.* New York: Harcourt and Brace.
McCall, George J., and J. L Simmon. 1978. *Identity and Interaction: An Examination of Human Association in Everyday Life.* New York: Free Press.
McClelland, David K. 1961. *The Achieving Society.* New York: Nostrand.

MacLeod, Jay. 1987. *Ain't No Makin' It: Leveled Aspirations in a Low-Income Neighborhood*. Boulder, Colo.: Westview Press.

McPherson, J. Miller, and Lynn Smith-Lovin. 1987. "Homophily in Voluntary Organizations: Status Distance and the Composition of Face-to-Face Groups." *American Sociological Review* 52:370–79.

Macy, Michael W. 1988. "New-Class Dissent among Social-Cultural Specialists: The Effects of Occupational Self-Direction and Location in the Public Sector." *Sociological Forum* 3, no. 3:325–56.

Magliulo, Bruno. 1982. *Les grandes écoles*. Paris: Presses Universitaires de France.

Mantoux, Thiery. 1985. *BCBG: Le guide du bon chic bon genre*. Paris: Editions Hermès.

Marceau, Jane. 1977. *Class and Status in France: Economic Change and Social Immobility 1945–1975*. New York: Oxford University Press.

Margolis, Diane R. 1979. *The Managers: Corporate Life in America*. New York: Morrow.

Marin, Bernd. 1988. "Qu'est-ce que 'le patronat'? Enjeux théoriques et résultats empiriques." *Sociologie du Travail* 4:515–43.

Marsden, Peter V., John Shelton Reed, Michael D. Kennedy, and Kandi M. Stinson. 1982. "American Regional Cultures and Differences in Leisure-Time Activities." *Social Forces* 60, no. 4:1023–47.

Martin, Bill. 1986. "From Class Challenge to Comfortable Collaboration?: The Politics of the Educated Middle Class in the United States, 1960–80." Paper presented at the annual meetings of the American Sociological Association, New York, August.

Maurice, Marc, F. Sellier, and J.-J. Sylvestre. 1975. *Shift Work: Economic Advantages and Social Costs*. Geneva: International Labor Office.

——. 1977. *Production de la hiérarchie dans l'entreprise: Recherche d'un effet social, Allemagne-France*. Aix-en-Provence: Laboratoire d'Économie et de Sociologie du Travail.

Mayer, Nonna. 1982. "The Middle Classes and Politics in Contemporary France: A Bibliographic Introduction." *European Journal of Political Research* 10:437–44.

——. 1986. *La boutique contre la gauche*. Paris: Presses de la Fondation Nationale de Sciences Politiques.

Mazataud, Pierre. 1987. *Géopolitique d'une région: L'Auvergne. Allier, Puy-de-Dome, Cantal, Haute-Loire: Les faits, les chiffres, les hommes. analyses, synthèses, prévisions*. Nonette: Editions Creer.

Mehan, Hugh. 1992. "Beneath the Skin and between the Ears: A Case Study in the Politics of Representation." In *Understanding Practice*, edited by Jean Lave and Seth Chaiklen. Cambridge: Cambridge University Press.

——. In press. "Understanding Inequality in Schools: The Contribution of Interpretive Studies." *Sociology of Education*.

Merelman, Richard M. 1984. *Making Something of Ourselves: On Culture and Politics in the United States*. Berkeley: University of California Press.

Mermèt, Gérard. 1988. *Francoscopie, les Français: Qui sont-ils? Ou vont-ils?* Paris: Larousse.

Merton, Robert K. 1949. *Social Theory and Social Structure*. Glencoe, Ill.: Free Press.

——. 1957. "Patterns of Influence: Local and Cosmopolitan Influentials." In *Social Theory and Social Structure*. New York: Free Press, 387–420.

Meyer, John W. 1980. "The Effects of Education as an Institution." *American Journal of Sociology* 83:55–77.

——. 1986. "Myths of Socialization and of Personality." In *Reconstructing Individualism: Autonomy, Individuality, and the Self in Western Thought*, edited by Thomas C. Heller, Morton Sosna, and David E. Wellbery, with Arnold I. Davidson, Ann Swidler, and Ian Watt. Stanford: Stanford University Press, 208–21.

Meyer, John W., John Boli, and George M. Thomas. 1987. "Ontology and Rationalization in the Western Cultural Account." *Institutional Structure: Constituting State, Society,*

and the Individual, edited by George M. Thomas, John W. Meyer, Francisco O. Ramirez, and John Boli. Beverly Hills, Calif.: Sage, 12–37.

Meyer, John W., F. Ramirez, J. Rubinson, and J. Boli-Bennett. 1977. "The World Educational Revolution 1950–1970." Sociology of Education 50:242–58.

Michelat, Guy, and Michel Simon. 1977. Classes, religion et comportement politique. Paris: Editions Sociales.

———. 1985. "Déterminations socio-économiques, organisations symboliques et comportement électoral." Revue Française de Sociologie 26:32–69.

Miles, M. B., and A. M. Huberman. 1984. Qualitative Data Analysis: A Sourcebook of New Methods. Beverly Hills, Calif.: Sage.

Millman, Marcia. 1980. Such a Pretty Face: Being Fat in America. New York: W. W. Norton and Co.

Mills, C. Wright. 1953. White Collar: The American Middle Class. New York: Oxford University Press.

———. 1963. Power, Politics and People: The Collected Essays of C. Wright Mills, edited by Irving Louis Horowitz. Oxford: Oxford University Press.

Mishler, Elliot G. 1986. Research Interviewing: Context and Narrative. Cambridge, Mass.: Harvard University Press.

Mitchell, Timothy. 1990. "Everyday Metaphors of Power." Theory and Society 19:545–77.

Moffatt, Michael. 1989. Coming of Age in New Jersey: College and American Culture. New Brunswick: Rutgers University Press.

Mohr, John, and Paul DiMaggio. 1980. "Patterns of Occupational Inheritance of Cultural Capital." Paper presented at the meeting of the American Sociological Association.

Mollenkopf, John Hull. 1988. "The Postindustrial Transformation of the Political Order in New York City." In Power, Culture and Place: Essays on New York City, edited by J. J. Mollenkopf. New York: Russell Sage Foundation, 223–57.

Morrill, Calvin. 1991. "Conflict management, Honor, and Organizational Change." American Journal of Sociology 97, no. 3:585–621.

Murphy, Raymond. 1988. Social Closure: The Theory of Monopolization and Exclusion. Oxford: Clarendon.

Nemeth, G. 1983. "Reflection on the Dialogue between Status and Style." Social Psychology Quarterly 46, no. 1:70–74.

Newman, Katherine S. 1988. Falling from Grace: The Experience of Downward Mobility in the American Middle Class. New York: Free Press.

Ortner, Sherry. 1978. The Sherpas through their Rituals. Cambridge: Cambridge University Press.

———. 1991. "Reading America: Preliminary Notes on Class and Culture." In Recapturing Anthropology: Working in the Present, edited by Richard G. Fox. Seattle: University of Washington Press.

Ostrander, A. 1984. Women of the Upper Class. Philadelphia: Temple University Press.

Palmer, Michael. 1987. "Media and Communications Policy in France under the Socialists, 1981–86: Failing to Grasp the Correct Nettle?" In Contemporary France: A Review of Interdisciplinary Studies, edited by Jolyan Howorth and George Ross. London: Frances Pinter Publisher, 130–55.

Paradeise, C. 1980. "Sociabilité et culture de classe." Revue Française de Sociologie 21, no. 4: 571–97.

Parkin, Frank. 1974. "Strategies of Closure in Class Formation." In The Social Analysis of Class Structure. London: Tavistock, 1–18.

Parmentier, Patrick. 1986. "Les genres et leurs lecteurs." Revue Française de Sociologie 27: 397–430.

Parsons, Talcott. 1949. "The Professions and Social Structure." In *Essays in Sociological Theory, Pure and Applied*. Glencoe, Ill.: Free Press, 34–49.

Pavalko, Ronald M. 1988. *Sociology of Occupations and Professions*. Ithaca, Ill.: F. E. Peacock Publisher.

Pells, Richard. 1985. *The Liberal Mind in a Conservative Age*. New York: Harper and Row.

Perin, Constance. 1988. *Belonging in America*. Madison: University of Wisconsin Press.

Pernoud, Régine. 1981. *Histoire de la bourgeoisie en France*. Vol. 2. *Les temps modernes*. Paris: Editions du Seuil.

Perrot, Marguerite. 1982. *Le mode de vie des familles bourgeoises*. Paris: Presse de la Fondation Nationale de Sciences Politiques.

Perry, Lewis. 1989. *Intellectual Life in America: A History*. Chicago: University of Chicago Press.

Peterson, Richard A., and Michael Hughes. 1984. "Isolating Patterns of Cultural Choice to Facilitate the Formation of Culture Indicators." In *Cultural Indicators: An International Symposium*, edited by F. Melischek, K. E. Rosengren, and J. Stappers. Wien: Verlag der Osterreichischen Akademie der Wissenschaften, 443–52.

Phillips, Kevin P. 1982. *Post-Conservative America: People, Politics and Ideology in a Time of Crisis*. New York: Random House.

Piesman, Marissa, and Marilee Hartley. 1985. *The Yuppie Handbook*. New York: Pocket Books.

Pinçon, Michel. 1987. *Désarrois ouvriers*. Paris: L'Harmattan.

Pinçon, Michel, and Monique Pinçon-Charlot. 1989. *Dans les beaux quartiers*. Paris: Editions du Seuil.

Pinto, Diana. 1988. "Toward a Mellowing of the French Identity?" In *Contemporary France: A Review of Interdisciplinary Studies*, edited by Jolyan Howorth and George Ross. London: Frances Pinter, Publisher.

Pinto, Louis. 1984. *L'intelligence en action: Le Nouvel Observateur*. Paris: A. M. Métaillé, 1988.

Pitt-Rivers, Julian. 1966. "Honor and Social Status." In *Honor and Shame: The Values of Mediterranean Society*, edited by J. G. Peristiany. Chicago: University of Chicago Press, 19–77.

Pitts, Jessie. 1957. "The Bourgeois Family and French Economic Retardation." Ph.D. diss., Department of Sociology, Harvard University.

Pizzorno, Alessandro. 1991. "On the Individualistic Theory of Social Order." In *Social Theory for a Changing Society*, edited by Pierre Bourdieu and James S. Coleman. New York: Russell Sage and Westview Press, 209–31.

Le point économique de l'Auvergne (April 1977): no. 2.

Poulantzas, Nicos. 1978. *Classes in Contemporary Capitalism*. London: Verso.

Powers, Brian. 1987. "Second Class Finish: The Effect of a Working Class High School." Ph.D. diss., Department of Sociology, University of California, Berkeley.

Press, Andrea. 1991. *Women Watching Television: Gender, Class and Generations in the American Television Experience*. Philadelphia: University of Pennsylvania.

Rainwater, Lee. 1974. *What Money Buys: Inequality and the Social Meaning of Income*. New York: Basic Books.

Ravitch, Diane, and Chester E. Finn, Jr. 1987. *What Do Our 17-Year-Olds Know? A Report on the First National Assessment of History and Literature*. New York: Harper and Row.

Rawls, James R., Robert A. Ullrich, and Oscar Tivis Nelson, Jr. 1975. "A Comparison of Managers Entering or Reentering the Profit and Nonprofit Sectors." *Academy of Management Journal* 18, no. 3: 616–23.

Reich, Robert B. 1991. "The Secession of the Successful." *New York Times Sunday Magazine*, 20 January.

Reinarman, Craig. 1987. *American States of Mind: Political Beliefs and Behavior among Private and Public Workers.* New Haven: Yale University Press.

Riccio, James A. 1979. "Religious Affiliation and Socioeconomic Achievement." In *The Religious Dimension: New Directions in Quantitative Research,* edited by Robert Wuthnow. New York: Academic Press.

Rieder, Jonathan. 1985. *Canarsie: The Jews and Italians of Brooklyn against Liberalism.* Cambridge, Mass.: Harvard University Press.

Riesman, David, with Nathan Glazer and Reuel Denney. 1950. *The Lonely Crowd: A Study of the Changing American Character.* New Haven: Yale University Press.

Ringer, Fritz K. 1979. *Education and Society in Modern Europe.* Bloomington, Ind.: Indiana University Press.

Robinson, John P., Carol A. Kennan, Terry Hanford, and Timothy A. Trippett. 1985. *Public Participation in the Arts: Final Report on the 1982 Survey.* College Park, Md.: Report to the National Endowment for the Arts, Research Division.

Robinson, Robert V., and Maurice A. Granier. 1985. "Class Reproduction among Men and Women in France: Reproduction Theory on Its Home Ground." *American Journal of Sociology* 91, no. 2 : 250–80.

Rosaldo, Michelle A. 1980. "The Use and Abuse of Anthropology: Reflections on Feminism and Cross-Cultural Understanding." *Signs* 5, no. 3 : 389–417.

Rosenbaum, James E., and Takehiko Kariya, Rich Settersten, and Tony Maier. 1990. "Market and Networks Theory of the Transition from High School to Work: Their Application to Industrialized Societies." *Annual Review of Sociology* 16 : 263–99.

Rosenberg, Morris. 1981. "The Self Concept: Social Product and Social Force." In *Social Psychology: Sociological Perspectives,* edited by Morris Rosenberg and Ralph H. Turner. New York: Basic Books, 593–624.

Ross, George. 1978. "Marxism and the New Middle Class." *Theory and Society* 5 : 163–90.

———. 1987. "The Decline of the Left Intellectual in Modern France." In *Intellectuals in Liberal Democracies, Political Influence, and Social Involvement,* edited by Alain G. Gagnon. New York: Praeger.

———. 1991. "Where Have All the Sartres Gone? The French Intelligentsia Born Again." In *In Search of the New France,* edited by James F. Hollifield and George Ross. New York and London: Routledge, 221–49.

Roudet, Bernard. 1988. "Bilan des recherches sur la vie associative." *La Revue de L'Économie Sociale* (April): 11–28.

Rubin, Lilian. 1976. *Worlds of Pain.* New York: Harper and Row.

Rudney, Gabriel. 1987. "The Scope and Dimensions of Nonprofit Activity." In *The Nonprofit Sector: A Research Handbook,* edited by Walter W. Powell. New Haven: Yale University Press, 55–64.

Rupnik, Jacques, and Muriel Humbertjean. 1986. "Image(s) des Etats-Unis dans l'opinion publique." In *L'Amérique dans les têtes: Un siècle de fascinations et d'aversions,* edited by Denis Lacorne, Jacques Rupnik, and Mari-France Toinet. Paris: Hachette, 101–23.

Ryan, John, and Larry Debord. 1991. "High Culture Orientation and the Attitudes and Values of College Students." *Sociological Inquiry* 61, no. 3 : 346–58.

Schatzman, Leonard, and Anselm Strauss. 1955. "Social Class and Modes of Communication." *American Journal of Sociology* 60, no. 4 : 329–38.

Schneider, David M., and Raymond T. Smith. 1978. *Class Differences in American Kinship.* Ann Arbor: University of Michigan Press.

Schudson, Michael. 1984. *Advertising, the Uneasy Persuasion.* New York: Basic Books.

———. 1989. "How Culture Works: Perspectives from Media Studies on the Efficacy of Symbols." *Theory and Society* 18 : 153–80.

Schutz, Alfred, and Thomas Luckman. 1989. *The Structures of the Life-World*. Vol. 2. Evanston: Northwestern University Press.

Schwartz, Gary. 1987. *Beyond Conformity and Rebellion: Youth and Authority in America*. Chicago: University of Chicago Press.

Schweisguth, Etienne. 1983. "Les salariés moyens sont-ils des petits-bourgeois?" *Revue Française de Sociologie* 24:679–703.

Scott, James C. 1990. *Domination and the Arts of Resistance: Hidden Transcript*. New Haven: Yale University Press.

Scott, Joan W. 1989. "The Sears Case." In *Gender and the Politics of History*. New York: Columbia University Press, 167–77.

Seeley, J. R., R. A. Sim, and E. W. Loosley. 1956. *Crestwood Heights: A Study of the Culture of Suburban Life*. New York: Basic Books.

Ségrestin, Denis. 1985. *Le phénomène corporatiste: Essai sur l'avenir des systèmes professionels fermés en France*. Paris: Fayard.

Sen, Amartya K. 1990. "Rational Fools: A Critique of the Behavioral Foundations of Economic Theory." In *Beyond Self-Interest*, edited by Jane Mansbridge. Chicago: University of Chicago Press, 24–43.

Sennett, Richard. 1976. *The Fall of the Public Man*. New York: Vintage.

Sennett, Richard, and Jonathan Cobb. 1973. *The Hidden Injuries of Class*. New York: Random House.

Service aux Associations. 1987. *Guide pratique des associations*. Paris: Service aux Associations.

Sewell, William, Jr. 1985. "Ideology and Social Revolutions: Reflections on the French Case," *Journal of Modern History* 57:57–85.

———. 1990. "Collective Violence and Collective Loyalties in France: Why the French Revolution Made a Difference." *Politics and Society* 18, no. 4:481–526.

———. Forthcoming. "Toward a Theory of Structure: Duality, Agency and Transformation." *American Journal of Sociology*.

Shonfeld, Andrew. 1969. *Modern Capitalism: The Changing Balance of Public and Private Power*, New York: Oxford University Press.

Shonfeld, William K. 1976. *Obedience and Revolt: French Behavior toward Authority*. Beverly Hills, Calif.: Sage.

Shortridge, James R. 1989. *The Middle West: Its Meaning in American Culture*. Kansas City: University Press of Kansas.

Shostak, Arthur B. 1969. *Blue Collar Life*. New York: Random House.

Showalter, Elaine. 1989. "A Criticism of Our Own: Autonomy and Assimilation in Afro-American and Feminist Literary Theory." In *The Future of Literary Theory*, edited by Ralph Cohen. New York: Routledge, 347–69.

Shweder, Richard A., Manamohan Mahapatra, and Joan G. Miller. 1987. "Culture and Moral Development." In *The Emergence of Morality in Young Children*, edited by Jerome Kagan and Sharon Lamb. Chicago: University of Chicago Press, 1–90.

Silver, Allan. 1985. "'Trust' in Social and Political Theory." In *The Challenge of Social Control: Citizenship and Institution Building in Modern Society: Essays in Honor of Morris Janowitz*, edited by Gerard D. Suttles and Mayer N. Zald. Norwood, N.J.: Ablex Publishing Co., 52–67.

Simmel, Georg. 1950. *The Sociology of Georg Simmel*. Translated, edited, and with an introduction by Kurt H. Wolff. Glencoe, Ill.: Free Press.

Singly, François de, and Claude Thélot. 1988. *Gens du privé, gens du public: La grande différence*. Paris: Dunod.

Smitherman, Genova. 1986. *Talkin' and Testifyin': The Language of Black Americans*. Detroit: Wayne State University Press.

Somers, Margaret R. 1991. "Political Culture, Property, and Citizenship: An Epistemological Exploration." Paper presented at the annual meeting of the American Sociological Association, Cincinnati.

Sperber, Dan. 1985. "Anthropology and Psychology: Toward an Epidemiology of Representations." *Man* 20:73–89.

Stinchcombe, Arthur L. 1975. "Social Structure and Politics." In *Handbook of Political Science* Vol. 3: *Macropolitical theory*, ed. Fred Grenstein and Nelson W. Polsby. Reading, Mass.: Addison-Wesley Publ., 557–622.

———. 1978. "The Deep Structure of Moral Categories: Eigthteenth Century French Stratification and the Revolution." In *Structural Sociology*, edited by Eno Rossi. New York: Columbia University Press, 66–95.

Stouffer, S. A. 1955. *Communism, Conformity and Civil Liberty: A Cross-Section of the Nation Speaks Its Mind*. New York: Doubleday.

Stryker, Sheldon. 1980. *Symbolic Interactionism: A Social Structural Version*. Menlo Park, Calif.: Benjamin/Cummings Pub. Co.

Suleiman, Ezra N. 1976. *Les hauts fonctionnaires et la politique*. Paris: Editions du Seuil.

———. 1979. *Les élites en France: Grands corps et grandes écoles*. Paris: Editions du Seuil. (English ed. 1978, *Elites in France*.) Princeton: Princeton University Press.

———. 1987. *Private Power and Centralization in France: The Notaires and the State*. Princeton: Princeton University Press.

Susman, Warren I. 1984. "Introduction: Toward a History of the Culture of Abundance." In *Culture as History: The Transformation of American Society in the Twentieth Century*, New York: Pantheon, xix–xxx.

Suttles, Gerald. 1968. *The Social Life of the Slum*. Chicago: University of Chicago Press.

Swidler, Ann. 1986. "Culture in Action: Symbols and Strategies." *American Sociological Review* 51:273–86.

Taylor, Charles. 1991. "The Politics of Recognition." Public lecture delivered at Princeton University.

Thelen, Ralph W., and Frank L. Wilson. 1986. *Comparative Politics: An Introduction to Six Countries*. Englewood Cliffs, N.J.: Prentice Hall.

Thélot, Claude. 1982. *Tel père, tel fils*. Paris: Dunot.

Thomas, George M. 1989. *Revivalism and Cultural Change: Christianity, Nation Building, and the Market in the Nineteenth-Century United States*. Chicago: University of Chicago Press.

Thomas, George M., and John Z. Meyer. 1984. "The Expansion of the State." *Annual Review of Sociology* 10:461–82.

Tilly, Charles. 1986. *The Contentious French: Four Centuries of Popular Struggle*. Cambridge, Mass.: Harvard University Press.

Tilly, Charles. 1991. "Domination, Resistance, Compliance . . . Discourse." *Sociological Forum* 6:593–602.

Tocqueville, Alexis de. 1945. *Democracy in America*. New York: Vintage.

Touraine, Alain. 1971. *The Post-Industrial Society: Tomorrow's Social History: Classes, Conflicts and Culture in the Programmed Society*. New York: Random House.

Tovell, Francois. 1985. "A Comparison of Canadian, French, British and German International Cultural Policy." In *Canadian Culture: International Dimensions*, edited by A. F. Cooper. Toronto: Canadian Institute of International Affairs, 69–82.

Turner, Victor. 1969. *The Ritual Process*. Chicago: Aldine.

Tyack, David, and Elisabeth Hansot. 1982. *Managers of Virtue: Public School Leadership in America, 1820–1980*. New York: Basic Books.

Tyree, A., M. Semyonov, and R. W. Hodge. 1979. "Gaps and Glissandos: Inequality,

Economic Development and Social Mobility in 24 Countries." *American Sociological Review* 44, no. 3:410–24.

Ulmann, André. 1946. *L'humanisme du XXe siècle.* Paris: Editions de l'Enfant Poète.

Ulrich's International Periodicals Dictionary 1990. New York: R. R. Bowker, 1990.

U.S. Bureau of the Census. *General Social and Economic Characteristics. 1983.* Connecticut, New Jersey, New York. Washington, D.C.: Government Printing Office.

U.S. Department of Commerce, Bureau of the Census. *Statistical Abstract of the United States 1987.* 107th ed. Washington D.C.: Government Printing Office.

———. *States and Metropolitan Area: Data Book 1986.* Washington D.C.: Government Printing Office.

U.S. Department of Education. Office of Educational Research and Improvement. *Digest of Education Statistics 1989.* Washington, D.C.: Government Printing Office.

Useem, Michael. 1984. *The Inner Circle.* New York: Oxford University Press.

Useem, Michael, and Jerome Karabel. 1986. "Pathways to Top Corporate Management." *American Sociological Review* 51, no. 2:184–200.

Vagogne, Joseph. 1984. *Les professions libérales.* Paris: Presses Universitaires de France.

Vanneman, Reeve, and Lynn Weber Cannon. 1987. *The American Perception of Class.* Philadelphia: Temple University Press.

Varenne, Hervé. 1977. *Americans Together: Structured Diversity in a Midwestern Town.* New York: Teachers College Press.

———. 1987. "Talk and Real Talk: The Voices of Silence and the Voices of Power in American Daily Life." *Cultural Anthropology* 2, no. 3:369–94.

Veblen, Thorstein. 1912. *The Theory of the Leisure Class.* New York: B. W. Huelsh.

Verdès-Leroux, Jeanine. 1983. *Au service du parti. Le Parti Communiste, les intellectuels et la culture (1944–1956).* Paris: Fayard/Minuit.

Verret, Michel. 1988. *La culture ouvrière.* St-Sebastien: ACL Editions/Société Crocus.

Veugelers, Jack, and Michèle Lamont. 1991. "France: Alternative Locations for Public Debate." In *Between States and Markets: The Voluntary Sector in Comparative Perspective,* edited by Robert Wuthnow. Princeton: Princeton University Press, 125–56.

Ville de Clermont-Ferrand. 1988. *Clermont-Ferrand en chiffres 1988.* Clermont-Ferrand: Services de Communications.

Villeneuve, A. 1978. "Les revenus primaires des ménages en 1975." *Economie et Statistiques* 103:59–72.

Wald, Alan. 1982. "The New York Intellectual in Retreat." In *Socialist Perspectives,* edited by Phylis Jacobson and Julius Jacobson. New York: Karz-Cohl Publishers, 155–84.

Wallace, Walter. 1990. "Rationality, Human Nature and Society in Weber's Theory." *Theory and Society* 19:199–223.

Walzer, Michael. 1983. *Spheres of Justice: A Defense of Pluralism and Equality.* New York: Basic Books.

Warner, R. Stephen. 1987. *New Wine in Old Wineskins: Evangelicals and Liberals in a Small-Town Church.* Berkeley: University of California Press.

Warner, R. Stephen. 1986. "The Evangelical Ethic and the Spirit of Parochialism." Paper presented at the annual meeting of the Society for the Scientific Study of Religion, Washington D.C.

Warner, W. Lloyd, J. O. Low, P. S. Lunt, and Leo Srole. 1963. *Yankee City.* New Haven: Yale University Press.

Warner, W. Lloyd, and P. S. Lunt. 1963. *Status System of a Modern Community.* New Haven: Yale University Press.

Waters, Mary C. 1990. *Ethnic Options: Choosing Identities in America.* Berkeley: University of California Press.

Watt, David Harrington. 1991. "United States: Cultural Challenges to the Voluntary Sector." In *Between States and Markets: The Voluntary Sector in Comparative Perspective*, edited by Robert Wuthnow. Princeton: Princeton University Press, 243–87.

Weber, Eugen. 1976. *Peasants into Frenchmen: The Modernization of Rural France, 1879–1914*. Stanford: Stanford University Press.

Weber, Henri. 1988. "Cultures patronales et types d'enterprise: Esquise d'une typologie du patronat." *Sociologie du Travail* 4:545–66.

Weber, Max. 1946. "The Protestant Sects and the Spirit of Capitalism." In *From Max Weber: Essays in Sociology*, edited by Hans Gerth and C. Wright Mills. New York: Oxford University Press, 302–22.

———. 1964. *L'éthique protestante et l'esprit du capitalisme*. Paris: Librairie Plon.

———. 1978. *Economy and Society*. Vol. 1. Berkeley: University of California Press.

Webster, G. 1979. *The Republic of Letters: A History of Postwar American Literary Opinion*. Baltimore: Johns Hopkins University Press.

Weil, Frederick. 1985. "The Variable Effects of Education on Liberal Attitudes." *American Sociological Review* 50:458–74.

Weisbrod, Burton A. 1980. "Private Goods, Collective Goods: The Role of the Nonprofit Sector." *Research in Law and Economics* 1:139–77.

Weiss, Robert. 1990. *Staying the Course: The Emotional and Social Lives of Men Who Do Well*. New York: Free Press.

Weitman, Sasha R. 1970. "Intimacies: Notes toward a Theory of Social Inclusion and Exclusion." *Archives Européennes de Sociologie* 11, no. 2:348–67.

West, Cornel. 1990. "The New Cultural Politics of Difference." October 53:93–109.

Westergaard, Barbara. 1987. *New Jersey: A Guide to the State*. New Brunswick, N.J.: Rutgers University Press.

Whyte, William H. 1956. *The Organization Man*. New York: Simon and Schuster.

Wickham, Alexandre, and Sophie Coignard. 1986. *La nomenklatura française: Pouvoirs et privilèges des élites*. 2d ed. Paris: Belfond.

Willis, Paul. 1977. *Learning to Labor: How Working Class Kids Get Working Class Jobs*. New York: Columbia University Press.

Wolfe, Alan. 1989. *Whose Keeper? Social Science and Moral Obligation*. Berkeley: University of California Press.

———. 1992. "Democracy versus Sociology: Boundaries and Their Political Consequences." In *Cultivating Differences: Symbolic Boundaries and the Making of Inequality*, edited by Michèle Lamont and Marcel Fournier. Chicago: University of Chicago Press.

Woloch, Isser. 1982. *Eighteenth-Century Europe: Tradition and Progress, 1715–1789*. New York: W. W. Norton and Co.

Wood, Michael, and Michael Hughes. 1984. "The Moral Basis of Moral Reform: Status Discontent vs. Culture and Socialization as Explanations of Anti-Pornography Social Movement Adherence." *American Sociological Review* 49:86–99.

Wright, Vincent. 1978. *The Government and Politics of France*. New York: Holmes and Meier.

Wuthnow, Robert. 1987. *Meaning and Moral Order: Explorations in Cultural Analysis*. Berkeley: University of California Press.

———. 1988. *The Restructuring of American Religion: Society and Faith since World War II*. Princeton: Princeton University Press.

———. 1989. *Communities of Discourse: Ideology and Social Structure in the Reformation, the Enlightenment, and European Socialism*. Cambridge, Mass.: Harvard University Press.

———. 1991. *Acts of Compassion: Caring for Others and Helping Ourselves*. Princeton: Princeton University Press.

Wuthnow, Robert, and Wesley Shrum, Jr. 1983. "Knowledge Workers as a 'New Class':

Structural and Ideological Convergence among Professional-Technical Workers and Managers." *Work and Occupations* 10:471–83.

Wylie, Laurence. 1973. *Village in the Vaucluse.* Cambridge, Mass.: Harvard University Press.

Wylie, Laurence, and R. Henriquez. 1982. "Images of Americans in French Textbooks." *Tocqueville Review* (Spring–Summer).

Yankelovitch, Daniel. 1981. *New Rules: Searching for Self-Fulfillment in a World Turned Upside Down.* New York: Random House.

Yin, Robert K. 1984. *Case Study Research.* Beverly Hills, Calif.: Sage.

Zablocki, Benjamin D., and Rosabeth M. Kanter. 1976. "The Differentiation of Life-Styles." *Annual Review of Sociology* 2:269–98.

Zelizer, Viviana. 1988. "Beyond the Polemics on the Market: Establishing a Theoretical and Empirical Agenda." *Sociological Forum* 3:614–34.

———. 1989. "The Social Meaning of Money: 'Special Monies.'" *American Journal of Sociology* 95, no. 2:342–77.

Zerubavel, Eviatar. 1991. *The Fine Line: Boundaries and Distinctions in Everyday Life.* New York: Free Press.

Zolberg, Vera. 1981. "The Happy Few-en Masse: Franco-American Comparisons in Cultural Democratization." Paper presented at the meeting of the American Sociological Association, Toronto.

Zukin, Sharon. 1982. *Loft Living: Culture and Capital in Urban Change.* Baltimore: Johns Hopkins University Press.

Zussman, Robert. 1985. *Mechanics of the Middle Class: Work and Politics among American Engineers.* Berkeley: University of California Press.

Zysman, John. 1977. *Political Strategies for Industrial Order: State Market and Industry in France.* Berkeley: University of California Press.

Bourdieu, Pierre (*continued*)
278*nn*63, 66, 72, 73, and 76, 279 *n*77;
contributions of, 5, 179, 181–88; on
class reproduction and inequality, 181–
88; on education, 234 *n*9, 253 *n*11; on familiarity, 51; on high culture, 107; on
mobility, 270 *n*47; on proximate structural
factors, 148, 275 *n*42; on social attainment, 274 *n*26; on working class, 243 *n*59
bourgeois culture, 108, 144, 278 *n*72; and cultural boundaries, 103, 170–71; defined,
200–201; and income, 160; and materialism, 69; role of humanism in, 49; values
of, 244 *n*67
bourgeoisie de promotion, 54
Bowles, Samuel, 290 *n*3
Brassens, Georges, 245 *n*79
Brel, Jacques, 245 *n*79
brilliance, 45, 51, 52, 93
Brint, Steven, 152, 158, 235 *n*23, 266 *nn*9 and
10, 268–69 *n*31, 273 *n*15
Bronfenbrenner, Ulf, 273 *n*10
bureaucracy, 48
Bureaucratic Phenomenon, The (Crozier), 49
Bush presidency, 173

cadre, 201, 284 *n*56
Cadres, Les (Boltanski), 73
Calhoun, Craig, 265 *n*77
Canard Enchainé, Le, 245 *n*79
Cannon, Lynn Weber, 273 *n*18
capitalists and capitalism, 54, 139, 151, 240 *n*24
Car and Driver, 95
career development, 33, 48, 134, 143, 160
Carroll, Raymonde, 251 *n*61
Cartesian intellectual tradition, 94, 134
Catholicism: as focus of French, xxv, 139, 170;
and humanism, 53–55, 244 *n*68; and disregard for money, 67; and work ethic, 47
Chamber of Commerce, 76
charity, xxvi, 56, 58–59, 61
charm, 167
Chartier, Roger, 275 *n*35
Cheek, Neil H., Jr., 254 *n*20, 258 *n*77
child care, 71
child-rearing values, 18, 117, 133, 168,
237 *n*57, 254 *nn*19 and 22
children, 42, 100, 272 *n*4
Christian humanist tradition. *See* humanist
tradition
Christian Science, 56–57
church, 56–58. *See also* religion
civil service, 47, 50, 269 *n*38
Clark, Priscilla Parkhurst, 142, 252 *n*5, 255 *n*32,
258 *n*71, 264 *n*60
class divisions, 189, 191–92, 281 *nn*21 and 22,

283 *nn*47 and 48; American views on,
78–79, 80; declining significance of,
10–11, 249–50 *n*39; French views on, 81,
86; and occupation, 78; and social identity, 64. *See also* lower classes; upper-
middle class; working-class culture
Clermont-Ferrand: compared with Paris, 132;
as interview site, 22, 212–15; similarity
of outlook with American Midwest, 51;
views on affluence, 66, 68
clientelism, 78
Closets, Francois de, 239 *n*8, 242 *n*54
Coleman, Richard, 237 *n*50, 246 *n*3, 259 *n*93,
271 *n*57
college education, 260 *n*95, 261 *n*22, 271 *n*52;
costliness of, 71, 282 *n*36; and conservatism, 266 *n*10; and cultural boundaries,
90–91, 109, 119, 280 *n*91; extracurricular
activities in, 260 *n*96; as predictor of occupational status, 11, 252 *n*3, 271 *n*53; and
tolerance, 80, 177
Collins, Randall, 133, 252 *n*3
comfort level, 69–70
communalism, 192
Communist party, 112
community, 15, 35, 76, 77
competence: in American workplace, 40, 41,
54, 60, 134, 242 *nn*41 and 42; in French
workplace, 44–46, 61, 98; linguistic, 90;
and mobility, 165; and moral character,
35, 44; valued by Americans, 92, 94, 97
competitiveness, 35; American stress on, 60,
95, 121, 138; in children, 42; as signal of
competence, 41, 41–42; French deprecia-
tion of, 46–47, 147
Confédération générale des cadres, 201
conflict avoidance: American emphasis on, 31,
35, 36–37, 60, 127, 128, 134, 143,
240 *n*26; French deemphasis of, 48, 50,
52
connections, 78
Consumer Reports, 95
consumerism, 68–69, 70, 141
control, 69
corporate executives, 35
corporatism, 147
cosmopolitanism, 89, 106, 107, 119, 124, 127,
168, 255 *n*28. *See also* anticosmopolitan
attitudes
Crane, Diana, 263 *n*49
Crawford, Stephen, 266 *n*14
Crittenden, Kathleen, 236 *n*40
Crozier, Michel, 49, 244 *n*64, 248 *nn*26 and 30,
252 *n*64
cuisine, 117, 258 *n*71
cultural boundaries: American tendency to sub-

ordinate, 13, 132–33, 178; and class reproduction, 176; defined, 4, 6, 234 n14; drawn by Americans, 94–100, 115–18; drawn by French, 13, 88–95, 127, 130–31, 138, 161–62, 278 n66; and high culture, 110; importance of, in French workplace, 46, 268 n30, 269 n36; importance of, to women, 133; and intelligence, 90–94, 96–97; and public sector, 190; role of education in, 140, 186; stressed by intellectuals, 152, 162, 268 n24, 278 n68; weakening of, 145. *See also* exclusion, cultural; loose-boundedness; tight-boundedness

cultural capital, 3, 33, 90, 188
cultural centers, 131–32
cultural categories, 1, 3–4
cultural codes, 6, 9, 103
cultural diffusion, 139–44
cultural diplomacy, 264 n58
cultural institutions, 141–42
cultural laxity, American, 114–27, 131, 178
cultural peripheries, 131–32
cultural resources, 7
cultural and social specialists, 150–63, 190, 265–66 n8, 268 nn26 and 31
curiosity, xx, 98, 100, 168, 176
current events, 95
curriculum, 94, 140

Darnton, Robert, 279 n80
data analysis, 221–23
Davis, Natalie Zemon, 275 n35, 279 n80
decentralization of authority, 52–53
Della Fave, L. Richard, 247 n14
democracy, 137
Democracy in America (Tocqueville), 8, 59, 86
Democratic party, 173
Derrida, Jacques, 8, 177, 189
deviance, 115, 178, 234–35 n16
diction, 96
Diderot, Jacques, 142
dieting, 99
differentiation, 118–20, 182
DiMaggio, Paul, 132, 234 n15, 235 n21, 255 n27, 256 n39, 257 n67, 259 n86, 260 n1
discretion, 102
dishonesty: descriptions of, 25–32; American views on, 25–27; French views on, 25, 27–30, 91
distancing behavior, 10
Distinction (Bourdieu), 181–82, 184–85, 186
divorce, 27
Donnat, Olivier, 254 n24, 256 n53, 258 n77
Douglas, Mary, 257 n66, 279 nn79 and 81

downward mobility, 7, 68, 163–65, 185, 246 n1, 270 n45
Durkheim, Emile, 9
dynamism, 35, 41, 42–43, 45, 60, 85

Eastern United States, xxv-xxvi, 119. *See also* New York
eating habits, 107. *See also* cuisine
eclecticism, 104
Ecole Nationale d'Administration, 94, 100
Ecole Normale Supérieure, 143
Ecole Polytechnique, 45
economic culture, 106
economic rationality, 151, 161, 163, 173
Economy and Society (Weber), 55, 151
education: and arts participation, 109; Bourdieu on, 234 n9; Catholic, 57, 171, 252 n7; and competitiveness, 47; and cultural boundaries, 4, 90, 141; as cultural resource, 7; and exclusion, 278 n65; and increase in managers, 193; in France, 45, 46, 47, 50, 57, 71, 104, 132, 141, 145, 186, 195–97; higher, 71, 91, 94, 141, 195–97; and humanist subculture, 53, 104; of interviewees, 219–20; and minorities, 263 n53; national differences in, 139–41; reasons for acquiring, xxii; pragmatic view of, 125–26; and social reproduction, 186; in United States, 71, 125–26, 195–97, 255 n33, 259 n89; upper-middle class and, 165; and work habits, 234 n12. *See also* college education; *grandes écoles*; teachers
educational homogamy, 11
efficiency, 45, 52, 98
egalitarianism, xxvi, 6, 74; American, 241 n34; class, 86; cultural, 8, 117, 125, 127, 131, 143, 177; and moral character, 240 n29; and moral exclusion, 176; occupational, 79; and socioeconomic boundaries, 137, 192
Elites in France (Suleiman), 45
elitism, 81, 86, 103, 142–44, 195
eloquence, 93–94, 97, 98, 176, 253 n10
entrepreneurship, 44
environmentalism, 151, 157
equality: and hierarchalization, 42
Erikson, Kai, 3
Erikson, R., 270 n41
Esquire, xxi
ethnicity, 10, 11, 80, 146–47, 177, 192, 220, 236 n33, 245 n75, 251 n50, 279 n77
European values/CARA surveys, 49, 60, 238 n5; on authority, 74; on conflict, 243 n58; on managers, 244 n70; on money, 65; on

home repair, 116, 120, 258n77
hommes de principes (men of principles), 53
homosexuality, 177
honesty, xxvi, 4; American views on, 35–36, 39; in American workplace, 35, 128; and competence, 40; contrast between French and American conceptions of, 27–28, 131; French views on, 28–30, 239n9; and reliability, 35; symbolic authority of, 184. *See also* dishonesty
honnête homme, 28, 29–30, 100–101
Honneth, Axel, 277n62
Horowitz, Ruth, 265n78
Hout, Michael, 260n97
Howe, Irving, 257n61
Hughes, Michel, 255n27
humanist tradition: American views of, 106; and education, 104, 260n95; importance in bourgeois culture, 49, 103–4; importance to French, 107, 244n68; and French moral traits, 53–54, 61, 94, 128
humanitarianism, 179
humanness, 56
humility, 37, 51
Hunt, Lynn, 275n35
Hunter, James, 265n6
Hurrelman, Klaus, 273n17

Iacocca, Lee, xxvii, 65, 75
impression management, 21, 34, 39
inadequacy, 165–66
inclusion and trust, 10
income, 70, 146, 157, 197–200, 237n51, 268n25, 283nn47 and 48, 285nn8 and 13
independence, 160
Indianapolis, 21, 119, 206–8
Indiana University, 76, 125–26
individualism, 6, 30, 35, 137, 139
inequality, 5–6, 9, 175–77, 184
inferiority, 94–95, 117, 237n56, 246n2
informality, 117
Inglehart, Ronald, 245–46n82, 253n17, 272n59
innovation, 115
integration in workplace, 38
integrity, personal, 4; American views on, 39; French views on, 31, 32, 49, 50–51, 52, 54, 60, 71
intellectual honesty, 25, 29
intellectuals and intellectualism, 89, 123, 127, 142–44, 147, 156, 256n41, 257nn56 and 61, 259n83; alienation of, 54, 113, 172; and capitalism, 151; and cultural boundaries, 162, 268n24, 278n68; influence of, 190, 264n65; subculture of,

110–14, 161, 256–57n54. *See also* anti-intellectualism
intelligence, xxi, 4, 90–94, 96, 127, 167
interpersonal relations, 67, 117, 243n60, 249nn33 and 37
interview procedures, 15, 18, 19–23, 32, 221
isolation, 77

Jackall, Robert, 35, 240n n27 and 30
Jackman, Mary and Robert, 200, 250n46, 279n83
Jacobinism, 137, 138
James, Estelle, 264n74
"Jeopardy," 96
Jesuits, 53
job security, 48, 176, 237n53
Jodi, Ellen, 236n43
Judeo-Christian morality, 28–29, 32, 60
Junior League, 76

Kalberg, Steven, 265n2, 269n38
Kanter, Rosabeth, 34, 60
Karabel, Jerome, 282n38
Katchadourian, Heran, 271n53
Keller, Suzanne, 234n7
Kerckhoff, Alan, 254n22, 272n4
Kohn, Melvin, 265n81
Kriesi, Hanspeter, 266n11

labor market, structure of, 52, 193
labor movement, 191
Ladd, Everett C., 268n28
Lambert, Wallace, 249n37
Landes, David, 242n47
language, 93, 127, 253nn9 and 16
Lareau, Annette, 234n11
Lash, Scott, 251n55
Laumann, Edward O., 250n45
lawfulness, 27
leisure-time activities, 96, 98, 100, 109, 110, 116, 120, 254n24, 258n77
Lévi-Strauss, Claude, 185, 257n66
Le Wita, Béatrix, 244n67
liberalism, 151, 152, 158, 235n23, 267n22, 268n28
lifestyle, 117, 119, 182
Ligue Notre-Dame, xxv, 55
linguistic competence, 90, 176
Lipovetsky, Gilles, 257n60
Lipset, Seymour Martin, 7, 8, 31, 86, 151, 234n6, 241n34, 263n47, 265n76
literary culture, 107, 109, 116, 142–43
Long, Elizabeth, 109, 122
long-term planning, 35, 41, 43, 60, 176

loose-boundedness, cultural, 115–16, 118–20; and art, 122–23; and formalism, 120–22; role of sports in, 121
losers, 35
lower classes, 79
loyalty, 50, 52, 243 n56
Luckman, Thomas, 236 n41
lycée St-Louis, 143
Lynd, Helen and Robert, 284 n1

McClelland, D. K., 247 n13
MacLeod, Jay, 272 n7
McPherson, J. Miller, 250 n49
Macy, Michael W., 265–66 nn7 and 8
magazines, 95, 108, 111, 142, 245 n79, 254 n24, 264 n60
mainstream culture, 101, 104, 113, 114, 118; and American intellectuals, 125, 158, 172, 259 n91; and cultural specialists, 158
managers and management, 272 n7; and cultural boundaries, 89, 151–52; income of, 197–98; increase in, 163–64, 193; intelligence of French, 97; and morality, 240 n30; nomenclature of, 283–84 n55; and power, 73, 74; professional associations of, 244 n65; selection of, 244 n70; traits valued by, 177; women as, 234 n7
manners, 4, 117, 167
Mantoux, Thiery, 272 n58
Maritain, Jacques, 244 n68
market mechanisms, 145
masculinity, 121
mass media, 7, 141, 142, 143, 176, 263 n49. See also magazines; television
materialism, 8, 85, 131, 139, 172, 189, 251 n60
maximization, 180, 185, 277–78 n62
Mechanics of the Middle Class (Zussman), 59–60
mediocrity, 99
membership, 64, 75–78
Men and Women of the Corporation (Kanter), 34
mental maps, 4, 12, 13, 14, 18
meritocracy, 175
Merton, Robert K., 247 nn14 and 15
methodology, 14–15, 18
Meyer, John, 139–40, 262 n34
Michelat, Guy, 244 n69
Michelin, 68
Midwest: anti-intellectualism in, 125; assets of, xxv; compared with New Yorkers, 132; New Yorkers' views of, 105–6, 255 n29; and professional success, 38; representative of mainstream culture, 284 n1; views of New Yorkers, 27, 83, 252 n64; views on affluence, 66
Miles, M. B., 286 n11
military leadership, 73

Millman, Marcia, 254 n18
Mills, C. Wright, 248 n21
mobility, 251 n57, 270 n49, 277 n55; barriers to, 145; and cultural exclusion, 270 n46; downward, 7, 68, 163–65, 185, 246 n1, 270 n45; in France, 81, 147; geographic, 8, 78, 86, 145–56, 190, 249 n34; and high culture, 127; intergenerational, 270 n41; intragenerational, 199, 260 n97, 265 n76, 270 n42; and moral boundaries, 164–65, 176, 185, 270 n47; professional, 38–39, 47–48, 52, 134, 163–64, 199–200, 243–44 n63; and socioeconomic boundaries, 270 n43
money, 138, 265 n82; American views of, 66, 69–71, 85, 161, 248 n20; French views of, 65–69, 72, 132, 159, 160, 171; as sign of ability, 64. See also income
moral boundaries, 261 n13; American stress on, 5, 13, 85, 274 n23; Bourdieu on, 184–85; defined, 4; and deviance, 234 n16; French stress on, 5, 132; and fundamentalism, 56; importance in periphery, 132; and mobility, 164–65; and public sector, 190; and religion, 139; and tolerance, 274 n24
moral character, 35; ambition and, 41; and class, 176; and egalitarianism, 240 n29; importance in American workplace, 43, 134; importance to Midwesterners, 131; and religion, 55–57; as status signal, 185
Moral Mazes (Jackall), 35
moral standards, 265 n6; Bourdieu on, 184, 277 n54; and competence, 44; concern for, xxiii, xxiv, 32, 184; as criterion for evaluation, 24, 137, 247 n5; Judeo-Christian, 28–29, 60; low, 25, 27–28, 32, 60; and social science literature, 33, 238 n1; and working class, 192
Mother Theresa, 186

narrow-mindedness, 89, 91
national character, 8, 47
national differences: Bourdieu on, 278 n67; in boundary work, 5–8, 13–14, 86–87, 130–34; in cultural boundedness, 127–28; in cultural innovation, 117; and cultural diffusion, 139–48; in exclusiveness, 105; in high culture, 8, 86; historical, 136–39; in income, 237 n51; in interclass dynamics, 85; in street names, 255 n32; mixed evidence for, 247 n16; in moral standards, 60–61; in political behavior, 191; research on, 234 n15; in volunteering, 50
National Endowment for the Humanities, 261 n11

Sperber, Dan, 135
sports, 99, 120, 121, 258–59 n82
Sports Illustrated, 95
Stanford University, 260 n95, 271 n53
status signals, 157, 189; and class, 175, 182;
    cultural, 88–89, 94, 131, 147; external,
    63; Faunce's work on, 247 n9; most highly
    valued, 183–84; socioeconomic, 64–65,
    138, 145, 192
stereotypes, 189
Stinchcombe, Arthur L., 235 n17
Strauss, Anselm, 272 n6
structural characteristics of society, 134–36,
    144, 275 n33, 280 n86; proximate, 152,
    157, 163, 172, 187
stupidity, 40, 91
subordination, 79
success: as criterion for assessing superiority,
    xxii, xxiii; French definitions of, 71–74;
    images of, xx; importance of, xxvii, xxix;
    and socioeconomic boundaries, 63, 85.
    See also professional success
Suleiman, Ezra, 45, 241 n40
superiority, xxi, xxvii, 117, 237 n56
Swidler, Ann, 235 n21, 262 n33
symbolic boundaries, 5, 157; as analytic tool,
    8, 128; autonomy from structural factors,
    135; defined, 9–10, 234 n14; expressions
    of, 157; formal features of, 6; and in-
    equality, 5–6, 175–77, 181; literature
    on, 6; and national character, 86; and
    power, 180; and socioeconomic inequal-
    ity, 178; and social structure, 187; varia-
    tions in, 7, 181

Tapie, Bernard, 65
taste, 4, 148; American view of, 116; impor-
    tance to French, 88, 89, 100–102, 182;
    and social structure, 187; women's stress
    on, 133
teachers, 93, 140, 159, 161, 263 n54
teamwork: American emphasis on, 31, 35–39,
    52, 60, 134; French deemphasis on, 48,
    49, 53
technical competence, 46
technology, 46
television, 96, 98–99, 258 n78; American
    fondness for, 116, 120–21; French, 132,
    141, 169; intellectuals and, 111, 113;
    programming, 107, 233 n2, 263 n56; and
    socioeconomic status, 100, 101, 233 n3
Ten Commandments, 27, 28, 29, 32, 54
Thélot, Claude, 242 n46, 252 n4
Theory Z, 73
Thomas, W. I., 8

Thompson, E. P., 275 n35
tight-boundedness, 123, 167, 170
Tilly, Charles, 239 n12
Time magazine, 265 n60
Tocqueville, Alexis de, 8, 59, 86
tolerance, 115–17, 139, 166–67, 176–77,
    257–58 n68, 271 n54, 274 n24, 278 n71
Trivial Pursuit, 96
Truffaut, François, xix
Trump, Donald, 65, 133, 176
trust, 243 n55; as hallmark of inclusion, 10; im-
    portance in workplace, 34–35, 36, 134,
    240 n23; and moral exclusion, 176; role of
    church in, 57

Union nationale des professions libérales, 202
universalism, 79, 86, 137, 175, 250 n42
university system, 126, 142, 143, 197. *See also*
    college education
upper-middle class: comparison of French and
    American, 194–203; defined, 14, 200;
    first-generation, 165–67, 271 n51; third-
    generation, 167–72, 271 n57
upward mobility, 7, 163–65, 185, 270 nn42
    and 47
Useem, Michael, 282 n38
utilitarianism, 143

vacation destinations, 107
valuation, 180
value rationality, 151, 159, 160, 161, 162
Vanneman, Reeve, 273 nn9 and 18
Varenne, Hervé, 35, 240 n29, 250 n42
Veblen, Thorstein, 103
Verret, Michel, 273 n19
Voltaire, 142
volunteerism, 58–60, 61, 245 n81, 246 nn83,
    84 and 87, 264 n74
voter apathy, 239 n16
vulgarity, 101, 119, 167, 176, 254 n23

Wald, Alan, 257 n64
Wang, Dr., 96
Warhol, Andy, xix
Warner, R. Stephen, 56
Warner, W. Lloyd, 103
Waters, Mary, 236 n33
wealth, 4, 67–68, 145, 171. *See also* money;
    patrimoine
Weber, Max, 11, 35, 180; on high status sig-
    nals, 240 n24; on rationality, 151, 163; on
    power, 237 n48; on religion, 55, 265 n1;
    on trust, 240 n23; on work ethic, 40, 47
Webster, G., 257 n54
welfare state, 71, 134, 144, 157, 163, 246 n82

versity of New York Graduate Center; the Culture Workshop of the University of Chicago; the Center for the Study for Social Transformation, University of Michigan; the Institute for the Humanities, University of California, Irvine; the Communication Studies consortium, Concordia University, Université de Montréal, and Université du Québec à Montréal; the Max Weber Seminar, Université de Paris 1—Sorbonne; the audience at various professional meetings and conferences. I want to thank the people who were kind enough to extend these invitations: Mitchell Abolafia, Steven Brint, William Buxton, Michel Dobry, Daniel Gaxie, Wendy Griswold, David Halle, Elizabeth Long, Ewa Morawska, Victor Nee, Andrea Press, Paul Rabinow, Barry Schwartz, Alan Wolfe, and Vera Zolberg.

My Princeton colleagues and the members of the Institute for Advanced Studies, some of whom participated in the Mellon Colloquium series on Culture, Religion, and Society in 1989–90 and/or in the sociology faculty discussion group on culture in 1988–89, provided me with intellectual stimulation that fed into the project. In particular, I want to thank Gene Burns, Miguel Centeno, Natalie Zemon Davis, Matthijs Kalmijn, Suzanne Keller, Sara McLanahan, Ewa Morawska, Sherry Ortner, Mark Schneider, Margaret Somers, George Thomas, R. Stephen Warner, Robert Wuthnow, and Viviana Zelizer. Thanks also to Robert Darnton for inviting me to join the European Cultural Studies program and for giving me the opportunity to teach in a wonderful environment. Princeton graduate students who worked with me and those who were involved in the culture and knowledge seminars or in the contemporary social theory seminar also contributed to this book. While thirty people should be thanked, I want to express my special appreciation for their enthusiasm and intellectual involvement to Raphael Allen, Matthew Chew, Timothy Dowd, Matthew Lawson, John Schmalzbauer, Libby Schweber, Jack Veugelers, Maureen Waller, Daniel Weber, and Marsha Witten.

Several social scientists have generously taken precious time away from their own research to comment on the manuscript as a whole or on specific chapters, or to review the book for one of the university presses that were interested in this book. They include Bennett Berger, Miguel Centeno, Randall Collins, Lewis Coser, Paul DiMaggio, Priscilla Ferguson, Marcel Fournier, Wendy Griswold, Joseph Gusfield, James Jasper, Seymour Martin Lipset, John Meyer, Paul Rabinow, Barry Schwartz, Ezra Suleiman, Hervé Varenne, Alan Wolfe, Eviatar Zerubavel, and Viviana Zelizer. Many thanks to all of them. Ann Swidler made me aware at an

many faux pas. His writings in comparative sociology have had a distinct influence on my own intellectual agenda.

A team of very competent research assistants who participated in the sampling, phone interviewing, and transcribing phases of the project have a large share of responsibility for its realization. They include, for Indianapolis, Richard Adams and Pamela Braboy (Indiana University, Bloomington); for the New York suburbs, Libby Schweber, Kei Sochi, Yvonne Veugelers (Princeton University) and Judith Darvas (New York University); for the Paris suburbs, Guy Campion, Julie Cheatley, Etienne Lisotte, and Mario Vachon (Université de Paris 5); and for Clermont-Ferrand, Aline Chiofolo (Université de Clermont 1). In Princeton, Laila Ahsan, Raymonde Arsenault, Vandala Gupta, Lisa Roche, Libby Schweber and Laurence Thébault transcribed the interviews while Raphael Allen, Terry Boychuk, Timothy Dowd, Gil McKennan, Rhonda Patterson, and Frank Small helped with computer work or assisted me in the final phases of the project.

The organization of the project was very complex and could only be accomplished with local assistance both in France and in the United States. Those who helped me solve specific organizational problems at various phases in the research include Pierre Ansart (Université de Paris 7), Alain Boyer (Centre National de Recherche Scientifique, Paris), Donna Eder (Indiana University), Daniel Gaxie (Université de Paris 1— Sorbonne), Judith Balfe (CUNY Graduate Center), and James Jasper (New York University). While I was on the road, several of my "native" friends invited me to share their homes for a few days or a few weeks: Warren and Julie McKellar (Indianapolis); Randy and Susan Hodson (Bloomington, Indiana); Mrs. Lee Huggins (Summit, New Jersey); Vera and Aristide Zolberg (Manhattan); Geneviève Lédée (Paris); and the Pitelet family (Clermont-Ferrand). The Institute for Social Research, Indiana University, made its phone facilities available to the project. Finally, Corinne Sérange, the "agent des relations publiques" of the Ville de Clermont-Ferrand, and Roger-Paul Cardot, directeur régional, Comité d'Accueil, Direction Générale Auvergne-Limousin, also were particularly helpful.

While working on the manuscript, I was given the valuable opportunity to present my arguments to various audiences. Each contributed to the final product by making me push my ideas further. These audiences include the sociology departments of Cornell University, the New School for Social Research, the University of Pennsylvania, and the City Uni-

ACKNOWLEDGMENTS

During the years that I was working on this project, I accumulated an impressive stock of debt. My first thanks go to the almost two hundred men and women who spent two or more hours of their busy lives sharing with me their intimate feelings and thoughts. I hope they will find that their trust has not been violated and that they will recognize their voices behind the sociological massaging of the data.

My second thanks go to the institutions that provided financial support for the research that led to this book: the Lilly Endowment, for providing the main funding for the project; the National Science Foundation and the American Sociological Association, for a small grant that in 1987 supported the pilot study that led to the book; and at Princeton University, the University Committee on Research in the Humanities and Social Sciences, the William Hallum Tuck '12 Memorial Fund, the Council on Regional Studies, the Center of International Studies (Woodrow Wilson School), and the Department of Sociology. Special thanks to Ezra Suleiman, director of the Council on Regional Studies, Henry Bienen, director of the Center of International Studies, and Marvin Bressler, until recently chair of the Department of Sociology, for providing crucial resources that made ends meet.

Third, I wish to express my appreciation to Seymour Martin Lipset who has helped me in so many ways since I first arrived at Stanford University in 1983 from Paris, having just completed a doctoral dissertation on the growth of the social sciences and the decline of the humanities. His total involvement with and love for his work, as well as his support, were crucial to me while I was learning to write in English and was familiarizing myself with American sociology and American society through

TABLES AND MAPS

CONTENTS

Ce livre est dédié à mon père et ma mère,
Jacques et Ninon.

MICHÈLE LAMONT teaches at Princeton University. She is the coeditor of *Cultivating Differences: Symbolic Boundaries and the Making of Inequality*, also published by the University of Chicago Press.

The University of Chicago Press, Chicago 60637
The University of Chicago Press, Ltd., London
© 1992 by The University of Chicago
All rights reserved. Published 1992
Printed in the United States of America

01 00 99 98 97 96 95 94 93 92   5 4 3 2 1

ISBN (cloth): 0-226-46815-1
ISBN (paper): 0-226-46817-8

Library of Congress Cataloging-in-Publication Data

Lamont, Michèle, 1957–
Money, morals, and manners : the culture of the French and
American upper-middle class / Michèle Lamont.
p.   cm. (Morality and society)
Includes bibliographical references and index.
1. Middle classes—United States—Moral and ethical aspects—Cross-
cultural studies.   2. Middle classes—France—Moral and ethical
aspects—Cross-cultural studies.   3. Social values—United States—
Cross-cultural studies.   4. Social values—France—Cross-cultural
studies.   I. Title.   II. Series
HT690.U6L36   1992
305.5'5'0944—dc20   92-7270
                                                   CIP

Money, Morals, and Manners

THE CULTURE OF THE FRENCH AND AMERICAN UPPER-MIDDLE CLASS

Michèle Lamont

THE UNIVERSITY OF CHICAGO PRESS   CHICAGO AND LONDON

MORALITY AND SOCIETY
A series edited by Alan Wolfe

Money, Morals, and Manners

Figures

Tables

Preface

The subject of hydrodynamic stability or stability of fluid flow is one that is most important in the fields of aerodynamics, hydromechanics, combustion, oceanography, atmospheric sciences, astrophysics, and biology. Laminar or organized flow is the exception rather than the rule to fluid motion. As a result, exactly what may be the reasons or causes for the breakdown of laminar flow has been a central issue in fluid mechanics for well over a hundred years. And, even with progress, it remains a salient question for there is yet to be a definitive means for prediction. The needs for such understanding are sought in a wide and diverse list of fluid motions because the stability or instability mechanisms determine, to a great extent, the performance of a system. For example, the under prediction of the laminar to turbulent transitional region on aircraft – that is due to hydrodynamic instabilities – would lead to an underestimation of a vehicle's propulsion system and ultimately result in an infeasible engineering design. There are numerous such examples.

The seeds for the writing of this book were sown when one of us (WOC) was contacted by two friends, namely Philip Drazin and David Crighton with the suggestion that it was perhaps time for a new treatise devoted to the subject of stability of fluid motion. A subsequent review was taken by asking many colleagues as to their assessment of this thought and, if this was positive, what should a new writing of this subject entail? The response was enthusiastic and revealed three major requirements: (i) a complete updating of all aspects of the field; (ii) the presentation should provide both analytical and numerical means for solution of any problem posed; (iii) the scope of the treatment should cover the full range of the dynamics, ranging from the transient to asymptotic behavior as well as linear and nonlinear formulations. Then, since the computer is now a major tool, the last need suggested that direct numerical simulation (DNS) must be included as well.

This challenge was accepted and with intensive collaboration, we have attempted to meet these goals. All prototype flows are considered whether confined (Chapter 3), semi confined (Chapter 3), in the absence of boundaries (Chapter 2) and both parallel, almost parallel or flows with curved stream lines (Chapter 6). In addition, the topics of spatial versus temporal stability (Chapter 4), compressible (Chapter 5) as well as incompressible fluids, geophysical flows (Chapter 7), transition and receptivity (Chapter 10), and optimization and control of flows (Chapter 12) are given full attention. Also, specific initial-value problems (Chapter 8) would be examined as well as the question of stability. In every case, the basics are developed with the physics and the mathematical needs (Chapters 1, 2) with emphasis on numerical methods for solution. To this end, in formulating the organization of the book it was decided that it would be beneficial if, at the end of each chapter that dealt with a specific topic, in addition to exercises for illustration, an appendix, when appropriate, would be attached that provided a numerical basis for that particular area of need. The reader would then be able to develop their own code. Nonlinear stability (Chapter 9) and direct numerical simulation, i.e., DNS (Chapter 11) are supplemented with a review of what is known from experiments (Chapter 13).

The book can easily be used as a text for either an upper level undergraduate or graduate course for this subject. For those who are already knowledgeable, we hope that the book will be a welcome and useful reference.

There are many friends who have helped us with the formulation and writing. Indeed, all have given us both criticism and advice when needed. Particular recognition should be given to Richard DiPrima, who was the mentor of one of us (TLJ) and was a person who provided more than a rationale to be engaged in the field of hydrodynamic stability with his teaching, expertise, and major contributions to the subject. In a similar manner, Robert Betchov provided the initial impetus for another (WOC). More recently, M. Gaster, C. E. Grosch, F. Hu, G. L. Lasseigne, L. Massa and P. J. Schmid have made their time available so that our writing would benefit and the contents be made to fit our goal. To each, we extend our sincere thanks. And, to the late Robert Betchov, Dick DiPrima, David Crighton, and Philip Drazin, a firm note of gratitude. The passing of our colleagues is a loss. Finally, we have had assistance from some who have helped with technical needs. In particular, Frances Chen, Michael Campbell, and Peter Blossey should be cited.

Chapter 1

Introduction and problem formulation

1.1 History, background, and rationale

In examining the dynamics of any physical system the concept of stability becomes relevant only after first establishing the possibility of equilibrium. Once this step has been taken, the concept becomes ubiquitous, regardless of the actual system being probed. As expressed by Betchov & Criminale (1967), stability can be defined as the ability of a dynamical system to be immune to small disturbances. It is clear that the disturbances need not necessarily be small in magnitude but the fact that the disturbances become amplified as a result and then there is a departure from any state of equilibrium the system had is implicit. Should no equilibrium be possible, then it can already be concluded that that particular system in question is statically unstable and the dynamics is a moot point.

Such tests for stability can be and are made in any field, such as mechanics, astronomy, electronics and biology, for example. In each case from this list, there is a common thread in that only a finite number of discrete degrees of freedom are required to describe the motion and there is only one independent variable. Like tests can be made for problems in continuous media but the number of degrees of freedom becomes infinite and the governing equations are now partial differential equations instead of the ordinary variety. Thus, conclusions are harder to obtain in any general manner but it is not impossible. In fact, successful analysis of many such systems has been made and this has been particularly true in fluid mechanics. This premise is even more so today because there are far more advanced means of computation available to supplement analytical techniques. Likewise the means for experimentation has improved in profound ways.

Fundamentally, there is no difficulty in presenting the problem of stability in fluid mechanics. The governing Navier-Stokes continuum equations for the

1

momenta and the conservation of mass that are often expressed by constraints, such as incompressibility that requires the fluid velocity to be solenoidal in a somewhat general sense, are the tools of the science. A specific flow is then fully determined by satisfying the boundary conditions that must be met for that flow. Other considerations involve the importance of the choice of the coordinate system that is best to describe the flow envisioned and whether or not there is any body force, say. Then, the important first step is to identify a flow that is in equilibrium. For this purpose, a flow that is in equilibrium need not necessarily be time independent but the system is no longer accelerated due to the balance of all forces. For such flows meeting these conditions very few, if any, remain that have not been theoretically evaluated using this approach but, because the governing equations of motion are a set of nonlinear partial differential equations, the results are most often the result of approximations. Nevertheless these flows are well established, many have been experimentally confirmed, and they are all laminar. In addition, a few exact solutions of the governing equations are known. In such cases, where more complex physics is entailed, such as compressibility or electrical conductivity of the fluid, similar arguments can be made and results have been equally obtainable.

Essentially there are three major categories of base mean flows, namely: (a) flows that are parallel or almost parallel; (b) flows with curved streamlines and; (c) flows where the mean flow has a zero value. Examples of the parallel variety are channel flows, such as plane Couette and Poiseuille flows where the flows are confined by two solid boundaries. There is but one component for the mean velocity and it is a function of the coordinate that defines the locations of the boundaries. In a polar coordinate system, pipe flow is another example of note. Almost parallel flows are of two main categories: (i) free shear flows, such as the jet, wake and mixing layer where there are no solid boundaries in the flow and (ii) the flat plate boundary layer where there is but one solid boundary. In these terms, (i) and (ii) have two components for the mean velocity and they are both functions of the coordinate in the direction of the flow as well as the one that defines the extent of the flow. In Cartesian terms, if U and V are the mean velocity components in the x and y spatial directions, respectively, then almost parallel assumes that $V \ll U$ and that the variation of U with respect to the downstream variable x is weak. Group (b) has flows such as that between concentric circular cylinders (Taylor problem) or flow on concave walls (Görtler problem). The cases where there is no mean flow (Rayleigh problem, Bénard cells, e.g.) are simply special cases of the more general picture. Whether from the standpoint of view of the physics or the mathematics needed to make analyses, each of these prototypes has its own unique features and it is the stability of same that is the question to be

Fig. 1.1. Laminar Boundary Layer (after van Dyke, 1975).

Fig. 1.2. Turbulent Boundary Layer (after van Dyke, 1975).

answered. It should be clear that the actual causes of any resulting instability will vary as well.

It should be again stressed that, regardless of the methods required for obtaining any mean flow, they are laminar and are in equilibrium or near equilibrium. But, unfortunately, just as the adage states, "turbulence is the rule and not the exception to fluid motion". In other words, laminar flows are extremely hard to maintain; transition to turbulence will occur in the short or the long term. One need only to observe the flow over the wings of an airplane, the meandering of a river, the outflow from the garden hose, or the resulting flow behind bluff bodies in both the laboratory and in nature to witness this predominance first hand. Laminar flow is orderly, can be well predicted, and is most generally desired. The illustrations of Figs. 1.1 and 1.2 vividly demonstrate the more than subtle differences for these two flows in the boundary layer setting. Here, a benefit of laminar flow is less drag when compared to

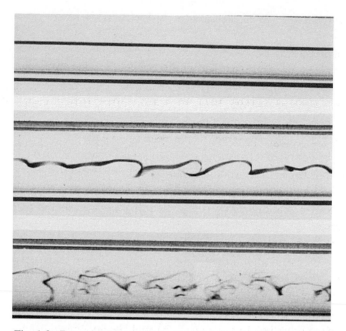

Fig. 1.3. Reynolds Pipe Experiment (after Drazin & Reid, 1984).

the turbulent state. Contrary to this, a case where a benefit from turbulent flow would be desired over laminar is mixing, for example. The goal of predicting or even approximating the process of transition has been a stated goal throughout the history of fluid mechanics and, it was once thought, stability analysis would be able to do this. Any success has been limited but stability analysis can explain – for almost all of the major cases – why a basic flow cannot be maintained indefinitely.

Figure 1.3 shows the classical experiment due to Reynolds for flow in a circular pipe. Here, dye was inserted and the mean flow run at different values. The original organized parallel laminar flow is seen at several stages with the ultimate breakdown and fully random three-dimensional motion transpiring. Ironically, this problem is one where stability theory has not been able to make any conclusions whatsoever and remains an enigma in the field. In short, linear theory has been used to investigate this flow in many ways and no solutions that predict instability have been found. This has been found to be true regardless of any added complexities that might be envisioned. For example, axisymmetric versus non-axisymmetric disturbances. Still, it is clear that this flow is unstable.

Drawings of vortices can be traced as far back as those of Leonardo da Vinci that were made in the 15th century! The first significant contribution to the theory of hydrodynamic stability is that due to Helmholtz (1868). The principal initial experiments are due to Hagen (1855). Later a major list of contributions can be cited. Reynolds (1883), Kelvin (1880, 1887a,b), and Rayleigh (1879, 1880, 1887, 1892a,b,c, 1895, 1911, 1913, 1914, 1915, 1916a,b) were all active in this period. Here, the birth of the Reynolds number as well as the first theorems due to Rayleigh appeared. As has been noted before, Lord Rayleigh was 36 when he considered the stability of flames and then published his work on jets. At 72 he began to do work in nonlinear stability theory! Unlike Reynolds' pipe experiment, which was intrinsically viscous, the exceptional theoretical work of Kelvin and Rayleigh was all done using the inviscid approximation in the analysis.

Independently, Orr (1907a,b) and Sommerfeld (1908) framed the viscous stability problem. Both workers were attempting to investigate channel flow with Orr considering plane Couette flow and Sommerfeld plane Poiseuille flow. Of course one case is the limit of the other and the combination has led to the Orr-Sommerfeld equation that has become the essential basis in the theory of hydrodynamic stability. But, even here, it should be remembered that it was not until 22 years after the derivation of this equation that any solution at all could be produced. Tollmien (1929) calculated the first neutral eigenvalues for plane Poiseuille flow and showed that there was a critical value for the Reynolds number. This work was made possible by the development of Tietjens' functions (Tietjens, 1925) and analysis of Heisenberg (1924) connected with the topic of resistive instability. Romanov (1973) proved theoretically that plane Couette flow is stable. Unlike pipe flow, there is no experimental controversy here. Plane Poiseuille flow, on the other hand, is unstable.

Schlichting (1932a,b, 1933a,b,c, 1934, 1935) continued the work of Tollmien and extended it even further. The combination of these efforts have led to the designation for the oscillations that are now the salient results for the stability of parallel or nearly parallel flows, namely Tollmien-Schlichting waves. It should be noted that such waves correspond to those waves where friction is critical and do not exist for any problem that does not include viscosity and are known to be present only in flows where a solid boundary is present in the flow. Also, in the limit of infinite Reynolds number, the flow is stabilized.

Prandtl (1921–1926, 1930, 1935) was active in problems related to stability in the hopes that the theory might lead to to the prediction of transition and the onset of turbulence. As mentioned, to date no such success has been achieved but the effort continues as the understanding makes progress. But, for the first

time during this period, a major boost to stability analysis was given by the work of Taylor (1923) where theory was confirmed by his experiment for the case of rotating concentric cylinders. Taylor himself was responsible for this and the work continues to be a model for understanding the stability of mean flows with curved stream lines.

The advent of matched asymptotic expansions and singular perturbation analysis brought new vigor to the theory. Lin (1944, 1945) made use of these tools and re-did all previous calculations, thereby confirming the earlier results that had been obtained by less sophisticated means. Experiments also gained momentum with the work of Schubauer & Skramstad (1943) in the investigation of the flat plate boundary layer setting the standard. Here, a vibrating ribbon was employed to simulate a controlled disturbance, that is a Tollmien-Schlichting wave, at the boundary. This method is still employed by many today. Theoretical calculations were confirmed and equally important, for the first time, it became apparent that the value of the critical Reynolds number meant the stability boundary for the onset of unstable Tollmien-Schlichting waves and not the threshold for the onset of turbulence. Figure 1.4, depicting the results of this experiment is a hallmark in this field. This conclusion has been further substantiated today. For example, Schubauer & Klebanoff (1955, 1956), Klebanoff, Tidstrom, & Sargent (1962), and Gaster & Grant (1975) performed even more extensive experiments for the boundary layer.

Investigating the stability of compressible flows was not done until much later with the theoretical work of Landau (1944), Lees (1947), and Dunn & Lin (1955) being the principal contributors at this time. Physically and mathematically, this is a far more complex problem and, in view of the time span it

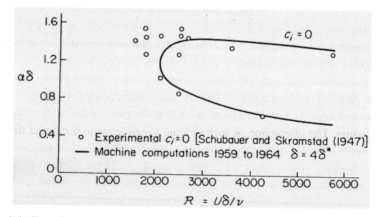

Fig. 1.4. Experimental and theoretical stability results for neutral oscillations of the Blasius boundary layer (after Betchov & Criminale, 1967).

took to resolve the theory in an incompressible medium, this was understandable. A wide range of problems have been investigated here, including different prototypes and Mach numbers up to hypersonic in value. Likewise, there are experiments that have been done for these flows: Kendall (1966).

The use of numerical computation for stability calculations was made with the work of Brown (1959, 1961a,b, 1962, 1965), Mack (1960, 1965a,b), and Kaplan (1964) being the principal contributions. Neutral curves that were previously obtained by asymptotic theory and hand calculations are now routinely determined by numerical treatment of the governing stability equations. Such numerical evaluation has proven to be more efficient and far more accurate than any of the methods employed heretofore. Furthermore, the complete and unsteady nonlinear Navier-Stokes equations are evaluated by the use of high order numerical methods in tandem with machines that range from the personal computer (PC) to supercomputers and the parallel class of machines. By numerical calculations, one of the earliest results for the full Navier-Stokes calculations obtained by Fromm & Harlow (1963) where the problem of vortex shedding from a vertical flat plate was investigated. Since this time, the complete Navier-Stokes equations are routinely used to study the vortex shedding process. Among others, Lecointe, & Piquet (1984), Karniadakis & Triantafyllou (1989), and Mittal & Balachandar (1995), for example, have all numerically solved the full equations in order to investigate instability and vortex shedding from cylinders.

Effort has been made to assess nonlinearity in stability theory. Meksyn & Stuart (1951), Benney (1961, 1964), Eckhaus (1962a,b, 1963, 1965) were all early contributors to what is now known as weakly nonlinear theory. Each effort was directed to different aspects of the problems. For example, the nonlinear critical layer, development of longitudinal or streamwise vortices in the boundary layer, or the possibility of a limiting amplitude for an amplifying disturbance were examined. The role of streamwise vorticity in the breakdown from laminar to turbulent flow has recently been explored using the complete Navier-Stokes equations. For this purpose, Fasel (1990), Fasel & Thumn (1991), Schmid & Henningson (1992a,b), and Joslin, Streett & Chang (1993) have introduced oblique wave pairs at amplitudes ranging from very small to finite values. The interaction of such oblique waves leads to dominant streamwise vortex structure. When the waves have small amplitudes, the disturbances first amplify but then decay at some further downstream location. When finite, the nonlinear interactions of the vortex and the oblique waves result in breakdown.

Since the experimental setting for probing in this field is almost unequivocally one where any disturbance changes in space and only oscillates in time,

thought has been given to the question of spatial instability so that theory may be more compatible with experimental data. The problem can be posed in very much the same way as the temporal one, but the equations must be adapted for this purpose. This is true even if the problem is governed by the linear equations. Direct numerical simulation also has major complexities when computations are made in this way. Nevertheless, this is done. For this purpose, reference to the summaries of Kleiser & Zang (1991) and Liu (1998) can be made where the use of direct numerical simulation for many instability problems has been given. More specifically, among this vast group, Wray & Hussaini (1984) and Spalart & Yang (1987) both investigated the breakdown of the flat plate boundary layer by use of a temporal numerical code. In other words, an initial value problem prescribed at time $t = 0$ and the computation of the disturbance development for later times. By contrast, when a spatial code is employed, and initial values are given at a fixed location and then the development thereafter downstream, the work of Fasel (1976), Murdock (1977), Spalart (1989), Kloker & Fasel (1990), Rai & Moin (1991a,b), and Joslin, Streett & Chang (1992, 1993) should be noted. For three-dimensional mean flows, where cross flow disturbances are present, Spalart (1990), Joslin & Streett (1994), and Joslin (1995a) studied the breakdown process by means of direct numerical simulation.

Stability theory uses perturbation analysis in order to test whether or not the equilibrium flow is unstable. Consider the flows that are incompressible, time independent, and parallel or almost parallel by defining the mean state as

$$\vec{U} = (U(y), 0, 0); \quad P$$

in Cartesian coordinates where $U(y)$ is in the x-direction with y the coordinate that defines the variation of the mean flow, z is in the transverse direction and P is the mean pressure. For some flows, such as that of channel flow, this result is exact; for the case of the boundary layer or one of the free shear flows, then this is only approximate but, as already mentioned, the U component of the velocity, $U \gg V$ or W, as well as U varying only weakly with x, and hence the designation of almost parallel flow. In this configuration, both x and z range from minus to plus infinity with y giving the location of the solid boundaries, if there are any. P is the mean pressure and the density is taken as constant.

Now assume that there are disturbances to this flow that are fully three-dimensional and hence

$$\vec{u} = (U(y) + u, v, w); \quad P + p$$

can be written for the velocity and pressure of the instantaneous flow. By assuming that the products of the amplitudes (defined nondimensionally with the measure in terms of the mean flow) of the perturbations as well as the products of the perturbations with the spatial derivatives of the perturbations are small, then, by subtracting the mean value terms from the combined flow, a set of linear equations can be found and are dimensionally

$$\frac{\partial u}{\partial x} + \frac{\partial v}{\partial y} + \frac{\partial w}{\partial z} = 0 \tag{1.1}$$

for incompressibility and,

$$\frac{\partial u}{\partial t} + U\frac{\partial u}{\partial x} + \frac{dU}{dy}v = -\frac{1}{\rho}\frac{\partial p}{\partial x} + \nu\nabla^2 u, \tag{1.2}$$

$$\frac{\partial v}{\partial t} + U\frac{\partial v}{\partial x} = -\frac{1}{\rho}\frac{\partial p}{\partial y} + \nu\nabla^2 v, \tag{1.3}$$

and

$$\frac{\partial w}{\partial t} + U\frac{\partial w}{\partial x} = -\frac{1}{\rho}\frac{\partial p}{\partial z} + \nu\nabla^2 w \tag{1.4}$$

for the momenta where ρ is the density of the fluid and ν is the kinematic coefficient of viscosity; ∇^2 is the three-dimensional Laplace operator.

It is more prudent to consider the equations nondimensionally and this will be done eventually but, for the purposes of the discussion of the basic concepts, they will here be considered dimensionally. When nondimensionalization has been done in this case, all quantities are redefined and the coefficient of viscosity is replaced with the reciprocal of the Reynolds number, defined in terms of the chosen length and velocity scales of the particular flow.

1.2 Initial-value concepts and stability bases

At this stage a temporal initial-value, spatial boundary-value problem has been prescribed and must be solved in order to determine whether or not the given flow is unstable. In this respect, it is well defined but, as will be seen, there are many difficulties in actually performing this task. There is, of course, more than one definition for stability that can be used but the major concern is whether or not the behavior of the disturbances causes an irreversible alteration in the mean flow. In short, if, as time advances from the initial instant there is a return to the basic state, then the flow is considered stable. There are various ways that instability can occur but it is first essential to understand

what means are possible for solving these problems in order that any decision can be made. At the outset it can already be seen that the order of the system is higher than the traditional second order boundary value problems of mathematical physics. As a result, some of the classic methods of exploration are of limited value; others that may be used require extensions or alterations in order to be employed here.

Any velocity vector field can be decomposed into its solenoidal, rotational, and harmonic components. For the problems being discussed here there is no solenoidal part due to the fact that the fluid is incompressible and $\nabla \cdot \underline{u} = 0$. On physical grounds the rotational part of the velocity corresponds to the perturbation vorticity with the harmonic portion related to the pressure. This analogy makes for better interpretation of the physics for, even though the boundary conditions must be cast in terms of the velocity, the initial specification can be considered as that of vorticity. In this respect, for each of the mean flows that have been cited, when the governing equations are written in terms of the vorticity, the vorticity is essentially a quantity that is diffused or advected from what it was initially and the velocity profile is the result of this action. The same reasoning can be made for the perturbation field.

The reasoning for the decomposition of the velocity can be best understood by actually using the definitions for the divergence and the curl. First, operate on (1.2) to (1.4) by taking the divergence and use (1.1) to give

$$\frac{1}{\rho}\nabla^2 p = -2\frac{dU}{dy}\frac{\partial v}{\partial x}. \tag{1.5}$$

The relation (1.5) is an equation for the perturbation pressure and has an inhomogeneous term that is effectively a source for the pressure due to the interaction of the fluctuating and mean strain rates. When neither is strained then the pressure is harmonic. If the velocity had not been solenoidal, then factors relating to the compressibility of the fluid would come into play.

Now, the definitions of the perturbation vorticity components are

$$\omega_x = \frac{\partial w}{\partial y} - \frac{\partial v}{\partial z}, \tag{1.6}$$

$$\omega_y = \frac{\partial u}{\partial z} - \frac{\partial w}{\partial x}, \tag{1.7}$$

and

$$\omega_z = \frac{\partial v}{\partial x} - \frac{\partial u}{\partial y}, \tag{1.8}$$

respectively, since $\vec{\omega} = \nabla \times \vec{v}$.

By using these definitions and the operation of the curl on the same set of equations for the momenta, the following are obtained:

$$\frac{\partial \omega_x}{\partial t} + U \frac{\partial \omega_x}{\partial x} - \nu \nabla^2 \omega_x = -\frac{dU}{dy}\frac{\partial w}{\partial x} = \Omega_z \frac{\partial w}{\partial x}, \tag{1.9}$$

$$\frac{\partial \omega_y}{\partial t} + U \frac{\partial \omega_y}{\partial x} - \nu \nabla^2 \omega_y = -\frac{dU}{dy}\frac{\partial v}{\partial z} = \Omega_z \frac{\partial v}{\partial z}, \tag{1.10}$$

$$\frac{\partial \omega_z}{\partial t} + U \frac{\partial \omega_z}{\partial x} - \nu \nabla^2 \omega_z = -\frac{dU}{dy}\frac{\partial w}{\partial z} - \frac{d^2 U}{dy^2}v = \Omega_z \frac{\partial w}{\partial z} - \frac{d\Omega_z}{dy}v, \tag{1.11}$$

where $\Omega_z = -dU/dy$ is the single component of the mean vorticity and is in the z-direction. Each of these equations has the expected transport by the mean velocity and diffusion but, in case there is also an inhomogeneous term that is due to the interaction of the fluctuating strain and the mean vorticity. Just as in the pressure relation, these interactions are needed for any generation of the respective fluctuating component. But, it is important to note, such generation here is due to three-dimensionality for, if there was neither the w component of the velocity nor the spatial dependence in the transverse z-direction, as it would be for the two-dimensional problem, then the fluctuating vorticity components, except for ω_z, could only be advected and diffused regardless of any initial input.

In order to seek a solution for this problem, the number of equations needs to be reduced. There are several ways to do this but one in particular is more than efficient. From kinematics it can be shown that

$$\nabla^2 v = \frac{\partial \omega_z}{\partial x} - \frac{\partial \omega_x}{\partial z}. \tag{1.12}$$

Thus, by combining equations (1.9) and (1.11) and using (1.12), then

$$\frac{\partial}{\partial t}\nabla^2 v + U\frac{\partial}{\partial x}\nabla^2 v - \nu\nabla^4 v = -\frac{d^2 U}{dy^2}\frac{\partial v}{\partial x} = \frac{d\Omega_z}{dy}\frac{\partial v}{\partial x} \tag{1.13}$$

can be obtained and, although still in a partial differential equation form, it is the Orr-Sommerfeld equation of stability theory. It is fortuitous that this equation uncouples in such a way as to only be fourth order and fully homogeneous in the v dependent variable. The solution of (1.13) is the first requirement that must be met. These solutions are then to be used in (1.10) for the solution of ω_y. In like manner, the results found for ω_y are combined with v and the problem is complete when these are used in (1.7) together with (1.1) to determine u and w. Finally, p can be evaluated from one of the momenta, (1.2) to (1.4). If

the initial data and boundary conditions are satisfied, the problem is complete and the query as to stability can now be answered.

One last observation should be noted here. Equation (1.10) is actually the Squire equation that is known to accompany that of Orr-Sommerfeld. In this form, however, the dependent variable is the component of the vorticity that is perpendicular to the $x - z$ plane and is only of interest in the full three-dimensional perturbation problem, strictly speaking. The importance of this cannot be stressed enough for it leads to the understanding of the physics of the problem and details of the flow. It is not necessary if only the stability of the flow is the requirement. This equation also provides the other two orders of the anticipated sixth-order system. Unlike (1.13), though, it is not homogeneous.

1.3 Classical treatment: modal expansions

The traditional classical method for solving (1.13) for v is by modal expansion (normal modes). First, it is recognized that the coefficients in (1.13) are functions of y only. Therefore, since the extent of the planes perpendicular to y defined by the x, z spatial variables is doubly infinite, v can be Fourier transformed in these two variables. Accordingly, define

$$\check{v}(\alpha; y; \gamma; t) = \int_{-\infty}^{+\infty} \int_{-\infty}^{+\infty} v(x, y, z, t)e^{i(\alpha x + \gamma z)} \mathrm{d}x\mathrm{d}z. \qquad (1.14)$$

With this step, the governing equation remains a partial differential equation in terms of the variables y and t but the far field boundary conditions in x and z, namely boundedness as $x, z \to \pm\infty$, are satisfied by the rigid conditions for Fourier transforms with α and γ both real. At this point, since the problem is linear, it would be natural to reduce the equation even further by employing a Laplace transform in time so that an ordinary differential equation for v results. This procedure will be reserved until later for it deserves its own treatment. Suffice it for the moment to note that this has been done by Gustavsson (1979). Instead, the classical method for solution has been made by assuming that the time dependence can be separated from that of y. Thus,

$$\check{v}(\alpha; y; \gamma; t) = \sum_{n=0}^{\infty} \hat{v}_n(\alpha; y; \gamma)e^{-i\omega_n t} \qquad (1.15)$$

is taken and, as noted, (1.15) should be the infinite sum of all such model solutions. Moreover, ω_n is taken as a complex frequency with a positive imaginary part indicating an unstable mode. The substitution of (1.15) into (1.13) after the Fourier decomposition that is prescribed by (1.14) has been done, then the

Orr-Sommerfeld equation is reduced to that of an ordinary differential equation for $\hat{v}$. Solutions are then required to meet the boundary conditions at the respective locations marked in terms of the y-variable; at y_1 and y_2, say. First, this means that $\hat{v}$ must satisfy conditions at y_1 and y_2. In Fourier space, the equivalent of (1.1) is $i\alpha\hat{u} + i\gamma\hat{w} = -\hat{v}'$, where $\hat{u}$ and $\hat{w}$ are defined in exactly the same manner as was done in (1.14) for $\check{v}$ as well as the solution form of (1.15). Thus, the conditions for $\hat{u}$ and $\hat{w}$ are now in terms of the first derivative of $\hat{v}$. The combination leads to the result that ω_n is a function of α, γ, and the Reynolds number of the flow for *every* n. From the point of view of the Laplace transform method, such solutions would be tantamount to finding poles in the complex Laplace space. But, in this way, the determination using (1.15) is more direct. Provided there are homogeneous boundary conditions in y, then the problem is that of the eigenvalue, eigenfunction variety with ω_n the eigenvalue. But, here the analogy to classical homogeneous eigenvalue, eigenfunction problems ends. First, as already noted, this differential equation is fourth order rather than second. Also, it is not self-adjoint, has a small parameter (reciprocal of the Reynolds number that is large compared to 1) multiplying the highest derivative thereby constituting a singular perturbation problem analytically or a stiff problem numerically. In short, neither the analysis nor the numerics are straightforward. Both of these topics will be treated in more detail. On the other hand, if only the question of stability is to be answered, then only **one** unstable eigenvalue need be found. But, no details of any specific initial-value problem or a determination of the full dynamics of any disturbance will follow in this way and it is not necessary for such a stability decision. But, if the modal expansions are to be used for this purpose, then all modes must be known and this includes those that are damped. The transient period becomes critical and it cannot be evaluated without this information. This topic will be presented in detail in Chapter 8 but, for now, it must be indicated that, among other things, it relates in part to the boundary conditions of the problem. Doubly bounded flows such as the channels have a different foundation in terms of the mathematics than those that have only one boundary (the boundary layer), or those without boundaries whatsoever as the jet, wake, and mixing layer.

After making the substitution given by (1.15), the more familiar Orr-Sommerfeld equation is found and is, for each mode,

$$(\alpha U - \omega)\Delta\hat{v} - \alpha\frac{d^2 U}{dy^2}\hat{v} = -i\nu\Delta\Delta\hat{v}, \tag{1.16}$$

where

$$\Delta = \frac{d^2}{dy^2} - \tilde{\alpha}^2, \tag{1.17}$$

and

$$\tilde{\alpha}^2 = \alpha^2 + \gamma^2 \tag{1.18}$$

with $\tilde{\alpha}$ the scalar polar wave number in the α-γ plane of Fourier space. This form of the equation, as indeed the one that is simply the result of the double Fourier transforms, offers some interesting properties. This is best seen by returning to the original set of equations (1.1) to (1.4) and making the transformation on all of the dependent variables and then using the modal form of solution or (1.15).

The ordinary differential equations that are obtained by the prescribed operations are

$$i(\alpha\hat{u} + \gamma\hat{w}) + \frac{d\hat{v}}{dy} = 0, \tag{1.19}$$

$$i(\alpha U - \omega)\hat{u} + \frac{dU}{dy}\hat{v} = -i\alpha\hat{p}/\rho + \nu\Delta\hat{u}, \tag{1.20}$$

$$i(\alpha U - \omega)\hat{v} = -\frac{1}{\rho}\frac{d\hat{p}}{dy} + \nu\Delta\hat{v}, \tag{1.21}$$

and

$$i(\alpha U - \omega)\hat{w} = -i\gamma\hat{p}/\rho + \nu\Delta\hat{w}. \tag{1.22}$$

Squire (1933) introduced what should be properly called an equivalent transformation. And, once this is done, the very useful Squire theorem in stability theory emerges. For this purpose, let

$$\tilde{\alpha}\tilde{u} = \alpha\hat{u} + \gamma\hat{w}, \tag{1.23}$$

$$\tilde{\alpha}\tilde{w} = -\gamma\hat{u} + \alpha\hat{w}. \tag{1.24}$$

Just as $\tilde{\alpha}$ was the polar variable in the α-γ plane, it should be clear that $\tilde{u}$ in (1.23) is the fluctuating component parallel to the wave number vector and $\tilde{w}$ of (1.24) is in the angular direction, $\varphi = \tan^{-1}(\gamma/\alpha)$ in terms of the polar coordinates defined in the plane and are therefore the polar components of the velocity in the α, γ plane. With the use of these definitions the set of equations (1.19) to (1.22) can be combined to give

$$i\tilde{\alpha}\tilde{u} + \frac{d\hat{v}}{dy} = 0, \tag{1.25}$$

$$i\tilde{\alpha}(\alpha U - \omega)\tilde{u} + \alpha\frac{dU}{dy}\hat{v} = -i\tilde{\alpha}^2\hat{p}/\rho + \nu\tilde{\alpha}\Delta\tilde{u}, \tag{1.26}$$

and

$$i(\alpha U - \omega)\hat{v} = -\frac{1}{\rho}\frac{d\hat{p}}{dy} + \nu\Delta\hat{v}. \tag{1.27}$$

Thus, if the additional changes of variables,

$$\tilde{v} = \hat{v}, \tag{1.28}$$

$$\tilde{p}/\tilde{\alpha} = \hat{p}/\alpha \tag{1.29}$$

are used along with

$$\omega = \alpha c, \tag{1.30}$$

$$\tilde{c} = c, \tag{1.31}$$

where $\tilde{c}$ or c is the phase speed in the Fourier space, then equations (1.26) and (1.27) read

$$i\tilde{\alpha}(U - \tilde{c})\tilde{u} + \frac{dU}{dy}\tilde{v} = -i\tilde{\alpha}\tilde{p}/\rho + (\nu\tilde{\alpha}/\alpha)\Delta\tilde{u} \tag{1.32}$$

and

$$i\tilde{\alpha}(U - \tilde{c})\tilde{v} = -\frac{1}{\rho}\frac{d\tilde{p}}{dy} + (\nu\tilde{\alpha}/\alpha)\Delta\tilde{v}. \tag{1.33}$$

Clearly these equations are analogous to those of a purely two-dimensional system except, that is, for the factor that multiplies the coefficient of viscosity. When the pressure is eliminated between (1.32) and (1.33) then

$$(U - \tilde{c})\Delta\tilde{v} - \frac{d^2 U}{dy^2}\tilde{v} = -i(\tilde{v}/\tilde{\alpha})\Delta\Delta\tilde{v} \tag{1.34}$$

with

$$\tilde{v} = \nu\tilde{\alpha}/\alpha = \nu/\cos\varphi \tag{1.35}$$

becomes the Orr-Sommerfeld equation in this notation. From (1.34), the well-known Squire theorem can now be identified. Except for the viscosity, the equations governing a three-dimensional and a two-dimensional perturbation are the same. The relation (1.35), when written in terms of the non-dimensional Reynolds number, Re, is simply $\tilde{Re} = Re\cos\phi$; $Re = \rho U_0 L/\mu = U_0 L/\nu$ with U_0 and L characteristic scales of the mean flow. Now, as was shown in Fig. 1.4, there is a minimum Reynolds number for the onset of instability. Although this result is for the flat plate boundary layer, it is also true for plane Poiseuille flow. Consequently, by use of the Squire transformation, the Squire theorem can be noted. The minimum Reynolds number for instability will be higher for an oblique three-dimensional wave than for a purely two-dimensional wave. Note that this statement does not rule out the possibility

that, for a high enough values of the Reynolds number, an unstable oblique oscillation is possible even though the purely two-dimensional one that has the same value of α is damped. This last point is one referred to by Watson (1960) as well as Betchov and Criminale (1967) but has not been exploited to date.

The equation for the other component of the polar wave velocity is found directly by combining the definition (1.24) with operations on the appropriate equation and is

$$i(\alpha U - \omega)\tilde{w} - v\Delta\tilde{w} = \sin\varphi \frac{dU}{dy}\tilde{v} \qquad (1.36)$$

which is nothing more than

$$i(\alpha U - \omega)\hat{\omega}_y - v\Delta\hat{\omega}_y = -i\gamma \frac{dU}{dy}\tilde{v} = -i\tilde{\alpha}\sin\varphi \frac{dU}{dy}\tilde{v} \qquad (1.37)$$

when written with the Fourier transform of the vorticity component that is in the y direction as the dependent variable as can be seen by taking the Fourier transform of (1.7) and using (1.20) and (1.22). Regardless of the choice, this equation has become known as the Squire equation in stability theory. It is important to notice that the inhomogeneous term depends upon the solution for $\tilde{v}$ and has the factor that is a measure of the obliquity of the wave. This term has been referred to as "lift up" by several authors and is attributed to Landahl (1980). When the angle of obliquity is perpendicular to the direction of the flow ($\varphi = \pi/2$), then the mean flow no longer has any influence and the equation, in this limit, can be solved exactly for $\hat{v}$ even without the assumption of modes.

The completion of the problem from this basis can be made by (i) solving for $\tilde{v}$ from (1.34); (ii) determining $\tilde{u}$ from the condition of incompressibility,

$$i\tilde{\alpha}\tilde{u} = -\frac{d\tilde{v}}{dy};$$

(iii) solving for $\tilde{w}$ from (1.36) and then inverting the transformations given by (1.23) and (1.24), namely

$$\hat{u} = \cos\varphi\tilde{u} - \sin\varphi\tilde{w}, \qquad (1.38)$$

and

$$\hat{w} = \sin\varphi\tilde{u} + \cos\varphi\tilde{w} \qquad (1.39)$$

to obtain the original Cartesian velocity components. And, as has already been shown, the pressure can be subsequently determined. From this summary, it can be seen that the central part of the analysis clearly rests with the success of solving both the Orr-Sommerfeld and the Squire equations if a full examination

is desired. This is far different than merely determining whether or not the flow is stable.

1.4 Transient dynamics

By comparison, the transient portion of the dynamics of perturbations has only relatively recently become a topic of some importance in stability theory. On the one hand, because of the many complexities in the mathematics and the lack of adequate computing in the early stages of the development, it was practically impossible to actually accomplish this task. At the same time, traditional thought on this matter did not indicate that this aspect could have any bearing on the ultimate behavior and was simply ignored. Today, it is now quite clear that the results of stability calculations in the modal form are really more for the purpose of predicting the asymptotic fate of any disturbance and the transient dynamics can have and do lead to events that make this part of the problem even more of interest than it ever was.

It can be recalled that the leading equations to be used in the stability analysis have different properties than those that are more common in initial-value, boundary value problems. For iteration, the principal ones, namely the Orr-Sommerfeld equation is fourth order and is not self adjoint. Thus, for a specific initial-value designation, there is the question of exactly how to express arbitrary functions or even what set of functions are to be used for expansion of these given functions. The Orr-Sommerfeld equation does not have a set of known functions. Of course, there are means to form inner products (cf. Drazin & Reid, 1984) in this case and therefore all constants needed can be evaluated. But, it is only the channel flows that have a complete set of eigenfunctions (cf. DiPrima & Habetler, 1969) so long as the problem is viscous. Inviscidly, there is only a continuous spectrum (Case 1960a, 1961), Criminale, Long & Zhu (1991). The boundary layer (Mack 1976) and the free shear flows have been shown to have only a finite number of such modes. But, regardless, the fact that there must be a continuous spectrum to make the problem complete is already a recognition of the salient fact that there can be temporal behavior that is algebraic rather than just exponential.

The use of the Laplace transform in time to transform the partial differential equations to ones that are but ordinary has been made by Gustavsson (1979) as an alternative to modal expansions for initial-value problems. In this way the problem is completely specified and, in principle, can be made tractable. Unfortunately, only general properties can actually be found using this approach since the ordinary differential equation that must be solved is the same as the Orr-Sommerfeld. However, the important algebraic behavior is shown to exist

along with the exponential modes and is due to the existence of a continuous spectrum because there must be branch cuts as well as poles when the inversion to real time is to be made. This method also closes the gap for those flows where is the lack of modes for the arbitrary initial-value problem and the continuous spectrum, together with the discrete modes, allows for arbitrary expansions. This approach, where both the discrete and continuous spectra are used, has been well described by Grosch & Salwen (1978) and Salwen & Grosch (1981). Thus, the method of the Laplace transform is a means whereby it is possible, at least in principle, to solve an arbitrary initial-value problem.

Then, there is yet another way in which algebraic behavior can arise. This can be seen by referring to the Squire equation where there is the one inhomogeneous term that is proportional to the normal velocity component, that is, the term attributed to lift up. This equation, unlike that of the homogeneous Orr-Sommerfeld equation, can be resonant if there is a matching of the frequencies of the respective modes of the normal velocity with the dependent variable of this equation. This phenomenon has been shown to be possible for plane channel flow by Benney & Gustavsson (1981) but, it was concluded, resonance is not possible for the boundary layer. The case for resonance in the free shear flows is yet to be determined.

Exactly how dominant the algebraic behavior might be depends upon the particular problem and, to some extent, whether or not the problem is treated with or without viscosity. For any of the cases where there is the existence of a continuous spectrum it should be noted that perturbations can increase algebraically to quite large amplitudes before any exponentially growing mode supersedes its progress. The algebraic growth is ultimately damped by viscous action if viscosity is included in the problem. Otherwise, for some problems, the portion that grows algebraically can do so without bound and thus the assumption of linearity is overcome long before the dominance of any exponential growth. Thus, the concept of stability needs to be put in the proper context and it would be better to ask such questions as the existence of (a) optimum or maximum growth of disturbances or (b) behavior of the relative components of the perturbation velocity or vorticity for example. Such undertakings have been and are continuing to be made.

1.5 Asymptotic behavior

As has been stated, one answer to the question of whether or not a given flow is stable is to determine whether or not there is at least one eigen mode that results in exponential growth. Then, regardless of the time scale, there will eventually be an unlimited increase of the perturbation amplitude and the flow

cannot in any way be stable. And, this may be possible with or without any early transient algebraic development. In short, it is the long time limit that must now be found. For this purpose there are numerous numerical schemes that can be used to make the determination in a reasonably efficient manner. The question of the many or an infinite number of modes does not actually need to be answered, for only one growing mode is required to answer the question. Typical results of this strategy results in an eigenvalue expression that has the complex frequency as a function of the polar wave number, angle of obliquity, and the Reynolds number if viscous forces are included. Or, because of the Squire transformation from the Cartesian to the polar wave number variables, the determination of these values can be made without resorting to the oblique angle value. If the behavior for three-dimensionality is desired, it can be inferred from the equivalent two-dimensional data by use of the transformation as was shown by Watson (1960) or Betchov & Criminale (1967), for example.

There are other means of assessing the asymptotic fate of a particular initial input in more detail. For example, in order to predict the complete spatial behavior of the initial distribution, then the Fourier transforms that were made in the x and z variables must be inverted for this purpose. In the asymptotic state any transient response has long been exceeded by the exponential modal behavior and thus the leading behavior of these double integrals is exponential in time and can be evaluated by the method of steepest descent. In this way, the general features of the evolving disturbance can be predicted as well as the maximum amplitude. Such features include the location and distribution of the maximum part of the evolving disturbance or, as is better known, the description of the wave packet. A very early attempt for this kind of analysis for a localized disturbance in the laminar boundary layer was made by Criminale & Kovasznay (1962) and it was found that a wave packet ultimately was formed with the wave fronts swept back (three-dimensional) and the wave numbers and frequencies those of the band of amplified Tollmien-Schlichting waves. The relative widths of the packet could also be determined by this method. The important point here is that modal expansions can and do provide the critical information required for the asymptotic behavior.

1.6 Role of viscosity

The role of viscosity in the stability of parallel or almost parallel flows has two parts and is both the cause of the instability and has the role of damping as well. This scenario is, in many ways, unique in fluid mechanics but the phenomenon is known to exist in other fields. It is best explained by analogy. First, as in many other physical problems, viscous forces do ultimately act as damping

but not necessarily at all times or in all situations in certain flows. An unstable Tollmien-Schlichting wave not only requires viscosity to be unstable but have only been shown to exist only in the presence of solid boundaries.

As suggested, an explanation as to why viscosity is destabilizing can best be illustrated by analogy. Such an analogy was suggested by Betchov & Criminale (1967) and it remains valid today. For an oscillator with mass m and a linear restoring force proportional to k but with a time delay τ, the equation of motion can be written as

$$m\frac{\mathrm{d}^2 x(t)}{\mathrm{d}t^2} + kx(t - \tau) = 0. \tag{1.40}$$

Then, for small values of the delay, τ, (1.40) takes the form

$$m\frac{\mathrm{d}^2 x(t)}{\mathrm{d}t^2} - \tau k\frac{\mathrm{d}x(t)}{\mathrm{d}t} + kx(t) = 0. \tag{1.41}$$

Thus, it is clear from this result that such action is destabilizing and it is essentially a question of phasing. Although the conclusions to be drawn from (1.41) may appear simple minded, it expresses the elements required. In the more subtle arguments that will be used to demonstrate this point more precisely, it will be expressed in terms of Reynolds stress and interaction with the mean flow but it is the certain phasing that must be correct in order for there to be an instability in the flow.

Still, there are many problems that can be investigated without viscosity and, historically, this is exactly what was done. Most notably the contributions of Rayleigh (1879, 1880, 1887, 1892) were all made by inviscid analysis. And, interestingly enough, when investigating these problems, Rayleigh only examined two-dimensional perturbations. The Squire transformation and theorem that demonstrates that the two-dimensional problem is all that needs to be considered in order to determine the stability came much later. Except for the much earlier work that is now referenced as Kelvin-Helmholtz (Helmholtz, 1868; Kelvin, 1871), this work provided much of the important bases that remains even to this day in the field of hydrodynamic stability. There are several theorems due to Rayleigh that are important both for the mathematics and to the understanding of the physics of such flows and this is true even if viscous effects are retained. However, the flows that were extensively examined in this manner by Rayleigh were those of the jet, wake, and the mixing layer.

One need only to return to the fundamental equations, (1.32) to (1.34), which were expressed as an equivalent two-dimensional system, as $\gamma = 0$ for no z-variation for true two-dimensionality, and neglect the viscous terms to derive the Rayleigh equation. This is straightforward where the pressure is eliminated

and it is found that

$$(U - c)\left(\frac{d^2\hat{v}}{dy^2} - \alpha^2\hat{v}\right) - \frac{d^2 U}{dy^2}\hat{v} = 0. \tag{1.42}$$

Unlike the Orr-Sommerfeld equation, (1.42) is second order and, although not self-adjoint, it can easily be so constructed and the more conventional rules for boundary-value problems can be used. Unfortunately, there is no set of known functions for this equation save for some special $U(y)$ distributions and, for the initial-value part of the problem, a continuous spectrum must be added since there are only a finite number of discrete eigen modes. If one is interested in the full three-dimensional problem, then the equivalent Squire equation must be included.

Comparison of (1.42) to (1.34), say, tacitly reveals another point that is well known in the theory. Just as the ignoring of viscous effects is tantamount to lowering the order of the governing equation and thereby making it singular, the Rayleigh equation can also be singular if $(U - c) = 0$ somewhere in the flow. For this to be true, then c must be purely real and thus the interpretation is that the phase speed for the mode, c_r, is equal to the value of the mean flow at some y-location in the flow. Likewise, this implies that the flow is neutrally stable in this case. Exploitation of this fact is the basis for many of the theorems due to Rayleigh. It is also part of the reasoning for the emergence of a continuous spectrum of eigenvalues, as demonstrated by Case (1960a, 1961). Chapter 2 is devoted to inviscid problems.

1.7 Geometries of relevance

The mean flows envisioned and described have been, at least tacitly, assumed to be those that are two-dimensional and unidirectional whether or not they are the true or approximate solutions to the Navier-Stokes equations. Under these restrictions this means the channel, the flat plate boundary layer or the free shear flows of the jet, wake, or mixing layer. Cartesian coordinates describe these situations quite well. But there is no reason that the parallel flow that exists in a round pipe or the wake or jet of a round nozzle cannot be explored in the same manner. Flow along curved walls is another similar analogy. Then, there is the flow that can exist between concentric cylinders. All of these are important and can be investigated but the respective governing equations in these cases are better cast in terms of polar or other coordinates. Such action has been taken and these problems generate still more surprises for the chain of logical thought. In short, a great deal of the physics can be transposed to the new geometries but the results are not nearly so satisfying. Some

of the failures can be explained but some are still enigmas; others yield even more salient conclusions. Examples for each of such flows will be examined in detail.

1.8 Spatial stability bases

As has been suggested, the major experiments that have been done in the investigation of stability in flat plate boundary layers for example, does not, strictly speaking, correspond to the theory defined by a temporal initial-value problem. Instead, exploration was made by introducing a disturbance at an initial x-location upstream in the flow. Then, subsequent measurements are made downstream from this location in order to determine the resulting flow. By definition, this is a spatial initial-value problem. The behavior in time is simply periodic and neither decreases nor increases. From the definition given by (1.15), ω must be purely real. As a result, some alteration in the formulation must be made so that this formulation has merit.

The set of equations, (1.19) to (1.22), are still valid. However, these were developed with the understanding that the respective wave numbers, α and γ, were real. For the spatial problem, these parameters are to be complex. But, if an initial value for the relevant quantity is to be given as a function of y and z at $x = x_0$, γ must be real in order to satisfy the far field boundary conditions as $z \to \pm\infty$. In like manner, the integral that defines the limits for the x-variable in (1.14) would only be for $x > x_0$, much in the manner of a Laplace transform in time with $t > 0$. The net result leads to an amended Orr-Sommerfeld equation in the sense that α is the eigenvalue with γ, ω, and the Reynolds number as parameters. Also, in this case, $\alpha_i < 0$ implies instability. The Squire transformation is still permitted and the theorem is valid since it implies the neutral locus where $\alpha_i = \omega_i = 0$.

A general problem can be constructed that combines both the temporal and the spatial bases. The boundary value requirements remain the same but now the resulting dispersion relation can be seen to be one where there are two complex variables, namely ω and α. The wave number γ remains real and the Reynolds number is again a parameter if the system is taken as viscous. It is for this reason that Gaster (1965a,b) offered an alternative when the question of spatial stability was originally proposed. In like manner, Briggs (1964) used this formulation in studying instabilities in plasmas. Here, solutions were sought by use of the normal modes decomposition and the dispersion relation that is developed once the boundary conditions have been met is taken as a function of the two complex variables ω and α. For many problems as the boundary layer, the amplification rates are small and this allowed Gaster to

make a local Laurent expansion and use the Cauchy-Riemann relations of complex variable theory to establish a correspondence between the temporal values that were already computed and the spatial quantities that were unknown. These relations have proven to be of major importance. When amplification rates are large, however, care must be taken and the complex eigenvalues must be computed directly, as shown by Betchov & Criminale (1966) for jet and wake problems. Mattingly & Criminale (1972) extended this work and added experimental confirmation results as well. Direct numerical calculations have also been made for the boundary layer by Kaplan (1964), Raetz (1964), and Wazzan, Okamura, & Smith (1966) and the agreement with the analytical continuation method of Gaster was shown to be quite accurate.

Once the spatial-temporal problem is established, then other issues must be considered. Briefly stated, means of instability – now known as convective and absolute instabilities – have been identified when viewed from the spatial initial-value construction. These concepts relate to the fact that, for convective instability, at a fixed spatial location, amplification can occur and then pass as it is convected downstream. Absolute instability is one that, when amplification has begun, does not cease, and local breakdown is inevitable. Chapter 4 will discuss such problems in detail.

Chapter 2

Temporal stability of inviscid incompressible flows

2.1 General equations

In this chapter the essentials for a good fundamental understanding of stability theory are presented. We limit our interest to two-dimensional incompressible flows and write the general equations along with certain derived equations that have special physical meaning. As was discussed in Chapter 1, for three-dimensional flows there exists a theorem that allows the discussion to be reduced to an equivalent two-dimensional problem. In this way the bases are provided for a discussion of the oscillations of uniform flows, shear flows away from walls (mixing layers, jets and wakes), and finally of shear flows along one or two walls. A shear flow along a single wall is generally called a boundary layer and is of special interest to aeronautical engineers. The oscillations of a boundary layer have played a large role in the historical development of stability theory because it lends itself relatively easily to experimental measurements and observation. The oscillations of boundary layers will be analysed in detail in the next chapter.

The two dimensional Navier-Stokes equations for an incompressible flow are

$$u_x + v_y = 0, \tag{2.1}$$

$$\rho(u_t + uu_x + vu_y) + p_x = \mu\nabla^2 u, \tag{2.2}$$

and

$$\rho(v_t + uv_x + vv_y) + p_y = \mu\nabla^2 v, \tag{2.3}$$

where $\nabla^2 = (\ )_{xx} + (\ )_{yy}$ is the two-dimensional Laplace operator. Note that partial derivatives have the format $u_x = \partial u/\partial x$, $u(x, y, t)$ is the fluid velocity component parallel to the x-axis and $v(x, y, t)$ is the fluid velocity component

24

parallel to the y-axis, and are typically expressed in units of m/s or ft/s for the velocity and m or ft for the axial directions. More precisely, u and v are the Eulerian velocity components. It is convenient to refer to the x-axis as the "horizontal" axis and to the region $y > 0$ as being "above" the region $y < 0$. This reference is a convention for drawing the axes and does not imply the existence of gravity forces. The function $p(x, y, t)$ is the fluctuation pressure, while ρ is the density assumed constant throughout the entire flow field. Equation (2.1) insures the conservation of mass for an incompressible fluid. Equation (2.2) states that any horizontal acceleration is produced by a combination of a pressure gradient and a viscous force proportional to μ, the coefficient of viscosity. Equation (2.3) plays the same role for the vertical acceleration.

It is assumed that μ is a constant and, in those cases in which μ varies with the temperature, it may become necessary to add additional terms. Some possibilities for the variable μ will be considered in Chapter 5.

The coordinates x, y and the time, t, are independent variables and the functions u, v, and p are the dependent variables and functions of x, y, t. Note that (2.2) and (2.3) are nonlinear, thereby making the solution of these equations nontrivial. As a result, theoretical assumptions or simplifications are made so that the nonlinear partial differential equations can be reduced to solving a problem of either linear partial differential equations or linear ordinary differential equations.

We now derive the equations that control the small oscillations of a parallel and steady mean flow. By parallel we mean that the dependent variables for the mean (or base) flow are at most a function of only one independent variable, while steady denotes that the mean flow does not change with time. This derivation is done in three steps: (i) separation of fluctuations, (ii) linearization, and (iii) recourse to complex functions. But first the system will be nondimensionalized so that a rational means of approximation can be made.

2.1.1 Nondimensionalization

To nondimensionalize the governing system of equations, the following scalings are introduced

$$u = u^\dagger / U_c, \quad v = v^\dagger / U_c, \quad p = p^\dagger / (\rho U_c^2), \tag{2.4}$$

for the velocities and the pressure. U_c is some characteristic flow velocity of the problem. The superscript $\dagger$ denotes a dimensional quantity. Whereas equations (2.1) to (2.3) were dimensional, the $\dagger$ was not used for convenience. The length

and time scales are chosen so that

$$x = x^\dagger/L, \quad y = y^\dagger/L, \quad t = t^\dagger/(L/U_c), \qquad (2.5)$$

where L is some characteristic length scale of the problem. Substitution of these variables into our original equations produces the following non-dimensional system:

$$u_x + v_y = 0, \qquad (2.6)$$

$$u_t + uu_x + vu_y + p_x = Re^{-1}\nabla^2 u, \qquad (2.7)$$

and

$$v_t + uv_x + vv_y + p_y = Re^{-1}\nabla^2 v. \qquad (2.8)$$

Henceforth, all variables will be assumed to be non-dimensional unless otherwise noted. The parameter, Re, is the Reynolds number, defined as

$$Re = \frac{\rho L U_c}{\mu}. \qquad (2.9)$$

It is extremely important to ensure that the units are consistent in all nondimensional parameters. When consistency in units is not maintained, then severe repercussions can result, as drawn out in the failure of the Mars Climate orbiter.

MARS CLIMATE ORBITER TEAM FINDS
LIKELY CAUSE OF LOSS[a]

A failure to recognize and correct an error in a transfer of information between the Mars Climate Orbiter spacecraft team in Colorado and the mission navigation team in California led to the loss of the spacecraft last week, preliminary findings by NASA's Jet Propulsion Laboratory internal peer review indicate.

The peer review preliminary findings indicate that one team used English units (e.g., inches, feet and pounds) while the other used metric units for a key spacecraft operation. This information was critical to the maneuvers required to place the spacecraft in the proper Mars orbit.

[a] NASA Press Release: 99–113, September 30, 1999

2.1.2 Mean plus fluctuating components

We now assume that the flow can be decomposed into a laminar basic flow and a fluctuating component that oscillates about the basic flow,

$$u = U(y) + \tilde{u}(x, y, t),$$
$$v = \tilde{v}(x, y, t),$$
$$p = P(x) + \tilde{p}(x, y, t), \tag{2.10}$$

where the tilde superscript indicates a fluctuation component and capital letters are the basic flow. If these relations are introduced into (2.6) to (2.8), and the mean flow equations are subtracted, we obtain the system

$$\tilde{u}_x + \tilde{v}_y = 0, \tag{2.11}$$

$$\tilde{u}_t + U\tilde{u}_x + U'\tilde{v} + \tilde{p}_x + \underline{(\tilde{u}\tilde{u}_x + \tilde{v}\tilde{u}_y)} = Re^{-1}\nabla^2\tilde{u}, \tag{2.12}$$

and

$$\tilde{v}_t + U\tilde{v}_x + \tilde{p}_y + \underline{(\tilde{u}\tilde{v}_x + \tilde{v}\tilde{v}_y)} = Re^{-1}\nabla^2\tilde{v}. \tag{2.13}$$

We have made use of the notation that $U' = dU/dy$ for simplicity. This system of equations is for the nonlinear disturbance equations. The underlined terms denote the nonlinear terms.

2.1.3 Linearized disturbance equations

In these equations the noted nonlinear terms are products of the fluctuating velocities and their derivatives, and correspond to an effect of a fluctuation on another fluctuation. If the fluctuation has a frequency ω, the coupled terms will have frequency 0 or 2ω. Therefore this interaction will either modify the non-fluctuating flow (often referred to as mean-flow distortion) and feedback to the fluctuating components or introduce higher harmonics. Such difficulties are removed if we assume here that the products of the fluctuations and their derivatives have small amplitudes. The terms that are underlined can then be neglected (in comparison with the other terms) because a small fluctuation multiplied by a small fluctuation results in an order of magnitude smaller term and no longer influences the equations to this order of approximation. Then we obtain the following set of linear equations:

$$\tilde{u}_x + \tilde{v}_y = 0, \tag{2.14}$$

$$\tilde{u}_t + U\tilde{u}_x + U'\tilde{v} + \tilde{p}_x = Re^{-1}\nabla^2\tilde{u}, \tag{2.15}$$

and

$$\tilde{v}_t + U\tilde{v}_x + \tilde{p}_y = Re^{-1}\nabla^2\tilde{v}. \tag{2.16}$$

From the linear system, if $\tilde{u}_1$ is a solution in combination with functions $\tilde{v}_1$ and $\tilde{p}_1$, and if $\tilde{u}_2$, $\tilde{v}_2$, and $\tilde{p}_2$ form another solution, any linear combination such as $3\tilde{u}_1 + 2\tilde{u}_2, 3\tilde{v}_1 + 2\tilde{v}_2, 3\tilde{p}_1 + 2\tilde{p}_2$ will be a solution as well. The same fundamental property of linearity occurs in acoustics, electromagnetics, and ordinary quantum mechanics, in which it is guaranteed that the simultaneous oscillations will evolve independently because the nonlinear terms that would permit interaction have been neglected in equations (2.14) to (2.16). In thermodynamics, ferromagnetism, electronics, and fluid dynamics nonlinear equations must often be retained to capture sufficient flow physics for engineering applications. Fortunately, the solution of the linear system is often sufficient for problems such as when very small disturbances are found to be fluctuating in a laminar basic flow. The amplitude of these disturbances in this case is much smaller than that of the basic flow. Later as these disturbances grow in energy, the nonlinear disturbance equations (2.11) to (2.13) are required to compute the subsequent disturbance evolution.

We now derive certain special relations from the basic equations of motion that will enable us to understand the physical processes occurring in such an oscillatory flow. More specifically, equations for the streamfunction, the pressure, and the vorticity will be developed.

(a) Velocity disturbance equation

A single equation for the tangential velocity disturbance $\tilde{v}$ can be obtained by taking the curl of the momentum equations (2.15) to (2.16) and substituting in the continuity equation (2.14). Or, differentiate (2.15) with respect to y and differentiate (2.16) with respect to x, and then subtract the resulting equations to eliminate the pressure. This results in two equations with two unknowns – the continuity equation (2.14) and the following equation

$$\frac{\partial}{\partial t}(\tilde{u}_y - \tilde{v}_x) + U\frac{\partial}{\partial x}(\tilde{u}_y - \tilde{v}_x) + U''\tilde{v} = Re^{-1}\nabla^2(\tilde{u}_y - \tilde{v}_x). \tag{2.17}$$

The next step is to differentiate the above equation with respect to x, and then eliminate $\tilde{u}$ by means of the continuity equation (2.14), to give

$$\left(\frac{\partial}{\partial t} + U\frac{\partial}{\partial x}\right)\nabla^2\tilde{v} - U''\tilde{v}_x = Re^{-1}\nabla^4\tilde{v}, \tag{2.18}$$

where $\nabla^4 = \nabla^2 \cdot \nabla^2 = (\ )_{xxxx} + 2(\ )_{xxyy} + (\ )_{yyyy}$ is called the biharmonic operator. This is a single partial differential equation for the dependent variable

$\tilde{v}$ and, in principle, can be solved given appropriate boundary and initial conditions.

(b) Streamfunction disturbance equation

An alternate form of the linear disturbance equation (2.18) can be derived using a streamfunction formulation. Define the streamfunction, ψ, in the usual manner with

$$\tilde{u} = \psi_y, \quad \tilde{v} = -\psi_x. \tag{2.19}$$

Take the curl of the momentum equations which leads to equation (2.17). Use of the streamfunction ψ that automatically satisfies the continuity equation (2.14) by definition exactly. Then substitute ψ into equation (2.17). The resulting single partial differential equation for ψ is found to be

$$\left(\frac{\partial}{\partial t} + U\frac{\partial}{\partial x}\right)\nabla^2\psi - U''\psi_x = Re^{-1}\nabla^4\psi. \tag{2.20}$$

(c) Pressure disturbance equation

The pressure appears in (2.7) and (2.8) as a scalar and, for incompressible flow is decoupled from velocity. One might attempt to arbitrarily select or impose a pressure solution as a sort of potential. However, an arbitrary pressure field might create a velocity field in the momentum equations that would violate the continuity equation (2.6). The fluid would accumulate in certain places and the density would be unphysically forced to be non-constant. In general, it takes great energy to alter the density. As long as the fluid velocity is much smaller than the speed of sound, the density physically should remain constant and (2.6) is always satisfied (for the moment this assumes that we do not have a density stratified flow, such as would occur in the ocean or in the atmosphere). This continuity equation and constant density impose a restriction on the pressure fluctuations which can be formulated in the following sense. Consider the linearized equations (2.14) to (2.16). Differentiate (2.15) with respect to x and (2.16) with respect to y (or the divergence of the equations), add the two equations, and simplify with equation (2.14). The end product is

$$\nabla^2\tilde{p} = -2U'\tilde{v}_x. \tag{2.21}$$

This equation is similar to that of an elastic membrane loaded with some external force $\phi(x, y)$. If the deflection of the membrane is η, the basic equation is

$$\nabla^2\eta = \kappa\phi.$$

Thus, just as the external force causes a deflection of the membrane, the product $U'\tilde{v}_x$ is the source of pressure fluctuations. In the absence of any "source"

the pressure obeys Laplace's equation and is determined solely by the boundary conditions.

Another convenient form of the pressure equation can be obtained by applying the linear operator

$$\frac{\partial}{\partial t} + U\frac{\partial}{\partial x}$$

to (2.21), and then using the momentum equation (2.16) to eliminate the time derivative of $\tilde{v}$. This results in the following equation

$$\left(\frac{\partial}{\partial t} + U\frac{\partial}{\partial x}\right)\nabla^2\tilde{p} - 2U'\tilde{p}_{xy} = -2U'Re^{-1}\nabla^2\tilde{v}_x. \qquad (2.22)$$

For an inviscid flow ($Re \to \infty$), the right-hand side vanishes, and this equation reduces to a single equation for the disturbance pressure. For the viscous problem note that, although an equation for the pressure is valuable to understand the physics, it is not useful for solving the boundary value problem. This is not necessarily true for the inviscid problem where the right-hand side of (2.22) vanishes and a partial differential equation homogeneous in the pressure emerges.

(d) Vorticity disturbance equation

Finally, we can derive a single equation for the spanwise vorticity component. In general the vorticity is a vector that indicates the rotation of a small mass of fluid with respect to the chosen coordinates. More precisely, consider a small surface element immersed in the fluid and define the circulation as the integral of the velocity along the perimeter. The circulation is equal to the flux of the vorticity through the surface; no vorticity implies no circulation. In a two-dimensional flow the vorticity vector is always perpendicular to the $x - y$ plane and, because its orientation is fixed, the vorticity can be treated like a scalar quantity because there is only the one component in two-dimensional flow. Thus for the disturbance vorticity, $\tilde{\omega}_z$, and the mean (basic) flow, Ω_z, we have

$$\tilde{\omega}_z = \tilde{v}_x - \tilde{u}_y, \quad \Omega_z = -U'. \qquad (2.23)$$

The vorticity fluctuations obey an important equation that can be obtained by taking the curl of the momentum equations to eliminate the pressure, resulting in

$$\left(\frac{\partial}{\partial t} + U\frac{\partial}{\partial x}\right)\tilde{\omega}_z - U''\tilde{v} = Re^{-1}\nabla^2\tilde{\omega}_z. \qquad (2.24)$$

This equation is analogous to that of the heat conduction-diffusion equation in the presence of sources and sinks of heat. Indeed, in a copper sheet of constant thickness and unit specific heat, the temperature T obeys the following basic equation:

$$\frac{\partial T}{\partial t} = \kappa \nabla^2 T + Q,$$

where κ is the coefficient of thermal diffusivity and $Q(x, y, t)$ is proportional to the rate of production or withdrawal of heat. If the copper is replaced by a layer of mercury moving with velocity $U(y)$, another term must be included to account for the convection of energy. The equation in this case becomes

$$\frac{\partial T}{\partial t} + U \frac{\partial T}{\partial x} = \kappa \nabla^2 T + Q.$$

In the absence of conductivity and production it has the solution $T(x - Ut, y)$, which shows that each particle of mercury retains the same temperature. In a comparison between the energy equation (in terms of temperature) and the vorticity equation (2.24), the term $U''\tilde{v}$ plays a comparable role as Q. However, unlike Q, the disturbance velocity $\tilde{v}$ is linked to $\tilde{\omega}_z$ (see equation 2.23).

2.1.4 Recourse to complex functions

We shall immediately take advantage of linearity and seek solutions in terms of complex functions. In this way we will be able to reduce the system of partial differential equations (2.14) to (2.16) to ordinary differential equations, making for an obvious facility in the analysis. Thus, one can hope to find normal mode solutions of the type

$$\tilde{u}(x, y, t) = \tfrac{1}{2}(\hat{u} + \hat{u}^*) = \frac{1}{2}\left(\mathbf{u}(y)e^{i\alpha(x-ct)} + \mathbf{u}(y)^* e^{-i\alpha^*(x-c^*t)}\right),$$

$$\tilde{v}(x, y, t) = \tfrac{1}{2}(\hat{v} + \hat{v}^*) = \frac{1}{2}\left(\mathbf{v}(y)e^{i\alpha(x-ct)} + \mathbf{v}(y)^* e^{-i\alpha^*(x-c^*t)}\right),$$

$$\tilde{p}(x, y, t) = \tfrac{1}{2}(\hat{p} + \hat{p}^*) = \frac{1}{2}\left(\mathbf{p}(y)e^{i\alpha(x-ct)} + \mathbf{p}(y)^* e^{-i\alpha^*(x-c^*t)}\right),$$

$$(2.25)$$

where $\hat{u}, \hat{v}, \hat{p}$ is a complex normal mode form and the $*$ quantities are the complex conjugates. Hence, the sum of the normal mode and its complex conjugate is the real disturbance quantity. In principle, since the complex conjugate values can easily be obtained from the quantities themselves, one need only solve for the complex quantities $\hat{u}, \hat{v}, \hat{p}$. In the above relations we identify $\alpha = \alpha_r + i\alpha_i$ as the non-dimensional wavenumber in the x-direction and

$c = c_r + ic_i$ as the wave velocity. The non-dimensional frequency of the disturbance is given by $\omega = \alpha c$, and the non-dimensional wavelength of the disturbance is given by $\lambda = 2\pi/\alpha_r$. In general both α and c, and hence ω, can be considered as complex numbers. Hence, the bases for a generalized temporal-spatial problem. The boldface symbols $\mathbf{u}$, $\mathbf{v}$, $\mathbf{p}$ are used to indicate a complex function of y only. As complex conjugate quantities, $c^* = c_r - ic_i$ and $\alpha^* = \alpha_r - i\alpha_i$. To be a physical solution for the disturbances, the normal mode form (2.25) must obey the continuity and momentum equations (2.14) to (2.16). After substituting (2.25) into these equations, we find that the resulting equations are no longer functions of x or t. Thus, the partial differential equations have been reduced to a system of ordinary differential equations in y.

The advantage of using complex quantities should now be evident; in general, an oscillation has an amplitude and a phase. This means that two numbers must be specified, and we may as well give the amplitude of the cosine and the amplitude of the sine components. This is just what the real and imaginary parts of a boldface quantity such as $\mathbf{p}$ can do. In a single complex quantity, the amplitude and the phase can be expressed for a fluctuation. The reader is reminded, however, that although complex quantities are used, the solutions to the original system are real and this fact must be borne in mind when describing the behavior of the original system. This particular approach of using complex quantities is usually called "the normal mode approach", and the solutions called normal modes. These points were also discussed in Chapter 1 from a somewhat different perspective.

To better explain the information contained in a complex normal mode analysis, let us look to an example solution. Suppose that we have a solution of the form

$$\hat{p} = \mathbf{p}(y)e^{4i(x-(0.7+0.2i)t)}, \quad \mathbf{p}(y) = 2y + 3y^2 i,$$

where we have assumed $\alpha = 4$ and $c = 0.7 + 0.2i$. Recall the relation $e^{i\theta} = \cos\theta + i\sin\theta$, $i = \sqrt{-1}$, and $i^2 = -1$. This leads to the real disturbance solution

$$\tilde{p} = \{2y\cos[4(x - 0.7t)] - 3y^2\sin[4(x - 0.7t)]\}e^{0.8t}.$$

The imaginary part of c leads to an exponential growth in time, the real part of $\mathbf{p}$ gives the amplitude of the cosine component, and the imaginary part of $\mathbf{p}$ gives the amplitude of the sine component except for a minus sign. We say that this function grows exponentially in time with growth rate of 0.8. The wavenumber of this function is given by $\alpha = 4$, and thus the wavelength is $\lambda = 2\pi/\alpha = \pi/2$. The phase speed is given by $c_r = 0.7$, which means that the

solution grows in time along the particle paths $x = 0.7t + x_0$, where x_0 is any constant along the real axis at time $t = 0$.

In our original problem, if $\alpha = \alpha_r + i\alpha_i$ and $c = c_r + ic_i$, we see that the amplitudes of the disturbance functions are proportional to

$$\tilde{v} \approx e^{-\alpha_i x + \omega_i t}, \tag{2.26}$$

and similarly for the other disturbance functions, with the complex frequency being given by

$$\omega = \omega_r + i\omega_i, \quad \text{where} \quad \omega_r = \alpha_r c_r - \alpha_i c_i, \quad \text{and} \quad \omega_i = \alpha_r c_i + \alpha_i c_r. \tag{2.27}$$

From (2.26) we note that the disturbance can grow exponentially in the positive x-direction if $\alpha_i < 0$, and increase exponentially in time if $\omega_i > 0$.

The use of the normal mode relationship for disturbances (2.25) substituted into the linearized disturbance equations (2.14) to (2.16) transforms the partial differential equations into ordinary differential equations. However, this transformation does not come without complications. Namely, with this substitution, the complex eigenfunctions **u**, **v**, **p** are unknown functions of y. The complex wavenumber $\alpha_r + i\alpha_i$ and frequency $\omega_r + i\omega_i$ introduce four additional unknowns, resulting in more unknowns than equations. Hence, one must make assumptions concerning these unknowns in order to obtain any solution. In one case, one may assume that the disturbance amplifies in space and not time with a fixed frequency. As such α becomes the unknown eigenvalue, $\omega_i = 0$, and ω_r is specified. As suggested in Chapter 1, this is referred to as spatial stability theory and will be discussed in some detail in Chapter 4. A second case could assume that the disturbances amplify in time and not space. Hence, ω becomes the unknown eigenvalue, $\alpha_i = 0$, and α_r is specified. This is referred to as temporal stability theory and will be discussed in detail in the remainder of this chapter and in Chapter 3. The intersection of temporal and spatial theories occurs at the neutral locations where disturbances neither amplify nor decay in space and time. That is $\alpha_i = \omega_i = 0$ and both theories yield the same normal mode solution. To restate, we have the following two limiting cases:

TEMPORAL STABILITY THEORY: $\alpha_i = 0$ and ω complex;

SPATIAL STABILITY THEORY: $\omega_i = 0$ and α complex.

To restate, temporal stability theory considers disturbances that grow in time, while spatial stability theory considers disturbances that grow in the positive x-direction. In temporal theory the wavenumber α is taken as real while the frequency ω is assumed complex; in spatial theory the wavenumber is assumed

complex while the frequency is taken to be real. These two limiting cases dominate the subject of hydrodynamic stability theory, and most publications and research fall into one of these two categories.

Historically, temporal theory can be traced to the time of Helmholtz (1868), Kelvin (1871), and Rayleigh (1879, 1880, 1887, 1892) in the late nineteenth century, while spatial theory originated in the 1950's. During this later time period spatial stability was recognized to be important for the case of parallel laminar flows, where various experimentalists observed that instability and transition to turbulence occurred by the growth of disturbances in the downstream x-direction (i.e., spatial instability; see review article by Dunn, 1960). The method was restricted to first computing temporal modes and then relating those to spatial modes by means of the phase velocity; i.e., $\omega_i = -c_r \alpha_i$. Such a simple relation is not valid in general, and very little progress was made as a result. Gaster put the concept of spatial stability on a firm theoretical foundation, and carried out the first (unpublished) spatial calculations as part of his doctoral thesis. Early spatial calculations confirmed the validity of the approach by comparing the growth rates obtained by numerics to those obtained by experiments. The more general case of space-time growth of disturbances, first published by Gaster (1962, 1965a, 1968), will be considered as a separate topic in Chapter 4.

To obtain an equation that describes the spatial-temporal amplification of disturbances, substitute the normal mode expression for $\tilde{v}$ (2.25) into the linear disturbance equation (2.18) to get

$$(U - c)(\mathbf{v}'' - \alpha^2 \mathbf{v}) - U''\mathbf{v} = (i\alpha Re)^{-1} (\mathbf{v}'''' - 2\alpha^2 \mathbf{v}'' + \alpha^4 \mathbf{v}). \quad (2.28)$$

This now-famous equation was first derived independently by Orr (1907a,b) and Sommerfeld (1908), and is known as the Orr-Sommerfeld equation. Note, that the partial different equation has become a fourth-order ordinary differential equation which requires four boundary conditions for closure. If the fluid is taken as inviscid ($Re \to \infty$) then the corresponding equation is

$$(U - c)(\mathbf{v}'' - \alpha^2 \mathbf{v}) - U''\mathbf{v} = 0. \quad (2.29)$$

Equation (2.29) was first derived by Rayleigh (1880) and is known as the Rayleigh equation[1]. The Rayleigh equation is a second order ordinary differential equation, requiring two boundary conditions for closure. The Orr-Sommerfeld equation governs the stability of parallel *viscous* flows, while Rayleigh's equation governs the stability of parallel *inviscid* flows. These two

---

[1] Rayleigh's equation is sometimes mistakenly referred to as the "inviscid Orr-Sommerfeld" equation; since Rayleigh derived his equation more than 25 years before Orr and Sommerfeld, we shall not use this terminology here.

equations mark the cornerstone of all hydrodynamic stability analysis and will be of primary importance for the remainder of this text.

The Orr-Sommerfeld and the Rayleigh equations can also be derived directly from the streamfunction equation (2.20). Let the streamfunction be represented by a normal mode form

$$\psi(x, y, t) = \frac{1}{2}(\hat{\psi} + \hat{\psi}^*) = \frac{1}{2}\left(\phi(y)e^{i\alpha(x-ct)} + \phi^*(y)e^{i\alpha^*(x-c^*t)}\right).$$
(2.30)

By substituting the normal mode form (2.30) into the linear disturbance equations (2.20) an alternative form of the Orr-Sommerfeld equation results, namely

$$(U - c)(\phi'' - \alpha^2\phi) - U''\phi = \frac{1}{i\alpha Re}(\phi'''' - 2\alpha^2\phi'' + \alpha^4\phi),$$
(2.31)

and an alternative form of the Rayleigh equation becomes

$$(U - c)(\phi'' - \alpha^2\phi) - U''\phi = 0.$$
(2.32)

This formulation is the one originally used by Rayleigh. Note that the Orr-Sommerfeld equation (2.28) governing the velocity disturbance **v** has the same form as the equivalent equation governing the streamfunction disturbance ϕ because of the relationship between **v** and ϕ in equation (2.19).

The proper boundary conditions for the Orr-Sommerfeld and Rayleigh equations depend on the configuration. For bounded flows, the boundary conditions require that ϕ and ϕ' vanish at the walls for the Orr-Sommerfeld fourth order equation, while the boundary conditions for the second order Rayleigh equation are that ϕ vanishes at the walls. Because, in this latter case the normal derivative can not be required to vanish, we see that the flow slips along the walls since $\mathbf{u} = \phi'$ is non-zero, in general, at the walls. For unbounded flows the perturbation solution is required to be bounded.

An alternative form of Rayleigh's equation can be derived by substituting the pressure normal mode form (2.25) into the linear disturbance equation (2.22). In the inviscid limit, the pressure disturbance equation becomes

$$\mathbf{p}'' - \frac{2U'}{U - c}\mathbf{p}' - \alpha^2\mathbf{p} = 0.$$
(2.33)

This equation often appears in the literature as an alternative means for solving the inviscid stability problem. The proper boundary conditions require that either **p** vanish at the walls or be bounded in the case of unbounded domains.

2.1.5 Three-dimensionality

The normal mode analysis can be extended from two to three-dimensions in a straight forward manner. Let $u(x, y, z, t)$, $v(x, y, z, t)$ and $w(x, y, z, t)$ be

the fluid velocities in the x, y and z-direction, respectively. Then the general non-dimensional equations for a three-dimensional incompressible flow are

$$u_x + v_y + w_z = 0, \tag{2.34}$$

$$u_t + uu_x + vu_y + wu_z + p_x = Re_{3d}^{-1}\nabla^2 u, \tag{2.35}$$

$$v_t + uv_x + vv_y + wv_z + p_y = Re_{3d}^{-1}\nabla^2 v, \tag{2.36}$$

$$w_t + uw_x + vw_y + ww_z + p_z = Re_{3d}^{-1}\nabla^2 w, \tag{2.37}$$

where $\nabla^2 = ()_{xx} + ()_{yy} + ()_{zz}$. Here, Re_{3d} is the Reynolds number associated with the three-dimensional problem, and we use the subscript to distinguish it from the Reynolds number associated with the two-dimensional problem. This notation is for convenience only, as will become apparent in the discussion below. Equation (2.34) is the continuity equation in three dimensions, (2.35) is the mass momentum equation in the x-direction, (2.36) is the mass momentum equation in the y-direction, and (2.37) is the mass momentum equation in the z-direction.

We again assume that the flow oscillates (or fluctuates) about mean values and use the tilde superscript to indicate a fluctuation. Thus we have the instantaneous quantities

$$u = U(y) + \tilde{u}(x, y, z, t),$$
$$v = \tilde{v}(x, y, z, t),$$
$$w = \tilde{w}(x, y, z, t),$$
$$p = P(x) + \tilde{p}(x, y, z, t). \tag{2.38}$$

When these relations are introduced into the Navier-Stokes equations (2.34) to (2.37), we obtain the nonlinear disturbance equations

$$\tilde{u}_x + \tilde{v}_y + \tilde{w}_z = 0, \tag{2.39}$$

$$\tilde{u}_t + U\tilde{u}_x + U'\tilde{v} + \tilde{p}_x + \underline{(\tilde{u}\tilde{u}_x + \tilde{v}\tilde{u}_y + \tilde{w}\tilde{u}_z)} = Re_{3d}^{-1}\nabla^2\tilde{u}, \tag{2.40}$$

$$\tilde{v}_t + U\tilde{v}_x + \tilde{p}_y + \underline{(\tilde{u}\tilde{v}_x + \tilde{v}\tilde{v}_y + \tilde{w}\tilde{v}_z)} = Re_{3d}^{-1}\nabla^2\tilde{v}, \tag{2.41}$$

$$\tilde{w}_t + U\tilde{w}_x + \tilde{p}_z + \underline{(\tilde{u}\tilde{w}_x + \tilde{v}\tilde{w}_y + \tilde{w}\tilde{w}_z)} = Re_{3d}^{-1}\nabla^2\tilde{w}. \tag{2.42}$$

The normal mode approach first linearizes the above system by neglecting the nonlinear terms (underlined), and then introduces the complex quantities

$$\tilde{u} = \frac{1}{2}(\hat{u} + \hat{u}^*), \quad \tilde{v} = \frac{1}{2}(\hat{v} + \hat{v}^*), \quad \tilde{w} = \frac{1}{2}(\hat{w} + \hat{w}^*), \quad \tilde{p} = \frac{1}{2}(\hat{p} + \hat{p}^*). \tag{2.43}$$

As before, let

$$\hat{u}(x, y, z, t) = \mathbf{u}(y)e^{i(\alpha x + \beta z - \omega t)},$$
$$\hat{v}(x, y, z, t) = \mathbf{v}(y)e^{i(\alpha x + \beta z - \omega t)},$$
$$\hat{w}(x, y, z, t) = \mathbf{w}(y)e^{i(\alpha x + \beta z - \omega t)},$$
$$\hat{p}(x, y, z, t) = \mathbf{p}(y)e^{i(\alpha x + \beta z - \omega t)}, \qquad (2.44)$$

where α is the complex wavenumber in the x-direction, β is the complex wavenumber in the z-direction, and $\omega = \alpha c$ is the complex frequency. With this notation, it is the real part of (2.44) that is the physical quantity. Substitution of (2.43) and (2.44) into the linearized version of (2.39) to (2.42) results in the following linear system of equations

$$i\alpha \mathbf{u} + \mathbf{v}' + i\beta \mathbf{w} = 0, \qquad (2.45)$$

$$i\alpha(U - c)\mathbf{u} + U'\mathbf{v} + i\alpha \mathbf{p} = Re_{3d}^{-1}(\mathbf{u}'' - (\alpha^2 + \beta^2)\mathbf{u}), \qquad (2.46)$$

$$i\alpha(U - c)\mathbf{v} + \mathbf{p}' = Re_{3d}^{-1}(\mathbf{v}'' - (\alpha^2 + \beta^2)\mathbf{v}), \qquad (2.47)$$

$$i\alpha(U - c)\mathbf{w} + i\beta \mathbf{p} = Re_{3d}^{-1}(\mathbf{w}'' - (\alpha^2 + \beta^2)\mathbf{w}). \qquad (2.48)$$

A single equation for $\mathbf{v}$ can now be obtained in a straightforward manner. The $\mathbf{u}$ momentum equation (2.46) is multiplied by $i\alpha$ and the $\mathbf{w}$ momentum equation (2.48) is multiplied by $i\beta$. The resulting equations are summed and the continuity equation (2.45) is used to replace the expressions $i\alpha \mathbf{u} + i\beta \mathbf{w}$ with $-\mathbf{v}'$, resulting in the equation

$$i\alpha(U - c)\mathbf{v}' - i\alpha U'\mathbf{v} + (\alpha^2 + \beta^2)\mathbf{p} = Re_{3d}^{-1}(\mathbf{v}''' - (\alpha^2 + \beta^2)\mathbf{v}'). \quad (2.49)$$

The pressure is eliminated by differentiating the equation (2.49) by y and then use the $\mathbf{v}$ momentum equation (2.47), resulting in a single equation for $\mathbf{v}$, namely

$$(U - c)(\mathbf{v}'' - (\alpha^2 + \beta^2)\mathbf{v}) - U''\mathbf{v} = \frac{1}{i\alpha Re_{3d}}(\mathbf{v}'''' - 2(\alpha^2 + \beta^2)\mathbf{v}''$$
$$+ (\alpha^2 + \beta^2)^2 \mathbf{v}). \qquad (2.50)$$

The above equation is the three-dimensional Orr-Sommerfeld equation, which is a fourth order ordinary differential equation. The number of unknowns has now increased to six, namely: α_r, α_i, β_r, β_i, and ω_r, ω_i.

2.1.6 Squire transformation

Squire (1933) recognized that, with a simple transformation, equation (2.50) can be reduced to a form equivalent to the two-dimensional Orr-Sommerfeld

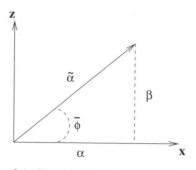

Fig. 2.1. Sketch of the polar representation.

equation. Define the polar wavenumber, $\tilde{\alpha}$, as

$$\tilde{\alpha} = \sqrt{\alpha^2 + \beta^2} \,, \tag{2.51}$$

and a reduced Reynolds number as

$$R_{2d} = \frac{\alpha R_{3d}}{\sqrt{\alpha^2 + \beta^2}} \equiv \frac{\alpha}{\tilde{\alpha}} R_{3d} = R_{3d} \cos \bar{\phi}, \tag{2.52}$$

where $\tan \bar{\phi} = \beta/\alpha$, the polar angle in wave space (Fig. 2.1).

The substitution of (2.51) and (2.52) into the three-dimensional Orr-Somm-erfeld equation (2.50) results in

$$(U - c)(\mathbf{v}'' - \tilde{\alpha}^2 \mathbf{v}) - U'' \mathbf{v} = \frac{1}{i\tilde{\alpha} Re_{2d}} (\mathbf{v}'''' - 2\tilde{\alpha}^2 \mathbf{v}'' + \tilde{\alpha}^4 \mathbf{v}), \tag{2.53}$$

which has exactly the same form as the two-dimensional Orr-Sommerfeld equation (2.28). Several remarks are in order here. First, the transformation that takes the three-dimensional problem and transforms it into an equivalent two-dimensional problem is now called the Squire transformation after H. Squire (1933) for this important contribution to stability theory. Second, for parallel flows, we need only study the two-dimensional problem for determining stability. Once $\tilde{\alpha}$ and Re_{2d} are determined from the two-dimensional problem, we can determine the true wavenumber α and Reynolds number Re_{3d} by inverting the transformation, for a given value of the polar angle $\bar{\phi}$. Third, since $\alpha \leq \tilde{\alpha}$, we see that the three-dimensional and the two-dimensional equations are the same except that the two-dimensional problem has a lower value of the Reynolds number. Finally, the phase speed, c, is unscaled and hence both the three-dimensional and the two-dimensional linear stability problems have exactly the same phase speed definition. These remarks were originally made by Squire, and we recast them in the form of the following theorem:

Squire's Theorem (1933): If an exact two-dimensional parallel flow admits an unstable three-dimensional disturbance for a certain value of the Reynolds number, it also admits a two-dimensional disturbance at a lower value of the Reynolds number.

The theorem could also be restated as, "To each unstable three-dimensional disturbance there corresponds a more unstable two-dimensional disturbance." Or, "To obtain the minimum critical Reynolds number it is sufficient to consider only two-dimensional disturbances." Because of the Squire transformation, we will henceforth only consider two-dimensional disturbances. However, it should be borne in mind that the theorem only applies to parallel flows; for more complicated mean flows, such as three-dimensional mean flows or for curved flows, three-dimensional disturbances are of utmost importance.

One final comment is in order here. The stream function approach to deriving the Orr-Sommerfeld equation is no longer useful in three dimensions, but the vorticity formulation can be used because the vorticity now has three components and these can be used to derive the counterpart of the Orr-Sommerfeld equation in three dimensions. These points were also outlined in Chapter 1.

2.2 Kelvin-Helmholtz theory

Before embarking on the solutions to the Rayleigh or Orr-Sommerfeld equation for the general case of parallel mean flows, it is instructive to depart somewhat at this point and consider the stability of piecewise constant flows. Helmholtz and Kelvin (see also Lamb, 1945) gave the first description of such flows, and the theory now bears their names in honor of their contributions. Consider an incompressible inviscid flow of two fluids with different velocities and different densities, as shown in Fig. 2.2. The dimensional mean variables that describe the flow are given by

$$U = \begin{cases} U_1 \\ U_2 \end{cases}, \quad \rho = \begin{cases} \rho_1 & y > 0, \\ \rho_2 & y < 0. \end{cases} \tag{2.54}$$

In this section all quantities will be considered dimensional because the results are easier to understand conceptually than the alternate non-dimensional analysis. As stated, Rayleigh's equation (2.29) governs the stability of the flow on either side of the interface $y = 0$, and has the general solution

$$\mathbf{v} = \begin{cases} Ae^{-\alpha y} & y > 0 \\ Be^{\alpha y} & y < 0 \end{cases} \tag{2.55}$$

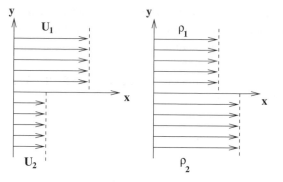

Fig. 2.2. Sketch of the piecewise constant approximation to a shear layer; the interface is located at $y = 0$.

that satisfies the $y \rightarrow \pm\infty$ boundary conditions. These solutions are those of a harmonic field. In order to complete the solution we need two conditions at the interface $y = 0$ to determine A and B^1. These are of the form of jump conditions, which we derive below.

2.2.1 Interface conditions

Two conditions are needed at the interface to complete the solution given above. The first condition comes from the requirement that the jump in the normal stress must be continuous. This condition is equivalent to saying that, for an inviscid fluid, the pressure is continuous at the interface, thus

$$[p] = 0. \tag{2.56}$$

Here, we use the notation $[\ ] = (\ )|_{y=0^+} - (\ )|_{y=0^-}$ to denote the jump across the interface located at $y = 0$. The interface condition can easily be obtained by first linearizing the jump condition (2.56) and applying the normal mode technique, then eliminating the pressure disturbance in terms of the vertical velocity component by combining the linearized continuity and x-momentum equations,

$$\rho\{(\omega - \alpha U)\mathbf{v}' + \alpha U'\mathbf{v}\} + i\alpha^2 \mathbf{p} = 0, \tag{2.57}$$

valid on either side of the interface, resulting in the jump condition

$$[\rho\{(\alpha U - \omega)\mathbf{v}' - \alpha U'\mathbf{v}\}] = 0 \quad \text{at} \quad y = 0. \tag{2.58}$$

---

[1] Alternatively, one can set $A = 1$ since the problem is homogeneous, but two conditions are still needed to determine B and the eigenvalue ω.

The second interface condition can be found by appealing to the motion of the interface. Let

$$F(x, y, t) = y - f(x, t) \tag{2.59}$$

describe the position of the interface[1]. The equation for the free surface is given by the material derivative

$$\frac{DF}{Dt} \equiv F_t + uF_x + vF_y = 0. \tag{2.60}$$

This equation states that the change in the quantity F along the particle path must be zero, and is also referred to as the kinematic condition at the free surface. After substituting for the definition of F, (2.60) becomes

$$-f_t - uf_x + v = 0, \tag{2.61}$$

or, in terms of the normal component velocity v,

$$v = f_t + uf_x. \tag{2.62}$$

Assume the shape of the surface can be written in terms of normal modes or

$$f(x, t) = ae^{i\alpha(x-ct)}, \tag{2.63}$$

with a the amplitude of the displacement of the interface from its mean position $y = 0$. By substituting (2.63) into (2.62),

$$v = \begin{cases} i(\alpha U_1 - \omega)a & y = 0^+, \\ i(\alpha U_2 - \omega)a & y = 0^-. \end{cases} \tag{2.64}$$

Since a is a constant, the jump condition becomes:

$$\left[\frac{v}{\alpha U - \omega} \right] = 0 \quad \text{at} \quad y = 0. \tag{2.65}$$

We now apply the two interface conditions to our solution obtained above. After substituting (2.55) into (2.58) and (2.65), then

$$-\rho_1(\alpha U_1 - \omega)A\alpha = \rho_2(\alpha U_2 - \omega)B\alpha, \tag{2.66}$$

$$\frac{A}{\alpha U_1 - \omega} = \frac{B}{\alpha U_2 - \omega}, \tag{2.67}$$

or, in matrix form,

$$\begin{bmatrix} -\rho_1(\alpha U_1 - \omega) & \rho_2(\alpha U_2 - \omega) \\ (\alpha U_2 - \omega) & (\alpha U_1 - \omega) \end{bmatrix} \begin{bmatrix} A \\ B \end{bmatrix} = \begin{bmatrix} 0 \\ 0 \end{bmatrix}. \tag{2.68}$$

---

[1] This equation is only valid if the shape of the interface is single-valued, as would be expected for small disturbances.

Since the system is homogeneous, a nontrivial solution exists if and only if the determinant vanishes, that is, we must have

$$\rho_1(\alpha U_1 - \omega)^2 + \rho_2(\alpha U_2 - \omega)^2 = 0. \qquad (2.69)$$

This equation determines our eigenvalue ω, and is called the dispersion relation for ω. The solution to the dispersion relation given by (2.69) is

$$\omega = \alpha \left\{ \frac{\rho_1 U_1 + \rho_2 U_2}{\rho_1 + \rho_2} \pm i \sqrt{\frac{\rho_1 \rho_2 (U_2 - U_1)^2}{(\rho_1 + \rho_2)^2}} \right\}, \qquad (2.70)$$

which is a linear function of α. Since one root of the imaginary part of ω is positive for $U_1 \neq U_2$, we see that the shear flow is always temporally unstable in an inviscid fluid and even if $\rho_1 = \rho_2$. The root corresponding to $\omega < 0$ is mathematically correct but cannot exist physically. This instability is a direct result of the fact that the dynamic pressure, $[P + \rho|\mathbf{u}|^2/2]$, is not equal on either side of the interface. Additional effects, such as buoyancy and surface tension, can be added. These effects will be considered in the exercise section at the end of this chapter and in Chapter 7.

The dispersion relation (2.70) also reveals another important point. In this discontinuous mean model, there is no characteristic length scale and therefore, as $\alpha \to \infty$, $\omega \to \infty$. Large α means small scales and this limit is physically not possible. This point will be made clear in the next section.

2.3 Piecewise linear profile

2.3.1 Unconfined shear layer

As an example of a piecewise linear profile, consider the unconfined shear layer with non-dimensional mean velocity defined by

$$U(y) = \begin{cases} 1 & y > 1, \\ y & -1 < y < 1, \\ -1 & y < -1. \end{cases} \qquad (2.71)$$

A sketch of the velocity profile is given in Fig. 2.3. Note there is now a length scale. The length scale L is taken to be half the shear layer thickness and the velocity scale is taken to be the freestream value.

In each region the equation for the disturbance is governed by Rayleigh's equation (2.29) with $U'' = 0$ from (2.71), namely

$$\mathbf{v}'' - \alpha^2 \mathbf{v} = 0. \qquad (2.72)$$

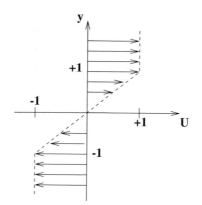

Fig. 2.3. Sketch of the unconfined piecewise linear shear layer.

Again **v** is a harmonic function. The general solution in each region can easily be determined in such a way to satisfy the far field boundary conditions where $y \to \pm\infty$. A convenient form is given by

$$
\mathbf{v}(y) = \begin{cases} Ae^{-\alpha(y-1)} & y > 1, \\ Be^{-\alpha(y-1)} + Ce^{\alpha(y+1)} & -1 < y < 1, \\ De^{\alpha(y+1)} & y < -1. \end{cases} \tag{2.73}
$$

We now apply the jump conditions (2.58) and (2.65) at $y = \pm 1$. First, the requirement that the pressure disturbance be continuous at the interfaces results in the following two equations

$$
A = B\left(\frac{\omega - \alpha - 1}{\omega - \alpha}\right) + Ce^{2\alpha}\left(\frac{\alpha - \omega - 1}{\omega - \alpha}\right), \tag{2.74}
$$

and

$$
D = Be^{2\alpha}\left(\frac{1 - \omega - \alpha}{\omega + \alpha}\right) + C\left(\frac{\alpha + \omega + 1}{\omega + \alpha}\right). \tag{2.75}
$$

The second interface condition, that the normal disturbance velocity be continuous across the interfaces, results in the following two equations

$$
A = B + Ce^{2\alpha}, \tag{2.76}
$$

and

$$
D = Be^{2\alpha} + C. \tag{2.77}
$$

Thus, we now have four equations for the four unknown constants A, B, C and D. We can rewrite the four equations in matrix notation

$$J \cdot \underline{x} = 0, \tag{2.78}$$

where

$$\underline{x} = (A, B, C, D)^T \tag{2.79}$$

and

$$J = \begin{bmatrix} 1 & -\left(\frac{\omega-\alpha-1}{\omega-\alpha}\right) & -e^{2\alpha}\left(\frac{\alpha-\omega-1}{\omega-\alpha}\right) & 0 \\ 0 & -e^{2\alpha}\left(\frac{1-\omega-\alpha}{\omega+\alpha}\right) & -\left(\frac{\alpha+\omega+1}{\omega+\alpha}\right) & 1 \\ 1 & -1 & -e^{2\alpha} & 0 \\ 0 & -e^{2\alpha} & -1 & 1 \end{bmatrix}. \tag{2.80}$$

As before, a nontrivial solution will exist if and only if the determinant of J vanishes. The determinant calculation leads to

$$|J| = \frac{e^{4\alpha}}{\omega^2 - \alpha^2}\{1 - 4\alpha + 4\alpha^2 - 4\omega^2 - e^{-4\alpha}\} \tag{2.81}$$

and, by setting (2.81) to zero, the eigenvalue relation

$$\omega = \pm\frac{1}{2}\sqrt{(1 - 2\alpha)^2 - e^{-4\alpha}} \tag{2.82}$$

results. This equation is the dispersion relation that relates the wavenumber α to the frequency ω, and was first obtained by Rayleigh (1894). Since α is real, we see that ω is either purely real (stable) or purely imaginary (unstable), depending on the sign of the square root term. The neutral mode can thus be found by setting the square root term to zero, resulting in the neutral mode

$$\omega_N = 0, \quad \text{for} \quad \alpha_N = 0 \quad \text{and} \quad \alpha_N = 0.639232. \tag{2.83}$$

The unstable region is given by $0 < \alpha < \alpha_N$, and a graph of the unstable region is given in Fig. 2.4. Contrast this with the previous example of Kelvin-Helmholtz where the unstable region is infinite with $\alpha > 0$. As mentioned, this is due to the fact that the Kelvin-Helmholtz model has no length scale and therefore unstable at all values of α. However, as α gets larger, the scale

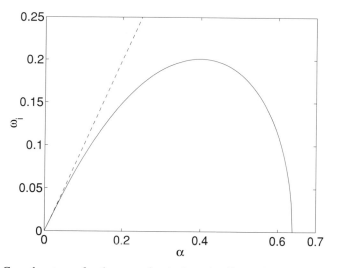

Fig. 2.4. Growth rate ω_i for the unconfined piecewise linear shear layer. The dotted line shows the growth rate from the Kelvin-Helmholtz theory with $\rho_1 = \rho_2$ and $U_1 = 1$, $U_2 = -1$.

decreases and viscous effects must be eventually considered. From this figure we see that the maximum growth rate, $\omega_{i,max} = 0.201186$, occurs for $\alpha \approx 0.39837$. The wavelength $\lambda = 2\pi/\alpha$ associated with the maximum growth rate is

$$\lambda_{max} = \frac{2\pi}{0.39837} \approx 15.772. \qquad (2.84)$$

In an experiment, all modes will be excited, but only that mode which has the largest growth rate will generally be observed. Thus, at large times one would expect to see a wave of length λ_{max} emerge that will continue to grow in amplitude in time, at least until nonlinear effects become important.

Extensions of the above analysis include Esch (1957), who included viscosity by solving the Orr-Sommerfeld equation using the piecewise linear profile given here. Esch showed that the inclusion of viscosity had a damping effect on the growth rate.

2.3.2 Confined shear layer

A similar analysis can be made for the confined shear layer where it is assumed that there is a wall at $y = \pm h$. The nondimensional mean velocity is

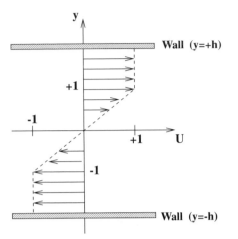

Fig. 2.5. Sketch of the confined shear layer.

defined by

$$U(y) = \begin{cases} 1 & 1 < y < h, \\ y & -1 < y < 1, \\ -1 & -h < y < -1. \end{cases} \qquad (2.85)$$

The length scale L is again taken to be half the shear layer thickness. With this scaling we have $y = y^\dagger/L$, $h = H/L$, where H is the location of the wall in dimensional units. The velocity scale is as before. A sketch of the configuration is shown in Fig. 2.5.

The solution to the reduced Rayleigh equation that satisfies the zero boundary conditions at the walls is given by

$$\mathbf{v}(y) = \begin{cases} A \sinh[\alpha(h - y)] & 1 < y < h, \\ B \sinh(\alpha y) + C \cosh(\alpha y) & -1 < y < 1, \\ D \sinh[\alpha(y + h)] & -h < y < -1. \end{cases} \qquad (2.86)$$

The two interface conditions, applied at $y = \pm 1$ leads to the following four equations:

$$(\alpha - \omega)[\alpha B \cosh\alpha + \alpha C \sinh\alpha] - \alpha[B \sinh\alpha + C \cosh\alpha] \\ = \alpha(\alpha - \omega)A \cosh[\alpha(h - 1)], \qquad (2.87)$$

$$-(\alpha + \omega)[\alpha B \cosh\alpha - \alpha C \sinh\alpha] + \alpha[B \sinh\alpha - C \cosh\alpha] \\ = -\alpha(\alpha + \omega)D \cosh[\alpha(h - 1)], \qquad (2.88)$$

$$A \sinh[\alpha(h - 1)] = B \sinh\alpha + C \cosh\alpha, \qquad (2.89)$$

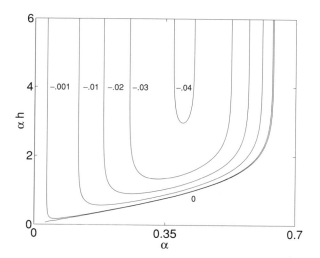

Fig. 2.6. Contours of $G(\alpha, \alpha h)$ showing the unstable region for the confined shear layer.

and

$$-B \sinh \alpha + C \cosh \alpha = D \sinh[\alpha(h-1)]. \qquad (2.90)$$

Again, we have four equations for four unknowns, and a nontrivial solution exists only if the determinant vanishes. After expanding the determinant, and equating it to zero the dispersion relation is

$$\omega^2 = \alpha^2 - \frac{\alpha(1+X^2)Y^2 + 2\alpha XY - XY^2}{(1+X^2)Y + X(1+Y^2)} \equiv G(\alpha, \alpha h), \qquad (2.91)$$

where

$$X = \tanh \alpha, \quad Y = \tanh[\alpha(h-1)].$$

We note that the flow is stable if G is positive, corresponding to ω real, and is unstable if G is negative, corresponding to ω imaginary. A graph of the contours of G is plotted in Fig. 2.6 in the $(\alpha, \alpha h)$ plane. Note that as $\alpha h \to \infty$, the zero contour, which corresponds to a neutral mode, shows that $\alpha \to 0.639232$, which is the neutral mode for the shear layer in the unbounded domain.

Similar analysis can be applied to other algebraic profiles, and some of these can be found in the exercise section at the end of this chapter.

2.4 Inviscid temporal theory

In terms of the stream function, recall that Rayleigh's equation for an inviscid fluid is given by

$$(U - c)(\phi'' - \alpha^2\phi) - U''\phi = 0, \tag{2.92}$$

where $c = c_r + ic_i$ is the complex phase speed and α is the real wavenumber. This equation is to be solved subject to the homogeneous boundary conditions

$$\phi = 0 \quad \text{at} \quad y = a, b, \tag{2.93}$$

appropriate for bounded flows. Presented in this section are several important results concerning Rayleigh's equation. It is important to remember that throughout this section we are concerned only with temporal stability; spatial stability is presented in Chapter 4. As a consequence, α is taken as real. Rayleigh used these facts to determine some very important results regarding such flows. Even more, he was able to establish theorems relating to the stability of the flows. Some of these theorems are given below, along with important contributions from other authors. In what follows we use the notation □ to denote the end of a proof. To avoid the use of mathematics beyond the scope of this text, only proofs that are construction in nature will be presented here. We also switch notation to denote a complex quantity: the superscript $*$ has been replaced by an overbar.

RESULT 2.1: Rayleigh's Inflection Point Theorem (1880). A necessary condition for instability is that the mean velocity profile $U(y)$ has an inflection point somewhere in the domain of the flow.

Proof: Assume $c_i > 0$. Then, multiply (2.92) by the complex conjugate $\bar{\phi}$ and integrate over the domain defined as $a \le y \le b$ to give:

$$\int_a^b \left[\bar{\phi}\phi'' - \alpha^2\phi\bar{\phi} - \frac{U''}{U - c}\phi\bar{\phi} \right] dy = 0. \tag{2.94}$$

The first term can be integrated by parts, giving

$$\int_a^b \bar{\phi}\phi'' dy = \bar{\phi}\phi'|_a^b - \int_a^b \bar{\phi}'\phi' dy. \tag{2.95}$$

After applying the boundary conditions and using (2.95), equation (2.94) becomes

$$\int_a^b [|\phi'|^2 + \alpha^2|\phi|^2] dy + \int_a^b \frac{U''(U - \bar{c})}{|U - c|^2}|\phi|^2 dy = 0. \tag{2.96}$$

By separating the real and imaginary parts of (2.96) we get two equations, namely:

$$\int_a^b [|\phi'|^2 + \alpha^2|\phi|^2]dy + \int_a^b \frac{U''(U - c_r)}{|U - c|^2}|\phi|^2dy = 0 \qquad (2.97)$$

and

$$c_i \int_a^b \frac{U''}{|U - c|^2}|\phi|^2dy = 0. \qquad (2.98)$$

From this last expression we can infer that either c_i is zero or the integral must vanish. If c_i is zero, we might expect some exceptional neutral solution, but the very existence of the integral often becomes questionable. When c_i is not zero, we see that the only way for the integral to vanish is for U'' to change signs somewhere in the interval (a,b). This implies that the velocity profile U must have a point of inflection; i.e., $U''(y_s) = 0$ for $a < y_s < b$. $\square$

We remind the reader that Rayleigh's Theorem states that if an inviscid flow is unstable, then the mean velocity profile U must have a point of inflection somewhere in the bounded domain. The converse is not necessarily true: "If the mean velocity profile has a point of inflection, then the flow is unstable." The negation of the theorem is, however, true: "If the mean velocity does not have an inflection point, then the flow is stable." The reader is cautioned against misapplying Rayleigh's Theorem.

A stronger version of Rayleigh's Theorem on the consequence of the inflection point in the mean velocity profile was noted by Fjørtoft (1950) (see also Høiland, 1953). This result is stated below.

RESULT 2.2: Fjørtoft's Theorem (1950). A necessary condition for instability is that $U''(U - U_s) < 0$ somewhere in the flow field, where y_s is the point at which the mean profile has an inflection point, $U''(y_s) = 0$, and $U_s = U(y_s)$.

Proof: Assume $c_i > 0$. Multiply the second condition (2.98) of Rayleigh's Theorem by $(c_r - U_s)/c_i$, where y_s is the point at which $U'' = 0$, and $U_s = U(y_s)$. Substitution into the first condition (2.97) results in the expression

$$\int_a^b [|\phi'|^2 + \alpha^2|\phi|^2]dy + \int_a^b \frac{U''(U - U_s)}{|U - c|^2}|\phi|^2dy = 0. \qquad (2.99)$$

Since the first integral is strictly positive, we must have $U''(U - U_s) < 0$ over some part of the flow field. $\square$

As in Rayleigh's Theorem, the converse is not necessarily true: "If $U''(U-U_s) < 0$ somewhere in the flow, then the flow is unstable." The negation of the theorem is, however, true: "If $U''(U - U_s)$ is not negative somewhere in the flow, then the flow is stable." The reader is cautioned against misapplying Fjørtoft's Theorem.

We note here again that, in terms of the mean vorticity for parallel flows,

$$\Omega_z = V_x - U_y = -U'(y), \qquad (2.100)$$

Rayleigh's Theorem shows that the mean vorticity must have a local maximum or minimum, while Fjørtoft's Theorem states a stronger condition in that the base vorticity must have a local maximum.

Some examples include plane Couette flow, where the mean velocity profile is given by

$$U = U_o \left(\frac{y}{L}\right), \quad -L < y < L. \qquad (2.101)$$

We see that $U'' = 0$ and hence $U''(U - U_s) = 0$, and the flow is inviscidly stable by applying the negation argument of Fjørtoft's Theorem. For plane Poiseuille flow

$$U = U_o(1 - (y/L)^2), \quad -L < y < L, \qquad (2.102)$$

we see that $U'' = -2U_o/L^2 < 0$, and the flow is inviscidly stable by the negation argument of Rayleigh's Theorem. Free shear flows, such as the jet, wake and mixing layer, all have points of inflection and thus these flows *may be* unstable to inviscid disturbances. The Blasius boundary layer flow, which does not have an inflection point on the semi-infinite domain $0 < y < \infty$, is also inviscidly stable. On the other hand, the compressible boundary layer will develop an inflection point at high Mach number due to viscous heating, and thus the flow may be susceptible to inviscid disturbances. We shall examine these examples in greater detail later.

RESULT 2.3: The phase velocity c_r of an amplified disturbance must lie between the minimum and the maximum values of the mean velocity profile $U(y)$.

Proof: Assume $c_i > 0$. We begin by defining the following function

$$f(y) = \frac{\phi(y)}{U - c}. \qquad (2.103)$$

Substitution of (2.103) into Rayleigh's equation, (2.92), gives

$$[(U - c)f']' - \alpha^2(U - c)^2 f = 0 \tag{2.104}$$

with $f = 0$ at $y = a, b$. We note that this equation is in standard Sturm-Liouville form. Multiplying by the complex conjugate $\bar{f}$ and integrating over the domain (a, b), we get

$$\int_a^b \{[(U - c)f']'\bar{f} - \alpha^2(U - c)^2 f\bar{f}\}\, dy = 0. \tag{2.105}$$

The first term can be integrated by parts, or

$$\int_a^b [(U - c)f']'\bar{f}\, dy = (U - c)\bar{f}f'|_a^b - \int_a^b (U - c)^2 f'\bar{f}', \tag{2.106}$$

and the boundary term is zero by the boundary conditions. For simplicity, let

$$Q^2 = |f'|^2 + \alpha^2|f|^2, \tag{2.107}$$

and equation (2.105) becomes

$$\int_a^b (U - c)^2 Q^2\, dy = 0. \tag{2.108}$$

Again, separating (2.108) into the real and imaginary parts, we get

$$\int_a^b [(U - c_r)^2 - c_i^2] Q^2\, dy = 0 \tag{2.109}$$

and

$$\int_a^b c_i(U - c_r) Q^2\, dy = 0. \tag{2.110}$$

Since $c_i > 0$, we see that the only way the last integral (2.110) can vanish is that $U - c_r$ change sign somewhere in the interval (a, b). Hence $U_{min} < c_r < U_{max}$. $\square$

Rayleigh (and later Tollmien, 1935) only stated the above result for neutral disturbances $c_i = 0$. Lin (1955) gave the extension of the theorem for excited flows (which is stated in Result 2.3), and the above proof follows his demonstration.

RESULT 2.4: Howard's Semicircle Theorem I (1961). If $c_i > 0$, then

$$U_{min} < \sqrt{c_r^2 + c_i^2} < U_{max}.$$

Proof: Assume $c_i > 0$. We begin by rewriting the expression (2.110) of Result 2.3 to get

$$\int_a^b U Q^2 \mathrm{d}y = c_r \int_a^b Q^2 \mathrm{d}y. \tag{2.111}$$

After substituting (2.111) into expression (2.109) we find that

$$\int_a^b [U^2 - (c_r^2 + c_i^2)] Q^2 \mathrm{d}y = 0. \tag{2.112}$$

For this last expression to be true, the term in the square bracket must change sign somewhere in the domain (a, b), that is,

$$U_{min}^2 < c_r^2 + c_i^2 < U_{max}^2 \tag{2.113}$$

or, assuming U to be positive in the domain (a, b),

$$U_{min} < \sqrt{c_r^2 + c_i^2} < U_{max}. \tag{2.114}$$

This is an equation of an annulus in the (c_r, c_i) plane, with c_i positive. $\square$

RESULT 2.5: Howard's Semicircle Theorem II (1961). If $c_i > 0$, then

$$\left(c_r - \frac{U_{min} + U_{max}}{2}\right)^2 + c_i^2 \leq \left(\frac{U_{max} - U_{min}}{2}\right)^2.$$

Proof: We begin by noting that $U_{min} \leq U \leq U_{max}$ so that the following inequality is true

$$(U - U_{min})(U - U_{max}) \leq 0, \tag{2.115}$$

where the first term is strictly non-negative and the second term is strictly non-positive, the product being negative or zero. Multiplying by Q^2 and integrating we get

$$\int_a^b (U - U_{min})(U - U_{max}) Q^2 \mathrm{d}y \leq 0 \tag{2.116}$$

or,

$$\int_a^b [U^2 - (U_{min} + U_{max})U + U_{min}U_{max}] Q^2 \mathrm{d}y \leq 0. \tag{2.117}$$

Now assume $c_i > 0$, and recall

$$\int_a^b U^2 Q^2 \mathrm{d}y = \int_a^b (c_r^2 + c_i^2) Q^2 \mathrm{d}y,$$

and

$$\int_a^b U Q^2 dy = \int_a^b c_r Q^2 dy. \qquad (2.118)$$

The substitution of the last two equalities into the inequality (2.117) gives

$$\int_a^b \left[c_r^2 + c_i^2 - (U_{min} + U_{max})c_r + U_{min}U_{max} \right] Q^2 dy \leq 0. \quad (2.119)$$

Since Q^2 is positive, the integrand must be negative or

$$c_r^2 + c_i^2 - (U_{min} + U_{max})c_r + U_{min}U_{max} \leq 0. \qquad (2.120)$$

After rearranging terms, (2.120) can be written as

$$\left(c_r - \frac{U_{min} + U_{max}}{2} \right)^2 + c_i^2 \leq \left(\frac{U_{max} - U_{min}}{2} \right)^2. \qquad (2.121)$$

This is the equation of a semicircle with radius $(U_{max} - U_{min})/2$ and coordinates $(c_r - (U_{min} + U_{max})/2, c_i)$. $\square$

The last four results can be summarized by referring to the following table. Let $A = U_{min}$ and $B = U_{max}$, then the above results can be restated as follows:

Unstable eigenvalue $c_i > 0$

Result 2.3 $A < c_r < B$

Result 2.4 $A < |c| < B$

Result 2.5 $\left(c_r - \frac{A + B}{2} \right)^2 + c_i^2 \leq \left(\frac{B - A}{2} \right)^2.$

Each of these results is graphed separately in Fig. 2.7. The left-slanted hatched region gives the exact region where all the discrete temporal eigenvalues of

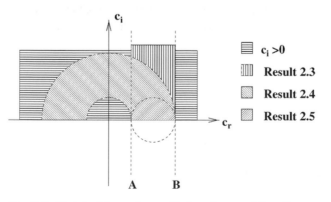

Fig. 2.7. Sketch of the regions with $A = U_{min}$ and $B = U_{max}$.

the inviscid, incompressible problem can be found. These are indeed remarkable results, and should be kept in mind when numerically searching for the
unstable eigenvalues for any inviscid problem. The reader is reminded, however, that these results only apply to the temporal eigenvalues, and cannot be
extended to the spatial problem.

As mentioned above, neither Rayleigh's nor Fjørtoft's Theorem give a sufficient condition for the instability of a general inviscid flow. A simple counter-
example was given by Tollmien for the mean velocity profile $U = \sin(y)$.
However, Tollmien did prove sufficiency for a symmetrical channel profile and
for monotone profiles and is given below.

RESULT 2.6: Tollmien (1935). If the mean velocity profile $U(y)$ is either
symmetric or monotone in y, then (1) there is always a neutral disturbance
given by $c_N = 0$, $\alpha_N = 0$, $\phi_N = U(y)$, (2) if $U''(y_s) = 0$ for $a < y_s < b$,
then there exists a neutral disturbance with $\alpha = \alpha_N > 0$ and $c_N = U_s =
U(y_s)$, and (3) for α slightly less than α_N there exists solutions with $c_i > 0$,
and for α slightly greater than α_N there are no solutions with $c_i > 0$.

Tollmien's result is remarkable because it gives us the exact value of the
neutral phase speed. The corresponding neutral wave number α_N must, in general, be determined numerically; there are very few examples of where α_N can
be determined by solving Rayleigh's equation analytically.

Tollmien proved the first two parts but was only able to heuristically prove
the third part by adding the further restriction $U'''(y_s) \neq 0$, and then constructing a series solution about the neutral point to show amplification for $\alpha < \alpha_N$.
An alternative to Tollmien's proof to the second part was given by Friedrichs
(von Mises and Friedrichs, 1971), while the third part was formally proved
by Lin (1945, Part II). Lin's proof, which removed the restriction on the third
derivative of U, is rather detailed, and the interested reader can consult the
original paper for details. Below we outline the proof of the second part of
Tollmien's theorem as given by Friedrichs. The proof of part one is trivial.

Proof: We begin the proof of (2) by considering the variational form of
Rayleigh's equation. This is

$$f'' + K(y)f + \lambda f = 0, \quad f(a) = f(b) = 0, \tag{2.122}$$

where f is any trial function that satisfies the homogeneous boundary conditions at $y = a$ and at $y = b$; $K(y) = -U''/(U - U_s)$, and $\lambda = -\alpha^2$. We
assume that the function $K(y)$ exists and is integrable over the domain (a, b).
Since K has no singularities this equation is in standard Sturm-Liouville form.

Thus, there is an infinite sequence of eigenvalues with limit point at $+\infty$, and any eigenvalue can be related to its eigenfunction by Rayleigh's quotient (e.g., Haberman, 1987)

$$\lambda = \frac{\int_a^b ((f')^2 - Kf^2)dy}{\int_a^b f^2 dy}. \tag{2.123}$$

This result can easily be obtained by first multiplying the above variational form of Rayleigh's equation by f, integrating the resulting equation over (a, b), integrating by parts the term involving the second derivative and applying the boundary conditions, and finally solving for the eigenvalue λ. The associated variational principle gives the least eigenvalue $\lambda_1 = \min \lambda$, where the minimum is taken over the entire set of trial functions. Now a neutral mode exists if and only if $\lambda_1 < 0$. We assume that $K(y)$ is non-negative and the mean velocity U vanishes at the boundaries but not between. This is equivalent to saying that the mean velocity profile is symmetric or is monotone in y. If we take for the trial function $f = U$, which lies in the space of admissible functions, then

$$\lambda_1 = \frac{\int_a^b ((U')^2 - KU^2)dy}{\int_a^b U^2 dy}$$

$$= -\frac{\int_a^b (UU'' + KU^2)dy}{\int_a^b U^2 dy}$$

$$= -\frac{\int_a^b (-UK(U - c) + KU^2)dy}{\int_a^b U^2 dy}$$

$$= -\frac{c \int_a^b KU dy}{\int_a^b U^2 dy}.$$

Since $K(y) > 0$, $U(y) > 0$, and $c = U(y_s) > 0$, it follows that $\lambda_1 < 0$, and so the existence of a neutral mode has been proven. $\square$

RESULT 2.7: Upper Bound On The Growth Rate. If there exists a solution with $c_i > 0$, then an upper bound exists and is given by

$$\alpha c_i \leq \frac{1}{2} \max |U'(y)|$$

where the maximum is taken over the open interval (a, b).

This result is due to Høiland (1953). The reader is asked to prove this last result in the exercise section at the end of this chapter. The outline of the proof will follow that given by Howard (1961).

2.5 Critical layer concept

If $U - c$ vanishes somewhere in the flow domain, Rayleigh's equation (2.29), or equivalently (2.32), becomes singular in that the term multiplying the highest derivative vanishes, unless $U''(y_c) = 0$. This occurs at a point y_c, say, when the phase speed c is real. Thus, y_c is a singular point and defines the location known as the critical layer. Note that when the phase speed is complex the expression $U - c$ is no longer zero, and Rayleigh's equation is no longer singular. To examine the solutions in a neighborhood about the critical layer, we first rewrite Rayleigh's equation as

$$\phi'' + p(y)\phi' + q(y)\phi = 0, \tag{2.124}$$

where

$$p(y) = 0, \quad q(y) = -\alpha^2 + \frac{U''}{U - c}. \tag{2.125}$$

Assume an extended series solution of the form

$$\phi = \sum_{0}^{\infty} a_n (y - y_c)^{n+r}. \tag{2.126}$$

Here, r satisfies the indicial equation

$$r(r - 1) + rp_0 + q_0 = 0, \tag{2.127}$$

where

$$p_0 = \lim_{y \to y_c} (y - y_c)p(y), \quad q_0 = \lim_{y \to y_c} (y - y_c)^2 q(y). \tag{2.128}$$

Note that $p_0 = 0$ by definition, and that $q_0 = 0$ only if $U'(y_c) \neq 0$. To see this, expand U in a Taylor series about y_c and note that the second term of q gives

$$\lim_{y \to y_c} \frac{(y - y_c)^2 U''}{(U - c)} = \lim_{y \to y_c} \frac{(y - y_c)U''(y_c)}{U'(y_c)} \to 0.$$

Since both p_0 and q_0 vanish in the limit as $y \to y_c$, the roots to the indicial equation are $r = 0$ and $r = 1$. We therefore say that y_c is a regular singular point with exponents of 0 and 1 (see, for example, Boyce & DiPrima, 1986). Consequently, there exists two linearly independent solutions, valid in some neighborhood about y_c, given by

$$\phi_1 = (y - y_c)P_1(y), \tag{2.129}$$

$$\phi_2 = P_2(y) + \left(\frac{U_c''}{U_c'}\right)\phi_1 \ln(y - y_c), \tag{2.130}$$

where

$$P_1(y) = 1 + \sum_1^\infty a_n(y - y_c)^n, \quad P_2(y) = 1 + \sum_1^\infty b_n(y - y_c)^n. \quad (2.131)$$

Here, ϕ_1 is the regular part of the inviscid solution, ϕ_2 is the singular part of the inviscid solution, and P_2 is the regular part of the singular inviscid solution. Substitution of these results into Rayleigh's equation shows that the first few terms of P_1 and P_2 are

$$P_1 = 1 + \frac{U_c''}{2U_c'}(y - y_c) + \frac{1}{6}\left(\frac{U_c'''}{U_c'} + \alpha^2\right)(y - y_c)^2 + \cdots \quad (2.132)$$

and

$$P_2 = 1 + \left(\frac{U_c'''}{2U_c'} - \frac{(U_c'')^2}{(U_c')^2} + \frac{\alpha^2}{2}\right)(y - y_c)^2 + \cdots. \quad (2.133)$$

We note that the singular part of the inviscid solution, ϕ_2, has a branch point singularity at $y = y_c$, and hence is multi-valued. The correct branch must be chosen, and is given by

$$\text{for } y > y_c, \quad \ln(y - y_c) = \ln|y - y_c|,$$
$$\text{for } y < y_c, \quad \ln(y - y_c) = \ln|y - y_c| - \pi i.$$

Also, the path of integration in the y-plane must pass *below* the singular point y_c.

Now suppose the mean velocity profile U has an inflection point at the critical layer y_c, that is $U_c'' = U''(y_c) = 0$. In this case, both ϕ_1 and ϕ_2 are regular and we can write the general solution as

$$\phi = A\phi_1(y) + P_2(y), \quad (2.134)$$

where we have normalized ϕ so that $\phi(y_c) = 1$. The two boundary conditions determine A and α. Since we have just assumed $U''(y_c) = 0$, according to Tollmien's result (1935) this corresponds to a neutral mode where

$$c_N = U(y_c), \quad \alpha_N, \quad \omega_N = \alpha_N c_N, \quad (2.135)$$

with eigenfunction $\phi_N = A\phi_1 + P_2$. Recall from Tollmien's result that, if the mean velocity profile is symmetric or is monotone in y of the boundary layer type, and if $U''(y_s) = 0$, then a neutral mode exists with $\alpha_N > 0$ and $c_N = U(y_s)$. Thus, the location of the inflection point and the location of the critical layer coincide, i.e., $y_s = y_c$.

2.5.1 Reynolds shear stress

The Reynolds shear stress defined in terms of an average over a wavelength, is

$$\tau = -\overline{\tilde{u}\tilde{v}} = -\frac{\alpha}{2\pi} \int_0^{2\pi/\alpha} \tilde{u}\tilde{v}\mathrm{d}x, \tag{2.136}$$

where $\tilde{u}$ and $\tilde{v}$ are the perturbed quantities. Now recall that, for the perturbation quantities,

$$\tilde{u} = \phi'(y)e^{i\alpha(x-ct)} + cc, \quad \tilde{v} = -i\alpha\phi e^{i\alpha(x-ct)} + cc, \tag{2.137}$$

or, equivalently,

$$\tilde{u} = [\phi'_r \cos(\alpha(x - c_r t)) - \phi'_i \sin(\alpha(x - c_r t))]e^{\alpha c_i t},$$
$$\tilde{v} = \alpha [\phi_r \sin(\alpha(x - c_r t)) + \phi_i \cos(\alpha(x - c_r t))] e^{\alpha c_i t}, \tag{2.138}$$

when using the streamfunction. Substitution of (2.138) into the integral (2.136) for the shear stress we have

$$\tau = -\frac{\alpha}{2}[\phi'_r\phi_i - \phi_r\phi'_i]e^{2\alpha c_i t} = \frac{i\alpha}{4}[\phi\bar{\phi}' - \bar{\phi}\phi']e^{2\alpha c_i t}, \tag{2.139}$$

where use of the trigonometric identities,

$$\int_0^{2\pi/\alpha} \cos(\alpha(x - c_r t)) \sin(\alpha(x - c_r t))\mathrm{d}x = 0,$$

$$\int_0^{2\pi/\alpha} \cos^2(\alpha(x - c_r t))\mathrm{d}x = \frac{\pi}{\alpha},$$

$$\int_0^{2\pi/\alpha} \sin^2(\alpha(x - c_r t))\mathrm{d}x = \frac{\pi}{\alpha}, \tag{2.140}$$

has been made. Let us now differentiate with respect to y the above expression and eliminate ϕ'' with the help of Rayleigh's equation or its conjugate. This leads to

$$\frac{\mathrm{d}\tau}{\mathrm{d}y} = \frac{\alpha c_i}{2} \frac{U''}{|U - c|^2} |\phi|^2 e^{2\alpha c_i t}. \tag{2.141}$$

If we now let $c_i \to 0$, $\mathrm{d}\tau/\mathrm{d}y$ vanishes except near the critical layer, where it diverges.

Several remarks are in order. First, for $c_i > 0$, integration of (2.141) gives

$$\tau|_a^b = \frac{\alpha c_i}{2} \int_a^b \frac{U''}{|U - c|^2} |\phi|^2 e^{2\alpha c_i t}\mathrm{d}y. \tag{2.142}$$

Since $\tilde{v}$ vanishes at the boundaries, and therefore so does τ, we see that the integral vanishes only if U'' changes sign somewhere in the interval (a, b); this is in fact Rayleigh's Inflection Point Theorem. The second remark concerns

the behavior of τ as $c_i \to 0$; that is, as we approach a neutral mode from the unstable side. With a small c_i we can consider that ϕ, U' and U'' are nearly constant through the critical layer, and an integration gives

$$[\tau] = \frac{\alpha \pi}{2} \frac{U_c''}{U_c'} |\phi_c|^2, \tag{2.143}$$

where $[\tau]$ denotes the jump $\tau(y_c^+) - \tau(y_c^-)$. The easiest way to derive this expression is to start with the definition of τ directly, and take the limit as $y \to y_c$ from above and from below. First recall that the eigenfunction ϕ can be written as a linear combination of ϕ_1 and ϕ_2 as

$$\phi = \phi_1 + \phi_c \phi_2, \tag{2.144}$$

where ϕ_c is the value of the eigenfunction at the critical layer and is, in general, complex. Now, as $y \to y_c$, we have

$$\phi_1 \to 0,$$
$$\phi_1' \to 1,$$
$$\phi_2 \to 1,$$
$$\phi_2'|_+ \to \frac{U_c''}{U_c'} \left(1 + \ln(y - y_c)\right),$$
$$\phi_2'|_- \to \frac{U_c''}{U_c'} \left(1 + \ln|y - y_c| - \pi i\right), \tag{2.145}$$

and thus the expression in the shear stress becomes

$$\phi_r' \phi_i - \phi_r \phi_i' = -|\phi_c|^2 \frac{U_c''}{U_c'} \pi, \tag{2.146}$$

and the result for the jump in the shear stress across the critical layer follows immediately. As discussed in Chapter 1, it is this critical phasing that leads to instability.

2.6 Continuous profiles

Continuous profiles are classified as those mean profiles which are infinitely differentiable. Examples include the class of free shear flows and boundary layer type flows. Free shear flows consists of jets, wakes and mixing layers in bounded or unbounded domains. This class of flows has inflection points and hence are susceptible to inviscid disturbances. We have already studied two different approximations to the mixing layer, the example of Kelvin-Helmholtz in Section 2.2 and the piecewise linear profiles of Section 2.3. In this section we will study two additional approximations, the hyperbolic tangent profile

and the laminar mixing layer profile. Each succeeding approximation, from the Kelvin-Helmholtz to the laminar profile, is more complex than the preceding one and is a more realistic representation to the actual flow of a mixing layer. Other continuous profiles will be considered in the exercise section at the end of this chapter.

2.6.1 Hyperbolic tangent profile

Consider the mixing layer given by

$$U(y) = \frac{1}{2}[1 + \tanh y], \quad -\infty < y < +\infty, \qquad (2.147)$$

where the length scale L is taken to be the half-width of the mixing layer and the velocity scale is taken to be the value of the freestream velocity at infinity. The temporal stability analysis of this profile was first investigated by Betchov & Szewczyk (1963) and Michalke (1964); much of this section draws from the latter reference.

The inflection point is found by setting $U'' = 0$, resulting in $y_s = 0$. This is also the location of the critical layer. The neutral phase speed is thus given by $c_N = U(y_s) = 0.5$. Note that $U''(U - c_N) = -0.5 \, \text{sech}^2 y \tanh^2 y < 0$, and so the profile satisfies Fjørtoft's Theorem, and thus the flow *may be* unstable. To find the neutral wavenumber α_N, we substitute $c_N = 0.5$ into Rayleigh's equation to give

$$\mathbf{v}'' - \left(\alpha_N^2 - 2 \, \text{sech}^2 y\right)\mathbf{v} = 0, \qquad (2.148)$$

which has the solutions

$$\mathbf{v}_1 = \alpha_N \cosh(\alpha_N y) - \sinh(\alpha_N y) \tanh y \qquad (2.149)$$

and

$$\mathbf{v}_2 = \alpha_N \sinh(\alpha_N y) - \cosh(\alpha_N y) \tanh y. \qquad (2.150)$$

The $\mathbf{v}_1$ solution is called the symmetric solution since it is an even function in y, while the $\mathbf{v}_2$ solution is antisymmetric. The general solution is a linear combination of the symmetric and the antisymmetric solutions, and the only combination which satisfies the boundary conditions $\mathbf{v} = 0$ as $y \to \pm\infty$ is

$$\alpha_N = 1, \quad \mathbf{v}_N = \text{sech} \, y. \qquad (2.151)$$

The corresponding neutral frequency is $\omega_N = \alpha_N c_N = 0.5$. For values in the unstable region away from the neutral mode, Rayleigh's equation must be

Table 2.1. *Phase speeds and frequencies as a function of the wavenumber α for the hyperbolic tangent profile.*

α	c_r	c_i	$\omega_r = \alpha c_r$	$\omega_i = \alpha c_i$
1.0	0.5	0.0	0.5	0.0
0.9		0.032693	0.45	0.029424
0.8		0.067334	0.40	0.053867
0.7		0.104321	0.35	0.073025
0.6		0.144162	0.30	0.086497
0.5		0.187511	0.25	0.093755
0.4		0.235225	0.20	0.094090
0.3		0.288447	0.15	0.086534
0.2		0.348728	0.10	0.069746
0.1		0.418227	0.05	0.041823
0.0		0.5	0.0	0.0

solved numerically. Table 2.1 shows the results of the numerical solution, and Fig. 2.8 plots the growth rate as a function of wavenumber.

It is of interest to also examine the vorticity distribution since it gives us a means to visualize the dynamics of the mixing layer. Define the spanwise vorticity in the usual fashion as

$$\omega_z = v_x - u_y. \tag{2.152}$$

In terms of the normal mode approach, we have

$$\begin{aligned}\omega_z &= -(U'(y) + \epsilon \tilde{u}_y(x, y, t)) + \epsilon \tilde{v}_x(x, y, t)\\ &= -U' + \epsilon(-\psi_{yy} - \psi_{xx})\\ &= -U' + \epsilon(-\phi'' + \alpha^2 \phi)e^{i\alpha(x-ct)},\end{aligned} \tag{2.153}$$

where ϵ is the initial amplitude of the disturbance. If we define

$$\tilde{\omega}_{z_r}(y) = \mathrm{Re}(-\phi'' + \alpha^2 \phi), \quad \tilde{\omega}_{z_i}(y) = \mathrm{Im}(-\phi'' + \alpha^2 \phi), \tag{2.154}$$

then the vorticity becomes

$$\omega_z = -\frac{1}{2}\mathrm{sech}^2 y + \epsilon e^{\omega_i t}[\tilde{\omega}_{z_r}\cos(\alpha(x - c_r t)) - \tilde{\omega}_{z_i}\sin(\alpha(x - c_r t))]. \tag{2.155}$$

A contour plot of the vorticity distribution is shown in Fig. 2.9 for two values of the wavenumber and for $\epsilon = 0.2$. The value of ϵ is chosen arbitrarily large to aid in visualizing the dynamics. One value of the wavenumber corresponds to the maximum growth rate ($\alpha_{max} = 0.4446$), and the other value

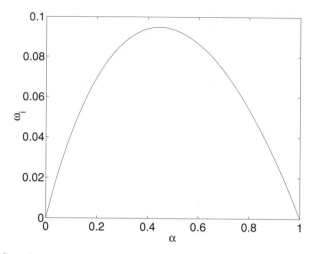

Fig. 2.8. Growth rate $\omega_i = \alpha c_i$ as a function of α for the hyperbolic tangent profile.

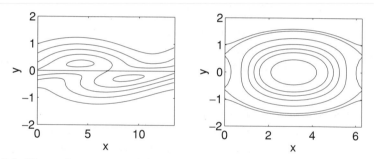

Fig. 2.9. Lines of constant vorticity for the wavenumbers of maximum amplification $\alpha_{max} = 0.4446$ (left) and of the neutral disturbance $\alpha_N = 1$ (right) at time $t = 0$ with a disturbance amplitude of $\epsilon = 0.2$. The contour levels for the left figure are $-0.6, -0.5, -0.4, -0.3, -0.2$, with the closed contours being -0.6 and increasing outward. The contour levels for the right figure are $-0.1, -0.1157, -0.2, -0.3$, $-0.4, -0.5, -0.7$, with the innermost closed contour being -0.7 and increasing outward. The mean flow is given by the hyperbolic tangent profile. (After Michalke, 1964).

corresponds to the neutral mode ($\alpha_N = 1$). Since the flow is periodic in the x-direction, the wavelengths of the disturbances are $\lambda = 2\pi/\alpha_{max} = 14.1322$ and $\lambda = 2\pi/\alpha_N = 2\pi$, respectively. Note that for the case corresponding to the maximum growth rate, there are two vortices within a single period. The vorticity distribution shows the initial stages of the roll-up of these two neighboring vortices, characteristic of Kelvin-Helmholtz instabilities. In contrast, in the case of the neutral mode there is only a single vortex which does not roll-up.

2.6.2 Laminar mixing layer

The hyperbolic tangent profile of the previous section is only an approximation to a real mixing layer since it does not satisfy the equations of motion. A more realistic approximation to the mixing layer, which does satisfy the equations of motion under certain assumptions, is what we call the laminar mixing layer profile. The derivation is based on the boundary layer approximation, and was first constructed by Lessen (1950), and extended to include different densities and viscosities by Lock (1951).

We begin by considering the non-dimensional equations of motion given by (2.6) to (2.8), and set the time derivatives to zero as is appropriate for steady flows. The boundary layer approximation assumes that variations in the normal direction y are small compared to variations in the streamwise direction (see White, 1974, for example). We therefore set

$$y = \frac{\overline{y}}{\sqrt{Re}}, \quad v = \frac{\overline{v}}{\sqrt{Re}}. \tag{2.156}$$

The leading order equations for $Re \gg 1$ are

$$u_x + \overline{v}_{\overline{y}} = 0, \tag{2.157}$$

$$uu_x + \overline{v}u_{\overline{y}} + p_x = u_{\overline{y}\overline{y}}, \tag{2.158}$$

$$p_{\overline{y}} = 0. \tag{2.159}$$

From the last equation we see that the leading order pressure term can at most be a function of x and is determined by examining the outer inviscid flow. Outside a boundary layer all variations in y are zero, and the momentum equation (2.158) reduces to

$$\frac{dp}{dx} = -u\frac{du}{dx}. \tag{2.160}$$

Thus we see that one can either specify a pressure distribution $p(x)$ or specify a streamwise velocity distribution $u(x)$. In this sense the pressure is considered a known function of x and is imposed on the boundary layer as a source term. Here we assume that the streamwise velocity in the freestream is constant ($u = 1$) and take $p = 1$.

The equations (2.157) to (2.159) are usually referred to as the boundary layer equations, and are parabolic in nature. One can numerically solve these equations directly by marching in the streamwise x-direction given some inlet profile[1] with appropriate boundary conditions in the y-direction. An alternative

---

[1] One can not start at $x = 0$ because in this region x and y are of the same order, and so the full viscous problem must be solved. An inlet profile is therefore assumed at some $x_o > 0$.

approach, and one that is commonly employed, is to assume that the solution can be written in terms of a similarity variable. Define

$$\eta = \frac{\bar{y}}{\sqrt{x}} \tag{2.161}$$

where η is the similarity variable[1]. The derivatives transform as

$$\frac{\partial}{\partial y} = \frac{d\eta}{dy}\frac{\partial}{\partial \eta} = \frac{1}{\sqrt{x}}\frac{\partial}{\partial \eta},$$

$$\frac{\partial}{\partial x} = \frac{\partial}{\partial x} + \frac{d\eta}{dx}\frac{\partial}{\partial \eta} = \frac{\partial}{\partial x} - \frac{\eta}{2x}\frac{\partial}{\partial \eta}. \tag{2.162}$$

The boundary layer equations in the similarity coordinate system are given by

$$u_x - \frac{\eta}{2x}u_\eta + \frac{1}{\sqrt{x}}\bar{v}_\eta = 0, \tag{2.163}$$

and

$$u\left(u_x - \frac{\eta}{2x}u_\eta\right) + \frac{\bar{v}}{\sqrt{x}}u_\eta = \frac{1}{x}u_{\eta\eta}. \tag{2.164}$$

We now assume that the streamwise velocity is only a function of the similarity variable, and set

$$u = f'(\eta), \tag{2.165}$$

where the prime denotes differentiation with respect to η. Substitution into the continuity equation (2.163) gives

$$\bar{v}_\eta = \frac{\eta}{2\sqrt{x}}f'', \tag{2.166}$$

and, upon integration, reduces to

$$\bar{v} = \frac{1}{2\sqrt{x}}(\eta f' - f). \tag{2.167}$$

In the integration process we assumed quite arbitrarily that the dividing stream-line is centered at zero, and thus $\bar{v}(0) = 0$ implying $f(0) = 0$. From the momentum equation (2.164) we now have

$$2f''' + ff'' = 0, \tag{2.168}$$

---

[1] An alternative definition is $\eta = \bar{y}/\sqrt{2x}$. Either definition is valid, but once a choice is made, care must be taken to be consistent throughout the entire subsequent analysis.

plus appropriate boundary conditions[2]. For the mixing layer the boundary conditions are

$$f'(-\infty) = 0, \quad f(0) = 0, \quad f'(+\infty) = 1. \tag{2.169}$$

Equation (2.168) with boundary conditions (2.169) were originally proposed by Lessen (1950) to describe the mixing layer when the Reynolds number is large. It remains a useful approximation today. Since the equation is third order and nonlinear, no analytical solutions have been found. Instead the solution is obtained numerically. There are several ways to do the integration and the one that we shall give here involves a Runge-Kutta method. We integrate, starting at $-\infty$, and integrate towards $+\infty$, using the asymptotic boundary condition (Lessen, 1950 ; Lock, 1951)

$$f = ag(\xi), \quad \xi = a\eta + b, \tag{2.170}$$

where

$$g(\xi) = -1 + e^{\xi/2} - \frac{1}{4}e^{\xi} + \frac{5}{72}e^{3\xi/2} - \frac{17}{864}e^{2\xi} + \cdots. \tag{2.171}$$

The value of a is determined by requiring $f'(+\infty) = 1$ and the value of b by requiring $f(0) = 0$. An iteration process is performed for each using a Secant method. Table 2.2 shows the numerical results at various values of η. The profile is shown in Fig. 2.10, and for comparison the hyperbolic tangent profile is also shown as a dashed line. From the table and figure we see that the tail of the laminar mixing layer profile is much longer than that of the hyperbolic tangent profile.

With the laminar mixing layer profile known at least numerically, the stability can be examined, and was first considered by Lessen (1950). We now note that the inflection point is located by setting $U'' = 0$, which is equivalent to setting $f''' = 0$. Since f''' is proportional to f, and $f(0) = 0$, we see that the inflection point is at the origin, $y_s = 0$. The neutral phase speed is thus given by $c_N = U(0) = f'(0) = 0.58727$. The corresponding neutral wavenumber and frequency must be found numerically; the result is the neutral mode where

$$c_N = 0.587271, \quad \alpha_N = 0.395380, \quad \omega_N = 0.232195. \tag{2.172}$$

For values in the unstable region away from the neutral mode, Rayleigh's equation must be solved numerically. Table 2.3 shows the results of the numerical solution and Fig. 2.11 plots the growth rate as a function of wavenumber. Comparing the growth rate curve of Fig. 2.11 for the laminar mixing layer to that of Fig. 2.8 for the hyperbolic tangent profile shows that the two results are in

---

[2] If $\eta = \bar{y}/\sqrt{2x}$, then one gets $f''' + ff'' = 0$. The boundary conditions remain unchanged.

Table 2.2. *Values for the laminar mixing layer profile with* $a = 1.238494$ *and* $b = 0.553444$.

η	f	f'	f'
-20	-1.23849	0.00000	0.00000
-18	-1.23847	0.00001	0.00001
-16	-1.23841	0.00005	0.00003
-14	-1.23821	0.00017	0.00011
-12	-1.23753	0.00060	0.00037
-10	-1.23516	0.00207	0.00128
-8	-1.22700	0.00710	0.00438
-6	-1.19905	0.02423	0.01477
-4	-1.10499	0.08046	0.04716
-2	-0.80602	0.24490	0.12599
0	0.00000	0.58727	0.19971
2	1.53515	0.91210	0.09794
4	3.47304	0.99588	0.00811
6	5.47115	0.99997	0.00009
8	7.47114	1.00000	0.00000

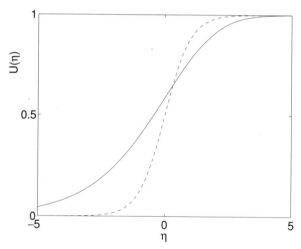

Fig. 2.10. Laminar mixing layer profile (solid) and the hyperbolic tangent profile (dash).

qualitative agreement, but do not agree quantitatively. In particular, the more realistic laminar mixing layer profile has a smaller growth rate, over a shorter range of wavenumbers. For experimentalists who wish to use Linear Stability Theory as a guide for flow control, it is imperative to use as realistic a mean profile as possible. However, for theoreticians, qualitative agreement is often sufficient.

Table 2.3. *Phase speeds and frequencies as a function of the wavenumber α for the laminar mixing layer profile.*

α	c_r	c_i	$\omega_r = \alpha c_r$	$\omega_i = \alpha c_i$
0.395	0.587271	0	0.232195	0
0.39	0.585880	0.004364	0.228493	0.001702
0.35	0.575833	0.037869	0.201542	0.013254
0.30	0.563940	0.082773	0.169182	0.024832
0.25	0.552682	0.131790	0.138171	0.032947
0.20	0.541923	0.186028	0.108385	0.037206
0.15	0.531497	0.247054	0.079725	0.037058
0.10	0.521205	0.317135	0.052121	0.031714
0.05	0.510807	0.399673	0.025540	0.019984
0.01	0.502215	0.478137	0.005022	0.004781

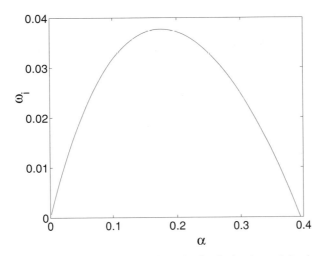

Fig. 2.11. Growth rate $\omega_i = \alpha c_i$ as a function of α for the laminar mixing layer profile.

2.7 Exercises

1. Substitute the instantaneous flow quantities (2.10) into the Navier-Stokes equations (2.6) to (2.8) and show how the linear disturbance equations (2.14) to (2.16) result.
2. Derive the linearized disturbance equation (2.18) in terms of the $\tilde{v}$ velocity.
3. Derive the linearized disturbance equation (2.20) in terms of the stream-function ψ.
4. Derive the linearized disturbance equation (2.22) in terms of the pressure $\tilde{p}$.

5. Derive the linearized disturbance equation (2.24) in terms of the vorticity $\tilde{\omega}_z$.

6. From the linearized disturbance equation (2.18) and the normal mode form (2.25), derive the Orr-Sommerfeld (2.28) and Rayleigh (2.29) equations.

7. From the nonlinear disturbance equations (2.39) to (2.42) and the normal mode form (2.44), derive the three-dimensional Orr-Sommerfeld equation (2.50).

8. Consider the two eigenvalue problems

$$(1) \quad y'' - \alpha^2 y = 0, \quad y(0) = 0, \quad y(h) = 0,$$

and

$$(2) \quad y'' - \alpha^2 y = 0, \quad y(0) = 0, \quad y(\infty) = \text{bounded}.$$

Determine the eigenvalues and show that the eigenvalues are different for bounded and unbounded regions. What happens in the limit $h \to \infty$ in the first case? Do the eigenvalues approach those of the second? Explain.

This example illustrates that care must be exercised when approximating unbounded regions by bounded domains for numerical considerations.

9. Consider the simple pendulum as shown in Figure (ix). The differential equation governing the motion of the pendulum is given by

$$mL^2 \frac{d\theta^2}{dt^2} + k\frac{d\theta}{dt} + mgL \sin\theta = 0,$$

where the first term is the acceleration term, the second term is the viscous damping term, and the last term is the restoring moment.

(a) Nondimensionalize the equation and show that only one parameter exists that governs the behavior of the system.

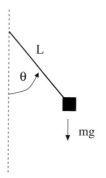

Fig. 2.12. Simple Pendulum

(b) Compute the two equilibrium states.

(c) Determine the stability of each of the two states.

10. Compute the temporal inviscid stability characteristics of the following piecewise linear profiles.

(a) Top hat (or rectangular) jet

$$U(y) = \begin{cases} 0 & L < y < \infty \\ U_c & -L < y < L \\ 0 & -\infty < y < -L. \end{cases}$$

Sketch the velocity profile. Note that there are two modes, one which is even about the $y = 0$ axis (i.e., $v'(0) = 0$), and one which is odd (i.e., $v(0) = 0$). Determine the eigenrelation for each mode.

Hint: Since v is continuous at the origin, it may make the calculations easier if you can show

$$v = \begin{cases} e^{-\alpha y} & L < y < \infty \\ A \cosh(\alpha y) + B \sinh(\alpha y) & 0 < y < L. \end{cases}$$

(b) Triangular jet

$$U(y) = \begin{cases} 0 & 1 < y < \infty \\ 1 - y & 0 < y < 1 \\ 1 + y & -1 < y < 0 \\ 0 & -\infty < y < -1. \end{cases}$$

Sketch the velocity profile. Again there are two modes, one which is even ($v'(0) = 0$), and one which is odd ($v(0) = 0$). Determine the eigenrelation for each mode, and plot the growth rate curve in the (α, ω_i) plane.

(c) Linear shear layer profile

$$U(y) = \begin{cases} 1 & 1 < y < \infty \\ \frac{1}{2}[1 + \beta_U + (1 - \beta_U)y] & -1 < y < 1 \\ \beta_U & -\infty < y < -1. \end{cases}$$

Here, $\beta_U = U_{-\infty}/U_{+\infty}$ is the ratio of freestream velocities. Sketch the velocity profile for several values of the parameter β_U. Determine the eigenrelation, and show that it reduces to that found by Rayleigh when $\beta_U = -1$. Plot the growth rate curve in the (α, ω_i) plane for $\beta_U = 0.5, 0, -0.5, -1$.

11. (a) Note that the equations of motion (2.1) to (2.3) for an inviscid flow, with gravity acting in the $-\hat{\jmath}$ direction, can be written as

$$\nabla \cdot \vec{u} = 0$$

$$\frac{\partial \vec{u}}{\partial t} + (\nabla \times \vec{u}) \times \vec{u} = -\nabla \left(\frac{p}{\rho} + \frac{1}{2}\vec{u} \cdot \vec{u} + gy \right).$$

where $\vec{u} = (u, v)$.

(b) Assume the flow is irrotational. Show for this case that there exists a potential function $\phi(x, y, t)$, defined by $\vec{u} = \nabla\phi$, which satisfies the equations

$$\nabla^2 \phi = 0$$

$$\frac{\partial \nabla\phi}{\partial t} + \nabla \left(\frac{p}{\rho} + \frac{1}{2}(\nabla\phi)^2 + gy \right) = 0.$$

Integrate the second equation to get

$$\frac{\partial \phi}{\partial t} + \frac{P}{\rho} + \frac{1}{2}(\nabla\phi)^2 + gy = c.$$

where c is a constant of integration. This last equation is Bernoulli's equation for unsteady incompressible flows.

(c) Using the above equations, we now wish to investigate the temporal stability characteristics for the following (irrotational) mean flow profile

$$U(y) = \begin{cases} U_1 & 0 < y < \infty \\ U_2 & -\infty < y < 0. \end{cases}$$

Assuming a normal mode solution, show that the eigenrelation is given by

$$\omega = \frac{\alpha(\rho_1 U_1 + \rho_2 U_2)}{\rho_1 + \rho_2}$$

$$\pm i \sqrt{\frac{\alpha^2 \rho_1 \rho_2 (U_2 - U_1)^2}{(\rho_1 + \rho_2)^2} - \frac{\alpha g(\rho_2 - \rho_1)}{\rho_1 + \rho_2}}.$$

Hint: Write ϕ in terms of normal modes, and then solve the Laplacian equation to determine the perturbation flow. Next, use Bernoulli's equation to get a jump condition that involves gravity.

(d) For internal gravity waves, set $U_1 = U_2 = 0$. Give the eigenrelation, and state the conditions for stability.

(e) For surface gravity waves, set $\rho_1 = 0$ and $U_1 = U_2 = 0$. Give the eigenrelation, and state the conditions for stability.

(f) If surface tension is present then the jump in pressure across the interface is no longer zero, but must be modified to

$$[p] = -T \frac{\partial^2 f}{\partial x^2}.$$

where T is the coefficient for surface tension and $F = y - f(x,t)$ gives the location of the surface. Show that the eigenrelation can be written as

$$\omega = \frac{\alpha(\rho_1 U_1 + \rho_2 U_2)}{\rho_1 + \rho_2}$$

$$\pm i \sqrt{\frac{\alpha^2 \rho_1 \rho_2 (U_2 - U_1)^2}{(\rho_1 + \rho_2)^2} - \frac{\alpha^2}{\rho_2 + \rho_1}\left[\frac{g(\rho_2 - \rho_1)}{\alpha} + \alpha T\right]}.$$

What role does surface tension play with regard to the stability of the flow?

12. Prove Result 2.7.

Use the following to aid in the construction of the proof.

(a) Let $G(y) = \phi(y)/\sqrt{U - c}$, and assume $c_i > 0$
(b) Show that G satisfies

$$\{(U - c)G'\}' - \left(\frac{1}{2}U'' + \alpha^2(U - c) + \frac{1}{4}\frac{U'^2}{U - c}\right)G = 0.$$

(c) Show

$$-\int_a^b \{|G'|^2 + \alpha^2|G|^2\}dy + \frac{1}{4}\int_a^b \frac{U'^2}{|U - c|^2}|G|^2 dy = 0.$$

(d) Note that

$$|U - c|^2 = (U - c_r)^2 + c_i^2 \geq c_i^2$$

and thus

$$|U - c|^{-2} \leq c_i^{-2}.$$

13. Why might using the Riccati transformation $G = \phi'/\alpha\phi$ instead of (2.173) not be a good idea (see the Appendix)?
14. Compute the temporal inviscid stability characteristics of the following continuous profiles. A numerical method for solving Rayleigh's equation is presented in the Appendix. In each case plot the mean profile, and give the location of the inflection point and the corresponding neutral phase speed.

(a) Error function profile

$$U(y) = \text{erf}(y) \equiv \frac{2}{\sqrt{\pi}} \int_0^y e^{-u^2} du.$$

The error function profile is sometimes used as an approximation to the laminar mixing layer downstream of a splitter plate. Compute the temporal stability and compare graphically the result you obtain with the result of Rayleigh as given by (2.83) and shown in Fig. 2.4.

(b) Hyperbolic tangent profile

$$U(y) = \frac{1}{2}[1 + \beta_U + (1 - \beta_U)\tanh y]$$

with $\beta_U = 0.5, 0, -0.2$. Here, $\beta_U = U_{-\infty}/U_{+\infty}$ is the ratio of free-stream velocities.

(c) Laminar mixing layer

$$2f''' + ff'' = 0, \quad f'(-\infty) = \beta_U, \quad f(0) = 0, \quad f'(+\infty) = 1$$

with $\beta_U = 0.5, 0, -0.2$.

(d) Symmetric jet

$$U(y) = \text{sech}^2 y.$$

Show that two neutral modes exist with

$$\phi_I = \text{sech}^2 y, \quad \alpha_N = 2, \quad c_N = 2/3$$

$$\phi_{II} = \text{sech}\, y \tanh y, \quad \alpha_N = 1, \quad c_N = 2/3.$$

(e) Symmetric wake

$$U(y) = 1 - Q\,\text{sech}^2 y.$$

with $Q = 0.3, 0.6, 0.9$. Here, Q is a measure of the wake deficit. Show that two modes exist, and plot the growth rate curves for each.

(f) Gaussian jet

$$U(y) = e^{-y^2 \ln 2}.$$

Show that two modes exist, and plot the growth rate curves for each. Compare the stability characteristics to that of the symmetric jet in (c) above.

(g) Combination shear + jet

$$U(y) = \frac{1}{2}[1 + \beta_U + (1 - \beta_U)\tanh y] - Q e^{-y^2 \ln 2}$$

with $\beta_U = 0.5$ and $Q = 0.4, 0.8$. Show that two modes exist if $Q > 0$, and plot the growth rate curves for each.

(h) Asymptotic suction boundary-layer profile

$$U(y) = 1 - e^{-y}, \quad 0 < y < \infty.$$

(i) Falkner-Skan flow

$$2f''' + ff'' + \beta(1 - f'^2) = 0, \quad f(0) = f'(0) = 0, \quad f'(\infty) = 1.$$

with the parameter β a measure of the pressure gradient (see, e.g., Acheson, 1990). The value of β can range from $\beta = -0.19884$ (flow separation), to $\beta = 0$ (Blasius), to 1.0 (2D stagnation-point profile). For values of $-0.19884 < \beta < 0$ show that the profile has an inflection point within the flow region, and hence may be unstable to inviscid disturbances. Compute the inviscid temporal stability characteristics, and plot the growth rate curve, for $\beta = -0.1$ and -0.16.

15. Derive the corresponding Rayleigh equation for an incompressible, density stratified flow

$$\mathbf{v}'' + (\rho'/\rho)\mathbf{v}' - \left[\alpha^2 + \frac{U'' + \rho'U'/\rho}{U - c} \right] \mathbf{v} = 0.$$

Hint: Assume that the mean density is a function of y, but ignore density fluctuations when deriving Rayleigh's equation. The same equation results for compressible flows in the limit of small Mach number, as will be shown later in Chapter 5.

Assume the mean flow profile

$$U(y) = \frac{1}{2} [1 + \beta_U + (1 - \beta_U) \tanh y]$$

$$\rho(y) = \frac{1}{2} \left[1 + \beta_\rho + (1 - \beta_\rho) \tanh y \right].$$

Solve the temporal stability problem for $\beta_U = 0.5$ and $\beta_\rho = 0.5$, 1.0, 1.5 and graph the eigenrelation in the (α, ω_i) plane.

2.8 Appendix: numerical computation

There are basically two different methods or approaches for determining the eigenvalues to Rayleigh's equation given a particular mean profile. The first method is called a global method in which Rayleigh's equation is discretized on a uniform mesh having M grid points, and all the eigenvalues of the resulting $M \times M$ matrix are found by an appropriate eigenvalue package. Care must be exercised when employing this method since the number of eigenvalues change as M is changed; i.e., as the mesh is refined the number of eigenvalues

increases. One must be able to distinguish between physical eigenvalues and unphysical ones associated with mesh refinement.

The second method is a local method in that Rayleigh's equation is solved by some numerical procedure and each eigenvalue is determined in succession. Since this method is most often quoted in the literature we present it here. One popular numerical procedure for solving Rayleigh's equation first involves a Riccati transformation or

$$G = \frac{\phi'}{\phi},$$

(2.173)

that reduces the second order linear equation to the following first order, nonlinear equation:

$$G' + G^2 = \alpha^2 + \frac{U''}{U - c}.$$

(2.174)

For unbounded flows where $\phi \approx e^{\mp \alpha y}$ for $y \to \pm\infty$, the appropriate boundary conditions are

$$G(\infty) = -\alpha, \quad G(-\infty) = \alpha.$$

(2.175)

Alternatively, one can first appeal to the pressure disturbance equation (2.33) and employ the Riccati transformation

$$G = \frac{\mathbf{p}'}{\alpha \mathbf{p}}.$$

(2.176)

By substituting (2.176) into (2.33) the first order nonlinear equation

$$G' + \alpha G^2 - \frac{2U'}{U - c} G - \alpha = 0,$$

(2.177)

with boundary conditions

$$G(\infty) = -1, \quad G(-\infty) = +1,$$

(2.178)

is found. The advantage of using (2.177) over (2.174) is that the boundary conditions (2.178) are no longer functions of α, which can cause numerical problems when the wavenumber becomes small. The results presented in Section 2.6 used (2.177) to (2.178) to compute the eigenvalues.

There are several advantages for solving the Riccati equation rather than Rayleigh's equation directly. These include:

- Rayleigh's equation is homogeneous and so has the trivial solution in its solution space. Unless one is close to the correct eigenvalue, the solution may converge only to the trivial solution. The Riccati equation is non-homogeneous and hence does not have the trivial solution in its solution space.

- Rayleigh's equation has exponentially growing solutions as $y \rightarrow \pm\infty$, and so care must be exercised to eliminate these non-physical solutions. The Riccati equation has finite conditions and so the problem of eliminating the growing solutions is avoided.

The numerical procedure for the determination of the eigenvalues is as follows:

Step 1: Fix a value of the wavenumber α and make an initial estimate on the phase speed c.

Step 2: Integrate the Riccati equation from L to 0 and from $-L$ to 0 (for the unbounded case, L is large and typically taken in the range of 6 to 8).

Step 3: Compute $[G]|_{y=0}$, the jump in G at the origin.

Step 4: If $[G] < tol$, where tol is a small number, then stop. The value of c is the required eigenvalue. If $[G] \geq tol$, compute an updated value of c by some numerical root finding procedure. Go to Step 2 and repeat until convergence.

For the integrator, a simple method is to use a fourth order, variable step Runge-Kutta method. For updating the eigenvalue, we typically use Muller's method, which is essentially a Secant method for complex eigenvalues. To start the procedure in Step 1, we must have a good estimate for c. This value is usually obtained by perturbing by a small distance from the neutral value. Recall that the neutral eigenvalue is given by $c_N = U(y_s)$, where y_s is the inflection point where $U''(y_s) = 0$. The value of α_N, and hence ω_N, can be found by integrating the Riccati equation numerically. However, a problem exists when integrating along the real axis since $U - cN = 0$ at y_s. To avoid this, we analytically continue the path of integration below the real y-axis (Lessen, 1950). That is, we let $y = y_r + iy_i$, and fix $y_i < 0$. However, care must be taken so that y_i does not pass through a branch point or singularity of the mean profile when analytically continued into the complex plane. For example, consider the profile $U = \tanh(y)$. Extending into the complex plane we get

$$U = \tanh(y_r + iy_i) \tag{2.179}$$

which has a singularity at $(0, -\pi/2)$ in the lower half plane.

Another numerical procedure for solving Rayleigh's equation involves the compound matrix method. This method has been shown to be essentially the same as the Ricatti method, but applied to Rayleigh's equation directly. Although it also offers the advantage of eliminating the exponentially growing solutions, we shall not discuss this method here but postpone the discussion until Chapter 3 where viscous disturbances are addressed.

Chapter 3

Temporal stability of viscous incompressible flows

3.1 Discussion

When a parallel or nearly parallel mean flow does not have an inflection point, viscous effects are important and the Orr-Sommerfeld equation (2.31) must be considered in order to determine the stability of the flow. This is in contrast to solving the much simpler Rayleigh's equation (2.32) where it is generally believed that, for flows with an inflection point, the most unstable mode is inviscid in nature.

In this chapter we will examine the temporal stability characteristics of various well known profiles. These profiles include bounded flows, such as plane Poiseuille and Couette flows, semi-bounded flows, such as the Blasius boundary layer and the more general Falkner-Skan family, and unbounded flows, such as jets, wakes and mixing layers. Other well-known profiles are given in the exercise section. We restrict our attention to two-dimensional disturbances, since according to Squire's theorem, if a three-dimensional disturbance is unstable, there corresponds a more unstable two-dimensional disturbance.

For bounded flows, DiPrima & Habetler (1969) proved that the spectrum of the Orr-Sommerfeld equation consists of an infinite number of discrete eigenvalues, and that the spectrum is complete. Contrary to this, if perturbations for this flow are considered inviscidly, then there are no discrete modes. As a result, only a continuous spectrum is possible. Thus, any arbitrary initial disturbance can be decomposed and expressed as a linear combination of the eigenfunctions. For unbounded flows, stability calculations for various flows have uncovered only a finite number of eigenvalues[1]. Since any initial disturbance cannot be written in terms of a finite number of modes, a continuum of modes must exist (Grosch & Salwen, 1978, and Salwen & Grosch, 1981).

---

[1] See, e.g., Mack (1976) for Blasius boundary layer flow.

Later, Miklavčič & Williams (1982) and Miklavčič (1983) proved rigorously that, if the mean profile decays exponentially to a constant in the freestream, then only a finite number of eigenvalues exists for any finite Reynolds number while, if the mean profile decays algebraically, then there exists an infinite discrete set of eigenvalues (see also the discussion by Herron, 1987). In the first case, a continuum must exist for a complete set to span the solution space, while in the latter case no continuum exists. Since the continuum is an important concept for receptivity, we present the ideas in the last section of this chapter.

3.2 Channel flows

Historically speaking, the study of channel flows has been an inspiration and a challenge to more than three generations of applied mathematicians. By definition, a channel flow is one confined by two walls, and therefore the boundary conditions are applied at two finite values of y. As a result, the problem is well posed and the mathematical analysis is considerably simplified.

It should be realized that the channel flows we are discussing are those of the fully developed variety in which U is a function of y only. In practice, however, there is a long entrance region beginning with a flow of constant velocity between two thin boundary layers along each wall. The stability of the entrance flow has been studied by Tatsumi (1952), for example.

Eventually the two boundary layers merge and the mean flow becomes truly independent of the variable x (save for the pressure). There are two well-known examples of this system: (a) Poiseuille flow, in which both walls are at rest and the flow is driven by a constant pressure gradient, and (b) Couette flow, in which there is no pressure gradient and the motion of the walls is a parallel flow of one wall with respect to the other.

3.2.1 Plane Poiseuille flow

The nondimensional plane Poiseuille flow is a parabolic flow due to the presence of a mean streamwise pressure gradient and is defined by

$$U(y) = y(2 - y), \quad \frac{\mathrm{d}P}{\mathrm{d}x} = \text{constant}, \quad \text{for } 0 < y < 2. \tag{3.1}$$

This is an exact solution of the system (2.1) to (2.3). We choose U_0, the centerline velocity, and L, the channel half-width, as our units to nondimensionalize the system. The temporal stability characteristics can be found by solving

the Orr-Sommerfeld equation (2.31) subject to the boundary conditions at the walls

$$\phi = \phi' = 0, \quad \text{at } y = 0, \ 2. \tag{3.2}$$

Any function can be represented as the sum of even and odd functions. By solving for the even and odd parts of the solution separately, it is possible to impose even or odd boundary conditions at the centerline of the channel and seek solutions only over half the range. That is, for the even part the odd derivatives are zero at the centerline, and for the odd part the function and even derivatives are zero at the centerline. We shall refer to the even modes as the Symmetric modes, and the odd modes as the Antisymmetric modes. This classification is with respect to the disturbance velocity $\tilde{u}$; see equations (2.19) and (2.30). Some authors classify the modes with respect to the disturbance velocity $\tilde{v}$; i.e., Symmetric modes have the function and the even derivatives set to zero, while Antisymmetric modes have the odd derivatives set to zero at the centerline of the channel. In this book we shall generally follow the first classification scheme. This lack of conformity among various authors can cause confusion and the student is advised to exercise much care when reading research articles and books. At the centerline of the channel we have

$$\text{Symmetric Mode: } \phi' = \phi''' = 0, \quad \text{at } y = 1$$
$$\text{Antisymmetric Mode: } \phi = \phi'' = 0, \quad \text{at } y = 1.$$

To solve the Orr-Sommerfeld equation we chose the Compound Matrix scheme of Ng & Reid (1979) because of its ease in implementation. The essential idea is to rewrite the Orr-Sommerfeld equation as a system of equivalent first-order equations, integrate from $y = 1$ to $y = 0$ using a standard Runge-Kutta constant-step size integrator, and then determine the eigenvalue c for a fixed value of α and Re that satisfies the wall boundary conditions to within a specified tolerance. The details of the method are outlined in the Appendix. This type of procedure is usually called a 'shooting method', since one guesses the eigenvalue, shoots (i.e., integrates forward) to the other end of the domain to see if it satisfies the proper boundary condition, and then updates the guess using a root-finding technique. The condition that must be satisfied is usually call the discriminate D. Unfortunately, the shooting method only determines one eigenvalue at a time, and the initial guess usually needs to be very close to the exact eigenvalue, that is not known a priori. A more systematic procedure for finding all of the eigenvalues in a given region of the complex c-plane is to compute D at enough points so that contours of $D_r = 0$ and $D_i = 0$ can be drawn (see, for example, Mack, 1976). Intersection points of the curve

$D_r = D_i = 0$ then reveal the eigenvalues. This method can be impracticable if there exists a large number of contours, but does have the advantage that all eigenvalues will be found within the given domain. The eigenvalues determined in this fashion are usually only accurate to a few significant digits, but can be used as the initial guess of a root-finding procedure which then computes each eigenvalue to within a prescribed tolerance (often termed 'polishing').

We have applied the above search algorithm for the Symmetric modes of the plane Poiseuille flow; the Antisymmetric modes are known to be stable[1]. Figure 3.1 shows the contour curves of $D_r = 0$ and $D_i = 0$ in the complex c-plane; the intersection points are identified by circles. These initial guesses are then substituted into the Orr-Sommerfeld solver to gain better accuracy. The eigenvalues for the Symmetric mode are displayed in Fig. 3.2 and listed in Table 3.1. The classification scheme is the one suggested by Mack, that three families of modes exist. The A and P families are finite, and the S family has an infinite number of stable modes. By varying the wavenumber α the maximum growth rate curve can be traced out in the (ω_i, α) plane, where $\omega_i = \alpha c_i$ is the temporal growth rate. The growth rate curve for $Re = 10\,000$ is shown in Fig. 3.3. This method was also used to identify the neutral stability boundary in the (c_r, Re) plane, shown in Fig. 3.4. The region inside the boundary corresponds to instability while the region outside the boundary corresponds to stability. Note that there exists a minimum Reynolds number, called the critical Reynolds number Re_{crit}, such that for all Reynolds numbers below this value the flow is stable to infinitesimal disturbances. The critical Reynolds number has been computed by a number of authors, and the accepted value is $Re_{crit} = 5772.22$ with corresponding values $\alpha_{crit} = 1.02056$ and $c_{crit} = 0.2640$ (Orszag, 1971). Degeneracies, eigenmodes of order two, are discussed by Koch (1986) and Shanthini (1989).

3.2.2 Plane Couette flow

For plane Couette flow the mean dimensional velocity varies linearly between two plates moving in opposite directions and with equal speed, U_0, with one plate located at $y = 0$ and the other plate located at $y = 2L$. Using the speed U_0 and the half-width of the channel L to nondimensionalize the system, we get

$$U(y) = y - 1, \quad P = \text{constant}, \quad \text{for } 0 < y < 2, \qquad (3.3)$$

---

[1] In the terminology of Mack, 1976, the modes are Antisymmetric and Symmetric, respectively.

Table 3.1. *First 30 eigenvalues of plane Poiseuille flow at* $\alpha = 1$ *and* $Re = 10\,000$; *Symmetric Mode.*

Mode	c_r	c_i	Mode	c_r	c_i
1	0.23753	0.00374	16	0.51292	−0.28663
2	0.96464	−0.03519	17	0.70887	−0.28766
3	0.93635	−0.06325	18	0.68286	−0.30761
4	0.90806	−0.09131	19	0.63610	−0.32520
5	0.87976	−0.11937	20	0.67764	−0.34373
6	0.34911	−0.12450	21	0.67451	−0.38983
7	0.85145	−0.14743	22	0.67321	−0.43580
8	0.82314	−0.17548	23	0.67232	−0.48326
9	0.19006	−0.18282	24	0.67159	−0.53241
10	0.79482	−0.20353	25	0.67097	−0.58327
11	0.47490	−0.20873	26	0.67043	−0.63588
12	0.76649	−0.23159	27	0.66997	−0.69025
13	0.36850	−0.23882	28	0.66957	−0.74641
14	0.73812	−0.25969	29	0.66923	−0.80439
15	0.58721	−0.26716	30	0.66894	−0.86418

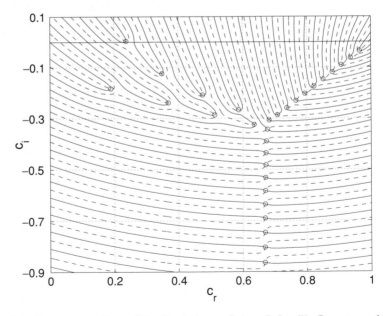

Fig. 3.1. Zero contour lines of the discriminate of plane Poiseuille flow at $\alpha = 1$ and $Re = 10\,000$; Symmetric Mode; $D_r = 0$ solid; $D_i = 0$ dash. The circles denote intersection points where $D_r = D_i = 0$. (After Mack, 1976).

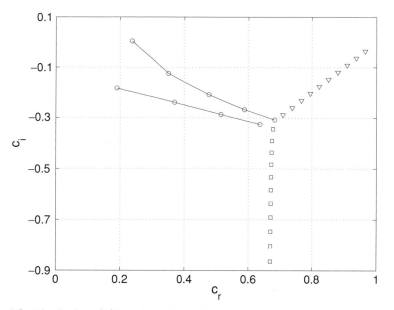

Fig. 3.2. Distribution of eigenvalues of plane Poiseuille flow at $\alpha = 1$ and $Re = 10\,000$; Symmetric Mode. $\bigcirc$, A family; $\triangledown$, P family; $\square$, S family. (After Mack, 1976).

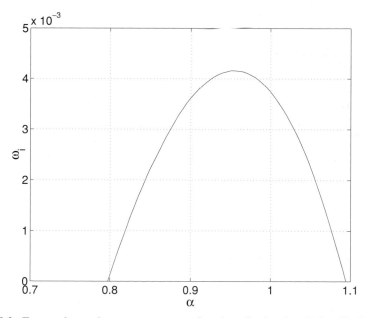

Fig. 3.3. Temporal growth rate $\omega_i = \alpha c_i$ as a function of α for plane Poiseuille flow at $Re = 10\,000$; Symmetric Mode.

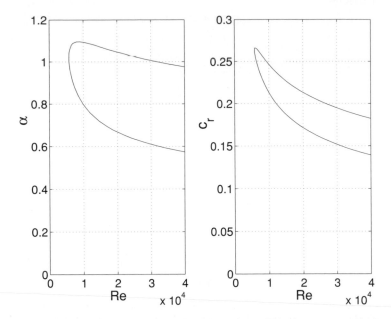

Fig. 3.4. Neutral stability curve in the (α, Re) and (c_r, Re) planes, respectively, for plane Poiseuille flow.

and an exact solution of (2.1) to (2.3). Because $U'' = 0$ everywhere, we immediately notice from equation (2.24) that there is no production of vorticity fluctuations. In fact, the vorticity fluctuations are merely transported and diffused. Therefore we should not be surprised that all stability studies for this problem point toward complete stability of this flow to small disturbances. This is borne out in Fig. 3.5 where we plot the contour curves of $D_r = 0$ and $D_i = 0$, similar to Fig. 3.1 for plane Poiseuille flow. Since $U(y)$ varies between ± 1 so does the phase speed c_r. Note that all eigenvalues lie below the $c_i = 0$ line indicating stable solutions. Indeed, Romanov (1973) proved theoretically that all modes are stable. There is, however, little doubt that this flow will in reality become turbulent at large enough Reynolds number. We discuss one possible mechanism for this in Chapter 8.

3.2.3 Generalized channel flow

The plane Poiseuille and Couette flows can be combined to yield a new flow, given by

$$U = Ay(2 - y) + B(y - 1), \quad P = c_1 + c_2 x, \quad \text{for } 0 < y < 2, \quad (3.4)$$

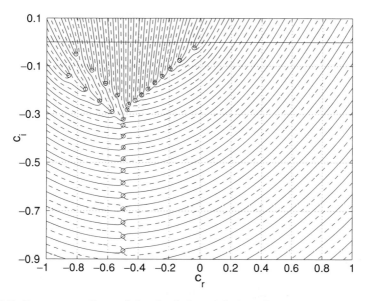

Fig. 3.5. Zero contour lines of the discriminate of plane Couette flow at $\alpha = 1$ and $Re = 10\,000$; Symmetric Mode; $D_r = 0$ solid; $D_i = 0$ dash. The circles denote intersection points where $D_r = D_i = 0$.

an exact solution of (2.1) to (2.3) (Deardorff, 1963), where c_1 and c_2 are constants. This two parameter family can be reduced to a one parameter family by requiring the maximum value of the mean velocity U to be one, leading to the constraint

$$B = \begin{cases} 1 & 0 \le A \le 1/2, \\ 2\sqrt{A(A-1)} & 1/2 \le A \le 1. \end{cases} \tag{3.5}$$

The temporal stability characteristics have been examined by Potter (1966), Reynolds and Potter (1967), and Hains (1967). When $A = 0$, $B = 1$ the profile corresponds to plane Couette flow and is stable. Thus, the critical Reynolds number is simply $Re_{crit} = \infty$. For $A = 1$, $B = 0$ the profile corresponds to plane Poiseuille flow, and the critical Reynolds number is $Re_{crit} = 5772$. Consequently, there exists an intermediate value of B, say B^*, for which the profile first becomes unstable; the region of instability then corresponds to $0 < B < B^*$ and occurs at $B^* = 0.341$, $A^* = 0.970$, which shows that only a modest component of plane Couette flow is sufficient to completely stabilize plane Poiseuille flow.

3.3 Blasius boundary layer

The Blasius boundary layer profile is given by

$$U = f'(\eta), \quad P = \text{constant}, \quad \eta = y\sqrt{\frac{Re}{x}}, \qquad (3.6)$$

where

$$2f''' + ff'' = 0, \quad 0 \le \eta < +\infty, \qquad (3.7)$$

subject to the boundary conditions

$$f(0) = f'(0) = 0, \quad f'(+\infty) = 1. \qquad (3.8)$$

No known analytical solutions exist and therefore the mean profile must be determined numerically. Although there are several methods from which to choose, the simplest method involves integrating (3.7) as an initial value problem starting with $f(0) = f'(0) = 0$, $f''(0) = a$. The value of a is determined by requiring $f'(+\infty) = 1$, and is found as part of an iteration procedure. The value of "$+\infty$" is taken to be 13, since then $f'(13)$ and $f''(13)$ deviate less than 10^{-9} from the asymptotic values of 1 and 0, respectively. Using a Runge-Kutta constant-step size integrator, it is found that $a = 0.332057336$.

With the Blasius boundary layer profile known at least numerically, the stability can be examined. The stability characteristics of this flow have a long history, beginning with approximations based on asymptotic methods, followed by a number of publications using machine calculations (for a brief history see, for example, Drazin & Reid, 1984, or White, 1974). Earlier results were shown in Fig. ??. Today the stability of the Blasius boundary layer is so routine that we only state the main results.

Mack has shown numerically that only a finite number of eigenvalues exist at any given Reynolds number and that this number increases as the Reynolds number increases with only one eigenvalue surviving in the limit of inviscid flow. The phase speed of all the other eigenvalues save this one approaches zero (Mack, 1976). Here we reproduce a subset of his results.

The Compound Matrix method, described in the Appendix, is modified to account for the unbounded domain by integrating the Orr-Sommerfeld equation, beginning in the far field with appropriate asymptotic conditions, and then integrating in toward $y = 0$ using a Runge-Kutta constant-step size integrator (Ng & Reid 1980). The eigenvalue c is then iterated on until the discriminate D at $y = 0$ is satisfied to within a prescribed tolerance or, if more than one eigenvalue is required, we compute D at enough points in a given region of the complex c-plane so that contours of $D_r = 0$ and $D_i = 0$ can be drawn. Figure 3.6 shows the contour curves for $\alpha = 0.179$ and $Re = 580$. The intersection points

Table 3.2. *Discrete eigenvalues of Bla-sius boundary layer flow at $\alpha = 0.179$ and $Re = 580$.*

Mode	c_r	c_i
1	0.36412269	0.00795979
2	0.28971430	−0.27686644
3	0.48392943	−0.19206759
4	0.55719662	−0.36534237
5	0.68626129	−0.33077057
6	0.79365088	−0.43408876
7	0.88736417	−0.41474479

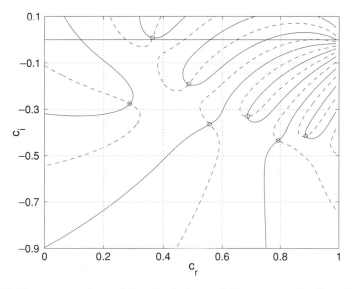

Fig. 3.6. Zero contour lines of the discriminate of Blasius boundary layer flow at $\alpha = 0.179$ and $Re = 580$; $D_r = 0$ solid; $D_i = 0$ dash. The circles denote intersection points where $D_r = D_i = 0$. (After Mack, 1976).

$D_r = D_i = 0$ (identified by circles) identify all the discrete eigenvalues in the given domain. These discrete eigenvalues are listed in Table 3.2 and compare favorably with those of Mack (1976). In addition to the finite discrete set of eigenvalues, there also exists a continuum located along the $c_r = 1$ line (see equation 3.26). The existence of this continuum will be explained in more detail in Section 3.6. Figure 3.7 plots the growth rate $\omega_i = \alpha c_i$ as a function of

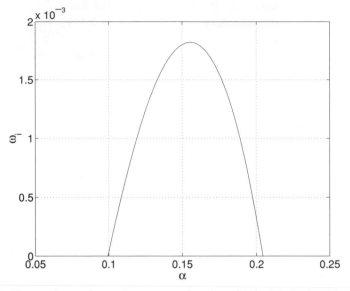

Fig. 3.7. Temporal growth rate $\omega_i = \alpha c_i$ as a function of α for Blasius boundary layer flow at $Re = 580$.

the wavenumber α at $Re = 580$. Figure 3.8 plots the corresponding amplitude of the normalized eigenfunction $\mathbf{u} = \phi'$ for $\alpha = 0.179$.

Figure 3.9 is a plot of the neutral stability boundary for the Blasius boundary layer flow. Instead of plotting the neutral stability boundary in the (α, Re) plane, say, it is customary to plot the neutral stability boundary in either the $(\alpha_\delta, Re_\delta)$ plane or the (c_r, Re_δ) plane, respectively, where $\delta = 1.72078764$ is the displacement thickness[1]. Here, we have the relationships $Re_\delta = \delta Re$ and $\alpha_\delta = \delta \alpha$. The critical Reynolds number and wavenumber are found to be $Re_{crit} = 301.641$, $\alpha_{crit} = 0.1765$; i.e., $Re_{\delta,crit} = 519.060$, $\alpha_{\delta,crit} = 0.30377$ (Davey, 1982). For a further discussion of the temporal stability of the Blasius boundary layer flow at even larger values of the Reynolds number (up to 10^6), see Davey (1982) and Healey (1995).

3.4 Falkner-Skan flow family

The more general Falkner-Skan boundary layer flow family is given by

$$2f''' + ff'' + \beta(1 - f'^2) = 0, \tag{3.9}$$

---

[1] The displacement thickness is defined by $\delta = \int_0^\infty (1 - f')d\eta$. If the scaling $\eta = y\sqrt{Re/2x}$ is employed, then the Blasius boundary layer equation becomes $f''' + ff'' = 0$, and we would chose $\delta = 1.72078764/\sqrt{2} = 1.2127806$ as the scaling parameter.

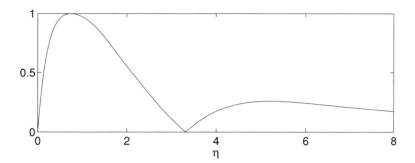

Fig. 3.8. Amplitude of the normalized eigenfunction $\mathbf{u} = \phi'$ as a function of η for Blasius boundary layer flow; Mode 1 of Table 3.2, $Re = 580$, $\alpha = 0.179$.

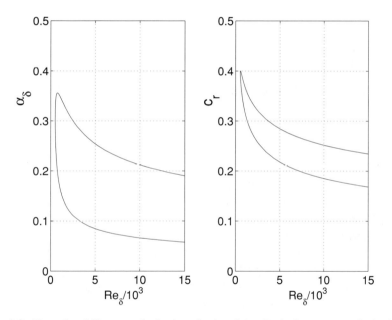

Fig. 3.9. Neutral stability curve in the $(\alpha_\delta, Re_\delta)$ and (c_r, Re_δ) planes, respectively, for Blasius boundary layer flow.

subject to the boundary conditions

$$f(0) = f'(0) = 0, \quad f'(\infty) = 1, \tag{3.10}$$

with the parameter β a measure of the pressure gradient (see, e.g., Acheson, 1990 or White, 1974). The value of β can range from $\beta = -0.19884$ (flow separation), to $\beta = 0$ (Blasius), to 1.0 (2D stagnation-point profile). A plot of the mean profile $U(\eta)$ is shown in Fig. 3.10.

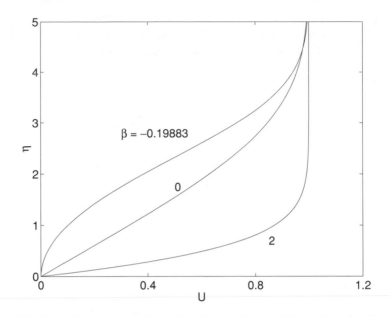

Fig. 3.10. Plot of the mean profile as a function of β for the Falkner-Skan flow family.

The temporal stability characteristics of the Falkner-Skan family was considered by Wazzan, Okamura, & Smith (1968) and Obremski, Morkovin, & Landahl (1969). Rather than generate a myriad number of stability plots as the pressure gradient parameter β is varied, it is more conventional to make a single plot that summaries the main findings. This is done by computing the critical Reynolds number for each value of β, and then plotting the critical Reynolds number against the shape function $H = \delta/\theta$, where δ is the displacement thickness and θ the momentum thickness[1]. The value of H is unique for each value of β. The critical Reynolds numbers are given in Table 3.3 as a function of β, and graphed in Fig. 3.11. We remark here that for values of $-0.19884 < \beta < 0$ the profile has an inflection point within the flow region, and hence, as we have noted, may be unstable inviscidly.

3.5 Unbounded flows

For unbounded flows, such as jets, wakes and mixing layers, where the mean profile has an inflection point, it is known that the largest growth rate is inviscid in nature, and that viscosity is only a dampening effect. For example,

---

[1] The momentum thickness is defined by $\theta = \int_0^\infty (1 - f')f'\,d\eta$.

Table 3.3. *Critical Reynolds number as a function of β for the Falkner-Skan family (Wazzan, Okamura, & Smith, 1968; the value at β = +∞ is from Drazin & Reid, 1984).*

β	Re_δ	Re_θ
$+\infty$	21675	10473
1.0	12490	5636
0.8	10920	4874
0.6	8890	3909
0.5	7680	3344
0.4	6230	2679
0.3	4550	1927
0.2	2830	1174
0.1	1380	556
0	520	201
-0.05	318	119
-0.1	199	71
-0.14	138	47
-0.1988	67	17

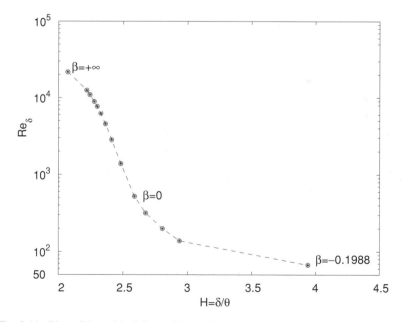

Fig. 3.11. Plot of the critical Reynolds number Re_δ against $H = \delta/\theta = Re_\delta/Re_\theta$ for the Falkner-Skan flow family.

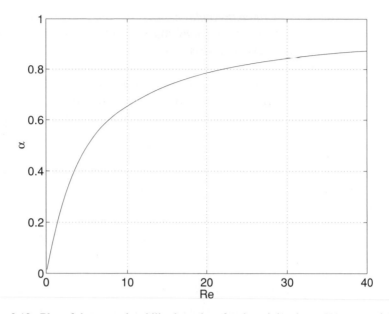

Fig. 3.12. Plot of the neutral stability boundary for the mixing layer $U(y) = \tanh(y)$ in the (α, Re) plane. (After Betchov & Szewczyk, 1963).

Betchov & Szewczyk (1963) have shown for the mixing layer that the effects of viscosity are felt below a Reynolds number of approximately 50, and that no critical value of the Reynolds number exists (see Fig. 3.12). For jets, Tatsumi & Kakutani (1958) and Kaplan (1964) found that viscosity has a stabilizing influence, beginning below a Reynolds number of 100. For this flow a critical Reynolds number does exist and was calculated to be approximately 4 with a wavenumber of 0.2. The same general observations are true for the wake profile. Because the largest growth rate is often of most interest, stability calculations for free shear layers are almost always restricted to solving Rayleigh's equation, and so we will not devote further space here.

3.6 Discrete and continuous spectra

For profiles on a bounded domain, DiPrima & Habetler (1969) have shown that there exists an infinite set of discrete temporal modes of the Orr-Sommerfeld equation, and that this set is complete. Since the normal modes span the solution space, any initial disturbance can be expanded in terms of them. Thus the complete solution can be described in terms of normal modes. For unbounded

domains, general completeness theorems do not exist. However, Miklavčič & Williams (1982) and Miklavčič (1983) did prove rigorously that if the mean profile decays exponentially to a constant in the freestream ($U \to 1 + O(e^{-ay})$, $a > 0$), then only a finite number of eigenvalues exists for any finite Reynolds number, while if the mean profile decays algebraically ($U \to 1 + O(y^{-a})$, $a > 0$), then there exists an infinite discrete set of eigenvalues (see also the discussion by Herron, 1987). In the first case, a continuum must exist for a complete set to span the solution space, while in the latter case no continuum exists.

The theory gives a solid foundation to previous numerical work, where it was shown that for various profiles that decay exponentially in the freestream, such as the boundary layer, the mixing layer, and the jet and wake profiles, only a finite number of discrete modes exist. Since a finite set of modes on the unbounded domain are not complete, they can not be used to describe an arbitrary initial disturbance. Therefore one must consider the presence of a continuum. Grosch & Salwen (1978) and Salwen & Grosch (1981) have shown that the set consisting of the discrete modes and the continuum is complete. Their work also provides the necessary mathematical foundation for the analysis of the receptivity problem, namely how acoustic disturbances or turbulence in the freestream interact with the boundary layer to excite instabilities. Since the work of Grosch & Salwen is of such importance for a proper understanding of the nature of the solution set of the Orr-Sommerfeld equation, we briefly present their analysis here. A review of these papers, and the implications to the receptivity problem, can be found in Hill (1995).

Recall from Section 2.1 that, for a two-dimensional flow, the disturbance velocity components $\tilde{u}$ and $\tilde{v}$ can be expressed in terms of a stream function, $\psi(x, y, t)$, in the usual manner with

$$\tilde{u} = \psi_y, \quad \tilde{v} = -\psi_x. \tag{3.11}$$

Use of the streamfunction ψ satisfies the continuity equation (2.1) exactly. By substitution of ψ into the momentum equations (2.2) and (2.3) and elimination of the pressure, then the single partial differential equation for ψ can be found to be

$$\left(\frac{\partial}{\partial t} + U \frac{\partial}{\partial x} \right) \nabla^2 \psi - U_{yy} \psi_x = Re^{-1} \nabla^4 \psi. \tag{3.12}$$

The boundary conditions at the wall are given by

$$\psi_x(x, 0, t) = -\tilde{v}(x, 0, t) = 0,$$
$$\psi_y(x, 0, t) = \tilde{u}(x, 0, t) = 0, \tag{3.13}$$

and, for unbounded flows, a finiteness condition at infinity must be imposed, or

$$\int_{-\infty}^{+\infty} \int_{0}^{+\infty} (\psi_x^2 + \psi_y^2) dx dy < \infty. \tag{3.14}$$

Physically this means the perturbation energy is finite. Mathematically, this inequality ensures that the Fourier integral expansion of ψ,

$$\psi(x, y, t) = \int_{-\infty}^{+\infty} \psi_\alpha(y, t) e^{i\alpha x} d\alpha \tag{3.15}$$

exists, where α is real, according to temporal stability theory.

We now assume that ψ_α is separable and has the form

$$\psi_\alpha(y, t) = \phi_\alpha(y) e^{-i\omega t}. \tag{3.16}$$

Here, ϕ_α is the solution to the Orr-Sommerfeld equation

$$(U - c)(\phi'' - \alpha^2 \phi) - U'' \phi = \frac{1}{i\alpha Re} (\phi'''' - 2\alpha^2 \phi'' + \alpha^4 \phi). \tag{3.17}$$

and ω is the complex eigenvalue. The discrete eigenvalues ω_n and the corresponding eigenfunctions $\{\phi_{\alpha_n}\}$ satisfy the Orr-Sommerfeld equation with boundary conditions

$$\phi_{\alpha_n} = \phi'_{\alpha_n} = 0 \quad \text{at} \quad y = 0, \quad \phi_{\alpha_n} = \phi'_{\alpha_n} \to 0 \quad \text{as} \quad y \to \infty. \tag{3.18}$$

For a particular mean flow the number of discrete modes, $N(\alpha)$, depends on both the Reynolds number and the wavenumber; $N(\alpha)$ can either be finite or zero.

Since the Orr-Sommerfeld equation is fourth-order and linear, there will be four linearly independent solutions $\phi_j(y)$; $j = 1, 2, 3, 4$. The character of each of these solutions can be determined by examining their behavior as $y \to \infty$. By writing

$$\phi_j(y) \approx e^{\lambda_j y}, \quad \text{as} \quad y \to \infty, \tag{3.19}$$

and substituting into the Orr-Sommerfeld equation (3.17), we see that

$$\lambda_1 = -Q^{1/2}, \quad \lambda_2 = +Q^{1/2}, \quad \lambda_3 = -\alpha, \quad \lambda_4 = +\alpha, \tag{3.20}$$

where

$$Q = i\alpha Re(U_1 - c) + \alpha^2, \tag{3.21}$$

and it is assumed that $Re(Q) \geq 0$. We have also assumed that $U \to U_1$, $U', U'' \to 0$ as $y \to \infty$. The constant U_1 is unity for a boundary layer, a mixing layer or a wake, and is zero for a jet. The eigenfunctions ϕ_1 and ϕ_2 are

called the viscous solutions since their asymptotic behavior at infinity depends on the Reynolds number while the eigenfunctions ϕ_3 and ϕ_4 are the inviscid solutions. Note that the eigenfunctions ϕ_2 and ϕ_4 are unbounded as y becomes large, and so must be dropped from the solution set. Thus, it is a linear combination of ϕ_1 and ϕ_3, the viscous and inviscid solutions, that must be required to satisfy the two boundary conditions at the wall $y = 0$. In the inviscid limit, the viscous eigenfunction ϕ_1 is not present and the solution to the Rayleigh problem is given only in terms of ϕ_3. For the more general case of an unbounded region $-\infty < y < +\infty$, such as a mixing layer, wake or a jet, we would keep ϕ_3 as the solution which decays as $y \to +\infty$ and keep ϕ_4 as the solution which decays as $y \to -\infty$, and enforce a matching condition at the critical layer.

The continuous part of the solution satisfies the Orr-Sommerfeld equation with boundary conditions

$$\phi_\alpha = \phi'_\alpha = 0 \quad \text{at} \quad y = 0, \quad \phi_\alpha, \phi'_\alpha \ \text{bounded as} \ y \to \infty. \qquad (3.22)$$

It is important to keep in mind that the difference between the discrete spectra and the continuous spectra is their behavior at infinity; the discrete spectra is required to vanish as $y \to \infty$, while the continuous part is only required to be bounded. We again look for solutions in the far field by writing

$$\phi_{\alpha_k} \approx e^{\pm iky}, \quad \text{as} \ y \to \infty, \qquad (3.23)$$

with $k > 0$ real and positive. Substitution into (3.17) results in the algebraic equation

$$(-k^2 - \alpha^2)(-k^2 - \alpha^2 - i\,Re(\alpha U_1 - \omega)) = 0. \qquad (3.24)$$

We see that this equation is a linear equation for ω in terms of the real parameter k and hence has one root,

$$\omega_k = \alpha U_1 - i\,\frac{k^2 + \alpha^2}{Re} \qquad (3.25)$$

or, in terms of the phase speed $c = \omega/\alpha$,

$$c = U_1 - i\,\frac{k^2 + \alpha^2}{\alpha\,Re}. \qquad (3.26)$$

The temporal continuum branch is shown in Fig. 3.13 for the specific case of Blasius boundary layer flow ($U_1 = 1$) and $\alpha = 0.179$, $Re = 580$; compare with Fig. 3.6. Note that, in addition to the continuum, there are seven discrete eigenvalues, one unstable and six stable. As noted by Mack (1976), as the Reynolds number decreases, one by one the eigenvalues move onto the

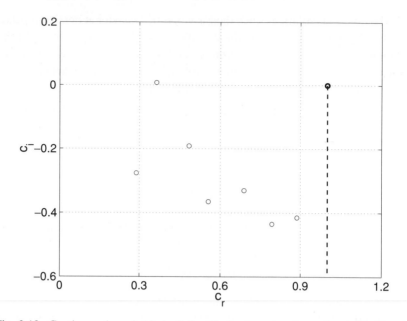

Fig. 3.13. Continuum branch (dashed) for Blasius boundary layer flow with $U_1 = 1$, $Re = 580$ and $\alpha = 0.179$. Also shown as circles are the associated discrete eigenvalues.

continuous spectrum until, when at some minimum value of the Reynolds number, there are no discrete eigenvalues[1]. Another way of stating this is, as the Reynolds number increases, new stable modes "pop off" the continuum. At least one of these new modes will move into the upper half of the complex c-plane, giving rise to unstable solutions. This behavior is shown graphically in Fig. 3.14 where we plot the location of the eigenvalues in the complex c-plane as the Reynolds number varies. Note that the number of eigenvalues decreases with decreasing Reynolds number, and that each eigenvalue disappears as it moves towards the continuum. So, for example, the unstable eigenvalue shown at $Re = 580$ (filled disk) moves into the stable region (defined as $c_i < 0$) between $Re = 350$ and $Re = 250$, then continues to move downward and to the right as Re further decreases ($Re = 150, 50, 25, 5, 4$), until it merges onto the continuum at a Reynolds number slightly less than 4[2].

---

[1] In contrast, for channel flows where the spectrum is an infinite set of discrete modes, the discrete modes approach zero as the Reynolds number goes to infinity.

[2] At such a low Reynolds number the Blasius boundary layer approximation ceases to be valid, but we ignore this here in order to make the above illustration clear.

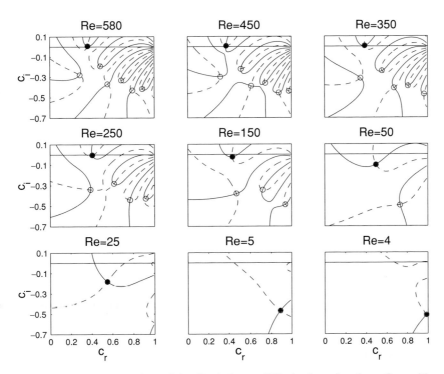

Fig. 3.14. Zero contour lines of the discriminate of Blasius boundary layer flow with $U_1 = 1$ and $\alpha = 0.179$ as a function of the Reynolds number; $D_r = 0$ solid; $D_i = 0$ dash. The circles denote intersection points where $D_r = D_i = 0$. The right domain $c_r = 1$, $c_i < 0$ corresponds to the continuum.

The continuum eigenfunction corresponding to ω_k is now given by

$$\psi_{\alpha_k}(y, t) = \phi_{\alpha_k}(y)e^{-i\omega_k t}. \tag{3.27}$$

The general solution in Fourier space is the sum of the discrete spectrum and the continuum, and can be written as

$$\psi_\alpha(y, t) = \sum_{n=1}^{N(\alpha)} \psi_{\alpha_n}(y, t) + \int_0^\infty \psi_{\alpha_k}(y, t)\mathrm{d}k$$

$$= \sum_{n=1}^{N(\alpha)} A_{\alpha_n}\phi_{\alpha_n}(y)e^{-i\omega_n t} + \int_0^\infty A_{\alpha_k}\phi_{\alpha_k}(y)e^{-i\omega_k t}\mathrm{d}k, \tag{3.28}$$

where the coefficients $\{A_{\alpha_n}\}$ and A_{α_k} are found by taking the inner products with respect to the eigenfunctions of the associated adjoint problem. Details and formulas for these coefficients can be found in Grosch & Salwen (1978)

and Salwen & Grosch (1981). The complete solution in physical space can be written as

$$\psi(x, y, t) = \int_{-\infty}^{+\infty} \left\{ \sum_{n=1}^{N(\alpha)} A_{\alpha_n} \phi_{\alpha_n}(y) e^{-i\omega_n t} \right.$$
$$\left. + \int_0^\infty A_{\alpha_k} \phi_{\alpha_k}(y) e^{-i\omega_k t} dk \right\} e^{i\alpha x} d\alpha. \qquad (3.29)$$

3.7 Exercises

1. Develop a numerical code based on the Compound Matrix method (see the Appendix) which solves the generalized fourth-order equation (3.30). Be sure to write the code in double precision (16 significant digits).

   (a) Verify the correctness of the new code by reproducing Figs. 3.1 and 3.2 and Table 3.1 for plane Poiseuille flow.
   (b) Extend the code to unbounded domains, and verify the code by reproducing Fig. 3.6 and 3.9 and Table 3.2 for Blasius boundary layer flow.
   (c) Compute the eigenfunction for plane Poiseuille flow with $Re = 10\,000$, $\alpha = 1$ and phase speed c corresponding to the unstable mode.
   (d) Compute the eigenfunction for the Blasius boundary layer with $Re = 580$, $\alpha = 0.179$ and phase speed c corresponding to the unstable mode.

   [Note: Verification and Validation are two important aspects of Computational Sciences. Verification asks the question, "Does the code solve the equations correctly?" This is usually answered by comparing the output of the new code to solutions generated by an older code, performing grid-resolution checks, or comparing numerical solutions to simple known analytical solutions. Validation asks the question, "Does the code have the right physics?" or, "Does the model you are trying to solve numerically have the correct equations?". Both aspects, verification and validation, should be kept in mind when dealing with numerical solutions.]

2. The Asymptotic Suction Profile is an exact solution of the Navier-Stokes equations under the assumptions

$$U(\infty) = U_0, \quad U(0) = 0, \quad V(0) = -V_s,$$

where U_0 is the freestream crossflow velocity, and V_s is the blowing ($V_s < 0$) or suction ($V_s > 0$) parameter.

(a) Assuming the mean profile is a function of y only, deduce the nondimensional solution

$$U = 1 - e^{-y}, \quad V = -1/Re, \quad P = const,$$

where the reference length is $L = \nu/V_s$, the reference velocity is U_0, and the Reynolds number is defined as $Re = U_0 L/\nu = U_0/V_s$.

(b) Using the Orr-Sommerfeld equation (2.31), compute the temporal stability characteristics. In particular, show that the critical Reynolds number is $Re_{crit} = 47,047$, with $\alpha_{crit} = 0.1630$ and $c_{crit} = 0.1559$ (see Hughes & Reid, 1965a, b; Drazin & Reid, 1984). Note that e^{-y} has a rather slow decay rate as $y \to \infty$, and so typically one must choose $y_2 = 16$ or larger. Note that $V_{s,crit} = U_0/Re_{crit} = 2.13 \times 10^{-5} U_0$, and so only a small fraction of the suction parameter is needed to stabilize the flow when compared to the Blasius boundary layer flow.

(c) Derive, from first principles, the modified Orr-Sommerfeld equation

$$(U - c)(D^2 - \alpha^2)\phi - U''\phi = \frac{1}{i\alpha Re}\{(D^2 - \alpha^2)^2 + (D^2 - \alpha^2)D\}\phi,$$

for the Asymptotic Suction profile (Hughes & Reid, 1965a,b). Here, $D = d/dy$ and prime denotes differentiation with respect to y.

(d) For the modified Orr-Sommerfeld equation, compute the continuous spectrum and sketch it in the complex c-plane.

(e) For the modified Orr-Sommerfeld equation, compute the temporal stability characteristics. Show graphically that there are a finite number of stable modes, and that the stable modes pop off the continuum as the Reynolds number increases (alternatively, show that the eigenvalues merge towards the continuum as the Reynolds number decreases, starting at a sufficiently large Reynolds number so as to have more than one mode). Finally, show that the critical Reynolds number is $Re_{crit} = 54,370$ with $\alpha_{crit} = 0.1555$ and $c_{crit} = 0.150$ (Hocking, 1975).

(f) Comparing the critical Reynolds number obtained in parts (b) and (e), discuss the reason for the differences. What lesson should be learned here?

3. Consider the Falkner-Skan family (3.9). Using asymptotic expansions, show that in the limit $\beta \to \infty$, the solution of (3.9) is given by

$$U = 3 \tanh^2 \left\{ \frac{z}{\sqrt{2}} + \tanh^{-1} \left(\frac{2}{3}\right)^{1/2} \right\} - 2,$$

where $\eta = z/\sqrt{\beta}$ is the scaled coordinate. Using this profile, compute the temporal stability characteristics using the Orr-Sommerfeld equation (2.31).

In particular, show that the critical Reynolds number is $Re_{\delta,crit} = 21,675$, with $\alpha_{\delta,crit} = 0.1738$ and $c_{crit} = 0.1841$.

4. Consider the Falkner-Skan profile (3.9).

   (a) Make a plot of the neutral stability boundaries in the (α, Re_δ) plane for $\beta = 10, \ 1, \ 0.5, \ 0, \ -0.1, \ -0.19$.

   (b) For the values of β just listed, confirm the critical Reynolds numbers with those listed in Table 3.3.

   (c) For the negative values of β, compute the inviscid limit using Rayleigh's equation (2.32).

5. Consider the constant mean profile

$$U = U_1, \quad V = 0, \quad P = const, \quad 0 < y < \infty,$$

which is a slip past a bounding plate at $y = 0$. Although the velocity does not vanish at the plate, assume that the disturbance velocity does.

   (a) Show that the general solution to the Orr-Sommerfeld equation (2.31) can be written as

$$\phi = Ae^{-\alpha y} + Be^{+\alpha y} + Ce^{-py} + De^{+py},$$

   where $p^2 = \alpha^2 + i\alpha Re(U_1 - c)$.

   (b) If $Re(p) > 0$, show that the only solution which satisfies the boundary conditions $\phi(0) = \phi'(0) = 0$ is the trivial solution.

   (c) Show that only a continuum exists if $p = ik, \quad 0 < k < \infty$ is purely imaginary, and deduce the solution

$$\phi_k = A\{e^{-\alpha y} - \cos(ky) + \alpha k^{-1}\sin(ky)\},$$

   with eigenvalue

$$\omega_k = \alpha U_1 - i(\alpha^2 + k^2)/Re.$$

3.8 Appendix: compound matrix method

Although many numerical methods exist that can be used to solve the Orr-Sommerfeld equation, e.g., initial-value, finite difference, Galerkin, spectral, etc., we shall present here only the Compound Matrix method because of its relative ease of implementation. Basically, one only needs to be familiar with Runge-Kutta methods to be successful in solving the Orr-Sommerfeld equation. Other methods require much more knowledge. We do not, however, pretend that the Compound Matrix method is as efficient as other methods; some methods work better than others given differing circumstances. The use of compound matrices to solve the Orr-Sommerfeld equation was first presented

by Ng & Reid (1979, 1980), and the presentation here draws from their work (the method is also presented in Drazin & Reid, 1984; see also Davey, 1980).

Consider the general fourth-order differential equation

$$\phi'''' - a_1\phi''' - a_2\phi'' - a_3\phi' - a_4\phi = 0, \quad y_1 \le y \le y_2, \quad (3.30)$$

where primes denote differentiation with respect to y, and $a_1 - a_4$ are coefficients which may be functions of the independent variable. This equation must be solved subject to appropriate boundary conditions at y_1 and y_2. For the particular case of the Orr-Sommerfeld equation,

$$a_1 = 0, \ a_2 = 2\alpha^2 + i\alpha Re(U - c),$$
$$a_3 = 0, \ a_4 = -\{\alpha^4 + i\alpha Re[\alpha^2(U - c) + U'']\}, \quad (3.31)$$

where $U(y)$ is the mean profile, α and Re are real parameters, and c is the complex eigenvalue.

Let ϕ_1 and ϕ_2 be any two solutions which satisfies the boundary conditions at y_2. We now consider the matrix

$$\Phi = \begin{bmatrix} \phi_1 & \phi_2 \\ \phi_1' & \phi_2' \\ \phi_1'' & \phi_2'' \\ \phi_1''' & \phi_2''' \end{bmatrix}. \quad (3.32)$$

The 2×2 minors of Φ, in lexical order, are

$$Y_1 = \phi_1\phi_2' - \phi_1'\phi_2, \ Y_4 = \phi_1'\phi_2'' - \phi_1''\phi_2',$$
$$Y_2 = \phi_1\phi_2'' - \phi_1''\phi_2, \ Y_5 = \phi_1'\phi_2''' - \phi_1'''\phi_2',$$
$$Y_3 = \phi_1\phi_2''' - \phi_1'''\phi_2, \ Y_6 = \phi_1''\phi_2''' - \phi_1'''\phi_2'', \quad (3.33)$$

and they satisfy the quadratic identity

$$Y_1 Y_6 - Y_2 Y_5 + Y_3 Y_4 = 0, \quad (3.34)$$

which is a useful check to the accuracy of the numerical integration. Differential equations for Y_1 to Y_6 may be found by differentiating (3.33) and using (3.30) to eliminate ϕ_1, ϕ_2, yielding the linear system

$$Y_1' = Y_2,$$
$$Y_2' = Y_3 + Y_4,$$
$$Y_3' = a_3 Y_1 + a_2 Y_2 + a_1 Y_3 + Y_5,$$
$$Y_4' = Y_5,$$
$$Y_5' = -a_4 Y_1 + a_2 Y_4 + a_1 Y_5 + Y_6,$$
$$Y_6' = -a_4 Y_2 - a_3 Y_4 + a_1 Y_6. \quad (3.35)$$

In general, we always integrate the system from y_2 down to y_1. The boundary conditions at y_2 depend on the mean profile. For channel flows we take $y_2 = 1$, the centerline of the channel. For symmetric disturbances we impose the condition $\phi'(1) = \phi'''(1) = 0$. This leads to the conditions $Y_2(1) = 1$ with all other quantities set to zero. The proper boundary conditions for the Blasius boundary layer is somewhat more complicated. We begin by noting that as $y \to \infty$, $U \to 1$, $U'' \to 0$, and

$$\phi_1 \to e^{-\alpha y}, \quad \phi_2 \to e^{-py}, \tag{3.36}$$

where

$$p = \sqrt{\alpha^2 + i\alpha Re(1 - c)}, \quad Re(p) > 0. \tag{3.37}$$

Substitution into (3.33) yields the asymptotic boundary conditions

$$Y_1 = 1, \; Y_4 = \alpha p,$$
$$Y_2 = -(\alpha + p), \; Y_5 = -\alpha p(\alpha + p),$$
$$Y_3 = \alpha^2 + \alpha p + p^2, \; Y_6 = \alpha^2 p^2, \tag{3.38}$$

where we have eliminated the exponential factors and normalized Y_1 for convenience. Typically y_2 ranges from 5 to 10, depending on the value of the Reynolds number.

When y_1 corresponds to a wall (as it does for channel flows and semi-infinite flows), the proper boundary condition is $\phi(0) = \phi'(0) = 0$. Examining (3.33) yields the condition $Y_1(0) = 0$ which determines the eigenvalue c; setting $D = Y_1(0)$ is then the discriminate. This condition is usually normalized by the largest growth rate of the variables $Y_i(0)$ to make the actual quantity finite when c is not an eigenvalue.

The numerical solution now proceeds as follows. Given a particular mean profile, we fix the values of α and Re and guess an initial value for the eigenvalue c. We then integrate the system (3.35) from y_2 to $y_1 = 0$ using a standard fourth-order Runge-Kutta scheme (although variable step schemes with error control would also work), and determine the value of the discriminate $D = Y_1(0)$. If the discriminate is not zero, we use an iterative procedure to update the value of c until $|D|$ is less than some prescribed tolerance; the value of c is then the required eigenvalue. The iterative method that we usually employ for finding complex eigenvalues is Muller's method (see, e.g., Press, Teukolsky, Vetterling & Flannery 1992). This procedure determines one eigenvalue at a time, and usually requires a sufficiently close initial guess to determine the eigenvalue. Alternatively, one can loop over some region in the complex c-plane, determine the value of D at each (c_r, c_i) point, plot the

contours of D_r and D_i, and write a short post-processing code which determines the intersection points. These then provide initial guesses which can be substituted back into the iterative method to determine the eigenvalues with more precision ("polishing"). The entire process can be written within a single code if desired.

Once an eigenvalue has been found, the Compound Matrix method can be used to determine the corresponding eigenfunction. Having found c and Y_i, we reason that there must exist constants λ_1 and λ_2 such that

$$\phi = \lambda_1 \phi_1 + \lambda_2 \phi_2. \tag{3.39}$$

By differentiating the above relation three times, and eliminating the constants λ_1 and λ_2, we obtain the following four relations

$$Y_1 \phi'' - Y_2 \phi' + Y_4 \phi = 0,$$
$$Y_1 \phi''' - Y_3 \phi' + Y_5 \phi = 0,$$
$$Y_2 \phi''' - Y_3 \phi'' + Y_6 \phi = 0,$$
$$Y_4 \phi''' - Y_5 \phi'' + Y_6 \phi' = 0. \tag{3.40}$$

The eigenfunction ϕ is then determined by integrating any one of the four relations from $y = 0$ to $y = y_2$. Since $Y_1(0) = 0$, the first two relations can not be integrated starting at $y = 0$ (Ng & Reid, 1979, showed that this is only a minor problem, and one can start at one grid point away from the origin). By trial and error, Davey (1984) noted that the third relation gave slightly more accurate results than the fourth for the specific case of Blasius boundary layer flow, with the normalization $\phi''(0) = (1 - i)Re^{1/2}$. We only remark here that the solutions Y_i need to be stored in tables, and then use these as reference tables as part of the integration scheme for ϕ.

Chapter 4

Spatial stability of incompressible flows

4.1 Discussion

So far we have only dealt with situations when the oscillations are periodic in space ($\alpha_i = 0$) and growing, decaying, or remaining neutral in time as $e^{\omega_i t}$. In reality, most fluid oscillations have an amplitude that is constant with time but grow, or amplify, in some spatial direction. Examples include the boundary layer and free shear flows, such as the mixing layer, jets and wakes. Hence, this situation corresponds to equations in which α is complex and the frequency ω is real, with the previous definition $\omega = \alpha c$. It should be noted that if α is complex, then ω cannot be real unless c is also complex. That is, if ω is real, then $\omega = \omega_r$, $\omega_i = 0$, and from (2.27) we have the relations

$$\omega_r = \alpha_r c_r - \alpha_i c_i; \quad \omega_i = \alpha_r c_i + \alpha_i c_r = 0.$$

From the point of view of mathematical analysis it is much more convenient to have a complex ω than a complex α. This becomes even more significant when viscous effects are considered. Furthermore, from a fundamental point of view, we note from the governing equations (2.1) to (2.3), that the time derivative is always first-order and has a coefficient of unity. On the other hand, when solved numerically, the transition to complex α adds only a few more operations to the program. We could modify the searching procedure in such a way that, given a particular ω, the code will search for the complex α that will satisfy the boundary conditions. Thus it is α that becomes an eigenvalue in place of ω.

It is important to note that, whether the growth occurs in time or in space, the neutral line is the same. Indeed, if $\alpha_i = c_i = 0$, we have $\omega_i = 0$.

In the context of hydrodynamic stability theory, the first correct treatment of spatial stability theory was done by Gaster (1962, 1965a,b)[1]. Prior to 1962, spatial stability calculations were carried out by first computing temporal

---

[1] Historically, the topic of spatial stability was a part of Gaster's dissertation but was never published because of little acceptance of the theory at the time. However, the concept of spatial

modes and then relating those to spatial modes by means of the phase velocity; i.e., $\omega_i = -c_r \alpha_i$ (see the review article by Dunn, 1960). Such a simple relation is not valid in general, and very little progress was made as a result. Gaster corrected the relationship by making use of the group velocity instead of the phase velocity. In the first paper Gaster noted that there exists an asymptotic relation between temporally increasing and spatially increasing disturbances. This relation is now referred to as the Gaster transformation in honor of this important contribution to hydrodynamic stability theory, and is presented in the section below. In the second paper a general discussion was put forward together with a specific example. The third work specifically demonstrated that the spatial problem corresponds more correctly to the experiments of Schubauer & Skramstad (1943) for the laminar boundary layer. Since this time there have been many important contributions to spatial stability theory, and we present some of these in subsequent sections.

4.2 Gaster's transformation

The general solution to the Orr-Sommerfeld equation at a fixed Reynolds number yields a dispersion relation between the wavenumber and frequency[1], given by

$$F(\alpha, \omega) = 0. \tag{4.1}$$

Suppose now that the frequency ω is an analytic function of the wavenumber α, so that $\omega = \omega(\alpha)$. Then, according to the Cauchy-Riemann equations, we have

$$\frac{\partial \omega_r}{\partial \alpha_r} = \frac{\partial \omega_i}{\partial \alpha_i}, \quad \frac{\partial \omega_r}{\partial \alpha_i} = -\frac{\partial \omega_i}{\partial \alpha_r}. \tag{4.2}$$

With these relations we can integrate over α_i from the S state shown in Fig. 4.1 to the T state, keeping α_r fixed. The S state corresponds to ω real and α complex, while the T state corresponds to ω complex and α real.

Integration of the Cauchy-Riemann equations gives

$$\omega_i \big|_S^T = \int_S^T \frac{\partial \omega_r}{\partial \alpha_r} d\alpha_i \tag{4.3}$$

and

$$\omega_r \big|_S^T = -\int_S^T \frac{\partial \omega_i}{\partial \alpha_r} d\alpha_i. \tag{4.4}$$

stability was previously noted in the physics literature (see Briggs, 1964), but apparently unknown to the fluids community until later.
[1] The following discussion is true for any homogeneous, nonconservative system where a dispersion relation is defined.

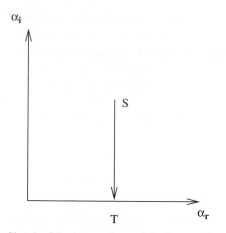

Fig. 4.1. Sketch of the integration path in the complex α plane.

Equation (4.3) can be simplified to

$$\omega_i(T) = \int_S^0 \frac{\partial \omega_r}{\partial \alpha_r} d\alpha_i, \qquad (4.5)$$

because $\omega_i(S) = 0$ and on the right hand side the T state corresponds to $\alpha_i = 0$. We thus have

$$\omega_i(T) = -\int_0^S \frac{\partial \omega_r}{\partial \alpha_r} d\alpha_i,$$

$$\approx -\frac{\partial \omega_r}{\partial \alpha_r}\bigg|_{\alpha_i^*} \alpha_i(S), \qquad (4.6)$$

provided the S state is close to zero; i.e., for an S state close to the neutral state where $\alpha_i = 0$ we can expand the integral in a Taylor series about S. Here, α_i^* is any value between zero and S. For dispersive systems we can define a group velocity as

$$c_g = \frac{\partial \omega_r}{\partial \alpha_r}, \qquad (4.7)$$

and thus the above equation can be rewritten as

$$\omega_i(T) = c_g \{-\alpha_i(S)\}. \qquad (4.8)$$

Equation (4.8) is called the Gaster transformation (Gaster, 1962) and relates the growth rate ω_i of temporal calculations to the growth rate $-\alpha_i$ of spatial calculations by means of the group velocity c_g. It is important to keep in mind

that this relationship is with respect to the group velocity c_g and not the phase speed c_r.

In a similar fashion, equation (4.4) can be simplified to

$$\omega_r(T) - \omega_r(S) = \int_0^S \frac{\partial \omega_i}{\partial \alpha_r} d\alpha_i. \tag{4.9}$$

Expanding the integral in a Taylor series, and then taking the maximum of both sides, results in

$$|\omega_r(T) - \omega_r(S)| \leq \max \left| \frac{\partial \omega_i}{\partial \alpha_r} \right| |\alpha_i(S)| + \cdots \tag{4.10}$$

Because the first term of the product on the right-hand side is bounded and the last term of the product is small near a neutral mode, we must therefore have

$$\omega_r(T) \approx \omega_r(S). \tag{4.11}$$

Thus, the real part of the frequency for temporal modes is approximately equal to the real part of the frequency for spatial modes provided one is in a small neighborhood about the neutral line.

One final comment is in order here. Caution must be exercised to insure that the group velocity is positive when attempting to apply the Gaster transformation for the usual type of flows considered here. Positive group velocities corresponds to waves traveling downstream, in harmony with the assumption that disturbances grow in the downstream direction. Negative group velocities travel upstream, and it would be incorrect to assume in this case that the flow is unstable.

4.3 Incompressible inviscid flow

In this section we present the spatial stability results of various mean profiles of incompressible inviscid flows. These include the mixing layer, jet, and wake.

4.3.1 Hyperbolic tangent profile

Consider the mixing layer given by the hyperbolic tangent profile

$$U(y) = \frac{1}{2}[1 + \tanh y]. \tag{4.12}$$

Michalke (1965) first considered the spatial stability for this profile, and much of this section draws upon his work. His primary motivation was that his earlier temporal stability calculations, presented in Section 2.6.1, did not agree well with the existing experimental data. In particular, the temporal calculations

Table 4.1. *Wavenumber and phase speed as a function of the*
frequency ω for the hyperbolic tangent profile.

ω	α_r	α_i	c_r	c_i
0.50	1.0	0.0	0.5	0.0
0.40	0.844361	−0.091617	0.468219	0.050804
0.30	0.649548	−0.180225	0.428845	0.118989
0.20	0.382625	−0.227690	0.386014	0.229706
0.10	0.128090	−0.120375	0.414570	0.389600
0	0.0	0.0	0.5	0.5

show that the phase velocity c_r was a constant and hence the wavenumber and
frequency were proportional to each other. This was found to be contrary to
what was observed experimentally. Thus, it was thought that perhaps spatial
calculations would better correlate to the physics. This was indeed the case, as
will be shown.

Recall from Section 2.6.1 that the neutral mode for the hyperbolic tangent
profile is given by

$$\omega_N = 0.5, \quad \alpha_N = 1, \quad c_N = 0.5, \tag{4.13}$$

with the corresponding eigenfunction

$$\mathbf{v}_N = \text{sech } y. \tag{4.14}$$

For values in the unstable region away from the neutral mode, Rayleigh's equation must be solved numerically. Table 4.1 shows the results of the numerical
solution, and Fig. 4.2 plots the spatial growth rate as a function of frequency.
We remark here that the phase velocity reported in Table I of Michalke (1965)
used the relationship $c_{ph} = \omega/\alpha_r$, a physically meaningful quantity that can
be measured in the laboratory. In contrast, the real part of the phase speed is
defined as $c_r = (\omega + \alpha_i c_i)/\alpha_r \equiv \omega\alpha_r/(\alpha_r^2 + \alpha_i^2)$, consistent with the definition
$\omega = \alpha c$ with ω real and α, c complex. Comparing the two, we see that c_{ph} and
c_r are not the same for spatial theory, and caution should be exercised so as not
to confuse the two. As mentioned, the phase velocity c_{ph} depends strongly on
the frequency, consistent with experimental observations.

Michalke also showed that the eigenfunctions ϕ_r and ϕ_i are neither symmetric nor antisymmetric about the origin, as was the case for temporal stability.
Thus, the derivatives ϕ_r' and ϕ_i' have zeros away from the critical layer located
at $y = 0$, implying that there is flow reversal away from the critical layer, again
consistent with experimental observations.

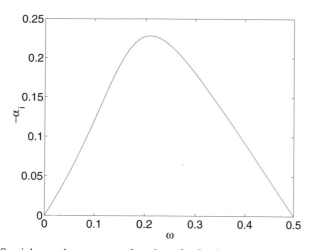

Fig. 4.2. Spatial growth rate α_i as a function of ω for the hyperbolic tangent profile.

The above discussion suggests that spatial stability theory, and not temporal theory, is better able to describe the observations seen in experiments.

As in the temporal case, it is of interest to examine the vorticity distribution since it gives us a means to visualize the dynamics of the mixing layer. Define the spanwise vorticity in the usual fashion as

$$\omega_z = v_x - u_y. \tag{4.15}$$

In terms of the normal mode approach, we have

$$
\begin{aligned}
\omega_z &= -[U'(y) + \epsilon \tilde{u}_y(x, y, t)] + \epsilon \tilde{v}_x(x, y, t) \\
&= -U' + \epsilon(-\psi_{yy} - \psi_{xx}) \\
&= -U' + \epsilon(-\phi'' + \alpha^2 \phi)e^{i\alpha(x - ct)},
\end{aligned} \tag{4.16}
$$

where ϵ is the initial amplitude of the disturbance. If we define

$$\tilde{\omega}_{z_r}(y) = \mathrm{Re}(-\phi'' + \alpha^2 \phi), \quad \tilde{\omega}_{z_i}(y) = \mathrm{Im}(-\phi'' + \alpha^2 \phi), \tag{4.17}$$

then the total vorticity can be written as

$$\omega_z = -\frac{1}{2}\mathrm{sech}^2 y + \epsilon e^{-\alpha_i x}[\tilde{\omega}_{z_r}\cos(\alpha_r x - \omega t) - \tilde{\omega}_{z_i}\sin(\alpha_r x - \omega t)]. \tag{4.18}$$

Note that the vorticity distribution is periodic in time and grows exponentially in the downstream direction. A plot of the normalized eigenfunction ϕ and perturbation vorticity $\tilde{\omega}_z$ are shown in Fig. 4.3, corresponding to the most unstable

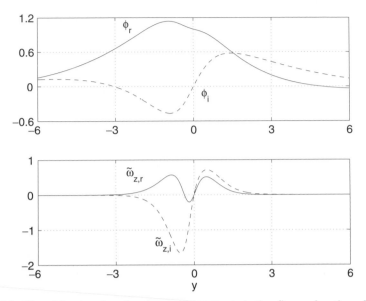

Fig. 4.3. Plot of the eigenfunction ϕ and vorticity perturbation $\tilde{\omega}_z$ as a function of y for $\omega_{max} = 0.2067$, $\alpha_r = 0.4031$, $\alpha_i = -0.2284$. The mean flow is given by the hyperbolic tangent profile. (After Michalke, 1965).

wave. A contour plot of the vorticity distribution is shown in Fig. 4.4 at two different times and for $\epsilon = 0.0005$. The value of the wavenumber corresponds to the maximum growth rate ($\omega_{max} = 0.2067$). Since the flow is periodic in time, the period is given by $T = 2\pi/\omega_{max} = 30.40$. Note that with increasing x, two peaks of vorticity are formed which will ultimately induce a rotational motion on the base flow, showing the mechanism of spatial instability.

4.3.2 Symmetric jet

The symmetric jet is given by the profile

$$U(y) = \text{sech}^2 y, \tag{4.19}$$

which can be obtained from a similarity analysis of the boundary layer type equations (c.f., White, 1974). Betchov & Criminale (1966) first considered the spatial stability of this profile, and much of this section draws from their work. The inflection point or critical layer is found by setting $U'' = 0$, i.e.,

$$U'' = -2\text{sech}^2 y(3\text{sech}^2 y - 2) = 0, \tag{4.20}$$

thus,

$$\text{sech}^2 y = \frac{2}{3}, \tag{4.21}$$

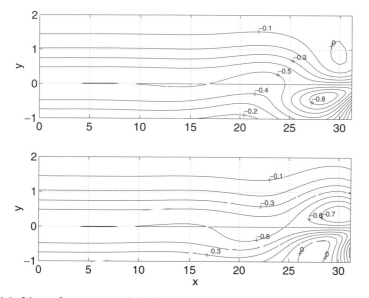

Fig. 4.4. Lines of constant vorticity for the case of maximum amplification $\omega_{max} = 0.2067$, $\alpha_r = 0.4031$, $\alpha_i = -0.2284$ at times $t = T$ (top) and $t = 1.5\,T$ (bottom) with $\epsilon = 0.0005$. The mean flow is given by the hyperbolic tangent profile. (After Michalke, 1965).

with solution $y_s = \pm 0.6585$. Thus, there are two neutral modes with phase speeds given by $c_N = U(y_s) = 2/3$. The neutral modes with corresponding eigenfunctions are given by

$$\text{Mode I:} \quad \alpha_N = 2, \quad c_N = 2/3, \quad \omega_N = 4/3, \quad \phi_N = \text{sech}^2 y,$$
$$\text{Mode II:} \quad \alpha_N = 1, \quad c_N = 2/3, \quad \omega_N = 2/3, \quad \phi_N = \sinh y \, \text{sech}^2 y.$$

Some authors classify Mode I as the even or symmetric mode since the streamfunction (and v) is an even function about the origin, while Mode II is classified as an odd or asymmetric mode. Other authors classify the modes with respect to u; through continuity we see that this is opposite for that of v; hence, Mode I would be classified as the odd or asymmetric mode while Mode II would be classified as the even or symmetric mode. We shall avoid confusion by simply using the notation of Mode I and Mode II.

For values in the unstable region away from the neutral mode, Rayleigh's equation must be solved numerically. The appropriate boundary conditions are

$$\text{Mode I:} \quad \phi'(0) = \phi(\infty) = 0,$$
$$\text{Mode II:} \quad \phi(0) = \phi(\infty) = 0.$$

Table 4.2. *Wavenumber and phase speed as a function of frequency ω for Mode I of the symmetric jet.*

ω	α_r	α_i	c_r	c_i
1.33333	2.0	0.0	0.666666	0.0
1.2	1.871369	−0.029338	0.641084	0.010050
1.0	1.668919	−0.078618	0.597864	0.028164
0.8	1.449709	−0.134110	0.547152	0.050616
0.6	1.203398	−0.194503	0.485895	0.078534
0.4	0.908688	−0.253103	0.408502	0.113783
0.2	0.516928	−0.269983	0.303981	0.158764
0.1	0.270462	−0.206506	0.233571	0.178338
0.0	0.0	0.0	0.0	0.0

Table 4.3. *Wavenumber and phase speed as a function of frequency ω for Mode II of the symmetric jet.*

ω	α_r	α_i	c_r	c_i
0.66667	1.0	0.0	0.666666	0.0
0.6	0.901124	−0.026220	0.665272	0.019357
0.5	0.741506	−0.059703	0.669960	0.053942
0.4	0.569285	−0.077614	0.689814	0.094046
0.3	0.396154	−0.070126	0.734273	0.129978
0.2	0.241420	−0.043023	0.802932	0.143088
0.1	0.110847	−0.014792	0.886360	0.118279
0.0	0.0	0.0	1.0	0.0

Note that the boundary condition $\phi = 0$ at $y = -\infty$ is replaced by boundary conditions along the centerline; the boundary condition for Mode I implies that we are searching for an even function about $y = 0$, while the boundary condition for Mode II implies that we are searching for an odd solution. Tables 4.2 and 4.3 shows the results of the numerical solution for each mode, and Fig. 4.5 plots the spatial growth rate as a function of wavenumber, respectively. As in the temporal case, Mode I is the most unstable since it has the largest growth rate.

4.3.3 Symmetric wake

The symmetric wake is given by the profile

$$U(y) = 1 - Q\operatorname{sech}^2 y, \tag{4.22}$$

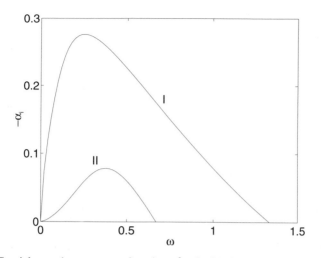

Fig. 4.5. Spatial growth rate α_i as a function of ω for Modes I and II of the symmetric jet.

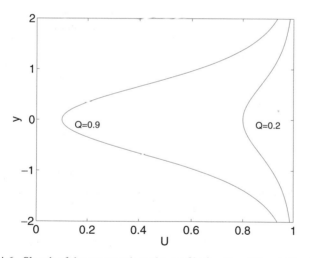

Fig. 4.6. Sketch of the symmetric wake profile for $Q = 0.2$ and $Q = 0.9$.

where Q measures the wake deficit. A sketch of the velocity profile is shown in Fig. 4.6. This profile can also be obtained from a similarity analysis of the boundary layer type equations (c.f., White, 1974). Note that Q is a parameter of the mean flow and in this sense the stability characteristics will change with changes in the value of Q. Betchov & Criminale (1966) first considered the spatial stability of this profile, and much of this section draws from their work.

Before we present their work, however, we note that the sech^2, as well as the Gaussian $1 - Qe^{-by^2}$, velocity distributions are the far-wake representation of the mean flow. Papageorgiou & Smith (1989) examined the wake stability characteristics of the near-wake region using a correct mean flow that satisfies the equations of motion for large Reynolds numbers (the wake boundary layer equations of Goldstein, 1930). The nonlinear development was analyzed in Papageorgiou & Smith (1988). The overall picture that emerges for incompressible wakes is that the disturbances grow linearly and two-dimensionally just downstream of the trailing edge of the plate. These two-dimensional disturbances then become nonlinear before three-dimensional effects lead to transition to turbulence. The important point of the work is that the stability of the wake is highly sensitive to the undisturbed flow. Since Gaussian or sech^2 profiles are far-wake representations of the mean flow, their range of applicability is limited. It is likely, therefore, that at positions where these profiles can be used rationally the flow is already nonlinear and a substantial history of the evolution is lost.

To find the neutral phase speeds we again find the value of y_s where U'' $(y_s) = 0$. This yields the same locations as in the symmetric jet described above, and thus $y_s = \pm 0.6585$. Setting $c_N = U(y_s)$ we see that there are two neutral modes with phase speeds given by $c_N = 1 - \frac{2}{3}Q$. The neutral modes with corresponding eigenfunctions are given by

$$\text{Mode I: } \alpha_N = 2, \quad c_N = 1 - \frac{2}{3}Q, \quad \omega_N = \alpha_N c_N, \quad \phi_N = \text{sech}^2 y,$$

$$\text{Mode II: } \alpha_N = 1, \quad c_N = 1 - \frac{2}{3}Q, \quad \omega_N = \alpha_N c_N, \quad \phi_N = \sinh y \, \text{sech}^2 y.$$

For values in the unstable region away from the neutral mode, Rayleigh's equation must be solved numerically. The appropriate boundary conditions are

$$\text{Mode I: } \phi'(0) = \phi(\infty) = 0,$$
$$\text{Mode II: } \phi(0) = \phi(\infty) = 0.$$

Tables 4.4 and 4.5 shows the results of the numerical solution for $Q = 0.9$, and Figs. 4.7 and 4.8 plot the spatial growth rate as a function of wavenumber for various values of Q. As in the temporal case, and similar to the symmetric jet profile results, Mode I has the largest growth rate for fixed value of Q.

Betchov & Criminale (1966) noted that for Mode I, spatial calculations could not be carried out for $0.94 < Q < 1$. To investigate the reason for this they plotted the eigenrelation in the complex (α, ω) plane for $Q = 1$, as shown in Fig. 4.9. From this figure we see the curves of constant α_r (and ω_r) and constant α_i (and ω_i) are orthogonal, implying that α (and ω) is an analytic function of ω (and α), except at some special points where the relationship is singular.

Table 4.4. *Wavenumber and phase speed as a function of the frequency
ω for Mode I of the symmetric wake with $Q = 0.9$.*

ω	α_r	α_i	c_r	c_i
0.8	2.0	0.0	0.4	0.0
0.7	1.669684	−0.398176	0.396682	0.094598
0.6	1.087681	−0.548301	0.439857	0.221732
0.5	0.696734	−0.376460	0.555467	0.300130
0.4	0.487767	−0.235489	0.665050	0.321080
0.3	0.336952	−0.138398	0.761815	0.312903
0.2	0.212425	−0.070076	0.849107	0.280107
0.1	0.102224	−0.023607	0.928719	0.214471
0.0	0.0	0.0	1.0	0.0

Table 4.5. *Wavenumber and phase speed as a function of the frequency
ω for Mode II of the symmetric wake with $Q = 0.9$.*

ω	α_r	α_i	c_r	c_i
0.4	1.0	0.0	0.4	0.0
0.3	0.784912	−0.064028	0.379682	0.030972
0.2	0.555653	−0.093738	0.349977	0.059041
0.1	0.312095	−0.083167	0.299171	0.079723
0.0	0.0	0.0	0.15	0.0

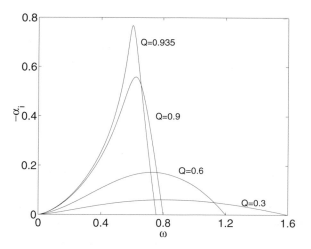

Fig. 4.7. Spatial growth rate α_i as a function of ω for Mode I of the symmetric wake
for various values of Q.

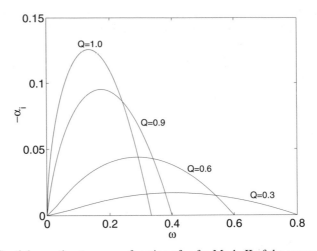

Fig. 4.8. Spatial growth rate α_i as a function of ω for Mode II of the symmetric wake for various values of Q.

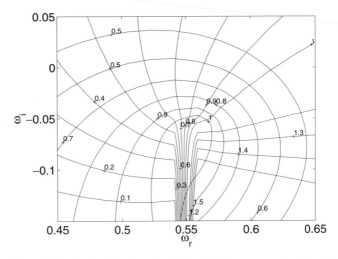

Fig. 4.9. Eigenrelation in the (ω) plane for Mode I of the symmetric wake with $Q = 1$.

A similar analysis for Mode II revealed that no such singularity existed in the eigen relation. Thus, for Mode I of the symmetric wake, we have

$0 < Q < 0.94$ singular point does not appear in the spatial calculations
$Q \approx 0.94$ singular point first appears in the spatial branch;
           cusp forms in the eigenrelation
$0.94 < Q < 1$ the spatial branch can no longer be calculated

We remark here that the singular behavior appears in the upper half plane for $Q < 0.94$, where spatial stability is valid, and then moves down into the lower half plane for $Q > 0.94$.

To investigate the singularity, Betchov & Criminale gave a possible explanation by carrying out the following simple analysis. Assume that ω is an analytic function of α. Then a Laurent series expansion yields

$$\omega = \omega_o + \left.\frac{d\omega}{d\alpha}\right|_{\alpha_o} (\alpha - \alpha_o) + \frac{1}{2}\left.\frac{d^2\omega}{d\alpha^2}\right|_{\alpha_o} (\alpha - \alpha_o)^2 + \cdots. \qquad (4.23)$$

Now assume that the first derivative vanishes at the point α_o

$$\left.\frac{d\omega}{d\alpha}\right|_{\alpha_o} = 0,$$

then the above expansion reduces to

$$\omega = \omega_o + \frac{1}{2}\left.\frac{d^2\omega}{d\alpha^2}\right|_{\alpha_o} (\alpha - \alpha_o)^2 + \cdots. \qquad (4.24)$$

Define $\triangle = (\ ) - (\ )_o$, then equation (4.24) can be rearranged to yield

$$\frac{2\triangle\omega}{d^2\omega/d\alpha^2\big|_{\alpha_o}} = (\triangle\alpha_r)^2 - (\triangle\alpha_i)^2 + 2i\,\triangle\alpha_r\,\triangle\alpha_i. \qquad (4.25)$$

Note that both the real and imaginary parts of the right hand side separately are constant along hyperbole. Thus there is a saddle point at α_o where the first derivative vanishes. But the first derivative is the definition of the complex group velocity; the saddle point occurs when the complex group velocity vanishes. Defining c_g to be the real part of the group velocity, we have

$$0 < Q < 0.94 \quad c_g > 0 \text{ the group velocity is positive}$$
$$Q \approx 0.94 \quad c_g = 0 \text{ the group velocity first becomes zero}$$

Betchov & Criminale state that *"The occurrence of the singularities was completely unexpected."* They suggested that these singular points had some special significance regarding likely modes of instability, but they were unable to explain in what way the flow was influenced by singularities in the eigenvalue relationships. The appearance of these singularities is the first reported occurrence of this behavior in hydrodynamic stability. Further discussion can be found in Mattingly & Criminale (1972) where experiment as well as calculations were made to confirm this result.

Gaster gave a simple interpretation of the singularities found by Betchov & Criminale in terms of an impulse function at $t = 0$ (Gaster, 1968). This work

is of such importance that we outline it in the next section. Today, the concept that singularities or saddle points can develop in the eigen relation as a physical parameter varies plays a pervasive role in our understanding of global instabilities, feedback mechanisms, and to some extent, flow control.

4.4 Absolute and convective instabilities

To explain the significance of the singularities found by Betchov & Criminale (1966) in the dispersion relation of the symmetric wake, Gaster (1968) considered the motion generated by an impulse

$$\tilde{v}(x, 0, t) = \delta(x)\delta(t), \tag{4.26}$$

where δ is the Dirac delta function. Such a disturbance will necessarily excite all modes, and thus any significant irregularities in the dispersion relation will be reflected in the flow. The solution of (2.18) subject to the initial condition given above, plus appropriate boundary conditions, will be an integral of traveling wave modes evaluated over all wavenumbers. Starting with this integral representation of the solution, Gaster then makes an asymptotic expansion in the limit as $t \to \infty$ using the method of steepest descent to explain the significance of the singularities. A more rigorous derivation can be found in Huerre & Monkewitz (1985). Below we briefly outline the main points of Gaster and Huerre & Monkewitz.

The solution to the impulse problem is given by

$$v(x, y, t) = \int_{C_\omega} \int_{C_\alpha} \frac{S(\alpha, y, \omega)}{D(\alpha, \omega)} \, e^{i(\alpha x - \omega t)} d\alpha d\omega, \tag{4.27}$$

where $D(\alpha, \omega)$ is the complex dispersion relation, $S(\alpha, y, \omega)/D(\alpha, \omega)$ is the solution in Fourier space, and the contours C_α and C_ω are the paths of integration for the inversion integrals in the α and ω planes, respectively (see Fig. 4.10). In general the dispersion relation D will have a finite number of zeros and branch cuts, giving rise to a discrete spectrum and a continuum (Grosch & Salwen, 1978; Salwen & Grosch, 1981). For the Fourier inversion to be valid, we first close the C_ω contour, which must lie above all the zeros and branch cuts of D, in the upper half plane $\omega_i > 0$ since then $e^{-i\omega t} = e^{-i\omega_r t} e^{\omega_i t}$ decays for $t < 0$; this satisfies causality in that no disturbances can originate from negative time. For $t > 0$, the contour is closed below C_ω as is shown in Fig. 4.10a and, as already mentioned, the solution can be written as a sum over all the discrete modes (poles in the complex plane) plus the continuum. Since for large time the continuum decays, the only contribution which remains is

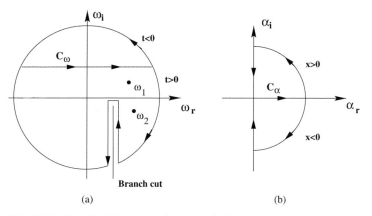

Fig. 4.10. Sketch of the integration paths in the complex ω and α planes.

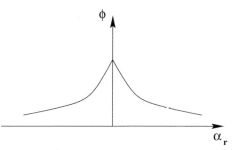

Fig. 4.11. Graph of $\phi = e^{-sgn(\alpha_r)\alpha_r y}$ showing the non-analytic nature at $\alpha_r = 0$.

that corresponding to the pole which has the largest, positive imaginary part, say $\omega_1(\alpha)$.

For the inversion in space to be valid we must close the contour as shown in Fig. 4.10b. The contour must be closed below for $x < 0$ since $e^{i\alpha x} = e^{i\alpha_r x}e^{-\alpha_i x}$ must decay, and must be closed above for $x > 0$ for the same reasoning. The reason why the quarter circle is chosen for the integration path instead of a semi-circle is because $S(\alpha, y, \omega)$ is non-analytic in α on the imaginary axis $\alpha_r = 0$. This stems from the fact that the far field solutions of Rayleigh's equation are $(D^2 - \alpha^2)\phi \approx 0$, or, $\phi \approx e^{-sgn(\alpha_r)\alpha_r y}$ as $y \to \infty$ and similarly as $y \to -\infty$. These solutions are not analytic at $\alpha_r = 0$ (see Fig. 4.11). Therefore, the contour C_α must be restricted to values of α with positive real part.

Applying the residue theorem to the integral over C_ω gives

$$\int_{C_\omega} \frac{S(\alpha, y, \omega)}{D(\alpha, \omega)} e^{i(\alpha x - \omega t)} d\omega = -2\pi i \frac{S(\alpha, y, \omega_1)}{\partial D / \partial \omega|_{\omega_1}} e^{i(\alpha x - \omega_1 t)}, \qquad (4.28)$$

and allows the solution to be rewritten as

$$v(x, y, t) = -2\pi i \int_{C_\alpha} \frac{S(\alpha, y, \omega_1)}{\frac{\partial D}{\partial \omega}\Big|_{\omega_1}} e^{i(\alpha x - \omega_1 t)}. \qquad (4.29)$$

The negative sign is because the convention is to close the contour in a counterclockwise fashion.

We now wish to examine the behavior of v as $t \to \infty$. For large values of t an asymptotic expansion of the integral in (4.29) can be obtained by the method of steepest descent, which involves expanding about the saddle point of the exponent where

$$\frac{d}{d\alpha}(\alpha x/t - \omega_1)$$

is zero; i.e., the saddle point is given by the relation

$$\frac{d\omega_1}{d\alpha}\Big|_{\alpha^*} - \frac{x}{t} = 0.$$

We begin by expanding about the saddle point $\alpha = \alpha^*$

$$\omega_1(\alpha) = \omega_1(\alpha^*) + \frac{d\omega_1}{d\alpha}\Big|_{\alpha^*}(\alpha - \alpha^*) + \frac{1}{2}\frac{d^2\omega_1}{d\alpha^2}\Big|_{\alpha^*}(\alpha - \alpha^*)^2 + \cdots, \qquad (4.30)$$

so that

$$i(\alpha x - \omega_1 t) \approx it\left\{\alpha^* \frac{x}{t} - \omega_1(\alpha^*) - (\alpha - \alpha^*)\left(\frac{d\omega_1}{d\alpha}\Big|_{\alpha^*} - \frac{x}{t}\right)\right.$$
$$\left. - \frac{1}{2}\frac{d^2\omega_1}{d\alpha^2}\Big|_{\alpha^*}(\alpha - \alpha^*)^2\right\}. \qquad (4.31)$$

With the definition of the saddle point, the solution (4.29) becomes

$$v \approx -2\pi i \frac{S(\alpha^*, y, \omega_1(\alpha^*))}{\partial D / \partial \omega|_{\omega_1(\alpha^*)}} e^{i[\alpha^* x - \omega_1(\alpha^*)t]} \int e^{-\frac{it}{2}\frac{d^2\omega_1}{d\alpha^2}\Big|_{\alpha^*}(\alpha - \alpha^*)^2} d\alpha$$

$$\approx -2\pi i \frac{S(\alpha^*, y, \omega_1(\alpha^*))}{\partial D / \partial \omega|_{\omega_1(\alpha^*)}} \frac{\sqrt{\pi} e^{i[\alpha^* x - \omega_1(\alpha^*)t]}}{\sqrt{\frac{it}{2}\frac{d^2\omega_1}{d\alpha^2}\Big|_{\alpha^*}}}. \qquad (4.32)$$

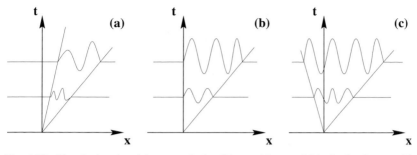

Fig. 4.12. Sketch showing (a) convectively, (b) transition, and (c) absolutely unstable flow.

The character of the solution can be described by defining

$$I(x,t) = \sqrt{\frac{2\pi}{t \, d^2\omega_1/d\alpha^2\big|_{\alpha*}}} \; e^{\Sigma t},$$ (4.33)

where

$$\Sigma = i\left(\alpha^* \frac{x}{t} - \omega(\alpha^*)\right).$$ (4.34)

The values of α^* can be found by satisfying the system of equations

$$\frac{\partial \omega_r}{\partial \alpha_r}(\alpha^*) = \frac{x}{t}$$

$$\frac{\partial \omega_i}{\partial \alpha_i}(\alpha^*) = 0,$$ (4.35)

which is just a restatement of the definition of the saddle point. Sets of $\{\alpha^*, \omega(\alpha^*)\}$ can now be found for any x/t. Once these have been determined, the real part of Σ gives the growth rate of the packet; the unstable region corresponds to $Re(\Sigma) > 0$, the neutral points at $Re(\Sigma) = 0$, and the stable region to $Re(\Sigma) < 0$. The values of $c_g = x/t$ which yield $Re(\Sigma) = 0$ yields neutral rays. The schematic shown in Fig. 4.12 show three possible cases, which are listed below.

1. $c_g > 0$ for both the leading and trailing edges of the wave packet. Wave packet moves downstream from the source as time increases. Flow is convectively unstable. See Fig. 4.12a.
2. $c_g > 0$ for the leading edge and $c_g = 0$ for the trailing edge of the wave packet. Transition case between a convectively unstable flow to an absolutely unstable flow. See Fig. 4.12b.

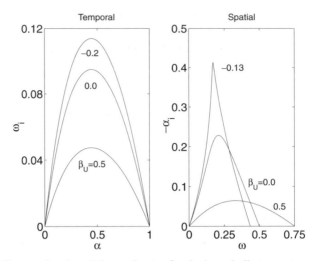

Fig. 4.13. Temporal and spatial growth rates for the hyperbolic tangent profile and for various values of β_U.

3. $c_g > 0$ for the leading edge and $c_g < 0$ for the trailing edge of the wave packet. Wave packet moves downstream and upstream from the source as time increases. Flow is absolutely unstable. See Fig. 4.12c.

Finally, the real part of I defines the wave packet while $|I|$ defines the envelope. Three-dimensional wave packets can be derived in a similar fashion (Gaster & Davey, 1968).

4.4.1 Mixing layer revisited

We return briefly to the mixing layer of Section 4.3.1, but add an additional complexity by means of a parameter β_U. Let

$$U(y) = \frac{1}{2}[1 + \beta_U + (1 - \beta_U)\tanh y] \qquad (4.36)$$

where the parameter β_U is the velocity ratio defined by the velocity of the freestream at $-\infty$ divided by the velocity of the freestream at $+\infty$. The case $\beta_U > 0$ corresponds to coflow, while if $\beta_U < 0$, the mixing layer has a region of reversed flow. This profile was originally considered by Monkewitz & Huerre (1982), and later by Huerre & Monkewitz (1985).

The neutral mode is given by

$$c_N = \frac{1 + \beta_U}{2}, \quad \alpha_N = 1, \quad \omega_N = \alpha_N c_N. \qquad (4.37)$$

The results of both temporal and spatial calculations are presented in Fig. 4.13

for various values of the velocity ratio β_U. Note that a singularity occurs in the spatial branch as β_U approaches the value -0.135. Thus, the flow changes from being convectively unstable to being absolutely unstable as $\beta_U \to -0.135$.

4.5 Incompressible viscous flow

In this section we present the spatial stability results for the Blasius boundary layer flow; the asymptotic suction profile and the Falkner-Skan family can be found at the end of this chapter in the exercises.

4.5.1 Spatial stability

The spatial stability characteristics for the Blasius boundary layer, given by (3.6) to (3.8), are given. As mentioned in Chapter 3, the profile must be determined numerically and, once this is done, the stability characteristics can then be examined. Of course the neutral stability boundary is the same for temporal or spatial theory, so Fig. 3.9 is still relevant. What is needed is to show how Figs. 3.6 and 3.7 are changed when going from temporal to spatial theory.

To compute the spatial stability characteristics for Blasius boundary layer flow, we modify the Compound Matrix method to allow the wavenumber α to be complex while fixing the frequency ω to be real. The eigenvalue that is to be determined is still the phase speed c. Thus, for spatial theory, we fix a (real) value of ω, and search for values of c, with $\alpha = \omega/c$, which satisfies the Orr-Sommerfeld equation with appropriate boundary conditions.

In Fig. 4.14 we plot contours of $D_r = 0$ and $D_i = 0$ in the complex c-plane for $Re = 580$ and $\omega = 0.055$[1]. The intersection points are shown as circles, and represent the eigenvalue for which $D_r = D_i = 0$. In particular, we see three distinct eigenvalues (listed in Table 4.6), one unstable and two stable. In addition, we also see a number of eigenvalues that seem to lie on a semicircle in the lower half plane. The significance of this is attributed to the presence of a continuum, and will be discussed in more detail in the next section.

Finally, in Fig. 4.15 we plot as the continuous curve the spatial growth rate as a function of ω for $Re = 580$. Note that the maximum growth rate occurs near $\omega_{max} \approx 0.05125$.

---

[1] The results presented here are in terms of the 'virgin' values Re and ω; in terms of the displacement thickness see the discussion in Section 3.3.

Table 4.6. *Wavenumber and phase speed for* $Re = 580$ *and* $\omega = 0.055$
for the Blasius boundary layer profile.

α_r	α_i	c_r	c_i
0.15515311	-0.00432824	0.35421288	0.00988133
0.07275631	0.05991724	0.45044992	-0.37096044
0.06729441	0.09298631	0.28092562	-0.38817839

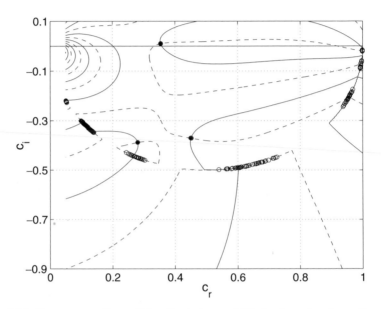

Fig. 4.14. Zero contour lines of the discriminate of Blasius boundary layer flow for
$\omega = 0.055$ and $Re = 580$; $D_r = 0$ solid; $D_i = 0$ dash. The circles denote intersection
points where $D_r = D_i = 0$.

4.5.2 Gaster transformation

The Gaster transformation (4.8) can be used to calculate the spatial growth rate
from the results of temporal theory. Recall that the spatial growth rate is related
to the temporal growth rate via

$$\alpha_i(S) = -\omega_i(T)/c_g, \tag{4.38}$$

where c_g is the group velocity defined by (4.7). We compute the group velocity
numerically as follows. First, fix a value of the virgin Reynolds number, 580
say. Then, from temporal theory, compute the complex frequency ω given a

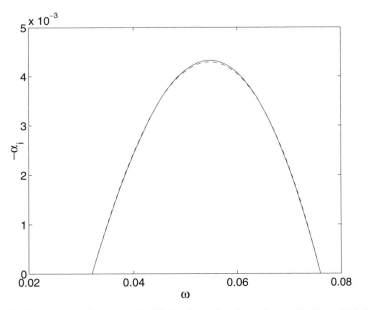

Fig. 4.15. Spatial growth rate for the Blasius boundary layer flow with $Re = 580$; from spatial theory (solid), from Gaster's transformation (dash).

real value of α that lies on the temporal growth rate curve; see Fig. 3.7. For each value of α on the curve, compute the group velocity as follows:

$$c_g = \frac{\partial \omega}{\partial \alpha} = -\frac{F_\alpha}{F_\omega}, \qquad (4.39)$$

where $F(\alpha, \omega) = 0$ is the dispersion relation, and the subscript denotes a partial derivative. The negative sign comes from expanding the dispersion relation about a point (α_0, ω_0),

$$0 = (\alpha - \alpha_0) F_\alpha + (\omega - \omega_0) F_\omega + \cdots, \qquad (4.40)$$

and differentiating to get the above result. We compute the derivatives using a standard second-order finite difference scheme,

$$F_\alpha = \frac{F(\alpha + \delta) - F(\alpha - \delta)}{2\delta}, \quad F_\omega = \frac{F(\omega + \delta) - F(\omega - \delta)}{2\delta}, \quad (4.41)$$

and we take $\delta = 1.0 \times 10^{-4}$. In general the group velocity, as computed above, will be complex. In applying (4.38) we simply take the real part as the true value for c_g. The result of computing the spatial growth rate from temporal theory is shown as the dashed curve in Fig. 4.15. Recall from (4.11) that

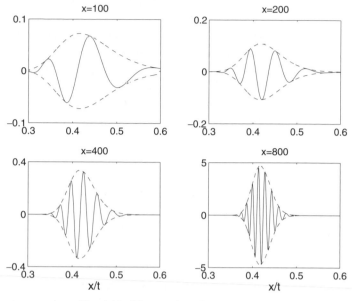

Fig. 4.16. Wave packets for $Re_\delta = 1000$.

$\omega_r(T) = \omega_r(S)$. Note the excellent agreement between the two curves, bearing in mind that Gaster's transformation is only a leading order approximation. For profiles that have an inflection point, the inviscid temporal growth rates are much larger by orders of magnitude than the temporal growth rates of the boundary layer. For this reason, the agreement between the spatial eigenvalues computed using Gaster's transformation and from spatial theory is not satisfactory. Gaster's transformation is of historical significance; today one simply calculates the spatial growth rate curve directly.

4.5.3 Wave packets

Insight into the transition process from laminar to turbulent flow can be gained via wave packets. To illustrate this we compute the wave packet for the Blasius boundary layer using (4.33) to (4.35). In general both α and ω are complex, except for the single point where the temporal amplification rate is a maximum (e.g., see Fig. 3.7 where $\partial\omega_i/\partial\alpha = 0$ at $\alpha = 0.1554$; the group velocity at this point is $\partial\omega_r/\partial\alpha \approx 0.424$.) This is done numerically as follows. For each (real) value of x/t, we wish to find α^* such that $d\omega/d\alpha = x/t$. The value of α^* is found by a root finding procedure, such as Muller's method for complex roots. We guess an initial (complex) value of α, compute the corresponding

ω (complex) from the Orr-Sommerfeld equation, use difference formulas to determine $dF/d\alpha$ and $dF/d\omega$, define $c_g = -(dF/d\alpha)/(dF/d\omega)$, and iterate until $c_g - x/t$ is less than some prescribed tolerance. This then defines a set of $\{\alpha^*, \omega(\alpha^*)\}$ pairs which can then be used in (4.33). Figure 4.16 shows the wave packets for four values of x. Note that, as x increases, the amplitude and frequency also increases. Gaster compared the wave packet determined from theory and that from experiments (Gaster & Grant, 1975) and found good qualitative agreement, at least for regions not too far downstream of the initial source disturbance.

4.6 Discrete and continuous spectra

For temporal stability, many existence and completeness theorems exist, some of which are mentioned in the previous chapter. We are unaware of any theo retical work about existence or completeness for spatial stability theory, either for a bounded or an unbounded domain. For profiles on an unbounded domain, such as the boundary layer, the mixing layer, and the jet and wake profiles, all numerical work to date suggests that there are only a finite number of discrete modes; in some cases there may be only one. Since a finite set of modes on the unbounded domain is not complete, they cannot be used to describe an arbitrary initial disturbance. Therefore one must consider the existence of a continuum. Grosch & Salwen (1978) and Salwen & Grosch (1981) have shown (but not rigorously) that the set consisting of the discrete modes and the continuum is complete. Their work also provides the necessary mathematical foundation for the analysis of the receptivity problem. In short, how do acoustic disturbances or freestream turbulence in the freestream interact with the boundary layer to excite instabilities? Since the work of Grosch & Salwen is of such importance for a proper understanding of the nature of the solution set of the Orr-Sommerfeld equation, we briefly present their analysis below.

Recall from Section 2.1 that, for a two-dimensional flow, the disturbance velocity components $\tilde{u}$ and $\tilde{v}$ can be expressed in terms of a stream function, $\psi(x, y, t)$, in the usual manner with

$$\tilde{u} = \psi_y, \quad \tilde{v} = -\psi_x, \tag{4.42}$$

which satisfies the continuity equation (2.14) exactly. Substitution of ψ into the momentum equations (2.15) and (2.16) and elimination of the pressure results in the single partial differential equation for ψ or

$$\left(\frac{\partial}{\partial t} + U\frac{\partial}{\partial x}\right)\nabla^2\psi - U''\psi_x = Re^{-1}\nabla^4\psi. \tag{4.43}$$

The boundary conditions at the wall are given by

$$\psi_x(x, 0, t) = -\tilde{v}(x, 0, t) = 0,$$
$$\psi_y(x, 0, t) = \tilde{u}(x, 0, t) = 0, \tag{4.44}$$

and, at infinity, a finiteness condition must be imposed

$$\int_{-\infty}^{+\infty} \int_0^{+\infty} (\psi_x^2 + \psi_y^2) dy dt < \infty. \tag{4.45}$$

This inequality ensures that the Fourier integral expansion of ψ,

$$\psi(x, y, t) = \int_{-\infty}^{+\infty} \psi_\omega(x, y) e^{-i\omega t} d\omega \tag{4.46}$$

exists, where ω is real according to spatial stability theory.

We now assume that ψ_ω is separable and has the form

$$\psi_\omega(x, y) = \phi_\omega(y) e^{i\alpha x}, \tag{4.47}$$

where α is the complex eigenvalue and the eigenfunction ϕ_ω is the solution to the Orr-Sommerfeld equation

$$(U - c)(\phi_w'' - \alpha^2 \phi_w) - U'' \phi_w = \frac{1}{i\alpha Re}(\phi_w'''' - 2\alpha^2 \phi_w'' + \alpha^4 \phi_w). \tag{4.48}$$

The discrete eigenvalues $\{\alpha_n\}$ and the corresponding eigenfunctions $\{\phi_{\omega_n}\}$ satisfy the Orr-Sommerfeld equation with boundary conditions

$$\phi_{\omega_n} = \phi_{\omega_n}' = 0 \quad \text{at} \quad y = 0, \quad \phi_{\omega_n} = \phi_{\omega_n}' \to 0 \quad \text{as} \quad y \to \infty. \tag{4.49}$$

For a particular mean flow the number of discrete modes, $N(\omega)$, depends on both the Reynolds number and the frequency. As in the temporal problem, $N(\omega)$ can either be finite or zero.

Since the Orr-Sommerfeld equation is fourth-order and linear, there will be four linearly independent solutions $\phi_j(y)$; $j = 1, 2, 3, 4$. The character of each of these solutions can be determined by examining their behavior as $y \to \infty$. Writing

$$\phi_j(y) \approx e^{\lambda_j y}, \quad \text{as } y \to \infty, \tag{4.50}$$

and substituting into the Orr-Sommerfeld equation (4.48), we see that

$$\lambda_1 = -Q^{1/2}, \quad \lambda_2 = +Q^{1/2}, \quad \lambda_3 = -\alpha, \quad \lambda_4 = +\alpha, \tag{4.51}$$

where

$$Q = i\alpha Re(U_1 - c) + \alpha^2, \tag{4.52}$$

and it is assumed that $Re(Q) \geq 0$ and $U \to U_1$, U', $U'' \to 0$ as $y \to \infty$. The constant U_1 is unity for a boundary layer, a mixing layer or a wake, and is zero for a jet. The eigenfunctions ϕ_1 and ϕ_2 are called the viscous solutions since their asymptotic behavior at infinity depends on the Reynolds number, while the eigenfunctions ϕ_3 and ϕ_4 are called the inviscid solutions. Note that the eigenfunctions ϕ_2 and ϕ_4 are unbounded as y becomes large, and so must be dropped from the solution set. Thus, it is a linear combination of ϕ_1 and ϕ_3, the viscous and inviscid solutions, that must be required to satisfy the two boundary conditions at the wall $y = 0$. In the inviscid limit, the viscous eigenfunction ϕ_1 is not present and the solution to the Rayleigh problem is given only in terms of ϕ_3. For the more general case of an unbounded region $-\infty < y < +\infty$, such as a mixing layer, wake or a jet, we would keep ϕ_1 and ϕ_3 as the solutions which decays as $y \to +\infty$, and keep ϕ_2 and ϕ_4 as the solutions which decays as $y \to -\infty$, and enforce matching conditions at the critical layer.

The continuum part of the solution satisfies the Orr-Sommerfeld equation with boundary conditions

$$\phi_\omega = \phi'_\omega = 0 \quad \text{at} \quad y = 0, \quad \phi_\omega, \phi'_\omega \text{ bounded as } y \to \infty. \quad (4.53)$$

It is important to keep in mind that the difference between the discrete spectra and the continuum is the behavior of ϕ at infinity; the discrete spectra are required to vanish as $y \to \infty$, while the continuum is only required to be bounded. We again look for solutions in the far field by writing

$$\phi_{\omega_k} \approx e^{\pm iky}, \quad \text{as} \quad y \to \infty, \quad (4.54)$$

with $k > 0$ a real and positive parameter. Substitution of (4.54) into (4.48) results in the algebraic equation

$$(k^2 + \alpha^2)[k^2 + \alpha^2 + i\,Re(\alpha U_1 - \omega)] = 0. \quad (4.55)$$

We see that this equation is a quartic equation for α in terms of the real parameter k and hence has four roots $\alpha^{(j)}$; $j = 1, 2, 3, 4$. It should be noted that, whereas the continuum has only one branch for temporal stability theory, the continuum has four branches for spatial stability theory. Two of these four roots, $\alpha^{(1)}$ and $\alpha^{(2)}$, satisfy the quadratic equation

$$k^2 + \alpha^{(j)^2} + i\,Re\left(\alpha^{(j)} U_1 - \omega\right) = 0, \quad (4.56)$$

or,

$$\alpha^{(j)} = \begin{cases} \frac{i\,ReU_1}{2}\left\{-1 \pm \sqrt{1 + 4\left(\frac{k^2 - i\,Re\omega}{Re^2 U_1^2}\right)}\right\} & U_1 > 0, \\ \\ \pm \sqrt{i\,Re\omega - k^2} & U_1 = 0. \end{cases} \tag{4.57}$$

We order the two roots by defining $\alpha^{(1)}$ with positive real part and $\alpha^{(2)}$ with negative real part. Note that these two roots have branch cuts in the complex α plane. The other two roots to the original quartic are

$$\alpha^{(3)} = ik, \quad \alpha^{(4)} = -ik. \tag{4.58}$$

The continuum of eigenfunctions corresponding to $\alpha^{(1)}$,

$$\psi_{\omega k}^{(1)}(x, y)e^{-i\omega t} = \phi_{\omega k}^{(1)}(y)e^{i(\alpha^{(1)}x - \omega t)}, \tag{4.59}$$

are waves propagating downstream from the source and decay in amplitude as they travel. In the same manner, the continuum eigenfunctions corresponding to $\alpha^{(2)}$ are waves propagating upstream and decaying. The continuum eigenfunctions corresponding to $\alpha^{(3)}$,

$$\psi_{\omega k}^{(3)}(x, y)e^{-i\omega t} = \phi_{\omega k}^{(3)}(y)e^{i(\alpha^{(3)}x - \omega t)}$$
$$= \phi_{\omega k}^{(3)}(y)e^{-kx - i\omega t}, \tag{4.60}$$

are standing waves that decay in amplitude downstream. In the same manner, the continuum of eigenfunctions corresponding to $\alpha^{(4)}$ are standing waves and decay in amplitude upstream.

The four branches for the continuum can be viewed graphically as follows. For the case $U_1 = 1$, we see that as $k \to 0$ with $\omega/Re \ll 1$

$$\alpha^{(1)} \to \omega + i\omega^2/Re, \quad \alpha^{(2)} \to -\omega - iRe, \tag{4.61}$$

and for $k \to \infty$,

$$\alpha^{(1)} \to 0 + ik, \quad \alpha^{(2)} \to 0 - ik. \tag{4.62}$$

The four continuum branches are sketched in Fig. 4.17. Note that the real axis does not cross any of the branch cuts. The circles denote the limit points as $k \to 0$. We also show the continuum branches, as well as the eigenvalues found earlier in Section 4.5, in Fig. 4.18 for the Blasius boundary layer with $Re = 580$ and $\omega = 0.055$. From this figure we see that the eigenvalues that formed a semicircle in Fig. 4.14 actually approximate the continuum. In this sense they are not discrete and should not be classified as 'eigenvalues'. Thus, for these particular values of the Reynolds number and frequency, there are only three

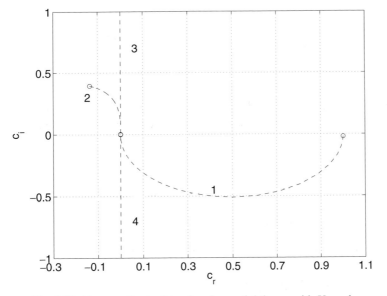

Fig. 4.17. Four continuum branches for spatial theory with $U_1 = 1$.

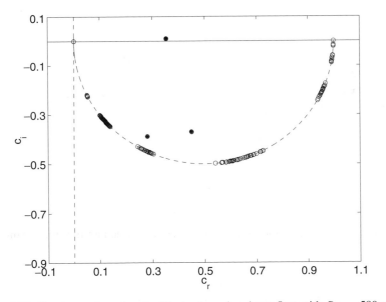

Fig. 4.18. Continuum branches for Blasius boundary layer flow with $Re = 580$ and $\omega = 0.055$.

discrete eigenvalues. This example shows that care must be exercised when computing the eigenvalues numerically. It is important to distinguish between those modes that are discrete and those that approximate the continuum (due to numerics). As in the temporal case, as the Reynolds number increases, more modes will move off the continuum and move into the stable regime.

For the case $U_1 = 0$, we see that

$$\alpha^{(1)} \rightarrow \frac{1}{\sqrt{2}}(1+i)\sqrt{\omega Re}, \quad \alpha^{(2)} \rightarrow -\frac{1}{\sqrt{2}}(1+i)\sqrt{\omega Re}, \qquad (4.63)$$

as $k \rightarrow 0$, and

$$\alpha^{(1)} \rightarrow 0 + ik, \quad \alpha^{(2)} \rightarrow 0 - ik, \qquad (4.64)$$

as $k \rightarrow \infty$.

The spatial eigenfunctions that form a complete set are formed from the sum of the discrete spectrum and the continuum, and can be written in Fourier space as

$$\psi_\omega(x, y) = \sum_{n=1}^{N(\omega)} \psi_{\omega n}(x, y) + \sum_{j=1}^{4} \int_0^\infty \psi_{\omega k}^{(j)}(x, y)dk$$

$$= \sum_{n=1}^{N(\omega)} A_{\omega n} \phi_{\omega n}(y)e^{i\alpha_n x}$$

$$+ \sum_{j=1}^{4} \int_0^\infty A_{\omega k}^{(j)} \phi_{\omega k}^{(j)}(y)e^{i\alpha_k^{(j)} x}dk, \qquad (4.65)$$

where the coefficients $\{A_{\omega n}\}$ and $\{A_{\omega k}^{(j)}\}$ are found by taking the inner products with respect to the eigenfunctions of the associated adjoint problem. Details and formulas for these coefficients can be found in both the Grosch & Salwen papers as well as that of Hill (1995). The complete solution in physical space can be written as

$$\psi(x, y, t) = \int_{-\infty}^{+\infty} \left\{ \sum_{n=1}^{N(\omega)} A_{\omega n} \phi_{\omega n}(y)e^{i\alpha_n x} \right.$$

$$\left. + \sum_{j=1}^{4} \int_0^\infty A_{\omega k}^{(j)} \phi_{\omega k}^{(j)}(y)e^{i\alpha_k^{(j)} x}dk \right\} e^{-i\omega t}d\omega. \qquad (4.66)$$

4.7 Exercises

1. For inviscid disturbances, modify your numerical code built in Chapter 2 for Rayleigh's equation to allow for spatial stability calculations. Be sure to

use double precision. Verify your code by computing the inviscid, spatial stability characteristics for the following flows and obtain the figures in this chapter.

(a) The symmetric jet
(b) The symmetric wake

2. For the Gaussian wake profile

$$U(y) = 1 - Qe^{-y^2 \ln 2},$$

compute the inviscid spatial stability characteristics for various values of the wake deficit parameter Q. Show that the flow becomes absolutely unstable when $Q \geq 0.943$ (scc Hultgren & Aggarwal, 1987).

3. Recall the laminar mixing layer of Section 2.6.2

$$u = f'(\eta), \quad \eta = y\sqrt{\frac{Re}{x}},$$

where

$$2f''' + ff'' = 0,$$

plus the following boundary conditions appropriate for the mixing layer

$$f'(-\infty) = \beta_U, \quad f(0) = 0, \quad f'(+\infty) = 1.$$

The profile was shown in Fig. 2.10.

(a) Compute the spatial growth rate curve for $\beta_U = 0$, and compare to that obtained using the hyperbolic tangent profile (4.12).
(b) Compute the value of β_U for which the flow first becomes absolutely unstable. Compare this value to that obtained using the hyperbolic tangent profile (4.36).

4. For viscous disturbances, modify your numerical code built in Chapter 3 for the Orr-Sommerfeld equation to allow for spatial stability calculations. Be sure to use double precision. Use the code to solve the following problems.

(a) Compute the spatial growth rate for the Falkner-Skan profile of 3.1.4. Take $\beta = 10, 1, 0.5, -0.1$ and -0.19 with $Re = 1000$. For one of the values of β, compute the temporal growth rate and use Gaster's transformation to compare to the curve obtained using the spatial code.
(b) Compute the continuum and the spatial growth rate for the Asymptotic Suction profile of Question 2 of Chapter 3 using the modified Orr-Sommerfeld equation.

Chapter 5

Stability of compressible flows

5.1 Introduction

The consideration of flows when the fluid is compressible presents a great many difficulties. The basic mathematics requires far more detail in order to make a rational investigation. The number of dependent variables is increased. And, regardless of the specific mean flow that is under scrutiny, the boundary conditions can be quite involved. Such observations will become more than obvious as the bases for examining the stability of such flows are established.

By their nature, the physics of compressible flows implies that there are now fluctuations in the density as well as the velocity and pressure. And, the density can be altered by pressure forces and the temperature. As a result, the laws of thermodynamics must be considered along with the equations for the conservation of mass and momentum. Consequently, a new set of governing equations must be derived. Moreover, this set of equations must be valid for flows than range from slightly supersonic to those that are hypersonic; i.e., M, the Mach number defined for the flow is of order one or larger. Flows that are characterized by a Mach number that is small compared to 1 and simply have a mean density that is inhomogeneous are those flows that satisfy what is known as the Boussinesq approximation and will be examined in Chapter 7. Suffice it for now to say that it is the force of gravity that plays a key role in such cases.

The stability of compressible flows was initially analytically studied by Lees & Lin (1946), Lees (1947), and Dunn & Lin (1955); a general review of this work has been given by Lin (1955). Later, theoretical work combined with numerical schemes was made by Reshotko (1960) and Lees & Reshotko (1962). A full numerical integration of the compressible stability equations was first achieved by Brown (1961b) and major work using numerical methods in this area is due to Mack (1960, 1965a,b, 1966). Experimentally, evidence for

instabilities in compressible boundary layers is due to Laufer & Vrebalovich (1957, 1958, 1960) and Demetriades (1958).

As mentioned, any general study of the stability of a compressible flow presents a most complicated problem because of the significant increase in the number of parameters that must be considered. For the compressible boundary layer, the mean velocity profile depends upon the conditions at the wall. For example, the wall can be insulated wall or there can be cooling at the wall, etc. The coefficients of viscosity and thermal conductivity are both functions of the temperature. The outer boundary conditions are also intertwined. In this way the basic thermodynamics is now essential to the posing of any problem in compressible flow. For the most part this means the assumption of a perfect gas for both the mean flow and the perturbations in order to form a closed set of equations for the dependent variables. The basic needs for this approach can be found in the example of Shen (1952) and a more detailed discussion is provided by Mack (1965a). Betchov & Criminale (1967) present the fundamentals.

Due to the complexities inherent with any discussion on the stability of compressible flows, we present in the following two sections the stability characteristics of the compressible mixing layer and the compressible boundary layer. Other compressible flows not examined here include, but not limited to, the recent studies of the compressible wake (Papageorgiou, 1990a,b,c; Chen, Cantwell & Mansour, 1989, 1990); the compressible jet (Kennedy & Chen, 1998); and the compressible Couette flow (Glatzel, 1988, 1989; Girard, 1988; Duck, Erlebacher & Hussaini, 1994). The *Journal of Fluid Mechanics, Physics of Fluids* and *Theoretical and Computational Fluid Dynamics* are good resources for the latest work on the stability of compressible flows.

5.2 Compressible mixing layer

In this section the inviscid stability of a compressible mixing layer, the interfacial region between two moving gases, is examined. The basic formulation of the theory for the stability of compressible shear flows, both free and wall bounded, is due to Lees & Lin (1946). Later, Dunn & Lin (1955) were the first to show the importance of three-dimensional disturbances for the stability of these flows.

Early studies of the stability of compressible mixing layers include those of Lessen, Fox & Zien (1965, 1966) and Gropengiesser (1969). The inviscid temporal stability of the compressible mixing layer to two-and three-dimensional disturbances was studied by Lessen, Fox & Zien for subsonic disturbances (1965) and supersonic disturbances (1966). Lessen *et al.* assumed that the flow was iso-energetic and, as a consequence, the temperature of the stationary

gas was always greater than that of the moving gas. In fact, because the ratio of the temperature very far from the mixing region varies as the square of the Mach number, the stationary gas is much hotter than the moving gas at even moderately supersonic speeds. Gropengiesser (1969) reexamined this problem without having to use the iso-energetic assumption. Consequentially, he was able to treat the ratio of the temperatures of the stationary and moving gas as a parameter. He carried out inviscid spatial stability calculations for the compressible mixing layer using a generalized hyperbolic tangent profile (see his equation (2.27)) to approximate the Lock profile for temperature ratios of 0.6, 1.0 and 2.0 and for Mach numbers between 0 and 3. Gropengiesser found that, for low and moderate Mach numbers, the flow becomes less unstable as the stationary gas becomes hotter. He also found that the spatial growth rates decrease with increasing Mach number over the range of Mach numbers that he studied. Gropengiesser also found a second unstable mode for two-dimensional waves in a narrow range of Mach numbers, $1.54 < M < 1.73$. Ragab & Wu (1989) recomputed many of the stability results of Gropengiesser, and verified the accuracy of the earlier numerical work.

Blumen (1970), Blumen, Drazin & Billings (1975) and Drazin & Davey (1977) investigated the temporal stability of a compressible mixing layer. Here, a hyperbolic tangent profile for the velocity was used and it was assumed that the temperature was a constant throughout the layer. Effects due to viscous heating were ignored. In these last two studies, multiple instability modes were found near a Mach number of 1. In particular, they showed that the hyperbolic tangent shear layer is unstable at each value of the Mach number, however large. These modes were investigated numerically and theoretically in the long-wave approximation ($\alpha \to 0$).

As a historical note, little else was done until the late 1980's when a flurry of theoretical studies on the stability of compressible free shear layers were conducted. The increased interest of such flows was due mainly to the projected use of the scramjet engine for the propulsion of hypersonic aircraft. It is impossible to give a chronological order of events since over 30 archival (and many more non-archival) publications appeared within a five-year time frame. We briefly comment on only a few publications that are directly relevant to the contents of this chapter, namely the inviscid stability of two-dimensional compressible mixing layers to two-dimensional disturbances, and present the rest of the publications as a list.

Earlier studies include that of Jackson & Grosch (1989) who examined the inviscid stability of a compressible two-dimensional mixing layer to two- and three-dimensional disturbances. The mean flow velocity was taken to be a hyperbolic tangent while the temperature was determined using Crocco's

relation. The classification of neutral and unstable modes over the Mach number range of 0 to 10 was determined, thus effectively extending and completing the results of Gropengiesser (1969). In particular, they verified the result that, for subsonic convective Mach numbers, only one subsonic mode existed (except at possible high angles of skewness of the disturbances) and that the growth rate decreased as the Mach number increased. These modes were classified as "Subsonic" modes. For supersonic convective Mach numbers, they clarified the second mode found by Gropengiesser (1969), Blumen, Drazin & Billings (1975), and Drazin & Davey (1977). Multiple modes were also found in a temporal stability analysis of the compressible mixing layer without invoking the assumptions of a hyperbolic tangent velocity profile and that of a constant temperature throughout the layer (Macaraeg, Streett, & Hussaini, 1988; see also Macaraeg & Streett, 1991). Jackson & Grosch's classification, relevant for supersonic convective Mach numbers where two unstable modes exist, are termed the "Fast" mode (with a corresponding phase speed greater than

$$c_N = \frac{\beta_U + \beta_T^{1/3}}{1 + \beta_T^{1/3}},$$

where $\beta_U = U_{-\infty}^*/U_{+\infty}^*$ and $\beta_T = T_{-\infty}^*/T_{+\infty}^*$ are the velocity and temperature ratios in the freestream at $-\infty$ to that in the freestream at $+\infty$, respectively, and c_N is derived from a vortex sheet analysis; see Section 5.2.4) and the "Slow" mode (with a corresponding phase speed less than c_N). The authors also indicated numerically how the two modes come about as the convective Mach number approaches 1, in general agreement with the theoretical findings of Blumen, Drazin & Billings (1975) and Drazin & Davey (1977). Zhuang, Kubota & Dimotakis (1988) also studied the mixing layer with the hyperbolic tangent profile and found decreasing amplification with increasing Mach number.

Ragab (1988) numerically solved the two-dimensional compressible Navier-Stokes equations for the wake/mixing layer behind a splitter plate, and then made a linear stability analysis of the computed mean flow. He found that increasing the Mach number leads to a strong stabilization of the flow and that the disturbances have large dispersion near the splitter plate and smaller dispersion downstream. Ragab & Wu (1989) examined the viscous and inviscid stability of a compressible mixing layer using both the hyperbolic tangent and Sutherland profiles. They found that, if the Reynolds number was greater than 1000, the disturbances could be calculated very accurately from inviscid theory. In addition, they reported that nonparallel effects are negligible. It seems that in this study their main interest was in determining the dependence of the

maximum growth rate of the disturbances on the velocity ratio of the mixing layer. They concluded that the maximum growth rate depends on the velocity ratio in a complex way, with the maximum growth rate appearing at a particular nonzero velocity ratio.

Tam & Hu (1989) examined the stability of the compressible mixing layer in a channel using the hyperbolic tangent profile. They showed that the presence of walls for supersonic convective Mach numbers introduces two new families of unstable modes. These new modes were classified either as "Class A" (those with phase speeds decreasing as the wavenumber and frequency increase) or "Class B" (those with phase speeds increasing as the wavenumber and frequency increase).

Additional investigations into the linear stability of compressible mixing layers include, but are not limited to[1]: (i) three-dimensional instabilities (Sandham & Reynolds, 1990); (ii) three-dimensional mixing layers (Grosch & Jackson, 1991; Macaraeg, 1991; Lu & Lele, 1993); (iii) effect of thermodynamics (Jackson & Grosch, 1991), (iv) effect of chemical reactions (Jackson & Grosch, 1990a; Shin & Ferziger, 1991; Planche & Reynolds, 1991; Shin & Ferziger, 1993; Jackson & Grosch, 1994; Day, Reynolds & Mansour, 1998a,b; Papas, Monkewitz & Tomboulides, 1999); (v) correlations of the growth rates with the convective Mach number (Ragab & Wu, 1989; Zhuang, Kubota & Dimotakis, 1990a; Jackson & Grosch, 1990b; Lu & Lele, 1994); (vi) absolute-convective instabilities (Pavithran & Redekopp, 1989; Jackson & Grosch, 1990b; Hu, Jackson, Lasseigne & Grosch, 1993; Peroomian & Kelly, 1994); (vii) effect of walls (Tam & Hu, 1989; Greenough, Riley, Soestrisno & Eberhardt, 1989; Macaraeg & Streett, 1989; Zhuang, Dimotakis & Kubota, 1990b; Macaraeg, 1990; Jackson & Grosch, 1990c; Morris & Giridharan, 1991); (viii) stability of binary gases (Kozusko, Lasseigne, Grosch & Jackson, 1996); (ix) nonhomentropic flows(Djordjevic & Redekopp, 1988); (x) high Mach number studies (Balsa & Goldstein, 1990;Cowley & Hall, 1990; Goldstein & Wundrow, 1990;Smith & Brown, 1990;Blackaby, Cowley & Hall, 1993); and (xi) the combined effect of a wake with a mixing layer (Koochesfahani & Frieler, 1989).

5.2.1 Mean flow

Consider the two-dimensional compressible mixing layer, with zero pressure gradient, which separates two streams of different speeds and temperatures, and assume that the mean flow is governed by the compressible boundary-

---

[1] We remark here that many of the papers listed can well fit into more than one category; we apologize to the authors for the over-simplification of their work.

layer equations. Let (U, V) be the velocity components in the (x, y) directions, respectively, ρ the density, and T the temperature. All of the variables are nondimensionalized using the magnitudes of the freestream values at $y = +\infty$; i.e., U_∞, ρ_∞, and T_∞. The mean flow equations are first transformed into the incompressible form by means of the Howarth-Dorodnitzyn transformation, namely

$$Y = \int_0^y \rho \, dy, \quad \text{and} \quad \hat{V} = \rho V + U \int_0^y \rho_x \, dy, \tag{5.1}$$

yielding

$$\rho T = 1, \tag{5.2}$$

$$U_x + \hat{V}_Y = 0, \tag{5.3}$$

$$U U_x + \hat{V} U_Y = (\rho \mu U_Y)_Y, \tag{5.4}$$

$$U T_x + \hat{V} T_Y = \left(\frac{\rho \mu}{Pr} T_Y \right)_Y + (\gamma - 1) M^2 \rho \mu U_Y^2. \tag{5.5}$$

Here, the viscosity μ is assumed to be a function of temperature. The nondimensional parameters appearing above are the Prandtl number $Pr = c_p \mu / \kappa$ where c_p is the specific heat at constant pressure and κ is the thermal conductivity, the Mach number $M = U_\infty / a_\infty$, and γ, the specific heats ratio. We note that the last term in the energy equation is due to viscous heating, and has an important effect when the Mach number is large.

Solutions to this system can be found by integrating in x subject to appropriate initial and boundary conditions. Alternatively, one can assume that a self-similar solution exists. We take the second approach, and seek solutions in terms of the variable

$$\eta - \eta_0 = \frac{Y}{2\sqrt{x}}, \tag{5.6}$$

which is the similarity variable for the chemically frozen heat conduction problem, and η_0 corresponds to a shift in the origin. For the case of both streams being supersonic, η_0 is determined uniquely from a compatibility condition found by matching the pressure across the mixing layer, while if both streams are subsonic, the compatibility condition is trivially satisfied and thus η_0 would remain indeterminate (Ting, 1959; Klemp & Acrivos, 1972).

Under the above transformations, with

$$U = f'(\eta), \quad \hat{V} = (\eta f' - f)/\sqrt{x}, \quad \text{and} \quad T = T(\eta), \tag{5.7}$$

equations (5.1) to (5.5) become

$$\left(\frac{\mu}{T} f'' \right)' + 2ff'' = 0 \tag{5.8}$$

and

$$\left(\frac{\mu}{PrT}T'\right)' + 2fT' + (\gamma - 1)M^2\frac{\mu}{T}(f'')^2 = 0, \tag{5.9}$$

subject to the boundary conditions

$$U(\infty) = f'(\infty) = 1, \quad U(-\infty) = f'(-\infty) = \beta_U, \tag{5.10}$$

$$T(\infty) = 1, \quad T(-\infty) = \beta_T, \tag{5.11}$$

where $\beta_U = U^*(-\infty)/U^*(\infty) \le 1$ and $\beta_T = T^*(-\infty)/T^*(\infty)$ are the velocity and temperature ratios, respectively with the asterisk denoting a dimensional quantity. It should be noted that the system (5.8) and (5.9) constitute
a fifth-order boundary-value problem, but that there are only four boundary
conditions. As stated earlier, a fifth boundary condition can be given if both
streams are supersonic. Here, we assume that the shift η_0 is such that the
dividing streamline lies at the origin, that is

$$f(0) = 0. \tag{5.12}$$

For a general viscosity law, solutions to the above equations can now be obtained numerically for any given value of the Mach number.

For the special case of the linear viscosity law $\mu = T$ and unit Prandtl number, the energy equation can be solved in closed form

$$T = 1 - (1 - \beta_T)(1 - \psi) + \frac{\gamma - 1}{2}M^2(1 - \beta_U)^2\psi(1 - \psi), \tag{5.13}$$

where

$$\psi = \begin{cases} (f' - \beta_U)/(1 - \beta_U), & 0 \le \beta_U < 1, \\ (1 + \mathrm{erf}(\eta))/2, & \beta_U = 1. \end{cases} \tag{5.14}$$

We further make the simplifying assumption that the mean flow can be modeled by a hyperbolic tangent profile

$$U = \frac{1}{2}[1 + \beta_U + (1 - \beta_U)\tanh(\eta)]. \tag{5.15}$$

In this way the entire mean flow is known analytically.

5.2.2 Inviscid fluctuations

In the absence of heat conductivity and viscous effects, the general equations
for the velocity, pressure, density, and energy are

$$\frac{\partial\rho}{\partial t} + \frac{\partial(\rho u)}{\partial x} + \frac{\partial(\rho v)}{\partial y} = 0, \tag{5.16}$$

$$\rho \left(\frac{\partial u}{\partial t} + u \frac{\partial u}{\partial x} + v \frac{\partial u}{\partial y} \right) + \frac{1}{\gamma M^2} \frac{\partial p}{\partial x} = 0, \tag{5.17}$$

$$\rho \left(\frac{\partial v}{\partial t} + u \frac{\partial v}{\partial x} + v \frac{\partial v}{\partial y} \right) + \frac{1}{\gamma M^2} \frac{\partial p}{\partial y} = 0, \tag{5.18}$$

and

$$\rho \left(\frac{\partial T}{\partial t} + u \frac{\partial T}{\partial x} + v \frac{\partial T}{\partial y} \right) - \frac{\gamma - 1}{\gamma} \left(\frac{\partial p}{\partial t} + u \frac{\partial p}{\partial x} + v \frac{\partial p}{\partial y} \right) = 0. \tag{5.19}$$

In addition to these equations we have the additional equation for a perfect gas or

$$p = \rho T. \tag{5.20}$$

In the usual fashion, these equations have been made dimensionless with respect to the freestream values U_∞, ρ_∞, T_∞, $P_\infty = \rho_\infty R T_\infty$ for the velocities, density, temperature and pressure, respectively. The length scale is referenced to L, and the time scale is L/U_∞. M is the Mach number, defined as U_∞/a_∞, where $a = \sqrt{\gamma p/\rho}$ is the speed of sound and γ is the ratio of specific heats. Our system is now closed, and we have five equations for the five unknowns ρ, u, v, p, and T.

Compressible Rayleigh equation

The flow field is perturbed by introducing two-dimensional wave disturbances in the velocity, pressure, temperature and density with amplitudes which are functions of y. Following the notation used by Lees & Lin (1946), we write

$$(u, v, p, T, \rho) = (U, 0, 1, T, \rho)(y) + (f, \alpha\phi, \Pi, \theta, r)(y)e^{i\alpha(x-ct)}. \tag{5.21}$$

Then the linearized equations for the fluctuations are

$$i(U - c)r + i\rho f + (\rho\phi)' = 0, \tag{5.22}$$

$$\rho[i(U - c)f + U'\phi] + \frac{i\Pi}{\gamma M^2} = 0, \tag{5.23}$$

$$i\alpha^2 \rho(U - c)\phi + \frac{\Pi'}{\gamma M^2} = 0, \tag{5.24}$$

$$\rho[i(U - c)\theta + T'\phi] - i\frac{\gamma - 1}{\gamma}(U - c)\Pi = 0, \tag{5.25}$$

and

$$\Pi = \rho\theta + rT. \tag{5.26}$$

The usual manipulation of the above set of equations (see the exercise section) results in the following relation for the pressure

$$\Pi'' + \left[\frac{T'}{T} - \frac{2U'}{U-c} \right] \Pi' - \frac{\alpha^2}{T} [T - M^2(U-c)^2] \Pi = 0, \qquad (5.27)$$

or, in terms of ϕ,

$$\left[\frac{\phi'}{\xi} \right]' - \left[\frac{\alpha^2}{T} + \frac{1}{U-c} \left(\frac{U'}{\xi} \right)' \right] \phi = 0, \qquad (5.28)$$

where

$$\xi = T - M^2(U-c)^2. \qquad (5.29)$$

These two equations are the equivalent counterpart of Rayleigh's equation extended to compressible flows. Although first derived by Lees & Lin (1946), we shall refer to either of the above equation as the "compressible Rayleigh equation" even though Rayleigh did not investigate compressible stability *per se*. For a discussion in terms of vorticity or pressure, see Betchov & Criminale (1967).

Temporal theory

Several important theorems concerning the compressible Rayleigh equation are presented in this section. The first result is due to Lees & Lin (1946) and extends Rayleigh's inflection point theorem (see Result 2.1) to compressible flows. The next three results are due to Chimonas (1970) and extends Howard's theorems, Results 2.4, 2.5, and 2.7, to compressible flows. (Result 5.3 was also proved by Blumen, 1970). The bounds presented below may not be the best possible because they are independent of both the Mach number and the temperature distribution. We are concerned only with temporal theory; extensions to spatial disturbances simply do not exist.

RESULT 5.1: Generalized Inflection Point Theorem. A critical layer exists at $U(y_c) - c = 0$, and, provided the disturbances decay exponentially in the free streams, the solution is regular if the following is true

$$\frac{d}{dy} \left(\frac{1}{T} \frac{dU}{dy} \right) \bigg|_{y=y_c} = 0, \quad \text{at } U(y_c) - c = 0,$$

otherwise the solution is singular. Thus, a neutral mode exists and is given by $c_N = U(y_c)$.

RESULT 5.2: The phase velocity c_r of an amplified disturbance must lie between the minimum and the maximum values of the mean velocity profile $U(y)$.

RESULT 5.3: Semicircle Theorem. If $c_i > 0$, then the real and imaginary parts of the phase speed c must lie inside the semicircle

$$\left(c_r - \frac{U_{min} + U_{max}}{2}\right)^2 + c_i^2 \le \left(\frac{U_{max} - U_{min}}{2}\right)^2.$$

RESULT 5.4: Upper Bound On The Growth Rate. If there exists a solution with $c_i > 0$, then an upper bound exists and is given by

$$\alpha c_i \le \frac{1}{2} \max |U'(y)|$$

where the maximum is taken over the open interval (a, b).

5.2.3 Linear stability

Formulation

Since the mean flow is given in terms of the similarity variable η, it is convenient to transform the compressible Rayleigh equation (5.27) so that one is working within a single coordinate framework. The compressible Rayleigh equation for the pressure disturbance in the transformed space is given by

$$\Pi'' - \frac{2U'}{U - c}\Pi' - \alpha^2 T[T - M^2(U - c)^2]\Pi = 0. \qquad (5.30)$$

The boundary conditions for Π are obtained by considering the limiting form as $\eta \to \pm\infty$. The solutions are of the form

$$\Pi \to \exp(\pm\Omega_\pm\eta), \qquad (5.31)$$

where

$$\Omega_+^2 = \alpha^2[1 - M^2(1 - c)^2], \quad \Omega_-^2 = \alpha^2\beta_T[\beta_T - M^2(\beta_U - c)^2]. \qquad (5.32)$$

If $\Omega_\pm^2$ are positive, then the disturbances decay exponentially in the freestreams. If Ω_+^2 or Ω_-^2 are negative, then taking a square root results in a complex value, and thus the solutions oscillates (i.e., bounded) in the respective freestream. In the former case, the equation in the freestream is elliptic, while in the latter case, the equation is hyperbolic. Thus, for the hyperbolic case the freestream solutions are acoustic waves, and hence supersonic in nature.

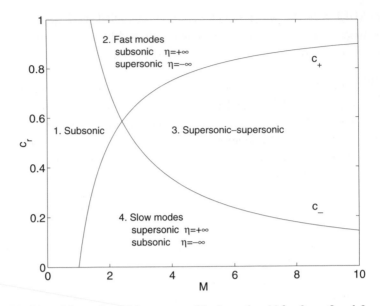

Fig. 5.1. Plot of the sonic speeds $c_\pm$ versus Mach number M for $\beta_U = 0$ and $\beta_T = 2$.

Let us define $c_\pm$ to be the phase speed for which $\Omega_\pm^2$ vanishes. Thus,

$$c_+ = 1 - \frac{1}{M}, \quad c_- = \beta_U + \frac{\sqrt{\beta_T}}{M}. \tag{5.33}$$

Note that c_+ is the phase speed of a sonic disturbance in the fast stream and c_- is the phase speed of a sonic disturbance in the slow stream. At

$$M = M_* = \frac{1 + \sqrt{\beta_T}}{1 - \beta_U}, \tag{5.34}$$

$c_\pm$ are equal.

The nature of the disturbances and the appropriate boundary conditions can now be illustrated by reference to Fig. 5.1, where we plot $c_\pm$ as a function of M. In what follows we assume that $\alpha_r^2 > \alpha_i^2$. These curves divide the $c_r - M$ plane into four regions, where c_r is the real part of c. If a disturbance exists with an M and c_r in region 1, then Ω_+^2 and Ω_-^2 are both positive, the disturbance is subsonic at both boundaries, and we classify it as a subsonic mode. In region 3, both Ω_+^2 and Ω_-^2 are negative and hence the disturbance is supersonic at both boundaries, and we classify it as a supersonic-supersonic mode. In region 2, Ω_+^2 is positive and Ω_-^2 is negative, and the disturbance is subsonic at $+\infty$ and supersonic at $-\infty$, and we classify it as a fast mode. Finally, in region 4, Ω_+^2 is negative and Ω_-^2 is positive so the disturbance is supersonic at $+\infty$ and

subsonic at $-\infty$, and we classify it as a slow mode. Note that the terminology 'fast' and 'slow' is in reference to the magnitude of the phase speed c_r. These modes are also referred to as 'outer' modes, see Day, Reynolds & Mansour (1998a,b).

If the disturbance wave is subsonic at both $\pm\infty$ (region 1), one can choose the appropriate sign for $\Omega_\pm$ and have decaying solutions. We therefore have an eigenvalue problem. If the disturbance is supersonic at either, or both, boundaries then the asymptotic solutions are purely oscillatory. These solutions are of two types. It is clear that the oscillatory solutions are either incoming or outgoing waves. If one assumes that only outgoing waves are permitted, the problem of finding solutions in regions 2, 3, or 4 is again an eigenvalue problem wherein one chooses, as boundary conditions, the solutions to the compressible Rayleigh equation that has only outgoing waves in the far field.

However if one permits both incoming and outgoing waves in the far field it is obvious that there are always solutions for any c in regions 2, 3, and 4. For a given ω, one can always find a continuum of α such that there is a solution to the compressible Rayleigh equation with constant amplitude oscillations at either or both boundaries. Lees & Lin gave a physical interpretation of this pair of incoming and outgoing waves as an incoming wave and its reflection from the shear layer. Mack (1975) also used this idea in developing a theory for the forced response of the compressible boundary layer. We will ignore these continuum modes in the remainder of this section.

One can now see that the appropriate boundary conditions for either the damped or outgoing waves in the free streams $\eta = +\infty$ and $\eta = -\infty$ are, respectively,

$$\Pi \rightarrow \exp(-\Omega_+\eta), \quad \text{if } c_r > c_+, \quad \Pi \rightarrow \exp(-i\eta\sqrt{-\Omega_+^2}), \quad \text{if } c_r < c_+,$$
(5.35)

and

$$\Pi \rightarrow \exp(\Omega_-\eta), \quad \text{if } c_r < c_-, \quad \Pi \rightarrow \exp(-i\eta\sqrt{-\Omega_-^2}), \quad \text{if } c_r > c_-.$$
(5.36)

Generalized regularity condition

Recall Result 5.1 where, if a neutral mode is to exist in region 1, the phase speed will be given by $c_N = U(\eta_c)$, where η_c is found from the regularity condition

$$S(\eta) = \frac{\mathrm{d}}{\mathrm{d}\eta}\left(T^{-2}\frac{\mathrm{d}U}{\mathrm{d}\eta}\right) = 0.$$
(5.37)

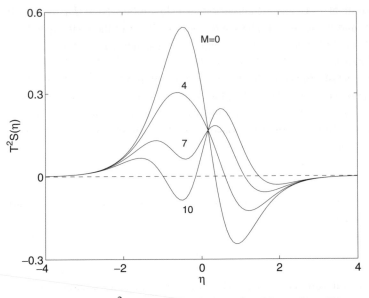

Fig. 5.2. Plot of $T^2 S(\eta)$ for $\beta_U = 0$, $\beta_T = 2$ and for various M.

The corresponding wavenumber α must be determined numerically. Note that this form differs from that given in Result 5.1 by a factor of T^{-1} because we have chosen to solve the equations in terms of the similarity variable η.

Figure 5.2 is a plot of S over a range of values of η for various values of M and fixed $\beta_U = 0$ and $\beta_T = 2$. From this plot one can see that, for low values of the Mach number, only one real root of S exists. But, as the Mach number increases, three real roots exist. For example, at $M = 0$ one zero exists at $y = 0.347$, at $M = 4$, $y = 0.601$, at $M = 7$, $y = 1.104$, while for $M = 10$ three zeros exist at $y = -0.981, -0.149$, and 1.478. For a root to correspond to a neutral mode, it must lie in region 1 of Fig. 5.1. Because the Mach number at which three real roots first appear is greater than M_* (for $\beta_U = 0$ and $\beta_T = 2$, we have $M_* = 2.414$; see equation 5.34), these cannot correspond to neutral modes.

However, Jackson and Grosch (1989) have shown, for three-dimensional disturbances, that the sonic speeds $c_\pm$ are functions of the angle of propagation of the disturbance. As the angle increases the sonic curves shift toward higher Mach number. Thus for any value of β_T, there will always be some angle of propagation for which all three zeros of S lie in region 1, and by Result 5.1, there are now three neutral modes with phase speeds equal to the value of U at the corresponding values of η_c. Thus, the significance of the three real

zeros of S only becomes apparent at very large angles of propagation. The relevance of these other modes at large angles of skewness have never been fully investigated.

There can also be supersonic neutral modes. Such modes do not satisfy (5.37) but are solutions of (5.30) with only outgoing or damped waves at $\pm\infty$. It is obvious that these are singular eigenfunctions. The singularity will be removed by the action of non-zero viscosity. Hence we can regard these singular modes as the limit of some viscous stability modes as the Reynolds number approaches infinity.

Results

To solve the disturbance equation (5.30), we first transform it to a Riccati equation by setting

$$G = \frac{\Pi'}{\alpha T \Pi}. \qquad (5.38)$$

The spatial stability problem is thus to solve the Riccati equation, subject to appropriate boundary conditions, for a given real frequency ω and Mach number M, with U and T defined by (5.15) and (5.13), respectively. The eigenvalue is the complex wavenumber α. Because the equation has a singularity at $U = c_N$, it is convenient to perform the integration in the complex plane, choosing for example the contour $(-L, -1)$ to $(0, -1)$ and $(L, -1)$ to $(0, -1)$, with $L \geq 6$, using a Runge-Kutta scheme with variable step size. We then iterate on α until the boundary conditions are satisfied and the jump in G at $(0, -1)$ is less than a specified small value (e.g., 10^{-6}). As is the case for all of our stability codes, all calculations are done in 64-bit precision.

The neutral phase speeds as a function of Mach number are shown in Fig. 5.3. Three different values of the temperature ratio β_T are taken. The top figure corresponds to $\beta_T = 0.5$, the middle figure to 1, and the bottom figure to 2. In all cases we set $\beta_U = 0$. For each value of β_T, there exists one or more unstable regions, bounded between two neutral curves. The classification for the neutral modes are: (1) subsonic, $\alpha_N \neq 0$; (2) subsonic, $\alpha_N = 0$; (3) fast, $\alpha_N \neq 0$; (4) slow, $\alpha_N \neq 0$; (5) constant speed supersonic-supersonic, $\alpha_N = 0$; (6) fast supersonic-supersonic, $\alpha_N = 0$; (7) slow supersonic-supersonic, $\alpha_N = 0$. The sonic curves are shown as dashed.

For $M < M_*$, there exists basically only one unstable region. The neutral curve labeled 1 corresponds to the value of c_N determined from the Lees-Lin condition, while the neutral curve labeled 2 has a neutral wavenumber of zero. The unstable region thus lies between curves 1 and 2. Because of the symmetry of the hyperbolic tangent profile with $\beta_T = 1$, curves 1 and 2 coincide;

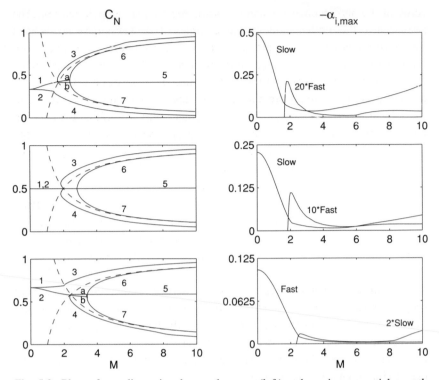

Fig. 5.3. Plots of two-dimensional neutral curves (left) and maximum spatial growth rates (right) for $\beta_T = 0.5$ (top), $\beta_T = 1$ (middle), and $\beta_T = 2$ (bottom) as a function of the Mach number M and for $\beta_U = 0$. The neutral mode classification is: (1) subsonic, $\alpha_N \neq 0$; (2) subsonic, $\alpha_N = 0$; (3) fast, $\alpha_N \neq 0$; (4) slow, $\alpha_N \neq 0$; (5) constant speed supersonic-supersonic, $\alpha_N = 0$; (6) fast supersonic-supersonic, $\alpha_N = 0$; (7) slow supersonic-supersonic, $\alpha_N = 0$. The sonic curves are shown as dashed. The spatial growth rates for the Fast modes for $\beta_T = 0.5$ and 1, and for the Slow modes for $\beta_T = 2$, have been scaled to better visualize the curves.

for more general profiles this is not true. For $M > M_*$, there exists more than one unstable region. For $M_* < M < M_{CR}$ and $\beta_T = 1$ (middle figure), the Fast modes lie between the neutral curves 3 ($\alpha_N \neq 0$, determined numerically) and 5 ($\alpha_N = 0$), while the Slow modes lie between the neutral curves 4 ($\alpha_N \neq 0$, determined numerically) and 5 ($\alpha_N = 0$). Mode splitting from subsonic to supersonic speeds at $M = M_*$ have been described by Drazin & Davey (1977). The upper limit M_{CR} of the Mach number is determined from an $\alpha \to 0$ asymptotic analysis, along the lines previously used by Miles (1958), Drazin & Howard (1962) and Blumen, Drazin & Billings (1975) in related studies; the analysis is presented later in the context of a vortex sheet. For $M_* < M < M_{CR}$ and $\beta_T \neq 1$ (top and bottom figures), the Fast modes lie

between the neutral curves 3 and 5a, while the Slow modes lie between the neutral curves 4 and 5b. Note that curves 5b for $\beta_T = 0.5$ and 5a for $\beta_T = 2$ are the continuation of the constant speed supersonic-supersonic neutral mode for Mach numbers below M_{CR}, while the curves 5a for $\beta_T = 0.5$ and 5b for $\beta_T = 2$ are the continuation of the subsonic neutral mode through the value of the phase speed where $c_\pm$ are equal, continuing to the minimum value where curves 6 and 7 join at M_{CR}. It is this mode that splits (or bifurcates) creating modes 6 and 7. Thus there is a small stable region between curves 5a and 5b, due to the non-symmetrical nature of the mean profile. For $M > M_{CR}$, the Fast modes lie between the neutral curves 3 and 6 ($\alpha_N = 0$), while the Slow modes lie between the neutral curves 4 and 7 ($\alpha_N = 0$). The unstable modes associated with the neutral phase speed labeled 5 for $M > M_{CR}$ have never been fully explored, nor has the possibility of neutral modes associated with the freestream speeds $c_N = \beta_U$ or $c_N = 1$ (these would be analogous to the non-inflectional modes of the compressible boundary layer found by Mack, 1984).

The corresponding maximum spatial growth rates as a function of Mach number are also shown in Fig. 5.3. For each value of the temperature ratio β_T, the maximum spatial growth rate of the subsonic mode decreases as the Mach number increases from zero to M_*. For Mach numbers greater than M_*, two unstable modes appear and remain relatively small as the Mach number is further increased. The curves also show that by increasing β_T, a decrease in the maximum growth rates results.

Convective mach number

A number of experiments (e.g., Brown & Roshko, 1974; Chinzei, Masuya, Komuro, Murakami, & Kudou, 1986; and Papamoschou & Roshko, 1986, 1988) and numerical simulations (e.g., Guirguis, 1988; Lele, 1989; Sandham & Reynolds, 1990; and Mukunda, Sekar, Carpenter, Drummond, & Kumar, 1989) have shown that the compressible mixing layer becomes less unstable with increasing Mach number. In order to correlate the experimental results, a number of experimentalists have used a heuristically defined "convective Mach number". This idea, first introduced by Bogdanoff (1983) for compressible flows, has permeated much of the work on the stability of compressible free shear layers since then. The basic idea is to define a Mach number in a moving frame of reference fixed to the large scale structures of the mixing layer (Bogdanoff, 1983; Papamoschou & Roshko, 1986, 1988). Thus, for streams of equal gases, the convective Mach number is defined as

$$M_c = \frac{U_1^* - U_2^*}{a_1^* + a_2^*} = \frac{M(1 - \beta_U)}{1 + \sqrt{\beta_T}}. \tag{5.39}$$

More general definitions include the effect of different gases (Bogdanoff, 1983 and Papamoschou & Roshko, 1986, 1988) or to defining the convective Mach number in terms of the most unstable wave (Zhuang, Kubota, & Dimotakis, 1988). These definitions were for unbounded flows. Tam & Hu (1989) have applied these concepts to a mixing layer in a channel. When a mixing layer is formed between two different gases some definitions will yield different values for the convective Mach number in the two gases. It is not obvious which value is the proper one to use in the correlation, or whether some average of the two is appropriate.

It is interesting to note that another interpretation of the convective Mach number exists. Extensive spatial stability calculations for the compressible mixing layer (Jackson & Grosch, 1989, 1991) suggested a way to rigorously derive from linear stability theory a single convective Mach number for a compressible mixing layer for both a single species gas and a multi-species gas (Jackson & Grosch, 1990b). In particular, the definition is based on the freestream Mach number in the laboratory frame and is independent of the speed of the large scale structures and the speed of the most unstable wave. From Fig. 5.1, we see that subsonic modes exist for $M < M_*$ and supersonic modes which radiate into one or the other stream exist for $M > M_*$, and thus one can define a convective Mach number as follows

$$M_c = \frac{M}{M_*} = \frac{M(1 - \beta_U)}{1 + \sqrt{\beta_T}}. \tag{5.40}$$

With this scaling, we see that subsonic modes exist for $M_c < 1$ and supersonic modes exist for $M_c > 1$. This definition is identical to (5.39) given by Bogdanoff (1983).

In order to present the variation of the maximum growth rates with M_c we normalize them by defining the normalized growth rate for spatial stability by

$$R = \frac{(-\alpha_i)_{\text{MAX}} (\beta_T, \beta_U, M)}{(-\alpha_i)_{\text{MAX}} (\beta_T, \beta_U, 0)}. \tag{5.41}$$

Figure 5.4 is a plot of R versus M_c for the three thermodynamic models and β_T of 0.5, 1, and 2. This data is taken from Jackson and Grosch (1991). It can be seen that with these scalings the data collapses onto essentially a single curve for $M_c < 1$, and a narrow band for $M_c > 1$. One should also note that the second unstable supersonic modes appear around $M_c = 1$. This curve is similar to that obtained by Ragab and Wu (1989) who use Bogdanoff's heuristic definition of the convective Mach number. However, in their graph the second supersonic mode is absent.

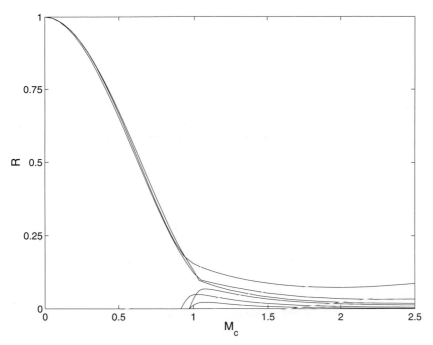

Fig. 5.4. Plot of normalized growth rate as a function of the convective Mach number for $\beta_T = 0.5$, 1, and 2, and for $\beta_U = 0$.

5.2.4 Compressible vortex sheet

Miles (1958) analyzed the compressible Rayleigh equation in the limit $\alpha \to 0$ for a vortex sheet. As will be shown below, this analysis also corresponds to determining the neutral modes of a compressible mixing layer.

The general solution to the compressible Rayleigh equation (5.30) is given by[1]

$$\Pi = \begin{cases} A_+ F(\eta) \exp(-\alpha\Omega_+\eta), & \eta > 0, \\ A_- G(\eta) \exp(+\alpha\Omega_-\eta), & \eta < 0, \end{cases} \tag{5.42}$$

where the equations for F and G are given by

$$F'' - \left(\frac{2U'}{U - c} + 2\alpha\Omega_+\right) F' + \left(\alpha^2\Omega_+^2 + \frac{2U'}{U - c}\alpha\Omega_+ - \alpha^2 g\right) F = 0, \tag{5.43}$$

---

[1] The analysis presented here follows that of R. Klein and A. Majda, and appears in the unpublished report by Grosch, Jackson, Klein, Majda, & Papageorgiou, 1991.

for $\eta > 0$, and

$$G'' - \left(\frac{2U'}{U-c} - 2\alpha\Omega_-\right) G' + \left(\alpha^2\Omega_-^2 - \frac{2U'}{U-c}\alpha\Omega_- - \alpha^2 g\right) G = 0,$$

$$(5.44)$$

for $\eta < 0$, where

$$g(\eta) = T[T - M^2(U-c)^2].$$ $$(5.45)$$

The appropriate boundary conditions are $F(+\infty) = 1$ and $G(-\infty) = 1$. In order for the above to be a uniformly valid solution over $(-\infty, +\infty)$, the Wronskian must vanish at $\eta = 0$, yielding the required eigen relation

$$F(G' + \alpha\Omega_-G) = G(F' - \alpha\Omega_+F).$$ $$(5.46)$$

Since we are interested in long-wave perturbations ($\alpha \to 0$), the appropriate expansions are found to be

$$F = F_0 + \alpha F_1 + \alpha^2 F_2 + \cdots,$$ $$(5.47)$$

and similarly for G. After substituting the above expansions, the solutions to the first two orders are

$$F_0 = 1, \quad F_1 = -\Omega_+ \int_\eta^{+\infty} \left[1 - \left(\frac{U-c}{1-c}\right)^2\right] d\eta,$$ $$(5.48)$$

and

$$G_0 = 1, \quad G_1 = -\Omega_- \int_{-\infty}^{\eta} \left[1 - \left(\frac{U-c}{\beta_U - c}\right)^2\right] d\eta.$$ $$(5.49)$$

The eigenrelation (5.46) is also expanded in powers of α, resulting in the following equations

$$F_0 G_0' = G_0 F_0'$$ $$(5.50)$$

to zeroth order, and

$$F_0(G_1' + \Omega_-G_0) + F_1 G_0' = G_0(F_1' - \Omega_+F_0) + G_1 F_0'$$ $$(5.51)$$

to the next order. The zeroth order equation is satisfied trivially, while the first order equation yields

$$\frac{\Omega_-}{(\beta_U - c)^2} = -\frac{\Omega_+}{(1-c)^2}.$$ $$(5.52)$$

Note that this relation is independent of the detailed form of U and T, and only depends on the basic flow characteristics at infinity. This is to be expected

from physical arguments since the length scale of the instability is much larger than the length scale over which the undisturbed flow is non-uniform. It is precisely this order that the vortex sheet results of Miles (1958) is recovered. Corrections can be obtained at the next order (Grosch, Jackson, Klein, Majda, & Papageorgiou, 1991.) Note that the above relation requires that both Ω_- and Ω_+ be complex, and hence the analysis is strictly limited to region 3 of Fig. 5.1. With the definitions for $\Omega_\pm$ then

$$\beta_T[M^2(\beta_U - c_N)^2 - \beta_T](1 - c_N)^4 = [M^2(1 - c_n)^2 - 1](\beta_U - c_N)^4,$$
(5.53)

which determines the phase speed c_N for a neutral mode. This equation is identical to (5.3a) of Miles (1958) if we re-express his result in our notation.

The following comments now apply:

1. A single real root of (5.53) exists for

$$M \geq M_* \equiv \frac{1 + \sqrt{\beta_T}}{1 - \beta_U},$$
(5.54)

with phase speed

$$c_N = \frac{\beta_U + \sqrt{\beta_T}}{1 + \sqrt{\beta_T}},$$
(5.55)

which is classified as a constant speed supersonic-supersonic neutral mode. Note that this solution is independent of the Mach number, and corresponds to the phase speed at which the two sonic speeds $c_\pm$ are equal. In this regime there is also a pair of complex conjugate eigenvalues corresponding to one unstable and one stable eigenvalue. The associated instability is analogous to the classical Kelvin-Helmholtz instability for subsonic vortex sheets (Artola & Majda, 1987). This instability vanishes as the Mach number increases.

2. A double root first appears at

$$M_{CR} = \frac{\left(1 + \beta_T^{1/3}\right)^{3/2}}{1 - \beta_U},$$
(5.56)

with phase speed

$$c_N = \frac{\beta_U + \beta_T^{1/3}}{1 + \beta_T^{1/3}}.$$
(5.57)

3. There are three distinct real roots for $M > M_{CR}$. One of the roots is (5.55), while the other two roots must be found numerically. For the special case

of $\beta_T = 1$, these roots are given by

$$c_N = \frac{1 + \beta_U}{2} \pm \frac{1}{2M}[M^2(1 - \beta_U)^2 + 4 - 4\sqrt{M^2(1 - \beta_U)^2 + 1}]^{1/2}.$$

(5.58)

The root that corresponds to the $(+)$ sign is classified as a fast supersonic-supersonic neutral mode, while that which corresponds to the $(-)$ sign is classified as a slow supersonic-supersonic neutral mode.

The phase speeds are plotted in Fig. 5.1 for $\beta_U = 0$ and various values of β_T. The classification scheme is given in the figure caption.

The neutral phase speeds given above are exact for $\alpha = 0$. In order to obtain the higher order corrections for $\alpha \neq 0$ the value of c must also be expanded in powers of α. When this was done it was found that the overall growth rate was $O(\alpha^2)$; Balsa and Goldstein (1990) also found, numerically, the $O(\alpha^2)$ growth rate for these modes. It was also found that the growth rate at $O(\alpha^2)$ becomes singular at M_{CR}. This singular behavior was studied by expansions about the singular value of M. A connection between the regimes $M_* < M < M_{CR}$ and $M > M_{CR}$ was found and yielded the transition from a stable/unstable pair of eigenmodes plus a supersonic neutral mode for $M < M_{CR}$ to three supersonic neutral modes for $M > M_{CR}$.

5.2.5 Bounded compressible mixing layer

The stability characteristics of a bounded mixing layer, that is a mixing layer in a rectangular duct, have been considered by Tam & Hu (1989), Greenough, Riley, Soestrisno & Eberhardt (1989), Macaraeg & Streett (1989), Zhuang, Kubota & Dimotakis (1990b), Macaraeg (1990), Jackson & Grosch (1990c), and Morris & Giridharan (1991). The effect of walls become apparent at supersonic convective Mach numbers because the coupling between the motion of the mixing layer and the acoustic modes of the channel produces two new instability modes. That is, with boundedness, there will always be incoming and outgoing waves and these must be properly accounted for, whereas for the unbounded mixing layer only outgoing waves are considered. This effect was clearly demonstrated by Tam & Hu (1989), who classified the new modes as Class A (those with phase speeds decreasing as the wavenumber and frequency increase) or Class B (those with phase speeds increasing as the wavenumber and frequency increase). Below we present a subset of the results of Tam & Hu, but within the framework presented above for the unbounded mixing layer.

We begin by considering the inviscid temporal stability of a mixing layer in a channel of width $2H$. We assume that the thickness of the mixing layer

is 2δ, with $\delta < H$. The stability problem can be formulated independently of the detailed form of the velocity and temperature profiles. A standard normal mode analysis again leads to the compressible Rayleigh equation (5.30). The appropriate boundary conditions are

$$\Pi'(\pm H) = 0. \tag{5.59}$$

The outer solution, valid in $\delta < \eta \leq H$ is given by

$$\Pi = \cosh[\alpha\Omega_+(\eta - H)], \tag{5.60}$$

and that valid in $-H \leq \eta < -\delta$ is given by

$$\Pi = \cosh[\alpha\Omega_-(\eta + H)], \tag{5.61}$$

where $\Omega_\pm$ is given by (5.32). Note that, when $\Omega_\pm$ are complex (i.e., the outer flow is supersonic), the outer solutions become cosine functions and thus represent acoustic modes.

The mean flow is given by (5.13) and (5.15). In the temporal stability calculations presented below we have taken $\beta_T = 1$, $\beta_U = 0$, and $M = 3.5$. In addition, we take $H = 12$ which is twice that of the shear layer thickness δ.

Figures 5.5 and 5.6 plots the phase speeds and temporal growth rates as a function of the wavenumber. In Fig. 5.5 we see that the phase speeds depicted in the top plot decrease as the wavenumber increases, and in the terminology of Tam & Hu (1989), are classified as Class A modes, whereas the phase speeds depicted in the bottom plot increase as the wavenumber increases, and are classified as Class B modes. The phase speeds of the two classes are a reflection of each other about the centerline $c_r = 1/2$ due to the mean profiles being symmetrical. The sonic speeds $c_\pm$ are also shown (dashed) and can be used as a reference when classifying the behavior of the disturbances at the walls with regard to Fig. 5.1 (for the bounded case, change the text "∞" to "H" in regions 2 and 3, and the figure then applies when walls are present). For example, Class A modes, which initially have a phase speed greater than c_+, are subsonic at $\eta = +H$ and supersonic at $\eta = -H$. As the phase speed decreases and eventually crosses the $c = c_+$ sonic line, the disturbances become supersonic at both walls. Similarly, Class B modes, which initially have a phase speed less than c_-, are supersonic at $\eta = +H$ and subsonic at $\eta = -H$. As the phase speed increases and crosses the $c = c_-$ sonic line, the disturbances become supersonic at both walls. Thus there is a continuous change in the character of the modes in that a mode which is subsonic at one boundary is transformed into a supersonic mode at that boundary as the wavenumber is increased. The growth rates for the Class A modes are shown in Fig. 5.6. Note that after an

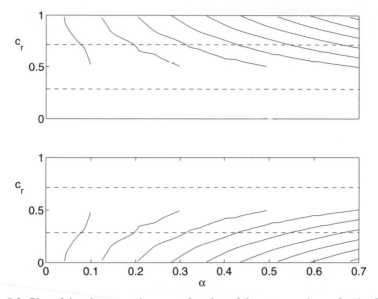

Fig. 5.5. Plot of the phase speeds c_r as a function of the wavenumber α for the Class A modes (top) and the Class B modes (bottom) at $M = 3.5$ and $\beta_T = 1$. The sonic speeds $c_+ = 0.714$ and $c_- = 0.286$ are shown as the dashed lines.

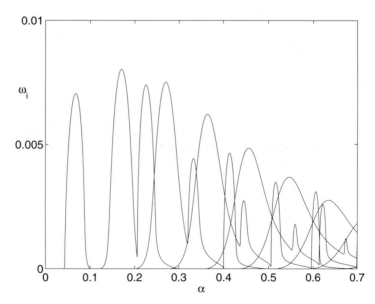

Fig. 5.6. Plot of the temporal growth rates ω_i as a function of the wavenumber α for both the Class A and Class B modes at $M = 3.5$ and $\beta_T = 1$.

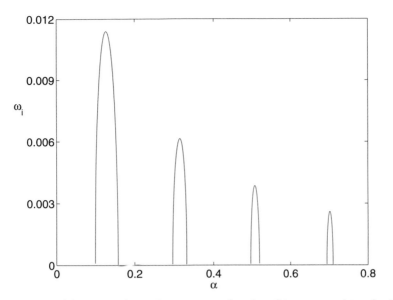

Fig. 5.7. Plot of the temporal growth rates ω_i as a function of the wavenumber α for the Class C modes at $M = 3.5$ and $\beta_T = 1$. The corresponding phase speeds are $c_r = 1/2$.

initial increase in the maximum growth rate, the maximum growth rates generally decrease as the wavenumber increases. It is clear from this figure that the spectrum is quite complicated, with multiple modes existing at higher values of α. Because the mean profiles are symmetrical, the growth rates of the Class A and B modes are identical.

In addition to the Class A and B modes, there exists another set of modes, all with phase speeds of exactly $1/2$, and is independent of α. We call these Class C modes. The growth rates of these modes are shown in Fig. 5.7. These growth rates are about 50% greater than those of Class A and B modes. Macaraeg & Streett (1989) and Macaraeg (1990) also found similar modes in their calculations. However, Tam & Hu (1989) did not report any such modes; perhaps this is due to the fact that their mean velocity profile was not symmetric; hence, these modes are likely of academic interest only.

5.3 Compressible boundary layer

The stability of compressible boundary layers has received considerable attention since the mid 1940's. In the early years, progress was slow because calculations were limited to asymptotic methods, and the results were often incomplete and sometimes contradictory. Substantial progress began in earnest

in the late 1950's and early 1960's as numerical calculations became routine. However, it still took over 20 years to unravel most of the subtleties of the stability characteristics of the compressible boundary layer. For a historical review, and results obtained up to the early 1980's, see Mack (1984, 1987). Our aim is to present the elementary basics while illuminating the richness of the subject; a complete review or summary of the subject is well beyond the intent of this book. Thus, in this section we consider only the two-dimensional compressible boundary layer on a flat plate subject to two-dimensional disturbances. More general configurations are presented in the review article by Mack (1984); see also the references contained therein. These extensions include both temporal and spatial theories, three-dimensional disturbances, and three-dimensional boundary layers (rotating disk, Falkner-Skan-Cooke boundary layers, swept wing). Finally, we note that the continuous spectra of the compressible boundary layer was discussed by Ashpis & Erlebacher (1990) and Balakumar & Malik (1992).

5.3.1 Mean flow

Consider the two-dimensional compressible boundary layer flow over a flat plate with zero pressure gradient. A description of the mean flow can be found in Mack (1965a), which is briefly presented here for completeness. Let (u^*, v^*) be the velocity components in the (x^*, y^*) directions, respectively, ρ^* the density, T^* the temperature, and P^* the pressure, a known constant. The dimensional equations governing the flow of a perfect gas are

$$(\rho^* u^*)_{x^*} + (\rho^* v^*)_{y^*} = 0, \tag{5.62}$$

$$\rho^*[u^* u^*_{x^*} + v^* u^*_{y^*}] = (\mu^* u^*_{y^*})_{y^*}, \tag{5.63}$$

$$\rho^*[u^* e^*_{x^*} + v^* e^*_{y^*}] = (\kappa^* T^*_{y^*})_{y^*} + \mu^* (u^*_{y^*})^2, \tag{5.64}$$

and

$$P^* = \rho^* R^* T^*, \tag{5.65}$$

where the asterisks refer to dimensional quantities. Here, μ^* and κ^* are the dimensional viscosity and thermal conductivity coefficients, assumed to be functions of temperature; R^* is the gas constant for air. The viscosity coefficient is computed from the Sutherland formula, namely

$$\mu^* = \begin{cases} \frac{1.458\, T^{*3/2}}{T^* + 110.4} \times 10^{-5} \text{ gm/cm-sec}, & T^* > 110.4\text{K}, \\ (0.693873 \times 10^{-6}) T^* \text{ gm/cm-sec}, & T^* < 110.4\text{K}, \end{cases} \tag{5.66}$$

while the thermal conductivity coefficient can be computed from the formula

$$\kappa^* = \begin{cases} \frac{0.6325\sqrt{T^*}}{1+(245.4/T^*)10^{-12/T^*}} & \text{cal/cm-sec-C,} \quad T^* > 80K, \\ (0.222964 \times 10^{-6})T^* & \text{cal/cm-sec-C,} \quad T^* < 80K. \end{cases} \tag{5.67}$$

The viscosity and thermal conductivity coefficients are related via the Prandtl number or

$$Pr = c_p^* \mu^* / \kappa^*, \tag{5.68}$$

which is a function of temperature. The enthalpy, e^*, is a function of temperature and is given in terms of c_p^*, the specific heat at constant pressure, by

$$e^* = \int_0^{T^*} c_p^* dT^*. \tag{5.69}$$

The equations assume that the temperature everywhere in the flow is below the temperature of dissociation. At high temperature, which can occur within the compressible boundary layer if the Mach number is large enough, the flow dissociates and, as a result, real gas effects must be considered.

In general, tables for a perfect gas are needed for the enthalpy-temperature relation and the Prandtl number. The specific heat, c_p^*, is then computed from (5.68). This is the approach taken by Mack, and subsequently used in all of his stability calculations. For purposes of clarity, we assume constant values for c_p^* and Pr; the thermal conductivity can then be omitted from active consideration, as well as the enthalpy in favor of the temperature via $e^* = c_p^* T^*$. Our stability calculations presented here will therefore differ only slightly from those of Mack.

To solve the mean flow equations, we first introduce the similarity variable

$$\eta = \frac{y^*}{x^*}\sqrt{R_x}, \tag{5.70}$$

where R_x is the x-Reynolds number

$$R_x = \frac{u_\infty^* x^*}{v_\infty^*}, \quad v_\infty^* = \mu_\infty^* / \kappa_\infty^*, \tag{5.71}$$

u_∞^* is the freestream velocity, and v^* is the kinematic viscosity coefficient. The partial derivatives thus transform according to

$$\frac{\partial}{\partial x^*} = \frac{\partial}{\partial x^*} - \frac{\eta}{2x^*}\frac{\partial}{\partial \eta}, \quad \frac{\partial}{\partial y^*} = \frac{\sqrt{R_x}}{x^*}\frac{\partial}{\partial \eta}. \tag{5.72}$$

The following dimensionless quantities are introduced

$$U = u^*/u_\infty^*, \quad V = v^*/u_\infty^*, \quad \rho = \rho^*/\rho_\infty^*,$$

$$\mu = \mu^*/\mu_\infty^*, \quad T = T^*/T_\infty^*, \quad \theta = \frac{T^* - T_\infty^*}{T_0^* - T_\infty^*}, \tag{5.73}$$

where the freestream stagnation temperature, T_0^*, is defined by

$$T_0^* = T_\infty^* + \frac{(u_\infty^*)^2}{2c_P^*}. \tag{5.74}$$

From the definition of the scaled temperature θ, we see that

$$T = 1 + \frac{\gamma - 1}{2} M^2 \theta, \tag{5.75}$$

where γ is the ratio of specific heats and M the freestream Mach number. Here we made use of the relations (see, e.g., White, 1974)

$$c_P^* = \frac{\gamma R^*}{\gamma - 1}, \quad M = u_\infty^*/a_\infty^*, \quad a^* = \sqrt{\gamma R^* T^*}. \tag{5.76}$$

We now assume that the horizontal velocity component and the temperature are functions of η only, and write

$$\rho U = 2g'(\eta), \tag{5.77}$$

where the prime denotes differentiation with respect to the similarity variable η. In these terms, the continuity equation (5.62) becomes

$$\rho V = \frac{1}{\sqrt{R_x}}(\eta g' - g) \tag{5.78}$$

for the normal velocity component. The momentum (5.63) and the energy (5.64) equations then reduce to

$$\frac{d}{d\eta}\left(\mu \frac{dU}{d\eta}\right) + g\frac{dU}{d\eta} = 0, \tag{5.79}$$

and

$$\frac{d}{d\eta}\left(\frac{\mu}{Pr}\frac{d\theta}{d\eta}\right) + g\frac{d\theta}{d\eta} = -2\mu\left(\frac{dU}{d\eta}\right)^2. \tag{5.80}$$

The appropriate boundary conditions are given by

$$\text{at } \eta = 0: \quad U = 0, \quad \begin{array}{l} \text{Case (i)} \quad \theta'(0) = 0, \\ \text{Case (ii)} \quad \theta(0) = \text{given}, \end{array} \tag{5.81}$$

$$\text{at } \eta \to \infty: \quad U = 1, \quad \theta = 0.$$

Case (i) corresponds to an insulated wall while case (ii) corresponds to a wall at a specified but fixed temperature. In the second case, the wall can either be cooled or heated, depending on the sign of $T_w/T_{ad} - 1$, where T_w is the wall

temperature and T_{ad} is the adiabatic wall temperature, the value of the temperature of an insulated wall; the adiabatic wall temperature is also sometimes referred to as the recovery temperature. We will focus our attention exclusively on case (i); for a discussion of case (ii) and its stability characteristics, see Mack (1984) and the references contained therein.

In the incompressible limit $M \to 0$ we see from (5.75) that $T = 1$, and hence $T^* = T^*_\infty$ from (5.73), $\mu = 1$ from (5.73), and (5.79) reduces to

$$g''' + gg'' = 0,$$

the well known Blasius profile.

The solution procedure is as follows. We begin by integrating the system (5.79) and (5.80) from $\eta = 0$ to $\eta = \eta_\delta$, where η_δ is the edge of the boundary layer. (Mack, 1965a, re-writes the system as four first-order equations so that a fourth-order Runge-Kutta integrator can be used, but this is merely a matter of preference.) Since the system is fourth-order, the integrator requires four boundary conditions to be specified. For the case of an insulated wall (the other case follows similarly), we use the boundary conditions

$$U(0) = 0, \quad U'(0) = U_0, \quad \theta(0) = \theta_0, \quad \theta'(0) = 0, \qquad (5.82)$$

where U_0 and θ_0 are determined by an iteration procedure so that the boundary conditions

$$U(\eta_\delta) = 1, \quad \theta(\eta_\delta) = 0, \qquad (5.83)$$

at $\eta = \eta_\delta$ are satisfied. The unknown function g is found by simultaneously solving

$$g' = \frac{U}{2T}, \quad g(0) = 0, \qquad (5.84)$$

with T defined by (5.75).

To complete the description of the mean flow, T^*_∞ must be specified in order to compute the dimensionless viscosity μ; see (5.73). One can either specify T^*_∞ directly, or specify the stagnation temperature T^*_0; see (5.74). Since it is customary to specify the stagnation temperature, we do so and compute T^*_∞ from the relation

$$\frac{T^*_0}{T^*_\infty} = 1 + \frac{\gamma - 1}{2} M^2, \qquad (5.85)$$

once the freestream Mach number is given. In all cases we assume "wind tunnel" conditions (in the nomenclature of Mack) by setting $T^*_0 = 311\text{K}$ until, with increasing Mach number, T^*_∞ drops to 50K. For higher Mach numbers,

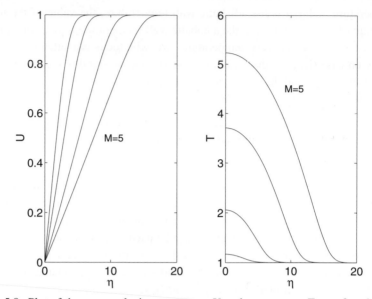

Fig. 5.8. Plot of the mean velocity component U and temperature T as a function of η and for $M = 1,\ 2.5,\ 4,\ 5$; insulated wall and wind tunnel conditions, $Pr = 0.72$, $T_0^* = 311$ K.

T_∞^* is held constant at 50K. In all calculations we use $\gamma = 1.4$ and set $Pr = 0.72$.

Figure 5.8 plots the mean flow quantities U and T as a function of the similarity coordinate η at various values of the Mach number. Note that as the Mach number increases, both the velocity and the temperature are defined over a broader and broader region, while at the plate the temperature increases due to viscous heating.

One final comment is in order here. In the original derivation of Mack, the density-weighted transformation was not used, as was the case for the compressible mixing layer presented earlier. There is no difficulty in employing such a transformation, and indeed some subsequent researchers found it convenient to do so. Here we chose to follow Mack, and there are at least three reasons for doing this. First, most of the work published on the stability of the compressible boundary layer is due to Mack, and it is therefore advantageous to follow his path. Secondly, if one stays in the physical coordinate system, physical insight and interpretation is easier than when working in the transformed space since the inverse transformation must be used to back out the solutions to the physical space. Thirdly, the viscous stability equations become slightly more complicated if the density-weighted transformation is used.

5.3.2 Inviscid fluctuations

For non-zero Mach numbers, the mean profile has an inflection point, defined by Lees & Lin (1946) when $(U'/T)' = 0$; see Result 5.1. Thus, the compressible boundary layer may be unstable to inviscid disturbances. We therefore begin the stability analysis of the compressible boundary layer by examining the inviscid case.

The compressible Rayleigh equation, either (5.27) or (5.28), governs the inviscid stability of the compressible boundary layer. The boundary conditions in this limit are

$$\Pi'(0) = 0, \quad \phi(0) = 0 \tag{5.86}$$

at the wall, and

$$\Pi, \phi \approx \exp(-\Omega_+ \eta) \tag{5.87}$$

in the freestream, where

$$\Omega_+^2 = \alpha^2[1 - M^2(1 - c)^2]. \tag{5.88}$$

Here we use the same general notation as that used for the compressible mixing layer, and so the subscript $+$ denote values in the freestream $\eta \to +\infty$. Let us define c_+ to be the phase speed for which Ω_+^2 vanishes. Thus

$$c_+ = 1 - \frac{1}{M}. \tag{5.89}$$

As in the case of the compressible mixing layer, the disturbances can either be subsonic ($c > c_+$) or supersonic ($c < c_+$) in the freestream. The sonic curve (solid) is shown in Fig. 5.9.

In addition to the sonic condition in the freestream, a sonic condition also occurs at the wall. This comes about by noticing that the compressible Rayleigh equation (5.28) is singular whenever $\xi = 0$. Evaluated at $\eta = \infty$ leads to the sonic speed c_+ defined earlier. However, ξ can also vanish within the compressible boundary layer. This will occur first at the wall and leads to the "wall" sonic speed $c_w = \sqrt{T_w}/M$, where $T_w = T(0)$ is the temperature at the wall (note that $U(0) = 0$). For an insulated wall, the wall sonic speed is shown in Fig. 5.9 as the dashed curve. As the Mach number increases, a supersonic region exists extending from the wall to the sonic line, located well within the boundary layer. Thus, disturbances can either be subsonic ($c < c_w$) or supersonic ($c > c_w$) in a region adjacent to the wall.

As in the case of the compressible mixing layer, the nature of the disturbances and the appropriate boundary conditions can be illustrated by reference to Fig. 5.9, where we plot the sonic speeds c_+ and c_w versus M. As before,

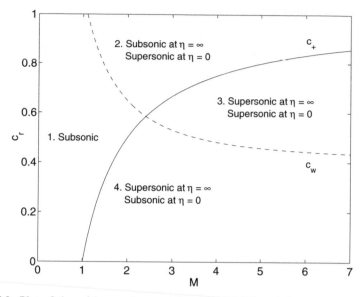

Fig. 5.9. Plot of the sonic speed $c_+ = 1 - 1/M$ (solid) and the wall sonic speed $c_w = \sqrt{T_w}/M$ (dashed) versus Mach number. The wall sonic speed is calculated for the case of an insulated wall and wind tunnel conditions.

there exist four regions in the (c_r, M) plane. In region 1, the flow is subsonic everywhere within the boundary layer and in the freestream. The phase speed of a neutral mode is thus given by the Lees & Lin condition $c_s = U(\eta_s)$, where η_s is the generalized inflection point found by solving

$$S(\eta) = (U'/T)' = 0.$$

Figure 5.10 is a plot of S as a function of η for various values of the Mach number. Note that as the Mach number increases, the point η_s also increases; i.e., the critical layer moves towards the freestream as the Mach number increases. The corresponding unique neutral wavenumber can be found numerically. In region 2 the flow is subsonic in the freestream, but has a supersonic region adjacent to the wall. The Lees & Lin condition still holds in determining the neutral phase speed, but now the wavenumber is no longer unique. In fact there is an infinite set of wavenumbers, called higher modes. These are primarily acoustic in nature, and represent sound waves reflecting from the wall and the relative sonic line. Following the nomenclature of Mack, we label the neutral wavenumbers in regions 1 and 2 as $\alpha_{s,n}$, where the subscript s indicates that the neutral phase speed c_s is determined from the Lees & Lin condition, and n is the mode number. Mack calls these "inflectional" modes.

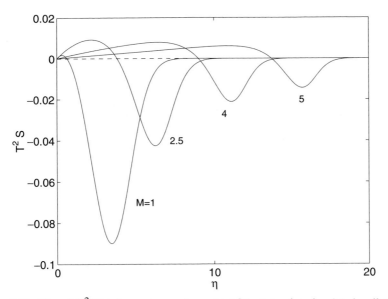

Fig. 5.10. Plot of $T^2 S(\eta)$ for various values of the Mach number; insulated wall and wind tunnel conditions.

Figure 5.11 is a plot of the neutral phase speed c_s. Note that at a Mach number of about 2.2, the neutral phase speed crosses from region 1 into region 2, where the neutral disturbances first become supersonic at the wall. The corresponding neutral wavenumbers are shown in Fig. 5.12. The associated eigenfunction can be computed for each neutral wavenumber, and it is found that the number of zeros of the eigenfunctions is one less than the mode number.

The maximum temporal growth rates for these modes has also been computed by Mack, and it was found that below a Mach number of $M = 2.2$, the maximum growth rates are so small that the compressible boundary layer is virtually stable to inviscid disturbances. Above $M = 2.2$, the second mode has the largest growth rate, and it is this mode that will first trigger nonlinearities. Above a Mach number of about $M = 3$, the maximum growth rate of mode 2 becomes larger than that computed from viscous theory. Thus, inviscid instability becomes dominant and viscosity is stabilizing at all Reynolds numbers, just as in free shear flows. It is this fact that allows the inviscid theory to be used to investigate most of the stability characteristics of the compressible boundary layer.

In addition to the inflectional modes described above for regions 1 and 2, there is also a set of "non-inflectional" modes having a neutral phase speed of $c_1 = 1$ of region 2. These modes are thus characterized because the requirement

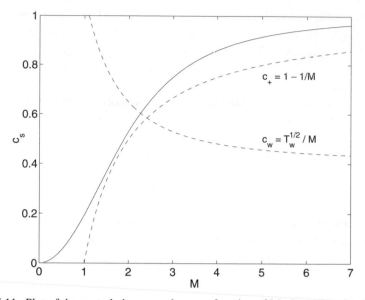

Fig. 5.11. Plot of the neutral phase speed c_s as a function of Mach number; insulated wall and wind tunnel conditions. The dashed curves correspond to the sonic speed c_+ and the wall sonic speed c_w.

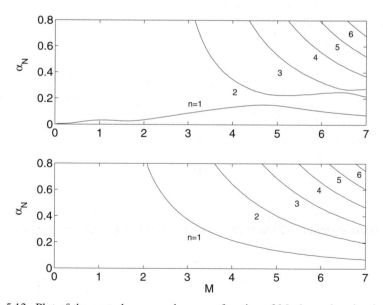

Fig. 5.12. Plot of the neutral wavenumbers as a function of Mach number; insulated wall and wind tunnel conditions. Top: inflectional modes $\alpha_{s,n}$ with phase speed c_s. Bottom: non-inflectional modes $\alpha_{1,n}$ with phase speed $c_1 = 1$.

for an inflectional mode, that $(U'/T)'$ vanish somewhere within the boundary layer, occurs only in the freestream. The corresponding neutral wavenumbers $\alpha_{1,n}$, where the subscripts 1 indicates that the phase speed is unity and n the mode number, are shown in Fig. 5.12. The importance of the neutral wave with $c_1 = 1$ is that the neighboring waves with $c < 1$ are always unstable. As in the case of inflectional modes, the number of zeros of the associated eigenfunctions for the non-inflectional modes is one less than the mode number.

In region 3 the flow disturbance is supersonic both in the freestream and within a region adjacent to the wall, while in region 4 the flow disturbance is subsonic everywhere within the boundary layer but supersonic in the freestream. The appropriate boundary condition is that only outgoing waves are allowed, as was the case for the compressible mixing layer. Although Mack did find solutions in these two regions, their associated maximum growth rates were much smaller than those of regions 1 and 2, and so little attention has been paid to them.

As a final note we comment here about the various solution techniques employed to compute solutions to the inviscid eigenvalue problem. One solution technique is to solve the compressible Rayleigh equation, either (5.27) or (5.28), directly with appropriate boundary conditions. Alternatively, one can employ the Riccati transformation

$$G = \frac{\Pi'}{\alpha T \Pi},$$

or some other equivalent form, to get a nonlinear first order differential equation, as was done previously for the compressible mixing layer. A final technique is to solve the two first-order equations

$$\Pi' = \frac{-i\alpha^2(U-c)\phi}{T},$$

$$\phi' = \frac{U'}{U-c}\phi + \frac{i\Pi}{U-c}(T - M^2(U-c)^2),$$

where the first equation is (5.24), and the second equation is easily derived from the system (5.22) to (5.26); the factor γM^2 has been removed by scaling. Note that in this formulation, only the mean flow temperature T and the velocity U and its first derivative are needed. In all cases the contour of numerical integration must be indented below the critical layer into the complex plane for neutral disturbances. The point is this: if one thinks of the solution as a topological surface, and the eigenvalues the zeros of that surface, then it is clear that different forms of the equations will lead to different topologies, and finding the zeros on one topological surface might be easier computationally

than on another surface. For this reason, it is generally advised to consider all the various forms of the equations; if difficulties should arise with one set of equations, then try another.

5.3.3 Viscous fluctuations

The dimensional equations governing the flow of a viscous compressible ideal gas in two-dimensions are

$$\rho_{t*}^* + (\rho^* u^*)_{x*} + (\rho^* v^*)_{y*} = 0, \tag{5.90}$$

$$\rho^*[u_{t*}^* + u^* u_{x*}^* + v^* u_{y*}^*] + P_{x*}^* = \frac{\partial}{\partial x^*}\left[2\mu^* u_{x*}^* - \frac{2}{3}\mu^*(u_{x*}^* + v_{y*}^*)\right]$$

$$+ \frac{\partial}{\partial y^*}[\mu^*(u_{y*}^* + v_{x*}^*)], \tag{5.91}$$

$$\rho^*[v_{t*}^* + u^* v_{x*}^* + v^* v_{y*}^*] + P_{y*}^* = \frac{\partial}{\partial x^*}[\mu^*(u_{y*}^* + v_{x*}^*)] + \frac{\partial}{\partial y^*}\left[2\mu^* v_{y*}^*\right.$$

$$\left. - \frac{2}{3}\mu^*(u_{x*}^* + v_{y*}^*)\right], \tag{5.92}$$

$$\rho^* c_P^*[T_{t*}^* + u^* T_{x*}^* + v^* T_{y*}^*] - [P_{t*}^* + u^* P_{x*}^* + v^* P_{y*}^*] =$$

$$(\kappa^* T_{x*}^*)_{x*} + (\kappa^* T_{y*}^*)_{y*}$$

$$+ \mu^*[2u_{x*}^{*\,2} + 2v_{y*}^{*\,2} + 2u_{y*}^* v_{x*}^* + u_{y*}^{*\,2} + v_{x*}^{*\,2}]$$

$$- \frac{2}{3}\mu^*[u_{x*}^{*\,2} + v_{y*}^{*\,2} + 2u_{x*}^* v_{y*}^*], \tag{5.93}$$

and

$$P^* = \rho^* R^* T^*, \tag{5.94}$$

where (u^*, v^*) are the velocity components in the (x^*, y^*) directions, respectively, ρ^* the density, T^* the temperature, and P^* the pressure. Here, μ^* is the viscosity, κ^* the thermal conductivity, c_P^* the the specific heat at constant pressure, assumed constant, and R^* the gas constant for air. We assume the Prandtl number $Pr = c_P^* \mu^* / \kappa^*$ is constant, and so eliminate the thermal conductivity from active consideration. For simplicity, the Stokes approximation of zero bulk viscosity has been assumed.

These equations are now rendered dimensionless with respect to the freestream values.

The flow field is perturbed by introducing two-dimensional wave disturbances in the velocity, pressure, temperature and density with amplitudes which
are functions of η. Following the notation used by Lees & Lin (1946), we write

$$(u, v, p, T, \rho) = (U, 0, 1, T, \rho)(\eta) + (f, \alpha\phi, \Pi, \theta, r)(\eta)e^{i\alpha(x-ct)}, \tag{5.95}$$

while for the viscosity we write

$$\mu = \mu(\eta) + s(\eta)\,e^{i\alpha(x-ct)}. \tag{5.96}$$

The linearized equations for the fluctuations now read as

$$i(U - c)r + i\rho f + (\rho\phi)' = 0, \tag{5.97}$$

$$\rho[i(U - c)f + U'\phi] + \frac{i\Pi}{\gamma M^2} = \frac{\mu}{\alpha Re}[f'' + \alpha^2(i\phi' - 2f)]$$

$$-\frac{2}{3}\frac{\mu\alpha^2}{\alpha Re}(i\phi' - f) + \frac{1}{\alpha Re}[sU'' + s'U' + \mu'(f' + i\alpha^2\phi)], \tag{5.98}$$

$$i\rho(U - c)\phi + \frac{\Pi'}{\alpha^2\gamma M^2} = \frac{\mu}{\alpha Re}[2\phi'' + if' - \alpha^2\phi]$$

$$-\frac{2}{3}\frac{\mu}{\alpha Re}(\phi'' + if') + \frac{1}{\alpha Re}\left[isU' + 2\mu'\phi' - \frac{2}{3}\mu'(\phi' + if)\right], \tag{5.99}$$

$$\rho[i(U - c)\theta + T'\phi] + (\gamma - 1)(\phi' + if) =$$

$$\frac{\gamma}{\alpha Re Pr}[\mu(\theta'' - \alpha^2\theta) + (sT')' + \mu'\theta']$$

$$+ \frac{\gamma(\gamma - 1)M^2}{\alpha Re}[sU'^2 + 2\mu U'(f' + i\alpha^2\phi)], \tag{5.100}$$

and

$$\Pi = \rho\theta + rT. \tag{5.101}$$

Here, primes denote differentiation with respect to η. In addition the viscosity
perturbation s can be related to the temperature perturbation via

$$s = \theta\,\frac{d\mu}{dT}. \tag{5.102}$$

The stability equations can be written in matrix form[1] as

$$(AD^2 + BD + C)\tilde{\Phi} = 0, \tag{5.103}$$

---

[1] The student is asked to compute the elements of the matrices B and C in the exercise section.

where $\tilde{\Phi} = (f, \phi, \Pi, \theta)^T$, and A is the 4×4 matrix

$$A = \begin{bmatrix} 1 & 0 & 0 & 0 \\ 0 & 1 & 0 & 0 \\ 0 & 0 & 0 & 0 \\ 0 & 0 & 0 & 1 \end{bmatrix}. \tag{5.104}$$

The appropriate boundary conditions are

$$\Phi_1(0) = \Phi_2(0) = \Phi_4(0) = 0, \tag{5.105}$$

at $\eta = 0$, and

$$\Phi_1, \ \Phi_2, \ \Phi_4 \to 0, \tag{5.106}$$

as $\eta \to \infty$.

Note that, although the mean profile assumes an insulated wall (i.e., $T'(0) = 0$), it is the temperature perturbation, and not its derivative, that is assumed to vanish (i.e., $\theta(0) = 0$). As pointed out by Malik (1990), this is equivalent to the assumption that the wall will appear insulated on the time scale of the mean flow but not on the short time scales of the disturbances. However, for stationary disturbances (such as crossflow and Görtler), one may need to replace $\theta(0) = 0$ in favor of its derivative or a combination thereof, depending on the physical properties of the solid and the gas.

The stability equations can also be rewritten as a system of first order equations[1], given by

$$Z_i' = \sum_{j=1}^{6} a_{i,j} Z_j, \quad i = 1, \dots, 6, \tag{5.107}$$

where

$$Z_1 = f, \quad Z_2 = f', \quad Z_3 = \phi,$$
$$Z_4 = \frac{\Pi}{\gamma M^2}, \quad Z_5 = \theta, \quad Z_6 = \theta'.$$

The appropriate boundary conditions here are

$$Z_1(0) = Z_3(0) = Z_5(0) = 0, \tag{5.108}$$

at $\eta = 0$, and

$$Z_1, \ Z_3, \ Z_5 \to 0, \tag{5.109}$$

as $\eta \to \infty$.

[1] The student is asked to compute the elements $a_{i,j}$ in the exercise section.

Various numerical methods have been presented to solve the compressible stability equations, either the system (5.103) or (5.107). These methods can be classified into initial value methods (IVM) or boundary value methods (BVM). In the IVM, one constructs the solution by integrating the system (5.107) from either $\eta = 0$ to $\eta = \infty$, or in the other direction from $\eta = \infty$ to $\eta = 0$. Initial conditions are needed, and the solution is advanced using a high-order integrator, such as a fourth-order Runge-Kutta method. The eigenvalue is determined by satisfying the appropriate final boundary conditions. Provided a sufficiently good initial guess is known, an iterative procedure can be used to determine the eigenvalue. Eigenvalues are thus determined one at a time. (This method has been extensively discussed in the context of incompressible flows in previous chapters.) An example of the IVM is described by Mack (1965a).

Alternatively, the BVM reduces the differential equations to algebraic equations using either a finite difference discretization or a spectral representation. The boundary conditions at both ends are included in a natural way as part of the method. The end result of the BVM leads to the eigenvalue problem of the general form

$$\bar{A}\Psi = \omega\bar{B}\Psi, \tag{5.110}$$

or, equivalently,

$$|\bar{A} - \omega\bar{B}| = 0, \tag{5.111}$$

which can be solved by standard matrix eigenvalue packages. Since the number of eigenvalues correspond to the number of grid points, care must be exercised to distinguish true eigenvalues from spurious ones. Various methods are reviewed and compared by Malik (1990).

The effect of the freestream Mach number on the neutral stability curve is shown in Fig. 5.13; for each Mach number, the corresponding inviscid neutral wavenumber is given by the first mode $\alpha_{s,1}$ shown in Fig. 5.12. Here, the Prandtl number is taken to be $Pr = 0.72$. Note that as the Mach number increases, the critical Reynolds number also increases. Note also that the neutral stability curve at $M = 1.6$ looks quite similar to the incompressible case, but at higher values of the Mach number the upper branch turns upward towards the inviscid limit; at a Mach number of 3.8 the viscous upper branch almost entirely vanishes and so the stability characteristics of the flow are governed by inviscid disturbances. As pointed out by Mack in his calculations, inviscid disturbances begin to dominate at $M = 3$ and the stability characteristics are more like those of a free shear layer than of a low-speed zero-pressure gradient boundary layer.

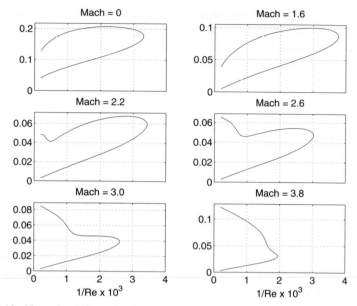

Fig. 5.13. Neutral stability curve in the wavenumber-Reynolds number plane for Mach numbers of $M = 0,\ 1.6,\ 2.2,\ 2.6,\ 3.0,\ 3.8$; insulated wall and wind tunnel conditions.

As a final comment, with the above neutral curves determined as a function of Mach number, the instability regions can be examined via either temporal or spatial theory. Early results relied on temporal calculations and used the Gaster transformation to relate the most unstable temporal growth rate to generate the most unstable spatial growth rates, but today one calculates the spatial growth rates directly. Since the boundary layer develops downstream, spatial calculations are more appropriate than temporal calculations.

5.4 Exercises

1. Consider the linear stability system (5.22) to (5.26).

   (a) Show that the system can be reduced to the two first-order equations

   $$\alpha^2 \rho (U - c)\phi = \frac{i\Pi'}{\gamma M^2}$$

   and

   $$(U - c)\phi' - U'\phi = \frac{i\Pi}{\gamma M^2}\xi,$$

   where ξ is defined in (5.29).

(b) Combine the two equations to get the second order equations (5.27) and (5.28).

(c) Following Gropengiesser (1969), introduce the transformation

$$\chi = \frac{i\Pi}{\gamma M^2 \phi}$$

and derive the following first-order nonlinear differential equation

$$\chi' = \rho \alpha^2 (U - c) - \chi \left(\frac{\chi \xi + U'}{U - c} \right),$$

where ξ is defined in (5.29). State the proper boundary conditions in the freestreams $y = \pm\infty$.

2. Write a numerical code that solves the compressible Rayleigh equation (5.30). Check the code by reproducing Fig. 5.3 using the hyperbolic tangent profile (5.15) with $\beta_T = 1$, $\beta_U = 0$ and $0 < M < 5$. Compare the results with those of the Lock profile by solving (5.8) with $\mu = T$ for the mean velocity and (5.13) for the mean temperature.

3. Use the steps outlined below to prove Results 5.2 through 5.4.

(a) Show that the compressible Rayleigh equation (5.28) can be written as

$$\left[\frac{\Omega^2 \psi'}{\xi} \right]' - \alpha^2 \Omega^2 \psi = 0,$$

where

$$\Omega = U - c, \quad \xi = T - M^2 \Omega^2, \quad \psi = \phi/(U - c).$$

(b) To prove Result 5.2 and 5.3, multiple the above equation by ψ^*, the complex conjugate of ψ, integrate over the region $[a, b]$, and set the real and imaginary parts to zero to get the desired results. It is helpful when proving Result 5.3 to use the relation

$$(U - U_{min})(U - U_{max}) \leq 0,$$

valid for monotone profiles.

(c) To prove Result 5.4 show that the above equation can be written as

$$\left[\frac{\Omega \chi'}{\xi} \right]' - \chi \left\{ \frac{1}{2} \left(\frac{U'}{\xi} \right)' + \frac{U'^2}{4\xi\Omega} + \alpha^2 \Omega \right\} = 0,$$

where

$$\chi = \Omega^{1/2} \psi.$$

Multiply by χ^*, integrate over $[a, b]$, and examine the imaginary part.

4. Rewrite the compressible Rayleigh equation (5.28) in terms of the similarity variable η.

5. Compute the elements of the matrices B and C of (5.103).

6. Compute the elements $a_{i,j}$ of (5.107).

7. Write a numerical solver using the method described by Malik (1990) for the compressible boundary layer with $Pr = 0.72$. Reproduce at least two panels of Fig. 5.13.

Chapter 6

Centrifugal stability

6.1 Polar coordinates

As has been mentioned earlier, there are many flows that require the formulation of the stability problem to be cast in coordinate systems other than Cartesian. For example, pipe flow is perhaps the most notable example. Then, there is the case that is now referred to as stability of Couette flow and has been examined both theoretically and experimentally by Taylor (1921, 1923). In this case, concentric cylinders rotate relative to each other to produce the flow. Free flows, such as the jet and wake, can be thought of as round rather than plane. If the boundary layer occurs on a curved wall, then Görtler vortices result. All of these examples can be described in terms of polar coordinates. And, at the outset, it should be recognized that, not only will the governing mathematics be different from that that has been used up to this point but the resulting physics may have novel characteristics as well.

The prevailing basis for the flows that have been examined heretofore has been that the flows are parallel or almost parallel. Then, the solutions for the disturbances were all of the form of plane waves that propagate in the direction of the mean flow or, more generally, obliquely to the mean flow. And, as we have learned, if solid boundaries are present in the flow, viscosity is a cause for instability. Now there are flows that will have curved streamlines and this leads to the possibility of a centrifugal force and its influence must be considered. For boundary layers on curved walls, this influence is also possible but the flow also has the elements for a secondary instability. Such a secondary instability is promoted by the fact that there is now curvature of the stream lines that are due to the Tollmien-Schlichting waves and hence the dual consequences.

As an illustration let us consider what may be the stability criterion when there is an effect due to a centrifugal force. For this purpose, consider the flow

of a constant density fluid in the absence of viscous effects that is described by curved streamlines. Assume also that a suitable curvilinear coordinate reference system has been established for examining the flow. Then, consider an element of fluid that has a velocity V and with the radius of curvature r for the streamline at that point. If ρ is the density of this element of fluid, a centrifugal force acting on it has the magnitude $\rho V^2/r$ and its angular momentum is rV. The question of stability here centers around the question: If the element of fluid is displaced a small distance in the radial direction to the point $r + \delta r$ where it will have a new velocity $V + \delta V$, will the fluid element return to its original position or not?

Under the assumed conditions for this flow, the angular momentum is conserved and hence

$$r\delta V + V\delta r = 0$$

or

$$\delta V = -(V/r)\delta r. \tag{6.1}$$

And, since $V = V + \delta V$ at the new position $r + \delta r$, use of (6.1) leads to

$$V = V - (V/r)\delta r. \tag{6.2}$$

With these relations, the centrifugal force, F, acting on an element is

$$F = \frac{\rho \left(V - \frac{V}{r}\delta r \right)^2}{(r + \delta r)}. \tag{6.3}$$

The force on this element due to the pressure gradient is

$$\Delta p = \frac{\rho(V + \delta V)^2}{(r + \delta r)}. \tag{6.4}$$

The question of the stability can now be resolved by examining the balance between these two forces.

With the expressions (6.3) and (6.4) we have

$$F - \Delta p = \frac{\rho \left(V - \frac{V}{r}\delta r \right)^2}{(r + \delta r)} - \frac{\delta(\nabla + \delta V)^2}{(r + \delta r)}. \tag{6.5}$$

Now, recognizing that $\delta r/r \ll 1$, (6.5) can be expanded and, to lowest order, this can be written as

$$F - \Delta p = -\frac{2\rho V^2}{r} \left(\frac{\delta r}{r} \right) \left[1 + \frac{r}{V}\frac{\delta V}{\delta r} \right]. \tag{6.6}$$

Stability here implies the pressure gradient resists the centrifugal force. If this is true, once the fluid parcel is displaced, it will return to its original location.

Since there is a negative sign in (6.6), the determination rests with

$$\left(1 + \frac{r}{V}\frac{\delta V}{\delta r}\right) \leq 0. \tag{6.7}$$

In short, if positive, stable; zero, neutral and negative, unstable.

6.2 Taylor problem

The problem that is familiarly referred to as the Taylor problem is that of determining the stability of the flow that exists between two concentric rotating cylinders. In some circles this is known as the stability of Couette flow. For others, it is the Taylor-Couette problem. Figure 6.1 is an illustration of exactly what Taylor was considering.

At the outset, the description for this flow should be cast in polar coordinates. For this purpose, let the x-y plane be defined by r and θ where $x = r\cos\theta$ and $y = r\sin\theta$; z will be the common axis along the length of the cylinders. In turn, u_r, v_θ, and w are the velocity components in the r, θ, and z directions respectively. With this description, the governing equations

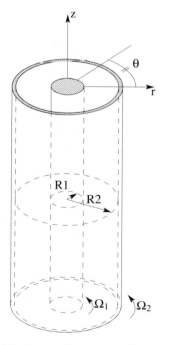

Fig. 6.1. Concentric rotating cylinders.

are

$$\frac{1}{r}\frac{\partial}{\partial r}(r u_r) + \frac{1}{r}\frac{\partial v_\theta}{\partial \theta} + \frac{\partial w}{\partial z} = 0 \qquad (6.8)$$

$$\frac{\partial u_r}{\partial t} + u_r\frac{\partial u_r}{\partial r} + \frac{v_\theta}{r}\frac{\partial u_r}{\partial \theta} + w\frac{\partial u_r}{\partial z} - \frac{v_\theta^2}{r} =$$

$$-\frac{\partial p}{\partial r} + \frac{1}{R_e}\left(\nabla^2 u_r - \frac{u_r}{r^2} - \frac{2}{r^2}\frac{\partial v_\theta}{\partial \theta}\right), \qquad (6.9)$$

$$\frac{\partial v_\theta}{\partial t} + u_r\frac{\partial v_\theta}{\partial r} + \frac{v_\theta}{r}\frac{\partial v_\theta}{\partial \theta} + w\frac{\partial v_\theta}{\partial z} + \frac{u_r v_\theta}{r} =$$

$$-\frac{1}{r}\frac{\partial p}{\partial \theta} + \frac{1}{R_e}\left(\nabla^2 v_\theta - \frac{v_\theta}{r^2} + \frac{2}{r}\frac{\partial u_r}{\partial \theta}\right), \qquad (6.10)$$

$$\frac{\partial w}{\partial t} + u_r\frac{\partial w}{\partial r} + \frac{v_\theta}{r}\frac{\partial w}{\partial \theta} + w\frac{\partial w}{\partial z} = -\frac{\partial p}{\partial z} + \frac{1}{R_e}\nabla^2 w, \qquad (6.11)$$

where

$$\nabla^2 = \frac{\partial^2}{\partial r^2} + \frac{1}{r}\frac{\partial}{\partial r} + \frac{1}{r^2}\frac{\partial^2}{\partial \theta^2} + \frac{\partial^2}{\partial z^2}. \qquad (6.12)$$

All variables have been nondimensionalized with respect to the gap width, $\ell = R_2 - R_1$ and a characteristic velocity U_0; the Reynolds number, $R_e = U_0\ell/\nu$ and the density, ρ, is a constant.

Now, the solution for the mean flow is one that is in the θ-direction and a function of r only or $V = V(r)$. Likewise, the mean pressure, P, is taken as only a function of r. Thus, $V = A r + B/r$ is the solution that meets these requirements and the pressure, P, can be obtained from the relation $\frac{1}{\rho}dP/dr = V^2/r$. The coefficients A and B are fixed by requiring the value of V to be that of the cylinders at $r = R_1$ and R_2 and are found to be $A = \frac{(R_2/R_1)^2\Omega_2/\Omega_1-1}{(R_2/R_1)^2-1}$; $B = -A$, when the cylinders rotate in the same direction. If the rotation is in opposite directions, simply replace Ω_1 by $-\Omega_1$.

Next, just as in the cases for parallel flows, small perturbations are introduced and the governing equations, (6.8) to (6.11), are linearized. In this way, with the notation for the velocity as $(u_r, V+v_\theta, w)$ and $P+p$ for the pressure, the linearized equations are

$$\frac{1}{r}\frac{\partial}{\partial r}(r u_r) + \frac{1}{r}\frac{\partial v_\theta}{\partial \theta} + \frac{\partial w}{\partial z} = 0, \qquad (6.13)$$

$$\frac{\partial u_r}{\partial t} + \frac{V}{r}\frac{\partial u_r}{\partial \theta} - 2\frac{V}{r}v_\theta = -\frac{\partial p}{\partial r} + \frac{1}{R_e}\left(\nabla^2 u_r - \frac{u_r}{r^2} - \frac{2}{r^2}\frac{\partial v_\theta}{\partial \theta}\right), \qquad (6.14)$$

$$\frac{\partial v_\theta}{\partial t} + \frac{V}{r}\frac{\partial v_\theta}{\partial \theta} + \frac{dV}{dr}u_r = -\frac{1}{r}\frac{\partial p}{\partial \theta} + \frac{1}{R_e}\left(\nabla^2 v_\theta - \frac{v_\theta}{r^2} + \frac{2}{r^2}\frac{\partial u_r}{\partial \theta}\right), \qquad (6.15)$$

and

$$\frac{\partial w}{\partial t} + \frac{V}{r}\frac{\partial w}{\partial \theta} = -\frac{\partial p}{\partial z} + \frac{1}{R_e}\nabla^2 w. \tag{6.16}$$

The solutions of these equations must satisfy the boundary conditions that all three perturbation velocity components vanish on both the inner and the outer cylinder walls.

With the original theoretical work of Taylor (1923) a general solution to this set of linear equations was not attempted because he had significant results from his experiments (Taylor, 1921) to justify further simplifications. First, only axisymmetric disturbances were treated and hence the θ-dependence is omitted. Second, it was assumed that the cylinders are fixed in such a way that the gap width, ℓ, is small or, in the sense of the nondimensional variables, $\ell/r \ll 1$.

When axisymmetry ($\frac{\partial}{\partial \theta} = 0$) is incorporated into the set of equations (6.13) to (6.16) and the pressure is eliminated, then the pair of coupled equations,

$$\left[\frac{\partial}{\partial t} - \frac{1}{R_e}\left(\nabla^2 - \frac{1}{r^2}\right)\right]\left(\nabla^2 u_r - \frac{u_r}{r^2}\right) = 2\left(\frac{V}{r}\right)\frac{\partial^2 v_\theta}{\partial z^2} \tag{6.17}$$

and

$$\frac{\partial v_\theta}{\partial t} - \frac{1}{R_e}\left(\nabla^2 v_\theta - \frac{v_\theta}{r^2}\right) = -\frac{dV}{dr}u_r \tag{6.18}$$

result. The set (6.17) and (6.18) bear a strong resemblance to those for perturbations in a parallel mean flow, namely Orr-Sommerfeld and Squire. In this case, however, the equations do not uncouple and it is clear at the outset that the full problem is sixth order. Solutions for u_r and v_θ can be obtained in terms of normal modes or $u_r(r, z, t) = \hat{u}(r)e^{\sigma t + i\lambda z}$, $v_\theta(r, z, t) = \hat{v}(r)e^{\sigma t + i\lambda z}$. As a result of this form for the solutions, (6.17) and (6.18) now become coupled ordinary differential equations.

Of course, in this form, even the general set of equations, (6.13) to (6.16), where the assumption of axisymmetry is not used, can be reduced to ordinary differential equations and the solutions can be expressed in terms of known eigenfunctions, namely Bessel functions. The resulting eigenvalue problem that determines the stability will be given as $F(\sigma, \lambda, R_2/R_1, \Omega_2/\Omega_1, R_e) = 0$.

The second approximation made by Taylor was to limit the analysis to the case where the gap width is small. In these terms, the operator, ∇^2 is of order $1/\ell^2$ and therefore the two terms, $\hat{u}/r$ and $\hat{v}/r$ as well as $1/r^2$, can, by comparison, be neglected. The net result of axisymmetry, the small gap approximation,

and the normal mode solutions reduces (6.17) and (6.18) to

$$\left[\frac{1}{R_e}\left(\frac{d^2}{dr^2} - \lambda^2\right) - \sigma\right]\left(\frac{d^2\hat{u}}{dr^2} - \lambda^2\hat{u}\right) = 2\lambda^2\left(\frac{V}{r}\right)\hat{v} \qquad (6.19)$$

and

$$\frac{1}{R_e}\left(\frac{d^2\hat{v}}{dr^2} - \lambda^2\hat{v}\right) - \sigma\hat{v} = -\frac{dV}{dr}\hat{u} \qquad (6.20)$$

with the boundary conditions $\hat{u} = \hat{u}' = \hat{u} = 0$ at the cylinder walls.

The small gap approximation also affects the variation of the mean velocity profile. Specifically, the part of mean flow that varies as $1/r$ can be neglected just as it was for the operators in the perturbation equations. Thus, $V(r) = Ar$, a linear variation, and is the reason that the flow has been referred to as Couette flow.

Equations (6.19) and (6.20) have been formulated in other ways by other authors (cf., Drazin & Reid, 1984) but the result is the same save for the designated nondimensional parameter. And, instead of the Reynolds number, Re, for example, it is more common to use the Taylor number, Ta. Moreover, no statement was made as to whether or not the cylinders are rotating in the same or in opposite directions. Then, as a minor point, in lieu of the velocity component u_r, a stream function is sometimes introduced and the two governing equations are in terms of the stream function and the velocity component in the θ-direction. These points will be clarified in more detail but, at this stage, this set of equations can be used to demonstrate what has become known as the principle of exchange of stabilities. Unlike the perturbations in parallel or almost parallel mean flows, it can be shown here that, if the disturbances are periodic in time, then they must decay in time. As a consequence, there are no traveling unstable waves and neutral stability corresponds to time independent or stationary behavior. It should be noted that Taylor's experiments verified these conclusions very well.

First, define $\epsilon = Re^{-1}$. Then, expand (6.19) and (6.20) so that all terms involving the fourth and second derivatives as well as the dependent variables can be grouped. These reordered equations are then multiplied by the respective complex conjugates of $\hat{u}$ and $\hat{v}$. Once this has been done, the product equation relations are integrated over r from R_1 to R_2. By integrating by parts and invoking the boundary conditions it is found that

$$\epsilon \int_{R_1}^{R_2} |\hat{u}''|^2 dr + (\sigma + 2\epsilon\lambda^2) \int_{R_1}^{R_2} |\hat{u}'|^2 dr + \lambda^2(\sigma + \epsilon\lambda^2) \int_{R_1}^{R_2} |\hat{u}|^2 dr$$

$$= \frac{2i\lambda V}{r} \int_{R_1}^{R_2} \hat{u}^*\hat{v} dr \qquad (6.21)$$

and

$$\epsilon \int_{R_1}^{R_2} |\hat{v}'|^2 dr + (\sigma + \epsilon\lambda^2) \int_{R_1}^{R_2} |\hat{v}|^2 dr = -V' \int_{R_1}^{R_2} \hat{u}\hat{v}^* dr. \quad (6.22)$$

By defining the integrals of $|\hat{v}''|^2$, $|\hat{v}'|^2$, and $|\hat{u}|^2$ as I_2^2, I_1^2, and I_0^2, all > 0, (6.21) can be written compactly as

$$\epsilon I_2^2 + (\sigma + 2\epsilon\lambda^2) I_1^2 + \lambda^2(\sigma + \epsilon\lambda^2)) I_0^2 = 2i\lambda \frac{V}{r} \int_{R_1}^{R_2} \hat{u}^*\hat{v} dr. \quad (6.23)$$

Analogously, for the integrals of $|\hat{v}'|^2$ and $|\hat{v}|^2$ as J_1^2 and J_0^2, all > 0, (6.22) becomes

$$\sigma J_1^2 + (\sigma + \epsilon\lambda^2) J_0^2 = -V' \int_{R_1}^{R_2} \hat{u}\hat{v}^* dr. \quad (6.24)$$

If $\sigma = \sigma_r + i\sigma_i$ and the respective right hand sides of (6.23) and (6.24) are similarly denoted as real and imaginary parts, then the following relations are obtained:

$$\sigma_r\left(I_1^2 + \lambda^2 I_0^2\right) + \epsilon\left(I_2^2 + 2\lambda^2 I_1^2 + \lambda^4 I_0^2\right) = -2\lambda \frac{V}{r} \int_{R_1}^{R_2} (\hat{u}^*\hat{v})_i dr \quad (6.25)$$

and

$$\sigma_i\left(I_1^2 + \lambda^2 I_0^2\right) = 2\lambda \frac{V}{r} \int_{R_1}^{R_2} (\hat{u}^*\hat{v})_r dr \quad (6.26)$$

for (6.23), and

$$\sigma_r J_1^2 + \epsilon\left(J_1^2 + \lambda^2 J_0^2\right) = -V' \int_{R_1}^{R_2} (\hat{u}\hat{v}^*)_i dr \quad (6.27)$$

$$\sigma_i J_1^2 = -V' \int_{R_1}^{R_2} (\hat{u}\hat{v}^*)_r dr \quad (6.28)$$

for (6.24).

The two imaginary relations for σ_i can be combined by recognizing the relations of complex conjugate pairs. This means the integrals on the right hand sides of (6.26) and (6.28) differ only by a minus sign and

$$\sigma_i \left[\frac{2\lambda(V/r)}{V'} - \frac{(I_1^2 + \lambda^2 I_0^2)}{J_1^2} \right] = 0 \quad (6.29)$$

results. For this to be true, either $\sigma_i = 0$ or the bracketed terms must balance. If $\sigma_i \neq 0$, then the disturbances are periodic in time. In turn, for this to occur, the ratio $2\lambda(V/r)/V' > 0$, implying that the mean profile must increase

outward. Certainly, if $V > 0$, $V' > 0$. Let us call the necessary relation as $2\lambda(V/r)/V' = P > 0$.

Now, the expression for the real parts of σ_r can be used. In fact, it is found that

$$\sigma_r = -\frac{(E + B/P)}{(D + A/P)} \tag{6.30}$$

where $A = (I_1^2 + \lambda^2 I_0^2)$, $B = \epsilon(I_2^2 + 2\lambda^2 I_1^2 + \lambda^4 I_0^2)$, $D = J_1^2$, $E = \epsilon(I_1^2 + \lambda^2 J_0^2)$. Thus, $\sigma_r < 0$ and consequently, a disturbance that is periodic in time must decay. The combination indicates that neutral stability corresponds to $\sigma = \sigma_r + i\sigma_i = 0$. This has become known as the principle of exchange of stabilities.

Again, unlike the results for parallel or almost parallel mean flows, neutrality is tantamount to a steady state.

By using the principle just established, the neutral solution for the Taylor problem can now be determined. After setting $\sigma = 0$ in equations (6.19) and (6.20) we have

$$(D^2 - \lambda^2)^2 \hat{u} = 2\lambda^2 \left(\frac{V}{r}\right) R_e \hat{v} \tag{6.31}$$

$$(D^2 - \lambda^2)\hat{v} = -V' R_e \hat{u}, \tag{6.32}$$

where the Reynolds number has been moved to the right-hand side for these relations. And, strictly speaking, for the narrow gap approximation, $V/r = V' = A$ with A an angular velocity in dimensional terms. These two equations can be combined to form one for $\hat{u}$, namely

$$(D^2 - \lambda^2)^3 \hat{u} = -2\lambda^2 R_e^2 \left(\frac{V}{r}\right) V'. \tag{6.33}$$

Now, the Taylor number emerges and is defined as $Ta = -2R_e^2(\frac{V}{r})V' \gg 1$ and, for the Taylor problem $V' < 0$. For the small gap approximation, (6.33) can be solved exactly. When the cylinders rotate in opposite directions, then $V = 0$ for some value of r between R_1 and R_2 and the solution must account for this fact and this has been done. Moreover, the flow in concentric cylinders has been investigated with arbitrary gap (Kirchgässner, 1961; Meister, 1962), a pressure gradient acting around the cylinders (DiPrima, 1959), and for non axisymmetric symmetric disturbances (DiPrima, 1961).

The role of viscosity in this system is simpler than that for parallel or almost parallel flows. In fact, its role is only damping and thereby stabilizing. If the Rayleigh (1880) criterion, namely that a necessary condition for instability for centrifugal flow is that the gradient of the mean vorticity must change sign

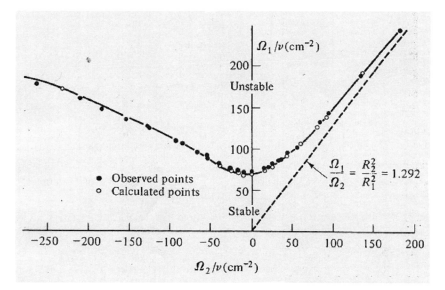

Fig. 6.2. Results for narrow gap calculations and experiment (after Taylor, 1923).

within the bounds of the flow is invoked, this can be seen directly. This need is essentially that of the inflection point criterion for parallel flow. In the inviscid limit, the criterion for the rotating cylinders was explicitly shown by Synge (1938) and requires

$$\frac{d}{dr}(r^2\Omega)^2 > 0, \tag{6.34}$$

where $\Omega = V/r$, the angular velocity. This result is the same as $\Omega_2 R_2^2 > \Omega_1 R_1^2$ and, in the inviscid limit, $\Omega_1/\Omega_2 = R_2^2/R_1^2$. For the values for Taylor's experiment, Fig. 6.2 vividly shows how well (6.34) is valid. The additional curve in this plot essentially shows the effects of viscosity and the plot is for both same and opposite directions of rotation of the cylinders.

With viscosity, and in terms of the Taylor number, there is also a critical value for this parameter. The value obtained is $Ta = 1708$ for $\lambda = 3.13$. When the critical value for Ta is exceeded, then there is instability and Taylor noted that the flow takes on a steady state where vortices, whose axes are located along the circumference with alternately opposite directions. Figure 6.3 illustrates this result, and it is for this reason that such vortices are now known as Taylor vortices. It should be noted here that there are several other problems that can be investigated within this same framework. One concerns that of the perturbation problem when there is no mean flow but there is a gravitational

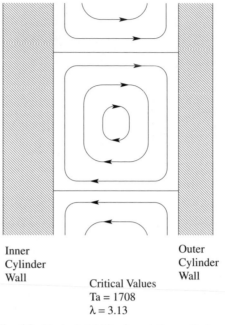

Inner
Cylinder
Wall

Outer
Cylinder
Wall

Critical Values
Ta = 1708
λ = 3.13

Fig. 6.3. Neutral stability for rotating cylinders.

field and a mean temperature field with density fluctuations. A second one is
that of the flow in an electrically conducting fluid and there are magnetic fields.
Neither of these cases will be considered here, but the flow over a wavy wall
will be analyzed, a problem that has become known as one that leads to Görtler
vortices (Görtler, 1940a,b).

6.3 Görtler vortices

A significant contribution was made by Görtler (1940a,b) when the problem
of the stability of a boundary layer on a concave wall was investigated. This
is a problem that involves centrifugal instability as well as the kind of disturbances that have already been shown to exist in boundary layers on flat walls.
Thus, unlike the Blasius boundary layer, both the mathematics for the linear
system as well as the consequential physics are different and the differences
are directly due to role of the centrifugal force in this flow. The problem has
subsequently been refined with the work of Smith (1955), Meksyn (1950),
Hämmerlin (1955), and Witting (1958) but the fundamentals remain the same.
Experiments in this kind of flow were made even earlier than the theory with
the work of Clauser & Clauser (1937) where the effect of curvature on the

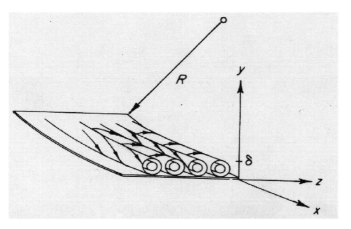

Fig. 6.4. Basic flow and coordinate system for Görtler vortices (after Betchov & Criminale, 1967).

transition of the boundary layer was considered. Then, the Görtler bases have since provided a means whereby secondary instability has been examined. In short, secondary instability can result in a flat plate boundary layer once Tollmien-Schlichting waves have been excited. The initial contributions that used this concept were due to Görtler & Witting (1958) and Witting (1958).

Reference is made to Fig. 6.4 that illustrates the basic flow and the coordinate system that is used. The linearized perturbation equations for this flow that were developed by Görtler (1940a,b) for the study invoked approximations in order to make the study: (1) The centrifugal force is neglected in determining the mean flow. As a result, the mean velocity, U, is taken as almost parallel, a common approximation in boundary layer stability analysis, and therefore $U = U(y)$ and there is no mean component in the y-direction. (2) The boundary layer thickness, δ, is taken to be much smaller than the radius of curvature, R. In fact, the equations are effectively developed with δ/R as the small parameter. The net result, save for the choice of independent coordinates, makes this problem effectively the same as the narrow gap concentric cylinder problem given by Taylor (1923) and discussed in Section 6.2. It is assumed that the perturbations are independent of x, making the analysis one that is local. The net result is a linear system that is a coupled sixth-order problem and can be expressed as the coupling of one fourth-order together with one second-order equation. With solutions given by normal modes where

$$(u, v, w, p) = (\hat{u}, \hat{v}, \hat{w}, \hat{p})e^{i\gamma z + \omega t}.$$

With δ and U_0 the basic scales, these equations, expressed nondimensionally,

are

$$\left(\frac{d^2}{d\eta^2} - \alpha^2\right)\left(\frac{d^2}{d\eta^2} - \alpha^2 - \sigma\right)\hat{v} = -2\alpha^2 \bar{Re} U \hat{u}, \qquad (6.35)$$

and

$$\left(\frac{d^2}{d\eta^2} - \alpha^2 - \sigma\right)\hat{u} = U'\hat{v}, \qquad (6.36)$$

with $\alpha = \gamma\delta$, $\eta = y/\delta$, $\sigma = \omega\delta^2/\nu$, and $\bar{Re} = Re^2(\delta/R)$; $Re = U_0\delta/\nu$. The boundary conditions require $\hat{v} = \hat{v}' = \hat{u} = 0$ at $\eta = 0$ and approaches zero as $\eta \to \infty$.

The analogy of this perturbation system to that of the narrow gap concentric cylinders is clear except, that is, for the boundary conditions. The condition of the principle of exchange of stabilities has been used although it is not, strictly speaking, a proven tool for this flow. Specific results for various values of the amplification factor have been obtained numerically for a range of specific mean velocity profiles, including Blasius, asymptotic suction, and a piece-wise linear profile. Although results can be expressed graphically in terms of a Görtler number as a function of the wave number, they can just as well be displayed as has been done for the Blasius boundary layer but where the Reynolds number is modified to include the δ/R ratio. Smith (1955) calculated the stability loci for the Blasius profile. Hämmerlin (1955) made calculations to compare the three mean profiles. Regardless, the important conclusion is the fact that even a moderately curved wall will lead to an earlier breakdown of the boundary layer than that on a flat plate.

The problem where there is flow in a curved channel has been termed Taylor-Dean flow. The linear system remains one that is the coupled fourth and second order and the boundary conditions are to be applied at the two boundaries. A general reference for results can be found in Drazin & Reid (1984).

6.4 Pipe flow

The stability of the flow in a pipe of circular cross section has been and continues to be an enigma in the field of hydrodynamic stability for, up to this time, it is a flow that that appears to be immune to linear disturbances. Yet this flow prototype is the one that was used by Reynolds to demonstrate the transition from laminar to turbulent flow as illustrated in Fig. **??**! And, it is a flow that is analogous to that of plane Poiseuille flow, a flow that is unstable. It is now believed that the cause of breakdown and transition in the pipe is due to nonlinearity. At the same time, it should be noted, the full three-dimensional problem

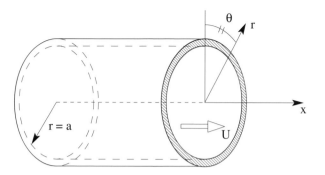

Fig. 6.5. Poiseuille pipe flow.

is rather involved and the linear system does not have the benefit of the Squire transformation even though this is a parallel flow, strictly speaking.

Consider pipe flow as shown in Fig. 6.5 where the mean flow is given as $\vec{U} = (U(r), 0, 0)$ with a pressure, P, that is a function of x only. The perturbation variables will be $\vec{u} = (u, v, w)$ in the x, r, and θ directions respectively. Also, $r^2 = y^2 + z^2$ and $\tan = z/y$ in this coordinate system. The mean flow variation is $U(r) = 1/4P(a^2 - r^2)$, where P is the pressure gradient in the x-direction and a is the radius of the pipe.

With this notation, the linearized perturbation equations in nondimensional form become

$$\frac{1}{r}\frac{\partial}{\partial r}(rv) + \frac{1}{r}\frac{\partial w}{\partial \theta} + \frac{\partial u}{\partial x} = 0 \tag{6.37}$$

$$\frac{\partial v}{\partial t} + U\frac{\partial v}{\partial x} = -\frac{\partial p}{\partial r} + \frac{1}{R_e}\left(\nabla^2 v - \frac{v}{r^2} - \frac{2}{r^2}\frac{\partial w}{\partial \theta}\right) \tag{6.38}$$

$$\frac{\partial w}{\partial t} + U\frac{\partial w}{\partial x} = -\frac{1}{r}\frac{\partial p}{\partial \theta} + \frac{1}{R_e}\left(\nabla^2 w - \frac{w}{r^2} + \frac{2}{r^2}\frac{\partial u}{\partial \theta}\right) \tag{6.39}$$

$$\frac{\partial u}{\partial t} + U\frac{\partial u}{\partial x} + v\frac{dU}{dr} = -\frac{\partial p}{\partial x} + \frac{1}{R_e}\nabla^2 u \tag{6.40}$$

with ∇^2 defined in polar coordinates, just as was done for the Taylor problem.

As can be seen, this set of equations bears a strong resemblance to those needed for the concentric cylinders. Thus, it is clear that they are fully coupled. However, if the assumption of axisymmetry is made together with normal modes for solutions, then some simplification does result. With the notation,

$$(u, v, w, p) = (\hat{u}(r), \hat{v}(r), \hat{w}(r), \hat{p}(r))e^{i\alpha x}e^{-i\omega t},$$

the above equations are

$$\frac{1}{r}\frac{d}{dr}(r\hat{v}) + i\alpha\hat{u} = 0 \qquad (6.41)$$

$$i(\alpha U - \omega)\hat{v} = -\hat{p}' + \frac{1}{R_e}\left(\Delta\hat{v} - \frac{\hat{v}}{r^2}\right) \qquad (6.42)$$

$$i(\alpha U - \omega)\hat{w} = \frac{1}{R_e}\left(\Delta\hat{w} - \frac{\hat{w}}{r^2}\right) \qquad (6.43)$$

$$i(\alpha U - \omega)\hat{u} + U'\hat{v} = -i\alpha\hat{p} + \frac{1}{R_e}\Delta\hat{u} \qquad (6.44)$$

with $\Delta = \frac{d^2}{dr^2} + \frac{1}{r}\frac{d}{dr} - \alpha^2$. These equations must be solved subject to the boundary conditions that $\hat{u} = \hat{v} = \hat{w} = 0$ at the boundary of the pipe ($r = a$, in dimensional form) and be finite at $r = 0$.

Observations: (i) the governing equation for the θ component of the velocity, $\hat{w}$, does uncouple from the others, making the problem one that is pseudo two-dimensional; (ii) the equations for $\hat{u}$ and $\hat{v}$ can now be combined to generate one fourth order ordinary equation; (iii) this equation would normally be in terms of the velocity component $\hat{v}$ as the dependent variable but, with the uncoupling, $\hat{u}$ and $\hat{v}$ can instead be replaced by a stream function, ψ, defined as $rv = \frac{\partial\psi}{\partial x}$, $ru = -\frac{\partial\psi}{\partial r}$. And, with the normal mode solution as $\Psi = \hat{\Psi}e^{i\alpha x}e^{-i\omega t}$, the governing equation is

$$(\alpha U - \omega)(D^2 - \alpha^2)\hat{\Psi} - \alpha r \left(\frac{U'}{r}\right)' \hat{\Psi} = \frac{i}{R_e}\left(D^2 - \alpha^2\right)^2 \Psi \qquad (6.45)$$

with $D^2 = \frac{d^2}{dr^2} - \frac{1}{r}\frac{d}{dr}$. The boundary conditions are now $\hat{\Psi} = \hat{\Psi}' = 0$ at the wall of the pipe but now $\frac{1}{r}\hat{\Psi}$ and $\frac{1}{r}\hat{\Psi}'$ must be finite at $r = 0$.

Equation (6.45) bears a strong resemblance to the Orr-Sommerfeld equation for plane Poiseuille flow. And, in like manner, this equation is one for vorticity, strictly speaking. Consequently, the flow could be expected to be unstable. But, for pipe flow, the analogy is somewhat deceptive in that a crucial term, namely that that represents the interaction of the mean vorticity with the perturbation field, $(U'/r)'$, is identically zero for the mean flow profile, $U(r)$, that varies as r. This being the case, then (6.45) is more like that for plane Couette flow, a flow that is well known to be stable. All eigenvalues that have been obtained for pipe flow are likewise all damped as shown by Davey & Drazin (1969) or Drazin & Reid (1984), for example.

6.5 Rotating disk

Because it involves a wealth of physics, the determination of the stability of the flow on a rotating disk is a problem that has interesting features. First, for the mean steady flow, it combines the flow of a boundary layer on a finite circular flat plate with the additional centrifugal force due to the rotation. As a result, the boundary layer is constrained and the solution for this flow is one that has an exact similarity solution of the Navier-Stokes equations (von Kármàn, 1921). In these terms, the mean profile is three-dimensional and the spatial dependence of the components is independent of the radius in these terms. This is also true for the boundary layer thickness. Then, just as we have seen for other problems where the centrifugal force is important, the perturbations must be analysed with full three-dimensionality in order to make meaningful conclusions. This flow is also unstable in the inviscid limit due to the fact that the mean velocity profile possesses at least one inflection point and thereby satisfies the criterion dictated by the Rayleigh theorem (Chapter 2, Section 2.4) for instability.

The original work in this area is due to Gregory, Stuart & Walker (1955) and included other related flows within this framework, such as that over swept wings or rotating boundary layers on curved boundaries as well as the more idealized flat disk. This collaborative work was both experimental as well as analytical. Since this time, there have been numerous additional contributions, even for the case of a flexible rather than a solid boundary and exploration of spatial as well as temporal stability. Among others of note are those due to Malik, Wilkinson & Orszag (1981), Wilkinson & Malik (1985), Malik (1986). Spatially, see Lingwood (1995, 1996); for the flexible wall disk, see Cooper & Carpenter (1997).

Consider the rotating disk and the coordinate system for this flow as defined in Fig. 6.6. From the list of references for this problem, the most illustrative is that due to Lingwood (1995) and will be followed here. The mean flow determined by von Kármàn (1921) is $\vec{U} = (U, V, W)$ and each component is a function of z, the coordinate normal to the plate due the similarity form of the solutions and defined relative to the disk. These three components, in dimensionless form, are defined as

$$\bar{U}(z) = U/(r\Omega), \quad \bar{V}(z) = V/(r\Omega), \quad \text{and} \quad \bar{W}(z) = W/\sqrt{v\Omega}. \quad (6.46)$$

Here, Ω is the constant angular frequency of the disk about the axis perpendicular to the disk and v is the kinematic viscosity. A mean length scale, L, is defined in terms of the kinematic viscosity and the angular frequency or

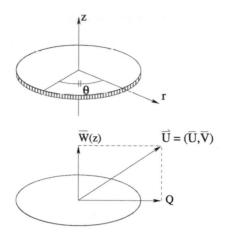

Fig. 6.6. Coordinate system for the rotating disk.

$L = (v/\Omega)^{1/2}$. Likewise, z is nondimensional with respect to L but r is the dimensional polar coordinate in the plane (along with the angle θ) of the disk. As determined by Lingwood, these three components of the mean velocity are shown in Fig. 6.7. A more revealing velocity profile is one that is defined in terms of ϵ, the angle between the radial direction of the flow and the direction of the rotation. Again, referring to Lingwood, this is defined as $Q(z)$, is termed the resolved velocity and is given by

$$Q(z) = \bar{U}(z) \cos \epsilon + \bar{V}(z) \sin \epsilon. \tag{6.47}$$

This is effectively the radial profile and is displayed in Fig. 6.8 for the full range of values for ϵ. It is clear that this profile is both inflectional and has reverse flow.

The stability analysis is performed by what is known as local. This means that perturbations are introduced at a specific value of the radius, $r = r_a$. Then, with a Reynolds number defined as $Re = r_a \Omega L / v = r_a / L$, the instantaneous velocity field and pressure are given by

$$u(r, \theta, t, z) = (r/Re)\, \bar{U}(z) + \tilde{u}(r, \theta, t, z),$$
$$v(r, \theta, t, z) = (r/Re)\, \bar{V}(z) + \tilde{v}(r, \theta, t, z),$$
$$w(r, \theta, t, z) = (1/Re)\, \bar{W}(z) + \tilde{w}(r, \theta, t, z),$$
$$p(r, \theta, t, z) = (1/Re^2)\, \bar{P}(z) + \tilde{p}(r, \theta, t, z). \tag{6.48}$$

These variables are substituted into the incompressible Navier-Stokes equations, linearized, and the mean flow subtracted so that a coupled set of perturbation equations are found. In order to proceed further, however, further

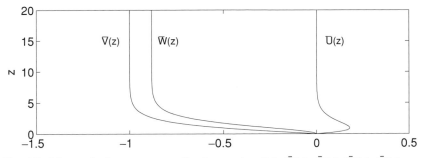

Fig. 6.7. Mean velocity components for the rotating disk: $\bar{U}(z)$, $\bar{V}(z)$, $\bar{W}(z)$; $\bar{U}(z) \to$ 0, $\bar{V}(z) \to -1$, and $\bar{W}(z) \to -0.8838$ as $z \to \infty$ (after Lingwood, 1995).

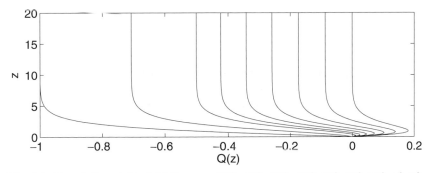

Fig. 6.8. From left to right, $Q(z)$ for $\epsilon = 90°, 45°, 30°, 25°, 20°, 15°, 10°, 5°, 0°$ (after Lingwood, 1995).

approximations are made, namely dependence of the Reynolds due to the radius is ignored. This must be done even though the thickness of the boundary on the rotating disk is constant. With this step, a separable normal mode form for the solutions of the perturbations can be assumed and becomes

$$\tilde{u}(r, \theta, t, z) = \hat{u}(z)e^{i\alpha r + i\beta\theta - i\omega t},$$

etc., for $\tilde{v}$, $\tilde{w}$, and $\tilde{p}$. Then, in addition to the linearization, all terms of $O(Re^{-2})$ are neglected and a set of coupled sixth-order ordinary differential equations must be solved subject to initial values and boundary conditions. Lingwood examined this set of equations in a thorough manner. First, all terms were collected, fixed in groups and noted as to the effects due to (a) viscosity, (b) rotation (Coriolis) and (c) streamline curvature, respectively.

If the rotation and streamline curvature effects are ignored, the set of equations uncouple and the more familiar Orr-Sommerfeld and Squire equations

are found. If viscous effects are further neglected, then the Rayleigh equation emerges. The only note is that the mean velocity in each of these cases is in terms of the sum of both the $\bar{U}$ and the V components, as suggested by the $Q(z)$ definition of (6.47) given earlier. Lingwood went on to numerically integrate the full set of linear equations subject to the initial input of an impulsive line forcing given as $\delta(r - r_s)\delta(t)e^{i\beta\theta}$. The analysis and the computations were performed as one that is a combination of the spatio-temporal stability basis.

Of special interest to Lingwood was the question of absolute instability (Cf. Chapter 4). When the system has absolute instability, then, at a fixed point, amplification continues without bounds. As a result, even a weak disturbance at a fixed point will amplify to quite large amplitude. For one that is amplified in the convective sense, it will be swept away and the boundary layer will recover. Lingwood did indeed find such an instability once a certain value of the Reynolds number, $Re > 510.625$, and if the parameter, $\beta/Re \approx 0.126$ are reached. The immediate effect of this is that the perturbations become nonlinear and transition is to be expected. Below this critical Reynolds number, the flow is unstable but not absolutely.

6.6 Trailing vortex

Another flow of significance that has received attention within the framework of centrifugal stability is that of the trailing vortex. Such a flow is most prominent at the tips of aircraft wings and the ensuing trail behind the aircraft. In short, the trailing line vortex. It is an important example of the class of flows denoted as swirling flows. And, just as other flows with such effects, such as the rotating disk, instability can be found inviscidly as well as in the viscous mode. This result represents a distinction from other free shear flows since viscosity normally has a damping effect (as in the jet, wake or the mixing layer, e.g.) and the instability that can be determined inviscidly is simply reduced in value when viscous effects are included. Viscous induced instability has required a solid boundary in in the discussions heretofore.

Investigation of swirling flows stems from the work of Howard & Gupta (1962) and was most general in that this effort dealt with both stratified as well non stratified flows and was fully three-dimensional. Sufficient conditions for stability were established together with a semicircle theorem for perturbations that are axisymmetric. This later result was extended to non-axisymmetric perturbations by Barston (1980). Numerical solutions for the inviscid stability problem were determined by Lessen, Singh & Paillet (1974). Then, Khorrami (1991) and Duck & Khorrami (1992) provided the work to show that this problem has instabilities that are caused by viscosity as well as those that were

found in the inviscid limit. Lastly, the presentation by Mayer & Powell (1992) makes an extensive survey and determines the stability of all possible modes numerically.

The basic mean steady flow that has been incorporated in the studies is that that was determined by Batchelor (1964) by means of a similarity solution for the line vortex far downstream of its origin of generation. With the z-axis as the coordinate that coincides with the axis of the vortex and (r, θ) are the polar coordinates in the vortex cross section, the similarity solution is two-dimensional and is given by $\bar{U} = (0, V, W)$ with V the azimuthal component and W is in the axial direction. When expressed in terms of the non-dimensional similarity variable, η, with $\eta \sim r/z^{1/2}$, these functions are

$$V(\eta) = q/\eta \, (1 - e^{-\eta^2}), \quad W(\eta) = W_\infty + e^{-\eta^2}, \qquad (6.49)$$

with q denoting the swirl intensity of the vortex and W_∞ a constant.

As mentioned, the stability analysis due to Mayer & Powell (1992) is one that has explored the full range of possibilities for this problem and will be the reference used here. When the fluid is incompressible, the set of linear equations for the perturbations can be found and solutions for this set are taken in normal mode form as

$$(\tilde{u}, \tilde{v}, \tilde{w}, \tilde{p}) = \big(i\hat{u}(\eta), \hat{v}(\eta), \hat{w}(\eta), \hat{p}(\eta)\big) \, e^{i\alpha z + in\theta - i\omega t}. \qquad (6.50)$$

Boundary conditions for these variables require finiteness at $\eta = 0$ and this will vary according to whether the value of n is zero, $|n| = 1$, or $|n| > 1$. As $\eta \to \infty$, all variables are required to vanish. Inviscidly, the result is a coupled third order system of ordinary differential equations. When viscous, the system is sixth order and there are no changes in the boundary conditions.

When inviscid, Mayer & Powell determined the most unstable eigenvalue numerically. It was found that $\omega = 0.0497186499174 + (0.2026281012942)i$ and is for the case when the parameters n, q, and α have the values $n = 1$, $q = -0.5$, and $\alpha = 0.5$, respectively. These authors have made extensive searches with extreme numerical precision and the most revealing graphics of this work have been provided by contour plots of the growth rates in the $\alpha - q$ plane for fixed mode number n.

As already noted, for the full viscous problem, Khorrami (1991) reported that there are instabilities that are due to viscosity and these were found when $n = 0$ and $n = 1$. For the $n = 1$ case, the lowest critical Reynolds number was 13.905, far in contrast to one of infinite value. Furthermore, the result for the inviscid instabilities when $n = 1$, was stabilized with increasing viscosity. More importantly, these new viscous instabilities occurred for values of the

parameters where no inviscid instability had been found. These results are especially significant for both the growth rates and the physical characteristics are in good qualitative agreement with observations in experimental studies of aircraft contrails at high altitudes.

6.7 Round jet

In many ways, save for the results, pipe flow can be thought of as the finite analogy to plane Poiseuille channel flow. Likewise, just as there are planar examples, such as the plane jet and wake, where the stability can be treated inviscidly, there are examples for flows that are labeled as round that also permit the stability investigation to be determined without viscous effects. It is only when there are solid boundaries present in the flow that viscosity can be a cause of instability; otherwise, viscosity leads to damping. In this sense, the round jet is an example of particular note. And, in fact, this problem even allows for the extension of results that follow theorems determined by Rayleigh for plane inviscid flows. More specifically, the extension deals with the mean velocity profile where, in Cartesian coordinates, an inflection point was needed somewhere within the region of the flow in order to have instability; this will be shown as the equations for the perturbations are developed. In fact, it was Rayleigh (1880, 1892, 1916) himself who noted the extension. The thorough stability analysis of the round jet was not, however, done until the work by Batchelor & Gill (1962).

Consider the coordinates and perturbations as those defined for pipe flow and illustrated in Fig. 6.5. When considered inviscidly and solutions for the perturbations are assumed to be of the normal mode form, where

$$(u, v, w, p) = (\hat{u}, \hat{v}, \hat{w}, \hat{p})e^{i\alpha x + in\theta - i\omega t},$$

with $\hat{u}, \hat{v}, \hat{w}, \hat{p}$ only functions of r, the system becomes

$$i\alpha\hat{u} + \frac{1}{r}\frac{d}{dr}(r\hat{v}) = 0, \tag{6.51}$$

$$i(\alpha U - \omega)\hat{u} + U'\hat{v} = -i\alpha\hat{p}, \tag{6.52}$$

$$i(\alpha U - \omega)\hat{v} = -\frac{d\hat{p}}{dr}, \tag{6.53}$$

and

$$i(\alpha U - \omega)\hat{w} = -\frac{in}{r}\hat{p}. \tag{6.54}$$

By eliminating $\hat{u}, \hat{w},$ and $\hat{p}$, just as was done for the system in Cartesian

coordinates, one equation for $\hat{v}$ can be found and this is

$$(\alpha U - \omega) \frac{d}{dr} \left[\frac{r(r\hat{v})'}{\alpha^2 r^2 + n^2} \right] - (\alpha U - \omega)\hat{v} - \frac{d}{dr} \left[\frac{\alpha r U'}{\alpha^2 r^2 + n^2} \right] r\hat{v} = 0. \quad (6.55)$$

It is from (6.55), with $n = 0$ (axisymmetric disturbances), that Rayleigh noted that a necessary but not sufficient condition for instability is the requirement that

$$\frac{d}{dr} \left(\frac{U'}{r} \right) = 0.$$

If it is recalled that $\omega = \alpha c$, this is fully equivalent to the need for the inflection point in the mean velocity profile when $(U - c) = 0$. When $n \neq 0$, then the generalization of this requirement is that

$$\frac{d}{dr} \left[\frac{r U'}{\alpha^2 r^2 + n^2} \right] = 0$$

at some point in the flow. An additional result was found by Batchelor & Gill (1962) for this condition by noting that, when the mode number, n, becomes quite large, then the flow is always stable because this term tends to zero everywhere. This result is precisely that that has already been observed for pipe flow in that it is no longer possible for there to be any generation of perturbation vorticity when the mean profile has such behavior.

Then, the most general conclusion derived for rotating flows is due to Rayleigh and is known as the circulation criterion. Again, for axisymmetric disturbances, if the square of the circulation, defined as

$$\frac{1}{r^3} \frac{d}{dr} (r^2 \Omega)^2,$$

where $U = r\Omega$, does not decrease at any location, then the flow is stable. Just as was outlined in the introductory Section 6.1, this argument is based on the physics of the flows that have centrifugal influence.

Batchelor and Gill used the top hat velocity profile to describe the round jet as well as for the case $U(r) = U_0/[1 + (r/r_0)^2]$, where r_0 is the scale of the extent for the jet. The solutions for $\hat{v}$ must vanish as the radius is increased and be finite for $r = 0$. Regardless of the choice for the mean profile, it was also found that only the mode $n = 1$ is unstable. Otherwise, all other modal solutions were found to be stable for these choices of the mean velocity variation.

Batchelor & Gill also showed that, by a unique transformation, that the equivalence of the Squire transformation can be formulated for this problem. In effect, the jet is cast in terms of a helix rather than the standard form of expression in polar coordinates. The helix is defined as $r = $ constant and, in

terms of the original coordinates, $\alpha x + n = $ constant. Once this is done, the perturbation variables are defined as

$$\bar{\alpha}\bar{u} = \alpha\hat{u} + \frac{n\hat{w}}{r},$$

$$\bar{v} = \hat{v},$$

$$\bar{\alpha}\bar{w} = \alpha\hat{w} - \frac{n\hat{u}}{r},$$

$$\bar{p}/\bar{\alpha} = \hat{p}/\hat{\alpha}, \qquad (6.56)$$

where, it should be noted, $\bar{u}$ is perpendicular to the radius and helix, $\bar{v}$ is parallel to the radius, and $\bar{w}$ is parallel to the tangent. The wave number, $\bar{\alpha}$, is now given by

$$\bar{\alpha} = (\alpha^2 + n^2/r^2)^2.$$

In these terms, the governing equations can be written as

$$i\bar{\alpha}\bar{u} + \frac{1}{r}\frac{d}{dr}(r\bar{v}), \qquad (6.57)$$

$$i\bar{\alpha}(U - c)\bar{u} + U'\bar{v} = -i\bar{\alpha}\bar{p}, \qquad (6.58)$$

$$i\bar{\alpha}(U - c)\bar{v} = -\bar{p}', \qquad (6.59)$$

and

$$i\bar{\alpha}(U - c)\bar{w} - \frac{n}{\bar{\alpha}r}U'\bar{v} = 0. \qquad (6.60)$$

Since the $\bar{w}$ component does not appear in the those for $\bar{u}$ and $\bar{v}$, the system (6.57) to (6.60) is similar to that for parallel or axisymmetric flow. In effect, a two-dimensional perturbation problem as the Squire transformation provides for three-dimensional perturbations in a parallel shear flow. And, although the actual problem considered was that of a round jet, such a mean profile can be adjusted so that it represents that of a round wake with the same conclusions.

Gold (1963) and Lees & Gold (1964) extended the Batchelor & Gill (1962) formulation for the jet and wake when the fluid is compressible. In this case, it was again found that the $n = 1$ mode is the most unstable but, unlike the incompressible problem, other modes are unstable and there is a strong influence from the temperature of the core in that an increase in the temperature of this part of the flow is destabilizing.

6.8 Exercises

1. Consider the problem where there is no mean flow. Instead, suppose the problem when there is a mean temperature and gravitational effects in the

vertical direction. In light of the Boussinesque approximation, then the perturbation velocity can be considered to one that is divergence free. Examine the stability for such a medium if it is contained between two boundaries in the vertical.

2. Determine the complete solutions for the Taylor concentric cylinder problem in the inviscid limit.

3. Repeat problem 2 for the viscous neutral limit.

4. What can be said regarding the vorticity for both the rotating cylinders and pipe flow?

5. Determine the governing equations for the perturbations for the rotating disk and indicate the terms that are due to viscosity, rotation and streamline curvature.

6. Determine the linear equations for the trailing vortex. Then, examine the energy equation and that for vorticity.

7. Determine the solution for the perturbations in pipe flow in the inviscid limit.

Chapter 7

Geophysical flow

7.1 General properties

From the class of flows that are termed geophysical, there are three that are distinct and these more than illustrate the salient properties that such flows possess when viewed from the basis of perturbations. First, there is stratified flow. In this case there is a mean density variation and it plays a dominant role in the physics because there is a body force due to gravity. At the same time, the fluid velocity, to a large degree of approximation, remains solenoidal and therefore the motion is incompressible. The net result leads to the production of anisotropic waves, known as internal gravity waves, and such motions exist in both the atmosphere and the ocean.

Second, because of the spatial scales involved, motion at many locations of the earth, such as the northern or southern latitudes, are present in an environment where the effects of the earth's rotation cannot be taken as constant. On the contrary, rotation plays a dominant role. Again, this combination of circumstances leads to the generation of waves.

Viscous effects can be neglected in the analysis for both the stratified flow and the problem with rotation but the presence of a mean shear in either flow – as we have already seen so often – does lead to important consequences for the dynamics when determining the stability of the system.

Third, there is the modeled geophysical boundary layer where the rotation is present but taken as constant and the surface is flat. In this case, viscous shear is important and the flow is known as the Ekman layer. The resulting mean flow solution also happens to be an exact solution of the full Navier-Stokes equations even if unsteady. The perturbation problem here leads to quite interesting results for, unlike the Blasius boundary layer, for example, the flow can be unstable inviscidly as well as having the viscous instability that is common for the boundary layer.

196

The concept of waves has been primarily investigated in terms of the effects of fluid compressibility, as was shown in Chapter 5, for example. For linearized perturbations in compressible flow, this is tantamount to acoustics when referring to the physics. In terms of the mathematics, it is clear that there must be a hyperbolic partial differential equation that governs the dependent variable of note in order to have waves. None of the stability problems discussed heretofore, save those dealing with compressibility, could have wave motion in this sense. The unique features of the geophysical flows have different bases for waves and, except for the physics, the concept is no different from the standpoint of the mathematics. The governing equation is hyperbolic but the waves that are produced are decidedly anisotropic. In addition, the flows can be unstable if there is a mean shear.

Many of the properties or results that have been found in the investigation of the more traditional shear flow instabilities, such as the Squire theorem, cannot necessarily be extended to these problems and it is the purpose here to probe such flows in more detail and, to not only indicate the novel effects, but to ascertain exactly what established results may or may not be used for these cases.

7.2 Stratified flow

Fluid motions that transpire in an environment where the density can vary are numerous in number and occur in nature to a large degree of approximation. Both the oceans and the atmosphere are harbingers of such action. For the ocean such a variation is due primarily to dissolved salts; in the atmosphere, this is due more to temperature variation. And, since gravity acts in only the vertical direction, a component of body force in this direction must be incorporated into the dynamics. This can be done and still have the motion remain incompressible. Such an assumption corresponds to motion of a fluid where it is difficult to change the density of a fluid parcel by pressure forces. The resulting governing equations within this framework are the result of what is known as the Boussinesq approximation. A full account of the details needed for this approximation can be found in the book on fluid dynamics by Batchelor (1967) but it will be useful to review the major points here.

Before proceeding, let the reader understand that the coordinate system for this section is different than that used in previous chapters. Here, instead of using $\mathbf{x} - \mathbf{y}$ as the primary flow direction and crossflow coordinate, $\mathbf{x} - \mathbf{z}$ will be used in this chapter because this is the conventional coordinate system that has long been established for such geophysical flow and is prevalent in the literature.

Basically, the Boussinesq approximation is tantamount to stating that the fluid velocity is solenoidal or $\nabla \cdot \vec{v} = 0$. This is the major basis for incompressibility. In order for this to be approximately true, then certain conditions should be met. Consider the spatial distribution of the velocity, $\vec{v}$, (and other flow variables as well) to be characterized by a length scale, L, and all variation will involve scales small compared to L. Similarly, a magnitude for the velocity is taken to be U_0. Thus, in these terms, it can be stated that $|\nabla \cdot \vec{v}| = O(U_0/L)$ and then $\vec{v}$ will be considered solenoidal if $|\nabla \cdot \vec{v}| \ll U_0/L$ or, because the divergence of $\vec{v}$ is coupled to variations in the density in the equation for the conservation of mass, this means $\left| \frac{1}{\rho} \frac{D\rho}{Dt} \right| \ll U_0/L$ must also be true. As shown by Batchelor (1967), this inequality leads to the following conditions that must be satisfied in order to assume that the Boussinesq approximation is valid: (1) the Mach number, defined as $M = U_0/a$, where a is the speed of sound, has the requirement that $M^2 \ll 1$. For reference air, at 15°C, $a = 340.6$m/sec and, for water at 15°C, $a = 1470$m/sec; (2) the ratio, $\omega L/a \ll 1$ as well, where ω is the frequency of a possible periodic flow. In this case, if $\omega \sim U_0/L$, then this ratio is simply that for the Mach number. Of course, when $\omega L/a = 1$, with L the wave length of sound waves with frequency ω, then compressibility cannot be irrelevant. (Sonar does work in the ocean!); (3) $gL/a^2 \ll 1$. This last condition is more sensitive for the atmosphere than the ocean since this inequality leads to what is known as a scale height. The consequences of all these conditions will be understood as we develop the necessary linear perturbation equations that govern the motion of disturbances in geophysical flows.

For a homogeneous, isentropic fluid that is in equilibrium with respect to the rotating earth, a reference state can be obtained from a hydrostatic balance, or summation of the forces on the fluid. Thus, neglecting viscous effects,

$$\rho_r \nabla G + \nabla p_r = 0. \tag{7.1}$$

And, if we recognize that the relative gravitational potential, G, is only in the vertical z-direction with $G = gz$, this relation becomes

$$\rho_r g + \frac{\partial p_r}{\partial z} = 0. \tag{7.2}$$

At once we see that

$$p_r = \rho_0 e^{-g \int_0^z dz/a^2}, \tag{7.3}$$

where $dp_r/d\rho_r = a^2$ has been used; ρ_0 is the value of the density at $z = 0$. For the ocean this would mean the value at the free surface or the mean oceanic density that is usually referred to as standard conditions. For pressure, this would be referred to as the ambient pressure. Note that this relation for the

reference state is characterized by the scale height (e.g., altitude or depth). Call the value $H = a^2/g$, say, and it is clear that we must require that any variation of the perturbation field in this direction or ℓ_z must satisfy the inequality $\ell_z/H \ll 1$.

The set of governing equations for such flows is obtained by subtracting the hydrostatic reference values from the momentum equations (2.34) to (2.37) yielding

$$\rho \frac{D\vec{v}}{Dt} = -\nabla(p - p_r) - (\rho - \rho_r)\nabla G \tag{7.4}$$

when, again, viscous effects are neglected.

Now, the difference between the actual and the reference states is small and typically $(\rho - \rho_r)/\rho_r \approx O(10^{-3}) \ll 1$. This suggests the replacing of ρ by ρ_r in the inertia term of the equations but not in the force due to gravity because the acceleration due to gravity, g, is $O(10^3)$. In fact, with $\ell_z/H \ll 1$, we can further assume that $\rho_r \cong \rho_0$. Finally, the equations of motion, under these conditions, are

$$\frac{D\vec{v}}{Dt} = -\frac{1}{\rho_0}\nabla \bar{p} - \frac{(\rho - \rho_0)}{\rho_0}\nabla G, \tag{7.5}$$

with $\bar{p} = (p - p_r)$. Along with (7.5) we have the continuity equation

$$\nabla \cdot \vec{v} = 0 \tag{7.6}$$

(or essentially zero) that is a result of the Boussinesq approximation. This means the relation for the conservation of mass uncouples and

$$\frac{D\rho}{Dt} = 0 \tag{7.7}$$

is also true in order to completely define a problem within this environment.

The system can now be perturbed and the necessary linear equations can be found for determining the stability. However, it should be noted that it is no longer necessary to maintain the notation with respect to the reference values. In short, density variations only appear together with the force of gravity and the uncoupled equations for the conservation of the density for a fluid particle. Thus, we assume a mean velocity in the ocean or atmosphere in the x-direction, $U(z)$, along with a mean pressure and a mean density varying in the vertical z-direction and then we write

$$u = U(z) + \tilde{u}(x, y, z, t),$$
$$v = \tilde{v}(x, y, z, t),$$
$$w = \tilde{w}(x, y, z, t),$$
$$\rho = \bar{\rho}(z) + \tilde{\rho}(x, y, z, t),$$

and

$$p = P + \tilde{p}(x, y, z, t). \tag{7.8}$$

After substituting (7.8) into (7.5) to (7.7), the following linearized disturbance equations result:

$$\tilde{u}_x + \tilde{v}_y + \tilde{w}_z = 0, \tag{7.9}$$

$$\tilde{u}_t + U\tilde{u}_x + U'\tilde{w} = -\tilde{p}_x/\rho_0, \tag{7.10}$$

$$\tilde{v}_t + U\tilde{v}_x = -\tilde{p}_y/\rho_0, \tag{7.11}$$

$$\tilde{w}_t + U\tilde{w}_x = -\tilde{p}_z/\rho_0 - g\tilde{\rho}/\rho_0, \tag{7.12}$$

and

$$\tilde{\rho}_t + U\tilde{\rho}_x + \bar{\rho}'\tilde{w} = 0, \tag{7.13}$$

with $()' = d()/dz$ and all variables denoted with tilde being the linear perturbations. As before, we will work with the disturbance or fluctuating components
and mean or basic state quantities, so the tilde can now be discarded.

Although not obvious in this form, these equations can be reduced to a set
for the stability analysis that is akin to those of the non-stratified problem. We
can easily show that the three momentum equations (7.10) to (7.12) can be
reduced to the following equation by taking the divergence and using (7.9) and
thus

$$\nabla^2(p/\rho_0) = -2U'w_x - g\rho_z/\rho_0. \tag{7.14}$$

Because of the variation in density, there is now a term for the source of pressure in addition to that that is prevalent for the constant density problem. Then,
operating on (7.12) with ∇^2, the three-dimensional Laplacian, and using (7.14)
and (7.13) to eliminate the pressure and density, the governing equation becomes

$$\left(\frac{\partial}{\partial t} + U\frac{\partial}{\partial x}\right)^2 \nabla^2 w - \left(\frac{\partial}{\partial t} + U\frac{\partial}{\partial x}\right)U''w_x + N^2(w_{xx} + w_{yy}) = 0, \tag{7.15}$$

where

$$N^2 = N^2(z) = -\frac{g}{\rho_0}\bar{\rho}' \tag{7.16}$$

is known as the Brunt-Väisälä frequency and, with the Fourier decomposition,
normal mode assumption for solution,

$$w(x, y, z, t) = \mathbf{w}(z)e^{i(k_1 x + k_2 y) - i\omega t}, \tag{7.17}$$

equation (7.15) can be reduced to an ordinary differential equation which is

$$w'' + \left(k_1^2 + k_2^2\right) \left\{ \frac{N^2 - (k_1 U - \omega)^2 - (k_1 U - \omega)U'' \frac{k_1}{k^2}}{(k_1 U - \omega)^2} \right\} w = 0.$$

(7.18)

One remark should be made here, namely the Squire transformation is still quite valid for this problem. This can easily be seen by using the same Fourier decomposition for the set of equations (7.9) to (7.13) and then recognizing the following:

$$k^2 = k_1^2 + k_2^2,$$
$$\tan \theta = k_2 / k_1,$$
$$k\tilde{u} = k_1 \hat{u} + u_2 \hat{v},$$
$$k\tilde{v} = k_2 \hat{u} - k_1 \hat{v}.$$

(7.19)

Substitution of these expressions into the three-dimensional set of equations that have been Fourier decomposed will result in an equivalent two-dimensional system. In other words, no z-dependence and no w component of the perturbation velocity in this direction as would be for the two-dimensional problem at the outset.

In order to illustrate some of the essential features of this kind of flow, let us consider the problem in the absence of a mean shear or $U = 0$. In this case, equation (7.15) reduces to

$$\nabla^2 w_{tt} + N^2 (w_{xx} + w_{yy}) = 0$$

(7.20)

and the ordinary equation is obtained by substituting the solution form of (7.17) into equation (7.20) and

$$w_{zz} + k^2 \left[\frac{N^2 - \omega^2}{\omega^2} \right] w = 0.$$

(7.21)

In this limit, the governing system is hyperbolic so long as the coefficient of w is positive. This result is that of internal gravity waves. The general properties for these waves are significant and will now be reviewed. From the point of stability, this is the same as a neutral dynamical system since there is neither amplification nor decay.

A local vertical length scale for the wave motion can be defined as

$$\ell_v = (\mathbf{w}/\mathbf{w}'')^{1/2}. \tag{7.22}$$

The horizontal length is $\ell_h = k^{-1}$ and the ratio of the two is

$$\frac{\ell_h}{\ell_v} = \frac{1}{k}\left(\frac{\mathbf{w}''}{\mathbf{w}}\right)^{1/2} = \left|\frac{N^2(z) - \omega^2}{\omega^2}\right|^{1/2}. \tag{7.23}$$

For low frequency internal gravity waves, $\omega/N \ll 1$ and, in fact

$$\frac{\ell_h}{\ell_v} \to \infty \quad \text{as} \quad \omega/N \to 0. \tag{7.24}$$

The horizontal length scale is therefore much larger than the length scale in the vertical, i.e., low frequency waves always have a horizontally elongated structure.

Suppose we now only consider wave lengths small compared to the scale of variation of $N(z)$. This input allows for the use of the WKBJ method for solving $\mathbf{w}(z)$. In fact, take $N(z)$ to be constant (e.g., the mean density varies exponentially in the vertical) and then a local solution can be found as

$$\mathbf{w} = a e^{i(\alpha_1 x + \alpha_2 y + \alpha_3 z - \omega t)}. \tag{7.25}$$

By substituting (7.25) into (7.21), a dispersion relation for the waves results and is

$$\omega = \pm N_0 \frac{k}{\alpha} = \pm N_0 \cos\theta, \tag{7.26}$$

where $\alpha = \sqrt{\alpha_1^2 + \alpha_2^2 + \alpha_3^2}$ and θ is the angle between the two and the three dimensional wave vectors. It is clear that the waves are anisotropic since the frequency depends upon the direction of the propagation and not just the magnitude of the wave number. Here, in the limit of $\omega \to 0$, $\theta \to \pi/2$. At the same time, for $\omega \to N_0$, the wave number approaches the horizontal. When $\omega > N_0$, the wave number is no longer real and wave motion ceases altogether.

An alternative form of the derivation of the dispersion relation can be given and thereby lends additional insight into this type of perturbation dynamics. Consider a plane of fluid, with an angle θ to the vertical, and displaced a distance ξ parallel to itself as shown Fig. 7.1. Because of the density gradient in the vertical, each element of fluid finds itself more dense than that of its surroundings, so that it has an excess in mass per unit volume of $\frac{d\bar{\rho}}{dz}$ times the vertical displacement $\xi \cos\theta$. There is an excess weight per unit volume of this times g, which acts vertically downwards or this multiplied by $\cos\theta$ in the

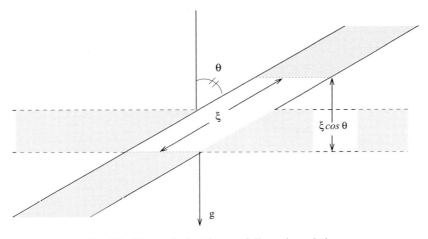

Fig. 7.1. Mechanical analogue of dispersion relation.

plane of the motion. This excess weight must be balanced by the acceleration and is given by Newton's second law of motion. Hence, in these terms,

$$\rho_0 \ddot{\xi} = -\left(g \frac{d\bar{\rho}}{dz} \cos^2 \theta\right)\xi.$$

The result is a linear oscillator with frequency $= \left(\frac{1}{\rho_0} \frac{d\bar{\rho}}{dz} \cos^2 \theta\right)^{1/2}$.

There are more salient points to this wave motion. The phase velocity, $\vec{C}_p$, is

$$\vec{C}_p = \pm \frac{N_0 \cos \theta}{\alpha^2} \underline{\alpha} = \pm \frac{N_0}{\alpha} \left(\frac{\alpha_1}{\alpha}\hat{\mathbf{i}}, \frac{\alpha_2}{\alpha}\hat{\mathbf{j}}, \frac{\alpha_3}{\alpha}\hat{\mathbf{k}}\right). \qquad (7.27)$$

The group velocity, $\vec{C}_g$, is defined in the usual manner and is

$$\vec{C}_g = \nabla_\alpha(n) = \frac{N_0}{\alpha^2}\left[\left(\alpha_1 - \frac{k\alpha_1}{\alpha}\right)\hat{\mathbf{i}}, \left(\alpha_2 - \frac{k\alpha_2}{\alpha}\right)\hat{\mathbf{j}}, \frac{k\alpha_3}{\alpha}\hat{\mathbf{k}}\right], \qquad (7.28)$$

where k is the absolute value of the wave vector in the plane or $\underline{k} = (k_1, k_2, 0)$. It can be seen that $\vec{C}_p \cdot \vec{C}_q = 0$ and hence these vectors are perpendicular. This is the consequence of the transverse nature of waves in an incompressible fluid. More specifically, for a single Fourier disturbance, the velocity vector must be perpendicular to the wave vector in order to satisfy the solenoidal property of the vector that is related to the condition of incompressibility. Thus, the energy flux, which is the product of the pressure with the velocity, is perpendicular to the same wave vector. In turn, the energy flux is proportional to the group velocity and therefore this phenomenon.

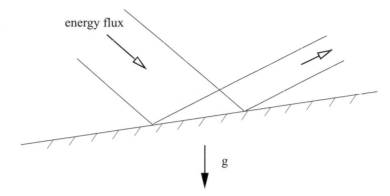

Fig. 7.2. Scaling change due to sloping bottom.

The above noted combination of results leads to curious effects that are common in anisotropic wave propagation and examples should be mentioned to illustrate same. First, consider the effect that ensues when internal waves reflect at a sloping bottom, say. Figure 7.2 depicts this situation.

The basic rule governing the reflection is that the frequencies of the incident and reflected waves are the same. This implies that the inclination of the wavenumbers to the *vertical* must be the same and the angle of incidence of the waves is not the same as the angle of reflection. The width of the reflected beam is less than that of the incident beam and the energy is concentrated and the scale is reduced. In spectral terms this corresponds to a transfer of energy to higher wave numbers and then it can be dissipated easier by viscous action. This kind of reflection is termed *anomalous* and it does not occur at a horizontal surface when the angle of incidence and reflection are the same. In this case, the wave number magnitude is conserved on reflection at a horizontal surface.

Second, suppose there is a source of disturbance at a constant frequency $\omega < N$ in a continuously stratified fluid. More specifically, consider the situation as in Fig. 7.3. Since the frequency is fixed, the wavenumbers of the disturbance produced are all at a fixed angle to the horizontal. As a result, the group velocity is at a fixed angle to the vertical since $\vec{C}_g$ is perpendicular to $\vec{C}_p$ and is determined by the frequency. Since the group velocity provides the direction of the energy flux, it follows that the energy radiated from the disturbance is confined to a set of of beams whose angle to the vertical is fixed by the frequency. The energy radiates away in these directions only and any disturbance in the dividing wedges is much less.

A last example is known as Brunt-Väisälä trapping. Suppose the buoyancy frequency has a local maximum. A wave, whose frequency is less than this

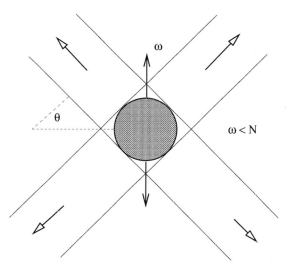

Fig. 7.3. Energy flux in a stratified medium.

value, will have a group velocity that is inclined to the vertical. As the wave propagates upwards, the local value of N decreases until it becomes equal to the wave frequency. As this happens, the direction of the group velocity turns towards the vertical and its magnitude decreases. And, when the local value of the frequency tends to be $\omega = N$ exactly, the group velocity is directed vertically but is vanishingly small. An accumulation of energy takes place at this region and the energy is reflected and returns downwards to be reflected again at a lower level where $\omega = N$. The net result is a trapping of energy in the layer where $\omega < N$. The energy propagates horizontally but is restricted vertically. This is depicted in Fig. 7.4 and is tantamount to a wave guide. Again, since viscosity is neglected, the reflection points here are cusps and hence all energy is contained within the bounds where $\omega = N$.

Whether the full three-dimensional Fourier solution is used or only the decomposition in the horizontal plane, there is still the question of proper boundary conditions. In any direction that extends to infinity, the Fourier modes are quite correct since these are bounded in these directions. In the z-direction of variation for the mean density, though, there is more than one possibility. First, there could be confinement between two solid barriers in z, indicating that $\mathbf{w} = 0$ at these locations. As a result, the solution is the same as any two-point boundary value, initial-value problem and there are an infinite number of discrete Fourier modes possible for the solution. The case where there are no solid boundaries or only one in the vertical, discrete modes are no longer the

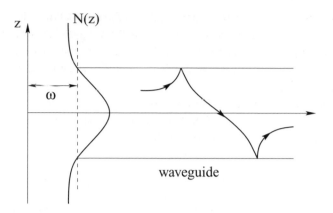

Fig. 7.4. Brunt-Väisälä trapping; Waveguide.

sole basis for the problem must resort to the use of a continuous spectrum as well. This result is no different from that of the nonstratified problem. And certainly problems that deal with free surface waves will require somewhat different boundary conditions. This is especially true if surface tension is to be incorporated into the analysis.

Now these waves do have vorticity and, for three-dimensional perturbations, all components can, in principle, be present. But since the fluid is taken as incompressible and there is no mean motion, then the component ω_z will be nonzero only if it is so specified initially, and then it will remain constant in time without further generation or diffusion since viscous effects are neglected. The other components, ω_x and ω_y, will be generated even if not given initial values but, like ω_z, cannot diffuse. This appraisal will be demonstrated more fully by examining the governing equations for the perturbation vorticity.

The definitions for the three vorticity components are, respectively,

$$\omega_x = w_y - v_z, \quad \omega_y = u_z - w_x, \quad \text{and} \quad \omega_z = v_x - u_y. \tag{7.29}$$

When there is no mean motion, the vorticity rests solely with the perturbations and the governing linear equations are

$$\frac{\partial \omega_x}{\partial t} = -g\rho_y, \tag{7.30}$$

$$\frac{\partial \omega_y}{\partial t} = g\rho_x, \tag{7.31}$$

$$\frac{\partial \omega_z}{\partial t} = 0. \tag{7.32}$$

As can be seen, generation of vorticity is due to the fact that there is a variation in the density field rather than a gradient in the velocity. This is known as baroclinic torque and, because of the assumptions on the mean density and pressure, the only generation possible is in the plane perpendicular to the line marking the stratification.

Consider the mean motion restored to the flow. It is now that competition in the dynamics emerges and, in fact, the flow has the possibility to be unstable. The equation that is equivalent to (7.15) for $\mathbf{w}$ is, with $U = U(z)$, is just (7.18) or

$$(k_1 U - \omega)^2 (\mathbf{w}'' - k^2 \mathbf{w}) - k_1 (k_1 U - \omega) U'' \mathbf{w} + k^2 N^2 \mathbf{w} = 0 \quad (7.33)$$

when rewritten, where $k^2 = k_1^2 + k_2^2$. In essence, this is just equation (7.15) written in terms of the modal form for solution. As (7.33) stands, however, it is not in the familiar format from the standpoint of stability. Instead of the Brunt–Väisälä frequency as the parameter, it is the Richardson number that is more meaningful here and it is defined as

$$\bar{R}_i = -g \frac{\bar{\rho}'}{\bar{\rho}} \frac{L^2}{U_0^2} = \frac{N^2 L^2}{U_0^2}. \quad (7.34)$$

As can be seen, this parameter can be interpreted as the ratio of the stabilizing influence due to the vertical stratification and the destabilizing influence due to the mean velocity and is a parameter of bulk form. Thus, after nondimension-alizing (7.33), the following equation becomes the center of the analysis:

$$(k_1 U - \omega)^2 (\mathbf{w}'' - k^2 \mathbf{w}) - k_1 (k_1 U - \omega) U'' \mathbf{w} + k^2 \bar{R}_i \mathbf{w} = 0, \quad (7.35)$$

where all quantities are nondimensional with respect to the mean length and velocity scales L and U_0. Now, unlike the case with no mean flow, the time behavior no longer has to be that of neutral wave motion. Such determination depends critically on the Richardson number. Often this criticalness is expressed in terms of the local Richardson number rather than the bulk value. If the mean velocity profile is approximated locally as a linear function of the z-coordinate, then the local shear value is a constant. In these terms, the Richardson number is

$$R_i = N^2 / (U')^2. \quad (7.36)$$

In many ways, this definition is more meaningful from the standpoint of stability since the mean shear is tantamount to vorticity. This point will now be put into perspective.

As has already been shown, the use of the energized form of the perturbation equations can be beneficial to indicating the means whereby there are sources

for amplification of the disturbances. This can be done here as well. Define the integrated value for the total energy to be

$$E(t) = \iiint \frac{\rho_0}{2}(u^2 + v^2 + w^2)dV \qquad (7.37)$$

and it is possible to show that, if the volume boundaries are passive, then the temporal balance for the perturbation energy is

$$\frac{dE}{dt} = \int -\rho_0 \overline{uw} U'dz + \int -g\overline{\rho w}dz. \qquad (7.38)$$

Thus, from previous considerations it is known that the Reynolds stress acting on the mean shear can, if the phasing is correct, lead to an increase in the energy. Counteracting such generation is the stabilizing effect of buoyancy because the fluid is stratified. Likewise, there can now be neutrality because the two mechanisms can be in balance.

In a similar fashion, the differential equations can be investigated directly as was done by Rayleigh (1883). Go back to the nondimensional equation for **w**, put $U = 0$, multiply by the complex conjugate of **w**, and integrate over the region of the flow variation. These operations will lead to

$$c^2 \int_{z_1}^{z_2} \{|\mathbf{w}'|^2 + k^2|\mathbf{w}|^2\}dz = \int_{z_1}^{z_2} N^2|\mathbf{w}|^2dz, \qquad (7.39)$$

where $c^2 = \omega^2/k^2$ has been used. First, the flow is stable so long as $N > 0$ everywhere in the flow regime. Second, for the case where where $N > 0$ everywhere, then the flow is unstable. In fact, such a flow is even unstable statically due to the fact that the more dense fluid is above that which is lighter.

Now, when $U \neq 0$, then Howard (1961) was able to extract a general stability criterion for stratified shear flow. Define a new variable, F, as $F = w/(U - c)^{1/2}$, and, in these terms, the equation is

$$\frac{d}{dz}\{(U - c)F'\} - \{k^2(U - c) + \frac{1}{2}U'' + \left(\frac{1}{4}U' - \bar{R}_i\right) \Big/ (U - c)\}F = 0. \qquad (7.40)$$

After multiplying (7.40) by the complex conjugate of F and integrating over the flow regime, then

$$\int_{z_1}^{z_2} (U - c)\{|F'|^2 + k^2|F|^2\} + \frac{1}{2}U''|F|^2 + \frac{(1/4U' - \bar{R}_i)}{(U - c)}|F|^2\}dz = 0 \qquad (7.41)$$

follows. The imaginary part of this expression is

$$-c_i \int_{z_1}^{z_2} \{|F'|^2 + k^2|F|^2 + \left(\bar{R}_i - \frac{1}{4}U'\right)|F|^2/|U - c|^2\}dz = 0 \quad (7.42)$$

and, if $c_i \neq 0$, then the local Richardson Number, R_i, has the requirement that

$$R_i = \frac{\bar{R}_i}{U'} < \frac{1}{4} \qquad (7.43)$$

somewhere within the flow regime. As a result, the flow is stable if the local Richardson number is everywhere $R_i > 1/4$. For most flows of this type, the frequency of the internal gravity waves is usually much less than N, the Brunt-Väisälä frequency, and hence they are probably in a stable environment.

One example for such flow should be given. Specifically, the flow that was perturbed was defined by $U = \tanh z$ and $\ell n \bar{\rho} = b \tanh z$ and is a stratified mixing layer. This choice leads to $N^2 = \operatorname{sech}^2 z$ and the flow is defined for $-\infty < z < \infty$. In terms of the neutral stability locus, the stability boundary was computed by Hazel (1972) for this flow and is shown in Fig. 7.5. As can be seen, the requirement for the Richardson Number is confirmed.

When treating the fluctuations inviscidly, the fundamental equation for w can be considered in much the same way as was done for v in the Rayleigh equation, (??), when there is no stratification. From kinematics, $\nabla^2 w = \frac{\partial \omega_x}{\partial y} - \frac{\partial \omega_y}{\partial x}$. In wave space, this is $ik\hat{\Omega}_\varphi = ik_2\hat{\omega}_x - ik_1\hat{\omega}_y$ and equation (7.15) can be

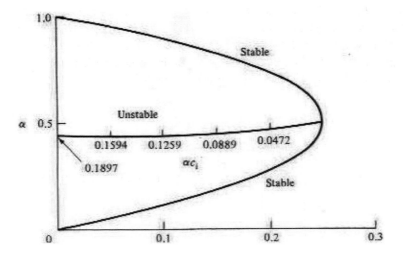

Fig. 7.5. Neutral stability boundary for stratified shear layer (after Hazel, 1972).

written as

$$\left(\frac{\partial}{\partial t} + ik_1 U\right)^2 \hat{\Omega}_\varphi = \left(\frac{\partial}{\partial t} + ik_1 U\right) \cos\varphi U'' \hat{w} + ikN^2 \hat{w}. \quad (7.44)$$

There are now two possible generating terms for the vorticity. First, the interaction with the mean vorticity and second, the baroclinic torque due to stratification. Now, similarly there is an equation for the component of the vorticity in the z-direction, just as done for the y-component in the constant density fluid. This equation has become known as the Squire equation and, in this case, is

$$\left(\frac{\partial}{\partial t} + ik_2 U\right) \omega_z = ik_2 U' \hat{w}. \quad (7.45)$$

Unlike (7.44) for $\hat{\Omega}_\varphi$, this relation is exactly as that for the constant density fluid where a mean shear and three-dimensionality are crucial to the full dynamical behavior.

More details of interest in flows that have variable density can be revealed by the use of an all encompassing simplified example in the manner of what is now known as the Kelvin-Helmholtz model. This technique was used in Chapter 2 as well. In other words, flows joined at an interface that has discontinuous mean properties. Consider the prototype as shown in Fig. 7.6.

In this case, both above and below the line of discontinuity, (7.33) reduces to

$$(k_1 U - \omega)^2 (w'' - k^2 w) = 0. \quad (7.46)$$

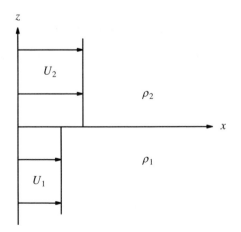

Fig. 7.6. Discontinuous stratified mean flow model.

And, unless there is an initial specification of vorticity, solutions of (7.46) are tantamount to a velocity field that is harmonic. Thus, the velocity can be replaced by $\nabla\phi$ where ϕ is the scalar potential and satisfies $\nabla^2\phi = 0$, just as w does in (7.46). The far field boundary conditions for $z \to \pm\infty$, are easily satisfied by the solutions for this equation and, in fact, the perturbations must vanish for these limits.

At the interface, $z = 0$, both a kinematic relation and a balance in the pressure (normal stress) must be insured. If $F = z - h(x, y, t) = 0$ defines the interface, then $DF/Dt = 0$ is the kinematic requirement. In linearized form this is

$$\frac{\partial h}{\partial t} + U\frac{\partial h}{\partial x} = w = \frac{\partial\phi}{\partial z} \tag{7.47}$$

and must be satisfied at $z = 0$. To do this, solutions for ϕ are obtained separately in the two regions $z > 0$ and $z < 0$. In so doing, the far field boundary conditions can be satisfied and the net results used in (7.47).

A relation for the pressure is derived from one of the forms of the Bernoulli equation. Since the perturbation field is harmonic, this means a Bernoulli equation that can be written for the pressure is

$$p/\rho + \frac{1}{2}|\vec{v}|^2 + gh + \frac{\partial\phi}{\partial t},$$

where g is the acceleration due to gravity. The balance at the interface $z = 0$ requires the pressure difference to be a consequence of the force due to surface tension. Simply stated, this requires $\Delta p = (p_2 - p_1) = T\left(\frac{\partial^2 h}{\partial x^2} + \frac{\partial^2 h}{\partial y^2}\right)$ where T is the coefficient for surface tension. Linearized, the expression for the pressure becomes

$$p/\rho + U\frac{\partial\phi}{\partial x} + gh + \frac{\partial\phi}{\partial t}. \tag{7.48}$$

This formulation results in three homogeneous equations for the unknown coefficients or simply an eigenvalue problem. In fact, assuming $h(x, y, t) = He^{ik_1x+ik_2y-i\omega t}$ and $\phi = Ae^{-kz}e^{ik_1x+ik_2y-i\omega t}$ for $z > 0$; $\phi = Be^{kz}e^{ik_1x+ik_2 2y}$ $-i\omega t$ for $z < 0$, then the eigenvalues are given by the determinant of the coefficients A, B, and H. This is

$$\begin{vmatrix} i(k_1U_2 - \omega) & 0 & k \\ i(k_1U_1 - \omega) & -k & 0 \\ (\rho_2 - \rho_1)g + k^2T & -i\rho_1(k_1U_1 - \omega) & i\rho_2(k_2U_2 - \omega) \end{vmatrix} = 0. \tag{7.49}$$

When expanded, (7.49) is

$$k\{\rho_2(k_1U_2 - \omega)^2 + \rho_1(k_2U_1 - \omega)^2 + k(\rho_2 - \rho_1)g - k^3T\} = 0. \tag{7.50}$$

The eigenvalue relation (7.50) is to be solved for the frequency ω ($k = 0$ is not of any interest) in order to determine whether or not there is an instability and, if the imaginary part, $\omega_i > 0$, the flow is unstable. The general result for the frequency is

$$(1 + s)\bar{\omega} = \cos\theta(1 + s\bar{U})$$

$$\pm i\cos\theta\left[s(\bar{U} - 1)^2 + \frac{(1+s)\bar{T} - (1 - s^2)\bar{g}}{\cos^2\theta}\right]^{1/2}, \quad (7.51)$$

where all the quantities have now been nondimensionalized and are defined as

$$\bar{\omega} = \frac{\omega}{kU_1}, \quad s = \rho_2/\rho_1, \quad \bar{U} = U_2/U_1, \quad \cos\theta = k_1/k,$$

$$\bar{g} = g/kU_1^2, \quad \bar{T} = \frac{kT}{\rho_1 U_1^2}.$$

The first observation should be directed to the fact that, if $\rho_1 = \rho_2(s = 1)$, then the force of gravity is no longer present. Second, the maximum amplification rate – when there is instability – is for $\cos\theta = 1$ or $\theta = 0$. Historically, if $\bar{T} = 0$, the general result is due to Kelvin; $\bar{T} \neq 0$ was considered by Stokes. More specific cases are:

(a) $s = 1, \bar{T} = 0$.

$$\bar{\omega} = \frac{(1 + \bar{U})}{2}\cos\theta \pm i\frac{(\bar{U} - 1)}{2}\cos\theta$$

This is the classical Helmholtz model where, unless $\bar{U} = 1$, the flow is always unstable.

(b) $\bar{U} = 1, \bar{T} = 0$.

$$\bar{\omega} = \cos\theta \pm \frac{[(1 - s^2)\bar{g}]^{1/2}}{(1 + s)}$$

In this case, there is no relative shearing motion but instability depends upon whether or not the heavier or the lighter fluid is in the upper location, i.e., $s \leq 1$.

(c) $\bar{U} = 1, \bar{T} \neq 0$.

Here, it is a question of the balance of the force of gravity with surface tension with the neutral focus, $\bar{\omega}_i = 0$, being given by

$$g/T = \frac{(1 + s)}{(1 - s^2)}k^2$$

when expressed in the original dimensional variables. But, since there is no natural length scale in a discontinuous model, it is the polar wave length,

k, that is of importance. As such, large values of k simply mean very small spatial scales and are non physical.

(d) With all effects considered, full neutrality is given by

$$(1 - s^2)\bar{g} = s(\bar{U} - 1)^2 \cos^2\theta(1 + s)\bar{T}$$

or a balance of all forces in the problem. Generally speaking gravity and surface tension tend to be stabilizing whereas relative motion (shear) destabilizes.

7.3 Effects of rotation

The basis for this problem concerns motions that are on the surface of the earth, in the atmosphere or perhaps on a rotating table in a laboratory. As such, the analyses have been made using what is known as the beta plane approximation for the fundamental model and it provides an excellent description for understanding such motions in the northern or southern latitudes of the earth where the value of the rotation varies as one moves from the equator to the poles. In this case, three-dimensionality is excluded because, in order to do this properly, stratification of the mean density must be incorporated in order to correctly model the full physics. (Cf. Drazin, 1978, among others for the full analysis.) Viscous effects can, however, be neglected to high order and the fluid is incompressible.

The perturbation equations for this problem can be written as

$$u_x + v_y + w_z = 0, \tag{7.52}$$

$$u_t + 2\Omega(w \cos\varphi - v \sin\varphi) = -\frac{1}{\rho}p_x, \tag{7.53}$$

$$v_t + 2\Omega u \sin\varphi = -\frac{1}{\rho}p_y, \tag{7.54}$$

$$w_t - 2\Omega u \cos\varphi = -\frac{1}{\rho}p_z + g, \tag{7.55}$$

for a constant density fluid and motion where the earth's rotation, Ω, plays a central role. The angle, φ, is measured from the equator in the northerly or southerly directions. Mean motion is neglected for the moment and, typically, $u, v \approx 200$cm/sec, $w \approx 1$cm/sec; $g = 10^3$cm/sec and $2\Omega = 1.456 \times 10^{-4}$/sec. Thus, rotation is essentially relegated to the x-y plane under these conditions. Once a location is established, in either the northern or southern latitude and not too near the equator, i.e., $\varphi > \pm 4°$, then it is also true that $|w \cos\varphi| \ll |v \sin\varphi|$ and $|\Omega u \cos\varphi| \ll g$.

Define $f = 2\Omega \sin \varphi$ as the Coriolis parameter and the reduced set of equations for the momenta are

$$u_t - fv = -\frac{1}{\rho} p_x, \tag{7.56}$$

$$v_t + fu = -\frac{1}{\rho} p_y, \tag{7.57}$$

and

$$w_t = -\frac{1}{\rho} p_z + g. \tag{7.58}$$

For hydrostatic balance to be valid, then $|w_t| \ll g$, with the centrifugal effect included in the definition of the pressure. In fact, if $w = \hat{w} e^{i\sigma t}$, then $|\frac{\sigma \hat{w}}{g}| \ll 1$ must follow or $|\frac{\sigma a}{g}| \ll 1$ with a the amplitude of any vertical motion. Hence, this assumption results in a condition on the frequency σ of the vertical motion. Under these conditions, equation (7.58) immediately reduces to

$$p_z \approx \rho g \tag{7.59}$$

and can be integrated to give

$$p = p_a + \int_z^h \rho g dz, \tag{7.60}$$

where p_a is the atmospheric pressure. If $\rho = \rho_0$, then $p = p_a + \rho_0 g (h - z)$ with h the height of the sea surface, say. The result is that hydrostatic balance allows for u and v to be independent of the coordinate z.

Continuity is expressed by the fact that the velocity must be solenoidal or (7.52). This equation can now be integrated in the vertical direction over the height of the fluid column and, in so doing, the pressure variable can be replaced by h, the surface height. Similarly, w can be replaced in the same way since there are boundary conditions both above and below that are given in terms of w. The combination of these operations leads to the new set of governing equations or

$$(u\bar{h})_x + (v\bar{h})_y + h_t = 0, \tag{7.61}$$

$$u_t - fv = -gh_x, \tag{7.62}$$

$$v_t + fu = -gh_y, \tag{7.63}$$

where $\bar{h} = h + s$; $z = s$ is the location of the bottom and taken independent of time; the atmospheric pressure is taken as constant. It is interesting to note that these changes have now changed the set of linear equations to ones that are again nonlinear. However, the approximation

$$\bar{h} = h + s = s \left(1 + \frac{h}{s} \right) \approx s; \quad \frac{h}{s} \ll 1, \tag{7.64}$$

must be used for consistency and then (7.61) becomes

$$(us)_x + (vs)_y = -h_t, \tag{7.65}$$

with $s = s(x, y)$ in general and is a known function in order to solve any problem.

There are several noted examples from the field of oceanography that use this set of equations:

(1) $s = s_0$, **a constant**. If rotation and the v-component of the motion are neglected, then the governing equation in terms of h as the dependent variable is nothing more than a one-dimensional wave equation and $\sqrt{gs_0}$ is just the shallow water speed for these waves:

$$\frac{\partial^2 h}{\partial t^2} = s_0 g \frac{\partial^2 h}{\partial x^2}. \tag{7.66}$$

(2) $s = s(x)$ **only**, constant rotation and in a narrow channel say. Solutions can be assumed of the form $h(x, t) = a(x)e^{i\sigma t}$, $u = U(x)e^{i\sigma t}$, $v = V(x)e^{i\sigma t}$ and the net equation will read

$$\frac{d^2}{dx^2}(sgU) + (\sigma^2 - f_0^2)U = 0. \tag{7.67}$$

As can be seen, wave motion is possible and depends upon the relative frequency when compared to the value of the rate of rotation.

(3) **Long progressive waves**. Here, $s = s_0$ and $f = f_0$, both constants. The more common solution for this problem is taken as

$$\{h, u, v\} = \{H, A, B\}e^{i(kx - \omega t) + \ell y} \tag{7.68}$$

and leads to a dispersion relation by substituting (7.68) into the set of governing equations (7.62), (7.63), and (7.65). This is:

$$\omega\left[\omega^2 - f_0^2 + gs_0(\ell^2 - k^2)\right] = 0. \tag{7.69}$$

Thus, either (a) $\omega = 0$ and is just the steady motion and is geostrophic or, (b) $\omega^2 = f_0^2 + gs_0(k^2 - \ell^2)$. In this case ℓ can be real or complex. If purely real, then Kelvin waves result but require $v = 0$ in order to satisfy the boundary conditions on the walls of the channel. If ℓ is imaginary, then the waves are known as Poincaré waves and the channel can be broad.

(4) **Rossby waves**. For this case, $s = s_0$, constant but $f \cong f_0 + \beta y$ and the assumption is known as the beta plane approximation. After eliminating u and v from the equations, an equation for h under these circumstances can be found. Furthermore, the temporal behavior remains periodic or $h(x, y, t) = \mathbf{h}(x, y)e^{-i\omega t}$, and the result becomes

$$(\omega^2 - f^2)\mathbf{h} + (gs_0)\nabla^2\mathbf{h} - i\frac{\beta}{\omega}(\beta s_0)\mathbf{h}_x = 0, \tag{7.70}$$

with ∇^2 the two-dimensional Laplace operator in x, y variables. The fact that this wave equation has a term involving an extra derivative with respect to x is the heart of Rossby waves, namely these waves have a westerly propagation since x denotes the east-west orientation. This point can be illustrated by using the WKBJ form for solution. To this end, let

$$\mathbf{h}(x, y) = a(x, y)e^{i\theta(x,y)} \tag{7.71}$$

with $i\theta = i\ell x + iny + \lambda x + \mu y$. And, for plane waves, λ/ℓ and μ/m are both $\ll 1$. To lowest order, the dispersion relation for these waves is

$$(\ell + \ell_0)^2 + m^2 = \ell_0^2 - \frac{(f_0^2 - \omega^2)}{(g s_0)} = r^2, \tag{7.72}$$

where $\ell_0 = \frac{1}{2}\frac{(f_0^2 + \omega^2)}{(f_0^2 - \omega^2)}\frac{\beta}{\omega}$. Again, the westerly nature of the Rossby wave is quite evident from (7.72).

Return to the set of equations (7.52) and (7.56) to (7.57) and insert the beta (or spanwise) plane approximation for f along with the restoration of the mean flow, $U(y)$. Elimination of the pressure from these equations will lead to the following nondimensional equation for v:

$$\left(\frac{\partial}{\partial t} + U\frac{\partial}{\partial x}\right)\nabla^2 v - \left(U'' - \frac{1}{R_0}\right)v_x = 0, \tag{7.73}$$

where all quantities have been nondimensionalized with respect to U_0 and L, mean flow values for the velocity and spatial scales. This governing equation is the analogue for that of internal gravity waves with shear except that the new parameter is known as the Rossby number, defined as

$$R_0 = U_0/\beta L^2 \tag{7.74}$$

and is the ratio of the relative values of inertia to the Coriolis force in the problem. In the limit, $R_0 \to 0$, the flow is in geostrophic balance as noted previously.

Equation (7.73), even with the addition of the Rossby number, is mathematically the same type of equation as that that was used by Rayleigh (1880) for the study of stability without rotation in the inviscid limit (equation (??)). This basis was recognized by Kuo (1949), Fjørtoft (1950), and Tung (1981), among others. Consequently it has led to a result that has become known as the Rayleigh-Kuo theorem for flows in this environment. The theorem is directly related to the necessity for an inflection point in the mean flow distribution. This can be demonstrated in a straightforward manner just as was done for stratified flow.

Normal mode solutions can be found for v as has been done throughout or $v = \hat{v}(y)e^{i\alpha x - i\omega t}$. Upon substitution of this form into equation (7.73), an ordinary differential equation for $\hat{v}$ is obtained:

$$\hat{v}'' + \left[\frac{1/R_0 - U''}{(U - c)} - \alpha^2\right]\hat{v} = 0, \tag{7.75}$$

where $c = \omega/\alpha$, the complex wave speed. Now multiply (7.75) by the complex conjugate of $\hat{v}$ and integrate the result over the range of the flow or from $y = y_1$ to $y = y_2$, say. With the boundary conditions such that $\hat{v} = 0$ or $\hat{v} \to 0$ for the y_1, y_2 values and, after integration by parts, this operation yields

$$\int_{y_1}^{y_2}\left[\frac{1/R_0 - U''}{(U - c)} - \alpha^2\right]|\hat{v}|^2 dy = \int_{y_1}^{y_2}|\hat{v}'|^2 dy. \tag{7.76}$$

The imaginary part of (7.76) is

$$c_i \int_{y_1}^{y_2}(1/R_0 - U'')\left|\frac{\hat{v}}{U - c}\right|^2 dy = 0. \tag{7.77}$$

Thus, a necessary condition for instability where $c_i > 0$ is that $(1/R_0 - U'') = 0$, the mean vorticity gradient, $((\beta - U'') = 0$, dimensionally) must change sign somewhere within the flow domain. In short, a generalized inflection point criterion and a result doe to Kuo (1949). In like manner, the real part of (7.76) was used by Fjørtoft (1950) to demonstrate that the generalized inflection point should be located exactly as that of the critical layer, $(U - c_r) = 0$, when there is a neutral disturbance, $c_i = 0$. These two results mimic those established by Rayleigh when there is no rotation ($\beta = 0$) and are particularly relevant to the bases of barotropic instability in zonal flows. Tung (1981) has further provided an extensive description of this type of flow and its instabilities.

There is still more to this problem other than the analogy to the non rotating case. In part, such inferences are directly related to the net value and sign of the coefficient $(\beta - U'')$. One extreme is for the case when there is no mean flow and it is only the effect due to the beta plane that dictates the perturbation motion. All relevant possibilities have been given and these are tantamount to linear wave motion. Then, there can be a finite mean flow which varies only linearly and thus the term U'' still vanishes. For the most part such flows are stable but, for flows in the geophysical environment, it is not just the mean velocity variation that dictates the salient nature of the problem but the specific boundary conditions that must be satisfied as well. The barotropic description is that of perturbations on the beta plane in the presence of a mean shear with $U'' \neq 0$ and the perturbation velocity is required to vanish at the boundaries. As has been shown, this flow can be unstable.

Another important problem deals with the stability of what is known as baro-clinic flow. In this case the boundary conditions are physically connected to the perturbation pressure instead of the velocity. Of course these conditions are, by use of the governing perturbation equations, easily set in terms of the velocity but such conditions are not simply the requirement that the velocity vanish and the results lead to far different conclusions. Work in this area was pioneered by Charney (1947) and Eady (1949). Both of these efforts considered only a linear variation for the mean velocity but, as has been mentioned, this is not a requirement and instability is still possible.

The Eady problem is also described by Drazin & Reid (1984) in fine detail and the underlying physics are presented. Then, these authors make note that there is an interesting mathematical equivalent of this problem to that for the stability of plane Couette flow of an inviscid constant density fluid where the boundary conditions require the pressure to be constant on the upper and lower boundaries in lieu of the vanishing of the velocity. For this purpose, however, the perturbation problem should be cast in a convective coordinate reference frame in order to fully make the analogy. In this way Criminale & Drazin (1990) examined the Eady problem – among other examples – in order to demonstrate an alternative method for solving the complete dynamics for per-turbations as well as determine the stability. A thorough presentation of this technique will be given in Chapter 8 but it is useful to apply the technique to the Eady problem now. And, since the inviscid plane Couette flow problem is perhaps the simplest of all modeled flows, the impact of the change in the boundary conditions is profound.

Consider the flow defined between $y = \pm H$ with $U(y) = \sigma y$. The inviscid perturbation equation for the v-velocity component is

$$\left(\frac{\partial}{\partial t} + U \frac{\partial}{\partial x} \right) \nabla^2 v = 0 \tag{7.78}$$

and the boundary conditions are that the pressure be constant for $y = \pm H$.

The convective coordinate transformation is defined by the change of variables[1]

$$T = t; \quad \xi = x - U(y)t; \quad \eta = y; \quad \zeta = z.$$

In these terms, equation (7.78) becomes

$$\frac{\partial}{\partial T} \nabla^2 v = 0, \tag{7.79}$$

where $\nabla^2 = \frac{\partial^2}{\partial \eta^2} - 2\sigma T \frac{\partial^2}{\partial \eta \partial \xi} + \sigma^2 T^2 \frac{\partial^2}{\partial \xi^2} + \frac{\partial^2}{\partial \xi^2} + \frac{\partial^2}{\partial \zeta^2}$. It can be immediately seen that there are two possible solutions for v. First, $\nabla^2 v = F(\xi, \eta, \zeta)$.

---

[1] In effect, characteristics for $\nabla^2 v$ as the dependent variable.

Second, $\nabla^2 v = 0$. These solutions correspond physically to whether or not there is an initial perturbation vorticity since all solutions for $\nabla^2 v = 0$ are those of a velocity field which has neither a divergence nor a curl and is thus harmonic.

Again, since the ξ and ζ variables are unbounded in both directions, Fourier decomposition is used and, with all solutions proportional to $e^{i\alpha\xi + i\gamma\zeta}$, (7.79) takes the form

$$\frac{\partial}{\partial T} \Delta\hat{v} = 0 \qquad (7.80)$$

with $\Delta = \frac{\partial^2}{\partial\eta^2} - i2\sigma T\alpha\frac{\partial}{\partial\eta} - (\tilde{\alpha}^2 + \sigma^2 T^2\alpha^2)$; $\tilde{\alpha}^2 = \alpha^2 + \gamma^2$. A further change of variables where $\hat{v}(\alpha; \eta; \gamma; T) = V(\alpha; \eta; \gamma; T)e^{i\sigma T\alpha\eta}$ and then

$$\Delta\hat{v} \equiv \left(\frac{\partial^2 V}{\partial\eta^2} - \tilde{\alpha}^2 V\right)e^{i\sigma T\alpha\eta}.$$

Immediately, $V = A(T)e^{\tilde{\alpha}\eta} + B(T)e^{-\tilde{\alpha}\eta} + V_p$ with V_p depending upon the choice for F, the initial vorticity.

An expression for the pressure in terms of the velocity can be obtained from the transformed equations for u and w. This is

$$-\tilde{\alpha}^2 \hat{p} = \frac{\partial^2 \hat{v}}{\partial T \partial\eta} - i\sigma T\alpha\frac{\partial\hat{v}}{\partial T} - 2i\sigma\alpha\hat{v}$$

and must be constant for $\eta = \pm H$. By applying these conditions two coupled first order ordinary equations for A and B result and can be written as

$$\begin{pmatrix} \tilde{\alpha}e^{-\tilde{\alpha}H} & -\tilde{\alpha}e^{\tilde{\alpha}H} \\ \tilde{\alpha}e^{\tilde{\alpha}H} & -\tilde{\alpha}e^{-\tilde{\alpha}H} \end{pmatrix} \begin{pmatrix} \overset{\circ}{A} \\ \overset{\circ}{B} \end{pmatrix} =$$

$$i\sigma\alpha \begin{pmatrix} (1 + \tilde{\alpha}H)e^{-\tilde{\alpha}H} & (1 - \tilde{\alpha}H)e^{\tilde{\alpha}H} \\ (1 - \tilde{\alpha}H)e^{\tilde{\alpha}H} & (1 + \tilde{\alpha}H)e^{-\tilde{\alpha}H} \end{pmatrix} \begin{pmatrix} A \\ B \end{pmatrix} + \begin{pmatrix} F_1 \\ F_2 \end{pmatrix}, \qquad (7.81)$$

where the pressure constant at the boundaries has been taken to be zero. Here, for notation purposes,

$$\frac{dA}{dt} = \overset{\circ}{A}, \quad \text{and} \quad \frac{dB}{dt} = \overset{\circ}{B}.$$

The functions F_1 and F_2 are defined as

$$F_1 = \hat{p}_p(\eta = H)e^{i\sigma T\alpha H}$$

and

$$F_2 = \hat{p}_p(\eta = -H)e^{-iT\alpha H},$$

with $\hat{p}_p$ is the pressure resulting from V_p. Inverting the matrix on the left-hand side of (7.81) produces a standard form or the system:

$$\frac{d}{dt}\begin{pmatrix} A \\ B \end{pmatrix} = \frac{i\sigma \cos\varphi}{2}\begin{pmatrix} (2 - q\coth q) & q/\sinh q \\ -q/\sinh q & -(2 - q\coth q) \end{pmatrix}\begin{pmatrix} A \\ B \end{pmatrix}$$

$$+ \frac{H}{q\sinh q}\begin{pmatrix} e^{\tilde{\alpha}H}F_2 - e^{-\tilde{\alpha}H}F_1 \\ -e^{+\tilde{\alpha}H}F_1 + e^{-\tilde{\alpha}H}F_2 \end{pmatrix} \qquad (7.82)$$

where $q = 2\tilde{\alpha}H$ and $\alpha = \tilde{\alpha}\cos\varphi$ have been used.

The homogeneous solutions for (7.82) are those of normal modes and, with the solutions proportional to $e^{\omega t}$, the eigen frequencies are

$$\omega = \pm\frac{i\sigma\cos\varphi}{2}(4 - 4q\coth q + q^2)^{1/2}. \qquad (7.83)$$

The system is dynamically neutral so long as $q > 2.4$ since ω remains purely imaginary. A and B are pure constants for $q = 0$, 2.4 or $\varphi = \pi/2$ since $\omega = 0$ for these values. For values $0 < q < 2.4$ the flow is unstable. These results are in contrast to those of plane Couette flow where there are no normal modes for the inviscid problem and $A = B = 0$ is the only possibility since it is the velocity that must vanish at the two boundaries in lieu of the pressure.

When an initial vorticity has been specified, the forced problem offers much more to either the Eady or the plane Couette flow problem. This is mathematically the result due to the continuous spectrum as discussed in Chapter 3. For inviscid plane Couette flow, the forced problem was done by Criminale, Long & Zhu (1991). The exact behavior for either problem will depend upon the choice for the forcing but it is significant to note that algebraic dependence in time evolves and dominates the early transient period of the dynamics.

In the case treated by Eady for baroclinic instability, the results for the homogeneous unforced problem are as the expression in (7.83) save for the fact that the relevant physical parameter is the Burger number, a number that involves the density variation, perturbation temperature, the acceleration due to gravity as well as the value of the rotation. The exact result for the forced problem will depend upon the initial input but, as for plane inviscid Couette flow, this part of the solution will involve the continuous spectrum.

7.4 The Ekman layer

The perturbation problem for the Ekman layer is remarkable for several reasons. First of all, the functions that define the mean flow that Ekman (1905) determined are known to be an exact set of solutions for the full Navier-Stokes

governing equations. In fact, this result is true for both the steady and the unsteady solutions for this flow. Ekman in essence considered this problem as one that approximated the planetary boundary layer and, to this end, it was assumed that the problem was local in that the surface was taken to be flat and the Coriolis parameter constant. Then, because of the important role that the rotation plays, this boundary layer is truly parallel. The mean flow vector is not, however, simply in one specified direction. On the contrary, it has two components that combine to form what is known as the Ekman spiral. If $\mathbf{U} = (U, V, W)$ defines the mean velocity vector, then the solution in dimensional terms is

$$U = U_g\left[1 - e^{-z/(f/2v)^{1/2}}\cos(z/(f/2v)^{1/2})\right],$$
$$V = U_g e^{-z/(f/2v)^{1/2}}\sin(z/(f/2v)^{1/2}),$$
$$W = 0, \tag{7.84}$$

where U_g is the geostrophic value of the velocity outside the boundary layer. Here, the z-coordinate is maintained for the geophysical flow examples and is the vertical coordinate perpendicular to the boundary. The velocity lies entirely in the x-y plane, is zero at the boundary and approaches the geostrophic value in the free stream ($z \to \infty$). The referenced spiral is defined in the x-y plane and can be evaluated by the ratio of U and V as a function of z and is shown in Fig. 7.7. The existence of the spiral nature also is the cause of notable features, such as the fact that the transport and the stress on the fluid at the boundary are opposed to each other, when viewed from the orientation of the vector $\mathbf{U}$. Figure 7.8 shows the velocity component solutions within the Ekman layer.

In nondimensional terms, the natural length scale is $(f/v)^{1/2}$. And, based on the considerations of the geophysical flows that have been presented, two

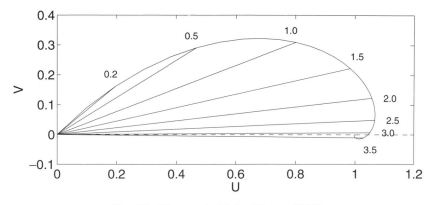

Fig. 7.7. Ekman spiral (after Ekman, 1905).

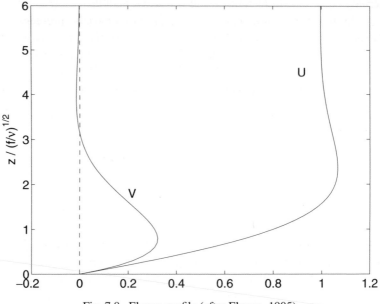

Fig. 7.8. Ekman profile (after Ekman, 1905).

parameters should be present in the governing equations, namely the Rossby number and one that assesses the effects of viscosity. The latter is known as the Ekman number in this context but is akin to the Reynolds number of non-rotating flows. In this case, however, the Rossby number fails to appear in the solution because there is no nonlinearity for an exact solution. More specifically, the Ekman solution is a direct consequence of a balance of the viscous force and the Coriolis acceleration and this is a linear problem.

This flow is now perturbed in a full three-dimensional manner. The linearized perturbation equations are

$$u_x + v_y + w_z = 0, \tag{7.85}$$

$$u_t + Uu_x + Vu_y + U'w - fv = -p_x/\rho_0 + \nu\nabla^2 u, \tag{7.86}$$

$$v_t + Uv_x + Vv_y + V'w + fu = -p_y/\rho_0 + \nu\nabla^2 v, \tag{7.87}$$

$$w_t + Uw_x + Vw_y = -p_z/\rho_0 + \nu\nabla^2 w. \tag{7.88}$$

Modal solutions combined with Fourier decomposition can be used as before to reduce this system to that of ordinary differential equations. Assume that all variables are a sum of modes written as

$$\{u, v, w, p\} = \{\mathbf{u}, \mathbf{v}, \mathbf{w}, \mathbf{p}\}e^{i\alpha x + i\gamma y - i\omega t}. \tag{7.89}$$

Then, with this ansatz, the pressure can be eliminated from (7.86) to (7.88) and the following pair of coupled equations must be solved as an eigenvalue problem.

$$(\tilde{\alpha}\tilde{U} - \omega)\Delta\mathbf{w} - \tilde{\alpha}\tilde{U}''\mathbf{w} + i\nu\Delta\Delta\mathbf{w} = f(\tilde{\alpha}\tilde{\mathbf{v}})', \qquad (7.90)$$

$$(\tilde{\alpha}\tilde{U} - \omega)(\tilde{\alpha}\tilde{\mathbf{v}}) + i\nu\Delta(\tilde{\alpha}\tilde{\mathbf{v}}) = i\tilde{\alpha}\tilde{V}'\mathbf{w} - f\hat{\mathbf{w}}', \qquad (7.91)$$

where $\Delta = \frac{d^2}{dz^2} - (\alpha^2 + \gamma^2)$ and full use of the Squire transformation has been used, namely

$$\tilde{\alpha}\tilde{U} = \alpha U + \gamma V, \quad \tilde{\alpha}\bar{\mathbf{u}} = \alpha\mathbf{u} + \gamma\mathbf{v}, \qquad (7.92)$$

$$\tilde{\alpha}\tilde{V} = \gamma U - \alpha V, \quad \tilde{\alpha}\tilde{\mathbf{v}} = \gamma\mathbf{u} - \alpha\mathbf{v}, \qquad (7.93)$$

in order to put the equations in this form. Originally, this was done by Lilly (1966) and later by Spooner & Criminale (1982) for a different purpose. But, it should be noticed that, even though (7.90) and (7.91) bear a strong resemblance to the classical Orr-Sommerfeld and Squire equations (exactly these equations if $f = 0$), this system is fully coupled. As such, it is now a sixth order system if one elects to obtain one governing equation.

Equations (7.90) and (7.91) can be better scrutinized in a nondimensional form. The basic velocity is taken to be U_g, the free stream geostrophic value and the Ekman length scale is chosen to be $L = (\nu/f)^{1/2}$. In this measure, the Ekman number becomes unity and the dominant parameter is again the Reynolds number, $Re = U_g L/\nu$. In this way, the governing equations are

$$\Delta\Delta w - iRe(\tilde{\alpha}\tilde{U} - \omega)\Delta w + i\tilde{\alpha}Re\tilde{U}''w = -i\tilde{\alpha}\tilde{v}', \qquad (7.94)$$

$$\Delta(i\tilde{\alpha}\tilde{v}) - iRe(\tilde{\alpha}\tilde{U} - \omega)(i\tilde{\alpha}\tilde{v}) = i\tilde{\alpha}Re\tilde{V}'w + w', \qquad (7.95)$$

where all quantities are now nondimensional. It is this set of equations that was numerically integrated by Lilly (1966), Faller & Kaylor (1967), and Spooner (1980) in order to determine the discrete eigenvalues for this flow. Unlike the Blasius boundary layer, where the instability requires viscosity to exist and is manifested by Tollmien-Schlichting waves, the Ekman layer has still other instabilities. Figure 7.9 displays the results in the conventional $\tilde{\alpha} - Re$ plane. Figures 7.10 to 7.12 depict surfaces in the Fourier space or cross sections of the data from Fig. 7.9 in order to better illustrate the possibilities. Such additional diagrams are the direct results from the fact that the system is a fully coupled sixth order system and the existence of an important new parameter that defines the orientation of the Ekman spiral. Figure 7.9 already reveals other possibilities for instability, particularly as $Re \to \infty$. It can also be seen that the phase speed of the perturbation can change sign. In Fig. 7.10, two maxima for the perturbation amplification are now possible. Figures 7.11 and 7.12 display such details in other ways.

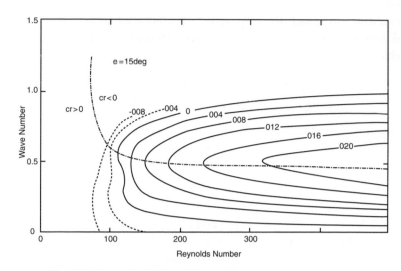

Fig. 7.9. Neutral stability of the Ekman layer (after Lilly, 1966).

Lilly explained the results that were obtained in terms of three distinct designations. First, the parallel mode. This instability is viscous and exists because the flow is rotating. This instability vanishes as $Re \rightarrow \infty$ and is more prevalent at low values of the Reynolds number. Second, as the Reynolds number is increased, dual regions of instability emerge. This is due to the lingering of the parallel mode and the viscous induced instability of the Tollmien-Schlichting type that is more common in the boundary layer. Third, there is an inviscid instability of the type that requires the mean profile to have an inflection. In terms of the physics, an inflection point in the velocity profile implies an extremum in the vorticity distribution (Lin, 1954) and follows exactly the bases established in Chapter 3. This can be made more lucid if equations (7.94) and (7.95) are considered at $Re = \infty$. Immediately there is an uncoupling and (7.94) is effectively the Rayleigh equation save for the particular distribution of the mean velocity.

The parallel instability that Lilly suggested was substantiated by a series of approximations to the set of governing equations. Although the approximations did demonstrate this type of instability, it was better done by a somewhat milder approximation made by Stuart (cf. Greenspan, 1969). Here, the mean flow was taken to be $\tilde{V}' = $ constant and $\tilde{U} = \tilde{U}'' = 0$ (and hence the designation of parallel mode) and then solutions of the approximate set of equations was sought by requiring that the solutions be oscillatory in z. This is possible, for the resulting sixth-order system is one of constant coefficients. Thus, if the

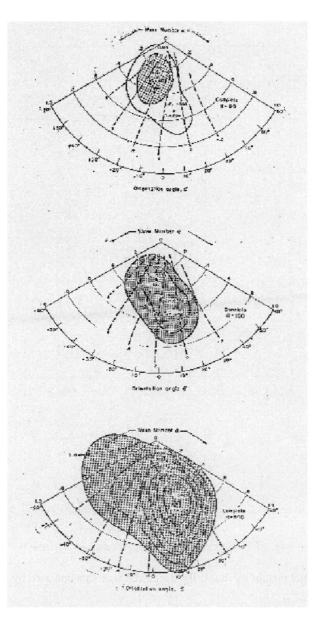

Fig. 7.10. Ekman eigenvalue display for fixed wave number as a function of spiral angle and Reynolds number (after Lilly, 1966).

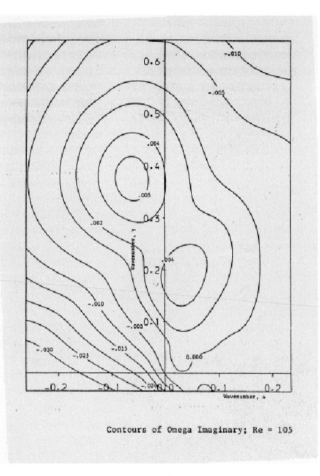

Contours of Omega Imaginary; Re = 105

Fig. 7.11. Contours of constant amplification for the Ekman layer at Reynolds number, $Re = 105$ (after Spooner & Criminale, 1982).

solutions are proportional to $e^{-i\beta z}$, then the following dispersion relation can be found:

$$\omega = \frac{i}{Re}\left[-(\beta^2 + \tilde{\alpha}^2) \pm \left(\frac{\beta\tilde{\alpha}\,Re\,\tilde{V}' - \beta^2}{\beta^2 + \tilde{\alpha}^2}\right)^{1/2}\right]. \qquad (7.96)$$

Consequently, the perturbations will be unstable if $Re > (\beta^2 + (\beta^2 + \tilde{\alpha}^2)^3)/\beta\tilde{\alpha}\tilde{V}'$. Again, the dependence on the parallel component of the mean velocity is essential for this mechanism. And, as mentioned, it is a viscous instability

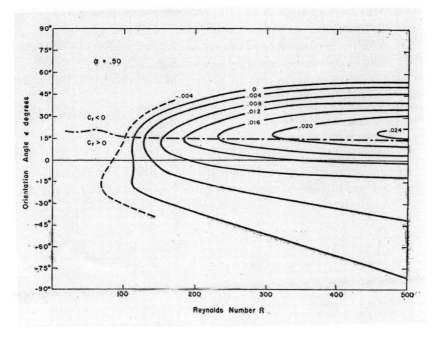

Fig. 7.12. Unstable regions for the Ekman layer as a function of wave number and spiral angle (after Lilly, 1966).

for, as $Re \to \infty$, the instability vanishes. The other viscous instability is that that has been discussed in Chapter 3 for the flat plate boundary layer.

It should be mentioned that Spooner (1980) has thoroughly examined all the modes for the Ekman layer and, not only were the eigenvalues that were obtained by others confirmed but the details of the eigenfunctions, the phasing, and the Reynolds stress distributions were given in addition. Such intense details were needed so that he could do an initial-value problem for the Ekman boundary layer, which was done by Spooner & Criminale (1982).

7.5 Exercises

1. Analyze qualitatively and quantitatively the stability of a flow that has a mean velocity, $\vec{U} = (\sigma z, 0, 0)$ with σ constant and is in an environment that is rotating with a value, f = constant about the z-axis. In making this analysis, answer the following questions:

   (a) What is the mean flow solution?
   (b) What can be said of the mean pressure?

(c) What are the relevant scales and parameters if the flow is (i) viscous, (ii) inviscid?

(d) Solve the problem when all fluctuations are independent of x and comment on the viscous versus inviscid solutions.

(e) Solve the problem by two different means and describe the type of instability – if one is present.

(f) Determine the energy and vorticity for both the mean and perturbation quantities.

(g) Compare to the Ekman-Blasius problem.

2. Investigate the stability of the flow illustrated below. Can the semicircle theorem and Richardson number $1/4$ criterion be used here? If so, explain.

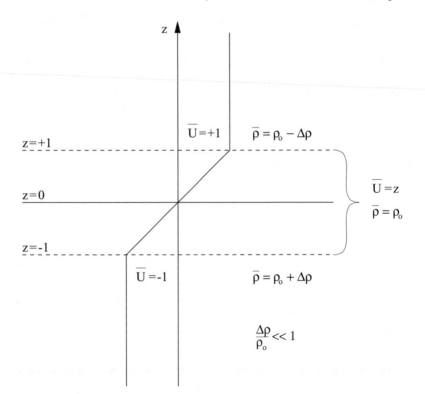

Chapter 8

Transient dynamics

8.1 The initial-value problem

The fundamental needs for specifying an initial-value problem for stability investigations are not in any way different from those that have long since been established in the theory of partial differential equations. This is especially true in view of the fact that the governing equations are linear. Thus, by knowing the boundary conditions as well as the particular initial specification, the problem is, in principle, complete. Unfortunately, in this respect, classical theory deals almost exclusively with second order systems and, as such, few problems in this area can be cast in terms of well known orthogonal functions. For the equations that are the bases of shear flow instability, however, it is only the inviscid problem that is second order (Rayleigh equation) and even this limiting equation does not have a detailed set of known functional solutions. The more serious case where viscous effects are retained, then the minimum requirement is an equation that is fourth order (Orr-Sommerfeld equation) and even this, as previously noted, is fortuitous. An a priori inspection would have led one to believe that the full three-dimensional system should be sixth order, such as that discussed for the case of the Ekman boundary layer, for example. The net result is one where there are neither known closed solutions nor mutual orthogonality. It is only the accompanying Squire equation, where the solutions are coupled to those of the Orr-Sommerfeld equation, that eventually makes for sixth order. These facts already form a sufficient basis for the necessity to inquire as to the early time as well as the long time behavior in the dynamics but, depending upon the particular flow under investigation, there are other considerations that must be included as well. All of these facts combine to strongly influence the initial temporal response and, in fact, under certain circumstances, can make the asymptotic behavior quite moot by comparison. And, although work dealing with this aspect of the problem did not make any

significant progress in the early years, both Kelvin (1887a) and Orr (1907a,b) had already recognized that the early time period contained significant information.

As has been demonstrated, there are three main categories for parallel shear flows, namely those (i) in enclosed channels, (ii) boundary layers and (iii) free shear flows that do not have any solid boundary influence in the flow. Physically, viscosity is critical to the understanding of the results for (i) and (ii) but not essential to (iii). Mathematically, (i) has only discrete eigen solutions and the set is complete (DiPrima & Habetler, 1969) whereas (ii) and (iii) must include the continuous as well as the discrete spectrum when one wishes to investigate the complete fate of an arbitrary initial disturbance. Grosch & Salwen (1978) and Salwen & Grosch (1981) have lucidly presented the details for these conclusions. In short, merely ascertaining that there may be at least one positive eigenvalue, and therefore the flow is unstable, is not sufficient. For example, Mack (1976) has long since shown that there are only a finite number of normal modes for the Blasius boundary layer and, as such, it would be impossible to represent any arbitrary initial distribution. A similar argument follows for free shear flows.

From the description of the mathematical complexities cited, it can be concluded that there are algebraic as well as exponential solutions in time. Specifically, there are three reasons for this. First, the nonorthogonality of the eigenfunctions is a reason for such behavior. Second, a possible resonance between the Orr-Sommerfeld and Squire solutions can lead to algebraic dependence. For channel flows, this is all that is possible for the viscous problem. With the boundary layer and free shear flows, then the continuous spectrum contributes to such behavior as well. Of the three, the nonorthogonality is ubiquitous and inherent in all of these flows when normal mode solutions are used for solving the equations. Resonance has been demonstrated to be possible for channel flow by Gustavsson & Hultgren (1980) and Benney & Gustavsson (1981) but, as the latter authors have further shown, this does not occur for the boundary layer. These conclusions are independent of any particular initial disturbance specification and are the consequences of the nature of the homogeneous set of governing equations and the respective boundary conditions.

Regardless of the underlying source that is the cause, the algebraic behavior translates to a linear dependence in the time variable. But, because there is viscous dissipation, any increase during the early period will eventually decay after reaching a maximum in finite time. Then, any exponentially growing mode, if one exists, will prevail as time increases beyond this point. If there is no growing mode, then the normal conclusion is that the flow is stable even though the initial algebraic growth may have increased to an amplitude that

violates the assumption of linearity for the amplitude. This point will be elaborated more fully as the methods are presented. And, towards this end, it will be seen that certain specific initial conditions can be made that will result in algebraic behavior that is stronger than just linear in time. In turn, initial input depends critically upon the physics of the problem. This thesis will be demonstrated in due course but, first, the fundamentals of the proper method for describing the initial-value problem should be reviewed.

The two major equations that are needed for determining the stability of any parallel or almost parallel flow are, in partial differential equation form (cf. Chapter 1):

$$\left(\frac{\partial}{\partial t} + i\alpha U\right)\Delta\hat{v} - i\alpha U''\hat{v} = \epsilon\Delta\Delta\hat{v}, \tag{8.1}$$

$$\left(\frac{\partial}{\partial t} + i\alpha U\right)\hat{\omega}_y - \epsilon\Delta\hat{\omega}_y = -i\gamma U'\hat{v}, \tag{8.2}$$

and are the Orr-Sommerfeld and Squire equations respectively in the two-dimensional Fourier (α, γ) space. In this way (8.1) and (8.2) can be used in a very general way in order to understand the needs of the temporal initial-value, boundary value problem. The Fourier decomposition assures the fact that all dependent variables are bounded in the x, z directions. Within the framework of the model assumptions, this is consistent in that these two variables range from $-\infty$ to $+\infty$. The remaining spatial variable, y, also requires boundary conditions to be met but the specifics are bound to the mean flow, $U(y)$, that is in question. In every case, the boundary conditions are requirements for the velocity that must be met. There is no reason, however, that initial data must be given in terms of the velocity. On the contrary, not only can it be given in terms of the vorticity mathematically, for example, but there is strong justification to do this in terms of the physics of the problems. Moreover, if the problem was one where the fluid is compressible, then the pressure might be yet another alternative. For the incompressible medium, however, this is not appropriate.

One of the original attempts to do an initial-value problem was made by Criminale & Kovasznay (1962). In this work, a localized disturbance was given in terms of the disturbance velocity in a Blasius boundary layer and the ensuing dynamics inferred from but a few normal modes. A similar effort was made by Gaster (1968) for the Blasius boundary layer and Spooner & Criminale (1982) considered the Ekman planetary boundary layer. In none of these cases was any consideration given to the need of a continuous spectrum. As a result, the results for these examples were limited and, in some ways, the work pointed more to the needs for the assumptions that were required then that are not, fortunately, needed today. For example, Breuer & Haritonidis (1990) and

Breuer & Kuraishi (1994) have since provided a modern treatment for the Blasius boundary layer. Still, even this work has assumptions that are needed in order to make the necessary numerical calculations but, generally speaking, it is a vast improvement over the earlier attempts. The noticeable weakness for these calculations has to do with the particular set of functions used to represent the vertical spatial variation. Chebyshev polynomials were chosen and these decay quite rapidly in the far field, a constraint that is too severe and loses the important physics that are related to the continuous spectrum.

The correct means of formulation is best given by the works of Grosch & Salwen (1978) and Salwen & Grosch (1981) as discussed in Chapter 3. In this work a completeness argument was shown that, any solution to (8.1), together with an initial-condition, can be written as

$$\hat{v}(\alpha, y, \gamma, t) = \sum_{j=1}^{N} A_j e^{i\omega_j t} \bar{v}_j(y) + V_c(y, t), \tag{8.3}$$

where N is finite and the number of discrete modes, $\bar{v}_j(y)$ are the eigenfunctions, and $V_c(y, t)$ is the continuum. The amplitude factors A_j and the frequencies ω_j are in general functions of $\tilde{\alpha} = (\alpha^2 + \gamma^2)^{1/2}$, $\phi = \tan^{-1}(\gamma/\alpha)$, and the Reynolds number, $Re = \epsilon^{-1}$. Once a choice for the initial value has been prescribed, use of the orthogonality principle between the eigenfunctions and the adjoint eigenfunctions allows for the determination of the amplitude factors and the continuum to be found. Unfortunately, although this procedure is mathematically correct, it is of limited use when actually studying transient behavior because of the underlying difficulties in the expansion process *per se* and the eigenfunctions for the system have been obtained numerically. Still, there are some important observations for this approach that should be noted.

For angles of obliquity, $\phi < 90°$, then N, the number of discrete modes, is finite with the number depending upon the value of the Reynolds number. For $\phi = 90°$, there are no discrete modes whatsoever ($N = 0$) and therefore only a continuum remains, regardless of the specific problem under investigation. The basic equations (8.1) and (8.2), when $\alpha = 0$ ($\phi = 90°$) are

$$\frac{\partial}{\partial t} \Delta \hat{v} = \epsilon \Delta \Delta \hat{v}, \tag{8.4}$$

$$\frac{\partial \hat{\omega}_y}{\partial t} - \epsilon \Delta \hat{\omega}_y = -iU'\hat{v}, \tag{8.5}$$

where $\hat{\omega}_y = -i\gamma \tilde{w}$ and $\Delta = \frac{\partial^2}{\partial y^2} - \gamma^2$ have been used. Equation (8.4) no longer has any dependence on the mean flow, $U(y)$. As a result, Salwen & Grosch (1981) have shown that the solution for v can be written as

$$\hat{v}(y, t) = \int_0^\infty a_k(\gamma) \bar{v}_k(y) e^{-\epsilon(\gamma^2 + k^2)t} dk. \tag{8.6}$$

The eigenfunctions are given by

$$\bar{v}_k(y) = \left(\frac{2}{\pi}\right)^{1/2} \frac{k}{(\gamma^2 + k^2)} \left[e^{-|\gamma|y} - \cos(ky) + |\gamma|k^{-1}\sin(ky)\right]. \quad (8.7)$$

The coefficients in (8.7) are found by use of initial data or

$$a_k(\gamma) = \int_0^\infty \hat{v}(y, 0)\bar{v}_k(y)dy. \quad (8.8)$$

Salwen & Grosch further showed that that this solution decays in time as

$$\hat{v} \sim t^{1/2} e^{-\epsilon\gamma^2 t} \quad \text{for} \quad t \to \infty. \quad (8.9)$$

Thus, in these terms, the Blasius boundary layer is asymptotically stable for all wave numbers and Reynolds numbers. Still, there is early transient algebraic growth and it is due entirely to the fact that there is an inhomogeneous term in the Squire equation (8.5). This result is not due to resonance, however, (cf. Benney & Gustavsson, 1981) and there is no contribution from non-normality of the Orr-Sommerfeld and Squire operators for this extreme angle of obliquity. It is only when the bounded channel flow is in question do these additional sources contribute to this kind of behavior.

Although the above outline provides a rationale for treating the initial-value problem, the actual details that are needed for the calculations are lacking and it suggests that an alternative means for analysis might provide a more expedient means for accomplishing this task.

8.2 Laplace transforms

Traditionally, when one wishes to solve an initial-value problem, a very powerful tool for this purpose is the Laplace transform in time. This is true even if the governing equations are partial differential equations and this method has been used in the study of shear flows as well. Of note are the contributions of Gustavsson (1979) and Hultgren & Gustavsson (1980). Earlier contributions are due to Eliassen, Høiland & Riis (1953), Case (1960a,b), and Dikii (1960).

The general problem using Laplace transforms can be applied directly to (8.1) and (8.2). With the definitions that

$$\bar{v}(y, s) = \int_0^\infty \hat{v}(y, t)e^{-st}dt \quad (8.10)$$

and

$$\bar{\omega}_g(y, s) = \int_0^\infty \hat{\omega}(y, t)e^{-st}dt,$$

then these two equations become

$$(s + i\alpha U)\Delta\bar{v} - i\alpha U''\bar{v} - \epsilon\Delta\Delta\bar{v} = [\Delta\hat{v}]_{t=0} \tag{8.11}$$

and

$$(s + i\alpha U)\bar{\omega}_y - \epsilon\Delta\bar{\omega}_y = -i\gamma U'\bar{v} + \hat{\omega}_y(y, 0). \tag{8.12}$$

It can be noted that the original partial differential equations have now been transformed to ones that are ordinary and, more significantly, both equations contain terms that are not homogeneous. For (8.12), the counterpart for the Squire equation, the term denoting the coupling to Orr-Sommerfeld remains but now there is a term that can be interpreted as that of vorticity or the polar velocity, as defined by the Squire transform. For (8.11), it is not the initial value of the normal component of the velocity but rather the initial value of the Laplace operator on v. In Fourier wave space, this is tantamount to vorticity. From kinematics,

$$\nabla^2\tilde{v} = \frac{\partial\tilde{\omega}_z}{\partial x} - \frac{\partial\tilde{\omega}_x}{\partial z} \tag{8.13}$$

in real space. And, when Fourier transformed, this is

$$\Delta\hat{v} = i\alpha\hat{\omega}_z - i\gamma\hat{\omega}_x \tag{8.14}$$

or the vorticity in the ϕ-direction in wave space as can be noted from the Square transformation. This result is not at all surprising for it was reviewed in Chapter 1 and the two major governing equations are the result of taking the curl of the governing linearized equations in order to eliminate the pressure. Thus, in any form, these are equations for components of the vorticity, strictly speaking. This observation further substantiates the claim that initial value specifications can be given for either physical variable. Regardless, solutions for (8.11) and (8.12) have the same requirements and consequences as those of the homogeneous equations that were obtained by the assumption of normal modes. In short, the equations in Laplace space do contain more information but are just as complex when consequences are to be determined. It will be expedient, then, to consider some limiting problems in this sense in order to better understand the needs for the initial-value problem.

The simplest problem of all the prototypical flows is that of inviscid plane Couette flow. In this case (8.11) and (8.12) reduce to

$$(s + i\alpha U)\Delta\bar{v} = [\Delta\hat{v}]_{t=0} \tag{8.15}$$

and

$$(s + i\alpha U)\bar{\omega}_y = -i\gamma U'\bar{v} + \hat{\omega}_y(y, 0), \tag{8.16}$$

with $U(y) = \sigma y$. Here, there is no problem for solutions to these reduced equations but, it must be remembered, there are boundary conditions that must be satisfied at the upper and lower boundaries, namely $\bar{v} = 0$ at these locations. If no initial value was given, then the solution of (8.15) that meets this requirement is $\bar{v} \equiv 0$. This result is identical to that that would come from normal modes. On the other hand, when there is an initial vorticity, there is now a nonzero solution. In fact, this solution will have the factor $(s + i\alpha U)$ in the denominator. Consequently, from the inversion of the Laplace transform, this implies the existence of a branch cut in the complex plane and therefore a continuous spectrum of eigenvalues that are related to the zeros of $(s + i\alpha U)$. From the basis of the differential equation, this is the same as a singularity, that is a condition where the coefficient of the highest derivative vanishes. It is for this reason that, when viscosity is added, the singularity is no longer present in the differential equation and only poles will be present in the complex plane. These become exponential solutions in time or normal discrete modes. The same argument is true for inviscid plane Poiseuille flow when compared to the viscous problem. More details can be found in Case (1960a, 1961) who was the principal author to analyze inviscid problems in incompressible flow in this way. Reference should also be made to Lin (1961) for a discussion of mathematical problems involved in the work of Case.

Similar conclusions can be made for the solution of (8.16) except that the real time inversion for $\bar{\omega}_y$ can lead to a power of time greater than that of linearity if $\bar{v}$ has a nonzero solution and already is proportional to time, for example. Otherwise the result mimics that of $\bar{v}$ with a non-zero initial value of the vorticity. A short review for this problem and its solution can be found in Drazin & Reid (1984) where the singular solution is given in terms of a Green's function and the Green's function needed for $\bar{v}$ is provided explicitly. The Squire equation is not included in any of these references but the general implications can be inferred.

Use of the Laplace transform has been used in the analysis for the stability of the Blasius boundary layer by Gustavsson (1979). The important aspect of this effort is again the fact that there is the existence of the continuum as well as the poles in the complex Laplace plane for the discrete spectrum that must be assessed when making the inversion of the transform to real time. Since one of the boundaries is at infinity, then this fact manifests itself in the evaluation of singularities in the complex plane with the results being that such disturbances (a) move with the value of the free stream velocity, (b) vary as waves in the vertical spatial variable and hence are bounded rather than decay exponentially in this direction, and (c) all eventually decay in time because there is viscous

dissipation. No specific initial input data was analyzed in this work and, again, the Squire equation was ignored.

As can be seen, the use of the Laplace transform is only marginally better than the traditional separation of variables using normal modes. And, unfortunately, since it is the consequence of specific initial data in the dynamics that is sought, then other strategies must be invoked or more succinct numerical treatment is required in order to arrive at this goal.

8.3 Moving coordinates and exact solutions

Explicit unsteady solutions for perturbations in plane Couette flow were initially found by Kelvin (1887a) and further developed by Orr (1907a,b). In addition to the class of exact solutions given by Craik & Criminale (1986), the history of such effort, together with many references of note in the development, are given by these authors. More recent work that uses the same or equivalent bases for solving initial-value problems in this manner are due to Criminale & Drazin (1990, 2000), Criminale, Long & Zhu (1991), Bun & Criminale (1994), and Criminale, Jackson & Lasseigne (1995). The particular problems analyzed range from free shear flows to the boundary layer.

In terms of the physics to this approach, the fundamental mechanism is that the vorticity of the disturbance is advected by the basic flow and the basic vorticity is advected by the disturbance. When viscous effects are retained, then the vorticity of the disturbance can also be diffused. If the basic flow is linear or piece-wise linear in the appropriate spatial variable, then the basic vorticity is constant or piece-wise constant. It is this last condition that ensures the fact that the solutions are exact for the full Navier-Stokes equations and the full ramifications have been elucidated by Craik & Criminale (1986) and later in a more general fashion by Criminale (1991), namely that a set of of basic solutions can be found for the linear perturbation problem that are (i) of closed form; (ii) contain both the discrete and continuous spectra allowing for arbitrary disturbances; (iii) the complications of critical layers or singular perturbation analysis are no longer required; (iv) even the near and far fields can be determined as well as the early and asymptotic temporal behavior; (v) Lagrangian descriptions can also be ascertained by using the solutions obtained for the velocity. This is a fringe benefit and allows for insight into mixing and vorticity physics.

The premise for this approach is to decompose the motion into a mean and a fluctuation part as

$$\vec{u} = \vec{U} + \vec{\tilde{u}}, \quad p = P + \tilde{p}, \tag{8.17}$$

where the underbar denotes a vector quantity. In this case the perturbations are not necessarily small and thus the governing Navier-Stokes equations are

$$\nabla \cdot \vec{\tilde{u}} = 0 \qquad (8.18)$$

and

$$\frac{\partial \vec{\tilde{u}}}{\partial t} + \vec{U} \cdot \nabla \vec{\tilde{u}} + \vec{\tilde{u}} \cdot \nabla \vec{\tilde{u}} = -\nabla(\tilde{p}/\rho_0) + \epsilon \nabla^2 \vec{\tilde{u}}, \qquad (8.19)$$

where it is assumed that the fluid is incompressible and $\vec{U}$ satisfies its own equations. A footnote here should be added. Incompressibility is required in the sense that the velocity field is solenoidal and not necessarily constant density (cf. Chapter 7).

In the special case for which the perturbation velocity can be written in the form

$$\vec{\tilde{u}}(\vec{x}, t) = f(\vec{x}, t)\vec{\hat{u}}(t), \qquad (8.20)$$

it follows that

$$\vec{\hat{u}} \cdot \nabla f = \nabla \cdot \vec{\tilde{u}} = 0. \qquad (8.21)$$

As a result, the nonlinear terms in the Navier-Stokes equations that are due to the fluctuations vanish identically for reasonable functions f and $\hat{u}$. Thus, the perturbation problem can be solved by a **linear** set of equations. If the velocity is initially in the same direction everywhere so that $\vec{\tilde{u}}(\vec{x}, 0) = f(\vec{x}, 0)\vec{\hat{u}}(0)$, then the linearized problem ensues and the results are exact solutions to the full governing equations.

For a steady basic flow, the linearized problem is customarily solved by the method of normal modes. This form is the same as the assumption of separation of variables and represents traveling waves so that

$$\begin{aligned} f(\vec{x}, t) &= F(\xi), \\ \hat{\underline{u}} &= e^{\int \sigma \, dt}, \\ \xi &= \vec{\alpha} \cdot \vec{x} + \int \omega \, dt. \end{aligned} \qquad (8.22)$$

Hence, along with the proper boundary conditions, this problem can in principle be solved as an eigenvalue problem where ω, σ, $\vec{\alpha}$ satisfy the eigenvalue relation. When $\vec{U}$ is not a function of time and the parameters are constants, the F is the exponential function and the eigenvalue relation is the traditional type in stability theory. This formulation also allows for a superposition of normal modes if $\vec{\tilde{u}}$ has the form given by (8.20). And, for an initial-value problem for $\vec{\tilde{u}}$ in the same direction, then all $\vec{\alpha}_N$ lie in the plane perpendicular to $\hat{u}$. This

point is significant because, although one Fourier mode is clearly a solution to the Navier-Stokes equations, a sum of Fourier modes is in no way a solution to the general nonlinear problem. However, with these constraints, this sum does become an exact solution.

One problem should be given for illustration and demonstration of the benefits of the technique. A good one for this purpose that demonstrates all the benefits is that of the mixing layer. The essential need for the method is a coordinate transformation that changes the set of linear partial differential equations to ones where the coefficients are at most functions of time. The general procedure is given by Criminale (1991); for various mean unidirectional flows that can be modeled as piece-wise linear, reference is made to Criminale & Drazin (1990). In this manner, Bun & Criminale (1994) modeled the incompressible mixing layer as shown in Fig. 8.1 and considered the perturbation problem inviscidly.

Here $\bar{U} = (\sigma y, 0, 0)$ in any of the regions. The moving coordinate transformation for such a parallel flow is

$$T = t, \quad \xi = x - \sigma yt, \quad \eta = y, \quad \zeta = z, \tag{8.23}$$

which is just a subset of the general transformation that can be used (cf. Criminale, 1991) if the mean flow can be written as

$$U_i = \sigma_{ij}(t)x_j + U_i^0(t). \tag{8.24}$$

With (8.22), the governing equation (Rayleigh equation (**??**)) reduces to

$$\frac{\partial}{\partial T}\Delta\bar{v} = 0, \tag{8.25}$$

where

$$\bar{v} = \int\int_{-\infty}^{+\infty} \tilde{v}(\xi, \eta, \zeta, T)e^{i\alpha\xi + i\gamma\zeta}\,d\xi\,d\zeta$$

and

$$\Delta\bar{v} = \frac{\partial^2\bar{v}}{\partial\eta^2} + i2\alpha\sigma T\frac{\partial\bar{v}}{\partial\eta} - (\tilde{\alpha}^2 + \alpha^2\sigma^2T^2)\bar{v}, \quad \tilde{\alpha}^2 = \alpha^2 + \gamma^2.$$

It should be noted that this transformation is not one of Eulerian to one of Lagrangian coordinates but should be thought of as a change to a moving set of coordinates. In this form, the far field conditions in the respective spatial variables are satisfied by finiteness of the dependent variables. Boundedness in the y (or η) direction is also required but, in view of the form the governing equations take, this will automatically be met and, instead, matching conditions will replace such at the locations where the mean velocity changes from one

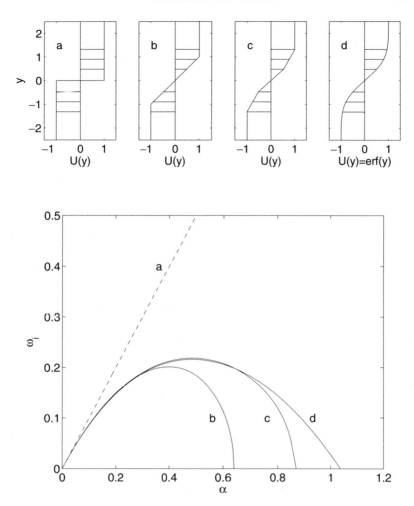

Fig. 8.1. Stability as a function of piecewise linear mean mixing layer profile (after Criminale, 1991).

linear variation to another or to a constant value. This means that $\bar{v}$ and the pressure are continuous at these locations in the inviscid limit.

The Squire transformation for the velocity components in wave space is just as valid here. Hence, if $\tilde{\alpha}\tilde{w} = -\gamma\bar{u} + \alpha\bar{w}$, then the Squire equation becomes

$$\frac{\partial\tilde{\omega}}{\partial T} = \sin\phi\bar{v}. \qquad (8.26)$$

Although (8.25) and (8.26) are written using velocity components as the dependent variables, it is again stressed that these equations are those for vorticity.

More specifically it should be noted that

$$\bar{\omega}_y = \bar{\omega}_\eta = -i\tilde{\alpha}\tilde{w},$$

$$\bar{\omega}_{\tilde{\alpha}} = \left(\frac{\partial}{\partial\eta} - i\alpha\sigma T\right)\tilde{w},$$

$$\bar{\omega}_\varphi = -\frac{i}{\tilde{\alpha}}\Delta\bar{v}. \tag{8.27}$$

In other words, the vorticity components in wave space can be transformed to polar dependent variables in the same manner as the velocity.

Every vector field can be decomposed into its solenoidal, rotational, and harmonic parts. Since the velocity is divergence free, there is no solenoidal component and thus only the rotational and harmonic parts are possible. And, as a result, both $\bar{\omega}_\eta$ and $\bar{\omega}_{\tilde{\alpha}}$ are in the η-direction normal to the α, γ (or $\tilde{\alpha}$, φ) plane. The solution of (8.25) can thus be interpreted as an initial source of vorticity if $\Delta\bar{v} \neq 0$ at time $t = 0$. When $\Delta\bar{v} = 0$, there is no vorticity and the resulting vector field is harmonic. In fact, the solution for the harmonic field is

$$\bar{v}_H = A(T)e^{\tilde{\alpha}\eta - i\alpha\sigma T\eta} + B(T)e^{-\tilde{\alpha}\eta - i\alpha\sigma T\eta}. \tag{8.28}$$

It should be especially noted that the coefficients can be functions of time and are proportional to an oscillatory factor that reflects the fact that these solutions are in the moving coordinate system.

The complete solution will then be the sum of (8.28) and a particular rotational component, $\bar{v}_R$ say. General considerations were made as to either initial velocity or vorticity by Criminale & Drazin (1990).

In the case of the mixing layer, modeled with a three section piece-wise linear mean profile, Bun & Criminale (1994) treated the problem by prescribing the vorticity initially and selected this as a combination of an oblique wave in the x-z plane and a localized pulse in the y-variable and located within the inner shear zone. Not only does this choice provide important physics but also makes for ease in inverting the double Fourier transforms to real space. In both the upper and lower non-shear regions, no initial value was given and the flow is irrotational in the outer flow. The solutions in the respective regions are established so that the conditions as $y = \eta \to \pm\infty$ are met. From (8.28) this means the solutions will exponentially decay in these regions. The remaining solutions then must allow for continuity of $\bar{v} = \bar{v}_H + \bar{v}_R$ and the pressure, $\bar{p}$, or

$$-\tilde{\alpha}^2\bar{p} = \frac{\partial^2\bar{v}}{\partial\eta\partial T} + i\alpha\sigma T\frac{\partial\bar{v}}{\partial T} + i2\alpha\bar{v}$$

when written in terms of $\bar{v}$, at the two locations where the mean velocity changes. This matching leads to a linear system of equations for the coefficients

of the unknown harmonic part of the velocity field and can be written in vector form as

$$\frac{d\vec{x}}{dt} = A\vec{x} + \vec{f},$$ (8.29)

where $\vec{x}$ are the coefficients of the irrotational components and $\vec{f}$ is due to the initial input of vorticity.

The system (8.29) has two solutions. First, the homogeneous problem and there are eigenvalues of A. The eigenvalues are those of the normal modes. The second solutions are the ones that are forced and can result in algebraic behavior in time and this is due to the continuous spectrum. The display of Fig. 8.1 shows the traditional results as those of normal modes. And, it is clear that the piece-wise linear model contains all of the essential features. And, although not shown, the inviscid problem has a damped mode for every growing one in the range of wave numbers where possible growth is to be found.

The initial value is completed in this way by further recognizing that, for the conditions given, this translates to $\vec{x}(0) = 0$ for (8.29). In other words, there are no normal modes at time $t = 0$ but, as time goes on such a mode will ultimately dominate asymptotically. Initially, it is the transient motion that is prominent. It was also demonstrated that three-dimensionality is strongly influential.

Another benefit from this means of solution for the problem comes from the fact that all the velocity components can be written as closed form functions of all spatial and temporal variables. Consequentially one can make a Lagrangian representation as

$$\frac{dx}{dt} = U + \tilde{u}, \quad \frac{dy}{dt} = \tilde{v}, \quad \frac{dz}{dt} = \tilde{w},$$

and then actually trace particle paths. The results of Bun & Criminale using these relations are shown in Figs. 8.2 and 8.3.

The classical roll-up process is equally robust under pure algebraic dynamics as it is for that combined with the maximum for normal mode growth. In addition, algebraic growth can lead to nonlinearity on a time scale shorter than the rate of growth for a normal mode. Then, the inclusion of three-dimensionality allows for the so called cross ribbing effect, as reported experimentally.

Criminale, Jackson & Lasseigne (1995) examined the case of the jet and wake mean flows when modeled in this manner and compared the results to the integration of the full linear equations with continuous mean profiles. And, although no specific feedback mechanism was determined, it was demonstrated how the disturbances could be delayed or enhanced.

Criminale, Long & Zhu (1991) considered the complete three-dimensional disturbance problem for plane inviscid Couette flow. As has already been noted,

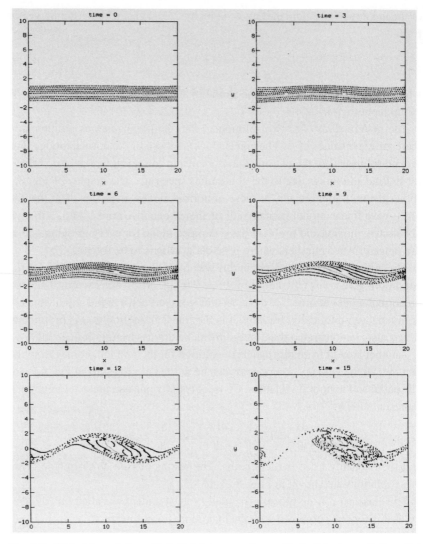

Fig. 8.2. Material particles with initial data $\varphi = 0$, amplitude 0.1 at $t = 0$, $\tilde{\alpha} = 0.4$ (normal mode maximum) (after Bun & Criminale, 1994).

there are no normal modes for this limiting problem. And, clearly the linear mean profile is no longer an approximation for the mean velocity. The results show that rapid algebraic growth can evolve and, again, three-dimensionality should not be neglected in the initial-value problem.

The viscous boundary layer was modeled in this way by Criminale & Drazin (2000). The piece-wise linear mean profile is used so that the governing

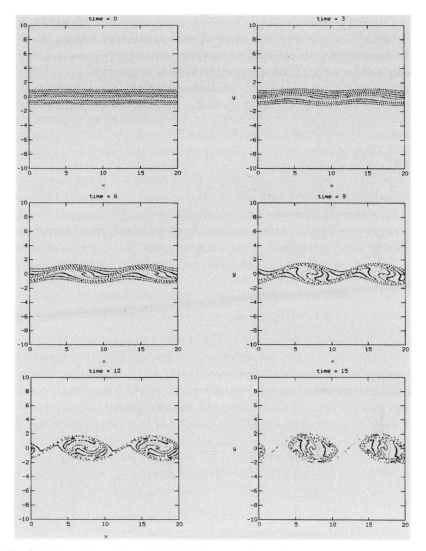

Fig. 8.3. Material particles with initial data $\varphi = 0$, amplitude 0.1 at $t = 0$, $\tilde{\alpha} = \tilde{\alpha}_s$ (zero growth normal mode) (after Bun & Criminale, 1994).

equations can be evaluated but now viscous effects are included and the problem is then solved by the method of matched asymptotic expansions for large Reynolds number. In this way the complete boundary conditions for no slip at the flat plate can be satisfied. The solutions are remarkably explicit although somewhat complicated. Various initial conditions are employed using both the velocity and the vorticity and the results substantiate once again that linear

disturbances may grow so much transiently as to excite nonlinear growth. The equivalent Orr-Sommerfeld and Squire equations for this case are

$$\frac{\partial}{\partial T}\Delta\hat{v} = \epsilon\Delta\Delta\hat{v} \tag{8.30}$$

and

$$\frac{\partial\bar{w}}{\partial T} = \epsilon\Delta\bar{w} = \sin\varphi\bar{v}, \tag{8.31}$$

where ϵ is the reciprocal of the Reynolds number. Both (8.30) and (8.31) are analyzed and it was shown that streamwise vortices are strongly amplified. The analytics also corroborates the use of the Laplace transform in time used by Gustavsson (1979) where it was established that algebraic growth was due to the continuous spectrum that stemmed from the branch cut in the complex plane and even complements numerical results that have been found for the evolution of specific initial perturbations.

8.4 Multiple scale, multiple time analysis

In spite of meaningful results that can be obtained *vis-à-vis* the determination of the dynamics of prescribed disturbances when the mean flow is modeled by a piece-wise linear distribution, there is still the question of the influence when the mean profile is continuous. In other words, how does one assess any errors that the approximation may invoke when the profile has discontinuous derivatives? A most recent work that is devoted to an analytical means for solving initial-value problems has been able to make a creditable response to this concern and it is due to Criminale & Lasseigne (2003). In summary: (1) it exploits the physics fully in terms of the vorticity; (2) uses a moving coordinate transformation in order to simplify the governing equations; (3) uses the partial differential equations directly for solution; (4) one is able to examine a fully viscous problem by regular rather than by singular perturbations. It also has all of the advantages cited for the moving coordinate transformation and has the additional asset that it can readily be extended to investigation of nonlinearity.

Once more the basis for the analysis is as that established for parallel or almost parallel flows. As a result, Fourier transforms in the x and z directions can be taken and all variables are assumed to be bounded in the far field. Thus, in this form the Orr-Sommerfeld and the Squire equations are

$$\left(\frac{\partial}{\partial t} + i\alpha U\right)\nabla^2\hat{v} - U''i\alpha\hat{v} = \epsilon\nabla^2\nabla^2\hat{v} \tag{8.32}$$

and

$$\left(\frac{\partial}{\partial t} + i\alpha U\right)\hat{\omega}_y - \epsilon\nabla^2\hat{\omega}_y = -i\gamma U'\hat{v}, \tag{8.33}$$

where $\hat{v}$ and $\hat{\omega}_y$ are the respective dependent variables for the velocity and vorticity components in Fourier space. Now in polar coordinates, $\alpha = \tilde{\alpha}\cos\varphi$, $\gamma = \tilde{\alpha}\sin\varphi$. Moreover, $\nabla^2\hat{v} = \frac{\partial^2\hat{v}}{\partial y^2} - \tilde{\alpha}^2\hat{v}$. Define this as $\hat{\Omega}$, which has already been shown to be the vorticity component in the φ direction in wave space. With these quantities substituted in (8.32) and (8.33), there will now be three equations or

$$\nabla^2\hat{v} = \hat{\Omega}, \tag{8.34}$$

$$\frac{\partial\hat{\Omega}}{\partial t} - \epsilon\frac{\partial^2\hat{\Omega}}{\partial y^2} = -i\tilde{\alpha}\cos\varphi U\hat{\Omega} + i\tilde{\alpha}\cos\varphi U''\hat{v} - \epsilon\tilde{\alpha}^2\hat{\Omega}, \tag{8.35}$$

and

$$\frac{\partial\hat{\omega}_y}{\partial t} - \epsilon\frac{\partial^2\hat{\omega}_y}{\partial y^2} = -i\tilde{\alpha}\sin\varphi U'\hat{v} - \epsilon\tilde{\alpha}^2\hat{\omega}_y. \tag{8.36}$$

Now, for purposes of illustration, consider the case of the Blasius boundary layer. Define new dependent variables as

$$\hat{\Omega} = e^{-\epsilon\tilde{\alpha}^2 t}e^{i\tilde{\alpha}\cos\varphi t}\bar{\Gamma}(y, t; \tilde{\alpha}, \varphi),$$
$$\hat{v} = e^{-\epsilon\tilde{\alpha}^2 t}e^{i\tilde{\alpha}\cos\varphi t}\bar{v}(y, t, \tilde{\alpha}, \varphi), \tag{8.37}$$
$$\hat{\omega}_y = e^{-\epsilon\tilde{\alpha}^2 t}e^{i\tilde{\alpha}\cos\varphi t}\bar{\omega}_y(y, t; \tilde{\alpha}, \varphi).$$

Equations (8.34) to (8.36) can now be written as

$$\nabla^2\bar{v} = \frac{\partial^2\bar{v}}{\partial y^2} - \tilde{\alpha}^2\bar{v} = \bar{\Gamma}, \tag{8.38}$$

$$\frac{\partial\bar{\Gamma}}{\partial t} - \epsilon\frac{\partial^2\bar{\Gamma}}{\partial y^2} = i\tilde{\alpha}\cos\varphi(U - 1)\bar{\Gamma} - i\tilde{\alpha}\cos\varphi U''\bar{v}, \tag{8.39}$$

and

$$\frac{\partial\bar{\omega}_y}{\partial t} - \epsilon\frac{\partial^2\bar{\omega}_y}{\partial y^2} = i\tilde{\alpha}\cos\varphi(U - 1)\bar{\omega}_y - i\tilde{\alpha}\sin\varphi U'\bar{v}. \tag{8.40}$$

The change given by (8.37) is one that shifts all quantities to move with the value of the free stream velocity and is a special case of the more general moving coordinate transformation; the other factor is merely an indicator of the net effect of viscosity in wave space.

In the new form, (8.39) and (8.40) have important implications when the question of the far field boundary condition in y is considered. In fact, as $y \to \infty$, then the right hand sides of these two equations will vanish since $U \to 1$ and $U'' \to 0$ in this limit. In turn, this means that the two equations are just those of classical heat diffusion in the free stream and are readily solvable.

As has been noted previously, the case when $\varphi = \pi/2$ reduces the system to one that can be solved explicitly.

The third observation of note deals with the moving coordinate transformation discussed in Section 8.3 as compared to just having movement with respect to the free stream. For the more general transformation, there would be terms as $T(t = T)$, $\tilde{\alpha}T$, and $\tilde{\alpha}^2 T^2$ in the Laplace operator. This fact has already been noted by Lasseigne, Joslin, Jackson & Criminale (1999) when investigating the early period dynamics for disturbances in the boundary layer. To supplement this is the established fact that the value of $\tilde{\alpha}$ is 0(1) at best, based on numerical computations of instability. Large values of $\tilde{\alpha}$ would imply very small spatial scales and these are heavily damped. It is also known that even the growth factors for normal modes are $O(10^{-3})$. These points suggest that there are multiple times as well as multiple scales in this problem. Indeed, for other mean flows as well. Thus, let

$$\bar{\Gamma}(y, t; \tilde{\alpha}, \varphi) = \bar{\Gamma}(y, \tilde{\alpha}y, t, \tilde{\alpha}t, \tilde{\alpha}^2 t^2; \tilde{\alpha}, \varphi)$$
$$= \bar{\Gamma}(y, Y, t, \tau, T; \tilde{\alpha}, \varphi) \qquad (8.41)$$

and similarly for $\bar{v}$, $\bar{\omega}_y$, indicating two spatial and three temporal scales are well suited for this problem. As a result, $\tilde{\alpha}$ is now the small parameter and viscous terms can be retained at the outset making for a straightforward means for satisfying boundary conditions in the y-direction. This is a regular perturbation problem.

Assume that the respective dependent variables can be expanded as

$$\bar{\Gamma} = \bar{\Gamma}_1 + \tilde{\alpha}\bar{\Gamma}_1 + \tilde{\alpha}^2\bar{\Gamma}_2 + \dots,$$
$$\bar{v} = \bar{v}_1 + \tilde{\alpha}\bar{v}_1 + \tilde{\alpha}^2\bar{v}_2 + \dots,$$
$$\bar{\omega}_y = \bar{\omega}_{y1} + \tilde{\alpha}\bar{\omega}_{y1} + \tilde{\alpha}^2\bar{\omega}_{y2} + \dots, \qquad (8.42)$$

with

$$\bar{\Gamma}(y, Y, 0, 0, 0; \tilde{\alpha}, \varphi) = \bar{\Gamma}_1(y; \tilde{\alpha}, \varphi),$$
$$\bar{\Gamma}_2 = \bar{\Gamma}_3 = \dots = 0 \text{ at } t = 0, \qquad (8.43)$$

and

$$\bar{\omega}_y(y, Y, 0, 0, 0; \tilde{\alpha}, \varphi) = \bar{\omega}_{y1}(y; \tilde{\alpha}, \varphi),$$
$$\bar{\omega}_{y2} = \bar{\omega}_{y3} = \dots = 0 \text{ at } t = 0. \qquad (8.44)$$

It is necessary that the series expansions begin as indicated so that all perturbations are ordered uniformly. This can be seen from the Square relations

(8.27) and incompressibility. The respective equations are

$$\frac{\partial^2 \bar{v}_1}{\partial y^2} = \vec{\Gamma}_1,$$

$$\frac{\partial^2 \bar{v}_2}{\partial y^2} = -2\frac{\partial^2 \bar{v}_1}{\partial y \partial Y} + \vec{\Gamma}_2,$$

$$\frac{\partial^2 \bar{v}_3}{\partial y^2} = -2\frac{\partial^2 \bar{v}_2}{\partial y \partial Y} - \frac{\partial^2 \bar{v}_1}{\partial Y^2} + \bar{v}_1 + \vec{\Gamma}_3, \qquad (8.45)$$

along with

$$\bar{v}(0, 0, t, \tau, T; \tilde{\alpha}, \varphi) = 0,$$

$$\bar{v} \quad \text{bounded as} \quad y \to \infty.$$

$$\frac{\partial \bar{\Gamma}_1}{\partial t} - \epsilon \frac{\partial^2 \bar{\Gamma}_1}{\partial y^2} = 0,$$

$$\bar{\Gamma}_1(y, Y, 0, 0, 0; \tilde{\alpha}, \varphi) = \bar{\Gamma}_0(y; \tilde{\alpha}, \varphi), \qquad (8.46)$$

$\bar{\Gamma}_1(\infty, \infty, t, \tau, T; \tilde{\alpha}, \Omega) = 0$ or bounded. The condition where the vorticity is zero precludes any value in the free stream. Then,

$$\frac{\partial \bar{\Gamma}_2}{\partial t} - \epsilon \frac{\partial^2 \bar{\Gamma}_2}{\partial y^2} = -\frac{\partial \bar{\Gamma}_1}{\partial \tau} + 2\epsilon \frac{\partial \bar{\Gamma}_1}{\partial y \partial Y} + i \cos\varphi(U - 1)\bar{\Gamma}_1 - i \cos\varphi U'' \bar{v}_1,$$

$$\frac{\partial \bar{\Gamma}_3}{\partial t} - \epsilon \frac{\partial^2 \bar{\Gamma}_3}{\partial y^2} = -\frac{\partial \bar{\Gamma}_2}{\partial \tau} - \frac{\partial \bar{\Gamma}_1}{\partial T} + 2\epsilon \frac{\partial^2 \Gamma_2}{\partial y \partial Y} + \epsilon \frac{\partial^2 \bar{\Gamma}_1}{\partial Y^2}$$

$$+ i \cos\varphi(U - 1)\bar{\Gamma}_2 - i \cos\varphi U'' \bar{v}_2, \qquad (8.47)$$

and

$$\frac{\partial \bar{\omega}_{y1}}{\partial t} - \epsilon \frac{\partial^2 \bar{\omega}_{y1}}{\partial y^2} = 0,$$

$$\frac{\partial \bar{\omega}_{y2}}{\partial t} - \epsilon \frac{\partial^2 \bar{\omega}_{y2}}{\partial y^2} = -\frac{\partial \bar{\omega}_{y1}}{\partial \tau} + 2\epsilon \frac{\partial^2 \bar{\omega}_{y1}}{\partial y \partial Y} - i \sin\varphi U' \bar{v}_1$$

$$+ i \cos\varphi(U - 1)\bar{\omega}_{y0},$$

$$\frac{\partial \bar{\omega}_{y3}}{\partial t} - \epsilon \frac{\partial^2 \bar{\omega}_{y3}}{\partial y^2} = -\frac{\partial \bar{\omega}_{y2}}{\partial \tau} - \frac{\partial \bar{\omega}_{y1}}{\partial T} + 2\epsilon \frac{\partial^2 \bar{\omega}_{y2}}{\partial y \partial Y} + \epsilon \frac{\partial^2 \bar{\omega}_{y1}}{\partial Y^2}$$

$$- i \sin\varphi U' \bar{v}_2 + i \cos\varphi(U - 1)\bar{\omega}_{y2}, \qquad (8.48)$$

$$\bar{\omega}_{y1}(y, Y, 0, 0, 0; \tilde{\alpha}, \varphi) = \bar{\omega}_{y0}(y; \tilde{\alpha}, \varphi),$$

$$\bar{\omega}_{y1}(0, 0, t, \tau, T; \tilde{\alpha}, \varphi) = 0, \quad \bar{\omega}_{y1} \quad \text{bounded as} \quad y \to \infty.$$

After the initial input of vorticity, the system of perturbation equations for the vorticity components become a series of forced heat equations whereas the equation for the vertical component of the velocity is forced at the outset. All equations can be solved in a most general fashion.

The work of Lasseigne, *et al.* (1999) essentially used this method to examine the transient motion for disturbances in the boundary layer and then compared the results to direct numerical integration of the linear partial differential equations. The agreement is very good, even to low orders of the expansion.

8.5 Numerical solution of governing partial differential equations

The partial differential equations (8.1) and (8.2) can be solved numerically by the method of lines (see e.g. Ames, 1977). This choice is a convenient numerical method; other techniques are possible. Given a mean flow with appropriate boundary conditions, the spatial derivatives are first centered-differenced on a uniform grid. By specifying arbitrary initial conditions, the resulting system can then be integrated in time by a fourth-order Runge-Kutta scheme. As with all our codes, calculations are to be carried out using 64-bit precision. Selected results for channel flows and for the Blasius boundary layer are briefly presented below.

8.5.1 Channel flows

In this section we consider both plane Poiseuille flow where

$$U(y) = 1 - y^2 \tag{8.49}$$

and plane Couette flow where

$$U(y) = y, \tag{8.50}$$

defined over the domain $-1 < y < 1$; see Criminale, Jackson, Lasseigne & Joslin (1997). The system (8.1) and (8.2) can now be solved by the numerical strategy described above. To validate the numerical procedure, numerical solutions were compared to those obtained from an Orr-Sommerfeld solver. For unstable modes, the two should agree. Table 8.1 shows the numerically computed temporal growth rate for plane Poiseuille flow as a function of grid points for $Re = 10\,000$, $\tilde{\alpha} = 1$ and $\phi = 0°$. Growth rates were computed by integrating the equations forward in time beyond the transient until the growth rate, defined as $\omega_i = \ln|E(t)|/2t$ where $|E|$ is the amplitude of the perturbation energy defined below, asymptotes to a constant value. The value given by an Orr-Sommerfeld solver is 0.00373967 (Orszag, 1971). Figure 8.4

Table 8.1. *Numerically computed temporal growth rate for plane Poiseuille flow as a function of grid points. $Re = 10\,000$, $\tilde{\alpha} = 1$ and $\phi = 0°$.*

Grid points	Growth rate
500	0.003726
1000	0.003736
2000	0.003739

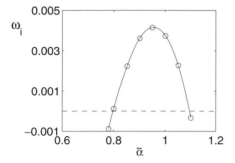

Fig. 8.4. Plot of growth rates as a function of wavenumber $\tilde{\alpha}$. The circles correspond to the numerically computed values from the partial differential equation, and the solid curve corresponds to the growth rate computed using the Orr-Sommerfeld equation. Results for plane Poiseuille flow with $\phi = 0°$ and $Re = 10^4$.

shows the growth rates as a function of wavenumber obtained from the numerical solution (shown as circles) and those obtained from the Orr-Sommerfeld equation (shown as the solid curve) for $Re = 10\,000$ and $\phi = 0°$. The agreement is excellent. The corresponding real and imaginary parts of the eigenfunctions from both the numerical solution (solid) and the Orr-Sommerfeld solution (dashed) are displayed in Fig. 8.5 for the case $\tilde{\alpha} = 1$ and $\phi = 0°$. Note that the two curves essentially lie on top of each other. Similar results are obtained at higher values of the Reynolds number, as well as for plane Couette flow.

8.5.2 Blasius boundary layer

We now consider the Blasius boundary layer, given by

$$2f''' + ff'' = 0, \tag{8.51}$$

Table 8.2. *Numerically computed temporal growth rate of a Tollmien-Schlichting wave as a function of grid points. Results for Blasius flow with* $Re = 1\,000$, $\tilde{\alpha} = 0.24$ *and* $\phi = 0°$.

Grid points	Growth rate
500	0.00285574
1000	0.00285181
2000	0.00284947
4000	0.00284961

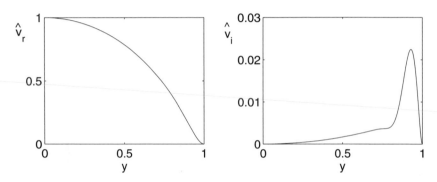

Fig. 8.5. The real and imaginary parts of the eigenfunction as a function of y for $\tilde{\alpha} = 1$. Results for plane Poiseuille flow with $\phi = 0°$ and $Re = 10^4$.

subject to the conditions

$$f(0) = f'(0) = 0; \quad f'(\infty) = 1, \tag{8.52}$$

with $U(y) = f'(y)$; see Lasseigne, Joslin, Jackson & Criminale (1999). As before, we validate the numerical procedure by comparing the numerical solutions to those obtained from an Orr-Sommerfeld solver. For a Tollmien-Schlichting wave, the two should agree. Table 8.2 shows the numerically computed temporal growth rate as a function of grid points for $Re = 1000$, $\tilde{\alpha} = 0.24$ and $\phi = 0°$. The value obtained from an Orr-Sommerfeld solver is 0.00284962. No effort was made to optimize the number of grid points by employing non-uniform meshes. If this were done, far less grid points would be needed. Figure 8.6 shows the growth rates obtained from the numerical solution (shown as circles) and those obtained from the Orr-Sommerfeld equation (shown as the solid curve) for three different values of the Reynolds number

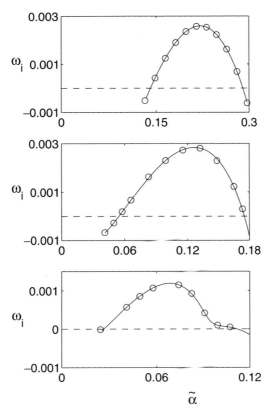

Fig. 8.6. Plot of the growth rate versus wavenumber for two-dimensional disturbances, $\phi = 0$. Circles represent growth rates calculated by numerical integration, and solid curves are growth rates obtained from the Orr-Sommerfeld equation (normal mode solution). Reynolds numbers: (top) $Re = 10^3$, (middle) $Re = 10^4$, (bottom) $Re = 10^5$.

and $\phi = 0°$. As was for the case of plane Poiseuille flow, the agreement is excellent.

We have shown, both for channel flows and Blasius flow, that the numerical method is capable of determining the temporal growth rate for any given value of wavenumber, angle of obliquity, and Reynolds number. If one is searching for the most unstable mode, this method works quite well and can be used in lieu of an Orr-Sommerfeld solver. Unfortunately, the numerical method can only select that mode which has the largest growth rate, or if the flow is stable, the least stable mode. If higher modes exist this method is not the proper choice. In this case it is best to resort back to the Orr-Sommerfeld solver. However, as will be shown in the next section, the numerical method can also be

used to investigate transient behavior for sub-critical Reynolds numbers. Thus, such a numerical method has significant advantages for understanding the flow characteristics in those regions of the wavenumber-Reynolds number plane where the Orr-Sommerfeld equation is not applicable.

8.6 Optimizing initial conditions

8.6.1 Perturbation energy

Of particular interest is the effects of various initial conditions and their subsequent transient behavior at subcritical Reynolds numbers. In order to examine the evolution of various initial conditions, the energy density in the $(\tilde{\alpha}, \phi)$ plane as a function of time is computed. The energy density is defined as

$$E(t; \tilde{\alpha}, \phi, Re) = \int_{-1}^{1} \left[|\hat{u}^2| + |\hat{v}^2| + |\hat{w}^2| \right] dy \qquad (8.53)$$

for channel flows, or

$$E(t; \tilde{\alpha}, \phi, Re) = \int_{0}^{\infty} \left[|(\hat{u} - \hat{u}_\infty)^2| + |(\hat{v} - \hat{v}_\infty)^2| + |(\hat{w} - \hat{w}_\infty)^2| \right] dy$$
$$(8.54)$$

for Blasius flow. The subscript denotes the value at infinity, which may be a function of time. Note that, in using (8.54), we have allowed for disturbances that are bounded at infinity. The total energy of the perturbation can be found by integrating E over all $\tilde{\alpha}$ and ϕ. A growth function can be defined in terms of the normalized energy density, namely

$$G(t; \tilde{\alpha}, \phi, Re) = \frac{E(t; \tilde{\alpha}, \phi, Re)}{E(0; \tilde{\alpha}, \phi, Re)} \qquad (8.55)$$

and effectively measures the growth of the energy at time t for a prescribed initial condition at $t = 0$. For cases where it is known that the solution is asymptotically stable for large time, we use the bases that, if $G > 1$ for some time $t > 0$, then the flow is said to be algebraically unstable; if $G = 1$ for all time, the flow is algebraically neutral; and, if $G < 1$ for all time, the flow is algebraically stable.

Various initial conditions can be specified to explore transient behavior at subcritical Reynolds numbers with the important issue here being the ability to make, in a simple manner, arbitrary specifications. For channel flows, a normal mode decomposition provides a complete set of eigenfunctions, and thus it is true that any arbitrary specification can (theoretically) be written in terms of an eigenfunction expansion. For the boundary layer, one must include the

continuum to form a complete set; see (8.3). However, there is nothing special about the eigenfunctions when it comes to specifying initial conditions, but they do represent the most convenient means of specifying the long-time solution. In addition, the use of the (non-orthogonal) eigenfunctions in the attempt to make any truly arbitrary specification introduces unnecessary mathematical complications that actually involve tedious numerical calculations. For channel flows, it would seem physically plausible that the natural issues affecting the initial specification is whether the disturbances being considered are (a) symmetric or anti-symmetric and, (b) whether or not they are local or more diffuse across the channel. The cases analyzed by Criminale, Jackson, Lasseigne & Joslin (1997) satisfy both of these needs and uses functions that can be definitively employed to represent any arbitrary initial distribution. This approach, of course, offers a complete departure from the specification of the initial conditions using normal mode decomposition, but, as previously stated, the use of an eigenfunction expansion to address the natural issues affecting arbitrary initial disturbances is mathematically infeasible. For the boundary layer there does not exist a complete discrete set of orthogonal functions, square integrable over $(0, \infty)$ with the function and its first derivative zero at the plate, that can completely describe all possible initial conditions. Thus, Lasseigne, Joslin, Jackson & Criminale (1999) considered three different subspaces, with different characteristics at infinity, to examine the effect of initial conditions.

The remaining salient question is whether or not the large optimal transient growth previously determined can be at all realized by an arbitrarily specified initial condition (which are the only kind of disturbances which occur naturally in an unforced environment). The analysis presented by Criminale *et al.* (1997) and Lasseigne *et al.* (1999) clearly show what properties that the initial conditions must have in order to produce significant growth. Furthermore, it should be asked whether or not the basis functions used for the expansion of the initial conditions have any predictive properties that can be exploited a priori in determining the optimal conditions. Because of the temporal dependence of the eigenfunctions, any eigenfunction taken individually does not provide any clue as to its importance in a calculation of optimal conditions; furthermore, some of the eigenfunctions are nearly linearly dependent in a spatial sense which can further cloud the issue of their importance. After identifying the initial conditions that are the most relevant to transient growth a straightforward optimization procedure can be used to show that the results of the transient calculations performed do indeed have a strong predictive property.

We begin by examining channel flows subject to specified initial conditions. Figure 8.7 plots the growth function G as a function of time for the initial

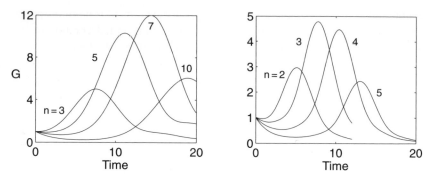

Fig. 8.7. The growth function G as a function of time for various values of n. Left: plane Poiseuille flow with $\tilde{\alpha} = 1.48$, $\phi = 0$, and $Re = 5000$. Right: plane Couette flow with $\tilde{\alpha} = 1.21$, $\phi = 0$, and $Re = 1000$.

condition

$$\hat{v}(y, 0) = \frac{\Omega_0}{\beta^2}[\cos\beta - \cos(\beta y)], \quad \hat{\omega}_y(y, 0) = 0, \qquad (8.56)$$

where $\beta = n\pi$, and for various values of n and $\Omega_0 = 1$. Note that this set is complete over the domain $[-1, 1]$, and so any arbitrary initial condition can be expressed as a linear combination of these modes. Other sets can be chosen, as shown by Criminale et al. (1997). For plane Poiseuille flow and with $n = 7$ the maximum value is 12, and for plane Couette flow and with $n = 3$ the maximum value of G is 4.8. In both cases, moderate transient growth is observed, with the maximum growth being lower than that obtained by Butler & Farrell (1992). For Couette flow, these authors have shown that the maximum optimal energy growth for this choice of $\tilde{\alpha}$ and ϕ occurs at $t = 8.7$. Here, we observe that the largest growth is for the initial condition with $n = 3$ and the maximum occurs at time $t = 7.8$. The same can be said of Poiseuille flow. Butler & Farrell have shown that the optimal initial conditions for Poiseuille flow produce a maximum at time $t = 14.1$ and the largest growth here is for $n = 7$ that has a maximum at time $t = 14.4$. It is easy to see how these solutions for different values of n can be combined to produce an optimal solution. This issue is explored further in the next section.

Figure 8.8 plots the growth function as a function of time for plane Poiseuille flow with $\tilde{\alpha} = 2.044$, $\phi = 90°$ and a Reynolds number of $Re = 5000$, and for plane Couette flow with $\tilde{\alpha} = 1.66$, $\phi = 90°$ and $Re = 1000$. In both cases the initial condition (8.56) is used with $\Omega_0 = n = 1$. The parametric values again correspond to those from Butler & Farrell (1992); the choice of $\tilde{\alpha}$ corresponds to the streamwise vortex with largest growth. In the case of plane Poiseuille

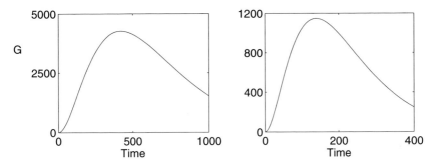

Fig. 8.8. The growth function G as a function of time for $n = 1$. Left: plane Poiseuille flow with $\tilde{\alpha} = 2.044$, $\phi = 90°$, and $Re = 5000$. Right: plane Couette flow with $\tilde{\alpha} = 1.66$, $\phi = 90°$, and $Re = 1000$.

flow the global optimal coincides with a streamwise vortex ($\phi = 90°$) but not so for Couette flow, where the global optimal was shown to be at $\phi \approx 88°$.

Comparing Figs. 8.7 and 8.8, we see that the transient growth is significantly larger for three-dimensional disturbances than it is for two-dimensional disturbances. For plane Poiseuille flow, the maximum is within 90% of the global maximum reported by Butler & Farrell. They point out that the presence of streamwise vorticity, while passive to nonlinear dynamics (Gustavsson, 1991), can cause the development of streaks which may themselves be unstable to secondary instabilities or possibly produce transient growth of other types of perturbations. For plane Couette flow, the maximum is within 97% of the maximum reported by Butler & Farrell. Thus, any initial condition with $\hat{v}$ velocity symmetric and no initial vorticity will give near optimum results when three-dimensionality is considered. This easily explains the growth observed by Gustavsson when only a limited normal mode initial condition was employed.

For Blasius boundary layer flow, we show similar results for the initial condition given by a Gaussian, namely

$$\hat{v} = e^{-(y-y_0)^2/\sigma}, \quad \hat{\omega}_y = 0, \tag{8.57}$$

centered at y_0 with width σ. The value of y_0 and σ are chosen so that the boundary conditions at $y = 0$ are essentially satisfied. Figure 8.9 is a plot of the normalized energy $G(t)$ for $\hat{\alpha} = 0.24$, $\phi = 0$, $Re = 1000$, $\sigma = 0.25$ and for various values of y_0; these parametric values corresponds to an unstable Tollmien-Schlichting wave. From this plot we see that for each value of y_0, the perturbation energy grows exponentially in accordance with classical stability theory. However, the time at which the eventual exponential growth sets in depends upon the location of the Gaussian initial condition. That is, as the location moves further out of the boundary layer (recall that the boundary

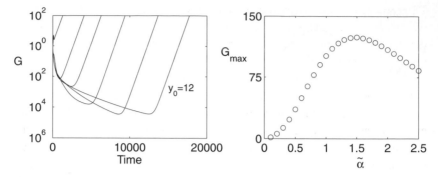

Fig. 8.9. Left: Normalized energy G versus time with $Re = 10^3$, $\sigma = 0.25$, $\tilde{\alpha} = 0.24$, $\phi = 0$, and $y_0 = 2, 4, 6, 8, 10, 12$ (increasing from left to right). Right: Maximum over time of normalized energy G versus wavenumber $\tilde{\alpha}$ with $Re = 10^3$, $\sigma = 0.25$, $\phi = 90°$, and $y_0 = 2$.

layer edge is at $y \approx 5$), the time at which exponential growth occurs also increases. What might not be expected is that even for $y_0 = 12$, which lies well outside the boundary layer, a Tollmien-Schlichting wave is still generated. This can be explained by appealing to the general solution given by (8.3). Since any solution can be expanded in terms of the normal modes and the continuum and since the initial condition is not entirely contained within the continuum, there must be a non-zero coefficient for the normal modes, no matter how small, which eventually gives rise to the observed exponential growth. This observation is further explained in the work of Hill (1995), and the reader is referred to that work for more details. And, more importantly, this point can be completely missed if one ignores the effect of initial conditions and relies entirely on the classical stability framework and might have critical consequences in the areas of receptivity and flow control. Also shown are results for $\phi = 90°$ (Fig. 8.9; right). Recall that at this angle only the continuum exists and there are no normal modes. We plot the maximum of G in time (denoted by G_{max}) for a given fixed wavenumber; the maximum does not increase without bound. The largest value of $G_{max} = 124$ occurs at $\tilde{\alpha} = 1.5$. The idea of determining the largest possible value of G_{max} for a set of initial conditions is explored further in Lasseigne, *et al.* (1999).

8.6.2 Optimization scheme

A mechanism for rapid transient growth when the initial condition is expressed as a sum of the eigenfunctions has been given by Reddy & Henningson (1993).

The concept is that a group of eigenfunctions are nearly linearly dependent so that, in order to represent an arbitrary disturbance (say), then it is possible that the coefficients can be quite large. Now, since each one of these nearly linearly dependent eigenfunctions has differing decay rates, the exact cancellations that produce the given initial disturbance might not persist in time and thus significant transient growth can occur. The mechanism can be (and is) taken a step further in order to determine the optimal initial condition (still expressed as a sum of the non-orthogonal eigenfunctions) that produces the largest relative energy growth for a certain time period. When this procedure is completed it can be seen to have the feature that the nearly linearly dependent eigenfunctions are multiplied by coefficients three orders of magnitude greater than the others. This optimal initial condition produces a growth factor of about 20 for the two-dimensional disturbance in Poiseuille flow. However, this optimal growth is nearly destroyed by not including the first eigenfunction (growth drops to a factor of 6 rather than 20) which seems to indicate that the prior explanation of (initial) exact cancellations by the nearly linearly dependent eigenfunctions is not the entire mechanism. Butler & Farrell (1992) also calculated optimal initial conditions in terms of a summation of the eigenfunctions (although they put no particular emphasis on the importance of using this approach) and reiterated the importance of near linear dependence of the modes to the transient growth. This work also explained the transient growth of the optimal initial conditions in terms of the vortex-tilting mechanism and the Reynolds stress mechanism, since these (physical) arguments apply no matter what the solution method.

By the method that we have been following, an optimization procedure can be determined without resorting to a variational procedure. We shall describe the optimization procedure for channel flows (Criminale *et al.*, 1997); the procedure for Blasius flow follows similarly and can be found in Lasseigne *et al.* (1999). A closer inspection of initial conditions (8.56) suggests that each of these disturbances is in essence a single Fourier mode of an arbitrary initial condition. If one were to consider an arbitrary odd function for the $\hat{u}$ velocity satisfying the boundary conditions written in terms of a Fourier sine series, then the initial condition in the $\hat{v}$ velocity is given by (8.56). Thus, if one wished to determine an optimal initial disturbance, a maximization procedure could be applied to an arbitrary linear combination of these modes, all of which are initially orthogonal and linearly independent. Clearly, if one wanted to also include nonzero initial vorticity in such an optimization scheme it would not be difficult to include (and these initial conditions are of course very important when modeling real disturbances as opposed to optimal disturbances). The results presented by Criminale *et al.* (1997) show that, if included

in the optimization procedure, the initial vorticity modes would not contribute to the optimal solution for the cases considered.

To start the optimization scheme, we consider the total solution $\underline{u} = (\hat{u}, \hat{v}, \hat{w})$ to be the sum

$$\vec{u}(y, t) = \sum_{k=1}^{N} (a_k + ib_k) \vec{u}_k(y, t), \tag{8.58}$$

where each of the vectors $\vec{u}_k(y, t)$ represents a solution to equations (8.1) and (8.2) subject to the initial conditions

$$\vec{u}(y, 0) = \left\{ \begin{array}{c} \cos\phi \sin k\pi y \\ \frac{i\tilde{\alpha}}{k\pi}(\cos k\pi - \cos k\pi y) \\ \sin\phi \sin k\pi y \end{array} \right\}. \tag{8.59}$$

In order to maximize the growth function, it is sufficient to maximize the energy,

$$E(t) = \int_{-1}^{1} \vec{u}(y, t) \cdot \vec{u}^*(y, t) \, dy, \tag{8.60}$$

subject to the constraint

$$E(0) = 1. \tag{8.61}$$

Therefore, we use Lagrange multipliers to maximize the function

$$\bar{G}(t) = \int_{-1}^{1} \vec{u}(y, t) \cdot \vec{u}^*(y, t) \, dy - \lambda \left(\int_{-1}^{1} \vec{u}(y, 0) \cdot \vec{u}^*(y, 0) \, dy - 1 \right), \tag{8.62}$$

that requires

$$\frac{\partial \bar{G}}{\partial a_k} = 0, \quad \frac{\partial \bar{G}}{\partial b_k} = 0, \quad k = 1, 2, \ldots, N. \tag{8.63}$$

The set of equations thus derived produces a $2N \times 2N$ generalized eigenvalue problem, and can be solved by any standard eigenvalue solver. A search over the eigenvectors gives the initial condition with initial unit energy that maximizes the function $\bar{G}$ at time t.

To illustrate the optimization procedure, we perform the calculations for the two cases reported by Butler & Farrell (1992). Both cases correspond to plane Poiseuille flow. The first is the computation of the two-dimensional optimal for $\tilde{\alpha} = 1.48$, $\phi = 0°$ and $Re = 5000$. In Fig. 8.10 we show the growth factor at $t = 14.1$ for each individual mode as well as for the optimal solution for various values of N. The convergence as $N \to \infty$ is well illustrated; compare with Reddy & Henningson (1993), e.g. Also shown in the figure are the magnitudes of the coefficients that produce the optimum with $N = 20$. There are no surprises. Each coefficient is of reasonable size, with the largest coefficient

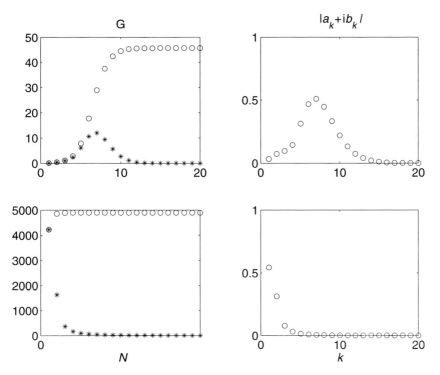

Fig. 8.10. Top Figure: Left: The growth function G at $t = 14.1$; individual mode results denoted by $*$; cumulative results from optimization procedure denoted by o. Right: The magnitude of the coefficients $a_k + ib_k$ from optimization procedure for $N = 20$. For plane Poiseuille flow with $\tilde{\alpha} = 1.48$, $\phi = 0$, and $Re = 5000$. Bottom: Same as above except $t = 379$, $\tilde{\alpha} = 2.044$, $\phi = 90°$, and $Re = 5000$.

being a factor of 10 greater than the first coefficient, and not a factor of 1000 as is the case when using eigenfunction expansions where a group of eigenfunctions is nearly linearly dependent and is not orthogonal. The magnitudes peak for $k = 6, 7$ and 8 which could be easily predicted from the previous graphs for the responses to each individual mode. The second calculation is for the optimal three-dimensional disturbance. The parameters chosen are $Re = 5000$, $\tilde{\alpha} = 2.044$ and $\phi = 90°$. The initial conditions that produce a maximum growth at $t = 379$ are found. The results are also shown in Fig. 8.10, and the composition of the initial conditions in terms of the modes chosen here could be easily determined from the individual responses of each mode.

It must be reiterated that, although it is possible and conceptually easy to reproduce the optimal initial conditions that have been previously found, the maximum transient growth is only a measure of what is possible and not what will actually occur as has been the difficulty in devising experiments. It is at least as important to investigate whether such large growth is possible

for arbitrary initial conditions. In this regard, the results presented by Criminale *et al.* (1997) produce a mostly negative answer to this question. For two-dimensional disturbances in Poiseuille flow, the transient growth observed for arbitrarily chosen initial conditions using this approach is, at best, only 25% of the optimal. When considering a fixed wavelength $\tilde{\alpha}$ and a fixed obliqueness ϕ, it is seen that very large relative energy growth of the perturbation can be observed in Poiseuille flow for oblique disturbances with arbitrary velocity profiles restricted to having zero initial normal vorticity, but the relative energy growth quickly decreases when arbitrary disturbances are combined with initial normal vorticity. Similar results are found for Couette and Blasius flows.

8.6.3 Concluding remarks

Plane Poiseuille and plane Couette flows in an incompressible viscous fluid have been investigated subject to the influence of small perturbations (Criminale *et al.*, 1997). In lieu of using the techniques of classical stability analysis or the more recent techniques involving eigenfunction expansions, the approach here has been to first Fourier transform the governing disturbance equations in the streamwise and spanwise directions only and then solve the resulting partial differential equations numerically by the method of lines. Unlike traditional methods, where traveling wave normal modes are assumed for solution, this approach offers another means whereby arbitrary initial input can be specified. Thus, arbitrary initial conditions can be imposed and the full temporal behavior, including both early time transients and the long time asymptotics, can be determined. All of the stability data that are known for such flows can be reproduced. In addition, an optimization scheme is presented using the orthogonal Fourier series and all previous results using variational techniques and eigenfunction expansions are reproduced. However, it was shown that the transient growth of the perturbation energy density is very sensitive to the presence of an initial normal vorticity perturbation.

The benefit of this approach is clear for it can be applied to other classes of problems where only a finite number of normal modes exist, such as the Blasius boundary layer (Lasseigne *et al.*, 1999). For unstable conditions, a localized initial velocity disturbance always excites the unstable Tollmien-Schlichting wave, even when the disturbance lies far outside the boundary layer. For stable conditions, the degree of transient growth was found to depend on the location of the localized disturbance, with localized disturbances within the boundary layer showing greater transient growth. For fixed disturbances, the transient growth was seen to depend greatly on the wavenumber and angle of obliquity. Since no complete infinite set of functions span

the flow, three subspaces were defined, with different flow characteristics in the freestream, for the optimization procedure. Using these orthogonal sets, it was determined what type of initial conditions were necessary to produce almost the same maximum growth that the governing equations allow; the contribution of the continuum to the initial conditions producing the maximum transient growth is properly included. Disturbances that are nonzero and non-localized in the freestream were found to produce the greatest transient growth. However, large transient growth was found only in response to disturbances with zero initial normal vorticity. When nonzero normal vorticity was included in the initial conditions, the transient growth either diminished or was eliminated.

Finally, this numerical approach was recently been successfully applied to free shear flows in an inviscid fluid (Criminale, Jackson & Lasseigne, 1995).

8.7 Exercises

1. Consider the flow of two fluids with the motion given by one fluid moving above the other and the force of gravity acting vertically downward. Also consider the motion inviscidly. With a coordinate system defined with x in the direction of the respective flows and y as the vertical direction, let the fluid above $(y > 0)$ be given as $u = U_1$ with a constant density ρ_1. Below $(y < 0)$, $u = U_2$ and a constant density ρ_2. Determine the stability of the motion.

2. Now, again consider an inviscid shear flow but with the density constant and equal everywhere. If the flow is given by the following diagram, determine the stability.

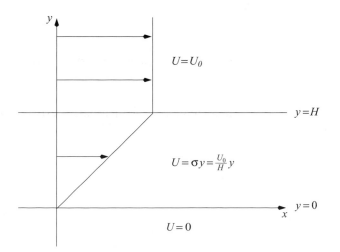

3. Examine the stability of motion on the β-plane for:

   (a) $f = f_0$ and $u = U_0$ where both f_0 and U_0 are constants and

   (b) $f = f_0$ constant and $u = \sigma y$.

4. Redo problems 2 and 3 using the moving coordinate transformation.

5. Consider inviscid plane Couette flow. Solve this limiting case by use of the moving coordinate transformation and with an initial distribution for $\Delta \hat{v} = \Omega \, \delta'(y - y_0)$ at time $t = 0$.

6. An idealized problem for internal gravity waves in the upper ocean can be modeled as show in the sketch below. With the additional assumption that the flow is inviscid, determine the fate of linear perturbations when the full equations for $W(z)$ is used and, above and below $z = -\frac{(d \pm \epsilon)}{2}$, $N = N_0 = 0$. Otherwise, $N^2 = -g\frac{\bar{\rho}'}{\rho} = -g\lambda$.

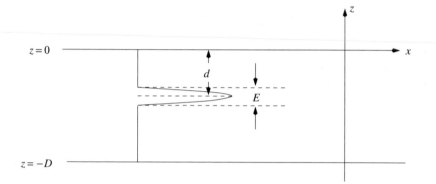

7. Redo the inviscid plane Couette flow with the boundary conditions requiring the perturbation pressure to vanish at $y = \pm H$.

8. Write a numerical code that solves the two-dimensional partial differential equation (8.1) by the method of lines. Verify the code by computing the temporal growth rate for plane Poiseuille flow for $\alpha = 1$ and $Re = 10^5$. Also, reproduce Figs. 8.4 and 8.5.

Chapter 9

Nonlinear stability

In this chapter, because energy can only be expressed as a nonlinear product, we examine the energy equation that is associated with disturbances that can decay, be neutral, or amplify, depending upon the attributes of the equation for the energy. Next, we extend the investigation by discussing weakly nonlinear theory, secondary instability theory, and resonant wave interactions. The chapter will close with a presentation of an all-encompassing theory that enables direct solutions for linear, secondary, and nonlinear instabilities within a single theoretical framework. This theory is now referred to as parabolized stability equation theory, denoted as PSE.

9.1 Energy equation

For the linear regime of stability theory, the Orr-Sommerfeld equation (2.28) provides a reasonable basis to describe the characteristics for the stability of the flow, particularly two-dimensional disturbances. Moreover, instability theory based on an energy equation is useful to help us understand the physical processes that lead from linear to a nonlinear instability basis and this has been demonstrated on several occasions.

Just as was done by Mack (1984), we define the kinetic energy for a two dimensional disturbance per unit density of an incompressible fluid[1] as

$$e = \frac{1}{2}(u^2 + v^2). \tag{9.1}$$

Note that the absence of nonlinear terms is not a weakness for this description. Specifically, the nonlinear terms only serve to shift energy between velocity components and can neither increase nor decrease the *total* energy. To obtain

---

[1] The assumption of two-dimensional disturbances is not critical and, in fact, the full three-dimensional case follows easily.

the equation for the kinetic energy, first multiply the x-momentum equation (2.12) by u, the y-momentum equation (2.13) by v, and add the two to give

$$e_t + Ue_x + uvU' = -up_x - vp_y + Re^{-1}(u\nabla^2 u + v\nabla^2 v), \qquad (9.2)$$

where only a parallel mean flow is considered. For temporally amplifying disturbances, equation (9.2) is integrated over the range of mean flow, from $y = a$ to $y = b$ say, and then averaged over a single wavelength in x. This leads to the equation

$$E_t = \int_a^b - <uv> U'\mathrm{d}y - Re^{-1}\int_a^b <(v_x - u_y)^2> \mathrm{d}y, \qquad (9.3)$$

where E is now the total kinetic energy per wavelength per unit density as defined by the integration of e in (9.1) over x and y. The right-hand side of equation (9.3) involves a total energy production component (over a wavelength) and a dissipation component (over a wavelength) due to viscosity. The production term consists of a Reynolds stress $<uv>$, and the dissipation term is the product of viscosity and the square of the disturbance vorticity ω_z since $\omega_z = v_x - u_y$.

For a fixed mean flow, the only term that can change sign is that due to the production term or the Reynolds stress $<uv>$. For disturbance amplification, the Reynolds stress must be such that it overcomes the dissipation; otherwise, the disturbance will either be neutrally stable (production balances dissipation) or decay (dissipation overcomes production).

From inviscid stability theory we have seen that a flow with a convex velocity profile has only damped instability waves. On the other hand, one of the most important convex profiles is the Blasius similarity solution for the boundary layer. In this case, the Reynolds stress associated with inviscid instabilities for the Blasius profile has $U'' < 0$ and can support amplifying disturbances provided the disturbance phase velocity is less than the free stream velocity in the region $y < y_c$, where y_c is the location of the critical layer. The critical layer is the distance from the wall to the point away from the wall where the free stream velocity matches the disturbance phase speed as shown by Rayleigh's Theorem (see Chapter 2). Therefore, amplifying disturbances can be present only if viscosity causes sufficient positive Reynolds stress near the wall. The mechanical analogue for such production was presented in Chapter 1, Section 1.6 in that even a linear spring force that has a time delay can lead to instability. In short, it is a question of phasing.

Because the Blasius boundary layer is a similarity profile governed by a single parameter (the Reynolds number) and there is no inflection point in the profile, the only possible convective instability is the viscous traveling wave

instability as described by normal mode solutions. Hence, we can study the viscous instability without potentially competing mechanisms. For the remainder of this section, we will use the Blasius profile and the associated viscous instability to study nonlinear effects.

For completeness and before we proceed with the next topic in this chapter, let us look at the energy equation for spatially amplifying disturbances. From the work of Hama, Williams & Fasel (1979) we find that, with the parallel flow assumption and averaging over one period in time, the energy equation will be

$$\frac{d}{dx} \int_0^\infty < e > U dy$$

$$= \int_0^\infty - < uv > U' dy - Re^{-1} \int_0^\infty < (v_x - u_y)^2 > dy$$

$$- \frac{d}{dx} \int_0^\infty < pu > dy + Re^{-1} \frac{d}{dx} \int_0^\infty < v(v_x - u_y) > dy. \quad (9.4)$$

Not surprisingly, the production term (first term on right hand side of equation) is the dominant process in determining whether a disturbance is amplified or decays. The second term on the right-hand side of equation (9.4) is the dissipation. The net total transfer of kinetic energy is governed by the last two terms of equation (9.4). Unlike temporal stability, for spatially growing disturbances, the production and dissipation terms do not balance. Moreover, for spatial disturbances, the $< pu >$ correlation plays a significant role in the energy balance and is always opposite to the trend of the fluctuations. When disturbances are amplified, it suppresses the energy; when disturbances are decaying, energy is supplied.

9.2 Weakly nonlinear theory

Squire's theorem states that, for every unstable three-dimensional mode, there is an unstable two-dimensional mode at a lower Reynolds number (see Chapter 2). However, Squire's theorem is only applicable for linear disturbances and is not valid when the disturbances are nonlinear. This fact was not recognized in early nonlinear studies, where the theory was restricted to two-dimensional perturbations. Fortunately, as is usually the case, beginning with the simpler two-dimensional approach can often shed significant light on our understanding of a subject before we approach the full three-dimensional system. A more careful nonlinear analysis must take into account three-dimensional perturbations.

Toward developing a framework for nonlinear stability, Watson (1960) and Stuart (1960) expanded the Navier-Stokes equations in powers of a

temporal disturbance amplitude, $A(t)$. This amplitude must satisfy the following equation

$$\frac{dA}{dt} = \sigma(Re, \alpha)A - \sum_{n=1}^{N} l_n(Re, \alpha)A^{2n+1}, \tag{9.5}$$

where $\sigma(Re, \alpha)$ is the small linear growth rate of a wave at a near-critical value of Reynolds number for wave number α. $l_n(Re, \alpha)$ are referred to as Landau coefficients (Landau, 1944). This weakly nonlinear theory is often referred to as the Stuart-Watson expansion and is often truncated at $N = 1$. As such, equation (9.5) becomes

$$\frac{dA}{dt}(Re, \alpha)A - l_1(Re, \alpha)A^3. \tag{9.6}$$

Solutions of the Stuart-Watson equation depend on both the linear growth rate σ of the disturbance and the Landau constant l_1. For $\sigma > 0$ and $l_1 > 0$, linear disturbances amplify but the amplitude, A, reaches a stable state $A \simeq \sigma/l_1$ as $t \to \infty$. Near the critical point, this is referred to as supercritical bifurcation. For $\sigma < 0$ and $l_1 > 0$, both linear and nonlinear disturbances are damped and $A = 0$ as $t \to \infty$. For $\sigma > 0$ and $l_1 < 0$, the disturbances are linearly unstable and grow unbounded. This type of behavior is referred to as sub-critical bifurcation. For $\sigma < 0$ and $l_1 < 0$, small amplitude disturbances decay; however, when the threshold amplitude ($A_0 \simeq \sqrt{\sigma/l_1}$) is exceeded, the disturbances grow unbounded. The amplitude A_0 itself is a finite-amplitude stable equilibrium condition. Note that this predicted unbounded growth results from truncating (9.5).

As the amplitude increases, the higher-order terms are no longer negligible and should alter the solution behavior. For an infinite Stuart-Watson expansion, the solutions should tend to the full Navier-Stokes solutions. However, no true minimum exists for equation (9.5).

For Poiseuille mean flow, $U(y) = 1 - y^2$, results from the truncated series (9.6) compared with full Navier-Stokes solutions indicate that sub-critical bifurcation should exist and that both linear and nonlinear neutral curves are possible.

For the study of instabilities in flows that are more complicated than the Poiseuille or Blasius flows, the Stuart-Watson expansion is replaced by an alternate equation. Based on the reaction-diffusion work of Kuramoto (1980) and the flame propagation modeling work of Sivashinsky (1977), the Kuramoto-Sivashinsky equation was identified as playing an important role in studying the linear and nonlinear instability (and potentially chaotic behavior) of non-traditional fluid mechanics problems.

The one-dimensional Kuramoto-Sivashinsky equation is given by

$$u_t + uu_x + u_{xx} + u_{xxxx} = 0, \tag{9.7}$$

with appropriate boundary conditions. Subsequent to their work, the equation has been used to study the thermal diffusive instabilities in laminar flame fronts, interfacial instabilities between concurrent viscous fluids, viscous film flow down vertical or included planes, the interfacial stress from adjacent gas flow, and the drift waves in plasmas.

We will not discuss the many uses of the Kuramoto-Sivashinsky equation, but have listed it for completeness sake.

9.3 Secondary instability theory

As we have discussed in Chapter 3, the viscous Tollmien-Schlichting wave instabilities of a boundary layer begins to amplify at rather long wavelengths at branch I (low frequency) of the neutral curve, amplify until branch II (high frequency) is reached downstream, and then once again decay. The transition from a laminar flow in boundary layers can begin with these seemingly harmless Tollmien-Schlichting waves. However, at some point, these two-dimensionally dominant waves begin to develop a three-dimensional, short wavelength structure reminiscent of a boundary layer transition to turbulent flow. The theory of secondary instabilities provides one understanding of this two-dimensional process becoming three dimensional and of the long wavelength dominant instabilities developing short scales.

The experimental observations and documentation of what we now know as secondary instabilities began with the early publications of Klebanoff, Tidstrom & Sargent (1962), who found that the Tollmien-Schlichting wave in the boundary layer evolves from a two-dimensional wave into an aligned arrangement of Λ (Lambda) vortices. Boundary layer transition soon followed the appearance of these Λ vortices. This alignment of Λ vortices, as shown in Fig. 9.1, is also referred to as peak-valley splitting whereby the peak of a wave is aligned with the peak of an adjacent wave. The valley of a wave is aligned with the valley of an adjacent wave. Later, Kachanov, Kozlov & Levchenko (1979) and Kachanov & Levchenko (1984) presented experimental results that showed two-dimensional Tollmien-Schlichting waves evolving to a staggered arrangement of Λ vortices and evidence of an energy gain forming a peak in the spectrum at near-subharmonic wavelengths. This staggered alignment of Λ vortices, as shown in Fig. 9.2, is referred to as peak-valley alignment because the peak of a wave is aligned with the valley of an adjacent wave.

Fig. 9.1. Sketch of peak-valley alignment secondary instabilities.

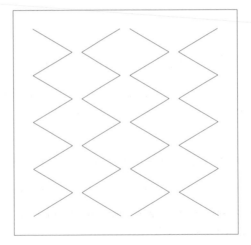

Fig. 9.2. Sketch of peak-valley spitting secondary instabilities.

The theoretical work of Herbert (1983) and Orszag & Patera (1980, 1981) led to the common state of the art in what is now known as *secondary instability theory*. This theory explains the process as to how a two-dimensional Tollmien-Schlichting wave evolves into either the peak-valley splitting (Fig. 9.1) or the peak-valley alignment (Fig. 9.2). The theory proposes that the three-dimensional disturbances originate from parametric excitation in the periodic streamwise flow that arises from the Tollmien-Schlichting wave when

it reaches finite amplitude. Whether peak-valley splitting or alignment results from this excitation depends upon a threshold amplitude for the Tollmien-Schlichting wave. For low finite amplitudes, subharmonic resonance and peak-valley alignment are predicted and verified in the experiments. As the threshold amplitude of the Tollmien-Schlichting wave is increased, the peak-valley splitting is predicted and observed in the experiments. The theory proposes that the growth of three-dimensional disturbances arises from vortex tilting and vortex stretching. A redistribution of energy in the spanwise vorticity near the critical layer causes the growth of secondary instabilities.

Similar to linear stability theory, secondary instability decomposes the velocity field and pressure field into basic state velocities $\vec{v}_2 = (u_2, v_2, w_2)$ and pressure p_2 and disturbance velocities $\vec{v}_3 = (u_3, v_3, w_3)$ and pressure p_3. The sum of these basic values plus disturbance quantities are substituted into the Navier-Stokes equations and, by subtracting the basic state equations, which are assumed exactly satisfied, we find

$$\nabla \cdot \vec{v}_3 = 0, \tag{9.8}$$

and

$$\left(Re^{-1} \nabla^2 - \frac{\partial}{\partial t} \right) \vec{v}_3 - (\vec{v}_2 \cdot \nabla)\vec{v}_3 - (\vec{v}_3 \cdot \nabla)\vec{v}_2 = \nabla p_3, \tag{9.9}$$

where $\nabla = (\partial/\partial x, \partial/\partial y, \partial/\partial z)$. The pressure can be eliminated by taking the curl of the momentum equations (9.9). In this way, equations for the vorticity result, namely

$$\left[Re^{-1} \nabla^2 - \frac{\partial}{\partial t} \right] \vec{\omega}_3 - (\vec{v}_2 \cdot \nabla)\vec{\omega}_3 + (\vec{\omega}_2 \cdot \nabla)\vec{v}_3$$
$$- (\vec{v}_3 \cdot \nabla)\vec{\omega}_2 + (\vec{\omega}_3 \cdot \nabla)\vec{v}_2 = 0, \tag{9.10}$$

where the streamwise, normal, and spanwise vorticity components $\Omega_i = \{\xi_i, \omega_i, \zeta_i\}$ $(i = 2, 3)$ are given by

$$\xi = w_y - v_z, \quad \omega = u_z - w_x, \quad \zeta = v_x - u_y, \tag{9.11}$$

for the basic state vorticity $\vec{\Omega}_2$ and the disturbance vorticity $\vec{\Omega}_3$. If we consider three-dimensional locally parallel boundary layers, the basic flow becomes a composite of the mean profile (U_b, W_b) and a two-dimensional or oblique Tollmien-Schlichting wave component (u, v, w), or

$$u_2(x, y, z, t) = U_b(y) + Au(x, y, z, t),$$
$$v_2(x, y, z, t) = Av(x, y, z, t),$$
$$w_2(x, y, z, t) = W_b(y) + Aw(x, y, z, t). \tag{9.12}$$

The mean flow (U_b, W_b) may be a similarity solution such as the two-dimensional Blasius solution or the three-dimensional Falkner-Skan-Cooke solution. The Tollmien-Schlichting solution is obtained from the Orr-Sommerfeld and Squire equations. The primary amplitude A is an input to the solution procedure and would directly reflect the maximum streamwise root-mean-square fluctuations in the flow, provided the profiles are normalized by the streamwise disturbance component. The mean basic state (U_b, W_b) is based on the choice of reference frame in which the solutions are are obtained. Hence, for a coordinate system moving with the free stream direction, $U_b = U$ and $W_b = 0$, or just the Blasius solution. For oblique primary waves in a Blasius flow, $U_b = U \cos \theta$ and $W_b = -U \sin \theta$, where θ is the angle the traveling wave is aligned relative to the free stream direction.

The primary instability is moving with a phase speed, defined with streamwise and spanwise components, as

$$c_x = \omega_r/(\alpha_r \cos \theta) \quad \text{and} \quad c_z = \omega_r/(\alpha_r \sin \theta), \tag{9.13}$$

where $\alpha_r = \sqrt{\alpha_r^2 + \beta_r^2}$ and α_r and β_r are the real parts of the streamwise and spanwise wavenumbers, respectively. In general, for flat plate boundary layers, the dominant primary mode is a two-dimensional Tollmien-Schlichting wave. However, for compliant (or flexible) walls that are used for drag reduction (see Chapter 12), the dominant primary instability is an oblique wave. This chapter will preserve the more general three-dimensional nature of the primary instability.

The equations are now transformed to a system moving with the primary wave according to Floquét (1883) theory. Hence, flow visualization of the Blasius flow together with Tollmien-Schlichting wave solutions would show a periodic state basic flow. Further, by assuming the primary wave as part of the basic flow solution for the secondary instability analysis, we are inherently assuming that the secondary instability amplifies much faster than the primary instability. This is a fundamental notion for the solution of the secondary instability equations as will be discussed later in this section.

By substituting (9.12) into the vorticity equation (9.10) and using the transformed reference frame, the normal vorticity for the secondary instability mode takes the form

$$Re^{-1}[\omega_{3,xx} + \omega_{3,yyzz} - \omega_{3,t} - (U_b - c_x)\omega_{3,x} - (W_b - c_z)\omega_{3,z}]$$
$$- U_b' v_{3,z} + W_b' v_{3,x} + A\{-u\omega_{3,x} - v\omega_{3,y} - w\omega_{3,z}$$
$$- u_3\omega_x - v_3\omega_y - w_3\omega_z + (\xi + v_z)v_{3,x}$$
$$+ (\zeta - v_x)v_{3,z} - v_z u_{3,y} + v_x w_{3,y}\} = 0. \tag{9.14}$$

By taking $\partial/\partial z$(streamwise vorticity equation) $- \partial/\partial x$(spanwise vorticity equation) for the secondary mode, the final equation, in the moving reference frame, is

$$\left[Re^{-1}\nabla^2\frac{\partial}{\partial t} - (U_b - c_x)\frac{\partial}{\partial x} - (W_b - c_z)\frac{\partial}{\partial z} \right]\nabla^2 v_3$$

$$+ U_b'' v_{3,x} + W_b'' v_{3,z} + A\left\{ -\left[u\frac{\partial}{\partial x} + v\frac{\partial}{\partial y} + w\frac{\partial}{\partial z} \right]\nabla^2 v_3 \right.$$

$$- \nabla^2 v_y v_3 - (u_{xx} + u_{zz} - u_{yy})v_{3,x} - 2v_{xy}v_{3,x}$$

$$+ (v_{zz} - v_{xx} + v_{yy} + 2u_{xy})v_{3,y} + (w_{yy} - w_{xx} + u_{xz} - v_{yz})v_{3,z}$$

$$+ (v_y + 2u_x)(v_{3,zz} - v_{3,xx} + v_{3,yy}) - 2v_x v_{3,xy} - 2(u_z + w_x)v_{3,xz}$$

$$- v_z v_{3,yz} - \nabla^2 v_x u_3 + 2(v_{zz} - v_{xx} + v_{yy} + 2u_{xy})u_{3,x}$$

$$+ 2(w_{xy} - v_{xz})u_{3,z} - v_x(u_{3,xx} + u_{3,zz} - u_{3,yy})$$

$$+ 2(v_y + 2u_x)u_{3,xy} + 2w_x u_{3,yz} + v_z u_{3,xz} - \nabla^2 v_z w_3$$

$$\left. + 2(u_{yz} - v_{xz})w_{3,x} - v_z(w_{3,xx} - w_{3,yy}) + 2u_z w_{3,xy} \right\} = 0. \tag{9.15}$$

This equation involves the secondary velocity components. To reduce the equation to normal velocity and vorticity representation only (similar to the Orr-Sommerfeld and Squire equations), normal modes are introduced.

Additionally, the primary amplitude, A, is a parameter in the equations and is assumed to be locally non-varying. As $A \to 0$ the Orr-Sommerfeld and Squire equations result. For the case of interest where $A \neq 0$, the primary eigenfunctions (u, v, w) appear in the equations as coefficients.

To solve the secondary system, an appropriate normal mode representation is sought similar to the linear stability normal mode assumption, and this is

$$v_3(x, y, z, t) = V(x, y, z)e^{\sigma t + i\beta(z\cos\phi - x\sin\phi)}, \tag{9.16}$$

where $\beta = 2\pi/\lambda_z$ is a specified spanwise wavenumber and $\sigma = \sigma_r + i\sigma_i$ is a temporal eigenvalue or is a specified real number for spatial analyses. $V(x, y, z)$ is a function that represents the class of secondary modes. Floquét theory suggests the form of solution for periodic systems and, for the present problem, this may be written as

$$V(x, y, z) = \tilde{V}(x, y, z)e^{\gamma(x\cos\phi + z\sin\phi)}, \tag{9.17}$$

where $\gamma = \gamma_r + i\gamma_i$ is the characteristic exponent and $\tilde{V}(x, y, z)$ is periodic in the (x, z) plane and may be represented by Fourier decomposition. Thus, the representation of the secondary instability for a three-dimensional basic

flow is

$$\{v_3, \omega_3\} = Be^{\sigma t + i\beta(z\cos\phi - x\sin\phi) + \gamma(x\cos\phi + z\sin\phi)}$$

$$\cdot \sum_{n=-\infty}^{\infty} \{\mathbf{v}_n(y), \omega_n\} e^{i(n/2)\alpha_r(x\cos\phi + z\sin\phi)}, \qquad (9.18)$$

where B is the amplitude of the secondary instability mode. This suggests a form of solution for the secondary disturbance based on a coordinate system oriented at an angle ϕ with respect to the mean flow and moving with the primary wave. If the coordinate system is aligned with the primary wave, or $\phi = 0^o$, then the solution for the secondary disturbance would follow the presentation presented by Herbert, Bertolotti & Santos (1985) who considered the case for two-dimensional primary wave.

If the secondary disturbance form (9.18) is substituted into equations (9.14) and (9.15), an infinite system of ordinary differential equations results. The dynamic equations are determined by collecting terms in the governing equations with like exponentials. The system consists of two distinct classes of solution because the even and odd modes decouple. Even modes correspond to the fundamental mode of secondary instability, and the odd modes are the subharmonic mode. Only a few terms of the Fourier series are retained since, as shown by Herbert, Bertolotti & Santos (1985), this provides a sufficiently accurate approximation for a two-dimensional disturbance.

The fundamental modes, v_f, and subharmonic modes, v_s, would satisfy

$$v_f(x + \lambda, y, z) = v_f(x, y, z) \quad \text{and} \quad v_s(x + 2\lambda, y, z) = v_s(x, y, z).$$
$$(9.19)$$

Thus, the fundamental modes are associated with primary resonance in the Floquét system and subharmonic modes originate from principal parametric resonance. This form of solution indicates two complex quantities, σ and γ, that lead to an ambiguity similar to that found with the Orr-Sommerfeld-Squire problem. There are four unknowns, σ_r, σ_i, γ_r, γ_i. Two can be determined while two must be chosen in some other way. For brevity in this text, only temporally-growing tuned modes are considered. The temporal growth rate is σ_r, and σ_i can be interpreted as a shift in frequency. In this case, $\gamma_r = \gamma_i = 0$. If $\sigma_i = 0$, then the secondary disturbance is traveling synchronously with the basic flow.

The rigid wall boundary conditions for the secondary disturbance are given as

$$\mathbf{v}_n, \mathbf{v}_n', \omega_n \to 0 \quad \text{as} \quad y \to \infty, \qquad (9.20)$$

and

$$\mathbf{v}_n, \mathbf{v}_n', \omega_n = 0 \quad \text{at} \quad y = 0, \qquad (9.21)$$

and are the same as those for the Orr-Sommerfeld and Squire equations.

Table 9.1. *Spectral convergence of temporal eigenvalues for the subharmonic $=$ mode of secondary instability for $Re_\delta = 880$, $F = \omega/Re \times 10^6 = 58.8$, $A = 0.00695$, $\beta = 0.214$, and $\alpha = 0.15488 - i0.005504$*

N	σ_1	$\sigma_{2,3}$
20	0.0039769	0.0007067 ± 0.010675
25	0.0041494	0.0011586 ± 0.010510
30	0.0041667	0.0011565 ± 0.010456
35	0.0041714	0.0011640 ± 0.010448
40	0.0041713	0.0011628 ± 0.010448
45	0.0041713	0.0011628 ± 0.010448

Solutions to the secondary instability equations can be determined by using whatever methods that are used for the primary Orr-Sommerfeld and Squire equations. For example, Joslin (1990), Joslin, Morris & Carpenter (1991), and Joslin & Morris (1992) have used Chebyshev polynomials and the Tau method together with the Gram-Schmidt orthonormalization approaches to solve both the primary Orr-Sommerfeld and Squire equations and the secondary disturbance equations.

The primary and secondary disturbance equations are nondimensionalized using the free stream velocity U_∞, kinematic viscosity ν, and a boundary layer scale. Here, the boundary layer displacement thickness δ^* is used and results in the Reynolds number $Re_{\delta^*} = 1.7207 Re_x^{1/2}$, where $Re_x = U_\infty x/\nu$ for the boundary layer similarity solution. An alternate Reynolds number often used in secondary instability analysis is $Re_\delta = 1.4 Re_{\delta^*}$.

Convergence of the subharmonic secondary instability eigenvalues are shown in Table 9.1 for the first three eigenmodes for a Reynolds number $Re_\delta = 880$, frequency $F = \omega/Re \times 10^6 = 58.8$, or $\omega = 0.051744$, and spanwise wavenumber $\beta = 0.214$. Here, spectral methods were used to compute the eigenvalues. For this test case, the primary wave has an amplitude $A = 0.00695$ and spatial wavenumber and growth rate of $\alpha = 0.15488 - i0.005504$.

To demonstrate how well the secondary instability theory models the physics of the true boundary layer transition problem, Fig. 9.3 shows a comparison of the velocity profiles from the shooting and spectral methods compared with experimental data of Kachanov & Levchenko (1984) for $Re_\delta = 608$, $F = 124$, and $b = \beta/Re \times 10^3 = 33$. Equation (9.22) shows the relationship between the disturbance profiles for the subharmonic mode and the eigenfunctions, namely

$$u_3 = B \cos \beta z [\mathbf{u}_1 \mathbf{u}_1^* + \mathbf{u}_{-1} \mathbf{u}_{-1}^*]^{1/2}, \tag{9.22}$$

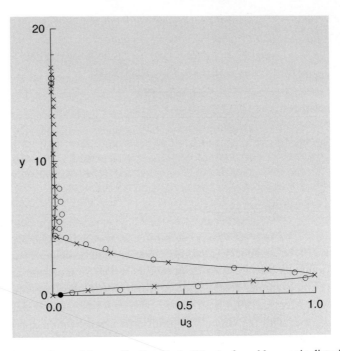

Fig. 9.3. Comparison of the u_3 distribution (solid, x) of a subharmonic disturbance at $Re = 608$, $F = 124$, $b = 0.33$ with experimental data of Kachanov & Levchenko (1984).

where $*$ indicates a complex conjugate. Note that the secondary instability theory matches quite well the experimental data.

To compute the amplification of disturbances with downstream location, we use the following relationships

$$A = A_o e^{\int_{x_0}^{x_N} \alpha_i dx} \quad \text{and} \quad B = B_o e^{\int_{x_0}^{x_N} (\sigma/c_r)dx}, \tag{9.23}$$

where c_r is the phase velocity. The amplification of both the primary and secondary instabilities, as a function of the downstream distance, are shown in Fig. 9.4 for comparison of the theory versus the experiments.

Note that A_o and B_o are somewhat arbitrarily chosen to match the initial values of the experiments. Again, secondary instability theory shows that the assumption of rather insignificant amplification of the primary mode (shape assumption) with the explosive secondary disturbance amplification is justified and that the theory agrees well with the experiments.

The analysis is repeated for the fundamental or peak-peak alignment mode. Again, the Reynolds number $Re_\delta = 880$, frequency $F = \omega/Re \times 10^6 = 58.8$,

Table 9.2. *Spectral convergence of temporal eigenvalues for the fundamental mode of secondary instability for* $Re_\delta = 880$, $F = 58.8$, $A = 0.00695$, $\beta = 0.214$, *and* $\alpha = 0.15488 - i0.005504$.

N	σ_1
20	0.00091129
25	0.00087073
30	0.00090107
35	0.00091794
40	0.00091743
45	0.00091831

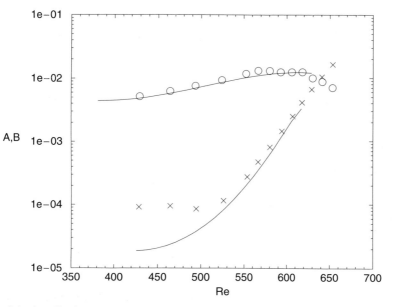

Fig. 9.4. Amplitude growth with Reynolds number of the subharmonic mode (x) of a two-dimensional primary wave (o) over a rigid wall at $F = 124$, $A_o = 0.0044$, $B_o = 1.86 \times 10^{-5}$, and $b = 0.33$. Kachanov & Levchenko (1984); solid, theory.

and spanwise wavenumber $\beta = 0.214$ are selected. The primary wave has an amplitude $A = 0.00695$ and spatial wavenumber and growth rate of $\alpha = 0.15488 - i0.005504$. With the spectral method, convergence of the fundamental secondary instability eigenvalues are shown below in Table 9.2 for the dominant mode.

In summary, the secondary instability theory discussed in this section has been shown to describe well the experimental amplification as a function of the downstream distance (Fig. 9.4). This theory represents a link between the two-dimensional Tollmien-Schlichting wave and the three-dimensional flow fields sketched in Figs. 9.1 and 9.2. The theory does tend to be less valid in the later nonlinear stages of breakdown. The difference between the experiments and theory in the highly nonlinear stages results from the assumptions made needed to obtain the simplified ordinary differential equations used to solve for the secondary instability modes. Specifically, the equations were linearized in the sense that all terms with A^2, AB and B^2 were neglected. Hence, secondary instability theory is a pseudo-nonlinear theory.

9.4 Resonant wave interactions

Numerous attempts have been made to explain the three-dimensional nature of boundary layer transition, which begins with the evolution of predominately two-dimensional traveling wave instabilities. Non-resonant models have been proposed which attempt to link a composite of Orr-Sommerfeld modes into a rational model for the onset of the three-dimensional experimental observations. Prior to the discovery of secondary instability theory, Benney & Lin (1960) proposed a link between the two-dimensional mode $(\alpha, 0)$ and a pair of oblique waves $(\alpha, \pm\beta)$ which would attempt to explain the observation of streamwise vortices (Klebanoff, Tidstrom & Sargent, 1962) in a laminar boundary layer downstream of the two-dimensional traveling wave amplification. The two-dimensional wave had the form

$$u(x, y, t) = Au_{2D}(y)e^{i\alpha(x-c_{2D}t)} + c.c. \qquad (9.24)$$

and the three-dimensional waves had the form

$$u(x, y, z, t) = [Bu_{3D}(y)e^{i\alpha(x-c_{3D}t)} + c.c.]\cos(\beta z) \qquad (9.25)$$

where A and B are the constants (amplitudes of the waves), c_{2D} and c_{3D} are the phase velocities of the waves, which were assumed to be equal. Benney & Lin found that a secondary flow was generated by this wave interaction and was proportional to $BA\cos(\beta z)$, $BA\sin(\beta z)$, $BB\cos(2\beta z)$, and $BB\sin(2\beta z)$. These terms which form the secondary flow make up streamwise vorticity and qualitatively show viability of how streamwise vortices develop in experimentally observed boundary layers.

Stuart (1960) argued against a flaw in the assumptions of the Benney-Lin model for describing the streamwise vortices. Whereas the Benney-Lin model assumed the two and three-dimensional wave speeds were equivalent, Stuart

noted that, for the Blasius flow, the real parts of the wave speeds differed by as much as 15%. A component of the flow generated by a nonlinear interaction of the fundamental modes make a frequency of 1/6th or 1/7th of the fundamental frequency. Stuart then argued that the oscillatory terms associated with $c_{2D} \neq c_{3D}$ undergoes a slow phase change relative to the fundamental mode. This phase change can have a reinforcing effect on the fundamental modes and streamwise vorticity. Landahl (1972) showed the presumed Benney-Lin mechanism could be responsible for breakdown using kinematic wave theory and the secondary wave riding on a primary wave.

For the model proposed by Craik (1971), a triad resonance occurs between the Orr-Sommerfeld Tollmien-Schlichting wave $(\alpha, 0)$ and a pair of oblique subharmonic waves $(\alpha/2, \pm\beta)$, whereby the oblique waves have twice the wavelength of the two-dimensional Tollmien-Schlichting wave. Resonance occurs only if the phase velocity of the two-dimensional Tollmien-Schlichting wave matches the phase velocity of the oblique wave pair. Resonant triads of this type have the same critical layer and hence the potential for powerful interactions can lead to amplification. A main feature of Craik's analysis was the inclusion of the nonlinear terms of the Navier-Stokes equations simplified using the linear analysis. Hence, the system is weakly nonlinear. Craik showed that the weakly nonlinear system can undergo an explosive (infinite) growth. Here we will use the more compact derivation of the weakly nonlinear theory of Craik (1971) as summarized somewhat differently by Nayfeh & Bozatli (1979, 1980) and Nayfeh (1987).

For the purpose of this text, the equations for the amplitudes of the resonant triad system follows Nayfeh & Bozatli (1979, 1980). For simplicity we assume a two dimensional mean flow field. The two-dimensional mean flow is assumed to be "slightly" nonparallel and is expressed as

$$U = U_o(x_1, y), V = \epsilon V_o(x_1, y), P = P_o(x_1) \tag{9.26}$$

where ϵ is a small dimensionless parameter characterizing the growth of the mean flow and $x_1 = \epsilon x$. The instantaneous velocities and pressure are

$$u(x, y, z, t) = U_o(x_1, y) + u'(x, y, z, t)$$
$$v(x, y, z, t) = \epsilon V_o(x_1, y) + v'(x, y, z, t)$$
$$w(x, y, z, t) = w'(x, y, z, t)$$
$$p(x, y, z, t) = P_o(x_1) + p'(x, y, z, t). \tag{9.27}$$

Substituting (9.27) into the three-dimensional Navier-Stokes equations (2.34) to (2.37) yields the following equations that include nonlinear and nonparallel

effects

$$\frac{\partial u'}{\partial x} + \frac{\partial v'}{\partial y} + \frac{\partial w'}{\partial z} = 0, \tag{9.28}$$

$$\frac{\partial u'}{\partial t} + U_o \frac{\partial u'}{\partial x} + v' \frac{\partial U_o}{\partial y} + \frac{\partial p'}{\partial x} - \frac{1}{Re} \left(\frac{\partial^2 u'}{\partial x^2} + \frac{\partial^2 u'}{\partial y^2} + \frac{\partial^2 u'}{\partial z^2} \right)$$

$$= -\epsilon \left(u' \frac{\partial U_o}{\partial x_1} + V_o \frac{\partial u'}{\partial y} \right) - u' \frac{\partial u'}{\partial x} - v' \frac{\partial u'}{\partial y} - w' \frac{\partial u'}{\partial z}, \tag{9.29}$$

$$\frac{\partial v'}{\partial t} + U_o \frac{\partial v'}{\partial x} + \frac{\partial p'}{\partial y} - \frac{1}{Re} \left(\frac{\partial^2 v'}{\partial x^2} + \frac{\partial^2 v'}{\partial y^2} + \frac{\partial^2 v'}{\partial z^2} \right) - \epsilon^2 u' \frac{\partial V_o}{\partial x_1}$$

$$= -\epsilon \left(V_o \frac{\partial v'}{\partial y} + v' \frac{\partial V_o}{\partial y} \right) - u' \frac{\partial v'}{\partial x} - v' \frac{\partial v'}{\partial y} - w' \frac{\partial v'}{\partial z}, \tag{9.30}$$

$$\frac{\partial w'}{\partial t} + U_o \frac{\partial w'}{\partial x} + \frac{\partial p'}{\partial z} - \frac{1}{Re} \left(\frac{\partial^2 w'}{\partial x^2} + \frac{\partial^2 w'}{\partial y^2} + \frac{\partial^2 w'}{\partial z^2} \right)$$

$$= -\epsilon V_o \frac{\partial w'}{\partial y_1} - u' \frac{\partial w'}{\partial x} - v' \frac{\partial w'}{\partial y} - w' \frac{\partial w'}{\partial z}, \tag{9.31}$$

with boundary conditions

$$u' = v' = w' = 0 \quad \text{at} \quad y = 0 \quad \text{and} \quad u', v', w' \to 0 \quad \text{at} \quad y \to \infty. \tag{9.32}$$

Introducing the parameter ϵ_1 to characterize the amplitude of the small but finite disturbance, both the nonlinear and the nonparallel contributions can be accounted for in one form with $\epsilon_1 = \gamma \epsilon$. If $\epsilon_1 \ll \epsilon$, the nonlinear effects are small compared with the nonparallel effects; if $\epsilon_1 \gg \epsilon$ the opposite is true. γ is taken as unity. The method of multiple scales is used to expand the disturbance quantities. Retaining only the first two terms of the expansion gives

$$u' = \epsilon u_1(x_0, x_1, y, z_0, z_1, t_0, t_1) + \epsilon^2 u_2(x_0, x_1, y, z_0, z_1, t_0, t_1)$$
$$v' = \epsilon v_1(x_0, x_1, y, z_0, z_1, t_0, t_1) + \epsilon^2 v_2(x_0, x_1, y, z_0, z_1, t_0, t_1)$$
$$w' = \epsilon w_1(x_0, x_1, y, z_0, z_1, t_0, t_1) + \epsilon^2 w_2(x_0, x_1, y, z_0, z_1, t_0, t_1)$$
$$p' = \epsilon p_1(x_0, x_1, y, z_0, z_1, t_0, t_1) + \epsilon^2 p_2(x_0, x_1, y, z_0, z_1, t_0, t_1), \tag{9.33}$$

where $x_0 = x$, $x_1 = \epsilon x$, $z_0 = z$, $z_1 = \epsilon z$, $t_0 = t$, and $t_1 = \epsilon t$. Note the following derivative relationship (van Dyke, 1975)

$$\frac{\partial u'}{\partial x} = \epsilon \left[\frac{\partial u_1}{\partial x_0} + \epsilon \frac{\partial u_1}{\partial x_1} \right] + \epsilon^2 \left[\frac{\partial u_2}{\partial x_0} + \epsilon \frac{\partial u_2}{\partial x_1} \right]. \tag{9.34}$$

Substituting the multiple scale approximation (9.33) into (9.28) to (9.32) and equating coefficients of ϵ, we obtain the following

$O(\epsilon)$ *First order (quasi-parallel) equations:*

$$\mathbf{L_1}(u_1, v_1, w_1) = \frac{\partial u_1}{\partial x_0} + \frac{\partial v_1}{\partial y} + \frac{\partial w_1}{\partial z_0} = 0, \tag{9.35}$$

$$\mathbf{L_2}(u_1, v_1, w_1, p_1) = \frac{\partial u_1}{\partial t_0} + U_o \frac{\partial u_1}{\partial x_0} + v_1 \frac{\partial U_o}{\partial y}$$

$$+ \frac{\partial p_1}{\partial x_0} - \frac{1}{Re}\left(\frac{\partial^2 u_1}{\partial x_0^2} + \frac{\partial^2 u_1}{\partial y^2} + \frac{\partial^2 u_1}{\partial z_0^2} \right) = 0, \tag{9.36}$$

$$\mathbf{L_3}(u_1, v_1, w_1, p_1) = \frac{\partial v_1}{\partial t_0} + U_o \frac{\partial v_1}{\partial x_0}$$

$$+ \frac{\partial p_1}{\partial y} - \frac{1}{Re}\left(\frac{\partial^2 v_1}{\partial x_0^2} + \frac{\partial^2 v_1}{\partial y^2} + \frac{\partial^2 v_1}{\partial z_0^2} \right) = 0, \tag{9.37}$$

$$\mathbf{L_4}(u_1, v_1, w_1, p_1) = \frac{\partial w_1}{\partial t_0} + U_o \frac{\partial v_1}{\partial x_0}$$

$$+ \frac{\partial p_1}{\partial z_0} - \frac{1}{Re}\left(\frac{\partial^2 w_1}{\partial x_0^2} + \frac{\partial^2 w_1}{\partial y^2} + \frac{\partial^2 w_1}{\partial z_0^2} \right) = 0. \tag{9.38}$$

The boundary conditions for the quasi-parallel equations are

$$u_1 = v_1 = w_1 = 0 \quad \text{at} \quad y = 0 \quad \text{and} \quad u_1, v_1, w_1, p_1 \to 0 \quad \text{at} \quad y \to \infty. \tag{9.39}$$

The quasi-parallel problem is simply that as described by the Orr-Sommerfeld and Squire equations.

$O(\epsilon^2)$ *Second-order equations:*

$$\mathbf{L_1}(u_2, v_2, w_2) = -\frac{\partial u_1}{\partial x_1} - \frac{\partial w_1}{\partial z_1}, \tag{9.40}$$

$$\mathbf{L_2}(u_2, v_2, w_2, p_2) = -\frac{\partial u_1}{\partial t_1} - U_o \frac{\partial u_1}{\partial x_1} - \frac{\partial p_1}{\partial x_1} + \frac{2}{Re}\frac{\partial^2 u_1}{\partial x_0 \partial x_1} + \frac{2}{Re}\frac{\partial^2 u_1}{\partial z_0 \partial z_1}$$

$$- u_1 \frac{\partial U_o}{\partial x_1} - V_o \frac{\partial u_1}{\partial y} - u_1 \frac{\partial u_1}{\partial x_0} - v_1 \frac{\partial u_1}{\partial y} - w_1 \frac{\partial u_1}{\partial z_0}, \tag{9.41}$$

$$\mathbf{L_3}(u_2, v_2, w_2, p_2) = -\frac{\partial v_1}{\partial t_1} - U_o\frac{\partial v_1}{\partial x_1} + \frac{2}{Re}\frac{\partial^2 v_1}{\partial x_0 \partial x_1} + \frac{2}{Re}\frac{\partial^2 v_1}{\partial z_0 \partial z_1}$$
$$- v_1\frac{\partial V_o}{\partial y} - V_o\frac{\partial v_1}{\partial y} - u_1\frac{\partial v_1}{\partial x_0} - v_1\frac{\partial v_1}{\partial y} - w_1\frac{\partial v_1}{\partial z_0},$$

$$(9.42)$$

$$\mathbf{L_4}(u_2, v_2, w_2, p_2) = -\frac{\partial w_1}{\partial t_1} - U_o\frac{\partial w_1}{\partial x_1} - \frac{\partial p_1}{\partial z_1} + \frac{2}{Re}\frac{\partial^2 w_1}{\partial x_0 \partial x_1} + \frac{2}{Re}\frac{\partial^2 w_1}{\partial z_0 \partial z_1}$$
$$- V_o\frac{\partial w_1}{\partial y} - u_1\frac{\partial w_1}{\partial x_0} - v_1\frac{\partial w_1}{\partial y} - w_1\frac{\partial w_1}{\partial z_0}.$$

$$(9.43)$$

The boundary conditions for the second-order problem are

$$u_2 = v_2 = w_2 = 0 \quad \text{at} \quad y = 0 \quad \text{and} \quad u_2, v_2, w_2, p_2 \to 0 \quad \text{at} \quad y \to \infty.$$

$$(9.44)$$

The disturbances can be represented by a linear summation of Tollmien-Schlichting waves. Here, we use three waves generalized as three-dimensional waves. Of course for two-dimensional waves, the corresponding spanwise wavenumber is zero. Thus,

$$u_1 = A_1(x_1, z_1, t_1)\hat{u}_1(x_1, y)e^{i\theta_1} + A_2(x_1, z_1, t_1)\hat{u}_2(x_1, y)e^{i\theta_2}$$
$$+ A_3(x_1, z_1, t_1)\hat{u}_3(x_1, y)e^{i\theta_3} + CC,$$
$$v_1 = A_1\hat{v}_1 e^{i\theta_1} + A_2\hat{v}_2 e^{i\theta_2} + A_3\hat{v}_3 e^{i\theta_3} + CC,$$
$$w_1 = A_1\hat{w}_1 e^{i\theta_1} + A_2\hat{w}_2 e^{i\theta_2} + A_3\hat{w}_3 e^{i\theta_3} + CC,$$
$$p_1 = A_1\hat{p}_1 e^{i\theta_1} + A_2\hat{p}_2 e^{i\theta_2} + A_3\hat{p}_3 e^{i\theta_3} + CC,$$

$$(9.45)$$

where CC is complex conjugate and

$$\theta_n = \int \alpha_n \mathrm{d}x_0 - \omega_n t_0 + \beta_n z_0,$$

$$\frac{\partial \theta_n}{\partial x_0} = \alpha_n, \quad \frac{\partial \theta_n}{\partial z_0} = \beta_n, \quad \text{and} \quad \frac{\partial \theta_n}{\partial t_0} = -\omega.$$

As before, α_n are complex streamwise wavenumbers, β_n are complex spanwise wavenumbers, and ω_n are frequencies.

Substituting (9.45) into (9.35) to (9.39) leads to

$$\mathbf{M_1}(\hat{u}_n, \hat{v}_n, \hat{w}_n) = i\alpha_n\hat{u}_n + \frac{\partial \hat{v}_n}{\partial y} + i\beta_n\hat{w}_n = 0$$

$$\mathbf{M_2}(\hat{u}_n, \hat{v}_n, \hat{w}_n, \hat{p}_n) = i(\alpha_n U_o - \omega_n)\hat{u}_n + \hat{v}_n\frac{\partial U_o}{\partial y} + i\alpha_n\hat{p}_n$$

$$- \frac{1}{Re}\left(\frac{\partial^2}{\partial y^2} - \alpha^2 - \beta^2\right)\hat{u}_n = 0$$

$$\mathbf{M_3}(\hat{u}_n, \hat{v}_n, \hat{w}_n, \hat{p}_n) = i(\alpha_n U_o - \omega_n)\hat{v}_n + \frac{\partial \hat{p}_n}{\partial y}$$

$$- \frac{1}{Re}\left(\frac{\partial^2}{\partial y^2} - \alpha^2 - \beta^2\right)\hat{v}_n = 0$$

$$\mathbf{M_4}(\hat{u}_n, \hat{v}_n, \hat{w}_n, \hat{p}_n) = i(\alpha_n U_o - \omega_n)\hat{w}_n + i\beta_n \hat{p}_n$$

$$- \frac{1}{Re}\left(\frac{\partial^2}{\partial y^2} - \alpha^2 - \beta^2\right)\hat{w}_n = 0 \qquad (9.46)$$

with boundary conditions

$$\hat{u}_n = \hat{v}_n = \hat{w}_n = 0 \quad \text{at} \quad y = 0 \quad \text{and} \quad \hat{u}_n, \hat{v}_n, \hat{w}_n, \hat{p}_n \to 0 \quad \text{at} \quad y \to \infty.$$
$$(9.47)$$

Similar to the linear stability equations used in the previous chapters, A_n are indeterminable because the first-order equations are linear; however, using the secondary order equations with a solvability condition, these amplitudes can be established.

For the second-order equations, equation (9.45) and a wave form for (u_2, v_2, w_2, p_2) are substituted into the second-order equations (9.40) to (9.44). The right-hand side of the resulting equations contain terms with

$$e^{\pm 2i\theta_n}, \quad e^{\pm i(\theta_n + \theta_m)}, \quad e^{\pm i(\theta_n - \theta_m)}, \quad e^{\pm i\theta_n}.$$

A combination of resonances can occur for these waves with

$$\theta_n - \theta_m = \theta_o, \quad \theta_n + \theta_m = \theta_o$$

for some combination of n, m, o waves.

Assume the triad wave form for the second order problem as

$$u_2 = \tilde{u}_1(x_1, y, z_1, t_1)e^{i\theta_1} + \tilde{u}_2(x_1, y, z_1, t_1)e^{i\theta_2}$$
$$+ \tilde{u}_3(x_1, y, z_1, t_1)e^{i\theta_3} + CC,$$
$$v_2 = \tilde{v}_1 e^{i\theta_1} + \tilde{v}_2 e^{i\theta_2} + \tilde{v}_3 e^{i\theta_3} + CC,$$
$$w_2 = \tilde{w}_1 e^{i\theta_1} + \tilde{w}_2 e^{i\theta_2} + \tilde{w}_3 e^{i\theta_3} + CC,$$
$$p_2 = \tilde{p}_1 e^{i\theta_1} + \tilde{p}_2 e^{i\theta_2} + \tilde{p}_3 e^{i\theta_3} + CC. \qquad (9.48)$$

After substituting (9.45) and (9.48) into the second-order equations (9.40) to (9.44) the following equations

$$\mathbf{M_1}(\tilde{u}_n, \tilde{v}_n, \tilde{w}_n) = a_n$$
$$\mathbf{M_2}(\tilde{u}_n, \tilde{v}_n, \tilde{w}_n, \tilde{p}_n) = b_n$$
$$\mathbf{M_3}(\tilde{u}_n, \tilde{v}_n, \tilde{w}_n, \tilde{p}_n) = c_n$$
$$\mathbf{M_4}(\tilde{u}_n, \tilde{v}_n, \tilde{w}_n, \tilde{p}_n) = d_n \qquad (9.49)$$

are found. The right-hand sides (a_n, b_n, c_n, d_n) will be derived as part of an exercise at the end of the chapter. The boundary conditions are

$$\tilde{u}_n = \tilde{v}_n = \tilde{w}_n = 0 \;\; \text{at} \;\; y = 0 \;\; \text{and} \;\; \tilde{u}_n, \tilde{v}_n, \tilde{w}_n, \tilde{p}_n \to 0 \;\; \text{at} \;\; y \to \infty.$$

(9.50)

The second-order system (9.49) to (9.50) have a non-trivial solution. These inhomogeneous equations have a solution if the inhomogeneous parts are orthogonal to every solution of the adjoint homogeneous problem, or

$$\int_0^\infty \left(a_n \hat{u}_n^* + b_n \hat{v}_n^* + c_n \hat{p}_n^* + d_n \hat{w}_n^* \right) dy = 0,$$

(9.51)

where the adjoint equations are

$$M_1(\hat{u}_n^*, \hat{v}_n^*, \hat{w}_n^*) = i\alpha_n \hat{u}_n^* + \frac{\partial \hat{v}_n^*}{\partial y} + i\beta_n \hat{w}_n^* = 0,$$

$$M_2(\hat{u}_n, \hat{v}_n, \hat{w}_n, \hat{p}_n) = i(\alpha_n U_o - \omega_n)\hat{u}_n^* + \hat{v}_n^* \frac{\partial U_o}{\partial y}$$

$$+ i\alpha_n \hat{p}_n^* - \frac{1}{Re} \left(\frac{\partial^2}{\partial y^2} - \alpha^2 - \beta^2 \right) \hat{u}_n^* = 0,$$

$$M_3(\hat{u}_n^*, \hat{v}_n^*, \hat{w}_n^*, \hat{p}_n^*) = i(\alpha_n U_o - \omega_n)\hat{v}_n^* + \frac{\partial \hat{p}_n^*}{\partial y}$$

$$- \frac{1}{Re} \left(\frac{\partial^2}{\partial y^2} - \alpha^2 - \beta^2 \right) \hat{v}_n^* = 0,$$

$$M_4(\hat{u}_n^*, \hat{v}_n^*, \hat{w}_n^*, \hat{p}*_n) = i(\alpha_n U_o - \omega_n)\hat{w}_n^* + i\beta_n \hat{p}_n^*$$

$$- \frac{1}{Re} \left(\frac{\partial^2}{\partial y^2} - \alpha^2 - \beta^2 \right) \hat{w}_n^* = 0,$$

(9.52)

with boundary conditions

$$\hat{u}_n^* = \hat{v}_n^* = \hat{w}_n^* = 0 \;\; \text{at} \;\; y = 0 \;\; \text{and} \;\; \hat{u}_n^*, \hat{v}_n^*, \hat{w}_n^*, \hat{p}_n^* \to 0 \;\; \text{at} \;\; y \to \infty.$$

(9.53)

Finally, use

$$\hat{A}_n = A_n e^{-\int \alpha_{n,i} dx_0 - \beta_{n,i} dz_0}$$

(9.54)

to obtain the final system of equations that can be used to obtain various resonant conditions. This lengthy derivation of the final system will be left to the student in the exercises.

Craik showed that, in finite time, the amplitudes become infinite. Contrary to the theory, the experimental results do not indicate this explosive instability amplification for perfectly tuned triad resonance. But, unlike the Benney-Lin model, the current resonant triad model does estimate a preferred spanwise wavelength and streamwise vorticity.

9.5 PSE theory

Herbert (1991, 1997) and Bertolotti (1992) developed a theory, now called the Parabolized Stability Equations (PSE), that sought approximate solutions to the unsteady Navier-Stokes equations by invoking a parabolic nature to the equations. Then, when parabolic, numerical solutions can be obtained by an efficient marching procedure. Generally, there are a number of ways to parabolize the Navier-Stokes equations. However, any acceptable approximation must be able to capture the physics of instability waves. The underlying notion of the PSE approach is to first decompose the disturbance into an oscillatory wave and a shape function. By properly choosing a streamwise wave number to resolve the wave motion, the governing equations reduce to a set of partial differential equations for the shape functions which vary slowly in the streamwise direction and their second derivatives are assumed negligible. These partial differential equations can be parabolized by neglecting the dependence of convected disturbances on downstream events and by neglecting the second derivatives $(\partial^2/\partial x^2)$ of the shape functions. Since most of the oscillatory wave motion is absorbed in the streamwise wave number and the terms neglected in the shape function equations are of order $1/Re^2$, the resulting system provides the desired results. A brief discussion of the theory is as follows.

For disturbances that are present in the flow field, periodicity is assumed both in time and in the spanwise direction. The total disturbance can then be described by the following Fourier-series expansion:

$$
\begin{Bmatrix} u \\ v \\ p \end{Bmatrix} (x, y, z, t) = \sum_{n=-N_z}^{N_z} \sum_{m=-N_t}^{N_t} \begin{Bmatrix} \hat{u}_{m,n} \\ \hat{v}_{m,n} \\ \hat{p}_{m,n} \end{Bmatrix} (x, y) e^{i(n\beta z - m\omega t)}, \qquad (9.55)
$$

where N_z and N_t are the numbers of modes retained in the truncated series, ω is an imposed frequency, and β is an imposed spanwise wave number. The disturbance form (9.55) is substituted into the Navier-Stokes equations so that a set of elliptic equations for the transformed variables $\{\hat{u}_{m,n}, \hat{v}_{m,n}, \hat{p}_{m,n}\}$ results. Because of the wave nature of these transformed variables, a further decomposition is made into a fast oscillatory wave part and a slowly varying shape

function:

$$\left\{\begin{array}{c} \hat{u}_{m,n} \\ \hat{v}_{m,n} \\ \hat{p}_{m,n} \end{array}\right\} = \left\{\begin{array}{c} u_{m,n} \\ v_{m,n} \\ p_{m,n} \end{array}\right\} (y) e^{i \int_{x_o}^{x} \alpha_{m,n} dx}. \tag{9.56}$$

In (9.56), the fast-scale variation along the streamwise direction x is represented by the streamwise wave number $\alpha_{m,n}$ and therefore the second-order variation of the shape function in x is negligible. In turn, this observation leads to the desired parabolized stability equations for the shape functions $\{u_{m,n}, v_{m,n}, p_{m,n}\}$. These equations are obtained by neglecting all second derivatives in the streamwise direction and the terms associated with upstream influence. Similar to the Orr-Sommerfeld and Squire equations, pressure can be eliminated by taking the curl of the Navier-Stokes equations. The resulting governing equations take the form of two equations that are given in matrix notation as

$$\mathbf{L_u} u_{m,n} + \mathbf{L_v} v_{m,n} + \mathbf{M_u} \frac{du_{m,n}}{dx} + \mathbf{M_v} \frac{dv_{m,n}}{dx}$$

$$+ \frac{d\alpha_{m,n}}{dx}(\mathbf{F_u} u_{m,n} + \mathbf{F_v} v_{m,n}) = 0, \tag{9.57}$$

where $\alpha_{m,n}$ is the complex wave number for mode m, n composed of a real part describing the growth rate and an imaginary part describing the wave number, the operators $\mathbf{L}$, $\mathbf{M}$, $\mathbf{F}$ depend on $\alpha_{m,n}$, the frequency ω, and contain derivatives only in y. The operator $\mathbf{L}$ contains the Orr-Sommerfeld and Squire operators that are well known in parallel flow stability theory. The term $F_{m,n}$ is the convolution that stems from the nonlinear products.

The matrices for the first equation are given by

$$\mathbf{L_u} = -2\alpha_{m,n} U_{xy} - 2\alpha_{m,n} U_x \frac{d}{dy},$$

$$\mathbf{L_v} = -Re^{-1}\frac{d^4}{dy^4} + V\frac{d^3}{dy^3} + \left[\alpha_{m,n} U - i\omega - \frac{2}{Re}(\alpha_{m,n}^2 - \beta^2) - U_x\right]\frac{d^2}{dy^2},$$

$$\mathbf{M_u} = -2U_x \frac{d}{dy} - 2U_{xy},$$

$$\mathbf{M_v} = -4\alpha \frac{1}{Re}\frac{d^2}{dy^2} + 2\alpha V\frac{d}{dy} + U\frac{d^2}{dy^2} - 2i\alpha\omega + 3\alpha^2 U - \beta^2 U$$
$$- 4\alpha Re^{-1}(\alpha^2 - \beta^2) - U_y + 2\alpha U_x,$$

$$\mathbf{F_u} = 0,$$

$$\mathbf{F_v} = -2i Re^{-1}\frac{d^2}{dy^2} + iV\frac{d}{dy} + \omega + i\alpha U - 6i Re^{-1}(\alpha^2 - \beta^2) - 2\alpha + iU_x.$$

For the second equation, the matrices take the form

$$
\mathbf{L_u} = -Re^{-1}(\alpha^2 - \beta^2)\frac{d^2}{dy^2} + V(\alpha^2 - \beta^2)\frac{d}{dy}
$$
$$
+ (\alpha^2 - \beta^2)\left[\alpha U - i\omega - \frac{1}{Re}(\alpha^2 - \beta^2) - V_y\right],
$$

$$
\mathbf{L_v} = -\alpha Re^{-1}\frac{d^3}{dy^3} + \alpha V\frac{d^2}{dy^2} + \alpha[\alpha U - i\omega
$$
$$
- \frac{1}{Re}(\alpha^2 - \beta^2) - V_y]\frac{d}{dy} - U'\beta^2,
$$

$$
\mathbf{M_u} = -2\alpha Re^{-1}\frac{d^2}{dy^2} + 2\alpha V\frac{d}{dy} - 2i\alpha\omega + 3\alpha^2 U - U\beta^2
$$
$$
- 4\alpha Re^{-1}(\alpha^2 - \beta^2) - 2\alpha V_y,
$$

$$
\mathbf{M_v} = -Re^{-1}\frac{d^3}{dy^3} + V\frac{d^2}{dy^2} + [2\alpha U - i\omega - Re^{-1}(3\alpha^2 - \beta^2)
$$
$$
- V_y - U_y\beta^2]\frac{d}{dy},
$$

$$
\mathbf{F_u} = -iRe^{-1}\frac{d^2}{dy^2} + iV\frac{d}{dy} + \omega + 3i\alpha U - iRe^{-1}(5\alpha^2 - \beta^2) - iV_y,
$$

$$
\mathbf{F_v} = iU\frac{d}{dy} - Re^{-1}2i\alpha.
$$

In order to solve the nonlinear problem, the nonlinear convection terms are placed on the right-hand side of the governing equation

$$
\vec{F}(x, y, z, t) = (\vec{u} \cdot \nabla)\vec{u}. \tag{9.58}
$$

For the PSE approach, the governing equations are solved in wave number space. The Fourier coefficients, that are obtained from the corresponding Fourier transform of $\vec{F}$ in (9.57), provide a nonlinear forcing for each of the linearized shape function equations. These inhomogeneous equations for the shape functions are solved by applying a marching procedure along the streamwise direction for each Fourier mode. If $\alpha_{n,m}$ are chosen (or computed) properly, the evolution of disturbances can be described by the parabolized equations for the shape functions. Equations (9.57) can then be marched in x using an Euler differencing for the x-derivative terms.

For the PSE theory boundary conditions, Bertolotti & Joslin (1995) showed that either asymptotic, Dirichlet, Neumann or mixed boundary conditions can be imposed at various distances from the wall. These are

Dirichlet conditions:

$$u_{m,n} = 0, \quad v_{m,n} = 0, \quad \frac{\partial v_{m,n}}{\partial y} = 0; \tag{9.59}$$

Neumann conditions:

$$\frac{\partial u_{m,n}}{\partial y} = 0, \quad \frac{\partial v_{m,n}}{\partial y} = 0, \quad \frac{\partial^2 v_{m,n}}{\partial y^2} = 0; \tag{9.60}$$

Mixed conditions:

$$\frac{\partial u_{m,n}}{\partial y} + \alpha_{m,n} u_{m,n} = 0, \quad \frac{\partial v_{m,n}}{\partial y} + \alpha_{m,n} v_{m,n} = 0, \tag{9.61}$$

$$\frac{\partial^2 v_{m,n}}{\partial y^2} + \alpha_{m,n} \frac{\partial v_{m,n}}{\partial y} = 0; \tag{9.62}$$

and

Asymptotic conditions:

$$\mathbf{x}_{m,n} \cdot \mathbf{B}^T \mathbf{e}_i = \mathbf{c}_{m,n} \cdot \mathbf{e}_i, \quad i = 1, 2, 3, \tag{9.63}$$

where the conditions for the highest derivative of $\hat{v}$ with respect to y are derived from the continuity equation. Here, $\mathbf{x}_{m,n} = \{u_{m,n}, u'_{m,n}, v'_{m,n}, v''_{m,n}, v'''_{m,n}\}$, the prime denotes differentiation with respect to y, and $\mathbf{e}_i$ denotes the unit vector in the $\mathbf{i}$, $\mathbf{j}$ and $\mathbf{k}$ directions, respectively. The matrix $\mathbf{B}$ can easily be derived from the full system. The mixed boundary conditions and the asymptotic boundary conditions are altered for the mean flow distortion term (i.e. $m = 0, n = 0$) to form

$$u_{0,n} = 0, \quad \frac{\partial v_{0,n}}{\partial y} = 0, \quad \frac{\partial^2 v_{0,n}}{\partial y^2} = 0. \tag{9.64}$$

To close the problem, a relationship for updating α must be obtained. One such relationship is given by

$$\alpha_{m,n}^{k+1} = \alpha_{m,n}^k - i \frac{\int_0^\delta u u_x^* dy}{\int_0^\delta u u^* dy}, \tag{9.65}$$

where $*$ refers to complex conjugates and k implies the level of iteration.

The solution sequence is as follows: (1) The x-derivative terms in equations (9.57) with the appropriate boundary conditions are first-order backward Euler differenced (e.g., $\partial u / \partial x = (u_{i+1} - u_i)/dx$, where the i solutions are known and dx is the step size in the x-direction). (2) To start the solution procedure, the initial solutions (profiles and wavenumber α) at $i = 1$ are obtained from linear stability theory. (3) The solutions at $i + 1$ are obtained by iterating on

equation (9.57) and (9.65) until the solution no longer changes with continued iteration. Then, depending on the algorithm, convergence can be obtained in three to four iterations.

Some sample two-dimensional PSE theory results are taken from Bertolotti & Joslin (1995). Here, the reference length is $\delta(x_0) = \sqrt{\nu x_0/U_\infty}$ that is defined at the streamwise location x_0. The corresponding Reynolds number at x_0 is $Re_0 = U_\infty \delta(x_0)/\nu = 400$. The non-dimensional frequency (Strouhal number) of the two-dimensional Tollmien-Schlichting wave is $F = 2 \times 10^6 \pi f \nu/-U_\infty^2 = 86$, and leads to an $\omega = 0.0344$.

The initial condition was composed of the single Fourier mode $m = 1$ obtained from the Orr-Sommerfeld equation. The arbitrary initial amplitude was selected to be 0.25 percent rms, based on the maximum of the u component of velocity.

At the wall, no-slip boundary conditions (i.e., homogeneous Dirichlet conditions) are enforced for the disturbance equations used by direct numerical simulations (DNS; see Chapter 11) and the Fourier-coefficient equations used by PSE theory. So, both DNS and PSE incorporate the same boundary conditions at the wall.

In the far field, homogeneous Dirichlet boundary conditions are imposed for the DNS computations.

This far-field condition is exact at infinity but, to computationally solve the system using DNS, the semi-infinite domain is truncated. For the PSE approach, homogeneous Dirichlet boundary conditions are used for all Fourier-coefficient equations except for the mean flow distortion equations. This non-zero component arises from assumptions of PSE theory. Unlike the DNS that solves the full Navier-Stokes equations, PSE theory reduces the equations to a simplified parabolic system in a manner as described in the previous subsection. As a result of the PSE simplification, the mean flow distortion equations are essentially of the boundary layer type. With boundary layer equations, the wall normal velocity component approaches a constant in the far field. Similarly, the mean flow distortion equation in PSE theory, that is the boundary layer equation type, incorporates a Neumann boundary condition for the wall normal velocity component. This Neumann condition allows the total normal velocity (mean flow + mean flow correction) in the far field as predicted by PSE theory to vary at infinity. Thus, the far field boundary conditions, used by both the DNS and PSE approaches, are approximate. The spatial DNS far-field boundary conditions cannot be changed to mimic the PSE approach because the DNS cannot accommodate an a priori Fourier modal boundary condition treatment as is present in PSE theory. When the Neumann condition is changed to that of Dirichlet, numerical instabilities in the PSE approach are generated.

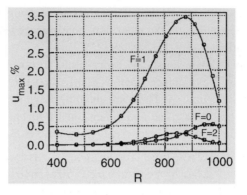

Fig. 9.5. Amplitude of $F = 0$, $F = 1$, and $F = 2$ modes from PSE (solid) and DNS (symbols) with Dirichlet boundary conditions (after Bertolotti & Joslin, 1995).

As a result, the far field boundary conditions for PSE theory are different from the boundary conditions employed for the DNS approach for the mean flow distortion equation. With the present boundary conditions, the PSE theory approximate far field conditions should prove more accurate for a far field boundary fixed close to the wall. The DNS conditions should prove more realistic for the boundary far from the wall.

Figure 9.5 shows the evolution of the disturbance amplitude based on the u component of velocity for the Fourier modes $F = 1$, $F = 2$, and their steady component $F = 0$ with a Reynolds number of $Re = U_\infty \delta(x)/\nu = \sqrt{x Re_0}$ for results calculated by both the PSE and DNS codes. Both codes enforced the Dirichlet boundary conditions at $y_{max} = 130$. The results agree well, indicating a reasonable equivalence of the two procedures for the flat-plate boundary layer problem.

Computations were conducted with PSE theory to compare the maximum amplitudes of $F = 0$ and $F = 1$ modes as functions of far field boundary locations. At the downstream location, that corresponds to $Re = 940$ (near the maximum amplification amplitude of the $F = 1$ mode), Table 9.3 shows the variation in the results by simply altering the boundary conditions. The exact values are 0.595% for $F = 0$ and 2.843% for $F = 1$. The results indicate that asymptotic and mixed boundary conditions yield the most accurate mean flow distortion and unsteady instability modes in comparison with the results obtained with either Dirichlet or Neumann conditions.

The use of a finite domain in y plus Dirichlet and Neumann boundary conditions eliminates some coding difficulties in direct Navier-Stokes simulation codes, but at the cost of error introduction. As in the case considered here,

Table 9.3. *Modal maximums (in percent of U_∞) at Re = 940.*

BC Type	$u_0(max)$	$u_1(max)$
Asymptotic	0.596	2.844
Mixed	0.598	2.858
Neumann	0.684	3.807
Dirichlet	0.298	1.895

the errors are small when the truncation location y_{max} is located well into the region of exponential decay of the disturbances. Exceptions are for the steady component $F = 0$, that does not decay in the free stream, and for which the error introduced by the use of Dirichlet conditions does not vanish as y_{max} is increased. A similar error is also expected for three-dimensional steady distur-bances because they decay slowly (i.e., as in $\exp(-\beta^2 y)$) in the free stream. On the other hand, the errors introduced in the calculation of traveling modes by either Dirichlet or Neumann conditions are negligible if a truncation location y_{max} is chosen sufficiently far from the plate. In contrast, asymptotic bound-ary conditions and mixed boundary conditions yield accurate results when im-posed beyond the 99.99% definition of the boundary layer edge. The asymp-totic conditions are exact but require a significantly greater amount of coding to implement.

9.6 Exercises

1. Derive (9.3) and state all necessary conditions and assumptions.
2. Derive (9.4) and state all necessary conditions and assumptions.
3. Derive the secondary instability theory equations as follows:

   (a) Substitute the secondary disturbance form (9.18) into the continuity equation (9.8) and definition of vorticity (9.11).
   (b) Substitute the secondary disturbance form (9.18) into the secondary in-stability equations (9.14) and (9.15).
   (c) Use the normal mode equations obtained from the normal mode conti-nuity equation and definitions of vorticity (part 1a) to reduce the equa-tions (part 1b) to normal velocity and vorticity only.
   (d) If $A = 0$ in the secondary instability equations, how do the terms which remain compare with the Orr-Sommerfeld and Squire equations?

4. In the discussion of the secondary instability results of Section 9.3, why are the frequency $F = \omega/Re \times 10^6$ and spanwise wavenumber $b = \beta/Re \times 10^3$ used?

5. By referring to equation (9.22) for the subharmonic profiles, derive the relationship between disturbance profile and eigenfunction for the fundamental mode profiles. (Note, use the $n = 0, \pm 2$ modes.)

6. From section 9.4, use the equations (9.46) to show that you can obtain the Orr-Sommerfeld and Squire equations.

7. Substituting equations (9.45) and (9.48) into the second order equations (9.40) to (9.43) leads to the equations (9.49). Determine the form of the right hand sides (a_n, b_n, c_n, d_n).

8. Derive the PSE equations for two-dimensional disturbances evolving in a two-dimensional basic flow.

9. Use the relation for $\hat{A}_n$ in equation (9.54) and the equations derived in the previous exercise to determine the final system from which resonant analysis can be performed.

10. Write a numerical solver for the linear PSE system and verify that the code works for the following initial conditions and basic flows.

    (a) Reynolds number based on displacement thickness ($Re = 900$) and non-dimensional frequency ($F = 86 = \omega/Re \times 10^6$) and the profiles from the Orr-Sommerfeld equation and Blasius basic flows are used for the initial conditions.

    (b) Compare the PSE results for parallel and non-parallel basic flows with the Orr-Sommerfeld solution.

    (c) Duplicate the results in Table 9.3.

11. Write a numerical solver for the secondary instability equations assuming a two-dimensional mean flow. Validate the code for the problem of Table 9.1.

12. Discuss the process you would follow using secondary instability theory to duplicate the results of Fig. 9.4.

Chapter 10

Transition and receptivity

10.1 Introduction

In this chapter, we discuss the breakdown of hydrodynamic instability, a theory that is initially characterized by a system of linear equations, as discussed in great detail in Chapters 2–8. Breakdown thus implies that the linear assumption is becoming invalid and the flow now has several modes interacting and amplifying. This interaction can then transfer energy to modes not yet dominant in the flow. The culmination of this breakdown process is a turbulent flow. One might suppose that the characteristics of the breakdown stage depends on the initial conditions – as receptivity – as well as freestream conditions such as vorticity and freestream turbulence. Today, we understand much about this initial stage and the linear amplification stage but have only limited knowledge for the nonlinear processes of many flows (cf. Chapter 9) because the complete Navier-Stokes equations must be solved and tracing measurements in this stage back to their origin to ascertain the cause and effect is challenging.

The major goal of this text has been to present the subject of hydrodynamic instability processes for many different engineering problems. The initial chapters demonstrated that this understanding can most often be achieved with linear systems. However, as was somewhat evident in Chapters 8 and 9, the transition from a laminar to turbulent flow is extremely complicated. This Chapter and the next will expose the reader to issues effecting hydrodynamic instabilities, the nonlinear breakdown of modes after linear growth, and we will summarize a condensed history of methods that have been used to predict loss of laminar flow and onset of transition to turbulence.

10.2 Influence of free stream turbulence and receptivity

Both experiments and computations in the field of transitional flows are plagued by uncertainly. This uncertainly comes primarily from external conditions.

Consider a box or volume of space where hydrodynamic instabilities are under study, such as a test section for either experiments or computations. This test section has a laminar flow that is subject to disturbances. The boundary layer may ingest these disturbances and, as a result, hydrodynamic instabilities may be induced. Such disturbances can take the form of acoustics, turbulent fluctuations, or organized vorticity. Furthermore, the plate may have small roughness discontinuities or joints that stem from the many parts to form a single plate. Any and all of these can induce instability modes. In addition, computations must deal with one additional mode, namely, numerical round off or loss of conservation in the governing equations. This artifact is inherent to various degrees in all computations. Furthermore, when attempting to compare numerical or theoretical solutions with the seemingly experimental counterpart, uncertainly in the differences between these external conditions must always be assessed.

Morkovin (1969) is usually given the credit for coining the term receptivity. By this, it is meant to describe the process by which free stream turbulence interacts with the boundary layer and it is believed by many to be a significant part in the transition process. Reshotko (1984) put forth a description of transition and the role of receptivity by stating: "In an environment where initial disturbance levels are small, the transition Reynolds number of a boundary layer is very much dependent upon the nature and spectrum of the disturbance environment, the signatures in the boundary layer of these disturbances and their excitation of the normal modes (receptivity), and finally the linear and nonlinear amplification of the growing modes."

Receptivity prediction tools provide the disturbance spectrum and initial amplitudes to be used by the linear or nonlinear evolution module, whether it be linear stability theory, PSE theory, etc. to predict the transition location or provide a means to correlate the transition location. Such capability already exists for the simplest of disturbance initiation processes as shown by Bertolotti & Crouch (1992).

Leehey & Shapiro (1980), Kachanov & Tararykin (1990), Saric, Hoos & Radeztsky (1991), and Wiegel & Wlezien (1993) have conducted receptivity experiments, and Kerschen (1987), Tadjfar & Bodonyi (1992), Fedorov & Khokhlov (1993), Choudhari & Streett (1994), Choudhari (1994), Crouch (1994) have conducted theoretical studies of receptivity in order to extend the knowledge base and capability for predicting the receptivity process. Acoustic noise, turbulence, and vorticity are free stream influences and couple with single and distributed roughness, steps and gaps, surface waviness, etc. to produce disturbances in the viscous boundary layer flow. For example, as shown in Fig. 10.1 the influence of the transition location with changes in Reynolds

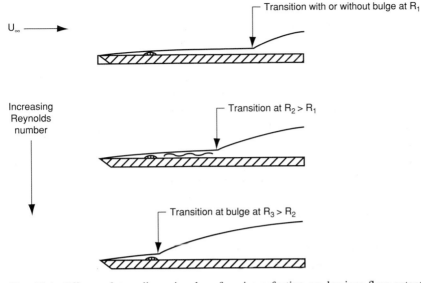

Fig. 10.1. Effects of two-dimensional surface imperfection on laminar flow extent (after Holmes, *et al.*, 1985a).

number is displayed. Here, the receptivity mechanism involves a roughness element.

These ingestion mechanisms are referred to as natural receptivity. In addition, there is forced as well as natural receptivity. Because the dominant instabilities in a boundary layer flow are of a small scale, the receptivity initiation must input energy into this part of the spectrum in order to result in the most efficient excitation of disturbances. As Kerschen (1989) pointed out, forced receptivity usually involves the intentional generation of instability waves by supplying energy to the flow at finite and selected wavelengths and frequencies that match the boundary layer disturbance components. Examples of forced receptivity include unsteady wall suction and blowing or heating and cooling, such as used for active flow control.

Forced theoretical and computational receptivity are linked to linear stability theory through a forcing boundary condition. This is done by introducing the boundary condition for the generation of a disturbance due to suction and blowing through a single orifice in the wall (or computational boundary) as

$$v = f(x)e^{-i\omega t}, \tag{10.1}$$

where ω is the frequency of the disturbance that one desires to initiate, $f(x)$ is the shape of the suction or blowing distribution, and v is the resulting wall

normal velocity component at the wall. Similar techniques can be used for unsteady thermal forcing and to excite disturbances in a wind tunnel experiment.

Natural receptivity is more complicated in that free stream acoustics, turbulence, and vorticity have wavelengths that are much longer than that of the boundary layer disturbance. In addition, complicating the matter is the fact that the free stream disturbance in nature has a well defined propagation speed and the energy concentrated at specific wavelengths. Hence, the free stream disturbance has no energy in wavelengths that correspond to the boundary layer disturbance. As a result, any mechanism must effectively and efficiently be able to transfer energy from the long wavelength range to that of the short scale wavelengths. Mechanisms to accomplish this transfer include the leading edge of a plate and wing and surface discontinuities, such as bugs or surface roughness, rivets, or other influence.

To determine the process of length scale conversion, Goldstein (1983, 1985, 1987) put forth a theory that showed that the primary means of conversion was through nonparallel mean flow effects. Hence, the two locations where nonparallel effects are strongest are (1) regions of rapid boundary layer growth such as at the leading edge where the boundary layer is thin and rapidly growing, and (2) downstream at a surface discontinuity such as a bump on the wall.

To determine the receptivity of the boundary layer in the leading edge region of a particular geometry to free stream disturbances, solutions of the linearized unsteady boundary layer equations are required. These solutions match downstream with the Orr-Sommerfeld equation that governs the linear instability and serves to provide a means for determining the amplitude of the viscous boundary layer disturbance.

Finally, the second class of natural receptivity involves the interaction of long wavelength free stream disturbances with local mechanisms, such as wall roughness, suction, or steps, for example, to generate boundary layer disturbances. In this case, adjustments made to the mean flow cannot be obtained with standard boundary layer equations and, instead, the triple deck asymptotic approximation to the Navier-Stokes equations is used. The triple deck produces an interactive relationship between the pressure and the displacement thickness due to matching of the requirements between the three decks. The middle deck or main deck responds inviscidly to the short scale wall discontinuities. The viscous layer or lower deck between the main deck and the surface is required to insure a no slip boundary condition at the wall. Finally, the rapid change in displacement thickness at the surface discontinuity induces a correction to the outer potential flow. This correction takes place in the upper deck. The mean flow gradients, due to the discontinuity, serve as forcing terms for the disturbance equations. So, although much understanding about receptivity has been

gained over the past few years, significant research must be conducted, especially in the three-dimensional effects and in supersonic flows before the tools can become widely used as transition prediction tools.

As has been mentioned, the principal difficulty in examining the role of receptivity in a boundary layer is due to the disparity of the scales when a linking to the free stream is needed. Although the triple deck formulation has had some success in assessing this connection, it is a rather complex method and it tends to imply that it is the leading edge where the boundary layer begins that is the major source for a connection. Along with this is the consequence of the boundary layer not being parallel. A similar appraisal can be made for the status for the understanding of by-pass dynamics for the boundary layer. For these reasons, recent efforts were made by Lasseigne *et al.* (1999, 2000) in order to provide alternative proposals and the results were most promising. This work was based on the complete understanding of initial-value problems as has been discussed in Chapter 8. Specifically, it was definitively shown that: (i) a transient disturbance in the free stream of the boundary layer can lead to the growth of an unstable Tollmien-Schlichting wave; (ii) a resonance with the continuous spectrum can provide a mechanism for bypass transition; (iii) the continuum modes of a disturbance feed directly into the Tollmien-Schlichting wave downstream through non-parallel effects. Not only was the importance of the continuous spectrum demonstrated but these results were correlated with DNS calculations.

10.3 Tollmien-Schlichting breakdown

The breakdown of Tollmien-Schlichting waves was discussed in great detail in Section 9.3 as an instrument for secondary instability. This section will briefly summarize the process so that crossflow vortex, oblique wave, and Görtler vortex breakdown can be better appreciated.

The viscous Tollmien-Schlichting wave instabilities of a boundary layer begin to amplify at rather long wavelengths at branch I of the neutral curve, amplify until branch II is reached downstream, and then decay. In a real flow, many other modes exist as well making it impractical to design many laminar configurations. However, the transition from a laminar flow to turbulent flow in boundary layers can begin with the Tollmien-Schlichting waves. At some point these two-dimensional dominate waves tend to be that of three-dimensional, short wavelength structure. The theory of secondary instabilities provides for understanding of this two-dimensional process becoming three-dimensional and of the long wavelength dominant instabilities developing short scales. When these secondary instabilities amplify, as discussed in Chapter 9, they

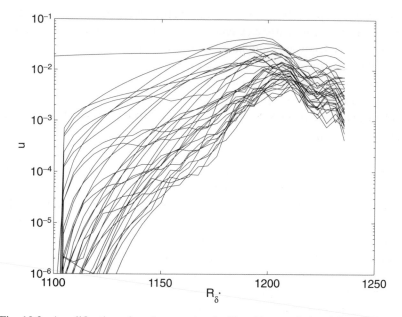

Fig. 10.2. Amplification of modes associated with subharmonic breakdown process.

amplify with a larger growth rate than that of the Tollmien-Schlichting wave. As the secondary mode amplitude approaches that of the Tollmien-Schlichting amplitude, the spectrum rapidly fills in a short spatial distance and breakdown occurs. This is shown in Fig. 10.2. Clearly at the end of the simulation the solution is under-resolved. The saturation of the modes is purely numerical due to the lack of resolution. The simulation was discontinued because of numerical instability.

10.4 Oblique wave breakdown

The oblique wave breakdown procedure is due to the linear or nonlinear interactions of a pair of oblique waves. This process is more likely to occur in high speed flows because, for low speed flows, the two-dimensional Tollmien-Schlichting mode dominates or has the largest growth rate, while for high speed flows, it is the three-dimensional Tollmien-Schlichting modes that dominate. We will briefly discuss this breakdown process because the modes interact in an unusual manner and induce stationary vortex structures. Because of nonlinearity, no adequate formal theory is available to explain the breakdown process. However, similar mechanisms have been studied by Hall & Smith (1991) using asymptotic methods. Specifically, Hall & Smith discussed vortex

wave interactions within a large wave number and Reynolds number limit. To further quantify the mechanisms of interest in the finite Reynolds number range, DNS (Chapter 11) and possibly PSE theory (Chapter 9) are just some options available to study the wave interactions.

Because this route or mechanism of transition is nonlinear, limited research has been done for oblique wave breakdown, but it is worth citing the salient work that has been done. Schmid & Henningson (1992a) studied bypass transition by introducing a pair of large amplitude oblique waves into channel flow. The evolution of the disturbances was computed with temporal DNS. They found that the development of the oblique waves was dominated by a preferred spreading of the energy spectra into low streamwise wave numbers and led to the rapid development of streamwise elongated structures. Schmid & Henningson (1992b) also looked at small amplitude wave pairs over a variety of parameters and suggested that the mechanism of energy transfer is primarily linear. Fasel & Thumm (1991) and Bestek, Thumm & Fasel (1992) computed such breakdown structure in a compressible boundary layer and described the physical structure as honeycomb like in order to identify a distinction from the secondary instability Λ-like structures discussed in Chapter 9. Chang & Malik (1992) used PSE theory to examine the breakdown of supersonic boundary layers because the dominant first mode is an oblique wave in supersonic flow. Chang & Malik found that even waves with amplitudes as small as 0.001 percent that are initiated at the lower branch can lead to transition in this breakdown scenario and depend on the frequency of the induced oblique waves. Here, we focus on the nonlinear flow breakdown process. A brief discussion is also presented in Chapter 11 because these results were obtained using DNS.

The profiles for the oblique wave pair are obtained from linear stability theory for the Reynolds number, $Re_{\delta_o^*} = 900$, frequency, $\omega = 0.0774$, and spanwise wave numbers, $\beta = \pm 0.2$. Details of the spatial DNS computations are included here in the event that they may be used as a test case. The grid consists of 901 uniformly spaced streamwise nodes, 61 wall normal collocation points, and 10 symmetric spanwise modes. In the streamwise direction, the outflow boundary is $465\delta_o^*$ from the inflow boundary; the far field or free stream boundary is $75\delta_o^*$ from the wall; and the spanwise boundary consists of a length equal to one half of the spanwise wavelength, or $\lambda_z/2 = \pi/\beta$. For the time marching scheme, the disturbance period is divided into 320 time steps. For the PSE computational approach, 100 wall normal grid points are used; 7 frequency modes and 7 spanwise Fourier modes are used; and the far field boundary is $58\delta_o^*$ from the wall.

The input modes consist of a pair of oblique traveling waves that were obtained from linear stability theory. The disturbance forcing consists of modes

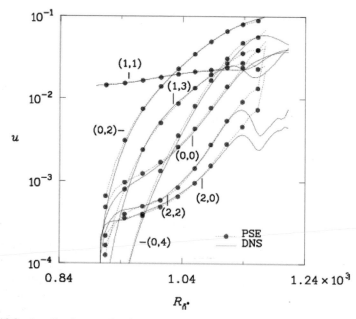

Fig. 10.3. Amplitude growth with downstream distance for a pair of oblique waves (after Joslin, Streett & Chang, 1993).

(1,1) and (1,−1), or (ω, β) and $(\omega, -\beta)$, and their complex conjugates (−1,1) and (−1,−1). Theoretically, if these modes self interact initially, then only certain higher modes are likely to be excited. These higher modes are: (0,0), (0,2), (2,0), and (2,2), etc.

The oblique waves are introduced with larger amplitudes $A^o_{1,1} = 0.01$. The computed primary disturbance (1,1) and higher modes are shown in Fig. 10.3. Again, the modes predicted by PSE theory are shown to be in agreement with the DNS results. The small wave number modes gain initial energy. The vortex mode (0,2) is clearly dominant. The self interaction of the wave pairs and the interaction with the streamwise vortex lead to a rapid cascade of energy to the other modes.

Rather than the meager growth and downstream decay, as occurs if the initial amplitudes are too small, these higher modes now grow with growth rate characteristics that are similar to the vortex mode. The vortex and harmonics rapidly overtake the introduced waves (1,1) and subsequent breakdown occurs. At breakdown, the spectrum is filled and both the DNS and PSE computations are under-resolved near the downstream end of Fig. 10.3. Further evidence that the onset of transition from laminar to turbulent flow has begun, and the skin friction curve begins to rise.

10.5 Crossflow vortex breakdown

In Section 6.5, crossflow vortex modes were introduced by way of the rotating disk flow problem. As discussed in Chapter 6, the crossflow instability occurs due to the existence of an inflection in the profile of a three-dimensional velocity profile as found in rotating disks and on boundary layer associated with a swept wing. For the boundary layer of a wing, the Tollmien-Schlichting process dominates until the wing is swept to 25-30 degrees. At that point, the inflectional profile properties cause the crossflow vortex mode to dominate with transition occurring very near the leading edge of a wing in most cases, depending on the pressure gradient and wing sweep.

Here, we discuss the breakdown process from results given by Joslin & Streett (1994) and Joslin (1995a). Again, because the breakdown process is of interest and is inherently nonlinear, the DNS code (Chapter 11) is used to obtain results for discussion. For the simulations no surface imperfections, such as particulates, weather condition effects, noise, or spanwise inhomogeneities, exist. Surface curvature is neglected to simplify the numerics and because the simulation is conducted on a chordwise region of the wing that corresponds to a relatively flat portion of a laminar flow airfoil. The base flow and most of the parameters used in the initial study by Joslin & Streett (1994) are used here to enhance the understanding of the transition process on swept wings.

The vortex packets are forcibly imposed into the boundary layer by steady suction and blowing through the wedge surface in the same manner as described by Joslin & Streett (1994). Suction and blowing techniques may be used because, as demonstrated by Kachanov & Tararykin (1990), the results from suction and blowing and roughness element disturbance generators correlate well and lead to disturbances that graphically coincide.

Consider the base flow given by the Falkner-Skan-Cooke profile. The pressure field used by Müller & Bippes (1988) is given by the following linear equation

$$c_p(x_c) = 0.941 - 0.845x_c. \tag{10.2}$$

The first simulation (SIM-I) is the case of Joslin & Streett (1994). This simulation has a grid of 901 streamwise, 61 wall-normal, and 32 spanwise grid points. The far field boundary is located 50δ from the wedge, the streamwise distance is 857δ from the inflow, with the spanwise distance 108δ. For time marching, a time step size of 0.2 is chosen for the three stage Runge-Kutta method. For all simulations, crossflow vortex packets are generated through a periodic strip of steady suction and blowing holes that are equally spaced on the wing surface and the shape of the wall normal velocity profiles at the wall have a half period

sine wave in the chordwise direction and a full period sine wave in the spanwise direction. This mode of disturbance generation would correspond to an
isolated roughness element within the computational domain. Stationary crossflow vortex packets are generated by steady suction and blowing with a wall
normal velocity component at the wall with an amplitude of $v_w = 1 \times 10^{-5}$.
The holes for SIM-I have a chordwise length of 8.572δ and a spanwise length
of 16.875δ.

The second simulation (SIM-II) has a grid of 901 streamwise, 81 wall-
normal, and 48 spanwise grid points. The far field boundary is located 50δ
from the wedge, the streamwise distance is 550δ, and the spanwise distance is
108δ. A time step size of 0.2 is chosen for time marching. Suction and blowing
with a wall-normal velocity amplitude of $v_w = 1 \times 10^{-4}$ is used to generate
stationary crossflow vortices. The holes for SIM-II have a chordwise length of
8.5δ and a spanwise length of 36δ and are aligned side by side in the spanwise
direction.

The final simulation (SIM-III) has a grid of 721 streamwise, 81 wall-normal,
and 64 spanwise grid points. The far field boundary is located 50δ from the
wedge, the streamwise distance is 440δ, and the spanwise distance is 108δ. A
time step size of 0.2 is chosen for time marching. Stationary crossflow vortex
packets are generated with steady suction and blowing with a wall-normal velocity component at the wall with an amplitude $v_w = 1 \times 10^{-3}$. The holes for
SIM-III have a chordwise length of 5.5δ and a spanwise length of 36δ and are
aligned side by side in the spanwise direction.

Distinct stages of disturbance evolution are found for crossflow evolution,
amplification, and breakdown. If the disturbances are generated by a local
means (e.g., roughness element), then the initial growth of individual disturbance packets occurs in isolation from adjacent packets. The individual packets coalesced at a chordwise location downstream depending upon the distance
between the suction holes, the directions of the disturbance evolution, and the
spreading rate. When the vortex packets reach sufficiently large amplitude in
the later stages of transition, the disturbance field becomes dominated by nonlinear interactions and vortex roll over. These stages are shown in Fig. 10.4,
where spanwise planar views of chordwise velocity contours viewed from the
trailing edge toward the leading edge, are shown. Note that the wing tip is to the
left and the wing root is to the right. For each simulation the contour results
show that, immediately downstream of the disturbance initialization point, a
distinct vortex packet evolves that is isolated from nearby disturbances. As the
disturbance evolves and spreads, additional vortices fill the span as a result of
the adjacent vortex superposition. This superposition process leads to apparent rapid increase in the disturbance amplitudes and phase adjustments. In the

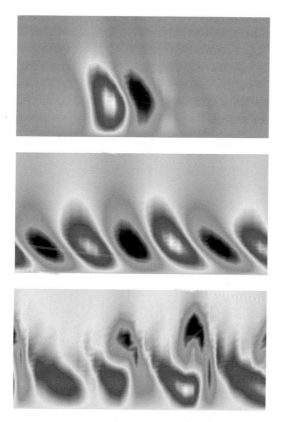

Fig. 10.4. Spanwise planes of disturbance velocity (u) contours at chordwise locations for swept wedge flow of SIM-I; $x_c = 0.25, 0.34, 0.45$.

later nonlinear stage of breakdown, the contours indicate that low speed fluid is dragged out and over the high speed fluid, which is then drawn toward the surface. Dagenhart & Saric (1994) observed this same phenomenon in their experiments.

The breakdown sequence of SIM-I may be typical for isolated roughness elements where initial energy resides in many instability modes but the evolution sequence can be more generalized by the following description. Instead of describing the first stage as a region of isolated growth that is specific to an isolated roughness, the initial growth stage should be described as linear or has an exponential growth. In both SIM-II and SIM-III, the initial amplitude levels of the disturbances are much larger than SIM-I and the disturbance initiation process imitates distributed roughness where initial energy resides in a single dominant mode. Still, all of the simulations have this linear growth stage. The second stage can be generically described as coalescence although, unlike

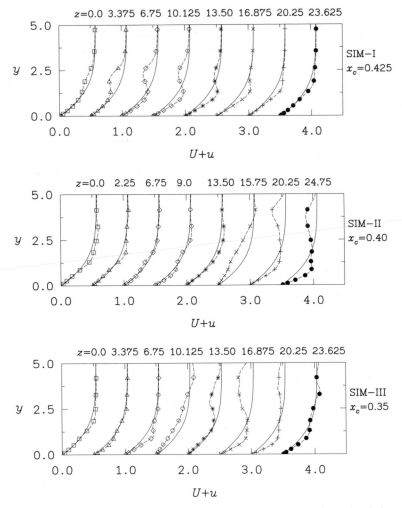

Fig. 10.5. Chordwise (base + disturbance) velocity profiles at various chordwise and spanwise locations for swept wedge flow.

SIM-I that is a linear superposition, the process may be nonlinear in SIM-II or SIM-III because of the much larger disturbance amplitudes. The final stage can be typically described as a nonlinear interaction because all of the simulations have very large amplitudes in this region.

In this nonlinear interaction region inflectional velocity profiles are observed in all of the simulations. Figure 10.5 shows the instantaneous chordwise velocity profiles $(U + u)$ for each simulation at a chordwise station that corresponds to the nonlinear vortex stage of roll over. The various profiles at each station correspond to adjacent spanwise locations. Across the span the flow is

accelerated in regions near the wedge surface and is retarded in other areas out in the boundary layer. The characteristic inflectional profiles have been observed in experiments by both Müller & Bippes (1988), Dagenhart, Saric, Mousseux & Stack (1989), and Dagenhart & Saric (1994). Dagenhart & Saric noted that the appearance of inflectional profiles was rapidly followed by the appearance of a high frequency instability and, subsequently, by transition.

The theoretical studies of Kohama, Saric & Hoos (1991) and Balachandar, Streett & Malik (1990) indicated that this high frequency instability in the experiments is reminiscent of secondary instabilities, that spawn from these inflectional velocity profiles. Thus, the late stages of crossflow breakdown, the most likely cause of transition, is the appearance of this secondary instability mode.

10.6 Dean-Taylor-Görtler vortex breakdown

Recall from Chapter 6, centrifugal instabilities were discussed using an analysis of a linear system of equations. Among others, centrifugal instability occurs for shear flows over concave surfaces. Rayleigh (1916b) determined the necessary and sufficient conditions for the existence of an inviscid instability. This instability is referred to as the Rayleigh circulation criteria and is a function of the circulation. As Saric (1994a) notes, there are three centrifugal instabilities that can occur with each sharing the same physical mechanism of generation. The Taylor (1923) instability occurs in flow between co-rotating cylinders; the Dean (1928) instability occurs in curved channel flows; and the Görtler (1940) instability occurs for open, curved plate boundary layer flows. Take note that, although the instabilities may have similar generation mechanisms, the mean flow states are quite different. However, these common vortex disturbances arise when the surface geometry becomes concave and are reminiscent of counter rotating vortex structures (see Fig. 6.4). Note the changes that occur in the flow due to the presence of these vortices. Low speed fluid near the wall is transported up and high speed fluid is transported down toward the wall. Such changes can then induce additional instability that effect a transition from a laminar to turbulent state.

The nonlinear breakdown process for these vortex-based flows can be quite complicated because additional traditional instabilities may become unstable. As discussed by Coles (1965) for the case of Taylor-Couette flow, with the inner cylinder having a larger angular velocity than the outer cylinder, the expected Taylor motion of periodic axial vortices developed followed by a secondary pattern of traveling circumferal waves. As these dual modes amplify, energy is observed in the harmonic modes. This process can be referred to as

cascade process whereby other modes gain energy from their parental modes until they have sufficient energy to interact nonlinearly. A catastrophic transition process may be observed when the outer cylinder has a larger angular velocity than the inner cylinder. Figure 6.2 shows the bounds between stable and unstable regions; however, the problem can become more complicated than simply stable-unstable regions. With both catastrophic and doubly period transition processes, more regions can be added. For doubly periodic, a region can be identified in the first quadrant with a region where only singly period flow is maintained. Also, for catastrophic transition, bands of turbulence mingle with the laminar flow. These turbulent regions can appear and disappear in a random manner or may form in a regular pattern in the form of a spiral turbulent pattern. To represent this appearance of turbulence, a boundary can be added to Fig. 6.2 above the Taylor bound. Above this line, the flow is turbulent and between these lines the flow is characterized as transitional.

Among others, Ligrani, Longest, Kendall & Fields (1994) examined a breakdown process for Dean vortex flow. Background or fluctuations in the flow trigger vortex initiation. The vortices meander in the spanwise direction as they are convected downstream with the flow. A splitting and merging of vortices is observed in the flow presumably because the flow supports a spanwise instability. The symmetric counter rotating vortex pair system encounters an instability. Then, after this encounter, the vortex pair experiences a strong up wash and the flow pattern now appears as an asymmetric mushroom like structure. This mushroom structure has been observed by Saric (1994a) as shown by Fig. 10.6.

Prior to this mushroom characteristic, vortex pairs can merge. As two pairs of vortices incur a decrease in radial extent, these pairs are observed to merge and form a single pair. This merging phenomenon is quite common. Additionally, two vortex pairs can split and result in three vortex pairs. The dynamics of this process involves an average preferred spanwise wavenumber. As a final note for the Dean vortex problem, the observations for the vortex splitting and merging process are very dependent on the free stream and initial conditions similar to crossflow vortex problem. Roughness induces more of a stationary vortex system, whereas fluctuations induce more of an unsteady vortex system.

The discussion by Saric (1994a) for Görtler vortex breakdown provides a consistent description of the formation of the symmetric counter-rotating vortex pairs. The action of the vortex pair induces up wash and down wash regions has been discussed. In the down wash region, high momentum fluid is drawn toward the wall and shear is increased while in the up wash region the low momentum fluid is ejected and the region has decreased shear. As the vortices amplify, the mean flow now encounters regions of large distortions similar to

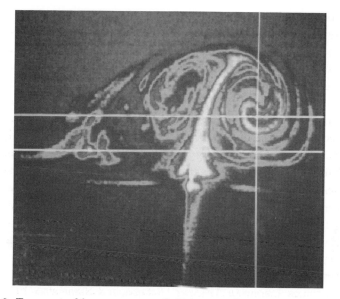

Fig. 10.6. Transport of low momentum fluid by a stationary vortex structure (after Peerhossaini, 1987; courtesy of Dr. W. Saric).

crossflow breakdown. The now highly distorted and inflectional mean flow is susceptible to inviscid Rayleigh or secondary instabilities. From computations and the experiments of Swearingen & Blackwelder (1986, 1987) it was concluded that Görlter breakdown was caused by a secondary instability associated with the spanwise velocity gradient and the strongly distorted mean velocity profiles. As measured by Winoto, Zhang & Chew (2000), transition is observed to start and become turbulent earlier in the up wash region when compared with the down wash region.

10.7 Transition prediction

Because the performance of a configuration is directly tied to the amount of laminar and turbulent flow present, it is imperative to be able to accurately predict and design for the transition location. This section reviews the transition prediction methodologies and focuses on the theoretical and computational aspects of the transition prediction. More detailed reviews of currently used approaches are provided by Cousteix (1992) and Reed & Saric (1998).

The reason why laminar flow is usually more desirable than the turbulent counterpart for external aerodynamic vehicles lies with the reduction of the viscous drag penalty. Do we have a sufficient understanding of the fundamental

flow physics for the problem to design an optimal, reliable, cost effective-system to control the flow? The answer is encouraging!

As has been discussed in Chapters 1 and 2, the first major theoretical contributions to the study of boundary layer transition were made by Helmholtz (1868), Kelvin (1880), Reynolds (1883), and Rayleigh (1879, 1880, 1887). Although these early investigations neglected the effects of viscosity, the second derivative of the mean velocity proved to be of key physical importance in explaining boundary layer instabilities. These fundamental studies proved to be the basis for future progress in the theoretical development. Viscous effects were added by Orr (1907a,b) and Sommerfeld (1908) who developed an ordinary differential equation that governs the linear instability of two-dimensional disturbances in channel flows. This was later extended by others to the incompressible boundary layer. Later, Squire (1933) accounted for three-dimensional waves by introducing a transformation from three to two dimensions. Tollmien (1929) and Schlichting (1932) provided the basis for convective traveling wave instabilities that are now termed Tollmien-Schlichting (TS) instabilities. Liepmann (1943) and Schubauer & Skramstad (1947) experimentally confirmed the existence and amplification of these instabilities in the boundary layer. One can visualize this disturbance by remembering the image of water waves created by dropping a pebble into a still lake or puddle. In this image, the waves that are generated decay as they travel from the source. Such is the case in boundary layer flow, except when certain critical flow parameters such as the Reynolds number are reached and the waves will grow in strength and lead to turbulent flow.

The improvements in aerodynamic efficiency directly scale with the amount of laminar flow that can be achieved. Hence, the designer must be able to accurately predict the location of boundary layer transition on complex three-dimensional geometries as a function of suction distribution and suction level or the accurate prediction of the suction distribution for a given target transition location. Pressure gradients, surface curvature and deformation, wall temperature, wall mass transfer, and unit Reynolds number are known to influence the stability of the boundary layer and transition location and must be reviewed.

This section describes the conventional and advanced transition prediction tools, some of which include prediction of perturbations in the laminar boundary layer, the spectrum and amplitudes of these perturbations, and the linear and nonlinear propagation of these perturbations that ultimately lead to transition. For literature focusing on the theoretical and computational aspects of transition prediction, refer to Cousteix (1992), Arnal, Habiballah & Constols (1984) and Arnal (1994).

10.7.1 Granville criterion

Granville (1953) reported a procedure for calculating viscous drag on bodies of revolution and developed an empirical criterion for locating the transition location associated with low turbulence flows. Low (or zero) turbulence characteristics of flight or low turbulence wind tunnels and high turbulence characteristics of most wind tunnels are the two problems considered relative to a transition criterion. The low turbulence case assumed that transition was Tollmien-Schlichting disturbance-dominated and began with infinitesimally small amplitude disturbances. Granville (1953) showed that a variety of flight and low turbulence wind tunnel data collapsed onto a criterion curve based on $(Re_{\theta,T} - Re_{\theta,N})$, the difference between the momentum thickness Reynolds number at transition and at the neutral point, versus $\overline{\theta^2/\nu dU/dx}$, which is the average pressure gradient parameter. This correlation was demonstrated for two-dimensional flows and is shown in Fig. 10.7. Granville used a transformation to convert this information to a body of rotation problem. The data was also correlated with the turbulence level in the free stream as shown in Fig. 10.8. Extrapolation of the criteria does work for a two-dimensional airfoil that is dominated by Tollmien-Schlichting waves (see Holmes, Obara, Gregorek, Hoffman & Freuhler, 1983) and the existing database included this form of transition. However, when the design configuration begins to significantly differ from the existing database, this transition prediction criteria fails.

10.7.2 C1 and C2 criteria

At ONERA[1], Arnal, Juillen & Casalis (1991) performed N-factor correlations with wind tunnel experimental results of a Laminar Flow Control (LFC) suction infinite swept wing. The motivation for the study was to gain fundamental understanding of the transition process with suction and to test the methodologies developed at ONERA/CERT[2] for three-dimensional flows. The streamwise instability criteria was based on an extension of Granville (1953). Two crossflow transition criteria have been developed by Arnal, Habiballah & Coustols (1984) at ONERA and are referred to as C1 and C2. The C1 criterion involves a correlation of transition onset integral values of the crossflow Reynolds number and the streamwise shape factor. The C2 criterion is a correlation of transition onset with a Reynolds number computed in the direction of

---

[1] Office National d'Etudes et de Recherches Aérospatiales; website http://www.onera.fr/english.html

[2] Centre d'Etudes et de Recherches de Toulouse; website http://www.cert.fr/index.a.html

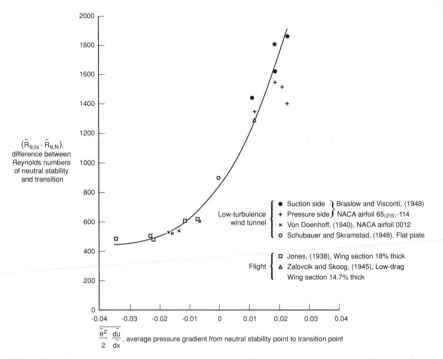

Fig. 10.7. Transition location as a function of average pressure gradient (after Granville, 1953).

the most unstable wave, the streamwise shape factor, and the free stream turbulence level. The results demonstrate that the transition criteria cannot be applied in regions where the pressure gradient is mild because there is a large range of unstable directions. In that region, one cannot only look at pure streamwise or crossflow instabilities. The C1 criterion leads to bad results with wall suction present whereas the C2 criterion correctly accounts for wall suction.

10.7.3 Linear Stability Theory and e^N

Although the growth or decay of small amplitude disturbances in a viscous boundary layer can be predicted by the Orr-Sommerfeld and Squire equations within the quasi-parallel approximation, the ability to predict transition using these results was first achieved in the 1950's with the semi-empirical method of Smith (1953), denoted as the e^N or N-factor method that correlates the predicted disturbance growth with measured transition locations. Although limited to empirical correlations of available experimental data, it has been the main tool that has been used throughout the 1990's. Moreover, linear stability

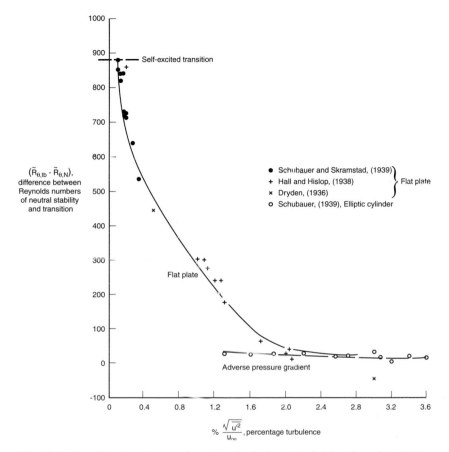

Fig. 10.8. Transition location as a function of turbulence level (after Granville, 1953).

theory represents the current state-of-the-art for transition location prediction for three-dimensional subsonic, transonic, and supersonic flows. To begin a transition prediction analysis, the steady laminar mean flow must first be obtained directly from Navier-Stokes solutions or the boundary layer equations. Then, the three-dimensional boundary layer stability equations are solved in order to determine the amplification rate at each point along the surface.

Significant advances have been made in the understanding of the fundamentals of two- and three-dimensional unsteady viscous boundary layer flow physics associated with transition (cf. reviews by Reshotko, 1976; Herbert, 1988; Bayly, Orszag & Herbert, 1988; Reed & Saric, 1998; Kachanov, 1994), Computational Fluid Dynamics (CFD) mean flow capabilities in complex geometries, turbulence modeling efforts, and in the direct numerical simulation of the

unsteady flow physics (Kleiser & Zang, 1991). However, the devised transition prediction methodology is considered state of the art and has been used by industry for LFC related design. This transition prediction methodology, termed the e^N method, is semi-empirical and relies on experimental data to determine the N-factor value at transition.

The disturbance evolution and transition prediction tools require an accurate representation of the mean flow velocity profiles. Either the velocity profiles can be extracted from Navier-Stokes solutions or are derived from solutions of a coupled Euler and boundary layer equation solver. Harris, Iyer & Radwan (1987) and Iyer (1990, 1993, 1995) have provided a solver for the Euler and boundary layer equations. Harris *et al.* (1987) demonstrated the accuracy of a fourth order finite difference method for a Cessna airplane fuselage forebody flow, flat plate boundary layer, flow around a cylinder on a flat plate, a prolate spheroid, and the flow over a NACA 0012 swept wing. In terms of computational efficiency, the Euler and boundary layer approach for obtaining accurate mean flows will be the solution of choice for most of preliminary design stages. Navier-Stokes solvers can be used for LFC design. A limiting factor for the Navier-Stokes mean flows is the demanding convergence required for the suitability of the results in the boundary layer stability codes.

For linear stability theory that makes use of the quasi parallel flow assumption, the mean flow $U(y)$, $W(y)$ are functions of the distance from the wall only and $V = 0$. Then, writing the velocities and pressure as a mean part plus a fluctuating part, substituting into the Navier-Stokes equations and linearizing, the following linear system results:

$$\frac{\partial u}{\partial x} + \frac{\partial v}{\partial y} + \frac{\partial w}{\partial z} = 0, \tag{10.3}$$

$$\frac{\partial u}{\partial t} + U\frac{\partial u}{\partial x} + v\frac{dU}{dy} + W\frac{\partial u}{\partial z} = -\frac{\partial p}{\partial x} + \frac{1}{Re}\left[\frac{\partial^2 u}{\partial x^2} + \frac{\partial^2 u}{\partial y^2} + \frac{\partial^2 u}{\partial z^2}\right], \tag{10.4}$$

$$\frac{\partial v}{\partial t} + U\frac{\partial v}{\partial x} + W\frac{\partial v}{\partial z} = -\frac{\partial p}{\partial y} + \frac{1}{Re}\left[\frac{\partial^2 v}{\partial x^2} + \frac{\partial^2 v}{\partial y^2} + \frac{\partial^2 v}{\partial z^2}\right], \tag{10.5}$$

and

$$\frac{\partial w}{\partial t} + U\frac{\partial w}{\partial x} + v\frac{dW}{dy} + W\frac{\partial w}{\partial z} = -\frac{\partial p}{\partial z} + \frac{1}{Re}\left[\frac{\partial^2 w}{\partial x^2} + \frac{\partial^2 w}{\partial y^2} + \frac{\partial^2 w}{\partial z^2}\right], \tag{10.6}$$

where the Reynolds number, $Re = U_o\delta/\nu$.

According to the conventional normal mode assumption used to derive the Orr-Sommerfeld equation, the eigensolutions take the form

$$\{u, v, w, p\} = \{\hat{u}, \hat{v}, \hat{w}, \hat{p}\}(y)e^{i(\alpha x + \beta z - \omega t)}, \qquad (10.7)$$

where α and β are the nondimensional wave numbers in the streamwise and spanwise directions, ω is the frequency, and $\{\hat{u}, \hat{v}, \hat{w}, \hat{p}\}$ are the amplitudes in y. Thus, using (10.7) in the linear equations (10.3) to (10.6), the Orr-Sommerfeld

$$\left[\frac{d^2}{dy^2} - \alpha^2 - \beta^2 \right]^2 \hat{v} - i\,Re \left[-\alpha \frac{d^2 U}{dy^2} - \beta \frac{d^2 W}{dy^2} \right.$$

$$\left. + (\alpha U + \beta W - \omega)\left(\frac{d^2}{dy^2} - \alpha^2 - \beta^2 \right) \right] \hat{v} = 0, \qquad (10.8)$$

and Squire

$$\frac{d^2 \omega}{dy^2} - [\alpha^2 + \beta^2 - i\,Re(\alpha U + \beta W - \omega)]\frac{d\omega}{dy} = i\,Re\left(\alpha \frac{dU}{dy} + \beta \frac{dW}{dy} \right) \hat{v}, \qquad (10.9)$$

equations result, where Ω is the vorticity in the y-direction. The wall boundary conditions are

$$\hat{v}, \frac{d\hat{v}}{dy}, \omega = 0 \quad \text{at} \quad y = 0, \qquad (10.10)$$

and, in the free stream,

$$\hat{v}, \frac{d\hat{v}}{dy}, \omega \to 0 \quad \text{as} \quad y \to \infty. \qquad (10.11)$$

Either spatial or temporal stability analysis may be performed with the temporal analysis less expensive and the spatial analysis more physical. In addition to the Reynolds number that must be prescribed, a stability analysis requires that the mean flow and its first and second wall-normal derivatives be determined very accurately. A small deviation in the mean flow can cause significant changes in the second derivative and contaminate the stability calculations.

Because the spatial formulation is more representative of the real boundary layer instability physics and the temporal to spatial conversion is only valid on the neutral curve, the remaining transition prediction methodologies will be described via the spatial approach. For the temporal approach see Srokowski & Orszag (1977) and Malik (1982). Malik also included the effect of compressibility in the equations. For the spatial approach in three-dimensional flows, the frequency (ω_r) is fixed, $\omega_i = 0$, and $\{\alpha_r, \alpha_i, \beta_r, \beta_i\}$ are parameters to be determined. While an eigenvalue analysis will provide two of these values, the main issue with the application of the e^N methodology to three-dimensional

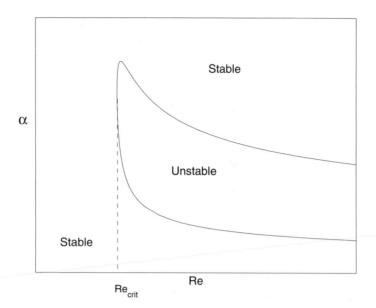

Fig. 10.9. Illustration of neutral curve for linear stability theory.

flows is the specification or determination of the remaining two parameters. Figure 10.9 illustrates the instability concept within linear stability theory. A certain parameter range exists whereby a certain combination of wavenumbers and frequencies characterize disturbances that decay at low Reynolds numbers, amplify over a range of Reynolds numbers, and then decay as the Reynolds number is increased. The Reynolds numbers nondimensionally represent the spatial chordwise location on a wing for example.

By assuming a method is available to determine the two remaining free parameters, the N-factor correlation with experiments can now be made. By integrating from the neutral point with arbitrary disturbance amplitude A_0, the amplification of the disturbance is tracked until the maximum amplitude A_1 is reached at which decay ensues. Since this is a linear method, the amplitudes A_0 and A_1 are never really used. Instead, the N-factor relation of interest is defined as

$$N = \ln \frac{A_1}{A_0} = \int_{s_0}^{s_1} \gamma \, ds, \qquad (10.12)$$

where s_0 is the point at which the disturbance first begins to grow, s_1 is the point at which transition is correlated, and γ is the characteristic growth rate of the disturbance. Figure 10.10 illustrates the amplification and decay of four disturbances (wavenumber, frequency combinations) leading to four N-values.

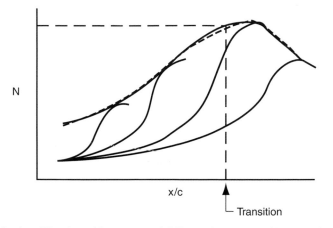

N

x/c

Transition

Fig. 10.10. Amplification of four waves of different frequency to illustrate the determination of the N-factor curve.

The inclusion of all individual N-values leads to the N-factor curve. By correlating this N-factor with many transition cases, the amplification factor for which transition is likely or expected for similar flow situations can be inferred. The resulting N-factor is correlated with the location of transition for a variety of experimental databases and is traced in Fig. 10.10. This information is then used to determine the laminar flow extent. Hence, this methodology is critically dependent on the value of the experimental databases and the translation of the N-factor value to a new design.

The saddle point, fixed wave angle, and fixed spanwise wavelength methods are three means that have been devised in order to determine the two free parameters for three-dimensional flows.

Strictly valid only in parallel flows, the saddle point method suggests that the derivative of $(\alpha x + \beta z)$ with respect to β equals zero. As noted by Nayfeh (1980) and Cebeci & Stewartson (1980), carrying out this derivative implies that $d\alpha/d\beta$ must be real, or

$$\frac{\partial \alpha_i}{\partial \beta_r} = 0. \tag{10.13}$$

The group velocity angle, ϕ_g, is given by

$$\phi_g = \tan^{-1}(\partial \alpha_r / \partial \beta_r). \tag{10.14}$$

The final condition needed to close the problem requires that the growth rate be maximized along the group velocity trajectory. Then, the N-factor or integrated

growth would be

$$N = \int_{s_o}^{s_1} \gamma\,ds \quad \text{where} \quad \gamma = \frac{-\left(\alpha_i - \beta_i \frac{\partial \alpha_r}{\partial \beta_r}\right)}{\sqrt{1 + \left(\frac{\partial \alpha_r}{\partial \beta_r}\right)^2}} \tag{10.15}$$

and where s_o is the location where the growth rate γ is zero and s_1 is the distance along the tangent of the group velocity direction.

For the second method, developed by Arnal, Casalis & Juillen (1990), the fixed wave angle approach sets $\beta_i = 0$ and the N-factors are computed with a fixed wave orientation, or

$$N = \int_{s_o}^{s_1} -\alpha\,ds. \tag{10.16}$$

Many calculations have to be made over the range of wave angles to determine the highest value of N.

Finally, the fixed spanwise wavelength approach proposed by Mack (1988) sets $\beta_i = 0$ and β_r is held fixed over the N-factor calculation, computed with

$$N = \int_{s_o}^{s_1} -\alpha\,ds. \tag{10.17}$$

Many calculations have to be made over the range of β_r in order to determine the maximum value of N. It is not clear what significance holding β_r to a constant has in three-dimensional flows.

A major obstacle in validating or calibrating current and future transition prediction tools results from insufficient information in both wind tunnel and flight test databases. For example, Rozendaal (1986) correlated N-factor tools for Tollmien-Schlichting and cross flow disturbances on a Cessna Citation III business jet flight test database. The database consisted of transition locations measured with hot film devices for points that varied from 5 to 35 percent chord on both upper and lower wing surfaces for Mach numbers that ranged from 0.3 to 0.8 and altitudes ranging from 10,000 to 43,000 ft. The results showed that cross flow and Tollmien-Schlichting disturbances may interact and that cross flow disturbances probably dominated. Cross flow N-factors were scattered around the value 5 and Tollmien-Schlichting N-factors varied from 0 to 8. The stability analysis showed no relationship between Mach number and disturbance amplification at transition. Rozendaal noted that the quality of the results was suspect because no information on the surface quality existed, an unresolved shift in the pressure data occurred, and an inadequate density of

transition sensors on the upper wing surface was used. Furthermore, the impact of the engine placement relative to the wing could be added as a potential contributing factor. The Rozendaal analysis reinforced that the N-factor method relies on creditable experimental data.

In a discussion of the application of linear stability theory and e^N method in LFC, Malik (1987) described the methodology for both incompressible and compressible flows and presented a variety of test cases. In situations where transition occurs near the leading edge of wings, the N-factors can be quite large compared to the N = 9 to 11 range applicable for transition in the later portion of a wing. Malik makes an important contribution to this understanding by noting that the linear quasi parallel stability theory normally does not account for surface curvature effects. However, for transition near the leading edge of a wing, the stabilizing effects of curvature are significant and must be included to achieve N-factors of 9 to 11. The remainder of this subsection documents samples of the extended use of the N-factor method for predicting laminar flow extent.

Schrauf, Bieler & Thiede (1992) indicated that transition prediction is a key problem of laminar flow technology. They presented a description of the N factor code developed and used at Deutsche Airbus that documents the influence of pressure gradient, compressibility, sweep angle and curvature during calibrations with flight tests and wind tunnel experiments.

Among others, Vijgen, Dodbele, Holmes & van Dam (1986) used N-factor linear stability theory to ascertain the influence of compressibility on disturbance amplification. They compared Tollmien-Schlichting disturbance growth for incompressible flow over a Natural Laminar Flow (NLF) fuselage with the compressible formulation and noted that compressibility has a stabilizing influence on the disturbances (first mode). For the NLF and LFC, an increase in Mach number (enhanced compressibility) is stabilizing to all instabilities for subsonic and low supersonic flow.

Nayfeh (1987) used the method of multiple scales to account for the growth of the boundary layer (nonparallel effects). The nonparallel results showed increased growth rates compared with the parallel flow assumption. These results indicate that nonparallel flow effects are destabilizing to the instabilities. Singer, Choudhari & Li (1995) attempted to quantify the effect of nonparallelism on the growth of stationary crossflow disturbances in three-dimensional boundary layers using the multiple scales analysis. The results indicate that multiple scales can accurately represent the nonparallel effects when nonparallelism is weak; however, as the nonparallel effects increase, multiple scales results diminish in accuracy.

Finally, Hefner & Bushnell (1980) investigated the status of linear stability theory and the N-factor methodology for predicting transition location. They noted that the main features lacking in the methodology are the inability to account for the ingestion and characterization of the instabilities entering the boundary layer (the receptivity problem).

10.7.4 Parabolized stability equations theory

Because the N-factor methodology is based in linear stability theory, it has limitations. Other methods must be considered that account for nonparallelism, curvature effects, and ultimately nonlinear interactions. The final method considered relative to the evolution of disturbances in boundary layer flow is the PSE theory or method. Unlike the Orr-Sommerfeld equation N-factor method that assumes a parallel mean flow, the PSE method enables disturbance evolution computations in a growing boundary layer. As first suggested by Herbert (1991) and Bertolotti (1992), PSE theory assumes that the dependence of the convective disturbances on downstream development events is negligible and that no rapid streamwise variations occur in the wavelength, growth rate, and mean velocity and disturbance profiles. At present, the disturbance $\Phi = (u, v, w, p)$ in the PSE formulation assumes periodicity in the spanwise direction (uniform spanwise mean flow) and time (temporally uniform) and takes the form

$$\Phi = \sum_{m=-N_z}^{N_z} \sum_{n=-N_t}^{N_t} \hat{\Phi}_{m,n}(x, y) e^{i(\int_{x_o}^{x} \alpha_{m,n} dx + m\beta z - n\omega t)}, \quad (10.18)$$

where N_z and N_t are the total numbers of modes kept in the truncated Fourier series. The convective or streamwise direction has decomposition into a fast oscillatory wave part and a slow varying shape function. Since the disturbance profile $\hat{\Phi}$ is a function of x and y, partial differential equations result and describe the shape function. These equations take the matrix form

$$[L]\hat{\Phi} + [M]\frac{d\hat{\Phi}}{dx} + [N]\frac{d\alpha}{dx} = f. \quad (10.19)$$

Because of the fast variations of the streamwise wavenumber, the second derivatives in the shape function are negligible. By the proper choice of $\alpha_{n,m}$, the above system can be solved by marching in x. For small amplitude disturbances, $f = 0$ while, for finite amplitude disturbances, f, in physical space, stems from the nonlinear terms of the Navier-Stokes equation, or

$$\vec{F} = (\vec{u} \cdot \nabla)\vec{u}. \quad (10.20)$$

After the initial values of $\alpha_{n,m}$ are selected, a sequence of iterations is required during the streamwise marching procedure to satisfy the shape function equations at each streamwise location.

Joslin, Streett & Chang (1992, 1993) and Pruett & Chang (1995) have shown that the PSE solutions agree with direct numerical simulation results for the case of incompressible flat plate boundary layer transition and for compressible transition on a cone.

Haynes & Reed (1996) investigated the nonlinear evolution of stationary crossflow disturbances over a 45-degree swept wing by computing with nonlinear PSE theory and compared the results with the experiments of Reibert, Saric, Carrillo & Chapman (1996). The nonlinear computational results agree with the experiments in that the stationary disturbances reach a saturation state, also confirmed with DNS by Joslin & Streett (1994) and Joslin (1995a), whereas the linear N-factor type results suggest that the disturbances continue to grow, Hence, the linear predictions inadequately predict the behavior of the disturbances.

Finally, theoretical and computational tools are being developed to predict a rich variety of instabilities that could be growing along the attachment line of a swept wing. Lin & Malik (1994, 1995, 1996) describe a two-dimensional eigenvalue method that predicts symmetric and asymmetric disturbances about incompressible and compressible attachment line flows that are growing along the attachment line. Such methodologies could provide important parametric information for the design of NLF and LFC swept wings. However, the costly eigenvalue approach has been superseded by an exact ordinary differential equation theory by Theofilis (in press). This new theory leads to identical results as those due to DNS and eigenvalue approaches.

10.7.5 Transition prediction coupled to turbulence modeling

In this final subsection, a relatively recent concept will be outlined that involves coupling transition prediction methodology with a two-equation turbulence model approach. Warren & Hassan (1996, 1997) posed the transition prediction problem within a nonlinear system of equations involving the kinetic energy and enstrophy. The exact governing equations provided a link between the laminar boundary layer flow instabilities, the nonlinear transitional flow state, and the fully turbulent flow fluctuations. By assuming the breakdown is initiated by a disturbance with a frequency reminiscent of the dominate growing instability, the simulations are initiated. The influence of free stream turbulence and surface roughness on the transition location were accounted for by a relationship between turbulence level and roughness height with initial

amplitude of the disturbance. The initial comparisons with flat plate, swept flat plate, and infinite swept wing wind tunnel experiments suggests a good correlation between the computations and experiments for a variety of free stream turbulence levels and surface conditions.

Then, building on the intermittency accomplishments of Dhawan & Narasimha (1958), the transitional flow region was modeled with an intermittency function Γ. The function ranges from $\Gamma = 0$ for laminar flow to $\Gamma = 1$ for fully developed turbulent flow. In between, the flow is intermittent and one function describing this process is

$$\Gamma = 1 - e^{-0.412\epsilon^2}, \tag{10.21}$$

where
$$\epsilon = max(x - x_t, 0)/\lambda,$$

x_t is the location where turbulent spots begin to form and λ is the extent of the transition region.

The viscosity can then be modeled using the following relationship between laminar and equivalent turbulent viscosity or

$$\mu = \mu_l + \Gamma\mu_t. \tag{10.22}$$

Warren & Hassan (1996) extended this model to include additional information on the fluctuation level where they introduce an expression for μ given by

$$\mu = \mu_l + [(1 - \Gamma)\mu_{lt} + \Gamma\mu_t], \tag{10.23}$$

where μ_{lt} is the contribution of the laminar fluctuations. Originally, the expression for μ_{lt} was determined using correlations from linear stability theory. Warren & Hassan (1997) extended this model so that μ_{lt} can be solved as part of the solution when the onset of transition is known (i.e., minimum skin friction, or some user-specified criteria). Such a link then removes the need for linear stability theory analysis altogether. As a result the individual instability modes do not directly play a role in the transition process. Further, the governing equations for the turbulent flow are not closed and stress-strain law modeling assumptions are required to close the system.

Finally, other researchers, such as Liou & Shih (1997), have been approaching the transition prediction and modeling process by a similar intermittency process. A significant difference results from the direct inclusion of free stream turbulence magnitudes and our understanding of the development of turbulent spots in flat plate turbulent boundary layers.

10.8 Exercises

By now the reader should be extremely familiar with the linear processes associated with hydrodynamic instability theory. Because this chapter is certainly more complicated and is a culmination of the amplification of linear modes, modal interactions, and subsequent breakdown, the exercises will primarily focus on essay types of assignments requiring you to think in a cause and effect manner. This cause and effect hypothesizing is consistent with what is required daily from the research engineer.

1. Outline all of the potential external factors that may impact or induce instabilities. Characterize which factors induce Tollmien-Schlichting waves versus other modes such as crossflow vortex modes.
2. Describe the similarities and differences between the Görtler, Dean and Taylor vortices.
3. Describe the similarities and differences between the Görtler and crossflow breakdown processes.
4. Generate a main routine to loop through frequency and Reynolds numbers so that you can make e^N calculations. For $Re_{\delta*} = 2240$, calculate the range of N values for each frequency over the neutral curve. What N-value do to you use to assess whether transition will occur?

Chapter 11

Direct numerical simulation

11.1 Introduction

Throughout this text various assumptions have been employed to simplify this mathematical system in order to extract theoretical insights into the physics of the problems or applications of interest. In this chapter, we return to the complete mathematical system to seek solutions without (or with minimal) a priori assumptions about the flow physics of the problem. The term direct numerical simulation (DNS) will be used hereafter to denote direct solutions of the Navier-Stokes equations; sometimes, DNS refers to Direct Navier-Stokes solutions. Inherently, high order methods for spatial and temporal discretization of the equations are employed and the grids and time stepping are such that all relevant scales of the flows of interest are sufficiently and accurately resolved. For linear hydrodynamic instability there might be one or a few scales of interest whereas, for fully turbulent flows, there are many orders of magnitude difference in the scales. In this chapter, we review aspects of the equations relative to the problem of hydrodynamic stability and provide some solution methodologies.

11.2 Governing equations

The Navier-Stokes equations can be written with the primitive variables using velocity and pressure, velocity and vorticity, streamfunctions and vorticity, or streamfunctions. For incompressible two-dimensional flows, the primitive variable formulation leads to

$$u_t + uu_x + vu_y = -p_x + Re^{-1}\nabla^2 u, \qquad (11.1)$$

$$v_t + uv_x + vv_y = -p_y + Re^{-1}\nabla^2 v, \qquad (11.2)$$

and

$$u_x + v_y = 0. \tag{11.3}$$

Here, the velocity vector is $\vec{u} = (u, v)$ and the scalar pressure is p in the Cartesian coordinate system $\vec{x} = (x, y)$. Unlike the compressible equations, the pressure in the above equations implicitly adjusts itself to satisfy the divergence free condition associated with incompressible flow. Hence, no initial conditions or boundary conditions are required for the pressure.

Vorticity is denoted as the curl of the velocity, or $\vec{\Omega} = \{\xi, \omega, \zeta\} = \nabla \times \vec{u}$. For two-dimensional flows, only the spanwise or z component of vorticity exists and is defined as $\zeta = v_x - u_y$. The dynamic equations governing vorticity can then be found by taking the curl of the momentum equations and thus

$$\zeta_t + u\zeta_x + v\zeta_y = Re^{-1}\nabla^2\zeta. \tag{11.4}$$

Note that the pressure is now absent from the dynamic equation of interest and that boundary conditions on vorticity must now be applied. However, there are no physical boundary conditions for vorticity. Such boundary conditions must be approximated.

For the streamfunction-vorticity formulation, a relationship between streamfunction (ψ) and velocity (u, v) and vorticity (ζ) is introduced. This is

$$u = \psi_y, \quad v = -\psi_x, \quad \text{and} \quad -\zeta = \nabla^2\psi. \tag{11.5}$$

This definition of streamfunction inherently satisfies conservation of mass in the continuity equation (11.3). The velocity-streamfunction relationships (11.5) are substituted into equation (11.4), leading to the streamfunction-vorticity equation or

$$\zeta_t + \psi_y\zeta_x - \psi_x\zeta_y = Re^{-1}\nabla^2\zeta. \tag{11.6}$$

The boundary conditions for the streamfunction become homogeneous Dirichlet and Neumann conditions.

Finally, by substituting the streamfunction relationship with vorticity into equation (11.6), the streamfunction formulation of the Navier-Stokes equations is obtained, or

$$\nabla^2\psi_t + \psi_y\nabla^2\psi_x - \psi_x\nabla^2\psi_y = Re^{-1}\nabla^2(\nabla^2\psi), \tag{11.7}$$

and two second order momentum equations become one fourth order equation with one dependent variable, ψ.

Each of the four formulations have distinct advantages and disadvantages when it comes to numerically solving the respective systems of equations.

Most often, either the primitive variables or the velocity-vorticity formulation
is used to represent conservation of mass and momentum for hydrodynamic
stability computations. For the remainder of this chapter, the discussion of
direct numerical simulation will focus on solutions of the primitive variable
formulation or (11.1) to (11.3).

In applications of hydrodynamic stability, it is customary to first obtain a
time independent (mean or basic state) solution and then compute the evolution of perturbations to that basic flow state. The final instantaneous solutions
are then a composite of the basic mean and disturbance solutions. The instantaneous velocities and pressure are given by

$$\{u, v\}(x, y, t) = \{U, V\}(x, y) + \{\tilde{u}, \tilde{v}\}(x, y, t)$$
$$p(x, y, t) = P(x, y) + \tilde{p}(x, y, t). \tag{11.8}$$

After substituting the instantaneous values (11.8) into the Navier-Stokes equations (11.1) to (11.3) and subtracting the mean values, the conservation of mass
and momentum equations for the disturbances result. These are

$$\tilde{u}_t + (U + \tilde{u})\tilde{u}_x + (V + \tilde{v})\tilde{u}_y + \tilde{u}U_x + \tilde{v}U_y = -\tilde{p}_x + Re^{-1}\nabla^2\tilde{u}, \tag{11.9}$$
$$\tilde{v}_t + (U + \tilde{u})\tilde{v}_x + (V + \tilde{v})\tilde{v}_y + \tilde{u}V_x + \tilde{v}V_y = -\tilde{p}_y + Re^{-1}\nabla^2\tilde{v}, \tag{11.10}$$

and

$$\tilde{u}_x + \tilde{v}_y = 0. \tag{11.11}$$

This disturbance formulation has a distinct numerical advantage over directly
solving equations (11.1) to (11.3) for the instantaneous quantities. Because the
basic state is typically many orders of magnitude larger than the disturbance
values (initially at least), round-off errors can be avoided by solving for the
basic state and disturbance solutions separately. Hereafter the tilde overbar will
be discarded from the disturbance quantities.

Before we proceed to solution methodologies for the Navier-Stokes equations and for completeness sake a summary of some comments by Zang (1991)
will be presented here relative to the form of the Navier-Stokes equations used
in numerical simulations. Zang discussed potential errors with the different
forms of the Navier-Stokes equations. While equations (11.1) to (11.3) are referred to as the convective form, additional forms include skew symmetric,
rotational, and divergence. The skew symmetric form is given by

$$u_t + \frac{1}{2}[(U + u)u_x + (V + v)u_y + uU_x + vU_y]$$
$$+ \frac{1}{2}[(2Uu + uu)_x + (Uv + Vu + uv)_y]$$
$$= -p_x + Re^{-1}\nabla^2u, \tag{11.12}$$

and

$$v_t + \frac{1}{2}[(U + u)v_x + (V + v)v_y + uV_x + vV_y]$$
$$+ \frac{1}{2}[(Uv + Vu + uv)_x + (2Vv + vv)_y]$$
$$= -p_y + Re^{-1}\nabla^2 v. \tag{11.13}$$

The rotational form of the Navier-Stokes equations is

$$u_t - v\zeta = -p_x + Re^{-1}\nabla^2 u, \tag{11.14}$$

and

$$v_t + u\zeta = -p_y + Re^{-1}\nabla^2 v, \tag{11.15}$$

where p is the total pressure in the rotational equations. Finally, the divergence form of the equations is

$$u_t + [(2Uu + uu)_x + (Vu + Uv + uv)_y] = -p_x + Re^{-1}\nabla^2 u, \tag{11.16}$$

and

$$v_t + [(Vu + Uv + uv)_x + (2Vv + vv)_y] = -p_y + Re^{-1}\nabla^2 v. \tag{11.17}$$

Zang (1991) concluded from his work, using a series of detailed numerical simulations, that the rotational form produces more aliasing errors which, in turn, contaminate the solutions compared with the convective, skew symmetric or the divergence form of the equations. However, all forms converge to the same solution as the grids are refined. Hence, caution must be exercised when using the rotational form of the Navier-Stokes equations with relatively coarse grids.

In the remaining sections of this chapter, the Navier-Stokes equations for the disturbances will be used to describe two fundamentally different solution approaches for hydrodynamic stability applications. Although the convective form of the equations (11.9) to (11.11) is used hereafter, all forms of the equations are quite similar and, in practice, it is quite easy to code all forms by employing a simple switching method with IF-THEN loops. For example, NFORM is an integer which the user prescribes at the beginning of a computation, whereby

IF NFORM $= 1$, THEN use convective form;
IF NFORM $= 2$, THEN use divergence form;
                        ELSE, use skew symmetric form.

11.3 Temporal DNS formulation

The temporal formulation for DNS parallels and complements the discussions in Chapters 2 and 3. A temporal formulation implies that the disturbances amplify or decay in time yielding complex frequencies. The spatial representation of disturbances are real and periodic. For most hydrodynamic stability applications of relevance, one or more spatial directions are non homogeneous. If one direction is non homogeneous, the temporal formulation can effectively and efficiently be used to compute the instability evolution. For two or three directions of non homogeneity, the temporal approach will give trends of behavior but with some quantitative deficiency because some important spatial features of the flow would be neglected. If quantitative accuracy is required, the spatial formulation may be required and is described in the next section. The temporal formulation may be well suited to the study of absolute instabilities where the disturbance amplifies in time and is fixed in space. In addition, if the spatial changes are of minor importance, then the temporal approach may yield results quantitatively close to the true physical results.

Consider here the case with only one non homogeneous direction. For example, channel flow between parallel plates or pipe flow are good examples. Let the non homogeneous direction be the y-coordinate; in this direction a variety of discretization approaches are available. Spectral collocation, finite difference, and compact difference methods have all been successfully applied to hydrodynamic stability. In the homogeneous direction (x or z coordinates), it is customary to use Fourier series for approximation of the flow because of the efficiency of the fast Fourier transform methods. Second order Adams-Bashforth with implicit Crank-Nicolson for the y diffusion terms or a low storage Runge-Kutta approach have all been used for time advancement. For the temporal formulation, these discretization approaches can reduce to the system for each spatial wavenumber, $k\alpha$, given by

$$\mathbf{L}(\underline{u}^{n+1}, p^{n+1})|_k = F(\underline{u}^n, p^n)|_k, \qquad (11.18)$$

where L and F are matrix operators and n are known solutions at current time $n \cdot t$ and $n + 1$ are desired (to be computed) solutions at the next time step. The system can be solved with either a direct or an iterative approach.

To visualize what is occurring with this temporal system, imagine a computational grid that has one or two temporal periods of the dominant instability mode and a grid in the y-direction. The x coordinate would be the streamwise direction. The Fourier series in the x coordinate suggests that this computational box moves downstream with time advancement. Effectively, the periodicity of the Fourier series means that the outflow in x winds back to become new inflow conditions. Hence, after the initial conditions are applied at the

beginning of the simulation, the system becomes a self sustaining system, which has only boundary conditions to enforce.

Because the temporal formulation has been used in the study of both hydrodynamic stability and turbulence since the 1970's, the reader can easily find additional solution strategies in the literature. Refer to Canuto, Hussaini, Quarteroni & Zang (1988), among others, for numerous references using the temporal formulation.

11.4 Spatial DNS formulation

The spatial formulation for DNS parallels and complements the discussions in Chapters 4 and 5. A spatial formulation implies that the disturbances amplify or decay in space and require complex wavenumbers for description. This formulation can be done for both two or three-dimensional directions. As such, truly non homogeneous features of the flow, such as non parallel effects, are captured in the computation.

However, the simulation of spatially evolving disturbances is available with a cost penalty. For this formulation, a sufficiently refined grid is required for all of the spatial length scales and for all of time. This means that, if the evolution of a disturbance over a length equal to 40 wavelengths is of interest, then the entire 40 wavelengths must be resolved throughout the computation. To defer some of this penalty, two approaches have successfully been applied in hydrodynamic stability. The first involves the use of a short domain (4-5 wavelengths) to compute the first few periods of disturbance evolution. Then, additional regions of the grid are gradually added in the downstream direction as the disturbance travels further in this direction. This step saves considerable computational cost, but care must be taken so that the disturbance does not reach the outflow of the computational domain prior to adding additional grid in the downstream direction. The second approach (as described by Huai, Joslin & Piomelli, 1999) involves saving all temporal information near the end of one shorter computational domain and using this information for the forcing of a second computational domain positioned downstream of the first. This is schematically shown in Fig. 11.1. This approach is optimal when the station in the first box, where temporal information is being stored for the second computation, has only a few modes of interest (i.e., there are only a few dominant modes in the frequency spectrum). Otherwise, a huge temporal database must be stored so that all of the energy containing spectrum is continued as the inflow of the second computational box.

Because of the cost penalties associated with the spatial formulation, this approach should be reserved for the situations where the spatial nonhomogenities are important or for the quantitative validation of proposed theoretical

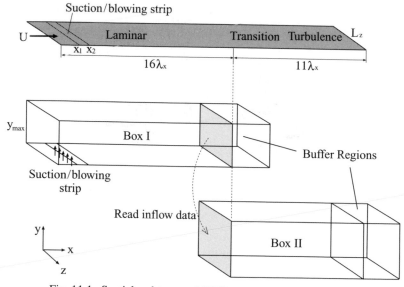

Fig. 11.1. Spatial and temporal DNS computational approaches.

methods. For example, a two-dimensional flat plate boundary layer has two non homogeneous directions and a swept wedge flow has three directions of nonhomogeneity. And, as shown in Chapter 9, the spatial DNS approach was invaluable in validating PSE theory. Additional PSE validation is demonstrated in Section 11.6 below. Because it is beyond the scope of this text to summarize all possible numerical methods of solution, we will focus on a combined use of spectral and high order finite difference techniques to formulate a spatial DNS code for three non homogeneous flow directions. The questions at the end of this chapter will contain some problems which will require the same kinds of procedures as outline here but with different numerical techniques and with the less complex one or two nonhomogeneous directions.

11.4.1 Boundary and initial conditions

Once the basic state or mean flow solution is obtained, a simulation for the disturbance equations can begin at time $t = 0$ with no initial conditions. Then, at time $t = t + \Delta t$, the disturbance(s) can be forced at the inflow using a theoretical solution(s) or with some unsteady wall condition. See Fig. 11.2 for different forcing regions and the outflow buffer domain sketched.

Because all of the applications in this chapter are of a boundary layer type, the boundary conditions that will be used at the wall and in the far field (free

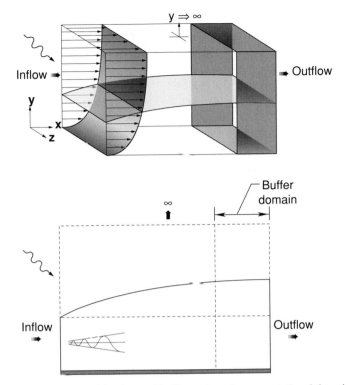

Fig. 11.2. Sketch of forcing and buffer regions for computational domain.

stream) are

$$u, v, w = 0 \quad \text{at} \quad y = 0 \quad \text{and} \quad u, v, w \to 0 \quad \text{as} \quad y \to \infty. \qquad (11.19)$$

Thus, the far field boundary conditions used by the DNS approach are approximate. The mean flow distortion component of a nonlinearly amplifying disturbance should change in the freestream, but DNS cannot accommodate an *a priori* Fourier modal boundary condition treatment as the PSE method of Chapter 9.

Time dependent inflow or wall boundary conditions may be used to generate or force disturbances. Solutions to either the Orr-Sommerfeld or PSE theory equations may be used for inflow forcing. As such, the inflow conditions for the spatial DNS approach appear as

$$\vec{u}_o = \vec{U}_o + \sum_{n=-N_z}^{N_z} \sum_{m=-N_t}^{N_t} A_{m,n}^o \cdot \vec{u}_{m,n}^o(y) e^{i(n\beta z - m\omega t)}, \qquad (11.20)$$

where $\vec{U}_o$ is the inflow basic component; $A^o_{m,n}$ the two and three-dimensional disturbance amplitudes; β is an imposed spanwise wave number; and ω is an imposed disturbance frequency. The terms $\vec{\mathbf{u}}^o_{m,n}$ are complex eigenfunctions found either by solving the Orr-Sommerfeld and Squire equations or obtained from a secondary instability theory (see Herbert, 1983). The eigenfunctions $\vec{\mathbf{u}}^o_{m,n}(y)$ are normalized with respect to the maximum streamwise velocity component such that the initial amplitudes of the induced disturbances are prescribed by $A^o_{m,n}$.

Disturbances can be forcibly imposed into the boundary layer by unsteady suction and blowing with the wall normal velocity component through the wall (harmonic source generators). An equal amount of mass injected by blowing is extracted by suction so that zero net mass is added to the boundary layer. Although the disturbances may be generated by random frequency input, disturbances of interest can be forced with known frequencies. Essentially, this disturbance generator is an alteration to the no slip boundary conditions that are conventionally used for the wall condition in a viscous flow problem. An example of a common boundary condition is

$$v(x, y = 0, t) = A \cdot \sin^2(\omega \cdot t) \sin(\pi x / \Delta x) \quad x_1 < x < x_2, \quad (11.21)$$

where ω is the frequency of the disturbance of interest, and $\Delta x = x_2 - x_1$ is a somewhat arbitrarily selected forcing region of the boundary. Typically, $\Delta x = \lambda/5$ is an effective means to initiate Tollmien-Schlichting waves. The half period sine wave for the shape of the forcing is somewhat arbitrary as well.

The buffer domain technique (see Figs. 11.1 and 11.2) introduced by Streett & Macaraeg (1989) is used for the outflow condition. Essentially, the elliptic equations (11.9) to (11.11) are parabolized in the streamwise direction using an attenuation function that varies smoothly from one at the beginning of the buffer region (end of physical region of interest) to zero at the outflow boundary.

This method is motivated by the recognition that, for incompressible flow, the ellipticity of the Navier-Stokes equations, and thus their potential for upstream feedback, comes from two sources, namely the viscous terms and the pressure field. Examination of earlier unsuccessful attempts at spatial simulations indicated that upstream influence occurred through the interaction of these two mechanisms; strong local velocity perturbations would interact with the condition imposed at the outflow boundary, producing a pressure pulse that was immediately felt everywhere in the domain, especially at the inflow boundary. Therefore both mechanisms for ellipticity have to be treated. To deal

with the first source of upstream influence, the streamwise viscous terms are smoothly reduced to zero by multiplying by an appropriate attenuation function in a buffer region, that is appended to the end of the computational domain of interest. The viscous terms are unmodified in the domain of interest. To reduce the effect of pressure field ellipticity to acceptable levels, the source term of the pressure Poisson equation is multiplied by the attenuation function in the buffer domain. This is akin to the introduction of an artificial compressibility in that region and locally decouples the pressure solution from the velocity computation in the time splitting algorithm. Thus, in effect the boundary layer equations govern the solution at outflow that are parabolic and do not require an outflow condition. Finally, the advection terms are linearized about the imposed mean or base flow solution in order that the effective advection velocity that governs the direction of disturbance propagation, is strictly positive at outflow even in the presence of large disturbances.

The attenuation function can be defined as

$$s_j = \frac{1}{2}\left[1 + \tanh\left\{4\left(1 - 2\frac{(j - N_b)}{(N_x - N_b)}\right)\right\}\right], \qquad (11.22)$$

where N_b marks the beginning of the buffer domain and N_x marks the outflow boundary location. As will be shown later, a buffer domain length of about three streamwise wavelengths is adequate to provide a smooth enough attenuation function to avoid upstream influence for most practical problems.

Alternatively, a moving downstream boundary may be employed to prevent wave reflections. For this boundary condition treatment, the domain is forever being increased in the downstream direction until sufficient results are obtained in order that the computations may be discontinued.

11.4.2 Time marching methods

For time marching, a time splitting procedure can be used with implicit Crank-Nicolson differencing for normal diffusion terms along with either an explicit Adams-Bashforth second order method or an explicit Runge-Kutta type of method for the remaining terms. Although the Adams-Bashforth approach is easier to code than the Runge-Kutta approach, an order of magnitude more time steps are required to reach the same point in time. This increase in the number of time steps for the Adams-Bashforth approach results from numerical instability of the method if the time step size is too large. Here, a third order three stage Runge-Kutta method (Williamson, 1980) is used for the remaining

terms. The pressure is omitted from the momentum equations for the fractional Runge-Kutta stage, leading to

$$\frac{\underline{u}^* - \underline{u}^m}{\Delta t^m} = C_1^m H^m(\underline{u}) + C_2^m Re^{-1} D^2(\underline{u}^* + \underline{u}^m), \qquad (11.23)$$

where

$$H^m(\underline{u}) = L(\underline{u})^m + C_3^m H^{m-1}(\underline{u}), \qquad (11.24)$$

and the operator is given by

$$L(\underline{u}) = (\underline{U} \cdot \nabla)\underline{u} + (\underline{u} \cdot \nabla)\underline{U} + (\underline{u} \cdot \nabla)\underline{u} - Re^{-1}(\underline{u}_{xx} + \underline{u}_{zz}). \qquad (11.25)$$

Here, $\underline{u}^*$ are disturbance velocities at the intermediate Runge-Kutta stages, $\underline{u}^m$ are velocities at previous Runge-Kutta stages ($m = 1, 2$ or 3), $\underline{u}^o$ are velocities at the previous time step, Δt is the time step size, and D is the wall normal spectral derivative operator. For a full Runge-Kutta stage, the momentum equations with the pressure are

$$\frac{\underline{u}^{m+1} - \underline{u}^m}{\Delta t^m} = C_1^m H^m(\underline{u}) + C_2^m Re^{-1} D^2(\underline{u}^{m+1} + \underline{u}^m) - \nabla \wp^{m+1}. \qquad (11.26)$$

After subtracting (11.23) from (11.26) we have

$$\frac{\underline{u}^{m+1} - \underline{u}^*}{\Delta t^m} = -\nabla \wp^{m+1}. \qquad (11.27)$$

By taking the divergence of (11.27) and imposing zero divergence of the flow field at each Runge-Kutta stage, a pressure equation is obtained or

$$\nabla^2 \wp^{m+1} = \frac{1}{\Delta t^m}(\nabla \cdot \underline{u}^*), \qquad (11.28)$$

which is subject to homogeneous Neumann boundary conditions. This boundary condition is justified in the context of a time splitting scheme as discussed by Streett & Hussaini (1991). The solution procedure is as follows: The intermediate Runge-Kutta velocities ($\underline{u}^*$) are determined by solving equation (11.23). The pressure correction ($\wp^{m+1}$) is found by solving (11.28). Then, the full Runge-Kutta stage velocities ($\underline{u}^{m+1}$) are obtained from (11.27). Upon solving the above system three consecutive times and full time step ($n + 1$) velocities are determined, where $\underline{u}^{n+1} = \underline{u}^{m=3}$. The Runge-Kutta coefficients and time steps given by Williamson (1980) are

$$\begin{pmatrix} C_1^1 & C_2^1 & C_3^1 \\ C_1^2 & C_2^2 & C_3^2 \\ C_1^3 & C_2^3 & C_3^3 \end{pmatrix} = \begin{pmatrix} 1 & 1/2 & 0 \\ 9/4 & 1/2 & -4 \\ 32/15 & 1/2 & -153/32 \end{pmatrix},$$

and

$$\begin{Bmatrix} \Delta t^1 \\ \Delta t^2 \\ \Delta t^3 \end{Bmatrix} = \begin{Bmatrix} 1/3\Delta t \\ 5/12\Delta t \\ 1/4\Delta t \end{Bmatrix}, \tag{11.29}$$

where the sum of the three Runge-Kutta time steps equals the full time step (h_t). For details of the time marching procedure, refer to Joslin, Streett & Chang (1993). The much simplified Adams-Bashforth time marching approach can be used in place of the Runge-Kutta approach, as documented in Joslin, Streett & Chang (1992).

11.4.3 Spatial discretization methods

For discretization in the streamwise direction, fourth to sixth order central and compact differences have been demonstrated in numerous studies to be sufficiently accurate. Here, fourth order central finite differences are used for the pressure equation. At boundary and near boundary nodes, third or fourth order differences can be used. For first and second derivatives in the momentum equations, sixth order compact differences are used. As described by Lele (1992), the difference equations are

$$\frac{1}{3}f'_{i-1} + f'_i + \frac{1}{3}f'_{i+1} = \frac{7}{9\Delta x}(f_{i+1} - f_{i-1}) + \frac{1}{36\Delta x}(f_{i+2} - f_{i-2}), \tag{11.30}$$

and

$$\frac{2}{11}f''_{i-1} + f''_i + \frac{2}{11}f''_{i+1} = \frac{12}{11\Delta x^2}(f_{i+1} - 2f_i + f_{i-1})$$
$$+ \frac{3}{44\Delta x^2}(f_{i+2} - 2f_i + f_{i-2}), \tag{11.31}$$

where Δx is the uniform streamwise step size, and f is an arbitrary function whose derivatives are sought. At boundary and near boundary nodes, explicit fifth order finite differences are used (e.g., Carpenter, Gottlieb & Abarbanel, 1993). The discretization yields a pentadiagonal system for the finite difference scheme and a tridiagonal system for the compact difference scheme, where both can be solved efficiently by LU decomposition with appropriate backward and forward substitutions.

In both the wall-normal (y) and spanwise (z) directions, Chebyshev series are used to approximate the disturbances at Gauss-Lobatto collocation points. A Chebyshev series is used in the wall-normal direction because it provides good resolution in the high gradient regions near the boundaries. Furthermore, the use of as few grid points as possible results in significant computational

cost savings. In particular, the use of the Chebyshev series enables an efficient pressure solver. Because this series and its associated spectral operators
are defined on $[-1, 1]$ and the physical problem of interest has a truncated
domain $[0, y_{max}]$ and $[-z_{max}, z_{max}]$, transformations are employed. Furthermore, stretching functions are used to cluster the grid near both the wall and
the attachment line. Here an algebraic mapping is used, namely

$$y = \frac{y_{max} s_p (1 + \bar{y})}{2 s_p + y_{max} (1 - \bar{y})} \quad \text{or} \quad \bar{y} = \frac{(2 s_p + y_{max}) y - y_{max} s_p}{y_{max} (s_p + y)}, \quad (11.32)$$

where $0 \le y \le y_{max}$ and $-1 \le \bar{y} \le 1$; y_{max} is the wall normal distance from
the wall to the far-field boundary in the truncated domain, and s_p controls the
grid stretching in the wall-normal direction.

The solution is determined on a staggered grid. The intermediate Runge-
Kutta velocities are determined on Gauss-Lobatto points. To avoid the use of
pressure boundary conditions, the pressure is found by solving the Poisson
equation on Gauss points and is then spectrally interpolated onto Gauss-Lobatto
points. Then, the full Runge-Kutta stage velocities are obtained from on Gauss-
Lobatto points with the updated pressure. The above system is solved three
consecutive times to obtain full time step velocities.

To satisfy global mass conservation, an influence matrix method is employed
and is described in some detail by Streett & Hussaini (1991), Danabasoglu,
Biringen & Streett (1990, 1991), and Joslin, Streett & Chang (1992, 1993).
For boundary layer flow, four Poisson-Dirichlet problems are solved for the
discrete mode that correspond to the zero eigenvalue of the system and single
Poisson-Neumann problems are solved for all other modes.

11.4.4 Influence matrix method

An influence matrix method is employed to solve for the pressure. Streett &
Hussaini (1991) used the method for the Taylor Couette problem and later
Danabasoglu, Biringen & Streett (1990) used the method for the two-dimensional channel flow problem. Instead of solving a Poisson-Neumann problem,
two Poisson-Dirichlet problems are solved.

The solution of the following Poisson-Dirichlet problem, which is the pressure like equation, is sought:

$$\nabla^2 \wp = F \quad \text{in} \quad \Gamma, \quad \wp_n = 0 \quad \text{on} \quad \partial \Gamma, \quad (11.33)$$

where Γ is the computational domain, $\partial \Gamma$ is the computational boundary, and
$\wp_n$ indicates a derivative of the pressure-like quantity normal to the boundary,
$\partial \Gamma$. To accomplish this, a sequence of solutions to the following problem is

first determined:

$$\nabla^2 \wp^i = 0 \quad \text{in} \quad \Gamma, \quad \wp^i = \delta_{ij} \quad \text{on} \quad \partial\Gamma \qquad (11.34)$$

for each discrete boundary point, $\underline{x}_j$. The δ_{ij} is the Dirac delta function defined as $\delta_{ij} = 1$ for $i = j$, and $\delta_{ij} = 0$ for $i \neq j$. Upon computing the vector of normal gradients $\wp_n^i$ at all of the boundary points, these vectors are then stored in columns, yielding a matrix that is referred to as the influence matrix, or

$$I_{NF} = [\wp_n^1, \wp_n^2, \ldots, \wp_n^{N_B}], \qquad (11.35)$$

where N_B is the number of boundary points.

The influence matrix, which is dense, is of order $N_B \times N_B$ for two-dimensional problems and of order $N_B \times N_B \times N_z$ for three-dimensional problems and is dependent on the computational mesh only. Since the matrix is dependent on the mesh, it needs to be calculated only once for a given geometry. The memory requirements for the influence matrix for a three-dimensional problem can quickly become overbearing and thereby eliminate the possibility of performing simulations into later stages of transition as a result of such insufficient memory.

The composed influence matrix gives the residuals of $\wp$ as a result of the unit boundary condition influence, or

$$[I_{NF}]\wp = \text{residual.} \qquad (11.36)$$

The value of one boundary condition is temporarily relaxed so that the problem is not overspecified. This is done by setting one column of the influence matrix to zero, except for the boundary point of interest, which is set to unity. The corresponding residual in (11.36) is exactly zeroed.

The Poisson equation with Neumann boundary conditions is equivalent to the following solution of a Poisson problem and a Laplace problem (or Helmholtz problems) with Dirichlet boundary conditions. First, solve

$$\nabla^2 \wp^I = F \quad \text{in} \quad \Gamma, \quad \text{and} \quad \wp^I = 0 \quad \text{on} \quad \partial\Gamma. \qquad (11.37)$$

Again, compute the gradients normal to the boundary, $\wp_n^I$. This gives the influence of the right-hand side, F, on the boundary. Then, solve

$$\nabla^2 \wp^{II} = 0 \quad \text{in} \quad \Gamma \qquad (11.38)$$

subject to the boundary constraint

$$\wp^{II} = I_{NF}^{-1} \cdot \wp_n^I \quad \text{on} \quad \partial\Gamma. \qquad (11.39)$$

The final solution that satisfies the original problem and boundary conditions is $\wp = \wp^I - \wp^{II}$.

Since the gradient or boundary condition at one discrete boundary point was relaxed in the influence matrix formulation, the desired condition ($\wp_n = 0$) may not hold at that boundary point. And, this may result since the discrete compatibility relation may not hold for the pure Neumann problem. In order to regain this boundary condition, the pressure problems (11.37) to (11.39) is resolved, but this time adding a nonzero constant (say 0.01) to the right-hand side of (11.37). A pressure correction ($\bar{\wp}$) results. The composite solution satisfies the boundary conditions at all discrete nodes and then consists of a linear combination of $\wp$ and $\bar{\wp}$. This combination is found by satisfying the following two equations:

$$a_1 \wp_n + a_2 \bar{\wp}_n = 0 \quad \text{on} \quad \partial \Gamma_i \quad \text{and} \quad a_1 + a_2 = 1. \tag{11.40}$$

The final pressure correction ($\wp^{m+1}$) is then given by

$$\wp^{m+1} = a_1 \wp + (1 - a_1)\bar{\wp} \quad \text{with} \quad a_1 = \bar{\wp}_n/(\bar{\wp}_n - \wp_n). \tag{11.41}$$

As a note, the corner points are not included in the discretization and are used in the tangential slip velocity correction only. The pressure at the corners are of minor significance and interpolations are sufficient to compute pressures used for the two-dimensional or zeroth wavenumber mode for three-dimensional problems.

To efficiently solve the resulting Poisson problem, the tensor product method of Lynch, Rice & Thomas (1964) is used in addition to the influence matrix method. The discretized form of the Poisson equation for the pressure is

$$(L_x \otimes I \otimes I + I \otimes L_y \otimes I + I \otimes I \otimes L_z)\wp = R, \tag{11.42}$$

where $\wp$ is the desired pressure solution; R results from the time splitting procedure; I is the identity matrix; L_x is the streamwise directed central finite difference operator; L_y and L_z are the wall-normal-directed and spanwise-directed spectral operators; and $\otimes$ implies a tensor product. By decomposing the operators L_y and L_z into their respective eigenvalues and eigenvectors, we find

$$L_y = Q \Lambda_y Q^{-1} \quad \text{and} \quad L_z = S \Lambda_z S^{-1}, \tag{11.43}$$

where Q and S are the eigenvectors of L_y and L_z, Q^{-1} and S^{-1} are inverse matrices of Q and S, and Λ_y and Λ_z are the eigenvalues of L_y and L_z. The solution procedure reduces to the following sequence of operations to determine the pressure $\wp$:

$$\wp^* = (I \otimes Q^{-1} \otimes S^{-1})R,$$
$$\wp^\dagger = (L_x \otimes I \otimes I + I \otimes \Lambda_y \otimes I + I \otimes I \otimes \Lambda_z)^{-1}\wp^*,$$
$$\wp = (I \otimes Q \otimes S)\wp^\dagger. \tag{11.44}$$

Because the number of grid points in the attachment line direction is typically an order of magnitude larger than the wall-normal and flow acceleration directions, the operator L_x is much larger than both L_y and L_z. Because L_x is large and has a sparse pentadiagonal structure and because Λ_y and Λ_z influence the diagonal only, an LU decomposition is performed for the second stage of equation (11.44) once and forward and backward solvers are performed for each time step of the simulation. The first and third steps to solve for the pressure from equation (11.44) involve matrix multiplications.

To obtain the attachment-line-directed operator L_x, central finite differences are used. To find the wall-normal L_y and flow acceleration L_z operators, the following matrix operations are required:

$$L_y = I_{GL}^G D_y \tilde{D}_y I_G^{GL} \quad \text{and} \quad L_z = I_{GL}^G D_z \tilde{D}_z I_G^{GL}, \tag{11.45}$$

where D_y is a spectral wall-normal derivative operator for the stretched grid, D_z is the spectral derivative operator that is grid-clustered in the spanwise region, and $\tilde{D}_y$ and $\tilde{D}_z$ are the derivative operators with the first and last rows set to 0. The interpolation matrix I_{GL}^G operates on variables at Gauss-Lobatto points and transforms them to Gauss points; the interpolation matrix I_G^{GL} performs the inverse operation. The spectral operators are described in detail by Canuto, Hussaini, Quarteroni & Zang (1988) and Joslin, Streett & Chang (1993).

The operators $\{L_x, L_y, L_z\}$, the eigenvalue matrices $\{\Lambda_y, \Lambda_z\}$, the eigenvector matrices $\{Q, Q^{-1}, S, S^{-1}\}$, and the influence matrix are all mesh-dependent matrices and must be calculated only once.

The above description of a DNS methodology is a rather general but complex code that permits solutions of hydrodynamic instability studies in three-dimensional non-homogeneous directions. Very often one or more of the directions are homogeneous and the solution approach can be simplified. For example, if the spanwise z direction was homogeneous, as is the case for the Blasius boundary layer, then Fourier series can be used to approximate disturbances in that direction. Then, one can essentially solve a set of two-dimensional equations for each mode of the Fourier series. Equation (11.28) simply becomes

$$\nabla^2 p^{m+1}(x, y) - \beta^2 p^{m+1}(x, y) = \frac{1}{h_t^m}(\nabla \cdot \underline{u}^*), \tag{11.46}$$

which is now a two-dimensional equation in Fourier transform space. Upon obtaining a solution, a Fourier transform yields the pressure needed to update the velocity in (11.27).

11.5 Large eddy simulation

Here, the Large Eddy Simulation (LES) methodology is discussed primarily for completeness sake with its relevance to hydrodynamic stability. LES implies that the large scales present in the flow are directly computed on a sufficiently fine grid and the scales smaller than this grid are modeled. Inherent in the approach is the assumed existence of a range of relevant scales and an adequate model for the smaller scales. Although the LES approach is most appropriate for the study of turbulent flows, the method has been used in hydrodynamic stability for the study of the highly nonlinear disturbance region associated with the transition from laminar to turbulent flow. Therefore, the basis of LES will be outlined here and some limited results will be presented in the next section.

While the application of LES to turbulent flows dates back to the 1960s where it was used to study atmospheric turbulence, only recently has this technique been used for the study of transitional flow. Piomelli, Zang, Speziale & Hussaini (1990), Piomelli & Zang (1991) and Germano, Piomelli, Moin & Cabot (1991) computed the transition in temporally developing boundary layer and plane channel flow. Their results indicate that, at the early stages of transition, the eddy viscosity must be inactive to allow the correct growth of the perturbations. The dynamic model (Germano, *et al.*, 1991) achieves this result without the *ad hoc* corrections required by other models; e.g., the Smagorinsky (1963) model.

As with the DNS approach, the present technique begins with the disturbance form of the Navier-Stokes equations (11.9) to (11.11). In LES, the large scale (i.e., grid-resolved) components of the velocity and pressure are calculated and the effects of the small, unresolved scales are modeled. By applying the filtering operation,

$$\bar{f}(\mathbf{x}) = \int_{\Gamma} f(\mathbf{x}')G(\mathbf{x}, \mathbf{x}')\mathrm{d}\mathbf{x}' \qquad (11.47)$$

to (11.9) to (11.11), where G is the filter function and Γ is the entire domain, the governing equations for the large scale velocity and pressure can be obtained:

$$\frac{\partial \bar{u}_i}{\partial t} + \bar{u}_j \frac{\partial \bar{u}_i}{\partial x_j} + U_j \frac{\partial \bar{u}_i}{\partial x_j} + \bar{u}_j \frac{\partial U_i}{\partial x_j} = -\frac{\partial \bar{p}}{\partial x_i} - \frac{\partial \tau_{ij}}{\partial x_j} + Re^{-1} \frac{\partial^2 \bar{u}_i}{\partial x_j \partial x_j}, \quad (11.48)$$

and

$$\frac{\partial u_i}{\partial x_i} = 0, \qquad (11.49)$$

where τ_{ij} is the subgrid scale (SGS) stress tensor given by $\tau_{ij} = u_i \bar{u}_j - \bar{u}_i \bar{u}_j$, which must be modeled.

The modeling of τ_{ij} remains a topic of considerable research for both transitional and turbulent flows. We will proceed no further with our discussion of LES since it goes beyond the scope of this text, but the student should take note of the similarities between the LES equations (11.48) to (11.49) and the DNS equations. As an LES computation uses a finer and finer grid, the term with the τ_{ij} component tends to zero and the computation becomes a DNS approach.

11.6 Applications

In this section some sample applications are explored using the spatial DNS approach described in Section 11.4 and the LES approach described in Section 11.5. However, the mean flow can be obtained using computational fluid dynamics (CFD). Because the first and second derivatives of the mean flow are required for theoretical investigations, significant computational cost results and it becomes more practical to use known analytical mean or basic states. With analytical basic states, the DNS and the theoretical analysis begin with the same mean flows. Here, disturbance evolution in a two-dimensional flat plate boundary layer flow and an attachment line flow are reviewed.

11.6.1 Tollmien-Schlichting wave propagation

By using the Blasius similarity profile to represent the flat plate boundary layer, we can quantify various transitional flow mechanisms of interest from the linear region to the nonlinear breakdown stage and provide a critical comparison of results for the spatial DNS and PSE theory. To date, this comparison offers the most rigorous test of the PSE approach for accuracy and the main focus will be to point out strengths and potential weaknesses of PSE theory as well as the impact of these weaknesses on the overall flow field prediction. To accomplish this goal, three test cases are computed by spatial DNS and then compared to PSE theory: (1) two-dimensional Tollmien-Schlichting wave propagation; (2) subharmonic breakdown; and (3) oblique wave breakdown.

The equations are nondimensionalized with respect to the free stream velocity U_∞, the kinematic viscosity ν, and displacement thickness δ_o^* at the inflow as the length scale. A Reynolds number is then be defined as $Re_{\delta^*} = U_\infty \delta_o^* / \nu$.

A Tollmien-Schlichting disturbance with a root mean squared (rms.) amplitude $A_{1,0}^o = 0.0025$ is introduced into the boundary layer by a forcing at the inflow for the DNS as well as for the PSE calculations. For reference, recall the definition of $A_{m,n}^o$ as given in (11.20). Through nonlinear interactions, all other harmonic waves including the mean flow distortion are generated for both DNS and PSE. Calculations are made with an inflow Reynolds number $Re_{\delta_o^*} = 688.315$ and frequency $F = 86$. To generate resolved benchmark data to test the PSE theory, the spatial DNS was computed on a grid of 2041

uniformly spaced streamwise nodes (60 nodes per disturbance wavelength) and 81 wall-normal collocation points. The outflow boundary is $442\delta_o^*$ from the inflow boundary, and the far-field (or free stream) boundary is $75\delta_o^*$ from the wall. The DNS parameters were chosen based on convergence studies by Joslin, Streett & Chang (1992). For the time marching scheme, the disturbance period is divided into 320 time steps. For the PSE computational approach, several numerical experiments have been performed by varying the grid, far-field boundary location, and the number of Fourier modes. These numerical experiments led to the choice of 100 wall-normal grid points, five frequency modes of series (11.20) ($N_t = 6$), and a far-field boundary located $58\delta_o^*$ from the wall.

Figure 11.3 shows the maximum streamwise amplitudes for the mean flow distortion u_o, fundamental wave u_1, and first harmonic u_2 predicted by PSE theory and compared to the DNS results with the downstream distance. Both the fundamental waves ($F = 1$) and the first harmonics ($F = 2$) are in good quantitative agreement throughout the initial linear region and the later weakly nonlinear region. The mean flow distortion components ($F = 0$) are in good agreement throughout the initial linear region. Later, however, a discrepancy begins to occur downstream at an apparent "notch" in the results at $Re_{\delta*} = 1400$.

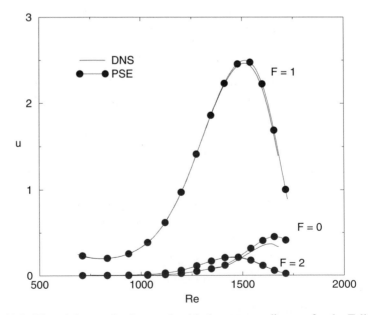

Fig. 11.3. Plot of the amplitude growth with downstream distance for the Tollmien-Schlichting mode ($F = 1$), the first harmonic ($F = 2$), and the mean flow distortion ($F = 0$).

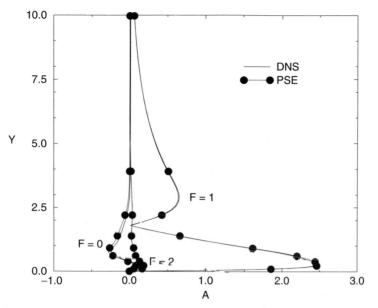

Fig. 11.4. Streamwise velocity profile for the Tollmien-Schlichting mode ($F = 1$), the first harmonic ($F = 2$), and the mean flow distortion ($F = 0$) at $Re_{\delta*} = 1519$.

At the local streamwise location $Re_{\delta*} = 1519$, Fig. 11.4 shows comparisons of the streamwise velocity component. The fundamental (Tollmien-Schlichting) wave and harmonics are in good quantitative agreement, even in regions of high gradients. A comparison of the streamwise velocity (u_o) profiles illustrates a comparable difference. The discrepancy in the mean flow distortion results identified in Fig. 11.3 arises from the change of profile contributions. This discrepancy is due to the homogeneous Neumann boundary conditions used in the far field for the mean flow distortion equations in PSE theory. As in the traditional boundary layer equations approach, this boundary condition leads to a nonzero, wall-normal mean flow velocity component in the far field, as discussed in some detail in Chapter 9.

In this first test problem of Tollmien-Schlichting wave propagation, the results from DNS and PSE theory agree very well for the fundamental and harmonic waves. However, a discrepancy exists in the mean flow distortion component. This discrepancy is a result of the difference in the treatment of the far-field boundary condition of the two approaches.

11.6.2 Subharmonic breakdown

A well understood breakdown scenario in an incompressible boundary layer on a flat plate begins with a predominantly two-dimensional disturbances that

emerges downstream into aligned and staggered three-dimensional distinct vortex structures through spanwise vortex stretching and tilting or some indistinct, non-unique combination of vorticities in the later stages. These vortex patterns are referred to as fundamental, subharmonic, and combination resonant modes, respectively, and may be described by secondary instability theory and PSE theory (Chapter 9). For the present study, the subharmonic mode of secondary instability breakdown will be computed and the results compared with the experiments of Kachanov & Levchenko (1984).

For spatial DNS, computations are performed on a grid of 1021 uniformly spaced streamwise nodes, 81 wall-normal collocation points, and five symmetric-spanwise nodes. In the streamwise direction, the outflow boundary is $442\delta_o^*$ from the inflow boundary, the far-field boundary is $75\delta_o^*$ from the wall, and the spanwise boundary consists of a length equal to one half of the spanwise wavelength, or $\lambda_z/2 = \pi/\beta$. Note that the spanwise computational length would be λ_z for the general, non symmetric computation. For the time marching scheme, the disturbance period is divided into 320 time steps and time is advanced using a three-stage Runge-Kutta method. For the PSE computational approach, 100 wall-normal grid points are used; seven frequency modes and three spanwise modes from series (9.42) are used, and the far-field boundary is $58\delta_o^*$ from the wall.

The prescribed primary and subharmonic disturbances are obtained at the Reynolds number $Re_{\delta^*} = 732.711$ and the primary frequency $F = 124$; values that correspond to the experiments. The primary wave has an inflow rms amplitude of $A_{2,0}^o = 0.0048$. The subharmonic mode has an inflow rms amplitude of $A_{1,1}^o = 0.145 \times 10^{-4}$ and corresponds to a mode with spanwise wave number $\beta = 0.2418$.

Figure 11.5 compares the maximum amplitudes predicted by PSE theory with the results from DNS. For this test case, note the extremely good quantitative agreement between PSE theory and DNS for the growth rates of the fundamental and the dominant harmonic modes. Even the mean flow distortion components are in good agreement. The DNS profiles are compared with the experiments in Fig. 11.6 at the local downstream Reynolds number $Re_{\delta^*} = 1049$. For this test case, it can be seen that DNS results agree with both the PSE predictions and the experiments.

11.6.3 Oblique wave breakdown

The final test case that uses both DNS and PSE theory is that of oblique wave breakdown. Oblique wave breakdown is due to the nonlinear interactions of a pair of oblique waves. Because of this nonlinearity, no adequate formal theory is available to explain the breakdown process. However, similar mechanisms

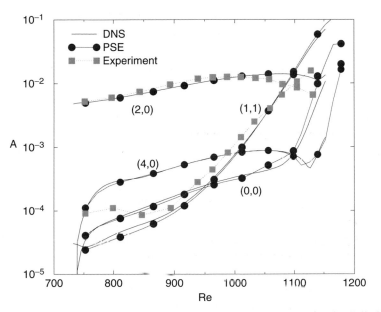

Fig. 11.5. Plot of the amplitude growth with downstream distance for the Tollmien-Schlichting wave (2,0), subharmonic (1,1), first harmonic (4,0), and mean flow distortion (0,0).

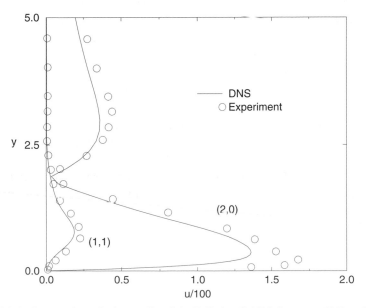

Fig. 11.6. Streamwise velocity profile of the Tollmien-Schlichting wave (2,0) and subharmonic (1,1) at $Re_{\delta*} = 1049$.

have bcen studied by Hall & Smith (1991) by use of asymptotic methods. Hall and Smith discussed the vortex wave interactions within a large wave number and Reynolds number limit. To quantify the mechanisms of interest in the finite Reynolds number range, DNS and possibly PSE theory are available to study the wave interactions.

Because this alternative route to or mechanism of nonlinear transition, limited research has been done for oblique wave breakdown. It is worth citing a few of the interesting papers on this topic that are available. Schmid & Henningson (1992a) studied bypass transition by introducing a pair of large amplitude oblique waves into channel flow. The evolution of disturbances was computed with temporal DNS. They found that the development of the oblique waves was dominated by a preferred spreading of the energy spectra into low streamwise wave numbers, and this led to the rapid development of streamwise elongated structures. Schmid & Henningson (1992b) also investigated small amplitude wave pairs over a variety of parameters. They suggested that the mechanism of energy transfer is primarily linear.

For this example problem, the profiles for the oblique wave pair are obtained from linear stability theory for the Reynolds number $Re_{\delta_o^*} = 900$, frequency $\omega = 0.0774$, and spanwise wave numbers $\beta = \pm 0.2$. Spatial DNS computations are performed on a grid of 901 uniformly spaced streamwise nodes, 61 wall-normal collocation points, and 10 symmetric-spanwise modes. In the streamwise direction, the outflow boundary is $465\delta_o^*$ from the inflow boundary. The far-field, or free stream boundary, is $75\delta_o^*$ from the wall, and the spanwise boundary consists of a length equal to one half of the spanwise wavelength, or $\lambda_z/2 = \pi/\beta$. For the time marching scheme, the disturbance period is divided into 320 time steps. For the PSE computational approach, 100 wall normal grid points are used, seven frequency modes and seven spanwise modes of series (9.42) are used and the far-field boundary is $58\delta_o^*$ from the wall.

The input modes are represented by (11.20) that are truncated to four terms. The disturbance forcing consists of modes $(1, 1)$ and $(1, -1)$, or (ω, β) and $(\omega, -\beta)$, and their complex conjugates $(-1, 1)$ and $(-1, -1)$. Theoretically, if these modes self interact initially, then only certain higher modes are likely to be excited (supplied energy). These higher modes are: $(0,0)$, $(0,2)$, $(2,0)$, and $(2,2)$, etc.

The oblique waves each have the small amplitude $A_{1,1}^o = 0.001$. In Fig. 11.7, the primary disturbance $(1,1)$ and the higher modes that were predicted by PSE theory are compared to the DNS results. The comparison shows that the modes are in quantitative agreement. Of the modes that were likely to be excited, all received energy initially. The streamwise vorticity component $(0,2)$ grows rapidly because of the self interaction of the oblique wave pair. All

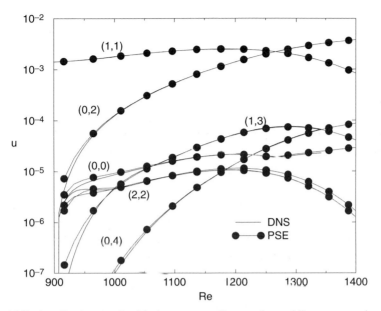

Fig. 11.7. Amplitude growth with downstream distance from oblique wave pair with initial amplitudes of $A_{1,1} = 0.001$.

other modes grow more slowly downstream than the streamwise vortex, and these other modes contain less energy by orders of magnitude. As a result of the rapid growth of the vortex mode (0,2), the oblique waves interact with the vortex and this leads to an amplified harmonic (1,3). This (1,3) mode gains sufficient energy to overtake the other initially excited modes but is insufficient to overtake the oblique waves. As shown in Fig. 11.7, the vortex modes self interact to supply energy to the (0,4) mode that has roughly the same growth rate as the (0,2) mode. Although the computations were discontinued, the disturbances will eventually decay and will not lead to transition because the primary oblique waves decay after they pass the upper branch of the neutral curve, and all other modes are decaying or becoming neutrally stable.

11.6.4 Attachment line flow

On a swept wing, many instability mechanisms exist that can lead to catastrophic breakdown of laminar to turbulent flow. Along the leading edge, Tollmien-Schlichting waves, stationary or traveling crossflow vortices, Taylor-Görtler vortices, or combinations of these modes are among the many mechanisms that can lead to such breakdown. In this section we only consider instabilities in the attachment line region.

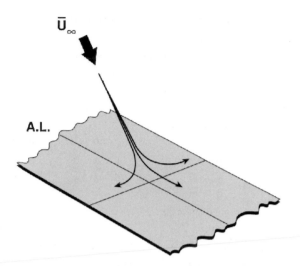

Fig. 11.8. Sketch of attachment line flow.

Figure 11.8 shows a sketch of the three-dimensional flow field representative of the attachment line region. The freestream flow approaches the leading edge of the wing and is diverted above and below the wing, thus forming an attachment line in the leading edge region. The exact location of the attachment line varies with geometry and angle of attack of the wing. When the wing is swept with respect to the incoming flow, a boundary layer flow forms along the attachment line, flowing from the root of the wing near the fuselage toward the wing tip. The stability or instability of this attachment line boundary layer flow is the topic problem for this section.

Contamination at the leading edge results from turbulence at a fuselage and wing juncture that travels out over the wing and contaminates otherwise laminar flow on the wing. If the Reynolds number of the attachment line boundary layer is greater than some critical value, then this contamination inevitably leads to turbulent flow over the complete wing. This phenomenon has been demonstrated by Pfenninger (1965), Maddalon, Collier, Montoya & Putnam (1990), and others. To correct this problem, Gaster (1965c) placed a bump on the leading edge to prevent the turbulent attachment line boundary layer from sweeping over the entire wing. This bump had to be shaped to create a fresh stagnation point without generating a detrimental adverse pressure gradient. Outboard of the bump, a new laminar boundary layer forms. With this fresh laminar boundary layer, we can study the stability of the flow.

For small amplitude disturbances introduced into the attachment line boundary layer flow, experimental results and linear stability theory indicate that

these disturbances begin to amplify at a momentum thickness Reynolds number of approximately 230 to 245.

By neglecting surface curvature, the governing flow simplifies to a similarity solution of the Navier-Stokes equations and is commonly referred to as swept Hiemenz flow. A Cartesian coordinate system $\underline{x} = (x, y, z)$ is used in which x is aligned with the attachment line, y is wall-normal, and z corresponds to the direction of flow acceleration away from the attachment line. The fluid comes obliquely down toward the wall and then turns away from the attachment line into the $\pm z$ directions to form a boundary layer. In the x direction, the flow is uniform. In the absence of sweep, U_o is equal to 0 and the flow reduces to the two-dimensional stagnation flow first described by Hiemenz (1911). A length scale (factor of the boundary layer thickness) is defined in the $y-z$ plane as $\delta = \sqrt{\nu L / W_o}$, a Reynolds number, $Re = U_o \delta / \nu = 2.475 Re_\theta$, and a transpiration constant, $\kappa = V_o \sqrt{L/\nu W_o}$, where $\kappa = 0$ for the zero suction case; U_o, V_o, W_o are velocity scales, and L is the length scale in the flow acceleration direction z. If the attachment line is assumed to be infinitely long, the velocities become functions of z and y only, and the similarity solution can be found.

The swept Hiemenz formulation was originally described by Hall, Malik & Poll (1984) where a linear stability analysis of the flow was performed. The respective velocities and pressure for swept Hiemenz flow are $\{u, v, w, p\}$, and the governing equations are given by

$$\frac{\partial U}{\partial X} + \frac{\partial V}{\partial Y} + \frac{\partial W}{\partial Z} = 0, \tag{11.50}$$

$$U\frac{\partial U}{\partial X} + V\frac{\partial U}{\partial Y} + W\frac{\partial U}{\partial Z}$$
$$= -\frac{\partial P}{\partial X} + \frac{1}{Re}\left[\frac{\partial^2 U}{\partial X^2} + \frac{\partial^2 U}{\partial Y^2} + \frac{\partial^2 U}{\partial Z^2}\right], \tag{11.51}$$

$$U\frac{\partial V}{\partial X} + V\frac{\partial V}{\partial Y} + W\frac{\partial V}{\partial Z}$$
$$= -\frac{\partial P}{\partial Y} + \frac{1}{Re}\left[\frac{\partial^2 V}{\partial X^2} + \frac{\partial^2 V}{\partial Y^2} + \frac{\partial^2 V}{\partial Z^2}\right], \tag{11.52}$$

and

$$U\frac{\partial W}{\partial X} + V\frac{\partial W}{\partial Y} + W\frac{\partial W}{\partial Z}$$
$$= -\frac{\partial P}{\partial Z} + \frac{1}{Re}\left[\frac{\partial^2 W}{\partial X^2} + \frac{\partial^2 W}{\partial Y^2} + \frac{\partial^2 W}{\partial Z^2}\right], \tag{11.53}$$

where the equations are nondimensionalized with respect to the attachment line velocity U_o, length scale δ, and kinematic viscosity ν.

A mean or steady solution of the Navier-Stokes equations is sought that obeys the following conditions. At the wall,

$$u = w = 0 \quad v = V_o, \quad \text{at} \quad y = 0, \tag{11.54}$$

and sufficiently far away from the wall,

$$u \to U_o, \quad w \to W_o \frac{z}{L} \quad \text{as} \quad y \to \infty. \tag{11.55}$$

The velocity field for this similarity solution is

$$U(Y) = \hat{u}(Y),$$

$$V(Y) = \frac{1}{Re}\hat{v}(Y),$$

$$W(Y, Z) = \frac{Z}{Re}\hat{w}(Y). \tag{11.56}$$

With the nondimensional velocities (11.56) in the Z momentum equation (11.53) we have

$$\frac{Z}{Re^2}\hat{v}\frac{d\hat{w}}{dY} + \frac{Z}{Re^2}\hat{w}^2 = -\frac{\partial P}{\partial Z} + \frac{Z}{Re^2}\frac{d^2\hat{w}}{dY^2}. \tag{11.57}$$

As $Y \to \infty$, the Z momentum equation, (11.57), reduces to

$$\frac{Z}{Re^2} = -\frac{\partial P}{\partial Z}, \tag{11.58}$$

with solution

$$P = P_o - \frac{1}{2}\frac{Z^2}{Re^2}, \tag{11.59}$$

where P_o is the constant pressure at the attachment line.

Substitute the velocity from (11.56) and the pressure from (11.59) into the Navier-Stokes equations (11.50) to (11.52). Then, after substituting the continuity equation into the momentum equations and subtracting the Y and Z momentum equations, the following system of ordinary differential equations for $\hat{u}$, $\hat{v}$, $\hat{w}$ results and is

$$\hat{w} + \frac{d\hat{v}}{dY} = 0, \tag{11.60}$$

$$\frac{d^2\hat{u}}{dY^2} - \hat{v}\frac{d\hat{u}}{dY} = 0, \tag{11.61}$$

and

$$\frac{d^3\hat{v}}{dY^3} + \left(\frac{d\hat{v}}{dY}\right)^2 - \hat{v}\frac{d^2\hat{v}}{dY^2} - 1 = 0, \tag{11.62}$$

subject to the boundary conditions given by

$$\frac{d\hat{v}}{dY} = 0, \quad \hat{v} = \kappa, \quad \hat{w} = 0 \quad \text{at} \quad Y = 0, \tag{11.63}$$

and

$$\frac{d\hat{v}}{dY} \to -1, \quad \hat{w} \to 1 \quad \text{as} \quad Y \to \infty, \tag{11.64}$$

where $\kappa = V_o/U_o$ is a parameter of the system. In the absence of sweep, the equations (11.60) to (11.62) reduce to the famous two-dimensional stagnation flow as first described by Hiemenz (1911).

Note that by virtue of the similarity solution, U and V are uniform along the attachment line and W varies linearly with distance from the attachment line. Because of the properties of this base flow, both temporal and spatial DNS approaches should yield equivalent results in the two-dimensional limit for small amplitude disturbances. However, the temporal DNS assumes that disturbances are growing in time and that there exists a linear transformation from temporal growth to the realistic spatially growing instabilities.

In general, disturbances on and near a three-dimensional attachment line region are of the three-dimensional nature, requiring solutions of the full three-dimensional Navier-Stokes equations. However, as assumed in the original theoretical study by Hall, Malik & Poll (1984) and confirmed in the DNS computations by Spalart (1989), a single mode in the attachment line region of swept Hiemenz flow can take the form that had a linear variation of the chord-wise velocity component with distance from the attachment line. In the present study, an alternate disturbance form is first used. Namely, the w-velocity component of the disturbance and the transverse shear of the mean flow are negligible; the disturbance becomes truly two-dimensional along the attachment line. This implies that $w = 0$ and $\partial w/\partial Z = 0$ on the attachment line. Although this simplification is not consistent with the equations of motion, it turns out that the neglected terms have little effect on the qualitative behavior of the computed disturbances. This assumption allows us to use a pre-existing DNS solver that has been tested for two-dimensional instabilities and three-dimensional spanwise periodic disturbances in two-dimensional and three-dimensional base flows. This two-dimensional assumption is arguably valid because the flow is overwhelming dominated by the flow in the attachment line direction.

Here, an assessment is made with regard to the value of linear stability theory (Orr-Sommerfeld and Squire equations) in attachment line flow. Note that
linear stability theory involves a quasi-parallel flow assumption (i.e., $V = 0$),
and that no amplitude information is included in the theory. The simulations
are performed on a grid of 661 points ($\simeq$ 60 points per wavelength) along
the attachment line and 81 points in the wall-normal direction. The far-field
boundary is located at 50δ from the wall, and the computational length along
the attachment line is 216.56δ. This attachment line length corresponds to 11
wavelengths for $Re = 570$ and $\omega = 0.1249$. For the time marching scheme,
the disturbance wavelength was divided into 320 time steps per period for
small amplitude disturbances and into 2560 time steps for large amplitude
disturbances (stability considerations). Disturbances for the first simulations
are forced at the computational inflow with an amplitude of $A = 0.001\%$ (i.e.,
arbitrary small amplitude). Disturbances that evolve in a base flow that complements the quasi-parallel linear stability theory assumptions ($V = 0$) and the
full, swept Hiemenz flow are computed with DNS. Figure 11.9 shows the computed disturbance decay rate and the wavelength in the quasi-parallel flow
agree exactly with linear stability theory. The disturbance that propagates in
the complete swept Hiemenz flow closely retains the wavelength predicted by

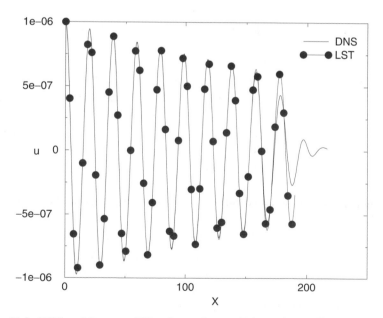

Fig. 11.9. DNS and linear stability theory for parallel attachment line flow ($Re = 570$, $\omega = 0.1249$; Samples at $Y = 0.86$).

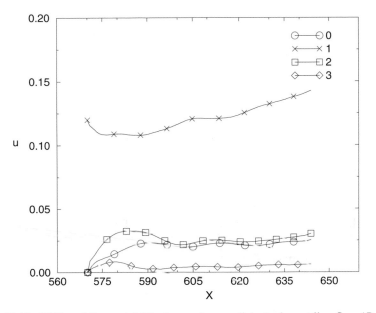

Fig. 11.10. DNS and linear stability theory for parallel attachment line flow ($Re = 570$, $\omega = 0.1249$).

linear stability theory but decays at a slower rate than that predicted by linear stability theory.

Hall & Malik (1986) utilized subcritically growing instabilities with a temporal DNS code and therefore the difference between the weakly nonlinear theory and the previous computations should not be attributable to the temporal DNS approximation. Although many previous studies have made use of the temporal approach because of the computational savings over the spatial formulation, the spatial and temporal formulations are only related in the linear limit, with the spatial formulation being more representative of the true physical problem.

Figure 11.10 shows the evolution of the fundamental wave, the mean flow distortion, and the harmonics from a simulation forced at the inflow with a large amplitude of $A = 12\%$ for the Reynolds number $Re = 570$ and frequency $\omega = 0.1249$. After a transient region of adjustment, the fundamental wave encounters subcritical growth that is in agreement with the weakly nonlinear theory. Contours of instantaneous streamwise ($U + u$) and wall normal ($V + v$) velocities are shown in Fig. 11.11. Because the disturbance amplitude is sufficiently large, notable distortions in the base flow are observed as a result of the unsteady disturbance forcing.

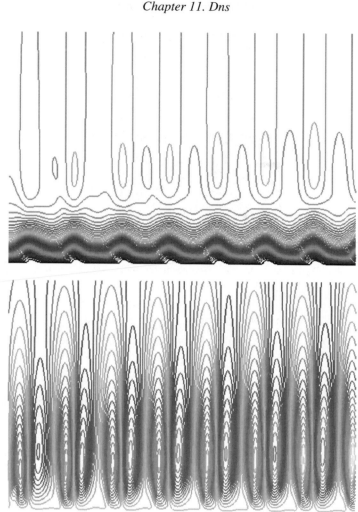

Fig. 11.11. Contours of streamwise (top) and wall normal (bottom) velocities for sub-critically growing disturbance in attachment line boundary layer at $Re = 570$ and $\omega = 0.1249$.

Finally, the spatial evolution of three-dimensional disturbances is computed by direct numerical simulation that involves the solution to the unsteady non-linear, three-dimensional Navier-Stokes equations. The simulations are performed on a grid of 661 points ($\simeq$ 60 points per wavelength) along the attachment line, 81 points in the wall-normal direction, and 25 points in the flow acceleration direction. The far-field boundary is located at 50δ from the wall, the computational length along the attachment line is 216.56δ, and the flow acceleration boundaries are located $\pm100\delta$ from the attachment line. For the

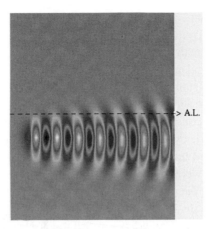

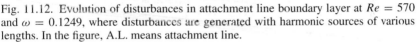

Fig. 11.12. Evolution of disturbances in attachment line boundary layer at $Re = 570$ and $\omega = 0.1249$, where disturbances are generated with harmonic sources of various lengths. In the figure, A.L. means attachment line.

time marching scheme, the disturbance wavelength was divided into 320 time steps per period.

To generate three-dimensional disturbances, the flow acceleration length of the harmonic source generator is reduced to enable a more direct transfer of energy to the w velocity component. Disturbances computed in the parameter regime were characterized by a Reynolds number $Re = 570$ and frequency $\omega = 0.1249$. The results of a disturbance generated with a harmonic source located at $-27.8 < Z < 0.0$ are shown in Fig. 11.12. The top view indicates that the harmonic source generates a local almost circular pattern that evolves along the attachment line with spreading both away from and toward the attachment line. The results imply that a disturbance generated off (but near) the attachment line can supply energy to the attachment region by the spreading of the wave pattern. In turn, this energy supply may feed an unstable mode on the attachment line. These results suggest that the flow accelerated shear away from the attachment line has insufficient strength to deter the spreading of the disturbance toward the attachment line. More details and results for this problem can be found in Joslin (1995b, 1997).

11.7 Summary

Here, PSE theory results were evaluated for accuracy in predicting convective disturbance evolution on a flat plate. PSE theory predictions were compared with spatial DNS results for two-dimensional Tollmien-Schlichting wave propagation, subharmonic breakdown, and oblique wave breakdown.

For two-dimensional Tollmien-Schlichting wave propagation, the modes predicted by PSE theory were in very good quantitative agreement with the DNS results, except for a small discrepancy in the mean flow distortion component that was discovered and attributed to far-field boundary condition differences.

For the test case of subharmonic breakdown, the PSE theory results were in very good quantitative agreement with the DNS results for all modes, even the mean flow distortion component. Also the present study supports the PSE and DNS comparison made by Herbert (1991) for subharmonic breakdown.

For the complicated test case of oblique wave breakdown, all modes predicted by PSE theory were shown to be in good quantitative agreement with the DNS results, even for the mean flow distortion component. Furthermore, these oblique wave pairs were shown to self interact to excite a streamwise vortex structure and agrees with the findings of Schmid & Henningson (1992a,b). If the initial wave amplitudes are above a threshold, the interaction of these waves and the vortex can lead to a breakdown that bypasses the secondary instability stage. Irrespective of the initial amplitudes, the streamwise vortex mode becomes the dominant, higher order mode. This dominance is significant because the presence of small roughness elements may generate oblique wave packets that can interact and lead to the increased presence of streamwise vorticity.

11.8 Exercises

1. From equations (11.1) to (11.3), derive the following

    (a) the vorticity equation (11.4),
    (b) the streamfunction-vorticity equation (11.6),
    (c) the velocity-streamfunction equation (11.7).

2. Beginning with the three-dimensional Navier-Stokes equations in primitive variables, derive disturbances equations in

    (a) convective form
    (b) skew symmetric form
    (c) rotational form
    (d) divergent form

3. Apply the filter (11.47) to the Navier-Stokes equations to get the LES filtered equations (11.48) and (11.49).

4. Develop a core set of subroutine modules that will be used to form a two-dimensional direct numerical simulation code.

    (a) Code fourth-order finite difference routines with homogeneous boundary conditions for first and second derivatives in the x-direction. Test this routine by using the function

$$f(x) = A \sin(\alpha x), \quad 0 \le x \le 4\pi.$$

Exercise this routine by varying the amplitude A and wavenumber α. Note that an exact solution exists to compare your numerical solution. These routines will serve to compute directions in the free stream direction.

(b) Code the sixth-order compact finite-difference schemes given by (11.30) and (11.31). Test the routines using the function

$$f(x) = A \sin(\alpha x), \quad 0 \le x \le 4\pi.$$

Exercise this routine by varying the amplitude A and wavenumber α.

(c) Integrate

$$\frac{dT}{dt} = \sin(t)e^{-t}$$

using the scheme (11.29). Compute the exact solution and compare to the numerical solution at $t = 1$ for various time steps Δt.

(d) Code Chebyshev collocation routines with homogeneous boundary conditions for first and second derivatives in the y-direction. Test this routine by using the function

$$f(y) = B \cos(n\pi y), \quad -1 \le y \le 1.$$

Exercise this routine by varying the amplitude B. Note that an exact solution exists to compare your numerical solution. These routines will serve to compute derivatives in the wall-normal direction.

(e) Code Fourier transform routines for first and second derivatives in the z-direction. To accomplish this, you must compute the Fourier transform of a function, perform the derivative operation in wavenumber space, and inverse Fourier transform back to physical space. Test this routine by using the function

$$f(z) = C + A \sin(\alpha z) + \cos(\beta z), \quad 0 \le z \le 4\pi.$$

Exercise this routine by varying the amplitude A and wavenumber α. Note that an exact solution exists to compare your numerical solution.

5. Develop a two-dimensional Navier-Stokes (DNS) code based on the temporal formulation of Section 11.3. Use either the Adams-Bashforth time marching scheme or the Runge-Kutta scheme given by (11.29), fourth-order finite differencing for the streamwise direction, and Chebyshev collocation for the wall-normal direction.

(a) Use $Re = 688.315$, $\alpha = 0.22$ from the Orr-Sommerfeld equation as initial conditions. Compare your solutions from the DNS code using parallel and non-parallel mean flows with the Orr-Sommerfeld solution.

(b) Show convergence of ω and the maximum u velocity versus time.

6. Develop a two-dimensional Navier-Stokes (DNS) code based on the spatial formulation of Section 11.4. Use either the Adams-Bashforth time marching scheme or the Runge-Kutta scheme given by (11.29), fourth-order finite differencing for the streamwise direction, and Chebyshev collocation for the wall-normal direction. Repeat the study of Tollmien-Schlichting waves in a Blasius boundary layer as discussed in Section 11.6.

11.9 Appendix: numerical methods

In this Appendix various numerical methods are outlined which may be of use to the reader for code development and in answering the exercise questions above.

11.9.1 Chebyshev series formulas

In this section the definition and listing of the Chebyshev polynomials are given. In addition, an example of how to represent a known function by a Chebyshev series is given. Many texts are available that outline these rules and relationships (e.g., Gottlieb & Orszag, 1986).

The Chebyshev Series

The Chebyshev polynomials, $T_n(x)$, are defined on the interval $x \in [-1, +1]$ and are derived from and related to the cosine function by

$$T_n(\cos \theta) = \cos n\theta, \qquad (11.65)$$

with the first few polynomials appearing as

$$T_0(x) = 1,$$
$$T_1(x) = x,$$
$$T_2(x) = 2x^2 - 1,$$
$$T_3(x) = 4x^3 - 3x,$$
$$\text{etc.} \qquad (11.66)$$

The following trigonometric identity can be obtained

$$\cos(n+1)\theta = 2\cos \theta \cdot \cos n\theta - \cos(n-1)\theta. \qquad (11.67)$$

This results in a Chebyshev recurrence formula for higher order polynomials

$$T_{n+1}(x) = 2x T_n(x) - T_{n-1}(x). \qquad (11.68)$$

The product formula is thus given by

$$T_n(x)T_m(x) = \frac{1}{2}[T_{n+m}(x) + T_{|n-m|}(x)],\qquad(11.69)$$

and the indefinite integral relation by

$$\int T_n(x)dx = \begin{cases} T_1(x) & n = 0 \\ \frac{1}{4}(T_o(x) + T_2(x)) & n = 1 \\ \frac{1}{2}\left(\frac{T_{n+1}(x)}{n+1} - \frac{T_{n-1}(x)}{n-1}\right) & n \ge 2. \end{cases}\qquad(11.70)$$

The series boundary conditions for a polynomial of order n are

$$T_n(\pm1) = (\pm1)^n\qquad(11.71)$$

and the differential relation for Chebyshev polynomials at the boundaries is

$$\frac{d^p}{dx^p}T_n(\pm1) = (\pm1)^{n+p}\prod_{k=0}^{p-1}(n^2 - k^2)/(2k + 1).\qquad(11.72)$$

Another efficient relation useful when performing the summation of a Chebyshev series to determine a functional value of x is given by

$$f(x) = \sum_{n=0}^{N}{}'a_n T_n(x) = \frac{1}{2}[b_0(x) - b_2(x)],\qquad(11.73)$$

where the prime signifies that the leading term is to be halved; i.e., the coefficients are $a_0/2, a_1, a_2, \ldots, a_N$.

The recurrence system required to evaluate (11.73) is

$$b_n(x) = 2xb_{n+1}(x) - b_{n+2}(x) + a_n$$
$$b_{N+1}(x) = b_{N+2}(x) = 0.\qquad(11.74)$$

A Chebyshev formula useful in approximating a known function in a Chebyshev series can be defined as

$$\Phi(x) = \sum_{n=0}^{N}{}'\phi_n T_n(x),\qquad(11.75)$$

where $\Phi(x)$ is a known function. The coefficients, ϕ_n, are given by

$$\phi_n = \frac{2}{N}\sum_{k=0}^{N}{}''\Phi(x_k)T_n(x_k),\qquad(11.76)$$

with

$$x_k = \cos\frac{k\pi}{N} \quad \text{for} \quad k = 0,1,2,\ldots,N.\qquad(11.77)$$

The double prime on the summation signifies that the leading and trailing coefficients are to be halved. This approximation of a known function is required for the mean profile and the primary eigenfunctions.

The final Chebyshev property that will be given prior to listing practical integral formulae is the approximation of the differential of a known function in Chebyshev series. The derivative is given by

$$\phi'(x) = \sum_{n=0}^{\infty} b_n T_n(x), \tag{11.78}$$

where

$$b_n = \frac{2}{c_n} \sum_{\substack{p=n+1 \\ p+n \, odd}}^{\infty} p a_p \tag{11.79}$$

and

$$c_n = \begin{cases} 2 & n = 0, \\ 1 & n > 0. \end{cases} \tag{11.80}$$

The coefficients, a_n, are obtained from the series approximation to the known function, $\phi(x)$.

To obtain the solution of a differential equation by a Chebyshev series approximation, it is convenient, although not necessary, to convert the differential equation to an integral form. As such, a function is represented by the following finite, Chebyshev series.

$$\phi(x) = \sum_{n=0}^{N} {}' a_n T_n(x). \tag{11.81}$$

By applying the integral relation (11.70) appropriately and repeatedly, the following relations are obtained:

$$1. \quad \int \phi(x) dx = \sum_{n=0}^{N+1} {}' b_n T_n(x), \tag{11.82}$$

where

$$b_n = \frac{1}{2n}(a_{n-1} - a_{n+1}) \quad \text{for } n \geq 1. \tag{11.83}$$

$$2. \quad \iint \phi(x) dx^2 = \sum_{n=0}^{N+2} {}' b_n T_n(x), \tag{11.84}$$

where

$$b_n = \left[\frac{a_{n-2}}{4n(n-1)} - \frac{a_n}{2(n^2-1)} + \frac{a_{n+2}}{4n(n+1)} \right] \quad \text{for } n \geq 2. \quad (11.85)$$

$$3. \quad \iiint \phi(x)dx^3 = \sum_{n=0}^{N+3}{}' b_n T_n(x), \quad (11.86)$$

where

$$\frac{b_n = a_{n-3}}{8n(n-1)(n-2)} - \frac{3a_{n-1}}{8n(n-2)(n+1)} + \frac{3a_{n+1}}{8n(n-1)(n+2)}$$
$$- \frac{a_{n+3}}{8n(n+1)(n+2)} \quad \text{for } n \geq 3. \quad (11.87)$$

$$4. \quad \iiiint \phi(x)dx^4 = \sum_{n=0}^{N+4}{}' b_n T_n(x), \quad (11.88)$$

where

$$b_n = \frac{a_{n-4}}{16n(n-1)(n-2)(n-3)} - \frac{a_{n-2}}{4n(n^2-1)(n-3)} + \frac{3a_n}{8(n^2-1)(n^2-4)}$$
$$- \frac{a_{n+2}}{4n(n^2-1)(n+3)} + \frac{a_{n+4}}{16n(n+1)(n+2)(n+3)} \quad \text{for } n \geq 4. \quad (11.89)$$

When the coefficients in the differential equations are non-constant, the Chebyshev product formula (11.69) is needed. Introducing a function, $u(x)$, representing the non-constant coefficient, the following is obtained

$$u(x)\phi(x) = \sum_{n=0}^{\infty}{}' d_n T_n(x), \quad (11.90)$$

with

$$u(x) = \sum_{n=0}^{\infty}{}' u_n T_n(x) \quad (11.91)$$

and

$$d_n = \frac{1}{2}u_n a_o + \frac{1}{2}\sum_{m=1}^{N}(u_{|m-n|} + u_{m+n})a_m \quad \text{for } n \geq 0. \quad (11.92)$$

Integrations are performed in a straightforward manner using the integral relation (11.70). The following integral relations prove useful for hydrodynamic

stability analysis.

$$1. \quad \int u(x)\phi(x)\mathrm{d}x = \sum_{n=0}^{N+1}{}' d_n T_n(x),$$

(11.93)

where

$$d_n = \frac{1}{4n}(u_{n-1} - u_{n+1})a_o + \frac{1}{4n}\sum_{m=1}^{N}(u_{|m-n+1|} - u_{|m-n-1|}$$

$$+ u_{m+n-1} - u_{m+n+1})a_m \quad \text{for} \ n \geq 1. \quad (11.94)$$

$$2. \quad \iint u(x)\phi(x)\mathrm{d}x^2 = \sum_{n=0}^{N+2}{}' d_n T_n(x),$$

(11.95)

where

$$d_n = \left[\frac{u_{n-2}}{8n(n-1)} - \frac{u_n}{4(n^2-1)} + \frac{u_{n+2}}{8n(n+1)} \right] a_o$$

$$+ \sum_{m=1}^{N} \left[\frac{u_{|m-n+2|} + u_{m+n-2}}{8n(n-1)} \right.$$

$$\left. - \frac{u_{m+n} + u_{|m-n|}}{4(n^2-1)} + \frac{u_{|m-n-2|} + u_{m+n+2}}{8n(n+1)} \right] a_m \quad \text{for} \ n \geq 2. \quad (11.96)$$

$$3. \quad \iiint u(x)\phi(x)\mathrm{d}x^3 = \sum_{n=0}^{N+3}{}' d_n, T_n(x)$$

(11.97)

where

$$d_n = \left[\frac{u_{n-3}}{16n(n-1)(n-2)} - \frac{3u_{n-1}}{16n(n+1)(n-2)} \right.$$

$$\left. + \frac{3u_{n+1}}{16n(n-1)(n+2)} - \frac{u_{n+3}}{16n(n+1)(n+2)} \right] a_o$$

$$+ \sum_{m=1}^{N} \left[\frac{u_{|m-n+3|} + u_{m+n-3}}{16n(n-1)(n-2)} - \frac{3(u_{|m-n+1|} + u_{m+n-1})}{16n(n+1)(n-2)} \right.$$

$$\left. + \frac{3(u_{|m-n-1|} + u_{m+n+1})}{16n(n-1)(n+2)} - \frac{u_{|m-n-3|} + u_{m+n+3})}{16n(n+1)(n+2)} \right] a_m \quad \text{for} \ n \geq 3. \quad (11.98)$$

$$4. \quad \iiiint u(x)\phi(x)\mathrm{d}x^4 = \sum_{n=0}^{N+4}{}' d_n T_n(x),$$

(11.99)

where

$$d_n = \left[\frac{u_{n-4}}{32n(n-1)(n-2)(n-3)} - \frac{u_{n-2}}{8n(n^2-1)(n-3)} \right.$$

$$+ \frac{3u_n}{16(n^2-1)(n^2-4)} - \frac{u_{n+2}}{8n(n^2-1)(n+3)}$$

$$\left. + \frac{u_{n+4}}{32n(n+1)(n+2)(n+3)} \right] a_o$$

$$+ \sum_{m=1}^{N} \left[\frac{u_{|m-n+4|} + u_{m+n-4}}{32n(n-1)(n-2)(n-3)} - \frac{u_{|m-n+2|} + u_{m+n-2}}{8n(n^2-1)(n-3)} \right.$$

$$+ \frac{3(u_{|m-n|} + u_{m+n})}{16(n^2-1)(n^2-4)} - \frac{u_{|m-n-2|} + u_{m+n+2}}{8n(n^2-1)(n-3)}$$

$$\left. + \frac{u_{|m-n-4|} + u_{m+n+4}}{32n(n+1)(n+2)(n+3)} \right] a_m \quad \text{for } n \geq 4. \quad (11.100)$$

These relations replace the appropriate terms in an integral equation in order to obtain a solution. The integral formulae require the order of the Chebyshev terms to begin with the order of the integral equation. The proof of this will not be given here, but can be found in Gottlieb & Orszag (1986).

11.9.2 Other numerical tools

In this section we present a number of diverse approaches which may be useful to solve some of the exercises in this text.

The following is a 5th-order Runge-Kutta method given by Luther (1966). Luther refers to this as a Newton-Cotes type, and is given by

$$y_{n+1} = y_n + \{7k_1 + 7k_3 + 32k_4 + 12k_5 + 32k_6\}/90, \quad (11.101)$$

where

$$k_1 = hf(x_n, y_n),$$
$$k_2 = hf(x_n + h, y_n + k_1),$$
$$k_3 = hf(x_n + h, y_n + \{k_1 + k_2\}/2),$$
$$k_4 = hf(x_n + h/4, y_n + \{14k_1 + 5k_2 - 3k_3\}/64),$$
$$k_5 = hf(x_n + h/2, y_n + \{-12k_1 - 12k_2 + 8k_3 + 64k_4\}/96),$$
$$k_6 = hf(x_n + 3h/4, y_n + \{-9k_2 + 5k_3 + 16k_4 + 36k_5\}/64). \quad (11.102)$$

where h is the step size.

The following are used for the shooting approach to find the zero of a function with Newton and three-point inverse Lagrange interpolations as listed by Burden & Faires (1985) and the False Position method listed by Gear (1978). These are

Newton:

$$\alpha_{i+1} = \alpha_i - (\alpha_i - \alpha_{i-1})\frac{\Delta_i}{\Delta_i - \Delta_{i-1}}. \qquad (11.103)$$

False Position:

$$\alpha_{i+1} = \frac{\Delta_i \alpha_{i-1} - \Delta_{i-1}\alpha_i}{\Delta_i - \Delta_{i-1}}. \qquad (11.104)$$

Inverse Lagrange:

$$\alpha_{i+1} = \frac{\alpha_i \Delta_{i-1}\Delta_{i-2}}{(\Delta_i - \Delta_{i-1})(\Delta_i - \Delta_{i-2})} + \frac{\alpha_{i-1}\Delta_i\Delta_{i-2}}{(\Delta_{i-1} - \Delta_i)(\Delta_{i-1} - \Delta_{i-2})}$$
$$+ \frac{\alpha_{i-2}\Delta_i\Delta_{i-1}}{(\Delta_{i-2} - \Delta_i)(\Delta_{i-2} - \Delta_{i-1})}. \qquad (11.105)$$

Here, α_{i+1} is the eigenvalue for the next iteration $(i + 1)$ and Δ is the matrix determinant of the numerical vector asymptotic matching which goes to zero as α converges to the proper eigenvalue.

In some circumstances a cubic spline can be useful. This is determined from the following

$$\begin{pmatrix} x_1^3 & x_1^2 & x_1 \\ x_2^3 & x_2^2 & x_2 \\ x_3^3 & x_3^2 & x_3 \end{pmatrix} \begin{Bmatrix} A \\ B \\ C \end{Bmatrix} = \begin{Bmatrix} p_1 \\ p_2 \\ p_3 \end{Bmatrix},$$

where x_i are the locations for the spline and p_i are the function values. These equations are solved simultaneously to obtain the coefficients

$$C = \frac{p_3 x_1^2 - p_1 x_3^2}{x_3 x_1^2 - x_3^2 x_1}, \qquad (11.106)$$

$$B = \frac{p_2 x_1^3 - p_1 x_2^3 - C(x_2 x_1^3 - x_1 x_2^3)}{x_1^2 x_2^2 (x_1 - x_2)}, \qquad (11.107)$$

and

$$A = \frac{p_1 - C x_1 - B x_1^2}{x_1^3}. \qquad (11.108)$$

Additionally, Simpson's rules are given by

$$\int_{x_o}^{x_2} f(x)\,dx = \frac{h}{3}[f(x_o) + 4f(x_1) + f(x_2)] - \frac{h^5}{90}f^{(4)}(\zeta), \qquad (11.109)$$

where $x_o < \zeta < x_2$, and

$$\int_{x_o}^{x_4} f(x)\mathrm{d}x = \frac{2h}{45}[7f(x_o) + 32f(x_1) + 12f(x_2)$$

$$+ 32f(x_3) + 7f(x_4)] - \frac{8h^7}{954}f^{(6)}(\zeta),$$

(11.110)

where $x_o < \zeta < x_4$.

Chapter 12

Flow control and optimization

12.1 Introduction

The previous chapters have outlined and validated various theoretical and computational methodologies to characterize hydrodynamic instabilities. This chapter serves to cursorily summarize techniques to control flows of interest. In some situations, the instabilities may require suppressive techniques while, in other situations, enhancing the amplification of the disturbance field is desirable. Similarly, enhanced mixing is an application where disturbance amplification may be required to obtain the goal. Small improvements in system performance often lead to beneficial results. For example, Cousteix (1992) noted that 45 percent of the drag for a commercial transport transonic aircraft is due to skin friction drag on the wings, fuselage, fin, etc., and that a 10–15 percent reduction of the total drag can be expected by maintaining laminar flow over the wings and the fin. Hence, flow control methods that can prevent the onset of turbulence could lead to significant performance benefits to the aircraft industry. For aircraft, as well as many other applications, the flow starts from a smooth laminar state that is inherently unstable and develops instability waves. These instability waves grow exponentially, interact nonlinearly, and lead ultimately to fully developed turbulence or flow separation. Therefore, one goal of a good control system is to inhibit, if not eliminate, instabilities that lead to the deviation from laminar to turbulent flow state. Because it is beyond the scope of this text to cover all possible flow control methodologies, this chapter will primarily highlight passive control techniques, wave-induced forcing, feed forward and feedback flow control, and the optimal flow control approach applied to suppression of boundary layer instabilities that maintains laminar flow. Detailed reviews of available flow control technologies can be found in Gad-el-Hak, Pollard & Bonnet (1998), Gad-el-Hak (2000), Joslin, Kunz & Stinebring (2000), and Thomas, Choudhari & Joslin (2002).

12.2 Effects of flexible boundaries

The literature is replete with techniques for passive flow control. The discovery of these techniques has primarily come from parameter studies using theoretical and computational techniques described in the earlier chapters and through an understanding of the governing flow physics of the application. For the two-dimensional flat plate boundary layer and flow over two-dimensional wings or engine nacelles, the viscous traveling wave (Tollmien-Schlichting) instability is a dominant mode effecting transition. It is well known that favorable pressure gradients stabilize the Tollmien-Schlichting wave and adverse pressure gradients destabilize the Tollmien-Schlichting wave. Hence, a passive method of flow control would be to effectively make use of the local pressure gradients the disturbance must encounter as it evolves in space. Other techniques may be pseudo-active in that, once they are employed, there is no time variance. For example, applying cooling or heating through a surface can stabilize or destabilize a Tollmien-Schlichting wave in air, while the opposite effects are realized in water. In addition, steady suction has been demonstrated through many wind tunnel and flight tests to suppress instabilities, enabling flow to be laminar in regions which would otherwise be turbulent (cf. Joslin, 1998, and Joslin, Kunz & Stinebring, 2000, for an overview of projects that used these flow control strategies). Finally, wall compliance is an additional passive technique that has primarily shown promise for underwater applications (cf. Carpenter, 1990, *vis-à-vis* compliant walls). With such a technique, the properties of the elastic-based wall are optimized to suppress the viscous traveling wave instability. However, the introduction of wall-induced instability modes is possible, destroying any benefit of using wall compliance to suppress Tollmien-Schlichting waves. This section will review some of the history of the use of flexible or compliant walls and derive the necessary boundary conditions for use with the Orr-Sommerfeld and Squire equations and secondary instability theory that was outlined in Chapter 9.

Research involving flow over flexible walls was started in the late 1950's by Kramer (1957, 1965). Experimentally, Kramer found significant drag reductions using rubber coatings over rigid walls. Investigators in the 1960's focused on the task of experimentally duplicating and theoretically explaining Kramer's results. The majority of these studies failed to produce any comparable results, but the theoretical results laid the foundation for all future studies involving flexible walls. Interest turned toward the use of compliant walls f turbulent drag reduction. In the 1970's NASA (Bushnell, Hefner & Ash, 19 and in the 1980's the Office of Naval Research (Reischman, 1984) spor investigations involving the use of compliant walls for the turbulent p

Although most of the results from this era were either inconclusive or unsatisfactory, the contributions, together with earlier results, did provide stepping stones to the understanding of the physically complex fluid/wall interaction phenomena.

In the early 1980's, Carpenter & Garrad (1985, 1986) theoretically showed that Kramer-type surfaces could lead to potential delays in transition. Further, they indicated deficiencies in previous investigations that may have prevented their achieving results comparable to Kramer's. Only recently, with the experiments performed by Willis (1986) and Gaster (1988) have favorable results been achieved using compliant walls. As outlined in the above-mentioned reviews, a number of investigations of the past 10 years have been conducted involving flexible walls. A main emphasis of these studies was to understand the physical mechanisms involved in the fluid and wall interaction for transitional and turbulent flows.

Most of the studies focused on the two-dimensional instability problem except for Yeo (1986) who showed that a lower critical Reynolds number existed for the isotropic compliant wall for three-dimensional instability waves. Carpenter & Morris (1989) and Joslin, Morris & Carpenter (1991) have shown that three-dimensional Tollmien-Schlichting waves can have greater growth rates over compliant walls than those that are two-dimensional. Even though three-dimensional waves may be dominant, it was demonstrated that transition delays are still obtainable through the use of compliant walls. For this study, they considered a compliant wall model used by Grosskreutz (1975) for his turbulent boundary layer experiments.

The remainder of this next section outlines boundary conditions for the primary instability problem using the Orr-Sommerfeld and Squire equations as well as the secondary instability problem of Grosskreutz (1975) for a wall model. Then, some limited results are presented that demonstrate the suppression of boundary layer transition using this method of flow control.

12.2.1 Primary wave model

The derivation of the boundary conditions and results for two- and three-dimensional primary instabilities over compliant and rigid walls have been given by Joslin, Morris & Carpenter (1991). The disturbances are represented as traveling waves that may grow or decay as they propagate. Nonlinear coupling is ignored so that individual components of the frequency spectrum may studied. Additionally, the quasi parallel assumption is made.

nsider the incompressible laminar boundary layer over a smooth flat wall. ier-Stokes equations describe the flow and the Blasius profile is used

to represent the mean flow. A small amplitude disturbance is introduced into the laminar flow. For this, a normal mode representation is given as

$$\{v', \omega'\}(x, y, z, t) = \{v, \omega\}(y)e^{i(x\alpha \cos \phi + z\alpha \sin \phi - \omega t)} + c.c., \quad (12.1)$$

where v and Ω are the complex eigenfunctions of normal velocity and vorticity, respectively. Here, α is the wavenumber, ω is the frequency, and ϕ is the wave angle. In general, α and ω are complex making for an ambiguity in the system. For temporal analyses, α is a real specified wavenumber and ω is the complex eigenvalue. For spatial analyses, ω is a real specified frequency and α is the complex eigenvalue. For the compliant wall problem, Joslin, Morris & Carpenter (1991) have shown that the use of equation (12.1) leads to an over-estimation of the growth of the wave as it propagates. The wave actually propagates in a nearly streamwise direction that is in the direction of the group velocity rather than normal to the wave fronts. The secondary instabilities were investigated using this simple representation of the primary instabilities. Since the present approach was conservative, it should exemplify the benefits of using compliant walls as a means to obtain transition delays. Also, a major emphasis and motivation of the present study was to determine the behavior or response of the phenomena of secondary instabilities to compliant walls.

If the normal mode relation (12.1) is substituted into the linearized form of the Navier-Stokes equations, the Orr-Sommerfeld (?? or 2.28) and Squire (??) equations result. The system requires six boundary conditions where the disturbance fluctuations vanish at infinity or

$$v(y), \quad v'(y), \quad \omega(y) \to 0 \quad \text{as} \quad y \to \infty. \quad (12.2)$$

The remaining boundary conditions are determined from the compliant wall model.

The compliant wall model was introduced by Grosskreutz (1975) in his experimental drag reduction studies with turbulent boundary layers. Here it was suggested that the link between streamwise and normal surface displacements would cause a negative production of turbulence near the wall. Although his results for the turbulent flow were disappointing, the surface does react to the fluid fluctuations in transitional flow in such a way as to reduce production of instability growth. Carpenter & Morris (1990) have shown by use of an energy analysis how the many competing energy transfer mechanisms are influenced by the presence of the compliant wall. Of note is the reduced energy production by the Reynolds stress that may cause the reduced growth rates. Further, Joslin, Morris & Carpenter (1991) predicted that transition delays of four to ten times the rigid wall transition Reynolds number were achievable with this

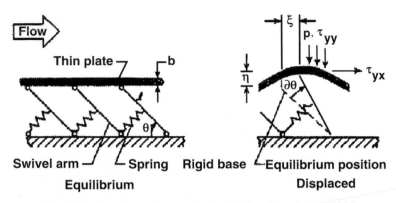

Fig. 12.1. Non-isotropic compliant wall (after Grosskreutz, 1975).

coating. As a result, the model has been extended to allow for a secondary instability analysis.

The mechanical model consists of a thin, elastic plate supported by hinged and sprung rigid members inclined to the horizontal and facing upstream at an angle, θ, when in equilibrium. A sketch of the mechanical wall model is shown in Fig. 12.1. The boundary conditions are obtained by enforcing a balance of forces in the streamwise and spanwise directions and the continuity of fluid and wall motion. These are given below in linearized form.

For small displacements of an element out of equilibrium, the mechanical surface can be thought to move in a direction perpendicular to the rigid swivel arm. The horizontal and vertical displacements (ξ, η) are linked to the angular displacement $(\delta\theta)$ as

$$\xi = \ell\delta\theta \sin\theta \quad \text{and} \quad \eta = \ell\delta\theta \cos\theta, \tag{12.3}$$

where ℓ is the length of the rigid arm member. Equations of motion for the element in the streamwise and spanwise directions may be obtained by a balance of the forces of the fluid fluctuations acting on the surface and the forces due to the wall motion. These equations are

$$\rho_m b \frac{\partial^2 \eta}{\partial t^2} + \left(B_x \frac{\partial^4 \eta}{\partial x^4} + 2B_{xz} \frac{\partial^4 \eta}{\partial x^2 \partial z^2} + B_z \frac{\partial^4 \eta}{\partial z^4} \right) \cos^2\theta$$

$$+ K_E\eta - E_x b \frac{\partial^2 \xi}{\partial x^2} \sin\theta \cos\theta$$

$$= -(p + \tau_{yy}) \cos^2\theta + \tau_{yx} \sin\theta \cos\theta, \tag{12.4}$$

and

$$\rho_m b \frac{\partial^2 \zeta_z b}{\partial t^2} + K_S \zeta - E_z b \frac{\partial^2 \zeta}{\partial z^2} = \tau_{yz}, \tag{12.5}$$

where

$$\{B_x, B_z\} = \frac{\{E_x, E_z\}b^3}{12(1 - \nu_x \nu_z)} \quad \text{and} \quad B_{xz} = \sqrt{B_x B_z}.$$

Here, ζ is the spanwise surface displacement, ρ_m and b arc the plate density and thickness, (B_x, B_{xz}, B_z) are the flexural rigidities of the plate in the streamwise, transverse, and spanwise directions, (E_x, E_z) are the moduli of elasticity of the plate, K_E, K_S are the effective streamwise and spanwise spring stiffness factors, p is the pressure fluctuation that is obtained from the fluid momentum equations, and τ_{yx}, τ_{yy} and τ_{yz} are the streamwise, normal, and spanwise viscous shear stress fluctuations in the fluid acting on the wall.

The terms on the left hand side of equation (12.4) refer to mechanical forces and the terms on the right refer to fluid motion forces due to viscous stress and pressure fluctuations. For the case where the ribs are aligned at $\theta = 0°$, the wall becomes isotropic and reduces to the theoretical model studied by Carpenter & Garrad (1985, 1986). Otherwise the wall is referred to as nonisotropic and the rib angle is determined by θ.

The continuity of fluid and wall motion is given in the streamwise, normal, and spanwise directions, respectively, as

$$\frac{\partial \xi}{\partial t} = u + \eta U', \quad \frac{\partial \eta}{\partial t} = v, \quad \text{and} \quad \frac{\partial \zeta}{\partial t} = w, \tag{12.6}$$

where (u, v, w) are the disturbance velocity components in the streamwise, normal and spanwise directions, respectively. For the Grosskreutz coating, $K_S \to \infty$ is assumed which, from equation (12.5), would result in zero effective spanwise surface displacement. From equation (12.6) this implies that $w(0) = 0$. Strictly speaking, if the assumption $K_S \to \infty$ is relaxed, the resulting instabilities have larger growth rates. This suggests that spanwise stiffeners are stabilizing to a disturbed flow. So, with the assumption enforced, a better coating for potential transition delays results. The surface displacement takes the same normal mode form as the primary wave given by equation (12.1). The normal modes are substituted into equations (12.4) to (12.6). These equations can be reduced to three equations in terms of the normal velocity and vorticity by performing operations similar to that of the Orr-Sommerfeld and Squire equations.

12.2.2 Primary instability results

The algebraic complexity of the dynamic equations for the secondary disturbance and the compliant wall equations requires that care be taken in applying
any numerical technique for solution. Because no theoretical or experimental
data are available for the compliant problem, both shooting and spectral approximations are used. Also, since Bertolotti (1985) has shown that for the
rigid wall problem with a two-dimensional primary instability, after the transformation from spatial to temporal has been made, the solutions are in good
agreement and only the temporal analysis is presented here.

For the spectral method, Chebyshev series are introduced to approximate
each mode of the Fourier series. An algebraic transformation is used to change
the Chebyshev spectral domain $[-1, 1]$ to the physical domain. Due to the
properties of the Chebyshev polynomials, the equations are recast in integral
form. Chebyshev polynomials are used to represent the basic flow in the series
that are substituted into the integral equations. For the basic flow, 35 polynomials provide sufficient resolution of the eigenfunctions. The series representing the secondary instability requires 40 polynomials for sufficient convergence to the dominant eigenvalue. For the shooting method, beginning with
the equations for the compliant wall, integrations of the disturbance equations
across the boundary layer are performed using a Runge-Kutta scheme. At the
edge of the boundary layer the numerical solution vectors are matched with the
asymptotic solutions. A very accurate initial guess is found to be required for
convergence using this method. To demonstrate the accuracy of the numerical
techniques, a comparison for the rigid wall case was made with Herbert (1983)
for $Re_\delta = 826.36$, $Fr = 83$, $\beta = 0.18$, and $A = 0.02$. Herbert obtained the dominant mode $\sigma = 0.01184$. In good agreement, the present spectral and shooting
methods lead to $\sigma = 0.011825$ and $\sigma = 0.011839$, respectively. Additional
rigid wall results can be found in Chapter 9.

For all of the results that follow the freestream velocity is 20 m/s, the density is 1000 kg/m^3, and the kinematic viscosity is 1×10^{-6} m^2/s. The coatings
considered consist of both isotropic and nonisotropic walls. Both walls were
optimized at $Re_{\delta*} = 2240$ for two-dimensional primary instabilities. The iso-
tropic wall has properties $\theta = 0°$, $b = 0.735$mm, $E_x = 1.385$MN/m^2, $K = 0.354$GN/m^3 and $\rho_m = 1000$ kg/m^3. The nonisotropic wall has properties
$\theta = 60°$, $b = 0.111$mm, $E_x = 0.509$MN/m^2, $K = 0.059$GN/m^3 and $\rho_m = 1000$ kg/m^3. The equations are nondimensionalized using the freestream velocity U_∞, kinematic viscosity ν, and an appropriate length scale. Convenient
lengths for the boundary layer scale with the x-Reynolds number, $Re_x = U_\infty x / \nu$. These include a thickness, δ, where the Reynolds number is defined

$Re_\delta = Re_x^{1/2}$ and a boundary layer displacement thickness, δ^*, where $Re_{\delta^*} = 17207 Re_x^{1/2}$.

A Reynolds number of 2240 was chosen because, for a boundary layer over a rigid wall, the disturbance with the critical frequency (in the e^N sense) reaches its maximum growth rate near this value of Reynolds number. Accordingly, this is a good choice of Reynolds number for optimizing the wall properties. In considering three-dimensional instabilities, the walls optimized for two-dimensional instabilities are used with the addition of isotropic plates. The properties of an isotropic plate are direction independent; that is, $E_x = E_z$. Although complete details of the optimization process and philosophy have been given by Carpenter & Morris (1990), a review is provided here.

With a flexible wall present, other modes of instability arise. And, changes in the compliant wall properties stable or marginally stable fluid and wall modes can become unstable and dominant. The present wall properties were varied to achieve an optimal specified condition. The desired condition was to achieve a minimum growth rate for a dominant two-dimensional Tollmien-Schlichting instability while keeping other modes marginally stable. For the secondary analysis, these "optimal" compliant walls led to no additional unstable modes. However, this is not to say that additional growing modes may not appear for different wall properties.

In this section the concept of stable and unstable regions is considered further. These regions indicate where the instability wave grows or decays. Illustrated in Fig. 12.2 are the neutral curves for the rigid wall, $\theta = 0°$ isotropic wall, and the $\theta = 60°$ nonisotropic wall for the two-dimensional Tollmien-Schlichting instability. The $\theta = 60°$ wall has a smaller region of instability located within the rigid wall case. As the Reynolds number increases, the lower branch approaches that of the rigid wall and the upper branch stretches midway between the rigid wall branches. The $\theta = 60°$ wall produces a curve that coincides with the rigid wall curve at high wave frequencies. As the Reynolds number increases, both branches approach the $\theta = 60°$ branches. Nothing is revealed as to the growth rates within the unstable region. Although the region of instability may be smaller for the compliant coatings, the growth rates may very well be greater than the rigid wall growth rates. This is not the case for the coatings under consideration as will be shown in the next section.

Some concern has been expressed with respect to the alignment of the ribs, or swivel arm. It has been suggested that the same solutions would be expected irrespective of whether the ribs are aligned upstream or downstream. Although Carpenter & Morris (1989) have shown that ribs aligned downstream, or in the direction of the flow, result in higher growth rates than coatings with ribs

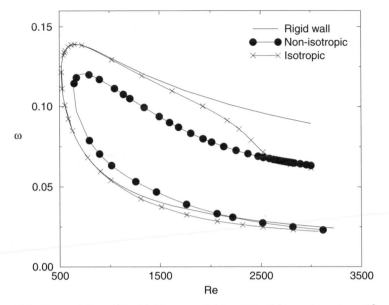

Fig. 12.2. Curves of neutral stability over rigid wall (solid curve); $x, \theta = 0°$; and $\bullet, \theta = 60°$ compliant walls for $Re_{\delta*} = 2240$.

aligned upstream. We will briefly examine this comparison for the neutral curve. Curves of neutral stability for the rigid wall, $\theta = 60°$ wall, and $\theta = -60°$ wall are shown in Fig. 12.3. These coatings result in distinctly different curves where disturbances propagating over the $\theta = -60°$ wall become unstable at lower frequencies and Reynolds numbers than those propagating over the rigid wall.

Figure 12.4 shows the growth rates for the two-dimensional waves for various frequencies for the compliant and rigid walls. For the $\theta = 60°$ wall, the maximum growth rate is about 25 percent of that for the rigid wall. The width of the unstable region in $\omega - Re_{\delta*}$ space is also reduced considerably for the compliant walls as compared to the rigid surface. Figures 12.5 and 12.6 show the growth rates as functions of frequency for various oblique waves propagating over the same two compliant walls. For both coatings, the maximum growth rates are found for three-dimensional waves traveling at oblique angles of 50–60° to the flow direction. For $\theta = 0°$ an approximately 60 percent increase in growth rate over the two-dimensional case is found. For the $\theta = 60°$ wall the dominance of the three-dimensional waves is considerably reduced but still quite marked. The reduced sensitivity of the non-isotropic compliant wall to three-dimensional waves compared to the isotropic case can be attributed to the effects of irreversible energy exchange between the wall and the

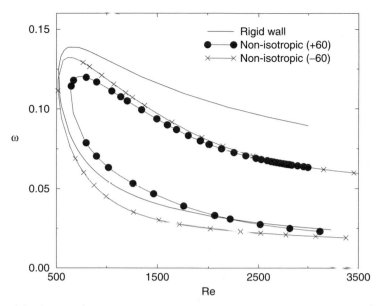

Fig. 12.3. Curves of neutral stability over a rigid wall (solid curve); $\bullet, \theta = 60°$; and $x, \theta = -60°$ compliant walls for $Re_{\delta*} = 2240$.

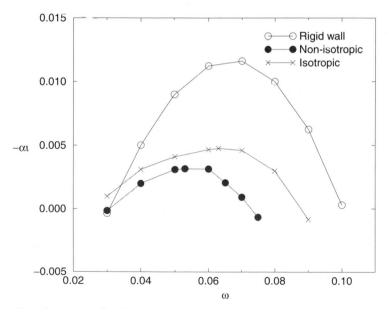

Fig. 12.4. Two-dimensional growth rates as a function of frequency for Tollmien-Schlichting waves over a rigid wall (solid curve); $x, \theta = 0$ wall; and $\bullet, \theta = 60°$ wall at $Re_{\delta*} = 2240$.

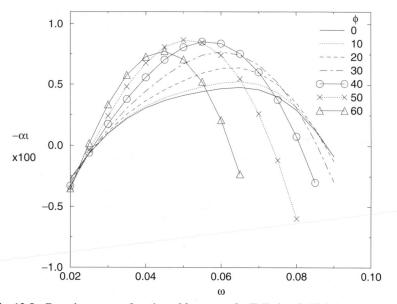

Fig. 12.5. Growth rates as a function of frequency for Tollmien-Schlichting waves over a $\theta = 0°$ wall/isotropic plate at $Re_{\delta*} = 2240$ for various oblique wave angles.

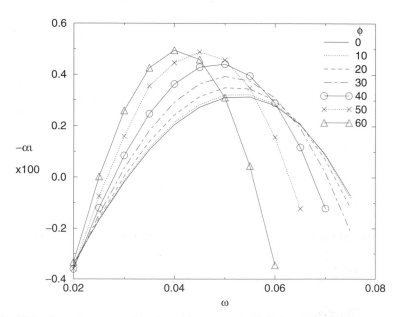

Fig. 12.6. Growth rates as a function of frequency for Tollmien-Schlichting waves over a $\theta = 60°$ wall/isotropic plate at $Re_{\delta*} = 2240$ for various oblique wave angles.

disturbance due to the work done by the fluctuating shear stress. Carpenter & Morris (1990) showed that this energy exchange has a relatively destabilizing effect on the Tollmien-Schlichting waves that grows as θ increases. This deleterious effect is reduced for oblique waves owing to the reduced magnitude of the fluctuating shear stress in the direction of wave propagation. Hence, the relative improvement is in terms of reductions in the three-dimensional growth rates and range of unstable frequencies for nonisotropic as compared to isotropic compliant walls.

For simplicity we consider the growth of disturbances initiated at the lower branch of the two-dimensional neutral curve for each coating. This is a somewhat more conservative approach compared to the approximate procedure used by Cebeci & Stewartson (1980) who begin their calculations on a sort of three-dimensional neutral curve that they termed the "Zarf." Since the growth rates for both two- and three-dimensional instability waves are small in this region, it is not expected that the predicted transition Reynolds number will be significantly different. The instability is then allowed to seek the angle of wave propagation in which it has a maximum growth rate. The wave is then traced as it convects downstream and the growth rates are used to determine the amplification of the wave. The amplification is given by

$$\ln \frac{A}{A_o} = - \int_{(x_o,z_o)}^{(x,z)} \gamma_i(x)\mathrm{d}(x,z),$$

where A_o is the initial amplitude of the disturbance at (x_o, z_o). The e^N method is based on the observation that, when the amplification of the disturbance reaches some value-N, transition occurs (or is imminent). As the waves travel downstream at fixed increments of the streamwise coordinate, x, values of the growth rate and the direction of wave propagation, ϕ, are retained. Although the spanwise incremental step is not known exactly, as it is a continuous function of x, a second order approximation is made with the known local values of ϕ and x. From this the spanwise increment is obtained and gives a possible error of ± 1 degree in the propagation angle for integrations in the low frequency range.

To confirm these local observations, e^N calculations have been performed. Figure 12.7 shows curves of maximum amplification for two-dimensional waves in the frequency range of interest for the compliant and rigid walls. The two-dimensional case agrees with Carpenter & Morris (1990). Some controversy exists as to which value of n is the proper indication of transition. But if we choose a conservative value of $n = 7$ a delay of approximately four to five times the rigid wall transition Reynolds number is realized. However,

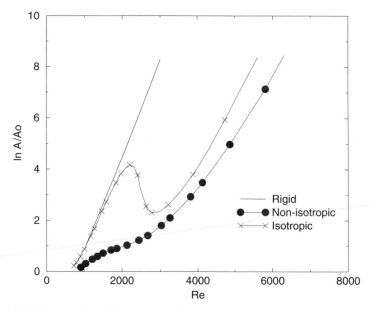

Fig. 12.7. Curves of maximum amplification for Tollmien-Schlichting instability waves over a rigid wall (solid); $\theta = 0°$ wall $(-\text{x}-)$; and $\theta = 60°$ $(- \bullet -)$ wall at $Re_{\delta*} = 2240$.

for higher values of n, the advantages of the wall compliance increase still more. Figure 12.8 shows similar calculations for the three-dimensional disturbances over the $\theta = 60°$ wall. Instabilities traveling over isotropic and orthotropic plates for the $\theta = 60°$ wall lead to similar maximum amplification curves. This is in agreement with the local calculations given above. A decrease from the two-dimensional transition delay occurs, but a transition delay remains compared to the rigid wall results. The same calculations for the $\theta = 0°$ wall illustrated in Fig. 12.9 show a notable difference between the isotropic and orthotropic plate cases. In fact, the results for the isotropic plate case approach the rigid wall results. No transition delay would be expected.

This concludes the presentation of the primary instability results. It can be concluded that three-dimensional primary instabilities dominate transition over the compliant walls considered and transition delays occur when compared with the rigid wall. In the next section, the effect of compliant walls on secondary instabilities that result from two and three-dimensional primary waves is discussed.

12.2.3 Secondary instability theory

In this section, boundary equations and conditions describing the compliant walls are introduced for secondary instabilities (cf. Chapter 9). The flow is

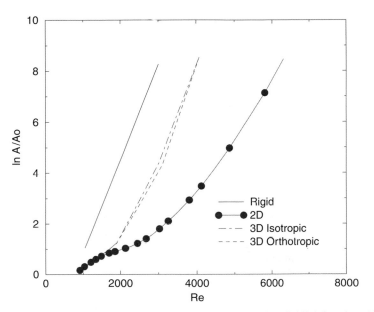

Fig. 12.8. Curves of maximum amplification for Tollmien-Schlichting instability waves over a 2D rigid wall; 2D $\theta = 60°$, 3D $\theta = 60°$ orthotropic plate, and 3D $\theta = 60°$ isotropic plate.

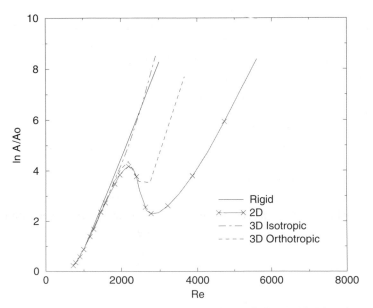

Fig. 12.9. Curves of maximum amplification for Tollmien-Schlichting instability waves over a 2D rigid wall; 2D $\theta = 0°$, 3D $\theta = 0°$ orthotropic plate, and 3D $\theta = 0°$ isotropic plate.

governed by the Navier-Stokes equations. Instantaneous velocity and pressure components are introduced and given as

$$\vec{v}(\tilde{x}, y, \tilde{z}, t) = \vec{v}_2(\tilde{x}, y, \tilde{z}, t) + B\vec{v}_3(\tilde{x}, y, \tilde{z}, t)$$
$$p(\tilde{x}, y, \tilde{z}, t) = p_2(\tilde{x}, y, \tilde{z}, t) + Bp_3(\tilde{x}, y, \tilde{z}, t), \tag{12.7}$$

where p_3 and $\underline{v}_3 = (u_3, v_3, w_3)$ are the secondary disturbance pressure and velocity in the fixed laboratory reference frame $(\tilde{x}, y, \tilde{z})$, and p_2 and $\underline{v}_2 = (u_2, v_2, w_2)$ are the basic pressure and velocity given by

$$\vec{v}_2(\tilde{x}, y, \tilde{z}, t) = \{U_o(y), 0, 0\} + A\{u, v, w\}(\tilde{x}, y, \tilde{z}, t),$$
$$p_2(\tilde{x}, y, \tilde{z}, t) = Ap(\tilde{x}, y, \tilde{z}, t). \tag{12.8}$$

The basic flow is given by the Blasius solution and eigenfunctions of the primary wave. Assume locally that the primary wave is periodic in time and periodic in $(\tilde{x}, \tilde{z})$ with wavelength $\lambda_r = 2\pi/\alpha_r$ and define a disturbance phase velocity as

$$\vec{c}_r = (c_x = \omega_r/\alpha_r \cos\phi, 0, c_z = \omega_r/\alpha_r \sin\phi).$$

Then, in a frame moving with the primary wave,

$$\vec{v}(\tilde{x}, y, \tilde{z}) = \vec{v}(x, y, z) = \vec{v}(x + \lambda_x, y, z + \lambda_z), \tag{12.9}$$

where (x, z) is the reference frame moving with the wave. With an appropriate normalization of the primary eigenfunctions (u, v, w) the amplitude, A, is directly a measure of the maximum streamwise rms fluctuation. This is given by

$$\max_{0 < y < \infty} |u(y)|^2 = |u(y_m)|^2 = 1/2. \tag{12.10}$$

As in Chapter 9, the instantaneous velocities and pressure are substituted into the Navier-Stokes equations that have been linearized with respect to the secondary amplitude, B. The disturbance pressure is eliminated, resulting in the vorticity equations and continuity. As with the primary problem, the final secondary disturbance equations take the form of a normal vorticity (9.14) and velocity (9.15).

The compliant wall equations give the remaining boundary conditions in the compliant case. Additionally, the primary amplitude, A, is a parameter in the equations and is assumed to be locally non varying. As $A \to 0$, the Orr-Sommerfeld and Squire equations result. For the case of interest where $A \neq 0$, the primary eigenfunctions (u, v, w) appear in the equations as coefficients.

The boundary conditions for the secondary disturbance are given as

$$\hat{v}_n, \hat{v}'_n, \hat{\omega}_n \to 0 \quad \text{as} \quad y \to \infty. \tag{12.11}$$

The analysis for the compliant boundary conditions for secondary instabilities follows the same route as was taken for the primary instabilities, except a number of additional terms arise due to the presence of the primary wave.

The fluid wall motion must be continuous in each direction. In addition, the equations of force (12.4) and (12.5) must balance in the streamwise and spanwise directions in the reference frame moving with the primary wave. Consistent with the fluid equations, the amplitude of the primary wave is assumed to be locally nonvarying. In deriving the final form of the wall equations, a significant difference between the primary and secondary form arises from the pressure contribution. The pressure for the secondary disturbance is determined from the momentum equations that are complicated by primary coupling terms.

The continuity of motion between the fluid and solid is given by

$$\frac{\partial \xi_3}{\partial t} = u_3 + \eta_3 U_o' + A\{(\vec{\xi}_1 \cdot \nabla)u_3 + (\vec{\xi}_3 \cdot \nabla)u_1\}, \tag{12.12}$$

$$\frac{\partial \eta_3}{\partial t} = v_3 + A\{(\vec{\xi}_1 \cdot \nabla)v_3 + (\vec{\xi}_3 \cdot \nabla)v_1\}, \tag{12.13}$$

and

$$\frac{\partial \zeta_3}{\partial t} = w_3 + A\{(\vec{\xi}_1 \cdot \nabla)w_3 + (\vec{\xi}_3 \cdot \nabla)w_1\}, \tag{12.14}$$

where

$$\vec{\xi}_i \cdot \nabla = \xi_i \frac{\partial}{\partial x} + \eta_i \frac{\partial}{\partial y} + \zeta_i \frac{\partial}{\partial z} \quad \text{for} \quad i = 1, 2, 3.$$

Equations (12.12) to (12.14) involve six unknowns for the velocity fluctuations and surface displacement in a highly coupled system. As with the primary boundary conditions, it is possible to derive a set of equations that represent the surface motion in terms of the normal velocity and vorticity only. This is algebraically very tedious. A complete derivation is given by Joslin (1990). Note that if $A = 0$ in the secondary wall equations, the primary wall equations result. This occurs with the fluid equations as well.

The compliant wall-dynamic equations for the secondary disturbance are extremely complex and tedious to implement numerically. Hence, we will move on to active control techniques for hydrodynamic instabilities. First, let us summarize the primary and secondary instability results for hydrodynamic instabilities over compliant walls.

The physical nature and makeup of the mechanisms in transition are not altered by the control device (i.e. compliant wall). Rather, only the response of that mechanism is changed. Three-dimensional primary instabilities theoretically dominate transition over the compliant walls considered, yet transition

delays were found compared to the rigid wall. As the primary amplitudes are
reduced, the excitement of the secondary instability is delayed. Thus, active
or passive devices that suppress primary instability growth should lead to corresponding suppression and delay of succeeding instabilities. The use of passive devices, such as compliant walls, leads to significant reductions in the
secondary instability growth rates and amplification, suppressing the primary
growth rates and subsequent amplification enable delays in the growth of the
explosive secondary instability mechanism.

12.3 Wave-induced forcing

The main deficiency of a passive control technique lies in the fact that the
control system has been optimized to operate at a single target design point,
whereas it is desirable to have efficient and effective controls over a range
of operating conditions. As such, a time-varying control system is required.
Also, for a given level of control, time-varying systems may require much
less power input than comparable pseudo time invariant systems. For example,
Liepmann & Nosenchuck (1982a) compared the effects of steady and unsteady
heating to suppress a Tollmien-Schlichting wave instability, and found that
steady heating demanded a 2000% increase in energy compared with an unsteady "wave cancellation" technique. Hence, unsteady control (i.e., 'active
flow control') may be more efficient for flow control applications. Wave-
induced forcing is one such time-varying approach.

For wave-induced forcing, the disturbance frequency, wavelength, phase,
and amplification rate are all parameters that may be used for control. This information can easily be obtained using two or more wall pressure transducers.
By using this disturbance information, a second control wave is forced to either
obtain disturbance suppression or enforcing the disturbance amplification. For
problems with the goal of instability suppression, the term *wave cancellation*
is commonly used since the goal of the second forcing wave is to cancel the
disturbance present in the flow.

To date, most of the experiments aimed at verifying the wave cancellation
concept were conducted on either a flat plate or an axisymmetric body. Many of
these experiments were conducted in water tunnels. Vibrating wires (Milling,
1981), hot strips (Liepmann & Nosenchuck, 1982a,b), suction and blowing
(Pupator & Saric, 1989; Ladd, 1990), electro-magnetic generators (Thomas,
1983), and adaptive heating element (Ladd & Hendricks, 1988) are some of
the methods that were used in experiments to generate the disturbance and
control waves. All of these input mechanisms gave the necessary control of the
phase and amplitude of the input wave. Among the more successful studies,

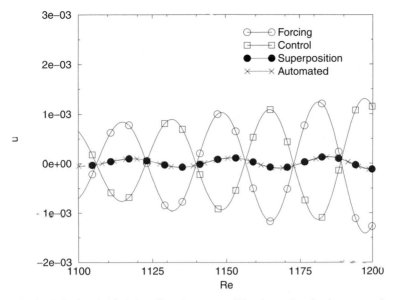

Fig. 12.10. Tollmien-Schlichting disturbance amplification using forcing, control, superposition, and automated (wave cancellation) methods.

Milling (1981) and Thomas (1983) achieved at least an 80 percent reduction in the amplitude of a two-dimensional disturbance.

Although intuitively obvious, until the work of Bower, Kegelman, Pal & Meyer (1987) and Pal, Bower & Meyer (1991), it was not known that perfect cancellation could be obtained within the context of linear theory for which the mean flow is independent of the propagating direction. They used the two-dimensional Orr-Sommerfeld equation to study and control instability wave growth by superposition, and showed that, within the limits of linear stability theory and the parallel flow assumption, both single and multi-frequency waves can be cancelled. Definitively, Joslin, Erlebacher & Hussaini (1996) performed a numerical experiment that served to unequivocally demonstrate the link between linear superposition and instability suppression. To ensure that linear superposition of individual instabilities was in fact responsible for the results found in previous experiments and computations, they carried out three simulations with (i) only the disturbance, (ii) only the control, and (iii) using both disturbance and control, which is the wave cancellation case. By discretely summing the control only and forcing only numerical results, they found that this linear superposed solution is identical to the wave cancellation results. These tests shown in Fig. 12.10 verify the hypothesis that linear superposition is the reason for the previous experimental and computational results. In

practice, the disturbance cannot be completely cancelled since some residual disturbance energy will remain in the flow. This residual energy has the potential to amplify and lead to a boundary layer somewhere downstream of the control point. Hence, the wave cancellation flow control strategy would again be required downstream of the initial control point. Incidentally, note that the phase of the residual wave is nearly the same as the original disturbance. This occurs because, at the point of control, the energy in the original disturbance is greater than that of the control wave. A nearly 180 degree change in phase would occur for the residual wave if the control wave had greater energy than the original disturbance at the point of control.

12.4 Feed forward and feedback control

The concept of feed forward or feedback control implies that some measurable quantity in the upstream or downstream location can serve to direct the attributes of the actuator so as to obtain a desired control goal, or objective (see Fig. 12.11). For unsteady flows, Joslin, Nicolaides, Erlebacher, Hussaini & Gunzburger (1995) considered feed forward control for instability suppression. Determining optimal feedback laws is a very difficult proposition, especially in the context of nonlinear problems, so that one usually has to be content with using sub-optimal feedback laws. In this section the wave cancellation problem is used to discuss feed forward and feedback control. As discussed by Joslin, *et al.* (1995), the computations consist of the integration of the sensors, actuators, and controller as shown in Fig. 12.11. The sensors will record the unsteady pressure or shear on the wall; the spectral analyzer (controller) will analyze the sensor data and prescribe a rational output signal; the actuator will use this output signal to control the disturbance growth and stabilize the instabilities within the laminar boundary layer. Although a closed loop feedback system could be implemented (using an additional sensor downstream of the actuator) to fully automate the control and to lead to nearly exact cancellation of the instability, the feedback will not be introduced here due to the added computational expense of the iterative procedure. The feedback control law would simply compare the measure energy in the residual disturbance and alter the actuation amplitude toward obtaining a near-zero residual. This section will describe a simple feed forward strategy for wave cancellation in order to maintain laminar flow.

Here, the term controller refers to the logic that is used to translate sensor supplied data into a response for the actuator based on some control law. For the present study, a spectral controller is used. Such a controller requires a knowledge of the distribution of energy over frequencies and spatial wave numbers. For the wave suppression problem, a minimum of two sensors must

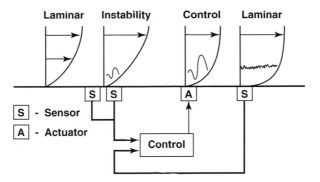

Fig. 12.11. Sketch of feed forward active control.

be used to record either the unsteady pressure or unsteady shear at the wall. By using fast Fourier transforms, this unsteady data can be transformed as

$$f(\omega) = \int_{-\infty}^{\infty} f(t)e^{-i\omega t}\,dt, \qquad (12.15)$$

where $f(t)$ is the signal and ω is the frequency. This transform yields an energy spectrum that indicates which frequencies contain energy and dominate the original signal.

The largest Fourier coefficient indicates which frequency should be used to control the disturbance even though the largest growth rate can be used instead of the largest coefficient. In addition to frequency information, the two sensors provide estimates of both spatial growth rates and phase via the relation

$$\alpha = \frac{1}{A}\frac{dA}{dx}, \qquad (12.16)$$

where A is the measured amplitude (complex Fourier coefficients of the dominant frequency mode). The temporal and spatial information are then substituted into the assumed control law or the wall-normal velocity boundary condition. We know that a functional control wave would have nearly the same amplitude but 180 degrees out of phase of the original disturbance at the point of control. This information provides a control law for the actuation. Namely, the computational actuator can be described by the following:

$$v_s(x, t) = v_w \left[p_w^1 e^{i(\omega + \phi_t)t + \alpha x_s} + c.c. \right]. \qquad (12.17)$$

Here, p_w^1 is the complex pressure (or shear) for the dominant frequency mode (or largest growth rate mode) at the first sensor; ω is the dominant mode determined from equation (12.15); ϕ_t is the phase shift parameter, t is the time, α is the growth rate and wave number information calculated from equation (12.16), and x_s is the distance between the first sensor and the actuator. Because the sensor information can be used only to approximate the actuator

amplitude and temporal phase, v_w and ϕ_t are parameters which must be optimized to obtain exact wave cancellation. This may be accomplished through a gradient descent algorithm and no attempt is made to demonstrate exact wave cancellation.

To demonstrate the effectiveness of feed forward control for wave cancellation, some sample results are presented from Joslin, *et al.* (1995). For the computations, the Reynolds number is $Re = 900$ (based on displacement thickness) and the disturbance frequency is $Fr = \omega/Re \times 10^6 = 86$, which is reminiscent of an unstable mode. The disturbance forcing slot has a length $5.13\delta_o^*$ and is centered $23.10\delta_o^*$ downstream of the computational inflow boundary. The first sensor is located $57.88\delta_o^*$ downstream of the inflow, and the second sensor is located $2.33\delta_o^*$ downstream of the first sensor. The actuator has a slot length $4.67\delta_o^*$ and is located $77.94\delta_o^*$ downstream of the inflow boundary. These separation distances were chosen arbitrarily for this demonstration. Ideally, the forcing, sensors, and actuator should have a minimal separation distance to improve the accuracy of the sensor information provided to the actuator.

A small amplitude disturbance ($v_f = 0.01\%$) is forced and controlled via the feed forward control law (12.17) without feedback. Figure 12.12 shows

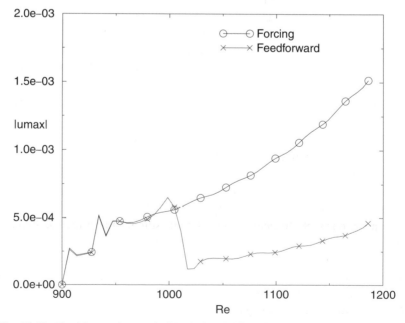

Fig. 12.12. Feed forward control of Tollmien-Schlichting waves in flat plate boundary layer.

the Tollmien-Schlichting wave amplitudes with downstream distance for the present spectrally controlled results compared with the control case ($v_w = 0.9v_f$; $\phi_t = 1.2\pi/\omega$) of Joslin, Erlebacher & Hussaini (1996) and the uncontrolled wave. The present results demonstrate that a measure of wave cancellation can be obtained from the feed forward system alone. Feedback is, however, necessary to optimize the control amplitude and phase for exact cancellation of the disturbance.

12.5 Optimal control theory

The optimal solution to suppress a single instability wave in a flat plate boundary layer is well understood and therefore would serve as a good test problem here to demonstrate the significant advantages of optimal control theory. Taken from the research of Joslin, Gunzburger, Nicolaides, Erlebacher & Hussaini (1997), a self-contained, automated methodology is presented for active flow control. This methodology couples the time-dependent Navier-Stokes system with an adjoint Navier-Stokes system and optimality conditions from which optimal states, i.e., unsteady flow fields and controls (e.g., actuators), may be determined. For wave cancellation, the objective of the control approach is to match the stress vector along a portion of the boundary to the desired steady laminar boundary layer value. Control is effected through the injection or suction of fluid through a single orifice on the boundary. The system determines whether injection or suction is warranted and at what point in time actuation is effected. The results for this sample test problem will demonstrate that instability suppression can be achieved without any a priori knowledge of the disturbance field, which is significant because other control techniques have required some knowledge of the flow unsteadiness such as frequencies, energy content, etc.

The goal of optimal control theory is to minimize or maximize an objective function in a robust manner. When the flow is time-dependent, and a strong function of initial conditions, it becomes difficult to establish the precise controls that will achieve the desired effect. Wave cancellation, as discussed above, only works well when the input wave fashion, or through a feedback mechanism, one seeks to cancel its effect while still in a linear regime. In practice, there are many waves that can interact nonlinearly in ways not always known in advance. Rather than try to cancel the incoming waves, one seeks appropriate controls in other ways. One means of achieving this, without an extensive search over the space of possible controls, is to postulate a family of desired controls. For example, an arbitrary time-dependent amplitude and a specified spatial distribution to find an objective function (i.e., stress over a region of the plate). Then, through a formal minimization process, one derives

a set of differential equations and their adjoints whose solutions produce the optimal actuator profile among the specified set. While the solution to this set of equations cannot be accomplished in real time, the results can be applied using standard passive or active control mechanisms. The advantage of this approach is that entire collections of controls can be studied simultaneously rather than one at a time. Optimal control techniques will not provide the real time control where there is ultimate interest but, by systematically computing the best control within specified tolerances and with a given objective function, it will be possible to develop strategies (active or passive) to control a wide variety of disturbances. For example, to effectively control boundary layer transition due to the interaction of a crossflow vortex and a Tollmien-Schlichting wave using periodic heating and cooling, optimal control would allow (1) a determination of the best objective function to use for a given type of control (some are better than others) and (2) provide insight into the relationship between the time dependence of the control and the input waves. This insight could then be built into a neural network, or other type of self-learning system, to allow effective control over a wide range of input parameters.

Optimal control methodologies have been recently applied to a variety of problems involving drag reduction, flow and temperature matching, etc. to provide more sophisticated flow control strategies in engineering applications. Computational fluid dynamics (CFD) algorithms have reached a sufficiently high level of maturity, generality, and efficiency so that it is now feasible to implement sophisticated flow optimization methods that lead to a large number of coupled partial differential equations. Optimal control theory is quite mathematical, and its formal nature is amenable to the derivation of mathematical theorems related to existence of solutions and well posedness of the problem. Only partial results of this type are possible in three dimensions since, in this case, the Navier-Stokes equations themselves do not enjoy a full theoretical foundation; in two dimensions, a complete theory is available. Two recent surveys of the mathematical theories of optimal flow control are Gunzburger (1995) and Borggaard, Burkardt, Gunzburger & Peterson (1995). A mathematical study of a simplified problem related to the one considered in this paper can be found in Fursikov, Gunzburger & Hou (1996).

12.5.1 Optimization methodology

In the present setting, an objective or cost functional is defined that measures the difference between the measured stresses, and the desired laminar values along a limited section of the bounding wall and over a specified length of time. One may interpret the objective functional as a sensor, i.e., the objective

functional senses how far the flow stresses along the wall are from the corresponding desired values. To control the flow, time dependent injection and suction are imposed along a small orifice in the bounding wall. Although the spatial dependence of the suction profile is specified (for simplicity), the optimal control methodology determines the time variation of this profile. However, unlike feedback control methodologies wherein the sensed data determines the control through a specified feedback law or controller, here the time dependence of the control is the natural result of the minimization of the objective functional. However, in the optimal control setting, the sensor is actually an objective functional and the controller is a coupled system of partial differential equations that determine the control that does the best job of minimizing the objective functional.

12.5.2 The state equations

Let Ω denote the flow domain which is the semi-infinite channel or boundary layer $[x \geq 0, 0 \leq y \leq h]$, where h is the location of the upper wall for the channel or the truncated free stream distance for the boundary layer. Let Γ denote its boundary and let $(0, T)$ be the time interval of interest. The inflow part of the boundary $[x = 0, 0 \leq y \leq h]$ is denoted by Γ_i. The part of the boundary on which control is applied (i.e., along which the suction and blowing actuator is placed) by Γ_a and is assumed to be a finite connected part of the lower boundary (or wall) $[x \geq 0, y = 0]$. Solid walls are denoted by Γ_w; for the channel flow, Γ_w is the lower boundary $[x \geq 0, y = 0]$ with Γ_a excluded and the upper boundary $[x \geq 0, y = h]$; for the boundary layer flow, Γ_w is only the lower boundary with Γ_a excluded. For the boundary layer case, the upper boundary $[x \geq 0, y = h]$, which is not part of Γ_w, is denoted by Γ_e. Controls are only activated over the given time interval $T_0 < t < T_1$, where $0 \leq T_0 < T_1 \leq T$.

The flow field is described by the velocity vector (u, v) and the scalar pressure p and is obtained by solving the following momentum and mass conservation equations (11.9) to (11.11) subject to the initial and boundary conditions:

$$(u, v)|_{t=0} = (u_0, v_0) \quad \text{in} \quad \Omega, \tag{12.18}$$

$$(u, v)|_{\Gamma_a} = \begin{cases} (g_1, g_2) & \text{in} \quad (T_0, T_1) \\ (0, 0) & \text{in} \quad (0, T_0) \quad \text{and} \quad (T_1, T) \end{cases}, \tag{12.19}$$

$$(u, v)|_{\Gamma_i} = (u_i, v_i) \quad \text{and} \quad (u, v)|_{\Gamma_w} = (0, 0) \quad \text{in} \quad (0, T), \tag{12.20}$$

and

$$(u, v, p) \to \text{base flow}, \quad \frac{\partial u}{\partial x}, \frac{\partial v}{\partial x} \to 0 \quad \text{as} \quad x \to \infty. \tag{12.21}$$

Here, the initial velocity vector $(u_0(x, y), v_0(x, y))$ and the inflow velocity vector $(u_i(t, y), v_i(t, y))$ are assumed given and the base flow is assumed to be Poiseuille flow for the channel case or the Blasius flow for the boundary layer case. The above system holds for both the channel and Blasius flow cases. In the latter case, the upper boundary is not part of Γ_w and the additional boundary conditions

$$u|_{\Gamma_e} = U_\infty \quad \text{and} \quad p - 2v\frac{\partial v}{\partial y}\bigg|_{\Gamma_e} = P_\infty \quad \text{in} \quad (0, T) \qquad (12.22)$$

are imposed, where U_∞ and P_∞ denote the free stream flow speed and pressure, respectively.

The control functions $g_1(t, x)$ and $g_2(t, x)$, which give the rate at which fluid is injected or sucked tangentially and perpendicularly, respectively, through Γ_a are to be determined as part of the optimization process. In order to make sure that the control remains bounded at T_0, it is required that

$$g_1|_{t=T_0} = g_{10}(x) \quad \text{and} \quad g_2|_{t=T_0} = g_{20}(x) \quad \text{on} \quad \Gamma_a, \qquad (12.23)$$

where $g_{10}(x)$ and $g_{20}(x)$ are specified functions defined on Γ_a. Commonly, one chooses $g_{10}(x) = g_{20}(x) = 0$.

12.5.3 The objective functional and the optimization problem

Assume that Γ_s is a finite, connected part of the lower boundary $[x \geq 0, y = 0]$ which is disjoint from Γ_a and that (T_a, T_b) is a time interval such that $0 \leq T_a < T_b \leq T$. Then, consider the functional

$$
\begin{aligned}
\mathcal{J}(u, v, p, g_1, g_2) &= \frac{\alpha_1}{2} \int_{T_a}^{T_b}\!\!\int_{\Gamma_s} |\tau_1 - \tau_a|^2 \, d\Gamma dt \\
&+ \frac{\alpha_2}{2} \int_{T_a}^{T_b}\!\!\int_{\Gamma_s} |\tau_2 - \tau_b|^2 \, d\Gamma dt \\
&+ \frac{\beta_1}{2} \int_{T_0}^{T_1}\!\!\int_{\Gamma_a} \left(\left|\frac{\partial g_1}{\partial t}\right|^2 + |g_1|^2\right) d\Gamma dt \\
&+ \frac{\beta_2}{2} \int_{T_0}^{T_1}\!\!\int_{\Gamma_a} \left(\left|\frac{\partial g_2}{\partial t}\right|^2 + |g_2|^2\right) d\Gamma dt, \quad (12.24)
\end{aligned}
$$

where g_1 and g_2 denote the controls and $\tau_a(t, x)$ and $\tau_b(t, x)$ are given functions defined on $(T_a, T_b) \times \Gamma_s$. Note that since Γ_s is part of the lower boundary of the channel or boundary layer wall, $\tau_1 = v\partial u/\partial y$ and $\tau_2 = -p + 2v\partial v/\partial y$ are the shear and normal stresses, respectively, exerted by the fluid

on the bounding wall along Γ_s and thus τ_a and τ_b may be interpreted as given shear and normal stresses, respectively. Then, the boundary segment Γ_s can be thought of as a sensor that measures the stresses on the wall. Thus, in (12.24), Γ_s is the part of the boundary Γ along which one wishes to match the shear and normal stresses to the given functions τ_a and τ_b, respectively, and (T_a, T_b) is the time interval over which this matching is to take place. Other than notational, there are no difficulties introduced if one wishes to match each component of the stress vector over a different boundary segment or over a different time interval.

The third and fourth terms in (12.24) are used to limit the size of the control. Indeed, no bounds are a priori placed on g_1 or g_2 and their magnitudes are limited by adding a penalty to the stress matching functional defined by the first two terms in (12.24). The particular form that these penalty terms take, i.e, the third and fourth terms in (12.24), is motivated by the necessity to limit not only the size of the controls g_1 and g_2, but also to limit oscillations. The constants α_1, α_2, β_1, and β_2 can be used to adjust the relative importance of the terms appearing in the functional (12.24).

The (constrained) optimization problem is given as follows:

> *Find u, v, p, g_1, and g_2 such that the functional $\mathcal{J}(u, v, p, g_1, g_2)$ given in (12.24) is minimized subject to the requirement that (11.9) to (11.11) and (12.18) to (12.21) and (12.24) are satisfied and, for the boundary layer flow case, (12.22) is also satisfied.*

12.5.4 The adjoint system

The method of Lagrange multipliers is formally used to enforce the constraints (11.9) to (11.11) and (12.19). To this end, the Lagrangian functional

$$
\mathcal{L}(u, v, p, g_1, g_2, \hat{u}, \hat{v}, \hat{p}, s_1, s_2)
$$
$$
= \frac{\alpha_1}{2} \int_{T_a}^{T_b} \int_{\Gamma_s} |\tau_1 - \tau_a|^2 \, d\Gamma dt + \frac{\alpha_2}{2} \int_{T_a}^{T_b} \int_{\Gamma_s} |\tau_2 - \tau_b|^2 \, d\Gamma dt
$$
$$
+ \frac{\beta_1}{2} \int_{T_0}^{T_1} \int_{\Gamma_a} \left(\left| \frac{\partial g_1}{\partial t} \right|^2 + |g_1|^2 \right) d\Gamma dt
$$
$$
+ \frac{\beta_2}{2} \int_{T_0}^{T_1} \int_{\Gamma_a} \left(\left| \frac{\partial g_2}{\partial t} \right|^2 + |g_2|^2 \right) d\Gamma dt
$$

$$-\int_0^T\!\!\int_\Omega \hat{u}\left[\frac{\partial u}{\partial t} + u\frac{\partial u}{\partial x} + v\frac{\partial u}{\partial y} + \frac{\partial p}{\partial x}\right.$$

$$\left.-2\nu\frac{\partial^2 u}{\partial x^2} - \nu\frac{\partial}{\partial y}\left(\frac{\partial u}{\partial y} + \frac{\partial v}{\partial x}\right)\right]d\Omega dt$$

$$-\int_0^T\!\!\int_\Omega \hat{v}\left[\frac{\partial v}{\partial t} + u\frac{\partial v}{\partial x} + v\frac{\partial v}{\partial y} + \frac{\partial p}{\partial y}\right.$$

$$\left.-\nu\frac{\partial}{\partial x}\left(\frac{\partial u}{\partial y} + \frac{\partial v}{\partial x}\right) - 2\nu\frac{\partial^2 v}{\partial y^2}\right]d\Omega dt$$

$$-\int_0^T\!\!\int_\Omega \hat{p}\left(\frac{\partial u}{\partial x} + \frac{\partial v}{\partial y}\right)d\Omega dt$$

$$-\int_{T_0}^{T_1}\!\!\int_{\Gamma_a} s_1(u - g_1)d\Gamma dt - \int_0^{T_0}\!\!\int_{\Gamma_a} s_1 u\, d\Gamma dt - \int_{T_1}^T\!\!\int_{\Gamma_a} s_1 u\, d\Gamma dt$$

$$-\int_{T_0}^{T_1}\!\!\int_{\Gamma_a} s_2(v - g_2)d\Gamma dt - \int_0^{T_0}\!\!\int_{\Gamma_a} s_2 v\, d\Gamma dt - \int_{T_1}^T\!\!\int_{\Gamma_a} s_2 v\, d\Gamma dt$$

$$(12.25)$$

is introduced. In (12.25), $\hat{u}$ and $\hat{v}$ are Lagrange multipliers that are used to enforce the x and y components of the momentum equation (11.9) and (11.10), respectively, $\hat{p}$ is a Lagrange multiplier that is used to enforce the continuity equation (11.11), and s_1 and s_2 are Lagrange multipliers that are used to enforce the x and y components of the boundary condition (12.19), respectively. Note that Lagrange multipliers have not been introduced to enforce the constraints (12.18), (12.20), (12.21) and (12.23), so that these conditions must be required of all candidate functions u, v, p, g_1, and g_2.

Through the introduction of Lagrange multipliers, the constrained optimization problem is converted into the unconstrained problem:

> *Find u, v, p, g_1, g_2, $\hat{u}$, $\hat{v}$, $\hat{p}$, s_1, and s_2 satisfying (12.18), (12.20), (12.21), and (12.23) such that the Lagrangian functional $\mathcal{L}(u, v, p, g_1, g_2, \hat{u}, \hat{v}, \hat{p},)s_1, s_2$ given by (12.25) is rendered stationary.*

In this problem, each argument of the Lagrangian functional is considered to be an independent variable so that each may be varied independently.

The first order necessary condition that stationary points must satisfy is that the first variation of the Lagrangian with respect to each of its arguments vanishes at those points. One easily sees that the vanishing of the first variations with respect to the Lagrange multipliers recovers the constraint equations (11.9)

to (11.11) and (12.19). Specifically,

$$\frac{\delta \mathcal{L}}{\delta \hat{u}}, \frac{\delta \mathcal{L}}{\delta \hat{v}} = 0 \Longrightarrow x\text{- and } y\text{-momentum equations (11.9) and (11.10),}$$

$$\frac{\delta \mathcal{L}}{\delta \hat{p}} = 0 \Longrightarrow \text{continuity equation (11.11),}$$

$$\frac{\delta \mathcal{L}}{\delta s_1}, \frac{\delta \mathcal{L}}{\delta s_2} = 0 \Longrightarrow x \text{ and } y \text{ components of (12.19),}$$

where $\delta \mathcal{L}/\delta \hat{u}$ denotes the first variation of $\mathcal{L}$ with respect to $\hat{u}$, etc.

Next, set the first variations of the Lagrangian with respect to the state variables u, v, and p equal to zero. These result in the *adjoint* or *co-state equations*. Note that for the channel flow, candidate solutions must satisfy (12.18), (12.20), (12.21), and (12.23), and thus

$$\delta u|_{t=0} = \delta v|_{t=0} = 0 \text{ on } \Omega, \quad \delta g_2|_{t=T_0} = 0 \text{ on } \Gamma_a,$$

$$\delta u|_{\Gamma_i} = \delta v|_{\Gamma_i} = 0; \quad \delta u|_{\Gamma_w} = \delta v|_{\Gamma_w} = 0 \text{ for } (0, T),$$

$$\delta p, \delta u, \delta v, \frac{\partial \delta u}{\partial x}, \frac{\partial \delta v}{\partial x} \to 0 \text{ as } x \to \infty \text{ for } (0, T). \quad (12.26)$$

Consider $\delta \mathcal{L}/\delta p = 0$ and

$$\alpha_2 \int_{T_a}^{T_b} \int_{\Gamma_s} \delta p \, (\tau_2 - \tau_b) \, d\Gamma + \int_0^T \int_\Omega \left(\hat{u} \frac{\partial \delta p}{\partial x} + \hat{v} \frac{\partial \delta p}{\partial y} \right) d\Omega dt = 0 \quad (12.27)$$

for arbitrary variations δp in the pressure. After applying Gauss' theorem to the above,

$$\alpha_2 \int_{T_a}^{T_b} \int_{\Gamma_s} \delta p \, (\tau_2 - \tau_b) \, d\Gamma - \int_0^T \int_\Omega \delta p \left(\frac{\partial \hat{u}}{\partial x} + \frac{\partial \hat{v}}{\partial y} \right) d\Omega dt$$

$$+ \int_0^T \int_\Gamma \delta p (\hat{u} n_1 + \hat{v} n_2) \, d\Gamma dt = 0, \quad (12.28)$$

where n_1 and n_2 denote the x and y components of the outward normal to Ω, respectively, along Γ by choosing variations δp that vanish on the boundary Γ but which are arbitrary in the interior Ω of the flow domain. Then,

$$\frac{\partial \hat{u}}{\partial x} + \frac{\partial \hat{v}}{\partial y} = 0 \text{ on } (0, T) \times \Omega. \quad (12.29)$$

Now, choosing variations δp that are arbitrary along the boundary Γ, shows that

$$\hat{u} n_1 + \hat{v} n_2 = \begin{cases} 0 & \text{on } (0, T) \times \Gamma \backslash \Gamma_s, (0, T_a) \times \Gamma_s, (T_b, T) \times \Gamma_s \\ -\alpha_2 \left(-p + 2v \frac{\partial v}{\partial y} - \tau_b \right) & \text{on } (T_a, T_b) \times \Gamma_s, \end{cases} \quad (12.30)$$

where $\Gamma \backslash \Gamma_s$ denotes the boundary Γ with Γ_s deleted. Note, that in the above

derivation of (12.29) and (12.30), as in the derivations found below, the boundary integrals at infinity do not make any contribution due to the last relation in (12.26).

Next, consider $\delta\mathcal{L}/\delta v = 0$, where the boundary and initial conditions (12.26) has been used to eliminate boundary integrals along Γ_i, Γ_w, and as $x \to \infty$, and an integral over Ω at $t = 0$. First, variations δv that vanish at $t = 0, t = T$, and in a neighborhood of Γ are chosen, but which are otherwise arbitrary. Such a choice implies that all boundary integrals in (12.26) vanish allowing for

$$-\frac{\partial\hat{v}}{\partial t} + \hat{u}\frac{\partial u}{\partial y} + \hat{v}\frac{\partial v}{\partial y} - u\frac{\partial\hat{v}}{\partial x} - v\frac{\partial\hat{v}}{\partial y} - \frac{\partial\hat{p}}{\partial y}$$

$$- v\frac{\partial}{\partial x}\left(\frac{\partial\hat{u}}{\partial y} + \frac{\partial\hat{v}}{\partial x}\right) - v\frac{\partial}{\partial y}\left(2\frac{\partial\hat{v}}{\partial y}\right) = 0 \quad \text{in} \quad (0, T) \times \Omega, \quad (12.31)$$

where equation (11.11) is used to effect a simplification. Next, variations that vanish in a neighborhood of Γ, but which are otherwise arbitrary, are chosen to obtain

$$\hat{v}|_{t=T} = 0 \quad \text{in} \quad \Omega. \tag{12.32}$$

Now, along Γ, δv and $\partial\delta v/\partial n$ may be independently selected, provided that (12.26) is satisfied. Also, $\partial/\partial n$ denotes the derivative in the direction of the outward normal to Ω along Γ. If $\delta v = 0$ and $\partial\delta v/\partial n$ varies arbitrarily along Γ, then

$$\hat{v} = \begin{cases} 0 & \text{on} \ (0, T) \times \Gamma\backslash\Gamma_s, (0, T_a) \times \Gamma_s, (T_b, T) \times \Gamma_s \\ \alpha_2\left(-p + 2v\frac{\partial v}{\partial y} - \tau_b\right) & \text{on} \ (T_a, T_b) \times \Gamma_s. \end{cases} \tag{12.33}$$

To see this, note that along the inflow, Γ_i, $n_2 = 0$ and $\partial/\partial n = -\partial/\partial x$ while, along the top and bottom boundaries $n_1 = 0$, $\partial/\partial n = \pm\partial/\partial y$, respectively, and, since $\delta v = 0$, $\partial\delta v/\partial x = 0$. Now (12.30) and (12.33) agree on the boundary segments where they simultaneously apply. Finally, δv is arbitrarily chosen along Γ_a to obtain

$$s_2 = -\hat{p}n_2 - \hat{v}(un_1 + vn_2) - v\left(\frac{\partial\hat{u}}{\partial y} + \frac{\partial\hat{v}}{\partial x}\right)n_1 - 2v\frac{\partial\hat{v}}{\partial y}n_2$$
$$\text{on} \ (0, T) \times \Gamma_a. \tag{12.34}$$

Next, consider $\delta\mathcal{L}/\delta u = 0$. By applying to the resulting equation the same process that led to (12.31) to (12.34) yields

$$-\frac{\partial\hat{u}}{\partial t} + \hat{u}\frac{\partial u}{\partial x} + \hat{v}\frac{\partial v}{\partial x} - u\frac{\partial\hat{u}}{\partial x} - v\frac{\partial\hat{u}}{\partial y} - \frac{\partial\hat{p}}{\partial x}$$

$$- v\frac{\partial}{\partial x}\left(2\frac{\partial\hat{u}}{\partial x}\right) - v\frac{\partial}{\partial y}\left(\frac{\partial\hat{u}}{\partial y} + \frac{\partial\hat{v}}{\partial x}\right) = 0 \quad \text{in} \quad (0, T) \times \Omega, \quad (12.35)$$

$$\hat{u}|_{t=T} = 0 \quad \text{in} \quad \Omega, \tag{12.36}$$

$$\hat{u} = \begin{cases} 0 \quad \text{on} \quad (0, T) \times \Gamma \backslash \Gamma_s, (0, T_a) \times \Gamma_s, (T_b, T) \times \Gamma_s \\ \alpha_1 \left(v \frac{\partial u}{\partial y} - \tau_a \right) \quad \text{on} \quad (T_a, T_b) \times \Gamma_s, \end{cases} \tag{12.37}$$

and

$$s_1 = -\hat{p} n_1 - \hat{u}(u n_1 + v n_2) - 2v \frac{\partial \hat{u}}{\partial x} n_1 - v \left(\frac{\partial \hat{u}}{\partial y} + \frac{\partial \hat{v}}{\partial x} \right) n_2$$

$$\text{on} \quad (0, T) \times \Gamma_a. \tag{12.38}$$

In deriving (12.37) we have used the assumption that Γ_s is part of the lower boundary of the channel so that along Γ_s we have that $n_2 = -1$. Again, there is no conflict between (12.28) and (12.37) along boundary segments on which both apply.

12.5.5 The optimality conditions

The only first order necessary conditions left to consider are $\delta\mathcal{L}/\delta g_1 = 0$ and $\delta\mathcal{L}/\delta g_2 = 0$. These conditions are usually called the *optimality conditions*. Now, since all candidate functions g_1 and g_2 must satisfy (12.23), it follows that $\delta g_1 = 0$ and $\delta g_2 = 0$ at $t = T_0$. Then, take $\delta\mathcal{L}/\delta g_2 = 0$ and apply Gauss' theorem to remove all derivatives from the variation δg_2. Choose variations δg_2 that vanish at $t = T_1$, but which are otherwise arbitrary and, using (12.34),

$$-\frac{\partial^2 g_2}{\partial t^2} + g_2 = -\frac{1}{\beta_2} \left(\hat{p} + 2v \frac{\partial \hat{v}}{\partial y} \right) \quad \text{on} \quad (T_0, T_1) \times \Gamma_a \tag{12.39}$$

results, where (12.33) and the assumption that Γ_a is part of the lower boundary so that, along Γ_a, $n_1 = 0$ and $n_2 = -1$, have been used. Now, choosing variations that are arbitrary at $t = T_1$ allows that $\partial g_2/\partial t = 0$ along Γ_a at $t = T_1$ so that, invoking (12.33), $g_2(t, x)$ satisfies

$$g_2|_{t = T_0} = g_{20}(x) \quad \text{and} \quad \frac{\partial g_2}{\partial t}\bigg|_{t = T_1} = 0 \quad \text{on} \quad \Gamma_a. \tag{12.40}$$

Note that, given $\hat{p}$ and $\hat{v}$, (12.39) and (12.40) constitute, at each point x on Γ_a, a two point boundary value problem in time over the interval (T_0, T_1).

In a similar manner, setting $\delta\mathcal{L}/\delta g_1 = 0$ leads to

$$-\frac{\partial^2 g_1}{\partial t^2} + g_1 = -\frac{1}{\beta_1} \left(v \frac{\partial \hat{u}}{\partial y} \right) \quad \text{on} \quad (T_0, T_1) \times \Gamma_a \tag{12.41}$$

$$g_1|_{t=T_0} = g_{10}(x) \quad \text{and} \quad \frac{\partial g_1}{\partial t}\bigg|_{t=T_1} = 0 \quad \text{on} \quad \Gamma_a. \tag{12.42}$$

12.5.6 Finite computational domains

Since we are still only considering the channel flow case, for the computations the semi-infinite domain Ω is replaced by a finite domain Ω_C defined by the introduction of the outflow boundary Γ_o given by $[x = L, 0 \leq y \leq h]$. Thus, we have that Ω_C is the rectangle $[0 \leq x \leq L, 0 \leq y \leq h]$. The outflow does not require the imposition of boundary conditions along the outflow boundary Γ_o because a buffer zone (Streett & Macaraeg, 1989) is attached to the end of the physical computational domain, where the governing equations are parabolized in this buffer region.

A similar treatment of the adjoint variables should have required consideration of an infinite domain $[-\infty < x < \infty, 0 < y < h]$. If this had been done, the boundary conditions (12.33) and (12.37) would not have been obtained along the inflow Γ_i. In fact, the inflow boundary Γ_i for the state equation is the outflow boundary for the adjoint equations and, conversely, the outflow boundary Γ_o for the state equation is the inflow boundary for the adjoint equations. This is easily seen by comparing the leading inertial terms of the state equations with t increasing and the adjoint equations with t decreasing. Now, on both Γ_i and Γ_o we have that $u > 0$ and $v \approx 0$ which is why Γ_i is an inflow boundary and Γ_o is an outflow boundary for the state. On the other hand, the fact that t is decreasing in the adjoint equations implies that now Γ_i is an outflow boundary and Γ_o is an inflow boundary for those equations.

Thus, to be consistent with the treatment of the state equations, the adjoint outflow Γ_i should be treated in a manner similar to the above treatment of the state outflow Γ_o. This treatment of the adjoint outflow does not require the imposition of any boundary conditions for the adjoint variables along Γ_i. Finally, since Γ_o is an inflow boundary for the adjoint equations, one has that

$$\hat{u} = 0 \quad \text{and} \quad \hat{v} = 0 \quad \text{on} \quad (0, T) \times \Gamma_o. \tag{12.43}$$

12.5.7 The optimality system for channel flow

We now have the full *optimality system* for channel flow whose solutions determine the optimal states, controls, and adjoint states. These are:

> *State equations – (11.9) to (11.11), (12.18) to (12.21)*
> *Co-state equations – (12.29) to (12.33), (12.35) to (12.37)*
> *Optimality equations – (12.39) to (12.42)*

Since (12.34) and (12.38) merely serve to determine the uninteresting Lagrange multipliers s_2 and s_1, they can be ignored.

The state equations are driven by the given initial velocity (u_0, v_0), the given inflow velocity (u_i, v_i), and the controls (g_1, g_2). Indeed, the purpose of this study is to determine g_1 and g_2 that optimally counteracts instabilities created upstream of Γ_a. The adjoint equations are homogeneous except for the boundary condition along Γ_s, the part of the boundary along which we are trying to match the stresses. The data in that boundary condition are exactly the discrepancy between the desired stresses τ_a and τ_b and the stresses $\tau_1 = v\partial u/\partial y$ and $\tau_2 = -p + 2v\partial u/\partial y$ along Γ_s, weighted by the factors α_1 and α_2. The equations for the controls are driven by the negative of the adjoint stresses along Γ_a, the part of the boundary along which we apply the control, weighted by the factors $1/\beta_1$ and $1/\beta_2$. Of course this division into equations for the state, the adjoint state, and the control is really obscured by the fact that equations are all intimately coupled.

12.5.8 The optimality system for boundary layer flow

If one follows a similar process to that used for the channel flow, one may derive an optimality system for the boundary layer. The only difference is that in the latter case Γ_w denotes only the lower boundary with Γ_a excluded and that the additional boundary condition (12.22) along the upper boundary Γ_e must be taken into account.

With the new interpretation for Γ_w, one can still define the Lagrangian functional (12.25) and use the constraints (12.26) on allowable variations. However, due to (12.22), allowable variations are further constrained by

$$\delta u|_{\Gamma_e} = \left(\delta p - 2v\frac{\partial \delta v}{\partial y}\right)\bigg|_{\Gamma_e} = 0 \quad \text{for} \quad (0, T), \tag{12.44}$$

which implies that, along Γ_e, one may not independently choose the variations in δp and $\partial \delta v/\partial y$. By simultaneously considering variations in p, v, and $\partial v/\partial y$ along Γ_e, one can show that

$$\hat{u} = 0 \quad \text{on} \quad (0, T) \times \Gamma_e. \tag{12.45}$$

Then, letting δv be arbitrary along Γ_e,

$$\hat{p} + 2v\frac{\partial \hat{v}}{\partial y} + v\hat{v} = 0 \quad \text{on} \quad (0, T) \times \Gamma_e. \tag{12.46}$$

The resulting system for the boundary layer now includes (12.45) and (12.46) in addition to the channel flow system.

12.5.9 Numerical experiments

The optimal control methodology (Joslin, *et al.*, 1997) was developed for the fully nonlinear Navier-Stokes system and thus is applicable to the case of non-linear and three-dimensional flow control. Here, we simply demonstrate the methodology for the wave cancellation problem because the optimal control is known a priori to be wave superposition and a single instability wave is evolving in a flat plate boundary layer.

The formidable coupled system is solved in an iterative manner. First, the Navier-Stokes equations are solved for the state variables, i.e., the velocity field (u, v) and pressure p with control information (i.e., no control $g_1 = g_2 = 0$ for first iteration). Then co-state equations are solved for the adjoint or co-state variables $(\hat{u}, \hat{v})$ and $\hat{p}$. Then, using these adjoint variables, the controls g_1 and g_2 are then found by solving the optimality equations. The procedure is repeated until satisfactory convergence is achieved.

The nonlinear unsteady Navier-Stokes equations and linear adjoint Navier-Stokes equations are solved by direct numerical simulation (DNS) of disturbances that evolve spatially within the boundary layer. The spatial DNS (Joslin, Streett & Chang, 1993; Joslin & Streett, 1994) approach involves spectral and high order finite difference methods and a three-stage Runge-Kutta method (Williamson, 1980) for time advancement. The influence matrix technique is employed to solve the resulting pressure equation (Streett & Hussaini, 1991). Disturbances are forced into the boundary layer by unsteady suction and blowing through a slot in the wall. The buffer domain technique (Streett & Macaraeg, 1989) is used for the outflow boundary treatment.

In the present study only normal injection or suction control is allowed, so that we set $g_1 = 0$ in (12.19), $\beta_1 = 0$ in the functional (12.24), and ignore (12.41) and (12.42). Also, we only match the normal stress along Γ_s so that we choose $\alpha_1 = 0$ in the functional (12.24) and in (12.37). The Reynolds number based on the inflow displacement thickness (δ_o^*) is $Re = 900$ and the nondimensional frequency for the forced disturbance is $F = \omega/Re \times 10^6 = 86$. The forcing amplitude is $v_f = 0.1\%$. The disturbance forcing slot Γ_f, the control or actuator orifice Γ_a, and the matching or sensor segment Γ_s have equal length $4.48\delta_o^*$. The forcing is centered downstream at $389.62\delta_o^*$. The Reynolds number based on the displacement thickness at that location is $Re = 1018.99$. The actuator is centered at $403.62\delta_o^*$ ($Re = 1037.13$) and the sensor is centered at $417.62\delta_o^*$ ($Re = 1054.97$). These separation distances were arbitrarily chosen for this demonstration. In practice, the control and matching segments should have a minimal separation distance so that the pair can be packaged as a single unit, or bundle, for distributed application of many bundles.

All simulations allow the flow field to develop for one period, i.e., from $t = 0 \to T_a = T_p$ before control is initiated. In the first series of simulations, the interval during which control is applied is arbitrarily chosen to be $T_a \to T_b = 2T_p$. Based on $\alpha_1 = \beta_1 = 0$, $\alpha_2 = 1$, and $\beta_2 = 10$, the convergence history for the wall-normal velocity and measured normal shear τ_2 are shown in Fig. 12.13. The velocities are obtained at a fixed distance from the wall corresponding to $1.18\delta_o^*$ and at the fixed time T_b. Convergence is obtained with four iterations. The results demonstrate that a measure of wave cancellation can be obtained from the DNS control theory system. The wall-normal amplitude of the modified wave at $Re = 1092.5$ is 40 percent of the uncontrolled wave. The control without optimizing the choice of α_1, α_2, β_1, and β_2 has led to a 60 percent decrease in the amplitude of the traveling wave. Clearly, Fig. 12.13 shows that a net reduction of the disturbance energy is obtained by energy input due to the control. This results in a delay of transition by way of a suppression of the instability evolution.

From the wave cancellation study of Joslin, Erlebacher & Hussaini (1996), the relationship between amplitude of the actuator (v_a) with resulting instability was similar to the channel flow wave cancellation study in Biringen (1984). The trend indicates that, beginning with a small actuation amplitude, as the actuation level is increased, the amount of wave cancellation by energy extraction from the disturbance increases. At some optimal actuation, nearly exact wave cancellation is achieved for the instability wave. As the actuation amplitude further increases the resulting instability amplitude increases. This was clearly explained in Joslin, *et al.* (1996) to occur because, in the wave superposition process, the actuator wave becomes dominant over the forced wave. At this point, the resulting instability undergoes a phase shift corresponding to the phase of the wave generated by the actuator. The relationship is encouraging for the DNS optimal control theory approach and suggests that a gradient descent type algorithm might further enhance the wave suppression capability of the present approach. Namely, an approach for the optimal selection of α_1, α_2, β_1, and β_2 might lead to a more useful theoretical and computational tool for flow control.

To simply demonstrate this concept, Lagrange interpolation (or perhaps extrapolation) is introduced for β_1 and β_2 based on imposed values for α_1 and α_2:

$$\beta_{1,2}^{n+1} = \frac{\beta_{1,2}^{n}\left(\tau_{1,2}^{*} - \tau_{1,2}^{n-1}\right) - \beta_{1,2}^{n-1}\left(\tau_{1,2}^{*} - \tau_{1,2}^{n}\right)}{\left(\tau_{1,2}^{n} - \tau_{1,2}^{n-1}\right)}, \qquad (12.47)$$

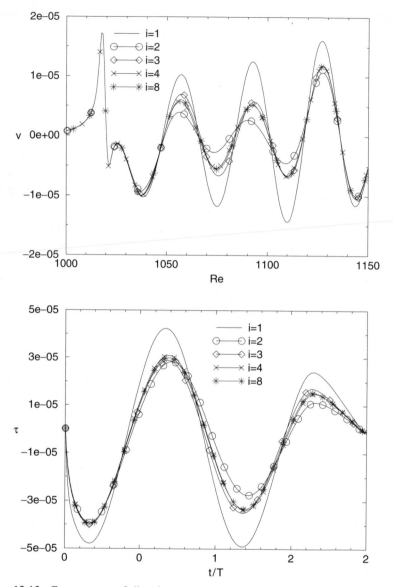

Fig. 12.13. Convergence of disturbance wall-normal velocity with downstream distance (top figure) and measured shear stress with discrete time (bottom figure) for control of Tollmien-Schlichting waves in flat plate boundary layer.

Table 12.1. *Normal stress for two values of β_2.*

β_2	normal stress
10	9.369×10^{-6}
11	8.814×10^{-6}

where $\tau_{1,2}^*$ are some desired values of the stress components and $\tau_{1,2}^n$ are the stress components based on the choice $\beta_{1,2}^n$. Although τ_1^* and τ_2^* may be equivalent to the target values τ_a and τ_b in the functional (12.24), this may lead to significant over/under shoots for the iteration process. Instead, τ_1^* and τ_2^* is the incremental decrease, or target value, for interpolation to more desirable β_1 and β_2 values. To illustrate this process, the $\beta_2 = 10$ and $\beta_2 = 11$ control results are obtained with the iteration procedure. The measures of normal stress are somewhat arbitrarily obtained at some time as measured by the sensor or matching segment Γ_s. The values of the normal stress are given in Table 12.1. These values are used for a desired normal stress τ_2^*, which in this case is 65% of the $\beta_2 = 11$ results.

Using the results for $\beta_2 = 10$ and $\beta_2 = 11$ in (12.47) yields the value $\beta_2 = 16.5$ which is used in a simulation to obtain a greater degree of instability suppression. The Wave Cancellation (WC) results and the enhanced optimal control solution are shown in Fig. 12.14. This interpolation approach based on relationship of Fig. 12.14 indicates that optimizing β_2 has led to results very close to WC. The solutions differ somewhat near $t = T_a$ and $t = T_b$ because of the conditions (12.40) and (12.42) that serve to control the levels of g_1 and g_2. For all practical purposes, the solutions obtained with the present DNS control theory methodology provide the desired flow control features without prior knowledge of the forced instability.

The adjoint system requires that the velocity field (u, v) obtained from the Navier-Stokes equations be known for all time. For the iteration sequence and a modestly coarse grid, 82 Mbytes of disk (or runtime) space are required to store the velocities at all time steps and for all grid points. For $T_a \rightarrow T_b = 3T_p$, 246 Mbytes are necessary for the computation. Clearly for three-dimensional problems the control scheme becomes prohibitively expensive. Therefore, a secondary goal of this study is to determine if this limitation can be eliminated.

Because the characteristics of the actuator (g_1 and g_2) and resulting solutions are comparable to WC, some focus should be placed on eliminating the enormous memory requirements discussed above. This limitation can easily

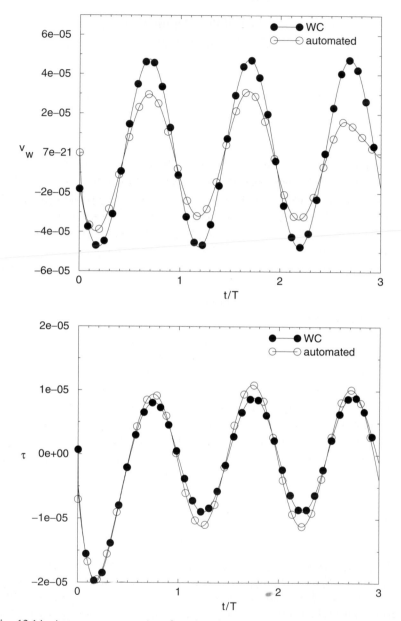

Fig. 12.14. Actuator response (top figure) and sensor-measured shear stress (bottom figure) for the control of Tollmien-Schlichting waves in a flat plate boundary layer.

be removed if the flow control problem involves small amplitude unsteadiness (or instabilities). The time-dependent coefficients of the adjoint system (12.31) and (12.35) reduce to the steady-state solution and no additional memory is required over the Navier-Stokes system in terms of coefficients. This has been verified by a comparison of a simulation with steady coefficients compared with the C2[1] control case. As expected, the results for both cases are identical. Additionally, if the instabilities have small amplitudes, then a linear Navier-Stokes solver can be used instead of the full nonlinear solver that was used in the present study. This linear system would be very useful for the design of flow control systems. However, if the instabilities in the flow have sufficient amplitude to interact nonlinearly, then some measure of unsteady coefficient behavior is likely required and then, depending on the amplitudes, the coefficients saved at every time step may be replaced with storing coefficients every 10 or more time steps thereby reducing the memory requirements by an order of magnitude. This hypothesis will require further study.

12.5.10 Summary

The coupled Navier-Stokes equations, adjoint Navier-Stokes, and equations for optimality were solved and validated for the flow control problem of instability wave suppression in a flat plate boundary layer. By solving the above system, optimal controls were determined that met the objective of minimizing the perturbation normal stress along a portion of the bounding wall. As a result, the optimal control was found to be an effective means for suppressing two-dimensional, unstable Tollmien-Schlichting traveling waves. The results indicate that the DNS control theory solution is comparable to the wave cancellation result but, unlike the latter, requires no a priori knowledge of the instability characteristics.

12.6 Exercises

Begin with the baseline solutions that you obtained from DNS and linear stability theory for Reynolds number based on displacement thickness ($Re = 900$) and non-dimensional frequency ($F = 86 = \omega/Re \times 10^6$) and the profiles from the Orr-Sommerfeld equation and Blasius basic flows for the initial conditions.

1. Introduce an oscillatory suction and blowing condition downstream of the wave forcing location (control actuator). Do a parameter analysis on the amplitude and frequency of the actuator, holding the forcing conditions fixed.

---

[1] See Chapter 10 for definition of C2 criterion.

Discuss your results. Did you observe any wave cancellation or suppression downstream of the actuator? Why or why not?

2. Write a simple routine to represent the feed forward strategy discussion in Section 12.4. Implement this strategy as discussion in the section using two grid points upstream of the actuator but downstream of the forcing wave generator. With two sensors, is it easy or difficult to cancel the wave? Why or why not?

3. Discuss the process you might use to introduce optimal flow control theory into your DNS code. Would you see these changes to the code as being extremely difficult, somewhat difficult, or easy to implement? Explain the rationale for your answer.

Chapter 13

Investigating hydrodynamic instabilities with experiments

This text has covered some historical and more advanced theoretical and computational techniques to predict the onset of transitional flows with linear methods, the amplification and interaction of these linear modes in the nonlinear regime, and the matching of these predictions with empirical models. Furthermore, some methods of control have been developed and discussed in the chapter on flow control. Here, we address issues associated with investigating hydrodynamic instabilities using experimental techniques. These issues include the experimental facility, model configuration, and instrumentation, all of which impact the understanding of hydrodynamic instabilities.

Because the authors have primary expertise in theory and computation, we readily acknowledge the topics in this chapter are based on literature from leading scientists and engineers in the field of transitional flows. This chapter serves as an introduction to the experimental process. The content of this chapter is primarily based on the review by Saric (1994b) and a text by Smol'yakov & Tkachenko (1983).

13.1 Experimental Facility

Because the theoretical and computational modeling of a hydrodynamic instability process is the goal, two key aspects of the flow must be carefully documented in the experiment before studying the instabilities. First, the physical properties of the flow environment must be understood within the experimental facility. The makeup of the facility dictates the background (or freestream) disturbances and the spatial-temporal characteristics of the flow environment.

The incoming freestream environment should be understood and characterized before commencing with a discussion of the use of artificial disturbances, that are typically the manner hydrodynamic instabilities are investigated. This freestream environment is dictated by the facility. Here, we will restrict our

401

discussion to wind tunnel facilities as opposed to free jet or water tunnel facilities. Typically, we design the experimental environment to mimic the environment that the application would encounter. For an aircraft in cruise flight this would be still air (low freestream turbulence and acoustic levels). For a turbine blade, this would be higher freestream levels associated with internal engine flows. As such, the wind tunnel must be constructed to achieve certain environmental goals to mimic the application. Most wind tunnels built to date have been designed for steady force balance measurements and typically have large freestream turbulence levels that make them inappropriate for use in hydrodynamic stability investigations. Such high turbulence levels overwhelm the potential existence and characterization of infinitesimal instability modes, making the background noise levels in the instrumentation far above the instability signal.

One of the first and now classical successful experimental investigations of hydrodynamic instabilities was conducted by Schubauer & Skramstad (1947) in a low turbulence tunnel ("Dryden tunnel") at the National Bureau of Standards. Additionally, Liepmann (1943) investigated hydrodynamic instabilities on curved walls. To minimize the turbulence levels, we now know that the diffuser design plays a significant role in the resulting flow characteristics. By introducing bends and a diverging diffuser the absence of sudden changes in the flow is ensured. Also, turbulence is damped by way of fine anti-turbulence screens as far upstream of the core measurement region as possible. For supersonic low disturbance wind tunnels, the turbulent boundary layer upstream of the chock location is removed by suction. The successful design of a low disturbance supersonic facility is extremely challenging because of the dominance of acoustic disturbances in the facility. The facility noise, such as vibration or the motor, must be suppressed to avoid contamination of the natural hydrodynamic modes with acoustically induced modes. Whereas the facility vibration can be inhibited with a mechanical vibration absorption means, the motor acoustics should be cancelled with mufflers. Finally, the air must be free from debris that could either stick to a model and act as a roughness element or impact or damage the instrumentation, that is typically very small and delicate. This can be accomplished using dust filters at the air intake point and upstream of the anti-turbulence screens.

The velocity fluctuations and turbulence levels should be documented in the free stream. Spatial correlations should be undertaken to decouple the turbulence and any existing acoustics fields. These measures will indicate whether the tunnel is a low turbulence or quiet facility. Although gaining an understanding of the facility attributes is essential to contributing to the study of

hydrodynamic instability, this step in the experimental process is often purposely not undertaken for two reasons. First, there can be considerable cost, in terms of funds and people, to perform this every time changes are made to the facility. Many contracts or grants will not cover the cost of such tests. The second rationale that may deter an organization from performing such a facility analysis resides with the meaning of the results. If the tunnel has extremely high disturbance levels, future business opportunities may be quenched because of the public knowledge of the tunnel deficiencies. So the topic of facility flow quality becomes a topic of debate. However, the characterization of the flow quality in the facility is key to understanding any hydrodynamic instability investigation.

13.2 Model configuration

Whereas the first key aspect of the flow was governed by the facility, the second salient aspect of the flow involves the installation of the model configuration in the facility and resulting basic state characteristics. For example, the leading edge of a flat plate model will have a nonzero pressure gradient. Downstream of the leading edge the measurements can indicate that the desired zero-pressure gradient field is present or a misalignment would yield an adverse or favorable pressure gradient. For a proper aligned, zero-pressure gradient flow, the now Blasius boundary layer will have an effective virtual leading edge which is different from the model's leading edge. If the measurements of instability modes in the flow do not account for this virtual leading edge, Reynolds number errors as high as 10-15 percent may result when comparing with theory. To ascertain a leading edge correction, one should measure the mean boundary layer and calculate the displacement thickness. From our understanding of the Blasius similarity scaling, the connection between the displacement thickness, streamwise location, and Reynolds number fall directly from the scaling.

In addition to the virtual leading edge correction that must be understood, small pressure gradients as small as fractions of 1 percent can significantly alter the stability or instability of traveling waves. To reduce this uncertainty and better understand the true characteristics of the basic flow, the shape factor should be measured using the boundary layer profiles at different stations in the downstream direction. Such minute pressure gradient features would become evident with changes in the shape factor. Further, any deviations in the spanwise direction should be documented because spanwise nonuniformalities can induce secondary instability modes.

13.3 Inducing hydrodynamics instabilities

As discussed in the previous sections, the facility and model directly impact the characteristics of experimentally observed hydrodynamic flow instabilities. Whereas turbulent flows are a robust and chaotic environment, the laminar counterflow is extremely sensitive to disturbances and, at the right flow conditions (e.g., Reynolds number), readily admit hydrodynamic instabilities. These instabilities can be induced by the natural tunnel environment or via more controlled artificial disturbance generators.

13.3.1 Natural disturbances

Although introducing artificial disturbances can be extremely beneficial to study numerous physical phenomena associated with the transition process, understanding the natural ingestion of disturbances has in recent years become a major research topic area. Under natural transition, the freestream turbulence, vorticity or acoustics can interact with the attributes of the model to introduce energy in the wavelength and frequency range relevant to the most unstable modes. This process known as receptivity has been discussed in Chapter 10. However, trying to understand what is measured downstream to the cause and effect attribute at disturbance inception is difficult and assumes that the direct receptivity mechanism can be inferred from downstream measurements.

13.3.2 Artificial disturbances

The process of hydrodynamic instability inception, amplification, and breakdown has been studied for over a century. While numerous techniques are available to study the later stages of this flow phenomena, the inception portion of this problem involves fluctuations too small to measure. Hence, comparisons between theory, computation, and experiments must recognize this deficiency in the comparisons. To minimize the unknowns in the upstream free stream environment and to control the experiment, artificial disturbances are introduced into the flow. As far back as the famous experiment by Schubauer & Skramstad (1947), artificial disturbances were introduced into a boundary by using a vibrating ribbon. In the presence of a stationary magnet, alternating current through the ribbon leads to a Lorentz force. This method leads to fluctuations with a prescribed dominant frequency and wavelength. A sufficiently long ribbon must be used or end effects from the ribbon can contaminate the flow. Even with a long ribbon, the end effects spread inwardly downstream at an angle of approximately 12 degrees. So, there is a cone of effectiveness that

is somewhat similar to side wall model and side wall end effects. Such end effects can alter the disturbance evolution process. The ribbon does not introduce a single mode but rather a disturbance whose dominant mode is the Tollmien-Schlichting wave for a flat plate boundary layer mean flow. This means a relaxation distance must be maintained until the more stable modes decay. This relaxation distance may be as much as 10 boundary layer thicknesses. The ribbon is an intrinsic device and so its presence may induce a wake that effects the basic flow state. Such an alteration of the basic state may induce otherwise less dominant instabilities. Furthermore, the disturbances induced by the vibrating ribbon may interact with other random disturbances already present in the flow and may potentially alter the amplification process as well as the nonlinear interactions in the nonlinear regime of the flow. The study of the nonlinear interaction of waves is complicated by the limitations of the disturbance generator. A large amplitude vibrating ribbon at a given frequency cannot introduce only these distinct and desired modes but rather the ribbon will introduce fundamental harmonics, and differences in the desired modes. Consequently the desired nonlinear instability study may be contaminated by the presence of additional modes that are related to the desired fundamental mode. Additionally, roughness elements can be placed at the branch I neutral point to maximize the receptivity in a flat plate boundary layer flow (King & Breuer, 2001). So similar to issues of natural disturbance induction, the artificial disturbance generation can lead to complications and requires care in the experimental study.

13.4 Measurement instrumentation

In this section, qualitative visual and quantitative measurement techniques are outlined for the study of hydrodynamic instabilities. Widely used techniques to visualize the instabilities include liquid crystals, smoke wire, and tracer techniques. Thermo-anemometry (hot wires and hot films) are discussed as quantitative measuring techniques.

13.4.1 Liquid crystals

Liquid crystals can be applied to a model using an air brush and should be applied evenly over the model. The approach is useful to measure abrupt changes in the surface shear stress properties by distinct color changes that can be recorded with a camera. Such abrupt changes of surface shear stress occur in flows that have separated or the onset of transition and are most relevant to our discussion. This robust technique is useful in the later stages of transition and

such information is a valuable aid to the placement of quantitative information and to visualize potential three-dimensionality in the flow transition process. The use of liquid crystals could induce additional instabilities within the flow due to the potentially nonsmooth application on a model. The flow could take this nonsmooth surface to be a rough surface which, in turn, contributes to the receptivity and amplification of infinitesimal modes. Also, chloroform is the solvent used to remove the remaining liquid crystals from the model and is somewhat cumbersome to use in a closed laboratory environment.

13.4.2 Smoke wires

The second flow visualization technique summarized here is the smoke wire. The smoke wire has a diameter typically ranging from 50 to 80 μm. A computer is used to initiate a set voltage with a time-delayed shutter release. The connected wire that has a coating of oil is heated via the voltage and generates a burst of smoke streaks. This smoke then travels downstream with the flow and is distorted with the flow. Problems can arise with the smoke wire similar to any intrusive measurement technique. Any upstream mode basing by the smoke wire will feel the interference of the wire. The traveling wave would involve a step like change in its amplitude resulting from the wire. Saric (1994b) also carefully notes that the quantitative measurements of a wave pattern should be acquired with the flow visualization technique in the flow. Furthermore, measurements within 15 diameters of the smoke wire should be interpreted with caution because of the wire-induced effects on the flow.

13.4.3 Bubbles and dyes

Finally, tracer techniques that have been successfully used to visually study transitional flows included hydrogen bubbles in water and dyes. The benefits and difficulties of these techniques are similar to the smoke wire technique, with the addition of possible buoyancy effects for bubbles.

13.4.4 Thermo-anemometry

Thermo-anemometry consists of a hot wire and hot film techniques. Shown in Fig. 13.1 are schematics of various thermo-anemometry concepts. For quantification of the fluctuations in the flow, the hot wire anemometer has been one of the most widely used techniques to date. A diameter for a hot wire is typically 3-5 μm and is therefore extremely delicate. The straight wire and slant wire pair can be used to accurately measure the streamwise and spanwise velocity

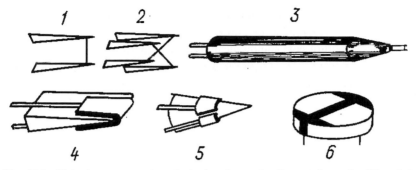

Fig. 13.1. Hot-wire anemometers: 1-single wire probe; 2-two wire probe (X-probe); 3-general appearance of probe and its body; 4-wedge-shaped film probe; 5-conical film probe; 6-thin film anemometer probe (flush mounted) (after Smol'yakov & Tkachenko, 1983).

fluctuations. For thin boundary layers, the wall normal cannot be measured due to the span of the wire. Because this technique relies on the correlation between temperature and velocity on a Wheatstone bridge, the temperatures during calibration and testing should be within a few degrees to avoid errors in the measurements. Similar to the visualization techniques, the hot wires or traverse mechanism may cause blockage and interfere with the flow field. The essential element of the hot wire is the miniature metal element that is heated by an electrical current. The metals most typically used are tungsten, platinum or platinum iridium. In a flow on situation, the cooling of the element or heat transfer to the fluid increase with increasing flow velocity. Hence, recording the cooling process with a bridge circuit leads to a relationship between the electrical resistance and the flow velocity. This relationship requires a calibration with a known velocity field. The sensitivity of the hot wire enables quantitative measures down to a few percent of the mean flow velocity.

A second technique to measure flow instabilities in a laminar flow (as well as turbulent flows) is the hot film. Here, the film is attached to the surface of the model and is used to measure the spectra and shear stress from the oncoming flow. Multiple films can provide phase and group velocity directions. This robust technique is often used in flight experiments primarily for shear stress measurements, ascertaining whether the flow is laminar, intermittent, or turbulent. See Fischer & Anders (1999) for a description of hot film usage in a supersonic laminar flow control flight experiment. The metals used for hot films are typically platinum and nickel.

For a better understanding of the mechanics of hot films, the discussion of Hosder & Simpson (2001) is summarized to describe how an experimental measurement is turned from a voltage signal into a shear stress. The hot film

sensors heat the near-wall region of the fluid by forced convection. The heat transfer gives a measure of the shear because of the similarity between the gradient transport of heat and momentum. The time-averaged voltage (v) and shear stress (τ_w) are connected through a constant temperature anemometer by King's Law or

$$\frac{v^2}{(T_w - T_\infty)} = A + B(\tau_w)^{1/3}, \tag{13.1}$$

where T_w is the sensor temperature and T_∞ is the free stream or tunnel temperature. The constants A and B are found by a linear regression through the calibration procedure. Hence, from this relationship, one can easily see that large changes in the fluid temperature during an investigation can lead to erroneous results or cause the experimentalist to re-calibrate the sensor.

Recently, advanced measurement techniques, such as laser Doppler velocimetry and particle image velocimetry, have successfully been used to measure two and three-dimensional fluctuations in turbulent flows. Such techniques have not been demonstrated for transition flows because of insufficient frequency response of the systems.

13.5 Signal analysis

The devices described above for obtaining quantitative information on hydrodynamic instabilities involve the transformation of a physical quantity into electrical current or voltage fluctuations. The electrical signals must then be processed to obtain velocities. This processing can be accomplished with analog or digital electronics. For analog systems, the continuous electrical signal is transformed in a similar fashion as an operator is applied to a mathematical function. An oscillatory electrical signal that is tuned to a specific frequency will transmit Fourier components of only that frequency, just as a Fourier transform. For a digital system, the continuous signal is encoded into a series of discrete levels. The more frequent the encoding, the higher the quantization frequency and the more detailed the correspondence between the discrete and continuous values. The quantization frequency is then extremely important and is usually referred to as the analog to digital conversion. The coded signals are then fed to computer memory for immediate or later analysis by a program. For a given quantization frequency, this post-analysis program dictates resulting statistics of the measurements. The discrete approach is advantageous because it does not depend on the origin of the data; however, highly fluctuating flow fields require large quantization frequencies and hence a large amount of stored data. So the analysis in a post-experimental program will lead to the

final spatial and temporal modal information for the disturbances. As such, we will not elaborate on various analysis approaches. However, one can easily begin a Fourier transform analysis routine to obtain dominant modal information; this analyzer is typically referred to as a spectral analyzer.

13.6 Summary

Many issues associated with experimentally measuring hydrodynamic instabilities have been discussed in this chapter. Because this text is primarily associated with theoretical and computational issues with hydrodynamic instabilities, this chapter is meant to be a cursory look at experimentation. The topic is extremely challenging and requires an understanding of the instability processes before moving to the laboratory.

References

[1] Acheson, D.J. (1990). *Elementary Fluid Dynamics*. Oxford Applied Mathematics and Computing Science Series, Oxford University Press.

[2] Ames, W.F. (1977). *Numerical Methods for Partial Differential Equations*. Academic Press.

[3] Arnal, D., Habiballah, M. & Coustols, E. (1984). Théorie de l'instabilité laminaire et critères de transition en écoulement bi- et tridimensionnel. *La Recherche Aérospatiale* N° 1984-2.

[4] Arnal, D., Casalis, G. & Juillen, J.C. (1990). *Experimental and Theoretical Analysis of Natural Transition on Infinite Swept Wing*. IUTAM Symposium Laminar-Turbulent Transition, Toulouse, France (ed. D. Arnal & R. Michel), Springer-Verlag.

[5] Arnal, D., Juillen, J.C. & Casalis, G. (1991). The effects of wall suction on laminar-turbulent transition in three-dimensional flow. *ASME FED*, 114, 155–162.

[6] Arnal, D. (1994). Boundary layer transition: predictions based on linear theory. *AGARD Rep.* 793.

[7] Artola, M. & Majda, A.J. (1987). Nonlinear development of instabilities in supersonic vortex sheets. *Physica D*, 28, 253–281.

[8] Ashpis, D.E. & Erlebacher, G. (1990). On the continuous spectra of the compressible boundary layer stability equations. In *Instability and Transition*, II, (eds. M.Y. Hussaini & R.G. Voigt), Springer, 145–159.

[9] Balachandar, S., Streett, C.L. & Malik, M.R. (1990). Secondary Instability in Rotating Disk Flows AIAA Paper 90-1527, June 1990.

[10] Balakumar, P. & Malik, M.R. (1992). Discrete modes and continuous spectra in supersonic boundary layers. *J. Fluid Mech.*, 239, 631–656.

[11] Balsa, T.F. & Goldstein, M.E. (1990). On the instabilities of supersonic mixing layers: a high Mach number asymptotic theory. *J. Fluid Mech.*, 216, 585–611.

[12] Barston, F.M. (1980). A circle theorem for inviscid steady flows. *Intl. J. Eng. Sci.*, 477–489.

[13] Batchelor, G.K. & Gill, A.E. (1962). Analysis of the stability of axisymmetric jets. *J. Fluid Mech.*, 14, 529–551.

[14] Batchelor, G.K. (1964). Axial flow in trailing line vortices. *J. Fluid Mech.*, 20, 645–658.

[15] Batchelor, G.K. (1967). *An Introduction to Fluid Dynamics*. Cambridge University Press.

[16] Bayly, B.J., Orszag, S.A. & Herbert, Th. (1988). Instability mechanisms in shear flow transition. *Ann. Rev. Fluid Mech.*, 20, 359–391.

[17] Benney, D.J. & Lin, C.C. (1960). On the secondary motion induced by oscillations in a shear flow. *Phys. Fluids*, 3(4), 656–657.

[18] Benney, D.J. (1961). A non-linear theory for oscillations in a parallel flow. *J. Fluid Mech.*, 10, 209–236.

[19] Benney, D.J. (1964). Finite amplitude effects in an unstable laminar boundary layer. *Phys. Fluids*, 7, 319–326.

[20] Benney, D.J. & Gustavsson, L.H. (1981). A new mechanism for linear and nonlinear hydrodynamic instability. *Studies in Applied Mathematics*, 64, 185–209.

[21] Bertolotti, F.P. (1985). Temporal and spatial growth of subharmonic disturbances in Falkner-Skan flows. M. S. Thesis, Virginia Polytechnic Institute and State University.

[22] Bertolotti, F.P. (1992). Linear and nonlinear stability of boundary layers with streamwise varying properties. Ph.D. Thesis, The Ohio State University.

[23] Bertolotti, F.P. & Crouch, J.D. (1992). Simulation of boundary layer transition: Receptivity to spike stage. NASA CR-191413.

[24] Bertolotti, F.P. & Joslin, R.D. (1995). The effect of far-field boundary conditions on boundary-layer transition. *Journal of Computational Physics*, 118, May, 392–395.

[25] Bestek, H., Thumm, A. & Fasel, H.F. (1992). Numerical investigation of later stages of transition in transonic boundary layers. In First European Forum on Laminar Flow Technology, March 16–18, 1992. Hamburg, Germany.

[26] Betchov, R. & Szewczyk, A. (1963). Stability of a shear layer between parallel streams. *Phys. Fluids*, 6(10), 1391–1396.

[27] Betchov, R. & Criminale, W.O. (1966). Stability instability of the inviscid jet and wake. *Phys. Fluids*, 9, 359–362.

[28] Betchov, R. & Criminale, W.O. (1967). *Stability of Parallel Flows*. New York: Academic Press.

[29] Biringen, S. (1984). Active control of transition by periodic suction-blowing. *Phys. Fluids*, 27(6), 1345–1347.

[30] Blackaby, N., Cowley, S.J. & Hall, P. (1993). On the instability of hypersonic flow past a flat plate. *J. Fluid Mech.*, 247, 369.

[31] Blumen, W. (1970). Shear layer instability of an inviscid compressible fluid. *J. Fluid Mech.*, 40, 769–781.

[32] Blumen, W., Drazin, P.G. & Billings, D.F. (1975). Shear layer instability of an inviscid compressible fluid, Part 2. *J. Fluid Mech.*, 71, 305–316.

[33] Bogdanoff, D.W. (1983). Compressibility effects in turbulent shear layers. *AIAA J.*, 21(6), 926–927.

[34] Borggaard, J., Burkardt, J., Gunzburger, M. & Peterson, J. (1995). *Optimal Design and Control*, Boston: Birkhauser.

[35] Bower, W.W., Kegelman, J.T., Pal, A. & Meyer, G.H. (1987). A numerical study of two-dimensional instability-wave control based on the Orr-Sommerfeld equation. *Phys. Fluids*, 30(4), 998–1004.

[36] Boyce, W.E. & DiPrima, R.C. (1986). *Elementary Differential Equations and Boundary Value Problems*. London: John Wiley, 4th Edition.

[37] Breuer, K.S. & Haritonidis, J.H. (1990). The evolution of a localized disturbance in a laminar boundary layer. Part I. Weak disturbances. *J. Fluid Mech.*, 220, 569–594.

[38] Breuer, K.S. & Kuraishi, T. (1994). Transient growth in two and three dimensional boundary layers. *Phys. Fluids* A, 6, 1983–1993.

[39] Briggs, R.J. (1964). Electron-stream interaction with plasmas. Cambridge, MA: MIT Press, Research Monograph No. 29.

[40] Brown, W.B. (1959). Numerical calculation of the stability of cross flow profiles in laminar boundary layers on a rotating disc and on a swept back wing and an exact calculation of the stability of the Blasius velocity profile. Northrop Aircraft, Inc., Rep. NAI 59-5.

[41] Brown, W.B. (1961a). A stability criterion for three-dimensional laminar boundary layers. *Boundary Layer and Flow Control.* 2, ed. G.V. Lachmann, 913–923. London: Pergamon.

[42] Brown, W.B. (1961b). Exact solution of the stability equations for laminar boundary layers in compressible flow. *Boundary Layer and Flow Control.* 2, ed. G.V. Lachmann, 1033–1048. London: Pergamon.

[43] Brown, W.B. (1962). Exact numerical solutions of the complete linearized equations for the stability of compressible boundary layers. Northrop Aircraft Inc., NORAIR Division Rep. NOR-62-15.

[44] Brown, W.B. (1965). Stability of compressible boundary layers including the effects of two-dimensional linear flows and three-dimensional disturbances. Northrop Aircraft Inc., NORAIR Division Rep.

[45] Brown, W.B. & Roshko, A. (1974). On density effects and large structure in turbulent mixing layers. *J. Fluid Mech.*, 64, 775–816.

[46] Bun, Y. & Criminale, W.O. (1994). Early period dynamics of an incompressible mixing layer. *J. Fluid Mech.*, 273, 31–82.

[47] Burden, R.L. & Faires, J.D. (1985). *Numerical Analysis*. 3rd Edition. Prindle, Weber and Schmidt.

[48] Bushnell, D.M., Hefner, J.N. & Ash, R.L. (1977). Effect of compliant wall motion on turbulent boundary layers. *Phys. Fluids*, 20, S31–S48.

[49] Butler, K.M. & Farrell, B.F. (1992). Three dimensional optimal perturbations in viscous shear flow. *Phys. Fluids* A, 4, 1637–1650.

[50] Canuto, C., Hussaini, M.Y., Quarteroni, A. & Zang, T.A. (1988). *Spectral Methods in Fluid Dynamics*. New York: Springer-Verlag.

[51] Carpenter, P.W. & Garrad, A.D. (1985). The hydrodynamic stability of flow over Kramer-type compliant surfaces: Part 1. Tollmien-Schlichting instabilities. *J. Fluid Mech.*, 155, 465–510.

[52] Carpenter, P.W. & Garrad, A.D. (1986). The hydrodynamic stability of flow over Kramer-type compliant surfaces: Part 2. Flow-induced surface instabilities. *J. Fluid Mech.*, 170, 199–232.

[53] Carpenter, P.W. & Morris, P.J. (1989). Growth of 3-D instabilities in flow over compliant walls. *Proceedings of the 4th Asian Congress of Fluid Mechanics*, Hong Kong.

[54] Carpenter, P.W. (1990). Status of transition delay using compliant walls. *Viscous Drag Reduction in Boundary Layers*, 123, pp. 79–113, ed. D.M. Bushnell & J.N. Hefner, Washington, DC: AIAA.

[55] Carpenter, P.W. & Morris, P.J. (1990). The effects of anisotropic wall compliance on boundary-layer stability and transition, *J. Fluid Mech.*, 218, 171–223.

[56] Carpenter, M.H., Gottlieb, D. & Abarbanel, S. (1993). The stability of numerical boundary treatments for compact high-order finite difference schemes. *J. Comp. Phys.*, 108(2), 272–295.

[57] Case, K.M. (1960a). Stability of inviscid plane couette flow. *Phys. Fluids*, 3(2), 143–148.

[58] Case, K.M. (1960b). Stability of an idealized atmosphere. I. Discussion of results. *Phys. Fluids*, 3, 149–154.

[59] Case, K.M. (1961). Hydrodynamic stability and the inviscid limit. *J. Fluid Mech.*, 10(3), 420–429.

[60] Cebeci, T. & Stewartson, K. (1980). On stability and transition in three-dimensional flows. *AIAA J.*, 18(4), 398–405.

[61] Chang, C.L. & Malik, M.R. (1992). Oblique mode breakdown in a supersonic boundary layer using nonlinear PSE. *Instability, Transition, and Turbulence*, (M.Y. Hussaini, A. Kumar, & C.L. Streett, eds.), 231–241. Springer-Verlag, New York.

[62] Charney, J.G. (1947). The dynamics of long waves in a baroclinic westerly current. *J. Meteor.*, 4, 135–162.

[63] Chen, J.H., Cantwell, B.J. & Mansour, N.N. (1989). Direct numerical simulation of a plane compressible wake: stability, vorticity dynamics, and topology. Ph.D. dissertation, Thermosciences Division, Stanford University, Report No. TF-46.

[64] Chen, J.H., Cantwell, B.J. & Mansour, N.N. (1990). The effect of Mach number on the stability of a plane supersonic wake. *Phys. Fluids* A, 2, 984.

[65] Chimonas, G. (1970). The extension of the Miles-Howard theorem to compressible fluids. *J. Fluid Mech.*, 43, 833–836.

[66] Chinzei, N., Masuya, G., Komuro, T., Murakami, A. & Kudou, D. (1986). Spreading of two-stream supersonic turbulent mixing layers. *Phys. Fluids*, 29, 1345–1347.

[67] Choudhari, M. (1994). Roughness induced generation of crossflow vortices in three-dimensional boundary layers. *Theor. & Comput. Fluid Dyn.*, 5, 1–31.

[68] Choudhari, M. & Streett, C.L. (1994). Theoretical prediction of boundary-layer receptivity. 25th AIAA Fluid Dynamics Conf., June 20–23, 1994. Colorado, CO. AIAA Paper 94-2223.

[69] Clauser, F.H. & Clauser, M.U. (1937). The effect of curvature on the transition from laminar to turbulent boundary layer. NACA Tech. Note 613.

[70] Coles, D. (1965). Transition in circular Couette flow. *J. Fluid Mech.*, 21, Part 3, 385–425.

[71] Cooper, A.J. & Carpenter, P.W. (1997). The stability of the rotating disk boundary layer flow over a compliant wall. Type I and Type II instabilities. *J. Fluid Mech.*, 350, 231.

[72] Cousteix, J. (1992). Basic concepts on boundary layers. Special Course on Skin Friction Drag Reduction, *AGARD Rep.* 786.

[73] Cowley, S.J. & Hall, P. (1990). On the instability of hypersonic flow past a wedge. *J. Fluid Mech.*, 214, 17.

[74] Craik, A.D.D. (1971). Nonlinear resonant instability in boundary Layers. *J. Fluid Mech.*, 50(2), 393–413.

[75] Craik, A.D.D. & Criminale, W.O. (1986). Evolution of wavelike disturbances in shear flows: a class of exact solutions of the Navier-Stokes equations. *Proc. Roy. Soc.* A, 13–26.

[76] Criminale, W.O. & Kovasznay, L.S.G. (1962). The growth of localized disturbances in a laminar boundary layer. *J. Fluid Mech.*, 14, 59–80.

[77] Criminale, W.O. & Drazin, P.G. (1990). The evolution of linearized perturbations of parallel flows. *Studies Appl. Math.*, 83, 123–157.

[78] Criminale, W.O. (1991). Initial-value problems and stability in shear flows. International Symposium on Nonlinear Problems in Engineering and Science, Beijing, China, 43–63.

[79] Criminale, W.O., Long, B. & Zhu, M. (1991). General three-dimensional disturbances to inviscid Couette flow. *Studies in Appl. Math.*, 86, 249–267.

[80] Criminale, W.O., Jackson, T.L. & Lasseigne, D.G. (1995). Towards enhancing and delaying disturbances in free shear flows. *J. Fluid Mech.*, 294, 283–300.

[81] Criminale, W.O., Jackson, T.L., Lasseigne, D.G. & Joslin, R.D. (1997). Perturbation dynamics in viscous channel flows. *J. Fluid Mech.*, 339, 55–75.

[82] Criminale, W.O. & Drazin, P.G. (2000). The initial-value problem for a modelled boundary layer. *Phys. Fluids* A, 12, 366–374.

[83] Criminale, W.O. & Lasseigne, D.G. (2003). Use of multiple scales, multiple time in shear flow stability analysis, submitted.

[84] Crouch, J.D. (1994). Receptivity of boundary layers. AIAA Paper 94-2224.

[85] Dagenhart, J.R., Saric, W.S., Mousseux, M.C. & Stack, J.P. (1989). Crossflow vortex instability and transition on a 45-degree swept wing. AIAA Paper No. 89–1892.

[86] Dagenhart, J.R. & Saric, W.S. (1994). Crossflow stability and transition experiments in a swept wing flow. (accepted) NASA TP, 1994.

[87] Danabasoglu, G., Biringen, S. & Streett, C.L. (1990). Numerical simulation of spatially-evolving instability control in plane channel flow. AIAA Paper No. 90-1530.

[88] Danabasoglu, G., Biringen, S. & Streett, C.L. (1991). Spatial simulation of instability control by periodic suction blowing. *Phys. Fluids* A, 3(9), 2138–2147.

[89] Davey, A. & Drazin, P.G. (1969). The stability of Poiseuille flow in a pipe. *J. Fluid Mech.*, 36, 209–218.

[90] Davey, A. (1980). On the numerical solution of difficult boundary-value problems. *J. Comput. Phys.*, 35, 36–47.

[91] Davey, A. (1982). In *Stability in the Mechanics of Continua* (ed. F.H. Schroeder), Springer, 365–372.

[92] Davey, A. (1984). A difficult numerical calculation concerning the stability of the Blasius boundary layer. Unpublished manuscript.

[93] Day, M.J., Reynolds, W.C. & Mansour, N.N. (1998a). The structure of the compressible reacting mixing layer: Insights from linear stability analysis. *Phys. Fluids*, 10(4), 993–1007.

[94] Day, M.J., Reynolds, W.C. & Mansour, N.N. (1998b). Parametrizing the growth rate influence of the velocity ratio in compressible reacting mixing layers. *Phys. Fluids*, 10(10), 2686–2688.

[95] Dean, W.R. (1928). Fluid motion in a curved channel. *Proc. Roy. Soc.* Ser. A., 15, 623–631.

[96] Demetriades, A. (1958). An experimental investigation of the stability of the hypersonic laminar boundary layer. California Institute of Technology, Guggenheim Aeronautical Laboratory, Hypersonic Research Project, Memo. No. 43.

[97] Deardorff, J.W. (1963). On the stability of viscous plane Couette flow. *J. Fluid Mech.*, 15, 623–631.

[98] Dhawan, S. & Narasimha, R. (1958). Some properties of boundary layer flow during transition from laminar to turbulent motion. *J. Fluid Mech.*, 3(4), 418–436.

[99] Dikii, L.A. (1960). On the stability of plane parallel flows of an inhomogeneous fluid. (in Russian) *Prikl.i Mekh.*, 24, 249–257 (English translation: *J. Appl. Math.Mech.*, 24, 357–369).

[100] DiPrima, R.C. (1959). The stability of viscous flow between rotating concentric cylinders with a pressure gradient acting around the cylinders. *J. Fluid Mech.*, 6, 462–468.

[101] DiPrima, R.C. (1961). Stability of nonrotationally symmetric disturbances for viscous flow between rotating cylinders. *Phys. Fluids*, 4, 751–755.

[102] DiPrima, R.C. & Habetler, G.J. (1969). A completeness theorem for non-selfadjoint eigenvalue problems in hydrodynamic stability. *Archive for Rational Mechanics and Analysis*, 34(3), 218–227.

[103] Djordjevic, V.D. & Redekopp, L.G. (1988). Linear stability analysis of nonhomentropic, inviscid compressible flows. *Phys. Fluids*, 31(11), 3239–3245.

[104] Drazin, P.G. & Howard, L.N. (1962). Shear layer instability of an inviscid compressible fluid. Part 2. *J. Fluid Mech.*, 71, 305–316.

[105] Drazin, P.G. & Davey, A. (1977). Shear layer instability of an inviscid compressible fluid, Part 3. *J. Fluid Mech.*, 82, 255–260.

[106] Drazin, P.G. (1978). Variations on a theme of Eady. In *Rotating Fluids in Geophysics*, eds. P. H. Roberts & A. M. Soward, 139–169.

[107] Drazin, P.G. & Reid, W.H. (1984). *Hydrodynamic Stability*. Cambridge: Cambridge University Press.

[108] Duck, P.W. & Khorrami, M.R. (1992). A note on the effects of viscosity on the stability of a trailing-line vortex. *J. Fluid Mech.*, 245, 175–189.

[109] Duck, P.W., Erlebacher, G. & Hussaini, M.Y. (1994). On the linear stability of compressible plane Couette flow. *J. Fluid Mech.*, 258, 131–165.

[110] Dunn, D.W. & Lin, C.C. (1955). On the stability of the laminar boundary layer in a compressible fluid. *Journal of the Aeronautical Sciences*, 22, 455–477.

[111] Dunn, D.W. (1960). Stability of laminar flows. Reprint of Article from *DME/NAE Quarterly Bulletin* No. 1960 (3), National Research Council of Canada, Ottawa, October 1960, 15–58.

[112] Eady, E.A. (1949). Long waves and cyclone waves. *Tellus*, 1, 33–52.

[113] Eckhaus, W. (1962a). Problémes non linéaires dan la théorie de la Stabilité. *Journal de Mecanique*, 1, 49–77.

[114] Eckhaus, W. (1962b). Problémes non linéaires de stabilité dans un espace a deux dimensions. I. Solutions péridoques. *Journal de Mecanique*, 1, 413–438.

[115] Eckhaus, W. (1963). Problémes non linéaires de stabilité dans un espace a deux dimenions. II. Stabilité des solutions périodqués. *Journal de Mecanique*, 2, 153–172.

[116] Eckhaus, W. (1965). *Studies in Non-linear Stability Theory*. Berline: Springer.

[117] Ekman, V.W. (1905). On the influence of the earth's rotation on ocean currents. *Arkiv för Matematik*, Astronomi, och Fysik, Band 2, No. 11.

[118] Eliassen, A., Høiland, E. & Riis, E. (1953). Two dimensional perturbations of a flow with constant shear of a stratified fluid. *Inst. Weather Climate Res.*, Oslo, Publ. No. 1.

[119] Esch, R.E. (1957). The instability of a shear layer between two parallel streams. *J. Fluid Mech.*, 3, 289–303.

[120] Faller, A.J. & Kaylor, R.E. (1967). Instability of the Ekman spiral with applications to the planetary boundary layer. *Phys. Fluids Supplement*, s212–s219.

[121] Fasel, H. (1976). Investigation of the stability of boundary layers by a finite-difference model of the Navier-Stokes equations. *J. Fluid Mech.*, 78, 355–383.

[122] Fasel, H. (1990). Numerical simulation of instability and transition in boundary layer flows. *Laminar-Turbulent Transition, IUTAM*, eds. D. Arnal & R. Michel. Berlin: Springer-Verlag.

[123] Fasel, H. & Thumm, A. (1991). Numerical simulation of three-dimensional boundary layer transition. *Bull. Am. Phys. Soc.*, 36, 2701.

[124] Fedorov, A.V. & Khokhlov, A.P. (1993). Excitation and evolution of unstable disturbances in supersonic boundary layer. *ASME FED*, 151, Transitional and Turbulent Compressible Flows.

[125] Fischer, M. & Anders, S. (1999) F-16XL-2 supersonic laminar flow control flight experiment. NASA TP.

[126] Fjørtoft, R. (1950). Application of integral theorems in deriving criteria of stability of laminar flow and for the baroclinc circular vortex. *Geofysiske Publikasjoner*, 17, 1–52.

[127] Floquét, G. (1883). Sur les équations differéntielles linéaires á coefficients périodiques. *Annales Scientifiques Ecole Normale Superieure*, 2(12), 47–89.

[128] Fromm, J.E. & Harlow, F.H., (1963). Numerical solution of the problem of vortex street development. *Phys. Fluids*, 6, 975–982.

[129] Fursikov, A.V., Gunzburger, M. & Hou, L. (1996). Boundary value problems and optimal boundary control of the Navier-Stokes system: the two-dimensional case. *SIAM Journal of the Control Optimizaiton*, 36, 1998, 852–894.

[130] Gad-el-Hak, M., Pollard, A. & Bonnet, J.P. (Eds.) (1998). *Flow Control: Fundamentals and Practices*. Springer-Verlag, New York.

[131] Gad-el-Hak, M. (2000) *Flow Control: Passive, Active, and Reactive Flow Management*. Cambridge University Press, Cambridge.

[132] Gaster, M. (1962). A note on the relation between temporally-growing and spatially-growing disturbances in hydrodynamic stability. *J. Fluid Mech.*, 14, 222–224.

[133] Gaster, M. (1965a). The role of spatially growing waves in the theory of hydrodynamic stability. *Progress in Aeronautical Science*, 6, 251–270.

[134] Gaster, M. (1965b). On the generation of spatially growing waves in a boundary layer. *J. Fluid Mech.*, 22, 433–441.

[135] Gaster, M. (1965c). A simple device for preventing turbulent contamination on swept leading edges. *J. Roy. Aero. Soc.*, 69, 788–789.

[136] Gaster, M. (1968). Growth of disturbances in both space and time. *Phys. Fluids*, 11(4), 723–727.

[137] Gaster, M. & Davey, A. (1968). The development of three dimensional wave packets in unbounded parallel flows. *J. Fluid Mech.*, 32, 801–808.

[138] Gaster, M. & Grant, I. (1975). An experimental investigation of the formation and development of a wave packet in a laminar boundary layer. *Proc. Roy. Soc.* A, 347, 253–269.

[139] Gaster, M. (1988). Is the Dolphin a Red-Herring? *Turbulence Management and Relaminarisation*, 285–304 (ed. H.W. Liepmann and R. Narasimha), IUTAM:Bangalore, India.

[140] Gear, C.W. (1978). *Applications and Algorithms in Science and Engineering*. Science Research Associates, Inc.

[141] Germano, M., Piomelli, U., Moin, P. & Cabot, W.H. (1991). A dynamic subgrid-scale eddy viscosity model. *Phys. Fluids*, 3, 1760.

[142] Girard, J.J. (1988). Study of the stability of compressible Couette flow. Ph.D. dissertation, Washington State University.

[143] Glatzel, W. (1988). Sonic instability in supersonic shear flows. *Mon. Not. R. Astron. Soc.*, 233, 795.

[144] Glatzel, W. (1989). The linear stability of viscous compressible plane Couette flow. *J. Fluid Mech.*, 202, 515–541.

[145] Gold, H. (1963). Stability of laminar wakes. Ph.D. Dissertation, California Institute of Technology.

[146] Goldstein, S. (1930). Concerning some solutions of the boundary layer equations in hydrodynamics. *Proc. Camb. Phil. Soc.*, 26, 1–30.

[147] Goldstein, M.E. (1983). The evolution of Tollmien-Schichting waves near a leading edge. *J. Fluid Mech.*, 127, 59–81.

[148] Goldstein, M.E. (1985). Scattering of acoustic waves into Tollmien-Schlichting waves by small streamwise variations in surface geometry. *J. Fluid Mech.*, 154, 509–529.

[149] Goldstein, M.E. (1987). Generation of Tollmien-Schlichting waves on interactive marginally seperated flows. *J. Fluid Mech.*, 181, 485–518.

[150] Goldstein, M.E. & Wundrow, D.W. (1990). Spatial evolution of nonlinear acoustic mode instabilities on hypersonic boundary layers. *J. Fluid Mech.*, 219, 585.

[151] Görtler, H. (1940a). Über eine dreidimensionale Instabilität laminarer Grenzschichten an konkaven Wänden, Nachr. Akad. Wiss, Göttingen Math-Physik Kl. IIa, *Math-Physik-Chem. Abt.* 2, 1–26 (Translation NACA Tech. Memo. 1375, June 1954).

[152] Görtler, H. (1940b). Über den Einfluss der Wandkrümmung auf die Enstehung der Turbulenz. *Z. Angew. Math. Mech.*, 20, 138–147.

[153] Görtler, H. & Witting, H. (1958). Theorie der sekundaren Instabilität der laminaren Grenzschichten. International Union of Theoretical and Applied Mechanics, Grenzschichtforschung, Freiburg, 110–126.

[154] Gottlieb, D. & Orszag, S.A. (1986). *Numerical Analysis of Spectral Methods: Theory and Applications.* Society for Industrial and Applied Mathematics: Philadelphia, PA.

[155] Granville, P.S. (1953). The calculation of the viscous drag of bodies of revolution. David Taylor Model Basin Rep. 849.

[156] Greenough, J., Riley, J., Soestrisno, M. & Eberhardt, D. (1989). The effect of walls on a compressible mixing layer. AIAA Paper 89-0372.

[157] Greenspan, H.D. (1969). *The Theory of Rotating Fluids.* Cambridge University Press.

[158] Gregory, N., Stuart, J.T. & Walker, W.S. (1955). On the stability of three-dimensional boundary layers with application to the flow due to a rotating disk. *Phil. Trans. R. Soc.* London. A, 248, 155–199.

[159] Gropengiesser, H. (1969). On the stability of free shear layers in compressible flows. *Deutsche Luft. und Raumfahrt*, FB 69–25. Also, NASA Tech. Transl. NASA TT F-12,786, 1970.

[160] Grosch, C.E. & Salwen, H. (1978). The continuous spectrum of the Orr-Sommerfeld equation. Part 1. The spectrum and the eigenfunctions. *J. Fluid Mech.*, 87, 33–54.

[161] Grosch, C.E. & Jackson, T.L. (1991). Inviscid spatial stability of a three dimensional mixing layer. *J. Fluid Mech.*, 231, 35–50.

[162] Grosch, C.E., Jackson, T.L., Klein, R., Majda, A. & Papageorgiou, D.T. (1991). Supersonic-supersonic modes of a compressible mixing layer. Unpublished manuscript.

[163] Grosskreutz, R. (1975). An attempt to control boundary-layer turbulence with non-isotropic compliant walls. *University Science Journal Dar es Salaam*, 1, 65–73.

[164] Guirguis, R.H. (1988). Mixing enhancement in supersonic shear sayers: III. Effect of convective Mach number. AIAA 88-0701.

[165] Gunzburger, M. (1995). *Flow Control*. Berlin: Springer.

[166] Gustavsson, L.H. (1979). Initial-value problem for boundary layer flows. *Phys. Fluids*, 22(9), 1602–1605

[167] Gustavsson, L.H. & Hultgren, L.S. (1980). A resonance mechanism in plane Couette flow. *J. Fluid Mech.*, 98, 149–159.

[168] Gustavsson, L.H. (1991). Energy growth of three dimensional disturbances in plane Poiseuille flow. *J. Fluid Mech.*, 224, 241–260.

[169] Haberman, R. (1987). *Elementary Applied Partial Differential Equations*. 2nd edition, Englewood Cliffs, New Jersey: Prentice-Hall, Inc.

[170] Hagen, G. (1855). Über den einfluss der temperatur auf die bewegung des wassers in rohren. *Math. Abh. Akad. Wiss.* (aus dem Jahr 1854), 17–98.

[171] Hains, F.D. (1967). Stability of plane Couette-Poiseuille flow. *Phys. Fluids*, 10, 2079–2080.

[172] Hall, P., Malik, M.R. & Poll, D.I.A. (1984). On the stability of an infinite swept attachment line boundary layer. *Proc. Roy. Soc.* A, A395, 229–245.

[173] Hall, P. & Malik, M.R. (1986). On the instability of a three-dimensional attachment-line boundary layer: weakly nonlinear theory and a numerical simulation. *J. Fluid Mech.*, 163, 257–282.

[174] Hall, P. & Smith, F.T. (1991). On strongly nonlinear vortex/wave interactions in boundary layer transition. *J. Fluid Mech.*, 227, 641–666.

[175] Hama, F.R., Williams, D.R. & Fasel, H. (1979). Flow field and energy balance according to the spatial linear stablity theory of the Blasius boundary layer. In: *Laminar-Turbulent Transition*, IUTAM Symposium (ed. E. Eppler and H. Fasel), Stuttgart, Germany, September 16–22, 1979, pp. 73–85.

[176] Hämmerlin, G. (1955). Über das Eigenwertproblem der dreidimensionalen Instabilität laminarer Grenzschichten an konkaven Wänden. *J. Rat. Mech. Anal.*, 4, 279–321.

[177] Harris, J.E., Iyer, V. & Radwan, S. (1987). Numerical solutions of the compressible 3-D boundary layer equations for aerospace configurations with emphasis on LFC. NASA Symp. on Research in Natural Laminar Flow and Laminar Flow Control, March 16–19, 1987. NASA Langley Research Center. NASA CP-2487, (eds. J.N. Hefner & F.E. Sabo), 517–545.

[178] Haynes, T.S. & Reed, H.L. (1996). Computations in nonlinear saturation of stationary crossflow vortices in a swept-wing boundary layer. AIAA Paper 96-0182.

[179] Hazel, P. (1972). Numerical studies of the stability of inviscid stratified shear flows. *J. Fluid Mech.*, 51, 39–61.

[180] Healey, J.J. (1995). On the neutral curve of the flat plate boundary layer: comparison between experiment, Orr-Sommerfeld theory and asymptotic theory. *J. Fluid Mech.*, 288, 59–73.

[181] Hefner, J.N. & Bushnell, D.M. (1980). Status of linear boundary-layer stability theory and the e^N method, with emphasis on swept-wing applications. NASA TP 1645.

[182] Heisenberg, W. (1924). Uber Stabilitat und Turbulenz von Flussigkeitsstromen. *Ann. Physik*, 74, 577–627. Translated as, On stability and turbulence of fluid flows. NACA TM-1291, 1951.

[183] Helmholtz, H. (1868). Über discontinuirliche flüssigkeits-bewegungen. *Akad. Wiss.*, Berlin, Monatsber., 23, 215–228. Translated by F. Guthrie, On discontinuous movements of fluids. *Phil. Mag.*, 36(4), 337–346, 1868.

[184] Herbert, Th. (1983). Secondary instability of plane channel flow to subharmonic three-dimensional disturbances. 26(4), 871–874.

[185] Herbert, Th., Bertolotti, F.P. & Santos, G.R. (1985). Floquet analysis of secondary instability in shear flows. In: *Stability of Time Dependent and Spatially Varying Flows*, August 19–23, 1985, 43–57.

[186] Herbert, Th. (1988). Secondary instability of boundary layers. *Annual Review of Fluid Mechanics*, 20, 487–526.

[187] Herbert, Th. (1991). Boundary-layer transition analysis and prediction revisited. AIAA Paper 91-0737.

[188] Herbert, Th. (1997). Parabolized stability equations. *Annual Review of Fluid Mechanics*, 29, 245–283.

[189] Herron, I.H. (1987). The Orr-Sommerfeld equation on infinite intervals. *SIAM Review*, 29(4), 597–620.

[190] Hiemenz, K. (1911). Die grenzschicht an einem in den gleichförmigen flüssigkeitsstrom eingetauchten geraden kreiszylinder. Thesis, Göttingen, *Dingl. Polytechn. J.*, 326, 321.

[191] Hill, D.C. (1995). Adjoint systems and their role in the receptivity problem for boundary layers. *J. Fluid Mech.*, 292, 183–204.

[192] Hocking, L.M. (1975). Non-linear instability of the asymptotic suction velocity profile. *Quart. J. Mech. Appl. Math.*, 28, 341–353.

[193] Høiland, E. (1953). On two-dimensional perturbations of linear flow. *Geofysiske Publikasjoner*, 18, 1–12.

[194] Holmes, B.J., Obara, C.J., Gregorek, G.M., Hoffman, M.J. & Freuhler, R.J. (1983). Flight investigation of natural laminar flow on the Bellanca Skyrocket II. SAE Paper 830717.

[195] Hosder, S. & Simpson, R.L. (2001). Unsteady Turbulent Skin Friction and Separation Location Measurements on a Maneuvering Undersea Vehicle. 39th AIAA Aerospace Sciences Meeting & Exhibit, 8–11 January 2001/Reno, NV AIAA Paper No. 2001-1000.

[196] Howard, L.N. (1961). Note on a paper of John W Miles. *J. Fluid Mech.*, 10, 509–512.

[197] Howard, L.N. & Gupta, A.A. (1962). On the hydrodynamic and hydromagnetic stability of swirling flows. *J. Fluid Mech.*, 14, 463–476.

[198] Hu, F.Q., Jackson, T.L., Lasseigne, D.G. & Grosch, C.E. (1993). Absolute-convective instabilities and their associated wave packets in a compressible reacting mixing layer. *Phys. Fluids* A, 5(4), 901–915.

[199] Huai, X., Joslin, R.D. & Piomelli, U. (1999). Large-eddy simulation of boundary-layer transition on a swept wedge. *Fluid Mech.*, 381, 357–380.

[200] Huerre, P. & Monkewitz, P.A. (1985). Absolute and convective instabilities in free shear layers. *J. Fluid Mech.*, 159, 151–168.

[201] Hughes, T.H. & Reid, W.H. (1965a). On the stability of the asymptotic suction boundary layer profile. *J. Fluid Mech.*, 23, 715–735.

[202] Hughes, T.H. & Reid, W.H. (1965b). The stability of laminar boundary layers at separation. *J. Fluid Mech.*, 23, 737–747.

[203] Hultgren, L.S. & Gustavsson, L.H. (1980). Algebraic growth of disturbances in a laminar boundary layer. *Phys. Fluids*, 24, 1000–1004.

[204] Hultgren, L.S. & Aggarwal, A.K. (1987). Absolute instability of the Gaussian wake profile. *Phys. Fluids*, 30(11), 3383–3387.

[205] Iyer, V. (1990). Computation of three-dimensional compressible boundary layers to fourth-order accuracy on wings and fuselages. NASA CR-4269.

[206] Iyer, V. (1993). Three-dimensional boundary layer program (BL3D) for swept subsonic or supersonic wings with application to laminar flow control. NASA CR-4531.

[207] Iyer, V. (1995). Computer program BL2D for solving two-dimensional and axisymmetric boundary layers. NASA CR-4668.

[208] Jackson, T.L. & Grosch, C.E. (1989). Inviscid spatial stability of a compressible mixing layer. *J. Fluid Mech.*, 208, 609–637.

[209] Jackson, T.L. & Grosch, C.E. (1990a). Inviscid spatial stability of a compressible mixing layer. Part 2. The flame sheet model. *J. Fluid Mech.*, 217, 391–420.

[210] Jackson, T.L. & Grosch, C.E. (1990b). Absolute/convective instabilities and the convective Mach number in a compressible mixing layer. *Phys. Fluids* A, 2(6), 949–954.

[211] Jackson, T.L. & Grosch, C.E. (1990c). On the classification of unstable modes in bounded compressible mixing layers. In *Instability and Transition*, II, (eds. M.Y. Hussaini & R.G. Voigt), Springer, 187–198.

[212] Jackson, T.L. & Grosch, C.E. (1991). Inviscid spatial stability of a compressible mixing layer. Part 3. Effect of thermodynamics. *J. Fluid Mech.*, 224, 159–175.

[213] Jackson, T.L. & Grosch, C.E. (1994). Structure and stability of a laminar diffusion flame in a compressible, three dimensional mixing layer. *Theoret. Comput. Fluid Dynamics*, 6, 89–112.

[214] Joslin, R.D. (1990). The Effect of Compliant Walls on Three-Dimensional Primary and Secondary Instabilities in Boundary Layer Transition, Ph.D. Dissertation, The Pennsylvania State University, August.

[215] Joslin, R.D., Morris, P.J. & Carpenter, P.W. (1991). The role of three-dimensional instabilities in compliant wall boundary-layer transition. *AIAA* 29(10), 1603–1610.

[216] Joslin, R.D. & Morris, P.J. (1992). Effect of compliant walls on secondary instabilities in boundary-layer transition. *AIAA J.*, 30(2), 332–339.

[217] Joslin, R.D., Streett, C.L. & Chang, C.L. (1992). 3-D incompressible spatial direct numerical simulation code validation study – A comparison with linear stability & parabolic stability equation theories for boundary-layer transition on a flat plate. NASA TP-3205, July.

[218] Joslin, R.D., Streett, C.L. & Chang, C.L. (1993). Spatial direct numerical simulation of boundary-layer transition mechanisms: Validation of PSE theory. *Theoretical and Computational Fluid Dynamics*, 4(6), 271–288.

[219] Joslin, R.D. & Streett, C.L. (1994). The role of stationary crossflow vortices in boundary-Layer transition on Swept Wings. *Phys. Fluids*, 6(10), 3442–3453.

[220] Joslin, R.D. (1995a). Evolution of stationary crossflow vortices in boundary layers on swept wings. *AIAA J.*, 33(7), 1279–1285.

[221] Joslin, R.D. (1995b). Direct simulation of evolution and control of three-dimensional instabilities in attachment-line boundary layers. *J. Fluid Mech.*, 291, 369–392.

[222] Joslin, R.D., Nicolaides, R.A., Erlebacher, G., Hussaini, M.Y. & Gunzburger, M. (1995). Active control of boundary-layer instabilities: use of sensors and spectral controller. *AIAA J.*, 33(8), 1521–1523.

[223] Joslin, R.D., Erlebacher, G. & Hussaini, M.Y. (1996). Active control of instabilities in laminar boundary-layer flow. An overview. *J. Fluids Eng.*, 118, September, 494–497.

[224] Joslin, R.D., Gunzburger, M.D., Nicolaides, R.A., Erlebacher, G. & Hussaini, M.Y. (1997). Self-contained, automated methodology for optimal flow control, *AIAA J.*, 35(5), May, 816–824.

[225] Joslin, R.D. (1997). Direct numerical simulation of evoluation and control of linear and nonlinear disturbances in three-dimensional attachment-line boundary layers. NASA TP-3623, February.

[226] Joslin, R.D. (1998). Overview of laminar flow control. NASA TP 1998-208705, September.

[227] Joslin, R.D., Kunz, R.F. & Stinebring, D.R. (2000). Flow control technology readiness: Aerodynamic versus hydrodynamic. 18th Applied Aerodynamics Conference & Exhibit, 14–17 August 2000/Denver, CO. (AIAA 2000-4412).

[228] Kachanov, Y.S., Kozlov, V.V. & Levchenko, V.Y. (1979). Experiments on nonlinear interaction of waves in boundary layers. In: *Laminar-Turbulent Transition*, IUTAM Symposium, Stuttgart, Germany. 135–152.

[229] Kachanov, Y.S. & Levchenko, V.Y. (1984). The resonant interaction of disturbances at laminar-turbulent transition in a boundary layer. *J. Fluid Mech.*, 138, 209–247.

[230] Kachanov, Y.S. & Tararykin, O.I. (1990). The experimental investigation of stability and receptivity of a swept wing flow. *IUTAM Symp. on Laminar-Turbulent Transition* (eds. D. Arnal & R. Michel), Springer-Verlag: Berlin, 499–509.

[231] Kachanov, Y.S. (1994). Physical mechanisms of laminar boundary layer transition. *Ann. Rev. Fluid Mech.*, 26, 411–482.

[232] Kaplan, R.E. (1964). The stability of laminar incompressible boundary layers in the presence of compliant boundaries. Massachusetts Institute of Technology, Aero-Elastic and Structures Research Laboratory, ASRL-TR 116–1.

[233] Karniadakis, G.E. & Triantafyllou, G.S. (1989). Frequency selection and asymptotic states in laminar wakes. *J. Fluid Mech.*, 199, 441–469.

[234] Kelvin, Lord (1871). Hydrokinetic solutions and observations. *Phil. Mag.*, 42, 362–377. Also, Mathematical and Physical Papers, 4, 152–165, 1910.

[235] Kelvin, Lord (1880). On a disturbance in Lord Rayleigh's solution for waves in a plane vortex stratum. *Nature*, 23, 45–46. Also, *Mathematical and Physical Papers*, 4, 186–187, 1910.

[236] Kelvin, Lord (1887a). Rectilinear motion of a viscous fluid between parallel plates. *Mathematical and Physical Papers*, 4, 321–330, 1910.

[237] Kelvin, Lord (1887b). Broad river flowing down an inclined plane bed. *Mathematical and Physical Papers*, 4, 330–337, 1910.

[238] Kendall, J.M. (1966). Supersonic boundary layer stability. (Abstract only.) 1966 Divisional Meeting of the Division of Fluid Dynamics, *Bull. Am. Phys. Soc.*

[239] Kennedy, C.A. & Chen, J.H. (1998). Mean flow effects on the linear stability of compressible planar jets. *Phys. Fluids*, 10(3), 615–626.

[240] Kerschen, E.J. (1987). Boundary layer receptivity and laminar flow airfoil design. NASA Symp. on Research in Natural Laminar Flow and Laminar-Flow Control, March 16–19, 1987. NASA Langley Research Center. NASA CP-2487, (eds. J.N. Hefner & F.E. Sabo), 273–287.

[241] Kerschen, E.J. (1989). Boundary-layer receptivity. AIAA 12th Aeroacoustics Conference, April 10–12, 1989. San Antonio, TX. AIAA-89-1109.

[242] Khorrami, M.R. (1991). On the viscous modes of instability of a trailing line vortex. *J. Fluid Mech.*, 255, 197–212.

[243] King, R.A. & Breuer, K.S. (2001). Acoustic receptivity and evolution of two-dimensional and oblique disturbances in a Blasius boundary layer. *J. Fluid Mech.*, 432, 69–90.

[244] Kirchgässner, K. (1961). Die instabilität der Strömung zwischen zwei rotierenden Zylindern gegenuber Taylor-Wirbeln fur beliebige Spaltbreiten. Z. Angew. *Math. Phys.*, 12, 14–30.

[245] Klebanoff, P.S., Tidstrom, K.D. & Sargent, L.M. (1962). The three-dimensional nature of boundary layer instability. *J. Fluid Mech.*, 12, 1–34.

[246] Kleiser, L. & Zang, T.A. (1991). Numerical simulation of transition in wall bounded shear flows. *Annual Review of Fluid Mechanics*, 23, 495–537.

[247] Klemp, J.B. & Acrivos, A. (1972). A note on the laminar mixing of two uniform parallel semi-infinite streams. *J. Fluid Mech.*, 55, 25–30.

[248] Kloker, M. & Fasel, H. (1990). Numerical simulation of two- and three-dimensional instability waves in two-dimensional boundary layers with streamwise pressure gradients. *Laminar-Turbulent Transition*, IUTAM, eds. D. Arnal & R. Michel. Berlin: Springer-Verlag.

[249] Koch, W. (1986). Direct resonances in Orr-Sommerfeld problems. *Acta Mech.*, 58, 11–29.

[250] Kohama, Y., Saric, W.S. & Hoos, J.A. (1991). A high frequency, secondary instability of crossflow vortices that leads to transition. *Proceedings of the Royal Aeronautical Society Conference on Boundary Layer Transition and Control*, Cambridge University.

[251] Koochesfahani, M.M. & Frieler, C.E. (1989). Instability of nonuniform density free shear layers with a wake profile. *AIAA J.*, 27(12), 1735–1740.

[252] Kozusko, F., Lasseigne, D.G., Grosch, C.E. & Jackson, T.L. (1996). The stability of compressible mixing layers in binary gases. *Phys. Fluids*, 8(7), 1954–1963.

[253] Kramer, M.O. (1957). Boundary-layer stabilization by distributed damping. *Journal of the Aeronautical Sciences*, 24(6), 459–460.

[254] Kramer, M.O. (1965). Hydrodynamics of the Dolphin. *Advances in Hydroscience*, 2, 111–130.

[255] Kuo, A.L. (1949). Dynamic instability of two-dimensional nondivergent flow in a barotropic atmosphere. *J. Meteorology*, 6, 105–122.

[256] Kuramoto, Y. (1980). Instability and turbulence of wave fronts in reaction-diffusion systems. *Progress of Theoretical Physics*, 63(6), 1885–1903.

[257] Ladd, D.M. & Hendricks, E.W. (1988). Active control of 2-D instability waves on an axisymmetric body. *Experiments in Fluids*, 6, 69–70.

[258] Ladd, D.M. (1990). Control of natural laminar instability waves on an axisymmetric body. *AIAA J.*, 28(2), 367–369.

[259] Lamb, H. (1945). *Hydrodynamics*. Dover Publications, New York.

[260] Landahl, M.T. (1972). Wave mechanics of breakdown. *J. Fluid Mech.*, 56, Part 4, 775–802.

[261] Landahl, M.T. (1980). A note on an algebraic instability of inviscid parallel shear flows. *J. Fluid Mech.*, 98, 243–251.

[262] Landau, L.D. (1944). On the problem of turbulence. *Akademiya Nauk SSSR Doklady*, 44, 311–314.

[263] Lasseigne D.G., Criminale, W.O., Joslin, R.D. & Jackson, T.L. (1999). Towards understanding the mechanism of receptivity and bypass dynamics in laminar boundary layers. ICASE Report No. 99-37.

[264] Lasseigne, D.G., Joslin, R.D., Jackson, T.L. & Criminale, W.O. (1999). The transient period for boundary layer disturbances. *J. Fluid Mech.*, 381, 89–119.

[265] Lasseigne D.G., Criminale, W.O., Joslin, R.D. & Jackson, T.L. (2000). In *Laminar Turbulent Transition*, Springer-Verlag, 85–90.

[266] Laufer, J. & Vrebalovich, T. (1957). Experiments on the instability of a supersonic boundary layer. *Proceedings of the 9th International Congress of Applied Mechanics*, 4, 121–131.

[267] Laufer, J. & Vrebalovich, T. (1958). Stability of a supersonic laminar boundary layer on a flat plate. California Institute of Technology, Jet Propulsion Laboratory Rep. 20-116.

[268] Laufer, J. & Vrebalovich, T. (1960). Stability and transition of a supersonic laminar boundary layer on an insulated flat plate. *J. Fluid Mech.*, 9, 257–299.

[269] Lecointe, Y. & Piquet, J. (1984). On the use of several compact methods for the study of unsteady incompressible viscous flow round a circular cylinder. *Computers & Fluids*, 12(4), 255–280.

[270] Leehey, P. & Shapiro, P.J. (1980). Leading edge effect in laminar boundary layer excitation by sound. IUTAM *Symp. on Laminar-Turbulent Transition*, Springer-Verlag, 321–331.

[271] Lees, L. & Lin, C.C. (1946). Investigation of the stability of the laminar boundary layer in a compressible fluid. NACA Technical Note 1115.

[272] Lees, L. (1947). The stability of the laminar boundary layer in a compressible fluid. NACA Tech. Rept. No. 876.

[273] Lees, L. & Reshotko, E. (1962). Stability of the compressible boundary layer. *J. Fluid Mech.*, 12, 555–590.

[274] Lees, L. & Gold, H (1964). Stability of laminar boundary layers and wakes at hypersonic speeds. I. Stability of laminar wakes. Fundamental Phenomena in Hypersonic Flow, *Proc. Internat. Symp. Buffalo, N.Y.*, 310–339, Cornell University Press.

[275] Lele, S.K. (1989). Direct numerical simulation of compressible free shear layer flows. AIAA 89-0374.

[276] Lele, S.K. (1992). Compact finite difference schemes with spectral-like resolution. *J. Comput. Phys.*, 103, 16–42.

[277] Lessen, M. (1950). On stability of free laminar boundary layer between parallel streams. NACA Report 979.

[278] Lessen, M., Fox, J.A. & Zien, H.M. (1965). On the inviscid stability of the laminar mixing of two parallel streams of a compressible fluid. *J. Fluid Mech.*, 23, 355–367.

[279] Lessen, M., Fox, J.A. & Zien, H.M. (1966). Stability of the laminar mixing of two parallel streams with respect to supersonic disturbances. *J. Fluid Mech.*, 25, 737–742.

[280] Lessen, M., Singh, P.J. & Paillet, F. (1974). The stability of a trailing line vortex. Part 1. Inviscid theory. *J. Fluid Mech.*, 63, 753–763.

[281] Liepmann, H.W. (1943). Investigation of laminar boundary layer stability and transition on curved boundaries. NACA Advisory Conference Report No. 31730.

[282] Liepmann, H.W. & Nosenchuck, D.M. (1982a). Active control of laminar-turbulent transition. *J. Fluid Mech.*, 118, 1982a, pp. 201–204.

[283] Liepmann, H.W. & Nosenchuck, D.M. (1982b). Control of laminar instability waves using a new technique. *J. Fluid Mech.*, 118, 187–200.

[284] Ligrani, P.M., Longest, J.E., Kendall, M.R. & Fields, W.A. (1994). Splitting, merging, and spanwise wavenumber selection of Dean vortex pairs. *Experiments in Fluids*, 18, No. 1/2, 41–58.

[285] Lilly, D.K. (1966). On the instability of Ekman boundary flow. *J. Atmos. Sci.*, 23, 481–494.

[286] Lin, C.C. (1944). On the stability of two-dimensional parallel flows. *Proceedings. National Academy of Science*, U.S., 30, 316–323.

[287] Lin, C.C. (1945). On the stability of two-dimensional parallel flows, Part I, II, III. *Quart. Appl. Math.*, 3, 117–142, 218–234, 277–301.

[288] Lin, C.C. (1954). Hydrodynamic Stability. *Proc. 13th Symp. Appl. Math*, 1–18, Amer. Math. Soc., Providence, Rhode Island.

[289] Lin, C.C. (1955). *The Theory of Hydrodynamic Stability*. London: Cambridge University Press.

[290] Lin, C.C. (1961). Some mathematical problems in the theory of the stability of parallel flows. *J. Fluid Mech.*, 10, 430–438.

[291] Lin, R.S. & Malik, M.R. (1994). The stability of incompressible attachment-line boundary layers. A 2D eigenvalue approach. AIAA-94-2372.

[292] Lin, R.S. & Malik, M.R. (1995). Stability and transition in compressible attachment line boundary layer flow. Aerotech '95, September 18–21, 1995. Los Angeles, CA. SAE Paper 952041.

[293] Lin, R.S. & Malik, M.R. (1996). On the stability of attachment line boundary layers. Part 1. The incompressible swept Hiemenz flow. *J. Fluid Mech.*, 311, 239–255.

[294] Lingwood, R.J. (1995). Absolute instability of the boundary layer on a rotating-disk boundary layer flow. *J. Fluid Mech.*, 299, 17–33.

[295] Lingwood, R.J. (1996). An experimental study of absolute instability of the rotating-disk boundary-layer flow. *J. Fluid Mech.*, 314, 373.

[296] Liou, W.W. & Shih, T.H. (1997). Bypass transitional flow calculations using a Navier-Stokes solver and two equation modesl. AIAA Paper 97–2738, July 1997.

[297] Liu, C. (1998). Multigrid methods for steady and time-dependent flow. Invited Review Paper, *Computational Fluid Dynamics Review*, 1, pp. 512–535, Edited by Hafez and Oshima, 1998.

[298] Lock, R.C. (1951). The velocity disturbution in the laminar boundary layer between parallel streams. *Quart. J. Mech. Appl. Math.*, 4, 42–62.

[299] Lu, G. & Lele, S.K. (1993). Inviscid instability of a skewed compressible mixing layer. *J. Fluid Mech.*, 249, 441–463.

[300] Lu, G. & Lele, S.K. (1994). On the density ratio effect on the growth rate of a compressible mixing layer. *Phys. Fluids*, 6(2), 1073–1075.

[301] Luther, H.A. (1966). Further explicit fifth-order Runge-Kutta formulas. *SAIM Review*, 8(3), 374–380.

[302] Lynch, R.E., Rice, J.R. & Thomas, D.H. (1964). Direct solution of partial difference equations by tensor product methods. *Num. Math.*, 6, 185–199.

[303] Macaraeg, M.G., Streett, C.L. & Hussaini, M.Y. (1988). A spectral collocation solution to the compressible stability eigenvalue problem. NASA Technical Paper 2858.

[304] Macaraeg, M.G. & Streett, C.L. (1989). New instability modes for bounded, free shear flows. *Phys. Fluids* A, 1(8), 1305–1307.

[305] Macaraeg, M.G. (1990). Bounded free shear flows: linear and nonlinear growth. In *Instability and Transition*, II (eds. M.Y. Hussaini & R.G. Voigt), Springer, 177–186.

[306] Macaraeg, M.G. (1991). Investigation of supersonic modes and three-dimensionality in bounded, free shear flows. *Comput. Phys. Commun.*, 65, 201–208.

[307] Macaraeg, M.G. & Streett, C.L. (1991). Linear stability of high-speed mixing layers. *Appl. Numer. Math.*, 7, 93–127.

[308] Mack, L.M. (1960). Numerical calculation of the stability of the compressible, laminar boundary layer. California Institute of Technology, Jet Propulsion Laboratory Rept. No. 20-122.

[309] Mack, L.M. (1965a). Computation of the stability of the laminar compressible boundary layer. *Methods in Computational Physics*, (B. Alder, S. Fernbach & M. Rotenberg, eds.), 4, Academic Press, New York, 247–299.

[310] Mack, L.M. (1965b). Stability of the compressible laminar boundary layer according to a direct numerical solution. *Recent Developments In Boundary Layer Research*, AGARDograph 97, part 1, 329–362.

[311] Mack, L.M. (1966). Viscous and inviscid amplification rates of two and three-dimensional disturbances in a compressible boundary layer. *Space Prog. Summary*, 42, IV, November.

[312] Mack, L.M. (1975). Linear stability theory and the problem of supersonic boundary layer transition. *AIAA J.*, 13(3), 278–289.

[313] Mack, L.M. (1976). A numerical study of the temporal eigenvalue spectrum of the Blasius boundary layer. *J. Fluid Mech.*, 73(3), 497–520.

[314] Mack, L.M. (1984). Boundary layer linear stability theory. Special Course on Stability and Transition of Laminar Flow, AGARD Report 709.

[315] Mack, L.M. (1987). Review of compressible stability theory. In *Proc. ICASE Workshop on the Stability of Time Dependent and Spatially Varying Flows*, 164, Springer.

[316] Mack, L.M. (1988). Stability of three-dimensional boundary layers on swept wings at transonic speeds. *IUTAM Symp. Transsonicum III*, Gottingen, (eds. Zierep & Oertel), Springer-Verlag.

[317] Maddalon, D.V., Collier, F.S., Jr., Montoya, L.C. & Putnam, R.J. (1990). Transition flight experiments on a swept wing with suction. *Laminar-Turbulent Transition*, (D. Arnal and R. Michel, eds.), Springer, Berlin, 53–62.

[318] Malik, M.R., Wilkinson, S.P. & Orszag, S.A. (1981). Instability and transition in rotating disk flow. *AIAA J.*, 19, 1131–1138.

[319] Malik, M.R. (1982). COSAL-A black box compressible stability analysis code for transition prediction in three-dimensional boundary layers. NASA CR 165925.

[320] Malik, M.R. (1986). The neutral curve for stationary disturbances in rotating disk flow. *J. Fluid Mech.*, 164, 275–287.

[321] Malik, M.R. (1987). Stability theory applications to laminar-flow control. NASA CP 2487, pp. 219–244.

[322] Malik, M.R. (1990). Numerical methods for hypersonic boundary layer stability. *J. Comp. Phys.*, 86, 376–413.

[323] Mattingly, G.E. & Criminale, W.O. (1972). The stability of an incompressible two-dimensional wake. *J. Fluid Mech.*, 51(2), 233–272.

[324] Mayer, E.W. & Powell, K.G. (1992). Instabilities of a trailing vortex. *J. Fluid Mech.*, 245, 91–114.

[325] Meister, B. (1962). Das Taylor-Deansche Stabilitätsproblem für beliebige Spaltbreiten. *Z. Angew. Math. Phys.*, 13, 83–91.

[326] Meksyn, D. (1950). Stabiliity of viscous flow over concave cylindrical surfaces. *Proc. Roy. Soc.* A, 203, 253–265.

[327] Meksyn, D. & Stuart, J.T. (1951). Stability of viscous motion between parallel flows for finite disturbances. *Proc. Roy. Soc. of London, Series A. Mathematical and Physical Sciences*, 208, 517–526.

[328] Michalke, A. (1964). On the inviscid instability of the hyperbolic-tangent velocity profile. *J. Fluid Mech.*, 19, 543–556.

[329] Michalke, A. (1965). On spatially growing disturbances in an inviscid shear layer. *J. Fluid Mech.*, 23, 521–544.

[330] Miklavčič, M. & Williams, M. (1982). Stability of mean flows over an infinite flat plate. *Arch. Rational Mech. Anal.*, 80, 57–69.

[331] Miklavčič, M. (1983). Eigenvalues of the Orr-Sommerfeld equation in an unbounded domain. *Arch. Rational Mech. Anal.*, 83, 221–228.

[332] Miles, J.W. (1958). On the disturbed motion of a plane vortex sheet. *J. Fluid Mech.*, 4, 538–552.

[333] Milling, R.W. (1981). Tollmien-Schlichting wave cancellation. *Phys. Fluids*, 24(5), 979–981.

[334] Mittal, R. & Balachandar, S. (1995). Effect of three-dimensionality on the lift and drag of nominally two-dimensional cylinders. *Phys. Fluids*, 7(8), 1841–1865.

[335] Monkewitz, P.A. & Huerre, P. (1982). Influence of the velocity ratio on the spatial instability of mixing layers. *Phys. Fluids*, 25(7), 1137–1143.

[336] Morkovin, M.V. (1969). *On the Many Faces of Transition. Viscous Drag Reduction*, C. Sinclair Wells, ed., Plenum Press, 1–31.

[337] Morris, P.J. & Giridharan, M.G. (1991). The effect of walls on instability waves in supersonic shear layers. *Phys. Fluids* A, 3(2), 356–358.

[338] Mukunda, H.S., Sekar, B., Carpenter, M., Drummond, J.P. & Kumar, A. (1989). Studies in direct simulations of high speed mixing layers. NASA TP.

[339] Müller, B. & Bippes, H. (1988). Experimental study of instability modes in a three-dimensional boundary layer. AGARD-CP-438.

[340] Murdock, J.W. (1977). A numerical study of nonlinear effects on boundary-layer stability. *AIAA J.*, 15, 1167–1173.

[341] Nayfeh, A.H. & Bozatli, A.N. (1979). Nonlinear wave interactions in boundary layers. AIAA Paper 79-1496.

[342] Nayfeh, A.H. & Bozatli, A.N. (1980). Nonlinear interaction of two waves in boundary Layer flows. *Phys. Fluids*, 23(3), 448–459.

[343] Nayfeh, A.H. (1980). Stability of three-dimensional boundary layers. *AIAA J.*, 18, 406–416.

[344] Nayfeh, A.H. (1987). Nonlinear stability of boundary layers, AIAA 25th Aerospace Sciences Meeting, Reno Nevada/January 12–15, 1987. (AIAA Paper 87-0044)

[345] Ng, B.S. & Reid, W.H. (1979). An initial value method for eigenvalue problems using compound matrices. *J. Computational Phys.*, 30(1), 125–136.

[346] Ng, B.S. & Reid, W.H. (1980). On the numerical solution of the Orr-Sommerfeld problem: asymptotic initial conditions for shooting methods. *J. Comp. Phys.*, 38, 275–293.

[347] Obremski, H.T., Morkovin, M.V. & Landahl, M.T. (1969). A portfolio of stability characteristics of incompressible boundary layers. AGARDograph No. 134, NATO, Paris.

[348] Orr, W.McF. (1907a). Lord Kelvin's investigations, especially the case of a stream which is shearing uniformly. *Proceedings Royal Irish Academy*, A27, 80–138.

[349] Orr, W.McF. (1907b). The stability or instability of the steady motions of a perfect liquid and of a viscous liquid. *Proceedings Royal Irish Academy*, A27, 9–138.

[350] Orszag, S.A. (1971). Accurate solution of the Orr-Sommerfeld stability equation. *J. Fluid Mech.*, 50, 689–703.

[351] Orszag, S.A. & Patera, A.T. (1980). Subcritical transition to turbulence in plane channel flows. *Physics Review Letter*, 45, 989–993.

[352] Orszag, S.A. & Patera, A.T. (1981). Subcritical transition to turbulence in plane shear flows. In: Transition and Turbulence, 127–146.

[353] Pal, A., Bower, W.W. & Meyer, G.H. (1991). Numerical simulations of multifrequency instability-wave growth and suppression in the Blasius boundary layer. *Phys. Fluids* A, 3(2), 328–340.

[354] Papageorgiou, D.T. & Smith, F.T. (1988). Nonlinear instability of the wake behind a flat plate placed parallel to a uniform stream. *Proc. R. Soc.* A, 419, 1–28.

[355] Papageorgiou, D.T. & Smith, F.T. (1989). Linear instability of the wake behind a flat plate placed parallel to a uniform stream. *J. Fluid Mech.*, 208, 67–89.

[356] Papageorgiou, D.T. (1990a). Linear instability of the supersonic wake behind a flat plate aligned with a uniform stream. *Theoret. Comput. Fluid Dynamics*, 1, 327–348.

[357] Papageorgiou, D.T. (1990b). The stability of two-dimensional wakes and shear layers at high Mach numbers. ICASE Report No. 90–39.

[358] Papageorgiou, D.T. (1990c). Accurate calculation and instability of supersonic wake flows. In *Instability and Transition*, II, (eds. M.Y. Hussaini & R.G. Voigt), Springer, 216–229.

[359] Papamoschou, D. & Roshko, A. (1986). Observations of supersonic free-shear layers. AIAA Paper No. 86-0162.

[360] Papamoschou, D. & Roshko, A. (1988). The compressible turbulent shear layer: an experimental study. *J. Fluid Mech.*, 197, 453–477.

[361] Papas, P., Monkewitz, P.A. & Tomboulides, A.G. (1999). New instability modes of a diffusion flame near extinction. *Phys. Fluids*, 11(10), 2818–2820.

[362] Pavithran, S. & Redekopp, L.G. (1989). The absolute-convective transition in subsonic mixing layers. *Phys. Fluids* A, 1(10), 1736–1739.

[363] Peerhossaini, H. (1987). L'Instabilite d'une couche limite sur une paroi concave (les tourbilons de Görtler). These de Doctorat. Univ. Pierre et Marie Curie, Paris.

[364] Peroomian, O. & Kelly, R.E. (1994). Absolute and convective instabilities in compressible confined mixing layers. *Phys. Fluids*, 6(9), 3192–3194.

[365] Pfenninger, W. (1965). Flow phenomena at the leading edge of swept wings. Recent Developments in Boundary Layer Research, AGARDograph 97, May 1965.

[366] Piomelli, U., Zang, T.A., Speziale, C.G. & Hussaini, M.Y. (1990). On the large-eddy simulation of transitional wall-bounded flows. *Phys. Fluids* A, 2, 257.

[367] Piomelli, U. & Zang, T.A. (1991). Large-eddy simulation of transitional channel flow. *Computer Physics Communication*, 65, 224.

[368] Planche, O.H. & Reynolds, W.C. (1991). Compressibility effect on the supersonic reacting mixing layer. AIAA Paper 91-0739.

[369] Potter, M.C. (1966). Stability of plane Couette-Poiseuille flow. *J. Fluid Mech.*, 24, 609–619.

[370] Prandtl, L. (1921–1926). Bemerkungen über die Entstehung der Turbulenz. Zeitschrift für Angewandte Mathematik und Mechanik, 1, 431–436; *Physik. Z.*, 23, 1922, pp. 19–23. Discussion after Solberg's paper, 1924; and with

F. Noether, Zeitschrift für Angewandte Mathematik und Mechanik, 6, 1926, 339, 428.

[371] Prandtl, L. (1930). Einfluss stabilisierender Kräfte auf die Turbulenz. Vorträge aus dem Gebiete der Aerodynamik und Verwandter Gebiete, Aachen, Springer, Berlin, 1–17.

[372] Prandtl, L. (1935). *Aerodynamic theory*, 3, (W.F. Durand, ed.), Springer, Berlin, pp. 178–190.

[373] Press, W.H., Teukolsky, S.A., Vetterling, W.T. & Flannery, B.P. (1992). *Numerical Recipes in Fortran*, 2nd. Edition. Cambridge University Press.

[374] Pruett, C.D. & Chang, C.L. (1995). Spatial direct numerical simulation of high-speed boundary-layer flows. Part II: Transition on a cone in Mach 8 flow. *Theor. Comput. Fluid Dyn.*, 7(5), 397–424.

[375] Pupator, P. & Saric, W. (1989). Control of random disturbances in a boundary layer. AIAA Paper 89-1007.

[376] Raetz, G.S. (1964). Calculation of precise proper solutions for the resonance theory of transition. I. Theoretical investigations. Contract AF 33-657-11618, Final Rept., Document Rept. ASD-TDR, Northrop Aircraft Inc., Norair Division, Hawthorne, CA.

[377] Ragab, S.A. (1988). Instabilities in the wake mixing-layer region of a splitter plate separating two supersonic streams. AIAA Paper 88-3677.

[378] Ragab, S.A. & Wu, J.L. (1989). Linear instabilities in two dimensional compressible mixing layers. *Phys. Fluids* A, 1(6), 957–966.

[379] Rai, M.M. & Moin, P. (1991a). Direct numerical simulation of transition and turbulence in a spatially-evolving boundary layer. AIAA 91-1607.

[380] Rai, M.M. & Moin, P. (1991b). Direct numerical simulation of turbulent flow using finite-difference schemes. *J. Comput. Phys.*, 96, 15–53.

[381] Rayleigh, Lord (1879). On the stability of jets. *Proc. London Math. Soc.*, 10, 4–13. Also, *Scientific Papers*, 1, 361–371, 1899.

[382] Rayleigh, Lord (1880). On the stability or instability of certain fluid motions. *Proc. London Math. Soc.*, 11, 57–70. Also, *Scientific Papers*, 1, 474–487, 1899.

[383] Rayleigh, Lord (1883). Investigation of the character of the equilibrium of an incompressible heavy fluid of variable density. *Proc. Lond. Math. Soc.*, 14, 170–177. Also, *Scientific Papers*, 2, 200–207, 1900.

[384] Rayleigh, Lord (1887). On the stability or instability of certain fluid motions. Part II. *Scientific Papers*, 3, 17–23.

[385] Rayleigh, Lord (1892a). On the question of the stability of the flow of fluids. *Phil. Mag.*, 34, 59–70. Also, *Scientific Papers*, 3, 575–584, 1902.

[386] Rayleigh, Lord (1892b). On the stability of a cylinder of viscous liquid under capillary force. *Scientific papers*, 3, 2–23, 1899.

[387] Rayleigh, Lord (1892c). On the instability of cylindrical fluid surfaces. *Phil. Mag.*, 34, 177–180. Also, *Scientific Papers*, 3, 594–596, 1902.

[388] Rayleigh, Lord (1894). *The Theory of Sound*, 2nd. edition. London: Macmillan.

[389] Rayleigh, Lord (1895). On the stability or instability of certain fluid motions. III. *Scientific Papers*, 4, 203–209, 1899.

[390] Rayleigh, Lord (1911). Hydrodynamical notes, *Phil. Mag.*, 21, 177–195.

[391] Rayleigh, Lord (1913). On the stability of the laminar motion of an inviscid fluid. *Scientific Papers*, 6, 197–204.

[392] Rayleigh, Lord (1914). Further remarks on the Stability of Viscous fluid motion. *Phil. Mag.*, 28, 609–619. Also, *Scientific Papers*, 6, 266–275, 1920.

[393] Rayleigh, Lord (1915). On the stability of the simple shearing motion of a viscous incompressible fluid, *Scientific Papers*, 6, 341–349.

[394] Rayleigh, Lord (1916a). On convection currents in a horizontal layer of fluid when the higher temperature is on the other side. *Phil. Mag.*, 32, 529–546. Also, *Scientific Papers*, 6, 432–446, 1920.

[395] Rayleigh, Lord (1916b). On the dynamics of revolving fluids. *Proc. Roy. Soc.*, Series A, 93, 148–154. Also, *Scientific Papers*, 6, 447–453, 1920.

[396] Reddy, S.C. & Henningson, D.S. (1993). Energy growth in viscous channel flows. *J. Fluid Mech.*, 252, 209–238.

[397] Reed, H.L. & Saric, W.S. (1998). Stability of three dimensional boundary layers. *Ann. Rev. Fluid Mech.*, 21, 235.

[398] Reibert, M.S., Saric, W.S., Carrillo, R.B., Jr. & Chapman, K.L. (1996). Experiments in nonlinear saturation of stationary crossflow vortices in a swept-wing boundary layer. 34th Aerospace Sciences Meeting & Exhibit, January 15–18, 1996. Reno, NV. AIAA-96-0184.

[399] Reischman, M.M. (1984). A Review of Compliant Coating Drag Reduction Research at ONR. *Laminar-Turbulent Boundary Layers*, 11, 99–105.

[400] Reshotko, E. (1960). Stability of the compressible laminar boundary layer. California Institute of Technology, Guggenheim Aeronautical Laboratory, GALCIT Memo. No. 52.

[401] Reshotko, E. (1976). Boundary-layer stability and transition. *Ann. Rev. Fluid Mech.*, 8, 311–349.

[402] Reshotko, E. (1984). Environment and receptivity. AGARD-R-709.

[403] Reynolds, O. (1883). An experimental Investigation of the circumstances which determine whether the motion of water shall be direct or sinuous, and of the law of resistance in parallel channels. *Scientific Papers*, 2, 51–105.

[404] Reynolds, W.C. & Potter, M.C. (1967). Finite amplitude instability of parallel shear flows. *J. Fluid Mech.*, 27, 465–492.

[405] Romanov, V.A. (1973). Stability of plane-parallel Couette flow. *Funkcional Anal. i Prolozen*, 7(2), 62–73. Translated in *Functional Anal. & its Applications*, 7, 137–146, 1973.

[406] Rozendaal, R.A. (1986). Natural laminar flow flight experiments on a swept wing business jet. Boundary layer stability analyses. NASA CR-3975, May.

[407] Salwen, H. & Grosch, C.E. (1981). The continuous spectrum of the Orr-Sommerfeld equation. Part 2. Eigenfunction expansions. *J. Fluid Mech.*, 104, 445–465.

[408] Sandham, N.D. & Reynolds, W.C. (1990). Compressible mixing layer: Linear theory and direct simulation. *AIAA J.*, 28(4), 618–624.

[409] Saric, W.S., Hoos, J.A. & Radeztsky, R.H. (1991). Boundary layer receptivity of sound with roughness. *ASME FED*, 114, Boundary Layer Stability and Transition to Turbulence, (eds. D.C. Reda, H.L. Reed & R.K. Kobayashi), 17–22.

[410] Saric, W.S. (1994a). Görtler Vortices. *Ann. Rev. Fluid Mech.*, 26, 379–409.

[411] Saric, W.S. (1994b) Low Speed Boundary Layer Transition Experiments. In: *Transition: Experiments, Theory, and Computations*. (eds. T.C. Corke, G. Erlebacher & M.Y. Hussaini), Oxford.

[412] Schlichting, H. (1932a). Über die stabilität deer Couetteströmung. *Ann. Physik* (Leipzig), 14, 905–936.

[413] Schlichting, H. (1932b). Über die enstehung der turbulenz bei der Plattenströmung. Gessellschaft der Wissenschaften, Göttingen, *Mathematisch-Naturwissenschaftliche Klasse*, 160–198.

[414] Schlichting, H. (1933a). Zur entstehung der turbulenz bei der Plattenströmung, Gesellschaft der Wissenschaften. Göttingen. *Mathematisch-Physikalische Klasse*, 181–208.

[415] Schlichting, H. (1933b). Berechnung der anfachung kleiner Störungen bei der Plattenströmung. *Zeitschrift fuer Angewandte Mathematik und Mechanik*,13(3), 171–174.

[416] Schlichting, H. (1933c). Laminar spread of a jet. *Zeitschrift fuer Angewandte Mathematik und Mechanik*, 13(4), 260–263.

[417] Schlichting, H. (1934). Neuere untersuchungen über die turbulenzenstehung. *Naturwiss.*, 22, 376–381.

[418] Schlichting, H. (1935). Amplitudenverteilung und Energiebilanz der kleinen Störungen bei der Plattengrenzschicht. Gesellschaft der Wissenschatten. Göttingen. *Mathematisch-Naturwissenschattliche Klasse*, 1, 47–78.

[419] Schmid, P.J. & Henningson, D.S. (1992a). Channel flow transition induced by a pair of oblique waves. In: *Instability, Transition, and Turbulence*. (eds. M.Y. Hussaini, A. Kumar & C.L. Streett), New York: Springer Verlag, 356–366.

[420] Schmid, P.J. & Henningson, D.S. (1992b). A new mechanism for rapid transition involving a pair of oblique waves. *Phys. Fluids* A, 4(9), 1986–1989.

[421] Schrauf, G., Bieler, H. & Thiede, P. (1992). Transition prediction – the Deutsche Airbus view. First European Forum on Laminar Flow Technology, March 16–18, 1992. Hamburg, Germany, 73–81.

[422] Schubauer, G.B. & Skramstad, H.K. (1943). Laminar boundary layer oscillations and transition on a flat plate. NACA Tech. Rept. No. 909.

[423] Schubauer, G.B. & Skramstad, H.K. (1947). Laminar boundary layer oscillations and stability of laminar flow. *Journal of the Aeronautical Sciences*, 14(2), 69–78.

[424] Schubauer, G.B. & Klebanoff, P.S. (1955). Contributions on the mechanics of boundary-layer transition. NACA Technical Note 3489.

[425] Schubauer, G.B. & Klebanoff, P.S. (1956). Contributions on the mechanics of boundary-layer transition. NACA Report 1289.

[426] Shanthini, R. (1989). Degeneracies of the temporal Orr-Sommerfeld eigenmodes in plane Poiseuille flow. *J. Fluid Mech.*, 201, 13–34.

[427] Shen, S.F. (1952). On the boundary layer equations in hypersonic flow. *J. Aeron. Sci.*, 19, 500–501.

[428] Shin, D.S. & Ferziger, J.H. (1991). Linear stability of the reacting mixing layer. *AIAA J.*, 29(10), 1634–1642.

[429] Shin, D.S. & Ferziger, J.H. (1993). Linear stability of the confined compressible reacting mixing layer. *AIAA J.*, 31(3), 571–577.

[430] Singer, B.A., Choudhari, M. & Li, F. (1995). Weakly nonparallel and curvature effects on stationary crossflow instability: Comparison of results from multiple scales analysis and parabolized stability theory. NASA CR-198200.

[431] Sivashinsky, G. (1977). Nonlinear analysis of hydrodynamic instability in laminar flames, Part I. Derivation of basic equations. *Acta Astronautica*, 4, 1117–1206.

[432] Smagorinsky, J. (1963). General circulation experiments with the primitive equations. I. The basic experiment. *Mon. Weather Rev.*, 91, 99–.

[433] Smith, A.M.O. (1953). Review of research on laminar boundary layer control at the Douglas Aircraft Company El Segundo Division. Douglas Aircraft Co. Rep. No. ES-19475, June.

[434] Smith, A.M.O. (1955). On the growth of Taylor-Gortler vortices along highly concave walls. *Quart. Appl. Math.*, 13, 233–262.

[435] Smith, F.T. & Brown, S.N. (1990). The inviscid instability of a Blasius boundary layer at large values of the Mach number. *J. Fluid Mech.*, 219, 499.

[436] Smol'yakov, A.V. & Tkachenko, V.M. (1983). The Measurement of Turbulent Fluctuations. An Introduction to Hot-Wire Anemometry and Related Transducers. Springer-Verlag, New York.

[437] Sommerfeld, A. (1908). Ein beitraz zur hydrodynamischen erklaerung der turbulenten fluessigkeitsbewegungen. *Proc. Fourth Inter. Congr. Mathematicians*, Rome, 116–124.

[438] Spalart, P.R. & Yang, K.S. (1987). Numerical study of ribbon-induced transition in Blasius flow. *J. Fluid Mech.*, 178, 345–365.

[439] Spalart, P.R. (1989). Direct numerical study of leading-edge contamination. Fluid Dynamics of Three-Dimensional Turbulent Shear Flows and Transition. AGARD-CP-438, 5.1–5.13.

[440] Spalart, P.R. (1990). Direct numerical study of cross-flow instability. *Laminar-Turbulent Transition, IUTAM*, eds. D. Arnal & R. Michel. Berlin: Springer-Verlag.

[441] Spooner, G.F. (1980). Fluctuations in geophysical boundary layers. Ph.D. Dissertation, Department of Oceanography, University of Washington.

[442] Spooner, G.F. & Criminale, W.O. (1982). The evolution of disturbances in an Ekman boundary layer. *J. Fluid Mech.*, 115, 327–346.

[443] Squire, H.B. (1933). On the stability for three-dimensional disturbances of viscous fluid flow between parallel walls. *Proc. Roy. Soc., Series A. Mathematical and Physical Sciences*, 142, 621–628.

[444] Srokowski, A.J. & Orszag, S.A. (1977). Mass flow requirments for LFC wing design. AIAA Paper 77-1222.

[445] Streett, C.L. & Macaraeg, M.G. (1989). Spectral multi-domain for large-scale fluid dynamics simulations. *Appl. Numer. Math.*, 6, 123–140.

[446] Streett, C.L. & Hussaini, M.Y. (1991). A numerical simulation of the appearance of chaos in finite-length Taylor-Couette flow. *Appl. Numer. Math.*, 7, 41–71.

[447] Stuart, J.T. (1960). On the non-linear mechanics of wave disturbances in stable and unstable parallel flows. Part 1. *J. Fluid Mech.*, 9, 353–370.

[448] Swearingen, J.D. & Blackwelder, R.F. (1986). Spacing of streamwise vortices on concave walls. *AIAA J.*, 24, 1706–1709.

[449] Swearingen, J.D. & Blackwelder, R.F. (1987). The growth and breakdown of streamwise vortices in the presence of a wall. *J. Fluid Mech.*, 182, 255–290.

[450] Synge, J.L. (1938). Hydrodynamic stability. *Semicentennial Publ. Amer. Math. Soc.*, 2, 227–269.

[451] Tadjfar, M. & Bodonyi, R.J. (1992). Receptivity of a laminar boundary layer to the interaction of a three-dimensional roughness element with time-harmonic free stream disturbances. *J. Fluid Mech.*, 242, 701–720.

[452] Tam, C.K.W. & Hu, F.Q. (1989). The instability and acoustic wave modes of supersonic mixing layers inside a rectangular channel. *J. Fluid Mech.*, 203, 51–76.

[453] Tatsumi, T. (1952). Stability of the laminar inlet flow prior to the formation of Poiseuille region. *J. Phys. Soc.* Japan, 7, 489–502.

[454] Tatsumi, T. & Kakutani, T. (1958). The stability of a two dimensional jet. *J. Fluid Mech.*, 4, 261–275.

[455] Taylor, G.I. (1921). Experiments with rotating fluids. *Proc. Camb. Phil. Soc.*, 20, 326–329.

[456] Taylor, G.I. (1923). Stability of a viscous liquid contained between two rotating cylinders. Philosophical Transactions. *Proc. Roy. Soc.*, Series A, 223, 289 343.

[457] Theofilis, V. (in press).

[458] Thomas, A.S.W. (1983). The control of boundary-Layer transition using a wave-superposition principle. *J. Fluid Mech.*, 137, 233–250.

[459] Thomas, R.H., Choudhari, M.M. & Joslin, R.D. (2002). Flow and Noise Control: Review and Assessment of Future Directions. NASA TM-2002-211631.

[460] Tietjens, O. (1925). Beiträge zur entsehung der turbulenz. Zeitschrift fuer Angewandte Mathematik und Mechanik, 5, 200–217.

[461] Ting, L. (1959). On the mixing of two parallel streams. *J. Math. Phys.*, 28, 153–165.

[462] Tollmien, W. (1929). Uber die Entstehung der Turbulenz. *Gesellschaft der Wissenschaften. Gottingen. Mathematisch-Naturwissenschaftliche Klasse. Nachrichten*, 21–44. Translated as, The production of turbulence. NACA TM-609, 1931.

[463] Tollmien, W. (1935). Ein allgemeines Kriterium der Instabilitat laminarer Geschwindigkeitsverteilungen. *Nachr. Wiss. Fachgruppe, Gottingen, Math. phys.*, 1, 79–114. Translated as, General instability criterion of laminar velocity disturbances. *NACA TM-792*, 1936.

[464] Tung, K.K. (1981). Barotropic instability of zonal flows. *J. Atmos. Sci.*, 38, 308–321.

[465] van Dyke, M. (1975). *Perturbation Methods in Fluid Mechanics*. Annotated edition. The Parabolic Press.

[466] Vijgen, P.M.H.W., Dodbele, S.S., Holmes, B.J. & van Dam, C.P. (1986). Effects of compressibility on design of subsonic natural laminar flow fuselages. AIAA 4th Applied Aerodynamics Conference, June 9–11, 1986. San Diego, CA. AIAA-86-1825CP.

[467] von Kármàn, T. (1921). Uber laminare und turbulente Reibung. *Zeitschrift fur Angewandte Mathematik und Mechanik*, 1, 233–252.

[468] Von Mises, R. & Friedrichs, K.O. (1971). Fluid dynamics. *Appl. Math. Sci. 5*, Springer-Verlag, New York.

[469] Warren, E.S. & Hassan, H.A. (1996). An alternative to the e^N method for determining onset of transition. AIAA 35th Aerospace Sciences Meeting & Exhibit, January 6–10, 1997. Reno, NV. AIAA Paper 96-0825.

[470] Warren, E.S. & Hassan, H.A. (1997). A transition closure model for predicting transition onset. SAE/AIAA World Aviation Congress & Exposition 97, Anaheim, CA. October 1997. Paper 97WAC-121.

[471] Watson, J. (1960). On the non-linear mechanics of wave disturbances in stable and unstable parallel flows. Part 2. *J. Fluid Mech.*, 9, 371–389.

[472] Wazzan, A.R., Okamura, T. & Smith, A.M.O. (1966). Spatial stability study of some Falkner-Skan similarity profiles. Proceedings of the Fifth U. S. National Congress on Applied Mechanics, ASME University of Minnesota, pp. 836.

[473] Wazzan, A.R., Okamura, T. & Smith, A.M.O. (1968). Spatial and temporal stability charts for the Falkner-Skan boundary layer profiles. Report No. DAC-67086, McDonnell-Douglas Aircraft Co., Long Beach, CA.

[474] White, F.M. (1974). *Viscous Fluid Flow*. McGraw-Hill, Inc.

[475] Wiegel, M. & Wlezien, R.W. (1993). Acoustic receptivity of laminar boundary layers over wavy walls. AIAA Paper 93-3280.

[476] Wilkinson, S.P. & Malik, M.R. (1985) Stability experiments in the flow over a rotating disk. *AIAA J.*, 21, 588–595.

[477] Williamson, J.H. (1980). Low storage Runge-Kutta schemes. *J. Comput. Phys.*, 35(1), 48–56.

[478] Willis, G.J.K. (1986). Hydrodynamic Stability of Boundary Layers over Compliant Surfaces. Ph.D. Thesis, University of Exeter.

[479] Winoto, S.H., Zhang, D.H. & Chew, Y.T. (2000). Transition in boundary layers on a concave surface. *J. Prop. & Power*, 16(4), 653–660.

[480] Witting, H. (1958). Über den Einfluss der Stromlinienkrummung auf die Stabilität laminarer Stromungen. *Arch. Rat. Mech. Anal.*, 2, 243–283.

[481] Wray, A. & Hussaini, M.Y. (1984). Numerical experiments in boundary layer stability. *Proc. Roy. Soc.* Series A, 392, 373–389.

[482] Yeo, K.S. (1986). The Stability of Flow over Flexible Surfaces. Ph.D. Thesis, University of Cambridge.

[483] Zang, T.A. (1991). On the rotation and skew-symmetric forms for incompressible flow simulations. *Appl. Numer. Math.*, 7, 27–40.

[484] Zhuang, M., Kubota, T. & Dimotakis, P.E. (1988). On the instability of inviscid, compressible free shear layers. AIAA Paper 88-3538.

[485] Zhuang, M., Kubota, T. & Dimotakis, P.E. (1990a). Instability of inviscid, compressible free shear layers. *AIAA J.*, 28(10), 1728–1733.

[486] Zhuang, M., Dimotakis, P.E. & Kubota, T. (1990b). The effect of walls on a spatially growing supersonic shear layer. *Phys. Fluids* A, 2(4), 599–604.

Author index

General index